JUDITH MICHAEL

Deceptions

and

A Tangled Web

POCKET BOOKS

New York   London   Toronto   Sydney

POCKET BOOKS, a division of Simon & Schuster, Inc.
1230 Avenue of the Americas, New York, NY 10020

This book is a work of fiction. Names, characters, places and incidents are products of the author's imagination or are used fictitiously. Any resemblance to actual events or locales or persons, living or dead, is entirely coincidental.

ISBN-13: 978-1-4165-0742-0
ISBN-10:   1-4165-0742-6

First Pocket Books trade paperback edition January 2005

10 9 8 7 6 5 4

POCKET and colophon are registered trademarks of Simon & Schuster, Inc.

Manufactured in the United States of America

For information regarding special discounts for bulk purchases, please contact Simon & Schuster Special Sales at 1-800-456-6798 or business@simonandschuster.com

These titles were previously published individually by Pocket Books

Deceptions

For Cynthia, Andrew and Eric

Part I

Chapter 1

Sabrina Longworth stood at the window of the Quo Fu Antique Shop on Tian Jin Road and debated whether she should buy the fantastically carved jade chess set or the bronze dragon lamp. She could buy both, but she hadn't even seen what was inside the shop. If she bought everything that took her fancy on a two-week trip through China, she'd go home a pauper.

When Stephanie arrived, she'd ask her what she thought. Maybe she'd buy the lamp for Stephanie. If, for once, Stephanie would let her buy her something.

From the shadows inside the dim shop, Mr. Su Guang watched the American lady, amazed at her beauty. Mr. Su, an artist and curator of antiques, had studied in America and had loved a fair-haired girl who took him to her bed and taught him to appreciate Western as well as Oriental beauty. But never had Mr. Su seen a lady as vividly beautiful as this one. Her deep auburn hair shone bronze and gold in the late afternoon sun and was held in a loose knot at the back of her neck by white enamel combs etched in gold. In the delicate oval of her face, her eyes were a dark midnight blue, wide-spaced, and her mouth was generous with the faintest downward curve at the corners giving it a vulnerable look. Watching her, Mr. Su wanted to offer his help. What man, he wondered, looking at

3

that lovely mouth, whether laughing or weeping or in repose, would not feel the same way?

She was not tall, he saw, but she held herself like a queen, slender and graceful against the background of crowds of people walking and bicycling home, carrying live chickens or ducks for their dinner or pulling their purchases on makeshift carts. Occasionally the lady glanced at them, but mostly she studied his window display. And of all the objects there, she had fastened on the two finest. Mr. Su decided to invite her in and take from locked cases precious antiques he showed only to those who could appreciate them. Smiling in anticipation, he stepped forward. Then, abruptly, he stopped, his mouth open in astonishment at the vision in his window: the lady had become two.

In every way they were the same, even to the silk dresses that Mr. Su recognized came from a shop not far from his. But he had no more time to wonder, for in the next minute the two ladies entered his shop.

Inside the door they hesitated, waiting for their eyes to adjust from sunshine to the half-light of candles and kerosene lamps. Mr. Su stepped forward and bowed. "Welcome. May I offer you tea?"

The first lady, who had led the way inside, held out her hand. "Mr. Su? I am Sabrina Longworth. I wrote to you about buying for Ambassadors, my antique gallery in London."

"Lady Longworth! I have been expecting you. Yet now I find not one but two of you!"

She laughed. "My sister, Stephanie Andersen, from America."

"America!" Mr. Su beamed. "I studied in America, at the Art Institute of Chicago."

Mrs. Andersen looked at her sister. "A small world," she said, and turned to Mr. Su. "My home is just north of Chicago, in the town of Evanston."

"Ah! I have been there also, visiting the university. Come, come, let us have tea." Mr. Su was excited by the luminous beauty of the ladies, brightening his shop as no candles could. Identical beauty, identical voices: low and soft, with a faint lilt he could not identify. How could one be from America and one from London when they both spoke with an accent vaguely European? They had been educated in Europe, Mr. Su decided, and, as he bustled about the tea table, he asked about their tour through China and the antique dealers' groups sponsoring it. "Lady Longworth," he said, offering her a cup. She laughed and looked at her sister. Embarrassed, Mr. Su looked from one lady to the other. "I have made a mistake." He bowed. "Mrs. Andersen. Forgive me."

She smiled. "There's nothing to forgive. Strangers often confuse us." She looked again at her sister. "The housewife from Evanston and the Lady from London."

Mr. Su did not understand, but he was relieved. They were not insulted. He resumed his chatter and, after they had drunk several cups of tea, he showed them his rarest treasures.

Lady Longworth, Mr. Su noted with approval, handled antiques with reverence and appraised them expertly. She was also, he discovered, an experienced bargainer. She knew intuitively when he had gone as far as he could within the price range set by the government, and she wasted no time in deciding to buy or to go on to the next piece.

"Sabrina, look!" Mrs. Andersen was kneeling before Mr. Su's collection of antique magic equipment. She turned the intricate pieces in her hands. "I'll buy one for Penny and Cliff. No, I'd better buy two, to keep peace in the house."

Working his abacus with swift fingers, Mr. Su added up Lady Longworth's purchases, including the jade chess set and bronze lamp from the window, plus the cost of shipment to London. Then he took from his magic cabinet an ivory carving and held it out to Mrs. Andersen. "With my compliments." At her look of surprise, he said, "You admired this but put it back when I told you the cost. Please accept it. You bought for your children; I would like you to have this for yourself."

She smiled with such delight that Mr. Su sighed for his lost youth. He bowed and held open the door as they thanked him, and he watched them until they disappeared around a corner in the narrow, twisting street.

"How do we get back to the hotel?" Stephanie asked. She was carrying the bronze lamp, and Sabrina had the chess set, trusting neither to the shipping company.

"I haven't the faintest idea," Sabrina said cheerfully. "I thought I remembered how we got here, but these streets are worse than the maze at Treveston. That'll teach us to escape our keepers and wander around Shanghai alone. We'll have to ask someone."

Stephanie took from its box the carved ivory Mr. Su had given her. "Did you see this?"

Sabrina handed her the chess set and stood still to study the delicate piece. It was made up of dozens of tiny, fancifully carved figures, interlocked to form an openwork cube. One piece moved under her finger. "It comes apart!" she exclaimed.

"I'm afraid to try," said Stephanie. "I'd never get it together again. But isn't it lovely? Ladies of the court, all intertwined."

"Clever Mr. Su, telling us he thought the two of us together are like one person. Where do you think we are?"

A bicyclist stopped beside them. "May I help you?" he asked in careful English.

"We've lost the Heping Hotel," Sabrina said.

"Lost? Ah, you have lost the way. It is indeed confusing. If you will follow me, I will lead you to NanJing Road East."

"Does everyone in China speak English?" Stephanie asked.

"We study in school," he said casually, and rode ahead slowly as they followed.

"You didn't buy anything for Garth," said Sabrina.

"I probably will. I told you, I'm not feeling very generous toward him right now. Anyway, we have another week. Oh—!"

"What is it?"

"Only one more week. Such a little time. Before I left, two weeks seemed forever. Now I've gotten greedy. I wish . . . Sabrina, did you ever wish you could just disappear for awhile?"

"Lately I wish it about once a day. But usually what I want to get away from is me, and wherever I went, I'd still be me."

"Yes, that's what I meant. You always know what I mean."

The bicyclist turned a corner, looking around to make sure they were following. "Maybe China is the farthest we can disappear," Sabrina said.

"Then perhaps I'll stay," said Stephanie lightly. "And really disappear. For awhile at least. No more Stephanie Andersen. I'll tell Mr. Su I'm Lady Longworth, staying on for a few weeks, and since you're his best customer, he'll be delighted to help me. That is, if you don't mind my temporarily disappearing into your name and title."

"Not at all, but if you're going to be me, I'd appreciate it if you'd go back to London and solve my problems."

"Only if you go to Evanston and solve mine."

6

They laughed. "Wouldn't that be a lark?" Sabrina said, and then the bicyclist turned again, pointing. "NanJing Road East," he said.

Before they could thank him, he was gone, blending into the hundreds of bicyclists, cars and pedestrians jamming the wide road. Stephanie walked slowly, staring with unseeing eyes at the shop windows. "It would be a fairy tale," she said. "Living your wonderful life. The only problem would be fighting off your Brazilian millionaire."

Sabrina looked at her. "I'd have to fight off your husband."

"Oh, no; no, you wouldn't. Garth mostly sleeps in the study. We haven't made love in . . . a long time. You wouldn't have any fighting to do at all."

They fell silent, passing the bookstore and walking on to the artificial-flowers store. Stephanie paused, gazing at the petals and leaves of colored paper and silk. "Do you suppose we could get away with it? I'll bet we could. Not for long, of course, but . . . we could do it."

Sabrina met her eyes in their reflected images overlaid with iridescent pink and red bouquets and nodded. "Probably. For a few days." She laughed. "Remember, in Athens, when you—"

"We could look at ourselves from far away, from another life, and figure out what we want to do—well, I mean, I could figure out what I want; you always know exactly—"

"Not exactly, and you know it."

"Well, then, we'd both have a chance to think about—"

"Ah, here you are!" Their guide, leading the tour group out of a nearby shop, began to scold them for wandering off on their own.

"Let's talk about it later," Stephanie had time to say before they were swept up and taken back to the hotel for dinner and a four-hour acrobatic show.

But it was the next afternoon before they had a chance to talk. Stephanie wanted to window-shop on the rest of NanJing Road East. "I keep thinking about it," she said. "Do you? Last night I was too tired to talk, but I thought about it, and this morning I haven't been able to think about anything else."

"I know." Since the day before, the idea had clung to the edge of Sabrina's thoughts. "It's one of those crazy ideas that won't go away."

"Not that crazy. Sabrina, I'm serious about it."

Sabrina looked at her. "It wouldn't solve anything—"

"How do we know? The main thing is that we'd get away from what we are now."

They were silent. Sabrina felt her blood quicken. Stephanie always knew what would strike home: to get away . . .

"And we could do it," Stephanie went on. "We know so much about each other's lives. We've talked about them and we think the same way—"

They did. They both knew it; they always had.

"Everything would be new, and we'd be able to think about ourselves in different ways. . . ." Her words tumbled out. "You can't do that when you're in the middle of a life that has no time for thinking. And you've said so often you'd like a taste of my life, it's so different from yours. . . . Listen, what do you have to do the first week you're home?"

"Not much." The idea had caught hold, and Sabrina's thoughts flew ahead. "I didn't schedule anything in case I needed to recover from China. There's nothing that really needs doing. Ambassadors could even stay closed for another week."

"And there's not much to do at my house, either," Stephanie said eagerly. "Penny and Cliff go their own way. You can call in sick at the office—Oriental dysentery or something. They all know about China; I had to get special permission to be gone for two weeks. Oh—but you'd have to cook for everybody at home."

Sabrina laughed. Her eyes were bright. "I'm a good cook. How do you think I eat when Mrs. Thirkell is on vacation?"

"They don't know what they're eating, anyway," Stephanie raced on. "They're always in such a hurry to be somewhere else. You'd really be alone most of the time."

They stopped at the paper-cuts store where intricate flowers, dragons, boats and hundreds of other folded creations were displayed. Sabrina could feel a familiar excitement building inside her, gathering itself, preparing to leap. She had felt it so often in the past, since she was a little girl: the pull of a challenge, the joy of a dare, the excitement of winning—gathering itself, preparing to leap. "To be someone else . . ." she murmured.

"To live another life," Stephanie said. "An adventure, Sabrina!"

They smiled, remembering—twenty years ago, Sabrina

thought. They were eleven, living in Athens. Their first great adventure.

They walked on. "A week," Stephanie said. "Just one incredible week."

"You might get greedy again," Sabrina said lightly.

"So might you."

A block from their hotel, in front of the Shanghai Cakes and Pastries Store, Nicholas Blackford bumped into them as he navigated with a stack of wrapped pastries. He smiled guiltily. "It seems so difficult to diet away from home. I should have brought Amelia. You must scold me, Sabrina, as you used to when you worked in my shop and monitored my bad habits. Or am I speaking to Stephanie? Do you know, I am ashamed to say this, and I assure you it is no reflection on either of you, but Sabrina—Stephanie—I really cannot tell you apart."

Sabrina and Stephanie looked at each other behind the bald and bouncing figure of Nicholas Blackford. Strangers often confused them, but Nicholas had known Sabrina for ten years. Her eyes dancing, Sabrina swept a low curtsy to Stephanie. "Lady Longworth," she said in a clear voice. "Welcome to Shanghai."

Stephanie stretched out her hand to help her up. "Mrs. Andersen," she said. "How glad I am to be here."

Chapter 2

They were always moving. It seemed barely the blink of an eye from the time they settled in a house and arranged their furniture and hung up their clothes to the time when the servants would begin packing everything into cartons for the trip to a new city with a different language and a school full of strangers. It started when they were two years old in Washington, D.C., and from then on they moved every two years: Norway, Sweden, Portugal, Spain—and now they were moving again.

"Not already!" Sabrina groaned when she came in from horseback riding and found her mother wrapping a fragile vase in a blanket. "We just got here!"

"Two years ago," said her mother. "And Daddy and I told you last spring we'd be moving to Athens in August."

"I don't want to go to Athens," Stephanie wailed. "I like Madrid. I like my friends. And we were going to get the best sixth-grade teacher in the school!"

"You'll make new friends in Athens," her mother said calmly. "The American school will have good teachers. And Athens is full of wonderful things."

"Athens is full of ruins," Sabrina grumbled.

"Which we will explore," said her mother, fitting the wrapped vase in a carton and stuffing crumpled newspapers

10

around it. "I'm sorry, girls, I know you don't like it, but we don't, either. It's just something we have to—"

"Daddy likes it," Sabrina said stubbornly. "Every time we move he gets more puffed up and important."

"That's enough, Sabrina," her mother said sharply. "The two of you go upstairs and start sorting your clothes and books. You know how."

"We've had enough practice," Sabrina muttered to Stephanie as they went upstairs.

In fact, she was already beginning to be excited about Athens, but she couldn't admit it because Stephanie was so miserable. Stephanie wanted to stay in one house and one school with one set of friends for years and years; she hated it when things kept changing around her.

But even if Sabrina was silent, Stephanie knew how she felt; they almost always knew what the other was thinking. "I get excited by new things, too," Stephanie said, throwing sweaters onto the bed. "But wouldn't it be wonderful to have a real home for awhile?"

"I don't know," Sabrina said honestly. "Since we've never had one."

She didn't think the rented houses had been so bad; Mother would walk in like a magician and make them beautiful and comfortable and soon they could hardly remember their old house. And that was exactly what happened when they moved to Athens in August. In a two-story white house that sparkled in the sun, with a garden and separate rooms for Sabrina and Stephanie, Mother filled the rooms with their furniture and rugs, putting everything in just the right places. Then, while their father went to the embassy to meet the staff and move into his new office, the three of them were driven in a limousine around Athens and its suburbs.

As they drove, the city crept through the windows of the car, making Sabrina quiver with anticipation. Everything was spread out, waiting to be discovered: strange smells and sights and sounds, new words to be learned and new songs to sing, folk tales to hear from the servants their mother would hire, new friends to trade stories with. She could hardly wait.

But Stephanie's unhappiness kept her quiet and even made her excitement fade away. She drooped and picked at her dinner their first week in Athens, just as Stephanie did, until their father put down his fork with a clatter, saying, "I have had enough of this. Laura, I thought you talked to them."

She nodded. "I did, Gordon. Several times."

"Evidently not enough." He turned to face them.

"We're going to get a lecture," Sabrina whispered to Stephanie.

"I will explain this one more time," Gordon began. "Our State Department rotates members of the diplomatic service to a new post every two years. We do not question that policy. Do you understand?"

"It's stupid," Sabrina said. "You're always starting over and then you can't do a good job."

"I hardly think," her father said dryly, "that an eleven-year-old girl is in a position to pronounce the US State Department 'stupid.' Or to say that her father cannot do a good job. I've told you before that rotation prevents our getting personally involved in the affairs of other countries. Our first loyalty must always be to America." He looked seriously at Sabrina and Stephanie. "I might add that it is good for you, too. How else would you get to know so many countries?"

"You mean," said Sabrina, as seriously as her father, "it's good for your career, so we'd better decide it's good for us, too."

"Sabrina!" Laura snapped, and held Sabrina's eyes with her own until Sabrina looked away.

"I'm sorry," she said.

Laura picked up her wine glass. "Tell us about your new school. You, too, Stephanie. No more pouting."

As Sabrina obediently described their math and science teachers and Stephanie listed the books they would read in literature and history, Laura watched them, frowning. They were becoming difficult to control. She was proud of them— her vibrant, spirited daughters, already beautiful and quick-witted—but too often they were also impudent and secretive, banding together in their struggle for independence. She had no idea what was the best way to handle them.

The problem was, she didn't have time. Her time belonged to the diplomatic career of Gordon Hartwell. She had vowed silently at their wedding to push him and help him until he became an ambassador, perhaps even Secretary of State, and nothing in the years that followed had stopped her, not even the unplanned birth of twin girls.

She was Gordon's partner, taking his place at meetings and receptions he was too busy or bored to attend; being at his side night after night at intimate dinners, banquets, tours for American senators, and entertaining American businessmen; and sitting with him in his study when he was thinking out loud to solve a problem.

He needed her. Once he had been poor and anonymous, a history professor in a small college in Maine. She had brought him her beauty and style, which added to his prestige, and also her wealth and sophistication, which eased him into the presence of the rich and powerful. Even now, when he had developed the smooth skills of a polished diplomat and had forged his own reputation as an expert on European cultural and political agreements, he needed her. They still had a long way to go, and he knew she would not let anything stop them.

Nothing ever stopped Laura when she made up her mind. She managed Gordon's career, their nomadic life in Europe, their social life and her daughters' upbringing. She concentrated on Gordon, but she made sure that competent servants cared for Sabrina and Stephanie and whenever possible took a few hours to guide their growing up herself.

From the first, she insisted they be brought up as separate individuals. Why should they be peas in a pod simply because they were identical twins? So their bedrooms were furnished in different styles, they dressed differently from each other and were given different presents to help them develop separate interests.

And once again Laura got what she wanted: her girls were different. She thought Sabrina was most like her, always eager to tackle the unknown, while Stephanie resembled Gordon: calmer and more cautious. Gordon saw that, too, and though he didn't spend much time with them, when he did it was Stephanie who got most of his attention while Sabrina watched with dark, somber eyes.

But they were not quite as different as Laura liked to believe. Even she could not deny that their minds worked together, often in startling ways, and the instinctive bond between them was so strong she knew no one could break it unless they did it themselves.

But that made their restlessness even more difficult to handle: two adolescents, not one, pushing for independence.

"Why can't we explore the city by ourselves?" Sabrina asked. "We've hardly seen any of it."

"You've had those school field trips," Laura said. She was brushing her hair at her dressing table and red glints flashed in the mirror.

"Ugh." Sabrina made a face. "We've seen every statue and church between here and heaven, but in a whole year we haven't met one real live person except at school—and they're Americans! Just let us go for a little walk. Just around the embassy. We never get to do anything!"

"No," Gordon said. He was adjusting his black tie at the triple mirror. They were going to dinner at the king's palace.

"Why not?" Sabrina wailed.

"Sabrina," Gordon said sharply. "Keep your voice down." Stephanie stood beside her father. "Why not, Daddy?"

"Because there are dangers," he said, ruffling her hair. "For young girls, and especially for American girls whose father is a member of the embassy."

"What kind of dangers?" asked Sabrina. "Mother goes out alone; she's a girl and she's related to you. Is she in danger? Why can't—?"

"Sabrina!" Gordon warned again. "If I tell you there are dangers, you will trust my word. I can tolerate the refusal of the premier of Greece to take my word for something, but I will not tolerate it in my daughter."

"But what can we do around here?" Sabrina ignored Stephanie's cautioning hand on her arm. "You go out and leave us stuck with the servants, you get to see Athens and meet people and have fun ... Everybody gets to be with you but us!"

Laura fastened jeweled combs in her hair. "We do spend time together—"

"We don't!" Sabrina burst out. "Mostly it's just when you're showing us off to old people from America!" Before Laura could make an angry response, Stephanie drew her attention away.

"Most of the time you're with Daddy or doing your own shopping. And Daddy's always working. Other families aren't like that. They have weekends together and they eat together and have a real family."

"The only family we have is us," Sabrina finished. "Stephanie and me—we're our whole family!"

"Silence, both of you!" Filling his pipe, Gordon spoke to

their reflections in the mirror. "Some professions take the co-operation of a whole family. We work for our country. It would be selfish to think of ourselves first."

"You think of getting promoted," Sabrina flashed, and then shrank back from her father's look.

"You know nothing about what I think and you will not comment on it here or anywhere else. Is that clear?"

Sabrina met her father's look. "If you talked to the Russians like you talk to us we'd have a war."

Laura stifled a laugh. Gordon flung down his tobacco pouch and Sabrina watched the shreds of tobacco fall like skinny worms all over the rug. "Leave the room," her father said.

"Just a minute, Gordon." Laura stood, tall and magnificent in black silk and long white strands of pearls. Sabrina hated her for being so beautiful and distant, and at the same time she wanted to crawl into her arms and be loved. But the only person who ever hugged her was Stephanie. Sabrina wondered if her parents ever hugged and kissed. Probably not. They'd wrinkle their beautiful clothes. But then her mother surprised her. "The girls do need more attention," she said. "I'm going to take them on some of my shopping expeditions."

"Oh—!" cried Stephanie.

But Gordon shook his head. "I think not."

Laura sighed deeply. "Gordon, I am doing the best I can. I know you don't approve of the places I go, but I assure you they are simple working-class neighborhoods, not dens of terrorists. And I have to go there to find the best buys."

"What terrorists?" Sabrina asked.

"There are no terrorists," said Gordon in exasperation, but he looked at his watch, and Sabrina knew that meant he had lost interest in them. "Take them if you insist, but use the limousine."

"Of course." Laura fastened her silk cloak. "Shall we go?"

The shopping expeditions began the next day after school. Trailed by neighborhood children who called them the three beautiful American ladies, they hunted for antiques and works of art in shops, markets and private homes. Laura called it her hobby, but it had long since become her passion. She studied in libraries, talked with museum curators, attended auctions and watched furniture and art restorers at work. Over the years their rented houses became showplaces of her purchases: gleaming woods and mosaics, sculptures and paintings, leaded glass and finely woven fabrics. By the time she began taking Sabrina and Stephanie with her, Laura had become an expert appraiser and bargainer, supreme in her own world, where Gordon never came.

She also had become an advisor to friends and the international set that mingled socially with diplomats. They called on her so often that, had she not been Gordon Hartwell's wife, she could have made a different life on her own. But she loved the glittering social life Gordon gave her, so she kept both her passions and taught them to her daughters.

Sabrina and Stephanie, eleven years old, for the first time became friends with their mother. They shared her private world; they spoke her private language. She poured out her knowledge and they absorbed it hungrily, as if it were love.

The three of them browsed in dingy shops where old people gossiped in corners and dust tickled their noses, and they visited homes where whole families gathered to show them rugs and paintings that had been theirs for generations. But best of all were the open-air markets, with row after row of stalls hung with rugs, baskets, tapestries, vases, even furniture, and standing in front of each someone shouting, "Buy this! Buy here! Such a bargain!" Sabrina and Stephanie wanted to buy everything, but their mother ruthlessly separated the fake from the genuine, brushing aside protestations from vendors who expected Americans to be gullible. Laura was in control, absolutely confident, and Sabrina and Stephanie watched her with wide-eyed wonder: this was a different woman from the one they knew at home, where she was Gordon's wife.

But those afternoons came only once or twice a week, and by spring Sabrina was chafing to see more of Athens. "Let's ask if today we can shop somewhere new," she said as they climbed into the embassy limousine after school.

Theo, the chauffeur, spoke to the rear-view mirror. "No shopping today, Miss. Your mother told me to bring you to the embassy."

"Oh, no!" Stephanie cried.

Sabrina struck her schoolbooks in frustration. "Daddy probably wants to show us off again. Well, I won't do it. I'm going to do my buck-teeth smile."

Stephanie brightened. "And I'll cross my eyes."

Grinning grotesquely, Sabrina hunched her right shoulder to her ear.

Eyes crossed, Stephanie stuck out her tongue and licked her chin.

They studied each other's demonic poses and imagined their father, tall and proper, saying to solemn visitors, "Meet my daughters," and they collapsed on the back seat in a fit of giggles.

"Damn, damn," grumbled Theo, and they looked up; what did they do wrong? But he was cursing a traffic jam caused by an automobile accident ahead. "We'll be here an hour," he said, throwing up his hands.

Sabrina and Stephanie looked at each other with the same wild, wonderful idea. Each of them reached out to a door handle and, without a word, pushed down, swung open the doors, slammed them shut and sped down the street, ducking around corners and pushing past shoppers. Theo, lumbering after them and shouting their names, was left far behind.

"We did it, oh, we did it," Sabrina sang. "Now we can explore by ourselves." The earth felt light and airy beneath her feet. "Oh, Stephanie, isn't it wonderful?"

"Wonderful," echoed Stephanie.

Hand in hand, they strolled through shops and crowded squares, chewing on sticky *baklava* they bought from a street vendor, reading Greek signs aloud to practice their vocabulary and pausing at butchers' stalls, where they listened in fascination to the gruesome sound of air whistling through sheeps' lungs frying in oil. Finally Sabrina looked at her watch and sighed. "Well, it's been half an hour; we'd better get back before Theo gets unstuck." But before they could turn, they heard shouts and a clatter of running feet, and Stephanie ducked as a stone struck the building near her head.

"Terrorists!" Sabrina exclaimed. She looked around, grabbed Stephanie's hand and pulled her down a flight of stairs to a heavy door that was partly open. They slipped inside, shutting it tightly behind them. The room was dark after the bright sun and it took them a minute to see three children huddled in a corner. When Sabrina came close, the baby began to cry. "Oh, don't," Sabrina said. She turned to the oldest, a thin boy about their age with straight eyebrows and a shock of curly black hair, and said in Greek, "Can we stay here a little while? Some men are fighting in the street."

The boy and his sister spoke rapidly in Greek and Sabrina

17

and Stephanie looked at each other helplessly; it was too fast for them to follow. But they recognized the boy's intent look as he stared at them; they had seen it many times. He smiled broadly, pointing at each of them. "You are a mirror," he said slowly in Greek, and they all laughed.

From the street above came loud crashes and men's voices shouting to each other. An acrid smell drifted into the room. Sabrina and Stephanie twined their fingers tightly together. They were all silent, listening. The smell burned in their noses, and then they heard gunshots.

The boy moved, herding his sister and the baby to a cot and covering them with a blanket. He was scowling in an effort to look brave. When Stephanie whispered, "What should we do?" he pointed to the door.

Sabrina became angry. "You know we can't go out there," she said in Greek. The shouts were louder. "Those are terrorists."

The boy looked at her defiantly. "It is a war of independence." Sabrina looked bewildered and he shrugged at her ignorance.

She ran to the high window and climbed on a box to look out, but the boy ran after her and pushed her away. She fell to the floor. Stephanie cried out, but Sabrina scrambled to her feet. "He's right. Somebody might have seen me. I just wanted to know what was making the smell."

"Burning cars," said the boy.

"Burning—? Why would they burn cars?"

"To block the street." He muttered, "Stupid American girl."

"How do you know we're Americans?" Sabrina asked. The boy threw up his hands in despair, and then they heard banging on the doors up and down the street.

"We've got to hide!" Stephanie said wildly. "They mustn't find us!"

"Where can we go?" Sabrina asked the boy urgently. "Please, we shouldn't be here. You could be in trouble if they find us. Is there another room?"

He hesitated, then pointed under the cot. They pushed it aside with the little girls still on it and saw a trapdoor in the floor. The boy put his fingers in a notch on one side and pulled it up. Taking a deep breath, Sabrina slid through the opening, holding out a hand for Stephanie to follow. The door slammed in place above them and they heard the cot scrape the floor as the boy pushed it back.

It was so dark they could not see each other or what was around them. The air was damp, with a cloying odor. A cellar, Sabrina thought, but the ceiling was too low; they banged their heads when they tried to stand up. There was knocking on the door of the room above and they stayed still, crouching in the damp blackness. Stephanie's fingernails dug into Sabrina's hand. With her free hand Sabrina swept back and forth in the darkness for a place to sit. She felt the hard-packed dirt of the floor and then something like burlap. Burlap with lumps. A sack of potatoes. That was the rotting smell: they were in a vegetable cellar.

They sat together, arms around each other, heads touching. A few inches above them boots clumped back and forth, and rough voices asked rapid questions. Sabrina heard the word "guns" and the boy's "No." But then she heard drawers being pulled out and crashing to the floor.

Shudders ran through Stephanie's body as she gasped for breath. Sabrina tightened her arm around her shoulders. "Wait," she breathed close to her ear. "They'll be gone soon. Hold on to me." She closed her eyes; it was less scary than not being able to see anything.

"My stomach hurts," Stephanie whispered. Sabrina nodded. So did hers. The smell of rotting vegetables stuck inside her nose and she could taste it deep in her throat. It made her gag. She buried her nose against her jacket and took a deep breath. That helped. Above them the men were arguing. The baby began to cry. And in the blackness Sabrina felt something crawling up her leg.

She jerked back just as Stephanie felt it, too, and gave a little scream, trying to stand up. Sabrina pulled her down. "Don't," she whispered. She thought the baby's crying had covered Stephanie's scream but she couldn't be sure. She brushed Stephanie's legs and her own. Spiders. One clung to her fingers and she crushed it against the dirt floor.

She was shaking all over. She'd tried so hard to be brave, but Stephanie's fear had seeped into her. Now with each footstep above them she felt herself being dragged into the open. They'd be raped. They'd be killed or held for ransom. They'd be cut up in little pieces and sent back to their parents one

19

piece at a time and Mother would cry. They had never seen their mother cry, and thinking about it made Sabrina start crying, as if the full terror of the afternoon only became real when she thought of her mother crying over them.

Then suddenly it was over. The boy said loudly, "My father." A man asked, "Where?" and the boy answered, "On Cyprus." The men's voices changed; one of them laughed and said, "A patriot." The footsteps moved out the door and up the steps to the street. The door closed. Only the thin wailing of the baby could be heard.

Sabrina was steadily brushing her legs and Stephanie's, holding Stephanie tightly with her other arm and breathing into her jacket. In the sudden silence she had a new fear: What if the boy kept them there? He probably hated them for hiding while he faced the men alone. What if he put something heavy on the door so they couldn't get out? She sprang up, hitting her head so hard it made her dizzy, but she pushed at the ceiling, trying to find the trapdoor. "Where are you?" Stephanie whispered frantically, but Sabrina was desperately moving her hands back and forth on the ceiling. Something sharp jabbed her fingers, and just as she realized it was a nail in the trapdoor the boy opened it. She blinked in the light, limp with relief and shame. He was as young and afraid as they were; how could she have thought he would hurt them?

When the boy had pulled them up, Sabrina and Stephanie stared at each other. They were filthy, their skirts torn, their faces streaked with tears and dirt. Sabrina's fingers were scraped and bloody, and when she moved a spider fell out of her hair. Seeing it, Stephanie violently ran her hands through her own hair. The boy was replacing the drawers the men had flung to the floor. On the cot, the little girl and the baby lay still, their eyes wide and blank.

Now that it was over, Sabrina became curious again. "What did they want?" she asked.

"Guns," said the boy. "They are Greek patriots fighting for independence in Cyprus."

Sabrina remembered something about it from school. "Why are they fighting here?"

"To get rid of the Turks." The boy spat out the word.

"But are the Turks here?"

"No. In Cyprus. Fighting Greeks. My father is there. I should be with him, fighting the Turks."

"Then who is in the street?" Sabrina demanded, stamping her foot in frustration.

"Greeks and Turks and police," the boy said, as if it were obvious.

Stephanie was feeling better. She knew Sabrina was ashamed because they had hidden, and she began to feel ashamed, too. "Where is your mother?" she asked the boy.

"Dead. My aunt was to be here, but she is late."

"Dead! Oh, Sabrina, we should—"

But Sabrina was looking at the boy intently. "Would you really fight?" she asked.

"If I had a gun," he answered, "I would kill."

Sabrina's eyes were dark with wonder. "What's your name?"

"Dmitri Karras." They stared at each other.

The room was quiet; outside, the noise had faded, leaving only the crackling flames of the burning cars. "Sabrina," Stephanie said. "It's late. Shouldn't we go? And maybe—if their mother is dead—we could—"

"—take them with us," Sabrina finished.

Dmitri drew himself up. "I take care of my sisters."

"Yes," Sabrina said. "But come for awhile. Come for dinner," she added as graciously as her mother in the embassy reception room. "Our chauffeur will bring you back whenever you want."

Dmitri could not take his eyes off her: so proud and beautiful. Like a queen. He hated her and he loved her. "Okay," he said at last.

And so it was that firemen arriving a few moments later came upon five children walking down the street—a Greek girl carrying a baby, and a Greek boy with eyes riveted on two identical American girls, scruffy with dirt but real beauties, their faces framed in auburn curls. The firemen took them to the police, who drove them to the address they gave, which the police knew was the American Embassy, and there was going to be hell to pay.

One of the policemen had telephoned ahead, and a crowd was waiting on the embassy porch. Laura flew down the walk to gather Sabrina and Stephanie to her, exclaiming in dismay at their torn, dirty clothes and the blood on Sabrina's hands. Gordon followed, his face like stone. As he reached them flashbulbs exploded on all sides from the cameras of thirty re-

porters who, like everyone else, had thought Cypriots had kidnapped the twin daughters of the American chargé d'affaires.

Sabrina leaned against her mother in the wonderful warmth
of her arms. Everything was all right. They were home. Then,
remembering Dmitri, she looked around and caught a glimpse
of him through the crowd of jostling reporters.

"Wait!" she commanded loudly. She and Stephanie pulled
away from Laura and went to Dmitri. "These are our friends.
They saved us. I've invited them to dinner."

"Sabrina!" Her father's voice lashed her. "Not another
word. You have done enough damage with your recklessness
and impudence. How many times must I warn you—?"

Sabrina stared, open-mouthed and stunned. They were
home. Why was Daddy scolding her? He hadn't even hugged
them. She hurt all over and she was so tired and she had felt so
safe when they saw the embassy and then Mother had held
them . . . Why was Daddy making her feel so awful? Tears
filled her eyes and spilled over. She tried to stop them, but
they ran down her cheeks and she tasted them on her lips.

"—a self-indulgence that shows you have no regard for my
career. This time you have dragged your sister into it and these
children, too, whoever they are. You are to go inside this instant; I will decide your punishment when—"

"That's not Sabrina! You've mixed us up!" Through her
tears Sabrina saw Stephanie hammering on Gordon's arm.
Stephanie was crying, too. "That's Stephanie, not Sabrina,
you've mixed us up, you can't blame her in front of everybody,
she didn't do anything and, anyway, we both had the idea, we
got out of the car at the same time, Theo will tell you, and then
the fighting started and we hid, and you can't blame Sabrina—Stephanie—either of us, it's not her fault!"

The reporters moved in, taking pictures. "Sir, if the young
ladies—Sabrina? or Stephanie?—would tell us what happened—"

Gordon, struck dumb, was looking from Sabrina to Stephanie and back again. Sabrina heard him mutter, "How the hell
am I supposed to—?" but Laura took over, stepping in front of
him.

"No interviews, please," she said. "The girls are exhausted
from their ordeal, and not well." She was not well herself, still
gripped by the paralyzing fears and guilt she had felt all afternoon: she had never done enough for her children, and now

they might be dead. But the clamoring reporters and the danger of a scandal touching Gordon aroused her to her duty, and she pushed her anguish down, out of sight. It would wait. Later, she would recover, in private.

"Sabrina, Stephanie, take these children inside. Get some food and wait for me in your father's office. Now!" she said, and they ran up the walk with lights flashing in their faces. Behind them, a recovered, suave Gordon promised the reporters a statement the next day.

But sensational stories appeared in the morning papers without Gordon's official version, each one featuring large pictures of Sabrina and Stephanie with the Greek children. By then the girls were locked in their separate bedrooms, but a Greek maid brought the newspapers with their breakfasts and later, when Gordon and Laura were out, unlocked their doors. Sabrina danced into Stephanie's bedroom, holding the paper. "I've never had my picture in the newspaper before. On the front page, just like Mother and Daddy! And it says they found Dmitri's aunt! Oh, Stephanie, isn't it amazing, so many things happening at once?"

Stephanie sat by the window. She was confused; everything seemed upside down. "Daddy fired Theo," she said.

Sabrina stopped in midflight. "I know." She sat in the window seat. "That wasn't fair. Daddy knows it wasn't his fault. I wish he hadn't fired him. But everything else is so exciting—"

"But what about the bad things?" Stephanie cried. "Mother and Daddy are furious and the ambassador told Mother we're uncontrollable and Americans aren't supposed to get involved in street fighting—"

"We weren't," Sabrina interrupted.

"And then it was our fault that Theo got fired and I feel bad."

"So do I." Sabrina looked out the window. The cuts on her fingertips hurt, and she pressed them against the cool glass. "Everybody's mad at everybody. We really made a mess. But, still, it was exciting, wasn't it? All shivery and—oh, I don't know—important. More real than school and books and movies. Dmitri cared about things so much. So did those men. It was an adventure, Stephanie!"

"I know . . . and it *was* exciting—now that it's over—"

"Everybody at school will see it in the paper—"

"—and be so jealous—"

"I'll bet they never had an adventure like that—"

"Even if they did, they'd be scared, not as brave as you."

"I was scared, and you know it. Every time they walked above us—"

"But you were brave, too, Sabrina. You always are. I wish I was."

"Don't be silly, of course you are. You told Daddy you were me."

"Oh, I had to do that, after I was such an awful coward in that cellar. At least now we're both being punished, instead of just you."

"Did you see Daddy's face? Was he confused!"

"Mother knew."

"She knows what clothes we wear."

"But Daddy hardly ever looks at us."

They fell silent, thinking about their father.

"Stephanie," Sabrina said slowly. "What if you couldn't have adventures without bad things and good things both? Would you want to give them up?"

"Oh, I don't know. I suppose not. I just wish I had some way of knowing ahead of time—"

"But we don't." They watched a bird light on a tree branch near the window, so close they could see each feather. Sabrina loved to sit like this, next to Stephanie, comfortable and peaceful. Sometimes she wished she was as calm as Stephanie and didn't talk back to her parents and teachers, or think danger was exciting. But she was so restless, and there were so many tantalizing things to try, that she couldn't sit still for long. And, strangely, she thought Mother secretly liked her best that way. So sometimes she talked back or tried something risky in gymnastics (with teachers yelling at her not to, which made it even more fun) just so Mother or other people would admire her and love her.

But mostly she got excited about doing different things because there was so much to discover. "What I think," she said to Stephanie, who was sitting quietly, waiting for her to go on, "is that I'd rather have some bad things happen than not have any adventures at all."

Stephanie thought about it. "Well," she said finally. "It's a good thing you're here. Because if you weren't, I probably wouldn't have any adventures. Ever. And I wouldn't like that, either."

DECEPTIONS

* * *

Later that year, they read about the settlement of the war in Cyprus. Dmitri and his sisters had gone away with their aunt, and Sabrina and Stephanie devoured stories in Greek newspapers and magazines, hoping to find news of anyone named Karras. But there was nothing, and in the fall they moved to Paris without knowing what had happened to them.

Gordon Hartwell was appointed chargé d'affaires of the US Embassy in Paris in the summer of 1960, the year President Makarios took office on the independent island of Cyprus and John F. Kennedy was elected President of the United States. But whatever changes occurred in the world, life for Sabrina and Stephanie was the same as in Athens. Their rented house was in an enclave of Americans; they attended the American school; they shopped in the famous flea markets on the edge of Paris only with their mother, never alone.

But Laura knew that explosive pressures were building in Sabrina and when the girls were fourteen she let them go to social events for the sons and daughters of diplomats from other embassies. There were picnics and swimming parties, dances, tours of the wine country, excursions to soccer games, horse races, tennis and bicycle races and ski holidays. They made friends from a dozen countries, and their speech soon blended the accents and vocabulary of all of them. It was as if they had their own country, separate from the rest of the world.

But then, once again, everything changed. At dinner one winter night their parents told them the great news that Gordon had been nominated by the President, and confirmed by the Senate, as ambassador to Algeria. But, Laura added, there was a problem. Speaking quickly so the girls could not interrupt, she reminded them that Algeria had just won its independence from France and it was still unsettled, possibly even dangerous for foreigners. It was certainly no place for teenage American girls.

"But there is a boarding school in Switzerland," she went on, "that we have looked into."

They had selected it from a dozen recommended schools. Juliette Institut International de Jeunes Filles was a high school of impeccable reputation. Under the amiable dictatorship of Professor L. E. Bossard, wealthy young women became cultured, superbly trained in sports and educated to the en-

25

trance standards of any French, American or English university. Its rules were strict, its students closely supervised. Professor Bossard would make sure that no scandal would attach to Juliette—or the parents of its girls.

Gordon would take up his new post in the spring, Laura told Sabrina and Stephanie. She would stay with them in Paris until the school year ended. Then Gordon would join them and they would drive to Switzerland to see the girls safely ensconced under Professor Bossard's wing.

Sabrina looked somberly at her parents. This was what her mother had worked for all these years: Gordon as an ambassador. And now that she had succeeded, she was sending them away. "It's not Algeria," she said. "It's because Daddy's an ambassador and you're sort of one, too, and you don't want to worry about us maybe doing something embarrassing to such very important people."

Laura slapped her face. It was the only time she had ever hit her, and she was ashamed immediately afterward. "Forgive me," she said to Sabrina. "But for you to talk to me that way—"

"She didn't mean it," Stephanie said quickly. "It's just that we don't want to go away."

"I meant it," Sabrina said. "And I do want to go away. I don't want to be with people who don't want me."

Laura's eyes flashed, but she said smoothly and emotionally, "Of course we want you; we'll miss you both terribly. But we can't turn down this appointment because of you. Algiers is a city still in turmoil, the schools are not—"

"It's all right," Sabrina said. "I understand." Her stomach was churning and she hated her mother, and her father, too—looking out the window as if he weren't involved at all. "It sounds like a wonderful school. We'll have a wonderful time, won't we, Stephanie? I guess we ought to practice our French some more; it is a French school, isn't it? We ought to start now, I guess. Stephanie, do you want to come upstairs with me and begin to practice our French?"

There was a long silence. The Hartwell family sat unmoving around the dinner table in the beautiful home that Laura had made for them in Paris. They were suspended on a breath of air, waiting to be carried in different directions.

Then Sabrina stood, followed by Stephanie, and the two of them went upstairs, to be together.

Chapter 3

At exactly 10:00 P.M., the mahogany doors of the grand ballroom in the Hotel Geneva swung open on a Venetian palace of papier-mâché and paint. Marbled columns supported a vaulted ceiling, and arched windows looked out on painted canals with gondolas and poling boatmen. The varnished ballroom floor was surrounded by a hundred round tables, each set with an orchid centerpiece and china and silver for four. As the doors opened the room became a kaleidoscope of four hundred young men and women in tuxedos and ball gowns crowding in for their graduation ball.

They came from ten select men's and women's schools on the shore of Lake Geneva, and they knew each other from years of chaperoned social events, trips to the great cities of Europe and sports competitions. Only that morning, they had competed in the annual Lake Geneva Sports Festival, their last chance before graduation to win trophies for their schools, their names etched impressively in brass or silver for victories in archery, sailing, fencing, swimming, horsemanship and soccer. From early morning until midafternoon, they struggled, hair slicked back, skin streaked with sweat and dust, muscles taut with the lust for victory. Now, polished and sophisticated, they mingled in the other kind of sports festival sponsored by their schools: finding a suitable partner for marriage.

Stephanie, in a froth of lemon yellow chiffon, her hair falling in heavy waves down her back, sat with Dena and Annie in the gilt armchairs at their table and watched for Sabrina to come in. She had to talk to her; so much had happened, so many new feelings danced inside her, and there was no one else she could share them with, not even her two closest friends.

It wasn't that she needed Sabrina as much as she used to; they had made separate lives, with separate friends. In the beginning, when they arrived and drove up the hill from the shore of Lake Geneva, they had huddled together, watching the road climb through vineyards of honey-green leaves edged with red and then, at the crest of the hill, pass through an iron gate into a park and on to the square stone castle that was Institut Juliette. Stephanie was assigned a room on the fourth floor with Dena Cardozo, Sabrina on the third with Gabrielle de Martel, where they lived and studied, along with one hundred and twenty other young women, for three years. It was the longest time they had ever lived in one place.

Where before Sabrina and Stephanie had been together all the time, at Juliette they began to go in different directions. They took art classes together and they both had joined the fencing team, but in their junior year Sabrina turned to sailing and captained her crew to first place in four Alliance races. Stephanie stayed with fencing and, on a team with Dena and Annie MacGregor, brought Juliette four trophies before the end of her senior year.

They studied and took up sports with different groups, but they always felt each other nearby, like a ribbon woven through their days. Whenever they could they snatched an afternoon or a holiday to go off together, apart from everyone else. "To make sense of things," Sabrina would say and settle back with a happy sigh to talk and listen.

"Hey," Dena said as a waiter filled their glasses with champagne. "You're dreaming again. Come back; I'm making a toast." She raised her glass. "To college, and the hell with it."

"Don't be silly, Dena," Stephanie said, turning her attention from watching for Sabrina. "You don't want to stay in high school."

"I want us to go on being roommates."

"Then come to Paris with Sabrina and me."

"You come to Bryn Mawr with me."

28

"I want to go to Paris, Dena—to the Sorbonne."

"Your parents enrolled you at Bryn Mawr."

"And we enrolled ourselves at the Sorbonne. One of these days they'll understand that we mean what we say."

Dena's eyebrows went up. "Tough talk."

Stephanie shook her head. Sabrina's determination had done it; alone, she would have given in to her parents, even though the money was theirs, left in a trust by their grandfather. Laura and Gordon wanted them at Bryn Mawr because Laura had gone there and because it was time, they said, the girls lived in America. But Sabrina and Stephanie wanted Paris; for years they had dreamed of Paris.

"Have you seen Sabrina?" Stephanie asked, becoming impatient. Soon the dancing would begin and then they would have no chance to talk.

"Not since the fencing match," Annie said. "But there is your Charles." She paused. "He has a nice face." She paused again so Stephanie could confide in them. When she was silent, Annie asked outright, "Where did you go this afternoon, after the match?"

"For a walk," Stephanie said vaguely, catching glimpses through the crowd of Charles, sitting with his senior class. She felt a pang of longing as his thin, serious face smiled at a friend, the way he had smiled at her that afternoon when he put his arm around her and led her out of the gymnasium, away from her disastrous fencing match.

They had gone to lunch in Lausanne. In a tiny café with red tablecloths and white curtains where they were all alone and, at last, away from spectators, she wept over a lost championship.

"Too *timid,*" she said through her sobs. "Putting everything I had into one attack to win a point and then when I needed one more—just one—to win the trophy, I couldn't follow through. I don't know why. Sabrina would have—"

But Charles told her how wonderful she was, and how he admired her grace and skill. "Everyone knows that technique is more important than strength," he said. "You don't have to be aggressive. Remember how they cheered you." He talked on and on until her sobs quieted and she began to feel less hopeless. She leaned against him, happy and trusting, thinking she was falling in love, and then his voice changed as he began to stumble over his words. Stephanie knew he was trying to

29

ask her to come with him to the small hotel next door, but it was his first time and he could not manage it and Stephanie, as inexperienced as he, had no idea how to help him. In all the late-night talk with her friends about sex, hours were spent on how to say yes or no, but not one minute on how to lead the way.

Looking at him through the crowd in the ballroom, Stephanie remembered his arm around her while they talked for hours and thought about the hotel next door until they had to separate to get ready for the graduation ball that night. I love Charles, she thought, and smiled to herself.

"Ah," said Annie expectantly, seeing the smile. "A very good walk." But still Stephanie was silent. The only one she could talk to about Charles was Sabrina. But Sabrina was nowhere to be seen.

With a flourish of trumpets, the directors of the ten Alliance schools were introduced to loyal applause. As the orchestra played the traditional medley of school anthems and then the first waltz, the lights slowly dimmed to a blue evening haze with hundreds of candles flickering like tiny stars. The ballroom swirled with color and young men crowded about Stephanie, claiming dance after dance. She glided about the room, dreaming, waiting for Charles.

"Too bad about the match," one of her partners said, bringing her to earth. She nodded shortly. "You're good to watch, though," he added soothingly. "Girls usually aren't interesting, but you're so beautiful I really enjoyed it."

Stephanie stopped dancing. "What an amazingly stupid remark."

"Hey," he said defensively. "I only meant—"

"I know what you meant." She wasn't interested in him; she wanted Charles. Where was he? Why hadn't he asked her to dance? "Excuse me," she said, and walked away, moving like a shadow between swaying couples, searching the room. And then she saw him. He was in a shielded nook, talking animatedly to a young woman. She stood with her back to Stephanie, wearing a shimmering ice-blue gown, her heavy auburn hair caught loosely at the back of her neck by a matching ribbon. Sabrina! Stephanie thought, and started forward eagerly. How amazing to find them both— She stopped as she saw Charles's expression—eager, fascinated, adoring. In their whole afternoon together, not once had he looked at her like that.

The music stopped and a young man approached Stephanie. She did not turn her head. All she saw was Charles and Sabrina.

"... this dance?" he asked, and reached for her. Still without looking at him, she shook her head.

"Why not?" he cried. "Stephanie, what's wrong?"

His plaintive voice calling her name rang out in the quiet moment before the conductor brought down his baton for the next dance. Charles swung about. For an instant Stephanie's eyes met his and then she fled, holding up her skirt and weaving between the whirling couples out of the ballroom.

Sabrina ran after her. Ignoring Charles's frantic questions, she pushed her way past curious dancers and through the mahogany doors. She caught a glimpse of Stephanie's yellow dress in the closing elevator and sped down the corridor to take the next one to the floor where the Juliette seniors were staying for the night of the dance.

"Stephanie?" She knocked on the door of Stephanie's and Dena's room. There was no answer. She waited, catching her breath. Her heart was pounding at the memory of the awful despair on Stephanie's face. I didn't know, she thought. I didn't know. But I would have, if I weren't so selfish. "Stephanie, please."

"It's open," Stephanie said.

She was curled on the couch, crying, and Sabrina ran to her, kneeling on the carpet to take her hands. "I'm sorry, I'm sorry. Why do I hurt you when I love you more than anyone in the world?" Stephanie tried to pull her hands back, but Sabrina clutched them. "Please, Stephanie, I didn't mean to hurt you. I wasn't flirting. He just came up to me—"

Stephanie jerked her hands away. "They're always 'just coming up to you,' " she said furiously. "Have you ever thought of saying no?"

Sabrina stared at her. "I do. But this was different. Charles—"

"Don't lie about it! It was just another—"

"Stephanie, stop. It *was* different. He thought I was you."

"That's not true," Stephanie said swiftly.

"It is. I got there late, I was alone, and when he came up I

31

didn't recognize him. I'd never seen him before this morning, at your match, and that was only for a minute, when the two of you were leaving. And he didn't say my name at first; we just started talking, and then all of a sudden he called me Stephanie, but I couldn't stop him—"

"You could have stopped him before then. You knew what was happening."

Sabrina's shoulders slumped. "Of course I did." She looked down at her beautiful dress and thought how wrong it was to look so pretty and feel so terrible underneath. She needed Stephanie; she'd come to the ball looking for her, desperate to talk about what had happened that afternoon, and now she'd hurt her and they were quarreling. "I guess I didn't want to stop him."

"Why not? Do you always have to show everyone you're better than me?"

"Stephanie!"

"Well, you are better, aren't you? Everyone knows it. You won the sailing championship this morning. You would have won my fencing match. You wouldn't lose a boyfriend. You never lose anything."

With a sinking feeling, Sabrina saw how wide the gulf was between them. "I didn't know he was your boyfriend," she said helplessly.

"You knew I left the gym with him. That was a clue." Stephanie's eyes were flat. "Why didn't you tell him who you were?"

Sabrina spread her hands. "Something happened today . . . I was looking for you, to talk about it, but you were dancing and then . . ."

In spite of herself, Stephanie was caught by the unhappiness in Sabrina's voice. "What happened?"

"Marco came in from Paris."

"I thought he couldn't come until tomorrow."

"He was anxious."

Stephanie heard the contemptuous note. "For what?"

"Some . . . games he thought I should play now that I'm grown up."

They looked at each other. "What did you do?"

"Threw a paperweight at him and told him to get out."

Stephanie laughed in reluctant admiration. "Did he?"

"All the way back to Paris, I guess."

"You don't think you'll see him again?"

"I know I won't. He called me a fool. Maybe I am."

Stephanie was about to ask what games Marco had suggested when the thought came that once again Sabrina had beaten her; *she* had been desired and pursued, while Stephanie couldn't even get Charles to take her to a hotel. "But why did you take it out on me?" she cried, and Sabrina felt as she had once when the calm eye of a hurricane passed and the furious winds returned.

She jumped up and began walking back and forth, rubbing her arms to warm them. She was ashamed of her trick on Charles and frightened by Stephanie's eyes. But worst of all was the gulf between them. How had they pulled so far apart?

"I didn't take it out on you. I'd never do that. I really didn't know he was important, and when I realized he'd mixed us up it was like a game. But it was only a few minutes; I was about to tell him when we heard your name. Stephanie, I would never hurt you—"

"It doesn't matter," Stephanie said wearily. "He liked you better than me, anyway. Whatever I try to do, you do it better."

"That isn't true."

"Then tell me why you left the fencing team."

"Why I—? That was a year ago. It has nothing to do with—"

"Because you were so much better than I was."

"I wasn't better, I was different."

"More aggressive, more formidable. Everyone knew it."

Sabrina stopped pacing. Stephanie's pain cut into her. "I wanted to sail. And I knew I could be captain."

"You knew nobody paid attention to me when you were fencing. That's why you left the team."

"No. I like sailing better than fencing. That was the only reason." She had never lied to Stephanie before. I'm sorry, she said silently. I just don't know what else to do. "Anyway, what difference does it make, it's all past. Unless you want us to fence together at the Sorbonne; why don't we do that—"

"It's easier for you to get good grades, too."

Sabrina shook her head. She felt sick. How long had Stephanie been hiding these feelings?

"Oh, yes, it is. You never study or cram and then you get *A*'s, and I'm always studying."

"And getting *A*'s."

"Yes, but everything comes to you, Sabrina, like grades and fencing and Charles, but I have to work at them and then hold tight or they'll get away." She was crying, and Sabrina knelt beside her again.

"Please, Stephanie, stop, please stop, I can't stand it if you cry because of me. I'm sorry about Charles, I'm sorry about fencing, but you're more important than anything." She was crying, too, for Stephanie and for herself, because she'd done everything wrong and Stephanie's anger was shutting her out. "I don't know what you want me to do, but I'll do whatever—"

"There isn't anything." Stephanie sat straight. "Sabrina, I've decided to go to Bryn Mawr instead of the Sorbonne."

Stunned, Sabrina stared at her. "Bryn Mawr?"

"It's a good school, and since I'm already enrolled there, thanks to Mother and Daddy, that's where I'll go."

"But we were going to Paris together."

"Sabrina, don't look so—lost! What are you worried about? You'll be fine. I'm thinking of me. I have to find out who I am separate from you. You're so bright and exciting, I just fade away when you're around. Nobody would notice me at all if you didn't step aside sometimes."

"No, no, no." Vehemently, Sabrina shook her head. "Of course people notice you, what are you talking about?" But Stephanie was silent, and Sabrina jumped up and began to pace again. Why hadn't they ever talked about these things? We're changing, she thought; we're talking in different ways. And so she told Stephanie something she had never even admitted to herself. "Stephanie, when I do exciting things, or crazy things, it's because everybody expects it. They tell me how wonderful I am and then I look for more things to do . . ." She paused. "I'm afraid if I don't, they'll stop loving me and thinking I'm wonderful. You're the only one I'm sure of who loves me just because I'm me. Everybody else talks about how beautiful I am, or how exciting it is that I win races and contests, how spectacular I am." She hesitated again, then burst out, "I need to be the center of attention. I wish I didn't."

Stephanie had stopped crying. "You'll have the attention all to yourself in Paris."

Sabrina stood still and gave her sister a long look. "I don't deserve that. I was trying to be honest."

"I'm sorry. I meant we'll each have our own attention. For the first time." Her eyes were bright. "It'll be an adventure, Sabrina. You always told me I should want them, remember?"

Sabrina searched those bright eyes for malice but found none. "I never tried to overshadow you," she said helplessly.

"Maybe not. But I still feel like I'm just Sabrina Hartwell's twin sister." She looked down at her hands. "We'll write to each other instead of talking."

Sabrina heard a new note in Stephanie's voice; she was beginning to waver. I could change her mind, she thought. If I pushed, if I reminded her of how often we needed each other the last three years, she'd come to Paris. We'd be close again. Once she had told her mother and father, "Stephanie and I are the only family we have." It was still true. I could convince her to come with me, she thought.

But she couldn't do it. Because Stephanie was right; she had to get away. Sabrina shrank from that awful fact—my sister doesn't want to be with me—but she couldn't deny it. She gloried in her own brightness and Stephanie had to escape, to find her own. I won't stop her from doing that, she thought. I won't make it any harder than it already is. I've done enough tonight to hurt her.

So she sat beside Stephanie on the couch and swallowed the tears welling in her throat. "What a lot of talking we'll do on summer vacations!" she said brightly. They sat together, not touching, their hands in their laps like proper young ladies. I love you, Sabrina said silently to Stephanie, and began that moment to live her life alone.

Chapter 4

The audience in the opera house stilled as the lights dimmed. Spotlights came up on the heavy gold curtain, the conductor swung down his baton and the sensual Spanish music of the overture wove through the hall, its gypsy lilt making Stephanie want to dance. She looked at Dena. "Thank you," she whispered, grateful for everything: New York at Christmas, shopping, theaters and the Cardozos' box for her favorite opera. Sighing happily, she let the music catch her up as the curtain majestically parted on a crowded scene of brilliantly dressed dancers and soldiers in bright red uniforms.

A commotion broke the spell; behind them, someone pulled open the door of the box, then stumbled against a chair. Stephanie and Dena swung about. "Sorry," a voice said. In the shadows Stephanie saw a tall man with dark hair trying to close the door and tug off his coat at the same time.

"Are you in the right box?" Dena asked.

He nodded and sat in the armchair behind Stephanie. Dena waited, but he said nothing more. She studied him for a moment, then looked at Stephanie, shrugged and turned back to the stage. "Rumpled," she murmured.

Stephanie gave a small laugh at Dena's swift judgment. Whoever he was, he was respectable, even though his jacket needed pressing. And he was self-confident enough to offer a single apology and then stop.

In the next minute she forgot him. On the stage, Carmen was singing with slow, taunting sexuality to the infatuated young soldier, Don José, and the song flowed through the audience like molten gold. Stephanie leaned forward, feeling its power. But she was distracted, aware of something besides the music. She turned around and met the eyes of the stranger, watching her.

She was the one who turned away, flushed from the steadiness of his gaze. He was older than she, with a strong face and a more direct look than she was used to in the men at colleges near Bryn Mawr. Turning her head slightly, as if she were looking at the side of the stage, she saw from the corner of her eye that he was still looking at her. He's missing the whole opera, she thought, and felt her lips curve in a smile. For the first time she wondered who he was and how he had a ticket for the Cardozos' box.

"Excuse me," he said. "Did you drop this?" Stephanie turned to look at the program in his outstretched hand and shook her head, her lips curving again. He knew she hadn't dropped it; he could see her program on her lap. Their eyes held for a moment and then she turned away again. But for the remainder of the first act, she could see him at the edge of her field of vision, watching her.

"Garth Andersen," he said, holding out his hand as the lights came up at intermission. Dena reached out quickly to take it.

"Dena Cardozo. Are you a friend of the Bartons?"

He chuckled at Dena's protectiveness, making her feel young and uncertain. He shouldn't do that, Stephanie thought, and as if he realized it himself he said quickly, "We're old friends. And I apologize for my noisy entrance. The Bartons neglected to tell me they shared the box and then I was late; I forgot the time at work and was afraid I'd miss the overture." He held out his hand to Stephanie. "We haven't met."

"Stephanie Hartwell." She fit her slender hand to his long, thin one. A musician, she thought. Or an artist.

"What work?" Dena asked.

"Research," he answered briefly and invited them to the lobby for a drink. He wondered why Dena asked all the questions. Did she always ask, and was Stephanie always silent? Or was Stephanie not interested?

As they drank their wine, Garth answered Dena's questions, telling them he was a molecular biologist, a professor at Columbia University, a researcher. "In what?" Dena asked, but he said it was too complicated for intermission talk. That was true, but he never talked about his work to strangers, fearing they would turn away, bored and uncomprehending. He didn't want to talk about himself, anyway; he wanted to ask his own questions about Stephanie Hartwell.

In the crowded lobby, reverberating with high-pitched laughter and rapid tongues, she was a quiet island, her body very still, her movements small and controlled. As Garth talked, he memorized her deep blue eyes, the delicate lines of her cheekbones and her wonderful mouth, wide and generous, surprisingly vulnerable, asking for protection.

Dena watched him, but not with jealousy. She was pleased he was interested in Stephanie because it was clear that Stephanie was interested in him. Lucky Stephanie, Garth thought, to have such a friend. And at the final curtain he asked if he could take them home. "We have a limousine," said Dena. She looked up suddenly, as if remembering. "Stephanie, I promised I'd call Mother before we left for home. I'll be right back."

When they were alone, Garth met Stephanie's smile with his own. "A nice thing to do."

"Dena is always doing nice things."

"I want to see you. Tomorrow?" She shook her head. "Then the next day."

"No. I'm sorry." Her eyes were clear and honest. "I'd like to. But I'm staying with Dena's family for the holidays and they've made plans for us. They're so wonderful to me that I can't just disappear and leave them with tickets and schedules. I'm sorry."

"And after the holidays?"

"I go back to Bryn Mawr."

"To graduate?"

She laughed. "Hardly. I'm in my second year."

He frowned. "You look . . . how old are you?"

"Nineteen."

"You look older."

"Isn't nineteen old enough?"

"I wouldn't have thought so," he mused. "But it will have to be."

Dena came back and they gathered their coats from the back of the box, friendly in their goodbyes. Garth stood in the shadows, feeling like a bumpkin at the side of the road as the royal carriage passed by. They had wealth, sophistication, style and all the world waiting for them. He looked at the opera stage where three hours of passion had just been sung and saw a vulnerable mouth and clear, honest eyes. He pulled on his coat and smiled to himself. This bumpkin was going to follow the carriage all the way to the castle.

Bryn Mawr College is tucked amid the hills and leafy splendor of Pennsylvania, an hour's train ride from New York. Stephanie had barely arrived and begun unpacking when Garth called.

"I'm going to be in your neighborhood this weekend," he said casually. "I thought I might drop by, if you'll be home."

She laughed. "What will you be doing in my neighborhood?"

"Spending the day with you."

They met at Pembroke Arch, the campus rendezvous, and shook hands formally. "Where are you taking me?" he asked, as they began to walk.

"I have to stop at the library for a few minutes and then I thought we'd have breakfast at Wyndham House. If that's all right? It's so early, I thought—"

"Too early for you?"

"No, I'm glad you're here." Snow had fallen during the night and they walked on shoveled paths, the dark lines bisecting sparkling white expanses dotted with gray, Gothic stone buildings.

Garth followed Stephanie through the library and down a staircase to the basement loading dock. "No one else could be here today," she said, "and they're delivering some furniture for the antique auction upstairs. As soon as I sign for it, we can leave."

A truck was backed up to the wide doorway and Garth watched as Stephanie talked to the driver. In a minute she came to him with a gesture of uncertainty. "He says his forklift won't work so he can't unload the crates. Do you want to go to breakfast while I hunt up a maintenance man? I don't know how long I'll be."

"I grew up with forklifts," Garth said. "Shall I have a look?"

She tilted her head to look at him. "Do scientists do research with forklifts?"

He laughed and went through the loading door to the flatbed of the truck. "Minnesota farm boys use forklifts. And fix them regularly." He conferred briefly with the driver, who found a toolbox in the cab of the truck, and then turned to Stephanie. "How long is breakfast served?"

"For three hours."

"I'll have an impressive appetite." He bent over the motor, working quickly and easily. "Try it," he said to the driver after a few minutes, and when the engine started he walked back, smiling, to Stephanie. "Science is wonderful."

"So are Minnesota farm boys." Reaching up, she ran her finger along his forehead and brought it away covered with grease.

He smiled ruefully and spread his blackened hands. "I never could work on an engine without carrying away half its grease. My mother used to comment on that. Where can I wash up?"

"Through there and down the hall."

"Don't go away."

"I won't."

He went off with long strides, still feeling her touch. And when he returned, he found her in the same place, signing the delivery slip.

For breakfast, Stephanie had gotten permission to take Garth to the dining room of Wyndham House, the best on campus, usually reserved, with the upstairs bedrooms, for visiting alumnae and parents. As they studied their menus beside a large window overlooking the campus, she snatched glimpses of him, taking pleasure in the strong lines of his face. His brown eyes were deep-set above prominent cheekbones, his mouth was wide, his strong chin marked with a cleft. When he smiled, fine lines radiated from the corners of his eyes, disappearing into his thick black hair. Everything about him was clearly defined; nothing was blurred or soft. Even his voice, deep and resonant, could reach the back of the largest lecture hall without straining.

"Do you still have your farm?" she asked when they had ordered.

"No. I gave it to my sister and her husband." Now that she was asking the questions, he talked easily, telling her about the farm carved out by his grandfather—wheat glistening gold beneath the sun, the feel of the earth when he worked it, the solitary hours he spent as a boy, dreaming of being a famous scientist, and the hours of close companionship with his father, learning all he knew so that when he retired, Garth could manage the farm.

"A peaceful, secure childhood," he told Stephanie as the waitress brought pancakes and sausages and filled their coffee cups. "A loving one. Everything in its place; no doubts about the future."

"But it all changed?" she asked when he fell silent.

"It all changed." He paused, remembering. "When I was eighteen I had a scholarship to college—I would have been the first of our clan to go. But I had to give it up to manage the farm when my parents were killed in an automobile accident."

Stephanie drew in her breath. "You say it so calmly—"

"I didn't at the time. It destroyed almost everything I believed in. But it was eight years ago," he added gently.

Eight years ago, she thought. He was eighteen, his parents were dead and he was running a farm. No wonder he thought I was young; I haven't done anything. "*Did* you run the farm?" she asked.

"For a year. My sister was still in high school, and I stayed with her; I was the only family she had. When she married right after graduation, I gave her the farm as a wedding present." He paused again, looking out at the snow-covered campus. "And then I came to New York, looking for another world where everything was in its place and there was a chance of predicting the future."

"Science," Stephanie ventured.

He nodded, smiling at her. She listened so carefully he thought she might hear all the unspoken words—about his poverty in New York, and his isolation, so different from that on the farm. He had no time for friends, holding three jobs while taking extra courses so he could graduate early and begin to teach. And lately, when he could go out, he didn't, because he was afraid of taking time from research, from preparation for his lectures, from anything that might slow down his progress in his field. Except for an occasional evening with a few close friends, he never went anywhere.

Until now.

He finished his coffee and sat back. "My turn. I don't know anything about you."

"But you haven't finished. Did you find a world where everything was in its place?"

"Almost everything. Where are you from? I can't place your accent."

"I grew up in Europe. But what is it you find? I don't know what a molecular biologist does."

Garth laughed, discovering the pleasure of having a beautiful woman insist that he talk about himself. "All right," he said. "We study the structure and behavior of molecules in living things. I specialize in the structure of genes and how we might alter them to eliminate genetic diseases."

Stephanie rested her chin on her hand, watching his eyes and his mouth. "If you change the structure of genes," she said hesitantly, "aren't you changing life?"

He looked at her curiously, like her professors when she asked a good question. "What does that mean?"

"Wouldn't you be tampering with—what makes life?"

"Well, I don't call it tampering; that sounds as if I'm screwing up the works. Look, those antiques you signed for; didn't craftsmen change the wood in making them? Doesn't a sculptor change marble?"

"But artists don't have power. A marble statue can't change the world. But you could, couldn't you, by changing genes?"

"Possibly."

"Well, somebody ought to control that."

"Who?"

She looked at him over her coffee cup. "The government?"

"Petty, untrustworthy, plodding, narrow-minded, no vision."

"Scientists, then."

"Probably just as bad. Most of us are a little crazy. The fact is, you can't limit research; it pops up every time you try to cut it down."

"I guess I have to think about that. What do you want out of your research?"

Back to the personal, he thought, admiring her tenacity. But the answer would take too long for today. He put it off. "To make a pile of money by inventing a boysenberry syrup for eternal youth."

She laughed. "What's wrong with cherry?"

"Run of the mill. No drama."

"Garth, you don't really want to make a pile of money."

"Oh, don't I."

"But do you expect to?"

"Oh, if you put it that way, no. Not in university research. Private companies pay well, but they're not my style."

She looked a question.

"I don't like commercial pressure. In a university, no one peers over my shoulder to see how close I am to discovering something that will make a profit. I like research for its own sake, being free to follow leads that might help—"

"Humanity."

"Something like that. You're right, though. It's unlikely I'll ever be able to afford you. Are we leaving?"

"Yes." Stephanie was taking bills from her wallet. "That is the silliest remark I've ever heard. I think it's wonderful that you care about research, about people, that you're willing to earn less so you can do what you believe in. That was a silly remark."

He caught her arm as she stood up. "Wait. Now wait a minute. First, I'm paying for breakfast."

"You're my guest. I invited you."

"I invited myself for the day. I may be only a lowly assistant professor who cares about humanity, but I can afford to take my friends to breakfast. Aside from my silly remark, why are we leaving?"

"I have to get back to the library to see if they need help setting up for the auction. It's less than a week away, and so many people have been sick that we're behind schedule. I'm sorry, because I promised you the whole day, but I have to do it—it's my job."

"Your job."

"I work for the art department and we run the auction."

"Why do you work for the art department?"

"To earn money."

"I thought—"

"Yes, I know you did."

Garth had paid for breakfast, and as they walked across campus he felt suddenly lighthearted, filled with energy. She doesn't live in a castle, he said to himself and, packing a snowball, threw an exuberant pitch at a gnarled tree, where it clung like a white star to the black trunk. He looked at Stephanie's bright face. "Tell me about the antique show. Do you know, I've always had a secret desire to fondle a nude statue. Could this be my chance? Will you have any nude statues?"

Stephanie laughed. What a wonderful day they were going to have. "We will have statues of nudes. If you want nude statues, you will have to undress them." It was his turn to laugh, and he took her hand securely in his as they walked up the steps of the library.

Garth had plenty of time to ponder the contradictions in Stephanie Hartwell before she visited his laboratory in New York. He spent nine Saturdays in Bryn Mawr through the winter and spring and learned about her twin sister and the break between them, still unhealed, and about her parents in Algeria, who would soon move to Washington when her father took up his new position as Under Secretary of State for European Affairs. He heard all about her posh, ridiculously expensive Swiss school, and he learned that her sophistication came in patches from a crazy upbringing that taught her enough about Europe to fill an encyclopedia but not enough about sex or men to fill one page of a diary. He knew about her quick intelligence, her quiet beauty and friends like Dena who clustered around her, offering places to stay over vacations: everyone wanted to give Stephanie a home. And so did Garth. Because he had fallen in love with her.

"I'll meet you at your office," Stephanie said when he called her at the Cardozos' apartment. "It's silly for you to pick me up. How do I get there?" He gave her directions and she skipped to her room to dress. Spring vacation in New York: a whole week with Garth, since the Cardozos knew about him and hadn't made plans for her. A week with Garth. She sang it to herself on the subway.

But as she walked to the university, the noise of a crowd cut across her thoughts. It seemed to come from all directions until, turning a corner, Stephanie found herself engulfed in it: the shouts of young people massed together, waving signs and cheering a freckle-faced boy who stood on a truck, yelling hoarsely through a bullhorn. A wall of policemen with linked arms stood between Stephanie and a four-story building whose windows and windowsills were crowded with shouting, gesturing men and women. Uncertain, she looked about, trying to find an address. She started to ask a policeman, but the noise drowned out her voice. Then, suddenly, Garth was there, his arm around her, walking her quickly past the occupied building and into the one next door.

They rode the elevator to the fourth floor. "Quite an introduction to my home-sweet-home," said Garth ruefully. "If I'd known beforehand, I wouldn't have let you come. But it seems to be a stalemate, so we'll have a quick tour and then get out."

"I've never been close to a demonstration; Bryn Mawr is so quiet—"

"We've been blessed with them like clockwork. They've almost become part of university life." He unlocked a door. "Come into my parlor."

The laboratory was partitioned down the middle by tall steel cabinets, and as they walked to one side Garth stood back to watch Stephanie's reaction. At first she was puzzled, then disappointed, then intrigued. It was a strange room, with no shiny equipment, no test tubes or flames or bubbling liquids, not even a microscope. Instead, crowded on a long soapstone bench were children's Tinkertoys: constructions of sticks, wires, balls, bits of plastic, string and paper, in all shapes, sizes and colors. On the floor, boxes overflowed with more material. Photographs of constructions covered the walls, and a large blackboard, gray with erasures, was filled with labeled diagrams of others. In the corner a desk and a battered typewriter were barely visible beneath piles of books and papers.

Garth grinned. "I am known in these parts as the Tinkertoy man."

"I'm not surprised," Stephanie said. "Garth, what is all this?"

He swung his arm to encompass the room. "My models. Works of art, each made by hand—"

"Garth. Be serious."

"You know, I am serious. These cockeyed models are my works of art."

"Tell me."

He smiled at her serious face. "Each model is a different

kind of molecule. The balls are atoms, the sticks are the forces that hold them in their different arrangements. You do know what molecules are."

She nodded. "They have them in Switzerland, too."

"Sorry, was I talking down?"

"A little. But I really don't know very much."

"Here." He erased the blackboard and sketched as he talked. "This is the cell, and inside it, the nucleus. Inside that, these ribbons are the chromosomes, made up of long strands of a particular molecule." He reached down to pick up a model, but just then a roar surged from the crowd below and he looked impatiently at the window. "We can come back another time."

"No, tell me now." She felt close to him in the silent laboratory; outside there was danger, but inside, with Garth, was safety.

"I'll make it short. The molecule that makes up the chromosomes is DNA. This is a model of it: something like a ladder twisted into a corkscrew. DNA is the molecule that controls heredity. It's a blueprint; the different kinds of rungs on the ladder are organized in special ways that make up a code, with all the information needed for the duplication of life. That's where I come in: trying to understand how this molecule, this ladder, is made."

"And when you do?"

"Then I might learn how to repair it when it's damaged." He returned the DNA model to the bench. "Kids are being born now with diseases we can't cure, because somewhere on their DNA ladder something went wrong with one or more of the rungs. If we knew how—"

He broke off. The shouting was louder; a girl's voice came through the bullhorn. "There's more to it, but that's the meat and potatoes. We'll get to the rest on a quieter day. Shall we go?"

As they were leaving Stephanie glanced at the other side of the laboratory. It was more familiar, with microscopes, test tubes, beakers, syringes, a sink. On one wall, beside a large window, dozens of white mice scampered in small cages. Looking over her shoulder, Garth said, "Bill and I trade information; he's working on inherited diseases in mice."

Stephanie smiled. "Tinkertoys and pet mice. Modern science—" Abruptly she screamed as an explosion threw her against him and fragments of glass shattered at their feet.

Garth cursed. "Don't talk," he said roughly. "And try to hold your breath."

"Why?" she asked, but his arm was muffling her face as he half-carried her into the hall and up a stairway. Suddenly she was violently ill: her eyes stung, tears streamed from under their swollen lids and her chest felt crushed as harsh gasps tore through her burning throat.

Then there was cool air and sunlight on her face, and Garth's strong arm steadying her. "I can't stop crying," she said. "I can't open my eyes."

His other arm came up to cradle her. "You'll be all right in a few minutes. It's only tear gas."

"Only—!"

"Not permanently damaging. Can you stay here alone? I'll get some water."

"Where are we?"

"On the roof. Be right back."

The burning lingered, but within ten minutes Stephanie could open her eyes and look over the parapet at the police dragging coughing, crying students into paddy wagons. "Why did the police throw one at us?"

"Not exactly at us; somebody had lousy aim. You'd think with all their practice they'd be in better form. Stephanie, I've got to go back and cover that broken window. Do you want to wait here?"

"I'll come with you."

But in the laboratory she shrank back from his rage. It welled up as he stood in the room, his face rigid, the veins standing out in his neck. "Bastards." The word ripped from him. "Goddamn bastards." She followed his gaze to the wire cages where, a short time before, she had laughed at the scampering mice. But none scampered now. They lay in limp piles, a breeze from the broken window gently stirring their flat white fur.

With a vicious kick Garth sent the empty tear-gas canister sailing through the air, scattering papers that lay in disarray on the floor. Glass crunched under his feet. "A year of Bill's work, a year of experiments and study—" His voice rose. "Remember those kids I told you about, born with diseases we

47

can't cure? They're at the end of a road that begins here. Do you see what this means? Do you see that this university thinks it's more important to clear out a bunch of students than to protect the work of its scientists?"

"I don't think you mean that," Stephanie said quietly. She was trembling, not from the tear gas but from Garth's anguish, the depth of his caring. He knew what was important; he knew what he wanted and where he was going. His world was far larger than hers.

Kneeling on the floor, she began to pick up the scattered papers, putting them in a box she found on the desk. Garth studied her bent head, the heavy auburn hair falling forward around her face. Wonderful, calm Stephanie. Wise beyond her years one minute; a young girl the next. Waiting. And who was he to think he could give her what she was waiting for? Beside her, he still felt like a bumpkin.

She stood up. "I think I've cut myself."

Blood ran down her hand. "All that glass," he said angrily. "Let me see."

She held out her hand like a child. Carefully he drew out a long sliver, found a gauze pad in a drawer and pressed it to the cut. She flinched. "Something still in there," he said. It was her turn to look at his bent head as he rummaged in the drawer again and found a tweezers. "All the comforts," he murmured. "Always cut yourself in a biologist's lab." He looked up and caught her watching him. "Do you know," he said conversationally, "you are probably the only woman in the world who can look beautiful after being teargassed? You have just passed the Andersen beauty test. We administer one canister of tear gas, and those whose beauty is only skin deep are transformed immediately into hiccuping toads. Why do you laugh? I am telling you that I love you and I want to marry you and I think I have found the splinter so if you will hold very still I will remove it."

He bent over her hand and probed in the wound. "Sorry," he said when she flinched again. "I would also like to take you home and make love to you, a desire I have had for several weeks in the less conducive atmosphere of Bryn Mawr. There. Done." Without looking at her he reached for more gauze and wrapped her hand in a neat bandage. "Boy Scout training in the wilds of Minnesota. What do you think?"

"About what?" she asked faintly.

"One or both of the above."

She moved forward confidently, knowing already the shape his body would take in enclosing hers. "Yes," she said. "To both of the above."

In May the bushes on Bryn Mawr's campus bloom densely pink and white and the ground is a carpet of petals that drop as new ones appear. A hot sun burns away the April rains and birds cluster in ancient trees. It is the season of weddings.

In the courtyard of Thomas Library, Laura stood beside Stephanie, casting a critical eye on the circular pond with its placid ducks, the neat rows of chairs beside it and the long tables set with food and drink. "It's not so much a wedding," she said thoughtfully, "as a garden party. Didn't you want something more formal, darling?"

"I wanted this," Stephanie said dreamily, watching her friends and Garth's gather in small groups, waiting for the ceremony to begin.

"Stand still, both of you," commanded Gordon and clicked his camera.

"And leaving school," Laura went on. "Are you sure, Stephanie?"

"Mother, if Garth is in Illinois, how can I stay here?"

"He could have waited two years."

"No, he couldn't. The job at Midwestern is too good." She kissed Laura's cheek. "We'll buy a big house with lots of bedrooms and you'll visit us. You've never been to Evanston, have you? Or Chicago?"

"Neither one."

"Well, now you will."

Stephanie saw Sabrina come into the courtyard and join Judge Fairfax and the Cardozos. "Excuse me," she said and crossed over to take her hands. "You look wonderful!"

"No, you're the one . . . is it possible to be as happy as you look?"

"When I come to your wedding I'll ask you that."

Sabrina smiled. "Judge Fairfax says he bounced us on his knee when we were babies in Washington."

"And predicted I'd preside at your weddings," said the judge. "I'm waiting for Sabrina's to give me an excuse to come to Europe."

Sabrina raised her eyebrows and once again changed the

subject. She never talked about herself, Stephanie thought; not even in her letters. She wrote like a good friend, describing her days, asking interested questions, but always a little remote, just as she was last summer when they were in Scotland with their parents. Then she had been quiet and withdrawn, reluctant to let others draw her into conversation, as if she were afraid someone would accuse her of attempting to outshine her sister. Stephanie understood, but she refused to make things easier. It evened things out, she thought, if Sabrina felt awkward for once. She was ashamed of being mean, but she did nothing to make Sabrina feel better and for the whole month neither of them had had a good time.

Once each of us was half of the other, she thought, watching Sabrina talk to the Cardozos. Now I don't know anything about her—whom she loves or what she dreams about. And she doesn't know me.

"Sabrina," she said, touching her sister's arm. They walked together, bending their heads to each other. Gordon caught them with his camera—his glorious daughters, identical but elusively more and more different: Sabrina strangely cool and quiet in a slim dress of dusty rose that subtly traced her body, her hair hidden beneath a matching cloche; Stephanie glowing in a white embossed gown edged in embroidered lace, a camellia nestled like carved ivory in the dark auburn of her hair. "I've got to apologize," she said.

"Don't," said Sabrina. "I think I understand."

"How can you? You left school early so we'd have a few days together, and I've done all the talking; you haven't told me anything about yourself."

"It doesn't matter. You look so happy; I've never seen you look so happy. Stephanie, I love you. Just enjoy your day."

"You do like Garth, don't you?"

"Of course I do. He's charming and he's in love with you. Stephanie, I'm happy for you. I'll talk about myself some other time. Not today."

Stephanie put her hands on Sabrina's shoulders and pressed her cheek to hers. She was glad Sabrina wouldn't talk about herself; that was the terrible truth. She didn't want to discover that behind Sabrina's casual letters was a life more exciting than hers. She had Garth; she didn't need Sabrina. "Thank you," she said to Sabrina, then stepped back as Garth came up. "You two never had a chance to get acquainted."

Sabrina and Garth exchanged a quick glance. "I'm sorry," he said. "I thought I could get here sooner. Too much to do. The end of the school year, the end of my teaching at Columbia. All that nostalgia to deal with. We'll get acquainted later."

Stephanie shook her head. "Not unless Sabrina leaves Paris and settles down in Illinois."

Sabrina smiled involuntarily at the idea, and Garth was struck by the imp that broke through her cool, remote lips. But she snatched it back; the imp disappeared. "We'll visit," she said. "Don't professors come to Europe for research and— whatever else they do?"

"Children," said Gordon. "The judge is ready."

Judge Fairfax stood before a bank of high bushes, Stephanie and Garth before him, with a friend from Columbia on Garth's left and Sabrina on Stephanie's right. As they arranged themselves, Garth whispered in Stephanie's ear. "She's cold. You're far more alive than she is. And much more beautiful."

In a sudden moment of illumination, Stephanie saw what her sister had done. Sabrina's wedding present, she thought: to diminish her beauty and subdue the vitality that makes her the center of attention. To stand in the shadows and leave the sunlight to me. She felt a wave of love and then of guilt. But I can't help it, she thought, if we're not close and she doesn't confide in me. We're making our own lives; we don't need each other anymore.

How do you know? a small voice asked. Have you asked her if she needs you?

Judge Fairfax began to speak and Stephanie pushed away her thoughts and her guilt. She only had time to think how amazing it was that just when she and Sabrina were farthest apart she had found Garth to love her, and then she concentrated on becoming his wife.

Chapter 5

The castle rose up from the green hills of Hampshire, its battlements and towers worn by the centuries to a pale gray, its windows cut deep into stone walls. Beyond, a forest of copper beeches loomed, like a gleaming bronze curtain rustling in the June breeze.

"Treveston Castle," Stephanie read in awestruck tones from Sabrina's letter. "Eighty rooms, twelve hundred acres of farms and parks ... Garth, look!" she cried, glancing up. "Peacocks!"

Garth slowed the car and looked at the two peacocks, the castle and the silver-blue lake that curved behind it, taking in what was once the moat. "A cozy cottage," he said ironically, but in spite of himself he was impressed. Straight out of a fairy tale, he thought; Minnesota farm boys and Midwestern professors have trouble believing such a thing is real. And, of course, it is ridiculous; it doesn't belong in the twentieth century. But still, it casts a spell: magnificent, beautifully proportioned, larger than life.

"Can you imagine Sabrina living here after the wedding?" Stephanie asked. "I'd feel ... dwarfed. As if I'd intruded in a house built for giants. I don't know how she'll do it."

"Ask her," Garth suggested, and stopped the car as a servant came up to open the doors and take their luggage inside.

Stephanie brought it up later as they took a tour of the grounds. "I think about the people," Sabrina said. "Not four hundred years of wars and knights and royal processions, but the family. Especially the black sheep."

The three of them walked on paths that wound among a thousand rose bushes as Sabrina told stories of the black sheep of the Longworth family. "I think they invented one every generation, partly to liven things up, but mainly so they could be as eccentric as they liked and still have someone more disgraceful to point to."

Stephanie laughed. "Is there one now?"

"Not that I know of. I think Denton would like to be one, but his father and the board of directors frown on publicity, much less scandal."

"I didn't know he worked. How does he—and have so much time to travel and be with you?"

"He works when the mood strikes. It seems he has a system . . ."

They walked on, talking, as Garth lingered behind, turning aside to look at the high hedges of the famous Treveston maze.

"Garth, we're going in," Stephanie called. "Do you want a tour of the house?"

"I'll catch up to you," he said. Stephanie had shown him a letter of Sabrina's that described the maze: a triangle two hundred feet long on each side, planted in 1775 by Staunton Longworth in a labyrinth of hedges where visitors could be lost for hours. Garth peered through the opening, pondering geometric patterns Staunton Longworth might have used. I'll try it later, he thought. Or tomorrow, after the wedding.

Inside the house, he followed the sound of his wife's voice. But, disconcertingly, he found it was Sabrina who was talking as he met them in the library. Odd, that over the years their voices remained identical even though they lived in different countries.

". . . restored the ceiling," Sabrina said, gesturing, and Garth began to pay attention, admitting to himself once again that even though it was an anachronism, more museum than home, it was as splendid as anything he had ever seen.

The rooms led one to another in stately grandeur, hugely proportioned and fabulously detailed, from parquetry and carved lintels to mullioned windows framed in ivory damask drapes with fringed velvet ties. The castle dated from 1575, when Sir William Longworth, member of Queen Elizabeth's Privy Council, built it in Treveston Village on land granted him for loyal service. Fifty years later his grandson hired England's greatest architect, Inigo Jones, to remodel the south front and add three state rooms and a Grand Staircase. Other descendants made more additions to a total of eighty rooms, and in the twentieth century the farms and parks were improved, including the addition of a narrow-gauge steam railway crisscrossing the estate.

Shakespeare's troupe entertained in Treveston's Great Hall, and generations of farsighted Longworths filled the castle with a priceless collection of Titians, Rembrandts and Gainsboroughs, rare books and prints and seventeenth-century tapestries and furniture.

"Of course, you can't just hang a picture or buy a new rug when you want to," Sabrina told Stephanie later as they sat on the balcony of her sitting room and bedroom. They were having tea while Garth tackled the maze. "That's the first rule. But isn't it exciting anyway?"

"You look so happy," Stephanie said. "Is it possible for anyone to be as happy as you look?"

They laughed in remembrance. Four years ago, Stephanie thought. Four years of being apart. In that time, while she was settling down in Evanston, Sabrina graduated from the Sorbonne, moved to London and went to work in Nicholas Blackford's antique gallery on Lowndes Street. She lived alone in a small flat, made new friends, helped organize two charity auctions. And in her letters to Stephanie she never mentioned her feelings. But now she might, Stephanie thought; because suddenly, it was so wonderful being together. She recalled Sabrina's look when they arrived. Love. And gratitude. "You are happy, aren't you?" she asked.

"Happy or excited," Sabrina said. "I think with Denton they're the same. He's so incredible—he strolls through the world as if it's one of his Treveston gardens. You can't believe how overwhelming it is."

"Oh, yes, I can," Stephanie said dryly, taking in the canopied bed covered with Sabrina's clothes, the maid folding and packing them for the honeymoon, the Regency dressing table and wardrobe, the French doors leading to the balcony where they sat.

"No, it's not money," Sabrina said. "I mean, of course the

money is wonderful—I've been living beyond my salary ever since I came to London. And it's not that Denton's father is a viscount, though that's part of it. Mostly it's the way Denton assumes he belongs wherever he goes. And he loves me, so by now I'm almost as confident as he is."

"You don't need Denton to make you confident."

"But I do, that's the trouble. You know how I've always tried to impress people so they'd like me ... well, look at Mother, how pleased she is with me and my spectacular marriage."

"Mother didn't need that to love you."

"Probably not, but have you ever seen her so affectionate?"

"No," Stephanie admitted.

But the next day, watching Sabrina after the wedding ceremony, Stephanie thought she had never seen anyone more sure of herself and in command. A queen, she thought. I'll never look like that. Or have a castle. She felt a quick flash of envy, and then it was gone as Sabrina looked her way and their eyes met. I just want her to be happy, she thought.

Sabrina's lips sent her a silent thank-you before Denton nudged her to turn back to the guests in the reception line.

"My dear Sabrina, you have taken London by storm," the Duchess of Westford said as she reached them. She beamed with the admiration only the very secure give to those younger and more beautiful than themselves, and Sabrina accepted it with a smile, in her gown of white silk and chiffon. Her slender neck rose above the triple strand of pearls and diamonds that was her husband's wedding gift; a matching strand glimmered like stars woven through her dark auburn hair. The duchess kissed her. "I don't blame Iris for capturing you for her son. I wish I'd found you first, for mine."

"But I captured her, you know," said Denton. "Mother only found her. She was looking for a desk and she found Sabrina."

"She found the desk, too," Sabrina said gaily. "I sold it to her and then she invited me to tea."

"Superb taste," said Lady Iris Longworth to the duchess. "Sabrina helped her mother furnish their home in Washington—of course, you've met her father, the under secretary of—?"

"Um," the duchess nodded, less concerned than her friend Iris with Sabrina's credentials.

"Duchess," said an impatient voice. "Can I kiss my old Juliette roommate?" And in a flurry, Gabrielle de Martel moved forward to kiss Sabrina's cheeks. "You look like a woman who has been swept off your feet by a handsome, debonair world traveler and bon vivant who quite properly adores you and has promised to give you a piece of the world for each birthday and Christmas."

"If I can't find anything better," Denton added.

"But what can I give you, then, except the moon?" asked Sabrina.

"Oh, forget the moon. I wanted it once, but now I have you." He held her hand, and Sabrina smiled at his cheerful round face and rosy cheeks and trim black mustache. His shrewd black eyes were often hard, but when he looked at her they softened and became eager. "I can't really believe even now that you belong to me."

The line moved on. "Sabrina, you'll both spend a week with us at Ranstead; do say you will, I'm counting on you. We'll just be a small group, twenty or thirty, so we can really get acquainted."

"But we expect you at Harleton House in August, Sabrina, don't forget."

"Sabrina, did Denton tell you we arranged for two weeks at Colburn Abbey in September?"

"Sabrina, have you hired a secretary yet? I can recommend—"

"When will your London house be ready, Sabrina? I've heard such wonderful things about it."

"Never."

"I beg your pardon?"

"We're going to be houseguests for the rest of our lives, swooping down on great homes and castles and perching awhile and then swooping on. We have so many nests to choose from, we don't need our own."

Iris Longworth tapped her arm, smiling in spite of herself at Sabrina's mischievous eyes. "You will be criticized if you jest about our friends' invitations. They take them very seriously."

Sabrina nodded. "Thank you." She knew her voice was not penitent, but at least she hadn't smiled, even though her laughter kept bubbling up because she was having such fun. She looked down the receiving line to catch Stephanie's eye again, but Laura was between them, nodding her approval as she saw Sabrina looking her way. I've given Mother the ultimate antique, Sabrina thought; an in-law with four hundred years of lineage. Gordon was less enthusiastic; he preferred Garth to Denton. "More solid," he said, "more serious." More like himself, he meant, but he was friendly to Denton, and Sabrina felt she had finally pleased both her parents at once.

And Stephanie? She stepped back to see her: calm, quietly friendly, as six hundred strangers greeted her and commented on her remarkable likeness to her sister. Gabrielle had reported that she was chatting comfortably with some of England's richest women about her two babies, life in a Chicago suburb and her husband's latest research grant.

Beyond Stephanie, Sabrina saw Garth watching her with a curiosity he made no effort to hide. She knew what he was thinking and gave a little smile, as if to apologize, before turning back to the guests.

Garth moved back from the receiving line to lean against a window. He was trying to fit his memories of Sabrina with this stunning, vibrant woman, shimmering in the mist of her gown, her warmth and vitality the center around which the party revolved. Where was the cold, distant woman who had attended his wedding four years earlier at Bryn Mawr, and the reserved sister-in-law who had made two brief visits, spent mostly with Stephanie, when their children were born?

Garth knew he had never met this woman. Either something had transformed her—or the Sabrina he had met in the past had been hiding her true self.

He looked at his wife. In a long, pink dress Sabrina had bought her in Paris, she was softly beautiful, a pastel portrait in the slanting afternoon sunlight. She said she'd gained weight, though Garth had not noticed, and she no longer had the regal posture drilled into them at Juliette, but she outshone every woman there except Sabrina, and she was holding her own with the aristocracy of England. Garth was proud of her.

"Clever man, to escape," Sabrina said with a low laugh, suddenly beside him. The reception line had wound to an end. "I wish I'd been able to. Let's get Stephanie and hide somewhere."

"And your husband?"

"Denton is discussing racing cars; he's investing in one for the Grand Prix. Do you know anything about the Grand Prix? Neither do I, but I have a strong suspicion I will soon learn.

For now, though, I deeply desire a hiding place where I may remove my shoes."

He chuckled as they rescued Stephanie from a plump earl "who kept talking about spaniels," Stephanie exclaimed, as they slipped into a small study. "He said the wedding reminded him of his last dog show!"

They laughed together. Sabrina pulled off her shoes and curled up on the couch with a happy sigh. "Oh, how I've missed you. Nobody else always laughs at the same things I do. Stephanie, how can you keep your shoes on? Two hours in that line—!"

At the other end of the couch, Stephanie shook her head ruefully. "I can't take them off. Not in a castle. I can talk to your lords and ladies and feast at your table, but I cannot take off my shoes. It's all right," she added quickly. "I think what you have is wonderful. It's just that I'm more comfortable in my own home, I'm happy to say."

Sabrina relaxed. "I'm so glad. I was afraid—"

"I'd be jealous?"

"Not exactly. That you'd think I'd grabbed a bigger spotlight."

"Oh. No, I don't. Isn't that strange? Maybe because I have my own now and I like it."

"No more being shoved in the shade?"

Stephanie thought about it. "Seems it's gone."

Garth looked at them with patient curiosity. "A code?" he guessed.

Stephanie started. She'd forgotten he was there. For a minute it had been just her and Sabrina, alone, as they used to be, their thoughts and words weaving together. She turned to him. "Once I told Sabrina her spotlight put me in the shade where no one noticed me."

"And then she went off to America," Sabrina said. "Leaving me alone with my spotlight."

Stephanie gazed out the window at guests drifting like flower petals through the gardens, accepting champagne and hors d'oeuvres that waiters presented on silver trays. Four years ago, standing before Judge Fairfax in a different garden, she'd brushed aside the thought that Sabrina might need her; she hadn't really wanted to know.

Well, now she knew. She heard the echo of Sabrina's voice: "Leaving me alone with my spotlight." So Sabrina had missed her. Sabrina had needed her. Maybe as much as she had missed and needed Sabrina, even though, with Garth and the excitement of getting settled in Evanston, it had taken her a long time to realize it.

On the lawn, the guests were beginning to congregate near the tent. Sabrina sighed. "If I don't get back, Denton's mother will say I'll be criticized." Groaning, she pulled on her shoes. "Weddings should be held in bed. That's where most of them begin these days anyway."

Garth chuckled. Stephanie turned from the window. "Sabrina, when are you and Denton coming to visit us? We have so much to talk about, so much time to make up—"

Something stirred in Sabrina. Stephanie's eyes, clear and shining, met hers without envy. Sabrina felt like singing. So much love to make up. "I'd come tomorrow if I could. I'll see what Denton has scheduled. He's full of plans to show me all his favorite places. But as soon as I can . . ." She held out her hands. Stephanie took them in hers and they held each other close, for a long moment, as they had in the far-off days when they were all the family they had. "As soon as I can," Sabrina whispered. "I'll be there. I promise."

Denton Longworth worked now and then in his family's shipping company, where he was vice president of finance and a member of the board of directors. To a point, he had done what his father expected of him, graduating from the university and immediately joining the company. But he had no intention of spending the decade between his twenty-fifth and thirty-fifth birthdays at a desk. Later he would settle in, but first there was a large world to enjoy. So he devoted one year to the office, building a dedicated staff capable of carrying on efficiently in his absence, and then he took off for the playgrounds of the world.

He worked when he felt like it. Rounding the corner of his thirtieth birthday, he discovered in himself a talent for reorganizing small, struggling companies his father acquired at bargain prices, and since that gave him pleasure—the yardstick by which he measured all his pursuits—he spent a few days a month at it.

Now, halfway through his thirtieth year, he assigned himself the happier chore of introducing his bride to his playgrounds and put his considerable energies to work on a grand tour.

Within a few months, at Biarritz and Cannes, Wimbledon and Buenos Aires, Minorca and Zermatt, jaded members of the international set were falling over themselves to entertain Sabrina Longworth and bask in her irresistible combination of beauty, sophistication, open delight in new discoveries and warm gratitude. For when had anyone in their circles last expressed the simple emotions of delight and gratitude? No one could remember.

Wherever they went, invitations awaited them, sent on by Denton's secretary in London. Denton would fan through them, letting some drop to the floor and handing the rest to Sabrina. "Pick out the ones that appeal to you, sweets. And toss out the rest." But he would watch her. "You're not throwing out Cora's invitation, are you? Wonderful hostess; no one misses her parties. And why did you—?"

So by the time they reached Monaco in May, almost a year after their wedding, Sabrina simply glanced at the invitations and handed them back to Denton. "You decide. I still don't know everyone."

He spread them on the coffee table in their suite, arranging them like a poker hand to fill the afternoons and evenings when they were not gambling in the Casino or watching the Grand Prix. "Well done," he told himself, having fit everyone in. "We'll even have time for Max."

"Who?"

"Max Stuyvesant. Amazing you haven't met him yet; he's all over the place. Pleasant fellow, something of a mystery, you'll like him. He wants us for a cruise on his yacht, four days, just after the race. Good idea; totally new experience for you."

"Why is he a mystery?"

"Because no one knows how he makes his money."

It was not that everyone hadn't tried to find out; they had. But no one got beyond Maxim Stuyvesant's own answer: he was "in art," which could mean anything. Some guessed he owned galleries in Latin America and Europe; others that he was an agent for wealthy clients. There was a rumor that he supported young artists, hiring people to bid on their paintings at auction to drive up the price and create excitement, then pocketing most of the inflated prices collectors paid for them. Cynics said he was a grave robber in the tombs of Egyptian kings.

However he made it, he spent his wealth lavishly, flying guests in his private plane high above Monte Carlo's fireworks displays, taking thirty friends for week-long African safaris, transporting two hundred people by train across Europe to a Yugoslavian dance festival. Sabrina hated him. He loomed above her, broad-shouldered, with a frizzled halo of red hair and flat gray eyes that guarded his secrets. Denton was surprised. "How can you not like him? You haven't talked to him; all you've done is say hello and make yourself at home on his boat."

"He's arrogant and brutal and I'll bet he doesn't know the first thing about art."

"How can you possibly—?"

"I feel sorry for his wife, too. She's like a puppy, waiting for him to pet her."

Denton was silent. Sabrina slipped on her evening gown of blue-black silk that settled about her like a delicate moth's wing, baring her shoulders and back. "You'd better dress, darling. Cocktails are at eight, and if we aren't prompt he'll stare at us with those awful eyes and turn us into statues. That's the kind of art he's in! He casts a spell on people and then sells them to their grieving families as mementos."

"Sabrina! Max is our host!"

"I'm sorry, Denton."

"I hope so. Where are my cuff links?"

Their stateroom was hung with a French tapestry over the king-size bed. The carpet was deep, the furniture pale ash with ebony handles, the bath blue and silver with a whirlpool in the tub. The *Lafitte,* 104 feet long, had six such staterooms and five crew rooms. Its decks were teak. In its salon thirty people could move about comfortably beneath a teardrop chandelier. Its chef and wine cellar were famous. Sabrina had learned never to ask the cost of anything, but Denton, planning to buy one like it, said the price, with furnishings, was two million dollars.

Five couples were the Stuyvesants' guests on the *Lafitte.* Over cocktails, Betsy Stuyvesant, Maxim's third wife, small and soft in cashmere and silk, her blond curls trailing wistfully about her ears, told them she was not allowed to interfere in the ship's operations. If they needed anything, Kirst, the head steward, was at their service. For going ashore, Maxim made all arrangements. She fell silent and did not speak again that evening.

61

They dined on fish soup with saffron and orange peel, followed by baby octopus in champagne sauce; the wine was a chilled white Palette from the hills above Marseilles. Max proposed a toast. "To a successful cruise." He smiled lazily at his dinner partner, a willowy blonde he had introduced as Princess Alexandra, from a country no one had heard of. Across the table, her husband, Prince Martova, looked fixedly at his plate.

Beside the Prince, a tanned, sleepy-eyed woman asked, "And where do we go tomorrow?"

"East," said Max, still looking at Alexandra. "Along the Italian Riviera di Ponente to Alassio and Genoa and back. Four days. A lifetime." Alexandra smiled.

Sabrina glanced at Denton and saw him smile lazily at Betsy Stuyvesant, as if he were trying to look like Max.

In the morning they found fruit, croissants and coffee in the small dining room. Max was their maestro. "Sunbathing on the afterdeck for those who want. Waterskiing at four. Games and stimulants in the salon at all times. Movies in the small theater; Kirst will run them if you wish. We lunch at one. Enjoy yourselves, *mes amis.*"

Denton stretched. "The salon first, I think. Then sunbathing. All right with you, sweets?"

Five people were in the salon, sifting through the cocaine and hashish and varicolored capsules in a corner cabinet. "Max is a lovely host," the sleepy-eyed woman said, and asked Sabrina, "What's yours?"

Denton stepped in. "Good of you, but I'll take care of my wife." He tapped a small amount of white powder into an empty vial and pocketed it. Watching, Sabrina tried to separate this Denton from the one who lived with her in London. That one hardly took a drink, never smoked or used drugs, never looked at women as he had looked at Betsy Stuyvesant last night. On their travels she had seen hints of this other Denton; now he was in the open. Preoccupied, she followed him from the salon and along the deck to the cluster of reclining chairs and chaise longues used for sunbathing by day and for drinks and snacks at night. Alexandra was there with her husband and two other couples, all offering their beautifully tanned nude bodies to the molten Mediterranean sun.

Denton barely glanced at them. "Come on, sweets," he said, dropping his robe. Sabrina felt foolish and clumsy in her reluctance. There was only one Denton, her husband, and he was showing her how he expected his wife to behave. "Totally new experience for you," he'd said of Max's invitation. And when had she been afraid of new experiences? She looked at the magnificent women's bodies spread out before her, oiled and glistening. Hers was better. She dropped her robe and lay beside Denton, letting his large hand oil her back.

But she shook her head when he took some of the white powder on his finger and offered it to her. One thing at a time, she thought, and he did not insist. He sniffed the powder into each nostril as the others sniffed theirs or smoked hashish. The sun beat down on the quiet deck and Sabrina drifted in it until a shadow crossed her eyes. She opened them to see Max standing above her. Her muscles instinctively tightened, but he was looking past her at Alexandra. And in a long languorous movement, Alexandra stood and went with him toward the staterooms.

As if she had been waiting, Betsy took Alexandra's place. Denton watched her stretch and pat oil on her white skin. She caressed her breasts, humming to herself, then lay back and in another minute was asleep, her hands clasped as if in prayer.

He turned and found Sabrina's eyes on him. "You're right," he said, smiling indulgently. "She's like a kitten. Cuddly. But not important."

Sabrina had said Betsy was like a puppy, but she let it pass.

At lunch in the port of Alassio, Alexandra maneuvered to sit beside her. "Honey," she murmured. "Relax. You're getting yourself all upset. They make the rules; we follow them. Everything's easier when you accept that." Sabrina toyed with her appetizer, bending her head to listen. "You see your Denton thinking about spreading little Betsy's legs, or doing it, you just close your eyes and soak up the sun or learn to snort coke or go off with a good book."

"How did you know—?"

"Now, see, that's something else you have to learn. Nothing is secret on this little canoe. You can do what you want—no limits—but whatever you decide, Max will know about it almost as soon as you do."

Sabrina wrapped a slice of pink prosciutto ham around a wedge of pale green honeydew melon. "Are you really a princess?"

Alexandra laughed heartily. "That's another lesson, honey. Everything around here is only partly true. You remember that when you're watching your husband watch someone else."

In the afternoon, as the *Lafitte* sailed east, they water-skied behind the high-powered speedboat that the yacht carried in place of one of its lifeboats. Sabrina and Alexandra skied side by side, skimming the water in a blue and gold mist. Sabrina felt young and strong and beautiful. I can do anything, she thought.

On the yacht, wrapped in bath sheets and drinking wine on the sundeck, Alexandra said, "You're a hell of a skier. Where'd you learn?"

"At school in Switzerland."

"Boarding school?"

"Yes."

"The privileged life. I went to high school in Los Angeles." She laughed at Sabrina's surprise. "My mother was a two-bit actress who taught me how to move up in the world. She made me a better actress than she was. Speaking of which, you've perked up. Is that an act?"

"I don't know. I just decided, out there on the water, that I could do anything. Even live like the rest of you."

"Honey, you said that as if it were a dose of arsenic. If you think we're poison, what are you doing here?"

Sabrina shivered in the breeze and pulled the bath sheet tighter. "I didn't mean you. I like you. But I don't like watching Denton ... being expected to watch ... damn, I sound stupid, don't I?"

"Just unprepared. Didn't he tell you beforehand? Everybody knows about Max's cruises."

"I didn't. And Denton never told me."

"And he's different in London? Cozy by the fire, tucked in by ten?"

Sabrina hesitated, watching the Italian shore come into view. "No. But I always know where he is when we go out separately."

"Do you, now."

Sabrina ignored her disbelief. "The trouble is, it doesn't really matter to Denton whether I like something or not."

"It doesn't matter to any of them, honey. That's the first rule."

"So I don't know whether I have a choice."

Alexandra nodded. "You're catching on. As long as you want what they provide, you haven't got one small god-damned choice. Now go make yourself glamorous. Dinner in Genoa tonight. Wonderful food."

As if he had heard their talk, Max organized the evening to demonstrate the life he and Denton could provide. Limousines whisked them along the highway far above Genoa to a restaurant with a sweeping view of the seacoast. After a leisurely dinner served by the chef and maître d', with a small orchestra playing in the background, they drove to a private party in a glass and wood home jutting out over the ocean, where they drank smooth ruby wines and gambled until three in the morning, when they returned to the yacht. Max took Sabrina's hand as she was going to her stateroom. "You honor us by being our guest. We will have many cruises together. Pleasant dreams, my dear."

Denton was in bed, keyed up, pleased with her. "You were smashing; they all loved you. And I won at *Trente-et-Quarante;* haven't done that for a long time. Come to bed, sweets; I'm waiting."

He pulled her to him, hastily stroking her body, straining and urgent with the excitement of winning and Sabrina's shining success. "They'll be talking about us for months," he murmured with satisfaction as he climbed on top of her. He centered himself and plunged in. "Mmmmm, nice and tight," he murmured with the same satisfaction, and closed his eyes.

Sabrina lay beneath him, moving as he liked her to move. He was in a hurry, so she knew this time would be like all the others; she was partially aroused and she would end up partially satisfied, rubbed and pounded to numbness. She had tried to talk to him about their lovemaking, but he had had so many women before her, grateful women, that he considered his technique a subject for applause, not discussion. Sabrina thought of telling him that women were grateful because he allowed them to be near—in fact, underneath—the future Viscount Treveston, but she was silent. Because he really believed he wanted to make her happy. "I never enjoy sex unless my woman enjoys it, too," he told her the first time they were in bed. And he meant it. As he meant it when he said he never enjoyed parties or hunting trips unless his companions and opponents also enjoyed what he had planned for his own pleasure.

And because he was generous when he got his way, and cruelly silent if he was disappointed, almost everyone lied and told him they were happy. Everyone fakes something with Denton, Sabrina thought as she deliberately quickened her breathing, tensed her legs for a minute and then grew limp. "That's my fine girl," Denton said, his satisfaction intact. And then he plunged deeply and forcefully to achieve the final satisfaction of his day.

When Denton was asleep, she went on deck and let her thoughts float on the cool air. It was four-thirty. The yacht had slowed and was rolling slightly as it sailed west; they were returning to Monte Carlo. Sabrina heard the muffled sound of a boat with its motor cut, and then in the light from the yacht she saw Max's speedboat, piloted by his secretary, Ivan Lazlo. She watched from the darkness as he and a crew member hoisted it on the yacht, then disappeared down the forward stairs to the crew's quarters. Odd, she thought, this far from shore; where could he have been? She toyed with it a moment, then shrugged. Ivan Lazlo had nothing to do with her. Nothing about Max had anything to do with her; she just wanted the cruise to end. Two more days. She let the breeze cool her until she was sleepy and then went back to lie beside Denton and fall asleep.

The next day they slept late and had breakfast in bed. Denton kissed her and Sabrina smiled at him, cozy and warm. He smiled back. "Sweets, I'm going to spend the day with Betsy. You can do what you want, but you ought to spend some time with Aldo Derona. He's interested in you, and he's a pleasant chap—"

She flung herself from the bed, putting space between them. "I am not available for loaning out."

"Now, sweets, that's a little harsh. You can't be surprised; you've known what was going on. I waited, but you didn't say a word, you adjusted beautifully. I'm proud of you. I hardly think I deserve harsh words."

She was stunned, as helpless as if they spoke different languages. She looked at Denton: he seemed to be speeding backward, away from her, receding to a small figure in the distance. "Sabrina?" said Denton uncertainly. His amiable eyes were worried as his wife looked at him in icy silence. He held out his hands. "Sweets, you're getting too excited, as if you think I don't love you. Of course I love you, I always love you." He waited. "None of this means anything, you know; it's not important, it's a game, something we do because—well, damn it, because it's different, but actually it's not, you know, you mustn't think it's different or special, it's not, it's no different really from bridge or waterskiing or any of the friendly things we all do together. Oh, thank heavens," he added, for she had begun to laugh, shaking her head and calling him a fool, but still she was his laughing wife again. "Waterskiing," she said. "Friendly things," and repeated them, putting her hands to her forehead. And because he was Denton, he did not hear or acknowledge the despair in her laughter.

For the remainder of the cruise Sabrina avoided Denton. She never knew whether he took Betsy to bed or not. Mealtimes were peaceful, and on the last night Max led a toast to Sabrina and Denton's first anniversary, which they would celebrate in America while visiting Sabrina's sister. Denton leaned over and kissed his bride, and Sabrina thought of their being alone finally to talk and work everything out. She put her hand on the back of his head to hold the kiss, and that made it easier to ignore the lingering thought that, after all, they were still playing by Denton's rules.

Chapter 6

Stephanie handed Denton a long, two-pronged fork and asked him to check the meat. He gripped the handle as if it was his golf club and sent a frantic prayer over the heads of the other guests to Sabrina, at the far end of the backyard. But she was talking to some professor, leaving Denton with two slabs of flank steak sizzling contemptuously at him from the Weber grill. How did one check meat? He poked tentatively at the slabs, then a bit harder, gathering courage, and finally plunged the fork through the meat, all the way to the handle.

"Voila!" said Stephanie at his elbow. "I used to know fencers who had that technique."

"Have I totally destroyed it? I'll buy more at the market if—"

She laughed. "You haven't destroyed anything. And you don't have to run away; I won't ask you to work again."

"It's just that I'm not very good at it, you know."

"Lack of practice. I'll take care of it, Denton."

"Well, then, I'll just find my wife." He wandered off.

Sabrina, glancing up, thought he looked like a tourist badly in need of a toilet, searching for someone who spoke his language. Stephanie was watching him, too; she met Sabrina's eye and they smiled together.

"The differences are cultural, perceptual and situational," Professor Martin Talvia was saying, sliding the words around his pipe. "Comparing your features one by one, you and Stephanie are identical. As whole individuals reflecting singular environments, you are quite separate and your being twins teases rather than shocks."

Sabrina nodded gravely. "You might say we look different because our lives are different."

He curved forward like a crane, peering into her eyes, deep blue, shining with honesty or gentle mockery. Of course she was making fun of him, but what a delight she was. "You might say that. But if you were a professor of sociology you would be ashamed to speak so simply."

She was laughing as Denton came up. He put his arm around her shoulders and squeezed. "What's the joke, sweets?"

Sabrina's muscles tightened. The yard was full of people Denton could talk to; why did he hover and clamp her against him whenever she was having a good time? Because he's not happy, she thought, as Martin asked a question about England and Denton answered with the jovial charm that meant he was bored. He's a stranger, and suburban barbecues aren't part of his life. But she was a stranger, too, she reminded herself. She'd lived in Europe since she was two, and she'd met Stephanie and Garth's friends only briefly when their children were born. Why was she having a good time?

Because she loved meeting new people, but Denton was always bored away from his own crowd.

"Aunt Sabrina?" She looked down into the small, wise face of four-year-old Clifford Andersen. "I'm supposed to tell everyone dinner is ready."

Sabrina bent down. "An important assignment."

He nodded seriously. "That's what Mommy said. But she said to hurry, and there are too many people. So would you pick me up, and if I'm tall everybody can hear me at the same time."

Sabrina laughed and lifted him in her arms. "As practical as your father. Ready?"

He took a deep breath and in a piercing voice shouted, "Dinner's ready! On the patio!"

At his son's raucous cry, Garth looked up to see Sabrina's vivid laughing face beside Cliff's small one, red with effort and self-importance. It was a picture he remembered, of Stephanie with Cliff when he was born.

"Aunt Sabrina, why didn't you let me tell them?" came a wailing cry from the yard, and Penny Andersen flung herself with the anguish of a disappointed three-year-old on the ground at Sabrina's feet.

"Can't anyone control these children?" Denton asked. Sabrina gave him a swift look and knelt with her arms around Cliff and his sister.

"How would it be if you announce dessert?" she asked Penny. A smile broke through and the little girl nodded vigorously. "Well, then, I'm starving. Who's going to sit with me at dinner?"

"I am!" they both cried, and led her to the patio.

On the patio and the lawn, small groups sat in nylon-webbed aluminum chairs, eating marinated flank steak, potato salad and thick slices of French bread, and drinking the red wine the guests had contributed. They talked about the coming political conventions that probably would nominate Richard Nixon and Hubert Humphrey, and they discussed their children's schools, crabgrass, food prices and the university, where most of them taught.

Darkness was falling, and Garth lit kerosene lanterns. Dolores Goldner leaned toward Denton. "Stephanie's told us so much about you both, but not the little things, like what you eat at home or where you shop. We really know so little about royalty."

"The nobility," Denton said stiffly.

"Oh, of course. I'm afraid we Americans don't take the class system as seriously as you do."

"Denton," Stephanie said hastily. "Tell us about Treveston, especially the history of your family and the castle."

"Aunt Sabrina sent me a picture," Penny said.

"Me, too; I'll get it," said Cliff and jumped up, knocking his plate off his lap and scattering his dinner to left and right. "Cliff!" Stephanie called, but he dodged through the door into the house. "That's not fair!" Penny cried. "I said it first!" She scrambled to her feet, tripped over Sabrina's foot and ran after her brother.

"Penny!" Stephanie's voice rose sharply, and she clenched her hands.

Sabrina stood. "Shall I calm them down?"

"It's all right," Stephanie said. "I told them they could stay up until after dinner. It is now after dinner as far as they're concerned. Go on without me; I'll get them started on the long road to bed."

She was trembling. Sabrina watched her go into the house. "Excuse me," she said, and followed her through the kitchen door.

Stephanie was already upstairs, and she waited in the kitchen. It was a wonderful old-fashioned room with a high ceiling, maple cabinets and countertops, and a Delft chandelier suspended over a worn sofa and low coffee table where the children often played. There was a large pantry next to a breakfast room with a round maple table and chairs and a maple corner cabinet filled with dishes. The furniture had been old and scarred when Stephanie bought it and restored each piece to its silken, honey-colored finish. "I wouldn't sit anywhere else," Sabrina said when she first saw the breakfast room. "I don't," Stephanie answered. "At least, this is where I sit when I have time to sit."

Sabrina was standing beside the round table when Stephanie came downstairs. She watched her stop in the kitchen to put something in the refrigerator and thought again, with the surprise she had felt when they arrived the week before, that she was not taking care of herself. She was heavier and had a faded look, the edges of her beauty smudged and dulled. Sabrina, slender and vivid in a red Italian peasant skirt and soft white blouse with full pleated sleeves, knew she was outshining her sister, but Stephanie seemed unaware of it. Or unconcerned. In her own home, with family and friends, what was most important to Stephanie?

"Can we sit for a minute?" Sabrina asked. "I could easily miss another rendition of Treveston history. I'll tell it to you if you like."

Stephanie sat down with a little smile. "Denton's mother told me at your wedding. I thought Denton would like a chance—"

"To have people listen to him."

"He does like it, doesn't he?"

"He does like it." They smiled together. Sabrina reached out her hand and Stephanie clasped it. "I'm sorry it took us a whole year to get here. I had a terrible time getting Denton to give up his international playgrounds for a week in an American suburb."

"And now that he's here, he's bored."

"Don't blame yourself, Stephanie. It's not your fault."

"Garth took him through the lab, but—"

"No, science isn't Denton's thing. He likes other kinds of experiments." Stephanie looked quizzical at the bitter twist in Sabrina's voice, but Sabrina went on. "Anyway, being apart isn't as bad as it used to be. Do you feel that? Just knowing we can write or call and understand each other after all those years when it seemed we couldn't—" She gave herself a little shake. "Tell me about you. Is there anything you haven't told me? About you and Garth? And the kids?"

"Nothing important. I've got what I always wanted, a home and a family. Permanence. When did we ever have that for more than the blink of an eye?" They laughed softly, thinking back. "Are *you* all right? I've felt all week that something was wrong."

"Oh, there was something, on the cruise, and we haven't talked about it yet. Denton overloads the schedule and we never have time to talk. I'll work it out. You were pretty upset just now with the kids."

"Was I awfully shrill? I wish I didn't get so excited. But Garth works day and night in the lab, and I'm alone with them so much my patience wears out. I didn't want them ruining the party for you."

"How could they ruin it? I'm having a wonderful time. I teased Martin about his awful academic sentences."

"They are awful, aren't they?"

"Yes, but funny. I like your friends."

"I'll trade them for your castle and that yacht you've been on."

"Stephanie, you don't mean that."

"No, of course not. I wouldn't know what to do with your life; it's so unreal to me. And I have everything I want. Except money; I do get tired of scrimping. No," she said quickly, seeing Sabrina's face. "You can't help us; Garth would be hurt. Anyway, the real problem is that he's not here, helping me. But that's not fair; he works so hard and everything really is fine. I don't know what's wrong with me tonight."

My red skirt, Sabrina thought; cruises you don't know anything about; my letters to you from fourteen countries in the last year; the issue of *Town and Country* on your night table that says Denton spends a hundred thousand dollars a year on clothes for each of us and that I spent half a million dollars furnishing our London house.

But she said none of that aloud. Instead, she let Stephanie know that she understood by saying lightly, "It's the strain of having Denton as a houseguest. He simply can't remember he has no servants at his beck and call. It's in his genes; I think Garth should study him. I made him hang up his towels this morning, and he called me a revolutionary out to overthrow the nobility."

Stephanie smiled. "Most of the time he's charming. And he takes care of you; you look marvelous."

"The Mediterranean sun. You could use some."

"I know. And I should lose weight. Maybe this summer. Is the sun the only reason you look beautiful and glamorous and happy?"

Sabrina looked thoughtfully at their clasped hands. "Do you know, in the last year I have met about nine thousand people, give or take a thousand, and haven't had a personal conversation with one of them?" Except, oddly enough, she thought, Alexandra, but she couldn't talk about Alexandra or the cruise to anyone, not even Stephanie. She was ashamed of it, as if she were to blame for the guests and their games. "I'm not used to talking about whether I'm happy."

"But you aren't talking. You're evading."

"I know." She sighed. "Remember once I told you I couldn't tell the difference between love and excitement with Denton? I still can't. And I have trouble talking about it." Because you love your husband, she added silently, and you have a place where you belong. And I can't admit that I envy you. I've only been married a year. I have to try harder. Maybe next year will be different. "But when I'm ready to talk, the best thing in the world is knowing you're here."

Stephanie's eyes were bright. "It is the best thing." She stood up and peered at her image in the darkened window, combing her hair with her fingers. "Time to hostess again, Sabrina," she said, leaning down to kiss the top of her sister's head. "I'm glad we're back."

Voices murmured on the patio; lanterns flickered over shadowed faces, red wine and black coffee, climbing roses and beds of snapdragons. Sabrina felt she was on a quiet island: a loving, relaxed, uncomplicated life. I have to remember it, she thought, until I come home again. And it did not seem at all strange that she called it home.

At midnight, Stephanie saw the last guest out. She came back to the jumble of food and dishes on the patio and shook her head wryly. "Does anyone know the magic words for making elves appear?"

"Those are the words," Sabrina said. "And we are your elves. Denton and I will clean up."

At the expression on Denton's face, Garth grinned. "There sits a terrified man. Don't worry, Denton; you're unskilled labor. I'll do it."

"Not by yourself." Sabrina began to stack plates. "I have to do something useful."

"You're unskilled, too," Garth said.

Stephanie stifled a yawn. "Well, I'm not. I can do it twice as fast as both of you. Anyway, Sabrina's a guest. Everybody go to bed."

Sabrina kissed Stephanie on the cheek and gently pushed her toward the door. "You worked all day; Garth and I will finish up. Go on. You can criticize our efficiency tomorrow. If you have the courage."

Denton watched with calm interest as Sabrina and Garth silently scraped plates and piled them on trays. He stepped lightly forward and kissed Sabrina's forehead. "I'll wait for you upstairs, sweets." She nodded, absorbed in stacking cups.

Garth eyed the pile appraisingly. "Risky."

She ignored him and lifted the tray. At the kitchen door the tall stack bulged in the middle and the cups toppled, shattering on the flagstone patio. Sabrina bit her lip and walked into the kitchen to find a broom. Garth followed with his tray of dishes and returned with a dustpan. They swept up the pieces in silence.

In the kitchen, Sabrina ran water in the sink. "I proved your point, didn't I? Unskilled labor."

"It was an unkind remark. I apologize."

"Why? You don't approve of me—of either of us, in fact. I've watched your face when we talk about our travels—"

"My fatal flaw. A wide-open face." He picked up a clean towel. "Sabrina, it isn't that I don't approve. I don't understand you. Your way of life, the things of your life, what you're looking for. They're so different from mine that I can't make

74

sense of them. That is, no doubt, another flaw in my character."

Sabrina moved her hands in the warm soapy water, remembering student days in a tiny apartment near the Sorbonne and working days in London before she married Denton. She hadn't washed a dish since then. She and Garth worked quietly, their voices low. Behind them, the honey-colored kitchen was in shadows and the house was dark and silent. She felt peaceful. "How do you know so much about our life?" she asked.

"Full reports from Stephanie, describing everything in rich detail. The key word there is rich. Let me ask you something." He dried a platter with careful attention. "Is Stephanie unhappy because I spend so much time at the lab, or because I don't give her your kind of life?"

"But she isn't unhappy, you're wrong—"

"I don't think so. Look, I'm asking for help. You know Stephanie better than anyone else. You'd know her real feelings—" He saw her face change. "I'm not asking you to betray any secrets, you know. I'm her husband. I love her. All right. We'll forget you're her twin. How about this? Pretend you're a scientist looking for explanations. The fact is: Stephanie is unhappy. What's the explanation?"

"Your work."

He picked up another platter. "Three in a row. You, Nat Goldner and Marty Talvia. They scold me regularly. I know it's hard on Stephanie; every day I vow to reform. But then the questions pull me back, the mysteries, the fascination—" He stopped. "Sorry; you wouldn't understand."

Sabrina let it pass. "You're a lucky man."

"Because of Stephanie? You don't have to tell me—"

"No. Well, of course because of Stephanie, but I meant—you have good friends who help you know who you are."

Intrigued, Garth stopped drying. Sabrina gazed unseeingly at the dark window. "Denton chases himself around the world to find out who he is, and he can't do it. Or even admit he's trying. People fawn over him because he's heir to Treveston, but a lot of them don't like him and he doesn't know why. He's bored a lot and he doesn't know why that is, either. He just escalates his fun. He won't listen to me because when I don't like something he does he says I'm unsympathetic. But if he had friends he might see himself through their eyes, what kind of a person he is, what he wants to do with his life. The way you do. That's what close friends do, isn't it? They value you and care about who you are instead of what you are. They help you discover your own worth."

His face was startled. "Well said."

She submerged a frying pan. "How nice that I've impressed you."

"I'm sorry. I didn't mean to insult you. But how did I know you have a head full of ideas? Your husband doesn't, and in your kind of life—"

"Why do you keep talking about our kind of life? You've already admitted you can't make sense of it. Parts of it are wonderful."

"And the other parts?"

"Some things we'll change. That happens in any marriage." Who am I, she thought, to lecture on marriage? "We won't keep running around the world forever; when we have children we'll stay at home in London. I want to meet different people, and work with art and antiques; I've been asked to help organize a new museum of primitive art ... so many things I want to do. And I want to entertain. You wait; we'll invite you and Stephanie and the kids to a barbecue on our terrace."

Garth smiled absently. "Sabrina, I don't think you should count too heavily on Denton's settling down."

She let the water out of the sink. "Why not?"

"Because I don't think he can."

"What are you talking about? You don't know Denton—"

"I know him better than you think; I've been his host for a week, remember? And the kind of life he makes you lead—"

"Oh, don't be so stuffy!" She stood with her back to the sink and glared at him. How dare he pass judgment on her! He was so solemn—no spark, no fire, and he didn't know how to laugh. He had a wonderful face, strong and sure, with warm deep eyes, but still he was dull. And smug. A smug, narrow-minded professor. "What makes you think I'm suffering? I have the most wonderful life in the world. You seem to have trouble understanding it, in your sterile laboratory, but to me it's exciting. It has crowds of people and new cities and scenery, parties, dances, different kinds of food, wonderful shops and markets, new clothes, books from all over the world, theaters—"

"Stop! You've convinced me. Sabrina, I admire you. I'm sorry I was stuffy and tried to knock down your castle."

She gave him a quick look before turning back to wipe the counter. "But you still don't think Denton is about to settle down."

Garth folded his arms and leaned against the refrigerator. "Sabrina, has Denton ever told you he thinks perfecting a life of pleasure is an art?"

"Oh, he talks like that—"

"An art that requires full-time attention, and as much involvement and careful planning as any job. If you pin him down, he'll say it *is* a job. Few men give up a job for a family. I don't think Denton is one of them. Many men assume their job comes before their families. I think Denton is one of them."

The room was silent, broken only by the soft swish of Sabrina's cloth as she wiped out the sink and polished the faucet. "You're wrong."

"I hope I am."

He hung up his towels. Sabrina's eyes were dark. These were the doubts she couldn't talk about to Stephanie, doubts she'd thought were locked within her. And now they'd been put into words by the unlikeliest person, one who had never seemed interested in her or Denton.

Garth went into the pantry to turn out the light. When he came back she asked, "Do you mean he might want to give it up but something keeps him from it?" Garth nodded. "Well, what something is it?"

"I'd call it passion."

"Oh, for heaven's sake, Garth, Denton isn't passionate about anything." She caught her breath. Now she'd given that away, too.

"Except his pleasure," Garth said. "His way of life. That's his passion. And he's consumed by it. I suppose he could conquer it, but it would be a struggle. Denton doesn't strike me as a man who welcomes struggle."

"Is that a scientific guess?"

"It's more than that." His voice roughened. "I looked at his eyes. There are many kinds of passion, Sabrina, but they recognize each other. Denton's eyes have the same look I see every time I look in my mirror. I knew it as soon as I saw him. Odd, but he's a kindred spirit."

Sabrina heard the painful honesty in his voice and thought of the glittering fixedness of Denton's eyes that she had tried to call eagerness. She turned her wedding ring on her finger, the circle of diamonds catching the light and throwing it back in flashes of color. "Thank you," she said quietly, and smiled. "I apologize for calling you dull. You're not."

"You called me stuffy. Dull, too?"

A laugh escaped her. "If I can't remember my insults, I shouldn't use them. I apologize for all my unkind words. You're not dull and you're not stuffy."

"And you're not empty-headed or unskilled."

They laughed.

"Shall I turn out this light?"

"I'll do it after I lock up. Good night, Sabrina."

"Good night, Garth."

She walked from the warm kitchen through the dark dining room and living room, feeling her way around the furniture. At the foot of the stairs she turned and looked down the length of the house to the lighted kitchen. His head bent in thought, Garth was at the back door, making his house secure for the night. Then he put his hand to the switch, and, as the room went dark, Sabrina slowly climbed the stairs to go to bed.

In the empty storefront, stripped to its bare walls, Sabrina held open the door as the carpenters carried in stacks of lumber. Her life had been stripped as clean as this empty space she was renting—and I'll build them both up together, she thought, smiling to herself at the idea. Fresh and new after I failed with Denton.

At the back of the shop, where the carpenters had set up their sawhorse, Laura was examining blueprints. Sabrina stood at the front door, watching rain beat down on the high black taxicabs crowding Brompton Road. Three years. That's all we could make it last. And then it took me another year to discover that nothing would ever be the same again.

"My lady," a carpenter called, his voice echoing off the walls. As Sabrina walked back to him, he drew a chalk line on the dusty floor. "Is this where you want the door, my lady?"

"That's fine," she said, and smiled ruefully at her mother. "I feel like an impostor; it isn't my title anymore."

"Oh, use it," said Laura. "It will help you. Even Americans love to roll titles on their tongues. Last month I gave a talk in a high school and someone called me Mrs. Madame Under Secretary of State."

"Much more impressive than mine."

"But yours is legitimate. Does Denton want you back?"

"I don't know. What difference does it make?"

"I thought you might be lonely."

"Oh." Sabrina picked up a blueprint and pretended to study it. Of course she was lonely. Lonely and scared. But she'd been that way for a whole year, beginning when she left Denton.

She had moved into a small ground-floor flat, seeing no one except when she was at work in Nicholas Blackford's antique gallery, where she had worked before her marriage. For six months she lived alone, besieged with telephone calls from Denton, his family, her parents, all telling her what a fool she was. Gabrielle called from Paris.

"Sabrina, he'll settle down now that his father's dead and he has the title and the estate."

"His father died a year ago," she said. "And he's still the same."

Other friends called. "He adores you, Sabrina. His playing around is just working off excess energy. He'll get over it. How many men adore their wives? You don't know how lucky you are."

I'm tired of his excess energy, she thought. I'm tired of living on a roller coaster with nothing solid beneath it. I want a home, children, a place to belong. But all she said was, "There are things I want to do with my life, and there's no room for them on Denton's social calendar."

Stephanie called. "Do you want me to come to London?"

"Not now," Sabrina said. "It's scary but manageable. I'll let you know. And Mother said she might come. Isn't that amazing?"

Laura had come, stayed awhile and returned to Washington. In November Sabrina and Denton had agreed on a settlement, and she had moved back to the house on Cadogan Square that she had restored and decorated with such excitement when they were married. Now it was hers. And then, from November to April, one whole London season, she had not seen or heard from anyone in Denton's circle—her circle, she once thought. She spent long hours working in Nicholas Blackford's shop and long nights alone in her exquisite, empty house. London had become cold and foreign; she had no one to talk to. Except Stephanie. But talking to Stephanie had become a luxury because she was worried about money: for upkeep on the house, for the shop she was planning to open, for living from day to day until the shop began to support her.

Yes, Mother, she thought, I have considered going back to Denton. To the protection of his family, to his circle. These days I never know what lies ahead. At least with Denton I always knew what he had planned. I even knew, most of the time, whom he was sleeping with.

"When you were here last winter," she said aloud, "before the property settlement, I felt like I was twelve years old, wanting to go shopping with you and Stephanie."

"You didn't tell me that."

"I know. If I'd talked about it I might have curled up on your lap and asked to be comforted. Wouldn't that have been awkward?"

"My lady, excuse me," said the carpenter. "Are the plans correct, that this wall is not to reach the ceiling?"

"Yes," Sabrina answered, looking at the blueprint he held. "But you'll hear sounds from the showroom even if you close your office door."

"I hope the sounds are customers and I hope very much to hear them."

"Ah. Of course. I hope so, too, my lady."

"Why would it have been awkward?" Laura asked.

"Because you never let me sit on your lap when I was a child. Why start now, when I'm grown up and can take care of myself?"

There was a long silence. Sabrina glanced at the lines in her mother's face and wished she had not spoken. Why recall the past when they were learning to be friends in the present? Laura was as proud and beautiful as ever, and Sabrina was happy with her—a beautiful woman with her beautiful mother. It was another step in growing up.

She broke the silence. "What do you think I should do with the new wall? Shelves or paintings?"

"Oh—perhaps both? Paintings mounted here and shelves in the corner? And maybe an easel or two in front, for other paintings."

"Easels. A marvelous idea. On a small rug. If the budget allows."

"Sabrina, why didn't you demand more money from Denton? By the time you finish here, you won't have much left."

"Enough for about six months if I'm careful. I couldn't ask him for more. He told me so often I belonged to him that I wanted to snap my fingers and walk away. Dramatic but not very practical. So I took just what I thought would get me started. You mustn't worry, Mother. I've given free decorating advice to Denton's friends and relatives for years; they know what I can do. How can I be anything but a smashing success?"

If they come, she thought. She hadn't told Laura she'd been ignored for six months; she was ashamed of it, as if somehow it was her fault. And she didn't want Laura worrying over her. I'll make them come, she vowed.

"Of course you'll be a success," Laura agreed. She ran her hand over the paneled wall. "Do you know, this was always my dream? A shop of my own, instead of picking things up on the fly."

"But you can have one now. You're in Washington for good."

"Oh, it's too late. I can't start from scratch; I haven't got your energy. I must have lost it somewhere between embassies. I'll just help now and then with Ambassadors. I was touched that you chose that name."

Sabrina put her arm around her mother and they watched the carpenters put up the office wall at the rear of the shop. The showroom was long and narrow, fronted with a square, paned window. The walls had dark oak wainscoting; the ceiling was molded in plaster octagons. Sabrina felt a shiver of delight and astonishment every time she walked in the door—that it was hers, that she was turning her dreams into reality, fitting her life to her own patterns and rhythms. I've never done that, she thought. I went from my parents to Juliette to the university to working for Nicholas and then to Denton. I've never made my own rules. Impulsively she spread her arms wide. "Isn't it wonderful!" she cried.

Laura smiled, and Sabrina again put her arm around her shoulders. It felt good to both of them. We need more touching, Sabrina thought, as we get older. And more love: giving it and finding it. "Mother, thank you for coming. You've made it more exciting. And less frightening."

"Thank you for asking me," Laura said. "Giving me a chance, after all these years, to make a shop. I guess if we wait long enough, we get most of the things we want. Sabrina, why don't you move to America? We would all be so glad. There's nothing keeping you in London."

"Yes, there is. Right now it's my home. And I know it better than any other city. The wealthy people, the markets, the competition. And the old people. Especially the sick ones. The ghoulish truth is that the only way to grab the best antiques and art is to know who's dying so you can have cash ready when their estates are auctioned. And I have friends in London."

"You have a sister and parents in America."

"Mother, please understand. I love all of you, and I miss you, but this is where I failed with Denton and this is where I have to succeed on my own. I want to find out what I can make of myself. Can't you understand that?"

"Yes," said Laura. She paused. "I think I may be envious." And, for the first time since Sabrina was fifteen and leaving home for boarding school, she put both arms around her daughter and kissed her. "I am so proud of you," she said. "And I love you."

Chapter 7

Lady Andrea Vernon had made Alderley House famous for its grand balls and when Sabrina stood in the doorway beside Nicholas and Amelia Blackford, she drank in the light and color and music as if she could never get enough. When a tanned young man with a lean face asked her to dance and they swept down the length of the wine and gold room, she felt young and carefree for the first time in months. Her taffeta gown swirled in an amber cloud as she turned and turned to the music, looking about her at the ballroom. It had been redecorated in the year since she had seen it last, and she admired the restoration of the gilded ceiling. But she stared in disbelief at the hundreds of light fixtures on the walls; they resembled the veined noses of alcoholics. Where in heaven's name had Andrea's designer dug them up? She shook her head, her fingers itching to sweep the walls bare and decorate them with a simple elegance to match the ceiling. "You don't agree?" the young man asked.

"Oh, forgive me, I was daydreaming. What did you say?"

She listened while he spoke, and listened to the man who cut in on him, but her thoughts kept drifting to Andrea Vernon's walls and other walls, other rooms she had thought once she would be called on to decorate.

83

"I heard someone say you'd opened a shop," her partner was saying. "What do you call it?"

"Ambassadors," she said.

"Good name," he said casually. "Doing well?"

"Doing well?" She steadied her voice. "Of course."

"Good," he said, and she knew he had not really listened to her, or he was ignoring the trembling in her voice to avoid asking if she was having problems. No one at a ball wanted to hear that a beautiful young woman had problems.

The truth was, no one anywhere wanted to hear; so no one did. Sabrina kept to herself the fact that her shop had no customers.

All around her were the aristocracy and business elite she had counted on. Once they had been her friends. She had gambled on that friendship. But in eight months, she had been proven wrong again and again. No one had come.

She had sent announcements to everyone she knew. Nicholas had said to watch especially for Olivia Chasson. "Where she goes, others follow. If you get her favor, you have nothing to worry about." Each day, eagerly, excitedly, Sabrina unlocked the shop door and waited in her office for Olivia Chasson and her friends to walk into the tapestry-hung room she and Laura had designed after the eighteenth-century salons of the great homes and castles of England. The eagerness and excitement faded; the feeling of adventure disappeared while she waited for the noise the carpenter had said she would hear from the showroom. Oh, for some noise, she prayed day after silent day, even the tiniest noise, like the tiptoe of a cautious duke. But only a few tourists came, wandering in off the street to browse but seldom to buy.

By now her money was gone. She had borrowed from the bank, and soon she would have to mortgage her house. After that . . . But she refused to think of that.

"Dinner," said her partner, who had been describing his polo game. "Shall we have something?"

They filled their plates at the buffet and sat on a couch in an alcove of drapes. They ate in silence. Sabrina wished for Stephanie. She wished for a friend to break up the long days and evenings and laugh with her and sometimes let her cry. She even wished for a few of the invitations she'd turned down when she was Denton's wife.

"But if she married Denton for his money," a woman's

voice said on the other side of the drapery, "why didn't she take a bigger settlement?"

Sabrina grew very still. When her partner began to speak, she put her finger to her lips.

A second voice answered, high and indignant. "How do you know what she took? Denton is too much of a gentleman to talk, but I know for a fact she demanded three million pounds and Treveston and the new yacht. Her own solicitor said that was outrageous. But you know how Denton adored her, so of course she got a fortune. He'd have given her everything he owned."

"Except Treveston," the first voice said dryly. It was puzzlingly familiar, but Sabrina could not place it.

"Well, my dear, he couldn't give away a national treasure like Treveston. You do know that she grabbed the London house."

"My sweet ballroom gossip," said a man's voice, joining them. "May I guess the subject of your sharp tongue? Could it be the beautiful Lady Sabrina Longworth, or have I stabbed more completely in the dark than you have stabbed her in the back?"

"Peter, that is grossly unfair," said the indignant voice. "We were simply discussing the settlement poor Denton had to make."

"Poor Denton," the first voice coolly mimicked, "gave up so little he probably charged it off to 'miscellaneous.' Sabrina didn't make a dent in his playtime."

"Then how did she get that shop on Brompton Road?" demanded the indignant voice. "I walked past it the other day, and she has an armoire in the window that I know for a fact is worth two thousand pounds at the very least."

"Rose! You walked past and didn't go in?"

"My sweet Rose wouldn't go in," the man's voice said, "unless everyone did. And the pack has decided Sabrina is a pariah, all of you who cozied up to her when she was Denton's wife—"

"Peter, don't be crude. If you looked past her face you'd know why she married Denton. She didn't even try to disguise it; she deserted him less than a year after his father died and he became viscount. But Americans are always obvious, aren't they?"

Sabrina sat rigidly in the corner of the couch, her eyes

lowered, as she tried to think about what she was going to do, tomorrow and the day after and the day after that.

She heard a chair scrape and the first voice came from a different location. "She's never played by your rules and you've never forgiven her. I think I may do something about that."

Sabrina tilted her head. She knew who the voice reminded her of: someone who'd told her long ago that she had to play by 'their' rules.

Her partner touched her arm. "Would you like me to take you home?"

She looked up, her eyes very bright. "That doesn't seem like a good idea." Her voice became stronger. "I think I'd like to dance some more." And think of how I'll fight them, she thought, now that I know what is happening. Why didn't I figure it out long ago?

His eyes admired her. "Brave lady. They're a bit vulgar, the Raddisons, especially Rose, but—"

"Well, now, fancy meeting you here, isn't life curious," said the cool voice that had been behind the drapery, and Sabrina turned to meet the lazy smile of Princess Alexandra Martova. "Will your friend forgive us?" asked the princess. "I'm about to take you under my wing."

Alexandra Martova was the owner of four floors of chic rubble. She had come to London alone, with nothing in the world but the proceeds from her divorce: a Swiss bank account, a house on the island of Minorca off the Spanish coast, an apartment in Paris, alimony of ten thousand dollars a month and a Great Dane she called Maxim, after an old friend. Tall, willowy, with light blue eyes turning up at the corners and blond hair falling sleekly to her shoulders, she had a decisive air she had not had when Sabrina met her on Max Stuyvesant's yacht. "I decided to make my own rules," she told Sabrina. "Looks like you did the same." She had come to London because she was bored. "Nobody knows how to give a good party. So I decided to show them how it's done. Honey, I am about to become the most famous hostess in Europe."

But first she needed a house. She found one in Belgravia, tall and narrow with high windows, like a Victorian lady with eyebrows raised in surprise. It had a red door with a lion's-head knocker. Alexandra loved the outside but hated the dim, cramped interior, so she had everything ripped out, leaving only the shell. "I want you to redo it for me," she said to Sabrina. "Top to bottom. Have some more wine."

She blew plaster dust from the bottle and refilled the cut-crystal glasses she had brought in a picnic basket. Sabrina sat on a packing crate, sipping the light fruity Beaujolais and surveying the rubble-strewn expanse that was Alexandra's second floor. With the interior walls gone, she had a straight view from front to back. All that remained of the original rooms was a marble fireplace with a chipped mantel. Streaks of sunlight, dancing with dust, cut across exposed beams and fragments of wood and marble that reminded Sabrina of the antiques her mother once bought, knowing they would shine with beauty when she polished them. Sabrina felt the same tingling desire she had had in those days when she watched her mother's sure hands with awe and envy. I can make this beautiful, she thought. Eyes shining, she turned to Alexandra. "Thank you."

Alexandra raised her glass. "I'm planning on us helping each other. You need a commission, but I need more: a house and respectability. I know everybody in London town, but, sad to say, they know me, too. After all those years and all those beds in Monte Carlo and points west, being a princess is not enough. I need to be launched, is what I need."

Sabrina shook her head ruefully. "I'm not the one to launch anybody. You ought to know that, after last night."

"Honey, you've learned more than that since you were tagging along behind Denton; you're just shook up by that little eavesdropping and you're not thinking straight. Now, you sit there and listen to me while I lecture at you. You are going to launch me as soon as I launch you. Didn't you hear me say I was taking you under my wing? You will do my house. We will present it to society with a grand party. And it will be such a sensation that within a week people will be saying that if Lady Sabrina Longworth won't lower herself to be your design consultant, you are nobody. And that will include the high and mighty Olivia Chasson."

Alexandra drained her glass and strode about the room, leaving footprints on the dusty floor as she skirted piles of plaster and wood. "And when your rocket goes off, mine does, too, right into respectable society, which by then is snuggling up to you again. Because I'll tell you, Sabrina, what you don't seem to understand is that people have always raved about you. You're absolutely gorgeous—more than me, which I'd never admit to anybody else—you're fun and nobody can predict what you're going to say or do. There's never been a breath of scandal about you and people who hate each other love you. Do you know when I started hearing about you? Right after you were married. Wherever I went—Rio, Cannes, Majorca—people talked about you. For a whole year I kept waiting to meet you so I could kill you. Then on Max's little boat you were so damned innocent and unhappy I couldn't believe it, and then I started to like you. Craziest thing."

She sat down on her crate and stretched her long legs. "Look, the only reason they're mad at you now is that nobody knows why you and Denton split and what you took him for. You ought to tell them—don't shake your head like that, I'm only saying I think you should. What they believe is that you appeared from nowhere and married one of them and took him for his title and God-knows-how-much money, and then opened a fancy shop as a hobby subsidized by poor Denton; and poor Denton is talking about his broken heart in every bed he can find his way into. I know what you got because it so happens you and I used the same solicitor for our divorces, and he was moaning about how much you gave up. It's your story, I'm not telling anybody, but most of them are waiting for you to prove them wrong because they're crazy about you. Sabrina, listen."

Alexandra poured the rest of the wine into their glasses. The sunlight had faded into late afternoon, and in the pale gray chill she looked like a marble statue. "You are the perfect person for me. You have class and style and independence. I give you this house to design; you stand at my side when I give my first party in it. What do you say?"

Sabrina had a faraway look. She had heard everything Alexandra said, but at the same time she was miles ahead, already designing the house, estimating dimensions and wall locations, furniture styles and arrangements, art works, draperies, rugs. She couldn't wait to begin. But she had to be sure of one thing. "Carte blanche?" she asked calmly.

Alexandra's eyebrows shot up in mock surprise. "Ho, what have we here?"

The grateful Sabrina of a few minutes before was gone; so was the bewildered one of last night. This Sabrina, professional and self-assured, looked beyond Alexandra at the shell of the house and asked, "How much are you willing to spend?"

"Whatever it takes to do it right."

Sabrina nodded. "Tell me the effect you want and I'll create it."

"Yes, ma'am." Alexandra grinned in admiration. "At your service, ma'am." They laughed and lightly touched glasses before drinking the last of the wine. "When can you start?" Alexandra asked.

Sabrina slipped into her coat. "I already have," she said.

They met for lunch and dinner and so many hours of talk that Alexandra finally moved from her suite at the Connaught Hotel into one of Sabrina's guest rooms. They talked about Alexandra, and as they talked Sabrina sketched rooms that would fit themselves to her. She hired the contractor who had remodeled Ambassadors to supervise the electricians and plumbers and plasterers. Specialists installed the intricate parquet floors she designed. In a few weeks the furnishings arrived: an eclectic unorthodox mixture far more daring than Alexandra realized.

There were neo-Rococo pieces from the 1850s in flowing curves and curlicues with mother-of-pearl inlays, gilt and painted flowers on a black lacquer background. This was the willowy, frivolous Alexandra of jewelry and parties. Sabrina alternated them with George Jack furniture from the 1890s: deceptively simple chests with inlaid designs of sycamore and other woods shading into each other. This was the Alexandra who talked wistfully of the "someday" when she could drop the act she put on for everyone, including herself. And finally Sabrina added a few striking modern Soriana chaises and ottomans by Scarpa: flat to the floor, made of soft leather squished into shape by chrome-plated steel tubing. "The Alexandra who is soft and hard at once," she said as the last chaise was moved into place. "Calculating and loving, earthy, sexy, holding back, but oh-so-comfortable once she relaxes with you."

Alexandra whirled through the rooms, up and down the stairs, touching and sitting and leaping up to run again. "I love it, I love it, I want to move in, I want to have a party. Can I move in today?"

Ceremoniously, Sabrina handed her the key she had been

using for four months and the guest list for the party she had drawn up the night before. The next day they began to plan Alexandra's launching.

It was a May Day ball, beginning at 10:00 P.M. on the first of May and ending with breakfast on the morning of the second. It was also the triumph of the 1976 season, the only social event given equal coverage on the society and architecture/home-furnishings pages of newspapers and international magazines.

"The educated eye finds the Martova house outrageous and chaotic," wrote Europe's most influential interior-design critic. "But only at first. In its remarkable ambiance, the eye soon discovers a design refreshing, enchanting, and uniquely the mark of a strong individual who knows herself and her client."

"As for the ball itself," wrote a society reporter whose story wound around photographs of the more prominent of the two hundred guests, "the orchestra was delightful, as were the love songs of the costumed singers and dancers in the salon. The clothes worn by the women were a galaxy of the world's great designers, and the tables were never empty of exotic food. Princess Alexandra was a statuesque goddess all in white with a necklace of emeralds. The star of the evening was Lady Sabrina Longworth, stunning in cloth of gold, a favorite of London society ever since her marriage to her former husband, Lord Denton Longworth, Viscount Treveston (who was not at the ball). Lady Longworth was responsible for the brilliant design of the princess' Belgravia abode. Among the guests were Peter and Rose Raddison of the automobile Raddisons, Lady Olivia Chasson and Gabrielle de Martel, daughter of the finance minister of France, who says she soon will be looking for her own London flat."

Sabrina moved from room to room in the house she had created. She forgot the reporters and barely noticed the guests clamoring to congratulate her on her design. She heard eager voices talk about "getting together soon" and knew that the evening was a triumph, but she moved on, not wanting to talk, just looking at the house, alive with light and talk and laughter, exactly as she had envisioned it. She had designed other places—the house Denton bought her on Cadogan Square, and Ambassadors—but they were done to her own desires. This was the first time she had created for someone else a place to live and love and grow.

DECEPTIONS

Stephanie would be proud of her, she thought; that afternoon she had sent her photographs of each room. One of them, a close-up, showed a small, personal touch, a gesture she could not resist. In a dim corner of the first-floor salon, she had lifted out five tiny sections of the parquet floor and replaced them in a new arrangement, a distinctive *S*, the only one in the house. No one would ever notice. But she had left her mark.

Sunday was a day of recovery. And on Monday morning, as she dusted the furniture in the showroom, Sabrina heard the small oriental chime that rang when the front door was opened. She looked up and then moved forward with a smile to welcome Lady Olivia Chasson to Ambassadors.

Chapter 8

Sabrina and Stephanie stood together on Cadogan Square in the chill October morning, near the end of a long row of five-story red brick Victorian mansions. Across the street was a locked park belonging to the owners of the mansions overlooking it. Sabrina's was one of them, embellished, like the others, with Gothic turrets and gables, balconies, pavilion roofs and pointed stained-glass windows.

Mrs. Thirkell took Stephanie's suitcases upstairs. "Do you want the grand tour now?" Sabrina asked, and Stephanie nodded, already feeling the cool elegance wrap itself about her as they walked through the ground-floor reception hall, dining room and kitchen. The drawing room took up the second floor; on the third floor a study and billiard room were separated by a bookshelf wall that swung open to make one large room; the bedrooms were on the fourth floor. Stephanie lingered in each room, in the harmonious balance Sabrina had achieved between sunlight and shadow, soft hues and brilliant colors, loose weaves, shimmering silks and sensual velvets, polished woods, muted wallpaper and glowing veined marble. "I could live here," she sighed. "My fantasy house come to life."

On the fourth floor she looked into Sabrina's bedroom suite, brown and gold when Denton was there, now peacock and ivory, and the two guest rooms. "Choose yours," Sabrina said, and Stephanie walked unhesitatingly into a room that was a spring garden in pale pinks and greens.

"The fifth floor is Mrs. Thirkell's apartment, and storage," Sabrina said, helping Stephanie unpack. "Now, how about lunch? It's so wonderful that you're here at last . . . what is it? What's wrong?"

Stephanie was standing before the tall pier glass, shocks of dismay running through her as she watched Sabrina bend and move. Once she had looked like that. But no longer. "Not even nicely rounded," she said with desperate honesty. "Just plain dumpy. And stoop-shouldered. At Juliette they'd say I don't look like a lady. And they'd be right. But they never taught me how to stand straight while I'm scrubbing floors or watching for stray crayons and hockey pucks that could kill me if I tripped over them." But there were other things, too. "My hair," she said mournfully. "My nails, my hands . . . well, I don't have the time you have to soak and steam in beauty salons."

It wasn't fair and she knew it. For three years, ever since designing Alexandra Martova's house, Sabrina had worked harder than anyone Stephanie knew, managing Ambassadors, buying at auctions all over Europe, visiting estates to design new rooms, even flying to New York, where Stephanie had met her twice for brief visits while she was buying for clients. And through it all she stayed vibrant and lovely while Stephanie, at home in Evanston, grew faded and worn.

Sabrina put her arm around her. "Can't you take some time? Don't you and Garth play tennis any more?"

"Not for ages. He used to ask, but I was always busy in the house or with the kids, so finally he got up some regular games with friends."

They were silent, looking at their images. "How did it happen so suddenly?" Sabrina asked.

"It wasn't sudden. It's been downhill since I saw you last year."

"But you didn't tell me you were having a bad year."

"I didn't know what to say." Her world had seemed so precarious; she had been afraid that if she talked about it, everything would collapse. Penny and Cliff were growing up and she hardly saw them; Garth was deep in his work. She had started her own business, organizing estate sales in the North

Shore suburbs. For awhile it had grown so fast she could barely keep up with it, but then it slowed down, and she didn't know why.

"How's the estate business?" Sabrina asked, and Stephanie jumped. "I was just thinking . . . not as good as it was." She turned to finish unpacking, and Sabrina sat on the arm of a chair.

"But you're good. You know what you're doing."

"With everything in a house except the people who live there. I keep thinking how good you'd be, telling Mrs. Somebody her soup ladle isn't Georgian, it's early Woolworth, and you're tagging it at one-ninety-five instead of a hundred and a quarter. Have I time to change before lunch?" Sabrina nodded. "Well, I don't feel comfortable enough to tell people they haven't got the fortune they thought they had. I hedge and tell them I'll get a second opinion, and after awhile I guess they think I don't know my business. Is this sweater and skirt all right? I feel so dowdy."

"You look fine. We're not going anywhere until tonight."

"Tonight?"

"There's a play and then a party to meet the author and the cast."

"Sabrina, I can't go; I haven't anything to wear."

"You can borrow one of—"

"Not anymore. Once I could, but now I'm two sizes too big."

"We'll find something. I thought you'd like to meet my friends and see some of London."

"Oh, I would. But—"

"Stephanie, we'll do whatever you want. Let's eat and then we'll talk about it. But first, tell me more about last year; what else happened?"

They walked downstairs. "It was an odd year. Nothing felt right and I guess I just let go. I didn't realize how far, though, until now."

Sabrina hesitated. "And Garth?"

Stephanie shrugged. "What about him? He's all wrapped up in his lab, he's on some kind of faculty committee, he counsels students and at night he goes back to the lab."

In the drawing room, on a round table beside a window, Mrs. Thirkell had set out oyster bisque and salad, white wine and winter pears. "You don't need Garth for tennis," Sabrina

94

said as they sat down. "Or to have your hair done or just to take time for yourself. Can't you think about yourself more?"

"What difference does it make? I mean, of course I don't like the way I look, but we never go anywhere that I need to dress up for—just to friends' houses or sometimes a movie. And if you really want to know about Garth, I can't remember when he last looked at me. And Penny and Cliff—oh, ten- and eleven-year-olds are so wrapped up in themselves. I'm like a piece of furniture they dodge around when they're dashing out to see their friends. What do they care whether I'm over-weight? I'm sorry, I shouldn't whine; I've got a family I love and a home that's a lot happier than most. We almost never fight. But as far as how I look, Sabrina, the truth is, nobody cares. And it doesn't seem worth the effort of diet and exercise and new clothes."

"I care," Sabrina said. "Because you're not being fair to yourself. If Garth is crazy enough to ignore you, shouldn't you pay twice as much attention to yourself?"

Stephanie looked at her sister and shook her head wonder-ingly. "I get so involved at home I forget how wonderful it is to be with you. Why did I wait so long to come to London?"

"Money, you said, and you wouldn't let me buy your ticket."

"No, I could slip into the habit of letting you buy me things, and that would be bad all around. But if Garth would accept more invitations to European conferences, I'd be here all the time, tagging along at half-fare. In fact, I just might move in. I did tell you, didn't I, that you've brought my fantasy house to life?"

"Excuse me," Sabrina said to Michel Bernard as Brian handed her a list of messages. She skimmed it. "Yes to Olivia Chasson; no to Peter and Rose Raddison; yes to the duchess, but tell her I can't begin the job until next month, possibly not until August; no to Nicholas and Amelia Blackford, but say I'd love to come for a weekend next month when things calm down. And Antonio says eight instead of eight-thirty? All right. After you take care of these, why don't you go home? I'll lock up."

She turned back to Michel. "Where were we?"

"Talking about my one newspaper story. You make me feel

like a sloth. Do you always have a dozen projects going at once?"

"Lately. Incredible, isn't it?"

"You're incredible. You know, we've been researching this story all over Europe, and we hear about you and Ambassadors wherever we go."

Sabrina took a deep breath. Dear Michel, to tell her that. A good friend, going back to college when he and Jolie Fantome, already living together, made her part of their small family whenever she was lonely. Now they wrote together and drifted in and out of Sabrina's life as they roamed the world for stories. She had not heard from them in months until Michel called to ask for background information on their investigation into the recent international wave of art forgeries involving small galleries.

Jolie and Michel were Sabrina's only friends who had to work for a living, as she did, and she relaxed with them, letting her enthusiasm show as she could not with wealthy customers and friends who expected her to be as casual about money as they were. "You've really heard about Ambassadors in other countries? I wondered; I had calls last week from Paris and Brussels. Oh, Michel, what do you do when all your dreams start to come true at once?"

"Revel in it. You've earned it. You did it all yourself."

"But sometimes I'm afraid it's happening too fast. Do you know there's an old Chinese superstition that if you look directly at something beautiful it will disappear? You can sneak a sideways glance but you mustn't stare, because beautiful things are fragile and fleeting and a hard look could destroy them. I feel that way about my life. If I talk about it, or look too closely, everything might collapse."

Michel shrugged. Superstition had no place in modern journalism. "You've made yourself one of the most successful, talked-of women in London. That isn't likely to collapse. Who's Antonio?"

"What?"

"Antonio. Eight o'clock instead of eight-thirty. Or am I prying?"

"Oh. A friend."

"Ah. I am prying. Well, leaving aside romance, you have success, fame and, no doubt, a handsome income. What more could you want?"

"Work. And I've got that, too. My own work that I love, and that I'm good at. That's the best thing."

"The best thing," said Jolie, coming into the office, "is independence. Especially after being led around by that little dictator you married."

"The best thing is money," said Michel. "Try buying groceries with independence."

"Oh, God, here we go a—"

"Don't let me stop you," Sabrina said, getting up as the doorbell chimed. "Just don't throw things until my customer leaves."

In the soft lights of the showroom, Rory Carr was admiring a tapered French pedestal clock, its round face surrounded by porcelain angels. "Very fine, my lady," he said, bowing low over her hand. "From the Comtesse du Verne's estate, perhaps?"

Sabrina smiled. "You always impress me, Mr. Carr. I did not see you at the auction."

"I have known the family for years, my lady. In fact I saw them last week in Paris, and the young Count sends you his regards. But today I am here on business, to show you something very special. If I may?" As Sabrina nodded, he lifted a leather case to the table and opened it. Lifting out a large parcel, he unwrapped it with slow, sweeping gestures. Sabrina admired his sense of drama. Impeccably dressed, with silver hair and soft pouches beneath his eyes, he was a showman, but he knew art, and in the past year he had sold her six superb eighteenth-century porcelains. Unlike some works that lingered in her shop, they had sold almost immediately.

Reverently Carr stood a chinoiserie group on the table: a pagoda-like summerhouse with a curved staircase and four young boys wearing straw hats and carrying butterfly nets and baskets of berries. The boys were dressed in white and yellow; the pagoda, with latticework and beading on the roof, was in brilliant primary colors. "Lück," Sabrina murmured. Long ago, in a Berlin museum, Laura had shown her and Stephanie groups made by Lück and other artists for the Frankenthal porcelain factory in the 1750s. Sabrina lifted the group to see the Frankenthal mark, a crown above a Gothic *F*, baked into the underside.

"The owners?" she asked. Carr handed her a rolled-up document and she skimmed it. "Only three?"

"So it seems, my lady. I would imagine it was sold only in dire circumstances. As you see, it is extremely fine."

Sabrina studied the group. "How much?"

"It's a bit dear. Four thousand pounds."

Not a muscle moved in Sabrina's face. "Three thousand."

"Oh, my lady, I really ... Well, for you, thirty-five hundred."

"I'll send you a check tomorrow," she said.

He bowed. "Admirable Lady Longworth. Would that everyone made decisions so decisively! I wish you good day."

"Sabrina," Michel said as the door closed behind Carr. "Do you deal with him often?"

She turned. "A few times in the past year. Do you know him?"

"Rory Carr, right?"

"You know him."

"We've come across him."

"Lately?"

He nodded. A chill touched Sabrina. She ran a finger over the cold porcelain: superb color, fine shading in the delicate construction of the little house. "How have you come across him?"

"His company. Westbridge Imports. High-class stuff from all over the world, new and antique, sold through small galleries like Ambassadors. And, it turns out, some bad apples in the barrel."

"Forgeries?"

"Seven so far that connect at some point to Westbridge—that's confidential, by the way."

"But that doesn't mean Rory Carr—"

"Right. He could have been taken in. But he's no fool, and he's the liaison with galleries. We'll know more when we find the moneyman behind Westbridge and some other import firms we're watching in America and Europe. All we know now is that Westbridge is owned on paper by a guy named Ivan Lazlo."

Sabrina repeated the name. "I've heard it, but it was a long time ago. France? Italy? I can't remember."

"Well, if you remember, let us know. And keep an eye on what Carr brings you. What about the stuff he's brought so far?"

She closed her eyes. "They had certificates of ownership.

DECEPTIONS

The ceramic marks were genuine. I always—as you put it—
'keep an eye' on what I carry. I wouldn't survive a week if my
customers doubted my judgment."

"Hey, I didn't mean—"

"My lady." Brian stood in the office doorway. "Señor Molena is on the telephone."

"The friend." Michel kissed Sabrina's cheek. "We'll be off."

Antonio Molena made dozens of telephone calls a day—in
Brazil, running his businesses, or in London, talking to his
managers in Brazil and arranging meetings in Europe with
financiers, friends and mistresses. A self-made millionaire with
the ruthlessness of his Portuguese father and the mysticism of
his Indian mother, he had waited fifty-one years to find the
right woman to grace his empire. When he met Sabrina at a
New Year's party at Olivia Chasson's country home, he made
up his mind in ten minutes as 1978 gave way to 1979—the
year, he decided, in which he would marry and have his first
son.

He banished his mistresses with appropriate gifts and
swooped upon Sabrina like the great bird of prey he resembled, pursuing her for five months with the single-mindedness
that had made him master of vast coffee plantations in Bahia
province and cattle ranches in the interior province of Serro de
Amambai. By now he had expected to be married, with Sabrina running their home in Rio de Janeiro and awaiting the
birth of their son. Instead, he was forced to tarry in London
and fit himself to her schedule until he could compel her to
accept him.

Because she could not make up her mind.

Her friends said he was everything a woman could want:
enormously wealthy and powerful, a modern prince who flew
his own plane, but scattered through his conversation ancient
folktales from the tribe of his mother and grandmother. "It is
better that you do not love me yet," he told Sabrina. "The
Guarani gods say love is the last thing, not the first. It grows
slowly through sharing and creating. When you live together
and build a family, love will come."

Society was waiting for Sabrina to marry again. At every
party she was paired with someone new in the tireless round
robin of matchmaking. Antonio stood above them all with his
determined courtship, his certainty about their future, his
powerful and mercurial personality—mystic and practical,

businessman and playboy. He and Sabrina were seen at many of the playgrounds Denton had proudly shown her, but he worked as hard as he played. Between film festivals and auto races, balls, derbies, hunts and country weekends, he would fly to Brazil to work twenty-hour days, or shut himself in his London apartment to make marathon telephone calls and dictate long documents for his staff of secretaries in Rio.

And each day he called, to remind Sabrina he was waiting.

But she was wary. "After all," she told Alexandra, "I thought marrying Denton was a good idea."

Alexandra snorted. "You were young and innocent. Dependent. Now you're on your own, with a business, a house and me to advise you."

"All right, advise me. Why should I marry Antonio?"

"Because, like all of us, you're happiest with a man around."

"Any man?"

"Honey, Sabrina Longworth doesn't have to settle for any man. Your Antonio is a very rare bird."

He was working on a plan to build villages, hospitals and schools for the peasants in the Brazilian provinces he dominated. His purpose was to keep them from organizing against himself and the other landowners, but publicly he said only that he wished to give dignity and comforts to the poor. It was important work that Sabrina would share. In addition to supervising the raising of their children and acting as his hostess, she would help him improve the lives of thousands of people.

"King Antonio the First," Sabrina joked to Alexandra, but not to Antonio. He was so serious, and how did she know those thousands of peasants wouldn't be better off with him arranging their lives?

"It's just that I don't want him to arrange mine," she said to Alexandra.

The first time she went to his bed, in his apartment in London, he surprised her with his gentle hands, caressing slowly, steadily, in a sensual rhythm as insistent as his courtship, until she was so open and longing she pulled him inside her. And when he let her lead him with her body, instead of forcing her to follow as Denton had done, he finally satisfied the arousal Denton had numbed. For the first time Sabrina understood what sexual gratitude meant.

"But if I marry again," she told Alexandra, "it won't be for gratitude. It will be for love."

She knew what love was: it was sharing. She had learned that with Stephanie. In her years of living alone, she had looked for someone who desired a companion, not a beautiful ornament; who would soothe her fears, not simply applaud her skills; who wanted caring, not the status of her poise and position in society; who would cherish her, not demand that she mold her life to his. She knew what sharing was, and it didn't seem to fit Antonio.

Then, just as Michel warned her about Rory Carr, Antonio telephoned. Maybe those Guarani Indians had something after all; maybe it was an omen. How did she know Antonio wouldn't share a problem and help her solve it? It was time she found out. With an eager step she went to take his call.

Garth opened his office window to the lake breeze as the morning sun climbed in the sky. Already it was hotter than usual for the end of May, and a few students dangled bare feet from the rocks along the shore, yelping as their toes met the forty-five-degree water. Frisbees sailed over huddled groups studying for finals, bicyclists passed lovers strolling beneath the trees, fingers tucked in the back pockets of each other's jeans. The air smelled of summer; a time to be outside. But Garth had an appointment. He rummaged for his file on Vivian Goodman. If he was lucky, he might get in a short walk before his two o'clock class. He was halfway to the door when the telephone rang.

"Garth," Stephanie said. "I have to talk to you about Cliff."

"I'm meeting with the dean. I'll call you back in—"

"No, this is my only time alone in the office, everybody went to lunch early. Please, Garth."

"Well, if it can't wait until tonight. What's he been up to?"

"I think he's been stealing things."

"Stealing—? I don't believe it. Why do you think so?"

"I found a radio and two calculators in his closet this morning, under a pile of clothes. I was going to wash them—"

"Under the clothes?"

"Yes. Still in their boxes. They've never been opened."

"I can't believe . . . He didn't steal them."

"Then how did they get there?"

"Maybe they belong to his friends."

"Garth, he *hid* them."

"Well, what do you think happened?"

"Someone in my office says kids are stealing things and selling them."

"What for? He has an allowance, and he's earned extra money all year cleaning basements and attics. Why would a sixth-grade kid need money, anyway? I thought even his richest friends have to wait until seventh grade for their first Mercedes."

"Garth, don't joke; it's not funny."

"It's not funny at all. Stephanie, Cliff is a solid, straight boy; he's not a thief. But it occurs to me that he could be envious of all the wealthy kids in his school. Or maybe ashamed. If some of his friends have taken up shoplifting as a hobby, they might have talked him into going along. Have you asked him how he feels about his classmates buying whatever their spoiled hearts desire?"

"Have *you* asked him?"

"If I had, I'd know the answer. Stephanie, I'm sorry, but I'm late for my appointment. We'll talk tonight."

"I want you to come home early and talk to Cliff. It *just occurred* to you he might be envious? It occurred to me a long time ago. You don't talk to him; you don't even know what he's thinking."

"Not always, but he should have secrets. I did, at his age; I thought parents were nosy intruders. Does Cliff know you go into his room?"

"No, and don't tell him. He's told me not to."

"Then how do I talk to him about the goods?"

"You'll think of something. We can't ignore it, Garth. When will you be home?"

"About six."

He raced up the stairs. William Webster, Dean of Sciences, was waiting for him, floating in a haze of pipe smoke behind his desk. Garth opened his file and sat down. "Bill, I'm asking you to reverse the tenure committee decision on Vivian Goodman."

"I figured." Webster leaned back, his chair creaking beneath his bulk. A happy man with a contented paunch and a bald head shining with satisfaction, he disliked controversy. For a week he had tried to deflect Garth to his assistant, but eleven years in a university had taught Garth its political maneuverings. Now he waited on the edge of Webster's protective smoke screen for the dean to talk about Vivian Goodman. "You held two meetings on her? You read her papers and her book on research techniques? You read the evaluations from other biochemists?" Garth nodded. "So you followed procedure. And the vote was eleven to nine to deny tenure, thus dismissing her from the faculty. Garth, you know that granting tenure is like a marriage: giving a professor a lifetime job, inviting him into your professional family forever. You have to be mighty sure of him to do that."

"Or her."

"I am told," Webster went on, ignoring the interruption, "that Mrs. Goodman's published papers are a bit sloppy and her book does not blaze new trails. Her most enthusiastic supporters seem to be her students. Which, of course, means very little. Dear me, nobody was more popular with students than you, my boy, but you would never have gotten tenure if your research and scholarship hadn't been first-rate. We're proud you're one of us. And students still like you and so does the faculty. Why, if you were ambitious, you might knock me out of my seat." He laughed heartily. "Lucky for me you prefer your laboratory. Well, I'm glad we had this chat; it's a pity Mrs. Goodman has to leave, but she'll find another job and we'll muddle along without her. Glad you came in, Garth."

Garth sat still as Webster rose through his smoke to escort him to the door. "Please sit down, Bill," he said quietly. Webster hesitated, frowned and sat down. "Vivian is as good a biochemist as most of those in the department. Her work isn't sloppy, it's meticulous. It's true that she's not a trailblazer, but how many in the department are? Most of the faculty that you tell me I am in some mystical way married to spend their time snipping away at old ideas, not whacking trails after new ones. The truth is, Vivian was voted out because she's a woman."

"Oh, come now, oh, shame on you, my boy, you know I do not tolerate prejudice; I will not be accused of it. Mrs. Goodman was treated like any other faculty member and the vote went against her. I will not be intimidated into granting tenure to someone just because she is a woman, ignoring her work—"

"I've told you her work is quite satisfactory."

"So you say. But others—"

"The evaluations from other universities agree."

"But your committee, Garth, your own committee voted. How could I overrule it? Now, I myself have not read Mrs. Goodman's work, but in my experience anyone with a home, a husband and two children to care for cannot possibly do the kind of work men produce with one hundred percent effort. This is not a criticism; I've met Mrs. Goodman, and she is attractive and seemingly intelligent. But we cannot ignore the many demands on her time. We have a responsibility to science."

Garth kept his voice even. "Bill, eleven men voted against the promotion of one woman who is as good a scientist as most of them and a better teacher. I can't pretend that's standard procedure. I am making a formal request that you reverse the decision." He held out the folder. "I've written the minority report, signed by all nine of us. It includes a list of women denied tenure in the last twelve years, with descriptions of their scholarship. I'll leave it with you and call back in a week to talk about it."

Webster kept his hands folded. "Ah, Garth, I won't be able to read it. I am truly sorry, but I leave tomorrow on a business trip."

After a moment, Garth drew back his hand. "I'll have to take this to the vice president, Bill, you understand that."

"Garth, what's gotten into you? Why are you playing cowboy on a white horse? Don't tell me you've got a thing going with this woman? You'll make a fool of yourself, going over my head; and if it comes to a battle, I can line up quite a force against you."

Garth stood, towering over the dean. His dark eyes were burning, but his voice was low. "You've called me a cowboy, a fool, a liar and an adulterer, all in less than a minute. That must be some kind of record, Bill. Enjoy your trip."

Webster called out "My boy—!" but Garth was gone, striding down the corridor, down a stairway, down another corridor to his office. In the corner beside his desk was his tennis racket, and he picked it up, slamming an invisible ball with furious strokes. "Damned idiot. Ass. Braying his monumental stupidity—"

"Oh, excuse me," said a startled voice, and he turned to see the rosy face of Rita McMillan, a senior in his two o'clock genetics class.

104

He grinned and lowered his racket. "It beats warfare. What can I do for you, Rita? Sit down; I'm harmless."

She sat on the edge of a chair. "It's . . . our final paper."

"You chose the paper instead of the exam?"

"Well, I thought I'd do better 'cause I sort of . . . freeze up in exams?" He nodded, wondering why students so often turned statements into questions, as if asking if they really meant what they were saying. "But now I'm having problems with the paper."

"Then take the exam. You can change your mind."

Tears filled her wide eyes. "I don't think I can do either one."

"You mean you want an incomplete so you can finish up this summer."

"No, then I wouldn't graduate, and my parents . . ." Tears rolled from her eyes in round droplets and she dabbed them with a tiny handkerchief.

Garth frowned. "What do you want to do, then?"

She looked at him carefully through her tears. "You know those times we had coffee and talked about my research project? I was thinking about them; they were, you know, just about the best nights I ever had. And then that time, you know, we had tea at the student union? We talked and talked and I could tell, you know, how much you liked me and . . . well, anyway, you know, some of the girls told me—not, you know, in this department, but in some . . . well, they're—I mean, their professors are . . . well, you know, we could have coffee again, is what I mean, at my apartment this time . . . and we could . . . and then I could . . . show you my paper? I mean, it's not finished, but you could give me—like, a C and, you know, I could graduate and . . . oh, don't look like that—!"

All the coiled anger Garth had carried from the dean's office exploded inside him. "You stupid little fool. You . . . whore." He paced to his window and back. "Selling yourself for a grade when there are women knocking themselves out for a degree, a job, a good salary, tenure . . . and getting trampled by self-righteous men. But you know how to get what you want, don't you? You don't need brains, just tears and a cunt—oh, my God." He took a long breath and flung himself past her to stand at the door. "You'd better leave. I'll give you an incomplete if you can't finish your paper or take the exam, but that's all I'll do. Now get out. Just get out of here."

She scurried around him, wide-eyed, but from astonishment, he noted, not fear. She had expected a different reaction. Had he really given her a reason to think—? His telephone rang and he snatched it up. "Andersen," he barked.

"Professor Andersen? One moment please for Mr. Kallen."

Kallen? Who the hell was—? "Professor Andersen, this is Horace Kallen, president of Foster Laboratories, in Stamford, Connecticut. You participated in a seminar we sponsored a year ago in Chicago."

"Mr. Kallen, I have a class in five minutes."

"Then I won't keep you. I'm going to be in Chicago next week, and I wondered if we could have lunch together."

Garth began to pay attention. Presidents of international companies did not call professors for lunch dates; their secretaries did that. "I suppose so," he said. "But if it's another seminar—"

"Oh, no." A chuckle came over the wires. "We'd like to talk to you about your joining us here in Stamford as director of our new research facility. We're interviewing several candidates, but you are definitely our first choice."

The bell in the administration building tolled twice. "When will you be here?" Garth asked.

"Tuesday. Shall we say one o'clock at the Ritz-Carlton?"

"Yes."

Later, sitting on the couch in the kitchen while Stephanie made dinner, he told her about it. "A year ago I wouldn't have considered it. But after Bill threatened me with a battle—"

"How much would it pay?" Stephanie asked. Her back was to him as she sliced vegetables.

"I don't know. Would you really want to move to Connecticut?"

"I'd move tomorrow."

He was taken aback by the vehemence in her voice. "You like Evanston. Our friends, the kids' school, your job—"

"The job is dull, we'd make new friends, I'm sure Stamford has fine schools." Opening the refrigerator, she took out lettuce, a red onion, cherry tomatoes. She looked at him. "It would be wonderful to have money. And be close to New York. Some excitement for a change."

Garth was beginning to feel uncomfortable. He had only made the lunch date because of his anger at Webster, fueled by the encounter with Rita McMillan; he had no reason to leave the university. But Stephanie had jumped at it. They knew nothing about the job, but already she was finding reasons to accept it while Garth, having cooled off from Webster, was losing interest even in the lunch. But of course he would go, if only to satisfy Stephanie.

"We'll see what Kallen says." He watched Stephanie turn back to the counter. "I didn't tell you about Rita McMillan. Damnedest thing—"

"Are you going to accept the job?"

"It hasn't been offered."

"If it's offered."

"I don't know. I told you I'd see what Kallen says. I started to tell you about Rita—"

"Mom!" Penny cried, running in. "We're starved!"

"Have you set the table?"

"It's Cliff's turn."

"Well, has Cliff set it?"

"He's doing it now."

"Make sure he remembers the napkins. And have both of you washed your hands?"

Stephanie took potatoes from the oven. The kitchen was silent. Garth waited, then shrugged and picked up the newspaper.

"Mom—!" Penny said.

"All right, Penny. Garth," Stephanie said. "Come to dinner."

"Stephanie—"

"Sabrina! I've been calling and calling—"

"I was in the country, and I gave Mrs. Thirkell all of July for her vacation."

"I've been worried that you might be in trouble."

"My bad dreams reached all the way to Evanston?"

"You are in trouble."

"No, but I thought I was. A couple of weeks ago I was afraid I might have bought a forged porcelain, but I checked it and it's genuine. No more bad dreams. How's your estate business? Have you found some wonderful antiques for me?"

"I . . . haven't done any for awhile."

"Oh, Stephanie, why not? You love it."

"Yes, but I didn't have any business. I'm working at the university now. Not as much fun, but it helps pay the mortgage.

Maybe I'll get back into estates if we move. Sabrina, Garth's been offered a job. Director of Research at a pharmaceutical company in Connecticut."

"Garth is leaving the university?"

"I want him to. It pays ninety thousand a year."

"Oh, Stephanie, how wonderful for you! No more worries about money; you can work at whatever you like. Why don't you open an American Ambassadors? We could trade customers across the ocean. And we can see each other more often! We'll take turns flying back and forth. It's the first time we'll both have enough money. Is Garth excited?"

"I think he's going to turn it down."

"But—why?"

"I don't know. He had lunch with the president of the company a couple of weeks ago, and he says he's thinking it over and we'll talk about it later. But he's not very enthusiastic. They want us to come to Stamford—I have to pass inspection, too—but Garth says he's too busy."

"He wouldn't be committing himself, would he?"

"No. Just visiting, talking to people, having a weekend with his wife. He might even look at me then and notice that I've lost weight."

"Have you really?"

"You'd be proud of me. After your lecture in London I turned a new leaf. Diet and exercise, and then I splurged at a place on Michigan Avenue that looks like a bordello. They used all the mud of the Mississippi on my face and styled my hair. Nobody noticed at home, but I was having such a good time I didn't care. If we looked in your mirror now, you'd wonder which is the famous European designer and which is the dull university housewife."

"Don't say that; it's not fair. You shouldn't make fun of your life; you don't know how often I wish I could have a taste of it."

"But not the whole meal."

"Stephanie, what else is wrong?"

"Oh, problems with Cliff that Garth somehow avoids discussing with him. And Penny wants special art classes and she's good, she deserves them, but they're awfully expensive, and that brings me right back to Garth's job offer, and I feel so ... helpless. Pinned down and trying to get away. Do you know what I did?"

"What?"

"Don't laugh. I applied for a visa to China. There's a tour in September sponsored by the International Antique Dealers, and I thought—"

"But so did I! It sounded so wonderfully far away that I—"

"You applied for a visa?"

"I had to. It takes—"

"Sixty days to get one."

"Oh, this is wonderful; we'll go together! Can you afford it? I would have asked you to go, but—"

"Of course I can't afford it. I mean, we have money in the savings account, but not for trips to China. I didn't tell Garth."

"Then you don't think you'll go."

"Probably not. I just felt very adventurous filling out the application, and it's fun to think about."

"I'm not sure I can go, either. September could be a busy time for me. But if we could figure out a way . . ."

"Oh, if we could—what a crazy, beautiful dream!"

After she hung up the phone, Sabrina sat in the stillness of midnight, curled in the deep cushions of the love seat in her bedroom, and thought about herself and Stephanie. Their lives were so different, yet somehow, miraculously, they were closer than ever. Alexandra and a few others were good friends, but Stephanie's was the only voice that sounded like her own.

The telephone rang. "My Sabrina, forgive me," said Antonio. "I knew you were not sleeping, for your telephone has been busy."

She felt a sharp dismay. "I thought you left for Brazil today."

"So I did. I am in New York. In two days I go to Rio. I am calling to wish you pleasant dreams. And when I return on August 15, you will give me your answer so we may plan our future."

She sighed with relief. He was really gone. For four weeks she could think about what she wanted to do without his smothering pressure.

But the weeks flew by, and Sabrina was just getting used to the freedom of his absence when he telephoned that he would be with her in two days. She was looking mournfully at her calendar when Michel and Jolie came to say goodbye. "We'll be in Berlin and New York," Jolie said. "The story grows bigger. We came to warn you about Rory Carr."

Sabrina shook her head. "That Lück summerhouse was genuine. I know you mean well, but try to understand. He could take his pieces to Adams or any other big porcelain dealer and perhaps get more for them, but he likes to help small galleries and I'm grateful to him. I don't believe he would sell a forged piece, and I know he hasn't tried it with me. I don't think he's involved at all."

"He's involved up to the pouches under his eyes," Michel said bluntly. "How many pieces have you bought from him?"

"Seven. And I've sold all of them but the summerhouse."

"Sabrina," said Jolie, "we've got to catch a plane, so we haven't much time, but please listen, we're trying to help you. We've traced five forgeries to Carr and Lazlo and Westbridge Imports, all sold through small elite galleries like Ambassadors."

"Five?" Sabrina repeated it. "You're sure?"

"Looks like. And what's more, it seems that some of the galleries may be collaborating with Westbridge to make a hell of a profit. They pay less because the pieces are forged; then they charge the going rate as if they were genuine. That's as far as we've gone, but it's a messy story. Since you've dealt with Carr, please check again the stuff he's sold you. Will you please do that? Look, we have to run. Here's our number in Paris. Why don't you call us there tonight? Sabrina?"

"What? I'm sorry, I didn't hear you." She felt sick and wished they would leave. Some of her wealthiest, most influential customers had bought the porcelains she'd purchased from Carr. Her head was pounding. "What did you say?"

"We'll call tonight to see how you are. And Sabrina? You'll check them out? And let us know what you find?"

She walked with them to the door. "I'll try. I'm not sure how I'll do it, but I'll try."

On the sidewalk, as Jolie hailed a cab, Michel asked idly, "By the way, did you ever remember where you came across Ivan Lazlo?"

"Oh, yes, but it was ages ago—seven years, I think. He was Max Stuyvesant's secretary. I met him on a cruise on Max's yacht."

Michel tilted his head. "Stuyvesant."

"That's ancient history," said Jolie as a cab pulled up. "His

110

secretary is Dennis something. I met him when I photographed Max's sculpture collection for *Art World.*"

"Oh, well," Michel said casually. "Probably nothing in it. Call you tonight, my dear." They waved goodbye as Sabrina walked from the blinding August sun into the dim coolness of her shop. Six porcelains to worry about and Antonio coming back. She looked at her calendar. Dinners, picnics, concerts, house parties. August was supposed to be the dull month when everyone went away. How could she think if she had no quiet time?

She sat at her cherry table. The telephone rang, and Brian came to the door. "My lady, Señor Molena—"

"No," she said. Not Antonio until she had to deal with him in person. "No calls for awhile. Take a message, please, Brian." She stared at her clasped hands until he reappeared.

"Señor Molena regrets that he cannot return for another week, my lady. He will see you on August 22 or 23 and will call you tonight."

A reprieve. "Thank you, Brian." How could she think of marrying a man who gave her the most pleasure by staying away an extra week?

But she would think about Antonio later; now she had time to check on the porcelains. Except that she had no idea how to begin. She couldn't go to Olivia Chasson and ask to borrow a porcelain figurine she had sold her without some explanation. She could be honest with Alexandra, but there would still be the other five to worry about. "Brian," she said suddenly, "let's lock up. It's summer and it's Friday and your vacation starts tomorrow. I'll see you in two weeks."

She walked home. The sun pressed down on her throbbing head and she shaded her eyes. Usually she loved this walk, but today she was hardly aware of it. The small, elegant shops and boutiques of Beauchamp Place, slumbering in the heat, did not tempt her, and even the outdoor fruit and vegetable stands that she loved failed to slow her pace. She was dizzy from the heat and suddenly very tired, but she walked more quickly, turning into the shade of Cadogan Square. In a few minutes she stood at her door.

Mrs. Thirkell opened it before she could use her key. "My lady! You didn't walk! In this heat!" But Sabrina barely heard her. She was looking at her polished brass door knocker in the shape of a hand holding a scroll. The certificates. She had copies of the certificates of ownership Rory Carr had provided with each porcelain; she could verify them. She had all next week, while Brian was away.

"My lady! You should rest!"

She smiled at Mrs. Thirkell. "A bath, I think. And then a light supper. I'm going to be working tonight."

Mrs. Thirkell sent Sabrina's regrets for the dinner party she was to attend that night while Sabrina went back to Ambassadors for the certificates. She spent the evening looking up telephone numbers in her office directories for Paris, Bonn, Geneva, Milan and Brussels, and the next morning she began making calls.

It took a long time; everyone seemed to be away. Sabrina thought of Europe in August as a huge chessboard, with populations moving from square to square. But servants and secretaries gave her forwarding numbers, and soon she was getting through.

In five days she had verified the ownership of four porcelains. On Wednesday she confirmed the ownership of the next figurine through six families. And on Thursday morning she turned to the last certificate, listing previous owners of a rare Meissen porcelain stork, and found they were names of people who did not exist.

For the next three days, in her silent office, she made dozens of calls, her heart racing, but there were no errors in spelling, no mistaken addresses. Every name was false.

And, therefore, so was the porcelain stork.

She stared blankly at a small landscape on the opposite wall. She had been careless. Five superb porcelain figures, the impeccable presence of Rory Carr and his friendships with the titled families of Europe, her customers' demand for fine objects—and she grew careless. Her success depended on her sharp eye and her knowledge, but somehow she had bought and then sold a porcelain without properly examining it.

When that became public knowledge, the sterling reputation that set her above so many design galleries would be tarnished. Customers who gave her open-ended commissions would look for different designers. A few might give her another chance, but most, even acknowledging that everyone makes a mistake now and then, would turn their backs on her. Failure was seldom tolerated by those with the luxury of unlimited choice.

Sabrina shivered. She would have to buy back the stork at its current market value. If she didn't have enough cash, Alexandra would probably help her. But money wasn't the problem. Exposure was the problem. She could not buy it back without telling the owner the truth.

Who was the owner? She read the invoice stapled to the certificate. Lady Olivia Chasson. "Why not?" she murmured. The best and the worst. Lady Olivia was Sabrina's best customer, spending fifty thousand pounds a year on redecorating her homes and on gifts. Frequently she sent new customers to Ambassadors, including foreigners who shopped by mail or telephone. She was one of Sabrina's most ardent supporters.

And she could destroy someone overnight if she felt she had been cheated.

But we know each other so well, Sabrina thought. I can talk to her. She is one of the few people with enough confidence in herself to keep the story quiet after I buy back the stork or replace it with another piece. I think it will be all right. We know each other so well. I think I can make it come out all right.

When the telephone rang she answered without thinking, her voice light and a little breathless with the effort to dispel her fear.

It was Antonio, back three days earlier than he had expected, telling her he would pick her up at eight o'clock for dinner.

Some people, Sabrina thought wryly, lead simple lives. But then, she added honestly, I didn't want a simple life. I wanted excitement, whirlwinds, adventures. Now all I have to do is cope with them.

Antonio first. And then Olivia. She could delay giving Antonio an answer, and as for Olivia, this wasn't three years ago; people knew and trusted her now; she had her own place in society—not a reflection of Denton's but one she had made for herself. Whatever happened, she could handle it.

For the evening, she chose a dress bare enough for August but not seductive and put up her hair with mother-of-pearl combs. She was surprised to discover that she was looking forward to seeing Antonio. His presence was so overwhelming that when he was gone he left an empty space in her life: something like an excavation for a building. She didn't want to fall in, but it was too big to ignore.

The trouble was, even when he was there, filling his space,

he did not give her what she needed. She thought of the time, months before, when she had tried to tell him about Michel's suspicions of Rory Carr. He deliberately led the conversation to other subjects until Sabrina gave up and did not try to confide in him again.

But tonight she would. Share with me, she murmured to his photograph on her dressing table. He knew Olivia; he might have an idea how to approach her. Sabrina was so glad she was going to see him, she thought perhaps she was falling in love with him after all.

But by the time they sat opposite each other at Antonio's favorite table at Le Gavroche, and Sabrina had listened to his problems with bankers, clerks, the postal service of eight different countries, coffee-pickers in Brazil, ship-loaders in New Orleans and United States government regulations on imported beef, she had lost all desire to talk about anything but the weather.

"Yes, yes, it may rain, my Sabrina," Antonio said impatiently, adding as an inspired afterthought, "It does not rain much in Rio."

That made her laugh, and for a moment she felt better.

"Ah, you are lovely," he said softly. "Like a queen. I have come back for your answer, Sabrina, to be my queen—so I may spread the world at your feet—"

A memory streaked past Sabrina: Denton saying he would buy her a piece of the world for each birthday. Why did the men she knew offer her things instead of feelings?

In the act of spearing veal and dipping it in three different mustards, Antonio saw Sabrina's frown. He put down his fork. "You cannot be surprised. I told you I would expect your answer tonight."

"Antonio, I want to talk to you." Rapidly, before he could stop her, she told him about Jolie and Michel's suspicions of Rory Carr and her discovery of the forgery. She ignored his deepening scowl. "Of course I'll buy it back from Olivia and tell her the truth. I'm sure she won't broadcast it; why should she? If you could help me decide how to tell her—"

"Sabrina." She waited. "Your friends say there have been five forgeries? And it appears that some galleries are collaborating with this Westbridge?" She nodded. "And your friends will publish their story in the newspaper. Exposing this Westbridge. And its bookkeeping."

Around her the softly lit room dimmed as the fears of the past week returned. "Of course," she said slowly. "Descriptions of every piece sold to every gallery, including Ambassadors."

"Ah, you are a child," he said. "You think you will ask Olivia to keep silent, but what you will be asking her to do is lie when all her friends read descriptions of her Meissen stork in a story on forged art. Why should she lie for you?"

Sabrina looked at the discreet crowd dining on the restaurant's famous veal and duck and spicy gossip. They would lie for their own protection, but few would lie for another. Some friends would lie to protect me, she thought: Alexandra, Antonio, a few others. No, she added with bitter humor; there's a limit to the number of times Alexandra can rescue me.

"My Sabrina," Antonio said, signaling the waiters to remove their plates and bring coffee. "I am glad you finally told me of these problems. I admire your strength and spirit, but there are limits to what any woman can do alone in the world of commerce. I will not allow you to suffer. I will hire solicitors to deal with this Westbridge, I will help you close your little shop and then I will take you far away, where you will have no more difficulties."

"Where you buy off the clouds so it will not rain."

"I beg your pardon? Is this some of your humor, my Sabrina?"

"No. I apologize." She could do it; she could marry him and let him carry her off to live where he was indeed like a king and she would be safe at his side. But always in his enormous shadow, and without her 'little shop.'

It wasn't enough. She held her glass of cognac to the light and looked into its amber glow. I want more than a protective shadow. I want someone who knows that that 'little shop' is a very big part of me, something I built, something I'm proud of. I want someone who will put his arms around me at night, in the quiet time when I wake up frightened about tomorrow or next week or next year, and hold me, and tell me I'm not alone. I don't know if Antonio would ever let me admit to fears when I am under his protection.

She put down her glass. She couldn't make a decision now; she refused to be forced into one when she was being pulled in so many directions. Antonio would have to be patient a while longer. And if he refused, then she would face that fact alone.

He was waiting for her to speak. She changed the subject, finishing her dinner with the poise and light conversation that had carried her through a number of complicated affairs, and then quietly told him that she was very tired and wished to go home.

He stood abruptly and reached for the chiffon scarf she had worn around her shoulders as the waiters, caught by surprise, rushed to help. "You make difficulties for me, my Sabrina. I wish only to help you." When they reached her front door, he said brusquely, "I will telephone you tomorrow."

In the quiet beauty of her drawing room, she sat beside a window reliving that long day, from the time she discovered the forged porcelain to the moment when she refused to answer Antonio, however bad the future might seem. She tucked her legs under her and put her head back against the chair.

Everything piled up. She was always running, as she had told Michel, afraid her life would get away from her. It took all her time and energy to keep her business going while keeping up with her crowd of friends, who were also her customers—wearing the right clothes, entertaining, taking time from Ambassadors for house parties and cruises. She loved it all—the brilliant, glamorous life of Sabrina Longworth, photographed and described in magazines around the world: aristocratic friends, luxurious homes, exotic foods, travel, clothes, her famous Ambassadors—a spinning world she could keep balanced as long as she was in control. But now she felt she was losing control.

She was so exhausted she ached all over. She felt hollow and alone. The clock on the landing struck ten-thirty. She hadn't been home this early in months. Now that she had time to think, she was too tired. All she really wanted to do was cry.

But that was for later. If she needed it. Because she wasn't alone. She calculated quickly—ten-thirty in London; four-thirty in Evanston. Stephanie would be home from work; Penny and Cliff would be outside playing. A good time to call. She reached for the telephone.

On her way to work, Stephanie stopped at the bulletin board to read the notice, dated August 18, that the office would be on a full schedule through September, even though classes would not start until the end of the month. Another reason she couldn't go to China. As if kids and house and money weren't enough. If she were a professor, the university would pay her way. Unlocking her desk in the room she shared with two other women, her anger flared as it did every time she thought of Garth spending a month in Berkeley and San Francisco.

He got a vacation while she stayed home and worked. He had a month near the ocean, an exciting city to explore; she had Lake Michigan, Evanston, two children, a house, a job. "It's not a vacation," he said. "I'll be at the university, working. No time for romping through the city or degenerating in its nightspots."

He joked about it, but he flew off and left her behind. And at the end of the summer session, worn down by office work and the humid August heat, Stephanie didn't think she could greet him with a cheerful face when he returned the next day. How could she keep her resentment from bursting out and ruining his homecoming for all of them? Well, she just wouldn't talk. Let the rest of them make conversation.

"Stephanie," said one of the secretaries. "Coffee?"

"No, thank you," she said. "I want to finish and leave early."

She organized her desk as secretaries from six deans' offices traded tidbits on the latest campus scandal. This one was nastier than most, accusing women students and professors of trading sex for grades. Whispers had floated around campus all summer, but lately their volume and ferocity had increased and Stephanie had begun hearing names mentioned by groups huddling in corridors. One of the names was their friend Martin Talvia. She would have to tell Garth when he got back.

Stephanie began to type up notes made by guidance counselors in sessions with students. But in a few minutes she stopped; the women were glancing at her furtively.

"What?" she asked. "What's happened?"

"Stephanie," said William Webster's secretary, "would anyone want to make trouble for you and Garth?"

"I can't imagine—" She stopped. "What is it?"

The secretary held out a piece of paper. "This was on my desk this morning. With Dean Webster's mail."

Stephanie took it. A letter, typed on pink stationery: "If you really want to know who gives grades for work between the sheets instead of in the classroom, take a good look at the famous Professor Garth Andersen, who talks like a monk but fucks like a monkey."

She read the words over and over. Childish, but ugly and very effective. Bile welled in her throat. She swallowed, feeling it burn. Not Garth. No one was more decent and honest than Garth.

But Garth stayed away most nights, "working," he said, and on those nights he slept in the study "to avoid disturbing" her. He never looked at her anymore; he hadn't noticed when she lost weight and changed her hairstyle and bought new clothes. He wouldn't take her to Stamford. How long had it been since they had a real marriage?

Carefully Stephanie folded the note and put it in the pocket of her sundress. "Stephanie," the secretary said. "It isn't true. Everybody knows Garth—"

"Thank you," she said and turned blindly back to her typewriter. She sat for a moment until her stomach settled and then worked steadily through lunch, until three o'clock, when she went home.

Penny and Cliff were visiting friends in Highland Park; she would pick them up the next day before going to the airport to get Garth. Alone in the rambling, quiet house, she rehearsed her argument with Garth, leaving out no detail of their courtship and marriage, reliving all that was good and all that was wrong with the past twelve years.

And she forgot most of it the next afternoon when they faced each other in their bedroom, while Penny and Cliff were playing outside.

Garth stood in the bay window overlooking the front yard, one foot resting on the long radiator curved to fit the bay. "It doesn't make sense for you to say you're not angry. You're so full of anger you can barely hold it in. But don't I have a right to be angry, too?"

Stephanie sat on the edge of the chaise near the window. "No. You go off and play with your friends and then expect us to greet you like Alexander the Great, home from conquering half the world—"

"I conquered more than I'd dreamed. But that doesn't interest you."

"Should it? Are you interested in us? Do you care about the things that happen around here, good and bad?"

"What is bad in your life?"

"If you have to ask that, after twelve years of marriage, I couldn't begin to tell you."

"Oh, for God's sake, this is absurd." He began to pace the length of the curved window. "Stephanie, I love you, I couldn't wait to get here and tell you about—"

"Garth, I've decided to go away for awhile."

He stopped. "You've what?"

"There's a tour of China in a couple of weeks—antique dealers—and I'm going. I've got my visa and I've paid a deposit."

"You did all this without a word—?"

"You wouldn't have listened. You would have nodded and said"— she deepened her voice—" 'Sounds all right to me.' "

"That isn't how I talk to you."

"Try listening to yourself for a change."

"I don't believe it. If I ever have, I'm sorry, but when was the last time you listened to what I was saying?"

"What should I listen to? Talk about the university? Did it ever occur to you that I'm sick of the university? But it's all you care about. You don't care about me. When did you last even look at me? We talk in the kitchen, we eat at the same table, we get dressed to go out, and you never once look straight at me. Or if you do, you look through me, thinking of something else—probably the university. If you closed your eyes, would you know what I look like? Would you know what your children look like? Do you have any idea what we think about? Do you remember how we used to make love, before it got to be a kind of routine exercise you perform when you do me a favor and sleep in here instead of in the study? You know one thing, you care about one thing—the university, and whatever it is you do there—"

"You know what I do. I tell you every—"

"And whoever you do it with."

"What does that mean?"

"You know what it means."

"I don't and I don't give a damn. What I do know is, you sit there and complain that I don't care about you, but you haven't once asked me about Berkeley, and when I try to tell you about it, to share one of the most important times in my life with you, you won't let me."

"How could I know it was so important? You never told me—"

119

"I told you a hundred times this last year, and then again and again, every phone call from Berkeley—"

"Talking about yourself all the time, not once asking about Cliff."

"Cliff?"

"You were going to talk to him—remember? Weeks ago when I told you I found some things in his room—a radio and—I forgot what—"

"I meant to. Stephanie, I'm sorry, I really meant to, but the last few weeks, getting ready for this seminar—"

"You keep talking about it as if it were something you never did before. You could do it in your sleep."

"I have tried to tell you in every way I could that this was different. Stephanie, please listen. I worked for two solid years for this. I know I neglected all of you, but there was so much to do to be ready to stand up in front of this group—the top geneticists in the world, Stephanie—and give the major paper of the seminar. I put together everything I've done for the last twelve years and then took a flying leap into the future, telling them what we should be doing in the years ahead. And then those eminent scientists dissected my every word so we could spend the rest of the month talking shop based on the conclusions of my paper. All that kept me going was that I learned to chant molecular formulas to calm my nervous stomach. The hotel staff thought they'd been invaded by mathematical Krishnas."

She laughed reluctantly. "Well? It went all right, you said."

"A little better than all right. It was, in fact, a triumph. Everything I ever hoped for—"

"That's wonderful. And it means you've finished your work here. You can take the job in Stamford."

Garth stared at her. "Is that job all you think about?"

"It's important to me. And it would be to you if you cared about what I want."

He moved from the window to stand behind a deep armchair where Stephanie curled up at night to read. He rested his hands on the back of the chair and looked at them. "I do care. But I can't wipe out my needs, even to give you what you want. I'm torn, Stephanie; I wish you could understand that it isn't an easy choice. There's the money—I know what it means to you; it means something to me, too; do you know what a budget I'd have for research and staff? But there's the other side—the freedom of the university, my teaching, which I love; you know how I feel about those things."

"We talked about those same things before we were married. Don't you think it's time you grew up and wanted other things?"

"Yes, by God, it is. And one of the things I'd like is a wife who gives a damn for my needs and provides some support when—"

"Don't you dare accuse me of not caring about your needs! I spend most of my life—when I'm not earning money to help pay for the house you live in—ironing your shirts, cooking your meals, cleaning your bathroom, making sure you have the kind of soap you like for your tender skin—"

"Damn it, that's not support, that's maid service. Stephanie, we used to talk about my dreams, and you encouraged me to hold onto them."

"That was a long time ago. I've given you twelve years; now you might give me a few. I want to get out of the Midwest and meet new people and live a different way. I want the excitement of New York—"

"For God's sake, you've been talking to your sister."

"What?"

"My Lady Sabrina, who dines at castles and dances until dawn. Every time she calls she gets you more dissatisfied. You never expected me to be a rich lord until Sabrina married one, and now you nag me to be something I'm not just so you can have the kind of pampered, parasitic life she has."

"She's not like that! You have no right—you don't know her—!"

"Well, whose fault is that? She hardly ever comes here; you run to meet her in New York or go off to London—by God, this crazy China thing is her idea, isn't it? She put you up to it."

"No, no, no!" Stephanie clasped and unclasped her hands as she walked around the room. "It was my idea. Sabrina doesn't know anything about it—it was because of Cliff and—"

"I've apologized for that. I will talk to him, I promise—"

"Oh, you and your promises. Well, when you do, you might ask him about cuff links and tie tacks and Cross pen sets."

"Good Lord. All in his room?"

"All under his dirty clothes. I suppose I should be grateful; a confirmed criminal would think of other hiding places."

"Stephanie, I am sorry. I'll talk to him tomorrow. It sounds as if he wants to be caught; he knows you'll find what's underneath those clothes when you do the wash. Have you talked to anyone else about this?"

"How could I? I tried to talk to Cliff, but he got hostile; and I don't want anyone else to know until we decide what to do."

"So you've carried it around by yourself."

"Oh, has that finally occurred to you? Has it finally penetrated your biologist's brain that I am lonely?"

"Now, wait a minute, you have close friends who—"

"I'm not talking about friends. I'm talking about someone who can put his arms around me at night, in the quiet time when I wake up frightened about tomorrow or next week or next year. I'm talking about someone to hold me and tell me I'm not alone."

Garth gave her a long look. "Don't you think I might want that, too? But you turn your back in bed, you move away when I put my arm around you, you turn your head when I try to kiss you."

"When have you last done any of those things?"

"Not for a long time. And I miss them. But I got sick and tired of being rejected."

"Well, you found another place for them, didn't you? Big scientists don't stay rejected long. They know where to go for fun and games, don't they, professor?"

"What the hell are you talking about?"

"About those sweet young things you make love to. Students!" She spat out the word. "Did you think you could keep it a secret? You and all the others, big men who don't need cash like those poor ordinary guys who find their prostitutes on the street; all you have to do is promise a passing grade—"

"Shut up!"

"Don't you dare talk to me that—"

"I'll talk to you any way I want. We've lived together twelve years and you actually believe that I would—oh, the hell with it."

He was trembling, his breath coming in short gasps. He folded his arms, holding himself in, then swung about and strode out of the room. Stephanie shrank back, frightened by his face and his rigid jaw. She heard him hesitate in the hall outside the bedroom door, and she waited for him to come back so she could find out the truth. She was confused. They had so many loose ends; they hadn't come to any conclusion. But in a moment she heard his footsteps running down the stairs, and after another pause the front door opened and slammed shut.

She looked around the room frantically. This was not happening; she and Garth would never do this to each other. They hadn't resolved anything, she couldn't see ahead, and that was terrifying.

But she could see one thing. She was going on her trip. She had to get away, and she'd told Garth she was going. He would take care of his children; she could count on him for that even if he had become a stranger in other ways. And when she got back they would work things out. She looked at her watch. Four-thirty. Ten-thirty in London. She was reaching for the telephone when, beneath her hand, it rang.

Chapter 9

A block from their hotel, in front of the Shanghai Cakes and
Pastries Store, Nicholas Blackford bumped into them as he
navigated with a stack of wrapped pastries. He smiled guiltily.
"It is so difficult to diet away from home. I should have
brought Amelia. You must scold me, Sabrina, as you used to
when you worked in my shop and monitored my bad habits.
Or am I speaking to Stephanie? Do you know, I am ashamed
to say this, and I assure you it is no reflection on either of you,
but Sabrina—Stephanie—I really cannot tell you apart."

Sabrina and Stephanie looked at each other behind the bald
and bouncing figure of Nicholas Blackford. Her eyes dancing,
Sabrina swept a low curtsy to Stephanie. "Lady Longworth,"
she said in a clear voice. "Welcome to Shanghai."

Stephanie stretched out her hand to help her up. "Mrs. Andersen," she said. "How glad I am to be here."

At the bubbling laughter in their voices, Nicholas strained to
see over his packages and sent pastries flying. "Oh," Stephanie
said, feeling somehow at fault, "let us help." She and Sabrina
gathered up the packages and carried them to his hotel room,
where he insisted they take a few "for being good Samaritans."

Stephanie shook her head, but Sabrina accepted them. "The
Guarani Indians would say they're an omen that our idea is
sweet. Or something like that. Thank you, Nicholas."

"Who are the Guarani Indians?" Stephanie asked as they walked down the hall to their room.

"A tribe in Brazil. Antonio's ancestors. He says. More likely he comes from a long line of Portuguese pirates, but he likes to quote Indians and it does lend a certain piquancy to country weekends in Derbyshire. You won't meet him because he's in Brazil for the month, but you might as well learn about the Guaranis while you're learning everything else."

Inside the room they looked at each other, touching their fingers, as if each were looking in a mirror. "Are we really going to trade places?" Stephanie asked.

"Do you really want to?"

"Oh . . . more than you, I'm afraid. To stop being me for awhile, to play at being you in your wonderful life, to live a kind of dream—I can't believe it's possible."

"Then let's do it. As long as you don't think you'll come home like the three bears and growl, 'Somebody's been sleeping in my bed.' "

"There wouldn't be anything to growl about. Sex just isn't a big part of our marriage anymore. Otherwise I wouldn't even think of—well, I know you wouldn't make love to Garth, he's my husband, and he isn't your type at all—I can't imagine anyone farther from a Brazilian millionaire than Garth—but there won't be any problem."

"After you've been apart for two weeks?"

"I don't think that would make any difference. Even if it did, you can say you have your period."

"Does that mean hands off?"

"Yes, of course. But it's not only then. There's never much hands-on in our house. I told you, Garth usually sleeps in the study."

"Stephanie, usually isn't always."

"Well, then, you just turn your back."

"Is that what you do?"

There was a pause. Stephanie walked around the ornate nineteenth-century beds and stood at the window, looking at the rippling water of the river below. "I get angry when he doesn't come near me for two weeks, three weeks, and when he walks into the bedroom, all I can think of is that he has no right to be in there. Or in me. He accused me of that when—" She stopped.

"When what?"

"Oh, we had a fight a couple of weeks ago, right after he got back from California, but it didn't last long. We smoothed it out. It wasn't anything unusual, just a quarrel; you and Denton must have had your share of them."

"A few," Sabrina said dryly. Stephanie was clasping and unclasping her hands, and Sabrina knew she was nervous because she wasn't being honest. She was afraid that, if she told the whole story, Sabrina would refuse to change places and walk into—what? A quarrel? Garth's refusal to take a trip to Stamford or decide about the job? It didn't seem very serious, at least from an observer's point of view, and that's all Sabrina was going to be for a few days: an observer. And then she'd leave.

"It's no good," Stephanie said abruptly. "I have no right to ask you to leave your wonderful life and step into mine; they're too different. I don't know why I let myself get so excited . . . we'll just forget the whole idea. It was crazy from the beginning."

Sabrina walked swiftly to her and put an arm around her waist. "Don't say that; don't sound so sad. Of course it's crazy, but we've done crazy things before. We said it would be a lark."

"But you can't really want to do it, Sabrina—you have a fairy tale and everything I have is ordinary. And there are things I haven't told you."

"Well, don't. Unless I absolutely have to know them to get through a week without giving myself away. I meant it, you know, when I told you I wanted a taste of your life. My life may look like a fairy tale from the outside, but it has its own dragons."

"Fire-breathing?"

"Fire-breathing."

"Well, I guess I don't want to know about them. Unless I have to."

"I don't think you do. I closed Ambassadors and gave Brian an extra holiday while I was gone; we'll just extend it a week. Antonio went to Brazil for the month to give me a chance to miss him, because I wouldn't let him arrange my life and I wouldn't give him a yes or no on marriage. He said he wouldn't even telephone. Which, knowing Antonio, is the greatest miracle of all. My calendar is clear; I wanted time to recover from China. Mrs. Thirkell is at the house, but she hardly ever looks up from whatever she's stirring on the stove. It will be a quiet week; all yours and all London to choose from."

"And a closetful of clothes. You don't mind?"

"Of course not. I'll be wearing yours."

"Blue jeans and shirts."

"A novelty. I haven't worn jeans in years. Stephanie, stop feeling ashamed of your life. Don't worry about me. We're talking about a one-week caper, not a lifetime."

"If you really want to ... I don't want you to lie about it."

"I'm not lying. Stephanie, don't you think I might want the same things you want? To stop being me for awhile? To live a different kind of life? I want the experience of a home, a family, a community where people know each other, a chance to slow down, to be alone, to think—I don't have any of those. And you and I are so close that I can have them with your family in a way I couldn't anywhere else. It's a fantastic idea. In fact, it's probably everybody's secret wish. For one glorious week we'll leave everything behind and discover strange and wonderful things by living a completely different life. And at the end of the week we'll turn up our coat collars, steal away to a mysterious rendezvous, whisper the secret password and trade places again. You'll go home and I'll fly back to London. *And no one but the two of us will ever know.* What could be simpler? What could be more fun?"

"Oh, Sabrina!" Stephanie threw her arms around her sister and hugged her. "Thank you. I love you."

Once again Sabrina felt the ripples of secrets in Stephanie's life, but she ignored them. Stephanie wanted this so badly, and it was something she could do for her. And it would be fun. The challenge had caught her imagination, and already she saw herself in her sister's world, blending into her family, settling into the rooms of her rambling old house. "Have you changed the furniture?" she asked. "Let's start there. We only have a week."

They left Shanghai the next morning and flew to Sian, where their small group stood on the edge of the great tomb of China's first emperor, who had died two thousand years before. Only recently discovered, the tomb was still being excavated, inch by inch, revealing an army of more than seven thousand larger-than-life terra-cotta warriors and horses the emperor had commanded to be made to accompany him to the afterlife.

In the Sian Museum they saw, close up, some of the giant figures from the tomb: noble, perfectly proportioned, serene. "Grand visions," murmured Stephanie. "I don't know anyone who has them today. Except perhaps Garth." She seemed surprised at her own words.

Sabrina looked at her quickly. "But that's wonderful."

"I suppose so. It's hard to live with."

The next day they drove through the magnificent countryside around Guilin. Limestone mountains thrust straight up from flat green plains, their craggy peaks hidden by swirling mists, their sides eroded by water into caverns and needle-sharp points. Water buffalo grazed between fields of sugarcane and grapefruit trees, and on the blue-green Li River floated hundreds of boats, from tiny rafts with single fishermen using rice as bait to crowded houseboats rocking beneath huge square sails.

Sabrina felt as if she were intruding on a painted scroll or an illustration in a book. But she was fascinated by the dreamlike beauty and peaceful, misty scenes of farmers, fishermen and small neat houses. "Do you think people are happier when they're surrounded by beauty?" she asked.

"If they have enough to eat," their guide answered, smiling, and led the group to a porcelain factory.

Sabrina and Stephanie stayed behind. "It's either the fourteenth or fifteenth of the tour," Sabrina said. "Whichever it is, we'll skip it."

They walked instead along the river. "What haven't we covered?" Stephanie asked. "Friends, time schedules, grocery stores, the office—you are going to call in sick, aren't you?"

"I'd better. I don't know how to type."

"But you shouldn't work anyway. A job in the dean's office of Midwestern University is nobody's definition of a great adventure. Ask for Ted Morrow, he's the dean, and tell him whatever strikes your fancy. He won't be happy, but ignore what he says; he's nicer than he sounds. If Penny asks about the art classes, tell her we haven't decided yet. I think Cliff has a soccer game that week, but he won't mind if you don't go."

"Why shouldn't I go? I've never seen Cliff play. I'd like to."

"Actually, he'd like it, too; one of us always tries to be there. The house will probably be filthy, because I can't imagine

Garth and the kids cleaning, but if you can stand it, don't worry about it. I'll do it when I get back."

"I can clean a house."

"When did you last clean house?"

"In the year one. But it's like bicycle-riding; once you learn, you never forget."

Stephanie laughed. "I didn't mean to sound as if you can't manage a house, only that it's not your responsibility."

"Stephanie, I'd like to do whatever feels right. How else can I have the experience of living your life?"

"I'm sorry. Of course you'll do what you want. You should. I don't know why I'm being so silly. I think I'm nervous. Two more days—"

"I know. I'm all tied up inside, too."

That evening they were in the crowded industrial city of Canton and the next day they went to its famous zoo. In that tropical paradise, an oasis in the dingy city, Sabrina had the dizzying sensation of being cut off from everything. She lagged behind and sat on a bench in the botanical orchid garden, surrounded by the riotous colors of exotic flowers. For two weeks she had been locked in a land and a society completely different from her own. For two weeks she had seen nothing familiar; even the flowers were different. And now, instead of going home, she was going to another strange place: a different land, a different society, a different house. She would live with strangers—for how well did she really know Garth or the children? She would have nothing to hold onto. But that's foolish, she thought. I'll only be gone a week longer than I'd planned, and then I'll be home. I've been away longer than that before.

Stephanie came looking for her, and they walked through the rest of the zoo, admiring the rare giant pandas. The next morning they boarded the train to Hong Kong. The tour of China was over.

Later, Sabrina regretted that she had been so tense with anticipation she hadn't been able to appreciate the Victorian grandeur of the train: an old-fashioned steam engine with enormous red wheels and a red cowcatcher, rolling on a track so smooth their tea had not a ripple. They sat on cushioned seats with white embroidered cloths behind their heads, a carpet beneath their feet and velvet curtains on the windows as they sped through a lush tropical countryside of heavy trees and dense vegetation. But they barely looked at it. They were absorbed in their game, repeating, memorizing, recalling people and places from past visits to each other. Stephanie clasped and unclasped her hands and Sabrina found herself doing the same.

"Money," Sabrina said. She opened her purse. "This is my Check Card; you can cash a check anywhere with it. And my checkbook; there's plenty in the account for a week. If you have an emergency, call Mr. Eccles at the bank; he'll transfer as much as you need. Write my name."

"What?"

"Write my name. As if you're signing a check."

"Sabrina, I'm not going to spend your money."

"Of course you are. I have only fifty pounds cash; you'll need more before the week is out. What will you do? I'll have all your dollars."

"There aren't many."

"We'll settle accounts later. Stephanie, don't worry about money; you can't have any fun if you do. I promise I will demand repayment of every pence after we're home again. Now sign my name."

Stephanie wrote, her lip caught between her teeth as she concentrated. "What do you think?"

"Lovely. Start a little higher on the *L* and make the final stroke of the *h* a little longer and you've got it. Now how about me? Do I cash checks?"

"At the grocery. I usually do it when I shop. I have about thirty dollars with me. You just cash more as you need it." She rummaged in her purse. "This is the card for Dominick's; this is for the Jewel. I keep them in the checkbook."

Sabrina confidently wrote Stephanie's name, and as the train followed a river through the rich, rolling country they talked about the Evanston post office, pharmacy, hardware store, self-service dry cleaner and Stephanie's house: a broken valve on the pressure cooker, garment bags with extra sweaters, bologna sandwiches, a bent latch on the washing machine, two overdue library books.

As the train approached Hong Kong, they talked of London: restaurants and pubs in Belgravia and Knightsbridge, Chelsea shops and boutiques, the Tate Gallery, Westminster Abbey, Portobello Road, Mrs. Thirkell's day off, emergency telephone numbers. Sabrina wrote down a name and telephone number and gave it to Stephanie. "If you have a real emergency, something so urgent it won't help to call me in Evanston, call this number."

Stephanie read it. "Alexandra Martova."

"You didn't meet her when you were in London because she was out of town, but I've told you about her. If you have to, you can tell her what we've done; you can trust her with anything."

"Thank you. I was thinking I'd be awfully alone."

"Not with Alexandra there."

Off the train the quiet trading of their lives went on in the midst of the chaos and noise of Hong Kong: streets so crowded they had to walk sideways, buildings climbing the mountains in vertical concrete slabs with windows reflecting the densely packed boats in the harbor, their masts a tangled forest swaying in the breeze. After dinner Sabrina and Stephanie walked from the Jade Gardens restaurant to their hotel. A crowd trailed behind them as they passed fortune-tellers, shoemakers, cooking stalls, salesmen with open valises of blue jeans and dealers behind folding tables spread with jade carvings and jewelry.

"Garth," said Sabrina.

"What?" Stephanie asked.

"Did you buy him anything?"

"Oh. No."

"Well, for peace in the family—" Sabrina looked at the jewelry displayed on one of the tables. "Excellent!" enthused the dealer in crisp English. She shook her head. "Very excellent stuff!" he insisted. She shrugged and turned. "Wait," he said. Bending down to a box between his feet, he brought out a small tray. "These?" She looked closely and pointed to a round tie tack that glowed softly under the garish streetlights. For the next ten minutes they bargained rapidly, bouncing prices back and forth like tennis balls. Finally Sabrina nodded and paid. The crowd applauded.

"Mother used to do that," Stephanie said.

"It's fun once in a while. It's a game. This seems to be my week for games, doesn't it?"

"I should have thought of buying Garth something."

Sabrina was thoughtful. "Isn't it strange? It's as if we've already traded places."

That night they slept fitfully and woke feeling still tired. "My heart is pounding," Stephanie said. "Like mine," said

Sabrina. They dressed in each other's clothes: Stephanie in Sabrina's dark blue suit with red piping, Sabrina in Stephanie's brown suit with white blouse. She left the top two buttons open but Stephanie, with a faint smile, did them up.

They went again through each other's purses and wallets, checking passports and airline tickets. They stood a last time before the mirror. "How strange I feel!" Stephanie said. Sabrina could only nod, caught between anticipation and the strange sense of loss she had felt in the orchid garden in Canton.

They turned to pick up their suitcases. "Oh!" Stephanie exclaimed. "I forgot—" She tugged at her finger and held out her wedding ring to Sabrina. Her hand was trembling. "This is the first time I've ever taken it off."

Sabrina touched her fingers as she took the ring. "I'll take care of it." She put it on, thinking how many years it had been since she had worn one of her own.

There was a knock on the door. "The bellboy," she said.

As he came in they picked up their shoulder bags. "One more thing," Sabrina said. "I've been saving it." She reached into her pocket and held something out to Stephanie.

Stephanie smiled. "So have I."

And in a sixth-floor room of the Furama Inter-Continental Hotel in Hong Kong, Sabrina Longworth and Stephanie Andersen handed to each other the keys to their front doors, in England and America. And then it was time to go.

Part II

Chapter 10

From the depths of the warm bed, Sabrina heard a door open, the rustle of clothes, the door gently shut. She frowned, coming out of her dark sleep: why was Mrs. Thirkell in her room so early? A drawer was pulled out, slowly, quietly. Sabrina opened her eyes and tensed in shock, her fist against her mouth. A tall man wearing pajama pants, his naked back to her, black hair tousled from sleep, trousers over his arm, a folded shirt in his hand.

Garth.

She closed her eyes again. Not Mrs. Thirkell. Not her own bedroom; not her own bed. Her sister's house, four thousand miles from London, a lifetime from—

"There's no bologna!" The indignant cry pierced the bedroom quiet.

Garth took two long strides to the door. His voice was low and muffled as he called down the back stairs. "Cliff, I told you to keep your voice down. I'll help you make your lunch in a few minutes. You are not to wake your mother."

Your mother.

Sabrina felt imprisoned in the bed. It was a lie. It was supposed to be an adventure, but it was all a lie. She felt ashamed and a little afraid. *I have no right to be here; I don't belong. These are real people and I'm a fraud.*

135

The night before, it had seemed like a game, careless and exciting, from the moment when she left the plane and saw, waiting for her—

The dresser drawer closed. Silence Then the brushing sound of bare feet on the carpet, a shadow across her sunlit eyelids, the warmth of a kiss on her cheek. She fought back panic, willing herself to lie still and breathe deeply and slowly. Last night he had slept in his study, but now—

The shadow moved away from her face. The bathroom door opened and closed, a light switch clicked, water sprayed from the shower. Sabrina burrowed into the protective cave of the bed. *I won't get up. I'll stay here the whole week, until Stephanie comes back. This is her life, not mine. What am I doing here?*

The night before, she had been so keyed up, so tense and watchful, that she never stopped to question what she was doing. It had not been difficult. Perhaps that was the trouble. Everything had seemed almost too easy, a little joke on all of them, until this morning, when Garth, the husband, came toward the bed. His bed, his house, his life.

They had been waiting at the airport when her plane arrived. Dinner time in Chicago, six-fifteen, and they were all there, standing on the glass-enclosed balcony above her as she inched ahead in the customs line. Penny and Cliff fidgeted and mouthed exaggerated hellos while Garth stood quietly, watching her. They were like an audience, waiting for her performance. Sabrina's hand shook as she moved slowly forward. I have stage fright, she thought.

But when, at last, she left customs, she forgot it in the midst of the family. Penny clung to her, arms around her waist, and even Cliff, tall for his twelve years, with flaming red hair, a pugnacious nose, and a pretense of cool disdain, kept touching her arm to assure himself she was really there. Behind them, Garth bent to kiss her, but she turned slightly as Penny spoke and his lips only brushed the edge of her mouth. "Welcome home," he said. His eyes were searching hers as she turned to Cliff and Penny, who were eyeing the box she had carried off the plane. "Is it a present?" Penny asked. She looked up at Sabrina with dark blue eyes; Stephanie's eyes, Sabrina's eyes. Her small face, framed in black curls like her father's, already had the vivid beauty that Sabrina and Stephanie had had at eleven. To Sabrina, it was like looking in a mirror that erased time.

"A present for the house," she answered. "A beautiful bronze lamp. I bought it in Shanghai from a little man named Mr. Su, who once lived in Chicago."

"For the house," said Penny, crestfallen.

"And," Sabrina went on casually, "Mr. Su had an amazing cabinet in his shop, filled with magic tricks. Somehow, probably by magic, two of them got into my suitcase."

Cliff's eyes brightened. "Chinese magic? What does it do?"

"It makes curious boys disappear," she said, bending to kiss the top of his head. "How can it be a surprise if I tell you about it now? Wait 'til we get home."

In the station wagon, the two of them perched on the edge of the back seat and fired questions at her about China. Garth drove silently; Sabrina could not tell if he was listening to the three of them or not. But in the twilight closeness of the car, excitement churned inside her: it felt so good to have a family waiting when she arrived; it felt good to be with them now, talking and laughing. And no one had noticed a thing. It's working, she thought. It's going to work.

"We wanted to order out Chinese food," Cliff said as Garth brought the luggage from the car. "But we thought maybe you'd had enough in China, so we changed it to pizza."

"And I'm cooking it!" Penny announced, turning on the oven.

"Finishing it," said Cliff.

"Cooking it!" She pulled two boxes from the freezer. "And since I'm the cook, Cliff does the dishes."

"You're not cooking, you're just putting them in the oven. And I cut up the salad stuff this afternoon, so I did more than you, so you're doing the dishes!"

"I'm not doing the dishes! I want to talk to Mommy."

"You can talk later."

"No I can't."

"You can too."

"You will both do the dishes," Garth said firmly. "I want to talk to your mother. Is the table set?"

"Yes," Cliff grumbled.

Sabrina knelt beside her suitcase. "How about presents before dinner?"

In the clamor—how do two children manage to sound like a dozen? she wondered—Sabrina pulled the wrapped gifts from the sweaters Stephanie had used to cushion them. She gave

137

Penny and Cliff theirs and, standing up, held out the third to Garth. He looked at her extended hand. "For me," he murmured as if to himself and met Sabrina's eyes. "Thank you."

"Take it," she said, puzzled by the strange note in his voice, and at last he reached for the small box and began to unwrap it. While Penny and Cliff were absorbed in their gifts, reading the instructions Stephanie had written in the hotel in Hong Kong, Sabrina watched Garth. He had aged in the three years since her last visit; the lines radiating from the corners of his eyes had deepened; his face was thinner, and his black hair was mixed with gray. But his eyes had a boyish eagerness, like Cliff's, as he unwrapped his gift, and then, as she watched, he grew thoughtful and a little sad, looking at the lustrous sphere of jade in his palm. He cupped his fingers around it. "A beautiful thing." He moved toward her. "I didn't think you—"

Confused by the expression in his eyes, Sabrina felt a spurt of anxiety. "The pizza!" she said quickly, and ducked away before he could kiss her. Opening the oven with one hand, she reached with the other to pull out the drawer beside it. Waxed paper and foil. She opened the next one down: towels. She opened the next.

"What are you looking for?" Garth asked.

"Where do you keep your potholders?" she asked absently. There was a moment of silence. Sabrina held her breath. *Fool. Fool.*

"Where we always keep them," Garth said.

"You mean you haven't reorganized the kitchen while my back was turned in Asia?" she asked gaily, and with a brief prayer opened the bottom drawer to find a neat stack of potholders and oven mitts.

"All these knots come untied at once, right?" Cliff said at her elbow. "And then sort of tie themselves up again? But I can't get them to do it. Did Mr. Su show you how?"

"I can't make my little man disappear," said Penny on her other side. "I pressed where the instructions said, but nothing happened."

"Mom, if you'd hold one end of the string—" said Cliff.

"No, first show me where to press on the box," Penny interrupted.

Feeling hemmed in and shaken by her slip over the potholders, Sabrina gripped the edge of the stove. "The line forms to the right," she said, trying to keep her voice low and steady.

138

"But not until we've eaten. I am not available until I've had my pizza."

Their mouths open, Cliff and Penny stared at her, and then at each other. What had she done? Sabrina was trying to think of something to say when Garth, after a quick glance at her face, said easily, "Now why didn't we think of that? Your drooping mother stands here starving and exhausted from traveling eighteen hours to get back to us from the wilds of Asia, and we don't even give her a chance to eat."

Gently moving Sabrina aside, he took the pizzas from the oven. "Penny, put the salad on the table; Cliff, pour milk or cider for the two of you. I'm going to open a bottle of wine to celebrate our traveler's return. Go on, now; I'll help you figure out your magic tricks later."

But the real magic, Sabrina thought, was Garth taking over. He moved them all to the dining room and brought everyone into the conversation.

When Sabrina described the rows and rows of men and women exercising in streets and factory yards before going to work, Garth asked Cliff and Penny to compare their school exercises. When Sabrina talked about the classes most people attended after work to study and improve their behavior, Garth said he knew of a few professors he'd like to send there, and Cliff said that was how they went over mistakes after soccer practice. When Sabrina told about a family in Canton living in two rooms—a grandfather, a mother and father and their three children—Garth led Penny and Cliff to imagine cutting down their ten-room house to two, bringing in their grandfather from Washington and another brother or sister, throwing out possessions to make room for everyone and then getting through a day's routine.

Sabrina was grateful to him; he made the talk easy, almost a game. How nice this is, she thought. The family. Sitting on four sides of a table, listening, talking, sharing the fun and strangeness of everything she told them, and in that way stretching out her trip, making it somehow larger. She was used to coming home to an empty house, sharing fragments of her experiences with friends. She sighed. This was nicer.

Then, in the space of a minute, exhaustion swept over her. "I'm sorry," she said after the tenth yawn. "I guess the traveling has caught up with me. Does anyone mind if I go to bed?"

Garth stood up. "Of course you should go to bed. By to-morrow you'll be yourself again."

And just who is that? Sabrina wondered wryly as he brought her two suitcases from the kitchen. She kissed Penny and Cliff good night. "We'll spend lots of time together tomorrow," she promised, and then she and Garth walked upstairs.

He put the bags inside the bedroom door. "I suppose—" he said with a strange diffidence. "Since you're so tired, I'll sleep in my study. Unless you've changed your mind—"

About what? she thought. About his coming to bed? Frowning, she remembered Stephanie saying, "We quarreled, but we made it up the next day." Did they? Or did they only agree on a truce—civility but no sex? If so, it made things easy for her; she'd simply assure him she hadn't changed her mind. But she did not even have to do that. Garth saw her frown and moved away. "We'll have to talk about this, you know," he said quietly. "We never went back to that quarrel before you left for China. It's still unfinished. Tomorrow, when you're rested—"

Oh, no, she thought. I can't finish your quarrel; you'll have to wait a week. And I'll have to find a way to stall.

"Good night, Garth," she said. "Thank you for the pizza."

He looked startled. "You're welcome." He kissed her quickly. "And you are more than welcome home. We missed you. Sleep well."

As soon as he was gone, she dropped her clothes where she stood, and slipped into bed. She barely had time to turn over before she was asleep.

And the next morning she listened to the sounds of a family getting ready for the day: water running, the rattle of dishes and silverware, Cliff and Penny alternately friendly and squabbling as they made their lunches, Garth's deep voice, their laughter. Then the slam of the back door, the turn of a key, and silence. They were gone.

Sabrina lay still, listening to the silence. Beyond the open window a dog barked, a woman called a child to breakfast, a distant driver honked his horn. But within the house nothing stirred. She had it all to herself.

Her panic was fading and, as it did, her confidence returned. There was nothing to worry about; Garth had behaved just as Stephanie had said he would. And last night she had slipped into the family as smoothly as she had planned. Now, for a week, she would play her part and then slip out, smoothly and silently, without leaving a mark. Anticipation began to bubble within her. It was time to begin.

First a shower. Then breakfast. She was starved; she'd been too tired to eat much the night before. And then an exploration of the house to make sure there were no more potholder mistakes. She had to call Stephanie's office, water the plants, pick the ripe tomatoes in the garden and think about dinner, which probably meant grocery shopping . . . She leaped out of bed; how could she waste time with a new life to learn?

She luxuriated in the shower, washing away the last of her fatigue, and dried herself in the folds of a velvety bath sheet she had bought at Harrods and sent to Stephanie last Christmas. As she combed her wet hair, she made a quick inspection of the linen closet and bathroom, pausing when she found a vial of sleeping pills prescribed for Stephanie. *Does she take them on nights when Garth isn't home, or when he is?* Then she went to the clothes closet in the bedroom.

Quiet colors; casual clothes. Blue jeans, linen pantsuits, shirtwaist dresses. Skirts, blouses, oxford-cloth shirts. The dress Stephanie had worn at the backyard barbecue for Sabrina and Denton seven years ago. The suit she had worn two years ago on a weekend trip to meet Sabrina in New York. Nothing had been thrown out or given away; each year Stephanie added one or two carefully chosen blouses, a dress or sweater, occasionally a suit, to her wardrobe. Always simple and always of superb quality; Laura had taught them how to shop on a diplomat's limited budget.

Pulling on blue jeans and a white cotton turtleneck shirt, Sabrina pictured Stephanie on Cadogan Square, dipping into her closet and bureaus filled with bright, frivolous designer clothes. She smiled to herself. What different weeks they had before them.

Downstairs, drinking tea, munching on the half-stale remains of a coffee cake, she explored the large kitchen, memorizing the contents of cabinets and drawers: mixer and blender, brightly enameled cast-iron pots and pans from France, wooden utensils from Portugal, clay roasters from Germany, glass pitchers, ironstone dishes from England, Swedish stainless silverware and small gadgets Sabrina had never seen and had no idea how to use. She shut the drawer on them. If she didn't know what they were for, she didn't need them. She refilled her mug and took it with her on an exploration of the rest of the house.

It was ninety years old, creaking and shabby; Stephanie often fretted about the repairs they could not afford to make. The walls looked like old porcelain, webbed with tiny cracks; in some rooms a single crack ran like a flash of lightning from ceiling to floor. The oak floors were dull and scratched. The walls and window frames needed paint, there were chipped tiles in the bathrooms, the carved moldings at the ceilings and on the walls at chair height needed restoring, the furniture needed new slipcovers.

And it was a warm, welcoming house that fitted itself snugly around Sabrina as she moved from floor to floor.

Stephanie had furnished the rooms in autumn colors, faded now to softness, as if touched by the slanting rays of a late-afternoon sun. She had found antique lamps at garage sales and flea markets and, after polishing and repairing them, had placed them everywhere—on end tables, suspended from the ceiling, standing beside chairs and couches—so that circles of light overlapped on the worn Oriental rugs, brightening their ancient flowers and designs.

It was nothing like Cadogan Square, yet Stephanie had made of it the same kind of sheltered retreat, serene and comforting, that Sabrina had made in London. "A home," Sabrina murmured, standing beside the curved radiator in Stephanie and Garth's bedroom. She looked through the wide curving window at the front yard below, where beds of bronze and yellow chrysanthemums bloomed in the shade of huge oak trees. Still, it was odd, she thought, that she felt so comfortable in a shabby house that was slightly rumpled, like a suit someone had slept in, when she was used to the gleaming order and elegance of her Victorian house in London.

The telephone rang.

She wasn't ready for telephone calls; she hadn't had time to think about them. It was only nine-thirty; who would call so early?

"Hello?" she said, but nothing came out. She cleared her throat. "Hello?"

"Am I speaking to the lady of the house? This is Lady Longworth in London, and I wish to speak to—"

"Stephanie!" At her sister's voice, lilting and mischievous, Sabrina laughed with relief and pleasure. "How wonderful! I was so busy memorizing your kitchen cabinets I forgot you were going to call this morning. Is everything all right?"

"Oh, I can't begin to tell you. Strange and wonderful. Unbelievable. Like a dream. But what about you? Does Garth suspect anything?"

"Nothing. Of course, we hardly talked . . . and he slept in his study. Penny and Cliff are fine, full of energy. They loved the magic tricks. Oh, I said the bronze lamp was a birthday present from you. Happy birthday tomorrow, Stephanie."

Stephanie laughed. "Happy birthday, Sabrina. What a strange way we're celebrating. You really didn't have any trouble?"

"Not a bit. They knew I was exhausted, and when I did something really stupid—"

"What?"

"Asked Garth where he kept his potholders."

"Oh, no."

"It was all right; I slid around it. Stephanie, we don't have to worry; it's amazingly easy. They have no reason to suspect anything, and I can handle little mistakes. I can handle all of it. When you come back everything will be waiting as if I hadn't been here at all."

"What does Garth . . . I mean, does he seem . . . What did he say about the tie tack?"

"He loved it."

"And you didn't have any problem with the office?"

"The office. Oh, damn, I forgot all about it. I'll do it right away. I'll say I've had Asiatic hiccups and couldn't talk until now."

"Where are you?"

"What?"

"Where are you sitting?"

"Oh. Your bedroom. I've been exploring, and I'm about to go grocery shopping. Your family ate everything in sight and didn't replace it."

"They never do. Be sure you buy—"

"Stephanie."

"Yes?"

"Don't worry about me or your family. You're too far away to change anything. Just enjoy your week. Now tell me what you've been doing. Have you gone to Ambassadors or called Brian for messages?"

Sabrina listened to Stephanie. Mostly she had just browsed in London; she'd run into Gabrielle and Brooks, who told her they were going to live together; Mrs. Thirkell was worried about— Sabrina grew impatient; it all seemed far away, and she had so much to do. Finally Stephanie said, "Well, then, unless something comes up I won't talk to you again until I see you in Chicago on Monday. At the airport."

"Have a wonderful week," Sabrina said, and was on her feet before she had finished saying goodbye. She hurried to the third-floor stairs to finish her tour. But she turned back. It could wait; she had to make a grocery list and call the office. She went downstairs and was walking into the kitchen when the telephone rang again.

She could ignore it, but that would only delay things. And after all, she thought, if I can fool the family, I can fool friends. She answered on the fifth ring. "Hello?"

"Hi, welcome home. Did I wake you? If you're still sleeping off your trip you can call me back."

Silence. *Close friends don't identify themselves on the telephone. We forgot about that. So what do I do now?*

"Stephanie? Are you there?"

Fake it. It's only the first of many.

"Yes, sorry, I was finishing some stale coffee cake. How are you?"

"We're all fine. Breakfast so late? Did China turn you into a lady of leisure?"

"Oh, everyone let me sleep this morning. I suppose it won't last."

"I suppose not. Was it a glorious trip?"

It was almost ten; she had to call the office. "What?"

"I said, was it a glorious trip? You *are* still asleep."

"No. I just remembered I haven't called the office about not going in today."

"Well, go ahead and call me back."

"No!" *How can I call her back when I haven't the faintest idea who she is?* "I mean, I've waited this long, I can wait a few more minutes. Tell me what's happened while I've been gone."

"Not much. School started, so the house is peaceful; Nat is at a conference in Minneapolis until tomorrow; and I've decided to overthrow the Evanston City Council for not putting a stoplight at the corner. Piddling stuff compared to China."

Sabrina laughed. Nat was Nat Goldner, so she was talking to Dolores Goldner and everything was fine.

"Oh, and you're coming to dinner tomorrow night," Dolores added. "Did Garth remember to tell you?"

"No. You're not having a party—?"

"In the middle of the week? Just the six of us. To celebrate your birthday and provide an audience for your exotic tales. Six-thirty?"

"Fine. I'll look forward to it."

There was a brief pause. "I should hope so," Dolores answered. "See you then."

A mistake: she had been too formal. But it wasn't serious. On the whole, a pretty good job.

Job. She dialed the number on her checklist for Stephanie's office and left a message at the switchboard that she was ill. Then, surveying the pantry and refrigerator, she made a grocery list, thinking up menus and snacks, becoming more and more ambitious. She was filled with energy and confidence, as if she had stepped into an adventure story and found everything she wanted—a home, a family, friends—and knew she could make them hers. For awhile.

The confidence carried her through the first roughness with the car—why couldn't governments agree which side of the road to drive on?—and the cavernous supermarket that would have held ten of the markets she frequented in London. She had never shopped for four people and, fearful of buying too little, bought four times what she ordinarily would. Her shopping cart looked as if she were supplying an army.

Driving from store to store, she used Stephanie's list as a guide to buy for a house and a family. Sabrina Longworth carrying bags of groceries, turtle food, toilet paper, detergent, OrthoSpray for the roses. She laughed to herself. What would Olivia think of her now?

The streets were full of cars driven by women doing the same errands. It did not seem to matter whether the stores were two or three blocks from each other, or two or three miles apart; everyone drove. And everyone bought so much. In Europe, shoppers carried string bags with enough food for the day. Here, every shopper was laden with what seemed to be enough for a month. Well, so am I, she thought. But surely everyone else hasn't just returned from two weeks in China? No. The difference is that these women have freezers. They can buy two or three of everything without worrying about spoilage.

The car was full of brown paper bags. Sabrina felt the thrill of victory. No one had questioned her signature on a check; the butcher smiled at her when she asked him to trim the steaks; at the dry cleaners they had given her Garth's sport jacket without hesitation; the clerk in the camera shop greeted her by name as she gave him her rolls of film, and said of course the pictures would be ready tomorrow; she must be anxious to show them off; it's not every day that people go to China. She had done it all.

At three o'clock Garth called. "I just wanted to make sure you were all right."

"Did you think I wasn't?"

"I thought you were tense last night, almost as if you weren't sure how to behave."

Some of her confidence ebbed away. *Stephanie didn't tell me he was a mind reader.* "Did I really act like that?"

"A little. Did you sleep well?"

"Yes, I feel better. I keep thinking I'm still a tourist, but I'll settle down. What time will you be home?"

"Five-thirty. You are all right?"

"Yes, of course. I'll see you then."

Cliff rushed in from school and Sabrina prepared to sit down and talk about his day. "Hi, Mom," he said, tearing open a bag of potato chips. "Penny says to tell you she has gymnastics and she'll be home at five-thirty. I'll be back later." He was halfway out the door before Sabrina caught her breath.

"Hold on!" Obviously friendly, parental, after-school chats were not part of the family routine. "Five-thirty for you, too," she said and Cliff nodded, slamming the screen door after him.

But it was all right, she thought; at least she would be alone and unobserved while she cooked her first meal for a family in a strange kitchen.

Garth was early and found her peppering the steaks. He had come through the house quietly and watched her from the dining room doorway. Slender as a young girl, in jeans and close-fitting pullover, she stood at the counter, her back to the door, murmuring to herself. "Mortar and pestle. There must be one somewhere."

Garth was puzzled. There it was again—that playacting: as if she'd been away much longer than two weeks and was seeing her house and her family for the first time. As if she no longer took anything for granted.

"No mortar and pestle," she murmured. "Well, a grinder, then."

Garth moved forward and Sabrina whirled about. "I didn't hear you."

"I just came in. What requires a mortar and pestle?"

"Peppercorns. But I can grind them."

"I have some at the lab, you know."

"Peppercorns?"

"Mortars and pestles."

"What do you do with them?"

"Crush peppercorns, of course."

"To study their genes?"

"To modify their genes so they grow on trees in little square cans with plastic lids."

"A peppercan tree."

"So far a peppercan't. It's a difficult project."

They laughed softly together. How beautiful she is, thought Garth. Has she always been this beautiful—or has something happened to change her? His eyes holding hers, laughter still on their lips, he moved toward her. Sabrina turned quickly back to the counter. "Did you have a good day?"

He stopped as if struck. "What?"

"I asked about your day."

Laughter one minute, her back to him the next, without rhyme or reason. He looked at her, but she was absorbed in pressing ground pepper into the steaks with the heel of her hand. He shrugged and sat on the couch, opening the newspaper. "Did you buy wine today?"

"Yes, I'll get it. Just a minute." She laid the steaks on a platter and covered them with waxed paper. From the pantry she brought a bottle of red wine, a corkscrew and two glasses. Garth looked at the glasses and his eyebrows went up, but Sabrina did not notice. "You didn't tell me about your day."

"You didn't tell me about yours. Dull and routine after your trip?"

"No. Peaceful and pleasant. I took a tour of the house and decided China has nothing to equal it, cracks and all. Shall we sit on the patio? It's a magnificent evening and I've hardly been outside all day."

Garth put down the paper. "Good idea. I haven't either." He led the way outside and opened the bottle. "It's been a long time since we sat together before dinner." He smiled at her as they sat at a small round table. Even if she was still angry from their quarrel before her trip, she was obviously trying to change their routine. Well, so was he, though she didn't seem to have noticed how early he'd come home and that he hadn't mentioned going back to the lab after dinner.

Sabrina gazed at the backyard. The late-afternoon sun, low in the sky, shone through tall honeysuckles at the far end. Its gold-flecked light spread over bronze chrysanthemums, rose bushes of deep red Mirandies and yellow Teas and the vegetable garden where glossy red tomatoes tangled with thorny raspberry stalks and yellowing cucumbers. No one had picked them while Stephanie was away.

The air was fresh and sweet; the sun lay like honey on Sabrina's face, and she felt at ease. "I've done all the talking, about my trip. You haven't told me what happened while I was gone."

"We missed you." He poured the wine and examined the bottle. "The house echoed and teetered on the edge of chaos. This is a new wine; are you experimenting?"

There was none in the house and Stephanie said you liked reds, so I bought one of my favorites. "Someone on the trip mentioned it. You don't mind trying something new?"

"Of course I don't mind." He sipped it and looked again at the label. "It's very fine. What else did you buy?"

"Just groceries. And I put petrol in the car. It was almost empty."

"Petrol?"

Sabrina gripped her wine glass. "Am I still doing it? There was an Englishman on the trip, an antique dealer named Nicholas Blackford, and we talked shop a lot and I started using his British terms. In Hong Kong I called our hotel elevator a lift, and Nicholas said that made me an honorary English citizen. I don't know why I picked up his phrases instead of his picking up mine—" *Stop babbling. You'll make things worse.* "—anyway, I guess I'm still doing it."

"Mom?" Penny was calling from inside the house.

Thank God for children. "We're out here," Sabrina called,

and in a minute Penny rushed through the door and flung herself on the chair next to Sabrina.

"Barbara says she's going to make the puppets."

"Oh?" said Sabrina cautiously. "How come?"

"Mrs. Casey told her she could." Tears filled Penny's eyes. "It's not fair!"

"Why did Mrs. Casey tell her that?"

"I don't know! You talked to her last year, at the end of school—didn't she say I could make them? Isn't that what she said?"

"I think so. Did she tell Barbara she'd changed her mind?"

"Barbara says she just told her to get started on them. But I already started and the puppet show is for Christmas so we don't have much time and I have so many good ideas and it's my project!" She burst into tears and Sabrina leaned close to her.

"Maybe Mrs. Casey just told Barbara to help you because she thought one person shouldn't do all of them."

"I've got three helpers—you know that! I told you a long time ago! Will you go talk to her?"

"Well . . . Mrs. Casey never talked to you about changing her plans?"

"No!"

"Well, I'll think about it. It certainly doesn't seem fair that she didn't talk to you about it, whatever her reasons."

"What are you doing out here?" Cliff asked, coming through the kitchen door.

"Having a quiet glass of wine before dinner," Garth said dryly.

"Can I have cider?" Cliff asked.

"Pour some for both of you," said Sabrina. "We'll eat soon."

"It's almost six-thirty," said Cliff. "I'm starved."

"Six-thirty?" Sabrina was surprised. "Weren't you supposed to be home at five-thirty? Both of you?"

"I was with Barbara," said Penny, sniffling.

"I was talking to Hal," said Cliff. "It was very important. I meant to call, but—"

"Sloppy time-keeping," said Sabrina. "You might improve on it in the future. Starting tomorrow. Now how about setting the table? We'll eat about seven."

Cliff and Penny looked at each other and turned and ran

into the house. Sabrina heard them whispering furiously together.

"No lecture?" Garth asked.

"Oh, it's too beautiful out here to lecture anyone." *I am not a good mother; not strict enough.* "Did I tell you about the weather in China? It was as if we were in three different countries, from cool highlands to the tropics." She talked rapidly, gesturing with her hands, making Garth laugh with tales of their Chinese guide. Then she stood up. "Dinner in just a few minutes. Shall we finish the wine with the steak?"

He nodded, and she went into the kitchen and breathed deeply. *Not too bad.*

At the table, his mouth full, Cliff made a face. "What happened to the steak?"

Sabrina's heart sank. "You don't like it."

"A new recipe?" Garth asked. "To go with the new wine?"

"I'm sorry," she said. "I found it in a cookbook—"

"Why are you sorry? It's excellent. Cliff, be daring and take another bite. Life is full of adventures. Penny, don't let him scare you; give it a try." He turned to Sabrina. "Does it have a name?"

"*Steak au poivre.* Steak with pepper."

"And what else?"

"Butter. Madeira. That's all. It's very simple."

"It tickles my tongue," said Penny. "I like it."

"It's all right," Cliff said. "Not as good as hamburger. I'll get it!" he added, scrambling from his chair as the telephone rang. In a minute he called from the kitchen, "Dad! For you!"

Garth left, and came back frowning. "I have to take over a seminar tonight; one of our bacteriologists has the flu."

"Poor fellow," said Sabrina. "Took his research home with him."

Garth smiled, but he was annoyed. "I didn't want to go out tonight." How would she know he was trying to do things differently, just as she was, if he spent another evening away from home? "If I can find someone else?"

"No, they need you," Sabrina said. This would take care of tonight, and tomorrow night they were going to the Goldners'. "Will you be late?"

"Probably about eleven. You'll be up, won't you?"

"I think so."

But she was not. She played Scrabble with Penny and Cliff,

then watched television in the living room while they did their homework. At ten o'clock she checked the front door, the patio door and the side door to make sure they were locked. Upstairs, after undressing and washing up, she slipped into one of the nightgowns folded in the top dresser drawer and pulled on the seersucker robe hanging in the closet. Then, curling up in the deep chair near the curved bedroom window, she took one of the books from the table beside it and began to read.

On the third page she looked up, as if suddenly awakened. What had she done? She had checked the doors, but no one had told her to. She had put on a nightgown, though she had not worn one in twenty years; she always slept nude. She had reached without looking to take the seersucker robe from its hook, but she couldn't remember noticing it when she looked through the closet that morning. And, without planning, she had come straight to this chair to read.

Stephanie must have told her these things. They'd described so many details to each other that last week in China, these must have been among them. Or, she thought, after a day of playing Stephanie, living in Stephanie's house, I'm becoming—just a little bit—my sister.

A wave of sleepiness swept over her. I'll think about both of me tomorrow, she thought, and then as she pulled back the covers and slid into bed, she smiled drowsily. *Both of me. What an extraordinary idea.* And then she fell asleep.

She woke at seven. The house was still. Sunlight flooded the room. Sabrina turned her head to the smooth sheet and pillow beside her. Had Garth come in last night and kissed her, as he had kissed her in the morning while she slept? She had heard nothing, felt nothing. She could not even remember if she had dreamed.

But it was a new day—Wednesday, her birthday, she suddenly remembered—a day when, in London, she might have felt melancholy at being thirty-two years old and alone, wondering what lay ahead. But today, in the midst of an adventure and a family, she was excited and full of energy. She sprang up, showered and was in the kitchen studying Stephanie's morning checklist when she heard the rest of the family beginning to stir.

But before she knew it they were in the kitchen, and her

carefully planned procedures fell apart. Everything had to be done at once: fixing breakfast, making lunches, finding schoolbooks and lost pencils, quizzing Cliff for his daily spelling test, helping Penny sew on a button. Sabrina felt she was stumbling over herself, searching for dishes and utensils, forgetting to put jam on the table, leaving napkins out of the lunch boxes.

"Didn't the paper come?" Garth asked.

"I don't know," Sabrina said, spreading mustard on Penny's sandwich.

"Mommy! You know I hate mustard!" cried Penny. "I won't eat it!"

"You didn't look outside?" asked Garth.

"No." *I didn't know about the paper. Stephanie told me about the mustard, but I forgot.* She tried to scrape the bread clean, then gave up and took a fresh slice.

Garth brought the paper from the front porch and began to read. Sabrina thought he was angry because she hadn't waited up for him last night, but there was no time or privacy to bring it up. In a hectic half hour they were all gone—Garth with his briefcase, Penny and Cliff with books and lunches—and the house settled with a sigh into peaceful stillness.

Sabrina felt triumphant. She had done it: gotten them fed, organized and out of the house on schedule without arousing suspicion. She was bursting to tell someone: look what I did; I took care of a family, and I've never done it before. But there was no one to tell, not even Stephanie. "You're proud of *what?*" Stephanie would ask. "I do that every morning of the year without giving it a thought."

But still Sabrina was proud of it. Even though no one in the family cared what she did. They hadn't even remembered her birthday. How could three people all forget a birthday? It doesn't matter, she thought. I'll make my own celebration. Sight-seeing in Chicago. And I'll buy myself a present.

She cleaned up the kitchen and decided with a glance at the downstairs rooms that they could wait a day for dusting. Upstairs, she made the beds. In the study, Garth had folded his bed back into a couch. Sabrina opened it. The sheets and blanket were neatly tucked in. He plans to sleep here again, she thought, and felt a flash of pique; didn't he find her desirable at all? She laughed at herself. Evidently not. For whatever reason—that quarrel Stephanie assured her they'd settled?—he didn't want her. And a good thing, too.

Ignoring the mess in Cliff's room, she dressed to go out. She put on a navy linen skirt, rummaged through the closet until she found a bright yellow silk blouse and then chose from Stephanie's jewelry box a stunning necklace of opaque amber glass in large, rough-cut chunks, so different from the rest of Stephanie's jewelry that she wondered where it came from. It was the kind of necklace she would buy for herself, and against the silk blouse it glowed like an autumn day. Pulling on a cream-colored linen blazer, she left the house.

In the glove compartment of the car she found a map and followed it to Lake Shore Drive and south to Chicago. She drove slowly, admiring the gardens of Lincoln Park on her right and the wide beaches and blue-green water of Lake Michigan on her left. The skyscrapers of the city appeared ahead, stark against the blue sky, and when she pulled into a parking lot they loomed above her, a mixture of the sculptured facades of the past and the sleek glass and steel of the present.

More than a thousand years younger than London, Chicago was loud and brash, everywhere selling itself. Sabrina felt homesick for London's privacy, its secretive closed-in mews and quiet storefronts, the careful distance maintained by people on the street.

But she liked Chicago for the aggressiveness that forced itself on visitors, insisting, "If you don't like me now, I'll make you like me." London welcomed visitors with civility and friendliness but also said clearly, "If you like me, fine; if not, I'll survive nicely, thank you."

I like them both, Sabrina thought. And I feel comfortable here. But why not? I live in Evanston. She walked on until she came to Grant Park and the Art Institute, where she climbed the broad steps between the two great lions guarding the glass entrance, to look for the exhibits Stephanie had urged her to see.

"Stephanie! What good luck to meet you here! I didn't know you were back from China!"

A tall woman, slouching, probably from trying to look shorter, with chestnut hair, large brown eyes behind round tortoiseshell glasses, pale lips. Wearing a plain brown suit and brown lizard shoes. Too much brown, Sabrina thought. She should wear red. At least a touch of red. She gave a friendly half-smile. "I got back Monday night."

"You look marvelous! Was it a great trip?"

"Wonderful." She paused. "How are you?"

"Better than when you last saw me. I've had a reprieve; they postponed the execution." Sabrina looked blank. "Sorry. Ghoulish humor; I use it to stave off despair. I meant I'm still on the faculty. Didn't Garth tell you? After he went over Webster's head, the vice president decided my case needed study, so I can stay for another year."

"I'm glad," Sabrina said. Another year? Why would they fire her? And why did Garth go over Webster's head, whoever Webster was?

"Glad is one word. Ecstatic is another. Hans just quit his job, which means I'm the only breadwinner on the premises. Still, to be safe, I'm applying at other schools for next fall." Her voice suddenly dipped on the last two words. "I don't want to leave, you know. We just bought the house, the children are settled in school and I've been so happy teaching here—"

Impulsively, Sabrina put her hand on the woman's arm. "Why don't we have lunch together? You can talk about—"

"No, no. I'm trying not to talk. I'll become a bore and my friends will run the other way when I appear. Anyway, I'm due back for a meeting at four. I'll call; may I? Perhaps we will have lunch one day. I've always wanted to know you better."

"I'd like that."

"Then I will." She turned to go, a brown, drooping figure. "One thing," she said, turning back. "I don't need to tell you, because of course you know, but I want to anyway, how wonderful Garth is. He's supportive and encouraging, and he listens in a way that makes others feel special. I don't know where I'd be without him. Will you tell him how grateful I am? Whenever I try he cuts me off. I'll call soon about lunch. You're a lot like Garth: a good listener."

Wandering through the exhibits, Sabrina thought about Garth. *He listens in a way that makes others feel special.*

On the ground floor she found a room of Early American quilts; some of them had a small but distinct initial in a corner of the design. She smiled, remembering her *S* on the floor of Alexandra's house, and thought of Garth. Supportive, the woman had said, and encouraging.

In the Art Institute store, she bought herself a birthday present, a lavishly illustrated book on Venice. Then, still thinking about Garth, she drove home, stopping on the way to pick up the pictures she had taken in China.

Garth. Three Garths: the indifferent husband Stephanie had described, a professional who would go over someone's head for a colleague, and the warm, humorous, companionable man Sabrina had lived with since Monday night. Which Garth was real? She didn't know. And she wouldn't have time to find out.

At home, Penny and Cliff buzzed conspiratorially while she made hamburgers and french fries for their dinner before she and Garth went to the Goldners'. Garth came home carrying a white box, which he placed like a mysterious centerpiece on the breakfast-room table. When he kissed Sabrina's cheek he touched her necklace, smiling with pleasure.

They all sat together as Penny and Cliff ate. "You haven't talked to Mrs. Casey," Penny said to Sabrina.

"I'll make an appointment," Sabrina promised.

Garth put up his hand for silence, and, more or less together, he and Penny and Cliff broke into a lusty, off-key "Happy Birthday." Sabrina felt a rush of happiness: they hadn't forgotten. She felt the family close about her. It was a new feeling. When she was growing up, her father's career had fragmented the family; later, Denton had refused to settle into one. On Cadogan Square she lived alone, luxuriously but without the embrace of people loving her, being part of her. Her face flushed and she was smiling. Until an inner voice whipped across her thoughts. They're singing to Stephanie, not you.

"Open the box!" cried Penny, bouncing in her chair.

Untying the ribbon, Sabrina found three boxes inside the outer one. The largest held a cake with an elaborately flowered heart surrounding a rosy S. The second, imperfectly wrapped, contained two round, smooth stones, one painted with her portrait, the other with a baggy clown.

She held the cool stones in her hands. The portrait was remarkably fine, the clown a rough caricature, both lovingly painted, varnished, wrapped in tissue paper and tied with gold cord. I wish they were for me, Sabrina thought.

"They're paperweights," said Cliff worriedly. "Don't you like them?"

Sabrina pulled the children to her and held them close.

"They're wonderful and I thank you. I'm going to show them off to everyone."

Penny beamed. "I could make more, if people wanted them. Like at your office."

"So could I," Cliff said. "But Penny's is better."

"It's more artistic," Sabrina agreed. "But yours would be a fine gift for puffed-up lords and ladies who don't know what silly clowns they often seem to the rest of us."

Penny and Cliff laughed.

"Lords and ladies?" Garth asked.

"Aren't you going to open Dad's present?" asked Cliff.

Thinking quickly as she unwrapped the slender box, Sabrina said, "Some of the rich people I met when I was doing estate sales reminded me of those lords and ladies we met in England at—at Sabrina's wedding. Not all of them; just the ones who think money makes them better than other people." Opening the box, she lifted out a porcelain bluejay about five inches high. She stared at it. Meissen. But how could Garth afford—? She turned it over and saw the mark on the underside: one of Meissen's own copies of its eighteenth-century originals.

"It's for your collection!" Penny said. "To go with the ones Aunt Sabrina sent you. Isn't it beautiful? We helped pick it out."

"Very beautiful," Sabrina said to Garth. "And very special. Thank you." No one could know that a porcelain bird reminded her of problems waiting to be solved; they were Sabrina Longworth's problems, not Stephanie Andersen's, and for Stephanie, Garth, like the children, had chosen a gift with love. I wish it were really for me, she thought again, and then it was time to go to the Goldners' for dinner.

On the white leather couch in the Goldners' living room, Sabrina handed around her Chinese photographs and talked about her trip. She was wound as tightly as a spring, trying to act at home with the Goldners and Martin and Linda Talvia—Stephanie and Garth's friends for twelve years—who had hugged her and welcomed her back and wished her a happy birthday, and who were closer than many families. She had given Dolores and Linda the silk scarves Stephanie has bought for them in Shanghai, and now she watched herself as she talked, and she watched the others watching her. As if she were at a play.

And that's just what it is, she thought, hearing herself describe porcelain factories and the jagged mountains of Guilin, shrouded in mist. It had been a play from her first stage fright in the airport. But now, strangely, though she was still on stage, she was also in the audience.

She was both Stephanie and Sabrina. One, sitting with her husband and friends in the Goldners' starkly modern living room, all leather, chrome and glass; the other, coolly, critically observing from a distance everything the other woman did.

"Wonderful pictures," Martin Talvia said, leaning forward, reminding her, as he had done at that long-ago backyard barbecue, of a tall, thin, pipe-smoking crane. "Did you take them all yourself?"

"We took turns," she murmured, leafing through the ones in her hand.

"Who took turns?" asked Linda.

"Oh, a few of us," Sabrina said quickly, but then she froze as she came upon three pictures Nicholas Blackford had taken in Hong Kong of her and Stephanie in their matching Shanghai silk dresses. Identical faces, identical figures. If Garth found out they had been together, how long would it be before he began to wonder about her mistakes and come to an obvious conclusion?

"What else?" cried Linda gaily, and reached for the pictures in her hand. Sabrina snatched them back. "Hey!" Linda said. She laughed uncomfortably. "What did I do?"

Sabrina's knuckles were white from clenching the pictures, and her face grew hot with embarrassment. "I'm sorry. These are ... they're pictures I took that aren't any good. I'm ashamed of them, I guess."

"You're too sensitive, Stephanie," Dolores said. "We could forgive you a bad photograph or two."

"But there were three," Sabrina said, making her voice light. "Linda, I'm sorry. Sometime when I'm feeling less sensitive, I'll show you my failures." But you just saw one, she thought. She was trembling. She had to think faster, be better prepared, never let herself relax; there were too many ways she could be caught—and ruin everything.

"Let's eat," said Dolores, and led the way to the dining

room, ablaze with flowers from her garden. Sabrina stood in the doorway, overwhelmed by the magnificence of the displays, each a work of art, from the delicate centerpiece of frail branches of mountain ash heavy with orange berries to huge baskets on the floor and sideboard bursting with chrysanthemums, late snapdragons and sprays of glossy red maple leaves. Olivia Chasson had always boasted of her flower arranger; she'd fire him in a minute and steal Dolores if she saw these. Sabrina turned to her. "They're the most incredible—"

"She won another prize with them," Nathan Goldner interrupted. "While you were gone. She's too modest to say so herself."

Sabrina breathed a silent *thank you* and changed her sentence. "—the most incredible you've ever done. Which prize did you win?"

"First place in the Midwest Fall Competition," said Dolores, serving baked chicken and rice. "I thought I told you I was entering."

"A wonderful pastime," Martin Talvia said. He turned to his wife beside him, small and neat, her dark hair cut close like a cap, her mouth pouting beneath a little pug nose. "You could do something like that. You're wonderfully creative when you try."

Linda looked at him coldly. "And when I don't try?"

"Then the house goes to pieces," he said amiably.

"There's nothing creative about cleaning house. It bores me."

"The way marriage bores you?"

She shrugged.

"More wine?" Nathan asked.

"Please," said Sabrina. She was uncomfortable.

He moved about the table, refilling their glasses. "Did I tell you—"

"The way *I* bore you?" Martin pressed on.

Linda shrugged again. "How lively is somebody who writes books on corporations?"

"How would you know? You never listen when I talk about them."

"I am not interested in corporations."

"Ah, but if you listened .... Today, for instance, I collated survey results on adultery among executives' wives. Wouldn't that be right up your alley? You do know about alleys, at least."

"Of all the filthy remarks! Why don't you just accuse me of something instead of hiding behind your textbooks?"

"Would you like that? Would you like me to spell it out?"

"Hey," said Nathan. "You're embarrassing us. Especially Stephanie, who's had two weeks to forget how you go on. I am changing the subject. Not to orthopedics, since I assume that fascinates no one but me, but to my hobbies. Which shall it be? My recent hike in the treacherous forests of southern Wisconsin, or the newest Venetian goblet in my glass collection?"

"The goblet," Sabrina said quickly, grateful to him for cutting off the wretched quarrel—though everyone else, she noted, seemed to take it in stride, as if it were a regular occurrence.

"A good choice," said Nathan, "considering your wondrous necklace. I've never seen it before. Where did it come from?"

Sabrina's eyes widened. "I don't know—"

"Sweden," Garth said quietly.

Oh. A present from Garth. Which, for some reason, Stephanie has never worn. So now Garth is pleased. Does he think I wore it for him?

"Where'd you find it, Garth?" Nathan asked.

"In Stockholm, when I was at the Genetics conference a couple of years ago."

Two years. Why hadn't Stephanie worn it? They were looking at her. "I never realized it was so beautiful," she said. "But this morning it looked like pieces of autumn sunlight, all golden and glorious like the day, and I felt so happy . . . I just decided to wear it."

Garth's face softened as he watched her. She looked away. Dolores and Linda were clearing plates, and in a minute, catching on, Sabrina pushed back her chair. "No," said Dolores. "It's your birthday. You don't work tonight."

They sang "Happy Birthday," presenting her with a Cuisinart food processor from all of them. "Use with caution," said Linda. "Or everything becomes baby food. You should see what I did to onions the first time."

"The idea was to chop them," Martin said. "Which took two seconds. One more and they were diced. In the flicker of an eyelash, they were minced, mangled, pureed and juiced. Fumes filled the house. We wept for a week."

He and Linda laughed with the others, their storm over. Sabrina cut the birthday cake, Dolores poured coffee and the talk turned to the neighborhood fight for a stoplight near the school.

Sabrina looked around the table. A quiet evening with simple food, friendship, shared experiences, even acceptance of a private quarrel. Nothing unusual. No suspicion, among a husband and four close longtime friends, that she was not Stephanie Andersen. How could that be? She made slips of the tongue; she couldn't answer some of their questions; her timing was off. Why didn't anyone see that something was wrong?

Because people see what they expect to see. No one has any reason not to expect me to be Stephanie. Whatever I do, they'll find a way to explain it or ignore it because otherwise it doesn't make sense. When people believe something is true, they work hard to make it seem true.

"You were so quiet over coffee," Garth said later as they walked home. "Was something bothering you?"

"Oh, no. I was just being comfortable. It was a nice evening."

He looked at her strangely but said nothing more until they reached their front porch. He put his hand on her arm. "I wanted to tell you—" She stiffened and he dropped it immediately, but she felt the force of his will, holding back words.

"I'm sorry," she said. "It's just that I'm not settled down yet. In a few days—"

He put out his hand and touched her necklace. "It meant a great deal to me that you wore this tonight. Stephanie, I want to understand you, what you're trying to do. If you can't talk about it now, I'll wait until you can. I won't push you, I'll stay away from our bed, if that's necessary for you now. But at some point we have to talk about where we are and where we're going. There are too many questions, too many unresolved angers. . . . What is it, why are you crying?"

"I'm not." But there were tears in her eyes. "I'm sorry," she said again. "Please just give me a few days—"

He kissed her forehead. "I think I'll stay out here for a few minutes. Why don't you go on upstairs? I'll lock up."

She nodded. "Good night, Garth." Briefly she touched his hand. "Thank you for a wonderful birthday."

DECEPTIONS

* * *

Thursday morning, after everyone had left, Sabrina climbed the stairs to explore the third floor. There were three rooms, each with an angled ceiling beneath the sloping roof. One was a storage room; the second, simply furnished with twin beds and a dresser, might have been a maid's room or a hideaway for Penny or Cliff when friends spent the night. But the third room tugged at her and she went in.

It was a sad room, empty except for a small desk and chair and some cardboard cartons covered with dust. Someone had cleaned it, hidden every sign of activity and left, a long time ago. Sabrina sat at the desk and opened the top drawer. Neat stacks of paper lay side by side, each labeled with the name of a North Shore suburb: detailed records of Stephanie's estate sales in the two years she had kept her business going. There were itemized inventories of the contents of her clients' houses, everything from paring knives to canopied beds, with the price she had assigned each item, the amount it had brought at the sale and her commission.

In the next drawer, Sabrina found color photographs Stephanie had taken of each client's house, inside and out, and of the rare and valuable silver, crystal, furniture and antiques in the sale. Leafing through them, Sabrina knew she could have found buyers for most of them among her customers in England and Europe. What a wonderful team she and Stephanie could have made! But when she had suggested it once, on the telephone, Stephanie had changed the subject. Perhaps she knew her business was failing and was already preparing to pack it away.

Sabrina touched the open drawers. She felt in her fingertips the tenderness with which her sister had neatly squared each stack of papers and photographs and placed it perfectly in line with the others. *And at the same time my bad years were ending and I was beginning to succeed. Stephanie, why didn't you tell me? We could have worked together and saved your business. Instead, you kept asking about Ambassadors and I kept telling you all my triumphs. How awful for you, to hear about my success while your own business was slowly failing. I should have known. I should have kept asking until you told me everything. I let you down.*

Downstairs, the doorbell rang. She jumped up and then realized she was crying. She wiped her eyes on the back of her hand. *As soon as I get home, we'll talk about working together. We need each other.* She wiped her eyes again and ran downstairs.

When she opened the door, Dolores Goldner walked casually through the house to the kitchen. Sabrina followed, astonished at the intrusion. But was it an intrusion? Dolores must do this all the time, she thought. As Stephanie probably does in her house.

In England, the closest friends wait to be invited inside. In America, where even strangers call each other by their first names, friends walk in without asking.

"We have to talk about Linda," Dolores said, sitting at the table in the breakfast room. She turned, looking for something.

"I was about to make tea," Sabrina said.

"The Chinese converted you to tea-drinking? That's why I see no coffeepot?"

Morning coffee. Sabrina remembered. She turned her back to make a fresh pot and her mouth curved in a small, wicked smile as she played with the truth. "You can't believe how strange coffee seems to me. I feel as if I've been drinking nothing but tea for years."

"Well, at least you didn't come back in blue trousers and jacket, or whatever it is they're wearing these days."

"No, but everything I put on feels strange, too. As if I'm wearing it for the first time."

"You're too impressionable. If you traveled more you'd get over that. Look what one trip did for you— drinking tea, hiding photographs ... you even look different somehow. Are you doing something new with your hair?"

"No, does it look new? I'm sure it's just what you said: I'm feeling different about who I am."

"Yes, well, let's talk about Linda. She and Marty are in trouble. We must do something."

Sabrina poured coffee into two mugs and sat down. "For example?"

"No cream? Good heavens, Stephanie, aren't you carrying this too far?"

"Sorry, I was thinking about Linda." At the refrigerator she hesitated, then decided against a pitcher and brought the carton to the table.

As Dolores talked about Linda, Sabrina's other self, the cool observer, watched: two women in a sun-filled breakfast room, drinking coffee, talking about their friend who was unhappy. The observer felt ashamed of herself, playing a reckless game of being Sabrina while Dolores was concerned about Linda. Sabrina disliked people who tried to arrange other people's lives—fleetingly, she thought of Antonio—but it was hard to dislike Dolores; she really cared about her friends. If she tried to manage them, it was because she wanted them to be happy.

"Stephanie? Are you with me? You look like you're a million miles away."

"No, I heard you. I was just thinking how nice it is that people care about each other."

Dolores looked surprised. "I should think so. Now how about it? Lunch next week with Linda and then the crystal exhibit at the Palmer House. She needs a chance to talk. Can you get off work one day?"

I won't be here. But Stephanie would want to do it. "I think so. Can I let you know on Monday?"

"Of course. We won't go without you." She got up and walked back through the house as casually as she had come in. "Will I see you at the soccer game this afternoon?"

"Yes."

Sabrina had promised Cliff she would be there, and she found the school athletic field a few minutes before the game began. Cliff was slouching nonchalantly with his team, but his face lit up as he saw her and ran over. "We're playing Lakeside. They're in third place. We'll win. The only one to worry about is the tall guy; he's their best forward."

Behind Sabrina, about forty women and a few men watched the play, the women tense and silent, the men shouting instructions or criticism at their sons. Dolores came to sit with her, but Sabrina barely noticed. She and Stephanie had grown up with soccer in Europe, and she had kept up with it in the last ten years; some of the men in her circle were top amateur players. She knew the game as well as most Americans knew baseball, and within a few minutes she was caught up in the action.

Cliff was good, she saw; he was alert and fast, and his teammates trusted him. "Go!" she breathed when another forward passed him the ball, and he moved it skillfully in short kicks toward the goal, twisting and darting around the Lakeside defenders. Sabrina jumped to her feet as if she ran with him, feeling the joy and excitement of the chase. Seconds later, with a thundering kick, Cliff sent the ball flying past the goalie to score for his cheering, shouting team.

"A prouder parent could not be found," said Garth, beside her.

She turned quickly. "I didn't know you were coming."

"Neither did I. But I recalled your just criticism of my missing past games. What's the score?"

"One to nothing. Cliff's point."

"I could tell that by looking at you."

A proud parent. She felt like one. "I'm glad you came," she said to Garth. "Cliff will be so pleased."

He was; Sabrina saw his grin from across the field as he ran to them at halftime. By then he had made a second goal. "Next half I'll do even better," he said. "Did you watch Pat Ryan? The tall guy? Is he mad! He made a bet with his team that he'd score more than me."

Pat Ryan made three goals in the second half. One of Cliff's teammates scored, but Cliff had been guarded fiercely and had not gotten near the goal. A few minutes from the end of the game, with his team tied three to three, he was angry and frustrated. Seeing the desperation in his face, Sabrina shook her head. "He's lost sight of the game." Garth started to say something when a shout came from the field.

"Cliff! Here!" A forward on his team was yelling at him, but Cliff, taking the ball down the field along the sideline, ignored him. The forward had broken free of the Lakeside defenders and had a clear shot at the goal. "Pass! Pass!" he screamed. No one from Lakeside was between them; it was a perfect play. Cliff looked up briefly and saw the play, but he also saw a small opening in his own path to the goal. "Pass!" This time his coach shouted it—an order. Cliff scowled, hesitated, then, keeping the ball in his control, feinted to the left to maneuver through the opening.

"Oh, he's good," Sabrina said. "He has wonderful control. But he can't . . . he's going to lose the ball."

Lakeside defenders had moved in to close Cliff's path to the goal, and one of them slid feet first into him, knocking the ball away. "Got it!" cried a teammate, and kicked it to the waiting Pat Ryan, who ran it down field, with none of Cliff's grace but with the lumbering determination of an eleven-year-old about to win a bet. And in the last seconds of the game, with a triumphant howl, he kicked the ball past the goalie, making the winning score for his team.

At first Cliff would not talk about it. "Coach chewed me out," he said once they were home. He sulked in his room while Penny set the table. Sabrina made a salad and took out the stew she had had cooking slowly in the oven all afternoon. Garth thought of asking when she had begun to enjoy soccer as a game instead of a duty, but he knew she could say bitingly, as in the past, that if he spent time with his family he might notice changes in them. So he let it go.

Cliff's sulking was a cloud over the dinner table. "Punishment or reprimand?" Garth asked, ready to sympathize.

"None of your business," Cliff said sullenly, his eyes on his plate.

"Clifford!" Sabrina was outraged. "How dare you! Look at me. Look at me, I said!" Startled, he looked up. "Who do you think you are to talk to your father like that? I thought we could talk about the game, what happens when you forget you're part of a team, but we won't talk about anything until you apologize. Now!"

"I didn't forget!" Cliff said hotly. "I was trying—"

"I'm waiting for your apology."

"Look, Mom, I had an opening to the goal—"

"Cliff!"

She stared him down. From the corner of her eye she saw Garth watching her. Apparently she had gone too far and wasn't behaving like Stephanie. But for the moment she didn't care. Garth had flinched at Cliff's rudeness, and she had reacted instantly. She would not have him hurt, not after last night, on their front porch, when he had given her understanding and affection, privacy—and time.

"Sorry," Cliff mumbled.

"I couldn't quite make that out," she said calmly.

"I'm sorry!" Cliff shouted. "I'm benched for the next game."

"Too rough," said Garth. "Half a game would have been sufficient."

"Yeah, sure, tell that to the coach."

"Maybe I will."

"No, thanks anyway, Dad, he'd just give me more shit if you did."

"Cliff!" said Sabrina.

Garth held back a smile. "Some words are better for the locker room than the dinner table."

"Yeah, okay, sorry." He turned to Sabrina. "What did you mean, I forgot I was part of a team?"

"You wanted to make Pat Ryan lose his bet, so you made a grandstand play, which a good team player wouldn't do."

"I did *not*—"

"You had a teammate with a clear shot at the goal. But all you cared about was scoring the winning goal yourself."

"But I thought I could. There was an opening—"

"With the whole other team closing in on it. And you knew it."

"I had a chance."

"With a miracle."

"So what? At least it was a chance. Aren't I ever supposed to take chances?"

"Of course you should." Sabrina smiled, almost to herself. "Taking chances can be wonderful. But you have to evaluate the risks. Know what you're getting into. Otherwise, you're just being foolhardy." She looked at him thoughtfully. "You're a fine player, Cliff. You move well; you have good control and timing. But if you act like a one-man team, you're sunk, no matter how good you are."

Cliff looked puzzled. "How come you know so much about soccer? I thought you didn't like it."

"I read a book. I felt silly not knowing what was happening." Quickly Sabrina turned to ask Penny about the history test she had quizzed her on at breakfast.

Garth watched his wife as she talked. How lively and animated she was, as she had been last night at the Goldners'. Lively and animated with everyone, in fact—except her husband. Probably she'd been that way for a long time, but he didn't think it had been so obvious before her trip. He felt diminished, not important enough for her liveliness, not even important enough anymore for her to pretend.

Sabrina glanced at him as she poured coffee. What was he glowering at? Which of her mistakes?

"What did you do today?" he asked.

"Oh—Dolores came over for coffee."

"Something special? Or just to talk?"

"She's mapping a campaign to make Linda happy. Isn't it curious how Dolores tries to arrange us the same way she arranges her flowers? Do you suppose one day she'll enter all of us in some contest like Midwest Marriages Fall Competition?"

He laughed. "Would we win?"

"Does Dolores ever lose?" she countered. "I did do something special today. I went upstairs to my old office."

"And what did you find?"

"Dust. Memories. But it was exciting to go through the records, and I was thinking maybe I could start up in business again. I read the *Evanston Review,* and there are estate sales all over the North Shore. I suppose it's inflation, and people moving back to the city, or into smaller places when their children go to college ..."

Her voice trailed away. Garth was looking past her, his face smooth and uninterested. He had glanced at her once, long enough to see her bright eyes that matched the excitement in her voice; long enough to think to himself that she had more enthusiasm for a defunct business than she had for him. "If that's what you want," he said distantly. "It seems risky, though, unless you know why you failed before."

A wave of fury swept Sabrina. She had cared enough about his feelings to risk giving herself away when Cliff was rude to him, but as soon as she mentioned the estate business he turned cold. He hadn't asked how she might make it succeed this time, or if he could help her. He reminded her of Antonio talking about her "little shop." Now she knew why Stephanie was angry at him; he cared for nothing but himself. She was surprised at how hurt and disappointed she was.

"I'm going to the lab," he said, pushing back his chair. "If you're up, I'll stop in later to say good night."

She nodded. Just what she wanted: a quiet evening at home. But still she had a sense of loss, and as the front door clicked shut, the house loomed around her and she felt very much alone.

The atmosphere was strained at breakfast; even Penny and Cliff were subdued. Sabrina quizzed Cliff for his daily spelling test, longer than usual since the Friday list included words from all week. Penny asked again about Mrs. Casey, and Sabrina said she would be seeing her next week. "Early dinner tonight, Mom, okay?" asked Cliff. "We both have parties to go to." Then they were gone and she and Garth were alone.

He opened and shut his briefcase. "I'm sorry about last night. I have no right to criticize you for lack of interest in my work if I show none in yours."

What lack of interest? she thought. Of course Stephanie is interested in your work. But she didn't want to quarrel; she missed the comfort of Garth's smile. "Thank you," she said.

"If you want to talk about it now—"

"It can wait." She looked at his briefcase. "Should you be going?"

He kissed her cheek. "Department meeting in half an hour. See you tonight."

At dinner Garth was restless. Penny and Cliff charged in and out, getting ready to go to separate parties, and as soon as they left he stood and went to the window. "How about a walk? I've been sitting in my office all day, watching students frolic by the lake. Do you recall why I decided to graduate those many years ago instead of remaining a perpetual student? I've forgotten."

"So you could *give* exams instead of having to take them."

He nodded. "I was a practical youth. Which reminds me, I brought you something." He left the room and came back with a paper bag. "Compliments of the university. Which asks only that you make that excellent steak often."

She pulled out a porcelain mortar and pestle. "Wonderful; of course I will. What is it used for in the lab?"

"I have no idea. I stole it from the chemists. You might boil it for two or three days before using it." Laughing, she took it to the kitchen. Garth followed, carrying their cups and the coffeepot. "How about that walk?"

"I should clean up; Penny and Cliff left in such a hurry—"

"It can wait. Please."

"You're not going back to the lab?"

"No, did you expect me to? Do you have other plans for the evening?"

"Of course not. I'd like to take a walk."

The sun was low on the horizon and the air was soft and warm, with the fresh smell of the lake and the dusky fragrance of fall flowers. As they crossed the park, the water stretched before them, calm and densely blue beneath the fading sky.

Far out, a few sailboats gleamed sharply white against the dark waves. Silent joggers ran past groups of boys playing touch football, and a small dog ran through the bushes, charging squirrels. Beneath the trees, lovers walked.

Garth took Sabrina's hand as they turned to follow the shore. In the slanting rays of the sun, their shadows stretched far over the water, mingling and separating. Sabrina leaned down to tie her shoe, and when she stood up she stepped to the side, a little distance from Garth. They walked that way, not touching.

"Vivian told me she saw you the other day," said Garth.

"Who?"

"Vivian Goodman. She said you met at the Art Institute."

"Oh. Vivian. I forgot to tell you. She said you'd been wonderful to her, but she's still worried. Can you do anything more or is it all up to the vice president now?"

He slowed and looked at her. "Did Vivian tell you the story?"

"Well"— *Stephanie didn't know about it? Why not?*—"she could tell that I was interested—"

"You pretended to be interested."

"I *was* interested." Her hands were cold. "She's very strong, but a lot of things are getting to her—she might have to move, her children would have to change schools, and"— *What was her husband's name?* —"and Hans just quit his job. I admire her and I like her. Of course I was interested." She plunged ahead, taking a chance. "If I didn't seem interested before, probably it was because it was different, hearing about it from you and hearing it from her."

"You didn't hear it from me. You weren't interested enough to listen."

"That's what I mean."

She knew that made no sense, but Garth let it pass. "I haven't talked to the vice president yet. Next week, I think." He began to describe the members of the tenure committee he headed. Sabrina listened and at the same time considered her sister's marriage.

Last night she had been furious at Garth's lack of interest in her estate business. But *was* Stephanie interested in Garth's work? She didn't know. If Stephanie wasn't interested, she must have good reasons. But I don't need to know them, Sabrina thought; they're between Stephanie and Garth. I won't even think about it. She concentrated on what Garth was saying; when he described William Webster she laughed at his pungent words and understood Vivian's admiration.

It grew dark, and they walked leisurely in the pale glow of the Victorian lampposts lining the lake-shore path. They were silent, but it was a comfortable silence. Sabrina felt the quiet strength of the man beside her, his undemanding presence. He was a companion. She was not alone, but still she was a separate person, allowed to be herself.

And just who is that? She smiled in the darkness. *For a little while longer, both of us.*

"Daddy says yes," Penny reported on Saturday morning, "if you say yes. A bike ride and a picnic. Please, can we go? I can collect leaves for my science class and Cliff wants to find a toad."

"Why not? It sounds like fun." I haven't ridden in years, she thought. But no one ever forgets how to ride a bike. They packed bread and cold meat, cheese and apples, and chilled cans of ginger ale.

"What about dessert?" Penny asked.

"We'll buy donuts on the way."

"You didn't forget! Cliff said you'd forget, but you didn't!"

Forget what? "Why should I forget?"

" 'Cause you've been forgetting things lately and Cliff said you'd forget that we always get donuts on picnics, but I said you wouldn't and I was right, so can we go now?"

"Yes." Sabrina handed her the baskets. "Will you and Cliff help your Dad fasten these on the bikes?"

"Aren't you coming?"

"As soon as I finish cleaning up."

As she put away the leftovers and wiped the counter, Sabrina mused about donuts. Had Stephanie told her? Or was it simply one more thing she couldn't explain?

"Mom!" Cliff bellowed, and she joined the three of them to begin her first bicycle trip in almost fifteen years.

She hadn't forgotten. And her legs were strong from playing tennis. Within a few blocks she knew she could ride as far and as hard as the rest of her family. Riding behind the others, she put her face up to the blue and gold sky and let her body find its own rhythm, muscles in harmony, while her mind drifted.

No one had told her about the donuts. Or the nightgown and bathrobe, or settling down to read in the bedroom armchair. Curious certainties. Was it because they were twins? She and Stephanie always read new studies and reports on twins, laughing at some because they were so foolish, recognizing the truth in others. But no one had ever tried the experiment of having twins take each other's place and live each other's lives. If they had, would one twin suddenly say, as she had on her second night here, "I'll think about both of me tomorrow"?

She wondered if Stephanie had felt the same in London. We'll talk about it, she thought, when we meet at the airport on Monday.

Monday. Day after tomorrow. The week was slipping away. It wasn't enough, really. She'd barely had a chance to get to know Penny and Cliff and feel part of a family. And she hadn't had a minute to look at her London life from this distance, to try to sort it out. Wasn't that the main reason she'd agreed to the switch? To slow down her roller coaster life—

"Stephanie! Watch out!"

"Mom! There's a—!"

"Mommy!"

Sabrina heard their shouts, and the squeal of tires, and swung her head to the right to see a pickup truck bearing down on her. She swerved, cutting her wheel sharply to the left, skidding in the dry dirt on the road. As she tried to straighten out, the truck nicked her back wheel, knocking the bike against the curb. She was flung through the air against a tree, her left hand twisted beneath her head. She heard something snap, heard Garth call her name, and then the golden day went black.

In the darkness of pain and shock, Sabrina caught a word, a question, a cry. She tried to tell everything to slow down and wait for her, but the pieces rushed past. Garth was holding her, whispering her name—not her name, her sister's, but she was shivering and couldn't tell him he had the wrong name. Strangers were telling Garth to wait in the other room—but she needed him; didn't they know that? She was lying on a cot, rolling along a smooth floor; then someone moved her left wrist and a stab of pain wrenched her whole body. "Don't!" she cried.

"Only be a minute, Stephanie; just hold on."

Nat Goldner's voice, then his smiling face. Blinding lights, her arm strapped down below a square black box. X-rays. But Nat had her name wrong, just as Garth had. "Wait." It came out in a whisper. Shivering, she cleared her throat. "Have to tell you—"

"Hold on, my dear," said Nat. "Better if you don't talk; just relax." She felt a needle in her right arm, and in a minute the shivering eased. And then she was too drowsy to worry about what they said.

"Mild concussion," Nat was saying to Garth when Sabrina began to pay attention again. She was on a cot in a small cubicle enclosed in light green curtains. And her left arm felt peculiar. She reached over with her right hand and touched a plaster cast. "Awake?" asked Nat. He and Garth looked down at her, Nat smiling, Garth's eyes dark with worry. Where were the children?

"Penny . . . Cliff," she said through dry lips.

"In the waiting room," said Nat. "I've told them you're fine. You can see them in a minute. In fact, you can go home soon if you follow orders. Here, drink this."

He put an arm beneath her shoulders and eased her up so she could drink. She had a terrible headache. "Now listen, Stephanie, I've told Garth what you need to do—"

"Wait." Why did they keep calling her by her sister's name?

"Just listen. You've got a fractured wrist and a mild concussion. No permanent damage; not even a scar. Now I've told this to Garth, but I'll tell you, too: take it easy for a few days. No work—office or home; let your family cook and clean house. You can shower if you keep the cast dry; wrap it in a plastic bag. Talk as little as possible for the next twenty-four hours. Drink six glasses of water a day and snack between meals. There's no medical reason for that, but it'll give you something to think about besides your headache. Which should be much better by tomorrow night. We'll X-ray the wrist again in four weeks; if it's mended we'll take the cast off then. Any questions?"

"Why do you call me Stephanie?"

"Because I've always called you Stephanie. Should I call you Mrs. Andersen just because you're my patient? I'll give you a few tranquilizers, enough for a week. You'll be all right; maybe disoriented for awhile, but nothing serious. Don't worry. Now rest for a few minutes. We'll be right back."

DECEPTIONS

She lay quietly, looking at the cracks in the ceiling. Mrs. Andersen. Stephanie. Garth. She raised her head and looked at the blue jeans and shirt she was wearing.

Stephanie's.

Stephanie in London. Without a broken wrist.

Oh, my God, I've got to call Stephanie.

Chapter 11

Chapter 11

When Stephanie's plane landed at Heathrow Airport and she took a taxi to Cadogan Square, it was almost ten o'clock at night. For sixteen hours she had traveled across continents and time zones while her imagination spun into a whirlwind around the week ahead, and by the time she moved through customs and settled into a taxi, she was in a trance of exhaustion. Resting her head against the seat, she watched the lights flashing past. She had seen them from the air: a sprawling mosaic that filled her vision as the plane came in to land. Now she saw them separately: shops, lampposts, the windows of apartments. The lights of London.

She had been here the year before, visiting her sister. Sabrina had met her plane and taken her to Cadogan Square, where she had unlocked the door of her wonderful house and welcomed Stephanie inside. Now, in the dark taxi, Stephanie opened the soft leather purse in her lap and took out a set of keys. This time she was not a visitor. This time she would unlock the door. This time she was going home.

But the door swung open just as she reached it. "Welcome home, my lady!" Mrs. Thirkell beamed. "You *have* been missed!" She had coins ready and tipped the cabbie before picking up the luggage he had dropped inside the door. "You'll find a small repast in the dining room; I made your favorite trifle, and a few other dishes to tempt you, though I'm sure you don't need tempting after all that foreign food. You must be starved for home cooking. I was sure you'd be skin and bones, but I must admit you do look fine. Oh, my lady, I am glad you're back. Will you go up first, or straight to the dining room?"

My lady. Through her exhaustion, Stephanie thrilled to it and what it meant. A house organized around her comfort, everything taken care of, everything in order. But she was so tired. Tomorrow she would be able to appreciate it.

"I'll go up," she said. "I'm really too tired to eat." She began to wish Mrs. Thirkell good night, but stopped at the stricken look on her face. She saw in it the hours of preparation that had gone into her "small repast," her affection for Sabrina, her happy anticipation of seeing my lady's gratitude for good English food after wandering in foreign lands. Stephanie had never had a maid or a housekeeper. Sabrina would have known immediately that Mrs. Thirkell's beaming face was more important than her own exhaustion.

"On second thought," she said softly, turning toward the dining room, "the trifle sounds wonderful. The Chinese have nothing to compare with it. I'll have something now, Mrs. Thirkell, and then perhaps tomorrow morning you'll indulge me with breakfast in my room."

"Oh, my lady, exactly what I planned. You go ahead now; everything is ready for you. I'll just take these bags upstairs."

The jelly and custard of the trifle drifted through her dreams that night, between Nicholas Blackford's pastries scattered on a Shanghai street and the roast she had cooked for her family the night before she left for China. Above the food floated Mrs. Thirkell's rosy smile, surrounded by the bright lights of London and the bronze door knocker, shaped like a hand holding a scroll, that led the way into Sabrina's house.

The images clung to Stephanie's memory, so that when she awoke in the morning she knew instantly where she was. She woke slowly, stretching like a cat between smooth sheets of Egyptian cotton as fine as silk. She had not been able to find any nightgowns when she undressed the night before and now, with the cool sheets caressing her skin, she was aware of her nude body as if for the first time. She stretched again and at last opened her eyes.

The bedroom was large and L-shaped, the walls covered in

striped silk of pale blue and ivory, a peacock-blue carpet on the floor. The high Louis XIV bed and night tables were in the small part of the room; a sitting room took up the large part, with a love seat and chaise before the fireplace, two French bureaus along one wall and a matching dressing table nearby. A round table with a floor-length damask cloth and two upholstered chairs were placed beside high windows overlooking the walled backyard and terrace four floors below. It was an exquisite room, at once soft and vivid, spacious and snug.

Stephanie walked nude about the room, surprising herself. How easy it was, how free and confident she felt. Brushing her fingers across silks and polished woods, the marble fireplace and velvet chaise, she came to the tall mirror beside the dressing table and stood on tiptoe before it, spreading her arms wide. "My lady," she said to her reflection, and smiled at the brightness in her eyes.

Excitement was spreading through her like a flower opening wide. She looked about the luxurious room and listened to the silence. No one was calling for breakfast to be made or a button to be sewed on; no dirty clothes were piled up behind doors, waiting to be washed; the office staff did not expect her. She was alone. She was free. She was Lady Sabrina Longworth.

She rang for Mrs. Thirkell and asked for breakfast in half an hour. What time was it? It didn't matter.

In the carpeted bath and dressing room, she turned on the shower and stepped into the triangular pale yellow tub bordered on one side by trailing green plants and on the other by a recessed shelf of oils, soaps, brushes and shampoos. Debating among the unfamiliar names, she chose one at random. As the perfumed steam swirled around her, she thought with a sigh of pleasure that she had a week to try them all.

But suddenly, as she sat at the small table in the window, wearing a flowered silk robe, her hair drying in the sun, watching Mrs. Thirkell arrange the breakfast dishes and morning newspaper before her, everything changed—as if a door had been opened, letting an icy wind cut through the cozy room.

"What will you be wanting this week, my lady?" Mrs. Thirkell was asking. "I'll arrange to have Doris come in if you'll be entertaining, and I think Frank should give us an extra day; that was a halfhearted job he did on the windows last time. Princess Alexandra called last night after you'd gone to sleep; she said she would call back today unless you care to call her. I'll be going to the market this morning, so if you will tell me your plans . . ."

Stephanie looked out the window, feeling helpless. She wasn't Sabrina Longworth; how could she pretend to be? Mrs. Thirkell knew more about this kind of life than she did. She had none of her sister's sophistication and confidence with servants; she was ill at ease in the world of wealth. She was exactly what she had called herself in Mr. Su's antique shop: a suburban housewife. About to make a laughingstock of both herself and her sister.

Mrs. Thirkell was waiting for instructions. Stephanie shivered in the icy wind that had shattered her excitement. There was nothing she could do with her week of freedom but hide in the house, where no one could see her and point a scornful finger.

"My lady, are you ill? Shall I close the window?"

"No." Stephanie shook herself. "It's all right, Mrs. Thirkell; the air is warm. But I think I did catch something in China—maybe an Oriental flu—so I'll be staying in for a few days. And no entertaining. I'll leave the shopping up to you; the usual things."

Worried lines creased Mrs. Thirkell's forehead. "Dr. Farr could come over this morning, my lady—"

"No, no . . . I'll call if I don't get better. But I'm sure I'll be fine. In a few days, a week, I'll be back to normal."

"And you won't be going to Ambassadors, my lady?"

"Not for a few days."

"Well, then, if you have everything you need—"

"Yes, thank you, Mrs. Thirkell; this all looks lovely."

"Then I'll leave you with your breakfast. Though it's probably cold by now; I can warm it up in a minute—"

"Mrs. Thirkell. Everything is fine."

"All right, my lady. If you say so. I'll be going then."

Stephanie picked up her spoon. If she had to be imprisoned, what more comfortable place, complete with a mother? Who feeds the prisoner well, she thought wryly as she ate sliced melon and strawberries. The coddled eggs and croissants were cool, but she was so hungry that she ate everything. By the time she finished the tea, still hot in its insulated server, she felt better. I can go sight-seeing, she thought. That would be safe.

But first there were the closets, and the two bureaus. The night before, she'd had a glimpse at the clothes inside them, a whiff of scent clinging to soft fabrics. She planned to try on a few each day, over the whole week, but once she began she could not stop. It was like having free run of a designer shop: silk and lace underthings, cashmere sweaters and silk blouses, suits, dresses, evening gowns, shoes and shawls. And jewelry, tucked into a velvet-lined Russian chest.

She was trying on a dinner dress when, once again, without warning, her mood changed. The dress was of lilac silk, closely following her body from narrow shoulder straps to a flaring hem at her ankles. Holding the matching jacket trimmed in purple braid, Stephanie walked to the mirror and looked at her reflection.

Sabrina gazed back at her.

How had it happened? She stood with Sabrina's regal poise, balanced lightly on her feet, head high, eyes bright, lips curved expectantly. Slipping her feet into wisps of black high-heeled shoes and holding the jacket over her shoulder with one finger, she tilted her head, smiled exultantly and made a deep curtsy to Lady Sabrina Longworth.

There is nothing, she thought, that I cannot do.

Filled with energy, she looked at the checklist Sabrina had written and called Ambassadors. "I'll be in to check the mail, Brian, but not much more; I'm a bit under the weather, and if there's nothing urgent, I'll stay home for a few days. What day would you like to take off?"

"Thursday, my lady, if that is satisfactory."

"Perfectly."

She listened to her voice. Smooth and controlled. She had never had an employee; never learned to talk to one. But to Brian it was a voice he knew. And on Thursday she would go in to check Sabrina's mail.

Mrs. Thirkell returned, full of worry, and found Stephanie emptying one purse and filling another. "I'm going to take a walk, Mrs. Thirkell. Your wonderful breakfast almost cured me. I'll want a quiet week, however, so you can expect me for dinner every night. Do you see my watch anywhere? I can't seem to find it."

"Wouldn't you have put it in its regular place, my lady?"

Stephanie paused. "I have no idea. I was so tired last night I hardly knew my own name. I remember that excellent trifle, but—"

"And here it is," said Mrs. Thirkell triumphantly. "You may have been tired, but you put it exactly where it belongs."

Stephanie looked at the watch nestled in a small lucite box on the dressing table. "Amazing," she murmured.

"Well, there," said Mrs. Thirkell comfortably. "Habit does wonderful things for us. Here you are, my lady."

Stephanie put on the watch and glanced at the time. Almost three-thirty. She was stunned. Where had the day gone? Penny and Cliff would be home any—no, of course they wouldn't—at least, not here. In Evanston. Sabrina would be waiting—Sabrina! She was supposed to call at—what time was it in Evanston? Nine-thirty in the morning. It was all right, then; she'd remembered in time.

But she'd almost forgotten. Guilt swept through her. How could she forget her family? How could she let almost a whole day go by without thinking of her own family?

"When would you like dinner, my lady?" asked Mrs. Thirkell.

"Oh. At . . . the usual time. I won't be out long."

She shut the bedroom door. Sitting on the chaise, the telephone in her lap, she closed her eyes. There was her house, speckled with shade from the oak trees in the yard. There was the kitchen, honey-colored in the sunlight, and her children, grabbing books and lunch boxes as they left for school. And there was her husband's back as he walked to the campus. Where was Sabrina? Alone by now; probably exploring the house. This might be her first telephone call. Stephanie smiled mischievously as she gave the operator her number in Evanston.

"Am I speaking to the lady of the house? This is Lady Longworth in London, and I wish to speak to—"

"Stephanie!" cried Sabrina, an ocean away. "How wonderful!"

Stephanie tucked her legs under her, as she always did when they had a long talk, and began to ask about Garth and the children and answer Sabrina's questions. "Sabrina," she asked. "Did you ever tell me about the box on your dressing table where you put your watch at night?"

"I might have. I don't remember. Why?"

"You probably did; I put it there last night when I was wandering around totally exhausted, and stuffed with Mrs. Thirkell's trifle."

Sabrina laughed. "She's so proud of her trifle. And she knows I love it. She'll probably make another one for your birthday."

"Should I call you then? You always call me, and Garth might wonder—"

"Why don't I just tell him we talked when you called to ask about my trip? Enjoy your week; don't worry about telephone calls."

Stephanie heard impatience in Sabrina's voice. "Yes, he'll believe that. Are you in a hurry?"

"Oh, it's just that I have so much to do—the house and grocery shopping—"

Stephanie knew: errands, chores, the daily routine. After they said goodbye, she pictured Sabrina moving about her rooms, cooking in her kitchen, talking to her family, eating breakfast with Garth, sitting across the dinner table from Garth . . .

She wanted to call back and talk some more, but Sabrina had been impatient. And, after all, thought Stephanie, it's her house right now; I shouldn't interfere. She's not interfering with me. She jumped up and ran down the three flights of stairs to the front door. The week would pass all too quickly; it was time she got acquainted with her neighborhood.

Skirting the park, she walked to Sloan Square, smiling at its contrasts: the old Royal Court Theater opposite the modern Peter Jones Department Store, and in the center a fountain with reliefs of Charles II and his mistress, Nell Gwynne, in happy dalliance. Respectable London, she thought; racy London. Letting visitors think what they like. Chicago tries harder to impress us.

She was looking for differences to make the week more of an adventure. Walking up the other side of Sloan Street, she admired the sleek window displays of art and antiques, fashion, shoes, jewelry and books. No shopping today, she told herself sternly, determined to watch her money— and then, unable to resist, bought a sampling of handmade candies at Bendicks, and a small vial of perfume at Taylor of London.

DECEPTIONS

Nibbling on a candy, Stephanie strolled unhurriedly. She felt light and untethered, as if she were floating. How odd to feel that way, she thought, but then, passing Children's Bazaar, she knew why. *No one knew where she was.* No one was expecting her. She was alone; she was anonymous; she was free.

She passed strangers, some with closed, private faces, some openly admiring her beauty, most simply absorbed in their own lives. No one looked at her as if she were an outsider, and suddenly she did not feel like one. She bought a magazine, handling the unfamiliar coins speedily enough to satisfy the clerk. Watching for landmarks, she easily found her way home. Her key worked smoothly in her front door the first time she tried it. Mrs. Thirkell, telling her the mail was on the desk in the study, peered closely into her face as she asked if her flu was really better and showed no suspicion that she was not three inches from Lady Longworth.

Stephanie hugged her delight to herself as she climbed to the third-floor study. There is nothing I cannot do, she thought again. And silently she thanked Sabrina.

"My lady, I forgot to tell you," said Mrs. Thirkell on the house phone. "Now that you're back the flowers are coming again."

"Flowers," she said cautiously.

"I put them in the drawing room, as usual."

"I see. Thank you." Stephanie walked down one flight and there they were, dominating the room, overwhelming, absurd, magnificent: three dozen red roses rising from a crystal globe. And nestled among them, like bits of luminous moonlight, a dozen great white orchids.

She had never seen anything like it. The scent of the roses reached her down the length of the room, and she walked toward them, thinking how ridiculous to do anything on such a scale, what a flagrant waste of money—and how impressive. She read the card.

Welcome home, my lovely Sabrina. You have asked me not to call, so I do not call. But I return to London next week, and I rely on your goodness and the pleasant hours we have spent together to move you to give me an evening and then, at last, your hand as my wife.

Antonio.

181

"My lady," said Mrs. Thirkell, as Stephanie tucked the card back among the flowers. "Princess Alexandra."

Alexandra walked in behind her, tall, blond, striking. Stephanie had never met her; when she had visited Sabrina the year before, Alexandra was in France. But, seeing her walk in, Stephanie recognized her as a character come to life from the pages of Sabrina's letters—the daughter of a bit player in Hollywood who lived out all her mother's dreams by marrying a prince and moving easily among European nobility. She made a mock curtsy to Stephanie. "Couldn't resist the chance to greet the returned traveler. Did it do the trick?"

"The trick?"

"Finding new ways of handling old dilemmas. Wasn't that what you said you were going off to China for?"

"I'm trying something new; I'm not sure yet it will do any good."

"Well, in the meantime, you can revel at my house tomorrow night. A small do in your honor."

"A small—?"

"Birthday party. Honey, I apologize. I wrote you about it, honest to God I did, but it just never got mailed. I don't know how these things happen in a house full of servants—they never happen to you, do they? Anyway, it doesn't matter, because you told me you weren't making plans for the week, so of course you're free and you know I wouldn't let your birthday pass without a celebration. Some of your friends are coming, I think about sixteen, and we'll call it a welcome-home party if you've stopped counting birthdays, so don't argue with me, just show up in casual finery at eight. I'm counting on you."

"I think I have some kind of flu; I shouldn't—"

"The best cure for flu is a party. Ask any sensible doctor."

"Well . . . I'll let you know."

Alexandra blew her a kiss. "See you tomorrow," she said, and was gone. But before Stephanie could think about the party, the phone calls began, each one announced by Mrs. Thirkell in a voice sternly disapproving of anyone who would force my lady to talk when she had the flu. Michel Bernard called from Paris to ask if Alexandra's party was still on; he and Jolie would be there. Andrea Vernon trilled that her ballroom, redecorated by Sabrina with a hundred new lamps, was being featured in an Italian magazine, and the editor wanted

Sabrina in the pictures they would be taking in two weeks. "I'll let you know," Stephanie said. Amelia Blackford called to ask if Sabrina would care to accompany Nicholas to the Chilton auction next week. "I'll let you know," Stephanie said.

Between calls, she opened the mail—a cornucopia of invitations. House parties, tennis matches, dinners, a fox hunt in Derbyshire, a luncheon in honor of a Comtesse in Paris, a dozen charity balls between October and May. To Stephanie they were as overwhelming as Antonio's flowers: too much— yet wonderful. And just as she had caught the fragrance of the roses from far off, she could imagine the brilliance and gaiety promised by the heavy parchment and elaborate lettering of each invitation.

Piling them neatly for Sabrina, she realized wistfully that, between telephone calls and the mail, Sabrina's calendar for months ahead was more crowded than her own for this one week. All she had was—she looked at the calendar—a hairdresser appointment and a fitting with the dressmaker. And Alexandra's party.

But was she going to the party? The idea terrified and tantalized her. She didn't want to go and make a fool of herself; but after seeing Sabrina's photographs, she wanted to see Alexandra's house. And how wonderful to be the guest of honor at one of her parties.

After dinner, curled up on the chaise in the bedroom with books on London from Sabrina's library, Stephanie thought about Alexandra's party. She thought about it as she fell asleep; she woke up thinking about it. I'll decide later, she told herself. After I do some sight-seeing.

But first, reluctantly, she telephoned Sabrina's hairdresser to cancel her appointment. He would know instantly that her hair had been cut by someone else. We can fool a husband, she thought wryly, but not a hairdresser. But I will go to the dressmaker; I've always wanted one, and this is my chance.

And Alexandra's invitation is my chance for a party this week. One party. To balance all those invitations. Why not? Climbing the steps of Mrs. Pemberley's flat on a warm September morning, Stephanie held her head high. I'll celebrate Lady Sabrina Longworth's thirty-second birthday in style, and no one will know I'm really celebrating the birthday of a suburban housewife who never even had a dressmaker.

Mrs. Pemberley adjusted the three-way mirror. "Madame

perhaps gained a pound or two on her Chinese excursion," she said through a mouthful of pins.

Stephanie looked down at her bent head and said nothing.

"But, of course," she added hastily, "madame's figure is so superb it does not matter." Her fingers, pinning a dart in the suede dress, trembled.

She's afraid, Stephanie thought, afraid I'll be offended and find another dressmaker. It was the first time she had ever felt the power that influential people have over those who serve them.

"Now if madame will look," said Mrs. Pemberley, getting to her feet. "I made a small change at the shoulder, here, so the sleeve moves more gracefully, but otherwise it is as madame wished. As you see—" She opened a glossy French magazine to a photograph of a model in a suede dress. And suddenly Stephanie understood the high fashion in her sister's closet—thousands of dollars worth of designer clothes costing a fraction of that because she had found a dressmaker who could copy photographs down to the smallest seam, modified to suit Sabrina's flair.

She looked from the magazine to her reflected image. "Marvelous," she murmured, and Mrs. Pemberley's face relaxed into a smile. She brought out another dress and then another, followed by an evening gown, two suits sleek enough to wear to dinner after a day of work, a floor-length wool paisley skirt with a velvet cloak and a pair of pants with a hacking jacket. As Stephanie tried them on, Mrs. Pemberley made adjustments and chatted about other customers, many of them obviously sent to her by Sabrina.

"—and Princess Alexandra tells me it is your birthday today, madame; my very best wishes. The party sounds quite festive."

"I beg your pardon?" Stephanie was startled. If she made a mistake tonight, how long would it be before everyone knew it?

Mrs. Pemberley's fear returned; she clamped her lips so that no further personal remarks would slip through. Stephanie felt sorry for her but said nothing, and the fitting ended in silence. "The garments will be ready in a week, madame," said Mrs. Pemberley as she was leaving.

Stephanie nodded. She felt guilty for causing her worry. "I'm very pleased with them," she said, and left quickly. She wasn't sure she liked having the power that Sabrina and her friends took for granted.

As soon as she left Mrs. Pemberley, Stephanie became anonymous again. Riding double-decker buses and the underground, with its clean-swept cars and velvet seats, she explored from Kensington Church Street to Gray's Mews in Bond Street. The buildings were not as tall as American skyscrapers, the shops smaller but more numerous, making Stephanie think of rooms in a vast museum filled with fabulous objects—antique furniture, porcelain, chandeliers, cut glass, clocks, dolls, jewelry and paintings. Gazing and dreaming, she felt like a young girl again, shopping with Sabrina and her mother in the enchanted world of open markets and small dusty shops. How simple everything had seemed when they were children! No complicated marriage, no worries about money, no search for a different kind of life.

But we ran away from the chauffeur, she remembered with a smile. Wanting to be free.

The statue of King George I in Grosvenor Square looked blankly past her as she remembered Athens. I've done it again, she thought. Run away to be free. Across the square stretched the block-long American Embassy where they had visited occasionally with their father. She walked toward it. First I ran away from my father, and then from Garth. She walked past it. But of course I'm going back to Garth.

She joined the crowds strolling on Park Lane along the green expanse of Hyde Park, nannies pushing baby carriages, dowdy dowagers, free-skirted young girls talking of discos, businessmen in derby hats, businesswomen in suits and white blouses. Harrods and then home, she decided, and quickened her walk until she saw the distinctive round awnings with scalloped edges and the store's name in bold handwriting—the largest department store in Europe and one of the most luxurious anywhere in the world, even boasting its own uniformed doorman.

She wandered happily through the aisles, looking for a gift she could leave behind for Sabrina when she went back to Evanston, and was in the Wedgwood room when, behind her, someone cried, "Sabrina!"

"Sabrina, isn't this amazing?" She was hugged and kissed on the cheek by an exquisite young woman, small and delicate, with a halo of ash-blond hair and wide gray eyes. "We're going to see you tonight and now here you are. Happy birthday!"

Stephanie stared. "Gabrielle! You haven't changed a bit!"

"In two weeks? I hope not. Unless you mean . . . have you already heard? Who from? We were waiting to tell you first."

"Heard what?" Stephanie's heart was racing; what a stupid thing to say. But she had been so surprised—Gabrielle de Martel, Sabrina's roommate at Juliette, here in the middle of Harrods. Stephanie hadn't seen her in almost fifteen years, but she looked just the same, though Sabrina had written that she was divorced and living in London, modeling for a cosmetics firm. Her voice was the same, too: light and a little breathless.

"Oh, good, you haven't heard. Here's my news."

Stephanie looked up as Gabrielle put her hand on the arm of a man standing behind her and brought him forward. He towered over her, handsome, broad-shouldered, muscular, with thick blond hair and impatient brown eyes, exactly as Sabrina had described him. Brooks Westermarck, president of Westermarck Cosmetics; wealthy, hardworking, a favorite of society reporters and photographers, always accompanied by a different beautiful woman.

"Welcome home, Sabrina," he said pleasantly. "Did you bring me my Chinese dancer?"

Dancer. Now what? Stephanie despaired. I can't keep up; there are too many— Then she remembered the carved jade figures Sabrina had bought in Peking. Which was Brooks's dancer? She didn't know. "Of course," she said easily. She could put off giving it to him for the week. "But I still don't know your news."

"We're living together," said Gabrielle. "You wouldn't advise me, so I made up my own mind. Now tell me, what would your advice have been?"

"To live with Brooks," said Stephanie instantly.

Brooks laughed. "Wise woman. Will you have dinner with us tomorrow night, Sabrina?"

"To celebrate," Gabrielle added. "At Annabel's. Brooks has been a member for years, but I've never been there. Do come."

"Oh, not this week; I really planned to stay home the whole—"

"Because Antonio is out of town? He wouldn't mind; we're quite respectable. And I've been waiting to celebrate until you got back. Please, I want you to."

"And what is more important than what Gaby wants?" asked Brooks, amused.

Well, why not? Stephanie thought. If Sabrina can have a full calendar, so can I. "I will, then; thank you. But since it's your celebration, I'll expect you to do all the talking."

"Wonderfully tactful, Lady Longworth," said Brooks, still amused. "You'll make Gaby the happiest woman at Annabel's."

The honeymoon, Stephanie thought, surprising herself with her bitterness. Just beginning. Once Garth and I were like that, our faces shining with happiness, as if we had a wonderful secret. And we did: we were in love. How long ago that seems. I don't even remember how it feels.

At home, Mrs. Thirkell brought her tea to the study as she went through the mail and telephone messages. And then she began to get ready for Alexandra's party.

In the bath, bubbles rising languorously about her, she heard the telephone and then Mrs. Thirkell coming upstairs to stand outside the bathroom door. "Princess Alexandra called, my lady. Her chauffeur will come for you at eight. What dress shall I put out?"

"I'll take care of it, Mrs. Thirkell," Stephanie said, wondering if she could ask her for a suggestion. She shook her head. Sabrina wouldn't do that. Sabrina would decide for herself. And whatever she chose would be right. Because if you are Lady Sabrina Longworth, who will tell you that you have on the wrong dress? Or that you are not clever enough to keep up with the people you meet?

And when she walked into Alexandra's salon, she knew she was right. She stood in the center of the room, poised, slender, as simple and elegant as a jewel in a full-length emerald-green taffeta skirt and a white satin blouse with tiny rhinestone buttons. Guests surrounded her with a confusion of smiles, kisses and birthday greetings; she saw Gabrielle and Brooks and was trying to match the other faces with Sabrina's descriptions when one lively voice rose above the others.

"And do you know, they bought identical Chinese dresses and I could not tell them apart? You would not have believed my bafflement! Now tell me," said Nicholas Blackford, smiling with genial wickedness at Stephanie as the other guests looked on. "Which one are you, really? 'Fess up! You're Stephanie, come to fool us all; isn't that right?"

Stephanie was stunned, the center of attention with nothing to say. She felt sick. Sabrina was successfully deceiving a husband and children, but she couldn't even fool casual friends. She lowered her eyes and caught the light flashing from her rhinestone buttons. In an instant her head came up. She knew she looked exactly like Sabrina; no one suspected anything. Nicholas was playing a game. I can play, too, she thought.

She had hesitated only a few seconds. Looking at Nicholas's small figure bouncing on the balls of his feet, she put on a worried frown. "Nicholas, you've confused me so much I'm not sure myself. But I've always trusted your judgment, so I put myself in your hands. You tell me who I am, and that's who I'll be."

Everyone burst into laughter and applause. "She's got you, Nicky," said Alexandra. "Who is she?"

Nicholas bowed over Stephanie's hand and kissed it. "Who else but our magnificent Sabrina? I never had a moment's doubt, my dear. In China I was confused because of that dreadful diet I was on. You know, I was starving the entire time I was there."

Stephanie smiled, the knot of tension unraveling inside her. "As I recall, the pastry-shop clerks heard all about your diet. Many times."

Amid the laughter, Alexandra led them to a buffet of hors d'oeuvres. Stephanie's breathing returned to normal. It was going to be all right. She was going to be all right.

"I wish I'd met your sister last year," Alexandra said. "Is she really your double?"

"No, of course not. We caught Nicholas with an armload of pastries, and he was so embarrassed he made up the first excuse he could think of." Stephanie listened to herself in amazement. How easily she lied. But she knew why it was easy. These people heard what they wanted to hear. Whatever she said, they would make it fit what they expected her to say, or wanted her to say. Did they really listen to her? Did they really look at her? Only as much as they wanted to. As she and Alexandra laughed together, she felt herself slide smoothly into place. The week was finally hers.

"Nicholas and his games," said Alexandra.

Stephanie, envying her statuesque beauty and flamboyant gypsy dress, had been trying not to stare; now, with her new confidence, she looked boldly at her. "You look magnificent. A gypsy queen."

"It was your idea, honey. And you were right, as always. Now look, you're not eating and it's your party. Fill up your plate: grape leaves, spinach something with pine nuts, flaming Saganaki—where's Arnold with the match?"

"Arnold?"

"The caterer, honey. Why can't you ever remember his name?"

"Maybe I don't like the way he combs his hair," Stephanie said, thinking: How incredible to have a caterer for only sixteen people. She'd given dinners for twenty or more with only Garth to help her clean up afterwards.

Arnold came from the kitchen with a long match and set aflame the squares of Saganaki cheese, fried in butter and surrounded with brandy. Stephanie looked at his hair, combed forward so that he looked like a sheep dog. How had she known? Had Sabrina mentioned a caterer named Arnold with sheep-dog hair?

"Sabrina, you look wonderful," someone said in a low voice. "No worries in China?"

She turned and met bright eyes in a pleasant face; a small man, ordinary looking; she would never notice him in a crowd. That was exactly the way Sabrina had described him: Michel Bernard.

"What should I worry about in China?" she asked.

"Nothing; you're absolutely right. But when we got your letter we were afraid your news might spoil the trip."

"Oh. Well, there wasn't time to think; our tour guide organized every minute—" She felt her way cautiously, with no idea what he was talking about. "What—what did you think of my letter?"

"We thought it was wonderful, of course; and you were wonderful to have the courage to write it." His voice dropped even lower. "Not many experts would admit they'd been taken in by a forgery. But I want you to know it helped us. Oddly enough, not the stork as much as the names on the certificate you sent. Some of those names have been used more than once—would you believe it?"

She shook her head.

"It seems to be their first real mistake. You'd think they'd be smart enough to make up different names for each fake certificate."

He paused, waiting for Stephanie to say something. She nodded.

"But the story's delayed by all this new information. We won't be ready to publish before November, middle or end of the month. That could help you, don't you think?"

"I think so . . ."

"Especially if you're going to try to get the stork back. Have you decided? Or don't you think the grand Olivia will keep your secret?"

"I don't know."

"If we can do anything to help—"

Stephanie was dizzy. "You could tell me what you've found," she said desperately.

"Since we talked last? Not much; mostly confirmation of what we already told you. But it's not a bad idea to go over the whole story; how about Monday? We'll be out of town until then."

"Not Monday." Monday morning she would be on her way to meet Sabrina in Chicago. Monday afternoon Sabrina would be flying back to London. "Can't we talk this weekend?"

"Maybe. We'll call you from Paris on Thursday or Friday when we know our schedule. What do I hear?"

Stephanie heard it, too, softly but growing louder: a lilting Greek melody strummed on a bouzouki. As the guests grew quiet, listening, Alexandra pulled aside a curtain at one end of the room to reveal a small orchestra with the bouzouki player in front, sitting cross-legged on the floor. At his signal the orchestra picked up the melody, following the tunes his quick fingers wove together.

The lights dimmed. Like silent shadows, waiters set up a low table surrounded with large tasseled cushions, and set it with gold plates and goblets, baskets of pita bread, steaming platters of lamb and onion kebobs, shrimp in wine sauce, cod with tomatoes and currants, lemon chicken, bowls of fresh fruit and bottles of red and white wines from the Island of Rhodes, all illuminated by flickering candles set in saucers of floating camellias.

Alexandra took Stephanie's hand and led her to the cushion at the head of the table. "The guest of honor."

Wide-eyed, Stephanie felt like an awestruck girl from the

country. How would Sabrina act? Pleased, but not overwhelmed; this was her world. She let herself look delighted and turned to Alexandra on her left. "It's marvelous. You've become an expert on Greece."

"Not me. Arnold has a Greek wife. I took her ideas and added a few of my own."

"But," said Stephanie, looking around the table, "where are the sheeps' lungs fried in oil?"

"I vetoed them. How do you know about such things?"

"A long time ago we lived in Athens. . . ." Stephanie told the story of the day she and Sabrina had escaped from their chauffeured limousine and walked into a street battle over Cyprus. Everyone fell silent, listening, and for a brief, clear moment she saw, as if from far off, the lavish table with its guests, and the small ghosts of two sisters huddled in a cellar, holding each other, while heavy boots tramped overhead. And in that moment she was both sisters: Stephanie living Sabrina's life; Sabrina describing a time when she and her sister Stephanie were frightened children, clinging together for protection.

"Poor things," said Amelia Blackford. "How terrifying for you."

"Sabrina gave me courage," said Stephanie softly. "She always—"

"*Who?*" said Jolie and Michel together.

Stephanie laughed slightly. "We gave each other courage."

"Well," said Amelia. "Nothing that exciting ever happened to me."

The spell was broken. The conversations resumed until the last of the baklava and thick black coffee was gone and Alexandra announced it was time for presents.

Everyone had brought something: Nicholas and Amelia, a nineteenth-century Saint Gobain hand mirror with a carved ivory handle; Michel and Jolie, a book of Greek art; Gabrielle and Brooks, a cashmere shawl from India; Alexandra, a set of crystal candlesticks. The other guests brought books, jeweled hair clasps, framed prints and a miniature porcelain dancer.

"And this," said Alexandra, handing her a slender, silver-wrapped box. "Antonio had it delivered. Do you want to open it now or at home?"

"Oh, now," said Gabrielle. "Do open it now."

Stephanie was uncertain. "Perhaps I'd better wait—" But the gift was already public. She tore off the paper and silently lifted from the box a gleaming strand of perfect star sapphires and diamonds. A note lay in the bottom of the box. She ignored it. There was a kind of brutality in Antonio's sending the gift to Alexandra's house, knowing it would likely be opened before a group of people—as if he had flung it in Sabrina's face, daring her to deny in public that he had the right to drape her in such jewels. Stephanie let the necklace drop into the box. The others felt her embarrassment and said nothing.

Alexandra clapped her hands once. Dancers appeared, the lights were turned up and waiters moved about the table with after-dinner drinks. Stephanie excused herself to Alexandra. She wanted to be alone, and to see the house. "I won't be long."

"Take your time, honey. You know your way around."

She didn't, but she remembered Sabrina's photographs. As the others watched the gyrations of a spectacular belly dancer, she slipped away and walked up the open staircase to the floor above.

She wandered from room to room in delight and pride. Sabrina had created an air of playfulness and exuberance that most designers, heavy-handed and pompous, never achieved, and now Stephanie could understand why the house was still being photographed for design magazines in America and Europe.

What luck, she thought enviously, to have such a chance— to take an empty house and create a home, an atmosphere, a place for parties and privacy and love ... oh, what a chance.

She stood before a whimsical Miro painting and gazed at the thick, childlike strokes, strong and full of purpose. What I wouldn't give for such a chance, she thought.

"Honey, you all right?"

She turned. "Yes. I've been rude. I'm sorry."

"It's your party and almost your house. If you want to be alone, don't apologize. What's he really like, your Antonio?"

"Occasionally crude."

"That I know. That we just saw. And?"

"Occasionally pleasant."

"How else could he keep you interested for almost a year? Okay, you'd rather not talk about him. Want me to show you something I discovered recently? You'll recognize it." She led Stephanie downstairs to a dim corner of the salon and pointed to the floor. "Isn't that amazing? Who do you suppose thought of such a thing?"

Stephanie bent down and looked at the small distinct *S* in the design of the parquet floor. "Clever," she murmured, smiling. Sabrina had sent her a photograph of it, thinking no one else would ever know.

"Clever, indeed. You know, honey, I'm so thrilled with this place, you could have carved it six feet high over the front door. You didn't have to hide it."

Still smiling, flushed with the pride and sense of ownership Sabrina had felt in completing the house, Stephanie touched the small letter with the toe of her shoe. "It's big enough," she said softly. "It was enough that I knew I had left my mark."

The next morning, haunted by her sister's mark in the floor, Stephanie went to Ambassadors. It was Brian's day off, and the shop was closed. She tried the keys on her ring until one of them opened the door.

She had been here before with Sabrina. Now she raised the shades on the front window and walked down the long narrow showroom modeled after an eighteenth-century salon. It was uncrowded and elegant, with a few fine pieces arranged in twos and threes, brightened by sunlight or the diffuse light of shaded lamps. At the back of the room, through a doorway, was Sabrina's office with the cherry table she used as a desk.

Stephanie sat at the table, taking in the long, low, crowded bookshelves, windows draped in antique velvet, oriental rugs and deep armchairs for visitors. Success and accomplishment were here, along with self-confidence, money, even power. She felt as small as her reflection in the silver tea service on a side table as she recaptured her feelings of the night before: pride, envy, ownership—and longing.

"I have to do something," she said to her reflection. "I've only done one thing, really: be a housewife. I've had one home for twelve years, one failed business, one man . . ." Wait, she told herself. Think about something to do, about getting back my own business. That's enough for now. Don't think about other failures. Only that one.

The chimes at the front door startled her. I forgot to lock it, she thought, and went to the showroom to explain that the shop was closed.

"Aha, someone home after all," said a heavyset man

hunched on a Regency armchair. He was taking off his shoes and massaging his feet. "Lucky for you; you almost lost a sale. You work here? Well, of course you do, what a question. And you are one beautiful girl, which I'm sure you don't mind my saying. You have what Betty— my wife, that is—calls an English complexion. The wife says one thing about me: I can spot a foreigner even before they open their mouth, and I would know you for English anywhere. I see you're looking at your little chair here. I had to sit down, the wife's been dragging me in and out of antique shops all day. Couldn't even see the changing of the guard at Buckingham Palace, I thought my feet would fall off. She's somewhere, I came in here, your door was unlocked. I won't break your chair, if that's what's worrying you."

"And what may I show you?" asked Stephanie, keeping her eyes lowered to hide the laughter in them. "You could surprise your wife with something quite remarkable. For instance"— she went to a back shelf and returned with a French beaded evening bag and a magnifying glass—"this dates from about 1690, a stunning piece of work—here, use the glass to look at it. Do you see the individual beads? And the stitching?"

He looked closely. The beads were no bigger than grains of sand, the stitches between them even tinier. Without the magnifying glass the floral design looked like a painting; under the glass it became a mosaic of wondrous delicacy.

"Not bad," the man said admiringly. "How the hell d'they do that?"

"I believe children made them. They probably suffered eyestrain, but the great ladies of the royal court had to have their evening bags."

"Not bad," he repeated. "Betty'd like to be a great lady. How much?"

"Six hundred pounds," said Stephanie, guessing from French bags she had seen in Bond Street.

"Don't give me pounds, give me dollars."

"Twelve hundred dollars."

He whistled. "You've got a nerve, little lady. Two hundred, and that's probably too much."

Stephanie was furious. How dare he try to bargain with her as if Ambassadors was a stall in a flea market? She wanted to make this sale; it was suddenly very important that she sell something from Ambassadors, but she would make it on her terms, not those of some crude bargainer. She smiled gently. "Where are you from, Mr.—?"

"Pullem. Omaha. I'm in meat."

Stephanie pictured him up to his chin in ground beef. "And you go to Chicago on occasion? San Francisco? New York? New Orleans?" He nodded each time. "And you take Betty."

"Course. Kids are grown, nothing for her to do at home."

"Do you know, Mr. Pullem, in all those cities, and in every other city in America, Betty will be the only woman with an evening bag like this one? Everyone will beg to look at it. Every woman will want one. But there is no other exactly like it anywhere in the world."

There was a pause. He turned the bag in his hands. "Six hundred."

"Is that in pounds?"

"Dollars! Dollars! Pounds are for meat, not money."

Gently, Stephanie took the bag from him. "I'm sorry, Mr. Pullem. I would have been pleased to help you make your Betty a great lady." She walked to the back of the store.

"Seven hundred!" he said. "Make it seven-fifty and that's it."

Stephanie turned. "Mr. Pullem. We do not bargain at Ambassadors." She was arranging the bag on the shelf when she heard him stand up.

"You drive a hard bargain. Shoulda been an American." He laid twelve one-hundred dollar bills on the table beside him. "Betty doesn't like it I can return it, right?"

Stephanie wrapped the bag in tissue and a small box she found in Brian's office. "Of course. I think you need not worry, however."

He put on his shoes and reached for the box. As Stephanie gave it to him, with a receipt, he held onto her hand. "You're one beautiful girl, you know. Hard bargains and all. Maybe I'll bring the wife in some day. When I make my second fortune." He winked as he left.

Jubilantly, Stephanie let out her breath in a long sigh. I did it, she sang to herself; I can do anything. She locked the front door and put the money with a note in Brian's desk and twirled from his office to the cherry table. Standing there, she looked with a different air around the office and into the show-room. Now she belonged here. Like her sister, she had left her mark.

Annabel's only seems noisy to those who want a quiet evening. For most, the music and talk mean excitement: marriages begun or ended, affairs budding or withering, agreements concluded, acquaintances struck. The membership of Annabel's is distinguished, and so is the menu. In any season diners can order raspberries, asparagus, truffles or snails, flown in from private sources and elegantly served. Annabel's is a place to dine and dance, but, more important, to see the ebb and flow of one's social world.

Maxim Stuyvesant often used Annabel's as a meeting place. The chatter and dim lights gave him more privacy than his office, and the staff would save his corner table for hours if they knew he was coming. In all the cities of the world where he conducted business and sought pleasure, Max looked for such a place. Annabel's, on Berkeley Square, was his favorite.

On Thursday night he arrived at nine with his guest, a small bearded man with piercing eyes magnified by round glasses and a cultivated air of boredom. As they settled themselves at Max's table, their waiter brought from the wine cellar a bottle of Chardonnay and opened it. Max sniffed the cork. "The fish tonight?"

"Swordfish in sea urchin sauce. Very delicate. Very fine."

He looked at his guest, who nodded. "For both of us," Max said. "Let Louis select the rest of the meal. Bring some paté now, and give us half an hour before you serve the soup."

"Louis?" asked his guest.

"The chef. He provides an excellent meal."

"With half an hour for business."

"With half an hour for pleasant conversation to put us in a proper mood for dining. Our business should take no more than a few minutes." He filled their wine glasses. "To the glories of the past."

Ronald Dowling nodded, sipped, raised his eyebrows at the quality of the wine and sipped again. "The vase is all you claimed. I am impressed. Even in your dingy warehouse—"

"Not mine. Westbridge Imports."

"They're the ones who brought it out? Across the Mediterranean to—where? France? Or directly on to Britain?"

Max smiled. "Annabel's is noisy tonight; I didn't hear you. The Etruscan vase you saw comes from the collection of a noble English family forced to sell one of its estates to raise money. Westbridge Imports handled the estate sale; when they saw the vase they called me, knowing my clients are interested in ancient treasures and can afford to pay for them."

Dowling smiled thinly. "I saw the listing in the catalogue you sent me. You may tell that story to others, Stuyvesant, but I flew in from Toronto especially to see this vase. I'm paying you a million and a half dollars for it, and in return I expect the truth, not a fairy tale."

"In art and sex one is never sure of the truth."

"I'm not joking, Stuyvesant."

"Ronald, if I told you an item was smuggled out of Turkey and listed as part of a duke's estate sale; that the duke was paid twenty thousand pounds to swear, if asked, that the item had been in his family for generations; and that the item will be smuggled into the country where its purchaser lives—would you not say that that sounds more like a fairy tale than my first story?"

Dowling's eyes gleamed. "I'd say it sounds like more fun than drilling for oil and gas in western Canada—and a damn sight more dangerous."

Max shrugged. "Life is full of dangers. Try getting safely across Fifth Avenue in New York. Or the Via Veneto in Rome."

They chuckled.

"All right," Dowling said. "Tomorrow I will deposit to your account in Switzerland ten percent of the purchase price in gold. When you deliver the vase to my home in Toronto, you'll receive the balance."

"Not quite, Ronald. When the vase reaches Canada, approximately four weeks after the deposit of the gold, you will be notified. You will wish to examine it. When you are satisfied, you will arrange for the balance to be paid. And then you take possession."

Dowling nodded. "I was told you were a careful man. I like that. I'll call my agent in the morning."

Max signaled to the waiter with his hand. "Another bottle," he said, and sat back, surveying the crowd. His survey stopped at a group of three people being shown to a table across the room. He gazed at one of them thoughtfully.

"—your other activities," Dowling was saying. "Real estate, you said? And art galleries? With so many legitimate—"

Max stood. "Excuse me one moment; I must speak to someone."

He moved smoothly between the tables and brass-covered pillars and was speaking as he reached the group. "My dear Brooks, good to see you again after all these years. And Sabrina." He lifted her hand to his lips. "I had heard you were in South America. A malicious rumor?"

Looking up, Stephanie saw only the man, his bulk blocking her view of the room. His dark suit was superbly cut and his bearing assured, even arrogant. Red hair shot with gray frizzled in a mock halo around his head, and his flat eyes reflected her image, revealing nothing of himself. Her hand closely held in his, Stephanie was conscious of his power, and excitement flared within her. She lowered her eyes to hide it, but his face subtly changed and she knew he had seen. She had no idea who he was and glanced at Brooks, who was introducing Gabrielle.

"Max Stuyvesant, Gaby. Max, Gabrielle de Martel."

Max deftly switched from Stephanie's hand to Gabrielle's, but the kiss he gave it was perfunctory. "I believe you came to London about the time I left for New York."

"Three years ago," said Gabrielle, examining him with open curiosity. "I've heard so much about you."

He smiled amiably and turned back to Sabrina. "Was it a malicious rumor that you were in Brazil?"

"Malicious or hopeful," she said. "Depending on who began it."

He laughed. "Your wit has not diminished. Later, after we have dined, will you dance with me?"

"I haven't—" she stopped. She hadn't danced in years, but had Sabrina? "I'm sorry; I don't think so."

"It would be a favor; I am assuming you would not criticize my lack of practice."

She looked up at him, at the small smile on his lips, the flat gray eyes, watching. "All right. I'd like to."

"Until then. Brooks, Gabrielle, a pleasant dinner." He bowed slightly and left.

"How odd," said Gabrielle as the waiter poured their wine. "You hear so many rumors about someone you feel you know him, and then he turns out to be completely different. You knew him years ago, didn't you, Sabrina? When you and Denton were married?"

"Yes," Stephanie said cautiously. Had Sabrina liked him? Loved him? She had never mentioned his name. "What rumors have you heard?"

"None that you haven't heard. He certainly seems more civilized than they make him out to be. But Brooks doesn't like him."

Brooks gazed at her. "You never fail to astonish me, Gabrielle. Was I impolite?"

"No. Impassive. The way you are when you disapprove of something I say or do, but you'll wait until later to spank me in private."

"And have I ever spanked you?"

"Only with words."

There was a pause. Brooks put his hand over Gabrielle's. "I apologize. I never thought of a spanking. And I promise I will not spank Max Stuyvesant, in public or in private."

Gabrielle laughed. "I hope not. He might turn the tables."

"Was there really an Annabel?" asked Stephanie. They were making her uncomfortable—childlike Gabrielle, who, surely, had been more grown-up long ago at Juliette, and Brooks, acting like a teacher, amused, critical, surprised when his student said something intelligent.

"I never met Annabel," said Brooks as the waiter served their soup. "But if you want to know the story of the club—"

"Where does he get his money?" asked Gabrielle.

Brooks sighed. "The fascinating Max Stuyvesant. No one really knows. He owns art galleries in Europe and the Americas, and he may be an agent, but none of that would account for his wealth. He's seen at auctions, and his private collection is considered one of the finest in the world. Beyond that, everything is rumor. He doesn't talk. And he's been gone for three years, so the rumors are no doubt even less reliable than usual."

"Will you, Sabrina? Brian can manage Ambassadors another day, can't he? He did the whole time you were in China. And we'll be back Sunday evening. Sabrina. Have you been listening?"

"No, I'm sorry; I seem to have—"

"Drifted away. Now listen: Will you come with us to Switzerland?"

"Switzerland?"

"I repeat, since you were not listening. Tomorrow Brooks is flying to Bern on business, and I'm tagging along. I shall be dreadfully bored while he is working, so I'm asking you to join us. There's plenty of room in the plane, and Brooks will take care of your hotel room. We'll be back on Sunday. Yes?"

Stephanie did not hesitate. "Yes."

Gabrielle clapped her hands. A waiter cleared their plates, another poured coffee, a third divided a sugared Grand Marnier soufflé among them as they talked together like old friends. Stephanie smiled with pleasure. And her smile met the answering smile of Max Stuyvesant as he made his way once more to her table.

The dance floor was crowded, and they moved in a narrow space. The rhythm of the music, slow with a steady heartbeat in the bass, slid into Stephanie's blood, and her body swayed as she followed Max's lead.

"How is it we have never danced?" he asked.

"How is it we have never talked?" she responded recklessly. She felt young and unfettered, and she saw in his smile that she was beautiful and that he desired her.

"Talked," he repeated. "For some time I had the impression that you would have found cozy chats with me distasteful."

"Which explains why we have never danced."

"My impression or your distaste?"

"Both."

"Very quick, Sabrina. Will you have dinner with me tomorrow night?"

"No."

"How abrupt. Not even an excuse? The South American, for example?"

"I'm sorry. I'll be away until Sunday."

"Sunday night, then."

"Late Sunday."

"I am free on Monday."

"On Monday I'll . . . be away again, for the day and evening."

The dance ended. He still held her. "We will find an evening. May I call you next week?"

Stephanie nodded, and they walked back to her table. She was shaken by her thoughts. She wanted him. A stranger—mysterious, arrogant, with cold eyes and an air of absolute assurance. So different from Garth, who was content to fill his own place in the world without demanding a larger one. How could she desire him? She had never desired anyone but Garth, and not even Garth, in this trembling way, for years. She breathed a sigh of thanks that she would be away for the next three days.

Which meant she would never see Max Stuyvesant again.

They reached the table. Gaby and Brooks were dancing and Stephanie hesitated. Well, then, she would never see him again. That was the best way to handle the feelings churning within her. "Goodbye," she said, unable to keep a regretful note from her voice.

He kissed her hand. "Until next week."

Stephanie watched him return to the table where his friend waited. She picked up her wine glass and a waiter rushed to fill it. The best way, she repeated to herself. She tasted the pale gold of her wine. Tomorrow they would leave for Bern.

The Lear jet was furnished with a built-in, curved leather couch, two armchairs and a long teak table used as a desk and for eating the Fortnum and Mason box lunches Brooks ordered for his trips. On the hour-and-a-half flight to Bern, Gabrielle and Stephanie feasted on French cheeses, bread and fruit, while Brooks read the reports of his managers in Bern.

"They're introducing a new line of cosmetics," said Gabrielle. "Or maybe an old line with new names. Brooks refuses to talk about it; you wouldn't believe the games they play with lipsticks and moisturizers and all the rest: passwords, codes, secret formulas, spies from other companies. It is big, big business."

Stephanie rested her arm along the back of the soft leather couch and looked through the window at the small, neat fields below, far different from the sprawling landscapes of America. But everything is different from America, she thought. Here is Stephanie Andersen, dashing off for a quick trip to Switzerland in a friend's private jet while her housekeeper tends her five-story town house and plans a tempting snack for Sunday night when my lady returns. "Nice," she said.

"What, the view? I like the Alps better. Do you know what I thought we might do? Visit Juliette. I haven't been back since we graduated, and it's less than an hour by train. What do you think?"

"I think I'd love it."

But when they were there, standing in the park and looking up at the school's balconies and red tiled roof, they were dismayed. Nothing had changed, but—"How small everything is!" they said. Professor Bossard's castle was just a large, handsome building in a pleasant park, neither as awesome nor as grand as it had seemed when they were students. "And look how young the girls are," Gabrielle marveled. "Not nearly as sophisticated as we were."

Stephanie smiled. "Maybe we weren't."

"Of course we were."

"I don't know. We sat up there on the fourth floor and dreamed about growing up—"

"Third."

"What?"

"We lived on the third floor. Your sister lived on the fourth, remember, with that girl, what was her name? The one from New York."

"Dena Cardozo. You're right." They wandered through the building—"feeling older every minute," Stephanie murmured. Professor Bossard was dead, his place taken by a rotund, white-bearded Santa whom they found in the gymnasium discussing tournaments with the fencing instructor.

Stephanie walked to the center of the room, imagining the foil in her hand, remembering a match she had lost, and a quarrel with Sabrina.

"Gaby," she said abruptly, "I'm starved. Let's go into town for something to eat."

They walked down the hill, through the vineyards. "I had a good time there," said Gabrielle. "But I was always disappointing people who expected too much of me. You knew you wanted to do something in art and antiques, but all I wanted was to find somebody to take care of me. To stand between me and the world and cherish me. Do you know what I mean?"

Stephanie nodded, her eyes on the choppy blue of Lake Geneva and the jagged Alps beyond the far shore. Wasn't that exactly what she had wanted with Garth? "And now you have Brooks," she said.

"Now I have Brooks. As long as I can walk the line that keeps him happy."

In the town, they found the small café that had been their

favorite when they were students. They sat outside in the sun and ordered lunch. "Walk what line?" asked Stephanie.

"The one you warned me about."

They were silent. "And was I right?"

"You were always right about Brooks. He wants a child-bride he can mold and be proud of and be adored by. And he also wants someone who can fuck like a professional and make smart conversation at dinner."

Taken aback, Stephanie said, "Did I really say that?"

"Not exactly. But close. And I didn't believe you and now I do. So I playact: One minute I'm a little girl, and then I'm a demimonde who's had a hundred lovers, and then I switch to the sharp lady who sees, for example, that he doesn't like Max Stuyvesant, even though he's trying to cover it up."

"Not easy."

"No. And I don't even know who I'm deceiving—him or me. But Sabrina, what can I do? I love him so much that I can't forget it for a minute; all I want is to sink into him and live there forever. And I'll do whatever I have to do to stay there."

With her finger, Stephanie traced the red checks on the tablecloth, thinking of Garth, remembering New York before they were married, and their early years when everything was new and wonderful. He had loved her for what she was, not for what she could pretend to be.

They ought to be able to find that love again; it couldn't have disappeared completely. If she went home and told him she wanted to go back to the beginning . . . but she couldn't go back. Not now, not today. How could she walk into her house and say, "Hi, everybody, I'm home!"—and come face to face with Sabrina cooking dinner? But it's only three more days, she thought. Then I'll be back with Garth and my family. Not even a full three days. Just the weekend. And then I'll be home.

And what will be waiting for me?

A filthy anonymous letter about my husband, worries about money, Penny wanting art lessons, Cliff's shoplifting, and trying to start a business again.

All of it. Waiting for me. But I don't want to think about it now; there's nothing I can do, and it would just spoil the rest of my week. There's plenty of time to think about it when I'm home again. Plenty of time to take care of everything.

Gabrielle talked steadily on the train back to Bern, giving Stephanie new information about Sabrina and her life, the kind of details people take for granted. It's too bad I'm about to leave, she thought wryly. With these facts I could play Sabrina for weeks.

Still, she was nervous when Brooks shepherded them to the Kursaal after dinner; she had never gambled, and she didn't want to learn on Sabrina's money. But Brooks and Gabrielle took it for granted that he would buy chips for the three of them. So all I have to worry about now, Stephanie thought, is pretending I know how to play *boule*.

But it was so easy—a simplified form of roulette—that within a few minutes she was betting cautiously with the chips Brooks had stacked in front of her. Gabrielle leaned close. "Brooks thinks you're being careful because you didn't buy your own chips. If you don't start being extravagant he'll be insulted. And very difficult to get along with."

"No," Stephanie said. "It's just that it doesn't make sense to—"

Brooks interrupted. "Of course, you're right; it can't compare with Monte Carlo, but it's the best Bern has to offer. We'll play for an hour or so and then Gaby wants to dance. Bet enough to make it interesting; all profits go to that new museum you're helping raise money for."

Profits, Stephanie thought. When I've never gambled in my life.

But she began to win, thinking all the while how foolish it was to bet money on where a tiny bouncing ball would come to rest among nine slots. Surrounded by serious players, she bet whimsically on the first digit of her telephone number in Evanston, and won. She bet on the first number of her address, the first number of Penny's birthday, and the first number of Cliff's, and won all three times.

Gabrielle's eyes sparkled. "What's your system?"

"Birthdays, addresses, telephone numbers."

"Whose?"

"It doesn't seem to matter."

"Sabrina, that's not a system; that's witchcraft."

"You're probably right. Next thing you know, I'll turn into someone else."

She bet the first digit of her London address. And she lost. It was so unexpected that she stopped short and stared at the little white ball that had betrayed her. She put a modest number of chips on the first digit of her London telephone number—and lost.

"Systems tend to do that," said Brooks. "So does witch-craft."

Gabrielle, who had won once and lost twice on Stephanie's system, stood up and swept her remaining chips into her hand. "These are for your museum, Sabrina. And I am for dancing."

When they cashed in their chips, Stephanie had won a little over a thousand dollars. "The system did well for the museum," she said casually and followed Brooks and Gabrielle to a table near the orchestra.

It hit her as she was dancing with Brooks. The system did well for the museum? A week ago a thousand dollars would have seemed a miraculous windfall for groceries, paying bills, sending Penny to art classes, perhaps buying a new dress for herself. I'm becoming Sabrina, she thought. Thinking like the rest of them in this fairy-tale world.

"Sabrina," said Gabrielle as they walked back to the hotel. "This has been so wonderful I don't want it to end."

"Neither do I."

But tomorrow was Sunday. Her last day.

"Come home with me," she suggested. "I'll call Mrs. Thirkell and tell her to expect us. She's only had me to feed this week, and she's happiest when she can show off for discriminating guests."

Did she really know that about Mrs. Thirkell? Of course she did. Because Sabrina knew it. And when they flew back Sunday evening and Stephanie led Gabrielle and Brooks upstairs into the drawing room, Mrs. Thirkell's smile was so delighted, and her buffet supper so ample, that Stephanie knew she had chosen the perfect way to end her week: entertaining in her Cadogan Square home—before she had to leave it for good.

Chapter 12

From the time Garth brought her home from the hospital, Sabrina had not a moment alone. All she could think of was calling Stephanie, but Garth hovered over her, and Penny and Cliff danced about trying to be useful and admiring the cast that extended from her palm almost to her elbow. They brought her tea, ice cream and toasted English muffins, but all she wanted was to be alone for five minutes with the telephone. She lay on the couch, feeling trapped, her head pounding, as her family bustled about, being helpful.

By eight o'clock her eyes were closing. She tried to stay awake, but her headache and the medication were like heavy, muffling blankets and the house faded away as she sank into sleep.

"Let's get you to bed," Garth said.

She jerked awake. "No, I can manage—"

"Tomorrow you'll manage." He lifted her and carried her upstairs to the bedroom, sitting her down on the bed. "Leave everything to me." He unbuttoned her blouse and slid the right sleeve off her arm, then eased the other over the cast. Half asleep, Sabrina closed her eyes. *I couldn't stop him even if I knew how. And it doesn't make any difference anyway.*

Supporting her with one arm, Garth pulled down her blue jeans and underpants, then unhooked her brassiere. He drew in his breath sharply as he saw the bruises covering the left side of her body. "Poor love, you must feel as if that truck ran over you." She opened her eyes, but he had moved to the bureau to take out a clean nightgown.

"I'm going to raise your arm; tell me if I hurt you." He slipped the nightgown over her head. Like a child, she put her other arm through the strap as he held it. "Now, stand up for a minute." He pulled back the blanket and sheet, helped her into bed and covered her. For a moment he stood quietly looking down at her. "If you're in pain, or need anything tonight, I'll be here. Just poke me and I'll wake up."

Unexpectedly, tears came to her eyes. *You are so good. And I do want you near me. I hurt all over and I wish you would hold me and comfort me. But you're Stephanie's husband. I can't even tell you I'm glad you're close by.*

"Good night," she said, and in a moment was asleep.

Garth was up and dressed before she awoke on Sunday morning. She had not heard him come to bed, had not been aware of him sleeping beside her, but when she opened her eyes he was there to help her dress, and he and the children stayed nearby for the rest of the day. Sabrina thought wryly of how she had told Stephanie she wanted the experience of a family. Well, she had it. But she wished she could have a few precious minutes of the aloneness of her London house.

In the afternoon Garth helped her upstairs to take a nap. As soon as he left the room she reached for the telephone, but it rang beneath her hand. Someone answered it downstairs, and before she could try again she fell asleep.

"Dolores called," Garth said, coming in as she awoke. "She's bringing dinner about six. And Linda has volunteered for Monday. If I go through town with my notebook, I may be able to sign up enough cooks for a year of dinners." He paused, but she only smiled. "Do you want to see Dolores when she comes?"

"Not today. Maybe I will tomorrow." She felt defeated, making plans for tomorrow. Monday. The day she was supposed to meet Stephanie at the airport and go back to London, to pick up her own life. *Our adventure is over,* she thought. *But how do I end it?*

At the dinner table she was quiet as Garth served Dolores's casserole and pumpkin pie and made conversation with the children. He was baffled by his wife's behavior. She never gave in easily to pain or illness. But now she not only showed pain, she showed fear—even something like panic. What was she afraid of? When he asked her, she shrank from him, shaking her head, so he dropped it. He felt helpless and angry. Why wouldn't she let him help her, let him be her husband instead of someone she feared or distrusted?

After dinner she refused his offer of a sponge bath and his helping hand to climb the stairs. "I can manage. But thank you."

She had stopped worrying about what Garth thought of her behavior; he would soon know the truth anyway. The problem was Stephanie. She would be leaving for the airport in a few hours. *I have to warn her, give her time to think about how she'll handle the mess I've made.*

She lay in bed, her mind spinning. She dozed, slept, woke when Garth came to bed, then forced herself to stay awake, watching the clock. One A.M., one-thirty, two. Eight A.M. in London. Garth's breathing was deep and regular. She slipped out of bed and crept down the stairs into the breakfast room, where she found the telephone in the dark and at last, in a low voice, gave the operator her own number.

The telephone rang in London; Sabrina could picture Mrs. Thirkell when she answered, and her bedroom when Stephanie came on the line.

"Sabrina! I was just getting ready to leave. Is anything wrong?"

Rapidly, Sabrina told her about her accident.

"Are you badly hurt?"

"Nothing serious. I look a mess, bruised and battered, and I have an awful headache—a mild concussion, Nat says. But the real problem is my wrist. I . . . fractured it. It's in a cast."

Stephanie said nothing. Sabrina, her head pounding, closed her eyes. "I had to warn you so you could think about it on the plane."

Stephanie's voice was faint. "Think about it?"

"How to tell Garth. Stephanie, I'm sorry, it's all my fault. At first I thought I could tell him and pave the way before you got here, but I can't, Stephanie; I'd only make things worse."

There was no answer. "Stephanie, don't you see, if you tell him right away, if the two of you talk about it together so he doesn't brood about it alone, you could work it out."

The static of the telephone line stretched between them. In

the peacock and ivory bedroom Stephanie listened to it, hunched over on the chaise, one arm held tightly across her stomach. "Sabrina, you've lived with him for a week; do you honestly think he'd go on as if nothing had happened?"

"No, things would be different, but that doesn't mean they'd be worse. If you love each other—"

"Love has nothing to do with it. He'll say we've made a fool of him—"

"Well, we have, haven't we? He isn't a fool, but we fooled him."

"*You* fooled him. And how do I make that all right? It's not like a quarrel—"

"No." In a quarrel, Sabrina thought, two people are equal. In a deception, one person knows everything and the other knows nothing. When Garth discovers that he's been trying to patch the problems of his marriage with a woman who is not his wife but his sister-in-law; that his wife and sister-in-law have played a monstrous joke on him . . . She slumped in her chair. "I thought I was giving you a gift. A week for yourself. But all I've brought is destruction."

"It's my fault. He's my husband. I didn't let myself think what would happen if he found out." Stephanie closed her eyes. He'd never understand why I did it, she thought, never forgive me. It would be the end of everything for us. "I can't tell him," she said.

"But if I do it—"

"No, that would be worse. Oh, I don't know what to do. If only we could . . . Sabrina! Why couldn't we fake it?"

"Fake—?"

"Tell Nat what we've done. I'll wear a cast and he could pretend to take care of me and no one would know the difference."

"I thought of that. But if you could see me . . . Stephanie, my whole side is black and blue and I have a cut on my forehead—"

"Oh." Stephanie suddenly felt very sleepy. All she wanted was to curl up and forget everything. "Just a minute," she said to Sabrina, and, putting the telephone in her lap, she rubbed her eyes with her fists like a child trying not to cry. Garth, I'm sorry, she said silently. I didn't realize what I was doing. And I'm afraid. I don't know what's going to happen. She looked at the telephone in her lap, connecting her to Sabrina, and through her to Garth. There was nothing else to do. She picked it up. "Will you be at the airport?"

Sabrina hesitated. "All right. Of course."

"What is it? Can't you drive?"

"Nat said I shouldn't, but there's no reason—"

"No, it's all right. I guess I can meet you at home. But what about Penny and Cliff?"

"Cliff has soccer practice, and Penny can go to Barbara Goodman's. I'll take care of it."

"I'll see you in a few hours." Stephanie hung up before either of them could say anything else.

Sabrina covered her face with her hands. In the dark silence the minutes passed. *Garth, I care about you. Forgive me. Stephanie, I love you, I wanted to give you*—

The telephone began to ring and she grabbed it. "Stephanie?"

"Sabrina, I can't do it, I can't do it. Please help me. I can't face him, I can't tell him. I can't do it!"

"All right." Sabrina took a deep breath. "I'll talk to him this morning, as soon as Penny and Cliff—"

"No!"

"But what do you want me to do, then?"

"Stay there. Could you do that? Would it be too terrible for you to stay until the cast comes off, or whatever happens next? Would it be very long? A couple of weeks? How long would it be?"

"Nat said four weeks." Sabrina sat up, her thoughts racing. *Stay here. But how can I? I have Ambassadors, my home, my friends, a future that I have to make. This is not my life.*

"What happens in four weeks?" Stephanie asked. Her voice was growing stronger.

"More X-rays. And, if my wrist is healed, Nat takes off the cast."

"Well, I could come back then. No one would ever know. Sabrina . . ." Stephanie's voice was still stronger, pleading but excited. "Everything is fine here; I can even take care of Ambassadors for you. I sold the French beaded bag—I'll tell you about it later. And you could manage, I know you could. We'd just go on doing the same things we've been doing, more of the same. Doesn't it make sense to keep on? Sabrina? Just four more weeks? Then no one would be hurt."

"Wait," Sabrina said. Her headache was pressing against

her eyes, and she tried to think. She probably could do it. The week had gone so quickly; four weeks wasn't a long time, and there still were things she wanted to do here. In fact, she liked it here. And it was Stephanie's decision. But— "Stephanie, I don't know if I can manage for four weeks . . . with Garth."

Stephanie sucked in her breath. The bedroom dimmed as clouds moved across the tall windows, broken here and there by a pale silver sun. "He's gone longer than four weeks without making love to me."

"Stephanie. Two weeks in China. One week just ended. And four more. Seven weeks. Do you really think—?"

"You can manage. I know you can. It means so much to me—to my marriage."

"What about later?"

"What about it?"

"If Garth finds out later, what will you tell him? The longer it lasts, the more impossible it is to defend. Stephanie, you could explain one week and go on from there, but would you have a marriage if he found out we'd played this joke on him for five weeks?"

The clouds scudded past the window, playing hide and seek with the sun. "I wouldn't have a marriage. But I don't think I'd have one now, either, if I came home this afternoon and told him. So what difference does it make? Sabrina, I'm *begging* you—"

A knot unraveled inside Sabrina, and a thought sprang full-blown within her: *I'll have a family for a while longer.* "All right. But we have to talk; there are so many things to talk about. Ambassadors, Antonio—will you call me later, when I'm alone?"

"Of course, whenever you want. Sabrina, I wish I knew how to thank you. I know it isn't your kind of life, it's dull and—"

"Stephanie?"

Garth's voice.

Sabrina cupped her hand over the phone. "I have to go; Garth is awake. Call me later, about ten my time."

"Yes, I will. Sabrina, thank—"

She hung up and was standing at the refrigerator when Garth came into the kitchen.

"Is anything wrong?" he asked.

"I was suddenly ravenous. Which probably means I've recovered."

"I wish you'd wakened me."

She smiled to ease the worry in his eyes. "I wanted to let you sleep. But now that you're here, shall we finish Dolores's pumpkin pie?"

"At the risk of Clifford's wrath," he said with a chuckle. And in the honey-colored breakfast room, with the house dark and silent around them, they sat together and ate from one plate.

Chapter 13

Garth looked at his Monday morning genetics class and saw instead the sleeping face of Stephanie. Alabaster skin flushed with rose, auburn hair tumbled against the white pillow, eyelids fluttering as she dreamed.

A student asked a complicated question and he answered briefly. Smartass, he thought, trying to impress the professor with a question that could fill a book. The professor is not impressed. Anyway, he's groggy from 3:00 A.M. pumpkin pie with his wife.

He dismissed the class early.

He'd call her, see how she was, then finish his paperwork so he could get to the lab before his next class. He took the stairs two at a time to his office. New gold lettering had appeared on the door: *Garth Andersen, Ph.D., Department Chairman*. He opened the door to tell his secretary to have it removed, then changed his mind. She had done it for him. For a year he'd resisted advertising himself while she argued that it was important for students and visitors to know he was chairman of the Department of Molecular Biology. Today, it seemed, she had ended the discussion by ordering the lettering on her own. He shrugged. It might make him seem more important to her and others; to him, the title simply meant more administrative work and less time in the lab.

He dialed his home number, but the line was busy. Beside the telephone was a reminder: "Call Ted Morrow." Damn, he'd forgotten. He called and told him about the accident, and that Stephanie could not work for a week. "And she won't be able to type for about four weeks, so if you hire someone else she says she'll understand."

"Not to worry, Garth; we'll wait for her."

Garth dialed his number again, but the line was still busy. He leafed through his mail. A bill for overdue books from the library, letters from biologists in Amsterdam and Stockholm, an advertisement for laboratory equipment, notice of a meeting with the vice president to discuss Vivian Goodman. If they kept going at this snail's pace, Vivian might get a life contract on her ninetieth birthday. And at the bottom of the stack, an airline ticket to San Francisco with his schedule for a week-long genetics conference in Berkeley beginning October 6. Less than two weeks away. Something else he'd forgotten.

He dialed Stephanie again. Busy. Probably everyone calling to see how she was. He looked through the conference schedule. There was no problem with his going to California. In two weeks Stephanie would be able to manage easily without him. But still, he shouldn't be gone for a week—not with everything between them so precarious. He picked up the phone and tried again to call her. Still busy. For the first time he thought something could be wrong. He looked at his watch. Plenty of time to go home and get back for his one-thirty class.

He found Stephanie in the breakfast room, talking on the telephone. "I'll call if I need you," she was saying, "and you should call anytime you want. I think we've covered the important things—"

Her body became very still. Garth thought of the squirrels in their backyard who froze, alert and ready to flee, when they sensed movement nearby. He came up and put his hand on her shoulder, feeling the muscles tense beneath his fingers. "When you're through," he said casually. "I was worried when I couldn't reach you on the phone."

"—and if anything else comes up, we'll talk about it," she said, finishing her sentence as if there had been no break in its smooth flow. "Take care of yourself and don't worry about me; I'll manage." She hung up and slowly turned around. Her

214

eyes were shadowed. "I'm sorry; I didn't think you'd try to call."

"It didn't occur to you that I might be concerned?" He paused. "Never mind. Who were you talking to?"

"My sister."

"All morning? Did she invite you to London to recuperate?"

"No, she—"

"Then no doubt she is sending over her maid to do the housework."

"No, Dolores is doing that."

"What?"

"Dolores is sending Juanita, her maid, for a couple of days this week. All paid for. Why are you angry at Sabrina?"

"I'm not angry. I shouldn't have said anything; of course you'd want to talk to her after your accident. Did it make you feel better? *Do* you feel better?"

"Yes, I do. Are you playing hookey from your classes?"

"Dignified professors never play hookey. They are called away on urgent matters—a golf game, a dentist appointment, a love affair. Or a wife who might need help. Is Dolores really sending you her maid? I wish I'd thought of it."

"You don't have a maid to send."

"I could have kidnapped Juanita and brought her to you wrapped in a red ribbon. When is she coming?"

"Tomorrow."

"Then how can I help you today? Grocery shopping?"

She laughed and opened the refrigerator. "Look." It was crammed with food. "From Dolores and Linda and a parade of good Samaritans. Even Ted Morrow's wife. How does news get around so fast?"

"Small town." He searched the refrigerator, sniffing under lids and pulling out packages. "Salmon salad, cheddar cheese, olives. Did anyone bring bread? Yes. And we have butter. Why don't you sit down and let me serve you? And then you should rest; you look pale."

"I might do that."

Garth filled a platter and put dishes and silver on the table. "What important things did you and your sister cover?"

Absently rubbing the cast on her arm, Sabrina watched his hands as he filled their plates. "Some ... problems. About Ambassadors. It seems fake porcelains are being sold to small

215

galleries. We talked about checking for authenticity—that sort of thing."

"It sounds like she bought one and discovered it was a fake after she'd sold it to a customer."

She gave him a swift glance. "Yes. If she asked your advice, what would you suggest she do?"

"Tell the customer the truth and buy it back as soon as she can. The longer she waits, the harder it will be to convince anyone, if the real story comes out, that she really meant to do the right thing."

She bit her lip. "Of course. The salmon is good, isn't it? Is there more?"

That was twice, Garth thought, that she'd changed the subject from her sister. Usually she related every detail of the glamorous London life that was a kind of endless fairy tale in her imagination. But now, instead of London, she was talking about the women who had come to the house all morning, bearing food.

"—and Vivian hadn't been here for ten minutes when Dolores turned into a pelican, quite haughty, with her neck growing longer every second. Vivian was completely bewildered, and she hadn't done anything, of course, except talk about people Dolores doesn't know. As soon as she left, Dolores unbent and became her other self, managerial but affectionate. Amazing how she puts up barriers when she's uncomfortable with someone."

"And who else was here?"

"Linda, with some kind of Italian casserole all round and rosy and bubbling. They looked so much alike I couldn't tell them apart, but Linda bubbled with gossip, not tomatoes, so I knew which one to talk to—"

Garth was chuckling as he cleared the table. Dolores as a haughty pelican and Linda as one of her casseroles. He couldn't remember Stephanie ever being so sharp, observing their friends in fresh ways, witty but not cruel. And she looked different this morning—more vivid and excited. More beautiful. But then, how often had she accused him in the past of not really looking at her? What strangers they had become.

But it occurred to him that she was putting on some kind of performance, to entertain him, distract him from something.

The phone call with her sister? Something else she didn't want him to know? New ideas about herself, her marriage, that made her tense, worried, perhaps frightened, unpredictable. "A few more days," she said after their dinner at the Goldners'. But then she'd had the accident. Well, he could wait until she was ready to talk to him, and, meanwhile, she was trying to change their routine—a glass of wine together before dinner, showing interest in Vivian and the university, even cooking steak a new way.

He bent down to kiss her forehead. "Take a nap. You'll need all your strength for dinner tonight; Penny and Cliff insist on cooking it."

She looked alarmed. "Can't they heat up Linda's casserole?"

"I'll recommend it. Call me if you need anything."

"When will you be home?"

"As soon as I can. I hope by four or four-thirty."

All through that afternoon and the next two days of meetings with graduate students, organizing his campus schedule and helping out at home, Garth thought about his wife. He had not thought about her this much in years—but then she had not puzzled him this much in years. He found himself hurrying home eagerly at the end of the day to be with her, and then he could not stop watching her. She would turn around and catch his steady gaze, and he would ask, quickly, how she was feeling.

"I'm much better," she said with some impatience as they sat at dinner on Wednesday night. "I shouldn't get so much attention. This is an excellent pot roast. Which of our benefactors made it?"

"Vivian brought it to the office this afternoon. She said she talked to you today."

"Yes, we made a lunch date for next week. And she brought me the new issue of *Newsweek*. Why didn't you tell us you're in it?"

"A few paragraphs in a long article."

"Dad's in *Newsweek?*" Cliff shouted. "Where is it?" He bolted from his chair.

"The living room," Sabrina called after him. "Even a few paragraphs," she said to Garth. "They're part of something so important. And incredible."

He looked at her curiously. "You read the whole article?"

"Well, of course. You were in it, even your picture. But I would have read it anyway; it's a fantastic story."

Cliff came back with the magazine folded to a page with photographs of three genetic engineering researchers: a blond woman at Harvard, a gray-haired professor from England and Garth in shirtsleeves in his laboratory. "So stern," Sabrina said, looking over Cliff's shoulder. "As if you're about to flunk the whole university."

Penny and Cliff giggled. "What's it about, Dad?" Cliff asked.

"Read it. It's not too complicated."

"Okay; but what's it *about?*"

As Garth took the magazine from Cliff and leafed through the article, Sabrina studied his face. Once, a long time ago, she had thought him stuffy and dull. Now, suddenly, he fascinated her. When she read the article that described him as one of the leading scientists in the field of genetic research, when she thought of him in the center of miraculous discoveries, he seemed to her like a being from another planet, mysterious and powerful, who knew things and did things she had never dreamed of. We're complete strangers, she thought. And without knowing why, she felt it was terribly important that she understand him.

"Yes, tell us," she said. "It isn't so simple. It's like a mystery with a new clue every time you turn the page."

"Well put." He smiled at her and she smiled back. "It's been a long time since you felt that way." Her smile faded, but Garth did not notice; he was pouring coffee. He looked up at his family and began to talk about his work.

When Garth had begun teaching, scientists had known little more than the structure of DNA and how it worked. But in the 1960s there was an explosion of knowledge in genetics and he found himself in the center of it. His calm manner and careful work, combined with daring leaps in his published papers, led to the invitation to participate in the month-long international seminar in Berkeley the August before Stephanie's trip to China. With that, he joined the ranks of the world's leading geneticists.

By now they were learning how to cut apart the DNA molecule, ten-thousandths of an inch long, and replace a missing or damaged part by splicing in a healthy part from another DNA molecule. *Gene splicing, genetic engineering, recombinant DNA*—the phrases were dry and dull, but as he described them Garth's voice lifted, ringing with excitement at the marvels behind them.

And his family listened, absolutely still, absorbed in his words. As he looked at them sitting around the table, the blood coursed through Garth's veins; he felt alive and powerful and hugely happy. A man needed to talk about his work, to share it with his family. If he couldn't, no matter how important it might be to the rest of the world, it became somehow insignificant—a part of his life that filled hours of every day but still could not attract the interest of the most important people in his life.

Garth put his hand over his wife's and smiled at her, grateful because she had done this for him. And then he went on to tell them what was happening in laboratories all over the world, the subjects of the conferences he attended and the seminars he taught.

First there was research into genetic disease. In hemophilia, for example, the instructions for making blood-clotting chemicals are absent or not complete in the DNA. Scientists would isolate one cell with the damaged DNA and one from a healthy person, remove the part from the healthy DNA that carried the instructions for clotting and fuse it to the damaged DNA. Then they would put the repaired cell into a culture to reproduce until there were enough cells to inject into the hemophiliac, where they would continue to reproduce. And that person would no longer be in danger of bleeding to death with every cut.

At the same time, they were learning to make vaccines against disease. They would remove from a cell certain genes whose function was to make antibodies against a particular disease and splice those genes into bacteria. In a culture, this new strain of bacteria would multiply by the billions, becoming a factory for the production of those antibodies. And the antibodies could then be used to make a vaccine against that particular disease. For example: interferon, ready for testing to fight viral infections and cancer.

Or they would splice genes that control hormone-making into bacteria. And when the bacteria multiplied and the hormones were removed, they were used to fight disease. For example: insulin, being produced for use against diabetes.

Sabrina looked puzzled. "I haven't read that hemophilia and diabetes have been cured."

"They haven't. What I've told you is what we will be able to do soon, when we answer the questions still remaining."

Sabrina looked at Garth's eyes, burning, intense, far-seeing, and heard in his voice the lure of limitless horizons. "Not easy to come home," she said lightly, "and cut the grass or change a broken faucet, after you've been cutting DNA and changing forms of life."

He gave her a long look. "Thank you." His voice was husky. "That means more to me than anything you might have said." He paused and looked around the table. "But I note with astonishment that the dishes have not been washed."

"We were listening to you," Cliff said indignantly. "Do we still have to clean up?"

"Have you created a new bacteria to do it?"

"You know I haven't."

"Then I regret to say that leaves only you and Penny. Go on, now, both of you. It's late."

It's late, he thought, leaning back with a sigh of pleasure. When did we last sit around the table, talking, being a family? I can't remember. But how hard have I tried lately to make it happen? He smiled at his wife. She had made it happen. "All clear to you now?"

"I want to read more about it. It seems a little scary."

"Awesome is more like it. The wonder of it, the leaps forward, the hope for people who never had hope before. . . . But, at the moment, the best part for me is that you read the article and got us talking, shared my work for once, so you could understand why I get caught up in it and sometimes forget my family. Though right now I find it impossible to believe I could ever forget you."

He went to her chair. Standing behind it, he put his hands on her shoulders and slid them down to enclose her breasts. Leaning down, he moved his lips along her hair, brushing it back from her ear. "I think—"

"No," she said tightly, and broke out of the circle of his arms to stand a little distance away.

She was very pale, her eyes averted, her face closed and frozen. "Not now, not yet, at least not—"

Garth was stunned, and furious. He had been teased, then slapped down and dismissed. His wife indulging her whims. He strode to the door to get out, to get away from her, but her voice caught him.

"I'm sorry. I am sorry." The words trembled, but she would not look at him. "It hurts when I move ... my bruises ... I thought you knew how much it hurts me—"

"Bullshit." He stood in the archway to the living room. "Dolores isn't the only one who puts up barriers, is she, when the situation gets uncomfortable? She could take lessons from you." His voice cut like steel. "You needn't worry; I won't trouble you again. Force doesn't amuse me. Or arouse me. I'll take care that you don't, either."

He slammed the front door and walked to the lake, breathing hard, damning his wife and himself for allowing her to fool him. What the hell did she want from him? If she didn't want him at all, why didn't she just say so?

He walked for miles, coming home late to a sleeping house with lights burning in the living room and kitchen. Someone had put a plate of cookies for him on the counter. He left it untouched and went to the study, worn out from his seething anger. He slept on the couch without bothering to open it into a bed.

The anger was still deep and harsh when he woke the next morning, early, before anyone was up. He left without breakfast and went to the cafeteria in the student union for coffee.

"Tennis is what you need," said Nat Goldner, startling him out of his thoughts. "Anything that furrows the brow so menacingly can be exorcised only by demolishing a ball or an opponent. I offer myself. Unless you'd rather talk."

"No, I'd rather demolish something. Good idea."

They were equally matched and played a fast game. After an hour Garth began to relax. Nat was admiring. "Good game. One of our best. Just think what we might have done if I'd been as furious as you. Do you have time for a second breakfast?"

"Lots of time; no classes today. But I want to get to the lab by ten."

At the Faculty Club, a Victorian frame house near the campus, they sat beside a bay window overlooking the lake. A freighter was on the horizon, riding low in the water. "Loaded with cargo," Nat said, attacking his eggs Benedict. "Coal for the coming winter. Hard to believe in winter on a day like this. How is Stephanie?"

Garth spread butter on his rye toast. "She's fine."

"No aches or pains or megrims?"

Garth looked up. "An old-fashioned word from a modern doctor."

"I like it. How else would I describe, in one word, depressed and irritable, with erratic behavior?"

"From just a broken wrist?"

"From trauma, or shock. Did Stephanie talk to you about the maid Dolores sent over? Juanita?"

"Only that she did a good job—when was it? Day before yesterday, Tuesday. It was good of Dolores to loan her out. Was there something else for her to tell me?"

"According to Dolores, who is quoting Juanita, 'That lady certainly know what she want; she give orders like royalty.' "

"Stephanie? Nonsense. She's uncomfortable ordering anyone around."

"I'm only quoting Dolores."

"Who is quoting Juanita. Who is probably exaggerating."

"Garth, relax. No one is attacking Stephanie."

"What else did reliable Juanita say via Dolores?"

"That Stephanie had her lunch on the patio while Juanita ate in the kitchen."

"So?"

"It seems the women eat with the maids around here. I never knew that, but I'm never home."

"Why should they eat together?"

"How do I know? Maybe the women want their maids to feel loved. Anyway, Stephanie didn't do it."

"She's not used to having a maid."

"Okay, I told you, I'm not attacking her. But, as her doctor, I ought to know about it if she's not acting like herself. She had one hell of a crack on the head, Garth, and she was frightened by it. Sometimes the fear lingers; patients think they're seriously hurt and the doctor is lying to them, having secret conferences with their family. All of which can make them act in tense, erratic, unpredictable ways. We can't deal with that if we don't know about it. So, does she?"

Garth left his toast unfinished and poured a second cup of coffee. "No. She says her bruises hurt, that's all."

Nat sighed. "If she did behave like that, it would likely disappear within a short time as she got better." Garth nodded. "If you need to talk, anytime, you know where I am."

"Nat, you're the one I'd come to. I value your sharp eye and your honest tongue. Even more, I value your friendship. And, of course, your tennis. When do our boys have their next soccer game? I forgot to ask Cliff this morning."

"Tomorrow. And next Tuesday ends the season. I don't like the way the coach handles them, but there's not much we can do about it—"

And, talking about their sons and soccer, they finished their coffee and left, looking, Garth thought, like two respectable professors with model families, secure reputations and no problems that couldn't be dealt with by a fast game of tennis and a friendly chat over coffee.

He looked at his reflection in the glass door of his laboratory. Am I that man, he wondered, with that family? How can I be, if I don't understand my wife and she can't seem to make up her mind whether to hold our marriage together or tear it apart? Or maybe something is happening to both of us and we are somehow changing—almost as if we are becoming different people.

Cliff dawdled on his way home from school. If Penny got there first, maybe she'd have the breakfast dishes washed before he arrived. He wished Mom would get her cast off so she could do things like she used to; though, come to think of it, he had a funny feeling that maybe she wasn't ever going to do things the way she used to, not exactly. It was kind of weird, because Mom used to do everything. Now they never knew what she'd do and what she'd tell *them* to do and what she'd just sort of forget.

But she didn't get mad as much as before. Actually, she didn't pay as much attention to him and Penny as she used to. Sometimes he kind of wished she would. But probably her wrist hurt. Or something.

At least she was cooking again, with Dad's help, which just proved she could do other things, too. It wasn't fair that he had to work in the house after school and soccer practice. Maybe he'd talk to Mom about it; these days she talked to him almost like a grown-up.

"Mom!" he shouted, slamming the screen door and dropping his books in the living room. He found her in the kitchen sitting on the couch with Penny.

"We're having a private talk!" Penny said.

"You didn't do the dishes," he growled with a disgusted glance at the sink.

"You're supposed to do them, too."

"I want to talk to Mom."

"I'm talking to her."

"Mom—" Cliff said.

"I could sell tickets," she suggested. Cliff was confused; he'd expected a scolding for arguing with Penny, but Mom didn't look mad at all; in fact, she looked happy. "Cliff, how about taking some cookies and milk to the backyard? It'll be your turn in a few minutes."

Penny watched him maneuver through the door with cookies and milk and a box of pretzels and then turned back to Sabrina. "The thing is, they make me feel so dumb—and kind of scared."

"Scared of what?" Sabrina asked.

"What they all talk about. At recess. You know."

"I'm not sure. What things do they talk about?"

"Well . . . oh . . . you know . . . fucking and screwing and masturbating and—"

"Penny!"

She shrank back. "I knew you'd be mad. Everybody says you can't talk to your mother. But I didn't know who else to talk to. Barbara's no help; she doesn't know any more than I do. And I can't ask a *teacher*—if anybody found out, I'd die!"

Sabrina nodded, remembering. You couldn't go to a teacher; that would betray the conversations of the other girls, and you couldn't ask the other girls because that would give away your ignorance. But Penny could wait a few days, couldn't she? Until Stephanie got home? It was a mother's job, after all. She looked at the embarrassment and worry on Penny's face and knew she could not.

"Hold on a minute." Sabrina went to the sink and ran a glass of water to gain time. What do I know about young girls? When we were Penny's age we didn't know anything. How come eleven-year-olds are talking about fucking and masturbating? Why aren't they thinking about ice cream sodas and swimming lessons?

She came back to the couch. "Penny, don't you have classes in health or something where you talk about your body and growing up?"

"There's sex ed, but that isn't the problem. All that talk about sperm and eggs and menstruating and venereal disease—everybody knows all that! That's not the problem!"

Sabrina gazed at Penny blankly. "What *is* the problem?"

"I don't want to do any of it."

In sixth grade? "Of course you don't. Why should you? No one has intercourse in sixth grade."

"But when they talk about it—what boys like best and what it would be like to screw with them—they make me feel dumb, like there's something wrong with me because *I don't want to do it!* Ever! It sounds awful. I don't want boys touching me there and sticking their penises in me. But when I said that, these girls laughed at me—"

"Which girls?" Sabrina asked.

"These girls in my class. They're menstruating and they wear bras and you wouldn't buy me one—"

"Well, but Penny," Sabrina said, looking at her flat chest.

"I know, but in the gym locker room I feel like a baby! And then they whisper and giggle and talk about—"

Sabrina listened, appalled, as Penny's artless chatter described a generation she knew nothing about. At eleven she and Stephanie had felt daring because they'd run away from a chauffeur. What did these children have to look forward to if they did everything in grammar school? Would they, at forty, take up hopscotch?

She sighed. It wasn't a joke. Penny was bewildered and forlorn, and looking for help.

"See," Penny said, "I don't care what they do. I mean, if that's what they want, it's okay, but I'd rather draw or work on puppet costumes or things like that. Does that mean there's something wrong with me? Am I abnormal or something?"

"No," Sabrina said quietly. "I think you're the most normal one of all."

"Really? Normal? Everything I said?"

"Not quite, because when you're older you'll change your mind about wanting to have intercourse—"

"You mean fucking."

"That's one word for it; it's not mine. I'll tell you why. You know, don't you, that intercourse is also called making love?"

"Oh, sure, everybody knows that."

"Really? But they prefer to call it fucking. Why do you suppose that is?"

"I don't know. I guess they just like it better."

"Penny, why is intercourse called making love?"

"Because . . . you love somebody and you do it."

"What if you do it with somebody you don't love?"

Penny frowned and then shrugged.

"You see, you can experiment with sex, and if you're lucky and things go well, it feels very good. You can do that with lots of boys and lots of times you'll feel good—like scratching a mosquito bite or eating a big meal when you're hungry. Or you can use sex only when you want to show a very special person how you feel. That's when it's called making love."

She looked through the window at a climbing rose, heavy with late blooms. "Making love is a way to show someone that you love him so much you want to be part of him. There are lots of ways to show you *like* someone: you talk and share private jokes; you smile at each other across a room; you hold hands and spend time together. But intercourse is more than all those things; it's the only way you can be as close to another person with your body as you can be with your mind."

Sabrina twined her fingers with Penny's. "Like this. Thoughts and bodies. And that's when you know you're in love. Do you think those girls in your class know the first thing about this? Or care about it?"

Penny looked at their hands and slowly shook her head.

"Penny, please listen. Wait for this. Whatever others do, don't let them shame you into trying to keep up with them. Don't turn lovemaking into fucking; don't make it as ordinary as a handshake. Wait until someone is so important in your life, so wonderful and special, that you want to share the things you are and the things you feel in this one way that is like no other way. Intercourse isn't an after-school sport or a way of scratching an itch. Intercourse is a language, Penny; it's using your body to say 'I love you.' Wait for that. Wait until you find somebody so wonderful you want to tell him you love him with your eyes and your mouth and then with your whole body."

Meeting Penny's eyes, wide with wonder at her intensity, Sabrina heard the echo of her words. Within her something fell away; she felt empty and desolate. *I haven't followed my own advice. I wish—*

"But, if it's so good, how come you and Daddy hardly ever do it?"

In the silence, Cliff's ball thumped rhythmically against the side of the house.

"Why do you think we don't?" Sabrina asked.

"Well, he hardly ever sleeps in your room anymore. Does that mean you don't love each other?"

"No," she said quickly, to smooth this new anxiety from Penny's face. "Sometimes grown-ups get complicated feelings that aren't easy to explain. They can love each other and still want to be apart now and then . . . sort of take a vacation from each other and think about themselves separately."

"Is that why you went to China?"

"That was one of the reasons."

"Lots of kids at school—their parents are getting divorced."

"Well, we're not." Too defensive, she thought, and added more quietly, "We're not going to, Penny."

"When you went to China, Cliff and I thought you were. 'Cause you went alone and Daddy was sad."

Sabrina put her arms around her and Penny nuzzled her nose against Sabrina's breast. "I love you, Mommy. Don't go away again." Sabrina kissed the top of her head—black curly hair, like Garth's—and felt a rush of love and protectiveness she had never known before. *Don't be afraid, Penny. I won't let you be hurt.*

"I love you, Penny," she said.

Outside, the thump of Cliff's ball was like a heartbeat. The thump stopped. "Hey," he said, appearing at the door. "Isn't it my turn?"

I'd like a five-minute break, Sabrina thought, but Cliff was peering through the screen like a refugee. "Yes, it is. Come on in."

"Can I stay?" asked Penny.

Sabrina looked at Cliff. "Is this a private talk?"

"I guess not." Cliff took the place of his sister, while Penny sat on the floor and began to draw in her sketch pad. "I . . . uh . . . it's about working in the house."

"Yes?" Sabrina smiled at him serenely.

"I don't like it," he blurted. "And I don't think I should

have to do it. I already go to school and practice soccer, and I have homework."

"Yes?"

"Well . . . that's three jobs."

"Two, if you really call them jobs. Student and soccer forward."

"Well, two. But if I work around here, that's three, and nobody has three jobs."

"What about me?"

"You? You're just a . . . a mother."

"Just a mother. Well, think about this. I clean house; that makes me a maid—hardly as much fun as soccer. I'm a cook; job number two. I drive you around, so I'm a chauffeur; job number three. I'm a laundress; that's four. A gardener; that's five. I refinish furniture and arrange it, so I'm a decorator; that's six. I'm a hostess for our friends; that's seven. I nurse you when you're sick; that's eight. I work at the university; that's nine." *Does Stephanie really do all this?* "And, of course, I am, as you say, a mother, which makes ten, and a wife, which makes eleven. I may have left out a few. How many jobs did you say you have?"

He stared. "But . . . you're supposed to do those things."

"Who says?"

He thought about it, mentally weighing answers. "The Bible?"

She laughed. "The Bible has women warriors who whack off men's heads with their swords. Shall I be like them?"

"No, but . . . well, maybe it's not in a book or a law, but everybody knows what mothers are supposed to do—what they've always done. Family things don't change."

She nodded seriously. "And what are sons supposed to do?"

"Go to school."

"Only in this century. All but the rich ones used to work twelve or fourteen hours a day in factories and coal mines. Earning money to help out their parents."

"But that's all changed—!"

She made a face of mock surprise. "A family thing changed?"

After a long moment Cliff grinned. "Oh," he said, and they began to laugh together. Sabrina, wanting to hug him, reached out to tousle his hair as their laughter grew, and that was how

Garth found them a moment later when he walked into the kitchen.

Sabrina's laughter stopped. "Cliff, we've talked away the afternoon, and what have we done for dinner?"

"We haven't done the dishes," he said, sliding off the couch. "Hi, Dad. Make any clones today?"

"I'm working on one for a respectful son," Garth said, but he was looking at Sabrina. "I brought a steak. If you'll tell me what you did last week, I'll do it this time."

"I can do it," she said, starting to get up.

"But I want to." He liked doing things for his wife, who had always doggedly done for everyone else, no matter how sick she felt. He liked being needed by her, for a change.

Sabrina sat back. Garth poured two glasses of wine and put them on the table in front of her. Then, following her directions, he crushed peppercorns with the new mortar and pestle and pressed them into both sides of the steak. Beside him, Cliff washed the breakfast dishes and talked about his science class. Sabrina watched them, father and son, working side by side. On the floor beside her, Penny hummed as she sketched, locked in her own world, unaware of the family. But Sabrina was keenly aware of it. She was not doing very well with Garth, but in spite of that she felt the force of the family holding her close, and she was content to be there, part of them, even though Garth's explosive anger of the night before hung unresolved in the air.

Garth sat beside her, and automatically she moved away from him. He ignored it, handing her a glass of wine. "I owe you an apology for last night. I talked myself into something simply because I wanted it. It was thoughtless and I'm sorry. Especially since it was such a wonderful evening until then. At least for me."

"For all of us. I should apologize, too—"

"There's no reason. It will take you a while to get back your equilibrium, and I should have known that. Instead, I was about as sensitive as a teenager on a back road."

Sabrina frowned. "Who said anything about my equilibrium?"

"Nat. Talking about the aftereffects of shock and concussion. We don't have to go into it; he simply made me aware that I'd been thinking of myself, not of you." He held out his hand, palm up, and after a moment's hesitation she put hers in it. "I don't like to think of myself as crude. I do apologize."

"Thank you." Gently she pulled back her hand. "I think I'd better do something about dinner."

"No, your job is to give orders and supervise. That way the responsibility for possible failure is shared. What do I do now?"

He enlisted Cliff and Penny, and they all worked while Sabrina, curled up on the couch, gave directions and let her thoughts wander. The days were settling into routine, but she was left in a strange limbo. Her brief adventure had collapsed, and she was no longer simply a visitor; this was home, this was her family. She was involved in the things they did today and planned for tomorrow, next week, two weeks from now.

But how could she make plans? She could not change the house or its routine; they weren't hers. She would begin things she would not have time to finish; she would make mistakes that could expose her at any minute; she would love Penny and Cliff and leave them; and Garth—

Garth. The biggest part of the future. The part she had to keep her distance from.

"Dinner," he said, smiling, and reached out a hand to help her up.

On Friday, Juanita came again. Dolores called first. "Go easy with her; she doesn't like to take orders."

"Dolores, I have to tell her what I want done."

"Don't. Just let her do what she wants. That's when she does best. You can make a suggestion now and then. As for lunch—"

"There's the doorbell. I'll talk to you later."

Silently, Juanita cleaned the rooms and changed the beds while Sabrina began some of the jobs Stephanie had told her she always did at the end of September: putting away summer clothes, bringing out winter ones from the garment bags in the hall closet. At noon Juanita came up to her. "What's for lunch?"

Oh, for Mrs. Thirkell.

"Anything in the refrigerator that appeals to you," she said, folding sweaters. Her cast made her clumsy, and she knocked two of them to the floor. Juanita picked them up.

"Mrs. Goldner and the other ladies fix something for me."

Sabrina took the sweaters from her. "Thank you. Do you cook for yourself in your own home, Juanita?"

After a pause, Juanita said, "Yes, ma'am," and went downstairs. An hour later, when Sabrina went down for her own lunch, she found on the breakfast-room table a plate of cold sliced roast beef, tomatoes and French bread, silverware wrapped in a napkin, and a glass of cider. As she looked at it, Juanita came in from the living room. "I thought you might have trouble fixing something, with your arm and all."

"That was kind of you. It looks lovely. Did you have enough to eat?"

"Yes'm." She went back to the living room.

Later, she found Sabrina in the backyard, pruning roses. "I have a free day every other Wednesday. If you want, I could come here."

"What do you charge, Juanita?"

"Thirty dollars plus carfare."

Could they afford it? She didn't know. Stephanie always did her own housework. But why should I do it? Sabrina thought. After all, I gave up Mrs. Thirkell. And it's only for the few weeks I'm here. Stephanie can decide what she wants to do when she returns. "All right. Next Wednesday or the one after?"

"Next."

"I'll see you then." She turned back to the roses. They had had a small contest of wills, she and Juanita, and both had won. Juanita cleaned house her own way; Sabrina managed lunch in her way. Except . . . who had the last word? Juanita. She decided what Sabrina would eat and drink. Sabrina began to laugh. Wait until I tell Garth, she thought.

At dinner, the last of the donated meals, she listened as Garth and Cliff talked about the soccer game he had played that afternoon, the first since he was benched. He had scored twice. "You shoulda seen it, Mom, it was great. You'll come next week to the last one, won't you? I like it best when you and Dad are both there."

"Of course," she said. "I think Penny might want to come, too." Then she sat back again, letting the others talk. Every few minutes Garth looked at her quizzically, waiting for her to join them or lead the conversation, as she had on other nights; but she was quiet. Let them be the family; she would watch.

"Headache still bad?" he asked after dinner.

"Only once in a while. Mostly it's like background noise; always there, but I get used to it."

"But you're so quiet. Wasn't it a good day?"

"Oh, it was. Something amusing—" Penny brought a carton of ice cream to the table, and while Garth scooped it into dishes and poured their coffee, she told about her contest of wills with Juanita. He chuckled, but he was surprised.

"You've always said you were uncomfortable giving orders; that was why you didn't want a maid."

"Oh. Well, it's amazing how a broken wrist and pounding head make it easy to give orders and get used to having a maid. As a matter of fact, that was the other way Juanita had the last word. After she chose my lunch, she got me to hire her."

Garth's eyebrows went up. "You hired her?"

"Only one day every other week." Sabrina was annoyed to find herself becoming defensive. She wasn't used to that. In London she never had to explain her decisions; she answered to no one but herself. Did Stephanie have to consult Garth whenever she wanted to spend money?

"Well, that's fine," he said. "You know how many times I've suggested it. I just assumed we'd discuss it first."

I don't discuss my plans with anyone.

But suddenly she thought of Antonio, sitting across from her at Le Gavroche, casually dismissing her problems, saying he would get rid of her "little shop" for her. Was it a luxury that she did not have to discuss her plans with anyone—or was it a burden, that she had no one to discuss them with?

"I'm sorry," she said to Garth. "The idea came up—"

The telephone rang and Cliff ran to get it, calling from the kitchen, "Mom! It's Aunt Sabrina!"

In the breakfast room, Sabrina tried to hear Stephanie through a bad connection and the clatter of Penny and Cliff clearing the table. Something about Antonio; Stephanie sounded upset. "I'll call you back," Sabrina said. "This weekend?"

"No." Stephanie's voice faded. ". . . away in the country."

"Monday, then," said Sabrina, adding, "Don't worry about Antonio." Whatever it was, it seemed far off and not very important.

Over the weekend, she almost forgot it. Imperceptibly, she had slipped completely into the family routine. She and Garth shared the house and yard work with the children, talking casually about family matters, and she was cooking again, choosing what she assumed were favorite recipes from spattered pages in Stephanie's cookbooks. She could not resist a few touches of her own, but she thought no one noticed until, over coffee on Sunday night, Garth said she made a more delicious meal with one good arm than most chefs did with two.

It was surprising how good that made her feel.

She thought about it later, when she and Garth were alone in the living room. They had watched a television show and then they read, sitting near each other in overlapping circles of light. Around them the house slumbered; music came softly from the record player. Sabrina looked up from her book and found Garth watching her. They smiled at each other—the only two people awake in the world. Abruptly she returned to her book, to break the spell.

At midnight, Garth said he was going to sleep—"Early meeting tomorrow with the vice president." And a little later, when she turned out the lights and went upstairs, she found him on the far side of the bed, eyes shut, breathing deeply. Holding her breath, trying to be invisible and weightless, she slipped into the near side. He did not stir, and before she could decide whether he was feigning sleep or not, she fell asleep herself.

On Monday Garth suggested she take a few more days off from her job. "I'll call Ted and explain," he said, and she let him. Coward, she thought. You'll have to go in sooner or later.

But some things could not be put off any longer. Sabrina finally had made an appointment with Penny's teacher, and after lunch she went to the school to meet her. "Intimidating," Stephanie had described her, and after one look at the small woman with perfectly waved gray hair, uncompromising mouth and rigid neck, Sabrina understood why.

"Do sit down, Mrs. Andersen. Penny told me about your accident; I'm so sorry. How is the wrist?"

"I hope it is healing."

"Of course, one cannot know what is happening beneath a cast. One can only hope. I want you to know, Mrs. Andersen, as I told you last year, I enjoy Penny. She's a lovely child and a fine student. She is, however, a bit willful; you must watch that in her."

Sabrina gazed calmly at Mrs. Casey. "Willful," she repeated.

"She likes her own way. Of course, all youngsters do, but Penny is too sure of herself. She needs to be taken down a notch or two."

"In what way?" asked Sabrina with interest.

"She must learn humility. Without it, Mrs. Andersen, children are uncontrollable. Penny, like all of them, must be taught to respect authority, to take her place in the orderly progression of authority. It is a simple fact that adults know more than children. If children begin to think their opinion is as valuable as ours, how can we keep them in their place? How can we teach them? Of course, you understand all this, but I bring it up because Penny tends to be . . . ah . . . assertive. I encourage independence, to a degree, Mrs. Andersen, but I do not encourage sedition."

Sabrina nodded impassively. "And the puppet show?"

"A good example. The show dramatizes westward expansion, the Mexican war, the gold rush. It is a teaching tool, not a game. Last spring I granted Penny's request to handle the costumes. When school began this fall she had already drawn a complete set of sketches, which showed admirable energy; but when I suggested certain changes she argued with me, and when I ordered her to make them, she refused, claiming the project was hers. Clearly, I could not tolerate that. There must be one central authority in a classroom or you have chaos. So I turned the costumes over to Barbara Goodman, who is—"

"Without discussing it with Penny."

"Ah. Yes, I grant you, that was a mistake. I meant to tell her, but something came up and by the next day it had slipped my mind. I can understand that the child is upset about that, and I will make a note to apologize to her. It sets children a good example when adults apologize for their mistakes. But I might add that if Penny had altered her sketches she still would have her little project and I would have no need to apologize."

"Mrs. Casey."

For the first time the teacher looked directly at Sabrina and saw the glint in her eyes. "Mrs. Andersen, this is a small matter. It will pass—"

"Please. It is now my turn." Sabrina let a long moment go by. "You are a tyrant," she said pleasantly. "Tyrants always have very definite ideas about the orderly progression of authority and keeping people in their place." She was so angry she was trembling, but she kept her voice even and good-natured. "If you were running your little show with adults I would ignore you. But you are lording it over sixth-grade children who haven't learned to defend themselves when someone in authority tries to stamp all confidence and independence out of them."

"You cannot speak to me this—"

"My taxes pay your salary, Mrs. Casey; you work for me. Please let me finish. As long as I am Penny's mother, I intend to do all I can to help her feel good about herself. I want her to feel confident that she can do things on her own, though not ashamed to ask for help when she needs it. I will not have her squashed into the subservient lump of humility you seem to require in order to feel powerful."

"How dare—"

"I am not quite finished. I give you two choices. I can have Penny transferred to another sixth-grade class and give a full explanation of my reasons to your principal. Or I will allow Penny to stay if you can convince me you will concentrate on teaching instead of tyrannizing."

Mrs. Casey was silent, twisting her hands in her lap. The rigid muscles of her neck had given way and her head trembled like a dried flower on a bent stalk. Sabrina, in the midst of her anger, felt pity. She had guessed that complaints already had been made about Mrs. Casey, and as the silence dragged on she knew she was right.

On impulse, she said, "Why don't we talk about this over a cup of coffee? Is there a place in the school—?"

Mrs. Casey looked up. "You know there is. The faculty lounge where you helped with our Christmas party last year."

"Of course. I meant a more private place."

"No one will bother us." She took a breath. "Mrs. Andersen, I have been a teacher for thirty years. Teaching is all I have. It is my only family; I have nothing else in the world. Of course, you cannot understand that; what do you know about being completely alone? We all need something to believe in. I believe in order and authority. But I have always wanted to be a good teacher. If I am not, then I have nothing at all."

Sabrina's anger vanished. Only pity was left. I believe in myself, she thought. Mrs. Casey has never been able to do that. She stood up. "Coffee? I think we can find a lot to talk about."

When Penny danced home from school on Tuesday afternoon she threw her arms around Sabrina, bubbling with the news that Mrs. Casey had put her in charge of the puppet costumes once again, with Barbara Goodman as her assistant. "And she said she was sorry and even smiled!"

"And what did Barbara say?"

"Oh, she was glad; she doesn't know anything about costumes. Why are you sitting by the telephone? Is somebody going to call?"

"I was calling someone. But she wasn't home."

"Then come see my drawings. Mrs. Casey says I can use all of them, but I have to change General Santa Anna. She showed me his picture in a book, so I know how to do it. Are you coming?"

Sabrina went upstairs slowly. She had been calling Stephanie to find out what she had been trying to tell her on Friday, but no one was home, not even Mrs. Thirkell. I'll call later, she thought; from the bedroom. No one will bother me.

At dinner Garth looked at her quizzically. "I heard a fascinating story today about my wife."

She tensed. "Oh?"

"From Vivian Goodman."

Vivian doesn't know anything. There's nothing to worry about.

"She told me she went yesterday to talk to her daughter's teacher about a project that had her daughter terrified—she couldn't do it and didn't have the courage to say so. When she got there, another mother was talking about the same project. It was so interesting she eavesdropped. You didn't tell me you called Mrs. Casey a tyrant."

Sabrina shook her head. She had decided not to tell Garth about that talk because she didn't know how Stephanie would have handled it.

"According to Vivian, you were cool, collected and devastating. I wish I'd been there. Usually your emotions run high about the kids."

Of course. Stephanie's anger would have overflowed. But it's easy to be cool and collected, Sabrina thought, when dealing with someone else's child. I can't take credit for being less involved than a mother would be.

"Why are you shaking your head?" Garth asked. "Didn't you call her a tyrant?"

"What? Oh. Yes. I . . . it just came out; she really was talking and acting like one—"

"Don't apologize. Vivian tells me Mrs. Casey has been terrifying her students for years. You're an amazing woman; I'm proud of you."

She flushed with pleasure, then felt a little tremor of alarm. She was beginning to depend on Garth for praise.

"I didn't realize Barbara was Vivian's daughter," she said, to shift the conversation. "I didn't connect the names."

"I thought you met them both at the class picnic last year."

"Did I? I don't remember."

And I'm getting tired of pretending, with no one to relax with, no one to talk to and just be myself. No one except Stephanie. And why isn't Stephanie home? Or Mrs. Thirkell?

Later, as she sat in the living room with Garth, reading and talking, the telephone broke the silence. "Long distance for you," Garth said, and she ran to the kitchen. *Stephanie. Finally.*

"Stephanie?" said her mother. "We just got back to Washington. How are you? And how was the adventure in China? I haven't been able to reach Sabrina in London, so you'll have to give me all the news."

Sabrina adjusted her thoughts from her sister to her mother. "I thought you were in Paris. Or Geneva. Or somewhere."

"Moscow, dear. Your father had a conference. But it ended early, so we came home. Now tell me about China."

Sabrina talked briefly about China, once more describing Mr. Su, the bronze lamp, the chess set, the intricate ivory carving Mr. Su had given her of ladies of the court.

How can I do this? How can I fool my mother? Doesn't she have any suspicion at all?

"You sound tired, Stephanie. Is everything all right?"

Don't mention a broken wrist; she might want to come and help with the housework. And I don't know if I could fool her close up. "I'm fine, Mother, just busy. You know how much there is to do after you've been away."

"You're sure that's all? Are you and Garth . . . getting along all right?"

"Yes, of course. Why shouldn't we be?"

"You don't have to be so defensive. I detected vibrations in

237

your last letter that caused your father and me some concern."

"Everything is fine, Mother. I hate housework and love the house."

Laura gave a surprised laugh. "Is that new?"

"Maybe it just seems new, coming back from China." Sabrina plunged ahead, letting the truth pour out; she hadn't had anyone to talk to for such a long time. "I hate the laundry and I love the garden. I've hired a maid one day every two weeks and I'm considering letting the house go to pieces in between."

"Stephanie, this is not like you."

"Probably not. I've felt different since the trip. I like the quiet rhythm of this life; I like not having to keep up with a social circle—"

"Is that a criticism of us, my dear?"

Sabrina paused. "No. I never even thought of you. Are you worried about keeping up?"

"We always worry about keeping up. You knew that from the time you were born. Sabrina understood it better than you, which is why she does so well in London. You could never have handled that pace."

"No. Where was I? Oh, yes. I like the people I know in Evanston and the way they're connected with the university and the town. I like the comfort of the shabby rooms in this big, wonderful house. I like my family around me. Lots of noise but lots of life. They keep me from drifting off."

"Stephanie, have you and Garth taken up drugs?"

"Mother!"

"Well, you certainly don't sound like yourself. Why am I getting this list of likes and dislikes?"

"Because I can talk to you, Mother. And I thought you would want to know how happy I am. And that Garth and I aren't getting a divorce."

"My dear, I never suggested—"

"That wasn't what you were worried about in my letter?"

"It may have been. In these days, one does worry about divorce. Look at Sabrina. I'm not sure which was her mistake— marrying Denton or divorcing him—but I don't think she's a very happy woman. Do you?"

Sabrina was silent.

"Stephanie? Do you?"

"Probably not. At least not a lot of the time."

"So you see, I worry. Well, my dear, your father is calling

me. We'll be at your house for Thanksgiving, as usual. Do you suppose we could get Sabrina to join us this year?"

"I doubt it."

"I'll ask her anyway."

Sabrina lingered in the breakfast room after hanging up. *What I didn't say, Mother, what I left out about my life, was this: I like being part of a community that accepts me for myself, not because of my looks and my sophisticated small talk, my elite shop, my social connections or my former marriage.*

Oh, come on, a small voice jeered. Who's the community accepting for being herself? Sabrina Longworth? Or Stephanie Andersen?

She didn't need to answer.

On Wednesday Sabrina tried again to call Stephanie. "Lady Longworth is out," said Mrs. Thirkell. "Shall I ask her to return your call, Mrs. Andersen?"

"Yes. I've been trying to reach her."

"Oh, I'm so sorry, Mrs. Andersen. I was visiting a sick sister in Scotland, and I believe Lady Longworth is redecorating a house on Eaton Square. But I shall make sure she returns your call."

A wave of depression swept Sabrina as she hung up. A door had slammed in her face. Lady Longworth working on Eaton Square. Mrs. Thirkell calling her Mrs. Andersen. As if she had lost her place in that life. *But I can't. I won't. Just because I like being here doesn't mean this is what I want. I'll talk to Stephanie tomorrow. Find out what is going on there.*

And remind myself of where I belong.

But the next morning Penny woke with a fever and a hacking cough that terrified Sabrina. It's my fault, she thought; I didn't pay attention to how they dressed when they went outside. She called the pediatrician on Stephanie's list. "Bring her in," said the nurse. "We'll take a look."

Sabrina looked again at the list. Cos Building on Ridge Avenue. "How do I get there?"

There was a puzzled silence. "Oh, is something wrong with your car?" the nurse asked. "Perhaps one of your friends—"

"Yes. Yes, of course. We'll be right there." Frantically she searched the map she had been using for three weeks and memorized the route to the medical center across the street from the hospital.

"Not like you to get so upset," the pediatrician said. She

DECEPTIONS

looked keenly at Sabrina. "You look like you're under a lot of strain. The wrist? Or something else?"

"Could we talk about Penny?" Sabrina asked.

"Sure. Penny, you've got bronchitis; not severe, but it could get nasty if you don't take it easy. Bed for a couple of days, a vaporizer in your room and a lousy-tasting syrup to keep your cough loose. You or your mom should call on Saturday to let me know how you're doing. Any questions?"

Penny shook her head.

"I'm sorry," said Sabrina, embarrassed by her rudeness. "A lot has been going on. We'll call on Saturday."

"Or before, if you need me. And relax. Penny's a tough little lady; she'll be well in no time."

In the car, Sabrina shook her head. A bad case of overreacting. *Stephanie would have taken it in stride. But I've never had a sick child before.*

That night she and Garth went to the Talvias' for dinner, leaving Penny cheerfully propped up in bed, sharing dinner on a tray with Cliff.

"We bought you a present," Linda said as they walked in.

"Another birthday?"

"Nope." Linda laughed. "But Dolores and I thought you needed cheering up, so we bought you this. It's cheerful."

It was a robe of smooth polished cotton splashed with brilliant flowers: brighter than anything in Stephanie's closet; the kind Sabrina loved best. Her face lit in a delighted smile that made Garth draw in his breath as she thanked Linda. "I think I'll wear it to work. It's too lovely to hide in a closet all day."

"You really like it? Dolores thought you'd say it's too loud."

"It's not loud, it's beautiful. What wonderful taste you have."

Linda beamed. "How did you know I picked it out?"

"Because Dolores thought it was too loud."

She wore the robe the next night, feeling more cheerful about everything. Penny's fever was down and her cough seemed better. Linda and Dolores had bought the robe for her, not Stephanie. In the past three weeks they had talked almost every day on the telephone and often met in one of their kitchens for afternoon coffee. Whatever name they called her, *she* was their friend. She still hadn't talked to Stephanie on the telephone, but it didn't seem so important now; if anything were wrong, Stephanie would have called.

240

DECEPTIONS

"A lovely robe," Garth said. "It almost does you justice."

She flushed. "Thank you."

"You look much better."

"I feel better. And Penny is getting well."

"No more headaches?"

"Not a one. And the bruises look bad but I hardly notice—"
She stopped.

"Good," he said easily. "I was going to sit out the conference, but I think, since you're doing so well, I'll go after all."

"Conference?"

"I told you about . . . I did tell you, didn't I?"

"I don't think so."

"October 6. Tomorrow. Berkeley for a week. Good Lord, did I really forget to tell you? That's unforgivable, how could I—"

"It's all right, don't be so upset. You probably told me and I forgot it." But I wouldn't have forgotten, she thought. A whole wonderful week. No need for excuses in bed after I was stupid enough to say I'm feeling fine. "I'm glad you're going," she added.

"A week to yourself."

She looked startled. How often did he know what she was thinking? "No, I meant, if it's something you want to do, I'm glad you don't have to worry about us. We'll be fine. We are fine."

"Are you going to the office on Monday?"

"I think so. Yes, of course. Why?"

"You'd rather not go at all."

"I didn't say that."

"You've thought it."

"I'll do what I have to do," she said almost angrily. "Anyway, I'll be socializing, too: I have a lunch date with Vivian. I meant to ask you: what's happening with Vivian's job?"

"Did I ever tell you my Theory of Universities? Like most institutions, each one is similar to a vat of molasses—slow and sluggish. If something goes wrong in one part, it spreads out and covers it up; if you try to make a dent in it, it oozes into the mark you think you've made. If you try to wade through it too quickly, you collapse from exhaustion; and if you try to beat it by plunging in and flailing away, you drown."

She was laughing. "But if you heat molasses it gets thin and moves quickly."

241

"Exactly. So we lit a small fire under the vice president. Lloyd Strauss. You've met him."

"And is he moving more quickly?"

"Like a tidal wave. In one week he has discovered that half the human race is female and has asked William Webster, whose paunch makes a formidable roadblock, to explain why our ivory tower resembles a club for men only."

"You'd like to get rid of Webster."

"Is it that obvious? I hope no one else sees that. It could look as if I want his job."

"But you don't."

"Lord, no. I want more time in the lab, not behind a desk."

"Would Foster Labs give you what you want?"

"I've been wondering when you'd bring that up again."

"I wasn't starting a debate; I only asked if it would satisfy you."

He gave her a long, thoughtful look. "I'm not sure."

"How will you find out?"

"I suppose I'll have to go there and look around."

She nodded.

"No comment?"

"What would you like me to say?"

"Damned if I know. You never lacked for something to say in the past. If I go for a look, will you come with me?"

"I don't think so. You should have a chance to think about it by yourself."

"That's new. Until now—"

She stood and shook out the folds of her robe. "I think I'll go up. I want to call my sister before I go to sleep."

"Since when is she awake at five-thirty in the morning?"

"It's not morning; it's late in the— No, how silly of me, you're right, I got it backwards. Of course she won't be up. I'll call tomorrow. I'll just go to sleep now."

"Without any more talk of Foster Labs?"

"I'd rather not. Not tonight."

He waited. "All right. I'll be up soon."

"Good night."

She climbed the stairs slowly, wondering how she could confuse the times in Chicago and London after she'd been here almost three weeks. She'd been uncomfortable with Garth—that was the reason. The easy intimacy of their talk troubled her. How did she know him so well that she knew what he was thinking? I don't want that, she thought.

But what did she want?

She wanted to keep distance between them—but she wanted his smile and his praise.

She tried to think of him as her sister's dull husband—but they laughed together and his work made him fascinating and powerful.

She reminded herself that Stephanie called him withdrawn and neglectful—but she warmed to the feeling he gave her of being protected and cherished.

Lying in bed, thinking about him, she heard him come upstairs. He was in the bedroom doorway when Penny began to cough.

Sabrina threw back the covers.

"I'll go," said Garth. He found Penny sitting up in bed, small and white-faced in the light from the hall. He poured a spoonful of cough medicine and she made a face as she swallowed it.

"Why is it so awful?"

"The worse it tastes, the faster you get well so you don't have to take any more. Snuggle down, now, and I'll tuck you in."

"Daddy, could you stay a few minutes?"

He put his hand on her forehead. No fever. "What, sweetheart?"

"I asked Mommy about art lessons. She said I could take them if it was all right with you."

"Did she? Well, I think we can manage it. When do they begin?"

"Right after Christmas. But—"

"But?"

"I need paints and brushes and charcoal and canvas. And they cost lots of money."

"Well, I don't know. I thought you could draw with sticks and mud on paper napkins. But if you insist on the same equipment Michelangelo used, we could make it an early Christmas present and get you everything you need."

"Oh, Daddy!" She struggled out of the blankets to throw her arms around him.

He held her close. "Now to sleep, don't you think? It's hard to paint a masterpiece if you're hacking away with a cough."

"Daddy?"

"Something else?"

"Why is Mommy so different lately?"

Garth sat down again. "How is she different?"

"Oh, you know. *Different*. Like she hugs us more than she used to, but she hardly ever scolds us. Sometimes it's like she doesn't even notice what we're doing. And sometimes she smiles at *you* and other times it's like she doesn't want to be close to you. And lots of times she looks far away and just . . . thinks. Like . . . like she's here and someplace else at the same time."

Garth smoothed back her hair. There was no sense in pretending. Children were oblivious to much that their parents did, but what they did see they saw with uncanny clarity and insight. "I think she's got a lot of things on her mind that she's trying to sort out. When you get to a certain age, usually in your thirties, you begin to wonder if you're doing what you really want to do, in the way you want to do it. So sometimes you stand back a little bit—"

"Like taking a vacation from everybody and thinking about yourself separately?"

He was surprised. "Yes. What made you think of that?"

"That's what Mommy said when I asked her."

"Did she. And what else did she say?"

"That you weren't going to get a divorce."

"That we weren't—"

"But I think maybe she's still thinking about it."

Garth sat very still, staring unseeingly at the light from the hall. Stupid ass. You stupid ass not to see it, to have to wait for your eleven-year-old daughter to tell you the obvious. His hand clenched an imaginary tennis racket; his muscles tensed to smash a ball across the room. Goddamned blind, stupid ass not to know that she's wanted to divorce you for—how long? Since her trip? Since before the trip? How long?

Penny knew. Penny had known for a long time, had even talked to her mother about it. "She's still thinking about it." Of course she was thinking about it. And who else knew, besides Penny? Who else saw his wife more clearly than he did? How many were not afraid, as he was, to see her clearly?

Because of course he'd known, in some part of him that he pushed out of sight whenever it poked its obscene head out, that she wanted to leave. Everything pointed to it, from running off to China to ignoring the laundry. Even when he tried to tell her that he'd talked to Cliff, as she'd nagged him to, about the loot stashed in his closet, she'd seemed indifferent. Worse; as if she didn't even know what he was talking about. As if she didn't care what he did. Everything pointed to it: she wanted to leave.

Except that she was still here. And wanted to stay. He had to believe that, too; how else could he explain the effort she was making to change, to be more lively and curious, more interested in all of them, more exciting? It wasn't just a shared glass of wine before dinner, or admitting she felt ill and letting him take care of her; it wasn't even a dinner table conversation about his work. She was trying to act differently in every way, forcing him to do the same. So they could begin again.

Sometimes. She acted like that sometimes. Other times she withdrew. As if her thoughts were pulling her to and away from him, hour by hour, day by day. She was thinking about divorce. But she hadn't decided.

He felt tenderness and admiration for her. He had not realized she was so strong, forcing him to court her again, forcing herself to court him, even while she wasn't sure what lay ahead, whether she would still have to leave him, to be—whatever she wanted to be. Whatever she thought she couldn't be as his wife.

He had to show her he understood, that he knew now he'd almost let her slip away from him in his absorption in his work, and that, with her, he would begin again if she would stay and give them a chance.

That was all he had to do.

"Daddy?"

"It's all right, sweetheart. Your mother and I are not going to get a divorce. Lots of married people think about divorce, and sometimes, when they have very serious problems, they have to separate. But not always. And do you know something?"

"What?" Her voice was warm and sleepy.

"I love your mother and you and Cliff more than anybody in the world. Do you think I'd be silly enough to let us all break apart, with so much love?"

"I love you, Daddy," Penny sighed, and slept.

Garth leaned down and kissed her forehead. Sometimes all

the love in the world isn't enough, he said silently. But I'll do my best.

Lying beside his wife in the dark, he said quietly, "I don't want to go to this conference. The past week has been so good; I've felt we were learning to know each other after being a long way apart. I know that was my fault far more than yours, and I've wanted to talk about it, but then it seemed that, lately, we were, in a real way, beginning again. Have you felt that? Stephanie? I know you're not asleep. Has it been a good week?"

Hidden by the dark, she gripped her hands. "Yes," she said reluctantly. The quiet evenings, his praise for things she did, the closeness of their talk and laughter, the way their eyes met when Cliff or Penny said something amusing, sharing the work of the house, her sense of being connected to him, to a family. . . . "Yes."

He slid his arm along the pillow, beneath her neck, and pulled her to him. "I want to know you again; begin again." His lips brushed her cheek and closed eyes. "Hold fast our good times and build on them. My love," he said, and his mouth covered hers.

She lay, taut and frantic, her mind in a turmoil, swept by the waves of happiness and depression that had battered her for days. As his hands slid the nightgown from her shoulders, her thoughts shouted at her, echoing and contradicting each other.

Stop him . . . tell him . . . what? Get out of bed. Push him away. Tell him . . . what? That he can't do this?

He is a husband in his own bed.

His hands and mouth moved on her body; his lips whispered on her breasts in slow kisses that shuddered through her. With her fingers she felt the bone and muscle of his shoulders, the smooth skin of his back, and realized she was embracing him. She tore her arms away. His body stilled, as if caught in flight, then bent to her again; he held her breasts and kissed the hollow of her throat.

Sabrina heard the small moan that tore from her and struggled against it. *We can't, we can't—* But his body moved against hers, demanding and already familiar, and beneath his insistent hands she felt herself letting go into dark languor and the desire that swept in heavy waves through the hunger of her body.

You must not do this. The cold voice slashed through the soft

246

darkness and she winced. Thinking he had hurt her, Garth pulled back, but her body, quite separate from the tumult in her mind, helped him move onto her and when he entered her, she was open to him, wet and smooth. In a sudden rush of joy that burst like a flame before she could smother it, she rose to meet him with such a passionate force that he, so long abstinent, could not hold back. With a low cry he came, deep inside her, and then lay still, pressing her beneath him into the bed.

She stretched the moment out, the feel of his strength upon her, then put her hands on his arms to push him away.

He lifted his head. "I'm sorry, my love." He slid his hand down. "Let me—"

"No," she whispered, torn by the pain of loss and guilt. She longed for him and was ashamed, and she turned her head away.

He lifted himself and lay beside her. Sabrina shivered, feeling bereft.

"I'll stay home this week," he said.

"No. I want you to go."

"Then I'll try to cut it short. We have so much to talk about, so much time to make up."

She heard a new note in his voice and tried to make it out. Not triumph; not satisfaction.

Anticipation.

"Good night, my love," he said.

"Good night." Her voice was barely audible. "Sleep well."

He reached out and took her hand, holding it tightly. And that was how they fell asleep.

Chapter 14

Stephanie and Max Stuyvesant walked together into the enormous white tent on the grounds of Chilton House. Holding her arm, he guided her through the crowd and they found seats near Nicholas Blackford and Alexandra just as the auctioneer mounted the rostrum. The chairs were closely packed, and Stephanie felt the pressure of his arm against hers as forcefully as she felt his commanding presence and his eyes on her face. She looked away as the auctioneer began a graceful speech of welcome.

The Chilton auction. The first highlight of the new social season. Three hundred bidders from Britain and the continent: wealthy, polite, dressed in country tweeds, seated in the carpeted tent and standing four deep along the sides. Outside, a hundred more watched through a raised flap of the tent, sitting on the smooth lawn or perched on walking sticks that opened at one end into a small seat. Sunlight filtered through high, thin clouds; the mild air smelled of cut grass and trimmed hedges.

The Chilton auction. The kind of high-flying, distant social event Stephanie always read about in newspapers.

And Max Stuyvesant. Whom she had met unexpectedly in the park outside the tent, and whose arm now pressed against hers, a constant reminder, even as she began to concentrate on the auction.

The auctioneer finished his history of Chilton house, built in the reign of Queen Anne, and a brief biography of its late owner, a renowned painter who had died without heirs. The executors were selling the house and its contents, as well as a separate studio, greenhouse, four garages, and ten acres of park. "I shall open the bidding on the house," said the auctioneer genially, "at two hundred thousand pounds."

A flurry of whispers rose from a group at the side of the tent. "The townspeople," said Max. "Worried about being saddled with an unacceptable neighbor. A momentous problem in a village of two hundred."

"Done," said the auctioneer, and a surprised murmur went through the crowd. In less than two minutes, the bidding had ended at two hundred fifteen thousand pounds. Stephanie heard Alexandra say disgustedly, "If I'd known it would go for nothing I would have grabbed it."

"The Earl of Wexon," someone whispered. "Bought it for his mother." A sigh of relief came from the townspeople, and many of them left as the real estate auctioneer stepped down and an auctioneer from Christie's of London took his place.

"Now the numbers will go up," Max murmured. "The contents always do better than the houses themselves. What are you bidding on?"

"The Meissen vases," Stephanie said, marveling at the calmness of her voice. In Sabrina's suede skirt and tweed jacket, a cashmere sweater caressing her skin, and the confident bulk of Max Stuyvesant beside her, she blended with the crowd; she belonged. She turned the pages of her catalogue. "The Louis XVI tulipwood bureau and the George III side table. Lord and Lady Raddison want the Regency breakfront, but I don't think we'll get it; they won't go above thirty-five hundred."

"You're buying for Peter and Rose? Did they come on hands and knees, or is this your season for forgiveness?"

Stephanie frowned. What was he talking about? Had Sabrina quarreled with Peter and Rose Raddison?

"An impudent question," Max said smoothly. "Allow me to change the subject. I will be bidding on the three fruitwood statues, which means you and I are not opponents. And I am delighted that I found you this morning."

She nodded, pretending to study the catalogue. She almost had not come. When Nicholas called her at Ambassadors yesterday, offering to pick her up, she had been slow and stupid. "What auction?"

"My dear Sabrina, the Chilton auction! Amelia called you about it, and, of course, Christie's sent you the catalogue. You must come; how could I venture into the depths of Wiltshire alone?"

She laughed. The blind leading the blind; she had never been in Wiltshire. She'd have to get a map and study it. "Of course, Nicholas; what time do we leave?"

"Eight, I fear. Absurd time, but what can one do?"

She found the catalogue and soon was swept up in its glossy pages, savoring the color photographs as she did whenever she read about items beyond her means. And then in a rush it came to her: she had the means. Ambassadors had a special bank account for auctions—and she had Ambassadors. In their long talk on Monday, Sabrina had told her to draw money for the shop as she needed it. For once she would participate in an auction instead of watching and dreaming like an outsider, or a child standing silently beside her sister as her mother bid.

Sabrina had told her to ask Brian anything about the shop. "We discuss most things and compare notes, so he won't suspect anything if you have questions." She had hesitated. "One thing he doesn't know. Don't buy anything from a slick gentleman named Rory Carr or his firm, Westbridge Imports. Tell Brian, will you? They may be playing around with forgeries; stay away from them until we're sure. Everything else, just ask Brian."

"Did you have any thoughts," Stephanie asked Brian, "about what we might want at the Chilton auction?"

They went through the catalogue together, and Brian suggested Meissen vases, a Louis XVI bureau and a George III side table. "Yes," Stephanie agreed. "Thank you. Would you bring me the auction records?"

She spread the thick books on the table, looking up the prices paid for those items and similar ones in previous auctions. Taking notes, she soon had a list of the highest figures she could bid on each piece and still give Sabrina a profit when she sold them. She felt buoyed up. For the first time since that incredible moment two days ago when Sabrina called to tell her about her broken wrist, she could think of this life as her own.

All day Monday and late into the night she had sat alone in Ambassadors, going through files and catalogues, learning about Sabrina's business and finding books on the shelves to fill gaps in her knowledge of antiques. I don't know half as much as Sabrina, she thought; but as she read, she found details coming back from studying for her estate sale business. It wasn't a complete failure, she thought wryly. It was preparation for becoming my sister.

In the stillness of Sabrina's office at midnight, she breathed the mingled odors of furniture polish, dusky velvets and brocades, and the carnations Brian had put on her desk that morning in a crystal vase. She touched the glass, her fingertips tingling. Four weeks. Ambassadors, Cadogan Square, Mrs. Thirkell. The shops and ancient streets of London. Theaters, restaurants, dinner parties; the tantalizing friendship of Alexandra and Gabrielle. Freedom.

The tingling stopped. She plunged into guilt, feeling as cold and hard as the glass vase. She was a wife and mother; what right did she have to freedom? Responsibilities pulled at her, and attachments. What had happened to them? Why wasn't she lonely, worried, anxious to get back where she belonged?

"Because I have no choice," she said aloud in the midnight quiet. "I can't go back. Everything would be destroyed if I went back now."

And you're *very* unhappy about it, jeered a small inner voice.

No, I'm not, she thought defiantly. I miss the children, but I know they'll be fine; they have Sabrina. I would have gone back, but now I've been given the time and I want to fill it with everything I've ever imagined. I'll never have another chance. Is it so terrible to want that? I'll go home soon and pick up the pieces and be everything I'm supposed to be. But not yet. Not yet.

On Tuesday, she gave Brian the list of purchases Sabrina had made in China. "The ones checked off are for display in the showroom; the others should be delivered as soon as they arrive to the customers listed on the back. You have addresses for all of them."

"Yes, my lady. I'll take care of it."

"And, Brian, I can't find the deposits for September."

"Oh, my lady, I'm sorry; the ledger is in my desk. Lady Vernon sent her check last week . . ." He waited. What for?

Some response. Surprise. Lady Vernon, perhaps, was not known for prompt payment.

"Did she indeed?"

"She did. And this time only six months late."

"An improvement."

"Considerably, my lady. It was eight months the last time."

"If we live long enough, Brian, we may see Lady Vernon pay on time."

He smiled. "I will have checks ready for you to sign day after tomorrow, my lady."

And then Rose Raddison had come in to ask about the Regency breakfront at Chilton.

It occurred to Stephanie, sitting beside Max in the auction tent, that she could try to find out what he knew about a quarrel with the Raddisons—he must have heard the story since returning from New York. But she gave up the idea. His secretive eyes and faintly smiling mouth made her feel young and ingenuous, and she knew he could outwit her and get more information than he gave.

The bidding was rapid, and a number of lots had been sold. Stephanie studied the bidders, especially Alexandra, who had made the trip with them at the last minute. She bid gracefully and boldly, without the gesticulations and twitchings of others, but it soon came to Stephanie that the real skill in bidding was to be unobtrusive; to keep others from knowing whom they were up against. Not knowing the wealth of other bidders, they had no idea how high they would have to go and might drop out. She remembered Garth and Nat Goldner talking about poker and smiled to herself. The Chilton auction was a high-class poker game.

When the Louis XVI commode was presented, the auctioneer described its provenance, or history of ownership, and opened the bidding at eighteen hundred pounds. He paused, his face alert, his eyes sweeping the tent. When his glance reached her, Stephanie lifted her chin. "Two thousand," he said.

She felt a surge of triumph. He had understood. "Any advance on two thousand?" he queried, and his dispassionate voice reeled off higher and higher sums at signals from other bidders. Then, in a delicate pause, as his glance again met hers, Stephanie touched the pin in her lapel. "Six thousand," he said, and added quickly as Stephanie touched it again, "I beg your pardon; seven thousand." There was a moment of confusion in the tent, and then two other bids. Stephanie heard the auctioneer's monotone announce "Eight thousand" and "Eight thousand five hundred," and she became angry. She would not be beaten on her first try.

Again the auctioneer scanned the crowd. When he came to her, Stephanie turned her head slightly to the right and then back. "Nine thousand," he said, but she was already turning to the left and back. "Ten thousand." He waited. There was a buzzing in Stephanie's ears; she was terrified.

"Sold," said the auctioneer, "to Lady Longworth for ten thousand pounds."

The crowd applauded. Stephanie stared at his bland face, too stunned to move. Ten thousand pounds. Over twenty thousand dollars. Twice what she earned in a whole year in her job at the university. Sabrina would never forgive her.

"Extraordinary, Lady Longworth," said Max, his flat gray eyes showing admiration. "Skillful, subtle and prudent. I hope never to find myself bidding against you."

She looked at him somberly. If he was making fun of her, everyone would soon know it.

"I should have guessed Sabrina Longworth was bidding," someone said nearby. "I saw her pull that trick before: making a bid, then raising herself before anyone else has a chance. Wonderful, how it knocks out other bidders."

How did I know? Stephanie wondered. She trembled. How did I know?

Max stood. "Will you have lunch with me?"

Instinctively she turned toward Alexandra and Nicholas, who were standing as the crowd began an exodus from the tent. "We can eat together," Nicholas said. "Amelia packed enough for all of Wiltshire."

He brought a picnic hamper from his car and spread the food on one of the dozens of tables set on the lawn with white paper tablecloths and green paper napkins. At a bar run by the owner of the town pub, Max bought ale for the four of them. They sat on folding chairs eating Amelia Blackford's smoked turkey, chutney, bread and cheese.

"Amelia wanted to come," Nicholas said between bites, "but she's at the shop. It's amazing, you know, the way she's taken hold there. Like a professional. Never knew she had it in her." He stood and began to bounce lightly on his feet. "Sabrina, my dear, I've been thinking. What would you say to a partnership? I don't have enough to do. Once Amelia was unleashed— oh, dear, an unfortunate way of putting it, but, in fact, she went considerably further than I anticipated in taking command. The truth is, I have very little to do. But I'm too old, or perhaps too comfortable, to start a new business, and I thought we might collaborate. You could handle interior design; I would manage the business end of Blackford's and Ambassadors."

No one will take Ambassadors from me, Stephanie thought, and aloud she said flatly, "No."

Nicholas' face crumpled, like a child who has been slapped when he expected praise. Alexandra looked surprised and Stephanie's heart sank. Sabrina wouldn't have been so clumsy; she would have handled the offer with grace and friendship.

Max put his hand under her elbow. "Some clarification is needed, Nicholas," he said smoothly. "Sabrina has—"

"Been very rude," Stephanie said, moving away. She didn't need Max Stuyvesant to cover for her. "Nicholas, I beg your pardon. My thoughts were elsewhere and I answered too quickly and impolitely. May I think about this for a few days? We can talk about it again later, if you still have kindly thoughts about me—"

"Kindly—! My dear Sabrina, I adore you! Take as long as you wish; I make the offer to no one else. Are we ready to go back in? I think the bidding is about to resume."

"I'm not ready to sit again," said Alexandra. "Sabrina, shall we let the gentlemen find us seats while we explore the grounds?"

Bless you, Stephanie thought, and they walked off across the smooth lawn, wending their way through groups of picnickers packing up lunch hampers and returning their dogs to their automobiles, where they would stay for the rest of the afternoon, watched over by tuxedoed car attendants. Everyone was dressed in tweeds that blended with the pale green grass and the aged red brick of the house beneath dark oaks, and Stephanie felt she was walking through a muted painting from some distant time. It seemed gentle and beautiful and perfect: a place without anxiety or unhappiness. How strange that Sabrina had wanted to get away from it.

"You all right, honey?" Alexandra asked.

"A little jumpy, for some reason."

"Delayed reaction from your trip. Maybe you need another one, to recover."

Stephanie laughed. "Not for awhile."

"Where's the Brazilian lover?"

"In Brazil, as far as I know."

"And Max?"

"What about him?"

"I wondered what you thought about his new look."

Max. The force of his presence struck her even when he was far off. "Have you known him long?" she asked absently.

"Honey, come back to earth; you haven't forgotten that famous cruise! If for no other reason than that's where you and I met."

"You know, I did forget for a minute. Now why would I do that?"

"Well, I hope not for me. I don't mind remembering it. Max has a lot of enemies, I guess, and maybe he deserves them—I don't know and I don't want to know. He and I had fun, we were good to each other, and we're still friends. Anyway, it was a long time ago and we've all changed, so I don't mind remembering."

They came to the small brick studio where the late owner had worked, and then to a row of garages. "Lady Longworth!" said a delighted voice, and Stephanie turned to see an impeccably dressed man with silver hair and soft pouches beneath his eyes. He bowed and kissed her hand. "I was hoping to see you here. You were in China, I understand."

Stephanie waited for a clue so she could introduce him to Alexandra.

"Were you buying for your fine gallery?"

He had glanced twice at Alexandra. Stephanie was embarrassed and angry; he was not helping at all. She looked at him coldly. "In part."

"Successfully, I hope," he said. "But may I hope, too, that you did not find all the porcelains you need? I expect to have some items in a few days that I think will impress you. May I bring them in?"

A salesman. Or a dealer. "Certainly," she said, relaxed now because she would have no reason to introduce a salesman to Alexandra. "I'll be glad to look at them." She nodded a dismissal and turned with Alexandra to walk on as he made another, smaller bow.

"Do all salesmen dress like French counts?" Alexandra asked.

"Only in England. In France they dress like English lords."

"And in Germany?"

"Like Italian dukes."

Alexandra laughed. "You mean they're all fakes."

"Probably," Stephanie said lightly. She felt daring; everything she did today was turning out well. "Do you really think Max has changed?" she asked casually.

"Mellowed. Like a pear: sweeter, smoother, maybe softer, but probably just as tough at the core, where it counts. If I didn't know him so well I'd think he was just what I'm looking for."

"Which is?"

"Oh, you know. Somebody who'll build me a castle, but let me be myself inside it. That doesn't mean fucking around; I don't have any trouble being faithful to one man; in fact, I like it. Men aren't all that different, you know; when you've fucked one, you've fucked them all, with minor and unremarkable differences. I see by your eyebrows you don't agree."

I have slept with one man in my entire life. "It might be debatable."

"I suppose. If you want to spend the time. Anyway, what I want is something to do besides fuck and be beautiful. I just don't know what that might be. So I'm waiting for somebody to show me a direction without ordering me to take it. Possible, do you think? Probably not. Perfection isn't around every corner." They had reached the tent. "I see our gallant men beckoning to us. What's Max bidding on?"

"The fruitwood statues."

"Probably for his new house. Watch his face when he bids; he always looks like he'd murder his opponents if he could."

As the crowd settled down with murmurs and the rustling of catalogues, the statues were offered. Stephanie unobtrusively watched Max. With each succeeding bid, his eyes grew darker and his high cheekbones sharpened like ridges in his bleak face. He made it a contest of wills, and two or three other bidders fought him until he wrestled them out by paying more than he or anyone else expected. If he had let her bid for him, Stephanie thought, she might have saved him thousands of pounds.

"So you think you could have done better," he said when the statues were his.

Caught by surprise, she laughed. "Was I so obvious?"

"You are never obvious, my dear Sabrina. But we both know you could have done better. Next time I will let you bid for me."

He watched with amusement and approval as she bought the George III side table for less than she thought she would have to pay. And then the Regency breakfront was offered, and Stephanie realized that was the piece she wanted the most. The Raddisons had done some harm to Sabrina—otherwise, why would she have quarreled with them?—and Stephanie did not want to go back in defeat.

The auctioneer began the bidding at two thousand pounds. At twenty-five hundred, Stephanie caught his attention. She repeated her signals of the morning, varying them slightly, more subtle because she was more confident. But she was also more combative and tried to hold herself back from bidding too high when she did not have to.

"Sold," said the auctioneer at last. "To Lady Longworth, for three thousand one hundred pounds."

Applause surrounded her as it had in the morning, and Max nodded, as if in confirmation. "Masterful," he murmured.

I beat them, Stephanie thought with triumph. If they thought they could give Sabrina trouble by limiting the price, I beat them. Wait 'til I tell . . . She looked around, bursting with pride, but in that entire throng there was not one person in whom she could confide. I'll call Sabrina tonight; wait until she hears what I did.

But she couldn't do that, either. How could she tell Sabrina, trapped in Evanston to protect Stephanie, about the excitement she was missing? She felt the glow of her triumph fade. She would have to savor it alone.

"My compliments once more, Sabrina," Max said. "Perhaps you will give me lessons some day."

She smiled. Max would enjoy the story of the deception; she wished she could tell him.

Why did she think that? Because there was an air of danger about him; as if he enjoyed taking risks himself and appreciated risk-taking in others. I probably wouldn't have liked that in a man, she thought, any other time but now. When I'm taking risks myself. And discovering how successful I can be.

"I have a new house," Max was saying. "On Eaton Square. Eighteenth century, once magnificent, but botched by owners who thought it needed improving." On the back of his catalog, he sketched the rooms with bold lines, describing each one. "In the last three months half a dozen decorators have pranced through the house. One gouged a piece from an over-mantle; another damaged a chandelier; a third suggested re-placing the oak banisters with wrought iron. The others were equally asinine. Will you rescue the house and me from these idiots?"

Stephanie looked at the sketches. A house to decorate. Since the birthday party at Alexandra's, she had been envying Sabrina's luck, longing for her own chance to do the same. Now here it was.

"I have the furniture," he went on. "Too much furniture. Too much art. Too many rugs, drapes, lamps. Everything from my old London house and my New York town house. I have a crew of workers. I need someone to tell them what to do; I need someone to tell me which furniture to keep and how to arrange it, which to give away, which to sell. I need you."

"No." She shook her head. "I'm sorry, but I can't do it."

"You can. I pay very well."

"Money has nothing to do with it." She clasped her hands tightly in her lap. At first she thought she was turning it down to keep her distance from Max, but that wasn't why. The real reason was that she was afraid of failing.

For years she had told herself she would be just as successful as Sabrina if she had her kind of life, with the same chances. Now Max offered her a chance, and she felt the fear rising in her throat. She shook her head and pushed the chance away. Let me keep my illusions, she thought.

"This is absurd," said Max. "I've seen Alexandra's house and Olivia Chasson's London house. You are the only one I want."

"But I am the seventh one you ask."

"Ah, you are insulted. That I can understand. The others were sent by incompetent friends. Forget them; they do not exist."

She laughed. "That's not the reason."

"Then what the devil is the reason?"

"I don't have time," she said a little wildly. And told the truth. "All I have is about four weeks."

"And then? You melt? You dissolve? You disintegrate?" She was laughing again. "If you have other commitments, you will do as much as possible in the time you have. I want you to do it. You will have a free hand and no limit on what you spend."

Stephanie finally could not resist. Studying his sketches, she pictured the rooms he had described, ideas already filling the spaces between his bold lines. "All right," she said, as the auction ended and they began to move out of the tent.

And I won't fail, she vowed silently. Any more than I failed today. Why should I? I can do as well as Sabrina. All I need is a chance.

As for Max, she would see only as much of him as she had to in order to remodel his house. And whenever she felt like it she could withdraw from the project, turn it over to someone else and never see him again.

"When can you start?" he asked as they said goodbye.

"I already have," she said.

The next morning Stephanie found a pile of checks on the cherry table, waiting for her signature. They were for expenditures Sabrina had approved before she went to China, and Stephanie memorized each of them so she could handle expenses in the coming month. She felt reckless, spending so much money. Not her money, but still—her signature on thousands of pounds' worth of checks in one morning.

She was on the last check when the telephone rang. In a moment Brian was in the doorway. "Señor Molena, my lady."

Stephanie's pen stopped moving. Sabrina had said Antonio would be away until the first week in October—at least another week. She grimaced; she would have to find a way to put him off until Sabrina was back.

"If my lady would like me to make an excuse—" Brian began.

"No," she said, reaching for the telephone. "But thank you, Brian."

"My Sabrina," Antonio said, his voice dark and intimate. "I finished my work in São Paulo and hurried back to see you. You will forgive my impatience? And this evening we will have dinner."

"No—"

"You have plans for this evening?"

She hesitated. This was absurd. She was always saying *no* as if she would be leaving in a few days. But that was no longer true. This was her home now, and she had to deal with it; she had nowhere else to go. "Dinner will be fine," she said.

"Eight o'clock, my Sabrina. It has been too long."

He picked her up in his car and they drove through twisting streets to Fulham Road. While Antonio spoke amusingly of someone he met on the flight from Brazil, Stephanie watched the neighborhood change. Antonio looked at her puzzled face as they turned right along Brompton Cemetery. "A surprise," he said, smiling, and parked the car. Following him down a flight of stairs, Stephanie looked at his dark face and hawklike nose. From Sabrina's descriptions she had expected a difficult, demanding man and an elegant dinner. What she seemed to have instead was a pleasant companion and a basement restaurant on a dingy cemetery road.

But inside, La Croisette was all she had imagined, and Antonio a charming host. His eyes gleamed when he saw that she wore the sapphire necklace, and his voice was possessive when he introduced her to Monsieur Martin, who had dared to open his restaurant on unfashionable Ifield Road and, within a few months, had made it one of the most fashionable and expensive in London. Then, ignoring Stephanie, they launched into a serious discussion of the best fish for their dinner.

Stephanie listened dreamily; neither of them seemed interested in what she wanted, and she did not care. She was content to settle back in the spell of the room: soft lights and fine fabrics, ubiquitous waiters holding her chair and helping her slip off the loose satin jacket she wore over a satin sheath, the discreet hum of wealthy men and women who believed that the world existed to give them pleasure. My world, she thought, and when the maître d' poured her wine she smiled, not because he did it but because he did it well.

Antonio talked of São Paulo and Rio de Janeiro, of costume balls and dinner parties, of the hospitals and schools being planned for the villages he was building. He was trying to impress her, and succeeding. He would have impressed Sabrina, Stephanie thought. However he had behaved in the past, if he had been like this she might have married him.

"I can't marry him," Sabrina had said in their long telephone call on Monday. "Everything would be easier if I could, but it wouldn't work; I can't be what he wants. But I'll tell him myself when I get back. Just tell him you need more time; I've kept him waiting so long—"

"Could you write to him?" Stephanie had asked. "I'm not clever enough to keep him waiting patiently for four more weeks."

"I might . . . yes, why not? I'll send the letter to you so you can mail it from there. I'll do it today; you should have it the first of next week. If he calls before then, just say you need a few more days. I think he'll accept that and not push you."

It was too soon for her to have Sabrina's letter, but Antonio seemed content to make casual conversation and look at her; he had not even pushed her to talk. When he did ask about her trip, Stephanie talked lightly and gracefully about Mr. Su, the terra-cotta warriors buried in the emperor's tomb at Sian, the houseboats on the River Li and the orchids in the zoo at Canton. Antonio asked about farm workers, and she told him about the little she had seen, not enough to satisfy his curiosity.

"Go yourself," she suggested. "You'd have a wonderful time."

"*We* will go," he said. "It will be wonderful if we go together."

He signaled to the waiter to bring both of them a cognac, and then he related a long Guarani legend about a search for rare jewels that seemed to have something to do with the search for love. But Stephanie listened only to the deep flow of his voice, relaxed in his easy companionship.

In the close darkness of the car she sighed and rested her head against the seat. "And your shop?" he asked. "Everything goes well?"

"Yes," she murmured. "Everything goes very well."

"With your newspaper friends, too?"

"What?"

"They have not published their story. I left word with friends to send it to me in Brazil, but it was not published. Have they changed their mind?"

"No." Jolted out of her dreaminess, Stephanie grew cautious, not knowing whether he knew more or less than she did. "It's been postponed for two months."

"Ah. Excellent. Then while Olivia still thinks her Meissen stork is genuine, there is time for me to help you."

"No," she said quickly, storing away the new information to think about later. Then, because he was being kind and she did not want to hurt him, she added, "Not for a few weeks."

"When you are ready, my Sabrina. But do not wait too long. I am concerned only for your welfare."

"Thank you," she said warmly, wondering how Sabrina could dismiss him so casually.

She turned her head to look at the shops and buildings they were passing. None of them were familiar. He was taking her home by a different route, but she could not ask him about it; Sabrina Longworth, at home in London, would know where they were.

She was framing a way to tell him, as soon as they reached Cadogan Square, not to call until he heard from her, when he pulled into a circular driveway and stopped the car in front of a sleek modern building. A uniformed doorman greeted him.

"You can put the car away," Antonio said.

"Yes, sir," said the doorman, walking around the car to open Stephanie's door.

She did not move. His apartment. His bed. Why hadn't she realized that was where he was going? Because she hadn't thought of going to bed with him. Because they weren't lovers. Sabrina and Antonio were lovers. Stephanie Andersen had never been to bed with any man but her husband.

"Sabrina," Antonio said, an edge of impatience in his voice.

"I thought you were taking me home," she said, feeling foolish as the doorman waited, his hand outstretched to help her.

Striding to her side of the car, Antonio reached past the doorman to grasp her arm and pull her out. "You saw where I was driving and you did not stop me. What is this game you are playing?"

"Not a game," she gasped, infuriated at the grip of his hand, at being pulled from the car, at her own stupidity. "I did not think I had to monitor your driving," she said icily. "That you would dare assume I would come here, without asking me—"

She stopped, conscious of the open interest on the doorman's face. Beyond him, across the street, was a small park. "Shall we walk for a few minutes?" Without waiting for an answer, she turned to the doorman. "Please don't put the car away."

"*Caramba!*" Antonio muttered, and moved off, still gripping her arm. "Leave the car here," he flung over his shoulder to the doorman.

In the park, Stephanie pulled her arm away. "Never have you done such a thing," Antonio fumed. "I do not expect such behavior from you. The woman who is to be my wife does not behave in this fashion. We had an arrangement—"

"Our only arrangement was that we would not see each other for a month. You returned before that time and I agreed to see you. I agreed to nothing else."

"You wore my jewels, you smiled, you were warm, soft, delicious. You were pleased with me and with our evening, and you behaved in ways that would please me. You will kindly remember that you said tonight I could soon get you out of this mess you have made for yourself in your little shop—"

"Little shop!" she blazed. She stopped walking. "The mess I have made? You are unforgivably insulting."

Astonished, Stephanie listened to herself. She ought to be careful; what if Sabrina changed her mind and didn't write the letter—decided to think about Antonio some more—perhaps even decided to marry him while Stephanie was driving him away? But anger overrode her caution. Stephanie and Sabrina were angry and insulted. Sabrina would not marry him, and Stephanie would tell him why.

"You treat me like a child. I will not tolerate that. I do what I want to do. No one forces me into anything."

"My Sabrina, I do not force you, I want only to care for you—"

"In your way, as you decide."

"What else? You foolish girl, are you doing so well by yourself? You would not be in trouble in your little—in this shop of yours if you had allowed me to manage your affairs. You are in danger of losing everything. I offer you security, position, wealth. And you fling at me some foolish idea of independence."

"Antonio, please take me home."

"What does that mean?"

"That my foolish idea of independence is very important to me and I will not give it up."

"You will not marry me?"

"No."

"You will. I would not have waited all these months if I was not sure of that."

"Will you take me home or must I take a taxi?"

"I will call you tomorrow."

"I will not be home."

"You will be home. By then you will be calm and reasonable."

Thank goodness for Mrs. Thirkell, she thought as they drove to Cadogan Square; someone to answer the telephone. This weekend I'll be away, and by next week Sabrina's letter will end it for good.

But, feeling guilty about what she had done, she called Sabrina that night. The connection was bad and they did not talk long; Sabrina seemed remote and uninterested. "Don't worry about Antonio," she said. Still, the next day, when Stephanie left for Olivia Chasson's weekend house party, she felt adrift, without guidelines or anyone to advise her.

Olivia, whom she was meeting for the first time, was a good antidote, shrewd and sharp-tongued. "No Antonio?" she asked when Stephanie arrived alone.

"Not at the moment."

Olivia nodded sagely. "I thought that would end. An overbearing man. I have observed that self-made men, not content with making themselves, are grandly determined to make everyone else as well to their own specifications. Men who are born to wealth seldom have that problem."

"Why is that?" Stephanie asked, laughing.

"Because growing up with wealth leaves them so bored they're satisfied only with large projects, such as saving the world. Look at the Rockefellers, for example. Oh, hell, I must greet the Raddisons; why do I invite them when I detest Rose?"

"Perhaps a thorny rose makes your other flowers seem sweeter."

Olivia threw back her head and laughed. The guests in the large salon turned and smiled with her. "You're a gem, Sabrina. How dull life would be without you. I would like you on my right at dinner."

"Of course," Stephanie said carelessly, and then saw, in Olivia's face, how important that was. "I'd be honored," she added quickly.

She watched Olivia cross the room and smiled as Rose Raddison waved gleefully in her direction. A waiter gave her a glass of champagne. Lights from chandeliers danced in the sparkling wine, scattering like jewels as Stephanie moved about, accepted and admired by everyone. Not one of the polished guests in that room challenged her right to be part of their world, where no one thought about the mortgage or grocery bills or whether the garbage had been taken out for the night. An enchanted place, she thought, where I belong.

The Chasson country house in Kent had large, square rooms and tall windows overlooking gardens, a croquet lawn and a small lake. The salon where Lord and Lady Chasson entertained before dinner was known for its painted ceiling and heavy chandeliers. The year before, Sabrina had redecorated it, upholstering the chairs in creamy suede and the couches in pale green velvet. She stained the parquet floor a rich, dark oak that reflected the chandeliers, so guests seemed to float between shimmering pools of light. A long, gleaming Chippendale commode held a collection of nineteenth-century porcelain dancers, and on a small console table at the far end of the room, reflected in its matching mirror, stood a tall, pure white Meissen stork.

Looking thoughtfully at the stork, Stephanie drifted down the room toward it, smiling serenely at the strangers who greeted her. She felt at ease. A letter had come from Sabrina and everything was fine at home; Dolores had even sent Juanita to help in the house. No problems, Sabrina wrote, adding, "I'm so bruised and stiff there's no question of doing anything in bed but sleeping."

Surrounded by brilliant lights and soft murmurs, Stephanie imagined Sabrina in Evanston, guarding her marriage so she could return to it without any harm being done. She looked down at Sabrina's white wool challis dress with its pattern of silver threads in the skirt and pictured her closet in Evanston. Sabrina in blue jeans cooking dinner. I owe her everything, she thought.

She picked up the stork and ran her fingers over the smooth glaze, the delicate lines of wings, feathers, talons, the small fish in its beak. Olivia thought the Meissen stork was genuine, Antonio had said. At Alexandra's party, Michel had talked about a forgery. About Lady Olivia. About "getting the stork back." Sabrina had told her not to buy from someone named Rory Carr because it seemed he dealt in forgeries.

Stephanie felt excitement rising within her. Sabrina had bought porcelains from Rory Carr, and at least one of them was a forged Meissen stork. Sold to Olivia Chasson. The stork she was holding was a Meissen; probably made by Kandler. She turned it over to see the mark on its underside. Yes. And it was superb; so perfect the wings seemed to flutter as she touched them. No wonder Sabrina had been fooled.

There is time to get back the Meissen stork, Antonio had said. She could do that for Sabrina; she held it in her hand. But how was she to get it back? She couldn't tell Olivia it was a forgery—only Sabrina could divulge that. She couldn't say it needed repair, because obviously it didn't. She couldn't sneak it out, because it was too big, and, anyway, the house was full of people. But somehow, before the end of the weekend—

"Sabrina, I'm so glad you're here!" Stephanie jumped. Rose Raddison had glided up behind her, braying directly in her ear. She was as thin as her nasal voice, with a narrow slice of a nose and a sharp, quivering chin. Her eyes were her best feature, and, to emphasize them, she made them up heavily. Stephanie thought she looked like an emaciated panda. "When you told me about the breakfront the other day, I was amazed, I confess it, and didn't properly thank you. Now I'm sure that silly rumor that you didn't like us isn't true."

"A strange rumor for someone to start," Stephanie said, thinking—Go on, go on, tell me why.

"Well, some people like to make trouble."

"But not little Rose," said a pleasant, colorless man appearing beside them. "My sweet wife dispenses only love and kindness. Did I say that correctly, my love?"

"Peter finds himself amusing," hissed Rose.

"And so she wonders, Sabrina," he went on, "why you avoid her. Could it be that after four years you still remember overhearing her slandering your good name at Andrea Vernon's ball?"

"Overhearing," Stephanie repeated neutrally.

"Peter is totally irresponsible," cried Rose. "Dear Sabrina, we would never accuse you of eavesdropping. Your friend Alexandra did mention recently that you happened to be nearby that night—*so long ago*—when we were saying how sad it was that you and Denton—"

"When you were saying," Peter interrupted, "that Sabrina

took Denton for everything he had. But, of course, Sabrina wouldn't remember something like that, would she, dear Rose?"

Rose stretched her neck. "Sabrina has manners, Peter. Your crudeness is quite foreign to her. If she believed that lie she would not have done so fabulously for me at the auction. However did you do it?"

Stephanie's eyebrows went up. Sabrina had never told her that story; how terrible it must have been. But now, talking about the auction, why was Rose Raddison's voice trembling with anger? "However did I do what?" she asked coolly.

"Get it, of course, at that incredible price. You are a wonder!"

Stephanie understood. Rose had set her up to fail, just as she had thought. Feeling properly malicious for Sabrina's sake, she said, "I wanted to save you the pain of being unhappy if I failed."

Laughter burst from Peter Raddison. "A direct hit, dear Rose."

Ignoring him, Rose met Stephanie's calm smile. "You've always been arrogant, for an outsider—"

And, at that moment, Stephanie knew what she was going to do with the stork, still resting cool and fragile in her hand.

"I beg your pardon?" she said softly. "I couldn't make out—"

Rose thrust her face forward. "I said you're an outsider—" Stephanie took a step backward and Rose followed —"and if you think you fool anyone—"

"Oh!" Stephanie cried. Stepping back, she had caught her heel in the fringe of the Persian rug. Off balance, falling, she reached out wildly to catch herself and the Meissen stork flew from her hand, falling to the parquet floor with a shattering crash.

"Oh, my God," breathed Rose. Stephanie, rubbing her ankle, looked calmly at the shards of white porcelain at her feet. Guests crowded about them. Peter Raddison backed away from his wife. Two servants materialized with brooms and dustpans. Olivia came up and Stephanie turned to her.

"I'm terribly sorry, I don't know what made me so clumsy—"

"You were on the defensive, my dear," said Olivia. "Any closer and Rose would have devoured you."

"We were having a conversation," Rose said through tight lips. "But if I was in any way responsible for Lady Longworth's becoming overexcited, you must send me a bill for the—it was a bird of some kind, wasn't it?"

"Olivia," Stephanie said quietly, "I will replace the stork. I may know of another Meissen quite similar—"

"You will do no such thing, my dear. We carry enough insurance to replace the British Isles if someone should lose them. Find me another, by all means, and we'll take care of the cost. Is your ankle badly hurt? Shall I call a doctor?"

"No, thank you, it's only twisted."

"Well, come and sit down."

"Olivia," said Peter Raddison in a carrying voice, "Rose is feeling ill. Will you forgive us if I return her to London? You know she gets such dreadful headaches. If she can manage at home, I may return alone, if that would not upset the symmetry of your party."

"As you please," Olivia said indifferently. "I'll see you out. Sabrina, sit down and rest."

Stephanie sat peacefully on a couch while voices swirled about her, dissecting the Raddisons, talking about the Chasson art collection in the upstairs gallery, a new play in London, a charity ball at Barchester Towers in December. Olivia disappeared through the double doors with Peter and Rose. The servants finished sweeping up the last of the Meissen stork.

I have become an expert at deception, Stephanie thought.

There was, she soon discovered, no routine in Sabrina's life. Ambassadors was a focal point for business and much of her social life, but Brian took care of the everyday running of the shop, leaving Lady Longworth free to attend auctions, visit homes she was decorating, go on week-long cruises, or work in the shop. After the fixed schedules of her life in Evanston, Stephanie felt, for awhile, at loose ends, always looking at her watch to be home on time, to begin dinner on time, to get to the grocery before it closed. Now when she looked at her watch, it was to plan the rest of her day or think about the evening. There was only one deadline, and it was on her calendar: Nat Goldner's X-ray of Sabrina's wrist in three weeks.

On Monday morning, the first day of October, she woke planning her meeting with the contractor at Max's house to check on his progress. That afternoon she and Max were going to the warehouse to look at his furniture. If they could keep to her work schedule, she would begin furnishing the top floors in two weeks.

Successive owners had long since demolished the original interior of the house, altering fixtures and walls, boarding up some windows, removing a chimney. During the past few years, when it had been used as a private school, students had covered the walls and ceilings of the fourth floor bedrooms with colorfully obscene limericks.

"Mr. Stuyvesant says they add a touch of humanity," said the contractor. "And not to paint them over."

Stephanie smiled. "I'll make a note of it."

They went through the house, checking the work against Stephanie's drawings. Each day she saw her ideas closer to completion, restoring the balance of walls and windows, using the angles of sun and shadow to bring the house to life. She felt she had never been happier.

It was in her face. "Pure happiness," Max observed that afternoon as they walked through the cavernous warehouse. "Always, with a new project? Or is this one special?"

"Always."

"Now I am disappointed."

"But not surprised," she laughed. She was glad to see him. Among the gossiping people of Sabrina's world, he was confident and casual, intriguing, private. He fended off personal questions, and his flat gray eyes were empty of emotion. There could be nothing personal between them, Stephanie thought. She was safe for the brief time she was here.

They were walking down an aisle lined with wooden lifts stacked to the ceiling, each six feet high, six feet deep, six feet wide, packed with furnishings. A lift truck lowered twenty-two of them, one at a time, to the concrete floor, and workers pried them open with crowbars. As they brought out the furnishings and Max checked them against his lists of contents, Stephanie watched, trying not to gawk.

It was not easy; she had never seen anything like it. Ranging through all the great periods of art and furnishings, from Russian samovars to William Morris chairs to Art Deco lamps, even including a disassembled fifteen-foot-high Jacobean canopied bed, Max's collection turned the dingy aisles into a dazzling palace.

"Did you rob a museum?" she asked lightly to hide her awe.

A light flickered in his eyes as he glanced up from his lists. "A dozen. Do you see anything you can use?"

That was carrying nonchalance too far. "Don't be absurd, Max. It's magnificent and you know it; much more than we'll be able to use."

"Good. And now I'm sorry, Sabrina, but I must go; I couldn't put off another appointment for this afternoon. I'll leave you to make your choices, and my chauffeur will return for you in half an hour; is that all right? He'll wait as long as necessary to take you home."

She turned away to hide her disappointment and took from a packing crate a porcelain canary perched on a spray of flowers. "Copenhagen," she murmured, remembering the day her mother had brought one home in triumph from a flea market in Paris. "Yes, of course," she said. "But I'll be here for hours. Your chauffeur shouldn't have to wait—"

"He is paid to wait. Will you have dinner with me Thursday night?"

"Yes."

He kissed her fingertips. "Until then."

The vast collection fired Stephanie's imagination, adding to her excitement. The house filled her thoughts, and she spent more and more time there, working closely with the contractor, whom Max was paying an exorbitant fee to meet her schedule. I have to see it finished, she thought; I can't leave without finishing it.

Max paved the way, too, for delivery of flooring, cabinetry, wallpaper, light fixtures.

"Is there anyone you don't know?" Stephanie asked when, with a telephone call, he assured delivery of handcrafted Swedish rugs for the bedrooms.

"I don't know you. Yet."

On Friday, Stephanie stopped at Ambassadors to go through the mail and reflect for a few moments on her dinner the night before with Max: friendly, casual, bantering, almost impersonal. Not once had they relaxed their guard in hours of conversation. I've taken up fencing again, she thought wryly. The chimes over the front door broke her thoughts, and she looked up to see the elegantly dressed elderly man who had greeted her at the Chilton auction. But he was not as smooth as he had been; Stephanie was puzzled to see that he was watching her closely, studying her. She held out her hand.

"My lady." He bowed. "I bring you something very special." Dramatically, he opened a parcel and unwrapped a porcelain statue of two figures: a regal Venus watching a small, mischievous Cupid, wings folded back, face bent over his arrows. The statue was made of biscuit porcelain in the pale rose pink called *rose pompadour;* with the thrill of discovery Stephanie recognized it as Sèvres, from the late 1700s, of enormous value.

He was watching her, and she kept her face smooth, hands clasped before her. More poker, she thought; just like the auction. "Very fine," she said calmly.

"My lady," he murmured reproachfully. "It is quite extraordinary. Sold privately in Germany last week; I was told in advance it would be offered. As soon as I saw it I thought of you."

Don't buy it. Stephanie tilted her head. Where had the thought come from? She looked past the statue through the front window, at the overcast sky and busy street, and let the silence stretch out.

The salesman adjusted his foulard, a small movement that betrayed nervousness. "We haven't discussed price, my lady, but of course you know the value." She slid her gaze slowly from the window to his face. He cleared his throat. "Perhaps you wish to think about it. I can leave it here; we trust each other . . ." She continued to look at him and saw him swallow, and swallow again. "I understand," he said, glancing around the shop, "that you had a sad accident at Lady Chasson's. A strange coincidence, breaking a piece you sold her yourself."

And suddenly Stephanie knew who he was. Rory Carr. He had come to find out about the stork—whether it had really been an accident.

"Mr. Carr," she said, testing it.

"My lady?"

Right on the button, she thought triumphantly. And you're the one who sold Sabrina that stork.

"I have no need for porcelains now." She let a note of genuine regret slip into her voice. "I must refuse this one, as fine as it is."

"But my lady, this is unexpected. We have dealt with each other for such a long and pleasant time—"

"Yes," she said firmly, feeling more confident as cracks appeared in his suave speech. "But not today. I bought many porcelains in China, and until I go through my inventory I will buy nothing more."

"My lady!"

"Nothing, Mr. Carr. And now, if you will excuse me—"

She saw a quick gleam of fear in his eyes. "My lady, perhaps I can change your mind."

"You can tell me nothing I don't already know," Stephanie said. That was probably rash, but she was swept along by a sense of adventure. By herself, she had solved the problem of the stork; now she was getting back at Rory Carr for cheating Sabrina. It served him right if he was afraid. Sabrina would have been afraid when she discovered the forgery. If only Sabrina had told her about it when it happened; she would have known enough not to encourage him at the auction.

But it didn't matter. It was over. He was leaving, and that would be the last of him.

"I will hold the Venus, my lady, and call in a few days."

"If I want to buy from you, Mr. Carr, I will call you."

When he was gone she went into her office, closed the door and called Sabrina. There was no answer. Ten o'clock on Friday morning in Evanston. She could be anywhere. Grocery store. Hardware store. Dry cleaner. Or at work. Was she going to the office this week? Stephanie couldn't remember. She closed her eyes, thinking back to their last phone call. What had they talked about? She couldn't remember. She was losing touch with her other life, her real life, her home.

I can't do that, she thought; I can't lose touch. It's the only real thing I've got. Behind her closed eyes she pictured the house, the porch, the living room. There's the new lamp, she thought; Penny's charcoal pencil, the tear on the couch that I meant to fix before I left for China. And in the kitchen, the new rack for mugs and—what's that on the counter? Oh, the Cuisinart I got for my birthday; Sabrina told me about it. And upstairs in the bedroom, the quilt on the bed and the striped wallpaper . . . No, no, the striped wallpaper is here, on Cadogan Square, with the blue carpet and . . . and what? In her mind the two bedrooms wavered and merged. Which was which? Which was real?

The trouble was, she was too tired to think. Trying to do everything, she was not getting enough sleep. Every night she went out to the dinner parties, theater parties and concerts that made up Sabrina's social life. She was collecting them, as if in a scrapbook—the elegance and color, the varied foods and entertainment that filled the hours. But she soon found it was as exhausting as it was exhilarating to keep up with the rapid-fire gossip, knowing glances and shared recollections of different groups of people whom she had trouble keeping separate. By the time she got home she was so keyed up that she slept restlessly, and the next day she had trouble distinguishing her dreams from her London life and both of them from her real life.

If it was real. "Which is my home?" she asked out loud.

"My lady?" Brian opened the door of his cubicle and stood, waiting.

Stephanie pushed back her thoughts. "Brian," she said, "I just told Rory Carr we would not be buying from him for awhile. Will you note that, please? There is some question about his honesty."

"In what respect, my lady?"

"He may deal in forgeries. Until we are sure, we will avoid him."

Brian restrained his curiosity, and Stephanie gathered her drawings and left for Max's house.

That night, Gabrielle telephoned. She and Brooks were having trouble, and fragments of quarrels and suspicions trailed through her talk. Each night, as Stephanie unlocked her door, the telephone was ringing, and she answered it to hear Gabrielle pour out new fears.

"He's changed," Gabrielle said a week after her first call. "He's cold and . . . I think . . . suspicious. He watches me; if I write a letter he looks over my shoulder. If I get a telephone call he has to know who it is. And now he's started going to the office at night. He's there now; I know because I called him—"

"Have you asked him what's wrong?" Stephanie asked.

"He won't tell me—he hardly talks to me at all. He doesn't come back 'til late, and I don't wait up for him. I'm afraid to, because he doesn't talk to me when he gets in. He makes me feel guilty just by looking at me, and I'd rather be asleep than face that. Then in the morning when I wake up he's leaving again."

Yes, Stephanie thought, I know how it feels to be with someone who barely knows you're there.

"I don't know what's happening," Gabrielle said, sounding like a bewildered child: Penny, tearful and clinging when she was frightened.

"Would you like me to come over and stay with you tonight?" Stephanie asked. It was midnight, and she really wanted to stay home; she had been out to dinner with Max for the third time in a week and was tired and exhilarated at the same time. She wanted to think. But the panic in Gabrielle's voice brought a rush of anxiety and protectiveness she had not felt in a long while.

"No, don't. Sabrina, you're wonderful, and I love you, I don't know what I'd do without you. But if Brooks comes home early, I don't want him to know I've told you about us. I'll call you tomorrow."

But the next day, instead of calling, she arrived on Stephanie's doorstep. "He told me I had to leave. He said I was a spy; that I sold the secrets of Westermarck's new line to another company, I don't even remember which one—" She looked up helplessly, and then, as Stephanie put her arms around her, she began to sob.

They sat on the sofa. Stephanie rocked Gabrielle in her arms, feeling her breast become wet with tears. She put her cheek against Gabrielle's clustering curls. "Hush, my dear Penny," she said, and caught her breath. But Gabrielle had not heard, and Stephanie said, "It will be all right, Gaby; we'll find out what happened, it will be all right," while she ached for Penny and tears came to her eyes.

She blinked them away. "Gaby, have you talked to *anybody* about Westermarck cosmetics?"

"No. I swear it. I don't know anything about them. I never even think about them except when I'm putting on makeup. Why should I? Anyway, I can't tell the difference between any of them. Westermarck, Revlon, Estee Lauder—they're all the same. Oh, God, don't tell Brooks I said that!"

Stephanie hid a smile. "Did you bring any clothes with you?" Gabrielle shook her head. "Well, we'll have to get your things."

"I can't. I can't go there until he calls—he will call, won't he?"

"If he doesn't, I will." Stephanie took Gabrielle upstairs to the pink and green bedroom she had used when she visited Sabrina the year before. "Take what you want from my closet, and then we'll talk about what comes next."

The telephone rang and she took it quickly. But it was not Brooks; it was Alexandra. "I have been asked to dine in splendor at a new Italian place in Soho, gracing it with my presence so it will become the new 'in' restaurant."

"A bit unsubtle of them. Does that happen often?"

"Honey? You all right?"

"Of course. Why?"

"Because either you are asleep or—oh, hell, are you in bed with someone?"

"No. What are you talking about?"

"I'm talking about us, you and me, getting these invites all the time. So what's bothering you?"

"Oh . . . we can talk about it later."

"Uh huh, there is something. Okay, how about dinner with me tonight? This one I'm accepting because the owner did me a favor once."

"What's the name of it?"

"Il Cocchio Oro. Could that possibly mean The Golden Cock?"

Stephanie laughed. "The Golden Coach. Your Italian needs polishing. What time?"

"Eight? I'll pick you up."

Before Stephanie could turn back to Gabrielle, the telephone rang again. This time it was Sabrina.

"I haven't got long, Stephanie, but I had to let you know."

"What's wrong?"

"Nothing, everything is fine. But Nat says he'll take X-rays on the twenty-second."

"The twenty-second? That's only a week away."

"Ten days. *Only?*"

"I mean, it seems so soon. Does your wrist feel better?"

"You can't tell when it's inside a cast. Wait a minute." Sabrina's voice turned from the telephone. "Yes, Cliff, of course you're going to the airport with me. Yes, Penny, you too. We're *all* going." Her voice came back, clear and exasperated. "When do you get to be *alone* in a family?"

"Not often," Stephanie said, remembering. "Who are you meeting at the airport?"

"Garth. He's been in Berkeley all week. Stephanie, I have to go. There's some mayhem downstairs. I just wanted you to know about the date. October twenty-second. Call me soon so we can talk."

Stephanie repeated it to herself. Ten more days. Sabrina had sounded so ... neutral. Not happy, not sad. How did she feel? How do *I* feel? she wondered. But there was no time to think about it; Gabrielle needed to talk, and she talked straight through to tea time.

By then Stephanie was so worried about her despair, and furious at the shabby way Brooks had treated her, that she called him and told him to meet her and Alexandra for dessert and coffee at Il Cocchio Oro. She did not wait for him to refuse.

"You don't mind?" she asked Alexandra later as they ate veal with almonds and raisins, baked mozarelle and scampi, while fending off a crew of waiters who had been ordered to make their meal memorable.

"Honey, after that story, I can't wait to see him. Do we use a horsewhip or hang him by his thumbs?"

"First we give him a chance. For Gaby's sake."

They smiled at each other, and the mirrored walls multiplied their images in the white and gold room—two stunning women, simply dressed and attended as if they were royalty. When Brooks arrived at ten, he did not have to look for them; they glowed like jewels in the center of the room.

"Zabaglione and espresso for three," Stephanie said to the waiter. She gazed, unsmiling, at Brooks. "Gaby is staying with me. I'll be coming for her things tomorrow. Please have them packed and ready."

He nodded. "I'm not happy about this, you know."

"Oh, my," said Alexandra. "I grieve to hear that."

Brooks ignored her. "I didn't act hastily. I have proof that she sold information to Rymer Cosmetics for a quarter of a million pounds."

"Ridiculous," Stephanie said automatically. "Gaby would never betray you. And she doesn't need money."

"She's in debt to everyone: dressmakers, shoemakers, beauty salons, a gymnasium. And she signed some notes in Monte Carlo a month ago that I knew nothing about until last week."

"Everyone is in debt," Alexandra said. "I'll bet you are, too."

"No."

"Then you're unnatural," she said flatly.

"What proof?" Stephanie asked.

"I was told by the man who bought the information. Rymer brought out its new line two weeks ago, beating ours by a full month, with identical brand names, colors and packaging. Not similar; identical. And all of it stolen. Do you know what it will cost us to formulate a new line? Do you know what we lose by coming in months behind Rymer and Revlon and the others?"

"No, but you're assuming that man is telling the—"

"Over a million pounds. Four times what Gabrielle got for her little job. If I'd known, I would have bought her off and saved three quarters of a million."

"You bastard, Brooks," said Alexandra.

Stephanie was silent as the waiter served their frothy zabaglione and espresso. Picking up the small lemon peel in her saucer, she dropped it in her coffee. "If I were you," she said to Brooks, "I'd look at my employees. Your friendly informant is protecting someone by accusing Gaby."

"For God's sake, this isn't a complicated spy story. Gaby has been acting guilty for a month, jumping every time I come near her, secretive about letters and phone calls. You would have acted exactly as I did if you had a million-pound loss and someone told you who was at fault. I love Gaby—"

"Oh, fuck," Alexandra said disgustedly. "My old-fashioned mommy always told me love means you trust somebody first and shoot second."

"I love Gaby," Brooks went on, less firmly. "But we all know she's like a child. And a child can be tempted—"

"But that's what you want, isn't it?" Stephanie asked. "For her to be like a little girl?"

Brooks gave her a startled glance. "I never asked her to be a child," he said, but he and Stephanie both knew they were remembering the night Gaby told him he spanked her with words.

"She wants to please you," Stephanie said. "That's all she wants."

"She would please me by telling me about her debts."

Stephanie shrugged slightly. "Maybe she doesn't like to ask permission to spend money."

"It has nothing to do with permission. I have to know what she is doing. In fact—"

"In fact," Stephanie said, suddenly understanding, "it's because you don't know for sure about Gaby that you're so angry."

"I was told—" He hesitated. "Perhaps I'll have a talk with her."

"Isn't it beneath you," asked Alexandra, "to converse with a traitor who leaks information?"

"She's not a traitor," he said coldly. "She may be in trouble. And if I was hasty—"

"Hasty, the man says. In such a hurry you scared her speechless. And now you're going to do her a favor and have a talk with her. How about finding your real spy first, and then maybe you'd be fit to crawl over and apologize. She's better off now with Sabrina."

"Sabrina," said a new voice, and Stephanie turned to see Antonio standing beside her. "How are you?" he said. "I have not called you."

She smiled. "I know." There was a brief silence. "Will you join us for a drink?"

He swung around a chair from the next table and sat down, greeting Brooks and Alexandra and ordering cognac for all of them. "If I am interrupting a personal talk—"

Again there was silence. "Plumbing," said Alexandra.

"I beg your pardon?" Antonio asked as Stephanie stifled a laugh.

"We were discussing leaks and evicting residents who are suspected of causing them. Do you know about such things?"

"Nothing. I have people to take care of them. Though lately I have been discussing them for the town I am building."

"What does that mean: building a town?"

"What it says. Is it not clear?"

"You start with empty land and build a town? Houses, stores, everything?"

"Everything. Schools, hospitals—"

"Where will you get the people?"

"They are there, living in hovels. I am building them a new life."

Alexandra's eyes gleamed. "I always thought towns just . . . happened."

"I make things happen."

Stephanie watched as Antonio and Alexandra looked at each other, talking, listening, each beginning to consider what the other might offer. They were alike, Stephanie thought; both coming from poverty to luxury by their wits and determination, using whatever and whoever was at hand. And both now anxious to find a place with another person that would make it all seem worthwhile.

"Alexandra," Stephanie said. "I have to be home early to make a call to America. Will you forgive me?"

Alexandra winked, so quickly no one saw it but Stephanie. "Call me whenever you want to talk about plumbing."

"I'll come with you," Brooks said. "I want to ask you—"

Their eyes met, and Stephanie's lips curved in a reluctant smile. She liked him. Even now, they could share an unspoken decision to leave Alexandra and Antonio alone together. If only he hadn't hurt Gaby, she thought; what good friends we all could be.

At home, she told Gabrielle about the evening. Huddled in an armchair, wearing one of Sabrina's robes, her eyes red, Gabrielle began to brighten as Stephanie talked. "I have to call him!" she cried. "He hates to admit he's wrong. And it was my fault; I should have asked him what was happening so we could talk about it."

"Gaby, that's not true." Stephanie sat on the arm of her chair. "Don't take the blame. You should have asked him, but his fault was worse: he heard a story and decided you were guilty without ever talking to you."

Gabrielle sighed. "I suppose. Sabrina, you know so much."

Look who knows so much, Stephanie thought after Gabrielle went to bed. Look who's giving advice on living with a man. She thought of Garth, sitting in their kitchen, reading the paper, while she stood with her back to him and cooked dinner. I should have talked long ago about what was happening to us. I shouldn't have believed that ugly letter any more than Brooks should have believed the story about Gaby. It was my fault as much as Garth's that we drifted apart. It was my fault as much as his that we didn't make love very often. I wanted to punish him. For what? For being Garth Andersen; for having a career and recognition and success while all I had was a failed business. And a family. Yes, but he had the family, too. He had everything.

Well, I got back at him, didn't I? Played a first-class joke on him; left him without his even knowing it; found out I can make a life on my own.

Not true, she thought quickly. I need my family. I just don't have time to think about them right now.

Business was picking up at Ambassadors; Stephanie accepted three new commissions for November and December. I won't be able to do them, she thought regretfully; Sabrina will. She went to another auction with Nicholas, and once again he raised the question of a partnership. "I'm thinking about it," she said. "I'll let you know soon."

On Friday she supervised the placement of furniture on the top two floors of Max's house. Mrs. Thirkell had packed a lunch, but she forgot about it until the movers were gone and she was alone, going from room to room with her checklist. It was almost five when she realized how hungry she was. The first meal in my new house, she thought, and, sitting cross-legged on the floor of the study, she opened the wicker basket.

She was eating scallop mousse from a plastic container when Max appeared in the doorway. "An inaugural picnic. And I wasn't invited."

Startled, she looked up. "How did you get in?"

"With my key. Was I indiscreet?"

She laughed. "Of course not. I'm sorry."

He looked at her keenly. "You forgot it was my house."

"So it seems." She kept her voice light. "I let myself get carried away. But I promise I won't go so far as to move in."

"The house would be lovelier if you did. May I sit down?"

"Of course." Her face was warm, and she busied herself filling a small plate with water biscuits, paté and mousse. "Your inaugural picnic. I'm sorry I have no wine."

"One moment." He left, returning with a bottle and corkscrew.

"Do you always carry a bottle of Beaujolais?" Stephanie asked as he pulled out the cork.

"Only today. A house is not furnished until it has a bed, a table and wine. You told me the first two would be delivered today. I provide the third. Now—do we have goblets?"

She held up her glass. "I apologize again. It was to be a picnic for one."

"Then we will share."

As they ate and drank, he told her about his plans for an art gallery that would sell tapestries from eastern Europe. "You must see them. Huge pieces, bold and vigorous. I'd like one in this house, on the long wall in the drawing room, if you approve."

"But you don't need my approval. If you want something in your home, you should buy it."

"Your judgment is important to me. Shall we have a guided tour of what you have done so far?"

"Certainly." She repacked the picnic basket, moving slowly, trying to recapture the private pleasure he had shattered. His presence filled the space she had actually begun to feel was hers, and now it was his house, silent about them, his silence as he stood above her. She took a deep breath to slow the beating of her heart.

But the house was part of her, and, walking through the rooms, she almost forgot Max. She knew she had failed to achieve Sabrina's lightness of touch, her witty combinations and unexpected contrasts in fabric and line—but then, Stephanie told herself, I've been designing for Max Stuyvesant, who is not known for lightness of spirit. Give me an Alexandra, and then see what I can do.

Still, the rooms had an unmistakable elegance and personality. Stephanie had made of each a separate setting with one or two massive pieces of furniture balanced by simpler ones, the walls covered in dark grasscloth or suede. The rooms blended together in dark woods and fabrics illuminated by recessed lights and occasional flashes of color to create an atmosphere both sensual and aloof, with a private, almost secretive air. Exactly like Max.

Standing in the center of each room, turning on lights against the October darkness, Stephanie hid her feelings of pride and possession as she described in dry phrases some finishing touches still to be done and the plans for completing the lower two floors. "I won't be able to do it all," she said quietly. "I have only until Monday. But most of the work is done."

Max was noncommittal, nodding as she spoke. When she finished, they were in the fourth-floor hallway, their shadows falling across the blocks of light from the bedroom doors. He took Stephanie's hands. "It is superbly done. There is nothing I would change." He kissed her palms, feeling with his lips the tremor that ran through her. Stephanie bent her head, resting it against his chest, and, with his arm around her, Max led her to his bedroom.

There was little time to think, but it did not matter. Max had been a shadow hovering over everything she had thought and done since she had danced with him at Annabel's, and she had known all afternoon, from the moment he appeared, that she was taking the last step away from the Stephanie Andersen who had come to London four weeks earlier. And why shouldn't I? she thought in a swift, defensive flash. Garth has Sabrina. It's crazy to pretend that by now they haven't ... Max tightened his arms around her, one hand on the back of her head, and she met his open mouth in a triumph of desire over caution.

Mine! she exulted silently. Mine! My house that I made; my lover. Sabrina's life. And mine.

Max stripped off her clothes and laid her on his bed before he took off his own. He stood above her, looking down at her slender body. "A long wait," Stephanie heard him murmur, and then he lay beside her, his large body and frizzled red hair a silhouette lit dimly from behind, a shadow with hard, cool hands. She moved toward him, but he shook his head. Taking both her hands in one of his, he pinned them to the bed above her head and, with his other hand, stretched her taut, slowly tracing the curves of her body until her muscles rippled beneath his touch. He lowered his head to take her nipples between his teeth and flicked his tongue across them like a fine and rapid whip, then ran it in a fiery line along her stomach to the mound of hair and shrinking flesh that tried to deny him.

"No ..." Stephanie moaned. She tried to move away or pull him on top of her, but Max still held down her hands. She closed her eyes, shame and desire mixed, as he took her into his mouth, taking small bites in the soft flesh. She tried to lie as rigid as her thoughts, to separate herself from the sharp pain and pleasure of his relentless mouth, but her hips moved of themselves, her neck arched, and then she cried out with the sudden release, astonished at the pleasure.

Dimly, within her body's response, Stephanie recognized the calculated skill of Max's hands and mouth, but she ignored it. When at last he freed her hands and lay on her, she looked up and met his flat gray eyes, watching her. He moved deliberately, entering her slowly until she could not wait; lifting her hips, she put her hands on his buttocks and fiercely pulled him deep inside her. The room was loud with the cacophony of her thoughts and her lips formed his name. And Max smiled.

* * *

"Honey," said Alexandra as Stephanie poured tea in her office on Monday morning, "you look tired."

Stephanie's lips curved. "I didn't get much sleep over the weekend. *You* look wonderful. I haven't seen you since our Italian dinner."

"I thought I'd talk to you about that. Can I talk to you about Antonio?"

"If it would please you."

"It would please me to know whether you're still thinking about marrying him."

"I'm not."

"No doubts?"

"No doubts. Alexandra, he expects ... No, I shouldn't inflict my feelings on you."

"Honey, how many times in the last year have you told me what he expects? And how many times have I told you what I'm looking for?"

Not knowing the answer, Stephanie looked at her in silence.

"I suppose you're thinking of my performance with Brooks last week." She held out her cup for more tea and bit into a croissant. "I did enjoy taking him apart, not because I like Gabrielle—actually, I think she's a fool—but because I get upset when I see self-satisfied men breaking their loyal little women in half. But the truth is, the whole time I knew he was the kind of man I wanted."

"Brooks?"

"Parts of Brooks. Not the bastard who wants his little girl to adore him, but the other one—successful, sure of himself, building an empire and protecting it. That's what I want. I could trust a man like that to build my castle and help me run my life. I've done it alone long enough, you know; I'm tired of it. Antonio's rich enough to buy anything we could ever want, and he'll let me run part of his empire. I'll be more than a plaything; I'll be helping to *build towns*—how could I resist that? If he demands in return that I concentrate on him, stay at his side, that's a fair exchange. After all, how long will I be thirty-five? Or look it? What the hell, honey, I want a place to belong and be taken care of and have something of my own to do. I want the works. Isn't that what we all want?"

Stephanie swirled the tea in her cup. A few leaves at the bottom clustered like a four-petaled flower. Or a family. It's Monday, she thought. October twenty-second. Sabrina's X-ray.

"Sabrina? You listening? You really do look tired."

"I was wondering where love comes in the exchange."

"Oh, love. Antonio says love comes later. It's an old Guarani legend. If we can be friends, I'll be satisfied. Maybe that's the best any of us can hope for."

"Forgive me, my lady," Brian interrupted, "but Monsieur Michel Bernard says it is important that he speak with you."

Alexandra stood in a whirl of energy. "I'll say goodbye, honey. We're off to Rio for a week."

"Already?"

"Well, don't tell Antonio, but Alexandra thinks it's a good idea to see the lay of the land before getting knee-deep into coffee beans and Guarani Indians."

"And what does Antonio think?"

"Antonio says he lost you because he was too patient. Forcefulness and speed are the order of the day, to sweep me into his arms. He told me a Guarani Indian legend to illustrate it. Too long to repeat. Come to think of it, too long to remember."

They laughed. Impulsively, Stephanie hugged Alexandra and kissed her cheek, feeling her surprised, reflexive pulling back. A mistake, she thought; they don't do that. But what difference does it make? I won't be here when she gets back. I may never see her again.

"I'll call when we get back," Alexandra said, and Stephanie nodded as she picked up the telephone.

"Michel? Weren't you going to call about four weeks ago?"

"I recall promising that and I apologize. I have been in Bonn and Jolie is in Turkey. I hear you had an accident at Lady Chasson's."

"Yes. I was clumsy."

"Truly amazing, for a graceful lady who knows fragile art so well. But then I heard also of a small contretemps with Rose Raddison."

"You heard all that in Bonn?"

"No, Paris. Lady Chasson was visiting friends. It is a little world we live in, yes?"

"Yes." With a rueful smile, Stephanie remembered how Sabrina's world had always seemed limitless compared to the narrowness of Evanston. "What is Jolie doing in Turkey?"

"Photographing a cache of vases confiscated as they were being smuggled out of the country. I am calling to ask for your

284

help. We are sure now that the forgeries are a sideline, not the main operation. The big money is in smuggling from countries where governments have banned the export of art and antiquities. Someone funds groups in these countries to rob museums and tombs and ancient temples, and then this someone smuggles the stuff out and sells it in Europe and America. You have heard of this?"

"Some . . ."

"Well, it does not affect you so much because you don't sell these things—art and jewelry from tombs in Turkey and Egypt, sculpture from temples in Cambodia, Thailand, Colombia; entire sections of the temples themselves—doorways, walls, altars."

"But how can I help you if I don't sell them?"

"We think that Ivan Lazlo, who is listed as the owner of Westbridge Imports, and his salesman, Rory Carr, store the smuggled pieces in their warehouse. Some are smuggled out for specific buyers; others are sold along with legitimate antiques. But it seems Ivan and Rory wanted to make money on their own. So they dabble in forgeries."

"But who really owns Westbridge?"

"Ah, that is our mysterious Mr. Big Man whom we have not yet found. When we do, the last piece is in place. But now we hear rumblings that the little men and the big one may be quarreling over money and also over the risk of the smuggling being exposed if the forgeries are discovered and account books examined and questions asked. Thieves always fall out, yes? So we thought you might hear something. Gossip about salesmen suddenly being fired or quitting, dealers finding new partners, maybe many rare items dumped on the market all at once. If you do, will you call us here in Paris? In two weeks we will be in London. Save us a night and we will take you to dinner. Yes?"

"Yes." I will be gone, she thought.

Brian brought in the mail. "Gabrielle de Martel called, my lady. She asks that you return her call. And may I bring you some lunch?"

"No, thank you, Brian, I may go out."

She leafed through the mail while dialing.

"Sabrina," said Gabrielle. "Brooks called."

There was a letter from Sabrina; she tore it open.

"I didn't talk to him; I told Mrs. Thirkell to say I was out."

News from Evanston; news of the family. Chatty, nothing personal.

"But now I think I should call him back. He gets angry when—"

How could that be? Nothing personal in a letter about her own family?

"But I didn't want to do anything until I talked to you. What if I do the wrong thing?"

No mention of Garth.

"It's just that I'm not sure what to say."

They hadn't talked for a week. Stephanie hadn't wanted to talk; her thoughts were too full of Max.

"Sabrina? Have you heard me?"

"Yes, Gaby." Beneath her thoughts, she had been listening. "I don't think you should call him back."

"You think I should wait for him."

"Don't you think you should? To make sure you both know what you're doing, and what you want to do? You shouldn't ... deceive each other. Or yourself."

Gabrielle sighed. "I suppose so. God, I hate being sensible."

It was not yet dawn in Evanston; hours before Sabrina's appointment with Nat Goldner, hours before she called to tell Stephanie what he had found. For awhile, then, Stephanie could think about Max. A weekend of Max, in his house, eating the food his butler brought from London's finest restaurants and served at the desk in the study. His maid had brought a suitcase for him and he wore a purple dressing gown, and Stephanie a blue velvet one that wrapped twice around her waist. She folded up the sleeves and tied them at her elbows with twine left by the movers. Her hair was tumbled, her eyes bright, every nerve alive to changes in temperature, a breath of air, the touch of sunlight on her skin and Max's hand on her breast, strong coffee in the morning and the dry bite of Burgundy wine at night, glowing darkly in the light of dying flames in the bedroom fireplace.

She glided on a fine edge of desire and excitement, flushed with the triumph of discovery. "Exquisite," Max said. "My stunning beauty."

"High praise, from a connoisseur," she said lightly, but the look of triumph was bright in her eyes.

But on Monday, sitting in her office—what triumph? she

286

asked herself. Not the triumph of intimacy or affection, or even friendship. The triumph of passion. And that, she realized, was the last item on my checklist. I wanted to do all that Sabrina had done, experience her life in all the ways it was different from mine. And this was the last: the calculated sensuality of Max Stuyvesant.

She shivered. Her pride in Ambassadors, the decorating of Max's house, her caring for Gabrielle, her affection for Alexandra. It was all a dream.

But even if I could keep it, she thought, it still wouldn't be enough. I want love and cherishing and commitment. Otherwise, I wouldn't have a place to belong.

Where do I belong? Wherever I can be connected to other people. Once I had that, or thought I did, and then I lost it. And now I've discovered that Sabrina's life isn't the one I want, either.

But how will I know what I want until I go back to Garth and find out? Garth. Penny. Cliff. My home. "I miss them," she said aloud, startling herself in the silence. "And I need them."

Have they missed me and needed me?

Don't be ridiculous.

They don't even know I've been gone.

The telephone rang. Brian was out, so she answered it herself and heard the smooth tones of Max's voice.

"Without planning it, I seem to have moved into my new house over the weekend. Now I'm stumbling over workers. I think I should disappear for a few days."

"Oh." A stab of dismay; she heard it in her voice.

"I thought a cruise would be pleasant. The Mediterranean is magnificent this time of year. The workers could then finish without obstructions."

"Yes."

"Can they finish without your direction?"

She sighed. She had forgotten one more item on the list of things she wanted to do: a cruise. Sabrina had had so many; all Stephanie wanted was one. Then I'll go back, she thought, to what is waiting for me. I'll go back to Garth and we'll find the love we used to have. I can do so much now. I've learned so much about myself. I will try. I promise.

But first I want one more dream. Only one.

"Brian can direct the construction crew," she said.

"We'll sail from Monaco to the Italian Riviera; about four or five days. Will that suit you?"

"Yes."

"Excellent. We'll take three other couples; you'll find them pleasant. We leave Wednesday morning, the 24th; can you be ready at nine?"

"Yes."

Hanging up, she moved her chair to look through the office door, down the length of the showroom to the street beyond the paned window. The day was overcast but warm, the silvery air like a screen between Stephanie and the people hurrying past. She would call Sabrina and find out about the X-ray; tell her she would be away for a few days. And then the adventure would end.

Everything was coming to a close. Mrs. Thirkell would watch over Gaby, and it was only a matter of time before Brooks came for her. Alexandra was with Antonio. The forged Meissen stork was broken and she had told Rory Carr to stay away. Ambassadors had done well under her care: she had sold some large pieces, earned an impressive fee for Max's house, taken on new commissions for next month.

When Brian came in she stood up and slipped on her jacket. There were things she had to do: call Sabrina, rearrange drawers and closets on Cadogan Square that she had made her own, decide what to pack for the cruise. She stood in the middle of the showroom, memorizing it, and then made a last, silent farewell to Ambassadors.

Chapter 15

Sabrina stirred, half awake. October 6, she thought. Garth is going to California. But when she opened her eyes she saw it was barely dawn, the first pale light turning the windows pearl gray. In the maple tree, a bird sang. Sabrina stirred again and felt her hand in Garth's, their fingers entwined. Then the night rushed back, enveloping her—Garth's mouth whispering against her breasts, his body covering hers, the passion of her response. Not a dream; she had let it happen. *But, no, I couldn't help—*

Garth's hand tightened in his sleep. Sabrina felt the warmth flowing between them and realized suddenly how changed the world could seem with a hand clasping hers in the darkness.

She was frightened. *Pull away. Your world has not changed.* But the thought faded as she slept again. When she woke, sunlight streamed through the clear, bright windows and she was alone in the bed.

She looked around the room. Garth's suitcase, packed but still open, was on the chair. I should get up, she thought, and see if he needs help. But she was afraid to face him. *Stephanie, please forgive me. I didn't mean it. Please understand . . .* Unexpectedly, she remembered the terrible joy of feeling him inside her and the swift feelings of loss and guilt that followed.

I will never know what we might have had.

But she had no right to think that and, ashamed, she closed her eyes again, like a child hiding from herself. Because she could not deny that she had wanted to make love to Garth. And she would never know if that was why last night, for the first time, he had turned to her not with a question but with the assurance of a husband.

But he wouldn't have waited indefinitely, she thought; we were foolish to think he would. The risk was always there; it just finally caught up with me. It meant nothing.

She heard his quiet footsteps on the stairs and quickly shut her eyes. He came to the bed, kissed her, picked up his suitcase and left the room.

And then he was gone. An extraordinary feeling of lightness swept over Sabrina. Last night had been an accident. She hadn't really felt anything; no more than a brief response. It wasn't important.

You wanted him and he knew it. Your arms held him, and all night long your hand was in his.

One episode, she told herself firmly. I was tired and let down my guard. That was the risk. It was no more than that.

Liar.

There is nothing for Stephanie to worry about. Whatever I felt, I can easily forget. I have a job to do here, and a time to leave. I am not involved in any other way.

She avoided her reflection in the mirror. *I won't let it happen again.*

And Garth will be gone for a week.

Linda Talvia called, inviting Sabrina and the children to dinner.

"Not for a few days," Sabrina said. "Maybe the end of the week?"

"The lady wants some time alone," said Linda. "I know the feeling. When Marty is gone I feel three feet taller and a hundred pounds lighter. The house to myself. Paradise."

That was my life in London, Sabrina thought. Responsible only to myself. What I wanted to get away from.

"But I want to see you," said Linda. "When does Garth get back?"

"Next Sunday."

"Could you come on Wednesday, or even Tuesday? Early? I thought we could talk for awhile."

She needs to talk, Sabrina thought. "Why don't we come tonight? I'd love to have somebody else do the cooking for a change."

"Would you really? Oh, Stephanie, what would I do without you? Come at four-thirty. Marty has an all-day seminar and won't be back 'til six. The kids can play in the yard."

"We'll be there," Sabrina said.

That afternoon she took Penny and Cliff shopping. She had put it off, hoping they could wait for Stephanie, but Cliff's shoes were falling apart, Penny was wailing that all the girls had something called Beene Jeans and she'd die if she didn't have some, too, and Sabrina finally ran out of excuses. I'm running out of excuses for everything, she thought; maybe I should break the other wrist.

At the shoe store the salesman measured Cliff's feet and brought out boxes of shoes. Cliff tried them on, looking from the shoes to Sabrina. What was he waiting for? "Which one feels best?" she asked. "Which do you like the best?" Hesitantly, Cliff picked up a heavy shoe, almost a hiking boot. "You don't think they'll be too warm, sitting inside school all day?" He shook his head. "All right, then. Let's go buy Penny some jeans."

"Mom!" Cliff burst out. "Can I really have these?"

Now what have I done? She picked up one of the heavy shoes, pretending to examine it. Evidently Stephanie would have said no, probably because they're for outside, not school, and maybe because of the price, but I don't know what boys' shoes cost. "If you want them, they're yours. I've decided we should buy whatever will last the longest. But you'll have to take care of them. Can they be waterproofed?" The salesman brought a waterproofing spray and, as Sabrina searched for one of Stephanie's charge cards, Cliff put on the new boots, grinning with delight.

Outside the store, he turned to go meet his friends at the playing field, then hesitated. "Mom? Thanks. A lot." And he ran off, leaving Sabrina flushed with pleasure.

At the entrance to Marshall Field's they saw Vivian Goodman with Barbara. "We are on the prowl for something called Beene Jeans," Vivian said.

"Amazing," Sabrina said dryly. "Geoffrey Beene has hypnotized the entire sixth grade."

"Mom," said Penny, "can I go with Barbara?"

"Why don't the two of you go alone while Vivian and I

wander by ourselves? Here's the Field's charge card. But only buy one pair for now."

Vivian looked at her curiously. "Am I behind the times? I've never sent Barbara off with a credit card."

"Penny's maiden voyage," Sabrina said, noting Penny's wide-eyed wonder. "I'm feeling reckless. But don't let me influence you—"

"On the contrary, I like it. Shall we have coffee?"

"If you don't mind, there's a new antique shop I'd like to see."

"That's right; Garth told me you like antiques."

It was a small shop called Collectibles, tucked between a high-priced luggage store and a restaurant specializing in crepes and homemade pastries. A perfect location, Sabrina thought; the owner knows what she's doing. Inside, dozens of small Oriental rugs overlapped to cover the floor of a square room crammed with furniture.

Vivian touched a leaded glass lamp shaped like a tulip. "How can people afford a Tiffany lamp these days?"

Sabrina glanced at it. "It's not Tiffany; it looks like Bohemian. They were wonderful imitators of Tiffany. If I were selling it, I wouldn't charge over fifty or sixty dollars."

"Indeed," said a new voice, and Sabrina saw a slender woman wending her way toward them. Her short hair was silver, brushed back from a thin, delicate face dominated by sharp, black eyes. With inexpensive clothes she achieved elegance and style, and Sabrina admired her; she does a lot, she thought, with not much money. And she owns the place. "And how much have *I* charged for it?" the woman asked.

Vivian read the small sticker on the base of the lamp. "Fifty-five dollars. That's amazing."

"Not for someone who knows Bohemian glass." The woman held out her hand to Sabrina. "Madeline Kane. Do you work with antiques?"

"Sa—Stephanie Andersen." They shook hands. "I have, in the past."

"Why don't you look around and tell me what you think. I've only been open for a week. Still getting organized."

Sabrina was nervous as they began to maneuver around the furniture. It was the first time she had slipped on her name, and she knew why: she was caught in the spell of the shop, the pungent fragrance of furniture polish, musty velvets and brocades, dust dancing in sunbeams that turned the grains of well-worn woods to gold. *I want to go home. I want to walk through Ambassadors, and sit in my office; I want my own work.* It was a piercing homesickness and her eyes filled with tears.

Vivian looked at her in alarm. "Stephanie? What is it?"

"Nothing." She blinked, and a magnificently ugly couch, tufted in purple, wavered through her tears. "An impossible thought."

"Is there anything I can do?"

"No, it's—oh, once I had my own business, managing estate sales, and I handled furniture like this, art and antiques, collectibles. It didn't work out; I had to close it and get another job. And I miss all this. The smell and look and feel of my own shop—"

"You had a shop?"

"Oh, no. But I always wanted one."

Madeline Kane had been following a little distance behind. There was something about this woman, she thought, that set her apart. The way she walked and held her head. The way she took in the shop with a swift glance, knowledgeable and certain. Her curiosity aroused, Madeline looked at her thoughtfully. "Perhaps you can help me. I'm trying to find some background information on this Duncan Phyfe table. Do you know anything about it? I know it has to be about 1850—"

"It's not Phyfe," Sabrina said bluntly. She ran her hand over it, bending to look at the feet. "It's Belter. Very early, 1840s, but Phyfe never handled rosewood that way; look at the carvings on the claw feet."

Madeline bent to look. "Yes," she mused. "Of course." She straightened up and pursed her mouth. "Stephanie, why don't you get back into the estate business?"

Sabrina looked at her coolly.

"You're thinking it's none of my business," Madeline said. "But I need someone to work for me, occasionally with inventory and in the store, but mainly to run estate sales. I used to do it, and I didn't like it; I prefer puttering around here. But there's good money in those sales, and it's the easiest way to add to my inventory. So I'm offering you a job. Part-time, if you have to be home with children. Now is it my business? Or is it our business?"

No, you wonderful, wonderful woman, it's Stephanie's busi-

ness. You just gave Stephanie a job. "Our business," Sabrina agreed with a smile. "When would you like me to start?"

"Yesterday."

"Then I'll be here Monday morning about ten."

"Ten is for customers, my dear. Nine would be better."

"Of course." *I've forgotten what it's like to work for someone.* "But I have to make a call first, to resign from another job. I'll be here as close to nine as I can make it."

"Fine. I take it you're not interested in salary."

"I beg your pardon?"

"You haven't asked about pay."

Sabrina laughed. "I'll be more practical when I manage estate sales. But it can wait until Monday, when we talk about how many hours I work and exactly what I'll be doing."

Madeline gazed at her, clearly puzzled, and Sabrina knew she had to be more careful. She was behaving like Lady Longworth instead of a housewife who had to work to help make ends meet.

"If that is all right with you," she added.

Madeline smiled faintly. "Of course. I'll expect you on Monday."

On their way to pick up Penny and Barbara, Vivian said, "Garth didn't tell me you were an expert."

"We don't talk about it much." Sabrina felt like skipping down the street. A job for Stephanie. And for herself as long as she was here. But her homesickness had not gone away; she wanted Ambassadors. I'll call Nat, she thought, and try to push up the date for the X-ray. If he can do it as soon as Garth gets back, I'll leave right away. She remembered waking up with her fingers twined in his. I have to leave right away.

"Mommy, look what I bought!" Penny cried. "And guess what? The saleslady didn't want to wait on us, but I showed her the card—here it is—and then she treated us like she treats you; she called us Miss!"

The girls turned their shining faces from Vivian to Sabrina. "What a wonderful thing you did for them," Vivian said. "I wish I'd thought of it. But eleven seems so young—"

I thought of it because I'm not a mother, Sabrina reflected. But when Penny hugged her and thanked her, she felt the same delight she had felt when Cliff thanked her for his shoes. She'd made them happy. And they loved her.

On the way home, Penny took her hand and held it tightly.

And a thought chilled Sabrina: When I leave, I'll leave this behind.

Penny scuffed the brown and rust leaves on the sidewalk, talking happily about the puppet costumes she was making. "I'll give you a fashion show in a few days," she promised. "And then I'll only have the last four to do. I need your help with those."

I won't call Nat right away, Sabrina thought. I don't want to seem in too much of a hurry. He might get suspicious.

Penny and Cliff were on their way to bed when Garth called from Berkeley on Sunday night. Sabrina, fumbling with needle and thread and Cliff's torn jacket, and blaming her clumsiness on her cast instead of the fact that she never learned to sew, let them take over the kitchen and bedroom telephones. From her chair in the living room she could hear them chattering as if Garth had been gone a month instead of two days, and once Penny went into peals of laughter that rang through the house.

"Mom!" Cliff called. "Dad wants to talk to you."

She went into the breakfast room, and, in a moment, Garth's voice was there, astonishingly close, low and warm, familiar. And as Sabrina's heart leaped she knew how much she missed him.

"It's beautiful here," he said. "I wish you were with me to watch the sun burn through the fog. The world turns green and gold and the water changes from gray to a wonderful silver blue."

"How do you see all that from a lecture hall?"

"The lectures begin tomorrow. All I've done so far is meet with the other seminar leaders to organize the week. I understand you gave Cliff and Penny a day to remember."

"Yesterday? We had a good time."

"And where did you go while Penny and Barbara were trying on bean bags?"

"Jeans," she said, laughing. What she missed was their companionship. Even as she had been pushing him away, they had become friends. She had happily looked forward to a week alone, to enjoy the family—*But it isn't a family without Garth.* "Did you call them bean bags to Penny?"

"I did. She found it amusing. Where *did* you go while she was trying them on?"

"To a new antique shop on Sherman Avenue. Owned by a very attractive, very sharp lady who, I think, gave me a test on what she called a Duncan Phyfe table."

"Did you pass?"

"With flying colors. And then she offered me a job. I start tomorrow morning."

"You quit the university job?"

"I will first thing tomorrow."

"Well. That's wonderful."

"Is something wrong? You don't think I should quit?"

"Of course you should; you might recall the times I've urged you to find something you like better. And, as you took care to point out not so long ago, you help pay the mortgage, so I have no right to tell you where to work."

"Garth, what is wrong?" She felt anxiety rising inside her. How had she made him angry? She tried to think of something to say, then caught herself. The job was for Stephanie; what did she care whether Garth was angry about it or not?

But I do care. Because when Garth is angry it usually means he's hurt. And I don't want him hurt.

"Garth, are you there?"

"Yes; I'm sorry I sounded—"

"No, I'm sorry. I should have talked to you about it, but I was so excited. . . . Do you know, I never even asked her what the job pays? I'll find out tomorrow, before I quit the other job, and then decide—"

"No, quit the job. If the new one doesn't work out, you'll find another."

We're trying to make each other feel better, Sabrina thought.

Garth was still talking. "What?" she asked.

"I asked how your dinner was, with Linda and Marty."

"Oh. Sad."

"Sad?"

"No, dinner was all right. But Linda asked me to come early so she could talk; she was so upset about . . . Garth, did Marty ever talk to you about having other women?"

After a moment, Garth said, "If he did, it would have been in confidence."

Oh, come on, nothing stays confidential for very long; everybody talks about these things.

But Garth isn't everybody.

"All right," she said, "but can you tell me if he thinks Linda is having affairs?"

"He's told her he thinks so."

"She wants him to think that. She isn't, you know, but she scatters clues around to make him jealous so he'll stop having the affairs she thinks *he's* having and love her more, or guard her more carefully from temptations—something like that. Honestly, I've never known two people more at cross-purposes, absolutely incapable of talking about what they're thinking—"

"Never?"

Oh, damn.

She ignored it; he wasn't going to trap her into discussing their marriage. "Garth, have you heard a rumor that some professors are giving passing grades to students they sleep with?"

This time the silence was longer. "Where did you hear that?" he asked finally.

"Linda heard it at the university bookstore. *Have* you heard anything?"

"Nothing I would credit."

"You've heard it, then. And Marty as one of the professors?"

"My God, no. Is that what Linda heard?"

"That's why she had to talk. Is it true?"

"The rumor? I think so. But I don't know who's involved. Accusations by themselves mean nothing; any student who's angry over a low grade could point a finger. But there's been some talk in the faculty club that sounds more serious. Have you talked about this to anyone else?"

"I am not in the habit of spreading rumors."

"I know. I'm sorry. What did you tell Linda?"

"To keep quiet until I talked to you."

"Did you really?"

"Well, why wouldn't I? I trust you more than anyone. And you understand better than anyone how to deal with the university. It's like all groups, isn't it? Everyone chewing on rumors for breakfast and dinner, as if they're the only real things in the world. I remember once Alexandra told me about a cruise—" She broke off.

"Alexandra?"

"Somebody at . . . on the China trip. She'd been on a cruise, and she said by the third day rumors were flying: sworn testimony about who was in whose bed and who was underneath taking notes. Something like the university, isn't it? Except I suppose at the university they use better grammar in their rumors."

He chuckled. "You're wonderful and I miss you. Why don't you fly out here for the end of the week?"

Oh, I'd like that. "I can't just up and leave the children."

"We could find someone."

"And my new job?"

"Yes. Of course. Well, what else is happening in Evanston?"

They talked, Sabrina discovered later, for an hour. "The university is paying for it," Garth said the next night when he called and she asked him. "But you're right; it is an unseemly extravagance. If you fly out here, we'd save the university hundreds of dollars."

She laughed but didn't answer. She would stay where she was. She missed him, but she was relieved that he wasn't there. It was better for everyone if she and Garth stayed two thousand miles apart.

Each morning she woke to the sounds of the children and the neighborhood and looked forward to the day. And each evening, when Garth called, she wondered where the day had gone.

She raced through the housework in the mornings, doing as little as possible. She was irrationally angry at Stephanie for forcing her into it; she would have ignored it entirely between Juanita's appearances, but there was too much to do. Even with Penny and Cliff helping she felt a slave to dust balls and dirty clothes and out-of-place objects.

After housework, Collectibles was like a holiday. She and Madeline were organizing the merchandise, tagging pieces with their history and price and arranging them to show off the best and improve the appearance of the ordinary. Sabrina liked Madeline; and even though she chafed at working for someone else, she was building up the job so that Stephanie could step into it when she came back. But before she knew it, it was midafternoon and she had to hurry home to supervise the invasion of the house and the raiding of the refrigerator when Cliff and Penny arrived, usually with friends.

Later the three of them ate dinner picnic-style on the patio. After Penny and Cliff did the dishes, Sabrina joined in a three-way game of Scrabble or Boggle, usually ended by Garth's telephone call. And later, when the house was quiet, Sabrina curled up to read in the quiet living room or the armchair in the bedroom until she found herself nodding to sleep.

On Thursday she brought home a wok and a cookbook and they made a Chinese dinner. Penny added two dozen hot dried peppers to the chicken when no one was looking. "You should have seen us, Daddy," she said when Garth called. "We were all crying. But Mommy said it was delicious anyway." She held the telephone out to Sabrina. "Daddy wants to talk to you and tell you he loves you."

Sabrina's heart took a little skip. "Is that what he said?"

"Not exactly, but isn't that what he tells you when he calls?"

Sabrina smiled and took the telephone.

"A corrosive dinner, I understand," Garth said.

"We'll remember it for a long time."

"I'm sorry I missed it."

"So am I."

"Will you make it on Sunday so I can share it? Peppers and all?"

"If you have the courage, and we don't grow faint of heart, we'll make it just for you."

"I can't wait. By the way, Penny was right."

"About what?"

"About my wanting to tell you I love you."

She felt her heart skip again, and then again. She was short of breath. But it's just because I'm tired, she thought; it's been a long day. I'll settle down as soon as I have some time to myself.

"And that my plane arrives at two in the afternoon on Sunday. Can you meet me?"

"Yes, of course."

"What are you doing tomorrow night? More Chinese food?"

"Dolores and Nat invited us for dinner."

"Give them my love."

"I will."

After dinner on Friday night, when Penny and Cliff went upstairs with the Goldners' three children, Sabrina repeated for Dolores and Nat Garth's descriptions of his lectures and the people he was meeting. "He won't say it outright, but it seems to me he must be the star of the show."

She caught the quick glance between them. "What's that all about?"

"Nothing," Nat said quickly.

Sabrina pressed her fingers to her forehead. Now what had she done wrong?

"No, Stephanie has a right to know," said Dolores. "We were just thinking that usually when Garth has some kind of success you bring up that job he's been offered in Stamford. And this time you didn't."

"Oh." *I keep forgetting how much that job means to Stephanie. I've got to ask Garth about it before I leave. I promised Stephanie I would.*

Nat lit his pipe. "You still getting headaches, Stephanie?"

"No," she said, startled. And then an idea came to her. "Well, yes, as a matter of fact. I wasn't going to say anything."

"Why not?"

She shrugged. "I knew I'd be seeing you soon to X-ray my wrist and if they were still bad—"

"Are they bad?"

"Sometimes."

"When?"

"Oh, evenings, mostly. It's probably just that I'm tired."

"Where's the pain? Show me, on your head."

She held her hand on the area where the headaches had been when she had had her concussion. I'm sorry, Garth, she said silently. I wish I had a more creative way of refusing to make love to you. But this is the easiest lie I can think of. And it's only for a few days, until Stephanie is back. Then the headaches will end.

"—should have stopped by now," Nat was saying. "I think you should check it out with your internist. Aren't we going to look at that wrist, too, pretty soon? When did you break it?"

"September twenty-second."

"I'd like to give it another ten days. Call the office and make an appointment for a week from Monday. If the X-ray looks good, we'll take the cast off then."

"All right." Now she knew. She'd call Stephanie tomorrow morning. Ten days. A long time to get through with Garth.

But he's coming home on Sunday, she thought; how wonderful it will be to see him. Then she concentrated on what

Dolores was saying and told herself she had not thought such a thing at all.

It was Wednesday before Garth caught up with his work at the university and had a chance to go through the mail that had accumulated while he was gone. He was restless and fed up with the nagging details of department administration that kept him at his desk. He'd come home from Berkeley like a schoolboy rushing to his first love, remembering Stephanie's warmth and laughter in their telephone calls, remembering that they had made love the night before he left. He'd come home looking forward to long hours with his family, and then, tied down at his office, the laboratory and classrooms, he'd barely seen them.

And his wife had almost encouraged him to stay away. He had found, with despair, her warmth muted, her wariness still intact.

It had not been that way at first. At the airport on Sunday her smile had welcomed him with such delight that he slowed as he walked toward her, stunned by her beauty. "My God," breathed a man behind him. "Wouldn't I like to be the guy she's waiting for?" His heart singing, Garth strode toward her, but as he came close her smile faded and her eyes grew shadowed, as if she had been as surprised as he by her open delight.

"Welcome home," she said, her voice controlled.

He kissed her mouth, her cool lips soft beneath his, a small tremor at the corners. And then, casually, she moved away, and he did not see the delight again until, at dinner, he unpacked his gifts. For Penny and Cliff there were models, to be assembled, of the wagons used by miners in the California gold rush. And for his wife, from a shop in Ghirardelli Square, a suede blazer, as soft as butter, simple but rich in a deep hunter's green with antique gold buttons. Eyes shining, she put it on and spun around, modeling it. "For *me*," she murmured as if to herself.

He was touched and saddened by her surprise. "For no one else."

She put her cheek against his. "Thank you. It's perfect."

"I thought it was the right size," he said, with only a touch of irony. "I don't think you have anything like it, but it seems to go with the different way you've been dressing lately."

"I'm dressing differently?"

"I think so. Aren't you?"

"How?"

"Brighter, it seems to me. Or different combinations of colors. Or maybe more casual. Didn't you used to button your blouses to the collar instead of leaving the top ones open?" She was laughing, and he shook his head. "All those times you accused me of not noticing what you wear. You were right; I'm sorry. However, I did notice the differences. And I like the new look, however you get it."

A happy family evening at home. And then she told him about her headaches; that she'd talked to Nat about them. And gradually she withdrew to the friendly distance she had maintained since her return from China. If anything, she seemed even more nervous.

Doggedly, he went through the mail on his desk. Near the top, dated two days ago, was another invitation from Horace Kallen, president of Foster Laboratories, to visit Stamford on October 23. Next Tuesday. Impossible; he couldn't cancel classes again so soon. But—Foster and Stamford were Stephanie's dream. And he knew they would have sophisticated facilities for more advanced research than he could do here. He could ask Vivian to take his classes; he'd only miss two. Without debating it further, he scribbled a note of acceptance and put it with the outgoing mail. Maybe that would please her.

The truth was, he was so torn by his wife's changing moods that he was beginning to think it would be better to force a confrontation at the risk of destroying everything than to go on indefinitely tiptoeing around her. A life of scientific research had taught him patience and a tolerance for the unexpected, but it had also taught him to expect results from the clues and information he had or to look for new clues and new directions. Either they were married, and would work things out together, or they weren't. And if they weren't, they would have to find a new direction, because they were living a lie.

His telephone rang, and when he answered it the vice president's secretary asked him if he would come to Mr. Strauss's office for a few minutes. It was a summons, not a request, and once again Garth put off going home early.

Lloyd Strauss was only a few years older than Garth, a tennis partner and a longtime friend. Small and compact, a dark bundle of energy always in motion, he had mastered the twists and turns of university politics to rise on a straight path to the vice presidency. Everyone knew that a majority of the board of trustees was ready to elect him president when the current president retired, and few challenged his decisions without careful thought.

"Well, the administrative board checked it all out," he said, pacing while Garth sat on the edge of his desk. "Went through your list of female rejects—sorry, lousy choice of words—your list of rejected female tenure-applicants. Looked into Webster's attitude toward women professors—actually, women in general—and interviewed other people in the sciences and on the tenure committee. No question, you were right; he's violated every equal-opportunity regulation on the books. Of course, we didn't have any until recently, so he's been a bastard, but a legal one, for most of his intolerant life."

Garth stirred, and Strauss put out his hand. "Hold on; let me finish. The administrative board is directing the tenure committee to review the application of Vivian Goodman. My prediction is she'll breeze through. The administrative board also, in its wisdom, has asked Dean Webster to take early retirement. He's sixty-two; we'll carry him for three years. Simplest way. He's been told that with the school year so young, we can hobble along if he leaves immediately. Since it would be crude to say he's been booted, I won't say it. So we're looking for a new Dean of Sciences."

He sat at his desk and riffled through a stack of papers. Garth swiveled to watch him, knowing what was coming. It would please Stephanie, he thought. More money and prestige, regular hours, more time at home. But he would have to give up his research. And teaching. The Dean of Sciences was an administrator; he had no time for anything else. I can't sit in an office all day, he thought, while others are exploring the locked worlds I've begun to discover. If I have to make a change to please Stephanie, Foster Labs would be better.

Strauss was on his feet again. "I don't need to tell you the first person we considered for the job was you. You have an international reputation for research and scholarship—good coverage, by the way, in *Newsweek;* amazing how your handsome puss in a popular magazine impresses the trustees more than a dozen scientific journals put together. So you'd bring prestige and dignity and fairness to the position. But I didn't think you'd want it."

Garth looked at him sharply. It was one thing for him to

303

decide he wouldn't take the job; it was another for Strauss to decide for him.

"Come on, Garth," Strauss grinned. "If I offered it, you'd thank me, shake my hand and tell me I could always count on you for help when I need it but you'd rather be in the lab and the classroom. You'd also offer to help find the new dean."

Garth laughed. "Agreed. But you're not going to give me the chance to make that handsome speech."

"I'm going to give you the chance to make another one. What would you say to the Directorship of our new Institute of Genetic Engineering?"

Garth's head came up, alert, weighing new information. "When was the decision made to build an Institute of Genetic Engineering?"

"Recently."

"Lloyd, I've been trying to get that institute for five years, and the answer has always been that there's no money. That's one of the reasons—"

"That you're considering Foster Labs," Strauss finished. "Have you visited them yet?"

"Next week."

"When they show you their stuff, you might compare it with this." He unrolled a set of blueprints. "Plus the director's salary, probably around sixty thousand, and any classes you want to teach."

Garth spread the blueprints on the desk and pored over them. "I see you've made a few changes. No auditorium."

"Can't afford it. No cuts in lab facilities, however."

"Where's the money coming from?"

"It was freed up."

He looked at Strauss. "It was always there? But not released?"

"There were other priorities—"

"Why wasn't it released?"

Strauss opened a file cabinet to reveal a small refrigerator. "I always like a drink this time of day. What will you have?"

"Scotch. Lloyd, I asked you—"

"Hold on and listen. You'd convinced us we had to have the institute to keep in the running for federal research funds and to develop products that we could license. But every time we put out a feeler for a director, in this country and Europe, we got back the same answer: the best man was right under our nose and why were we looking elsewhere?"

"And why were you?"

"Drink your Scotch."

"Well?"

"Garth, you couldn't have handled it. You're a brilliant researcher, but you were lousy with people. Impatient, bad-tempered—hell, we all knew how often you went to your office and swung your tennis racket at unseen fools or enemies . . . more Scotch?"

"No."

Strauss refilled both their glasses and added soda. "You had a reputation as the pure scientist who would have been happy in a world uncluttered with people. I see that you wince. You've heard it before?"

"No." But my wife used to hint as much, he thought, swirling the liquid in his glass. "So you wouldn't put me in charge and you couldn't or wouldn't bring in someone else. Until now. Has the time suddenly become ripe for pure but bad-tempered scientists who whack unseen enemies with tennis rackets?"

"I think you've changed in the last year or so, especially in the last few months. You've done a top-notch job as department chairman—we do look kindly, you know, on chairmen who bring in government research grants; your support of Vivian has been admirable and your testimony to the administrative board on your charges against Webster were pithy and indisputable. And then there was the kid who messed up the lab work while you were in Berkeley. My God, Garth, a few months ago you would have torn him to pieces and banished him to the School of Agriculture to shovel out stables for the rest of his life. Instead, you only gave him sinks and beakers to scrub: the ones nobody has gotten clean in a hundred and fifty years. More Scotch?"

"If I'm as mellow as you say, I don't need it."

"You don't. This one celebrates your new position."

"Wait a minute. I haven't accepted it."

"Garth, I have to report to the board of trustees—"

"Damn it, I told you I'm going to Stamford next week."

"You don't want to go to Foster Labs. That was a gun at our heads."

"Don't tell me what it was or wasn't. I'm going to Stamford next Tuesday. On Thursday or Friday I'll give you my answer."

"And if I have to know before?"

Garth hesitated briefly. "I want the position, Lloyd; you know how long I've cared about it. I hope I can take it. That's all I can tell you now. I have to visit Stamford."

"Oh. Stephanie. But, Garth, there's money and prestige in the directorship—"

"I know. And she'll know that too. But this is something I owe her. And I owe it to myself to look at the great world out there now and then. I'll give you my answer next week, Lloyd. I hope that's good enough."

"It's good enough. Can you let us know definitely by Friday?"

"Yes."

Sabrina woke to the reverberating racket of Penny and Cliff bumping into each other in the kitchen and squabbling over burned toast. Saturday morning. No school. She burrowed into the pillow. They could manage; she'd sleep awhile longer.

But she could not relax. Something was wrong; there was something she had to think about. She heard Penny and Cliff talking about apple orchards. "I'll pick a hundred bushels," Cliff announced. "They won't let you," Penny said. "There wouldn't be any left for the rest of the world." And then Sabrina knew what she had to think about. *Penny and Cliff in the kitchen. Saturday. Apple-picking. Saturday, October 20. Monday would be the 22nd.*

"We'll X-ray it then," Nat had said. "And if everything looks good, we'll take the cast off at the same time."

Time. There wasn't much more time. She opened her eyes. Garth was sleeping on his side, his face a few inches from hers. She gazed at him. He was so quiet, self-contained, sure of himself and where he was going. And even though he was not sure of her, often bewildered by the twists and turns of the past weeks, still he was gentle and loving even when she was cold, generous when she was stingy, giving her time, as he had promised he would, to find herself.

And who is that? she asked silently, and knew the answer

before the question was finished. A woman in love with her sister's husband.

How long had she loved him? She didn't know; it was not important. She knew it now with a certainty so powerful it swept her up and she felt the absolute joy of loving him before it was pushed aside by despair. Impulsively she put out her hand and touched his face, the high strong cheekbone and the rough stubble on his skin, the little nerve below his eye that jumped as her finger accidentally pressed it. She pulled back her hand, but Garth had opened his eyes and was watching her.

He saw the love in her unguarded face, but before he could reach out and take her in his arms, her face became neutral and he was looking once again at a friendly companion.

"Good morning," he said quietly, not moving.

She looked at him helplessly. Everything he did was right and whatever she did seemed wrong. Silently she said the words she wanted to say, *Good morning, my love,* when from the kitchen came a resounding crash and a ringing "I told you so!" in Penny's triumphant voice.

Sabrina leaped out of bed. Her nightgown caught on the corner of the chair and she swore at it—she would have abandoned Stephanie's nightgowns entirely, but they made it easier to share the bed with Garth—then pulled on a robe and ran from the room.

In the kitchen, Cliff stood at the edge of a lake of orange juice dotted with islands of broken glass. Penny had thrown him a roll of paper towels and he held it in front of him, unrolling it in a long ribbon that folded back on itself in the middle of the lake, slowly turning orange. When Sabrina came in he looked up, frowning in solemn concentration exactly as Garth frowned when working on notes at his desk. "How many *towels* do you think it will take," he asked seriously, emphasizing key words as his father did, "to *soak* this up so I can use the *wet* ones to pick up the pieces of *glass* and some of the *juice,* and then *dry* towels to get the *rest* of it?"

Sabrina burst out laughing. Penny was outraged. "Why is it funny?" she demanded, and Sabrina knew Stephanie wouldn't have laughed. Stephanie would have been concerned about broken glass, cut fingers, children slipping on the floor, a sticky mess. But Sabrina saw a different scene: the warm bed upstairs, her hand on Garth's face, his eyes meeting hers, followed not by words of love but by the spectacular crash of a quart of orange juice, a trail of paper towels in the morning sun and Cliff's scientific study of the problem, his face the picture of Garth's.

She shook her head firmly, stopping her laughter. "You're right, it's not funny. How did it happen?"

Cliff struggled a moment, then told the truth. "I was balancing the bottle on my head."

"The star forward of the hockey team doesn't know about balance?"

He shrugged glumly.

"Well, it's all yours. Use as many towels as it takes, wet and dry. If you run out, we have more. And I would say no apple-picking for you until the floor is washed clean."

"Mom! Men don't wash kitchen floors! I'll pick up the glass and soak up the orange juice, but—"

"In this house," said Sabrina calmly, "men wash kitchen floors." She started to leave, then turned back. "Come on, Penny. Let's talk about what kind of apples we're going to pick." She put her arm around Penny to urge her from the room, and over her shoulder she saw Cliff's swift look of gratitude for removing his sister so he could wash the floor without an audience.

As they walked upstairs, Penny looked at her curiously. "What did you mean—what kind of apples? This late in October there's only one kind we can pick."

Sabrina sighed. So many small details Stephanie hadn't told her. A lifetime of details.

"You're right," she said. "I guess I forgot."

"What's the damage?" Garth asked from the bedroom, and Penny ran to tell him while Sabrina went to the end of the hallway. The house was rounded there, like a turret, and a bench had been built in the curved wall beneath a circular window that looked out over the side yard. It was one of Sabrina's favorite niches, isolated from the activity of the house by a folding screen Stephanie had placed there. She sat on the bench and looked through the window at the flaming orange leaves of the sugar maple in the yard. Apple-picking. Fall.

In London and Paris and Rome, everyone had returned from summer travel; the dinner parties and balls were beginning; clients would be coming in to Ambassadors. What was she doing planning a day in an apple orchard when her real world was stirring with a new season? She had so much to do—Mrs. Pemberley would have finished her fall outfits by now; her hair needed shaping; clients were due in November to pick up items she hadn't even searched out.

I do not belong here. The words were harsh in the soft sunlit day. That other world across the ocean had not disappeared: Stephanie was living in it, and, no matter what news she told in letters and telephone calls, Sabrina knew now, better than ever, how many little details make up a life—more than could ever be covered from a distance. What was Stephanie doing in her world? What trail was she leaving as Sabrina Longworth that Sabrina would have to follow when she returned? *What is she doing with my life?*

She felt Garth sit down beside her, his arm around her waist. He pulled her to him and kissed her forehead, the corners of her eyes, the tip of her nose. "Good morning," he said again, his voice relaxed. "Can one get into the kitchen to make breakfast?"

Her thoughts were still in Europe. "I don't think we have any orange juice," she said, and was surprised when he laughed and tightened his arm around her. Then it all came back: the orange lake, her laughter, Cliff's grateful look. Her family. This world. Garth. Loving him, wanting him, needing him. One world balanced against another.

Trembling, she leaned back against his arm, and he drew a line of small kisses along her forehead and down her cheek. Within her, a tight knot loosened, and desire flowed through her, insistent, warm and heavy. She raised her face and opened her lips and kissed him for the first time as she wanted to kiss him, deeply, drinking him in, as she wanted to be kissed by him, as she knew now they were meant to kiss each other. He took his arm from her waist and encircled her shoulders, supporting her head as his mouth drove down on hers. With his other hand he pushed aside the film of her nightgown and cupped her full breast, drawing his fingers up along the curve to the nipple, taut beneath his touch.

Sabrina was dizzy, her thoughts spinning away from the hunger of her body. Tears stung her eyes and she pulled back, shaking uncontrollably. "I can't do this!" she cried. *Stephanie, forgive me. I didn't mean to love him.* She shook her head. "I can't. I can't."

"What the hell is the matter with you?" Garth roared.

"Oh, don't!" Penny wailed and Sabrina looked up to see her standing in her bedroom doorway at the other end of the hall. *Too much is going on; how can I make sense of anything?* But Penny's face was twisted with fear and Sabrina went to her. She knelt and put her arms around her.

From below, Cliff shouted, "Is Dad yelling at me? What did I do now?"

"Damn it!" Sabrina exploded. She was still shaking with desire and guilt. "Does everyone have to get in on every act? Isn't anything private in this house?" Penny began to cry, and Sabrina felt the morning slide away from her as she ruined one thing after another. "I'm sorry," she said. She turned and called downstairs, "Nobody's yelling at you, Cliff." She turned back to Penny. "I'm sorry, love. Don't be afraid. Everything is all right. It's all right," she repeated, wondering whether she was reassuring Penny or herself or Garth. "I'll bet we sounded like you and Cliff, didn't we?"

"Daddy sounded so *mad*," Penny said, awed and fearful. "He hardly ever yells at anybody."

Sabrina waited for Garth to say something, but he was silent. He could help me, she thought, but he's too angry. She smiled at Penny. "Well, sometimes you and Cliff sound like you could cheerfully pound each other to a pulp."

A small laugh escaped Penny. Sabrina knew she was thinking that parents aren't supposed to sound like their children, and perhaps she was even thinking of her friends whose parents fought and sometimes divorced.

"Yelling isn't a great thing to do," she said lightly, "but it does clear the lungs for cheering at soccer games." Penny laughed again. "Come on, now. You're not even dressed yet. We have to check on Cliff's scrubbing talents and then eat and get out of here or all the Jonathans will be gone before we get to the orchard."

"Golden Delicious," said Penny automatically. "I told you, that's all they let you pick by now. *You* knew that."

"So far, there is nothing delicious about this morning," Sabrina said, kissing Penny's cheek, "except you. Go on, now; get some clothes on."

After Penny went to her room she remained kneeling, waiting for Garth to tell her, as she had told Penny, that everything was all right. But he sat silently beside the window where she had run away from him. For a long moment they stayed that way, separated by the length of the house and a terrible gulf of misunderstanding. Sabrina looked up and met his eyes. "I'm so sorry," she said. Her words traveled down the hall and touched him with the same tender caution with which her fingers had touched his sleeping face less than an hour earlier.

Garth smiled then, a smile so loving she caught her breath. "It's all right," he said at last, and added, "I thought you might have made up your mind."

Sabrina heard him, but the words made no sense. Made up her mind to what? To make love to him? To tell him why she swung between coldness and warmth? To confess? If he knew or suspected something, why didn't he just say so? "I must get dressed," she said hurriedly and went to their room, closing the door behind her. *I won't think about it now; I'll think about it later. I don't want to know what he meant.* She pulled on a pair of Levi's, a pale yellow Oxford-cloth shirt and a russet boatnecked sweater that made her look, in the full-length mirror, only a few years older than Penny. For the briefest of moments she felt very young—untouched by time and the complicated maneuvering of adults.

She pulled back her heavy auburn hair, tying it at her neck with a brown velvet ribbon. Tendrils at the sides escaped, framing her face with wisps of curls that made her look more like a mischievous gamine than a grown woman.

She looked at the gamine in the mirror and recalled other mirrors, in palaces and estates, where she had dressed in gowns of tulle and lace and silk for Europe's most famous balls, and then had swept down staircases or through great doorways, bringing a hush to the most sophisticated of the world's beautiful people.

Where was she now, that stunning woman? In a three-story frame house in Evanston, Illinois, in faded Levi's and bare feet.

She went to breakfast in bare feet.

On the curved bench at the end of the hall, Garth watched his wife go into their bedroom and close the door; watched her ten minutes later leave the room and, without looking in his direction, go barefoot downstairs. He was amazed at her stubbornness; again and again she refused to let herself settle back comfortably into their marriage. For each step forward, she took half a step back into the hard shell she had worn since her trip.

And what did she expect of him while she huddled inside her shell, refusing to let him join her private debate over leaving him? Was she hoping he would force the issue, demand that they talk about it, make her face her own failures as well as his? Was she waiting for him to tell her, whether she wanted to hear it or not, that he was in love with her almost as if for the first time?

"Daddy!" Penny called, and he went downstairs to breakfast.

The kitchen floor was clean. In a corner, the wastebasket bulged with soggy orange paper towels. Cliff and Penny had set the table, poured glasses of grapefruit juice and piled a plate with doughnuts. The coffee was made. His family was sitting peacefully at the table, smiling at him.

"Have I walked into the wrong kitchen?" he asked. Penny giggled. He raised his juice glass. "To a delicious day."

Sabrina met his eyes. "Thank you," she said softly.

And in the car he felt her relax beside him. "What a nice way to spend a Saturday," she said. As if she had never done it before. And maybe, he thought, she hasn't. Not in this way, caught in her own arguments over her future. Our future, he added silently; I'll have to remind her of that.

In the back seat, Penny and Cliff were competing in identifying approaching cars. Garth was withdrawn in his thoughts. Left to herself, Sabrina watched the passing scene: neatly plowed fields stretching to the horizon; sleek cattle standing or lounging in small groups like guests she had seen at balls clustering with their friends; white farmhouses, cherry-red barns, bright yellow tractors, their colors burned into the blue sky. And around it all, the rich brown of the soil and the brilliance of autumn foliage.

European farms were smaller, older, more weathered. To Sabrina, these American farms radiated expansiveness and endless progress, dominion, from the road to the horizon and beyond. Everything seemed open and free, harmonious, settled, and she wanted to reach out and grasp it, to press it in a scrapbook, to remember.

The apple orchard lay in a countryside of small lakes. The larger ones were surrounded by homes, boat docks and parks, with weekend crowds spilling everywhere. Garth was cursing the traffic; the closer they came to the orchard the longer it took them to reach it. Cliff groaned. "Can we get *out?* We'll race you there. And beat you."

"Better yet," Garth said. "You drive. High time you did the work while I play. Your mother and I will stroll happily to the orchard while you and Penny fight traffic."

"Do you mean it, Dad?" Cliff said eagerly. "Will you let me drive?"

Garth shook his head. "The law says no. When you're fifteen you'll learn in school."

"They never teach anything," Cliff said scornfully.

"If that's true, I'll teach you then, but not before. You'll be behind the wheel soon enough, and your mother and I will be waiting up fretting whenever you're ten minutes late getting home. Don't push time away—for us or yourself."

Their voices seemed far away to Sabrina. *I won't be here when Cliff is fifteen. Garth and I will never stroll happily while Cliff and Penny fight traffic for us.* They'll go on, growing and changing, long after I leave. And—it struck her suddenly—*they won't even know I'm gone.* Garth's wife, Penny and Cliff's mother, would still be part of their lives, their quarrels and jokes and family talks, their waking and sleeping. Their love. Only Sabrina would be gone.

As Garth pulled into the mass of cars in the parking lot, he glanced at her, smiling. Then his face changed. "What is it?"

She shook her head quickly. "Nothing. Shall we go?"

They picked up a bushel basket and walked into the orchard. The air was heavy with the scent of fallen ripe apples carpeting the trampled grass beneath the trees. Above them branches bowed down with the weight of hundreds more, perfect globes ranging from pale yellow-green to deep gold tinged with red. All around them, apple-pickers were filling baskets and plastic bags, but they walked on until they came to a quiet section. Cliff took one look at the gnarled trees and with a whoop of joy leaped up and climbed with sure hands and feet through the tangled leaves and branches. "First cousin to a monkey," said Garth with amusement.

Penny began to follow, but Cliff called down, "Wait; I'll toss you the ones I pick, and then we'll trade places and I'll help you up."

Sabrina was touched. They squabbled, but Stephanie had taught them to share, too. She and Garth watched as they found a rhythm of picking, throwing and catching. "Can we walk awhile?" she asked.

"Nothing better." He took her arm and waved to Cliff in the tree. "We'll be back. If you fill a bushel, start another. The only limit is the number of apples you're willing to peel at home."

Cliff paused, arm outstretched, then nodded. As they walked off, Sabrina heard him say to Penny in awe, "Mom didn't even tell us to be careful."

Garth and Sabrina walked down the path, the trees lush and heavy on either side, sounds of family groups a murmur in the air about them. Dark leaves and yellow apples shone against the deep blue sky; a breeze waved the tendrils of Sabrina's hair. She lifted her face to the sun and took a deep breath. Nothing had happened—nothing exciting, nothing glamorous, nothing that put her in the spotlight of attention among people of wealth and power. Nothing had happened except that she was in love with the man beside her. And she was happy.

The path intersected another that warned against trespassing. Here were rows of Jonathan, McIntosh and Red Delicious trees whose apples were being saved for sale in the orchard store and a final fate as cider and applesauce. "Let's trespass," said Garth. "With respect for the flora and fauna."

Their arms were linked and they walked slowly, warmed by the October sun, breathing the fragrance of apples and clover and cut grass from nearby fields. "You make me wonderfully happy," Garth said quietly. "I don't tell you that often enough."

She looked up at him.

"And," he added, "you are gloriously beautiful. I don't tell you that often enough, either."

She continued to look at him in silence.

He turned her to him and held her face between his hands. He felt her stiffen. "Don't run away, my love. I know what's bothering you and I'm trying not to force you into anything. But you must know that I won't sit by indefinitely—after all, I have a stake in bringing things into the open—"

He was stopped by the alarm in her eyes. Was she afraid of him—or of herself? "Stephanie," he said gently, his words oddly formal because he was being so careful, "I will not hurt you. I would never hurt you. Whatever you decide, I suppose I would have to accept it. But I love you more now than I ever have, and I need you—as, of course, the children do—and it would mean everything to me if you stay with us."

A late red apple fell with a soft plop on the ground near their feet. A dragonfly darted past, its translucent wings glinting in the sun; a chipmunk scattered a mound of dry leaves. Sabrina was silent. Garth's warm hands on her face kept her from turning away, and their eyes met, his probing, hers dark with uncertainty. She was bewildered by much of what he said, but one phrase echoed again and again—*more than I ever have; I love you more now than I ever have.* It reverberated with the desire he had aroused that morning, still pulsing through her body, beating strongly, steadily, glowing in her blood as the melting sun glowed through her eyelids when she closed them.

"Look at me," Garth said roughly, but she shook her head. Whatever he knew, it was not the truth—could not be the truth or he would not have called her Stephanie—but somehow he had come to believe she might leave him and it was true, it was true, though he would never know why, or what it really meant. *My dear love, there is nothing I can tell you.*

He dropped his hands. Her face felt cold and naked, as cold as Garth's bleak look when she opened her eyes. She searched for words to recapture the harmony of a few minutes before, but there was nothing to say. "We should turn back—the children—"

"Soon," he said shortly, and turned onto another path. Sabrina kept pace with him. "We owe each other some time," he said casually. "When did we last go away together?"

"I don't know," she answered, grateful for the chance to tell a simple truth.

"This week, then. I meant to tell you, I finally accepted Kallen's invitation to visit Foster Labs. We'll fly out Tuesday morning, stay in New York that night and come back on Wednesday."

Sabrina reacted automatically. "No." When he frowned, she fumbled for reasons. "The children. My job. My wrist. The money."

He ticked them off. "The kids will stay with Vivian; I've already asked her. Your antiques got along without you for a hundred years; they'll manage another two days. You told me the cast comes off Monday. Foster is paying the whole tab, including the hotel in New York. Look, you've pushed me for months to take this job. That's why I said we'd go."

Sabrina picked up an apple and polished it on her sleeve. It was perfect, without a bruise or soft spot. She bit into the flesh, its sharp tang crisp on her tongue. To travel with Garth, to be alone with him—*Oh, I'd love it,* she had thought when he asked her to join him in Berkeley. But how could she travel with Garth? How many intimacies could she share with him and keep on rejecting him?

But she could not tell him to forget the job when Stephanie so desperately wanted him to take it, and she'd even promised Stephanie she'd try to convince him to visit Stamford. So, reluctantly, she nodded. She would go with him to Connecticut. He put his arm around her as they turned to go back to Penny and Cliff. "It's about time we had a chance to be alone," he said, "and find out who we really are."

Chapter 16

Nathan Goldner snapped the X-ray into place on the illuminated panel and stood back so Sabrina could view it with him. "Couldn't be better," he said. "You can go back to beating Garth and the kids and whipping up your famous cakes. Now let's get that cast off."

He bent over Sabrina's arm, then looked up. "No cries of joy at getting back your very own wrist?"

She smiled faintly, locked in her thoughts, seeing in her mind not her left wrist lying on the table, still encased in plaster, but two left wrists, healthy and identical: Stephanie's and Sabrina's wrists, once again interchangeable. "Stephanie?" Nat said. "Are you all right?"

I'm fine; that's the trouble. "I'm sorry, Nat. I was thinking of three bushels of Golden Delicious apples at home. If you could leave the cast on for a few more weeks, I could delegate the pies and strudel and applesauce to the rest of the family."

A joke: "If you could leave the cast on for a few more weeks . . ." Would she like that? As much as she missed London and wondered what was happening to her other life, would she like a few more weeks? She didn't know. That was the crazy part: she really didn't know. But what difference did it make? She had no choice.

317

But to Nat it was a joke. "Condemned to strudel," he said, and bent once again to cut open the cast.

When it was off, Sabrina saw her arm white and frail, newborn. "Should I keep it bandaged? Or not use it too much?"

He shook his head. "Can't get out of it, Stephanie. You can peel apples from now until Christmas, or move all the furniture in that shop where you work. In fact, use the wrist as much as possible, to strengthen the muscles. The bone is even stronger now than before."

I'm stronger than before, she said to herself as she went to her car. She thought of Garth. And more easily hurt.

She was taking the morning off from work, and, at home, she opened the patio door to let in the breeze and the spicy fragrance of late roses still blooming against the house. She gazed thoughtfully at the three heaping baskets standing in a row next to the back door where Garth had set them down the evening before. I should do something with them, she thought. Make a dent, at least.

Instead, she made a cup of coffee and sat at the table. Her wrist felt strange in the warm air. She flexed it—how weightless it was!—picked up her cup, pressed the bones, testing for pain. Nothing. She was cured. Sabrina Longworth, in one piece again, ready to take on the world. And then the telephone rang.

She knew it was Stephanie before she picked it up. "Sabrina," said Stephanie in a rush, her voice a little breathless. "How are you? How are Penny and Cliff?"

"Wonderful." Sabrina was puzzled. Not only breathless, she thought. Wary. As if she's afraid of what I might say. "We went apple-picking, and they turned into a couple of harvesting machines. Stephanie, what do I do with three bushels of apples?"

Stephanie's laugh had a wistful note that Sabrina caught instantly. "They always get carried away. How come you didn't tell them to stop?"

"We weren't there—"

"Weren't there?"

"We went for a walk. I . . . didn't feel like picking, the cast was clumsy, so we let them do the work."

There was a brief silence. "How is Garth?"

"Fine. He's . . . fine. I told you last week, he's spending more time at home, and that makes Penny and Cliff happy. We're all . . . fine."

"And?"

Sabrina took a deep breath. "And this morning I had—"

"No, I was asking about Garth. I was wondering if maybe, when he got back from California, he might have wanted to make love. Sort of a welcome home."

Her voice was different again, as if she was trying to put distance between them. Sabrina was uneasy. "Is that what he used to do?"

"Yes. And he did this time, didn't he? It's all right, you know. You can do what you want. It's too much to expect someone to live a whole life without doing . . . some things that are . . . different. After all, five weeks is a long time . . ."

Her voice trailed away, and suddenly Sabrina understood. Who's the man? she wondered. It must have happened very suddenly. "It isn't so long," she said cautiously. "A lot has been going on—"

"He did want to, didn't he? Sabrina, how many times have you and Garth made love? Five? Ten? How many? *Don't lie to me.*"

"Once," said Sabrina, stung, her guilt rushing back. She heard Stephanie take a sharp breath. "The night before he went to California. I couldn't avoid it. But, Stephanie, it had no meaning. It—didn't mean anything at all."

"It did to Garth." Sabrina said nothing. Sighing, Stephanie curled up on the chaise in her bedroom, wishing she had someone to talk to. Gaby would be back soon, but she couldn't talk to her. Or anyone else. Not even her sister, who had made love to her husband.

"I hate this," she said, but she didn't mean Garth and Sabrina as much as she meant her own wild swings of emotions. She had called to tell Sabrina about the cruise. Hearing about apple-picking, she wanted to be home. When Sabrina admitted making love to Garth, she wanted Max.

"I know you hate it," Sabrina answered. "But I didn't seduce him, you know. I just happen to sleep in a bed that happens to be his. I wouldn't even have told you—"

"Why not? Do you think it makes any difference to me? You can make love to Garth all you want."

"I don't need to have you offer me your husband," Sabrina

said coldly. "It only happened once, and I won't let it happen again. Not because of you, but so I can live with myself."

"Sabrina, wait, don't be angry. I'm sorry; I didn't mean . . . Sabrina, listen, I feel so far away; nothing I do here has anything to do with that life, and I get confused. Sabrina? Are you there?"

"Yes. I'm listening. What's wrong, Stephanie?"

Stephanie heard the love in Sabrina's voice and wanted to tell her everything, but her thoughts were too tangled to sort out. "I don't know. . . . Jitters, I guess, because sometimes I don't know who I really want to be. No, that's not true—of course I know. All this will pass as soon as I'm back where I belong, but—it's hard to describe. So many odd feelings."

In the noon sunlight of the breakfast room, Sabrina ran her finger along a scratch in the round table and gazed at a dead leaf dangling from an avocado plant that Penny refused to throw away. As clearly as she could see the table and the plant, she could picture each room at Cadogan Square; she could feel their quiet serenity and privacy, the beauty she had created.

Absentmindedly, she bent down and picked up a baseball trading card Cliff had dropped. She put it on the sideboard, thinking that she'd forgotten to take the pot roast out of the freezer for dinner. "I know," she said. "I'm going through the same things you are."

"In Evanston?" Stephanie asked, with such genuine surprise that Sabrina laughed in a rush of love for her sister.

"Even in Evanston," she said. "A lot goes on here."

"Yes, indeed," Stephanie said flatly. "You told me."

All right, Sabrina thought. It's over. I don't know why she hasn't asked about the X-ray—she knew it was supposed to be today—but I have to tell her and then get out. It doesn't matter whether I want to or not; it's her family and I'm the destructive outsider.

"Stephanie, I had an appointment with—"

"We've been busy at Ambassadors," Stephanie interrupted.

"Oh, have you? What did you sell?"

"The Petuntse porcelain you bought in China." Stephanie's voice was elated. "It arrived three days ago, and before Brian and I even had it all unpacked a salesman from Bonn bought it—Brooks sent him over. And a lawyer from Manchester bought the Grendly daybed, the mahogany one with scrolls. Oh, and Lady Stargrave came in—she wants a Chippendale lacquered cabinet for her new town house. I said I'd get it, but I don't know where."

"Thomas Strang may have one in his shop. He bought two last year. If not, he'll probably have a Gillows, and Bettina would be satisfied with that; they're so similar in technique she'll never know the difference. But I can—"

"I'll call him," Stephanie said, and raced on. "Gabrielle is fine, though she moons around like a teenager about Brooks and won't go out with anyone else. I thought I'd ask her to help Brian in the shop while I'm away."

Silence. "While you're what?"

"Just for a few days. Sabrina, I've met someone—not the kind of man I'd want to be with for a long time, but exciting, and different from anyone I've ever known, and enormously wealthy." She laughed lightly. "The perfect fantasy. He wants me to go on a cruise in the Mediterranean for four or five days, on his yacht, and I've decided to go. It's just this once, this one chance, and I don't want to turn it down."

That's why you forced me to say Garth and I had made love. You wanted to know; you wanted the excuse. And that's why you're not letting me tell you about my wrist. Quiet Stephanie, who had worried about being overshadowed; cautious Stephanie, afraid to take risks, who had met Garth so early and married and settled down—and now was having a daring romance. Sabrina smiled to herself at the twist their lives had taken. I'm having *my* daring romance, she thought, because I met Garth so late.

But—a cruise, a yacht, the Mediterranean. That was Sabrina's world, and thinking of it triggered her appetite as no other memory could. She knew those cruises: self-contained worlds of luxury and sensuality cut off from time and space. A blinding white yacht cutting through a blue-green sea, hazy islands like mirages on the horizon, molten sun, cool staterooms, and dark, dreamlike sex weaving through the days and nights. *Oh, I miss it, I miss it, I need it.*

"But you've done all that," Stephanie said, as if she heard Sabrina's thoughts. "And you will again. This is my only chance."

"A last fling?"

"A last fling." It was a promise, made to both of them.

Sabrina took a deep breath. Another week. Another week with Garth. "Who's the man?" she asked casually.

Stephanie hesitated. "Max Stuyvesant."

"No."

"Don't be so quick. He's changed. Even Alexandra says so. Anyway, when did you see him last? He's been in New York for three years."

"Alexandra says he's changed?"

"She says he's mellowed. Like a ripe pear."

Sabrina laughed. "That sounds like Alexandra. Stephanie, you can't know much about Max. Did you ask Alexandra about him?"

"I didn't need to. I decorated his house. Top to bottom. The way you did Alexandra's. I didn't tell you because I was afraid I'd fail and have to bring in someone to rescue me. But I didn't. Sabrina, I know all I need to know about Max. I'm not asking for permission, you know; I've already said I'd go with him. And you're hardly in a position to tell me to stay out of his bed."

"I don't deserve that." *Don't you? You're in love with her husband.*

"I suppose not," said Stephanie carelessly. "What's the real reason you don't want me to go? It can't be Max. Are you so bored you can't wait to get back? It's only a few more days, you know. And it's not as if I'm asking a favor; we don't have any choice. Do we, Sabrina? Nat hasn't taken the final X-rays, has he?"

She wants me to lie. "No. No, he hasn't. He changed it to the end of this week. About the time you get back from your fling."

"Well, then, everything is fine, isn't it? I'm not making you wait any longer at all. I'll get my plane ticket for next Monday. Sabrina . . . don't be angry with me. I need you. I know I'm going back, and I'll live in my house and take care of my children and try to work things out with Garth, and everything will be all right. I just can't picture myself at home yet. I'll be able to later, after the cruise. And I'll have your help, won't I? Because I guess by now there are things you can tell *me* about my family so I can take over again. I will have your help, won't I, Sabrina?"

Sabrina was crying. "Yes. Any way I can." She closed her eyes, blotting out the sun. She could hear the strain in Stephanie's voice and knew she was dreading coming back as much as she was anticipating it. But it didn't matter. Whatever happened between Stephanie and Garth, Sabrina would have disappeared and it would be Stephanie who was in Garth's arms, a world away from Max and his yacht. And Stephanie would have forgotten the fantasy of that yacht long before Sabrina had stopped aching for Garth.

Next Monday. But until then, let Stephanie have her cruise, her fling. I owe it to her. Let her go without knowing about the trip to Connecticut, without knowing that the cast is off. Let her go. There is plenty of time for the truth.

Sabrina watched Chicago tilt below them as the plane climbed through the early-morning haze and banked to the east. Lake Michigan glittered below, the skyscrapers of the city clustered on its shore. She could make out Evanston and the university campus, the green expanse and turning leaves of Lincoln Park, the wall of high-rise apartments along the pale ribbon of beaches lapped by long, slow waves. A few hardy sailors had their boats out, tall white sails snapping and billowing above the water striped blue and green beneath sunlight and shifting clouds.

"The end of the season," Garth said, looking with her out the window. He put his arm around her. "What a lovely autumn we've had."

She held out her wrist, flexed the hand with its gold wedding band. "A strange autumn."

Her burnished hair curled against his shoulder; the perfect curve of her cheek, her clear skin and long curved eyelashes were inches from his lips as his arm held her. He thought back to last year when they had flown together to Amsterdam and she had gone on by herself to London to visit her sister. Had they spent any time together on that trip? He couldn't remember. Probably not. They hadn't done many things together in those days. Why not? He looked at the beautiful woman beside him and could not think of an answer.

They had climbed above the clouds. Below them, moving with them on the white landscape, was a perfect circle of a rainbow with the shadow of their plane in the center. "It's called a pilot's halo," Garth said when she pointed it out to him.

"Are we in the middle of a rainbow, too?"

"Not that I know of. Why?"

"I was wondering if our plane might look like a shadow in-

323

side a rainbow to the people in another plane, far above us."

He chuckled. "You think we might be only shadows, then?"

"If we were, I wonder if we'd know it."

He put his lips to her hair. "I wouldn't care, as long as you were this real to me."

Sabrina was silent. Garth took his arm from her shoulders and opened his book to read; a minute later she did the same. When they had landed in New York and were in the limousine Foster Laboratories had sent to drive them to Stamford, he said wryly, "My first trip with my wife in over a year, and I have to spend the day with a bunch of pharmaceutical executives. Doesn't make sense."

"I have to spend it with their wives," she countered. "Does that make more sense?"

"No. Shall we run away? Go back to New York and have our own holiday and forget all about Stamford?"

"We can't."

"No." His voice changed. "Of course not. I forgot how important this is to you."

It's important to Stephanie. "I meant that we'd accepted their invitation and they've made plans for us. Garth, what am I going to do with all those wives?"

"Nothing. Just follow them around. They're the ones with something to do—entertain you, I gather, and make you think Stamford is the earthly Garden of Eden so you can't wait to move there."

"But I have no idea how to behave with them."

"Any way you want."

"Garth, what do *you* want? I can be wide-eyed and eager, or cold and disdainful, or cool but friendly—what would you like?"

"Look, my love, you're not playing a role. I just want you to be yourself."

She looked at him, her lips slightly parted. "I'll do my best."

There were three of them waiting in the president's reception room when the limousine pulled up to the executive headquarters of Foster Laboratories in Stamford, a town much like Evanston, some thirty miles from New York. The steel and glass building rose from a marble plaza floating in a sea of grass with fountains, groves of pine trees and undulating chrysanthemum beds lining the half-mile-long driveway.

The women wore wool suits, blue and brown and green.

They stood in a row in the huge, rosewood-paneled reception room, sinking slightly into the wool pile beneath their feet. Nearby, massive suede couches curved around a glass table resting on chromium scrolls. Here and there on the expanse of carpet stood illuminated lucite pillars with objects displayed inside them like rare jewels: hypodermic needles, time capsules, packets of pills, bottles of colored liquid.

The women gave Sabrina and Garth time to be awed by the dazzling scene. Garth said nothing. Sabrina knew he was unimpressed by carefully staged grandeur; in fact, he barely noticed it. He was more interested in a well-equipped laboratory, or even the inner workings of their new food processor, than in all the rosewood in Connecticut.

But she knew their hostesses expected the Andersens to be overwhelmed, so she turned her head to take in the entire room. "Grand," she murmured. "Opulent."

The women smiled and held out their hands to her, with sidelong glances at Garth, who turned out to be younger and far more handsome than expected. When he was whisked away by their dark-suited husbands, they concentrated on Sabrina. "We meet again," said one. "Welcome to Stamford."

It took Sabrina by surprise. Stephanie hadn't visited Stamford. This woman must have been in Evanston, then. Why hadn't Garth mentioned it? "We're glad to be here," she said, but there had been a perceptible pause.

"Too many new faces," said another of the women casually, coming to Sabrina's aid. "Of course you remember Irma Kallen—"

"President," Irma Kallen put in quickly.

"From the time she was passing through Chicago on her way to Los Angeles," went on Sabrina's savior, supplying details. "And I'm Freddie Payne, vice president, finance."

"Angie Warner," chimed the third, "vice president, manufacturing."

This time Sabrina was quicker, understanding that they were identifying themselves with their husband's titles. She smiled. "Stephanie Andersen, professor." Freddie Payne grinned but shook her head slightly in warning. Bad beginning, Sabrina thought. Try again. "We've been so looking forward to our visit."

"Ah," said Irma Kallen. "We wondered. It has been postponed so many times."

"We want you to love our town," Angie Warner said quickly. Short and plump, she had the angelic face and rosebud mouth of a peacemaker. "We want you to love us. We thought a short tour on the way to lunch at Irma's, and then a visit to the school and the Women's Club, if that seems all right ... if that pleases you ..."

Sabrina bowed her head in agreement. How could she disagree with Angie Warner? Or, at the moment, with any of them? Their husbands earned upwards of three hundred thousand dollars a year; her husband earned thirty-five thousand. On their home ground, using their yardsticks of power and prestige, Sabrina was at a distinct disadvantage. She told herself to remember it.

Irma Kallen led the way to her car, a Silver Shadow that glided through wide, peaceful streets past churches two centuries old and a village green where a battle of the Revolutionary War had been fought. She pulled into the driveway of a three-story brick mansion with newly added rooms jutting out on all sides—like a demented chicken flapping its wings, Sabrina thought. She had taken a strong dislike to Irma Kallen. But she's the president's wife, she told herself. Show respect.

Irma Kallen was tall and angular, long-chinned, with brown eyes that went in two directions, each unconcerned with what the other chose to look at. This caused difficulties for those around her who never knew which eye to meet in conversation. Sabrina chose the left and found herself in focus about half the time. Such a woman, whose looks made others nervous, and whose temper was short, would not take kindly to a visitor who was not only young and beautiful but also made light of her husband's title and, worse, forgot a previous meeting.

But Irma Kallen had a magnificent home, decorated with sophisticated imagination. Sabrina walked through the rooms, impressed with the blend of two styles of simplicity: spare Shaker furniture and the more massive but still simple turn-of-the-century oak pieces of Philip Webb, stained with the green that was his trademark and decorated with lacquered leather or raised silver designs. She ran her hand over the delicate tracery on the piano. "Webb," she murmured. "How marvelous."

326

Irma looked startled and pleased. For a moment both eyes focused on Sabrina. "How did you know that?"

"I know furniture," said Sabrina. "I work with antiques."

"Oh," cried Angie Warner, "then you'll love Silvermine." Sabrina looked a question. "An artists' colony in Norwalk. Just a few miles away. We go there for shopping and lunch at least once a week."

Freddie Payne chuckled. "I have a feeling Stephanie is way ahead of Silvermine. She probably knows more than anyone there. Even more than you, Irma."

Sabrina looked alert. A private war. She had seen a skirmish earlier, in the car. "It's Frederique," Freddie had said, explaining her name. She was tall and striking, with thick black hair cut bluntly and heavy-lidded hazel eyes beneath dark brows. "Frederique, from some unknown French ancestor. But that doesn't go over big in Stamford. One does better as a Pilgrim. Irma is a Pilgrim, aren't you, Irma? Or rather, since even Irma is not that well preserved, more likely one of her pirate ancestors was." Irma ignored her.

At lunch, angelic Angie worked at keeping the peace between Irma and Freddie. The women held the rank of their husbands, so Irma, as president, was clearly chief officer of the meal and of their entire social life; but she often allowed Angie to smooth edges made jagged by her temper.

Sabrina ate her broiled grapefruit and turkey Florentine and watched with amusement the same kind of small, swift, daggers-drawn drama she was used to among her circles in London. Of course, she thought, it exists everywhere, even in Evanston. But I never thought about it because I never thought of Evanston as anything but temporary.

Nothing with Garth is permanent.

She felt the familiar stab of pain at the thought. Irma's voice broke through. "What?" Sabrina said. "I'm sorry; I was thinking of something else."

"I said," Irma rapped out, "we've planned a small dinner for this evening, at the club, so that you and your husband can meet all of us. You should know that we are a close-knit group. Many of the men in Stamford commute to New York, but we feel our duty is here. Foster is Stamford's most prestigious institution, and those of us who are its leaders are also leaders of the community. We strengthen Stamford; we do not take our money to New York. This is a responsibility we bear gladly, but it is effective only if we stay together. Freddie thinks this is foolish—she has a number of strange friends—"

"Whose husbands aren't executives," Freddie said solemnly to Sabrina.

"But Freddie never wanders too far," Irma continued. "Because we all need each other, as you will discover when your husband joins us. And with our help you will learn quickly how to be one of us. The fact that you have much to learn need not embarrass you. Coming from the Midwest you could not be expected to know our ways."

Sabrina listened, wide-eyed and silent, as Irma went on. "Our way of life filters slowly to the rest of the country. Often, of course, by the time others pattern themselves after us, we have developed new styles."

Angie looked embarrassed; Freddie winked at Sabrina. Sabrina looked steadily at Irma's precise mouth. "We take as our model the cultured centers of Europe. We dine later, for example, than you do: eight o'clock; even, on occasion, nine. Six o'clock, of course, is proper for the children. We do not eat in backyards; we do not barbecue our food in clouds of foul smoke. We do not wear one-piece clothes such as jumpsuits and overalls. We support the public schools as essential to our town, but we do not send our children to them. You have children, of course."

"Two," Sabrina said automatically. She was fascinated, almost mesmerized, by Irma's chant. "A boy and a girl."

"And you are raising them as good Christians."

"I think we are raising Cliff to be a soccer forward," said Sabrina. "We're not sure yet about Penny."

Freddie burst into laughter; Angie giggled. Irma seemed frozen, coffee cup raised halfway to her mouth. "Those of us who are blessed with material wealth take our responsibilities seriously."

"It's all right, Stephanie," Angie said brightly, aware that Irma was making a fool of herself. Angie didn't know exactly what it was—maybe the way Stephanie identified the Webb piano, or her steady, unimpressed gaze on Irma's face, or the regal way she held her head. Or her beauty, which Angie envied simply and good-naturedly, the way she envied one woman's cooking or another's needlepoint. Whatever it was, Angie knew Stephanie was no country girl, and she didn't want her to judge them by Irma's treating her like one. "Irma's always serious with new people, but in our group she's lots of fun. She plays tennis, and I really have to work to keep up with her, and sometimes we get her on the volleyball court. Not often," she added with sad honesty, "but sometimes."

"We don't play too much volleyball in the Midwest," Sabrina said earnestly, leaning forward and addressing Irma's left eye. "Though progress has brought tennis right to our doorstep. But we do work hard to learn how to be sophisticated. Some of us occasionally wear Karl Lagerfeld or Perry Ellis designs. Now and then we serve wine with dinner—Montrachet, or perhaps a Brouilly if red seems appropriate. And lately our more daring hostesses have begun serving the salad after the entrée rather than before. Of course we have to work very hard at it. But you may be sure we are grateful for all you allow us to learn from you."

There was a long silence. Angie tried to smile, but her lips were trembling. Freddie said, "Well, I'll be damned. Over to you, Irma. On second thought, never mind." She turned to Sabrina. "Irma told us you were a shy little housewife from the sticks. Irma, love, you must send your first impressions to bed without any dinner. They have failed you badly." She pushed back her chair. "Stephanie, let's look at the terrace."

Sabrina sat still. *Damn. Oh, damn. What is wrong with me? Stephanie would have worried about Garth; she would have been quiet and sweet and let the president's wife feel superior. Now I've messed it up. Stephanie would have acted for Garth. I acted for myself. Why in heaven's name did I let this silly woman get to me?*

"Stephanie?" Freddie said. Sabrina excused herself and followed her through the folding doors. The two women sat on a low brick wall surrounding the flagstone terrace. Huge redwood planters with late roses and asters stood beside white wrought-iron furniture not yet stored for the winter. Beyond the wall a crew of gardeners raked fallen leaves and planted bulbs for next spring's tulips and hyacinths. Another crew was fitting a tarpaulin over the swimming pool while a third rolled up the nets in the tennis courts. It was a peaceful scene of abundance—so perfect, Sabrina thought, it might have been staged to illustrate the benefits of joining the Foster team.

"She can be harmful, but not really dangerous," Freddie

said. "Unless you give her that power. The trick is to understand that she is a fool who must be taken seriously."

Sabrina shrugged. "I would only take her seriously if Garth asked me to."

Freddie was surprised. "Why else are you here?"

"To look around. To be looked at. Why do you all assume it's settled? Isn't there any room for doubt?"

"Look, sweetie, I don't know what your husband told you, but he is not here for an interview. This is a formal session for the men to work out the details of the job, and for us to make sure your little heart flutters with delight at becoming one of us. From what I've heard, you're moving here when the current school quarter ends."

Sabrina felt betrayed. Garth hadn't told her it was decided. Would he really take the job without talking it over with her? They always talked things over.

"Hey," Freddie said. "It's okay. Ignore Irma. She's a small piece of the scenery. Though I suggest, to make things easier when you move here, that you revive the act you put on for her in Chicago. You'll have a few required exercises: dinner parties with the correct guests, a few luncheons, sponsorship of a couple of charity affairs and some command appearances at Irma's parties—you do have to get along with her. But the rest of the time you can be yourself. As long as you're discreet, you can be anything you want, with anyone you want. It's not a bad way of life, you know."

"I know." Sabrina stood and brushed off her skirt. Stephanie could manage it; she could be what Irma expected, without getting angry but also without sinking into their little group as Angie, and even Freddie, had done. Stephanie could have a good time here.

She thanked Freddie. "You rescued me twice; I'm very grateful. But now I think I'd better mend my own fences." And returning to the dining room she made her apologies. "So rude of me . . . too many new impressions . . . lunch was delicious . . . the conversation so pleasant . . ."

Irma put a hand to her perfectly smooth hair and smoothed it. "We accept your apology. My husband thinks your husband will be a great asset to the Laboratories. Shall we have our little tour now?"

They drove through the town, inspected the new high school, visited the hospital where Irma was director of volunteers, parked along the shore of Long Island Sound and watched sailboats that made Sabrina think of home. Then they returned to the headquarters of Foster Laboratories and picked up Garth and the husbands of Sabrina's hostesses and went to dine at the club, so Sabrina and Garth could meet the people they were supposed to know.

Later, in the limousine taking them to the Plaza Hotel in New York, where they would spend the night before catching a morning plane to Chicago, Garth took Sabrina's hand. "Wined and dined and flattered. Duck for lunch. What did you have?"

"Turkey. Dried out, then drowned in sauce."

"And lobster for dinner. What was that we had for dessert?"

"Hazelnut mousse with raspberry puree."

"Do you suppose professors eat this way whenever they come to Connecticut?"

"Do you suppose their wives get a lecture on how retarded Midwesterners can learn the high style of the East Coast whenever they come to Connecticut?"

"Intriguing. Who gave the lecture?"

She described the lunch, sparing herself nothing. "I didn't do you any good at all. But if Freddie was right and you've already decided—"

"I haven't." He was still holding her hand; he put his other hand over it and faced her. "I agreed to come out here because I thought it was necessary for us. I would never make the decision without you. It occurs to me," he went on carefully, "that by letting Irma Kallen have it with both barrels, you may have been saying you didn't want me to take the job."

Sabrina closed her eyes. All the lies, all the deceptions, all the guilt and tangled feelings of the past five weeks piled up between them in a wall she could not break down. *My love, I want to help you. I want you to be happy. But I owe this to Stephanie.* Her hand was warm between his. "Garth, it's your decision. I can't make it for you."

Tired and depressed, he took his hands from hers. If she no longer cared what he did, she was not planning a future with him. Yet she loved him. He had seen it in her face, heard it in her voice. She loved him.

But still she shut him out. So often they had come close to warmth, to love, to shared feelings—and she had pulled back, turned away. All those lost opportunities to talk. As if she were afraid that if she listened to him she might be swayed, by his arguments or her own feelings, and not be able to make her own decision to go or to stay.

How the hell did a man fight that? For, of course, he intended to fight. He had told her in the orchard he would accept her decision, but that was absurd. He would fight to keep her. But until he understood why she deliberately withdrew from him, why she refused to make love to him, why she had even relaxed her close vigilance of the children, he could not decide how to begin—or foresee how it would end.

They made the rest of the trip in silence, and in silence rode the hotel elevator to the suite that had been reserved for them. Sabrina stood at the window looking on either side of the leafy darkness of Central Park at the lighted windows of buildings that never slept.

Garth locked the door. "I don't want the job," he said abruptly. On a round table a bottle of champagne nestled in a bucket of ice; a card around its neck wished them a pleasant evening from the Kallens. Garth eased the cork out with his thumbs. "Even if it means lobster every night and champagne at bedtime."

"Why not?" she asked.

He filled two tall, slender glasses and handed one to her. "How long has it been since you and I were in a hotel room?" he wondered aloud.

We have never been in a hotel room. She sat at one end of a striped silk couch. "A long time. Why don't you want the job?"

"Because the only subjects my hosts talked about today were the market, the consumer, dollars-per-research-hour, return on investment. Because to them gene splicing means a product, as if I'd be directing a team of chefs inventing a new breakfast cereal. Because what they want to do is what they are supposed to do: make money. Because what I want to do is what the university expects me to do: research and teach. Because I don't want to have to explain why I'm following a promising new lead in research even though it might not result in a product for years—if ever. Because I can't look at the problems of genetics and see the bottom line of a corporate profit and loss statement. Because, damn it, I don't belong there. More champagne? It's on the house."

She held out her glass. He refilled it and sat in a wing chair near the other end of the couch.

"Two other points," he said. "One, as I said before, I don't think you belong there, either. Maybe you did once, or thought you did, but not anymore. If this were two or three months ago you wouldn't have jumped on Irma Kallen; when she was in Chicago last spring you treated her like a first cousin to Queen Elizabeth. You've changed since then. You've changed since your trip." He paused, waiting, but she ignored the opening he offered.

Garth could not bear to look at her. He had never been so aware of her nearness—or of how far from him she went when she withdrew into silence. He drained his glass. "And one of the changes I like best is that you can put down a pompous, small-town queen mother like Irma Kallen without being afraid that she won't like you, or me, afterward. Which means one of two things. You have a lot more confidence than you've ever had before . . ."

Sabrina watched the bubbles streaming upward in her glass. "Or?"

"Or you've decided you don't give a damn what I do or what happens to me. Or us."

The room was hushed. Soft light from the table lamp glinted off melting ice in the champagne bucket and the dark green bottle as Garth tilted it above their glasses. The rest of the room was in shadow. A doorway led to the bedroom, where a single lamp illuminated the bed, turned down for the night by a maid who had left a gold-wrapped chocolate centered on each pillow. Nearby, their two overnight bags stood side by side, touching, like lovers.

They had not been alone, away from the children, in the five weeks Sabrina had been there. In the muffled quiet she was conscious of Garth's presence with such force that her skin felt his touch though he was a dozen feet away. She saw each detail of his face though she was not looking at him. Her mouth felt his mouth on hers though they had not kissed for three days, since the moment in the hallway at home when she had broken from his arms in a panic of love and guilt.

He has become a part of me.

"And finally," he said when she did not answer, "I have been offered the directorship of the Institute of Genetic Engineering at Midwestern, to be built this spring and in operation by next year."

"Garth!" She looked up, her eyes shining. "But that's wonderful! It should have been your first reason—your only reason! Nothing else matters. Does it?"

"It might."

"Why didn't you tell me? Oh, now I know what Vivian was talking about when I took Penny and Cliff over there yesterday. She said to give you her congratulations. I thought she was talking about your committee granting her tenure, that you'd won. But she wasn't; she knew about your appointment."

"She knew I'd been offered the position. I haven't taken it."

"But why not? Isn't it everything you want?"

"I don't know if it's what you want. The pay is about two-thirds of what Foster would pay, much less when you add bonuses, stock options, travel, company car, country club membership—all the perks that universities never heard of. I know how worried you've been about money—worried enough, probably, to make Irma Kallen tolerable."

"But all those reasons you gave for not—"

"I said I don't want to take it. But if you want me to, if you would share it with me—"

"But you would hate it."

He shrugged. "A lot of it. I'd concentrate on the research and learn to deal with the rest of it." He leaned forward in his chair. "Stephanie. Listen to me. I love you. I can't imagine making a life without you. Nothing I do means a damn thing if I can't bring it home to you—if I can't say your name and hear you answer—if I can't go to sleep at night knowing that when I open my eyes in the morning I'll find you next to me. All the wonder of my work disappears when I look at the wonder of you. The discoveries are there, even the excitement is there, but it's empty, it doesn't mean a damn thing to me without you. I am not complete without you. Don't you understand that? Don't you understand that I would do anything to keep your life woven into mine? If you ask me to take this job—"

"I wouldn't. I don't want you to take it. Of course I don't want you to take it."

He looked at her somberly. "I don't know what that means."

It means I love you. I love you. I want you to be happy. I want you to do what is best for you even if I'm gone, even if I'll never share it, never be with you when you wake up in the morning.

He watched her lips move silently and tears fill her eyes. He stirred, wanting to go to her, but he forced himself to wait. "I don't know what your tears mean, either," he said harshly.

Sabrina put her hands over her face and let the tears come. She had been holding them back for so long that now they came with relief and a kind of exhilaration. *I can't help it, I'm sorry, I can't help it. I can only do so much. And I did try.*

"What do they mean?" he repeated. He went to her and pulled away her hands. Her face was wet with tears and her mouth trembled; her eyes were shining as they had been on that morning when he awakened and caught her in an unguarded moment.

"That I love you," she said at last, the words finally freed, and his arms caught her up, enfolding her in an embrace so confident she felt she had at last come home.

He would have picked her up, but she shook her head. She would share this with him; her decision as well as his. They walked to the bedroom and undressed each other, hurrying, touching the skin they bared as children explore a new discovery to make sure it is real, and really theirs.

Garth removed the ivory combs in her hair and the heavy waves fell over her shoulders, bronze in the dim light. He looked at her slender body and passed his hands along the clear, silken skin as if he had never seen it before. Her ripe fullness lifted toward him, her head high and proud as he gazed at her. *I am a part of us,* her eyes said, *and my beauty is greater because you desire me.*

Once again he gathered her into his arms, her softness curving against the muscles of his arms and stomach and legs, the warmth of her body merging into his. They held each other, treasuring their desire, for now they knew it would be fulfilled. At last he bent his head to her uplifted face and kissed her, tasting the coolness of champagne in the warmth of her mouth.

"Dear love," Sabrina whispered against his lips. They lay on the bed, Garth's full weight upon her. He raised his head and his eyes, dark and intense, met hers, deeper than he had ever imagined, with a blue flame in their depths.

"My love," he murmured. "My dearest, newfound love." The room was bright from the luster of her body. He closed his eyes, but the brightness was still there and he knew then that it was everywhere, that in rediscovering his wife he had discovered light and life, and they were part of him, as she was.

"Yes," she said, and with the passion they had denied for so long he thrust into her. She moved against him, enclosing him, her bones against his, her skin against his, one body, one rush of blood.

This is where I belong, she thought, and then she let go of the solid room, let go of herself, and disappeared in the darkness of sensation, her mind finally stilled, nothing left but feeling and an overwhelming gratitude for what she was discovering of herself and of him in their flesh, the meeting of their mouths and the worlds they saw in each other's eyes.

The gilt-wrapped chocolate lay crushed on the pillow. Carefully, Garth unwrapped it, and Sabrina took it into her mouth from his hand. "Where is yours?" she asked, and they hunted until they found the other on the floor where it had fallen.

"But I'm still hungry," he said after nibbling it from her fingers. "What shall we demand of room service?"

"Nectar. Robins' eggs. Rose petals with dew."

Garth dialed. "Champagne; omelet; salad. And grapefruit sorbet."

Sabrina was laughing. "Grapefruit sorbet?"

"I forgot to tell you. A new passion I discovered in California. Robins' eggs take half an hour. I would like to make love to you again."

"Yes." *These are our years together; these hours. They are all we have.* Garth bent over her, kissing her mouth, but she put her hands on his chest, pushing him firmly until he lay back, and then she was kissing him, her lips trembling along his throat and through the dark hairs of his chest, slipping softly, lingeringly over his smooth, flat stomach. She curled up beside him, her hands on his thighs, and raised her head for a moment, meeting the darkness of his gaze, telling him, with her eyes and her strong hands, to lie still and let her give him pleasure. Languidly, with her tongue, she caressed the tip of his penis extended before her, and then she brought him slowly into her mouth, along her tongue, into her throat. He filled her: smooth, firm, a strong, solid force pulsing with life, and Sabrina felt an exaltation, a freedom, a kind of love and giving she had never known before.

Garth groaned with the waves of pleasure that flowed through him in widening circles, thinking this was something else she brought him for the first time in so many years, thinking he could sink into her, drown himself in the tenderness and strength of her mouth. But finally he needed to give to her, and he pulled out of her mouth to bring her beside him.

He kissed her closed eyelids and followed with his lips the shape of her face, the long line of her slender throat, her rounded breasts, heavy against his cheek, and took into his mouth first one nipple and then the other, until they grew erect beneath his tongue.

Slowly, slowly, his lips moved along her body, drinking in her silken scent, brushing with light kisses the luminous skin, alive beneath his mouth, down her belly to the cluster of curling hair and within it the warm, pliant flesh that trembled as he reached it. Sabrina thrust her fingers into the thick black hair of his head and opened her legs as she felt him take her with his tongue and lips. All her senses were drawn to that one yielding place. Then suddenly, fiercely, he thrust his tongue deep inside her, possessing her throbbing dark center until it contracted, poised on a thin precipice, then leaped, pulsing wildly as she cried out and shuddered beneath his hands.

He was smiling at her when she opened her eyes. Her mouth formed a silent Oh and she smiled up at him. "My love—" she began, when a knock came at the door and a hearty voice bellowed that room service had arrived.

Garth leaped from the bed. "Dunce," he muttered. "If he's so energetic at three in the morning, why isn't he serenading us with Italian love songs? Do you know what? I forgot to pack a robe."

He looked at Sabrina, sitting cross-legged on the bed, her face radiant, laughing at him. "Here," she said, holding out the quilt and as he made a toga from it he began to laugh with her, and their laughter filled the room.

Nothing was settled, but everything was changed. Sabrina sat beside an airplane window looking at a landscape of towering clouds as she had only twenty-four hours earlier and knew that the game was over. She would have to leave today.

She had had her moment of love, and from now on everything in her life would be different because of it; but no matter how she relived the past twenty-four hours, they were not hers; they were Stephanie's.

What had begun in mid-September as a careless lark had grown by the end of October to a complex web of passion and need and commitment to a shared future. Which was impossible for Garth and Sabrina, but essential for Garth and his wife. And even if Sabrina had wanted to forget that, she could not. Because Garth's wife was the other half of herself.

Beside her, Garth shook his head as a stewardess offered him a magazine, and leaned back in his seat. "It's hard to believe how much has happened since your trip."

She clasped her hands in her lap and turned to him, letting herself look fully at him in the brilliant sunlight above the clouds, memorizing the tiny lines that radiated from the corners of his dark eyes, his strong cheekbones and wide mouth, the cleft in his chin, the gray hairs mixed with black at his forehead.

"A turning point," he mused. "Did you know it would be? Or did you just run away and then later realize it might be the first step of the final step out the door? I think that was it. And then you came back, trying in so many ways to be different, as if you were determined to remake our marriage, forcing me to see what had happened to us. I've wanted for some time to tell you how grateful I am, though you must know. I want you to understand that I'm aware of what you've done, how hard it is to change, how hard you've tried. And you were the one to do it. I didn't know how. I didn't even know what had to be done."

He took her hand. "That was some of what I was trying to tell you last night. I suppose you knew most of it already. What I'm saying now is that I won't let you slip away again. You've taught me—Stephanie, what is it? What's wrong?"

She bent her head. "I don't know. I'm so dizzy, all of a sudden. Could you get me a cup of tea?"

He rang for the stewardess, and Sabrina put her head back against the seat. "Thank you." Her voice was shaking; her body was shaking. What's wrong with me? she thought wildly. It's not Garth, it's something else. Something is wrong, something terrible, and I don't know what it is.

Reaching across to pull down the tray in front of her, Garth felt the violent trembling of her body. "Good God, what is it? Stephanie, my love, what can I do—?"

"I don't know," she whispered, and buried her face in his shoulder. Garth put his arms around her, holding her tightly until the stewardess came with a pot of tea.

"Is there anything I can do?" she asked. "A blanket—?"

"I don't think so," Garth said. Gently, he disengaged himself. "Stephanie, can you manage some tea?"

She nodded and took the cup in both hands, sipping the scalding liquid.

Garth looked at his watch. "Eleven-thirty; we'll be landing in half an hour. Penny and Cliff will be at the airport, you know, with Vivian."

"Yes. Just give me a few minutes."

Shivering, Sabrina drank the hot tea. As Garth refilled her cup, she saw through the window a plane, in the far distance, traveling in the opposite direction. Yesterday I was on that plane, she thought. Talking about shadows.

She forced herself to think of Garth and what he had been saying when the dizziness began. She understood now why he had not seen through the deception. Garth the trained scientist, the astute observer, who had been married to the same woman for twelve years, had not guessed he was living with his wife's twin sister because he convinced himself she was deliberately changing her behavior to save their marriage. If she and Stephanie had written a scenario to protect them, they could not have found a better one. How clever we were, she thought through her despair. And look where it got us.

She had to leave. Today. And that meant calling Stephanie, telling her to catch the first plane—but Stephanie wasn't there. Stephanie was on Max's yacht. Until Friday or Saturday.

I can't stay that long. I can't do that to any of us.

But I can't just disappear, either.

She closed her eyes. She would have to stay a few more days. Stephanie would call as soon as she got back to Cadogan Square, and on Monday they would meet at the airport in Chicago and reverse the procedure they had gone through so lightheartedly in China: exchange clothes and purses, hand over a wedding ring, trade keys to their front doors. And it would be over.

It will be over. The words rang in her head. They echoed through the excited greetings of Penny and Cliff at the airport;

echoed through the sounds of the house—a door slamming, Cliff dropping a tray of cookies and Penny shouting at him to clean up the mess, Garth walking from room to room talking of storm windows; echoed through the sizzling of the steaks Sabrina cooked for dinner, the burbling of the coffeepot, the tales that Penny and Cliff took turns relating: a stray cat, a school contest, plans for a Thanksgiving parade.

It will be over echoed through the rattling of dishes as the children cleaned the kitchen, echoed through the ringing of the telephone, echoed through Garth's words calling her to say that it was long distance; someone named Brooks Westermarck wanted to speak to her.

And then the echo stopped as Brooks's voice, from the other side of the ocean, began heavily, "Mrs. Andersen . . . Stephanie . . ." and went on, crying, to tell her they had just heard the news that Max Stuyvesant's yacht had exploded and gone down in the Mediterranean about eleven-thirty Chicago time. Everyone on board, including her sister, Lady Sabrina Longworth, had been killed.

Part III

Part III

Chapter 17

The mourners came early to Kensington Cemetery. Some wept and others murmured together as they stood near the open grave. Sabrina heard them behind her, like rustling leaves, but she did not turn around; she was watching her sister's coffin, her own coffin, settle into the grave as the Vicar gave a short prayer and began to speak.

"Lady Sabrina Longworth, vivid with life, brought us love and joy—"

Heavy, pale clouds hung low over the earth and grass, draining their color, leaving them gray beneath the supplicating branches of bare trees. A light October mist drifted from the Thames, touching the mourners with chill fingers. Sabrina was numb, but still she shivered, and Garth tightened his arm around her shoulders.

"She was young and beautiful and awake to the beauty around her—"

In the circle of Garth's arm, Sabrina was very still, but a scream clawed in her throat. *Stephanie.*

"In the midst of life we are in death."

Stephanie was dead.

She was cold, so cold, and her skin hurt, stretched across her bones: a thin, taut membrane holding in her pain and the invisible tears that would not stop, even when she slept.

Come back, Stephanie. We'll go back to the beginning, we'll do it all differently, and everything will be all right.

"The Lord is my shepherd, I shall not want . . ."

But the only beginning she could think of was the phone call from Brooks, the beginning of the nightmare. His voice had come across the ocean, crying, and as he talked the room darkened around Sabrina, receded to a small pinpoint of light, then surged back, crushing her. She could not breathe. The crash of the falling telephone brought Garth and the children running; she remembered Penny and Cliff, fearful and still, watching, as Garth cradled her and with his other hand picked up the telephone to talk to Brooks, his voice level, making arrangements. He was the steady center of that crazily spinning room, a whirlpool that would have sucked her down if Garth had not held her. She clung to him. Garth, my love—

But he didn't know, he didn't know what had happened. "Wait." She struggled to pull away from him. "It wasn't Sabrina. It wasn't Sabrina. It wasn't Sabrina who died."

"Sssh, dear love, just hold me; you don't have to face it yet."

"But it wasn't Sabrina, it wasn't Sabrina—" And then the tears came, wrenching sobs that drowned her words while she struggled to tell them. "Not . . . Sabrina . . . who died." Until Nat came, with a hypodermic needle. "No! Let me cry! Don't take that away from me, from both of us—!"

But the needle slid smoothly into her arm and slowly, shudderingly, she calmed, dimly hearing Nat's voice as she fell asleep. "My God, my God, what a dreadful thing. Garth, what else can I do?"

Thursday was a blur of faces and voices. The telephone rang steadily. Doors opened and closed; people brought flowers and food. Why was everyone so busy when Stephanie was dead?

Garth took care of everything. He had called her parents; she heard him calling Brooks again. ". . . register the death at the American consulate in Marseilles and fly the body—"

Not "the body," you fools, it's Stephanie!

"—back to England . . . at the undertaker's—yes, give me the address. T. C. Dryden and Sons, Regent Street, Mayfair—"

Near home; Stephanie will be near home.

"—leaving this afternoon; we'll see you tomorrow morning, Friday . . . of course, at Sabrina's house; that's where Stephanie will want to be."

Home. I'm going home.

She let Garth do everything. He drove the children to Vivian's house, packed for both of them and held her close when they reached the airport and walked through the echoing concourse to their plane.

Garth is the center of my world, she thought; all I have left. She tried to shake off her lethargy. I have to tell him; he still doesn't know. I'll tell him as soon as we settle down. Brooks just called; I can wait a few minutes until we're ... no, Brooks called—when?—I can't remember. Yesterday? A few minutes ago?

On the plane, Garth took the magazines the stewardess offered, giving Sabrina her privacy. She pushed back her seat and closed her eyes, trying to think, to go back to the beginning, while waves of sleepiness swept over her.

If I hadn't traded places, she thought, drifting in and out of sleep. Or broken my wrist. Then everything would be all right. Or if I'd insisted we end the deception then, tell the truth, instead of letting it go on. Or later, if I'd refused to give Stephanie another week, so she could have her cruise and I could stay a little longer with Garth.

If I hadn't fallen in love with Garth.

I caused my sister's death.

She was awake for the rest of the flight, her face turned from Garth. *Everything I did led to her death. But I didn't know—*

At the airport, she insisted on going straight to the undertaker's. "I want to see my sister. I have to see my sister."

She went in alone, to the small room at the back of T. C. Dryden and Sons, and knelt beside the coffin. "Stephanie?"

Her sister slept, cold and remote, her beauty as fragile as parchment. Sabrina watched over her, at last going back to the beginning, all the way back—the cities where they had grown up, schools and rented houses, chauffeured limousines and servants, the sleek figures of Gordon and Laura leaving them alone, the two of them, alone, making their own family.

She remembered one summer vacation when they were seven or eight. She and Stephanie had run off to find a waterfall, and Stephanie had slipped on some rocks and broken her ankle. Sabrina had raced back to find Gordon and Laura, and while Gordon worked to free Stephanie's ankle from the rocks, Sabrina had gripped her hand, to help ease the pain. That night, in bed, Stephanie had said drowsily, "We'll always help each other, won't we? Whenever we're hurt or lost, we'll always be there."

"Yes," Sabrina said.

"Promise."

"I promise."

"I promise, too," Stephanie had said.

In T. C. Dryden's silent shadowed room, lit by candles and small lamps, heavy with the fragrance of tall bouquets of flowers, Sabrina watched her sister. "We promised, Stephanie. We promised."

She was crying, the tears cold on her cheeks, and she rested her forehead on the polished wood of the coffin. "I love you, Stephanie. I never meant to hurt you. It didn't seem important—one more week. I wanted to love your family for a few more days and you could have your . . . one last fling . . ."

She closed her eyes. "It's all my fault, and now I'm left alone to tell them. We didn't plan that; we were so careless, we never thought we might have to tell anyone, and now I don't know how to do it, or how I'll bear all their anger. I did try to tell them, but no one listened and I have no one to talk to about it. All these last weeks, when I didn't have anyone in Evanston, it didn't matter because I had you and we understood each other. But now . . . Stephanie, *there is no one who will understand.*"

Sabrina reached out to smooth her sister's hair and a gleam of gold caught her eye—the wedding band she wore, glinting against the dark strands. Swiftly she pulled it off. "This is yours, Stephanie. I have no right to it." She slipped it on Stephanie's finger, her warm hand holding her sister's marble one. "It's always been yours. If I'd remembered that, you would have come home sooner and none of this—"

She clasped her hands in her lap, thinking. If I'd remembered that, I would have told everyone the truth by now. I never had any right to this family. And I have to tell them that. Alone. Without Stephanie's help when they turn their anger on me. Alone. I'd better get used to it.

She leaned forward again to say goodbye to her sister. She felt drained, as lifeless as Stephanie. *Because part of me is gone. I am burying my sister, who is also myself.*

"No," she said aloud. "No, they can't bury us. I won't let them. No. No. No!"

"Stephanie," said Garth. She had not heard him come in, but he was kneeling beside her, his arm around her shoulders. Huddled beside the coffin, Sabrina felt the life in his arm, the life in her body, and trembled. Who lay in the coffin? To this man she was Stephanie, she lived with him in Stephanie's house, caring for Stephanie's children, loving them, loving Stephanie's husband. And she was in London to bury Stephanie's sister. What have I done? she thought frantically. I've caused us both to die. A low cry tore from her throat, and then Garth was helping her into a taxi to take her to Sabrina's house.

"My love," Garth said as they moved slowly through the afternoon traffic. "I'll help you all I can, but in the end you have to face this yourself." His voice was gentle but unsparing; he could not do it all for her. "Are you sure you want to stay at Sabrina's house?" She nodded. "Do you want to use a guest room instead of her bedroom?" She shook her head. "It might be less painful for you."

"No," she said. "It's my room; I'll stay in it."

"Whatever you want," he said. "I'll do anything I can to help you."

No, you won't. Not when I tell you. When we get home and we're alone and I tell you the truth.

At Cadogan Square, Mrs. Thirkell, crumpled with grief, met them at the door and gestured toward the upper floors. "Mrs. Andersen, your father arrived a few minutes ago; he's very ill, and your mother is—"

Sabrina flew past her up the stairs, leaving Garth to follow. She found Gordon and Laura in the third-floor study, her father sitting in a leather chair, his face gray and pinched, her mother at the telephone. "Stephanie, thank goodness you're here. Do you know how to call an ambulance? I don't suppose you do, but—"

"Dial 999. I'll do it." She dialed and turned to her father as Garth came into the room. "What happened?"

He was bewildered. "My chest and arm . . . thought it was indigestion. Airplane food." His voice was shallow.

Laura paced angrily. "His doctor said he shouldn't come to London. He's already had two of these—"

"An ambulance," Sabrina said into the telephone. "For St. George's Hospital." She gave the address on Cadogan Square.

"The home of Lady Longworth. Please hurry; her father may have had a heart attack." She looked at her parents. "You never told me about other attacks."

"Incidents," Gordon murmured. "Not the real thing."

"The doctors say they're warnings," said Laura. "What luck that you knew about the hospital. How did you know?"

"I've been here before." Sabrina dialed on the house phone. "Mrs. Thirkell, an ambulance will come for Mr. Hartwell. Please call us as soon as it arrives."

Garth was watching her thoughtfully as she leaned over Gordon, who seemed small and frail, clinging to her hand like a child. Where was the tall powerful father of her childhood? She pushed aside her mourning and knelt before him. "Is the pain bad?"

"Better. Would you bring me a shot of Scotch?"

"No."

"Stephanie," said Laura. "What has happened to you?"

Gordon smiled palely. "She is being as strong-willed as Sabrina. But an obedient daughter would not deny her father a small medicinal Scotch."

"An obedient daughter would not kill her father," Sabrina said, trying to keep her voice light. "How do I know what Scotch would do to an uncooperative heart?"

Mrs. Thirkell called to say the ambulance had arrived. "They're bringing up the stretcher, my lady." Her embarrassment came over the telephone. "I'm sorry, I meant Mrs. Andersen. I can't get used to—"

"It's all right," Sabrina said. "I understand."

As the attendants came in, Gordon stood up, pushing his hands against the arms of the chair. "I'll walk, Stephanie."

"No," she said. "It's three flights." As he hesitated she took his arm. "Don't argue; we're trying to help you."

He peered at her. "How fierce you have become." But he let them wrap him in a blanket and strap him down before carrying him out.

"We'll follow in a taxi," Sabrina called after them, but as soon as they were gone her knees buckled. Garth was there in an instant, holding her. He sent Laura in a taxi to the hospital and settled Sabrina on a love seat in the drawing room.

Then people were everywhere, purposeful, bustling about. Everyone but Sabrina. Restless and confused, she followed them, watching, and now and then they moved her from one place to another, like a puppet, heavy and numb. Like Stephanie.

We're in the way, she thought wryly. No one needs us; they all have jobs to do. I have something to do, too. But I can't remember what it is.

She remembered it at the cemetery as the Vicar came to the end of the service. "I will lift up mine eyes unto the hills from whence cometh my help."

The crowd was still except for the rustle of its weeping. Behind Sabrina, Alexandra stood with Antonio, tears streaming down her face; next to her, in front of Brooks, Gabrielle sobbed into a handkerchief. Jolie held hands with a stony-faced Michel, and Nicholas Blackford bounced in agitation while Amelia tried to keep him still. Everyone was there: the American ambassador and his staff; a cluster of art dealers, some of whom had flown in from Paris and Rome; the nobility who had been clients and friends; servants, waiters and shop clerks who remembered a smile and a word of thanks. They were all there, even Mrs. Pemberley, standing behind a stunned and motionless Brian, and Mrs. Thirkell, clutching wet handkerchiefs to her crumpled face, and Olivia standing in a group that included the dim figures of Lady Iris Longworth and Denton Longworth. How strange that they had come, Sabrina thought. The Raddisons had not.

She felt the strength of Garth's arm around her shoulders. Standing at the edge of the grave, she heard the Vicar's cadenced voice.

"May we yet see the radiance of a new day."

On this day she was burying her sister, her father was in the hospital and her mother stood trembling beside her, clutching her hand.

"Earth to earth, ashes to ashes, dust to dust." The Vicar looked at her, telling her with his sad eyes that it was time for her to throw the first handful of earth on the coffin. Everyone was waiting. All of them, waiting, and the Vicar looking at her. The first handful of earth on the coffin. The first handful of earth. And Sabrina remembered. *You haven't told them. This is your last chance. Tell them now. You can't put it off any longer. Tell them. TELL THEM!*

A long shudder ran through her body and Sabrina fell to her knees beside the grave. "It's not Sabrina!" she cried. She heard gasps behind her, and a moan from Laura. She looked at the coffin and then pleadingly at the Vicar. "It wasn't Sabrina who died, it was Stephanie! *Stephanie died!* Or perhaps it was both of us, sometimes it seems that . . . Sometimes I *feel* like Stephanie but I'm not, I'm Sabrina, I've always been Sabrina. I've only been Stephanie since we—"

"Stop, my love." Garth was raising her, his voice urgent, his arms holding her tightly against him. "I'm going to take you home."

"No, wait, listen." She pushed against his arms. "Listen to me—!"

Brooks was beside them and Garth met his eyes. "You and the Vicar can finish the service?"

"Of course. We'll see you at the house. There's a Dr. Farr, by the way—"

"Stop, please, stop!" Sabrina cried. "Listen to me. Don't you understand, I'm trying to tell you—"

"—who could give her something; his number is in the book."

Garth nodded and led his wife away. The Vicar's voice followed them. "And may God have mercy on her soul."

"I think we should call Dr. Farr," Garth said as they walked to the limousine. "To help you through these first few days."

Sabrina stumbled beside him, sick and empty, angry at herself. If it hadn't been for her confusion, when she wasn't sure who she was, they would have believed her. "You didn't let me finish," she said despairingly. "I was trying to tell you the truth and you wouldn't listen."

"Later."

"You didn't believe me."

"Later, my love."

Garth remembered when his parents died, feeling anger and grief because they had left him. But his wife's mourning was more frantic: she was distraught, as if her whole being had been ripped from her. Even knowing that it was her twin sister who had died, he was puzzled that the strong woman he knew, who had taken command when her father was ill, could collapse into incoherence and overwhelming despair.

He knew that, in grief, people often took refuge in denial, refusing to acknowledge that a loved one had died. But if that were the case she would say her sister was alive, traveling, and they would be together soon. Instead she pretended to be her sister. Why? To make up to her for something? Or was it that, in spite of physical separation, the twins had been far closer, more innately parts of a whole, than he realized?

At Cadogan Square, Sabrina refused to see Dr. Farr. "He'll give me something to put me to sleep. Why can't you let me have my grief?"

"You should have grief. But not hysteria."

"I'll try to avoid that," she said with a trace of her own dry humor, and Garth let her have her way. She was right; it would be best if she could pull out of it herself.

Brooks and Olivia had arranged the funeral, and now the lunch guests they had invited were filling the house. Mrs. Thirkell threw all the energies of her grief into directing the activities of the hired staff, and within a short time platters of meat and fish, cheeses, patés, breads, pastries and tortes covered long tables in the dining room and drawing room. Sabrina moved among the guests with Garth at her side, watching her. Pale and aloof, her head high, she moved easily through the rooms as if she belonged in them, or was taking Sabrina's place. Everyone commented on the resemblance between them and how natural it seemed to see her there, and she listened to them politely, as if trying to understand what they had to do with her.

Garth felt, painfully, that he had never loved her as much as now, when she seemed both lost and at home, needing him yet apart from him. Grief cloaked her in mystery and vulnerability; he wanted to draw her close and kiss her despairing eyes, and listen closely to everything she said, whether it made sense or not, so that he could understand what it meant to lose someone who was so deeply a part of her.

But she said very little and so, while keeping watch over her, he listened to those around them talk about the accident. Brooks had told the story to a few, and it had spread rapidly. No one knew what caused the *Lafitte* to go down, but the rumor was that the fuel tanks had exploded just as it left the harbor at Monte Carlo. Denton Longworth had been gambling in the casino that week, and, when he heard it was Max Stuyvesant's yacht, he called the coast guard to offer his services. He was there when the first bodies were pulled from the water; one of them was Sabrina, and it was Denton who identified her.

The police had called London for the names of Lady Longworth's next-of-kin, but Gabrielle, who took the call, told them to call Brooks. And a good thing, Garth thought, for he had handled the complicated arrangements, involving Monaco police, the French coast guard and police, British Airways and British police, quietly and smoothly. Garth liked Brooks. Wary at first of his imperiousness, he soon found himself responding to his honesty. "I'm going to miss Sabrina," Brooks had said when the two men sat late over drinks the night before the funeral. "I've got a problem on my hands—we needn't go into it—and Sabrina made me see that it might be partly my fault, or, rather, that I might be looking at it the wrong way. She was a very whole person who knew what she believed in and was impatient with those who pretended they were something they weren't. I suppose she was as capable of pretending as the rest of us, but I always felt, when she told me something, that it was honest—it was the way she really felt."

Garth had looked around the study and pictured the other rooms of the house with their quiet beauty and harmony, their interplay of serenity and wit. He had never been there before. If he had, he would have known much more about his sister-in-law, for the house was a reflection of a woman in many ways like his wife, not the woman he had imagined Sabrina to be. "I never really knew her," he said to Brooks. "I wish I had."

And the next day, after the funeral, as he stood with his wife, listening to Sabrina's friends talk about her, he thought again how much he did not know.

"She worked very hard," Olivia recalled, taking a bite of torte.

"For a long time she was afraid of failing," said Alexandra.

"Nonsense. I never knew a woman more sure of herself. She had a way of listening to my ideas and nodding pleasantly, and then telling me just as pleasantly why I was wrong. I'm amazed when I think of how often she did that and how I took it from her."

Jolie turned to Olivia. "You don't think she was afraid of failure in the beginning? When everyone ignored her?"

"Why talk about bad times?" Nicholas interrupted. "When she became successful and had her choice of clients, she worked for love—the love of beauty, the love of creating with her impeccable style, the love of—"

"Money," Alexandra said with a small chuckle. "Don't forget that. Unlike the rest of us, she had to earn her own living."

Garth saw his wife listening with interest. "I'm sorry," he said to her softly. "All the times I criticized her ... I didn't really know her, which is exactly what you kept telling me."

She nodded. "Yes, but it doesn't matter, does it? Once I thought there was plenty of time for the truth, but I was wrong. Lies and mistakes keep growing, and it's so hard to stop them; and then it doesn't seem to matter so much."

He had no idea what she was talking about, but before he could respond, a stranger came to them: tall, dark, with heavy brows in a thin face, and black, intense eyes. "I'm sorry," Sabrina said as he took her hand. "I don't—"

"Dmitri Karras," he said, smiling slightly. "We met once a long time ago in—"

"Athens!" she cried, her face coming to life. "When you hid us! But isn't this amazing! After all these years! Do you live in London? Are you working here? Wait until I tell Stephanie—" She stopped abruptly.

Garth saw sidelong glances on all sides—pity, embarrassment, curiosity. He held out his hand to Dmitri. "Garth Andersen. Stephanie has told me about you."

Dmitri took his hand in gratitude. "Yes. We had an adventure, the three of us." He turned to Sabrina. "I remember your sister so clearly: her courage, and her eyes—so eager, demanding to see everything. I called her three days ago when I arrived, but she was away. Perhaps, before you leave, if you have time, we could have tea?"

"Perhaps," Sabrina said, anxious to get away. He reminded her of a time when everything was simple. A dream time that was dead.

She was trembling. I can't tell Stephanie I met Dmitri, she thought. I can't tell Stephanie anything ever again. I can't even talk about her to anyone else. Because I'm still Stephanie. *And I can't find a way to tell the truth.*

"And how long are you here?" Dmitri asked. Sabrina turned, but he was speaking to Garth.

"I'm not sure."

"Why not?" she asked abruptly. "Your ticket is for tomorrow."

"I won't leave if you need me."

"I don't need you."

353

"You may not be the best judge of that."

Dmitri began to retreat. "I will call, then, about tea—if you are still here—"

"I'll be here," Sabrina said. "My father is in the hospital, my mother is here and I have my own affairs to handle."

"My dear," urged Nicholas, coming close. "I would like to talk to you about Ambassadors. Lady Longworth and I had talked about a partnership. How long will you stay in London?"

In an instant, Sidney Jones was at her elbow: Sabrina's solicitor, who had gotten her divorce from Denton, who had drawn up her will. "I can arrange an appointment. I would, of course, be present. Lady Longworth would have wished that, since I drew up her will. And I have already spoken to Mrs. Andersen about her inheritance of the estate."

The whole thing, Sabrina thought. Left to Stephanie Andersen. I've left everything to myself. And the foolish, sad joke brought tears to her eyes.

But a spark of curiosity had been aroused. Stephanie had talked to Nicholas about a partnership? What else had she done, besides get involved with Max Stuyvesant? For the first time Sabrina realized that she knew almost nothing of what Stephanie had done in London. And now Stephanie could not tell her.

She looked at Antonio and Alexandra, standing nearby, the sexual pull between them so strong Sabrina could feel it. When did that begin? Stephanie had broken with him only a little while ago. But it was a good match. How clever of Stephanie, if she had encouraged it. At the buffet Michel and Jolie were heaping a plate with chicken paté and cornichons. Stephanie hadn't mentioned them since the birthday party at Alexandra's. Sabrina would have to find out about their newspaper story without giving away her ignorance. More playacting. *There is no end to a deception once it begins.*

"My dear," said Sidney Jones, "may I get you a cup of tea?" He cocked a superior eyebrow at Garth to show him who knew best how to take care of fragile women.

"Not tea," Sabrina said smoothly. "Garth, would you get me a glass of wine?"

Garth smiled at her, his heart lifting as she came out of her grief to put this supercilious snob in his place. "I love you," he said, kissing her cheek, thanking her. "I'll be right back."

Sabrina saw Brooks come into the room and go to Gabrielle. Those nearby, their faces alert for a quarrel, inched closer to listen. Sabrina shook her head. Nothing changes, she thought. Some of them will miss me for awhile, but everything will go on just as it always has. Nothing changes.

But when I tell the truth, everything will change for Garth and the children.

Unless I don't. The thought whipped in so quickly it was a moment before she grasped it and realized she had thought it before. Unless I don't. If I told the truth today or tomorrow, or a month from now, or next year, what difference would it make? Or if I never did. We could just go on as we have been. What difference would it make to anyone?

But if I don't tell anyone the truth, how can I ever be Sabrina again?

Garth returned, followed by a waiter bearing a tray with canapés and wine. "He wouldn't let me do my own serving. I gather he thinks of me as an outsider trying to bust his union." Sabrina gave a small involuntary laugh, and he felt he had won a victory.

They sat together in quiet companionship, surrounded by noise. "Nothing changes," Garth murmured, eyeing the crowd.

Sabrina looked at him quickly. "But you don't know them."

"Do I need to? Look at them. They came here solemn and respectful, whispering, and within two hours they're thrashing around in their endless entanglements. Listen to them."

Everything goes on, she thought again, listening to the high-pitched chatter of a cocktail party.

"Amazing resemblance; I could swear it was Sabrina."

"No, it's quite superficial. The mouth is different, and the eyes; you just aren't very observant."

"I'll ask her; she'll tell you I'm right—they're really identical."

"Oh, for God's sake, you're not going to ask her! One more scene like the one at the grave and I'll take to my bed for a week. So chilling; my God, I couldn't bear another."

Garth kept an eye on his wife, but she seemed indifferent to the chatter. She was very pale, but calm and alert; the look of the sleepwalker was gone. In fact, though she had let Brooks and Olivia arrange the funeral and buffet lunch, she behaved like the owner of the house with Mrs. Thirkell and the staff.

And, though she clung to him for support, she would still, at odd moments, suddenly and unexpectedly withdraw into her shell and look at him as if she was not sure who he was, or what she had to do with him.

"What I would like," Garth said, "is a Scotch."

"I'll get you one," Sabrina said, as if glad to have something to do, and before he could stop her she was gone.

"Restless," said Nicholas Blackford knowingly. "Usually happens in mourning. Take her awhile to get over it. The two of them were so close in China that I can't imagine them apart."

China? What the hell was the man talking about? They hadn't been together in China. But Blackford had been there; Garth remembered Stephanie saying she'd picked up British phrases from him. "They did have that time together, though," he said probingly.

"Right, exactly right; I hope you help Stephanie see it that way. Two whole weeks together, when otherwise Sabrina might have—oh, dear, how does one say it—died without their having been together for a year. Mysterious ways, the fates work. I was thinking of the pictures I took of them, in those identical silk dresses they bought in Shanghai. Do you know, I never saw those pictures. Did they come out?"

"Yes," Garth said thoughtfully as his wife came up to them with a bottle and a glass with ice cubes.

"I foiled the union," she said with a small smile. "But I only brought one glass. Nicholas, if you'd like some—" She looked into Garth's face. "What's wrong?"

"Nothing. Where did you locate the Scotch?"

"In the study upstairs. I . . . Sabrina kept a few bottles there. Something *is* wrong."

Nicholas fidgeted, alarmed by hints of a domestic squabble. "Perhaps I will get a drink. If you'll excuse me—"

Garth poured the amber liquid into his glass. "Nicholas was telling me how close you and Sabrina were in China. He took pictures, he said."

Her face froze with a bleak emptiness. "Yes," she said finally. "In Shanghai. Near the hotel. The day before he spilled his pastries all over the street. That isn't important, of course, I just remembered it. I meant to tell you all about it, everything, from the beginning, but so much has been happening, and I've been confused, and I kept putting it off . . . I was going to tell you tonight, when we were alone, so you'd know before you caught your plane tomorrow—at least, I think that's what I was going to do, but we can do it now if you want—"

Her voice was a monotone of such loneliness and despair that he was alarmed. "No, not now. It can wait. In fact, you don't have to tell me at all. Whatever it was—were you afraid I'd be angry if I knew? You were right; I probably would have been. Because I didn't really know her. I only wish you hadn't been afraid of telling me, as if I was the ogre in the castle who had to be lied to or he'd eat everyone up. Was I really like that?"

She bent her head and shook it slowly back and forth, her hair hiding her face. "No, don't say that. You're not an ogre. I love you."

"Then nothing else matters. What the hell do I care if you were with Sabrina in China? Let's talk about something else. Can you tell me, for example, why these guests, who must collectively own half the wealth in England, are gorging themselves on lunch as if they are destitutes with no hope of dinner?"

She laughed, looking up at him. "Maybe to remind themselves they're still alive."

He brushed a lock of hair from her forehead. Even preoccupied with sorrow, he thought, her mind was quick. "Or to make sure they haven't missed anything. Funerals remind them of the uncertainty of tomorrow."

They smiled softly at each other, as if saying they were the lucky ones whose tomorrow was certain. And Garth began to believe they would soon find again what they had discovered in New York the night before Brooks called from London.

That night, as they lay in bed, he held her hand and offered again to stay with her for a few more days. But she refused to consider it. "My mother is here, and all my . . . Sabrina's friends, and Mrs. Thirkell—if I need company or help, they're all here. The children need you, and you shouldn't miss any more classes and lab work. And didn't you plan to meet with the architects for the Genetics Institute?"

"Yes, yes, and yes. But if you need me, I would stay here."

She turned to him. Her eyes, in the soft light from the bedside lamp, studied him as if memorizing the lines of his face. "I was going to tell you tonight about the China trip, the whole story—"

"I don't want to hear it. Unless you think it would help you work out your feelings about your sister. But I can't tell you how to do that, you know. However you felt about her when she was alive, you have to be yourself now, separate from her and separate from her memory. You can't slide back and forth from one to the other—" She drew a sharp breath. "What is it?"

"What you said—that's what I have to tell you. But every time I begin, I can't go on."

"Then don't. Damn it, I don't want to hear it if it's so difficult for you." He was afraid to hear it; afraid he would have no weapons against decisions she made in her grief. "Wait until later, when we're home. Then you can tell me if you still think you must."

"But it isn't—"

"Stephanie, I don't want to hear it. It can wait." He raised himself on his elbow and kissed her. "It's late and you're exhausted. Why don't you try to sleep?"

She hesitated. He was giving her time. Why not take it? She'd already decided it made no difference. Put it off a little longer. She touched his face. "I thought you'd want to make love."

"I want to do what you want," he said.

She moved toward him and he pulled her close; they lay still in each other's arms. Garth felt her stir and his hands caressed her. "My love, shall I stay in London a while longer?"

"No. But make love to me now."

She stirred against him and her breathing quickened; he lay on her, letting himself melt into the scent and touch of her body. As he was about to enter her he looked into her eyes and stopped abruptly. Without a word, he moved away and lay on his back beside her.

"Garth—what—?"

"You didn't want to make love. You were faking it, weren't you?"

After a moment, eyes closed, she nodded.

"Why? Do you think my pleasure is so important to me that I'd want to get it that way?"

"I wanted to make love to you."

"That's not true."

"*I* wanted to make love to you. My mind wanted to make love to you. I don't know why I couldn't get my body to respond ... I tried, but it wouldn't, so I pretended. Because I wanted to make love to you. Don't you understand? I wanted to feel you inside me. I didn't care whether I had an orgasm or not. I wanted you inside me."

"Then why not say that? Why fake it?"

She shuddered. "I'm sorry. I don't know why I can't tell you everything."

He took her hand. "Go to sleep. When you get home, we'll talk; you can tell me anything you like."

She burrowed her head into the pillow. "You're going back tomorrow?"

"Yes." He leaned over her and kissed the small corner of forehead he could see. "Good night, my love."

"Good night."

He turned off the lamp. In the darkness, her voice reached him like a soft caress. "I love you, Garth."

On Sunday morning, Gordon lay propped up in his hospital bed reminiscing about the past. Sabrina kept her eyes on his thin face, but she was thinking of Garth, on his way back to America. Gordon's voice grew louder.

"Then in Algeria, there was so much to do ... of course, my heart was fine in those days—I could go eighteen hours at a stretch ..."

"And did," Sabrina murmured. "Leaving us with the servants."

"Stephanie," said Laura sharply.

Sabrina shrugged. "It was a long time ago."

"Then why bring it up? Your father always did the best he could, for his country and his family. I must say, I'm surprised. It wasn't you who complained in the past; it was always Sabrina."

Her voice broke on Sabrina's name. "I'm sorry," Sabrina said.

Gordon's forehead creased as he looked at her. "Your mother told me what happened at the cemetery. It's no good, you know, trying to be Sabrina. That won't bring her back."

Sabrina met his eyes boldly, daring him to recognize her, but she knew he would not; if he hadn't done so earlier, how could he now, when he was concentrating on the steady beating of his heart?

"And you don't owe her anything, either. She was different

from you and lived a different life. I'm not saying it was good or bad . . ." He coughed, and immediately Laura was standing over him.

"Don't excite yourself. The doctors said you'd be all right if you kept quiet. We'll be here indefinitely if you don't do as they tell you."

"I wasn't excited," Gordon said mildly. "I was simply pointing out that Stephanie needn't be ashamed to be herself."

"You were implying that Sabrina's way of life had something to do with her death. You had no right—I'm sorry, Gordon, I shouldn't say that. Stephanie, what will you do about Ambassadors?"

"Your mother is changing the subject," Gordon said to Sabrina. "But I loved your sister, you know. Even when I thought her wild and reckless; even when she married that pompous ass what's-his-name duke—"

"Viscount," Laura said. "But I thought we weren't going to talk about Sabrina."

"I always loved her. I just didn't feel as close to her as I do to you. Do you understand that?"

"Don't," Sabrina said softly. "Please don't." Her face was hot and she wanted to run away.

"I was uncomfortable with her because I always felt she was about to spring out of her chair and go off and . . . *do* something. Run a race or explore some caves or shoot at a fox or be the belle of the ball. I loved her, there was no one like her, but I couldn't relax with her because I could never predict what she would do next."

His voice was rising. Sabrina forced herself to sit still.

"I always worried about what she might do to the reputation of the embassy. We tried to tell both of you that we were symbols of America and my career depended on the image we presented to the world. I never had to worry about you, but Sabrina, with her high spirits, seemed uncontrollable. Do you understand why I was sometimes harsh with her, fearing she would do something foolish or dangerous? Why we decided to send you both to Juliette? Why I may have seemed not quite . . . fatherly all the time?"

Sabrina was silent.

"But I loved her. She was fire and light and love. So much energy and curiosity. So much life. I regret that I never told her that." Gordon's voice began to fade. "Even when we settled in Washington, I didn't tell her. She was running about as much as ever, getting married and divorced, building up that shop of hers, going on hunts and cruises. She'd even taken up with some Brazilian at the end. But I loved her as much as I love you. And I wish I had told her so."

Laura was crying, her head averted. Gordon's eyes were closed, his slight figure rising and falling with shallow breaths beneath the white coverlet. In the stillness, Sabrina heard footsteps and low voices of other Sunday afternoon visitors to the hospital.

Parents, she thought. She was thirty-two years old, and still they had the power to make her feel guilty about disappointing them. Gordon was trying to explain away a lifetime of neglect and, at the same time, tell her he didn't want her to act like Sabrina. And Laura, who had felt closest to Sabrina, was trying not to show that she resented his preference for Stephanie.

"She knew you loved her," Sabrina said to Gordon's closed eyes, wishing she could find a way to convince him. "Even when she knew she disappointed you."

Gordon nodded. Absorbed in his own health, he was easily convinced that all was well. "I'll take my nap now," he said.

Laura took Sabrina's arm as they left the hospital. "I feel I ought to apologize for what your father did just now."

"What did he do?"

"Dismissed us as soon as he made his point and got some agreement. That's his way. It seems very effective in diplomacy, but it's not easy to live with."

"Isn't it comforting, though, to know he's consistent? Even in grief?"

Laura looked sharply at her daughter. "That's the kind of double-edged remark Sabrina would have made. It's not kind to your father."

Sabrina sighed. "Mother, you're as hard to deal with as he is."

Parents, she thought again. But we keep loving them and wanting their approval, no matter how old we are. How was she going to have the courage to tell them the truth when Gordon recovered? Rejoice, Mother, Sabrina is not dead. Intensify your mourning, Father; it was your beloved Stephanie who died.

Neither of them would ever forgive her.

"I was hoping," Laura said the next morning as Sabrina put her key into the door of Ambassadors, "that you wouldn't sell it. Of course, it may not be fair to ask you that—I know you and Garth could use the money—but I was hoping you would keep it."

Sabrina did not answer. She had been away so long, and now, walking through the dusky showroom, she breathed deeply, touching familiar pieces, and felt as she had when she walked into the house on Cadogan Square: she was back where she belonged. A shop, a home. Every inch of them hers; created by her, held together by her work. "Of course I'll keep it," she said.

"But what will you do with it? If you can't run it—"

"Of course I'll run it; what are you talking about, Mother?"

"Stephanie, I'm asking how you plan to run Ambassadors from Evanston. Unless—are you suggesting you might not be in Evanston? That you and Garth—?"

"No." Standing with her mother at the door to her office, Sabrina came back to earth. "I'd work something out with Nicholas Blackford. He's interested in a partnership."

"Then you'd come over now and then. Well, that might work out. But, of course, Ambassadors really was Sabrina; it would take someone with her brilliance to keep its reputation. You could do it, though, if you study, or work in a small shop in Chicago to get some experience. And I would help you." She put her arm around Sabrina. "Oh, there is so much I could teach you! Wouldn't it be wonderful? Now my suggestion is—"

"Mother."

Laura drew back at the coldness in her daughter's voice. "If you don't want to talk about it now—"

"I don't want to talk about it now." Sabrina felt the pressures building inside her. Last night she had not slept, thinking of Stephanie, and, alone in bed for the first time in weeks, she had felt lonely and vulnerable without the comfort of Garth's arms. But mostly she was angry at her mother: how dare she insult Stephanie by assuming she couldn't handle Ambassadors? All her life she'd favored Sabrina, and now she was doing it again, acting as if Stephanie would automatically fail if she were to take over the shop.

Wait, this doesn't make sense, she thought. Am I Sabrina,

defending Stephanie, who is dead? Or am I Stephanie, angry because my mother doesn't believe in me?

"I don't want to talk about it now," she said to Laura. "I have to meet with Sidney Jones and Nicholas and Brian, and in a few days I'll know better what I'm going to do." She was walking toward the front door, bringing Laura with her. The shop was closed for the week; she'd come back alone the next day and think about the future.

By the next day she had another reason for coming to Ambassadors: it was her only private place. Laura and Gabrielle both were living in her house, wanting to talk to her. Mrs. Thirkell found little tasks on the upper floors so that she could find someone to talk to about Lady Longworth. The telephone rang constantly; everyone wanted to entertain Sabrina's American sister before she left London, and though she told Mrs. Thirkell to refuse them all, more kept coming. Flowers, letters and telegrams arrived daily. Sabrina retreated to the dim quiet of Ambassadors.

Alone, she went through the account books and files, reading letters and scanning catalogues that had come while she was away. Stephanie had recorded the sale of the Grendly daybed, the French beaded bag and several other pieces. In a notebook on the shelf behind the cherry table, she had listed three interior decorating commissions she had accepted for November and December. Sabrina was about to put the notebook away when she saw a letter tucked in the back. "Dearest Sabrina," it began. Dated October 23. The day before the cruise.

"I've been wondering," Stephanie had written, "what present I can leave you when I go back to Chicago, to thank you for the most wonderful time of my life. I could buy you something, but I've just thought of a better gift than anything Harrods has to offer. It's a story I've kept secret, and I'm writing it now for you to discover when you return. I'll have such fun imagining your face when you read about it, and then your telephone call. . . .

"It began at a party at Olivia Chasson's some time ago. I was talking to Rose Raddison when a sad accident occurred. . . ."

How wonderful, Sabrina thought, reading about the broken stork. Such a simple solution. Why didn't it occur to me when

I was trying to figure out what to do? Maybe now, after living with two rambunctious kids, I would have thought of it. She picked up the letter to finish it.

"That's about all, except that Rory Carr did come in later, after I'd seen him at the Chilton auction, with a magnificent Sevres piece that it broke my heart to turn down. But by then you'd told me not to deal with him. He wasn't here to sell, anyway, not really. He'd heard about the stork and was fishing for information. When he kept prying, I did a small imitation of a police officer and said, 'There isn't anything you can tell me that I don't already know.' That shook him up—he kept adjusting his cravat with elegant nervousness, and speedily departed. Oh, there's the front bell. I'll try to finish this tomorrow."

But tomorrow she was dead.

Alexandra walked in and found Sabrina carefully folding a handwritten letter. "Mrs. Thirkell gave away your hiding place; you don't mind if I invade your privacy?"

"Of course not. Please sit down. I'm not getting much done anyway."

"Thinking about Sabrina."

"Thinking about Sabrina and Stephanie."

"Funny, I never realized how close you two were."

There was a silence. "Shall I make us some tea?" Alexandra asked.

"Oh, how rude of me. I'll make it."

Sabrina put the kettle on the hot plate in Brian's office. "I'm afraid we have only biscuits to eat."

"Biscuits will be fine." There was another silence. "Are you still worried about your father?"

"No, he's much better. He'll go home Sunday."

"And you with him?"

"I . . . think so. Probably."

They sat in silence. "I'm sorry, honey," Alexandra burst out at last. "I can't get used to it. Are you a ghost? Sabrina told me the two of you didn't look alike."

"But—why would she say that?"

"How do I know? I thought she said it because it was true. Nicholas had played a little game, accusing her of being Stephanie—that you'd switched places in China, or something like that—and Sabrina was great; she frowned so seriously and told Nicholas to tell her who she was because he'd gotten her

364

so confused she couldn't remember. You know, I loved that lady, though I don't think I ever actually told her so. Anyway, after Nicholas proclaimed her Sabrina, I asked if you two really were identical and she said, no, he just thought so because of his pastries or his diet or some such thing."

Sabrina laughed. *Oh, Stephanie, good for you. You were saving that, weren't you, to tell me when we met in Chicago. So we could laugh about it together.*

But they couldn't laugh about it together. She stood up quickly. "I'll just see what's happening with the kettle."

"Damn," said Alexandra, following her into Brian's office. "I'm a damn fool. Please forgive me, I don't mean to upset you. It's just that I can't get used to the resemblance; it's uncanny, you know—people must tell you that all the time. Oh, why can't I shut up and leave you in peace?"

"No, don't shut up. I'm fine." The chatter helped; she made the tea with a steady hand and filled a plate with biscuits. She picked up the tray to carry it into her office. "Napkins," she said to Alexandra, tilting her head toward a cupboard in the corner.

"There! See? That's exactly what she did, only a week ago. See why I'm having trouble?"

Stephanie did that a week ago. But I've never done it before.

Sabrina poured the tea and spread jam on a biscuit, taking her time, thinking. Of all the people she knew in London, Alexandra was the most trustworthy, the one closest to her—and the toughest. There wasn't much that would shock Alexandra. But she was proud. Would she be such a close friend when she knew she'd been tricked?

It didn't matter. I have to tell someone, Sabrina thought. It's been so long since I had anyone to talk to—I have to tell someone. It will be my rehearsal for telling Garth. And everyone else.

"I'm going to tell you a story," she said slowly, "if you promise to listen to the whole thing without interrupting and not make a judgment until you've heard it all."

"Intriguing. Possibly wicked. I can't wait."

"Promise?"

"You want me to draw blood and sign my name?"

Sabrina smiled. "No. I wouldn't be telling you if I didn't trust—" The bell over the front door rang as someone opened it. "I'll be right back; I thought I had a *Closed* sign in the door."

A tall man was silhouetted against the front window; Sabrina saw his graying hair, a slight stoop, the thin cane he carried. She could not make out his features. "Mrs. Andersen?" he asked.

"Yes. But the shop is closed. If you'll come back next week—"

"I'm from Scotland Yard, Mrs. Andersen." He showed his identification. "Detective-Sergeant Thomas Phelps. I'd appreciate a few minutes of your time to talk to you about the death of your sister."

"Scotland Yard?"

He walked past her. "If we could sit down?"

Sabrina turned blindly and led the way into her office. Somehow they'd found out. They knew she was Sabrina. She wouldn't be able to tell the story in her own way after all. Everyone would learn about it in a jumble from the police, reporters, gossip columnists . . . and Garth would hear about it, too, from the police when they called—when they called to tell him his wife was dead. In London society it would be a scandal; at home in Evanston there would be pain and anger and tears. . . .

"My God," cried Alexandra, looking at her face as she came into the office. "What is it?" She looked at Phelps and stood up. "If you think I should leave, honey—Stephanie—"

"No, would you mind staying? I'd like it if you stayed."

"This is confidential, Mrs. Andersen," said Phelps.

"Then it will be confidential for Princess Martova," Sabrina said coldly. "I am asking her to stay."

He hesitated, then shrugged. It would be all over London in no time, anyway; one more society gossip wouldn't make a difference. He sat down and opened a notebook. "In the course of our investigations," he began, "we've learned that some of the people on Mr. Stuyvesant's yacht were not what they seemed to be."

Sabrina looked at him fixedly, waiting for his flat deliberate voice to call her Lady Longworth. "How did you discover—?"

"Please, Mrs. Andersen, let me begin at the beginning."

Mrs. Andersen. He had called her Mrs. Andersen. She watched him, waiting for the moment when he would try to trap her.

"Let me tell you what we've learned so far. Lady Longworth flew with Max Stuyvesant and two other couples to Nice on October 24. From there they drove to Monaco. They spent some time in Monte Carlo while Mr. Stuyvesant's yacht, the *Lafitte,* was being provisioned. At approximately 4:30 P.M. they boarded the yacht and left the harbor. When they were about two miles out—this would be at 5:30 P.M.—the yacht exploded and caught fire."

As Sabrina shrank back, Alexandra moved over to sit on the arm of her chair. "Are these details necessary?" she asked.

"I would not give them if I thought otherwise." Phelps consulted his notes. "By the time rescue boats got to the scene, the yacht was sinking. They concentrated on searching for survivors or bodies; they found three immediately, one of which was Lady Longworth. I'm sorry, ma'am, I know this gives you pain, but I'm trying to explain why the yacht itself was not examined until a few days ago."

"What difference does it make?" Sabrina asked, wondering why it was taking him so long to expose her. Was it something they found on the yacht? Something Stephanie had with her?

Phelps was reading from his notes. "Positive identification, made by Lady Longworth's former husband, Viscount Longworth, was made at 1:00 A.M., and I'm told you were told the news about an hour later, around dinner time in America. By this time the yacht had sunk, and several of those aboard with it. It wasn't until two days ago that divers were able to raise it. What we found, Mrs. Andersen—what the French police found, that is—was a large hole in the side of the *Lafitte* below the waterline in the area of the staterooms. They reported that—"

"The staterooms?" Sabrina leaned forward. "The staterooms are nowhere near the fuel tanks. So they couldn't have been the cause of the explosion."

Phelps was disconcerted. The revelation toward which he was building was being taken from him. "That is precisely the point. We'd assumed it was a fuel tank. Now we know it was not. We think, in fact—"

"You think it was a bomb, set to go off in a stateroom."

Phelps sat back, defeated. He was a low-level investigator who did the preliminary work for higher-ups to evaluate; there was little excitement in his job and no glamour. His only enjoyment came when a gasp ran through his audience as he sprang an unexpected bit of information on them. Now, just when he was prepared to spring, this pale beauty, too smart for her own good, took his moment away from him.

"But that means they were murdered," she was saying, and he looked at her with reluctant admiration.

"It seems likely, ma'am. So we're trying to discover if Mr. Stuyvesant or his guests had any enemies. Now, I'm not suggesting that Lady Longworth had enemies, but we received information from two writers—Michel Bernard and Jolie Fantome—that they had recently learned Mr. Stuyvesant was the owner of a company called Westbridge Imports, and they also said that Lady Longworth occasionally bought—Mrs. Andersen!"

But Alexandra held her and kept her from collapsing while Stephanie's letter echoed in her mind: *I did a small imitation of a police officer,* and said, "There is nothing you can tell me that I don't already know."

There is nothing you can tell me that I don't already know.

There is nothing you can tell me—

They were after me. They thought I knew about their forgeries.

Phelps was satisfied. He had achieved his effect. "I have a few questions, Mrs. Andersen," he said gently.

Sabrina raised her head. They didn't know who she was. They were after something far worse. "All right."

Phelps was curious. There's something else on her mind, he thought. She's scared. Of what? Something about Westbridge. But what could it be? She lives in America; she has nothing to do with them. "First," he began, "did Lady Longworth talk to you about Max Stuyvesant?"

"Only that she was going on a cruise with him."

"And what did she say about the cruise? Anything about the other guests? Where they were going?"

"No. Nothing."

"She didn't mention enemies that Stuyvesant might have had?"

"Mr. Phelps, my sister never spoke to me about Max Stuyvesant's business or the people he dealt with."

Phelps was puzzled. He would swear she was telling the truth. So what was she afraid of? He went on, using his notes. "Michel Bernard came to us when he heard we suspected a bomb on the yacht. He told us there'd been a falling out between Stuyvesant and the people at Westbridge. Did Lady Longworth ever talk to you about Westbridge Imports or Rory Carr or Ivan Lazlo? Buying from them?"

There was a pause. "She mentioned Carr occasionally, along with dozens of other salesmen and dealers. I don't think she had bought from him lately. At least not a major piece."

They were silent. Well, Phelps thought, this time she's lying about something. But damned if I know what. There's not a shred of evidence that this shop was involved in any smuggling or in collusion on forgeries. But something's bothering her. Trying to identify it, he continued to ask questions about people Sabrina knew and others she did not. He went on and on, pointlessly it seemed, and then at last closed his notebook.

"We're looking for Carr and Lazlo, and no doubt we'll know more when we find them. Do you have anything else you think might help us, ma'am?"

"No," Sabrina said wearily. When they found Rory Carr, he probably would implicate her, but she couldn't do anything about it now. For the moment Ambassadors' reputation was safe, and so was her own secret. But she was so tired, as if she had run a race and finished barely a step ahead of everyone else. It was too late to tell Alexandra the truth; with Scotland Yard involved she could not make her a part of the half-lies she had told. She was more alone than ever. I want to go home, she thought. I want to be with Garth.

"Where can we reach you, Mrs. Andersen?" Phelps asked, pocketing his notes. She gave them her number at Cadogan Square. "And in America?"

"I'll let you know when I return. I plan to be here for a while."

Alexandra saw him out. She held in her questions while Sabrina pulled the shades on the front windows and locked the door. "Do you want to talk, honey?" she asked, as they flagged down a taxi. Sabrina shook her head. "No. But thank you. Maybe later . . ." At Cadogan Square she got out alone, still holding Stephanie's letter. As she unlocked her door and went inside, she was still repeating one line of it, over and over, in her mind.

The nights were the hardest times—the slow quiet hours when Sabrina was alone, thinking of Stephanie, aching for Garth, her thoughts skipping wildly between her two worlds.

The days were better; she kept busy and thought only about what she was doing from one minute to the next.

Each morning, she visited Gordon and then had lunch with Laura at Grenadier, a pub tucked away among mews houses behind the hospital. Afterward, Sabrina walked to Ambassadors to plan the decorating jobs Stephanie had accepted and to study auction catalogs. But she never stayed long; restless and impatient, she would escape as soon as she could to be alone in the crowds of the city. All week she took long, solitary walks through the villages that make up London's neighborhoods. At tea time she returned home to Mrs. Thirkell and Gabrielle and listened to Gabrielle talk from tea time through dinner about London gossip and Brooks. Without knowing it, she filled Sabrina in on everything that had happened while she was in America.

"I don't suppose you're interested, Stephanie, since you don't know most of these people. But you're so much like Sabrina—"

"It's all right. Of course I'm interested. They're your friends, and Sabrina's. Of course I'm interested."

"I feel so odd talking to you. Eerie. It's so amazing, how you look . . . as if Sabrina hadn't died. The last few weeks, you know, she was the only one who really cared about me. And now—I know it's not fair to you, but you're all I have. And not even you, really, because you've got a family to worry about and you've lost Sabrina, too—"

When Gabrielle's eyes filled with tears, she looked like Penny, small and disconsolate. Sabrina led her to the couch in the drawing room and put her arms around her, and by the way Gabrielle relaxed against her, she knew that was what Stephanie had done.

Would she have held Gaby this way a few months ago? Probably not, or at least not so easily. She would have been self-conscious about displays of affection and nurturing, as were her friends. But here sat Sabrina Longworth, comforting Gabrielle de Martel without embarrassment or discomfort; in fact, feeling perfectly natural.

It was Penny and Cliff, Sabrina thought; living with them changed me so that this seems right. And important. She could close her eyes and see them: Penny sitting quietly in a corner, drawing and humming to herself, or sitting close, touching, confiding something special; Cliff chanting words for a spelling test, or sitting with her, eyes bright as they joked together. Oh, she missed them; she missed their trust and love and even the chaos they brought into a house. Her arms felt empty. Holding Gabrielle, they still felt empty.

On most nights Gabrielle was restless and soon would find a party to fill her evening while Sabrina went upstairs to the quiet of her room. Mrs. Thirkell would have lit a fire, laid out her robe and left a snack of cake and a silver thermos of tea. Sabrina would sit beside a small lamp, reading and thinking—about Stephanie, about Garth, about the children, about a future she could not predict. And each night, almost exactly at ten, Garth called. In Evanston it was four o'clock; he was home from the university and Penny and Cliff were with him in the breakfast room, clamoring for the telephone so they could talk for a few precious minutes.

"When are you coming home?" they asked each night, and finally, when Gordon had been told he could leave the hospital, Sabrina had an answer.

"We're leaving on Saturday," she told Garth. "I'll fly to Washington with my parents and then to Chicago on Monday."

"Monday," he said, passing the news to Penny and Cliff, and Sabrina heard their shouts of delight.

But it won't last, she thought, watching the flames in the fireplace and the long, distorted shadows they threw on the walls and ceiling. Because she was going back to tell them the truth. For a week she had been acting as Stephanie in Sabrina's world, and by now she felt she was no one. Garth had been right: she could not drift back and forth; she had to be one or the other; she had to be Sabrina. So she would tell them the truth, and then they would hate her. When Garth knew his wife was dead, when Penny and Cliff knew their mother was dead, that Sabrina had deceived them for weeks, they would turn away from her. She couldn't even tell them she loved them. They wouldn't want her love. She would be left with no one to give it to.

When they said goodbye and she had put down the telephone, Sabrina sat in the silent room until she was tired enough to fall asleep before the longing for Garth began to pulse through her. It was not making love that she craved—she didn't let herself think of that at all—but just his presence, close beside her, sharing the small space that was theirs alone.

But she was too tired even to reach out to touch the warm dream that was not there. She turned off her light and went to sleep.

"Are you coming back?" Alexandra asked when she stopped in at Ambassadors on Friday. She had brought a stack of photographs and fanned them out on the table. "These were taken at a new restaurant where Sabrina and I had dinner one night. Brooks joined us there later. So did Antonio, in fact— the launching of our passionate romance. I thought you'd like a set. *Are* you coming back, do you think?"

"Yes, of course," said Sabrina, studying the photographs in silent amazement. How had Stephanie done it? In the tilt of her head, her posture and cool, public smile, she had become Sabrina. And what about me? Sabrina asked herself. What did I become? "Yes, of course I'm coming back," she said absently. "This is home."

"Home? What about America?"

"I meant, this is Sabrina's home and I haven't decided what I'll do about it. So I'll be back soon. What about you? Will you be here or chatting in Portuguese with contractors and jungle-clearers?"

Alexandra gave her a swift glance. "Sounded like your sister there, honey. Looks like I may be chatting. But not in Portuguese. It took me a long time to learn proper English, and I'm not going to start another language for anybody. I can make Antonio understand that."

"Why don't you find a Guarani legend that says the home tongue is the best and quote it whenever he asks you to learn Portuguese?"

"Now that is a brilliant . . . What do I do if there isn't one?"

"Make one up. He'll be ashamed to admit he's never heard of it."

Alexandra burst into laughter. "God damn, honey, I'll do it. You're wonderful, you're as sharp as Sabrina. Do they ever let you out of Chicago? Come visit us. In our lavish hut in the middle of nowhere, or our condominium in Rio. Or here, when we're in London. Will you come? You and your husband, of course. If he's interested."

"I might."

"We'd make you welcome. For your sister's sake, as well as your own." She pulled on her coat and stood in the doorway.

"She was a very special lady, and you are, too. I think we'd get along fine."

"So do I. Will you write and tell me about yourself? I'll miss . . . I'll miss having a chance to get to know you."

"Honey, I never write. The words pile up in my head and won't come out. They get so crowded they give me a headache and I give up. But I'm terrific with a telephone; what's your number in Evanston?"

Sabrina hesitated. "I may be here. You should call Ambassadors first, or at Cadogan Square."

Alexandra looked at her keenly, began to say something, then changed direction. "Whatever you say. Take care of yourself, Stephanie."

"Goodbye, Alexandra."

On Friday afternoon she told Nicholas and Sidney Jones she was going to America for a few days. "I'll be back as soon as I get my father settled in Washington and spend a few days with my family. I'm keeping the shop closed, and I've told Brian the same thing I'm telling you; I won't make any decisions until I talk to both of you. Until then, nothing is to be done with Ambassadors or my house. Is that clear?"

What would they say, she wondered, when she came back and told them the truth? They wouldn't care much; their lives would not change.

But she was gentler that night when she told Gabrielle and Mrs. Thirkell. "I'll be back soon, so neither of you should think of leaving. This is your home, Gaby, as long as you want it, and yours, too, Mrs. Thirkell. I want you to keep it in good order until I come back. I'll let you know when to expect me."

They will care, she thought, when I tell them the truth. Because they have relied on me in different ways.

And who else would care? Scotland Yard. Because someone blew up Max's yacht to kill her and would probably try again when it became public that it was her sister, not Sabrina Longworth, who had been killed.

Maybe I won't come back, she thought. It's safer in Chicago.

Flying at thirty-five thousand feet through bright Saturday sunlight, a week after Stephanie's funeral, Gordon sat between his daughter and his wife, planning the future. He and Laura talked about selling their house, buying a smaller one without stairs and hiring an assistant to help him research and write his book on American foreign policy in Europe. How much they've aged, Sabrina reflected; arranging their time to do less, have more help, smooth their days. And she realized she could not tell her story to both of them at the same time. She would tell her mother first; Laura would know how to tell Gordon.

But first she had to tell Garth. She would stay with her parents in Washington over Saturday and Sunday night, and fly to Chicago on Monday. Monday noon, while Penny and Cliff were in school. She couldn't bear to see them, and she couldn't talk to Garth while they were there. So, at noon, when they were safely in school, Garth would meet her plane and they would go—where? Not home. Not that wonderful, protective shabby house that was home. A restaurant. Some place where Garth need never go again and hear echoes of that terrible moment when she looked at him and finally told him the truth.

Then, that same afternoon, she would go back to Washington to tell her parents, and the next day she would return to London. And it would be truly over. She would never see Penny and Cliff again. Never see Garth again. Never see Dolores and Nat, Vivian, Madeline Kane, Linda and Martin, Garth, Garth, Garth . . .

"Stephanie, what is it?"

She wiped her eyes and leaned over to kiss her father. "Just thinking."

Gordon peered at her. "You're sure you're all right?"

"I'm fine," Sabrina said, pleasing him. "Don't worry about me; I'll do my thinking less damply."

You'd think I'd be dried up by now, she thought. How can one person have so many tears? But she knew there would be more when she confessed to everyone. And anger. But only then, when it was all out, would it be time to put this life behind her and pick up the pieces in London where she had left them in September.

If you can. Her eyes flew open at the thought. What makes you so sure you can simply pick up the pieces? Things have happened since you left. Will your London friends be overjoyed when they hear how you and Stephanie made fools of them, even letting them weep at a funeral for the wrong woman? Will they laugh in high good humor at such a jolly prank? Or will they walk away from you and Ambassadors because they don't like to be the butt of someone's joke? Especially in public.

Alexandra wouldn't do that.

Alexandra will be in South America most of the time.

Gaby wouldn't do that.

But Gaby and Brooks will get back together soon, or she'll find someone else. And how much time will she have for an ostracized Sabrina Longworth?

Olivia—but, of course, Olivia would do just that.

And how pleased will Scotland Yard be when they discover you lied about who was killed on that yacht near Monte Carlo? An international incident—Monaco, France, England.

No one will want to have anything to do with you.

You can't live in Evanston and you can't live in London.

I'll have to live somewhere else, she thought. Start again somewhere else. New York. I could open a shop in New York.

And who will you be?

Not Stephanie Andersen. You're going to tell everyone Stephanie is dead.

Sabrina Longworth.

Yes. Sabrina Longworth, starting a new life in New York, opening a new shop called—what will you call it?

No Deceptions.

Very amusing. Any other ideas?

No.

The plane followed the sun across the ocean. In the cabin, stewards cleared lunch trays, brought pillows, poured drinks. Laura read. Gordon closed his eyes and slept. Sabrina moved to an empty seat and rested her head against the cool window, looking at the pale merging of water and sky. *Stephanie, I miss you.*

Garth, dear love . . .

Any other ideas?

No.

Chapter 18

Sunlight glinted off the Potomac River as Sabrina's plane banked and climbed for its flight to Chicago. Early November: the trees of Virginia flamed with yellow, russet and orange across the river from Washington's clustered stone and marble monuments.

She caught a glimpse of Georgetown before the plane finished its turn. Laura and Gordon would be in the study, thinking of lunch. By nightfall I'll be back, she thought, shattering their tranquility with my story. Garth is first.

I have something to tell you; could we go somewhere for a cup of coffee?

No, not home. A restaurant.

These last few weeks, since September, I haven't been what you think—

These last weeks, when you thought I was . . .

I have something to tell you . . . in a restaurant . . . You see, last September, in China, Stephanie and I decided, for a lark—

No, that wasn't a mistake. I meant to say Stephanie. That's what I want to tell you. When we were in China, Stephanie and I decided to change places for a week.

Far below, the black tangle of Indiana's steel mills moved into view. And then there was the curved shore of Lake Michigan. *I have something to tell you; can we go to a restaurant?*

376

When they had landed, she walked with the other passengers from the plane to the waiting area and paused, scanning the crowd.

"Mom! Here we are!"

"Mommy!" Penny flung her arms around Sabrina. "I'm glad you're back, I'm glad you're back, I don't *like* it when you're gone." Cliff reached up to plant a vigorous kiss on her cheek. Stunned, Sabrina stared at them and over their heads at Garth.

"Why aren't you in school?"

Cliff grinned. "Dad said we could stay out to meet your plane. Aren't you glad to see us?"

Slowly Sabrina nodded. With Penny's arms tight around her and the imprint of Cliff's warm kiss on her cheek—oh, yes, she was glad to see them. But this wasn't the way she had rehearsed it; it had never occurred to her that Garth would bring them. Which shows, she thought, how much I know about being a mother. "Speechless with delight," she said, kissing them. "And surprise."

"Make some room, you two," said Garth. He took her in his arms, holding her close, and Sabrina felt the shape of her bones fit into his. "Hello," he said quietly. "Welcome home."

She looked at the strong lines of his face and the glow in his dark eyes. *Oh, I've missed you, I've missed you.* She rested her head against him.

Enclosed in his arms, her face against his chest, she heard his heartbeat and felt his lips touch her hair. And in that moment, she knew, with absolute certainty, that she could never tell him the truth.

She could never tell him he had been tricked into loving and cherishing a woman who was a fraud. She would not fling her lies in the face of his tenderness.

Then stay. Live with him and his family—my family. Stay. This is home.

But the thought did not make it so, and neither did the desire. This was not her place; her home and life were elsewhere. And even though she had seen her London world all too clearly after Stephanie's funeral, with its gossip and jealousies and idle entanglements, it was a world she knew, where she moved with confidence. And Ambassadors and Cadogan Square—built by her, maintained by her efforts and her own social and business contacts—were where she belonged.

But as Garth's arms held her she knew there was another reason she could not stay: the most important reason. They could not build a life together based on a deception. He had been honest and open with her, trusting her with the self he kept hidden from others. In return she had lied and kept her private self hidden from him. She could not see any way out of that, except deeper into lies. *And I can't do that—to either of us.*

She would have to find a reason, any reason, tell it to him and leave, just as she'd planned, right away, before their love drew her into their life again. "I have to tell you something, but not with the children—"

"And I have a great deal to tell you, but not with the children. Shall we pack them off somewhere?" With his arm around her they were walking through the terminal, and he scanned the airline gates. "Denver. Seattle. Fairbanks . . . how about Fairbanks? They can explore Alaska while we explore each other."

"Garth, I'm serious."

"So am I. We need to be alone. I thought we'd go to Wisconsin this weekend, just the two of us, find a lodge, do some hiking, sit in front of the fire. Sound all right?"

She shook her head.

"Think about it; we have all week to decide."

Chattering steadily, Penny and Cliff skipped beside them to the car. Then, as Garth drove, Penny asked a question about London and Cliff hushed her sharply. Sabrina turned around.

"It's all right. You can ask about London. And anything else."

"Daddy told us about the funeral," said Penny. "It sounded very impressive."

"Indeed it was."

"All those noble people."

"The nobility, Penny. To be noble takes more than a title."

Garth chuckled and relaxed, no longer worried that the questions would upset her. They talked about the Vicar and the people who came to Cadogan Square, Gordon's heart attack and the ambulance, Mrs. Thirkell, Alexandra and the Guarani Indians, Ambassadors. And, through it all, Sabrina listened in disbelief.

Two months ago, when she arrived from China, Garth wanted to have a serious talk and she would not give him a chance. Today, when she arrived from London and wanted to have a serious talk, no one would give her a chance.

But soon they would be home. Not home, she thought quickly. The Andersens' home. Then Penny and Cliff would go off somewhere and she would tell Garth she was leaving. She wouldn't even sit down or take off her coat; she would tell him immediately, take a cab back to the airport and still be in Washington before her parents went to bed.

"You're very quiet," Garth said, as he parked the car. Sabrina was looking at the house.

"It looks so different—all the leaves are gone."

"We had a spectacular thunderstorm one night that sent both kids scurrying to our room—pretending they wanted to watch the lightning with me—and it stripped the trees clean. Autumn came to a crashing end."

I've never seen it look so bare. And unprotected.

Garth carried in her suitcase and put on a pot of coffee. Penny and Cliff took cookies from the jar. "Five-thirty, Mom?" Cliff asked.

I won't be here. "Yes. Can I have a quick hug?"

They held her tightly. "It's *awful* when you're not here," Penny said. "I *hate* it. The house is so *empty.*" She looked quickly at Garth. "I'm sorry, Daddy, I didn't mean . . ."

Garth chuckled and kissed her. "I know what you meant, my sweet. It seemed empty to me, too. Are you off somewhere?"

"I told Barbara I'd come over when we got back from the airport."

"Go on, then. Five-thirty for you, too."

And in one swift moment, Sabrina and Garth were alone in the breakfast room.

Sabrina did not sit down. "Garth, I have to leave. I wanted to tell you at the airport and not come home at all, but I couldn't with Penny and Cliff there. I'm going back to London, to be alone, to find out what I really want, I can't stay here—"

"Wait." Incredulous, Garth had swung his head to look at her, and now he put out his hand—a barrier to stop her voice. "I'll see if our coffee is ready. I think you should sit down."

Sabrina was shaking. She pulled out a chair and fell into it, gripping her hands and staring through the window at the bare, wintry backyard. Empty: the way she felt. Garth came back with the coffeepot. "I don't think that's a good idea," he said carefully. Sabrina saw the stiffness of his movements; he was holding himself in. He sat beside her and took her cold hands between his, warming them. "You can't run away from yourself. You can't live Sabrina's life. Nothing would be solved by leaving: Penny and Cliff and I would always be here, waiting, like an unfinished story. You'd have two half-finished lives instead of one."

The front doorbell broke into his words. "Goddamn it, there aren't five quiet minutes . . . I'd better see who it is. Don't go away, I'll be right back. You won't go away? You'll wait?"

"Yes." Alone, Sabrina looked around the honey-colored room. Home. An unfinished story. A half-finished life. She couldn't argue with him because he was right, but he only knew part of the story and she couldn't tell him the rest. She would just have to get up and walk out. And whatever pain he felt when she left would be far less than the pain of the truth.

Faintly she heard Dolores's voice from the front porch. Don't let her in, she prayed silently to Garth; I can't face her. On the sideboard was a stack of mail addressed to Stephanie. Mechanically she began to tear open the envelopes. A condolence card from Vivian. Another from Linda and Martin. A note from Juanita. Three cards from people she'd never heard of. A pink envelope with no return address, and inside a short, typed note.

How come those stories about students fucking profs for passing grades leave out Garth Andersen—the fuckingest of them all? A regular gene-ius at fucking students, that's our Professor Garth!

She read it twice and then again, frozen in the cold wave of fury that swept through her. How dare someone—! This filth, these obscene lies—how dare anyone accuse Garth of them! Who would do this—try to destroy a man who was more honorable than anyone she had ever known?

Everything else dropped away; the past week receded, and all she saw was the letter and what it could do to Garth. Energy surged through her, buoying her up from the despair that had dragged at her since Stephanie's death. Someone was trying to ruin Garth, viciously, anonymously . . . and whoever it was would succeed; he could be irreparably damaged if they didn't fight. They had to find out who —

Wait, wait, she thought. What about leaving? I've told Garth I'm leaving.

She brushed it aside. Yes, of course, of course I have to leave. Nothing has changed that. But I can't right now, not this minute, because there's something I have to do first. I owe it to Stephanie; I owe it to Garth, because I deceived him. Nothing has changed; I'll still leave—I'm just putting it off for a little while until this is cleared up. Because it's obvious that—

"I told Dolores you'd call tomorrow," said Garth, coming in. "I'm sorry I was so long; I feel as if I'd been in combat with a tornado. You haven't poured the coffee." He sat down and filled their mugs. "Now maybe we can—my God, Stephanie, what is it?"

Wordlessly, she handed him the letter. He scanned it, the lines in his face hardening as he read it a second time. "I didn't know they'd drag me into it." A thought struck him. "Unless . . . you've gotten one of these damned things before, haven't you? This is what you were talking about when we quarreled just before you went to China. Why didn't you show it to me? All that anguish, when I didn't know what the hell you meant—"

"I don't want to talk about the past," Sabrina broke in impatiently. "We have to think about what we're going to do now to stop it before it goes any further." She was thinking quickly. "If copies were sent to the trustees or officers of the university, and they believe it, or even if they don't but they're afraid of a scandal, you could be hurt; couldn't it even affect your appointment as director of the Genetics Institute?"

"Yes. But wait a minute." Events were whipping past Garth, and he tried to slow them down. A few minutes ago, answering the doorbell, he left behind a drooping, anxious figure determined to run away. He came back to a vividly alive woman sitting on the edge of her chair, a warrior charging to his defense, recognizing with perfect insight what damage the letter could do. Six months ago, concerned with herself and less interested in the politics of the university, she would not have been so quick. He was stirred by the bright anger in her eyes, the taut line of her slender neck as she held her head high, ready for battle. For him. "You don't believe the letter," he said.

"*Believe* it? Garth, you can't be serious. No one who knows you would believe this trash. Someone wants to destroy you; we have to find out who it is."

He looked at her thoughtfully. She had believed it in September. Now she didn't. "I'm a little slow today," he ventured. "I thought I heard you say you were leaving, going back to London."

"You're not slow and you know it; don't play games with me."

"And if I ask the same of you?"

"I'm not playing games! What is the matter with you? Can't you see how things have changed? If other people get this letter and I'm not here, they'll assume I've left you because what it says is true. No one will believe I left for other reasons; if I leave now, you would be condemned no matter what you said."

So she had seen that, too, Garth thought. She had seen it all. He went to her and took her face between his hands. "I thought of that when I saw the letter. Thank you."

"You didn't say anything."

"Such as?"

"Asking me to stay because of the harm that would be done if I left."

"If you left. My dear love, if you left, the wreckage would extend far beyond a campus scandal. It would destroy this house, this family, three hearts and minds and spirits—"

"Don't, please don't—"

He kissed the tears from her eyes. But her body was tense, as if she was clamping down the possibility of desire, and he moved away. They had time now. As long as she was staying, they had time. Her grief and despair in London had been so terrible, and her loneliness for her sister so much more than he could imagine, that he felt demands on her would be intrusions in a healing process he could support but not direct.

But now he asked for one more assurance. He took her hands in his. "You are staying? Whatever your reasons were for wanting to leave, I don't have to wonder each morning if I'll find you here at the end of the day?"

"I'll help you get through this," she promised.

"That isn't what I asked."

"Garth, can't we take it one step at a time? So much has happened in such a little while ... I'm trying to do what is right for everyone."

"You can't make that decision alone. It involves all of us."

She bent her head. Garth began to say something, then stopped. In the silence, she felt him turn over the hand he was holding. Her left hand. "You aren't wearing your ring."

A chill touched her. "No."

"Where is it?"

She hesitated, swinging between lies and the truth. "In London."

"Damn it, who are you to take all these steps on your own? You decide you won't have a family anymore, so you take off your ring and that makes it official? Then all you have to do is say a quick goodbye?"

She felt relief and guilt. One lie or another, she thought. But better this than the truth: that she'd returned the ring to Stephanie. "I thought it would be—"

"A symbol," he said. "And it is. But I happen to believe in symbols. Where is it now?"

"I suppose ... in the house on Cadogan Square."

"Then Mrs. Thirkell can send it back."

"If she can find it."

"Write to her."

"All right."

"And if she can't find it, we'll buy another."

I won't be here long enough.

"And I'm asking you, Stephanie—are you listening to me?" She nodded. "I'm asking you to let me help you at the same time you're helping me. Damn it, we're part of each other and we'll help each other. Agreed?"

"Agreed," she said, wishing he could, knowing he could not. She picked up the letter. "What does this mean—'those stories about students—'?"

"I'll show you." He left the room and brought back the university newspaper. "Last Wednesday's *Standard.* Our journalism students outdid themselves."

Sabrina read the banner headline, "Sex for Grades," and beneath it, "Or Vice Versa."

"The *Standard* doesn't know who makes the first offer," she read. "But three professors and a passel of fair female students have been summoned to V.P. Lloyd Strauss's office for an air-ing of charges that they've been trading favors, with payment in grades—the only thing more valuable than money hereabouts. It may have been going on since last spring quarter; a nasty tale that could affect class standing and even graduation in some cases. Not to mention the academic future of the professors."

"Written like a gossip column," Garth muttered. "Somebody ought to teach those kids that journalism is serious business. They're dealing with people's lives."

"Which people?" Sabrina asked.

"Melvin Blake, someone named Millburn and Marty Talvia—"

"Not Marty. You mean those rumors were—? I don't believe it. Oh, poor Linda."

"—and now, it seems, Garth Andersen."

"But it's all absurd. You and Marty wouldn't—"

"And Blake and Millburn?"

"I don't know them. I suppose if any of the rumors are true—"

"The problem is, my love, that if you admit the possibility of one, you admit the possibility of all."

"But Garth, I know you wouldn't, and Marty . . . *would* Marty?"

"I think he and Linda had a bad time a few months ago. He didn't confide in me; I think he tried to once or twice and then backed off."

"When you were in California I asked you once on the telephone—"

"He's had other women. He talks about them, long after the fact, ashamed of himself for behaving like a kid who sneaks candies even when he's not hungry. But I would have thought he'd keep away from students."

"What did he tell Lloyd Strauss?"

"All of them denied it."

"And then?"

"That's as much as I know. I assume Lloyd is doing some checking; I haven't talked to him lately. I will now. Would you like more coffee?"

"No, I ought to be thinking about dinner." How naturally she said it; how natural it was to slip back. Sabrina looked at Garth, close to her in the warm room. How natural it was to love him.

He met her look. "And I love you," he said. "As for dinner, we'll go out. The larder is bare. We didn't want to function too successfully without you. But there is wine."

Sabrina watched him open a bottle and fill two glasses. "I think we should make some waves on the social scene," she mused. "I think we should be highly visible. Garth and ... Stephanie Andersen, in the open, with nothing to hide."

He handed her a glass. "Who is it you're trying to convince?"

"Whoever wonders about our marriage and what you do with your free time."

He laughed. "If you think it will help. I'd rather find the letter-writer."

"Oh, yes," she said calmly. "We'll do that, too. We should make a list of students you've failed in the past year. Or any who got a lower grade than expected. Or anyone you yelled at. Why are you laughing?"

"The list is getting very long."

"How long? You think of names and I'll start writing."

Half an hour later, when Penny and Cliff came in, they found their parents still at the breakfast room table, talking. Dad was relaxed in his chair, legs stretched out before him, a quiet smile on his face. Mom sat straight, writing, her eyes bright. Penny sighed and touched Cliff's arm. "Right," he said, and they both knew what he meant: their home was back together again.

When Sabrina unpacked that night, she discovered Mrs. Thirkell had filled the suitcase with Lady Longworth's clothes. Her closet in Evanston was now a mixture of Stephanie and Sabrina—like our lives, she thought. I wonder how much longer I'll be able to tell them apart. Putting everything away, she slid into the familiar four-poster bed, feeling the weariness of a day that had gone through a dozen transformations since she left Washington in the morning.

She saw Garth's silhouette in the doorway before he disappeared into the bathroom. There was something special about that; she tried to think what it was. And in a moment she had it: this was their first night together in a routine of family life since the night in New York when she had acknowledged her love for him. Since then they had been separated, first by her grief and then by the ocean. Now, she had agreed to stay. As his wife. And she could not pretend that night in New York had never happened.

She lay still, waiting for him, remembering the hours of longing that had filled her nights in London. And then he was beside her, silently gathering her to him.

"My sweet love," he murmured. "This bed grew emptier and wider each night you were not in it."

She laughed, a low, contented laugh, moving her lips against his. "So did mine. If we had waited long enough, they might have met in the middle of the Atlantic."

"No. We waited long enough. Too long."

His hands moved over her slender form, and hers answered along the harder lines of his body. Their lips spoke against each other, murmuring, laughing, making small wordless sounds, while their eyes met. When they came together, it was with the incandescence they remembered: joy and delight, the intensity of pleasure given and received, a sense of belonging, of coming home. They were strong in what they could give each other; they were both vulnerable, without shame, in what they needed from each other.

Wonderingly, Garth gazed at her beauty, at the brightness it cast. "You fill the room with light," he said.

"And life and love," Sabrina said softly. She traced the lines of his face with tender fingers. "I remember a poem: 'Love makes one little room an everywhere.' That's what I've found with you."

"What we have found," he said. They lay still in the lamplight, holding hands, Garth's arm cradling her, Sabrina's head on his shoulder as she drifted in the pleasure of the last hour and the comfort of his flesh, so much a part of hers there seemed no division between them.

She gazed at the reflection of the moon in the mirror, a clear white crescent caught in the black branches of an oak tree. As I am caught, she thought drowsily, in my love for this man, and his for me. She remembered with a smile one of Antonio's Indian tales. It was not important, he had said, if she did not love him before she married him. "The Guarani gods say love is the last thing, not the first. It grows slowly through sharing and creating. When you live together and build a family, love will come."

"Do you know," Garth said ruefully, "reluctant as I am to admit it—"

"—You're hungry," Sabrina finished, laughing. "Well, come on. Let's see what we can find in the bare larder. It won't be the first time you and I have made something from nothing."

Garth handed Lloyd Strauss the letter, in its envelope. "Add it to my official biography for university press releases. BA, MA, PhD, director of the Genetics Institute and lecher."

Strauss took a similar envelope from his desk drawer and held it out to Garth. "Came yesterday."

Garth felt a stab of helplessness: an invisible presence, vindictive and persevering, on a campus of thirty thousand students—assuming it was a student who was behind it. He pulled out the letter, identical to his. "Are there others?"

"Not that I know of. The president didn't get one."

"How come you got the honor?"

Strauss shrugged. "The story in the *Standard?* My strong arm summoning Talvia and Blake? Somebody wants you summoned. And lo and behold, here you are."

"Not through a summons."

"You beat me to it."

"Lloyd, you're not taking this seriously."

"I take all accusations seriously."

Garth gave him a long look. "Something else is new, I gather."

"Talvia and Blake resigned from the faculty today."

Garth swore softly and began to pace the office. "Forced out? To make it look as if the university was cleaning house?"

"They confessed, Garth. I had weeping girls in here, outraged parents, remorseful professors ... more drama than Shakespeare. The guy who started it—called the president, bellowing about his little girl being corrupted—happens to be a big contributor to the new football stadium. It would be football, wouldn't it? Can't ignore football. So the stink spread, and the president ordered me to clear it up before word got out. Word, of course, got out; the *Standard,* damn its industrious student hide, got the details into last week's paper before I'd even arranged my Shakespearean session. By the time I did, I was getting telephone calls from, as they say, the media."

Sitting on the edge of the window seat, arms folded, Garth shook his head. "Poor Marty. You think you know someone, you think you've built trust, and then, when it's too late, you find there are still gaps. I hardly know Blake; wasn't there another one?"

"Millburn. I'll have his resignation tomorrow. And—you."

"Oh, for God's sake, Lloyd—an anonymous letter. You know me well enough to know what shit that is—"

"Right. I know you; I know what shit it is. Does the *Chicago Tribune* know it? Does *Time?* Does *Newsweek?*"

"What the hell—" Garth stopped in disbelief. *"That* media?"

"That media. This is juicy stuff, my friend. 'What dark doings really go on behind those ivy-covered walls? Tune in tomorrow, or buy tomorrow's paper or next week's magazine.' We set ourselves up for this, you know, acting as if we're above the crowd: scholars, researchers, keepers of the truth. So, of course, the public loves to hear that we're as fucked up as the rest of them, and out of the woodwork come the reporters, to tell them all about it. So even though I'd like to burn anonymous letters, I can't do it. How do I know who else got them? How do I know who's blabbing all kinds of crap to reporters? You're my friend and colleague, and I trust you, but my first responsibility is to the university."

"Which means an investigation."

"That's what it means. It's already started. I hired a topnotch firm this morning."

"And just what are they going to investigate?"

Strauss jumped up and paced the length of his office. "You, other professors, students. Maybe we have it all, maybe this is only the tip of an iceberg. But when someone makes a specific charge, we have to look into it. They'll find out who wrote the letter, talk to people about your reputation and character—"

"My reputation and character!" Garth swept up his briefcase and strode to the door. "Listen, you son of a bitch, I don't have to defend my reputation and character to you or anyone else. You know me well enough to handle this yourself without bringing in professional spies. If you don't, you shouldn't be announcing my appointment to the Genetics Institute next week."

Strauss looked at him in silence. Garth held the door half open. "You *are* announcing it next week."

"It's been postponed. Garth, *I've got to cover my ass.* And you know it. It's not just money for a goddamn football stadium; it's the whole university. We have to be pure as a virgin when we apply for government research grants or ask donors to fund a new theater, a music building, the library addition, an international studies center. ... I have to show that I am doing my damnedest to keep this a safe place for people to send their kids or give money to so their name can be on a building. That's my job. If it means hiring a detective to ask people if Garth Andersen screws between seminars, I'll do it. And, since your job is to teach and do research, *and be the director of a new Genetics Institute,* you'll answer every one of their fucking questions. What do you have to hide? You'll be here a lot longer than they will."

"Has it occurred to you that it might affect my reputation just to have those fucking questions asked at all?"

"It has. I considered it. The university's reputation comes first. Yours will survive. Garth, for Christ's sake, you were a hero in *Newsweek* not so long ago; that's your reputation. You don't need to be in the same magazine again under a cloud of suspicion."

Helplessness swept Garth again. First an invisible foe, now a stranger investigating him. He opened the door. "I can't stop you from playing hide-and-seek with your detective. But you could have asked us first. My wife, who believes in me without the guidance of a top-notch agency, is helping me look for the person responsible—"

"Garth, I'd rather you didn't do anything. We'll take care of it, swiftly and discreetly."

"That sounds like the motto of your detective friends."

Strauss looked sheepish. "I think it is. But they know what they're doing, and they won't frighten anyone off. You and Stephanie might. Just hold on until we see what they come up with. We're on your side, Garth. We want to clear you."

"You can't clear me if I haven't been charged with anything. But that's the difference between us. We're looking for a vicious liar who writes letters; you're looking for proof of my virtue. If we discover that I am of moral and upright character before you do, we'll be sure to let you know."

"Oh, fuck it, Garth," Strauss said wearily. "You know I have complete faith in you."

"Good. So does my wife. So do my children. Can your Dick

Tracy and the media be far behind? But I still think we'll try to see what we can do on our own. I'll talk to you soon, Lloyd; I'm off to buy a magnifying glass."

Madeline Kane had managed to create disarray in every corner of Collectibles in the two weeks Sabrina had been gone. "I'm not sure exactly how it happened, Stephanie," she said on Wednesday morning with a perplexed air. "I just turned around one day and everything was out of place. Do you think I was trying to show how much I missed you?"

"I would have believed you if you'd just told me," Sabrina said dryly. "Shall we start with the breakfront and move outward from there?"

They worked silently, saving their energy for moving the heavy furniture. "Coffee," Madeline gasped finally, and they walked to the back of the shop. "Has it been a very bad time for you?" she asked as they sat at her small desk.

"Yes."

"Is there anything I can do?"

"You did it. You messed up Collectibles. Physical labor is good therapy for someone in mourning."

"Tell me when you need it again. I seem to do it with no trouble at all. What will you do about your sister's shop in London?"

"Keep it going, at least for now. There's an assistant manager who's been there for some time and an antique dealer who wants to buy into it. I've told them to open the shop, and I've set a limit on what they can spend at auction."

"But surely, without supervision—"

"They're both highly professional and competent. And my solicitor keeps an eye on the funds and handles the accounts for my housekeeper as well."

"But how can he? I mean, I don't mean to pry, but if he has no authority—"

"I've sent him my power of attorney."

"I see," Madeline said.

Sabrina stood up. "Back to work, I think."

"And your sister's house?" Madeline asked. "Will your solicitor sell it?"

"No. The housekeeper will maintain it. A friend is living there until she gets her own affairs in order."

"Ah. It's all yours now—the shop and the house?"

"Yes."

"Ah. Valuable furnishings and property, I gather."

"Yes."

"I don't mean to pry."

"Of course you do, Madeline; you want to know everything about my affairs in London. Why?"

"No reason. I just . . . oh, the truth is, it all sounds quite glamorous and—forgive me, Stephanie, but you seem to belong in that kind of life. I've never quite believed that *you* work for *me*."

Sabrina looked at her quizzically. "I haven't done a good job?"

"You know that's not what I mean. *Are* you going back?"

"Of course I am." She chose her words carefully. "To see my solicitor, and Nicholas, who's running Ambassadors, and my housekeeper."

Madeline sighed. "You see, I've come to depend on you. You're very special, and I don't want to lose you. In fact, while you were away, I contracted for five major estate sales, which will probably require an assistant anyway. If you're gone—"

"Right now, I'm going only as far as lunch. Five estate sales? What a businesswoman you are, Madeline! Tell me about them after lunch. Shall we lock the shop or are you staying in?"

"Staying; I brought a sandwich. Will you be long?"

"I don't know. It's a solace session for a friend whose husband just resigned from the university."

"Talvia or Blake?"

Pulling on her coat, Sabrina sighed. "Does everyone know everything—?"

"I read the *Standard*. What a marvelous coat. Real leather?"

"The real thing. I brought it back from London. It was my sister's." She settled on her shoulder the strap of the matching bag she also had brought back. "Do you hear campus rumors, too?"

"No. Am I missing much?"

"Not much. I'm late; I'd better run."

She was meeting Dolores and Linda at Café Provençal, and she walked there quickly in the brisk wind whipping off the lake. She found them at a table in the back. Linda was wearing dark glasses.

"I've been crying a lot."

"I don't mind your looks, Linda; I can't talk to dark glasses."

She took them off and, looking at her swollen eyelids and blotched cheeks, Sabrina ached for her, not so much for her unhappiness as for the cowed look of shame in her eyes. "It's not your fault," she said, taking Linda's hand. "You didn't know anything about it."

The waitress took their order and Dolores leaned forward. "Exactly what I told her."

Linda shook her head. "He wouldn't have done it if I'd been nicer to him, if we weren't always fighting, if I didn't tell him . . ." Her mouth worked for a moment. "He doesn't always satisfy me. He says it isn't his fault, that I'm too busy criticizing his performance to relax. And he's probably right, he's always right about everything; but I still blame him and make him feel like he isn't really a man. So I guess he goes to young girls who tell him what he wants to hear."

"That's absurd," Sabrina said flatly. "You can't blame yourself because Marty got taken in by a couple of young girls who set him up and then blackmailed him into giving them passing grades."

"Who said it was only a couple?"

"Garth."

"Did he really? Marty refused to tell me. But it doesn't make any difference, does it? Even one means I'm a failure. I've always known I'd be a failure with Marty. I don't have a college degree, you know. I haven't read half the books he has, and I keep wondering if he wouldn't rather have someone who's smarter than me. And I can't talk to him about it. I wish I could, but I keep putting it off and the longer I wait the harder it gets, because I don't know where to begin. Marty says if you really want to talk about something you'll do it, not make up excuses. He's always right, so I guess I don't really want to talk. But now he's found college women to make him happy, so I know I'm a failure."

Sabrina was looking at her intently. "You're nothing of the kind. Give Marty credit for being a unique individual with his own problems and his own ways of working them out. Are you so powerful you're responsible for everything he does?"

Linda finished her salad, her lips pouting in thought. "It sounds different when you say it that way."

Dolores ordered dessert. "What you need, Linda, is something to do. You'll need an income until Marty finds a job, and it will occupy your mind. You come with me to the next meeting of the garden club; those women know when their husbands need secretaries."

"I don't want to be a—"

"You don't have so many choices, Linda; you'll do what you have to do. You'll hear about a number of openings at the meeting, and I'll help you put together a résumé—all those secretarial jobs you held in the past—and I can go with you to your interviews, to bolster you up—"

"Dolores, *please stop arranging my life!*"

Heads swiveled at other tables. Dolores flushed. "I'm sorry. I thought you needed a friend."

"I do, I do, I don't mean to sound ungrateful . . ."

"I'm going to order coffee," Sabrina said. "For all of us."

Dolores straightened in her chair. "I always go a little too far, don't I? I never know I'm doing it until it's too late."

"We'll be glad to tell you," Sabrina offered, easing the tension, and they laughed.

Dolores frowned. "You've changed, Stephanie. You never used to be the one to take charge."

"Oh, we're all mixed up by everything that's happened . . ." Sabrina said vaguely. "Linda," she added. "We need an assistant at Collectibles, to help with estate sales. Why don't you try it?"

"I don't even know what an estate sale is."

"We organize the sale of homes and their furnishings, everything from oil paintings to paring knives. You'd learn how to price items, how to make up a catalogue, how to advertise the sale and then how to run it—which means you have to be there the whole time, hovering over customers who try to sneak off with silver and snuffboxes and anything else portable."

Linda's eyes brightened. "It sounds like fun."

"It is. Exciting, dusty, aggravating, and always different. Interested?"

"If you're offering it just because we're in trouble—"

"I'm offering it because less than two hours ago Madeline told me she's got five estate sales lined up, and we can't handle them without an assistant."

"Somebody without a college degree?"

"Linda, I'm asking you if you want to try it. I didn't ask you anything else."

"Yes, yes, yes, it sounds wonderful! Oh, Stephanie, how can I repay you?"

"By becoming better at it than I am. Then, if I ever have to leave, you'll keep it going."

"Leave? What are you talking about? Are you and Garth moving? You're not going away, Stephanie!"

"No, I didn't mean—" *What is the matter with me?* "I meant if I ever get another job. But that's a long way off. Now I've got to get back to work or I won't even have this job."

"Should I come too?" Linda asked.

"Not today. I'll talk to Madeline and call you later. Dolores, is ten dollars enough for lunch? I really have to run."

"No, lunch is my treat; it was my idea."

Sabrina leaned over and kissed her on the cheek. "Next time I'm buying."

She looked back at them from the door: Dolores talking and Linda looking dreamily at a picture on the wall. She thought of Alexandra and Gabrielle. How strange, the many ways we help each other, she thought. And for a moment she wondered who would help her when she finally left for good. They would all be so busy. Oh, but there was one. She smiled faintly as she opened the door to Collectibles. There was always Mrs. Thirkell.

On Friday afternoon Sabrina left the shop early to take Linda a stack of books on the history of furniture and decorative arts.

"You don't need to memorize them," she said when she saw the dismay on Linda's face. "But you have to know how to use them to look up a piece. And you ought to have an idea of the way furniture styles have changed and how fads affect the market in collectibles. Right now it's political posters and lacquerware; I have a feeling dolls will be next. Anyway, read through these, and we'll talk on Monday."

Walking up the front steps of the house, she sighed with anticipation. An hour alone before Penny and Cliff arrived; a little time to herself without the demands of family and friends and work. But the door was unlocked. No time after all, she thought; which one of them had come home early?

The living room was empty. "Cliff?" she called. "Penny?" There was no answer. Curious, Sabrina went upstairs and found Cliff sitting on his bed, desperately shoving into a plastic bag a jumble of pocket calculators, FM radios, pen-and-pencil sets, wallets, tie clips, cuff links and gloves.

"You look like a pirate with his loot," she said lightly from the doorway.

Cliff spun around. "I thought you got home at four."

"I thought you got home at four-thirty."

"Well, I came home early—"

"So did I. Did you plan to hide everything before I got here?"

He looked up with such fear and shame that Sabrina wanted to rush to him and tell him not to be afraid, she would help him, everything would be all right. But it was clear that something was very wrong, and she stayed across the room. Pulling out his desk chair, she sat down. "I think you'd better start at the beginning and tell me all about it."

"But I told Dad. When you were in China. Didn't he tell you?"

No one told me anything, she thought. But Stephanie did talk about problems with Cliff.

"It seems he decided to keep it between the two of you. I wonder if you appreciate that. From the evidence, I doubt it."

Cliff looked at his shoes.

"Well?" Sabrina pressed. "Did you promise him then that you'd stop whatever you were up to? I suppose you did. What happened next? Cliff, you're going to have to answer me sooner or later; why not save a lot of time and do it now? Before Penny gets home."

His eyes brimming with tears, Cliff looked up. "I did stop. I told them my dad knew about it and I couldn't hide any more stuff for them. But last week, when you were in England, they brought over this whole load and told me I had to keep it, and I didn't know what to do."

"Where was Garth—your dad?"

"At a meeting, and Penny was at school working on her puppet show, and they came over—"

"Cliff, who are 'they'?"

"These kids, they're in eighth grade, and they sort of, you know, run the school. They choose the teams and they're always the captains and they go through the cafeteria first even if the rest of us are ahead of them in line ... you know. And they rip off stores. They'll say, 'I'm going over to Radio Shack to rip off a calculator.' Like that. They used to do it just for themselves, but then they started selling the stuff to kids in Chicago when they were down there dealing drugs. So they needed a place to keep things before they sold them, and one day they asked me if I'd help them out. I thought they liked me ... I mean, I felt ... good about it ..."

Flattered, Sabrina thought. The little tin dictators ask for your help. Join the elite. "You thought then *you'd* be able to go first through the cafeteria," she said.

Cliff looked startled. "How did you know that?"

She smiled at him. "When I was in high school most of the girls were very rich, looking way down their noses at St—at Sabrina and me. We always felt they were doing us a favor by asking us to help them with their homework. Then, later, when we began to win prizes for classwork and trophies in fencing and sailing, they started looking up to us and suddenly they weren't special or awesome at all. Pretty ordinary, in fact. What did this gang promise you for helping them?"

"I could take something for myself once a month, or they'd pay me fifteen dollars a week. I took the money. I was going to buy a stereo for my room."

"Expensive. It sounds like a lot of fifteen-dollar weeks. Are you sure you were a reluctant partner?"

Cliff studied his shoes again. "Sometimes I was, and then I guess sometimes I wasn't." Sabrina's careful mildness had reassured him, and he talked with relief and growing confidence. "It's better to be friends with those guys than against them. You never win if you're against them. And I thought, when they asked me, I'd be part of their group ... and I'd get money, too, and ... so that's what happened."

"Did it ever occur to you that you were aiding and abetting criminals?"

"Mom! They're not criminals! They just rip off stores. It's not like murder or robbing a bank or something. Anyway, they said the stores make so much money they don't even notice when a few things are missing."

"Oh, don't they? Cliff, stealing is wrong, wherever it's done, and whether it's noticed or not. But it usually is discovered. Did you ever hear of taking inventory?"

"No."

"That's when stores count their stock and check it against what they bought and sold. When the figures don't match, they know what's been stolen. It's called shrinkage. And then, to make up their losses, they raise the price of everything else in the store. So the rest of us, who don't believe in stealing, end up paying for your pals' thievery."

There was a pause. "I never thought of that."

"And your friends never told you."

"They're not really my friends."

"I thought you said you'd be part of their group."

"I did. But . . . they don't really want me, Mom. They don't like me at all. Oh, shit." The tears had come back and he brushed them away fiercely. "I'm sorry, I know you don't like me to say that, but nothing's the way I thought it would be. They never talk to me like friends; they make fun of me."

"For what?" Sabrina asked gently.

"Liking books and getting good grades."

"Well, we're proud of you for that. But why did you stay with them if they made fun of you? Was it the money?"

"No, it was . . . If you really want to know, I'm scared of them. They said they'd beat me up if I told on them, and last week they said if I didn't hide this stuff they'd tell the principal *I'd* stolen it. Dad wanted to go to the police, but I asked him not to and I wouldn't tell him their names. I can't tell anybody. And I can't stop helping them, either, because even if they don't beat me up they'd keep me off the teams. They'd keep people from talking to me, even my friends, and I'd be out of everything and *alone.* They can do that, Mom, and I'm sorry, but I'm scared of them, and whatever I do, things will be bad. I know you can't understand that, because you always know what to do, but I don't. I don't know *what* to do."

Sabrina went to sit beside him as he slumped on the bed. *I understand exactly how you feel.* She put her arms around him, and after a minute he put his head on her shoulder. "I'm sorry, Mom."

"For what?"

"Crying."

"We all cry when we're sad and afraid; you shouldn't apologize. I'd rather you were sorry for not telling us when this mess started again. Are you more afraid of us than these bullies?"

Cliff ducked his head. "I *wanted* to."

"And?"

"Dad trusted me."

"And you didn't want him to know you had failed him?"

"I didn't want him to know I'd lied. Every once in a while he asks if they ever tried to get me in with them again, and I always say no. So I let him down and then I lied. Now I guess you'll tell him, but there still isn't anything anybody can do."

"Oh, I think there is."

"What? Mom, they'll beat me up or oster . . . ostra . . ."

"Ostracize. They won't do either one. I'm going to ground you for a month."

"Ground me! Mom!" He pulled back and glared at her through reddened eyes. "That's not fair!"

"Is it fair to work for these bullies? Or to get beat up and ignored? Or to be accused of shoplifting to the principal?"

"But—"

"If your parents say that for one month you have to come straight home from school every day, you can't have friends over and you can't go out at night, what better excuse do you have for not working with these fellows? You can tell them honestly that you have no choice. And, after a month, you'll say your parents are suspicious and you don't want to get grounded again so you have to stay away from them. But that may not be necessary. Because while you're grounded, I think we'll alert the police to put some detectives in Radio Shack and other places you'll tell us about. That way, you won't have to give us any names. It shouldn't take long to spot them and break up their ring; they sound fairly stupid to me."

Cliff's eyes were round with admiration. "Mom, that's not bad! That's pretty clever!"

"Yes, I thought so. Considering I've never done anything like it before."

"Sure you have. You grounded me—"

"I try to forget past punishments."

"Mom? I've got an idea. If you help me get rid of this stuff now, we wouldn't have to tell Dad. He'd never have to know."

"You mean you'd lie to him again."

"No, I just wouldn't say anything at all."

"But hiding the truth is just a different kind of lie. If you let him believe something that you know isn't true—" She stopped and stared into space. *Who am I to give advice?*

"Mom?"

Slowly Sabrina turned back to him. "Cliff, there are some

empty cartons in the storeroom. If you'll get a couple of them, we'll pack everything up and your Dad and I will deliver them to the police when we talk to them."

"But then they'll know I had it all here."

"We'll find a way to keep you out of it." As he stood uncertainly, she lost her patience. "You'll just have to trust us. Now go get those boxes!"

Mumbling, Cliff went off, and Sabrina stood up, trying to slow the beating of her heart. She started to go to her room—maybe now she could have a few minutes alone—just as the front door slammed and Penny's voice danced ahead of her into the house.

Garth had gone through his records and listed eleven students who had complained in the last year about low or failing grades.

"What about this one?" Sabrina asked. "The one with a question mark after her name."

"Rita McMillan," said Garth. "Only a possibility. Didn't I tell you about her last June?"

"I don't think so."

"I thought I did. She offered her charms in return for a passing grade, and I chased her out with my tennis racket. Something like that. I believe I may have called her a whore. It was the week Vivian had been turned down by the tenure committee, and I was not favorably impressed with young women trading on their anatomy. I didn't flunk her, though; she took an incomplete, and I gave her permission to take Vivian's class this quarter so she could graduate. But it was all six months ago; I can't believe she'd be involved now."

Sabrina repeated the name. "Young women have long memories. Especially when their crown jewels are rejected."

He smiled. "Rita might think of it that way. Well, now, what shall we do with this list? I must say it makes me feel ridiculous—as if someone handed me a toy gun and told me to play cops and robbers. I'm better at hunting an elusive bacterium."

"And I'd rather look for a lost Wedgwood."

He chuckled. "Bacteria and Wedgwood. Cops and robbers. What a couple we are."

They were a couple. Sabrina made sure of that. They were seen everywhere. Wednesday night, two days after she returned, they attended a film preview and a reception for the director. On Thursday they went to a cocktail party, where the president of the university was attentive and admiring. "Rightfully so," said Garth. "You've never been so beautiful."

She was vividly beautiful, dressing all that week, for the first time, with the brilliance of Sabrina Longworth. In vibrant greens and blues, in wine velvet, in striped silk, her heavy hair falling in waves of shimmering bronze below her shoulders, poised and quick, she was a beacon, drawing others to stand in her orbit. And she was never far from Garth. On Saturday night they appeared at the opening of the new university art museum, where Sabrina talked to artists and sculptors and collectors in their language, drawing on all her years of experience. She was exhilarated by the surroundings and the people, and Lloyd Strauss, finding her for a rare moment alone, was effusive.

"You're magnificent, Stephanie; it's wonderful that you can do it, so soon after your loss."

"I am doing it for Garth," she said clearly, and met Strauss's gaze, daring him to doubt Garth's innocence or call her naive. He did neither; instead, he invited them to dinner the following night.

"You're never home!" Penny wailed as Sabrina brushed her hair at her dressing table on Sunday evening.

"Our social season," Garth said wryly, adjusting his tie and talking to Penny's reflection in the full-length mirror. "In the line of duty, my sweet."

A tag end of memory caught Sabrina, and she turned to see Penny's woebegone face. "We hardly have a family any-more—we never even see you!"

The bedroom faded. Sabrina and Stephanie Hartwell stood before a triple mirror in a bedroom in Athens, watching their parents dress for an embassy ball. "Everybody gets to be with you but us! The only family we have is Stephanie and me—we're our whole family."

She remembered it so clearly. But for a week she had forgotten it. For a week, with Garth, she had filled the calendar, going out each night after working each day, just as she had done in London: hours crammed with dinners and conversation and new faces. She hadn't realized how much she missed it. And sometimes, standing in a group beneath bright lights, talking, holding a glass of wine, hearing music and laughter on all sides, she forgot for a brief moment who she was; her worlds merged, and she would touch Garth's arm as he stood beside her, loving him, loving the way others looked at them, as a couple, as husband and wife.

But the crowded calendar was not fair to Penny and Cliff, and Sabrina knew it. They need a family, she thought, and I should help them have one. I'll be gone soon enough.

"You're right, Penny," she said. "We should slow down and stay home more."

Bemused, Garth looked at her. "I thought this was your campaign."

"But you only do it because I think we should."

"On the contrary. I'm having a very good time."

"Daddy!" Penny cried, and Sabrina looked at him in surprise.

"It's true, we've overdone it a bit," he said, enjoying his wife's startled silence. "But after years of telling me we didn't go out enough, you've shown me how much I've been missing. I might," he said, seeing the shadow in her eyes, "stay home four or five nights out of seven, but no more."

She laughed softly. "Not excessive; we could arrange that."

"But what about tonight?" Penny asked.

"Tonight we go out; we are expected. Tomorrow we stay home. Can we manage that, Stephanie?"

"Yes." She smiled as Penny ran out of the room and Garth put his arms around her. "Tomorrow we stay home."

She canceled the party they were to attend on Monday, and the four of them spent a slow, quiet evening together. After Penny and Cliff had gone to bed, Sabrina and Garth sat in the living room, talking, reading, thinking separate thoughts. How had she done it, Sabrina wondered—slipped so comfortably back into the life of the family? It had not been effortless; each morning she woke to the shattering realization of Stephanie's death and the precariousness of her life with Garth. But then, as the hours passed in a web of people and activities, she was pulled away from guilt and sadness over Stephanie toward the life of the family and community around her. And each day the pull of life became stronger. For the first time she could remember, she felt she had found the place where she belonged.

But then she would be pulled up short. This was not where she belonged; it was based on a lie, it all depended on a lie. She sat in the living room with Garth and reminded herself of that, repeating it to keep it real. Because beneath the touch of his hand, the weight of his body, the love in his eyes, she knew she could lose sight of what she had to do, or the strength to do it.

She turned back to her book just as the doorbell rang. Garth answered it and brought into the living room a small, middle-aged man who introduced himself as Karl Jenks, the special investigator hired by Lloyd Strauss to look into anonymous charges against Professor Andersen.

"I've been talking to some folks," he began, settling into an armchair in the living room and looking around. "Nice room." His small features, tucked beneath a high forehead, gave him a permanently suspicious look, and when he wrote in his note-book he puckered his mouth in concentration, like a child having trouble with spelling. "Anybody mad at you, professor? You take somebody's job, or flunk somebody, or borrow a lawnmower and forget to return it?"

"No."

"Nobody's mad at you? Nobody at all in the whole very wide world? You are universally loved?"

Garth looked steadily at Jenks until the small eyes slid sideways. "We've made a list of students who may have felt badly treated by me. I'll get it for you."

"In a minute. You help with the list, Stephanie?"

Sabrina raised her eyebrows. "Have we met before?"

"What? Before tonight? I don't think so; why?"

"Because, Mr. Jenks, only my friends use my first name."

There was a pause. "Oh, ho," Jenks said finally. "Excuse me, madam. Or perhaps you prefer *my lady.*"

Sabrina smiled and said nothing.

"Well, then, how about this list, my lady? You help make it up?"

"No."

"You believe it?"

"Believe what? It's simply a list."

"Might be you think your hubby didn't include everybody."

"That is absurd."

"Ah." He wrote. Sabrina and Garth exchanged glances. Nothing they had said seemed worth recording.

"You play tennis, professor?"

Garth looked up from his thoughts. "Yes. Does that apply to your investigation?"

"Might. Do you, Mrs. Andersen?"

"Yes."

"Played together lately?"

"No," said Garth. "My wife's sister died recently, and she is in mourning."

"My condolences. Busy life you have—parties and museum openings and such. That part of your mourning?"

"What a busy bee you've been, Mr. Jenks," Sabrina said pleasantly. "Investigating our social life. Garth, do you think we should discuss our social life with Mr. Jenks?"

"I think if Mr. Jenks doesn't talk about anonymous letters, there is no reason for him to be here."

"Nice little rugs," Jenks said, swiveling his head. "From China?"

"Yes," said Sabrina.

"You get them in China?"

"No."

"The professor go with you to China?"

"That's enough," Garth said, standing up. "I'll show you out."

"Professor, I'm conducting an investigation. Under orders from your boss."

"You're not investigating; you're fishing."

"That's what an investigation is, professor. We toss out a bunch of worms and see who bites. You'll just have to be patient with me. You were in Stamford lately. Connecticut."

Garth stood beside a bookcase, resting his arm on a shelf. "That's right."

"Didn't take the job, though, right?"

"Evidently you know the answer already."

"Right. Professor Andersen go with you to China, Mrs. Andersen?"

"No. I traveled with an association of antique dealers, and my husband generously made the trip possible by taking care of our children while I was away."

Jenks wrote, puckering his mouth. "This Talvia—you've been friends for a long time?"

"A long time," Garth said evenly.

"They fight a lot, he and the little lady."

Garth and Sabrina were silent.

Jenks wrote. "Too bad about marital discord. Makes for wandering. And all those young lovelies you teach."

Sabrina caught Garth's eye and shook her head slightly.

"You don't agree, Mrs. Andersen? About wandering, or about those young lovelies?"

"I don't agree that you're a fool."

Jenks was thrown off his stride. He pulled a stick of chewing gum from his pocket and folded it into his mouth. "Blake, now. How well d'you know him?"

"He and I have met," Garth said. "Briefly. My wife doesn't know him."

"Now, there's a reputation for you. He likes 'em all ages and sizes, from what I hear."

Sabrina looked at him pensively. "What an unpleasant job you have, Mr. Jenks."

"Then there's Millburn."

They were silent.

"You don't know him at all, I gather. Someone wrote a letter—there you are, professor, I'm talking about anonymous letters—and I checked him out for your boss. Mathematician. Fools with numbers. When he's not fooling with young lovelies."

"Is that based on the anonymous letter?" Sabrina asked coldly.

"No, ma'am, it's based on his confession. He says it only happened once, but who knows? His wife was his student when he married her. He likes the young ones. And I must say"— a wistful note entered his voice—"they are indeed lovely. So tempting."

The room was still. From upstairs, Sabrina heard Cliff's radio.

"You have office hours, professor."

"Of course."

"You see one student at a time or a group?"

"One at a time. We discuss confidential matters—grades, the quality of their work, their plans for the future."

"One at a time. With the door closed?"

"Sometimes." Sabrina could see rage building in him from being forced to treat seriously Karl Jenks and his slithering questions.

"Mrs. Andersen, you have many dinner guests?"

"Occasionally."

"Ever invite any of the professor's students?"

I have no idea. Sabrina looked at Garth.

"No," he answered for her. "We have an open house in June for all my students and lab assistants."

"Mrs. Andersen couldn't say that herself?"

"Mrs. Andersen does not have to answer anything she doesn't want to. Especially if she thinks you are trying to trap her."

Jenks chewed his gum. "Professor, I've just come from Talvia's house. Everything hunky-dory, lovey-dovey; you'd never guess they have a reputation for fighting at parties. I come here, there's a houseful of sweetness and light, but the wife has been running off to China and England and the husband dashes to California whenever he gets a chance, and there's a very specific letter accusing the professor of screwing those tempting lovelies and making payment with grades, and I have a strong suspicion, professor, that you did not look the other way when the treats were offered."

Swiftly Sabrina crossed the room and stood beside Garth, putting her arm around the rigid muscles of his waist. Her breast was against his arm, and she could feel him gradually relax.

"I could throw you out," he said conversationally. "But that would take more energy than you deserve. Lloyd Strauss told me you were brought in to find an anonymous letter-writer and get a confession, or whatever is required, to clear my name. Instead, in your own mind, you have tried and convicted me, on what information I have no idea. You did not come here to investigate, as you claimed, but to entrap. Therefore, you are here under false pretenses; you are impersonating an investigator, and that is a crime under statute 44-C-1 of the City of Evanston, for which you can lose your license. I will decide whether to call the police or the university, or both, in the morning. It will depend in part on how quickly you leave my house. I will give you sixty seconds. Beginning now." He put his arm around Sabrina and brought up his other wrist to look at his watch.

"You can't intimidate me, professor."

"I'm sure I can't. Forty-five seconds."

"Your wife knows that an innocent man would not try to kick me out of his house."

"Thirty seconds."

"Bluffing. That's all you're doing—"

"Twenty seconds."

405

Jenks shot out of his chair and bolted to the front door. "I'll be back; your boss will be very interested to know that you kicked me out. An innocent man wouldn't—"

"Out!" roared Garth, and Jenks yanked open the door and was gone.

Sabrina's laughter rang out. "Garth, how ridiculous."

"I know." Laughing with her, he took her in his arms. "You were wonderful."

"There's no Evanston law against impersonating yourself."

"Of course not. The man is stupid. You were right—he's too sly to be a fool, but he is most certainly stupid."

She stopped laughing. "You're worried about him."

"Yes. Aren't you?"

"Yes."

The next morning Garth called Lloyd Strauss. "You've put my career in the hands of a stupid son of a bitch who's already decided I'm guilty. I warn you, Lloyd—"

"Garth, don't warn me. I'm taking enough heat from the president on this, I'll be damned if I'll take any from you. Has it occurred to you that you aren't the only one with a job and a future on the line? I want this whole fucking mess out of the way so we can get back to normal, and if you think I'm going to call off an investigator just because he rubbed you the wrong way . . . Oh, shit. Listen, I don't like him, either. But I needed an agency in a hurry, and his was recommended by someone who'd used it. I'll call to see if they can put someone else on the case. Good enough?"

"Good enough." And he hung up before Strauss could tell him again not to do anything on his own. Because they had decided, after Jenks was gone, that they would begin to talk to the students on Garth's list. Someone, they thought, would give away something. And even if not, it was intolerable to sit by and do nothing.

He called his wife at Collectibles. "I just wanted to hear your voice. And tell you I love you. I talked to Lloyd, who will try to replace our stupid friend. And Marty Talvia finally called, full of apologies, saying he let us all down. I told him to take care of Linda; we'd survive. Is she there with you?"

"Yes, we're planning a sale. And Thanksgiving dinner. Marty has a new job."

"He told me. That was the reason he finally called. He

didn't feel he could face us until he was earning a living again. So Thanksgiving will be a celebration."

"For them. Not for us, yet. What time will you be home?"

"About five. You'll be there?"

"Of course."

Sabrina went home for an hour at noon to call London. "Nicholas, it's Stephanie Andersen. I haven't heard from you about Ambassadors."

"Ah, my dear Stephanie, I meant to write; your dear sister would be so pleased, everything is so excellent."

"What does that mean, Nicholas?"

"We bought at auction the chaise and ormolu clock you mentioned before; we bought the Regency chiffonier from—"

"Nicholas."

"Yes, Stephanie."

"What have you sold?"

"Ah, sold. There is a slowing down this time of year—"

"There is no slowing down this time of year, Nicholas; what do you take me for? This should be the height of the season for our customers. What about your own shop?"

"We are doing—well."

"Is that because of Amelia?"

"My dear Stephanie, you sound exactly like Sabrina. How sad you make me feel, remembering."

"Nicholas, perhaps you will call Brian to the telephone."

"No, no, Stephanie, there is no need. In fact, we sold the French clock, the one with the angels, you recall, and both pieces you bought at the Chilton auction. And I believe I will put the George V secretary in Lady Stargrave's new country house."

"How much for the clock?"

"Three thousand."

"It might have brought four. And the Chilton pieces?"

"Twenty-three thousand for both."

"Excellent. I can't believe you were going to keep that from me."

"No, no, my dear, of course not. It was to be a surprise. But you dragged it out of me. How could I keep things from you, even if it entered my mind? Sidney Jones looks over my shoulder every day. By the by, he asks when you'll be here again."

"Soon. Am I needed now?"

"Of course, dear Stephanie, since final decisions at Ambassadors still depend on you. Olivia was saying the other day that you remind her so much of Sabrina she wishes you would move here and we could all pretend ... oh dear, how crude that sounds; somehow it didn't seem that way when Olivia—"

"Yes, Nicholas, I know. Olivia has a way of making outrageous statements in the most ordinary way."

"Goodness, did Sabrina really tell you such small details about us?"

"Often." I can stop this pretending, she thought, as soon as I get back and tell them the truth. She and Nicholas talked about her December decorating commission, and she gave instructions on two auctions and the sale to Bettina Stargrave. Nicholas listened to her now; he no longer treated her like an ignorant provincial who could be disdainfully brushed aside. Finally she hung up, but before she could leave the breakfast room a new thought came to her and she sat down again. *As soon as I get back and tell them the truth.* But how can I do that? How can I tell my parents or anyone else that I'm Sabrina if I don't want Garth to know? If anyone knows, even one person, eventually it would get back to him.

She got up and began to walk around the kitchen, arms crossed, nervously running her hands up to her shoulders and down again.

I can't tell Garth the truth.

I can't tell anyone.

But if I don't, I'll be Stephanie Andersen for the rest of my life.

Sabrina Longworth will be dead.

As, of course, she is. We were all at her funeral.

Oh, Stephanie, look what we've done.

Chapter 19

Snow fell on the morning of November 20, a light dusting like a whispered warning of what lay ahead. The sky was steel gray, hanging low over the yard, over black tree limbs furred with snow and bushes as delicate as spider webs. Garth turned up the furnace, Sabrina helped locate missing gloves and Penny and Cliff took careful steps on their way down the front walk, admiring their footprints.

When they were gone, Sabrina stood at the front window, finishing her coffee. The yard was a tapestry of grass and chrysanthemum stalks jutting through the snow; the white street was striped with dark automobile tracks. Powdery snow clung to roofs, chimneys and windowsills. A light wind caught the branches of trees, and now and then, with a soft sigh, snow fell in a spray to the ground.

Winter. The seasons were changing, and they were no nearer to clearing Garth's name. She had helped by standing by him and being seen with him in a social whirl that was now bringing invitations in each day's mail to rival the number she used to receive in London; but they hadn't yet begun talking to the students on his list. They'd been too happy. Loving, living together with no holding back for the first time since she returned from China. Trusting, joyful, alive.

Because my sister is dead.

She turned from the white world outside and walked back through the house to the kitchen. There it was again. She would let the truth slip to the back of her mind and begin to think, in small snatches, of perhaps finding a way to stay with Garth, as if somehow the truth could become part of a past that had nothing to do with the present.

Deceiving herself. She had promised never to do that. *Because I will not profit from my sister's death.*

She could not change that even if she could forget it for small bits of time. *Someday, when we least expect it, it would catch up with us. And destroy us.*

The telephone rang; Garth calling from the university. "My calendar reminds me I have a meeting in New York in December. Can you arrange with Madeline to get away? I want you with me."

"When in December?"

"The third. For three days. I'll ask Vivian if Penny and Cliff can stay at her house. We're going to have to board her kids for six months to make up for all the times she's done it for us. You will come?"

"Yes, I'd love to." How strange that he should call, just now, when she was reminding herself why she had to leave. "Would you mind if I went on to London from there to take care of some business?"

There was a barely perceptible pause. "Of course not. Would you want me to come along?"

"No. I want to go by myself." *Because I won't be coming back.*

"If you want to go alone, of course you should. How long will your business take?"

"I don't know. But I'll probably stay on for a bit, once I'm there, in the house . . ."

This time the pause was longer. Garth had almost convinced himself she no longer thought about living in her sister's house, following in her sister's footsteps. But now, suddenly, she was talking again of leaving them to playact in another life. It seemed when things were best between them she thought of running away. He considered reminding her that she had promised to stay at least until the letter-writer was found. But he would not whine or beg. "We can talk about it later," he said. "But you will arrange to come with me to New York?"

410

"Yes. And I'm having lunch with Vivian, so I'll talk to her about Penny and Cliff."

"You look so somber," said Vivian, joining her in the restaurant at noon. "Like our premature winter. Is there anything I can do?"

"Talk about cheerful subjects. Your tenure, for one. Garth says the committee vote was unanimous. Have I thoroughly congratulated you?"

"You should thoroughly congratulate your husband. He outwitted our former dean, outmaneuvered a timid committee and turned a century-old policy on its head. And that was just on campus. He also made it possible for the Goodman family to stay put, since I don't have to look for another job. That's called security. First time I ever had it. Did he tell you I have dubbed him Saint Garth?"

Sabrina shook her head, laughing. "No doubt modesty prevented him."

"He is modest, isn't that amazing? Anyone with his reputation and popularity has a right to take a bow now and then. His students are so proud of him, you know. Oh, let me tell you what one of them said—a girl in my genetics class. We were talking about Garth's work, and she said—here, let me write it, it's more amusing that way." On a paper napkin, Vivian wrote a single word and showed it to Sabrina.

"Gene-ius," Sabrina read, and reread it. *Bingo.*

"Clever," she said casually. "What's her name?"

"Rita McMillan. And clever describes her. Not a good student, not at all interested in learning, but clever. The kind who finds shortcuts to get where she wants to go. Wherever that is. Now, tell me, does your somber face have anything to do with an anonymous letter about Garth?"

Sabrina was caught off guard. "Have you seen it?"

"I wasn't even sure it existed until this minute. There are rumors all through the department. And some pasty-faced fellow is going around asking determinedly rude questions, which all of us are determinedly not answering. No one believes Garth is involved in that mess; he's not only too ethical, he's too smart. Tell me what's happening."

Sabrina described Jenks's visit and the way Garth got rid of him. They laughed together and went on to talk about their jobs and the books they were reading.

"I'm due back at work," Sabrina said at last. "Oh, I almost

forgot. Can we prevail on you once more to take Penny and Cliff, for three days this time? Garth has a meeting in New York on December third, and he wants me to go along."

"Of course I'll take them; they're wonderful to have around, and our kids love them. I think Barbara's secret wish is to be Penny Andersen. When will you leave?"

"I'll let you know. You're a good friend, Vivian."

"I *have* good friends. I'm off to class. See you soon."

"Vivian?"

"Yes?"

"Is that the class with Rita McMillan?"

"Yes; why?"

"Just curious. I enjoyed our lunch."

Sabrina called Madeline and told her she would not be in for the rest of the day. "Too bad," Madeline said. "You'd enjoy watching Linda—she's been following me around, examining different woods and carvings and memorizing shapes and construction techniques. She's a quick learner, and she's beginning to believe in herself. That was your good deed, bringing her here." Yes, Sabrina agreed silently. And it will go on long after I've left.

She debated stopping at Garth's office to tell him about Rita, but she knew he would want to talk to the girl himself. *I* want to handle it, she thought. This is what I stayed here for—to do this for him, and for Stephanie.

Outside Vivian's classroom, at the end of the hour, Sabrina stopped a boy and asked him to point out Rita McMillan. When he did, she went directly to her.

"Stephanie Andersen." She held out her hand. The girl, blond and lithe, with pale blue eyes, reluctantly touched Sabrina's hand with limp fingers. "I want to talk to you. The faculty club is across the street; we can be private there."

"I don't think—"

"This is very important." Smoothly, she steered Rita down the hall. "I understand you studied genetics with my husband last year."

She felt the quick alarm that brought a flush to the girl's face. Neither of them spoke again until they were in the faculty club. Sabrina had been there before with Garth, and the receptionist leaped up to greet her.

"Mrs. Andersen! How nice to see you again." After a brief glance at Rita, he turned to Sabrina with admiring eyes. "Coffee hour begins in the living room in a few minutes; would you care for fruit or dessert?"

"Would it be possible to have tea?"

"Tea! Of course. There is no one upstairs now," he added. "You'll have it to yourself."

Sabrina smiled at him, offering no clues to satisfy his curiosity. Upstairs, she led Rita to a corner of the long, high-ceilinged room, crowded with desks, couches and chairs. They sat in two wing chairs, almost touching. Sabrina, folding her hands in her lap, gazed steadily at Rita, taking her measure, noting the puzzlement in her round eyes. Not used to being ignored by men, she thought, while an older woman is admired. And how old I must seem to her, at thirty-two! It would be amusing if she hadn't tried to destroy Garth.

The girl was beginning to fidget under Sabrina's steady gaze. "Well?" she demanded truculently. "I'm here; what do you want?"

"I thought it would be a good idea for us to get acquainted. You're about to graduate, aren't you?"

"Yes," Rita said, perched on the edge of the chair.

"But weren't you supposed to graduate last June?"

"I . . . changed my plans."

"And what will you do after graduation?"

"I don't know. Travel, maybe get a job."

"What kind of job?"

"I don't know. Something exciting. Designing clothes, maybe. Interior decorating. Something like that."

"And become famous?"

"Sure; why not?"

"Your tea, Mrs. Andersen." The headwaiter from the dining room appeared with a rolling cart. Every afternoon the faculty club served rolls and coffee, but for Sabrina they had worked a miracle. "Sliced jelly roll," said the waiter, lifting a napkin with a flourish. "Torte. Cookies. If there is something else you would prefer—"

"This is perfect," Sabrina said, smiling at him. "And very special. Thank you."

He returned the smile, lingering a moment before crossing the room to set up the coffee urn. Nat Goldner, walking through from the library on the third floor, stared in amazement at the cart as he greeted Sabrina with a kiss. "Did you mesmerize the kitchen staff?"

"The magic word seems to be tea."

"Not if I'm the one who says it. May I join you?"

"Not this time, Nat. Will you forgive us? This is a private talk."

"Another time, then, if you promise to work your magic for me. And I gather we'll see you at Thanksgiving. Your house or ours?"

"I've convinced Dolores to make it ours."

"I'll bring the wine." He nodded to Rita and kissed Sabrina's cheek. "See you soon."

Rita had slid back in her chair, watching with undisguised envy. "You sure wind them around your finger."

"I treat people with respect," Sabrina said gently, handing her a cup of tea. "So," she went on thoughtfully, "you want to become famous. You'll make a lot of friends if you do."

Rita nodded with satisfaction. "I know."

"But probably a few enemies, too. It seems that the more people you know, the more chances you have of making someone angry or jealous—without even realizing you're doing it."

"I don't know anything about that."

"Of course, I'm sure you'll have many more friends than enemies, but you have to be prepared for both. Because when you're famous, you never know how people feel about you, or how they talk about you to others. You're prepared for that, of course."

"What?"

"For the fact that people might say things about you that aren't true." Sabrina was relaxed now, her anger controlled. "When that happens, we call it a rumor. You know about rumors; they're found everywhere. Did you ever wonder why they start? Sometimes for excitement or on a dare, sometimes for someone to feel important, sometimes just to see how people react, but probably most often for revenge. More tea?"

Rita's blue eyes were fixed on her. "No."

She filled her own cup. "Of course, anyone interested in a career like dress designing or interior decoration would never take a chance of starting a rumor. After all, you know from your history classes that rumors have started wars and panics and revolutions . . . who could ever trust someone who had started even one rumor? A dangerous person, careless with a whisper or a little joke—or an anonymous letter."

The pale eyes blinked. "Are you trying to scare me?"

"Why would I do that?"

"Because you don't like me."

"I don't know you; I neither like nor dislike you." Sabrina reached over to fill Rita's cup and met her wary eyes through the tendrils of steam rising between them. "But it is true that our interests and loyalties have clashed."

Rita looked uncomprehending.

"Your interest is what pleases you; your loyalty is to yourself. Ordinarily that would not concern me, since I find self-centered people boring and easily forgettable. But when your self-interest threatens my husband, in whom I have a strong interest and loyalty, that puts us on a collision course."

"I don't know what you're talking about." The pouting lips had turned sullen. "You're crazy."

"That was a mistake," Sabrina said softly. "You should not be antagonizing me, but trying to gain my sympathy."

"I don't care about your—"

"Yes, you do. Or you should." She leaned forward, holding the girl's eyes with her own. Her voice was low, but her words whipped like steel between them. "Because I am going to expose you for what you are, and I am going to make it impossible for you to graduate."

"You can't do that! There's no way you can do that! Just because your husband hates me—!"

"My husband hates you? Why?"

"Because ... because I wouldn't go to bed with him," Rita said defiantly.

Sabrina shook her head slowly. "You little fool. Couldn't you just once use your head instead of what you have between your legs? How long do you think you can buy your way by being a woman? How good a bargain can you get? And how many friends will you have, when every time you sell yourself you make it harder for women who are relying on their brains?"

"He told you to say that; that's what he said to me last June."

Sabrina pushed aside her cup. "Now, you listen to me. My husband does not know I am talking to you. You are dealing with me, and we will settle this between us. But even if he knew I was here, he would not tell me what to say. *No one* tells me what to say. *I* decide what I will say, and I ask no one's permission. You would understand that if you believed in yourself as a person instead of a motorized sex machine." She paused. "But we were talking about other things, weren't we? Your graduation. Anonymous letters. And the kind of genius who writes them."

There was a long silence. Sabrina watched expressions move across Rita's face as the girl tried to think of a response and then slowly crumpled.

"Are you going to tell on me?"

Tell on me. As if she were three years old, Sabrina thought. "What did you think I meant when I said I was going to expose you?"

"I didn't know. I didn't know you knew about the letters." She waited. "But you can't tell on me! They'd suspend me, or even expel me, and then I couldn't graduate!"

Exasperated, Sabrina said, "Of course you can't graduate! I told you I would make it impossible."

"But I have to graduate! My parents told me they wouldn't give me any more money if I didn't graduate this time. And I haven't got any of my own, so I have to graduate."

Perfect logic, Sabrina thought. "And how do you intend to graduate?"

"I have a *C* in my class, and that's all I need."

"No, you also need to have me on your side."

Nibbling a fingernail, Rita looked bewildered. "But there's nothing I can do for you."

"Think about it," Sabrina suggested. "Since I have no desire to go to bed with you, what might you offer that would interest me?"

Rita nibbled, glancing vaguely around the room, then looked at Sabrina in dismay. "You want me to tell them what I wrote isn't true! But then I'd have to say I wrote the letters! I can't do that! They'll kick me out! I won't graduate!"

"Well, I think that's negotiable," Sabrina said with a sigh. "I'll go with you to the vice president's office; if you confess the whole story, I'm sure the three of us can work something out." She pushed the tea cart away and leaned closer to Rita. "Now. Why don't we go over exactly what it is you are going to say?"

Snow fell again on Thanksgiving morning and continued all day. "It's all right," Dolores said briskly. "We need the moisture. It was a dry summer and fall."

"How grateful the snow must be," Nat said, putting an affectionate arm around her shoulders. "For your permission to keep on falling."

Dolores smiled calmly. "You'll notice I don't ask it to stop." She winked at Linda as she went back to grinding cranberries.

Linda clutched Sabrina's arm. "Did you see that?" she asked in an audible whisper. Her cheeks were crimson from the heat of the oven, and her black eyes were sparkling. "Have you ever seen Dolores wink before?"

"No," answered Sabrina honestly. She was cutting oranges and handing them to Dolores to be ground with the cranberries, while Linda grated nutmeg for the sweet potatoes. The pungent odors filled the warm kitchen, mingling with the pervasive smell of the stuffed turkey roasting in the oven and the spicy fragrance of cooling pumpkin pies. At the other end of the counter, Garth and Marty were making corn pudding from a recipe of Garth's great-grandmother's that he was trying to recall from memory as they went along, debating proportions and the scientific properties of baking soda and sour milk. Nat decanted wine and basted the turkey and circled the room, tasting everything.

Sabrina listened to the talk and laughter and breathed deeply, as if she could draw in the scents and sounds with her happiness and store them for the future. Since Gordon's doctor had ruled against his traveling, Sabrina was spared the sharp eye of her mother and could relax in a celebration of her first Thanksgiving dinner since she was fifteen. It was the first time she had spent such a day with a group of friends: cooking together, decorating the rooms with the flowers and Indian corn Dolores had brought, listening to the giggles and chatter of all their children setting the table while, outside, snowflakes fell, dark against the gray sky, piling in soft drifts on the ground. My first and my last, she thought, and it shouldn't even be mine; it should be Stephanie's day. Sadness slid through her happiness and a tear splashed on the orange she was cutting.

"I thought only onions did that," Nat said, beside her. "First time I ever saw oranges have that effect. Shall I take over?"

Sabrina shook her head. "It will pass."

"Mourning always does, though memories don't. You haven't had much time. And then you had this business with

417

Garth to worry about. Which reminds me." Picking up an open bottle of wine, he filled six glasses and handed them around the room. "Ladies and gentlemen, I propose the first toast of the holiday, no doubt the first of many. We hope the first of many." He paused as they turned to him. "We have, of course, countless blessings, but at the moment three special ones, and so I offer a toast. To Marty Talvia, the new senior editor at Fairbanks Publishers, who will revolutionize textbooks by ensuring that they are written in English instead of jargon; and to Garth Andersen, for his victory over scurrilous lies that only a heteromorphic pinch-mouthed, dim-witted, imbecilic investigator would believe."

"It means unnatural," Marty said as Linda and Dolores demanded a definition. Looking up, Sabrina saw the six of them reflected in the dark window, close together in the honey-colored kitchen as the early winter night closed in. She held the picture with her eyes, fixing it in her mind. Mourning passes; memories don't. *I'll have my memories. Of Stephanie. And of her friends and family. Because, for a little while, they were my friends and family, too.*

"But what's the third blessing?" Dolores asked.

Nat turned to Garth. "Your turn."

"My wife," Garth said, and took Sabrina's hand. "Who discovered our anonymous letter-writer and, through a conversation she will not describe to me, cowed the young woman into accompanying her quite meekly to Lloyd Strauss's office, where a full confession was written in ink and signed. And who kept her promise to the letter-writer by convincing Lloyd he should allow her to graduate. And who then, after the young woman departed—Lloyd told me this himself—gave him a scolding he will not soon forget and stood over him while he read a statement to his secretary to be telephoned to the media. And who finally, as Lloyd also told me, refused to leave until he set the date for the announcement of my appointment as director of the Genetics Institute."

He touched his glass to Sabrina's. "My wife. My dearest love."

Linda's eyes brimmed with tears. "Stephanie, you never said a word. That's the most wonderful story I ever heard."

"Poor Lloyd," Nat said wryly. "Facing Stephanie's wrath. He must have been terrified."

"He deserved it," said Dolores scornfully.

"I wish," Linda said to Marty, her voice low, "I wish I'd done something that wonderful for you."

"You did," he said. "You stayed with me."

In the golden, fragrant room, Sabrina lay her palm against Garth's cheek. "I love you."

He put his arms around her, his mouth close to hers. "My life, my world, my whole being."

She closed her eyes. *I can't, I can't; don't make me leave him.* In a moment, she opened her eyes. "I have a toast, too."

"I should hope so," said Nat. "My glass is empty." Her tears were gone, he saw; she looked magnificent. Stunningly beautiful—strange how they all got used to it and then suddenly would see her as if for the first time and be taken aback by her beauty. Today, flushed from the heat of the kitchen, her hair casually held back by a gold band, she was at once a lovely woman and a young girl radiantly in love. And why not, after Garth's words? Looking at her, it was hard to believe in the confused, incoherent, grieving woman Garth had described after the funeral. But Nat still heard her stumble occasionally, thinking of herself as Sabrina, and he knew she had not yet resolved her confusion—though at the moment she seemed to know exactly who she was.

Thinking about her, he had missed her toast. To Garth, he gathered, for being elected to the National Genetics Research Advisory Council. A high honor for a man not yet forty; no wonder they were pleased.

"—Council meeting next week in New York," Garth was saying.

"Stephanie, too?" Linda asked. "But the estate sale—"

"Madeline will help you," Sabrina said. "And I'll work with you this week, before I leave. You've learned so much; you'll be wonderful and you know it. Madeline thinks you're amazing. And so do I."

"Mom, we're starved!" Cliff said, coming into the kitchen. "When do we eat?"

"My God, the bird!" Nat cried. "I've abandoned my duties as a baster." He opened the oven. "When *do* we eat?"

"One hour," Dolores said. "If Garth and Marty get that corn concoction in the oven right away."

"Can we have some pretzels?" Cliff asked.

"Go easy," said Sabrina. "There's a feast ahead of us."

As everyone moved about the kitchen to different tasks, she

took a quick glance at the window. It was smooth and dark; all the reflections were gone.

After dinner the next night Sabrina climbed the stairs to the third floor and sat at Stephanie's desk. The room was bare but no longer dusty; Juanita's determined hand had been at work. And its sad air of defeat was gone, too; it was just a room where projects had been stored and now were about to be revived. She emptied the drawers of the records and photographs Stephanie had kept from her estate business and slipped them into large envelopes for Linda. In the years to come, she would continue the business that Stephanie had begun.

In the strange quiet, so rare in that house, Sabrina looked at the pile of envelopes. One by one she was completing the unfinished pieces of Stephanie's life. Cliff was free of his gang and so relieved about it that he was tolerating almost cheerfully a month of restrictions. He had gone to Garth with the whole story, and the two of them had reached their own understanding; all Sabrina knew about it was Garth's comment later, in bed. "Someday Cliff will appreciate what you've done for the two of us, helping us to be friends. I appreciate it now. I appreciate *you.*"

She had seen Garth through the ugliness of the anonymous letters; the story already was fading and he was deep in discussions with architects and contractors on the new Genetics Institute. She had helped Linda when she needed it, as Stephanie would have done. Soon Penny's art classes would begin, and next month the costumes she had designed and made would be seen in the class puppet show—

I won't see it. And I promised—

"Mom? You coming down?"

"In a few minutes, Cliff," she called. Opening the desk drawers to make sure nothing was left behind, she ran her hand to the back of each one. They were all empty. Picking up the envelopes, she reached for the light to turn it off.

"Mom!"

"Yes, Cliff, right—"

"Telephone, Mom! From London!"

London? At this hour? Something must have happened; it was three in the morning there; who would call—?

She swept up the envelopes and ran downstairs to the telephone in the bedroom.

"Mrs. Andersen, this is Michel Bernard; we met at Sabrina's funeral, if you remember."

"Of course, I remember. What is it? Ambassadors? Has something happened—?"

"No, it's something else. We wanted you to know as soon as we did. We heard today from Scotland Yard that Ivan Lazlo and Rory Carr have been arrested for placing a bomb on Max Stuyvesant's yacht. It seems they—"

"Wait. Please, wait a minute."

"Oh, damnation—forgive me—Jolie told me not to rush into—hey!"

"Mrs. Andersen, this is Jolie Fantome. Michel is a boor and I apologize for him. This is not the way to tell you."

Sabrina sat on the edge of the bed. "It's all right; I knew there had been a bomb; it was just suddenly hearing it. It all seems so far away from here. What else have they found?"

"This is what we know. It will all be in our story when it is published in December. You know about Max Stuyvesant's smuggling? And that Lazlo and Carr stored his smuggled goods and also had a little sideline of selling forged art mixed in with the real thing? You know all that from Sabrina?"

"Yes. But what about Ambassadors?"

"Almost nothing. It is listed in the books at Westbridge as a customer; but reporters want drama, and a few forged art works are not dramatic. The reporters are interested in Lazlo and Carr because they put a bomb on Stuyvesant's yacht. *That* is dramatic. And it has nothing to do with Ambassadors."

"But it does. If Sabrina was killed because of what she knew—"

"No, that is not correct. We thought you feared that, but we could not say for sure you were wrong. Now we can. Carr and Lazlo are babbling on and on, blaming each other for everything, but it all comes down to a quarrel with Stuyvesant over the forgeries; he said they could be discovered, which would open the door to exposing his smuggling operation. Carr and Lazlo thought he was planning to get rid of them, so they simply beat him to it."

"It wasn't Sabrina—it was Max they were after?"

"That is what I'm telling you. Years ago, Lazlo spent some time on the *Lafitte* as Stuyvesant's secretary and also doing a

421

little smuggling for him, making deliveries along the Italian Riviera."

A boat, Sabrina remembered, near dawn, when she had gone on deck for some air and to get away from Denton. Ivan Lazlo in a motorboat, helped on board by a crew member, disappearing down the stairs to the crew's quarters without seeing her.

"So," Jolie went on, "he knew some of the crew members still there from those days, and he went aboard to see them in the Monte Carlo harbor. At some time while he was there he put a bomb in the stateroom. It went off too soon, he had not set it properly, which is why the boat was only two miles out and the French divers were able to raise it so quickly. Otherwise, we might never have known it was not an accident."

"They killed all those people—"

"They didn't care. They wanted it to look like an accident." There was a pause. "Stephanie, does this make you feel better or worse?"

"A little of each."

"I thought it might. They were an unpleasant bunch, but Stuyvesant had great charm and knew the art world better than anyone. He and Sabrina had known each other for years; she decorated his London house; and we think she may have gone on the cruise on legitimate business, perhaps to buy for her gallery. He had been at Chilton and all the major fall auctions; he would have had a good selection for her to choose from. Honestly come by."

She is defending Sabrina Longworth to her American sister, thought Sabrina. Explaining her presence on that yacht. "Thank you," she said. "I'm grateful for that."

Jolie talked on, mentioning casually that Sabrina's little friend Gabrielle had been seen several times at dinner with Brooks Westermarck; Sabrina was grateful for that, too. Life goes on, Jolie was saying, and yours will, too. "Goodbye, then," Jolie said.

"Thank you," said Sabrina. "And thank Michel."

"Oh, Michel I shall strike on the rump for being so abrupt with you."

A small laugh broke from Sabrina. Those two, she thought affectionately, as she used to think when she was Sabrina and lived in London. She wondered if the three of them could be as close now that she was Stephanie as they had been when she was Sabrina.

The pile of envelopes lay on the bed beside her. Tomorrow she would give it to Linda. And that would mean there was nothing left for her to do. There was not even an obstacle to her returning to London anymore: the forgery story was public and Ambassadors was not part of it; she needn't fear damage to its reputation or to Sabrina's memory. Nor was she in any personal danger; in fact, she never had been.

Nothing was left for her to do; there was no longer any reason for her to stay.

"Mom? Is everything all right?"

She steadied her voice. "Yes, Cliff. Everything is all right."

"Could we have a quick game of Monopoly then?"

"There is no such thing as a quick game of Monopoly. That's a ploy to stay up until midnight. How about Scrabble?"

"Sure. Are you coming now?"

"Right away."

No reason for her to stay. She sat on the bed and felt time slow down, everything slow down, coming gradually to an end. Around her, every object was clear and sharp; ordinary pieces of furniture seemed to glow and burn themselves into her memory, joining the pictures from Thanksgiving. One last chance to memorize them so that when she closed her eyes she could see them still and know she would for a long time to come. In three days, on Monday, she would leave. First to New York with Garth and then, alone, to London. Stephanie Andersen going home to Sabrina Longworth's life.

We'll always be here, Garth had said; an unfinished story.

The one part of Stephanie's life, and my life, that I cannot finish.

Two half-finished lives, Garth had said.

Yes. But still better than wounding you with the truth. Or living a lie with you, founded on my sister's death.

"Mom!"

Don't think about it. Enjoy these last few days. "Yes, Cliff," she said, and went downstairs.

Later Sabrina would remember those three days as a haze of voices and gestures. She would try to recall single moments, but they slipped from her. All she had was the blurred memory of a time when her feelings swung wildly from piercing happiness to dark despair, and the hours escaped her as she tried to hold them back.

On Friday night Lloyd Strauss hosted a dinner for university trustees, faculty members and scientists from around the country. Penny and Cliff were there, sitting near the front, awed by the talk about their father and the glowing elegance of their mother in an antique gold full-skirted dress with a matching short embroidered jacket. The room was brightly lit and crowded. "Lloyd's apology," Garth said, amused but touched. "For our investigative friend."

Watching, saying little, Sabrina let the evening carry her along, loving Garth for his quiet acceptance of praise from scientists older and more famous than he and congratulations from trustees and faculty members. After dinner, sitting at the head table, she listened to the president describe Garth's background—telling her much she never knew about him—and then make the formal announcement of his appointment as director of the new Genetics Institute.

Keeping her face serene through the applause and flashes from reporters' cameras, Sabrina thought, I helped this happen. It all may have happened without me, but I helped. He will always have that to remember.

Beside her, Garth stood and made a brief speech on his goals for the Institute and its staff and thanked those who were helping make it a reality. "But in my smaller, personal sphere," he added, "I want to thank two people who helped me reach this night. Lloyd Strauss, who has balanced friendship and his responsibility to the university as few others could, and my wife, who has never failed me in love and encouragement and in challenging me to look as far and as high as possible without losing sight of the wonders of our family and our life together." He looked down at Sabrina's shining eyes. "Stephanie Andersen."

Everyone stood, applauding, as Garth sat down and took Sabrina's hand. "Who is also," he added to her alone, beneath the applause, "the most desirable woman I have ever known, and whom I would much rather be in bed with than in this large and very public room."

She laughed, buoyant with joy and love. "Soon," she promised. "As soon as I can seduce you from all your other admirers." Nothing was real but Garth's eyes on hers, his hand holding hers, his lips lightly on hers before the university president took him away to talk to a local businessman who wanted to contribute to the Institute building fund.

That was all she remembered of that night, though she talked to dozens of people, and later, when the children were in bed, she and Garth made love. They made love as they had learned to in these last weeks: slowly, leisurely, as if all the time in the world was theirs, savoring each urgent moment as they came wondrously alive, still exploring, still learning what they could give and share and take from each other.

But she only remembered the rightness of it, the sense of completeness, not the individual moments when they filled each other's vision and nothing else mattered. Those moments were blurred, part of the darkness of the night and the glaring brightness of the morning when Penny and Cliff woke them with a reminder of the weekend's plans.

"You didn't forget! We're going cross-country skiing at the Goldners'!"

"There is a difference," Garth said sternly from his pillow, his hand, beneath the covers, on Sabrina's breast, "between forgetting and beginning one's weekend at a civilized hour." But, urged on by the children, they bestirred themselves, and within a short time were on their way to Michigan.

Dolores and Nat had been inviting them to their country house at Lakeside in the dunes since Thanksgiving. When the time came, Sabrina had not wanted to go. *I want it to be just the four of us; it's the last weekend we'll ever have together.* But she could not say that, and Penny and Cliff were so excited that she gave in.

The weekend was as blurred as the rest of those last few days. Her memory could recapture the whiteness: snow-covered dunes against a pale sky, the lake shining like pewter under the slanting rays of the sun, the white shadows of their ski tracks snaking up and down the low slopes. She could recall Garth's face close to hers when the children had pulled ahead and they were alone, her mouth opening beneath his and his whispered "I love you" before Nat and Dolores caught up to them. She remembered a lazy dinner before the Goldners' huge fireplace and quiet talk late into the night, the four of them watching the flames die to glowing, shimmering coals. And she could remember the freezing bedroom where she and Garth undressed quickly and slipped into the icy bed, shivering, until the two of them, clasped in each other's arms, grew warm, and, almost without moving, Garth was inside her.

But that was all, except for the sharp pain of happiness and the dull despair that lay just beneath it.

Early Monday morning, they packed for the New York trip and said goodbye to Penny and Cliff at breakfast. "Don't forget," Sabrina said. "After school you go to the Goodmans' house."

"Mom," said Cliff, "you've told us that fifty times. That's what we did when you went to Connecticut, so how come you think we'll forget?"

"I don't like the idea of your coming home to an empty house."

"We *won't,* I told you. We're not *babies.*"

"I know." She smoothed Penny's curls and straightened the strap of her jumper. "It's just that I'm going to miss you—" Her voice broke, and she turned abruptly away.

"Mom?" Cliff was alarmed; she could hear it in his voice as Garth came into the kitchen.

"Something wrong?" he asked.

"I think Mom's sick."

Garth moved quickly toward her, but Sabrina stood up before he reached her. "Small upset stomach," she said lightly. "Nothing that breakfast won't cure."

He studied her face. "Nothing else?"

"Nothing else."

They bustled about. "You'll remember—"

"—to go to the Goodmans'," Cliff and Penny said together, and they all laughed.

"Mom," said Cliff, "could you get me a suit of armor in England?"

"A suit of— Cliff, do you know what they weigh?"

"No, how much?"

"Over a hundred pounds. Knights had to be lifted onto their horses with a crane."

"How come the horse didn't fall down under them?" Penny asked.

"That would have been a knightmare," said Cliff and collapsed, laughing, on the floor.

"Not bad," said Garth, chuckling. "Now get yourself together before you're late for school. And we have a plane to catch, Stephanie. Are you almost ready?"

"Yes. Just these dishes—"

Garth was upstairs and Penny and Cliff were in their coats when she found them at the living room door. Penny gripped her with both arms. "Don't stay in England long." She dropped her voice to a whisper. "Daddy said not to nag you, there are things you have to do, but you have things here, too. You won't stay long, will you?"

Sabrina kissed Penny's smooth cheek and held her close. "I don't want to. I don't want to leave you at all. I love you, my Penny. Don't ever forget that. I love you and I'm proud of you. You are my very special girl."

"Mom," Cliff said. "We're late. Can I kiss you goodbye?"

She tried to let Penny go, but her arms would not move. *Don't go. Please don't go.*

"Mommy, don't cry," said Penny. Her hand began to pat Sabrina's shoulder. "You'll be back soon. Don't cry."

"I didn't mean to. I guess trips sometimes do that to people. Your turn, Cliff."

He gave her a quick hug. "If you can't bring me some armor, could you get me a sword like King Arthur's?"

She laughed shakily. "I'll find you something. Does it have to be destructive?"

"Well, since I'm reading about King Arthur . . ."

"I'll see what I can do. Cliff, take . . . take care of Penny and yourself, will you?"

"Sure. I always do. You'll bring her something, too, won't you?"

"I'll send presents as soon as I get there. How will that be?"

"Okay. 'Bye, Mom. Have a good trip." He kissed her cheek. Sabrina put her arms around him and kissed him on both cheeks. "The French do it that way," he said.

"I do, too," said Sabrina, kissing him again. "I'm going to miss you, my star soccer player. Especially your awful puns. And your dear face and smile—"

"Come on, Mom!"

"Sorry," she said, wiping her eyes. "I didn't mean to start up again. Off with you now, or you really will be late. Have a good time at the Goodmans' and give my love to Vivian."

They ran down the walk. Sabrina watched them. At the corner they turned and waved. She raised her arm and waved back and watched them disappear through the mist of tears in her eyes.

Chapter 20

The streets of New York were slick with rain. Lunchtime crowds scurried under black umbrellas that bobbed and bumped against each other like an awning whipped by the wind. Young boys and old men sat in doorways selling umbrellas for those who had left home unprepared, and messengers on bicycles were almost hidden in ballooning yellow slickers that dripped rain onto the puddles in the street.

Sitting in the taxicab with Garth, Sabrina thought of winter tears, cold and gray, dropping from the dark clouds that had settled on the tops of skyscrapers. Windows shone as if it were night. In front of every hotel a doorman raised his arm, as if saluting a parade, and blew his whistle to stop a cab in flight, but none stopped; they all had passengers.

"Don't matter, though," their driver grumbled as they sat in the middle of a crosstown street, immobilized by a mass of traffic. "Sun shines, nobody rides. It rains, everybody rides but nobody moves."

"Shall we buy an umbrella and walk?" Garth asked Sabrina.

"Helluva long walk, mister," the driver answered.

"I know. I used to teach there."

"You hold on and keep dry. We get to the corner we're all right. Uptown is faster than crosstown."

"I know."

"Right. You useta teach there. My kid teaches third grade. She likes it, but she don't make much."

Garth looked at Sabrina, but she was gazing out the window on her side. She had barely spoken since they had left home. On the plane, he had asked what she would like to do in New York, but she had answered briefly and absently, and he knew she was barely aware of him. Thinking of London, of her sister's life. Of adopting that life? He had no idea and would not ask her. If it came to that, he would find her wherever she was and try to bring her back, but he would not anticipate a crisis where, so far, none existed. If the bond with her sister was so strong it withstood death, he would not try to break it, even if he thought he could, unless he saw it destroying his marriage.

"Have you bought your ticket?" he asked as lunch was being served, and she looked surprised.

"No. I've . . . been so busy. I will in New York."

When they reached the Plaza, Garth watched her face. "Oh," she said. "I didn't know, you didn't tell me—"

"We had a very special night here about six weeks ago. I liked the idea of coming back."

"Yes." She looked at him, her eyes so lonely he cried out. "My love, what is it?"

He watched the effort she made to push her thoughts aside, and he marveled at her strength, even more because at other times he had seen it fail her. She took his arm as the bellhop unlocked the door of their room. "What are you going to do now?" she asked.

"You and I are going for a quick visit to Columbia. I want to poke my nose into my first lab and have a moment of nostalgia. For both of us." When she made no response, he said, "Do you want to unpack? Hang some things in the closet?"

"Not now."

Garth surveyed the room. "Not the suite the Kallens provided, but it will do very well. I'm looking forward to crushing chocolates on the pillow again."

"And losing one on the floor," she murmured, remembering with a small smile. "Shall we go?"

In the rain, it took them an hour to get to Columbia, but they still had time to visit the lab before Garth's lecture to a graduate seminar. "A favor to an old friend," he said as they entered the building. "Since my meeting isn't until tomorrow,

429

he asked if I'd mind dispensing wisdom to his students for a couple of hours this afternoon. You can sit in, or would you rather shop?"

"Shop, I think. There are some antique dealers I'd like to meet."

"Then I'll meet you at the hotel about five-thirty or six."

They rode the elevator to the fourth floor. "Quieter than the last time you were here," said Garth.

Sabrina had no idea what he was talking about. A month ago, a week ago, she would have tried to cover her ignorance, but now it seemed unimportant. She had said goodbye to the children and had taken a last walk through the house; now she could feel herself withdrawing steadily from Garth. In an hour she would buy her ticket for London and tomorrow she would tell him she would not be coming back.

She walked ahead of him into the laboratory, a large room partitioned down the center by tall steel cabinets. They went to one side, and Garth looked at the bare soapstone bench. "Gone are the Tinkertoys. Ah, but look there. They don't get rid of me so easily."

Still not understanding him, Sabrina followed his gaze and saw on the wall framed drawings that did indeed look like Tinkertoy constructions. Now she knew what he meant: models of molecules. She had seen others like them in his lab at Midwestern.

"I did those just before I left," he said. "They still look pretty good. But how little we knew then; what incredible miles we've traveled in twelve years! Let's see what Bill's successor is up to."

On the other side of the cabinets, Sabrina saw cages of scampering white mice stacked on a wall beside a large window. "Not a bit different," Garth said, smiling. "I think Bill may still be on the premises. He may even still have a stock of tweezers and gauze bandages for unexpected wounds."

Sabrina was looking at the mice. "I wonder if that window seems like protection, or a view of a world they can't ever touch."

"Give me your hand," Garth said roughly.

Puzzled, she held it out to him. "Why?"

"To see if I can jog your memory."

"Jog my—" Mentally, she shook herself. "I'm sorry, please forgive me; I'm being absentminded and rude." Her hand, held out to him, was trembling. "Shall we reenact the scene?" *I'll do the best I can; just give me some clues.*

"No, we don't need to relive the past. I do remember, though, how you looked when I told you I wanted to marry you and make love to you."

"How?" she asked faintly.

"As if I'd given you a gift. Your eyes were red and swollen from that damn tear gas, but they shone so brightly that I remember wondering how a pair of midnight-blue eyes could look as if they held the sun within them. And then you frowned, as if you were wondering what gift to give me in return."

"And what did I give you?"

"Yourself. The most I have ever wanted. And what incredible miles *we've* traveled since that day." He drew her to him and kissed her. "Stephanie, whatever is troubling you, I promise you we'll remedy it. Two such fine gift-givers have no place in their life for troubles."

"Good God, would you believe it?" A tall gray-bearded man with horn-rimmed glasses came into the lab. "It isn't enough they have their own bedroom; they still make out in the lab. What an example for the younger generation!" He stretched out his hands to Sabrina. "Rolf Taggart. I thought Garth was exaggerating when he described you in his letters. Now I find he didn't do you justice. Welcome." He shook Garth's hand. "And welcome home."

Garth smiled. "Rolf does not admit I could have another home, even after twelve years."

"I still miss you, even after twelve years; best researcher I ever worked with. Are you prepared to face the sharp questioning of my sharpest students?"

"Probably not, but I'll do my best. Stephanie, five-thirty at the hotel? Six at the latest."

"I'll be there. I hope it goes well."

As she took the elevator to the cabstand, Rolf said, "Garth, she's stunning, but that pallor . . . is she ill?"

"She's troubled about going to London. I'm not sure why." In their correspondence over the years, Garth had written to Rolf about matters he could not discuss with Nat or Marty, simply because it often was easier to confide in a friend one did not see every day. But he could not tell Rolf, any more than anyone else, that his wife might still be thinking of leaving him. "She's always identified strongly with her sister; as long as I've known her she's had fantasies about being Sabrina, or at least living her kind of life. Now, since Sabrina's death, she's been confused, off and on, about whether she's Stephanie or Sabrina. As if she feels a compulsion to live both their lives or choose between them. But lately, in the most extraordinary way, we'd finally come together, found each other for the first time in the way all of us dream of—"

Garth rubbed his forehead. They had reached the door of the seminar room, and he looked apologetically at his friend. "I didn't come here for a therapy session, Father Rolf. Why didn't you stop me?"

"Because you needed to talk and I wanted to hear. But now there's this damn seminar. Can you face these young animals whose favorite sport is trying to show professors youth knows more than middle age?"

Garth squared his shoulders. "Let's show them our tricks."

The room was full; Garth's name was a magnet. He looked at the sixty faces before him, alert and expectant, and felt renewed. However unsure he felt about his future with Stephanie, here in this room he was absolutely confident and excited about the contact with students. Pacing back and forth, he talked easily, relaxed and humorous, but technical; he did not talk down to students. At the same time, he made them feel they were part of a community of scientists, free to ask questions or make comments as he talked.

It was almost four-thirty when he paused and then said, casually, "I want to talk now about immortal antibodies." A stir went through the class; the phrase caught their imagination, and the inflection in Garth's voice told them it was something big. He let the suspense build, enjoying it.

"What we are working on," he said, leaning on the desk with both hands, "is the ability to make the human immune system immortal. That implies exactly what you think it does: perpetual production of antibodies. We are looking at the potential for fusing two human cells—one that produces antibodies and one that reproduces itself forever. The result is a hybrid that will produce an endless supply of antibodies, vastly strengthening the body's natural defense system, which, by itself, often is not effective. In other words, an immortal immune system. In addition, the antibodies would be used to make a broad spectrum of vaccines against disease."

A hand went up. "Sir, hasn't this kind of cell fusion been done in mice?"

Garth nodded. "For about ten years. But you know that when we treat human disease with vaccines made from animal antibodies, there are drastic side effects. Those of you who've had the vaccine for rabies, which is made from horse antibodies, know how painful it is. But humans can accept human antibodies, as they do in blood transfusions, without those side effects. When we perfect the technology, we expect to produce unlimited amounts of them, specific to various diseases."

"Which ones, sir?"

"At the moment, tetanus, erythroblastosis—a cause of jaundice in babies—and malignancy of the white blood cells in children, or childhood leukemia. We're probably seven or eight years away from availability of these vaccines for treatment, but clinical tests may begin within a couple of years."

"Professor, what chemical is used to fuse the cells?"

"Ethylene glycol, inexpensive and readily available."

"Sir, have you compared actual nucleotide sequences between the original hybrid and succeeding ones to determine that they are truly identical? How many generations have you followed, and what methods do you use to keep track of the original hybrid cell?"

There's always a show-off, Garth thought, trying to impress the professor and the class. "We've compared a number of the DNA nucleotide sequences through several generations, and so far they've been found to be identical in every respect. With identical cells, there is, as you point out, the problem of distinguishing the original from the copy. We've found the most efficient method is to use a radioactive tracer to give the original cell a special identification. This is sufficient, even when all other aspects are identical, to distinguish it from a copy—"

He stopped. The words echoed in his mind: Distinguish it from a copy. Original. Identical. Copy. Distinguish the original from—Identical. Copy. Identical. Original. Copy . . .

A blank look in the laboratory; no recollection of tear gas and a cut hand. Wine before dinner. "I don't want you to take the job at Foster Labs." Deflating Irma Kallen. Intimidating Mrs. Casey and Rita McMillan. Hiring a maid, taking a new job, without discussion. "It wasn't Sabrina who died . . ." A funeral: "I'm Sabrina . . ." China. *China.*

The copy can be determined from the original.

"Professor Andersen has another appointment." Rolf was at his side—where had he come from?—completing the answer to the question, bringing the seminar smoothly to a close. The students were standing, applauding. A few came up with questions poised on their lips, but Rolf turned them away. "A tight schedule, not this time, perhaps a return visit . . ." And then they were alone in the empty room.

"Come on, I'll get you to a doctor."

Slowly, Garth focused on him. "Do I look that bad?"

"Like you'll pass out any moment. Where's the pain? Chest? Arm?"

He laughed shortly. "Head and heart. But not a heart attack, Rolf. Just an attack of reality; enough to wake me up." He looked at the high dark windows, raindrops running crazily down their length, and heard his voice go on and on. He could not stop it. "Amazing, isn't it, how we keep ourselves deluded long past the time when we should have forced our eyes open? We see things, we hear them, and they don't fit, but we force them to make sense, we push them into the shapes we want, we don't even allow ideas to reach the surface of our minds because they're impossible to accept, too awful to contemplate. I sound like a psychologist. Maybe I'm in the wrong profession. God knows I'm in the wrong marriage."

"Garth, what the hell—!"

"Oh, fuck it, don't pay any attention to my ravings, Rolf. I have no right to burden you with a delayed awakening. I'm going for a walk; think some things out."

"In this rain? And aren't we meeting later, for dinner?"

"Not tonight. Rolf, I let you down. I'm sorry. The seminar—"

"The seminar was terrific. An abrupt ending, but that wasn't important. You can't tell me about your waking up? Sometimes it's easier to have the eyes forced open if a friend shares the view."

"I can't. I'm not even sure I'm right. But there may be a time . . . I'll let you know." They shook hands. "I owe you another seminar."

"Forget it. Let me get you a cab."

"I'll find one."

But there were no cabs. The rain was as steady as before, and, after walking a few blocks, he gave up and ran down the subway stairs. He stood on the platform, jostled by riders positioning themselves to leap through the train doors when they opened. The air smelled of wet wool. He was in no hurry; he stepped back.

He could be wrong. He had no proof. Scientists insist on proof or overwhelming evidence. Observation, controlled experiments, documentation, replication. All he had was the sudden flood of light that had blinded him in the seminar room, as if a curtain had been ripped aside. Everything fit together; he was certain she was Sabrina.

There were no empty seats on the train. He stood in the packed aisle, swaying, grasping the steel loop above his head, shaped like a hangman's noose, he noted, or a teardrop. Fooled him. How well she had fooled him. The scientist, the careful observer, with an international reputation for the purity of his experiments and the thoroughness of his documentation. Couldn't even tell he was living with his wife's twin sister. Sleeping with his wife's twin sister. Excused her mistakes; convinced himself she was trying to improve their marriage; gave her the benefit of every doubt; helped her make a fool of him. Again and again, helped her make a fool of him, *helped her* and loved her while doing it.

Fool.

In the hotel lobby he slowed his steps. But it was only when he was in the crowded elevator, stopping at every floor, that the full impact hit him and he doubled over as if struck in the stomach.

His wife was dead.

"You getting off here?"

Garth looked up. The elevator doors had opened at his floor and a young girl was holding them back with her hand.

"Yes," he said hoarsely. He cleared his throat. "Thank you."

She watched him shuffle along the flowered carpet. "You got somebody to take care of you?"

"Yes. Thank you." No. No one. But it doesn't concern anyone else. Only Sabrina and me.

Outside the door of their room, he leaned against the wall. Cold tremors ran down his legs and arms and crushed his chest; his breath came in gasps. He stood there, in that frozen vise, waiting for the tremors to stop. Guests passed with curious glances. A waiter pushed a cart loaded with drinks and hors d'oeuvres to a room down the hall. And from the other side of the door beside him, Garth heard the telephone ring, and heard it answered. So she was there. Waiting for him.

He stood away from the wall. He had to face her. He might, after all, be wrong. An infinitesimal, unscientific hope. He put his key in the door and went in.

Sabrina was curled up in a chair beside the window. Lamplight turned her hair red-gold and her skin a pale translucence; she looked fragile and vulnerable, and reflexively Garth's arms began to reach out to her. *No!* he cried silently, and stayed beside the door as Sabrina said, "Rolf called, wondering how you—"

She stopped as she saw the set of his mouth and the deep lines of his face. And she knew that he knew the truth. Briefly she wondered how he had discovered it. Her stupidity in the lab that afternoon, some other mistake or, at last, his analytical mind putting everything together? What difference did it make? It was too late to make a difference.

She was frightened, but she also felt a strange sense of relief. It was out of her hands. She had not been able to tell him herself, but *she had wanted him to find out;* she wanted to leave with the truth between them, not layer upon layer of lies . . .

The silence stretched like a fuse between them. They were hesitating, each reluctant to say the words that would alter their lives forever. At last Garth walked stiffly to a floor lamp and turned it on. "No shadows. We've had enough shadows, haven't we, Sabrina?"

She did not recognize her name on his lips; it was a stranger's name.

No, not a stranger's. Her own. A stranger to Garth.

"Well?" he asked, and she heard in his voice the desperate thread of hope that perhaps he was wrong.

"No," she said, so quietly he had to strain to hear her. "You aren't wrong."

"Sabrina."

"Yes."

His body spun about, as if flung by an explosion, and he strode the length of the room and back, not looking at her. "What was it, a game? You wanted to play housewife for awhile and needed an instant family, some simpletons who would lie back and play dumb and let you walk all over them? Life was dull in London, so you told your rich friends to hold the fort while you dabbled in genteel poverty? Nothing like a little diversion, is there, to make the time pass more—"

"Garth, stop it, stop, please stop, it isn't true, none of it—"

"And the professor, the stuffy professor, does tricks, sits up and begs for Lady Sabrina Longworth while she plays him for a fool. The greatest fool of all time."

"Please, that isn't—"

He kicked his suitcase aside. "Now why would the Lady Sabrina do that? What did she want? Just to play housewife? Probably not. She wanted something more. What could that be?" He perched on the arm of a sofa near Sabrina. "Could it be, could it possibly be, that she wanted to show up her sister at being a housewife? Was that it? Lady Longworth, bored with her rich friends, decided to show her sister there was nothing she couldn't do. She'd already beat her at everything else—money, success, freedom, lovers . . . oh, my God . . ." His voice trailed away and he stared vacantly at his hands, opening and closing them as if reminding himself they had nothing to hold. "Stephanie is dead. My wife is dead. *You knew that. You stood beside me at her funeral. You let me bury my wife and never told me what I was doing.*" He stood over her, and she shrank back in her chair. "You damn bitch, how could you stand there while they put that coffin in its grave and *not tell us who was in it?*"

"I told you! I tried to tell you! You wouldn't listen to me, I told you I was Sabrina—!"

He began to pace again. "You did. Now that is true. How hard did you try? How many times? *How soon after the news came of her death?*"

As he heard himself say it, he flinched and his body froze, while a jumble of images tore through his mind: Penny and Cliff laughing, their upturned faces filled with trust; his family at dinner, listening as he talked about his work; Thanksgiving and a kitchen crowded with friends; a cemetery, a coffin, Stephanie trembling within the curve of his arm . . . no, damn it, no—not Stephanie; Stephanie was dead; he had comforted Sabrina and watched the Vicar bury his wife. "My God, you took that telephone call, you flew with us to London, you spent two days before the funeral weeping prettily and never told us, *never told us* who was dead."

"That's enough! How dare you!" She leaped up and stood beside the window, her head high. "Whatever else happened, how dare you imply I was not really mourning my sister? How dare you accuse me of taking her place to show her I was better than she was? I wasn't better, I never thought I was; we were the same, we were part of each other and I loved her more than anyone in the world. I loved her more than you did—at least I cared about her as a person and not just as *a wife;* I wanted her to have love and attention, and you gave her neither; you were so wrapped up in yourself you barely looked at her for years, you didn't listen to her ... oh, Garth, I'm sorry, I'm sorry, I don't mean that. I know it was more complicated than that, things are never so simple between two people. ... But I loved her so, and I miss her, and we never intended any of this, we thought it would just be a week—"

"We? What are you talking about?" Pacing the room, he touched each piece of furniture as if they were the only solid supports in his shifting world. "Stephanie would never be a part of a filthy trick—"

"Of course she was; how else would we change places? I'm sorry, I didn't want you to know, I didn't want you hurt—"

"Hurt! Are you mad? After weeks of lying to me, playing me for a fool, you didn't want me hurt?"

"I know how it sounds." She looked through the cold window at the lights of the city, distorted by the rain. "But I told you, we never expected it to last more than a week. Stephanie felt she had to get away for a few days, to think about problems with Cliff, and with you, worries about money, about the job in Stamford—"

"Did she broadcast all our intimacies?"

"Of course not. She didn't even go into details. But I knew she needed to get away, and so did I; there were pressures in my life, too—problems I had to think about. And then we had the idea of spending a week in each other's lives—"

"Who had the idea?"

"I did," she said swiftly. Too swiftly.

"You're lying. It was her idea, wasn't it?"

"I don't remember. What difference does it make?"

"Can't you for once in this whole stinking mess tell the simple truth?"

"It was Stephanie's idea. But I agreed."

"To change places. And then?"

"We thought we could look at our lives from a different angle, understand ourselves better—where we were and where we wanted to go. And then we'd change back. No one would have known. I told Stephanie I wouldn't make love to you, and she said it happened so seldom—"

His face darkened, the lines deep and harsh about his mouth. "But you did, didn't you? And my God, weren't you good at it? That was quite an act you put on; I even brought us back here, like a damned romantic fool. . . . You had a good time, didn't you, night after night, and I believed it all, fell for it—"

"It wasn't a lie. Don't you understand? Garth, please try to understand. *I fell in love with you.* I didn't want to; I tried not to, but I loved you for a long time before I even admitted it to myself. And then, when I realized it, I wanted to go back to London right away, but Stephanie wanted to go on a—but my wrist wasn't healed, and we were afraid if we changed then you'd discover—"

"Where did Stephanie want to go?"

"She wanted to come home to you. But until my wrist—"

"Where did she want to go before she came home to me and her children?"

"It doesn't matter."

"Goddamn it, don't treat me like a child who can't be told the truth. That's what you've done from the beginning. It's a little late for that now. *Where did she want to go?*"

"On a cruise. Because I'd been on so many and she never had."

"With whom?"

"A group of people."

"In other words, she'd found someone else."

"Garth, what difference does it make? She's dead. She loved you and the children, she wanted to come back and stay with you and make your marriage a good one, and then she was killed. Nothing else matters."

"Nothing else matters. Isn't that convenient? Is that how you live with yourself? I'll tell you what matters: three god-damned months. Three months of lying to two children who loved you and trusted you. Three months of lying to friends who worried about you and helped you when you broke your damned wrist. Three months of lying while I explained away your behavior and believed you were trying to reshape our marriage. Three months of smiles and kisses and some remarkably passionate lovemaking. Three months of a deception—and you did it well, I must say, I congratulate you on a remarkable—"

"Stop, stop, don't you see, *I wasn't always sure who I was.*"

He was arrested in his pacing. His face took on a look of curiosity—the scientist hearing something new and intriguing—but he shoved it aside; he even made a movement with his hands, pushing it away and letting his anger return, as if she had not spoken. "And how much longer were you going to play your little deception? Until the novelty wore off? Until the kids and I got on your nerves? Until you decided it was time to get back to your glamorous friends and the social whirl?"

"That's not fair," she whispered. She turned back to the window and said aloud, "It was over." Her breath misted the glass, and she watched the circle of moisture shrink and disappear.

"What does that mean?" He swung a chair around and straddled it. "Turn around, damn it; look at me when you talk to me."

The pain in his voice knifed into her, and Sabrina felt she was bleeding from his anger and grief. Her knees gave way; she moved shakily to the sofa. "You knew I was flying to London from here. I bought my ticket this afternoon while you were giving your lecture. I was going to tell you tomorrow that I couldn't live with you anymore, that I didn't think we could make our marriage—"

"Not ours, lady!"

"I'm trying to tell you what I was going to say. That I didn't think we could make our marriage work and I was going to stay in London permanently."

"After that remarkable faked loving, in bed and out, after tackling Rita McMillan, after such a good job of acting that you really succeeded in making us a family—" His voice caught and he had to stop for a minute. "After all that," he went on huskily, "and carrying on as if we did indeed have a marriage, you were going to say it wouldn't work."

Her hands were cold and stiff, and, crossing her arms, she tucked them into her armpits. "I never faked anything, or acted with you and Penny and Cliff. I wasn't carrying on. I love all of you so much I hurt from it. But it was over." Her voice grew stronger. "After the funeral I came back to tell you the truth, to end all the deceptions, and then I was going to tell my parents, and then go back to London. But you brought the children to the airport, and I couldn't tell you in front of them, and later, at home, I saw the letter, and I knew I had to stay and help you."

"I didn't ask for your help. I didn't need it or want it."

"Yes, you did. You were worried, and it didn't matter what name you called me, you loved me and wanted me to stand with you. Garth, my love—"

"Don't call me that!"

She flinched as if he had struck her. "No, of course, I have no right. But I'm trying to tell you that by then the only deception was my name. Everything I felt for you was the truth. I love you, and we had a wonderful marriage—"

"We had no marriage at all! *What kind of monster are you that you would profit from your sister's death?"*

Sabrina broke. Sobs wracked her body, and she curled into a ball on the couch, her face in her hands. Garth tensed in his chair, torn apart, wanting to hold her and comfort her, remembering her body, her laughter, the love in her eyes—and despising her, despising himself.

"Get up," he said, his voice empty. "And get out of here. I can't bear to look at you. Go back to your own kind; that's where you belong."

"No. Not anymore." She walked blindly to the bathroom, and Garth heard the splashing of water. In a few minutes she came back, her face washed, the deadly pallor of her skin looking like wax. Tendrils of damp hair curled about her forehead. "Sabrina Longworth is dead. She died when the *Lafitte* went down. I'm someone different now; I don't even know who. I was going to London as Stephanie, so no one would ever know what had happened; that way, I knew the truth wouldn't accidentally get back to you and the children. I was going to keep it a secret, and I will, for the children, unless you decide to tell the truth. But that would be your decision. Because, either way, I've become someone else."

She put on the green suede blazer Garth had bought her in San Francisco and then pulled on her coat. "I want you to know that I love Penny and Cliff. They are so dear to me, their love meant so much to me ... I never had children, and I didn't pretend with them; it was so wonderful to love them and know they loved me—" She bent her head and waited until she could control her voice. "And I love you, my darling, with all my heart, more than I can ever tell you. I know you don't want to hear it, but you are my life and all my dreams, all I ever hoped I might someday find, and I wanted to make you happy. It was all wrong, I know; I did a terrible thing to you, and I knew from the beginning it could never end well, but before I left I wanted to be able to help you one last time, to do what I could—"

Garth's head was averted, his forehead resting on his hand. "Get out," he said, and he was crying.

Sabrina reached for her suitcase, then straightened. Most of what it contained was Stephanie's. She left it on the floor beside Garth's, picked up her shoulder bag and opened the door. She stood there a moment, looking at the back of his head, the thick dark hair mixed with gray, seeing in her mind the lock that fell over his forehead when he leaned forward that way.... *My love, my love, forgive me.*

Garth thought she was gone and turned to find her watching him. "Goddamn it, get out!" he cried through his tears. "And let me mourn my wife!"

Swiftly she left and pulled the door shut behind her, leaning against it, her heart pounding. It was over. She touched the door with her fingertips. "I love you," she said softly, and turned to walk down the flowered carpet to the elevator. She forced herself to stand straight, her head high, as she left the hotel in the rain.

Chapter 21

Mrs. Thirkell was just returning from the market, maneuvering her dripping umbrella and damp packages through the front door, when the cab from the airport pulled up. "Mrs. Andersen!" she cried, and stood in the pouring rain, holding the door while Sabrina paid the driver and ran into the house. "Come in, come in, oh, I am so glad to see you! And won't Miss de Martel be pleased! Let me take your coat and hat; there's a fire laid in the drawing room and one in my lady's . . . in your bedroom, and I'll bring you tea. Where would you like to go first?"

"My room, Mrs. Thirkell. And muffins and jelly with the tea, please. Is Miss de Martel in?"

"No, my lady, you just missed her." Mrs. Thirkell's forehead creased in confusion. "I'm sorry, I meant Mrs. Andersen. You're so alike—"

"It's all right; you needn't apologize." Stephanie turned to the stairway. "Many others have been unable to tell us apart."

"But, Mrs. Andersen! Where is your luggage?"

"I have none. When you bring the tea, Mrs. Thirkell, please bring the mail and today's *Times.*"

"Yes, my lady."

Sabrina smiled faintly and climbed the stairs to her room, pausing on the third floor to examine a bouquet of pink and

443

red carnations on the piano. "Until tonight," the card read. Gabrielle had an admirer. Brooks? Jolie had said they'd been dining together. Well, Gabrielle would soon tell her. In detail. She looked about the quiet drawing room, gleaming in soft lamplight. Mrs. Thirkell had not been idle; everything was exactly as it should be.

Except that it was empty, without the laughter of children and the caressing voice of a husband.

In the fourth-floor bedroom, she knelt to light the fire and then found she could not get up. She was so tired, her limbs dragging her down, that she stayed where she was, leaning against an ottoman and watching the leaping flames through half-closed eyes. Her thoughts were heavy and slow, creeping away from a hotel room in New York and slowly fastening on today and tomorrow and all the weeks to come, barren weeks without her family, long hours of making a new life that was neither hers nor Stephanie's. *How do I make a life for a person who never existed before?*

When Mrs. Thirkell knocked and brought in the tea tray, she got up and sat at the round table beside the window. She glanced at the small stack of mail. "Has Sidney Jones taken care of the rest of it?"

"He collects it every few days." She stood uncertainly. "Mrs. Andersen, may I ask . . . will you be staying long? Or entertaining? Or have you come back to sell this house? I don't know what plans I should make, do you see—"

Sabrina looked at her curved reflection in the silver teapot and the teapot's reflection in the rain-streaked window. There were two of everything. *Once there were two of me.* "I'll be staying permanently, Mrs. Thirkell." It was the first time she had said the words aloud; they were sharp blows, hammering down a lid. "I hope you will stay with me as you did with my sister."

"Oh, I will, of course I will, there's nothing I'd like better. But—your husband, ma'am? Your children? Your home in America?"

"This is my home," Sabrina said dismissively. "The children are with their father and in school, where they belong." *I have to say more; I can't let people think I've just abandoned them.* "Perhaps this summer they'll join me here. I don't see the *Times* on the tray."

"Oh, dear, I forgot, there seem to be so many things, all at once. I'll bring it, ma'am, and then I'll go back to the market, since I didn't buy enough for—will you be entertaining?"

"Not at first. But I'll be eating in."

Mrs. Thirkell left, returned with the newspaper and left again, admirably subduing her curiosity. When she returned an hour later to remove the tea tray, Sabrina had changed into a soft wool robe and was lying on the chaise in front of the fire. "Mrs. Andersen, it would be an honor for me to stay with you. I had the highest esteem and affection for Lady Longworth, and I miss her deeply. If I can stay with you, it will be almost as if I had not lost her."

"Thank you," Stephanie said. "I appreciate that more than I can say."

And neither of them ever again touched on the strangeness of Stephanie Andersen's unheralded arrival from America, without luggage, to make her permanent home in London and live her sister's life.

Yet there was another home, with shadowy rooms, footsteps and voices, that clung to the edges of her thoughts whatever she did. All night, restless between the silken sheets, she reached for Garth's hand or turned toward the remembered warmth of his body and the sheltering circle of his arms whenever she began to doze. But there was nothing, nothing, and each time she would come awake with a start of realization and remembrance, and a sinking emptiness within her that matched the emptiness of the bed and her silent, dark house.

But in the morning, on her way to work, she planned the first day of her new life: Nicholas and Brian at Ambassadors, a conference with Sidney about finances, lunch with Gabrielle and shopping. And in a few days she would begin to call her friends to let them know she was here.

At Ambassadors, Nicholas and Brian were discussing a small crack in a red-painted tulipwood cabinet and chest dated 1766. The drawers of the chest were decorated with square, Sevres porcelain plaques; the cabinet above it had round plaques centered in its doors; and atop the chest was a gilded clock with gold candelabra extending on each side, like arms in prayer, and two ebony figures perched on top. From the doorway Sabrina gazed in amusement at the absurd beauty of the piece. "Wherever did you find it?" she asked, walking in. "I haven't seen a Carlin for years."

Nicholas scrambled up, his hand on his chest. "My dear Stephanie! What a start you gave us! We had no idea . . . you should have let us know . . ."

"Brian," said Sabrina, "are you having trouble with your heart, too?"

"No," he said, smiling as he took her hand. "I'm glad to see you."

She nodded thoughtfully. "Nicholas, please come into my office. Brian, you'll take care of the showroom?"

"Of course."

"And I'd like to talk to you in a few minutes."

"Of course."

"Amiable fellow," said Nicholas, following her. "But tell me, dear Stephanie, however do you know the furniture of Martin Carlin? Sabrina never told us your knowledge was so extensive. I *am* impressed; it seems there is much about you we don't know."

She sat at the cherry table, running her fingers over its polished surface. "Nicholas, I understand your concern. You're afraid I'll interfere with your running of Ambassadors or sell it to someone else. Let me clarify things for you. First, Ambassadors is not for sale, to you or anyone else. Second, I intend to manage it, as Sabrina did, but with your participation. So you see, you need have been only half as worried as you were."

"My dear lady—"

"Excuse me." She went to the door. "Brian, could we have tea, please? And croissants." She returned to her chair and gazed at Nicholas. "In our recent telephone calls I had the impression you might be planning to conceal some inventory and financial matters from me."

"My dear Stephanie!"

"Of course, since Brian keeps the books and Sidney keeps an eye on Brian, you would have to be clever. But we both know you are clever. I thought a private discussion might make it unnecessary for me to speak to Brian or Sidney."

There was a pause. Nicholas's bouncing energy was stilled. "You understand, Stephanie, we had no idea when you would be back, or for how long, or, indeed, if at all. Even now, though you say you will manage the shop, I fail to see how you can do that from America. We are the ones with the day-to-day responsibility for—"

"I am here to stay, Nicholas. Living in my house on Cadogan Square and running Ambassadors."

"You have left your husband? And your children?"

"I am here to stay. We need not discuss it further. As for the partnership you wanted with Sabrina, I suggest this arrangement: you will supervise Ambassadors and Blackford's and buy from dealers. I will buy at auction for both shops and handle all home decorating and restoration. Brian will run the office—invoices, bank statements, correspondence, and so on—for Ambassadors, as Amelia does for Blackford's. Division of finances between us will be worked out with Sidney Jones. Does that meet with your approval?"

Speechless, Nicholas nodded.

"I will retain an auditor to check Brian's and Amelia's bookkeeping, since our finances will be intertwined. You and Brian and I will consult regularly on buying and selling, combining operations where possible for economy. Does this seem feasible to you?"

"Stephanie." Nicholas cleared his throat. "In China you were so quiet. Have you changed because Sabrina did not trust me?"

"On the contrary. She did trust you. But in the last few weeks, on the telephone, I found you evasive. I will not tolerate that."

"I assure you, Stephanie—"

"I'll have Sidney begin work on the partnership papers tomorrow. Will that be satisfactory?"

"Quite uncanny, you know—you are so like Sabrina. Uncanny. Did the two of you often think alike?"

"Often." She stood and held out her hand. "Nicholas, will we be friends?"

He jumped up. "Yes, yes indeed. Haven't we always been friends? In fact, I could not agree so readily to a partnership with anyone else. But you are quite extraordinary, my dear. And then, I must tell you, these last weeks I have discovered what a remarkable reputation Sabrina built for Ambassadors. If your skill is like hers, as your self-confidence seems to be, we have an amazing future. Indeed, there is no telling how far we can go."

"Yes, I thought you felt that way." She smiled so pleasantly that it was several minutes before Nicholas realized how well she had understood his hunger for a share in Ambassadors.

"Now, before I talk to Brian, what would you suggest for his salary? Perhaps a small percentage of ownership?"

Nicholas was confused. After taking the initiative, as Sabrina would, she asked his advice, as Stephanie would. Or, he realized, as if they already were partners. He made a suggestion. When she encouraged him, he made another, and soon they had worked out an arrangement that pleased them both. "I'll bring him in," Nicholas said, and then swiftly stood on tiptoe and kissed her cheek. "Remarkable," he said, and left the office.

Waiting for the two of them, Sabrina stood beside the table, feeling the blood course through her veins. She had taken a chance, guessing that Nicholas, in keeping back information, was preparing to try to wrest Ambassadors from her. And, because she'd been right, she was now fully in control, her energy, determination, and knowledge intact. With the security of two shops and Nicholas and Brian sharing the work, she could specialize in restoration and decorating and fill her evenings with a selective social life, seeing only those people she really wanted to see, not everyone who might be good for business.

And if she concentrated on all that, she could build a new life and keep hidden in a small corner of her thoughts the laughter of two children and the caressing voice of a husband.

"Lunch?" Gabrielle said, interrupting her thoughts. "I'm sorry to interrupt your work, Stephanie, but I thought you might have forgotten. And I've been looking forward to it all morning."

"It's all right, Gaby. We can go now."

They walked to Le Suquet because Gabrielle wanted fish. "We'll split the *fruit de mer* platter, shall we? It's too much for me but so beautiful I can't resist it. Oh, you don't know how happy I am you're here. You don't know how awful it is with no one to talk to. Oh, damn, of course you know, what am I saying? Stephanie, do you want to banish me or shall I just shut up and eat?"

"Neither." Sabrina found herself laughing. Gabrielle's mixture of cultivated childishness and genuine vulnerability was just what she needed. It's good for me, she thought, to have someone besides myself to worry about. "Tell me about Brooks," she said.

Gabrielle divided the seafood platter between them and buttered a second roll. "I'm amazingly hungry. For weeks I didn't eat, and now I eat all the time. He wants to marry me. I told him I had to talk to you first."

"Why?"

"Because to me you're the same as Sabrina, and of course she must have told you about me, and I don't have anyone else. There's Alexandra, but she's in Rio, and she never liked me anyway. I was going to call you in America, but now here you are. Don't you miss your children?"

"Yes."

"And your husband?"

"You were going to tell me about Brooks."

"That's right, I was. Well, he found his spies. One in the London office sold trade names and marketing strategy to Rymer Cosmetics, and another one in the Bern plant sold them chemical formulas. That's why it took Brooks so long to find them; he knew one person wouldn't have both kinds of information—except for me."

"But why did he believe you did it?"

"The one in Bern, the spy, told somebody I was selling information to Rymer. When the rumor spread, someone wrote to Brooks. Then Rymer came out with Brooks's fall line of cosmetics and he lost millions and he blamed me because I had access to his personal files. He put it all together and kicked me out. I don't know what I would have done without Sabrina. I never had the confidence in myself that she had, or your strength. The two of you always could get through bad times, I suppose because you had each other. I never had any—oh, damn, I'm sorry, Stephanie, I did it again. You must miss her terribly."

Sabrina was silent, waiting for the rush of pain and loneliness to subside. The maître d' approached and bent to her. "Mrs. Andersen, we wish to convey to you our condolences. We all admired Lady Longworth; she was gracious and unfailingly kind to everyone."

Sabrina bowed her head in acknowledgment. The pain had settled back to the dull ache she carried all the time—Stephanie, Garth, Penny, Cliff, a thousand might-have-beens. "Would you like to be married at Cadogan Square?" she asked Gabrielle.

"Oh, Stephanie, may we? How wonderful! I thought of it, but, of course, it was impossible without you, but now that you're here, it would be perfect."

"Come to dinner with Brooks on Friday, and we'll plan your wedding. Mrs. Thirkell will need to know the number of guests."

"And you'll stand up with me in the ceremony? I always wanted Sabrina to do it.... Stephanie, do you mind if I think of you as Sabrina? The two of you—it's very confusing, you know."

"I know."

After lunch, Sabrina had one more promise to keep. At Peter Dale, in the Royal Opera Arcade in Pall Mall, she browsed among antique suits of armor. "Not an entire suit," she explained to the proprietor. "Something smaller—"

"One moment. I have it." He had known Sabrina, and, after offering his sympathies in a voice that creaked like the armor he sold, he vanished into the back of the tiny shop to bring out a small shield brilliantly decorated with a griffin protecting a castle keep. "Used by one of the Cecils in practice jousts when he was about ten." It was perfect, Sabrina thought, and, as she wrote a check, she imagined Cliff showing it off and then hanging it on his bedroom wall to remind him he once had a mother who loved him.

At Falkiner's she put together a collection of artist's papers for Penny—Japanese parchment, watercolor, marbled sheets in fantastic designs and vellum with fine deckle edges. At Winsor and Newton she bought one of their largest boxes of oil paints, then, caught up in her vision of Penny's delight, she stopped at Collet's for a set of Oriental brushes and ink sticks.

"Brian," she said, when she returned to Ambassadors, "how does one ship this unwieldy mass to America?"

"The same way we ship unwieldy art. Leave it to me, Mrs. Andersen."

"Wait. One thing more." She disappeared into her office and returned in a moment with a sealed envelope. "It all goes to this address."

A shield, art supplies, a letter.

"My dearest Penny and Cliff: I think of you and I miss you, and every time I close my eyes I see you very clearly. I can't reach across the ocean to hug you, so instead I'm sending you the presents I promised, for now and an early Christmas. I love you both. I love you both."

And a note for Garth.

"Whatever you decide to tell Penny and Cliff, please let them have these gifts. I won't write to them again, or send them anything else, unless you tell me I may, but I promised to send them presents as soon as I arrived in London. Please let me keep my promise. It is the last favor I will ask of you."

She had nothing more to do for her family now except long for them and wait for the pain of her longing to diminish. But she had forgotten her mother.

Laura called on Saturday noon as Sabrina and Gabrielle were going out to buy a wedding dress. "Stephanie, what in heaven's name is going on? Garth says you're staying in London indefinitely. Just what does that mean?"

"What it sounds like, Mother. I'm living here now."

"And Garth and your children?"

"Mother, you know the answer to that. They're in Evanston."

"You've left your children?"

"I left . . . Yes. They're with Garth."

"And you've left him?"

"Yes."

"For how long?"

"For . . . as long as necessary."

"Necessary! To do what? To destroy a wonderful marriage, a fine home, the lives of two—"

"Please, Mother, don't . . ."

"Why shouldn't I? Do you know what you've thrown away? The best—"

"Mother, stop it. Please. Garth and I both decided I should leave. We have more than enough pain without your making it worse. Someday I may be able to tell you the whole story, but I can't now. You'll just have to trust me, that I'm doing what I have to do."

"Stephanie," Gordon said on the extension phone, his voice like a frail thread. "You don't love Garth anymore?"

I love him with all my heart. I love him more with every mem-

ory that haunts me and clings to me through the long endless nights. "There are problems I can't talk about," she answered. "You'll have to believe that. And trust me. I'm sorry I've caused you unhappiness—"

"So soon after Sabrina!" Laura cried. "You might have waited and dealt us just one blow at a time."

"Yes, Mother. It was thoughtless of me. I apologize."

"I don't need your sarcasm—"

"What will you do?" Gordon interrupted. "Alone in London."

"I've formed a partnership with Nicholas Blackford to run Ambassadors. I'll keep Sabrina's house, make friends, make a life for myself."

"Terrible," Laura moaned. "Terrible. The last thing we ever would have expected. We were so sure of you."

"Yes. I'm sorry. I let you down."

"But you'll go back, of course. You'll think things over and then go back to your family. Women are doing that these days; you read about it all the time: someone who seems perfectly happy suddenly ups and decides she needs space, whatever that is. I don't understand what these women mean when they say they need space. Most of them mean they want a lover. Is that what you want?"

"No."

"Well, if it is, have one and get it out of your system and then go back to your family. If you're not looking for a lover, what are you looking for? A career? You had one, that little place, what was it, Collectibles. Are you looking for a new career?"

"No."

"Then what are you looking for? What do you expect to find by living in Sabrina's house and running her shop?" Sabrina did not answer. "Stephanie? Stephanie, are you trying to pretend you're Sabrina? I remember you always talked about her glamorous life in London, her successes . . . and I suppose I encouraged you . . . is that what you're trying to do? Finally, after all these years, to turn yourself into Sabrina?"

"Mother." Sabrina's voice caught between an involuntary laugh and a sob. "I am trying to be myself."

"Do you know who that is?" Gordon asked.

"Not always," she said. "But I'm finding out."

How simple that sounded: *Finding out.* And I will, she told herself the next day as she took a taxi to Kensington Cemetery. *It will just take a little while.*

She walked slowly toward the small rise in the ground where they all had stood not so long ago. The cemetery was gray and damp, as she remembered it, wavering in a mist that made the stones seem to soften and change shape. The trees wept clear drops, and puddles on the walks were small flat mirrors reflecting the scudding clouds, gray on gray.

She stood beside the grave, letting her memories weave in and out—childhood, school days, Juliette, visits in New York, visits in London, childhood again, servants packing, the strangeness of new schools, two sisters always holding hands. But soon the dampness cut through her coat and the suit beneath it, and, shivering, she turned and left.

Near the gate, a tall man got out of a waiting car. "Your housekeeper told me you were here," Dmitri said. "May I drive you home?"

She looked at his thin face, dark eyes beneath fierce brows, deep lines on either side of his firm mouth. His arm was extended to help her into the car. She remembered a young boy forcing himself to be brave while men in heavy boots searched his room and clomped above the cellar where he was hiding two American girls. *He wants to protect me,* she thought. But his eyes were gentle and undemanding. He was offering friendship. "Yes," she said. "I'd like a ride home."

Chapter 22

No one met Garth's plane from New York; no one expected him for two more days. He had left the hotel early Tuesday, phoning Rolf from LaGuardia to say he would not be at the executive committee meeting, and flew back on the first plane leaving for Chicago. He had not slept, and in his fatigue everything seemed exaggerated: too loud, too bright, voices clattering off hard walls and floors. But at home, when he unlocked his door and stepped inside, the silence overwhelmed him. An empty house. Penny and Cliff at school. His wife dead. Her impostor in London. A silent, empty house.

He stood in the center of the kitchen and wondered what to do. Nothing that he could think of seemed worth doing. He looked about at the neat kitchen, at the couch and low table where Penny's sketches lay beside a book Stephanie had been reading, at the breakfast-room table. A picture sprang to Garth's memory: nighttime, very late, the house dark and hushed. Penny and Cliff were asleep, and he and Stephanie sat together at the round table, eating pumpkin pie from a single plate. Only it hadn't been Stephanie. That had been—

"NO!" he cried, a long anguished note that echoed through the empty rooms. Snatching her book from the table, he

454

hurled it at the wall. Its pages fluttered as it fell to the floor, and Garth sank to the couch, weeping for his wife and the shattered pieces of his world.

Exhausted, he fell asleep, and when he woke it was dark. Confused, he fumbled for the light and looked at his watch to discover it was only five o'clock. He shivered; they had turned the furnace down when they left, and the house was cold. Then he remembered everything that had happened, and he could feel his anger settling, spreading through his body in a cold viscous mass, inseparable from the flow of his blood and the pumping of his heart and the roar in his ears.

He had to move, act, occupy his mind. "At least be practical," he said aloud, and called Vivian to tell her the meeting had been shorter than expected; he would pick up Penny and Cliff in an hour.

"Come for dinner," she urged. "And tell us about New York."

"Not this time. Give me a rain check."

"Then let your offspring eat before you pick them up. They helped make the food; I think they should be compelled to eat it."

"All right. Eight o'clock?"

"Eight o'clock. Garth, whatever it is, eat something. You'll feel better."

So it was in his voice. Well, why not? How much anger could one person contain before it spilled over into public view? He unpacked, washed his face, changed his shirt and downed two quick Scotches. Refilling the ice cube tray, he saw that the refrigerator was full. How thoughtful; the bitch had left them well taken care of before she flew the coop to go back to her European playground.

He paced the house, his thoughts flying wildly like debris from an explosion; nothing was whole, nothing was solid. Why hadn't he suspected her? He'd been over it time and time again, trying to understand how he had been so thoroughly taken in. Looking back, remembering slips of the tongue and quick recoveries, atypical behavior, lapses in memory, he could not understand it. He was a trained observer, a man who collected facts and analyzed them. Why had he been so easily deceived? He didn't know. Nothing made sense; he had nothing to hold onto except his house and his children, and that was why he had to see them as soon as possible; they were all he could be sure of.

He left early for the Goodmans' house, driving slowly on snow-packed side streets. He was rehearsing.

I have something to tell the two of you; it's not easy, it's not very nice—

Sit down, both of you, I want to talk to you about your mother—

I have to tell you, some time ago your mother was in an accident—no, not on the bicycle, another accident, on a yacht, in Europe; you see, the woman who's been living here, the one who had the accident on the bicycle—

The woman who's been living here, making fools of us, laughing at us for loving her and needing her while she was playing a game—

How the hell did a man tell that to his children?

He brought Penny and Cliff home, and the three of them sat in the breakfast room, eating ice cream and pretzels.

"Mom doesn't think this is a great combination," said Cliff. "But I like it."

"It's ice cream and dill pickles she really doesn't like," Penny said. "And I think she's right."

"I do, too," Cliff admitted. "Dad, can we call her in London?"

"No."

"Why not? You called every night when she was there after Aunt Sabrina's funeral."

"That was different."

"Why?"

"She was very unhappy then . . ."

"Well, maybe she's unhappy now, missing us."

"No, Cliff."

"But why? Does it cost a lot?"

"More than a dollar a minute. Are you willing to pay for it?"

"Yeah, if you won't. If that's the only way I can talk to Mom."

"Daddy?" Penny said. "Why are you mad? Are you mad at Mommy? Is that why you came home early? Is she mad at you?"

Through the coldness that gripped him, Garth felt a flash of wry humor. We take pride in our intelligent children, and then we have to live with the fact that they see through us.

But why didn't these intelligent children see through that woman and know she was not their mother?

Because they are innocent and trusting and she took advantage of them.

"Daddy?"

"It's true, Penny, I am angry. I'll tell you why." He searched for a way to begin. His children watched him, their bright, curious faces just beginning to be apprehensive. Garth let the moment drag on, unable to say the first word. Finally, he opened his hands and dropped them in resignation. He could not do it. Later, perhaps, when the time was right. But not now. "I'm angry because your mother is off in London instead of being here with us. And because she thinks she has to stay there for awhile, to think about her life away from everything here."

"But she already did that," said Penny, biting her lip. "In China."

"That's right, she did. And remember, when we talked about it, I said that often people need to get away from their everyday lives to think about themselves in different ways. But sometimes they have to do it more than once, or for a longer time."

"But when we talked you said you weren't going to get a divorce."

Garth felt a wave of nausea and clenched his teeth. No divorce; a surgical operation: cut her out of our lives. "We're not talking about divorce, Penny. Look, it's late; don't you two have homework?"

"We did it this afternoon," said Cliff. "Is Mom coming back?"

"I don't know."

"She is!" Penny screamed. "She is! I know she is! You're lying!"

"I'm not lying!" Garth said, more sharply than he intended. He lowered his voice; he had to make them understand. "Penny, sometimes people do things that may not seem right or sensible to you, but that doesn't mean they're wrong. Your mother and I had a ... disagreement about something, and she thought she'd go back to London for awhile. You knew she was going anyway, to take care of her sister's business. The only change is that she's going to stay longer than she thought—"

"How long?"

"I don't know."

"You do! You and Mommy decided and you're lying about it! It's not fair, nobody asked Cliff and me what *we* wanted and we live here, too, and she's *our* mother, and I'm going to tell her we're waiting for her to come home and you can't stop me!"

She dashed from the room and up the stairs. Cliff looked at his father and spoke carefully, trying to be more grown up than his sister. "She is coming back, isn't she? I mean, you said you don't know, but isn't that what scientists always say when they don't know *exactly* what's going to happen?"

Garth nodded. "That's what scientists say."

"Dad." Cliff squirmed in his chair. "Dad, you *want* her to come back, don't you?"

"It's . . . complicated, Cliff. I can't give you a simple answer."

Cliff squeezed his eyes shut. "Bullshit."

"Now, that's enough! I don't talk to you that way, and I expect the same courtesy from you. Do you think I like this? Damn it, things are happening that I can't help. Can you begin to understand that? If you're old enough to tell your father he's talking bullshit, you're old enough to listen when I tell you that *I can't control everything that happens to me.*"

"Well, you can't blame us if you screw up your life!" Shocked at his own words, Cliff drew back. "I'm sorry, Dad, I'm sorry. I didn't mean it."

Garth felt the ground pull out from beneath him. His children never spoke to him like this; Stephanie wouldn't allow it. Stephanie held them all together. Now things fell apart—the center did not hold. He started to say something, then let it go. He pushed back his chair, wanting a drink.

"Dad?"

"Yes, Cliff."

"Do you love Mom?"

In the silence they could hear the humming of the electric clock and the refrigerator. "Do you know," Garth said, "when we were married, your mother was so beautiful everyone stared at her; they thought I was the luckiest guy in the world. And when we moved here and you were born—"

"Why won't you answer?" Cliff shouted. *"We* love her; how come you don't? She loves you, too. What's wrong with you? Oh, shit." He rubbed his eyes. "I guess I don't want to talk about it. I'm going to write to Mom. I suppose you don't like *that,* either."

We're going to cut her out of our lives, Garth thought. That means no communication. He kept his voice even. "Maybe we should leave her alone, let her have some time without any contact from us. Maybe that's what she wants."

"How do you know? You don't care what she wants. Anyway, you told me scientists shouldn't make decisions until they have as many facts as possible. Shouldn't Mom have facts, too?"

"What facts?"

"That we love her," Cliff said reprovingly. "And we want her to come back. And," he added in a burst of inspiration, "if she doesn't come back, we'll go to London and *get* her!"

Crushed between his anger and love for his children, Garth tried to speak, and no words came out.

"Well," Cliff said, emboldened by his father's silence, "I don't get this whole thing, but I'm writing to Mom. Penny and I can mail our letters together. I might even call her one of these days. Out of my allowance."

"We'll talk about it again tomorrow, Cliff. All right?"

"Yeah, but we're still going to write to her tonight."

Garth nodded. "I'll be up to say good night to both of you later."

Bitch, he thought, and repeated it, the vicious word like a hammer blow as he sat alone and poured himself a drink. Look what you've done to them. They'd be better off if they knew you were dead.

If *who* was dead? he asked himself. And answered unclearly: I don't know.

Nat called him in his office the next day. "Just heard you were back. Good meeting?"

"I didn't go. A change in schedule."

"And Stephanie? Did her schedule change, too?"

"No."

"So she's in London now?"

"Yes."

"When does she get back?"

"She doesn't."

"She— What does that mean?"

"She's staying there. Nat, I don't want to talk about it."

"So I gather. Dolores will ask me questions."

"If you'll forgive my saying it, Dolores's questions are your problem, not mine."

"An indisputable fact. I have a couple of days off next week; we could go ice-fishing."

"You are inventing a couple of days off."

"So I am. But my patients will survive. Shall we take some time in the wilds and perhaps get a new perspective on the world?"

"I don't want to leave Penny and Cliff."

"For a day or two?"

"Nat, let me get used to being a single parent."

There was a pause. "Right. Then how about dinner with us? Dolores will ask that, too."

"You come here. I'll cook something in a wok. Did you know that almost any idiot can make an acceptable meal in a wok?"

"Dolores would prefer cooking for you."

"And I prefer cooking for her. Tell her I'll call soon. And Nat—thank you."

Others called as the days passed, asking when Stephanie would be home; and they asked, too, in the faculty club, the library, even in the grocery store. "She must feel lost in London," said Linda, inviting Garth and the children to dinner. "And I'm lost without her. We have an estate sale coming up just after the first of the year and I need her. She'll be home soon, won't she? After all, it's getting close to Christmas."

To everyone, he answered that he did not know.

Liar, he lashed out at himself at night, in the silence of his bedroom. Coward. Perpetuating the lie. How much longer will you keep it up? Who are you to talk about deception when you're as guilty of it as they were?

He heard Penny and Cliff talking in Cliff's room as they wrote another letter to London.

The three of us—Sabrina, Stephanie and I—caught in their damned deception, entangled in it as the days pass, until there seems no way to end it without inflicting pain on those we would protect.

He understood that now.

At night he lay alone in the four-poster bed in a room filled with ghosts: the fragrance of her clothes, the sound of her laughter, memories of a woman who had become his light and life. He held himself carefully still along the edge of the bed, for every movement sent ripples of longing through his muscles and set his blood pounding until he forgot his anger and reached out unthinkingly to pull her warm body to his. He could feel her against him, hear himself tell her he loved her and feel the warm whisper of her breath as she answered him, again and again: *I love you.*

But his arm found empty space, the sheets cold and taut, and with a cry of fury he flung the blanket away and left the bed, pulled on a robe and sat for hours before the dead coals in the living room fireplace. He would read until a memory touched him: the two of them sitting here, reading, looking up to share a glance in a quiet so deep it seemed they were the only two people alive in the world. Then, sick with loneliness, he would close his book and stare at the gray landscape of the cold fireplace, brooding and growing fearful of something that was happening to him.

He was having trouble separating his wife from the woman who had lived with him for the past three months.

His wife of twelve years was dead, but how did he mourn her when he had only lost her a few days ago?

Who are you mourning? he asked his reflection in the dark living room window a week after his return. My dead wife. Who died twice. Once off the Mediterranean coast and once in a hotel in New York.

Two separate women. One left him; the other casually took her place, toyed with their lives and kept her secret long past the time when she should have revealed it.

But she had said she wanted to end the deception. All the deceptions, she had said.

Then why hadn't she?

Garth stood at his front window, gazing at the ghostly sphere of the Victorian streetlight through his transparent reflection. He was not able to tell his children the truth. Had she faced the same indecision, trying and failing, saying, as he did, "Later, when the time is right"?

He didn't know. But one thing he now believed. His wife of twelve years had wanted more than a brief trip to the Orient. Oh, yes, he believed that now. She had wanted to be on her own, loose and free, shed of her husband and family. For as long as it pleased her. There was no rush to return. After all, her sister was filling in.

Why hadn't she come to him, to talk, to see what they could salvage together instead of planting her sister and taking off on an experiment that shut him out completely?

Because he would have chalked it up as another example of her dissatisfaction—with him, with his job and salary, with Evanston, with the life she led, especially when compared with the glittering star of Sabrina's London life. He would have accused her of wanting to be Sabrina.

And he would have been right. Because that was exactly what she did want. And finally got. Sabrina's life, ready-made, a home, wealth, social life, status, friends—and lovers.

His mourning for her was subtly shifting to anger, and at the same time his thoughts were turning to Sabrina. It had been Stephanie's idea to change places. Did Sabrina come to Evanston as a game—or as a favor to Stephanie? It was the first time he had asked that question.

On Monday, he came home from the university just as Penny and Cliff arrived, and together they all saw the strange-shaped package from London on the porch. He watched as they excitedly untied knots, ripped off heavy tape and tore open the layers of protective wrapping paper.

"Oh, Dad," Cliff breathed as he lifted the shield. He studied it from all angles, then slipped it on his arm, positioning it to cover his body. "I'll hang it on the wall in my room, okay?"

"Look, look," Penny bubbled, setting out the packages of colored papers in a circle around her, with the box of oil paints in the center beside a bundle of Japanese brushes and ink sticks. "Mommy knew, she knew exactly what I wanted, I never told her I wanted the ink sticks, but she knew, oh, Daddy, look how many kinds of paper, here, feel the edges of these . . . Oh, look, this is for you."

Garth touched the envelope. His name was on it. Penny pushed it into his fingers and slowly he opened it and read the brief message. ". . . Please let me keep my promise. It is the last favor I will ask of you."

The words wavered before his eyes. He could hear her voice and see her mouth; he could see the light in her eyes when she looked at the children.

She loves them.

Chapter 23

Alexandra flew in from Rio and came for tea, unashamedly curious. "I heard you were here for good, that you dealt smartly with Nicholas and are now doing business with him and that you have had dinner twice in a row with a handsome, unknown male of distinguished bearing."

Sabrina laughed with a delight that cut through the numbness of the past two weeks. She may have thought her life lay in pieces, but some things stayed the same; here was Alexandra to prove it. "His name is Dmitri Karras and he hid me in a cellar when I was eleven."

Alexandra's eyes gleamed. "You told part of that story at your birthday party. Do I get the rest of it some time? Or will it be like the one you never finished the day Scotland Yard intruded?"

"This one I promise to finish. How long will you be in London?"

"Long enough to close Antonio's flat, catch up on gossip—"

"Which you are doing admirably."

"And buy out Harrods, Zandra Rhodes and Fortnum and Mason."

"Are there no stores in Rio?"

"Honey, you wouldn't believe the stores in Rio. Everything anyone could want. But I want London, and London it isn't. I suppose I'll get used to it after awhile, but until then, if I can buy out a few stores and ship everything across the ocean, why not? Do you have time to shop with me, or are you too busy marrying off Gaby and Brooks?"

"Is there anything about me you haven't heard?"

"I haven't heard how you feel about leaving a couple of kids back in the States with their father."

Sabrina put down her cup with a shaking hand. Everyone mentioned it, obliquely or carefully—you must miss them, my dear; it must be difficult for you—but no one spoke out with Alexandra's bluntness; no one had challenged her to a direct answer. And no one knew that Penny's and Cliff's letters lay on her bedside table, read and reread each night and answered in her thoughts but never on paper, not until Garth gave her permission to write to them. "I don't discuss my feelings," she said.

"I know, honey, or I would have heard about it. But I thought you might like a sympathetic ear. Sabrina and I never talked about feelings much, but when we said goodbye, just before that damned cruise, she kissed me. Surprised me—it wasn't like her, and I pulled away. I think it hurt her; she was being honest about her feelings and I didn't let her. I thought about that after she died. That's why I'm keeping my house for when we visit London. Antonio wanted to keep his apartment, but I won't sell my house; it's Sabrina's, too. Which reminds me—while I'm here I could introduce you to some people for business and pleasure, get you started, help take your mind off our kids."

"I really just want to be quiet and alone."

"Brooding. An unhealthy pastime. Are you going to see them soon?"

"You don't give up, do you?"

"Come on, lady, you must miss them. And also your handsome if slightly stuffy husband. Don't you want to unburden?"

"I can't. It hurts to talk. It hurts all the time, I miss them so much, and if I had any tears left I'd walk around in a pool of my own making. What good does it do to talk? I want them close to me, I want the feel of a place with people who love me and need me . . . oh, damn, look what I've done, I've started and now I can't stop. Have some more tea; I'll be back in a minute."

"No, stay. My God, I'm sorry, I didn't know it was that bad. But then why did you leave?"

"I had to."

"He kicked you out?"

"I had to leave. I had no choice. I can't go back, and I can't talk about it."

A shudder swept her, like the trembling of a leaf, and Alexandra said quickly, "Honey, I didn't know. I won't bring it up again. I don't know anybody who feels that way about families; most of them leave it all to servants and boarding schools. I find it pretty scary, if you want to know. I'm not sure I want a family of my own if there's so much . . . *emotion* involved."

In spite of herself, Sabrina laughed. "There is if you want it."

They sat together in friendly silence. "Well," Alexandra said, "what about Dmitri of the cellar? How do you have dinners with him and still be quiet and alone?"

"Dmitri is a friend."

"So am I."

"Then I'll have dinner with you, too."

"I'd like that. I wish we had more time; I have this crazy feeling I've known you for years, because of Sabrina, but then I want to get to know you better. What the hell am I going to do in the middle of Brazil without you? Come to my wedding! Will you? You've got to come; I won't consider it legitimate unless you're there."

"When is it?"

"Christmas Eve or Christmas Day, whichever suits the Guaranis. Can you imagine waiting for permission to get married from a bunch of Indians who have to consult the stars or the moon or the shape of ant hills, or some such thing? Do you think I'm crazy?"

"No. I think you're doing what you want to do."

"You're the only one with sense enough to say that and not ask me if I'm in love. Say you'll come to the wedding."

"I can't, Alexandra. I have to stay in one place for awhile until I get straightened out."

Alexandra nodded. "I thought you'd say that. But you'll be here, whenever I'm in London?"

"Where would I go?"

"Back to America, to your husband and children."

The smile faded from Sabrina's face. "No. I'll be here. And I'll be glad to see you. I hope you come often."

"As often as I can. If you change your mind, you can just show up at the wedding, you know, without warning."

Sabrina shook her head. "I won't change my mind. But I'll give you my blessing and kiss you. And this time you won't pull back."

They looked at each other. "You know, honey, if I walked in here right now, for the life of me I couldn't say whether you were Sabrina or Stephanie."

"I know," Sabrina said. "That's the way it should be."

Others said the same; invitations poured in from hostesses who declared Stephanie the sensation of the season for taking Sabrina's place with such panache. And then a new story obliterated all others. On December 17, the *Times* of London featured a front-page article on art thefts and forgeries written by Michel Bernard, with photographs by Jolie Fantome. The article appeared simultaneously in the international edition of the *Herald Tribune* published in Paris, *Die Welt* in Germany and *The New York Times*. Within hours of its appearance, a tempest of whispers and telephone calls swept it through restaurants, clubs, boutiques and every art and antique gallery in London. Sabrina was awakened with the news by a frantic early-morning call from Nicholas, who remembered seeing Westbridge Imports and Rory Carr listed in Ambassadors' ledgers.

"All I ask, dear Stephanie, is are we involved? Blackford's is not. I recall meeting this Carr several times, but I never bought from him. Sabrina did; there are several porcelains listed—"

"Which porcelains, Nicholas?"

He read the descriptions. Dancers, animals, figures, birds. No Meissen stork. Of course not; the record and invoice had been destroyed soon after the stork was broken. Somewhere in the books at Westbridge, Ambassadors would be listed with dozens of other galleries, but Michel and Jolie's story did not mention Ambassadors at all and there was no reason to connect them. No one would even be interested in such a small detail when the story was already splashed in sensational headlines: multi-millionaire Max Stuyvesant, his personal art collection, his smuggling network and dealings with forgers, murder on the Mediterranean and so many dead, among them the beautiful Lady Sabrina Longworth.

"We are not involved," Sabrina said. "The porcelains Sabrina bought from Westbridge were genuine; she told me she checked their provenance."

"But are you sure?" Nicholas persisted. "I don't like to press you, Stephanie, I know this brings back dreadful memories—"

"Nicholas, I will say it once more. We are not involved. There is no danger. But rumors can be deadly and if I ever hear you question Ambassadors' reputation or integrity, I will not hesitate to dissolve our partnership and purchase your half. That should set your mind at rest."

"Good heavens, Stephanie, I never meant to imply ... I trusted Sabrina; I admired her. But she was on that yacht; I had to make sure—"

"And now you have. So there is no need for further discussion."

"None. Of course, none. Will you be in the shop today?"

"Of course."

She was in her office every day, catching up on the past three months, poring over auction records, preparing for the time when she would begin buying and decorating again. She felt she was wandering in an unmarked land between past and future, building a barrier between her work and life of today and her memories of a sister, a husband, children, a home. She lived one day at a time. To plan ahead was to admit that the door was locked on the past. She knew it was, but, still, it was easier to live in the present.

Olivia Chasson was part of the present and she called, inviting her to dinner. "Just a small party; I was Sabrina's friend and patron, and I want to get to know you as well as I knew her."

"I'm sorry, I'm having dinner with a friend—"

"Bring him, my dear. I assume he would be comfortable with us?"

Is he our kind? Sabrina translated silently. "His name is Dmitri Karras—"

"Oh, international banking. We met at lunch after Sabrina's funeral; we have several friends in common. Do bring him."

Fourteen people sat down to dinner in Olivia's house near Belgrave Square. They greeted Sabrina eagerly, getting through their condolences as quickly as possible so they could ask her for inside information on the smuggling and forgery

467

scandal; the second installment had appeared in that morning's paper.

They discussed it with the relish reserved for the downfall of the powerful but also with wariness, since they all were collectors investing in art and antiques and no one knew what revelations lay in future installments.

Over the consommé, they asked Sabrina about detecting forgeries. She answered briefly, describing types of clay, glazes, paints and designs. She explained how ultraviolet light could sometimes detect false or double glazing but not always, and less and less reliably with improved glazes. "Much of it is instinct," she said. "If you study details, you begin to get a feel for style and treatment that often makes it possible to distinguish an original from a copy"— she hesitated for a fraction of a minute, and then went smoothly on —"by examining them. Usually, though, we first check the provenance of an object, looking for clues that help us tell our clients whether a work is an original or a forgery. In my experience, few forgeries go undetected in the long run."

Her low, clear voice had captured the guests' attention. "Fascinating," someone said as she listened to the echo of her words. "But that wasn't Max's line, was it?"

Dmitri put his hand on her arm, but Sabrina did not need him. She raised her chin and looked coolly down the length of the table. "I do not discuss Max Stuyvesant or any of his activities."

"Well, really!" said the same voice, but whispers cut across it.

"Don't be so stupid; her sister—"

"Just a few weeks ago—"

"Really quite idiotic of you to bring it up."

Olivia's strong voice overrode the whispers. "Stephanie is my guest, not a hired art expert. We are welcoming her to London." She turned to Sabrina, on her right. "My dear, you will answer no more questions. Will you have more wine?"

Sabrina and Dmitri exchanged a smile. "You have forbidden me to answer you," she said to Olivia. Laughter rippled around the table; someone asked about a new game in Monte Carlo, and Dmitri began to tell Sabrina about the villa he had just bought outside Athens, near the villas of his sisters and their families. She listened in silence, relaxed and grateful for his presence. He reminded her of Garth in his quiet way, ready to help her if she needed it but not forcing himself upon her. Even the light in his eyes . . . But no, nothing was the same as the light in Garth's eyes. "It is quite lovely," Dmitri said of his villa. "The air smells of flowers, thyme and oregano. No one gossips and we do not discuss business. There is music, and stories of gods and goddesses and the glories of the past. We pretend the present does not exist. Will you come one day and see it for yourself?"

She smiled. "Perhaps, one day."

After coffee and cognac, Olivia invited Sabrina and Dmitri to view her art gallery. "I want it enlarged and redecorated," she said. "With better lighting. And I want you to do it, Stephanie."

They stood in the doorway, looking down the long, arched room. "Sabrina was after me for years to modernize it, but I never cared until now. It won't do for my new sculptures."

"What kind are they?" Dmitri asked.

"Modern. Ten, fifteen, twenty feet high. Frankly, they look like plumbers' nightmares and carpenters' drunken binges, but I only say that privately. Experts call them art and good investments. Some museum in Boston has already offered to call them the Chasson collection if I leave it to them in my will. What would you do with them?"

"Forget the museum," Dmitri suggested. "Build the Olivia Chasson playground. Children can climb on them."

Olivia laughed and clapped him on the shoulder. "You finance it; Stephanie will design it."

"And name it," Sabrina said. *"Cacher et chasser."*

Dmitri chuckled at the pun on Olivia's last name. "Hide-and-seek," he said, as Olivia laughed delightedly. "Wonderful," she said. "Wonderful. I feel I haven't lost Sabrina at all. You can begin remodeling the gallery after the new year, my dear Stephanie." And she returned to her guests, happily repeating the French words.

Dmitri took Sabrina's hand. "A callous woman. *She* does not feel she has lost your sister."

"But she hasn't," Sabrina said, moving away as she began to walk the length of the gallery. "With only a brief interruption, she has before her a woman who looks the same, treats her as an equal and will help redecorate her house. What more could she want?"

"A real person."

"Really? Most people are satisfied with the surface."

Dmitri followed her, and they gazed at the Chasson collection of French and German oil paintings. "I would like to get to know you better, if you would let me. You are a remarkable woman."

Sabrina turned from a brooding portrait of a long-dead wool merchant and looked into the living warmth of Dmitri's eyes.

"We've had dinner together three times," he said, "and we are no closer than when I first saw you."

"I hope we're friends," she said quietly.

"Friends. Of course. I want much more than that, you know. But I am in no hurry."

"How thoughtful," she murmured dryly. "Since I am still married."

"It is not necessary to remind me. You are also still in love with your husband."

She froze, then turned to walk back the way they had come. "I think we need not discuss that."

"Please." He put his hand on her arm. "I apologize. There is such a difference between us, in the way we see each other. In a way, you know, I've spent a lifetime thinking about you. One memorable afternoon, and you have been clear in my mind ever since; I never forgot you or your sister."

They strolled on, and Sabrina relaxed as Dmitri talked about himself, especially about the reporter who had "adopted" him and his sisters after photographing them at the embassy. "He had no children, and we became his family. He got my father a new job, sent us to school, helped me get a scholarship to Cambridge, even tried to find me a wife." He smiled. "There he failed."

They neared the end of the gallery. "I know I stayed in your past," Dmitri said. "But you must understand that you and your sister have been in my dreams since I was a child, weaving through my life, appearing at odd times when I least expected you—sometimes, you will forgive me, at awkward times."

"You mean when you were with other women."

"Even then." He continued talking, but Sabrina was no longer listening. He had described her dream of Garth, and his words brought the dream back: Garth's touch on her hand, his mouth covering hers, his quiet voice, his eyes desiring her, the warmth of their bodies when they lay together after making love. Loneliness swept her; she felt lost. *Oh, my love, my dear love, I miss you so, I need you, I can't bear* ... and then she clamped down her silent cry and listened again to Dmitri.

"... your beauty and courage," he was saying. "And your joy in being alive. I suppose I have always loved you because you showed me those things when I was young, and from then on no one else ever showed them to me in the same way. I always hoped I would find you some day and give you a dream to match mine. I never thought I would find you through a tragedy."

Suddenly she felt smothered by his insistence on bringing back the past. *I have to get away, I can't breathe, I can't think ... I want my sister. I want my family. I want Garth.*

"Stephanie, what is it? What have I said?"

Breathing quickly, she tried to smile. "Too much talk of the past when I'm supposed to be building a new life. Shall we go back to the others?"

"But wait, we are friends? If I promise not to talk about the past, we will be friends?"

"Yes. Of course." Why did everyone push her so? Why did they try to shape her to their own desires? Couldn't they leave her alone to be herself? *I would have shaped myself to Garth's desire because he never demanded it. He did not even ask. And never will.*

"Of course we are friends," she said, returning to the party. But she forgot him as Gabrielle's wedding day approached and, to keep from thinking about Garth, she forced herself to concentrate on details that Mrs. Thirkell could have handled admirably. And when the guests began to arrive, she knew she had succeeded in creating a setting Gabrielle would love, even if she had failed in pushing Garth from her thoughts.

In the drawing room, bouquets of violet orchids and white roses from Olivia's greenhouses glowed softly in the light from white candles in silver candelabra as fifty guests sat on velvet chairs listening to duets played on a harp and piano. "Exactly the way Sabrina would have done it," the guests said again and again. "How wonderfully well you have kept her spirit alive."

Gabrielle wore ivory peau de soie with a satin cape trimmed in ivory and gold braid. She admired herself in the tall mirror in Sabrina's bedroom. "It's as close as I can come to white without pretending I'm a virgin. But I feel virginal. Silly, isn't it?"

"No," said Sabrina beside her, wearing coral velvet. "You look lovely. As if you're standing at the beginning of the world."

"But that's exactly how I feel! How on earth did you— Oh, how stupid, forgive me, Stephanie. You shouldn't have to listen to my sentimental ravings when your own marriage is—"

"Gaby, I'll listen to your ravings if you promise not to talk about my marriage."

"That's fair. But now I feel guilty about raving."

"Then I'll run downstairs for a word with Mrs. Thirkell. We should start in about five minutes, I think."

In the drawing room, Brooks stood before the fireplace with its bower of white and lilac, calmly surveying the room; a friend from Paris stood at his side. Alexandra sat in the first row; she was leaving the next day to join Antonio in Rio, and three days later, on Christmas Eve, they would be married.

I am surrounded by romance, Sabrina thought. For years no one got married; everyone was getting divorced. Now my house is filled with love and marriage. The words echoed within her and she wanted to send everyone home, to curl up in the silence of her room and spread out her memories, one by one, like photographs that could not be taken away. *Soon enough. They'll all be gone soon enough.*

She stood beside Gabrielle during the ceremony, listening to the traditional words and responses and thinking of Garth. I took this from you, she said to him silently. The ceremony, its dignity and mystery and faith, I took from you. I made it a joke in your eyes. That was one of the worst things I did to you. And I never knew it until now. I wish you and I were standing here, saying these words. I would promise you that what I would build with you is marriage—not a game, not a diversion, not a brief adventure. I would pledge to you my heart and my hand and my love, but you are so far away, and so angry—

"Stephanie," Alexandra said. "Are you all right?"

She turned. Brooks and Gabrielle, arm in arm, married, were greeting their guests. She apologized. "I seem to have let my thoughts get the better of me."

Alexandra put her arm around her. "You're so pale. What can I do?"

"Help me feed everyone and keep the gossip light and pleasant."

"I meant, what can I do to make you happier?"

For the briefest of moments, Sabrina rested her forehead on Alexandra's shoulder. Then she stood straight and smiled. "Come back to London often. It will be good to have that to look forward to."

And they went downstairs to supervise the wedding feast.

Chapter 24

Garth was in the university library when the headline of the December 17 *New York Times* caught his eye. Snatching it from the librarian's neat arrangement, he took it to an armchair in a corner of the periodical room and sped through the story, then went back to the beginning and read more slowly. His heart was pounding. Here in Michel Bernard's precise words was the whole story of the conniving and maneuvering, the rivalries and vast sums of money, the art thefts and forgeries that had led to the murder of Max Stuyvesant.

And of his wife.

He went through it a third time, and still it did not seem real. He was reading about the death of his wife, but her name was not mentioned. He was learning about her lover, who had not even known her true identity. He was reading about the life and death of a woman he was no longer sure he knew.

The other night he had told Cliff how she had looked at their wedding. That was clear in his mind. And he remembered their early years when the children were young and they were becoming a family. But when he tried to recall the last year, everything slid away from him. The only image in his mind was of the woman he had known for the past three months.

And he could not ignore the truth about that woman any

longer. He loved her with a passion he could not eradicate or contain, though he still fought to destroy it, night after night, pacing alone and exhausted in his cold living room.

Which woman was he mourning? Both. Both. He no longer tried to deny it.

But he tried to forget. So many people were asking when Stephanie would return that he withdrew from the social contacts she had so carefully built and buried himself in work and activities with his children. He was supervising three new research projects in the laboratory, meeting daily with architects and contractors for the Genetics Institute, making preliminary plans with Lloyd Strauss for the ground-breaking ceremony scheduled for March, teaching an extra graduate seminar and gathering material for his paper on an immortal immune system in humans. He drove himself through the hours of each day, barely pausing to eat, never allowing himself to think about anything but the work he was doing.

And at home he drove himself with Penny and Cliff: cross-country skiing in the lakefront parks in Evanston and Chicago, going to movies and hockey games, playing word games at the dining room table, helping them with homework and working together on projects around the house that had been neglected for years. He refused to talk about their mother. "We'll talk about her soon. It isn't time yet. I'm sorry; I'm not any happier than you are; you'll just have to trust me on this."

What was he waiting for? He didn't know. But as each day passed and he did not expose the deception, he knew that the deeper its roots, the more real it became.

Which, he now understood, was exactly what Sabrina had discovered.

An air of quiet sadness clung to Penny and Cliff, even when they were praised at school or brought home a paper with a high grade. Even their squabbling was subdued. They fell into it automatically now and then but always stopped quickly, as if afraid of losing each other as they had lost their mother. They no longer rushed to see each day's mail in the hopes of finding a letter from her, but Garth knew they had written to her at least twice and he was not surprised when, at dinner on the same day he had seen the story in the *New York Times,* Cliff told him they were going shopping the next day for presents. "If we mail them tomorrow, will they be in London in time for Christmas?"

"It's possible. If they're small we can send them airmail and a week might be enough. But it will be close."

"Why didn't you tell us earlier how long it would take?" Penny demanded. "You know more about it than we do! You don't want us to buy presents for her!"

"Maybe not," he said, trying to be honest before their accusing eyes. "Maybe I think we should only have Christmas here."

"That's mean," Penny said flatly. "I think you're awful."

But, later, when he came to say good night and found Cliff in her room, they both put their arms around him. "We don't think you're awful," Penny said. "We think you're crying inside just like us. Daddy?"

"Yes, sweetheart."

"Cliff said we shouldn't bug you, but why won't Mommy write to us? Or come home?"

"She's doing what we both think is best, Penny."

"But if you think that, too, why are you crying inside?"

"Because often we can't have what we want."

"If you want it bad enough, you can," Cliff said.

"Look, both of you—" Garth heard the angry impatience in his voice and stopped. Leave me alone, he pleaded silently to his two children, who had done nothing wrong and needed reassurance as much as he did. I can't talk about it, I can hardly bear to think about it. I love her, I love her; not a moment goes by that I don't cry out for her. But more than an ocean lies between us, and I don't see any way in the world that we can cross it.

But he could say none of that aloud. "Listen, now," he said gently. "Your mother and I have problems that I still can't talk about. You have a right to know, as soon as I sort things out, but for now, all I can tell you is that they keep us apart, like a broken bridge. How we feel isn't as important as the destruction between us. Can you understand that?"

"No," they said together.

Garth sighed. "I'm not surprised." He put his arms around them and held them close, feeling them burrow against him as if looking for a hiding place. He bent his head and his voice was low and strained. "I know I'm not doing a very good job at this, and I'm sorry. I'm sorry for the mistakes I make, and for the times I seem cruel, but, my dear ones, I don't know what to do. I know I make it harder for you by not telling you everything, but I can't do it, not yet. Can you trust me on that? Can you believe that I'll tell you as much as I can, as soon as I can? Please believe that, please believe in me. I need that. And I need your love. Because I love you, you know. More than anyone in the world—"

"More than Mom?" Cliff demanded.

"Oh, Cliff," Penny scolded, and put her hand on Garth's cheek, for a brief moment becoming a woman, comforting a man. "Don't cry, Daddy. We'll wait until you tell us. But—" And she was a little girl again. "I just wish Mommy would come home."

Garth kissed them and stood up. "Get to sleep now, it's late. I love you both."

The next day Penny and Cliff went shopping, and when Garth got home they handed him two small wrapped packages, asking him to mail them right away. He did not ask what was in them and they did not tell him.

On the last day of school Penny's puppet show was presented in the lunchroom and Garth left the university early so he could be there. In the front of the room, students from other classes sat cross-legged on the floor; in the back, parents sat on folding chairs, Garth and Vivian among them. Penny and Barbara Goodman were behind the stage with Mrs. Casey, supervising the puppets before their classmates put them in action. Afterward, while Cliff stocked up on punch and cookies served by the sixth-grade food committee, Penny stood beside Garth, gravely accepting compliments from the audience. "My mother can't be here," she said to everyone. "Her twin sister died in London and she has to be there to take care of the grave and things like that. She wanted to be here, but she couldn't. She helped me with the costumes. I didn't do them myself. She helped me."

Vivian brought Garth a paper cup of punch. "It tastes awful, but it's wet. Is Stephanie coming back?"

"No."

Silently she looked at Penny, in earnest conversation with another parent about her mother's twin sister.

"It's not enough," Garth said angrily. "You can't rebuild a ruined marriage just because your children are unhappy."

"Is it a ruined marriage?" Vivian asked. "I never saw any signs of it, or got any clues."

"It isn't even a marriage." He looked at her worried face.

"I'm sorry, Vivian; I can't talk about it. Thank you for the punch."

He counted the passage of each day, not knowing what he was waiting for. He and the children bought a Christmas tree, smaller than usual—"since our family is smaller this year," Penny said—and decorated it, putting their wrapped packages beneath it. Dolores invited them to their country house for cross-country skiing, but Penny and Cliff refused to go. "I won't do it again without Mom," Cliff declared. When school and the university closed for the holidays, the three of them spent a day painting the upstairs bedrooms. "Won't Mommy be amazed?" Penny exclaimed again and again. "Everything looks so *bright*. Won't she be amazed?"

And finally, though he had turned down every other invitation to holiday parties, Garth gave in to Nat and Dolores's insistence that he join their annual gathering three days before Christmas. He sat with Penny and Cliff while they ate dinner, saw them settled in the living room with books, television and popcorn and walked alone to the Goldners' house.

It was always a large party. Dolores was determined to combine the university and the town into one happy community, and when Garth arrived he saw her steering local lawyers, insurance agents, store owners and physicians to small groups of faculty members. "They complain they have nothing to say to each other," she confided to Garth as she brought him a glass of wine. "But after half an hour they're all talking about sewage problems and schools and Dutch elm disease. They have a wonderful time, thank me for introducing them to everyone and then go their own ways and never cross paths again until next year in this room. Can you explain it?"

Garth laughed with her. "How often do most of us want to be in unpredictable situations? Once a year is plenty. The rest of the time we stay with comfortable places and people. Fewer surprises."

"Surprises are lovely," she protested.

"Only when they don't shatter everything that is familiar," he said with such gravity that she stared, for once speechless.

Nat appeared. "I've enlarged my library. Come have a look."

Garth turned to apologize to Dolores for leaving, but as she exchanged a look with Nat he realized they had planned this:

478

Nat was to have a talk with him. The conspiracies of happily married couples, he thought, to solve the problems of their friends.

"You're in one of those unpredictable situations, aren't you?" Nat said, switching on the light in his upstairs library. "But uncommunicative as a double agent. Is she or is she not coming back?"

"She's not."

"So you said. So others have said. I didn't believe it." He pulled two leather armchairs together. "Have a seat. There's wine and Scotch in that cabinet. You two were closer than I've ever seen you the last couple of months. So what happened so suddenly?"

"I thought we came here to see your enlarged library."

"So we did. You're looking at it. What happened so suddenly?"

"Nat, do I ask you about your marriage?"

"No. You're more polite than I am. Also, you aren't a doctor. I am; therefore, I am accustomed to prying."

"Into bones and ligaments, not—"

"Despair."

"Do I seem to be in despair?"

"Why the hell do you think I'm prying? I'm worried about you; we're all worried about you. For God's sake, Garth, what happened between you and Stephanie?"

"I found out she wasn't the woman I thought she was."

"Well, what does that mean? If you're saying that after twelve years you've discovered things about your wife you hadn't suspected, I wouldn't be surprised. Stephanie is in many ways a private person. I would be surprised if you had discovered depravity or criminal behavior, but, knowing Stephanie as a friend and patient, I'd say the chances of that are nonexistent. So is it *what* you have discovered, or simply the fact that there was something you hadn't known that has hurt you?"

Garth sat back in the leather chair and watched the wavering reflection of lamplight in the deep red of his wine. He was very tired, and Nat's words drifted to him from far away.

After twelve years you've discovered things about your wife you hadn't suspected.

A little more serious than that. But still, something to think about. "Nat," he said. "Would you do me a favor?"

"Ask."

"Let me sit here alone for awhile. No interruptions. I'll join the festivities later."

"Whenever you're ready." Nat opened the cabinet and brought out a bottle of wine and a box of crackers. "Everything you need for profound thoughts. Dinner is at ten-thirty."

Garth barely heard him leave. Is it *what* you have discovered—? What had he discovered besides the fact that he'd been deceived for three months into thinking he was living with his wife? He refilled his glass, and for the first time in weeks relaxed the rigid control he had kept over his thoughts. Images poured in: pictures, memories, recollections—a kaleidoscope revolving before his eyes.

He saw the woman who led the family to talk about his research at the dinner table and who encouraged him to turn down Foster Labs and stay where he would be most happy. He saw the woman who tore into Mrs. Casey for damaging Penny's belief in herself and later found a way to ease Cliff out of his gang of thieves. He saw the woman who got Linda a job at Collectibles to give her a way to succeed on her own. He saw the woman who cowed Rita McMillan, marching her off to Lloyd Strauss's office to clear Garth Andersen's name and pave the way for his formal appointment as director of the Genetics Institute.

Why? Because she was having fun playing a role? Or because she cared about the people she was helping? Because she had fallen in love?

She loved his children. He knew that now.

The door opened, and Garth looked up to see Madeline Kane. "Excuse me," she said. "Dolores wonders if you will join us for dinner."

"I don't think so. I have some . . . work to do at home. Dolores will understand."

"Before you go, could you tell me—I don't mean to pry, but—could you tell me when Stephanie will be back?"

Garth hesitated. "I don't know. I can't tell you. Would you make my apologies to Dolores?"

He found his coat and left by the side door. The night was brittle with cold, and in the silent streets his footsteps crunched on hard-packed snow. He plunged his hands into his pockets and turned into the park along the lake, lengthening his stride across the unbroken white expanse shimmering beneath a full moon.

His wife of twelve years had cared about people, loved them, worried about them. But, no matter how involved she became in their lives, when there was a crisis she became fearful and withdrew. She could not have backed Mrs. Casey into a corner or frightened Rita McMillan into a confession or even confronted Cliff when she thought he had been shoplifting.

And I knew that, Garth thought; I knew it, but I let myself think that was one of the ways she was changing to help us rebuild our marriage.

But Sabrina, Lady Sabrina Longworth, who had no family and no responsibilities, who lived a life of extravagance that skimmed the surface of friendships and love affairs and even marriage ... she could dominate, she could confront, she could speak out. In fact, Stephanie had envied Sabrina for the courage to speak out and take the offensive when a wrong needed correcting. But was Lady Longworth the kind of woman who would have cared enough to take the trouble? Would she have loved Penny and Cliff? Would she have loved Garth Andersen?

His face felt frozen and his fingers in his coat pockets were numb. Garth turned toward home, slipping sideways on patches of ice as he broke into a run on the last block. The house was quiet; Penny and Cliff had left him half a bowl of cold popcorn and gone to sleep. Shivering, he laid a fire and lit it, then ran upstairs and changed into an old pair of jeans and a turtleneck sweater. In the kitchen, he fixed a tray of cornedbeef sandwiches and beer, put on a pot of coffee and carried it all into the living room where the fire crackled and leaped up the chimney. Pulling up an armchair, he sat down with his tray on a table beside him, looking at the flames, letting the warmth seep into his skin. He realized suddenly that he felt extraordinarily good.

Why? he wondered. And knew the answer even as he asked it. Because, as a scientist, he was making progress, making discoveries, and spiraling in on the central one, the heart of the puzzle. The woman he had lived with for the last three months was neither his wife nor her sister, but a different person, just as she had said she was in New York—a woman with the caring and loving of Stephanie and the independence and strength of Sabrina. *That was why he had not seen through the deception.*

There had been far more to his blindness than the explanations he clutched in order to avoid disquieting suspicions; trying to believe she wanted to renew their marriage, or was in shock after the accident, or was mourning and identifying with her sister. The fact was, Sabrina Longworth had not lived with them very long before she began to act as much like her sister as herself. Twins, Garth thought. In each other's homes, in each other's thoughts. Within a few weeks the best of Sabrina merged with the best of her sister; she was Stephanie Andersen in so many important ways that the suggestion that she was someone else would have seemed absurd.

And as that happened to her, she became as much a victim of the deception as he—loving him and unable to tell him so until she was sure it was over. She had been caught, and neither of them had realized it.

And then, of course, there was one more reason why he was content to believe this woman was his wife; he had fallen in love with her. She had deceived him for three months, yet for almost every moment of that time she was more than he had ever dreamed of finding and loving and making a part of his life. And even now, knowing what he did, he thought of her as his wife.

The sandwich plate was empty; the beer was gone. More than I've eaten in three weeks, Garth thought. He poked the fire, adding more wood, and then poured a cup of coffee. Holding it between his hands, he watched the orange flames, tinged with yellow and blue, as they licked the cherry logs and sputtered and hissed when they reached a hidden drop of sap. There was no one left to hate, no more room for anger. He mourned the woman he had married years ago, who had fled their house to find something of herself, only to find death. He remembered the love they once had, and he thought with sorrow of the misunderstandings and failures they had brought to each other in their years together.

But out of the tangle that she and her sister had created when they took each other's place, Garth found a single strand: a new beginning. We might have found it anyway, he thought. After twelve years, both of us were changing; perhaps we were almost at the place where we could have built a new kind of love and marriage.

Instead, her sister came and stayed and became both of them. My dearest love. My wife.

In the quiet room, he smiled at the softly whispering flames. We'll have to get married, he thought.

Chapter 25

Each morning, Dmitri called. Two days after the wedding, as Sabrina was closing Ambassadors for the holidays, he came to take her to lunch. "I thought you might be melancholy, seeing your friend married and being without your family at Christmas."

In the pub, a group was singing a French carol. "I know that song," Sabrina said. "We sang it at Juliette, my sister and I."

"I want to talk about you," he said. "How can I give you what you want if you won't tell me what it is?"

"I told you, Dmitri. Friendship."

"And that means someone to share feelings as well as talk and a lunch. All right," he went on as she was silent. "I will talk about my villa in Athens. As it is near the homes of my sisters and their husbands and their children, too numerous to count, it is a good place to spend Christmas." He took her hand. "We could be private and see no one, or be part of a large family with much noise and kissing and music. We would do whatever you wish. Come with me, Stephanie. I would make no demands on you; only that you enjoy friends and a family instead of being alone."

The group ended its Christmas carol on a soft chord and began another. Dmitri smiled. "We would teach you our Greek songs."

Temptation tugged at her. To be with a family, even one that was not hers; to have a change of scene with no reminders of a sister who was gone . . . But it was not fair to Dmitri. She was not a whole person. And though she had told him that many times, if she went with him to Athens he would think it a first step, not a single time shared by friends. She shook her head. "Someday I might, Dmitri, but not yet."

"You should not be alone," he insisted.

"Sometimes being alone is important. How else do we have conversations with ourselves to make decisions about the future?"

"Friends can help you make decisions. Stephanie, I would make no demands on you."

She took her hand from his to pick up her glass of ale. She wanted very much to believe him. "May I let you know tomorrow?"

His face lit up. "I'll call you in the morning. We would leave in the afternoon of the twenty-fourth. Would that suit you? Never mind," he added hastily. "You can tell me tomorrow." And, as they finished lunch, he talked about his family and Greek friends and neighbors. "And you could help me decorate my villa," he said as they left the pub, as if looking for one last incentive for her to come with him.

"Perhaps," she answered, smiling, and they talked about the brilliant white sunlight of southern Greece, so different from the light of other countries, while walking through London's damp gray afternoon, brightened only by Christmas lights.

Christmas lights: even the December mist could not dim them. They walked along Oxford Street, past Selfridges, where crowds stood at the windows, watching the story of Pinocchio acted out by puppets in miniature villages; and through Piccadilly Circus to Trafalgar Square, where the huge spruce, given each year to London by the city of Oslo, glittered as if stars had settled on its dark branches. Farther on, past Hyde Park Corner, every lintel, archway and window of Harrods, even its high dome, was outlined in pale gold lights like hundreds of small moons in the misty air.

Dmitri was silent, leaving Sabrina with her thoughts. She told herself the holiday meant nothing to her, that the lights and songs of carolers left her unaffected; but each time she saw a family group, with two children looking up and talking eagerly to the adults beside them, she turned quickly away, fixing her gaze elsewhere. It was then that she was grateful for Dmitri's undemanding companionship and his graceful withdrawal at her door on Cadogan Square.

Inside, she found Mrs. Thirkell gazing happily at a small tree in the drawing room. "I thought it might cheer you up, my lady, but I'll put it in my apartment upstairs if it brings back too many memories."

"No, leave it," Sabrina said. "Will you decorate it?"

"I will, my lady, but I thought we might do it together."

My lady. She no longer corrected Mrs. Thirkell; often she barely heard it. Nor did it seem important; it made Mrs. Thirkell happy, and they were both used to it.

The telephone rang. Sabrina's hands clenched. Each time it rang she thought . . . but it never was. "Another invitation," Mrs. Thirkell predicted.

"If so, another refusal," Sabrina responded, and they smiled at each other. It was curious, she thought, as Mrs. Thirkell went to answer it, how close they had become. Lady Longworth could not have done it; too many social barriers lay between them. But now, even though Mrs. Thirkell called her "my lady," she also thought of her as an American who had never been married to a viscount. They still were not quite friends, but they were two women sharing a home, and Sabrina felt less isolated than she had feared she would.

It was Mrs. Thirkell who handled the torrent of invitations that came in the week before Christmas—for house parties, trips to the south of France, skiing at St. Moritz, New Year's Eve balls—telling everyone that Mrs. Andersen was accepting no invitations for the holidays.

The calls were still coming the day before Christmas. "You're the rage of the season," said Mrs. Thirkell with satisfaction as the telephone rang in the late morning. "Because you're something of a mystery. Not quite real, if you know what I mean."

Yes, Sabrina thought as Mrs. Thirkell left the room. I know what you mean. But she was listening. Each time the telephone rang, she could not help herself; her body grew still, waiting.

"It's Mr. Karras, my lady," Mrs. Thirkell said, returning. "And if you don't mind my saying so, I think you should go to Greece with him. It would do you good."

Sabrina touched the needles of the small spruce tree they

had decorated. It smelled of forests and mountains; of serene, private places. "Perhaps I will," she said, and went to talk to him.

But her face was clouded when she hung up; his delighted, eager voice, saying he would pick her up at four o'clock, made her feel guilty. It was not fair, it was not fair. I only want Garth, she thought; how will I talk and laugh with other people when I keep turning to the telephone to see if Garth is calling?

Mrs. Thirkell found her a while later in the study. "The post, my lady. Mostly cards, but also these packages."

Sabrina knew what they were before she opened them. Two. One from Cliff, one from Penny. Nothing from Garth. Nothing. Not even a note. She unwrapped the packages, each colorfully wrapped, each with its own note. "Mom, have a Happy Christmas," Cliff wrote. "With lots of food and presents. I hope you find what you're looking for. I wish I knew what it was. I love you. Your loving son, Cliff."

"Dearest Mommy," wrote Penny. "I hope you like this and it makes you happy. I'd rather give it to you but I can't so Daddy will mail it. We're all fine but sad and Cliff and I talk about you a lot. I love you, I miss you, I love you. Love, Penny."

I will not cry. I knew this might happen and I was prepared for it. I will not cry. Gently, she refolded the notes, pressing the creases with her fingertips, and then she opened the boxes. Cliff had sent a pin: a pair of yellow enameled birds on an enameled branch with two small leaves of green jade. A note inside the box said, "These are you and Dad."

Penny's box, long and narrow, held a silver pen and pencil set engraved with the letters *S A.* A small note beneath them read, "For writing letters."

The best extortionists, Sabrina thought, are children. She picked up the house phone. "I'll have lunch in my room, Mrs. Thirkell." Carrying her presents, she climbed the stairs. Rain drummed against the windows, and her room was dark and chilly. She lit a fire, curling up before it on the chaise with an angora afghan over her lap, and looked at the enameled birds and the pen and pencil set and at the bright, dancing flames.

She should be packing for Athens, but, instead, she sat still, seeing in the flames all the dreams that haunted her days and nights.

They had been so careless, she and her sister, so incredibly careless of others. But what if it had ended differently; what if, somehow, there had been a way for her to love Garth and receive his love without guilt, a way to live with him and build a life with him? We could have had a child, she thought. A surprise for Penny and Cliff. A small smile curved the corners of her mouth as she pictured the two of them tossing a coin to see who got to feed the baby.

She could have gone into partnership with Madeline, decorating and restoring old buildings, while Linda handled estate sales. What a team the three of them would have made, especially if they joined Collectibles to Ambassadors and had the best art and antiques of two continents to choose from.

She and Garth would have the money from her sale of the Cadogan Square house and she would lure Mrs. Thirkell to America. Then they could travel—to London, to Paris, where Gaby and Brooks would be living part of the time; even to Rio, to see Alexandra and finally meet some Guarani Indians. They could combine the whirl of her London social life with the home and community life she loved in Evanston. They could afford it all. They could even fix up the house. At least, they could finally paint the bedrooms. And she could buy Garth the leather jacket he'd been eyeing at Mark Shale one day when they were browsing together.

Jacket. Packing. She had to get ready. Taking her small suitcase and makeup case from the closet, she began to look through her clothes to choose what she would pack for Athens. But each dress meant gaiety and people, laughter and lights, and as she ran her fingers across them she knew she could not do it. Not yet; not when Garth was still a part of her, so real she felt she could reach out and touch his face and put her lips to his; so much a part of her deepest self that all she longed for was to tell him she loved him and wanted to be with him for the rest of her life—only him, no one else.

She called Dmitri and told him she could not go. Perhaps another time; perhaps they had a future. She did not know. It was not fair; she heard the disappointment in his voice and knew it was not fair. Whatever she did caused pain. Perhaps she would just sit in her room, alone, and eventually fade away. Then they would both be gone. Sabrina and Stephanie Hartwell: grew up together; later traded places; still later, disappeared.

She poked the fire, putting on another log, and went back to the chaise, the afghan on her lap. Her dreams were still there, in the flames, brighter than ever. They don't go away, she thought; they don't even fade. The days and weeks pass, the telephone rings and presents come from two loving children; the days go by and people come and go in our lives, and the dreams remain, vivid and alive.

She heard Mrs. Thirkell climbing the stairs. Lunchtime, she thought. Then I'll do some work; I brought so much with me from Ambassadors—catalogs to read, books to study, letters to answer. Enough work to fill all the holidays. If I concentrate, I can forget everything else, at least for awhile.

Mrs. Thirkell knocked and appeared in the doorway, breathless, red-faced and beaming. "My lady, there's a visitor to see—"

But before she could finish, following closely behind and overtaking her, Garth strode into the room, his face alight with love.

With a cry, Sabrina leaped up, but Garth had stopped, hesitant and watchful halfway across the room, the memory of their violent words echoing between them. Sabrina held out her hands, her voice barely a whisper. "I dreamed of you . . . all the time . . ."

As if her words had released him he was suddenly beside her, catching her up, enfolding her tightly in his arms, her cheek against his heart. Dimly, she heard Mrs. Thirkell leave the room, and then she heard only Garth's wild heartbeat and his voice, murmuring as his lips moved against her hair. "My love, my dearest love, all the empty days without you—"

She stirred within his arms, turning up her face, and her mouth met his. Through closed eyes she saw the orange glow from the fireplace; she smelled the damp wool of his coat and felt with her fingertips the raindrops clinging to his hair. *These are real; no longer a dream; not ever again.*

Garth felt her slender bones beneath his hands and breathed the silken fragrance that had haunted him for weeks. In the deepest part of him he felt his aching restlessness subside; he had come home.

"Yes," she breathed, as if he had spoken, and opened her eyes to meet his, dark and intense. "A place to belong . . ."

But not yet. We haven't . . . She put her hands on his chest, between them. "Garth, we haven't talked . . . so much is unfinished . . ."

"No, my love." He kissed her eyes, her mouth, the hollow of her throat. "Not unfinished. Begun. And not with lies; with the truths you've told."

"Truths! I deceived you—"

"Shamefully. But did you deceive me in the way you felt about Penny and Cliff? Or me? Or our life together?"

She shook her head. "But beneath it all—"

"Beneath it all was love. Dear one, you made a marriage, you made us a family, and that is the truth you gave us. Except—" He laughed slightly. "It is not quite the truth. My dearest love, I want to marry you, I want to take you home, to make the past and the present one life, our life together . . ."

She took his face between her hands and searched his eyes for traces of the bitterness and hurt of their last meeting. But they were gone; he had resolved them, and there was only the warm caress of the times they had loved without restraint. She kissed him then, a long, slow kiss, pledging her heart and hand and love. Garth's arm tightened around her; his hand held her breast. "Dear heart—" she said, a low sigh deep in her throat, and her body curved to his as if already taking him inside her. Together, they turned to the bed.

"Oh . . . wait." She held him back. "We forgot . . . What did you tell Penny and Cliff?"

Garth looked at her radiant face, her eyes bright with anticipation, and knew they mirrored his own. All the dreams were coming together at once. "That I would try to bring you home," he said.

"Are they at Vivian's?"

He nodded, his love for her so powerful it made him tremble, stopping the words in his throat.

She picked up the telephone and dialed and when Vivian answered, she settled back in the curve of Garth's arm. "Vivian," she said, "it's Stephanie. Could I talk to my children, to tell them I'm coming home?"

A Tangled Web

Once more, for Cynthia, Andrew and Eric

"I think it's the most special blessing of all: to like our children as companions."

—Garth Andersen

"Oh, what a tangled web we weave,
When first we practice to deceive!"

—Sir Walter Scott

Part I

CHAPTER *1*

---

*S*abrina took a deep breath and blew out the birthday candles—thirty-three and one for good luck—closed her eyes and made a wish. *Please let everything stay the same. My children, my dearest love, my friends, my home: close and safe. And truly mine.* She opened her eyes, smiling at everyone around the table, and picked up the antique silver cake cutter she had brought back from her last trip to London.

"What'd you wish, Mom?" Cliff asked.

"She can't tell us," Penny said. "Wishes don't come true if you tell them."

"They don't come true anyway," Cliff declared. "Everybody knows that. It's all a myth."

"Oh, too cynical," Linda Talvia said, putting her hand on Marty's arm. "Lots of my wishes came true."

"And all of mine," Garth said, his eyes meeting Sabrina's down the length of the table. "Even one or two I hadn't thought of."

"They can't come true if you don't wish them," Cliff scoffed.

3

"Sure they can," said Nat Goldner. "Dolores and I didn't even know we wanted to get married, all those years ago, and then all of a sudden we were and it was exactly right."

"And I wished for wonderful children," Sabrina said, "smart and fun and full of love. Was that a myth?"

"Oh. Well, sometimes they come true." Cliff grinned as the others laughed. "I mean, if you make the right wish . . ."

The right wish.

I made a wish once. So did Stephanie.

Oh, Stephanie, look where it took us.

Sabrina folded into herself as the others talked, remembering Stephanie, longing to hear her voice, to look into her eyes and see her own eyes gazing back at her, her own face, her mirror image, her identical twin. *It's your birthday, too, Stephanie, not just mine; you should be celebrating today; you should be—*

Here. She should be here. If Stephanie were alive, she would be sitting at this table surrounded by the family and friends that were hers long before she and Sabrina dreamed up their plan to switch places. It had been a mad and careless idea, though at the time it had seemed like a lark, a daring adventure. One year ago, only a year, they both had had troubles in their separate lives and lightheartedly wished for a chance to live a different life, just for a little while.

And then it became serious. And so, at the end of a trip to China, Sabrina went home as Stephanie Andersen, to a husband and two children and a shabby Victorian house in Evanston, just outside of Chicago. And Stephanie became Sabrina Longworth, divorced and living alone in the elegance of a Cadogan Square town house in London. Just for a week, they said, one week of escaping into another life, and then they would switch back, with no one the wiser.

But they had not switched back. Sabrina broke her wrist in a bicycle accident, and Stephanie, her marriage to Garth

4

already shaky, pleaded with Sabrina to stay in Evanston until her wrist was healed, the final X-ray taken. Then, when once again they were identical in all ways, they could safely return to their own lives.

But the weeks of healing turned their lives upside down. Sabrina fell in love with Garth with a passion she had never known, and found a deep love for Penny and Cliff, while Garth discovered a wife quite different from the one who had been drifting away from him, whom he had barely looked at for many months. He found her enchanting and exciting, and told himself she was consciously changing herself since her trip to China, to save their marriage.

Stephanie, in London, made new friends, and began an affair with Max Stuyvesant, a man of wealth and mystery and social connections who was involved with the world of art and antiquities. And she managed Ambassadors, Sabrina's exclusive antique shop, growing more self-confident with each day that she pretended to be her glamorous sister. Still, they would have changed back, but first Stephanie begged for just a few more days for a cruise with Max on his yacht. One last fling, she told Sabrina. One last fling.

And then she was dead. The yacht exploded off the coast of France, and the news came that everyone on board, including Lady Sabrina Longworth, had been killed. Sabrina and Garth went to London, where everyone mourned the loss of her sister, and in the funeral home Sabrina said goodbye to Stephanie, almost blinded by tears of loss and guilt. At the funeral, trying to tell the truth, she fell to her knees beside the grave, crying, "It wasn't Sabrina who died . . . It wasn't Sabrina . . . !" But no one would listen; they said she was unbalanced by grief. And Sabrina, in a turmoil of despair and confusion, could not fight them.

And so she returned to Stephanie's family. She knew it could not last—she could not build a life on a deception—but for the next three months, weaving through her grief was a happiness greater than any she had ever dreamed of:

passionate love with a strong man; warmth and cherishing and humor with two bright, loving children.

But by Christmas, almost four months after the sisters switched places, before Sabrina had gathered the strength to tell Garth she was leaving, he unraveled the deception himself. Enraged, he ordered her out of his life, out of his children's life. She fled to London, her world in ruins from that mad act she and Stephanie had so carelessly committed.

But, alone in his home, Garth slowly came to understand the depth of Sabrina's love for him and his children. He understood that she, too, had been trapped by the deception. And he knew that he loved her more deeply than he had ever loved before.

"Stephanie? You still with us?"

Sabrina started slightly and saw Nat Goldner looking at her with concern. Nat, the close friend, the doctor who had set her wrist when she broke it one year ago, looking at her with affection. "I'm sorry," she said with a small smile. "I guess I drifted away."

Garth came to sit on the arm of her chair. "It's usually professors who get accused of that, not professors' wives." He put his arm around her. "This isn't an easy time."

"You're thinking about Aunt Sabrina, aren't you?" Penny asked. "It's her birthday, too."

"I miss her," Cliff said. "She was lots of fun."

Tears filled Sabrina's eyes, and Dolores Goldner leaned forward. "How awful for you, Stephanie; such a happy day, but filled with sadness, too."

"I guess I need to be alone for a few minutes," Sabrina said, standing up. "Cliff, you're in charge of cutting more cake." She leaned down and kissed Garth lightly. "I won't be long."

She heard Cliff taking orders for seconds as she climbed the stairs to the bedroom. The bedside lamps were on; the sheet was turned back on either side of the four-poster bed; their clothes had been put away. Wonderful Mrs. Thirkell,

Sabrina thought. I brought her from Cadogan Square in London, where her only concern was Lady Sabrina Longworth, and plunged her into a family of four in an old three-story house that always needs repairs, and in the eight months she has been here she has never once seemed flustered.

Lady Sabrina Longworth. Sabrina sat on the curved window seat and looked into the front yard, palely lit by streetlights and the windows of neighboring houses. There is no such person as Lady Sabrina Longworth anymore, she thought. Mrs. Thirkell calls me, from habit, "My lady," to the children's endless amusement, but Sabrina is dead; to the world, she died on a cruise with Max Stuyvesant last October. To me, she died when I realized I could never go back to my own identity, because that would give away the deception to Penny and Cliff. They would know that their mother had thought it would be a lark to pretend to be Sabrina Longworth, free and on her own in London while her sister took her place at home. They would know that their mother had been traveling with a man not their father when she was killed. I could not let them know that. And so there is no more Sabrina Longworth. And often I miss her, miss being her, miss living her life.

But she had been Stephanie Andersen for a year of love and discoveries, and most of the time she missed her other life simply as a child misses a bedtime fairy tale: something dreamlike and perfect, not real. Not real, Sabrina told herself. Not real. Below, on the dark grass, she spotted Cliff's T-shirt, tossed to the side that afternoon in the heat of an impromptu soccer match. That's what is real: all the little things and the big ones that make a family. That was my wish, a year ago, when I wanted to live Stephanie's life. And it came true.

But it came true with a terrible dark side.

Because Stephanie died. And because she was murdered.

"You're not responsible," Garth said from the doorway. "You couldn't know what would happen, and there

7

was nothing in your life that led her inevitably to her death.''

"I tell myself that," Sabrina said, her voice low. "But I keep wondering . . . How did the police know that the bomb was put on the ship just to kill Max? What if it was to kill Stephanie, too? Because to them she was Sabrina and she might have gotten involved in something. Once, when I was at Ambassadors after the funeral, I was sure that was what happened, that she had said something that made them feel threatened. I don't know. I just don't know. But if I hadn't been so happy here, I might have pushed her to tell me what she was doing, what Max was doing, and whether she knew anything about it. Maybe I could have warned her. I *knew* those people and she'd just met them. But all those months I was living her life, happier than I'd ever been and turning my back on everything over there. *I never asked.*''

Garth sat behind her on the window seat, his arms around her, and Sabrina rested against him. "Maybe I couldn't have done anything. I don't know. But I do know that all I really cared about was you and the children—''

"Listen to me, my love.'' His voice was patient; they had gone over this so many times, but still he went through it each time as if it were the first. "You told me you'd talked to her about the forged artworks and she handled the whole thing brilliantly. She kept Ambassadors out of that scandal; she protected its reputation as if it were her own shop. You did warn her to stay away from Max, not because he was the head of a smuggling operation—none of us knew that until it was too late—but because you'd never liked him or trusted him. She had plenty of information from you, and she probably had learned a lot more that you didn't know. She was a smart, grown-up woman who chose her own path. You can't hold yourself responsible for the choices she made.''

"I know, I know. But"—she looked around the room— "I have all this, I have everything, and she—''

"Yes, I think of that.'' Garth turned her in his arms and

kissed her. "My dear love, I think of that more than you know. But I cannot feel guilty for what we have found."

"Mommy, don't you want to open your presents?" Penny stood in the doorway, her eyes wide and worried. "Are you sick or something? Everybody's worried about you."

Sabrina smiled. "Everybody?"

"Well, Cliff and me. 'Cause if you forgot about your presents . . ."

"I must be sick." She laughed and hugged Penny, her somberness lifting.

Garth gazed at her beauty and thought of all she had been to him since last Christmas, when he had brought her back from London. She had played the shabbiest trick that could be played on someone close and vulnerable, but it had not been done from malice, and in the end, she had been trapped by her love for them and theirs for her. And who could have foreseen that? he mused. We'd never even liked each other very much.

But she had changed in the years since he had first met her, and she changed again, living with them, so that, after a while, she truly was not always sure which sister she was, and that was another way she was trapped. Once Garth realized that, he let himself love her with a passion greater than any he had ever known with Stephanie or anyone else.

"So can we go?" Penny asked. "We've been waiting and waiting . . ."

"You're right, it's time," Sabrina said. "But where are the presents?"

"We hid them in the best place! Guess where!"

"Oh, Penny, can we play guessing games later? Why don't you just put them in the living room? Then Mrs. Thirkell can clear the table."

"Okay. On the coffee table or the couch or . . . ?"

"You decide," Garth said firmly. "We'll be down in a minute."

Penny gave them both a swift look, seeking reassurance, then gave a little nod and dashed out. Sabrina turned again to Garth and kissed him. "I love you. I'm sorry I get so . . . lost, sometimes."

"It's not something you choose. But it is getting better, isn't it?"

"Yes. Oh, yes, of course. Time, and so much love, and wonderful kids who demand a lot of attention . . . Do you know, I find myself thinking about Stephanie and then I tell myself, 'I'll think about her later, after I have my conference with Cliff's teacher or take Penny shopping or help Linda with an estate sale . . .' and I do, in snatched minutes, but then you come home and everything seems wonderful because you're here . . ."

Garth's arms tightened around her. "Everything *is* wonderful. And I won't allow us to deny what we've found, and that it gets more astonishingly wonderful all the time."

"Do you know what I wished when I blew out the candles?"

"Penny says you're not supposed to tell anyone."

"You're not 'anyone,' you're my love, and I can tell you anything. I wished that everything would stay the same. You, the children, this house, our friends. I want it all to stay just as it is." She gave a small laugh. "Dolores would say that's because no woman wants to have any more birthdays past thirty."

"But the truth is, you wished it because it took us so long to find what we have. I wish it, too, you know, every night when I'm falling asleep with you in my arms. I'd hold back the clock for you, my love, but that's not my branch of science. Come on, now, we'd better get to those presents. Mine isn't there, by the way. I'll give it to you later, when we're alone."

"Is it so private? The children will be disappointed. Remember when I tried that with your birthday present."

"Oh, Lord, I suppose you're right. Where do children get these ironclad ideas about appropriate family behavior? Well, okay, but it is private and special; you'll understand when you see it.'

"How mysterious." Sabrina took Garth's hand and they walked down the stairs and into the living room, where the others waited.

"Thirteen years married and still holding hands," said Marty Talvia. "We should drink a toast to that. And it so happens that I brought a special port for the occasion." He reached over the back of the couch and retrieved the bottle he had hidden there. "And the admirable Mrs. Thirkell has provided glasses, so I shall pour while Stephanie opens presents. You'd better start, Stephanie, or your kids will explode with waiting."

Penny had placed three packages on the coffee table, and Sabrina removed the wrapping paper from the two top ones, opening them at the same time. "Oh, how lovely!" she exclaimed. "I've been wanting a new necklace, Penny, how did you know? And is this candleholder made of walnut, Cliff? It's perfect with our new tablecloth; we'll use it tomorrow night."

"We made them in school," Cliff said. "Dad said it was better to make things than buy them."

"Of course it is. I love whatever you give me, but it's special when you make something yourself. And I love you. More than anybody in the whole—"

"Except for Dad," said Cliff.

"Always except for Dad." Over their heads, Sabrina met Garth's eyes. "Always."

"Port," said Marty Talvia, handing small glasses to the six of them. "Penny and Cliff, you'll have to wait a few years."

"Mom lets us take a sip," Cliff said. "She never used to, but all of a sudden, you know, lately she started—"

"It's because you're twelve," Garth said.

"But I'm only eleven and I get a sip, too," said Penny.

"Those are the magic ages: eleven and twelve," Sabrina said lightly, sliding past another observation—one of so many in the past year—that she did things differently from the way Stephanie had done them. "Now, what's going to happen to that large, elegantly wrapped gift still sitting on the coffee table?"

"Open it!" cried Cliff.

"Please open it," Linda Talvia said. "I'm going crazy, waiting."

"So am I," Dolores said. "We bought it together. Of course you can buy any of these things for yourself now, but we thought—"

"Not necessary," said Nat, his hand on her arm.

Sabrina pretended to be absorbed in working open the gilt wrapping paper. There had been difficult moments among the six of them when the others became aware of how much money and property the Andersens now had, since Sabrina's will had left everything to her sister. *I've left everything to myself,* Sabrina had thought, frantic with despair and bitter humor the previous October, in those awful weeks after Stephanie's funeral. But she and Garth were careful to keep their life much as it had been except for a few changes. They had had the house painted, and she had gradually brought in some fine antiques from London and from Collectibles, the shop in Evanston where she had become a partner. She had linked Collectibles to Ambassadors, and occasionally she went to London to buy at auction and to watch over her shop. She and Garth took more short trips together, and of course Mrs. Thirkell was there, the perfect housekeeper, the envy of everyone.

Those had been the only changes, and as the months went by, everyone seemed to forget that Garth and Stephanie Andersen had become wealthy, at least compared with other academics in Evanston.

But now Linda said, "We think about it, though, buying you things. It used to be so different. Remember when we bought you that bathrobe? Dolores thought it was too loud, but I said you'd been wearing brighter colors since you got back from China, so we bought it and you loved—"

"Oh, wonderful," Sabrina breathed, lifting from its

cushioned box a Penrose Waterford decanter. From the early nineteenth century, it was etched with eight-pointed stars, its stopper shaped like a small umbrella above three doughnut-like rings. "It's absolutely perfect. Where did you find it?"

"The Charteris estate sale. I knew you liked Waterford."

"Oh, I do. And I've never had a Penrose."

"You've never had Waterford, period. Until lately, that is."

"That's true." Sabrina barely noticed her small slip; no one else did, either. By now she did not guard her tongue as she had in the beginning; if she spoke occasionally from Sabrina's background and experience, or did not know what they were talking about when they reminisced together, the others found ways to explain it away. They explained everything away; they always had, from her first night home when they were in the kitchen and she'd asked Garth and the children where they kept the pot holders. After that there had been dozens of mistakes and slips of the tongue, but no one was suspicious or even curious because, Sabrina realized, people see what they expect to see and they find reasons for oddities to protect the comfortable order and predictability of their lives.

Now, in her living room, she set the decanter on the coffee table and stretched her arms wide. "What a wonderful birthday. The best I've ever had. It's so perfect, being here with all of you, knowing this is where I belong . . ."

"Dad, you didn't give Mom a present," Cliff said accusingly.

"Where is it?" Penny demanded. "You told us you got it."

Garth grinned at Sabrina. "Right again." He pulled a small velvet box from his shirt pocket and put it in her hand. "With all my love. For now, for always."

Sabrina kissed him, then opened the box. A long sigh broke from her.

"What is it? What is it?" Penny cried.

"Hold it up, Mom!" said Cliff.

"It's a ring," Nat said, looking into the box over Sabrina's shoulder. "Stunning. A star sapphire, yes?" he asked Garth.

"Yes," Garth murmured, his eyes holding Sabrina's. She put her hand along his face. "My engagement ring."

"But you're already married," Penny protested.

"I never had an engagement ring," Sabrina said.

"Neither did I," said Dolores. "Probably for the same reason: Nat couldn't afford it."

"Neither could Marty," Linda said. "Garth, what a nice idea."

Garth pulled off Sabrina's gold wedding band and slipped the engagement ring and wedding band together onto her finger. Sabrina closed her eyes. This ring was for a wedding the others knew nothing about. This was for a rainy December day when Garth had come to London to say he loved her and wanted her and it no longer mattered what she and her sister had done; and for another rainy day two days later, when they took the train to Canterbury, where no one knew them, and bought two gold wedding bands and found a magistrate to marry them. The narrow streets and stones of that ancient town were dark gray, streaked and dripping in the steady downpour, but Sabrina wore a red raincoat and rain hat and she bought Garth a red carnation for his lapel, and when their eyes met as each slipped a ring onto the other's finger and the magistrate said "husband and wife," they saw in each other the sun, and spring, and hope.

"Thank you," Sabrina said, her lips close to Garth's. "It's the most wonderful gift I could have imagined. And the most private; you were right about that. So when we're alone . . ."

The telephone rang, and abruptly she began to tremble. She knew Penny and Cliff were watching, but she could not stop. She could not hear a late night ring without

14

recalling in terrible detail the night last October when Brooks had called from London, crying, to say that Max Stuyvesant's yacht had gone down and everyone on board . . . everyone on board . . . everyone on board—

"It's all right." Garth drew her tightly to him. "It's all right, my love, we're all here, it's all right."

"My lady," Mrs. Thirkell said from the doorway. "There's a call for you, from London—"

"No," Sabrina cried involuntarily.

"—Miss de Martel. Though of course she's Mrs. Westermarck now; I must try harder to remember that."

"Gaby," Sabrina said. She forced her body to stillness. "At three in the morning London time. What in heaven's name is she up to? Excuse me," she said to the others, and left the room behind Mrs. Thirkell's ample back, her muscles tight, her heart pounding.

"Gaby," she said, picking up the telephone in the kitchen. "It must have been quite a party, if you're just getting home."

"I haven't been to a party in two weeks." Gaby's high voice was clear and close. "We've been in Provence, bicycling. I've had an inordinate amount of fresh air; I can't believe it's healthy for anyone to have that much all at one time. You didn't tell me you'd be there; we could have spent some time together."

"That I'd be where?"

"In Provence. Avignon, to be exact. About a week ago."

"I wasn't there, Gaby, I was here. What are you talking about?"

"Oh, God, am I being indiscreet? Stephanie, were you there to see somebody? I can't believe it; I thought you were head over heels for your professor. Have you got something going on the side? You can trust me, you know; I'd do anything for you because you're Sabrina's sister and I adored her and she saved Brooks and me when—"

"I'm not having an affair; I haven't got anybody but Garth. Gaby, what is this all about?"

There was a silence. "You weren't in Avignon last week?"

"I just told you. No."

"But I saw you. Or your double. It was some festival or other, hordes of people—"

Or your double. Sabrina was trembling again. Once she had had a double. Once she had had a sister.

"—and I couldn't get to you—you were across the square, walking in the other direction, with a guy, very handsome, very attentive—and you took off your hat, one of those wide-brimmed straw ones with a long scarf tied around the crown, red and orange, and you were brushing back your hair—you know, combing it with your fingers?—and then you put on your hat again and you were gone."

Brushing back your hair. She and Stephanie had done that all their lives: taken off a hat, combed their hair with their fingers, feeling the air lift and cool it, then replaced the hat. Their mother had not approved; a lady kept her hat on, she said. But Sabrina and Stephanie went on doing it long after they were grown up and far away from their mother's strictures. *Brushing back your hair.*

"My lady?" Mrs. Thirkell pulled a chair up and put her hands on Sabrina's shoulders, settling her into it. "I'll get you some tea."

"So either you've been identical triplets all this time, without telling anybody," Gaby said, "or something very weird is going on."

"Of course we weren't triplets, don't be absurd." She was trembling again; she could not hold herself still. It was as if the earth were shifting beneath her feet. "This whole thing is absurd," she said, biting off her words. "You saw someone who reminded you of me, that's all; I can't imagine why you'd make something of it—"

"Stephanie, listen, I'm not joking, this is very weird and a little scary. I've known you and Sabrina since she and I were roommates at Juliette; I lived in her house on Cadogan Square when Brooks and I broke up, and she and

16

I talked every night; she even took me on her lap once, and I cried like a baby, and I loved having her hold me, and I loved her, and I know what the two of you look like and I'm telling you, I saw you, or her—oh, God, how could it be her, she's dead—*but I know what I saw, and it was you or her. Or a ghost.*"

*N*oontime crowds filled the streets of London, and Sabrina merged with them, a Londoner again, Sabrina Longworth again, free and independent, on her way to Ambassadors, the exclusive antique shop she had created after her divorce from Denton. She never thought of Denton except when she was in London, and she thought of him briefly now: his round, rosy face, his fascination with himself and his pleasures, his love of women and gambling. He had been gambling in Monaco when Max Stuyvesant's ship went down; he was the one who identified the body of Sabrina Longworth. Max's body had never been found.

Sabrina's hands were clenched. Beneath a cool, early-October sun, she walked along Pont Street, wearing a black and taupe plaid skirt and matching cape that furled about her with each step. She wore a black narrow-brimmed hat angled low over her eyes, and fine black kid gloves. She looked sophisticated, purposeful and calm, but beneath the cape she was tense and withdrawn, her thoughts swinging from the past to the present, from one

18

life to another, from Stephanie to herself, from the memory of a funeral to Gaby's telephone call, and always, always, to Garth.

She had told him about the call, but made light of it. "She saw someone who looked like me and wondered why I hadn't told her I'd be in Europe. I'll call her next time I'm there." And then, casually, she had added, "I think I'll go next week. I want to check on Ambassadors and . . . just be there. Would you mind?"

"And our October trip?" Garth asked.

"Oh, of course we'll do that." She had planned her trip to Ambassadors for the end of October, while Garth gave a paper at the International Biogenetics Conference in The Hague; then they would meet in Paris for a week to themselves. "Of course we'll go; I wouldn't give up a week in Paris with you. But I'd like to be there now, too. I was thinking of next Monday; would you mind?"

Of course he said he would not mind. Garth had always given her plenty of space in which to merge her two lives. "We miss you more each time you go," he said, "but you've given us the formidable Mrs. Thirkell, and if anyone can ease the pain, she can."

Mrs. Thirkell had taken firm control of their house, keeping it so well lubricated that none of them could imagine how they had functioned without her. And so when Sabrina moved up her trip to London, there was only a brief conversation with Mrs. Thirkell to go over shopping lists, schedules, the window washer, who was due on Tuesday, and the landscaper, who was coming in a week to cut back the gardens for winter. And then she asked, as she always did, if there was anything she could bring back from the London house.

"Why not bring the dessert forks, my lady? You don't entertain there anymore, and we seem to be doing more all the time here, and what a shame to keep such handsome silver locked away."

"A good idea." Sabrina thought of the steady westerly movement of possessions from Cadogan Square to Evanston, matching the steady fading of Lady Longworth into Stephanie Andersen.

"And then there's the fish poacher, my lady; I certainly could use that."

Sabrina laughed. "I am not about to carry a fish poacher across the ocean. Buy a new one, Mrs. Thirkell; I'm surprised you haven't already."

"You do get a fondness for certain familiar things. But of course I'm sure I'll get attached to a new fish poacher, too."

It doesn't take long to get attached to new things, Sabrina thought, approaching Ambassadors, already missing Garth and the children even though her plane had landed only that morning. But she was still attached to Europe, too, where she and Stephanie had grown up. Their life had been nomadic as they moved from city to city whenever their father was assigned to a new embassy. They had learned half a dozen languages, speaking all of them, including English, with a faint, unidentifiable accent, and they had become experts in antiques and decorative arts during leisurely afternoons browsing with their mother in castles, stately homes, and out-of-the-way shops where they would come away with dusty hands and some wonderful piece that their mother would clean up to reveal its hidden beauty and value.

Then their father was named U.S. ambassador to Algeria. Their parents decided the country was a dangerous place for American girls, and sent them to Juliette high school in Switzerland, where Sabrina roomed with Gabrielle de Martel and Stephanie with Dena Halpern. They earned blue ribbons in fencing and sailing, and then, in their last year, they quarreled, bitterly and painfully, over Stephanie's feeling that she was always in Sabrina's shadow, outshone by her more dramatic, more adventurous sister.

And so they separated, Stephanie to Bryn Mawr College in America, Sabrina to the Sorbonne in Paris. And then they found each other again, after Stephanie married

Garth and Sabrina married and divorced Denton. The ties that bound them, so that each felt her sister was the other half of her, could not be torn apart for long, and in the years that followed, they visited in America and London and talked for hours on the telephone. And then they joined a group of antique dealers on a trip to China, and while they were there, away from everything familiar, Stephanie—it was Stephanie, the less adventurous one, who thought of it—suggested changing places.

Such a simple idea; such a lark. They spent a week memorizing details of each other's life, and on the last day of the tour, in a Hong Kong hotel, they exchanged clothes and luggage, Stephanie took off her wedding ring and gave it to Sabrina, and they handed each other the keys to their houses. And then they went home.

Home, Sabrina thought, turning the doorknob of Ambassadors. It wasn't my home then; it was Stephanie's. But it became the most wonderful home I've ever had. The only home I ever want. She opened the door into the softly lit warmth of the shop, waiting for her eyes to adjust after the brightness outside. "Mrs. Andersen!" said Brian, coming forward. As he came closer, he sucked in a sharp breath of surprise. "Forgive me, Mrs. Andersen; it's still such a shock, seeing you. You could tell me you're Lady Longworth, back from the dead, and I'd believe you."

"Yes, Brian." She began to walk around the shop as if she were a customer. The room was patterned after an eighteenth-century salon, long and narrow, fronted with a square-paned window. The walls had dark oak wainscoting; the ceiling was molded in plaster octagons. Sabrina made a circuit of the room, then stood in the center, turning in place, eyeing the placement of furniture, the arrangement of small objects on shelves, the lighting.

"Very good, Brian," she said at last and heard his quick sigh of relief. Every time she walked in the door, Brian held his breath, even now, almost a year after Ambassadors had been taken over, as far as he knew, by Lady Longworth's sister from Evanston.

At first he and Nicholas Blackford had been condescending to the housewife from America, but Sabrina had stopped them cold. She had behaved like Sabrina, which confused them, and she had recklessly demonstrated her vast knowledge of antiques and even of London and the people in it. And they had accepted it. Everyone accepted it.

Because London was just like Evanston. Here, too, everyone found ways to explain away her mistakes. Well, they thought, Sabrina must have told her sister everything; she must have talked about us all the time. How else would Stephanie Andersen know so much? And while they were amazed by that astonishing conclusion, they were also satisfied by it.

So Brian sighed with relief and Sabrina went into her office and sat at the cherrywood table she used as a desk. *I could call Gaby now. That's what I'm here for, the only reason I came to London now instead of waiting until the end of the month. I'll call her now; she might be home.*

"There is a fair bit of mail I haven't had a chance to forward to America," Brian said, and brought in a basket piled high with letters, announcements of sales, and even invitations, on the off chance that Stephanie Andersen would be in London for various balls and dinners and country weekends.

It can wait; after all, it's not really urgent, it's just something I'm curious about.

She spent the afternoon at her desk. When the front bell rang and Brian left to take care of the casual customers who wandered in, mostly tourists at this time of year, Sabrina stayed behind the partition, refilling her teacup, nibbling on crackers, deep in the affairs of the shop. It was a place she loved, a place she had created when Denton's circle was snubbing her, calling her an American adventuress who had taken Denton for huge sums of money. In fact, she had refused money from him and when society ignored Ambassadors she had been in despair. But Princess Alexandra Martova rescued her. She hired Sabrina to renovate and furnish her new town house, and Sabrina's brilliant design won such wide attention and lavish praise that society could no longer ignore her. And Alexandra gave a series of parties that made her house and her character—once thought irrevocably tarnished because of the men in her past—respectable and intriguing. From that beginning they had grown to be the closest of friends, Alexandra became the center of London society, and Ambassadors was a stunning success.

Almost done. I can call in a few minutes. But . . . not from here. I'll call from home.

Of course it wasn't urgent, so she methodically worked through the pile of papers on her desk, then stood and fastened her cape with its single ebony button. "I'll be in tomorrow, Brian, but I don't know what time. I may stop in at Blackford's on the way."

Outside, beneath the streetlights that had come on in the early dark, she merged again with the crowds, this time office workers rushing to their tube stations to go home. She would stroll home, she thought, and call Gabrielle. Not the minute she got there; there was no reason to do it immediately, since it wasn't urgent. She would hang up her cape, put her hat in its box in the cloakroom, pour a glass of wine, climb the stairs to her fourth-floor sitting room, perhaps make a fire in the fireplace, settle herself on the chaise, then reach for the telephone.

But as she walked, her steps grew faster until she was out of breath when she reached her front door, and as soon as she was inside, she sat down at the telephone, still wearing her hat and cape, and called Gaby.

"I'm sorry, Mrs. Andersen," the secretary said, "Mr. and Mrs. Westermarck are driving through Italy; I can't even tell you how to reach them. They should be calling in, but I don't know when."

"Ask Mrs. Westermarck to call me," Sabrina said. "I'll be here for a few days; at least until Thursday or Friday."

She hung up, frustrated and more disappointed than she

would have expected. *What do I think she'll tell me?* She removed her gloves and hat and took them to the cloakroom, nestling them in their tissue-lined boxes, then hung up her cape. It doesn't matter, she told herself, it's just a day or two; I'm sure she'll call in a day or two.

She was sharply aware, as she was each time she came to London, of the emptiness of the house without Mrs. Thirkell bustling about to make her comfortable. Four floors of large, perfectly proportioned rooms filled with the finest antiques from England and the Continent: the walls covered with silk, the floors with Oriental rugs, the furniture with shantung and velvet and loose cashmere throws. A warm, sensual house, but empty, with a chill in the air. Mrs. Thirkell would have banished the chill. Mrs. Thirkell would have stored Sabrina's gloves and hat and hung up her cape; she would have said, "You look tired, my lady, why don't you go upstairs and I'll bring you a good tea in a little while. I'll wager you had no lunch; you don't take proper care of yourself."

But Mrs. Thirkell was now taking proper care of Sabrina's family, so Sabrina gathered up the mail she'd found scattered on the floor inside the front door, poured a glass of wine, and climbed the stairs to her sitting room. The velvet drapes were closed and the room had a hushed stillness that made her feel alone. She settled herself on the chaise and looked at her watch. Five-thirty. Eleven-thirty in the morning in Evanston. Maybe, she thought, and dialed Garth's office number.

In a minute she heard his voice. "Andersen," he said absently, absorbed in whatever he was doing, barely aware of the telephone, faintly annoyed at being interrupted.

"Are you too busy?" Sabrina asked, smiling, knowing the answer. "Shall I call back?"

"Never too busy, you know that. How are you? God, it's wonderful to hear your voice. I was thinking about you."

"You were thinking about science. At least I hope you were; I'd hate to hear about other scientists forging ahead while Professor Andersen daydreams about dalliances with his wife."

"Ah, but I wasn't daydreaming; I was thinking scientifically. I calculated the percentage of space that you occupy in our house, the space that's empty right now. It turns out to be one hundred percent. The house is empty, no matter how much we dash from room to room to create the impression of purposeful activity and therefore of occupancy. I miss you. We all miss you."

"There's a lot of empty space here, too." Sabrina could feel his arms around her, his body fitting itself to hers in bed. "What have you been doing?"

"We went to Nick's Fishmarket for dinner; I thought it was the only restaurant in Chicago that would be a match for Cliff's appetite. But I was wrong; he cut a swath through his plate like a tornado and asked for more. Penny ate like a lady, and made conversation like one. She's a good companion. Almost as good as her mother. And almost as beautiful. Did you find everything all right at Ambassadors?"

"So far. They sold a desk and a commode for good prices, even though the economy here is slow, and they've bought a few new pieces that are very fine. And the shop looks lovely, warm and attractive and inviting. I felt very good about it."

There was a pause. "Like coming home."

"Oh." She was still taken by surprise at how well he knew her: better than anyone ever had, except Stephanie. "No, not home, it can't be that, ever again, for me; not the shop or my house. But they're more than just a shop and a house; I've got a lot invested in them in time and energy and emotions; it's not as if I'm a tourist."

"They were home to you, for a long time. So they have familiarity. And freedom."

Sabrina winced slightly. *If I hadn't thought it this morning, he wouldn't have picked up on it.* "If you mean freedom from you, I don't want it. I want to be with you, I want to live with you and be part of you and make love to you. I miss your arms around me and your eyes smiling at me and the way we laugh together—"

"Wait a minute." Sabrina heard him put down the telephone; she heard a door close, and then he was back. "I don't want anyone to see the distinguished professor looking lovelorn, woebegone and awash in tears."

"Oh, my love." She caught her breath at the note in his voice and blinked back her own tears.

"Well." She could hear his voice change; he was settling back in his chair. "Tell me more about London. Have you seen any of your friends?"

"No. I may not even try; I'd just like to be quiet. I did call Gaby, but she and Brooks are driving through Italy. Did Penny get her art project in this morning? She didn't like it; she said the assignment was too restrictive . . . my fierce little free spirit—" Her breath caught again.

"She showed it to me; it was fine. Not her best, but she's learning that she can paint what someone tells her to paint and still be herself, with her own style, and that's not a bad lesson. And Cliff actually wrote a longer book report than he was assigned; he got energized when I suggested he compare one character's crisis to a game of soccer."

"Oh, wonderful; what a good idea. If it's soccer, it has to be interesting and important. Oh, Garth, I miss them. I miss you. You sound so close, as if you're around the corner."

"I wish I were." There was a pause. "When are you coming home?"

He was always reluctant to ask, but he always did. "As soon as I can." *As soon as I talk to Gaby. I know it's crazy, but I can't leave until I talk to her.* "There are a few things I have to do; I'll let you know. I hope in a couple of days. Garth, don't you have a class about now?"

"My God, what a memory. Yes, but I can be late."

"You hate to be late. You think professors have an obligation to give their students the full hour of class and all their attention."

"This woman forgets nothing. That's why I can never

26

lie to you; I'd forget which lie I told when, and with what degree of fervor, but you never would. Goodbye, my love; shall I call you next?"

"I'd like to talk to Penny and Cliff; I'll call tomorrow around breakfast time if that's all right."

"Hectic, as you know, but very much all right. Until then. I love you."

"I love you, Garth."

She sat very still after they hung up, as if, by not moving, she could freeze the moment and prolong the spell of their talking: the warmth of Garth's voice, the palpable feeling of his arms around her. I could go home tomorrow, she thought. There's nothing to keep me here.

Nothing but Gaby. And if I don't talk to her, I'll never get that phone call out of my mind: it will jump around inside me and keep me from thinking of more serious things. Just the way it is now.

But Tuesday and Wednesday came and went and Gaby did not call. "I haven't heard from them, Mrs. Andersen," the secretary said when Sabrina called on Thursday morning. "I'm sure Mrs. Westermarck will call as soon as she knows you're waiting to hear from her."

By Thursday noon she was so impatient she could barely sit still in her office. She thought of Garth and the children, and the three breakfast conversations they had had. *I want to go home. I want to be with my family.*

Well, then, forget it, she told herself. It was exactly what I told Garth: Gaby saw someone who looked like me. That's all it was. It was crazy for me to come to London, to try to talk to her . . . there's nothing she has to tell me.

She gazed at the yellow leaves swirling around the entrance to Ambassadors and, beyond them, gardens of russet and gold chrysanthemums across the street. A year ago she had watched the leaves turn in Evanston; it had been a glorious week of crisp fall days and she had moved smoothly through them, thinking it would be her only time there before returning to London. That was before she broke her wrist, before she knew Stephanie was having an affair with Max, before Stephanie wanted one last fling with him on his yacht. Before Stephanie was killed.

I know what I saw, and it was you or her. Or a ghost.

But it wasn't any of those. Not Sabrina, of course not Stephanie, and they all knew there were no ghosts.

You could tell me you're Lady Longworth, back from the dead, and I'd believe you.

"Stop it!" she said aloud. Ridiculous, crazy imaginings; what was wrong with her?

Something was driving her, something that would not leave her alone. *Jumping around inside me, keeping me from thinking of more serious things.*

I could go look, she thought.

Look for what?

I don't know. Someone who looks like me. A ghost.

And then she knew that all week she had been moving to this point; that it might be ridiculous and crazy—of course it was ridiculous and crazy—but she was going to try to find out for herself whom Gaby had seen.

She was going to Avignon.

CHAPTER 3

There was a plane to Marseilles early the next morning, and then the TGV to Avignon. Sitting on the upholstered seat of the high-speed train, Sabrina barely saw the landscape; she was telling herself how foolish she was. But even as she repeated it, she knew there was nothing else she could do. And when she stood in front of the small brick train station fronting on a circular drive jammed with cars and taxis, she knew exactly what her schedule would be. The hotel first, she thought. And then a tour.

The old walls of Avignon encircle the city, the huge stones worn by centuries of rain and wind to an indeterminate brown. Broad gates that had seen processions of Roman legionnaires, popes and their retinues, favor seekers, bandits, marauders, farmers, merchants, refugees and settlers now look down on traffic jams and strolling tourists, their heads tilted back to see the watchtowers spaced along the walls and, in the distance, the great towers of the Palace of the Popes. The narrow, twisting streets open onto small, intimate squares or large public ones; the stone buildings hide their secrets behind shutters of wrought iron or wood mottled with flaking paint.

Sabrina left her small bag in her room at L'Europe, barely glancing at the antiques with which it was furnished, or at the view, beyond paned windows, of the square that could be glimpsed through huge trees in the hotel courtyard. She walked out onto the Place Crillon, then stood in place, getting her bearings. She had never been to Avignon, but she had studied maps and books on the plane, and now, in search of a hat, she turned toward the Place de l'Horloge. *You took off your hat, one of those wide-brimmed straw ones with a long scarf tied around the crown, red and orange, and you were brushing back your hair . . .*

She had searched for such a hat in London, but no shops had summer hats in October and so, beneath the blazing Avignon sun, she walked to the shopping enclave, free of autos, just off the Place de l'Horloge and found Mouret, where every wall, floor to ceiling, was filled with every kind of hat ever dreamed of, from fur hats and hunting hats to opera hats and walking hats, summer hats, winter hats, and hats for every holiday.

Sabrina took three wide-brimmed ones and tried them on, angling them differently while the shopkeeper made admiring comments and adjusted the mirror for her. "Fine," she said, choosing one, "but I need a scarf as well."

"Alas, Mouret has no scarves," the shopkeeper said, "but DJ Boutique on Rue Joseph-Vernet . . ."

So she doubled back, almost to her hotel, and found the shop, where a riot of sun-drenched colors greeted her. She bought a long narrow scarf and wound it around the crown of the hat, letting the ends float free, just as she and Stephanie had done all the years they were growing up in Europe, just as their mother had taught them to do on a limited budget: to change a hat with scarves, feathers, flowers, so it always looked new.

She went out into the slanting rays of the late afternoon

sun, softer than before. People walked more slowly here than in Paris or London; they stopped to chat and gave way when others approached. Children in school uniforms with book-filled backpacks walked hand in hand or ran across the squares, chased by yapping dogs. *You were across the square, walking in the other direction.* Which square? There were several, linked by narrow streets or gracious esplanades, and Sabrina walked slowly, looking into people's faces, beginning at the highest part of the city, where, almost six hundred years earlier, a succession of seven popes had made Avignon their Rome, building a huge palace of domes and spires and great windows fronting on an enormous square that dwarfed everyone in it. So many people, Sabrina thought as she walked across the square; so many families, so many generations standing on these granite slabs, all with their own stories, their own problems, hoping for answers. And so am I.

She went into the small hotel at the edge of the square; she walked in and out of shops in the streets leading from it. What did she expect to find? Someone who would look at her with recognition; someone who would greet her. But no one did; she was anonymous. And so she went on, leaving the palace behind, walking purposefully, as if she knew exactly where she was going, and found herself once again at the Place de l'Horloge with the great clock for which it was named.

This time she paused and let herself enjoy the scene. It was the largest square in Avignon, like a small town lined with trees and shrubs, outdoor cafés and shops, with the magnificent white stone theater at one end and, nearby, a carousel of brightly painted horses and elephants and great throne-like seats, turning to the accompaniment of hurdy-gurdy music. Sabrina stood beside it, wishing Penny and Cliff were there, wishing she and Garth could sit on a matched pair of elephants and circle in stately grace for hours with no past, no telephones, nothing to break their private rhythm, while people came and went, filling the square with shifting colors and the soft French pronunciation of the south.

A stillness came as evening fell: the carousel still revolved, but the children went home to their supper, taking the dogs with them; shopkeepers swept up and straightened their shelves with slow, dreamlike movements; in the cafés people sat at small metal tables in a kind of reverie, reading newspapers and talking softly while waiters glided among them with trays held high.

Sabrina found a table and sat down. She felt she was waiting for something. No one questioned her being alone, as did the maître d's in London; cafés were a place for those who had no one with whom to share a meal. But I have a family to share my meals, Sabrina thought. A whole family, waiting for me.

Not yet, not yet. She was the one who was waiting now.

The next morning she had a brioche and coffee in the courtyard of her hotel, then went out again and walked again, up and down the streets, looking into shop windows, looking into people's faces, asking directions. She was waiting for someone to recognize her. But no one did; she wore her hat, grateful for it in the hot sun, and walked through Avignon, a stranger.

Just before noon, she walked on the cobbled street along the Sorgue River, cooler than the open squares, admiring the mossy waterwheels on the river's edge and the antique shops on the other side of the Rue des Teinturiers. Almost as mossy as the waterwheels, she thought with a smile, and went into a secondhand bookshop, a shop that offered embroidered waistcoats and decorative fabrics, and then into one crammed with antique maps. She had never dealt with maps and knew nothing about them, but she went in.

No one was in the small room, though she heard rustling and footsteps beyond a doorway in the corner. She moved slowly around a large table, idly lifting heavy folios, each map encased between protective sheets of plastic. The air was cool and musty, the only sounds the rustle of papers in the other room and Sabrina's steps on the dark wood floor as she moved to a wall of shallow drawers and began to pull them out, glancing at the maps inside. She had no reason to be there; she had no idea of the value or rarity of the maps she saw in drawer after drawer, but she did not want to leave. Twice she thought about it—*there are other places to go; it's a big town and I have only today*—but both times she stayed where she was.

"Good morning, madame, may I be of service?" A small man came through the doorway, stooped over a cane. His white hair was in disarray; his white beard was trimmed to a neat point. "I'm sorry I kept you waiting; I was wrapping some maps for a customer— Ah, madame, have you come for the Tavernier? Perhaps your friend could not wait to have it shipped; it is not surprising: he was so excited about it. I have it wrapped for you; I will get it."

Sabrina's heart began to pound; she felt herself sway.

"Madame! Here, a chair, oh, I'm so sorry, only a stool, but still . . . please, please, madame, it is perhaps the heat outside?"

He was holding her arm, but Sabrina gently moved away. "Thank you, I don't need to sit down; I'm fine." A map had fallen from her hand and she saw its delicate traceries and pale colors waver as she stared at it.

"There is a doctor, madame, not far from here; I can take you to him."

"No, really, I don't need a doctor." She smiled at him. "You're probably right; it was the heat." She paused, then made a decision. "However, I must tell you that I am confused. I was not here recently; I have never been in your shop. Whoever was here must have been someone who looked like me."

He was frowning at her. "Madame makes some kind of joke? Everything is the same, the hat, the scarf, the hair . . . and the face! Someone so beautiful, madame, so in love, so eager to learn, is not quickly forgotten. And your friend, who knows so well the world of maps; I do not forget him either." He bent to retrieve the map from the floor. "It was a pleasure to talk to him; not many these days have such knowledge. And he is a painter, not a cartographer! It astonishes me still."

Sabrina shook her head. "There is some mistake. Did they tell you their names?"

"You are asking me if you told me your name, madame? You did not. I asked your friend if he had a card, but he said no and made a little joke, that painters have canvases but not cards. No, madame, your friend did not tell me his name and neither did you." He looked at her pointedly, waiting for her to tell him, and end whatever game she was playing.

Whoever they were, Sabrina thought, they had some reason for not telling you. A long conversation about a shopkeeper's wares, a possible purchase, almost always led to an exchange of names.

"My name is Stephanie Andersen," she said, "but that is not the name of the woman who was in your shop."

"Madame!" he exploded. He turned away to replace the map in its proper drawer, then turned again to face her. "If you have changed your mind about buying the Tavernier, that is one thing. I understand that you are not especially interested in maps—that you deal with antique furniture instead—but . . ."

"What?"

"I beg your pardon, madame?"

"You said antique furniture."

"*Mon dieu!* Madame, I am baffled that you insist on playing this very strange game; it is nothing to me what your name is—"

"Did they say where they live? What neighborhood in Avignon, or nearby town?"

He flung up his hands. "No, madame, you did not tell me that."

"What kind of painter is he?"

"As you know, he did not tell me."

"Did you watch them after they left your shop? Where did they go?"

34

"I do not know where you went, madame. Nor am I interested in finding out. Now, if you will excuse me, I have work to do." Furious with her, he returned to the other room.

Sabrina stood indecisively, then slowly left the shop and retraced her steps along the river and returned to the center of town. The shops would be closing soon for the afternoon break, and by the time they reopened, she would be on her way to Marseilles to catch her flight to London; otherwise she would miss the morning flight to Chicago. But what difference did it make whether the shops were open or closed? If this woman, this *impostor*—for what else could she be?—was determined not to tell her name to shopkeepers, and her friend was determined, too, what good would it do to go from shop to shop to try to find out who they were and what they were doing and why?

But he's a painter. If he was telling the truth about that, he would have wanted to go to galleries. Or maybe he needed more supplies.

Suddenly filled with energy, she went to the tourist office on Cours Jean-Jaurès and got a list of art galleries and artists' supply shops. There were only two supply shops, and the first, Monet Fournitures Artistiques, was a few blocks away. She walked quickly, ignoring the heat, her face shaded by her hat.

"Ah, madame, I am so glad you return," said the tall woman behind the counter. She had broad shoulders, her cheeks were round and full, and she wore oversize glasses that made her look like an amiable owl. "I left out one brush in wrapping your package; I have it here." She brought a narrow box from behind the counter and held it out to Sabrina with a wide smile. "Otherwise I would have had to go looking for you, which would have been a long process, since I did not know where to look."

Sabrina avoided the truth; it was too difficult. "I didn't tell you where I live?"

"No, madame, the subject did not come up." The woman tilted her head and contemplated Sabrina's pale face calmly and with sympathy; she was prepared to accept any kind of infirmity or eccentricity. "Did you think you did?"

Sabrina laughed. "No, I know I didn't. Did I tell you my name?"

"No, madame, and neither did your companion."

Sabrina frowned slightly. "How do you know he was not my husband?"

"In fact, madame, at first I thought he was, from your closeness, your joy at being together, so very evident, especially to someone recently widowed, but I overheard a conversation when I left the room for a moment and it was clear that someone else was the husband."

Their eyes met. They liked each other. "I'm sorry about your husband," Sabrina said gently, and the woman bowed her head in acknowledgment. Her hands gripped each other; tears were in her eyes. A loving woman, Sabrina thought. So loving that she was willing to indulge a stranger in a bizarre conversation rather than issue a challenge and perhaps cause distress. A wonderful woman, a caring woman.

And Sabrina knew she could not intrude with her own concerns on memories of a dead husband.

Slowly, reluctantly, she turned to go. But the woman's voice stopped her. "Madame asked me if you told me your name."

She turned back. "Yes."

"As I said, you did not." In gratitude for Sabrina's sympathy, the shopkeeper no longer spoke as if it had been Sabrina in her shop. "The woman did not tell me her name. But when I was in the other room—I was searching for a kind of gesso that I thought I had, and indeed I did—she and her friend were talking together and he called her by her name. And she spoke her husband's name."

Sabrina looked at her, waiting.

"Her name was Sabrina," the woman said. "And the husband's name was Max."

Part II

CHAPTER 4

*T*he explosion ripped open the *Lafitte*'s staterooms, flinging debris in a wide arc above the Mediterranean. The roar echoed off the white and pink buildings on the shore, causing cries of alarm in the streets and cafés of Monte Carlo. Those who had binoculars grabbed them, but saw little in the turbulence of waves and wreckage. On the ship, within seconds, water flooded the elegant quarters where Max Stuyvesant had entertained and made love, and the crew's quarters below, and within minutes the ship began to sink. It was five-thirty in the afternoon of an overcast October day.

Stephanie and Max were flung across the lounge by the force of the explosion. Stephanie's head struck a corner of a steel-and-glass cocktail table, and she lay beside it like a rag doll. Max was thrown against the end of the mahogany bar, and he huddled there, trying to catch his breath, the words *the bomb, too early, the bomb, too early . . .* pounding through his head.

He heard no screams or cries for help, only an eerie silence broken by the angry slapping of waves against the ship as it rocked and shuddered beneath him. *Christ, blew the whole thing . . . .* He forced himself up on all fours and shook his head like a dog shaking off water. Pain shot through his left shoulder, and he shifted his weight to his right arm as he tried to stand. He fell back and, muttering a steady stream of curses, crawled across the room to the high, wide window, not thinking of anything now but getting away. He pulled himself up to the windowsill, grunting, swearing, soaked with sweat. The glass was shattered; he had a clear way out.

With his right arm he pulled himself up to the sill, then he swiveled and swung one leg out. And as he turned, he saw Stephanie on the floor, her eyes closed, blood running down her face.

"Sabrina—" It came out as a gasp. *My God, they've killed her.* He wiped away the sweat running into his eyes and thought he saw her move. Or it might have been the rocking of the ship. "Christ!" he burst out. He swung his leg back into the lounge to go to her, then stopped. He couldn't wait; he had to get away. She was dead and he was alive; his men would be waiting for him, and he had to get the hell out of here before the ship went down. He pushed his other leg through the window and tensed to leap into the water.

But he could not stop himself from taking one quick look back, and when he did he saw Stephanie's head roll to the side into a thin stream of water trickling in beneath the door. As he watched, the water flowed faster and then the force of it burst the door open and a torrent gushed in. Max knew he could not leave her like that. He had to know if she was alive, and if she was, he had to keep her with him.

He swung his legs around and dropped back into the room, gasping with the pain. Broke something, he thought. No, probably not that bad. He knelt in the water beside Stephanie. "Sabrina! God damn it, Sabrina, wake up, help me . . .

"*Merde.*" He was cursing now in whatever language

broke through the panic building inside him. He held his fingers against Stephanie's neck and found the thread of a pulse. Alive. God damn, she's alive. A wellspring of joy sprang up within him, so powerful it stunned him. Wait. Think about it later. Got to get us out of here.

He gripped Stephanie's hands and, crawling backwards through the water, dragged her to the window, fighting dizziness and the pain in his leg and left shoulder. She was deadweight, and he slipped on the wet floor as he struggled to push her up until she lay over the windowsill like a burlap sack. Gasping, coughing, he pulled himself up to sit beside her and catch his breath. No time, he thought; no time to breathe. He pulled off his shoes, and Stephanie's, then lifted her and shoved her through the window and into the sea. And as she dropped, he dove in, just behind her.

It had been two minutes since the explosion.

He hit the water clumsily and fought his way to the surface. Debris churned around him in the waves rolling outward as the ship went down; he felt a piece of metal cut his hand, another struck his thigh. Treading water, he looked around. He was on the side of the ship away from shore, and except for some small boats speeding in his direction, he seemed to be alone. "Sabrina! Sabrina, for Christ's sake . . ." Sputtering, coughing, he took a few lurching sidestrokes, favoring his bad shoulder, and found himself at the stern of the ship. He saw the hole in its side—*the bomb, the fucking bomb, wasn't supposed to go off until*—and then he saw Stephanie, floating face down in water red with her blood, shards of wood and metal swirling around her.

He reached her in an instant and twined his fingers in her thick hair to yank her head back and out of the water. He rolled her over, then hooked his left arm beneath her chin and swam with his other arm away from the ship. His clothes dragged him down, the water was colder than he had imagined; his head and shoulder throbbed, and he had to force his legs to keep moving. "*Bastardos,* fucking *bastardos,''* he said aloud, meaning all of them, the ones who had set the bomb to kill him, and his own men who should have been there by now to pick him up.

Stephanie floated, her face colorless, pale veins tracing across her dead white eyelids. Max could see the gash in her forehead now; he thought it was not as bad as all the blood had made it seem. She'll be all right, he thought. She'll be fine. She's tough; I always liked her toughness.

But he was so tired he could barely stay afloat. It would be easier without her. Easier alone. He'd known that all his life: it was easiest to go alone. But he held on to her. He remembered that spurt of joy when he knew she was alive, though he could not recapture it now. *Verfluchen,* he swore wearily. Sons of bitches. Said they'd be close by . . .

The motorboat was beside him before he saw it; the men had cut the engine and maneuvered through the debris to come close without setting up high waves. "Sorry, boss," one of them said. "Didn't think it'd go off this early. You want her, too?"

"Fuck it!" Max exploded.

"Okay, right." The two men reached down and dragged Stephanie into the boat. "Grab my arm," the first one said to Max, and pulled him in as the other man started the engine. The small boat leaped away, its prow high out of the water. Max lay beside Stephanie in the bottom of the boat, out of sight, while the men kept fishing poles and nets raised high and looked straight ahead as they tore through the water.

Max slid a life preserver beneath Stephanie's head, then ripped off his shirt and pressed it to the bleeding gash in her forehead. Holding it there, he lay back again, breathing deeply. Now, he thought; now I can breathe. But then he heard one of the men say, "She's gone," and he raised himself and looked behind them. He stared at the widening circle of debris and the motorboats bobbing a little distance away. Rescue boats were approaching from shore. That was all he saw. The *Lafitte* was gone.

"A beaut, that bomb," one of his men said cheerfully.

Max looked at him until the man's cheer faded. "Why the fuck did you wait so long to tell me about it?"

"I didn't wait! I told you as soon as I knew! I didn't hear word one about a bomb, about any *plans* for a bomb, until today. I don't know; maybe they were starting to wonder about me—"

"I pay you so they don't wonder about you. I pay you to make them trust you. I pay you to get information to me in time for me to use it."

"Well, you did; you got out in—"

"None of us should have been on board in the first place."

"I didn't hear a thing until this afternoon, boss, honest to God. I called you on your plane, but you'd landed and the pilot said you'd just left for the dock. I got down there as soon as I could, but you were gone, so I called you on the ship's radio; what else could I do?" There was a silence. "So you went forward, right? I mean, when you knew the bomb was under your stateroom . . ."

"We went forward."

The others had been unpacking in their rooms, but Max had insisted on going to the lounge. "You can unpack later, Sabrina," he had said. "I want a drink; I want you to see Monte Carlo in this light." And they had gone forward.

In fact, he'd thought he had plenty of time. His man, who had worked his way into Denton's organization, had told him the bomb was set to go off at seven, when everyone was dressing for dinner. But Max was not one to sit calmly on top of a bomb without doing something about it. He had planned to leave the lounge after a few minutes and get the engineer to go with him to find the bomb. But then it had occurred to him that the engineer could be part of the plot. Whoever brought the bomb on board and found a place to hide it and then left the ship without anyone being suspicious . . . whoever did that couldn't have managed it without help from someone on the crew.

He had been thinking about that while pouring drinks in the lounge. "It looks like a little girl's birthday cake," Stephanie had said, looking at the pastel colors and rococo designs on the buildings of Monte Carlo, stepping up the hill from the shore.

Max brought her a drink and saw the sudden cloud that shadowed her face. "What is it?"

"I was thinking about little girls' birthdays," she said, and he grasped her hand, angry at her for letting her thoughts take her away from him. He put her glass in her hand and curved her fingers around it. And then the bomb went off.

In the small motorboat, Max cradled Stephanie's head against him to protect her from the pounding vibration of the engine. They were racing west, toward Nice, the beaches and harbors of the Côte d'Azur on their right. The sun was still bright, but the beach was emptying as bronzed men and women gathered possessions, packed them into brightly striped raffia bags, and strolled to the hotels lining the shore.

"Almost there, boss," said the man at the wheel. "Burt's waiting at the dock; he took care of the helicopter. Trouble is, we didn't know you'd need a stretcher or an ambulance or, you know, so there won't be anybody waiting when we get to Marseilles."

"Burt can call from the helicopter. An ambulance and a hospital."

"Right; he'll know where to go; he's lived there all his life."

Nice was a jumble of buildings behind the forest of ships' masts in the harbor; the cafés on the Promenade des Anglais were crowded with people settling in for late afternoon drinks. Max looked at them, thinking that that familiar life was closed to him for a long time. Then he turned away as his small boat chugged slowly to a deserted part of the harbor near a cluster of squat warehouses, and eased into place at the far end of the dock.

A black Renault was parked close to the dock; beside it

stood a short, slender priest with a brown beard. He squatted as Max's men tied the boat to the dock. "I heard you were coming in today; I came to greet— *Mon Dieu*, Max, you're hurt!" He leaned into the boat, his hand extended. "But who is this? She's bleeding . . . Max, what happened?"

"An explosion; the ship went down." Max grasped the priest's hand and clambered out of the boat, gritting his teeth against the pain that shot through his arm. "I'm glad to see you, Robert. We'll need a hospital in Marseilles."

"You need one now. We'll forget Marseilles for today; it can wait—"

"It can't wait. Another half hour, Robert, that's all. Do you know a doctor in Marseilles?"

"Of course. But, Max, this is not wise; we don't know how badly she—" He saw Max's face darken. "Well, then, to Marseilles. Gently, my friends!" he said as the men in the boat lifted Stephanie's inert form and laid her on the dock. The gash on her head was bleeding again, her sodden hair dripped water mixed with blood, and bruises and small cuts covered her swollen face and arms. "Into the car. Max, you first, the back seat, and hold her when we put her in . . . Now, my friends, lift her gently but speedily; the helicopter is waiting."

Stephanie lay against Max, her head rolling from side to side as Robert careened around corners until Max held her tightly to his chest. He watched the buildings that seemed to race past on both sides, the palm trees and flower gardens and policemen directing traffic, but his eyes were dulled by exhaustion and a low, throbbing anger that held him in its grip. *Fool, fool, to let them get ahead of me.*

They had never been able to do it before; they'd never been able to touch him. I got lazy, he thought, stupid, let down my guard; didn't give a damn about anything but—he looked at the woman in his arms—about anything but Sabrina.

It wasn't quite true: he had conducted his business and made careful plans to wind up his activities in England and disappear when the time was right, but for the past few weeks he had let himself be distracted from business and the survival and prosperity of Max Stuyvesant; he had been absorbed by thoughts of this woman, so different from the Sabrina he had known years before, when she was married to Denton.

As if she mesmerized me, he thought: Max Stuyvesant so mesmerized by Sabrina Longworth that I forgot to keep looking over my shoulder, forgot to watch and wait and listen . . . and so the bastards almost killed me. Almost killed both of us.

He tightened his hold. She was alive. He let himself recapture the joy he had felt on the ship when her pulse had fluttered beneath his fingers. She was alive and she was his. And he knew he was more than mesmerized. He was fiercely. possessively in love with her.

"All right, Max," said Robert, and they pulled up beside the helicopter. Two men were waiting; they helped Max and Robert bring Stephanie inside, and in a moment the blades were spinning in the muggy air, singing a high, sustained pitch and lifting the helicopter from the ground.

They flew low, over the hotels and villas of the Côte d'Azur, one of the great playgrounds of the world, to the dense, industrialized sprawl of Marseilles and, directed by Robert, to the roof of a hospital built in the shape of a cross. The helicopter door was opened and a team of men and women in white coats took Stephanie from Max, lifting her onto a stretcher. He did not see her again until the next day.

She lay in a narrow bed in a narrow whitewashed room, with the morning sun streaming in. She wore a white gown beneath a white coverlet; a wide white bandage was wound around her forehead; a clear, shiny ointment and small white patches were on the cuts and bruises all over her face and arms. Her eyes were closed, the eyelids quivering as she slept. Her magnificent hair had been cut short; it was a curly halo, chestnut gleaming red and gold in the sun, the only color in the room.

Max sat in a hard metal chair beside the bed. He took her hand from beneath the coverlet and held it between his. Tubes ran from her other hand to three clear plastic bags hanging from a metal stand at the foot of the bed. Max could see the slow drip of fluid from the bags into the tubes, and he thought of the other time he had seen that, when he was nine years old, sitting beside his mother's hospital bed in London. He had not thought of his mother for years; he had not thought of himself as a boy since his father had disappeared when he was twelve. Max had been a man all his life.

But the clutch of fear he felt as he watched the fluid drip into the plastic tubes brought back the child he had been, and he had to wrench his thoughts away from that terrified boy and away from his mother. She had died; this woman would live. He sat in the metal chair as the hours passed and the nurses replaced the empty bags with full ones, and the drops moved slowly down their channels, agonizingly slowly, into the veins of the pale hand lying motionless on the bed, and he held the other hand, moving away only when the doctor made his twice daily examination. Each time, as soon as he was gone, Max moved back to the hard chair and again took that unresponsive hand in his.

He was willing her to live and recover, even as he spent the hours trying to figure out what to tell her if she did. They had to go into hiding and change their names; he had already used her new name when he filled out the forms admitting her to the hospital. They had to go into hiding and stay there until he found a way to eliminate those who had set the bomb. Until he knew they were safe.

He had made plans for hiding. He had known for some time that he would have to leave England and change his operations. When newspaper stories began appearing on the smuggling of antiquities, he had known it would have to be soon. At the same time, he was being pressured by Denton to expand their operations just when he knew he had to cut back or stop altogether, at least for a while. And then, because the damn fools who worked for him had started a little sideline of selling forged art to galleries, and the reporters were after that story, too, he knew another spotlight could be turned on him. Every week he moved up the date for disappearing. He had made plans and everything was in place . . . but the plans were for one person, not for a couple.

Now he had to rethink all of it. He could handle their living arrangements: Robert would help him find a larger place for them to live than the small apartment he had rented for himself in Aix-en-Provence. But to keep her with him, to persuade her to give up her life in London, her antique shop, her friends, her very identity, required either that she loved him so passionately that nothing else mattered—loved him as he knew now he loved her—or that she was afraid.

She did not love him. He knew that. But he was sure she would, if they had time. And so he would have to convince her that she was in danger, and that safety lay only in staying with him.

His thoughts raced, then settled on this solution while he sat beside her and watched her as the hours passed. He ate, dully and automatically, the food the nurses' aides brought him, and answered their questions in his fluent but oddly accented French that made them look at him curiously, wondering where he came from; and he dozed through the nights on a cot they put beside the bed. And then, on the third day, Stephanie opened her eyes.

Max felt again that leap of joy and he leaned over her, his hands clasping hers, and started to say her name. But then he stopped. She was staring straight up, at the ceiling, not moving, and something about that blank stare and the stillness of her body made him fearful and kept him silent. He tightened his grip on her hand, and waited.

The minutes stretched out. Finally, very slowly, she turned her head. Their eyes met in a long look, and Max knew that she had no idea who he was.

In an instant, everything changed. It might be only temporary—a few days, perhaps only a few hours—but if it was not, if she really had lost her memory and it held, it would be as if he had been given a gift. Max had lived a lifetime on his wits, on the ability to incorporate new information instantly and adapt it to that moment's situation. Now, meeting Stephanie's blank stare, he knew that this was far better than his other solution. He would not know for sure for a while yet, but he had an alternative now, and if it worked out, he could not have planned events more perfectly. "Sabrina," he said, and watched her face.

She frowned and echoed it, her voice thin and tentative. "Sabrina . . ."

"You don't remember?" He spoke in French, silently willing her to reply in French. Her command of the language was as good as his and her accent was better, and he assumed that if, indeed, she had no memory, she would follow what she heard and saw. He would make sure that she followed him in everything, and clung to him, and belonged to him. "Well, if you don't remember, we won't worry about it now; we'll deal with it later. You've had a shock, you've been hurt." He bent down and kissed her cheek, then kissed her lightly on the lips. "You'll be all right, Sabrina; you'll be fine."

"Sabrina." She tested it on her tongue, then shook her head. *"Je ne comprends pas . . ."* Max let out his breath. Perfect. Stephanie's eyes widened as the enormity of it struck her—*I don't understand*—and she began to cry. "I don't understand. I don't know anything. Why don't I know?"

"If you please, monsieur." The doctor was behind Max. "If you will wait outside . . ."

Max did not look at him. "I'm staying with my wife."

Stephanie's eyes widened. She stared at him.

"This is my patient, monsieur; I intend to examine her."

After a moment, Max relinquished Stephanie's hand and backed away from the bed. He leaned against the wall, making it clear, by his folded arms and unwavering stare, that that was as far as he would go.

The doctor fastened a blood pressure cuff around Stephanie's arm. "You do not know your name, madame?"

"Go away." Still crying, Stephanie rolled her head back and forth, as if trapped, then looked away, through the narrow window at the blue-white sky. "Go away, go away, I don't want you here. I don't want anybody here."

"Madame has had an accident," the doctor said calmly. "It is necessary that we discover the extent of the damage, physically and mentally." He bent over Stephanie, holding her eyes open to shine a tiny flashlight into them. He took her pulse, pulled out his stethoscope to listen to her heart, thumped her chest. He pulled back the coverlet and struck her knees and Achilles tendon with a tiny hammer. He raised and lowered her arms and legs, examining her bruises, then covered her again, neatly, laying her hand gently at her side on top of the coverlet.

Stephanie lay still, unresponsive, almost unaware, staring at the ceiling past the doctor's fringe of gray hair. She winced when he began to unwrap the bandage around her head. "Ah, *très bien,* this will heal," he murmured, and rewrapped the wound with fresh gauze.

He gazed at Stephanie's profile. He could not place her nationality. She spoke perfect French, but with a faint, unidentifiable accent that made him sure she was not French. The man most assuredly was not French; he spoke fluently but with an accent that was vaguely German. Two people who probably have spent their lives in many places, the doctor mused; intelligent people who are quick with languages. The world has more of them every day: sophisticated chameleons. The woman, even bruised and injured, was extraordinarily beautiful, and her beauty and fearfulness drew him, but he knew he could help her only as much as the husband permitted.

"So, madame." He spoke to Stephanie's profile, aware of Max's unwavering stare on his back. "Physically, you improve. You are a fortunate woman; your wound will heal, your hair will grow and cover the scar, your bruises will disappear. We have superb plastic surgeons who can repair the damage to your face. But now we must talk about the other injury, to your memory. There are many things you do not remember?"

Stephanie did not reply.

"Your name, madame. Tell me your first name. And your maiden name."

She stared at the ceiling.

"Or any name that comes to you, madame, a friend's name, perhaps, an acquaintance, someone who works for you; it might lead you closer to your own. Madame, I cannot help you unless I know the extent of the problem. Can you tell me your name? Or anything else about yourself, your friends, your life in . . . where is it you come from, madame?"

"I don't know, I don't know, I don't know!" Stephanie held up her hands, one of them trailing the plastic tubes, and turned the palms toward her, then away, then toward her again. "Hands," she said. "My hands." Her gaze raced around the room. "Wall. Window. Sky. Bed. Hands. Is that right? Doctor," she said, and pointed at him. She pointed. "Left. Right. Up. Down. Is that right? Was everything right?"

"Yes, madame, yes, yes," the doctor said. "What else do you know?"

"Ceiling," Stephanie said. "Door. Sheets. Pillow."

"And your name is Madame . . ." The doctor let the word dangle. "Quickly, madame. Your name is Madame . . ."

Stephanie shook her head. "I don't know. I know *things*. Why is that? Why don't I know anything else? What am I going to do?"

"You'll get well," Max said. "You'll be with me and you'll get well." He came to the bedside and spoke to the doctor. "How soon can you arrange for the plastic surgeon? Everything else I can take care of."

The doctor ignored him. "Something has made you forget many things, madame. Perhaps not for long, and perhaps not everything; I would like to help you find out. It may have been the blow to your head or the trauma of the accident—"

"What accident? Nobody said anything about an accident."

The doctor looked at her closely. "A few minutes ago I said madame had had an accident. You do not remember that?"

"No. You said an accident? I don't remember. What accident?"

"Your husband said your motorboat rammed the end of a dock and there was a fire . . ." He turned to Max. "You're sure that was what happened, monsieur? A ship exploded off Monaco last week; you were not involved in that?"

"I told you what happened. I didn't hear about a ship exploding; when was it?"

"Oh, Monday or Tuesday, I don't remember. It must have been about the time of your accident. But of course you could not have been in that other one; I understand there were no survivors. A terrible thing." He turned back to Stephanie. "You remember nothing about a motorboat?"

"No." Stephanie turned her head to look at Max. "My husband." She held up her hands again, spreading the fingers wide, looking at the bare third finger on her left hand.

Max moved in, bringing Stephanie's hands down to the bed, holding her free one between his. He had had time, standing there, to think everything through, and now it was all in place; everything that he had planned for the past year reformulated to a new life not just for Max Stuyvesant but for Sabrina Longworth as well. He spoke to Stephanie, but his words were for the doctor, too. "We met five days ago, at a party in Cap-Ferrat; we were married the next day, and we went for the boat ride that afternoon. You've been unconscious for three days. We didn't take the time to buy a ring; we planned to wait until we found the perfect one. We planned a honeymoon, too, and we'll have it, and you'll have your ring, but first we'll get you well and take you home."

Stephanie was watching him through the tears still welling in her eyes. "I don't know who you are."

"Max Lacoste."

"And I—?"

"Sabrina Lacoste."

"What was madame's name before she was married?" the doctor asked.

"Robion," Max said promptly.

The doctor sighed. "There must be half a million Robions in France. But you, monsieur, you can tell madame who she is, where she comes from, who is her family . . ."

Max was shaking his head, still looking at Stephanie. "We didn't talk about our past; we thought there was plenty of time for that. We talked about the future. We had so many ideas about what we would do together, so many hopes and dreams . . . and all of them can still come true."

"Sa-bri-na." She said it as she had before, testing it. "Sabrina. Sabrina. Sabrina." She shook her head. "It doesn't seem right."

"Where do you live?" the doctor asked Max.

"Not far. I asked you about a plastic surgeon for madame; I'm anxious to get her home."

"I want to give her a week to get her strength back; then we'll have the plastic surgeon come in. But I also urge you to let me bring in a psychologist for counseling. She should be evaluated—"

"If we're married," Stephanie said, "what was my name before?"

"I told you," Max said. "Robion."

"You did? Robion? That was my name?" Her eyes widened. "When did you tell me?"

53

"A few minutes ago; it isn't important."

"It is, it is." Her voice rose. "I can't remember *any-thing?*"

"You must not be alarmed," the doctor said quickly. "This is not unusual, this form of amnesia; it often occurs after a trauma. It is called anterograde amnesia and it almost always disappears within a few days. But, madame, you also have a kind of amnesia known as retrograde amnesia, which can be more persistent. I think you should be fully evaluated by skilled professionals who can diagnose the particular form your amnesia has taken and help you with the trauma you have undergone, perhaps help you find ways to jar loose your memories."

"My wife and I will deal with her trauma," Max said.

"But there are those, monsieur, who are so familiar with cases like this . . ."

Leave me alone! The thought was in English, not French, and as she realized it Stephanie was engulfed in a wave of terror. She jerked her hand from Max's grip and slid it beneath the coverlet; she closed her eyes and shut both men out. Their voices rumbled above her, deep and antagonistic, but it was like trains going by—trains, Stephanie thought; was I on a train? Where did I go?—a rush, a roar, with no meaning, and she lay stiffly beneath the sound, her hands clenched, afraid to move. She was alone in emptiness—a fog, a cloud, the sky, all of space, infinity—with nothing to gaze upon or touch or grasp. She tried to think of a place where she belonged—a house, a room, a chair, a bed—but there was nothing. She tried to picture a town, a neighborhood, a street, but there was only emptiness: no scenery, no roadway, no guideposts. Only a muffling, terrifying emptiness.

Sabrina. Sabrina . . . what? What did he say my last name was? He told me, didn't he? Oh, God, I can't . . .
She began to shiver. The name Sabrina meant nothing to her, and she could not remember her last name.

"What is my last name?" she asked without opening her eyes.

"Lacoste," said Max.

Sabrina Lacoste. And he is . . . he is . . . Max. He said Max. Max Lacoste. Her shivering would not stop. That name meant nothing to her, either. She felt she was falling soundlessly through that terrible fog of nothingness, absolutely alone, unconnected to anything or anyone. She saw herself reaching out her hand, searching for someone to clasp it, but there was no one. Oh, help me, she cried silently, tears stinging behind her eyelids. Help me find a place to belong.

"Sabrina." Max's voice was the only sound in the room, and she opened her eyes. He towered above her, tall and broad-shouldered, with shaggy red eyebrows and frizzled red hair. He had slightly bulging gray eyes, a heavy, sensual mouth, and large, well-shaped hands. He carried himself with purpose and moved with a restless energy that seemed to create eddies in the air around him, unsettling the room. *My husband.* The thought sank into the muffling fog, and Stephanie repeated it, trying to make it seem right.

"We'll go home soon." His voice was relaxed; he seemed to control everything around him, and Stephanie stared at him, conscious of his strength. "I'm going to buy a house in Cavaillon." The idea had come to him just a few minutes before; he knew the area, a perfect one for privacy, and Robert ran a Catholic school there; he would find them a house. "You'll love it; it's very beautiful and quiet."

"Cavaillon?"

"Where we're going to live."

"Did you tell me that, too?"

"No, why should I, in front of the doctor? No one needs to know where we're going. You'll like the town and our house; you'll be very happy."

"I don't want to go there."

"Indeed. Where would you like to go?"

There was a long silence. The tears came again, running soundlessly along her cheeks, wetting the pillow and disappearing into the emptiness where she was suspended, alone. "I don't know."

"Of course not. And in fact, where else would you go but home, with your husband, where you belong? Listen to me, Sabrina. I love you. And you love me. You belong with me, and you'll stay with me, and do as I say; that's the only way I can guarantee your safety and your happiness. Do you understand that?"

His voice pierced the thick fog that swirled around her. *Safety. Max will keep me safe.*

From what? she wondered. But then it was gone, and all she knew was that she was not alone after all. Someone would be there when she reached out her hand. Max would be there. Max loved her. And Max would keep her safe.

*F*or two months the hospital was Stephanie's whole world. The people she talked to were doctors and nurses and other patients in the solarium, but much of the time she was in her own room on the top floor, where Max had had her moved after the first week. At one end of the room stood a brightly patterned armchair and chaise and a low table with books and magazines, and after each of the three operations on her face, Stephanie spent the days curled up in the armchair, reading, or lying on the chaise. She would gaze for hours at the blue of the Mediterranean blurring into the blue of the sky, and at the boats moving in and out of the harbor while great gulls swooped around them in widening circles and then, with a flapping that could be heard above the creaking of the ships' masts and the boisterous calls of fishermen, flew out to sea and disappeared in the mist.

Twice a week a psychologist came to her room after Max finally allowed it. Max did not join her for any of their talks, though Stephanie often asked him to; his excuse was that he had a great deal of work to do. And it seemed that he had: he had begun leaving the hospital as soon as she moved to her new room, at first for an hour or two, then for a whole day and, once, for almost a week.

He had put off going because he thought she would die without him there to watch over her. He had come to believe that it was only his presence that kept her alive: he had saved her when the ship exploded, and now he was saving her again, hour by hour, day by day, by willing her to live. The first time he left to go to the warehouse on the dock with the sign Lacoste et fils over the door, he had fought with himself the whole time not to rush back. But he told himself it was a weak, childish fantasy, and because he abhorred anything that was weak or recalled childish fears, he pushed the thought from him and stayed away all that day, and next morning left again and did not look back after saying goodbye.

In fact, he had to go; he had no choice. He had to know what had happened to the people on the yacht, and what the police had found. He had told the doctors that the accident had occurred in a motorboat when it struck a dock, but he maintained that fiction only within the hospital; he needed Robert, and so Robert had to know the truth.

The day after Stephanie awakened, when for the first time he had let himself think of something else, he had asked Robert to go to Monaco for him; now Robert had returned, and they were to meet in a café in a corner of town where no one would know them. The newspapers had reported almost nothing beyond the bare story of an explosion on the French-registered *Lafitte* with apparently no survivors. The doctor in the hospital had said the same thing. *No survivors.* How could they know that? No one in Monte Carlo knew how many were on the ship, or who they were. The *Lafitte* was registered under the name of Max's French company, Lacoste et fils, and his crew chief signed either Max's name or his own when registering with the dockmaster. If he had signed Max's name and the police had found bodies in the water but not Max's, why wasn't that in the newspaper stories? None of it made sense, and Max chewed on the ambiguities while Robert made arrangements to go to Monte Carlo and then was there for three days.

"Max." Robert took his hand and held it, searching his face. "You look much better than the last time I saw you. How is the lady we took to the hospital?"

"Still there; she'll be there for a while." They sat in a booth and the waiter brought them two beers. "I want to talk to you about her, Robert, but first tell me what you've found."

"Yes. Well, you've read the newspapers; you know that the police reported that everyone on the ship was killed." His gaze was fixed on Max's face. "They're not absolutely sure about you; they say you are missing and presumed dead."

Max spread his hands. "You think I should call the police in Monte Carlo and tell them I'm alive."

"Of course I do. Why would you not? You must have family who will worry about you—"

Max shook his head. "No one."

"Well, then, friends. And the authorities must keep open the investigation into the explosion until they know for sure that you are alive or dead. Why would you not tell them?"

"Because it suits me right now to have people think I am dead."

Robert contemplated him. "What caused the explosion?"

"I don't know. I suspect a malfunctioning boiler; we'd had trouble with it before."

"A malfunctioning boiler is no reason to keep secret the fact that you are alive." He waited. "Max, listen to me. You know very well that I cannot continue to be your friend if you are hiding a crime."

"I am not hiding a crime. I was in a business in London that others were trying to take over. I've shut that business down, but I don't want them to know where I am."

Once more Robert waited. "You could provide more details."

"I'd rather not. Robert, we've been friends ever since I started my company here, over a year ago. Do you have reason to think I'm not worthy of your friendship?"

"Ah, what a cleverly phrased question. No, my friend, I have had no reason to doubt it, in our relationship. But now what you are doing goes far beyond our relationship. Pretending to be dead . . . that means you are in hiding, yes? And the lady in the hospital? She hides with you?"

"Of course."

There was another silence. "I've overlooked much secretiveness in you, Max," Robert said at last. "Your wariness, your caution, what I thought was your occasional prevarication . . . But the world is full of secretiveness and lying, and it does not have many men who are as good and kind and generous as you. And I like you. I suppose nothing has really changed, except that I have one more piece of information about you. You understand, however, if someone should ask me, I could not lie to keep your secret."

"I understand that. I don't think anyone will ask you."

"And one more thing. I will not be used by you."

"I wouldn't do that. I think the reverse may be true, however."

"You think I am using you?" Robert grinned. "I am using your money, which you give willingly. Men who do good works always turn to those who have money; where else would they turn?"

"Perhaps to prayer."

"Well, yes, of course, and I do. And one of my prayers is that you remain wealthy and generous."

Max chuckled. "You're a practical man, Robert. It's one of the traits I find most admirable in you." He nodded to the waiter who brought two more beers. "Now tell me what else you learned."

"Well, the bodies of the crew were found and identified, and seven others, presumably the guests, were found and also identified. I don't understand—" ·

"Seven? There were nine of us."

"The police said the ship had four staterooms."

"One couple brought a friend; they made up a bed for her in the sitting room off their stateroom."

"Well, they are assuming there were four couples in four staterooms, and they have accounted for three of the couples and one single woman, a Lady Longworth, who—"

"What? What are you talking about?"

"—who would have been your companion, is that right? But then, Max, I don't understand. Who is the lady we took to the hospital?"

Max was staring past Robert, his mind racing. "Who identified her?"

"Denton Longworth. Her former husband. He happened to be in Monte—"

"Jesus Christ."

"Max."

"Sorry." He sat stiffly in his chair, locked in a fury of frustration. What the hell was Denton up to? He knew damn well the woman he identified was not Sabrina; why would he . . . ? Or *did* he know? One of the women on the ship had looked vaguely like Sabrina—in fact, they all had teased her for mimicking Sabrina, wearing her hair the same way, copying her makeup, buying her clothes and jewelry at Sabrina's favorite shops—but a former husband would not have been misled.

Unless . . . He recalled the scene in the water, and Sabrina's face when he held her in the motorboat: colorless, swollen, blood running from her forehead and oozing from dozens of small cuts. A man might be misled if a woman who looked vaguely like his former wife was so badly bruised or burned or cut by debris that he could not be absolutely sure. And he most definitely would assume—

"Max?"

—definitely would assume it was his ex-wife if he wanted to believe she was dead. And Denton wanted very much to believe Sabrina Longworth was dead, she and Max both, because they knew too much.

"Max? The woman who was with you . . . ?"

Max Stuyvesant missing and presumed dead. The body of Sabrina Longworth identified by her former husband.

No one would be looking for them. Max and Sabrina Lacoste, living quietly in a small town in Provence, were home free.

He turned back to the priest. "She's my wife, Robert. We were married in Cap-Ferrat the morning of the explosion. Her name is also Sabrina; it was Sabrina Robion. The other people on the ship were from London and Paris, not close friends, simply companions for a few days."

"Your wife." Robert smiled and covered Max's hand with his. "You once told me you would never . . . Ah, but we should not remind ourselves or our friends of rash statements in our past. I am very happy for you, my friend. But she was gravely injured, Max; will she recover?"

"She will, I think, physically. But she has no memory."

"You mean, of the accident?"

"Of anything except the names of objects. But she's a remarkable woman, very strong; she'll make a new life here, I'm sure of it. In fact, I'm looking forward to it."

"But you can tell her her past, and the more you tell her, the more likely that she will remember all of it."

"I don't know it. We were acquainted only a few days before we were married. But she doesn't miss her past, Robert. She has a new life to create, a completely new life; most of us would give everything we have for that chance."

Robert's eyebrows rose. "Would we? I think, my friend, you'll find that she misses it very much."

Max shrugged. "She'll do what she has to do. That's true of all of us. Robert, I have another favor to ask. The last one, I hope."

Robert smiled. "Another rash statement. What can I do?"

"You know I rented an apartment in Aix. It won't do for both of us. I need a house. I want to buy one, and I was thinking of the plateau above Cavaillon."

"A beautiful spot. You want me to look for one."

"A private one; you know I don't like being crowded."

"You mean I must remember that you're in hiding. Well, I'll see what I can do. The father of one of our students sells houses in the Lubéron; I'll ask him. Now I must go; tomorrow morning is our weekly faculty meeting." He looked closely at Max. "If you need to talk sometime . . ."

"I would not burden our friendship. It's all right, Robert, I've never needed to talk about my problems, or my successes, either. You understand"—he hesitated, a man who had difficulty expressing emotion of any kind—"my friendship with you is the closest I've ever had. I appreciate it." He stood up, as if he had said too much. "When Sabrina and I are in our own home, you'll dine with us. I want her to meet you."

"And I want to meet her. May I visit her in the hospital? I would be pleased to."

"No, I'd rather wait. They've got doctors and psychologists running in and out of her room; she's barely alone and she's exhausted from all of it. You'll come to our home."

"Fine. But if you change your mind . . . priests are good at hospital visits, you know."

Max nodded, barely hearing; he was suddenly frantic to get back. He sped through the streets, repeating his words to Robert. *She will, I think, physically. She will, I think, physically.* But he had been away from her for two hours, and in that time . . .

He raced to her room and found her sitting in her chair, talking comfortably to a doctor he did not know. There were always new doctors in her room, sometimes chatting about the weather or sailing in the Mediterranean or dining

63

at fine restaurants, but most often asking questions, giving Stephanie tests, noting with approval the steady healing of the gash on her head. Much of those conversations she did not remember from day to day, or even hour to hour, but the doctors were patient: they always began again.

"Your amnesia, madame," said one doctor, "is of two kinds. The anterograde, which causes you to forget what I said this morning, will pass, I can positively assure you. But the other, the retrograde, that is more serious. I cannot make any predictions about how long it will last."

"No one told me that," Stephanie said.

"Your first doctor did. You forgot. It happens."

"We find it puzzling," said another doctor to Stephanie on a day when Max was there, "that your type of memory loss does not fit the usual pattern of posttraumatic amnesia. We think it possible that you are primarily suffering from psychogenic amnesia—that is, an amnesia that results when a patient attempts to hide from an overwhelming psychic trauma by totally dissociating the self from the environment. In which case your amnesia would have little to do with the accident on the boat."

Stephanie stared at him. "Are you saying I *want* to forget everything? I'm keeping myself from remembering?"

"You are not consciously preventing yourself from remembering, madame, but it is possible that your unconscious is doing just that. You may have been involved in circumstances that caused you much conflict, that you had not resolved, that, in fact, caused so much pain when you tried to resolve them that it took only a blow on the head to make you cut yourself off from them entirely."

She shook her head, then stopped because it made her headache worse. "What kind of circumstances?"

"I have no way of knowing, madame."

"Something . . . criminal?"

"It is possible."

"It is not possible," Max cut in. "She's not a criminal; she's not capable of criminal acts. I think we've had

enough of this; we won't have any more of these sessions.''

"Why do you think that?" Stephanie asked the doctor.
"That I'm repressing the personal parts of my whole life.

He looked at her with interest, noting the level of intelligence that allowed her to reformulate his theory in that
way. "Your memory, madame. It is intact regarding language—in fact, we now know that you speak Italian, English and French with equal fluency—and it is intact
regarding the names of objects and how to perform many
functions. You buttoned your blouse this morning.''

Stephanie looked down at the white buttons on the blue
and white striped silk blouse Max had brought her the day
before in a large box that also contained a dark blue skirt,
underclothes, silk stockings, high-heeled blue shoes. "I
didn't realize I was doing it.''

"Precisely; it was automatic. Something you knew from
before. But what of the rest of your life, madame? Can
you think back to buttoning your blouse at other times,
perhaps when you were a child and your mother was helping you? Think about your mother, madame, holding you
on her lap—yes?—and showing you how to button your
blouse. Or taking you to the store to choose a blouse, or
perhaps not a blouse, perhaps a doll or a coloring book. Or
anything else. You and your mother shopping together,
think about that, madame, you and your mother in a shop,
choosing something to buy and take home, can you think
about that, can you concentrate on that? Think about your
mother, madame, and doing things together, shopping together, going in and out of shops, or it does not have to be
shopping, it could be—''

"Laura," Stephanie said.

"Madame!" Excitedly, he took her hand. "Is that your
mother's name? Don't stop, madame, please go on, concentrate: your mother is Laura and your father is . . .
Come, madame, tell me the name of your mother and
father.''

"I don't know.''

"Come, I will help you. Your name is Sabrina. Your mother's name is Laura. Your father's name is . . ."

"I don't know! I don't know if Laura is my mother's name; I don't even know if Sabrina is really my name. Max says it is, but it doesn't feel like my name—"

"What does feel like your name, madame?"

She shook her head then stopped, as she always did, because the pain became worse when she moved her head in any direction, and then she said no more.

In January, Max took her home. The doctors and nurses said goodbye with affection and regret: they had wanted to help her, no matter how long it took, but she was still locked in her empty space, with no past, and her husband said she would not return to them.

Stephanie looked back at the hospital as they drove away. "Home," she murmured. It was the only one she knew, the doctors and nurses and other patients her only friends. She clasped her hands in her lap and sat quietly in the velvet interior of a dark blue Renault driven through streets completely strange to her, by a man who said he was her husband, toward a future he had arranged. She wore a country tweed suit he had given her, part of a complete and lavish wardrobe he had brought to the hospital over the past two months, and as she watched him maneuver easily through the traffic of Marseilles and into the rolling countryside, she felt like a child in a small boat carried by the current to a place so distant it could not be guessed at or even imagined.

They did not stop when they reached Cavaillon, but drove through the town and beyond it on a road that climbed to a plateau overlooking the valley. On the plateau, a large plaque, mounted beside stone gates, commemorated the history of the village and the plain. Max turned into the gates and drove past homes spaced widely apart, set back from winding roads amid tall trees and shrubs, each one shielded from its neighbors. Within that small discreet community Robert had found for them the most discreet spot of all, a stone house set within wooded

66

acres at the end of a road, well hidden behind a high stone wall with a wrought-iron gate.

"Home," Max said, echoing Stephanie's word of two hours earlier, and opened her door to help her out.

And then, almost without effort, she was living there. Madame Bessèt, the housekeeper, unpacked and put away her clothes; the gardeners touched their caps and one of them gave her a bronze chrysanthemum from the greenhouse. The maintenance man pulled a chaise to a protected corner of the terrace where she could look down upon the town with its orange tile roofs crammed together between narrow, angled streets and bustling squares, its slender church steeples silhouetted against the fields beyond. The terrace was made of white stones, pale beneath the winter sun and the deep blue sky; behind Stephanie the stones of the house were smooth and warm; below, a cliff fell away in huge rock outcroppings surrounded by dense shrubs and pines that clung tenaciously to the steep slope.

I could jump, Stephanie thought the first time Max settled her in the chaise and she gazed over the low wall bordering the terrace. I could just float off the wall and disappear. No one would miss me because they wouldn't know I'd died.

She shivered in the pale rays of the January sun. *No one who ever knew me knows where I am.*

Each day she lay on the terrace and listened to Madame Besset's purposeful clattering in the kitchen, the low rumble of Max's voice on the telephone in his office, the gardener pushing a wheelbarrow to and from the greenhouse, the maintenance man whistling as he repaired some broken tiles on the roof. Those were the only people she had heard since she arrived in Cavaillon. No one came to see them; they did not go out. "We will when you're strong," Max said. "There's no hurry, and in the meantime this is hardly an unpleasant place to be."

It was a beautiful place, the stone house bleached white by the sun, with bright blue shutters, red and pink geraniums on the windowsills, and strings of garlic and dried herbs hanging in the kitchen. Stephanie's bedroom was on the ground floor, a small room with a high four-poster bed, a painted dresser, and fresh flowers brought every day by Madame Besset to her bedside table. Max had taken her to the room when they arrived. "While you recover," he said.

And so she divided her time between her bedroom and the terrace with its sheltered corner and its view of the roofs of Cavaillon, listening to the sounds from the house and the garden. She lay on the chaise, and the sun settled deep within her, easing the last, lingering pain from surgery. She wore a hat to keep the sun from making her headache worse and to protect the sensitive skin grafts on her face, and the days merged into each other as she lay motionless for hours at a time, listening to the silver trills of the birds and the snapping of clippers as the gardener trimmed the holly hedge, and smelling saffron and garlic in the bouillabaisse Madame Besset was preparing, and the fragrance of the red rose Max had brought her that afternoon.

She took the rose from its vase and held it to her nose, breathing deeply of the heady fragrance. *Roses. I've cut roses . . . with a scissors, a silver scissors, and put them in a vase, a tall vase with a design . . . some kind of design . . .* But Max's voice from the study grew louder, repeating something to make a point, and she lost the thought.

His voice wove through her days. Every morning and afternoon he was in his study, on the telephone. But he joined her at lunch and dinner and after dinner, when they sat on the couch in the living room, finishing their wine while Max talked. He told her about his travels, his acquaintances on four continents, his art collection, his childhood in Holland, Belgium and Germany. "I was always a loner; I never stayed anywhere long enough to make friends."

"I moved around, too," Stephanie said.

"Where?" he asked quickly.

"I don't know." She looked at him with puzzled eyes. "I don't know."

They were sitting at either end of the long couch, and all the living room lights but one had been turned off. The room was large and high-ceilinged, with a floor of square white stone tiles and scattered Bessarabian rugs patterned in bold flowers in oranges and greens and browns. Hand-hewn beams ran the length of the ceiling, the slipcovered furniture was deep and soft, and paintings of the lavender fields and vineyards of Provence hung on the walls. One large painting, a wild scene of the Alpilles range signed with the bold signature of Léon Dumas, stood in the most prominent place, on an easel near the fireplace. It was almost midnight and the house was quiet, the housekeeper and gardener gone, the birds still.

"What did I wear?" Stephanie asked abruptly. "When you met me, what was I wearing?"

"A long skirt and a blouse, off the shoulders, I think."

"What color were they?"

"I don't remember. I don't notice that much about clothes."

"That's not true. You've bought everything I have and it's all the right size and the styles are right for me and so are the colors. Max, please, what colors was I wearing? What was the skirt made of? And the blouse?"

"Cotton. The blouse was white and the skirt was striped red and black."

"Where did I buy them?"

"I have no idea. Probably in France."

"You didn't see a label on them?"

"No." He contemplated her. "You didn't ask any of these questions in the hospital."

"I didn't think of them then. Did you see labels on any of my clothes?"

"You unpacked a Valentino evening dress on the ship, and two Christian Dior blouses."

"That's all?"

"We didn't finish unpacking. I wanted you to see the

skyline of Monte Carlo from the lounge and we went forward.''

''That was all you saw? No private label?''

''What made you think of that?''

''If I had a dressmaker, she would know me.''

''There were none.''

Stephanie was frowning, studying his face. She did not believe him. Something was wrong; she knew it, even though she had no idea what it could be or why he would lie to her. She felt ungrateful, doubting him after all he had done for her, but she could not shake this certainty. ''Did I have a purse?''

''Of course, but I wasn't in the habit of rifling it.''

''Did I wear makeup?''

''A little. Not very much. You didn't need it.''

''What was my hair like?''

''Long. Magnificent. You can let it grow again, if you like.''

''I think I will.'' She looked at her hands. ''You said I hadn't been married. When did I tell you that?''

''Soon after we met. Why?''

''I don't know. I think . . . maybe . . . it might not be true.''

''Indeed. Why do you think that?''

She fell silent, suddenly reluctant to confide in him the new thoughts that came to her each day. ''What did you do after your mother died?''

He paused, wondering if he should pursue his question. Not necessary, he thought; the less we talk about it, the better. ''My father and I kept moving: Spain for a while, then London. I told you about my mother yesterday. You remembered.''

''Oh.'' She sat forward. ''Max, I remembered!'' For the first time since she awoke in the hospital, she smiled, a slow smile that caused Max to draw in his breath on a wave of desire that made him dizzy. He had wanted her every minute of the past week, since coming to Cavaillon, but he had held back and given her her own bedroom, put

70

off by the distant look in her eyes when she turned to him: the look of a stranger, the look of someone who had no desire to be close to him. He knew that was not true of her; their affair in October, in the weeks before the yacht exploded, had been the most passionate he had known in a lifetime of sexual encounters.

They had met again, in London, years after Max had first met her, when she and Denton, newly married, were guests on his yacht. She was unused to their ways then, resisting the drugs and casual sex that the rest of them took for granted. When he saw her again, at the end of September, sitting with Brooks and Gabrielle at Annabel's, there had been a hunger in her eyes for adventure, and a kind of recklessness, as if she were trying to squeeze everything into a short time. He had liked that; it was the way he had always lived.

He had asked her to decorate and furnish his new town house, and she had done it brilliantly, and then she had made it hers as well by staying there for a weekend that had struck him with that same kind of intense recklessness: as if it were to be their only time together.

He had fallen in love with her then; her presence haunted him after she left. But at the same time he had been preoccupied with his company, Westbridge Imports, with Denton's trying to take it over, with rumors of reporters working on stories about smuggled antiquities and forged works of art. He had been busy winding up his London operations, setting up Lacoste et fils in Marseilles, and getting out of England while he could, to make a new life with a new identity in France, and so he did not recognize the fact that he had fallen in love with her and, in fact, probably would have asked her to marry him if the explosion on the yacht had not happened.

Now, in Cavaillon, seeing her smile, seeing her eyes come to life, he could not wait any longer. He took her in his arms. "My beautiful, adorable Sabrina," he said, and covered her mouth with his.

She let him hold her, but her mouth was slack beneath

his and her hands stayed in her lap, and after a moment he let her go. "What we had was so memorable," he murmured, but then he realized the irony of it. Nothing was memorable to this woman, and that was the way it had to be: they could go on together only if she remained locked in her amnesia, believing she was his wife and knowing nothing of the bomb on the yacht, or that it had been put there to kill not only Max Stuyvesant but Sabrina Longworth as well.

"Memorable," Stephanie said wryly. "It would have had to be a lot better than that."

"It was better, and we'll have it again. Listen to yourself, Sabrina: this is the first time you've been able to look at yourself with humor. You're getting better." He took her unresisting hand. "If you still want to wait, if you insist on sleeping downstairs . . ."

"Yes."

"Well, for a time." He kissed her fingers and her palm. "I adore you, Sabrina; you're everything I want. You'll come to me, and I promise you we'll be everything to each other. We don't need anyone else; all we want, all we need, is here."

Stephanie gazed at the top of his head as he kissed her hand. She felt his lips brush her skin, but that was all. *I ought to feel something if he's my husband. I ought to want him.* And she knew then that she knew what sexual desire was and that she had felt it once, but felt nothing now.

Two weeks after they arrived, the weather changed: the sky lowered into a solid gray and the wind rose, bending the trees and making the shutters creak. Rain spattered on the white stones of the terrace, and chill air crept into the house. For the first time, Max and Stephanie ate lunch indoors, in a small room off the kitchen with a round olivewood table and four cushioned wicker chairs. Madame Besset had been making bread, and the room was fragrant and snug while the wind flattened the grass beyond the windows.

Something let go within Stephanie. The tense fearfulness of the past two weeks began to ease, her body relaxed against the flowered cushions of her chair, and she picked up her glass and saw how beautiful was the pale gold of the wine in the golden light from the chandelier. I'm alive and I'm getting better, she thought. And if·I keep getting better, pretty soon I'll remember everything. I'm already remembering things that happened yesterday and the day before, and I do know some things about myself. She ticked them off in her mind. I knew someone named Laura and she may have been my mother, and I cut roses with a silver scissors and I moved around a lot. She felt a sudden sinking. It isn't much. It really isn't anything.

"Sabrina?" Max was looking at her.

"I'm sorry. I didn't hear you."

"Dreaming again." He looked up as Madame Besset came in.

"There is a man waiting to see you in your study. Very serious, very intense. He calls himself Father Chalon, though you would not know he is a priest to look at him, and he says he will wait until you have finished your lunch."

"No, bring him here; he'll join us for lunch. A good friend," Max said to Stephanie. "I've been wanting you to meet him."

Stephanie looked up as he came in: he was short and slender, with a neatly trimmed brown beard shot with gray and dark brown eyes set close together above a thin nose. He bent over her hand. "I'm so pleased to meet you. Max speaks of you often."

"Join us," Max said. "Madame Besset is bringing a plate."

"Thank you." Robert sat down, his eyes still on Stephanie. Quite young, he thought. Thirty? Perhaps thirty-one or -two. Slender, holds herself well; perhaps she has been an athlete. He recognized the clothes she wore: the white turtleneck sweater and blue jeans that Max had bought on a shopping trip in Marseilles. Robert had been with him, watching with amusement Max's sureness with sizes and styles: he knew how to dress a woman.

But more than anything, Robert was struck by her beauty, a vibrant beauty enlivened by the curiosity and intelligence in her eyes. That had not been visible when he helped bring her to Marseilles; he had known only that she probably had once been beautiful. Now, looking at her as if he were viewing a Botticelli in the Uffizi, or one of Titian's glorious women in the Louvre, he felt the tug that beauty exerts: the desire to draw close to it, to absorb some of its perfection, to believe that, because it exists, the world can become a place without pain or sorrow or grief. He became aware that the silence was stretching out and he said, "I am delighted to see you so much improved."

Sabrina looked at Max questioningly.

"Robert accompanied us to Marseilles and to the hospital," he said.

"And would not have predicted such a rapid recovery. I can see that your bruises have faded, as has the swelling; how is the wound on your head? That frightened us very much."

Instinctively, Stephanie's hand went to the scar, hidden by her hair. "It's much better. I'm getting better."

"And remembering, too?"

"No." She looked swiftly at Max. "You promised you wouldn't—"

"I told only Robert because he's very close to us. We'll tell no one else; I promise you that."

"Close to us?" Stephanie waited as Madame Besset arranged a plate and cutlery for Robert and placed a casserole nearby so he could serve himself. Max poured his wine as Robert broke off a chunk of bread from the large round loaf in the center of the table.

"Robert and I do some work together," Max said. "It's something that would not interest you. But—"

"Why not?"

"Well, it might, someday, but not today. Anyway,

74

Robert has had a most unusual life; he might tell you about it.''

"If madame would be interested," said Robert.

"Oh, not 'madame,' " Stephanie said. "It doesn't sound like me."

"Ah, thank you. Sabrina, then. A very lovely name. If indeed you are interested . . .''

"Yes." And to her surprise, she was. It was the first time since she had been in the house that she had felt a spark of curiosity. She had not opened any of the books that filled the library; she did not look at *Figaro* when it arrived each day on their doorstep, nor had she read *Madame Figaro*, the glossy magazine that came with the Friday edition. She had thought idly of going into Cavaillon, especially on market days, but Max said they could not go yet, and she did not care enough to press it.

But today the wind howled, the breakfast **room** was cozy, and it was exciting to talk to someone who was not a doctor or a nurse or Max. Today, over the deep sadness that lay like a weight inside her, and over the terrors of emptiness that haunted her nights, she felt a ripple of being alive and of being glad that she was. She smiled at Robert. She liked him. He wore corduroy pants and a dark blue sweater over an open-necked shirt, and his raggedly cut hair reached his collar. He looked like a schoolboy. "How old are you?" Stephanie asked.

"Forty-one," he said promptly. "Forty-two next month."

"You look younger."

"I feel younger. Probably from bicycling up Mont Ventoux once a week. Perhaps you'll do it with me one day."

"I don't know if I know how to ride a bicycle."

"The easiest way to find out is to start pedaling. If you find you can't do it, I'll gladly teach you."

Stephanie looked at Max. "I'd like to try. Is it all right? May I buy a bicycle?"

"Of course, if that's what you want. We'll wait," he said to Robert, "until she's stronger."

"She's strong enough now for many rides around here. The postal roads that circle the vineyards and cherry orchards—empty except once a day when the postman comes in his car—even you could do them."

Max smiled. "I thought you'd given up trying to turn me into an athlete. But if Sabrina wants it, of course she'll have it."

Stephanie felt like a child between two grown-ups. They knew everything, and she knew nothing. She imagined curling up between them, letting them take care of her. Then, perversely, she felt stirrings of anger. *Don't treat me like a child.*

But in a powerful way, she really was like a child. She had no history, no framework of experience in which to maneuver and hold her own and make decisions about the future.

Then I'll pretend, she thought, and said to Robert, "You were going to tell me your story."

"And so I will." He wiped his plate with his bread, finished his wine, and sat back. "My father was a pirate." He smiled at Stephanie's expression. "It amuses me to say that, and in fact, when I was growing up, that was what he told me and my brothers: he was a pirate on the high seas. But he was something less dramatic: a clever and rather lucky thief who worked as a steward on a very posh cruise line. He was quite short, but extraordinarily handsome and well-muscled, and he charmed everyone; I never knew a man before or since who was so loved—adored, really—by everyone. Including, of course, his wife and six sons."

"That I hadn't known," Max said. "Six boys. No girls?"

"My mother often said her character was forged by having to hold her own against seven men. And she was indeed a woman of admirable fortitude. She was a maid in the Hôtel Fouchard, an elegant place with a restaurant that Michelin gave three stars every year. That was my favorite place in the world, that kitchen."

"What did your father steal?" Stephanie was leaning forward, her chin on her folded hands, for the first time happily absorbed in someone else.

"Whatever he could. Small amounts of money that were not likely to be missed; jewelry, always from women who had brought such an enormous cache of gold and jewels on board that a bracelet or brooch or jeweled hair clip might not be missed until they were back on shore. It was highly risky and stupid, because his tips were extremely generous, and of course it was immoral, but he was convinced he could not support his family in fine style in any other way. And then, you see, he had so many successful years that it all began to seem quite normal. After a while he saw himself as an entrepreneur; his business, with regular routines and accounting systems and steady hours, was piracy."

Stephanie laughed. Max and Robert looked at her as if she had been transformed. And in a way she had: her face was alight as it had not been before. For Max, it was as if the woman he had known in London had come back to him, exuberant, vivid, living life as if everything she found was new and wonderful. For Robert, the moment when Stephanie laughed was the moment when he began to love her with the protective love of an adult for a child caught in a world filled with dangers.

Of course her world is filled with dangers, he thought. Why else would Max pretend to be dead? From whom was he fleeing? What if these people, whoever they are, found out that he was still alive? Where could this child-woman go? To whom could she run for help? She would come to me, Robert thought. And I would take care of her.

It was a promise.

"Where is your father now?" Stephanie asked.

"Dead, for many years. It becomes a sad story. You see, for all his legendary charm, my father was a man of vicious temper. My mother kept him under control at home, but away from his family he was a coiled spring, waiting to explode at any provocation. It did not happen

77

often, but it happened a few times that I knew about before the last time, when I was sixteen. Some man tried to blackmail my father into sharing his loot. They had a fight. The man had a knife, and my father was killed."

Stephanie was staring at him, wide-eyed. "He was very young. And your mother was left with six boys to bring up."

"Spoken like a mother," Robert said, smiling.

Stephanie gave a small gasp, and Max said, "Sabrina has no children."

"How do you know?" Stephanie demanded.

"You told me you'd never been married. I assume you had no children. You never mentioned any. I got the impression you didn't want any."

There was a pause. "You never told me that. What else did I say that you haven't told me?"

"A few things, nothing that would help us fill in your background. I was waiting until you were better to tell you all of them; I thought if they triggered some memories, you would handle them more easily if you were stronger."

"Max, I'm strong now."

"You're still recovering. We'll go over everything, Sabrina, at the right time. You said you would trust me; I expect you to do that." He refilled their wineglasses. "Robert, finish your story."

Robert looked from Max to Stephanie. He saw Stephanie clasp her hands—in despair? he wondered, or resignation?—and he pulled his chair closer to the table to drink the coffee Madame Besset had served. "Well, then, my mother was left with six boys. I was the oldest and by then I was earning a little money, so I could help her."

"But you were in school," Stephanie said.

"No, I left school when I was twelve. I made a fuss and my mother did not argue. I was not a good student; what I really wanted was to be in the kitchen of the Hôtel Fouchard. So I would go to work with my mother, and while she cleaned the rooms, I hung around the kitchen. I washed dishes, I folded napkins and polished cutlery, I ran errands, and then one day the sous chef said I could help cut up vegetables. I did that for all of my fourteenth year. When I was fifteen I was allowed to help make salads. By the time I was sixteen, when my father was killed, I was assistant to the pastry chef and they were paying me, not much, but something.''

"And then?'' Stephanie asked.

"Well, eventually I became a chef with my own three-star restaurant. I had a reputation equal to that of the Troigrois brothers, Paul Bocuse, Michel Guérard . . . all the masters of French cuisine. We were all good friends, compatriots, dedicated to our art. And after a while I had a wife and a child.''

"Oh. But then . . .''

"But then, one day, just ten years ago, I was working late and someone came to rob the restaurant. And my life changed.''

He paused, and Stephanie murmured, "Another thief.''

Robert gazed at her with pleasure. "You understand how curious it is that my life was shaped by two thieves. Well, yes, another thief. He broke in a side door while I was at my desk off the kitchen. I heard a sound—he was breaking open the safe in the maître d's office—and when I confronted him we fought. And I killed him.''

Stephanie gasped. "You had a knife. From the kitchen.''

"Ah, my dear, you are quick. Yes, this time I was the one with the knife. But he had a gun, and though he had no chance to use it, everyone agreed that I had been defending myself and therefore should not be convicted. So I was free and my restaurant had a soupçon more publicity, and all should have been well. But it was not. Because, you see, when I fought with that man I discovered in myself a fury I did not know I had, and a great joy in the attack. I became my father, exploding into murderous rage, and nothing, *nothing* could have stopped me from killing. When it was over, I understood my father and I understood that I was indeed his son.''

There was a silence. Robert was looking at his hands,

clasped on the edge of the table. "I understood, too, that all of us harbor some seed within us that is fundamental to our being even though we have no suspicion it is there, something so deeply a part of us that even when we claim, in our arrogance, that we can predict how we will behave in this circumstance or that, and can control our actions, in truth we do not have the proper eyes to see that seed, nor do we have the self-knowledge that would allow us to plumb deep enough to reach it. And so we know only a part of ourselves and often cannot control even that part. I did not know the man who killed that thief. His name was Robert Chalon and he inhabited my body, but he was unknown to me. That terrified me. And I thought then that it was essential to learn who I was, and to use my knowledge to help others know truly who they are, to help them understand their fundamental nature and use it for good."

"You've upset her," Max said, and Robert looked up to see tears glistening on Stephanie's face.

"Ah, Sabrina, forgive me." Robert held her hand between his. "I did not realize . . . Of course, that is your loss, too: you do not know the person who inhabits your body. Well, then, let me help you, let us try together to bring back your past and return to you your true self."

"I don't know how," Stephanie said.

"Nor do I, but perhaps we can learn together. And do you know what else? I will teach you to cook. Shall I? I would make a bet that you knew how in the past, and it may come back and help us find the rest of you. What do you say to that?"

"Madame Besset will not be happy," Max said, and Stephanie knew that though he said it lightly he was not pleased with the discussion.

"I'd like that," she said firmly to Robert, not looking at Max. "I'd like that very much."

"Then we'll do it. Perhaps two mornings a week? Would that be all right?"

She smiled ruefully. "I'm not busy; that would be won-

derful. But I don't want Madame Besset to find out that I
have no memory."

"Can you give her the day off?"

"Oh, yes, that would be perfect; I'll tell her she can
have two mornings— Oh." She turned to Max. "I'm
sorry. Is it all right? We could give Madame Besset two
mornings a week off, couldn't we?"

"If it would make you happy."

"Thank you," Stephanie said, and no one commented
on the fact that twice, during lunch, she had asked Max's
permission as if, indeed, she were a child.

Robert stood up. "I must leave. I thank you for lunch;
it was excellent. We should decide on which mornings—"

"Why didn't you say anything about God?" Stephanie
asked abruptly. "If you wanted to help people find themselves, you could have become a psychologist or a psy-
chiatrist; you didn't have to become a priest."

He sat down again. "You know about psychologists
and psychiatrists."

"From the hospital."

"And you know much more than that, I'm sure. Well,
you want to know about God. Long ago, in ancient times,
when men tried to map the world, they would draw as
much as they knew from sailing along the coastlines of
countries, but without airplanes, they could not know all
there was. And so the rest of the map was left blank. In
that blank space they drew dragons and other fire-
breathing creatures, and wrote, 'Where you know nothing, place terrors.' After I killed that man, when I knew
that I knew nothing, my world was filled with terrors. And
the only way I could live with my ignorance and those
terrors was to acknowledge that there are mysteries that
pervade our lives and we will probably never understand
them. People like to think they can understand everything,
given enough time and money, but of course that is not
true. So I accepted the great mystery in what makes us
human and unique, and, like others throughout history, I
gave it the name of God. And within that name lie all the

unknowns and powers and potentials that make us what we are; the fears and dreams and terrors that visit us; the love we give and the love we are so grateful to receive; the spirit that lets us soar—unless we fail to nurture it, and so we sink. I could not look inside myself or help others to do the same without acknowledging the dominance of that mystery in my life. Psychiatrists and psychologists seem able to do it; I know many of them are sensitive and superb in their helping professions. But I cannot. Does that answer your question?''

"What happened to your wife and child?''

"My wife died two years ago. My child lives with a family in Roussillon. Sometimes we count our gains in losses. We will talk about that sometime. Now I will say goodbye, my dear Sabrina. And I will see you . . . day after tomorrow? At nine in the morning?''

Stephanie looked at Max. "Fine,'' he said. "I'll see you out, Robert.''

She watched them go. She heard the shutters creak and the house groan beneath the onslaught of the wind and she saw the trees whip wildly, like dancers gone mad. *Sometimes we count our gains in losses.* She had lost her past, but the house sheltered her, and within it Max and Madame Besset cared for her. She was alive; her body grew stronger each day; she remembered someone named Laura and the smell of roses, and a silver scissors, and moving around a lot, and she knew about psychiatrists and psychologists.

And now she had a friend who would help her remember the rest.

CHAPTER *6*

*S*abrina and Garth stood in the round, dimly lit main room of the Shedd Aquarium, greeting their guests. It was February, almost four months after Stephanie's funeral, and by now Sabrina found it so natural to be with Garth, to stand beside him hosting a university function, that she no longer wondered at her life, or her sureness in making it her own. Her grief over Stephanie's death was a permanent part of her, clutching her at unexpected moments, but her love for Garth and the children was more powerful, always new and wondrous, a kind of magic she had never known.

In the aquarium, she and Garth stood close together, smiling and greeting everyone by name. On the circular wall around them large windows looked into the bright underwater worlds of exotic fish, crustaceans, corals, and undulating plants that made the aquarium on Chicago's lakefront famous. Garth had chosen it as a unique place for a reception to honor major donors to the Institute for Genetic Engineering, and to welcome potential ones, and now he watched the guests move from window to window, murmuring through their sophisticated veneer at the wondrous iridescent colors of rare fish and the fantastic shapes of crustaceans from all the oceans of the world. He and Sabrina shared a smile. "I'm glad you're here," he said. "Even with the fish, it would have been as dull as every other reception, without you."

"It wouldn't be dull for me," Sabrina said. "I love to watch you work a crowd and make speeches, and I love you, and there's nowhere else I'd rather be right now."

Their guests commented on what a striking couple they were, Garth in his tuxedo and Sabrina in a gold sweater and long white satin skirt she had brought from her closet in London, and when Claudia Beyer, the president of the university, arrived, she eyed them with approval. "Stephanie, Garth, you do us proud. Do we have a goal for tonight?"

Garth shook his head. "We're just making everyone feel wanted and loved. We'll go after them in the next six weeks, the end of the campaign, I hope. February and March are good times to ask for money; by then most people have forgotten how much they spent on Christmas."

Claudia smiled. She was tall and very thin, curved like an archer's bow, with slicked-back gray hair and oversize tortoiseshell glasses. She wore a black pants suit with a ruffled white blouse and was almost a twin to her tall, thin husband, a professor of French history. "And the goal for the end of the campaign?" she asked.

"Three million four," Garth said patiently, knowing that she knew exactly how much everyone in the university was seeking at every moment of the year. "That will bring us up to fifteen million and we won't have to ask for any more until we decide to expand."

"It's taken a lot of entertaining," Claudia mused.

"All of it in the budget. We haven't gone over."

"I know. It's a very big budget. But tonight looks like a good evening; I like your idea of the aquarium."

"I can't take credit for that," Garth said, glancing at Sabrina.

"Ah." Claudia nodded. "I always did like Stephanie's ideas. I'll call you about another lunch, Stephanie; there's something I'd like to talk to you about. Shall I call you at your shop?"

"Yes. If I'm not there, Madeline will be. I'd like lunch; I enjoyed our last one."

"Good." She left as abruptly as she had arrived, moving purposefully to a group of guests watching a school of anglerfish glide through the darkened water, their bands of color as luminous as neon.

"What did she mean about a very big budget?" Sabrina asked.

"That we're spending a lot to raise a lot and she'd rather spend a little to raise the same amount. I'd do it if I could, but I haven't found a good way to get someone to write a six- or seven-figure check without some socializing to smooth the way."

"Claudia ought to do it. You should be thinking about science and running an institute, not going around with your hat in your hand."

"She does do it, and she's one of the best, but people who write checks with lots of zeroes usually want to see the person who's going to spend them. I can understand that. You look extraordinarily beautiful tonight. You look wonderful in gold, and I like your hair; you've cut it, haven't you? It looks shorter."

She was laughing. "I have cut it and it is shorter, and I'm glad you like it." But beneath her laughter a sudden stab of grief cut through her and she shrank into herself, almost breathless with pain. Stephanie had had long hair; the two of them had always worn it tumbling loose to their shoulders and when one of them felt like braiding it or pinning it up, the other had done the same. Why did I cut my hair? she wondered suddenly. I started thinking about it in January and I knew it was the right thing to do. Why was that? Why am I so sure it was right?

85

"My love," Garth said gently.

"I'm sorry." She put her hand on his arm. "I don't mean to go off like that and leave you."

"I know you don't; it's not something you can control. I think we should leave as soon as possible; how do you feel about that?"

"Wonderful."

But Garth and Claudia Beyer were hosts for the evening and so they stayed, through dinner and brief speeches, and then dancing. "We're stuck," Garth said as he and Sabrina moved in a smooth rhythm at the edge of the dance floor. "I can't leave until Claudia does."

Sabrina slid her hand farther around his shoulders. "I love to dance with you. I'm very happy where I am."

"I'm very happy with where you are, too."

They danced in silence. "Sometimes I miss Ambassadors, though," Sabrina said slowly, almost tentatively, knowing Garth did not like to talk about the past. "That whole crazy business of antiques in Europe, the competition, so much more fierce than here."

Garth's eyebrows rose. "You want more tension in your life?"

She laughed. "I can't imagine why I would. But I've been thinking about Ambassadors, Garth; I think I ought to go there, just for a few days. It's been two months since I was there, and that was Christmas and they were so busy . . . Anyway, I don't think I should stay away more than two months at a time."

"You don't trust Nicholas and Brian?"

"I trust Brian; he's worked for me for a long time. But I've never worked with Nicholas and there's so much going on, merging his shop with Ambassadors and both of them with Collectibles in Evanston, it almost feels as if I'm starting over again, and I don't feel I have any real control unless I can be there, at least once in a while. I want to make this work; it means a lot to me."

"I know it does. Of course you should go. And you've got your house to stay in; that makes it easier."

"And Mrs. Thirkell. I've decided to bring her here, Garth. She has nothing to do there and—"

"Bring her here?"

"It's that or let her go, and I don't want to do that; she's been with me even longer than Brian has. And why shouldn't we have someone full time to take care of the house, and all of us? You know how wonderful she is; she'd make everything a lot easier."

The music stopped and they stood still, holding each other lightly. Garth looked beyond Sabrina, at the other dancers. "There's a lot of hostility on a campus when professors seem to be living higher than they should."

Sabrina stiffened. "Who decides how high they should live?"

"No one; you know that. It's a kind of unwritten community standard that everyone recognizes. And it's not always a bad—"

"So everyone who lives in that community has to fit that standard, is that right? What if I hired Juanita for two days instead of one, or served better wines, or bought a fancier car—would the tongues start wagging? Would somebody paint a hex sign over our front door?"

"Look, I didn't make this up. It's part of the world we live in. And it's not always a bad thing. When you're part of a community you don't lord it over everyone else or give them reasons to think you are. I have more important things to do with my time than deal with whispers and wounded egos. I'm not saying they're inevitable, but—"

"You said, 'There's a lot of hostility.' "

"Well, it's happened. It isn't a sure bet that it would this time, but it's a possibility. And why chance it? Hostility makes a lousy atmosphere for research and building a new institute, especially if the people who are hostile know they're not likely ever to have the kind of resources we have."

"Garth, this is ridiculous; I can't believe you're saying this. If they can't afford a full-time housekeeper, they can't afford one. That's all. It isn't a commentary on their character or scientific brilliance; all it says is that different people have different bank accounts. And we don't judge people by their bank accounts. At least I don't.''

They had walked a little distance away from the dance floor to a quiet corner, their heads close together, their voices low. Their bodies were tense, and no one interrupted them.

''You haven't lived on a campus,'' Garth said impatiently. ''You might try to understand how people feel when they make just enough to support a family without a wagonload of frills.''

''I might try to understand? There was a time when I didn't earn enough to support anyone but myself, and sometimes I wasn't sure I could do that. It took me a long time to make Ambassadors a success; there were a lot of years when I didn't have one frill, much less a wagonload. And I never stopped being careful. You know that; I've told you about it. Are you accusing me of being extravagant or profligate, Garth? Do you think I've been throwing our money around?''

''No, but you don't know—''

''I know enough to run your house, and I have no intention of lying down and letting a bunch of hidebound professors tell me how to do it with their unwritten rules and regulations. I haven't—''

'' 'No intention'? What does that mean? That you'll do what you want, come hell or high water? That you don't give a damn what's important to me?''

''You know how much I care what's important to you. I think I pay a lot of attention to that. I haven't failed, you know; I've done a pretty good job with your family.''

''It's your family, too.'' He took a deep breath. ''What the hell are we talking about?''

''The elegant, high-toned, exclusive Mrs. Thirkell.''

Their eyes met and they burst out laughing. ''Well, she's more homey than high-toned,'' Garth conceded. ''Christ, I'm sorry, my love; I went overboard, didn't I?''

"I'm sorry, too. I shouldn't have gotten angry. I'm never angry at you; how did I do this?"

"Maybe you've got the tension you were looking for. I don't know what got into me, though."

"I think you're under a lot of pressure about the institute and you worry too much about fitting into your community. But you're good enough to be whatever you want to be, Garth. Everyone likes you and admires you; why are you afraid to be different? What would happen if some people think that we're living too high for our station in life?"

"They could make life unpleasant. It's a very small community, you know, and we all need each other, for support, for getting funding, for bouncing ideas off each other, even for convincing the administration we need another secretary. It isn't as simple as it seems to outsiders."

"Am I an outsider?"

"No, my God, no. Look, go ahead; bring her back from London if you want. It won't cause an earthquake, just a small shift in the earth's crust. Everyone will get used to it."

"Fine." They were silent. "Have we really been talking about Mrs. Thirkell?" she asked.

"Well, not entirely. I suppose I'm jealous of London. You tend to wrap a place around you, my love, and make it part of you, and it was your home for a long time. I think of you there with your friends, and nothing to remind you of us, and it's occurred to me—it occurs to me often—that they might seduce you into coming back."

She put her hand along his face. "Not one chance in a million. The only seduction I'm interested in is my husband's. If we were home now, I could prove that with a few very interesting moves."

He chuckled. "I'll hold you to that." The music began again and they moved into each other's arms and onto the dance floor. "So, let the marvelous Mrs. Thirkell come to

Evanston; you're right, it would be wonderful for you, and I think the kids would love her.''

"I think so, too.''

"When do you want to go?''

"In a week or two. I may do some buying while I'm there, if Madeline agrees. I don't want her to think I'm taking over, but we have clients who are looking for particular pieces that I might be able to find.''

"Let her go next time.''

"She doesn't know Europe. I'll have to do it a few times a year. You really don't mind?''

"I'll miss you. But of course you should go.''

Her hand curved around the back of his neck. "Would there be a lot of hostility if I kissed you here? Would people say it wasn't appropriate for your station in life?''

"If they do, the hell with them.'' They kissed lightly, smiling. "It is amazing and wonderful to me how much I love you,'' Garth murmured, and then Claudia Beyer came up to them and Sabrina and Garth had no more time alone until almost midnight when, finally, everyone left, buttoning fur and heavy wool coats against the bitter end-of-February wind that whipped in off the lake and buffeted them as they walked down the broad steps to their waiting limousines.

"Nice of Claudia to do this,'' Garth said as he and Sabrina saw the limousine waiting for them. "I like her style.''

"I like her,'' Sabrina said. "We had a good talk at lunch last week. She's smart and she cares about people and she cares intensely about the university.''

The driver held the door and Garth slid into the back seat after Sabrina. "More than she cares about people?''

"You mean, would she sacrifice people for the good of the university? I don't know. I'm not sure she does. I hope she doesn't have to make the choice.''

"I hope not.'' Garth put his arm around her and held her as the limo merged with the traffic on Lake Shore

Drive. "If you had married a rich man you could travel like this all the time."

Sabrina did not say that she had married a rich man once, and it had not been enough. There was no reason to talk about Denton; he no longer had any part in her life, and she had had no reason to think of him for years. "I like the man I married," she said, "with or without limousines. Do you think tonight was a success?"

"I know it was. They all loved you, you know; they think if you're connected with the institute it's well worth their hard-earned or hard-inherited money. But right now I want to stop thinking about money and just think about us."

He pulled her closer and they kissed, a long kiss of familiarity and contentment, and of a love and passion that grew with each day they were together. Five months, almost six, Sabrina thought, settling back against Garth in the warmth of the car as snowflakes began to streak past the windows. Almost six months since I came here, deceiving everyone, and stayed and stayed and fell in love and then Stephanie . . .

Stephanie.

It was a low cry within her. Stephanie was gone, and it felt to Sabrina as if the place where she had been was a vast emptiness, a fog, a cloud, all of space, infinity. All that was left was a memory, a longing, a love.

But there were many other loves—Garth, the children, her work, a way of life. She felt she was living on two planes, pulled in two directions: My sister is dead, but for the first time I have more than I ever dreamed could be mine.

"Do you know," Garth mused, his voice a soft murmur at her ear, "once in a very rare while there comes a time when our lives settle into perfect balance, when everything is in its perfect place. I never really believed that could happen. Now I know that it can. Because right now, my love, now is our perfect time."

"Yes." The word was a long breath, like a prayer of

thanksgiving. The flare-up with Garth, all the little flare-ups and tensions of learning to live together while pretending to the world that they had been married for twelve years, all faded away. They were not important. What was important was that even though she had lost the person closest to her in all the world, she had found Garth, and a family, and a love between a man and woman beyond imagining. *I don't know how that can be. Unless somehow I've become both of us in a way that's beyond logic. If that's true, then, look, Stephanie, we both have short hair now.*

She sighed, a little ashamed of her fantasy, and settled deeper into Garth's arms as the car headed north to Evanston, and the snowflakes streamed past the window, blotting out the lights of the city and the rest of the world.

"Sounds like a fishy evening to me," Cliff said and guffawed as he poured a small pond of syrup over his waffle.

"It sounds like fun," Penny said wistfully. "Like, if nobody talked to you, you could look at the fish and they'd keep you company."

Sabrina gave her a swift glance. "Has that happened lately? People not talking to you?"

"Oh, sometimes. You know."

"No, I don't know," Garth said. "You and Barbara were best friends, I thought. What's going on, Penny?"

"Nothing." Penny looked at her plate. "It was just, you know, I was just thinking about the fish."

Cliff stuffed waffle into his mouth. "A lot of your friends look sort of like fish; you know, mouths going all the time, and staring at you like they're looking for dinner."

"They're not like that!" Penny cried. Tears appeared in her eyes. "They're my friends."

"I thought you just said they don't talk to you."

"They do! It's just . . ."

"Okay," Sabrina said, "I think we've talked enough

about Penny's friends. Maybe Penny and I can talk about them later, by ourselves.''

Trouble here, she thought as Penny threw her a quick, grateful glance, but we'll take care of it. Whatever it is, it hasn't been around long enough to become deep-rooted or I would have heard of it.

She watched Cliff spear a piece of waffle on his fork and swirl it around his plate, making figure eights through the pool of syrup. He looked absorbed, but something about the tilt of his head told her he was listening. He's waiting for us to say something, she thought. About what? About last night?

"It *was* fun," she said. "Everybody said it was the best place to have a party because it was so different, even a little mysterious. You know how they keep the rooms dark so the fish tanks show up better; it's probably the only university party where people were in the dark.''

Garth smiled. "Some people say academics are always in the dark.''

"Not the academic in this family," Sabrina said.

"Was what's-his-name there?'' Cliff asked. His voice was casual, but Sabrina saw his grip on his fork.

"What's-his-name?'' Garth echoed.

"You know, Lun or Lon or Loony or whatever.''

"*Lu*," Penny said. "Lu Zhen. He's only been here for dinner a hundred times.''

"Six or seven," Sabrina said. "And you do know his name.''

"*Was* he there?'' Cliff asked Garth.

"No. There weren't any students. Would it make a difference if he had been?''

Cliff shrugged. .

"You're jealous," Penny said.

"I'm not! I just was *wondering*; you don't have to make a big deal out of it.''

"More waffles?'' Sabrina asked. "Cliff? Do you want another piece to sop up all that syrup?''

"Sure.''

"Cliff doesn't like him," Penny said.

"I never said that!"

But you don't, Sabrina thought. You don't like your father's star graduate student and maybe that shouldn't surprise us. Another piece of trouble to watch out for; I guess we'll have to talk about it before we invite Lu to dinner again. "What I want to know is, what is everybody doing this afternoon?"

"We could go to the aquarium," Cliff said brightly. "That's a good thing to do on Sunday afternoon."

"Good idea," Sabrina said quickly, to forestall the impatient exclamation she saw Garth about to make. "I didn't get to see much last night; we were too busy talking to people. You'd better bundle up, though; it's unbelievably cold walking there from the car."

"We're really going?" Cliff asked in disbelief.

"It's okay with me if it's okay with everybody else."

"Can I take my paints?" Penny asked.

"They're too messy to carry around, Penny. Take crayons or chalk. You can paint at home. Garth? Is the aquarium all right?"

"Only if Cliff can find me a coelacanth."

"A what?" yelped Cliff.

"I'll show you." Garth took out a pencil and pad of paper and began to draw. Penny and Cliff hunched near him, and Sabrina watched the three of them. *There comes a time when our lives settle into perfect balance, when everything is in its perfect place.* Wonderfully true, she thought. Because Penny's and Cliff's problems are part of growing up and children grow up bumpily, not smoothly—that's something I've learned in the last five months—and one of the perfect parts of our life is sharing our children's growing up: shaping, nudging, helping, guiding. Something I never had and always wanted. And, Stephanie, these are such lovely children, so full of love and life, so bright and curious and eager to learn. You did that. You and Garth. Before I ever got here.

"Well, I think it's ugly," Penny said. "You can look

for one if you want, but I'm only going to look for beautiful things that I can draw. I only want to draw beautiful things.''

"There's lots of unbeautiful things in the world, though," Cliff said.

"But I don't have to paint them. Do I, Mommy?"

"Not now," Sabrina said. "Maybe, if you decide to be an artist when you grow up, you might paint more of the whole world, the good and the bad, the beautiful and the ugly, and the happy and the sad, too."

"You don't do that," Penny objected. "You and Madeline don't buy ugly antiques; you only buy beautiful ones."

Sabrina met Garth's amused glance. "That's true. But do you think I'd have a lot of customers if I bought ugly things?"

"No, but nobody would buy my paintings if they were ugly, either."

"I think it's different with art. Artists give us their visions of the world and we look at them to find whatever we can in their paintings or sculptures and books. Every work of art probably has as many meanings as it has people looking at it, because each of us sees it in our own way. Sometimes what we see helps us understand the world a little better, or maybe understand ourselves better, know who we are and what we want . . ."

Penny was watching her intently, trying to grasp it all. "It's more complicated than antiques," Sabrina finished. "One of these days we'll talk about it again." She spooned a few strawberries from a glass bowl to her plate. "But I did want to talk about antiques, and maybe this is a good time."

"Gonna watch television," Cliff said and pushed back his chair.

"No, I want you here," Sabrina said. "And you don't watch television in the morning, ever, you know that."

"Yeh, but, Mom, *antiques.*"

"I know they're not your thing, but I want you to stay

95

because what I really want to talk about is my shops."

"Collectibles," Penny said.

"She said *shops*," said Cliff.

Sabrina nodded. "Collectibles and Ambassadors and Blackford's."

"Yeh, but those other ones are in London," Cliff said. "You don't work in them; you work in Collectibles."

"But I own half of each of them. So I have to keep track of what we buy and sell, and how much money we make, all that sort of thing. And it isn't enough to do it on the telephone; owners have to check out what they own in person, at least once in a while."

The breakfast room was silent. Then Penny cried out, "You can't! You can't go there!"

"You're going to London?" Cliff demanded. "You can't; you have to stay here!"

Penny burst into tears. "Mommy, don't go! Please don't go! Please stay here!"

Garth and Sabrina exchanged a look. We should have expected this, they told each other silently. "Hey, you two," Garth said firmly, "listen for a minute. Your mother is going to London for a few days, three or four, that's all, and then she'll be back."

"Last time you went to London you didn't come back," Cliff said loudly. "You sent presents, but you didn't come back. You didn't even write to us."

"I did come back," Sabrina said quietly.

"Well, yeh, finally, but it took forever and Dad had to go over there to get you."

"He won't this time," Sabrina said.

"Dad, are you going to let her go?" Cliff demanded.

"I won't try to stop her, if that's what you're asking."

"I'd stop her if she was my wife!"

"You couldn't!" Penny wailed. "Husbands can't stop wives from doing things anymore."

"Then ask her!" Cliff cried to Garth. He glared at Sabrina. "If you really loved us, you wouldn't go. No-

96

body else has a mother who goes to London; they all stay home."

"You sent me those paints and things," Penny said through her tears, "and I loved them but I didn't want them, I mean, I didn't want them if that was all I could have, I mean, *I wanted you and you were gone and you didn't even call us!*"

Because your father thought you should forget me, Sabrina told her silently. Because I was the interloper, taking the place of the mother you did not even know was dead, and I had no right to be here . . . until he came to understand how I loved you, how I loved him, and that the three of you had become my whole life. And then he came to bring me home.

"—few days," Garth was saying. "I told you: three or four, that's all. It's a business trip; it's the same as when I go to conferences. I always come back, right? And your mother will come back."

"There's no scientific proof of that," Cliff said flatly.

"*Listen to me.*" Sabrina held her hands toward them. In a minute Penny and Cliff each put a hand in hers. "You and your dad are the most important people in the world to me. My work is important and that's why I'm going on this very short trip and that's why I'll go again, a few times a year, probably, but I promise you this—are you listening?" She waited until they nodded. Their eyes were fixed on hers, Penny's filled with tears, Cliff's intent and somber. "I promise you I will always come back to you. I will never leave you for good. You are my whole life and nothing could ever make me give you up. I love you, I love you, and nothing will ever change that."

Penny jumped up and threw her arms around Sabrina. "I love you, Mommy."

Over Penny's head, Sabrina met Garth's eyes again. "I love you," she said quietly.

"Hey, Mom, listen, are you in trouble or something?" Cliff asked. "I mean, are your shops losing money? 'Cause we could help, like maybe work after school at

Collectibles and you wouldn't have to pay us as much as somebody who isn't in your family, and if you save money, maybe you wouldn't have to go over there.''

"Oh, Cliff, you're wonderful." My sweet, mercurial son, she thought: one moment a child, the next so close to being a man. "No, I'm not in trouble, but I appreciate your offer, and if things get bad, we'll talk about it. All right?"

"Right." Cliff jumped up. "I've got an idea. We'll go with you!"

Sabrina laughed, marveling at his stubbornness. "It's a wonderful idea and one of these days you will, and we'll see a lot of London and maybe other places, too. That's another promise."

"When are you going?" Penny asked, still anxious.

"In a few days. But something wonderful is going to happen before that. I was going to keep it a secret, but I've changed my mind; I'd rather you knew about it now. We're getting a present for our house named Mrs. Thirkell.''

"She doesn't belong here," Cliff declared, automatically opposed to anything that had to do with London. "She lives over there and she takes care of Aunt Sabrina's house. We don't need her here."

"Will she make our beds?" Penny asked.

Cliff wheeled in place. *"Will* she? And set the table and do the dishes?''

Sabrina smiled. "She'll help us as much as we want her to, but I think she'd be very unhappy if she thought she was taking away all your jobs."

"No, she wouldn't; she doesn't have to know we do those things."

"Let's talk about it when she gets here," Garth said. "Right now, since she's not here, you have to clean up your rooms by yourselves and if you get going we can go to the aquarium."

"Yeh, but—"

"Now, Cliff. No more talk."

Cliff gave an exaggerated shrug and he and Penny turned to go. Sabrina and Garth watched them run up the stairs. "I should clean up the kitchen."

"They'll do it before we leave. You were wonderful with them. It's astonishing how much reassurance children need. Did I need that much? I can't remember. Did you, do you think?"

"Probably, because we moved around so much we never felt we belonged anywhere. Until Juliette; four years of high school in one place. But we made most of our own reassurance: we always had each—" The words caught in her throat.

Garth drew her out of her chair and onto his lap, and held her like a child. His love for her was so deep and encompassing that he could not imagine life without her, but he did not know how that had happened. Two women, he thought, two halves of one woman, and now somehow both of them are here, part of me in a way Stephanie never was when we were married. There is a mystery to this: to what they were individually, and to what Sabrina is now that Stephanie is dead, and to what Sabrina and I have forged. And though it is hard for me, a scientist, to say this, perhaps this is a mystery that we will never understand. This is a mystery we will live with, and in our more fanciful moments we will call it magic.

"I'm all right," Sabrina said, her face against his shoulder. "Thank you, my darling. Thank you for everything." She sat up. "We really should plan a trip to Europe for all of us: London and Paris, maybe Provence. Do you know, I've never been to Avignon or Arles or Cavaillon . . . Oh, Garth, let's plan a trip."

Garth smiled. "All those places in one trip?"

"No, we can't; you're right. But let's think about it. Maybe spring vacation? Or this summer?"

"One of the above. Or October; I have a conference in The Hague. We could keep the kids out of school . . . except that I want some time for the two of us."

"Oh, so do I. But we can't just go off after I've promised . . ."

"We'll do both. We'll figure it out." They smiled at each other. *So many plans; so much time for so many wonderful plans.*

She was still thinking about that two weeks later as she drove to Chicago: that once she had thought she was only borrowing this family, but now she knew she would have them always. And stay with them, she thought, amused, because she had put off her trip to London again and again and finally had abandoned it for the foreseeable future. She had too much to do here, and London no longer seemed urgent or attractive, especially since Mrs. Thirkell had arrived and had plunged into organizing their house and their family.

The great organizer, she thought, smiling, as she walked into the Koner Building and saw a man leaning against a pillar, waiting for her. "Koner," he said, and held out his hand. He was short and square, with a flat, pugilist's nose, black eyes constantly darting back and forth, heavy whiskers, and a custom suit and shirt that he wore with dark blue suede shoes. A gold watch chain stretched across his generous paunch.

Sabrina shook hands with him. They had talked on the telephone, but she had never met him, and now they looked at each other for a long moment, to see if they liked what they saw enough to take the next step to working together.

William Koner had bought the abandoned ten-story warehouse in Chicago's Printer's Row neighborhood a few months earlier. It had been renovated once in its long history by Ethan Chatham but then had fallen into disrepair, and Koner had hired Vernon Stern, an architect, to design the renovation, with shops on the ground floor and loft apartments above, and he had asked Sabrina, in a telephone call, to do the interiors. This was the first time Sabrina would meet both of them and walk through the building.

Koner paced, waiting for Stern, anxious to start. Sabrina, wearing faded jeans, a black turtleneck sweater and a tan corduroy blazer, perched on a windowsill littered with paint and plaster chips. "Why do you want me for this job, Mr. Koner? I've never done a building of this size; I haven't worked with loft apartments at all."

"Right, I know all that." He pulled out a pipe and stuck it between his teeth. "Madeline Kane took me to the house you're doing in Lake Forest. Good job. Old on the outside, old and new all mixed up on the inside. I liked it. My wife liked it. And Madeline says you're the best."

"And you'd give me this job because of one home I've designed and Madeline's recommendation?"

"Why not? My first two wives bought a lot from her; they said she knew her stuff. My wife, my current wife, says you've made that shop world class and you've got some kind of deal with a couple of shops in London, so you know Europe, too. I'd say you're ambitious and smart and you've got class; I don't need a wife to tell me that. So why shouldn't you do this job?"

Sabrina laughed. "I think I should."

They smiled at each other. "And cut out this 'Mr. Koner' business," he said. "My friends call me Billy. And I call you Stephanie, unless you have a problem with that."

"I have no problem with that."

The door swung open and Vernon Stern arrived. He was tall, blond, tanned, as perfectly handsome as if he had stepped from the pages of a magazine. His hair was carefully tousled, he wore jeans and cowboy boots and a tweed jacket over a purple silk shirt open at the neck; he was impeccably casual. Sabrina found herself smiling. He had designed some of Chicago's most striking buildings, but it seemed that his most loving creation was himself.

His eyes widened when they were introduced, as men's eyes always did when they met her; she barely noticed it anymore. But he also made their handshake last longer than necessary and studied her as if he were evaluating a painting. "Beautiful," he said. "It's rare these days to find beauty that hasn't been carved out by a plastic surgeon or layered on with cosmetics. A pleasure to meet you, Stephanie."

"I admire your buildings," Sabrina said and slipped her hand from his.

He nodded, still gazing at her, then unhurriedly unrolled the set of plans he carried. Sabrina took out her clipboard and pencil and a steel tape measure and they began to walk through the building. Koner's secretary had arrived and trailed invisibly behind them, taking notes. When they reached the ninth floor, Sabrina stopped at a window. "What an amazing view of the city. We ought to do something spectacular up here. May I see the plans for this floor?"

Stern spread them on the floor and the three of them knelt in the dust and littered plaster to bend over them. "But it's the same as the other floors," Sabrina said.

"Your job is to make it spectacular," Koner said.

"What did you have in mind?" Stern asked Sabrina.

She looked again at the vast space. "I was thinking of two apartments instead of four. It's hard to find five- or six-thousand-square-foot apartments in the city." She looked at the high ceiling. "Or you could get the same size apartments by making them two stories, with a two-story living room, the windows extended all the way, and—maybe a winding staircase? Then you'd get the full impact of the view, and incredible light."

"Good idea," Stern said dryly.

Sabrina drew back. "I'm sorry. This is your field, not mine."

"You'd be good in it. I presented both of those ideas to Billy and he vetoed them."

"I want the most apartments I can get," Koner said. "Two thousand square feet is plenty big enough for a city apartment, and there's more money in four on a floor than two."

"Not necessarily," Stern said. "We talked, if you recall, about how much of a premium you could get for larger apartments on the top two floors. In fact, I brought those plans, just in case." He flipped through the plans to the last few pages.

Sabrina leaned over them. "Oh, I like this; you found a way to combine them. But how would they share a central foyer and elevator?"

"This way." Stern took out his pencil, and he and Sabrina bent closer to the drawing. "We'd enlarge the foyer here and add an elevator behind the existing one . . ."

She nodded as he talked and sketched in bold, swift lines. After a moment she made a tentative sketch of her own in a corner of the sheet. Stern frowned, changed it, changed it again, then smiled. Their voices were murmurs, their pencils busy. Sabrina forgot everything except the joy of creating a space, envisioning it, and manipulating it with her pencil and her imagination. She followed Stern's lead, but whenever she offered a suggestion, he treated it seriously and once flashed her a smile that made her flush with pride. But then Koner, standing above them, broke in. "I told you: four apartments to a floor."

"Which is exactly what you'll get if you insist," Stern said, clipping his words. He stood and slapped dust off the knees of his jeans. "But Stephanie has some fine ideas and I think you should consider them very seriously."

"You think they're fine because they agree with you."

Stern grinned. "I inevitably admire people who agree with me."

Sabrina stood with them, holding the plans. "The Koner Building could get a lot of attention with this design. And Billy Koner would be called a visionary."

"That doesn't buy groceries," Koner said.

Sabrina met Stern's eyes and saw an impatience and frustration that matched her own. All designers and architects probably wish they could do without clients, she thought; at least some of the time. "Well, maybe you're right," she said at last. "Maybe ordinary apartments sell more easily than dramatic ones."

"Ordinary is exactly what people want," Koner said. "They don't want surprises; they want things they're comfortable with." He watched Sabrina roll up the plans. "I can get three hundred thousand for a twenty-five-hundred-square-foot loft apartment in this neighborhood; it's hot now; young couples like lofts and they like the city."

"I imagine they're adventurous, too," Sabrina said casually. "Maybe they like surprises instead of always being comfortable. Maybe they'd choose your building over another one if it was exciting: something that's fun to furnish and to show off to their friends."

Koner contemplated the empty space. He stood for a long time, his head bent in thought. Sabrina met Stern's eyes, and they waited, willing Koner to change his mind. "Well, maybe," he said at last. "The right people, if you can find them, pay for prestige. They don't enjoy paying for ordinary. I'll give it some thought; massage some numbers in my office. I'm not promising anything, but maybe."

Sabrina and Stern exchanged a smile. "Well done," Stern murmured. Then he said to Koner, "We'll put together ideas for the lower floors while you play with your numbers, but let us know as soon as you can."

Koner nodded. "Right. Absolutely. No time to lose."

"I have to finish the house in Lake Forest," Sabrina said quietly.

He frowned. "How long?"

"Two to three weeks."

"But that's finishing up a job; it's not full time, right? You could be meeting with Vern at the same time."

"Finishing a job is often the busiest time. I'll do what I can, but I won't have much time until April."

"This is a big job, Stephanie. People make time for big jobs."

She took a breath. "I have a family. I run Collectibles with Madeline; I have a project in Lake Forest that I intend to finish in the best way I can. I'll do my best, Billy; that's all I can promise."

He peered at her. "Maybe you're not hungry enough. Maybe I need somebody who's willing to toss everything else over to do my job."

"Maybe you do," she said, her voice turning cold. "I've never let anyone down, I've never had a project run over in cost or time unless my clients made too many changes, but I can't guarantee any of that unless I have control over when I start a new job. If that isn't good enough for you, I suggest you find someone else."

Scowling, he tried to stare her down, then nodded, as if to himself, and stuck out his hand. "I don't want anybody else. Vern? You okay working with Stephanie?"

"Very much so."

"Well, so okay." They shook hands. "So that's done."

"I'll send you my contract," Sabrina said. "You'll want your lawyer to look at it."

"Shouldn't be too complicated, should it? You're not the architect, after all; you're doing the simple part: paint and carpets. That shouldn't take more than a simple contract. Fixed price, too; we talked about that."

"And I said I didn't work that way." Sabrina walked to the center of the vast open space. The painted brick walls were flaking, long cracks ran like lightning through the plaster, electrical conduit hung from steel beams in the exposed ceiling, the window frames were splintered and most of the windows were broken, the lavatories had been vandalized, the painted steel columns that marched from one end of the building to the other were pitted and peeling, the floor was a wild mosaic of linoleum, carpet strips, paint, and the original wood planks.

"The simple part," she repeated thoughtfully. "I'll tell you what, Billy. I'll send you my contract, which is probably pretty standard, and when I've gone over Vern's plans I'll give you an estimate of the number of hours I'll spend on it—an estimate, not a fixed-price bid—and when we're finished, if you think I've made the job overcom-

plicated or billed you for too many hours, I'll refund ten
percent of my total charge.''

"You mean you're making a bet?"

"Something like that."

"Who decides how complicated it was or how many
hours it should have taken?"

"You do."

"How about that. Well, it's a deal. You're okay,
Stephanie. You believe in yourself. I like that."

"So do I," Stern said. He shook Sabrina's hand. "I'm
looking forward to working with you."

She drove home in a haze of euphoria. *Oh, Garth, I
can't wait to tell you . . .* That was the core of her life
now: that at the end of a wonderful day, or any kind of
day, what she wanted most of all was to share it with her
husband. *I'll always need this: to tell you all of it so we
can make it ours, not just mine.*

She treasured her excitement as she drove home and
pulled into the driveway, but as she came to a stop she saw
Penny flying toward her, sobbing. *Oh, not now. Later, but
not now; I really want this time just to be happy with
Garth . . .* But she saw that his car was not in the garage,
and then, the minute she opened the car door, Penny was
in her arms, so she pushed her exhilaration aside and knelt
on the driveway, holding Penny close. "Hush, hush,
sweet Penny. We'll take care of it, whatever it is."

After a moment, Penny's shudders eased and her breathing slowed. "Let's go inside," Sabrina said. "Otherwise,
we'll freeze to the driveway and Daddy will have to chisel
us loose. I'd like a cup of tea; how about hot chocolate for
you?"

Penny nodded. "She wanted me to have tea."

"You mean Mrs. Thirkell? Well, she's only been here
for a few days and I guess nobody told her that the best
thing in a crisis is hot chocolate. Come on, love, then
we'll talk."

Sabrina made hot chocolate while Mrs. Thirkell made
fresh tea and then Penny and Sabrina carried their mugs to

the living room and curled up in one of the deep couches
near the bay window. The wind had risen and tree branches
whipped against the house as low clouds gathered.
"Doesn't Chicago have springtime in March?" Sabrina
murmured. "Well, I ought to be used to it; London
doesn't, either."

"What?" Penny asked.

"Nothing important, sweetheart. Now tell me what happened."

But Penny, clutching her mug, was suddenly unable to
talk. Her face grew flushed, she huddled in the corner of
the couch, and then she was crying again.

"Penny," Sabrina said sharply. "I can't help you if
you don't tell me what it is. Is it about school? Or . . ."
She looked at Penny's drooping figure and remembered
their dinner conversation two weeks earlier. *Like, if nobody talked to you, you could look at the fish and they'd
keep you company.* "Is it your friends?"

"They're not my friends! They don't want me!"

"Well, why don't you tell me about that?"

"I can't. They just, well, you know, they get together
and talk and look at you, you know, like they're talking
about you and they laugh but you don't know why, or
what they're saying . . ."

"Where, Penny?"

"Oh, all over, but mainly the playground, at recess.
They stand real close together, you know, sort of bunched
up, all the girls, and the boys, too, and they smoke, you
know, they roll these cigarettes, grass, and they say these
things . . . like they're going to some kid's house after
school and do I want to come, and I can't—I mean, I want
to but I'm scared, so I say I have to go shopping with you
or something and the girls call me a baby and say I'm not
their friend and then . . ."

Through her anger, Sabrina said quietly, "Then what?
What happened today, Penny?"

Penny struggled with it and then the words poured out.
"Greg, he's one of the boys, gave me his cigarette, there

was just a little piece left, and I took it because . . . you know . . . I didn't want them to laugh at me, but I couldn't put it in my mouth, it smelled and it was soggy and *I couldn't do it*, so he grabbed it back and said in this disgusted voice, 'oh, shit'—I'm sorry, Mommy, but that's what he said, and then he pushed me backwards until I was against the fence and he rubbed against me, you know, down here, and he said I need a lot of teaching and he called me Henny Penny and then everybody called me that and they were laughing and pointing and I started to run away but Greg grabbed me and he put his hand here and said how flat I am and then he . . . he sort of threw me to Wally and Wally pushed me to Cal and they all did that, like I was a . . . a *football* or something, and I got dizzy and I was crying and then the girls said they should leave me alone and then I ran away.''

Sabrina was cradling her, so enraged she could not speak. She kissed Penny's forehead and her wet, closed eyes and rocked with her.

"So I went to the bathroom and washed my face, I didn't know what else to do, I was so hot, Mommy, but I was cold, too, and my teeth kept chattering, and then in math Mrs. Thorne asked me if I was sick and I said no and in history Miss Daley said I looked sick but I said I was okay and then when I came home you weren't here and Mrs. Thirkell said I should have cookies and some tea, but I just wanted you.''

Sabrina held her, rocking gently, sick with anger and fear. What can we do, she thought: how can we protect her? Every day she leaves this house and the people who love her and try to make her feel good about herself, and she goes into the world and it's so big and harsh, and there are only the two of us, Garth and me, trying to protect her. How can we do it?

Penny's tears had stopped; now and then she hiccuped. Sabrina brushed her heavy black hair back from her forehead and saw, as if for the first time, how beautiful she was, her face a perfect oval, her deep blue eyes wide spaced over high cheekbones, her hair a mass of black curls. Her body was wiry and tough; she was a strong swimmer and was becoming a fine tennis player, but all Sabrina saw was a fragile child who needed protection.

"Penny, do you want to be friends with those girls?"

"Well, sure. I mean, everybody does."

"Why?"

"Because they're the best." Penny looked up at her earnestly. "They know more than anybody else about everything, and they're so grown up and they decide who gets first in line at lunch and who goes inside first when it's raining . . . you know, all those things. If you're their friend you always get the best and you have the most fun, 'cause they have the most fun of anybody."

"Do they get the best grades?"

"No, but that isn't . . . I mean, I get good grades, but I'm not popular the way they are."

"But they don't sound very nice."

There was a pause. "They're nice if they like you."

"Well, anybody can do that. It's harder to be nice to people you *don't* like a lot. The people who can do that are the people I admire and want to be friends with."

Penny sighed and was silent.

"How many boys and girls are we talking about?" Sabrina asked.

Penny closed her eyes and counted. "Six boys and five girls."

"That's not very many. What about all the others in your class? Don't you want to be friends with them?"

"They're okay. They're just not . . . exciting."

"What about Barbara Goodman? She was your best friend a couple of months ago."

"We still are, sort of. She kind of hangs around them sometimes, and then she says she just wants to be with me . . . it's sort of confusing. I don't think she knows what she wants."

"Have you talked to her about it?"

Penny shook her head. "I mean, how can I tell her I

want her to like me better than them when I . . . sort of
. . . want to like them better than her?''

"It sounds as if neither one of you is sure of what you
want.''

Penny nibbled on a fingernail.

"Well, let's talk about the rest of it." Sabrina moved
back a little so she could watch Penny's face. "They use
drugs at school and also, I'm sure, after school, and that's
what they're asking you to do when they ask you to come
with them to somebody's house. Is that right?''

"I guess. I've never gone, but they talk about it.''

"And they drink, too?''

"Mostly beer. At least that's what they say. And Scotch
sometimes.''

"And what else do they do after school?''

There was a long pause. Penny reached for her mug of
hot chocolate and drained it. "They have sex," she said.

Sabrina drew in her breath. *These are eleven-year-old
children. What has happened to speed up their lives so
that they've become children who have no childhood?*

She and Penny had talked about this in October, on
another day when Penny had come home from school
embarrassed and afraid that her classmates would think
she was a baby "because," she had said, "in the gym
locker room they whisper and giggle and talk about . . .
you know . . . fucking and screwing . . . and I don't want
to do it! Ever!''

Sabrina had let pass for the moment the words Penny
used. There were more important things to talk about.
"You will, Penny," she had said. "But wait for it. Don't
turn lovemaking into fucking; don't make it as ordinary as
a handshake. Wait until someone is so important in your
life that you want to share the things you feel in this one
way that is like no other.''

And Penny had seemed to accept it, to understand that
she could have her own ideas and feelings about lovemaking and not be ashamed if they were different from those
of her classmates.

But when they had had that talk, in October, Penny had been worried about what the others in her class were talking about, not what they were doing. Now, it seemed, they were doing it.

Sabrina looked through the window at the sedate street where they lived. Tall, serene elms and maples formed a long tunnel of bare branches with the first spring buds just beginning to push their way to the sun; solid houses were lined up on both sides, all of them exactly the same distance from the street, all of them neatly painted, roofs tight against rain and snow, windows hung with shades or drapes, lawns free of weeds, sidewalks free of cracks. Everything looked snug, settled, secure, protected. But the children of those houses, and of other houses on streets that looked just like this one, were making their own way in a world that was not settled or protected, and who could predict what way that would be? *What was I doing when I was eleven?*

Oh, we were so insulated, she thought. There must have been drugs at Juliette, but no one that we knew used them, at least not openly; Stephanie and I didn't know anyone who drank more than a daring glass of champagne at school dances; we didn't know anyone who had any serious plans for sex, at least before we graduated. Somehow we thought we wouldn't be grown up until we graduated from high school. Penny's classmates think they're grown up at eleven.

"Mommy?" Penny was looking at Sabrina, her eyes wide with worry. "Are you mad at me?"

"No, sweetheart, of course not. I'm thinking about those boys and girls in your class. If you don't want to do those things—"

"I don't! I told you a long time ago—remember?—only now they're always talking about it and if you don't do what they do, they make fun of you and it *hurts,* and they don't talk to you and they walk right into you, you know, like you're not even *there,* you're just nobody . . ."

"Or they throw you around," Sabrina said when Penny

fell silent. "Why didn't you come home when they did that to you?"

"I couldn't. They would have laughed at me and called me a baby and told everybody."

"Yes," Sabrina murmured. Power plays and mocking peer pressure had been a fact of life even at exclusive Juliette. "But, Penny, you said you wanted to go with them after school, but you were scared. Does that mean you're thinking about doing the things they do?"

There was a long silence. Penny twisted a strand of hair around her finger, frowning fiercely in concentration.

"Penny?"

"No," she said at last.

Sabrina sighed. "Have you ever lied to me, Penny?"

Tears filled Penny's eyes. She shook her head.

"How about now?"

Penny twisted her hair and looked at her lap and was silent.

Sabrina finished her tea but held on to the mug, as if for support. *I've never had a daughter; I've never helped anyone grow up. What if I say the wrong things?* She saw herself earlier that day, with Vernon Stern, excited by her own competence, proud of her ability. Now she was filled with anxiety. It's easier to design a building than to help a young person grow up, she thought ruefully. She looked at Penny's lowered head and nervous fingers, the tense line of her neck, the slim body curled tightly in the corner of the couch. *What does Penny want me to say?*

The back door slammed and Cliff came in, pulling off his backpack. One sleeve of his soccer shirt hung loose, ripped at the shoulder. "Mom, can you fix this? I need it for tomorrow."

"You could say hi," Sabrina said over her shoulder.

"Oh, yeah, hi. Hi, Penny. Are you guys having a private talk?"

"Yes," Sabrina said.

"Can you fix my shirt?"

"Later. Do you have much homework?"

Cliff shrugged.

"What does that mean?"

"A little bit. It won't take long."

"Even in science?"

"Okay, okay, I'll do it. Shall I leave my shirt?"

"Put it in the washing machine. I can't sew through mud."

"Okay. What's for dinner?"

"I don't know. Why don't you ask Mrs. Thirkell?"

"How come you don't cook anymore?"

"Because I'm having a private talk."

"*Okay.*" He turned to go. "Wash the shirt," he mumbled, "talk to Mrs. Thirkell, do my homework . . . God, they really keep me busy around here."

Sabrina stifled a laugh. She turned back to Penny and took in her doleful face and tense posture. *Still waiting.* But Cliff had provided a respite and Sabrina's anxiety had faded. She was Penny and Cliff's mother and they trusted her and loved her, and the best she could do was tell them what she felt was right and important. And if she made mistakes, she hoped they would someday forgive her.

"Penny, I think you aren't telling me the truth. I think you want this group to like you so much that you're on the way to joining them even if it's scary." Penny sat still, the muscles in her neck and arms taut and quivering. Sabrina took a breath. "Well, you're not going to do that."

Penny's head shot up; her eyes were wide.

"It's illegal for young people to use drugs and alcohol, but besides that, it's incredibly stupid. You've got good bodies and clear minds, but you can mess them up before you've even begun to know who you are and how you can be part of all the worlds that are waiting for you. Everything is waiting for you—friendship and learning and adventures and love—but you have to come to them gradually, making discoveries all along the way and learning how to fit them into your life. But those kids in your school are willing to put all that at risk because they think it's cool to pretend to be grown up. And they don't even know what that means.''

Penny was staring at her, and Sabrina realized how intensely she had been speaking. "Sex isn't for eleven-year-olds, Penny," she said quietly. "They can brag about it from here to the next county, but they don't know the first thing about it. They're too young. I told you last time we talked about this that intercourse isn't an after-school sport or a way of scratching an itch; intercourse is a language, it's using your body to say, 'I love you.' You remember that, don't you, Penny? Well, those kids in your school haven't the vaguest idea how to do that; they're like Tinkertoys that somebody put together with a few gears that turn, but they have nothing inside—''

A giggle broke from Penny, but Sabrina was in full flight and barely noticed.

"They're not all put together yet, their hearts and their heads, their emotions and their understanding of themselves and the world; they have no insight into the value of their bodies. They're going through motions and thinking they're pretty great, but they're not finding out how to make intercourse loving and joyful and fun. And I am not going to let you mess up the wonders of sex and everything else that's waiting for you just because a bunch of kids talk big and laugh at you. They may talk big, but they're babies. In fact, I'll bet they're laughing because they're just as scared as you are, but they've gotten in too deep to admit it.''

Penny's lips were parted; she had not taken her eyes from Sabrina's face.

"So if I find out that you've gone to anybody's house, even your girlfriends' houses, without my permission; if I find out you've been doing drugs or drinking or having sex—and I'm very good at finding things out, Penny, you know that—I'm grounding you for a year. Not a week or a month; a year. No more art classes or art supplies, no more friends over to spend the night, no more movies on Saturday afternoons or trips to the Art Institute or the planetarium or the aquarium or the Field Museum with Daddy and Cliff and me. Is that clear?''

"That's not fair," Penny said, but it came out weakly: not a cry of defiance but a standard complaint so intrinsic to adolescence that young people could utter it in their sleep. Penny's rigid muscles, Sabrina saw, had relaxed; she was no longer quivering.

"I think it's fair because I think it's right. And I think it's important for your growing up. When you're ready to leave home you'll make your own decisions about what's fair and right and important, and your father and I won't be a part of it, but until then—"

"I don't want to leave home!" Penny flung herself into Sabrina's lap. "I want to stay here forever, with you and Daddy and Cliff and our house and everything just the same!"

Sabrina laid her cheek on Penny's hair. "You'll grow up, my sweet Penny, and you'll create your own life; you'll believe in yourself and trust your decisions, and you'll know who you want to be and how you're going to become that person. But for now we're all here, we're together in our family and our house, and it's going to stay that way for a long time. I promise you that."

She looked up. Garth was standing in the doorway, carrying his raincoat and briefcase, watching her. He raised his eyebrows in a question, and Sabrina shook her head. "No, you're not interrupting; we've had a good talk and we've just about covered everything. Haven't we, Penny?"

Penny sat up. "I guess."

"But?" Sabrina asked.

"I don't know what to say when they . . . you know."

"Say your mother told you you'd be grounded for a year if you go with them. I did that with Cliff last fall and it worked like a charm."

"With Cliff? You did? Why? What did he do?"

"Well, that's between Cliff and me. But it worked for him and I'm sure it will work for you. In fact, now that I

think about it, it's amazing how a few basic ideas can be
used in dozens of situations, like ingredients in recipes. It
makes being a parent a lot easier than one would think.''

Garth chuckled. ''It's only easier when you're smart
enough to figure out how to use the ingredients. Penny, I
saw two of your puppets in a display in Kroch's window
today; you didn't tell us they'd be there.''

Penny leaped up, everything else forgotten. ''In the
window? My puppets? Why?''

''There was a precariously balanced tower of books on
arts and crafts, and in front of it were two extremely
beautiful puppets and a sign saying they were made by
Penny Andersen. I told everyone who was walking by that
that was my daughter. They were very impressed.''

Penny was jumping from one foot to the other. ''Can
we go see them? Mrs. Casey must have loaned them, but
she never told me. Can we go? Please? Right now?
Please?''

Garth and Sabrina exchanged a quick look. Five o'clock
was their time, a quiet hour for a glass of wine and talk
about their day. ''Okay,'' Garth said, ''a very quick trip to
Kroch's, and then your mother and I want some time
together.''

''Okay, but can we go *now?*''

Sabrina watched them go, Garth tall and lean, his hair
a little too long, his jacket patched at the elbows, his shoes
scuffed. We have plenty of money for him to buy a new
everything, she thought, but we don't do that because he's
still worried about comments from his colleagues. Peer
pressure. Not so different from what Penny faces. Maybe
we never escape it: wondering what others see when they
look at us, what they want to see, what we want to show
them. Poor Penny, to have to deal with all of that at her
age. But when Penny and Garth returned, Penny was talking only about the display and the manager who had com-
plimented her on her artistic skill. ''I'm famous! They're
going to put my picture in the paper! I have to tell Cliff!''

When she had run upstairs, Garth sat with Sabrina on

the couch. Mrs. Thirkell appeared, and set a bottle of wine and two glasses and a gold-rimmed platter of hors d'oeuvres on the table before them. "There were a number of calls today, my lady; the messages are on your desk. I would have told you earlier, but I didn't want to interrupt you and Penny."

"Thank you, Mrs. Thirkell. Seven-thirty for dinner, please; we're running a little late. And would you make sure that Cliff really washes his hands? He seems determined to keep part of the soccer field with him at all times."

Mrs. Thirkell smiled. "I have a photo of England's top cricket player accepting an award with impeccably clean hands. I'll show it to Cliff." She made minute adjustments to the placement of the wine bottle and the platter, made a swift survey of the living room to see that nothing else required her attention, and then was gone.

Garth poured the wine. "Does she lie in wait like a cat, watching for the perfect moment to pounce?"

"She probably timed it to Penny's going upstairs." Sabrina contemplated him. "Are you really annoyed? I know she hasn't been here long, Garth, but she's settled in so completely and it's so wonderful to have her, I can't believe you're upset."

"It doesn't bother you that she stands around and chatters when we ought to be having our own time?"

"She chattered, as you call it, for a little less than one minute."

"And why the hell does she hang on to her royalist 'my lady'? It doesn't belong in this country and the kids don't understand it."

"The kids find it vastly amusing. She's always called me that, Garth, and it seems to give her pleasure to go on doing it."

"She has never called Stephanie Andersen 'my lady.' "

"No, but she looks at me and thinks I look exactly like Lady Sabrina Longworth, and maybe she doesn't want to think of that woman as being dead. Maybe she'll get over

117

it after she's been here awhile, but if she doesn't, I don't think it's anything to worry about. What is it that really bothers you? Is it being waited on?" She gazed at him. "That is it, isn't it? Deep inside, the Minnesota farm boy feels guilty because he's living like a capitalist and therefore he must be exploiting labor. Good heavens, Garth, Mrs. Thirkell is doing a job she loves and does superbly; her job is no different, really, from yours at the university or mine at the Koner Building. Why not let her enjoy it and let yourself enjoy the fruits of it?"

"The Koner Building. I meant to ask you about that as soon as I got home. Was it a good day?"

"Yes." Sabrina felt a spurt of anger. "Damn it, it was a wonderful day, and I couldn't wait to tell you about it—"

"I'm sorry." Garth put his arm around her. "You were right about there being too much going on, and I'm more wound up than I think. But I don't mean to take it out on you."

Sabrina slid her hand to the back of his head and brought his lips to hers, and they kissed with an intensity and passion that was the greater for the tensions that sprang up between them. "I love you," Garth said. "I never want to hurt you; what we're building is so good, if I thought I was destroying it—"

"You couldn't do that. All the way home this afternoon I kept thinking that nothing I did was complete until I'd shared it with you; I felt I'd explode with all the things I had to tell you. And I want to hear about your day, everybody you talked to, and I want to know when what's-his-name from the congressman's office is coming—"

"Dinner, my lady," said Mrs. Thirkell from the doorway.

Sabrina felt Garth's muscles tense. She stayed still; he would have to handle this himself. "Good timing," he said after a moment, with an irony that only Sabrina caught. He put his lips beside her ear. "And you and I, *my lady*, my dearest lady, will sit before the fire later on, just the two of us, while the rest of our world sleeps, and whatever we need we will give to each other with no one's help.''

Sabrina gave a low laugh. She turned her head and kissed him lightly. ''You are a most wonderful man, and I love you, and I am so very glad that I have a lifetime to share with you.''

Turning back to the kitchen, Mrs. Thirkell nodded with approval. It was a wonderful thing how love grew. She had reason to know it: already she loved Mrs. Andersen fully as much as she had loved Lady Longworth. And in fact it was as if Mrs. Andersen *was,* in a strange way, her sister. Mrs. Thirkell was not a mystic; she prided herself in seeing clearly what was what, but the truth was that she saw both sisters in Mrs. Andersen and if that was strange and impossible to understand, then that was the way it was. And thank goodness, Mrs. Thirkell thought, carrying the soup tureen to the sideboard in the dining room. This family is better for it, and heaven knows, so am I. ''Penny,'' she said, ''how about helping me serve the soup?''

*S*tephanie was alone. Max was in Marseilles, Madame Besset was at the market, and the house was silent, except for the drumming of a hard early March rain on the tile roof. "I'll only be a couple of days," Max had said that morning as he packed a small bag, and after he left, Stephanie wandered through the rooms, trailing her fingers along the furniture, catching glimpses, through the rain-streaked windows, of the misty hills in the distance. "My house," she said aloud. "This is my house."

She liked the silence. It was the first time she had been alone since she and Max had arrived, a month earlier, the first time she could listen to her own thoughts for a whole day, without interruption. "I live here. Even if I don't know anything about myself, I have these rooms where I belong, and a name—Sabrina Lacoste, even if it feels somehow wrong—and a housekeeper, a gardener, a maintenance man, and . . . a husband."

In the kitchen, Madame Besset had left a platter of baked Provençal tomatoes and sliced roast veal for Stephanie's lunch; the table in the breakfast room was set for one, with a bottle of wine and an espresso maker ready to be switched on. The kitchen was immaculate, the house was clean, the laundry folded and put away, the plants watered. There was nothing left to be done.

Stephanie walked out of the kitchen and up the stairs to the large bedroom Max had been using, alone, for a month. Madame Besset had been here, too: the bed was made, the clothes put away, the bathroom scrubbed. But Max's presence hung in the room, in the book on his bedside table, his hairbrush and a tray of tie tacks and cuff links on the dresser, a pile of coins on the rolltop desk—he never carried loose change, Stephanie had learned—beside an embossed pen rising from a heavy gold penholder and Stephanie's picture, snapped by Robert in front of the fire in the living room, framed in silver.

Idly, Stephanie pulled up on the handle of the closed rolltop. It was locked. How odd, she thought; I guess he doesn't trust me. Or Madame Besset. She tried the drawers; they were all locked. Maybe he doesn't trust anybody.

When, at breakfast, he had told her he would be taking a trip, on business, she had asked, "What business?" "Exports," he had said briefly, and changed the subject. "No, but I really want to know," Stephanie had insisted. "You said once that you and Robert work together, but when I asked him about it, he said you meant that you give money to some of his causes. You're both so secretive; I hate that."

"Not secretive; I thought you'd find it boring. I export farm and construction equipment to developing countries. Tractors, forklifts, backhoes, whatever they need and can pay for."

"Do you go there, to all those countries?"

"Sometimes. Usually not. I use my office and warehouse in Marseilles, and I work from here."

"But what do you *do?*"

"I just said—"

"No, I mean, if you don't travel to those countries to make sales or negotiate contracts, and you don't type up the contracts or go out and buy the tractors and forklifts yourself—at least I assume you don't—and you don't deliver them in person to your customers, what do you do?"

He chuckled. "Not much, it seems. Well, I do make sales and negotiate contracts, as it happens, usually by phone; I have local agents who take care of the details. But mostly I deal with government agencies. The poorer the country, it seems, the more devious and obstructionist the government is, and even the best governments are a hierarchy of agencies staffed by people committed only to holding on to their jobs. Usually they're someone's brother or cousin or nephew, and that gives them a certain confidence; those are the ones who get things done. The ones without connections are usually the smartest and most interesting ones, but they spend their time protecting themselves by tying knots in every step of every negotiation to a degree of complication so dense that no one but they can unravel it. I spend my time unraveling their knots."

Stephanie was smiling. "I like that. I like listening to you; you make everything a story."

His face changed and he reached for her hand. "I don't like leaving you. I'd take you, but I couldn't spend time with you."

"What about Robert? He said you work together."

"Robert has assigned himself the task of saving the youth of the world. He has a few cohorts, priests in various countries, and they go about educating and training and finding jobs for young people. I give him money; that's all I do; it's very simple."

Simple, Stephanie thought, standing in his bedroom with her hand on the rolltop of his desk. Very simple. So why does he lock everything up?

She sat on the edge of the bed and gazed at her picture on the desk. "I love you," Max said every night when he kissed her on the forehead and cheek and let her go to the small first-floor room she still made her own. The night before, he had embraced her, holding her tightly before giving her that chaste kiss on her cheek and forehead. And when he had released her, Stephanie had felt, for the first time, a sense of loss, and had almost reached out to return to the warmth of his arms.

But she had not. Because nothing else had changed: she still believed he kept things from her. And she still could not trust him.

Sitting on his bed, she listened to the drumming of the rain. She was beginning to feel uncomfortable with the silence that she had treasured only a little while before. The air in the bedroom seemed heavy, stifling the sound of the rain; Stephanie clapped her hands, and the sound was muffled. She began to tremble. It was as if once again she was lost in the fog that had enveloped her when she was in the hospital.

"I don't want to be alone," she said aloud. "I've never been alone and I don't want to be now." She drew in her breath. *I've never been alone.* Was that really true? If it was, then she must have lived with her parents until she went to college—*if* she went to college—and then gone on living with them or gotten married right away—*if* she had gotten married; Max said she'd told him she hadn't been married—and then lived with her husband . . . and children? But Max said she didn't have children.

And then what? How did she get from there, wherever that was—parents, maybe college, maybe marriage—to being Max's wife, on a yacht off the coast of France?

The fog closed in, the silence wrapped itself around her. *Oh, please come back! My past—my own life—my self— please come back! I want to know who I am!*

She jumped up and ran down the stairs. Her soft shoes made almost no sound on the polished wood, and in the crushing silence she ran faster, back to the kitchen. She turned on the faucet and listened to the splashing of water; she opened the freezer and dropped ice cubes into a glass, the clink loud and comforting. On the counter, her lunch waited for her. She took the platter of tomatoes and veal to the breakfast room and sat at the place set with blue-glazed Provençal dishes and a country wineglass, heavy and solid in her hand. She served herself and poured a glass of wine, then sat still for a long time, holding the glass and looking at the heavy raindrops bouncing as they struck the terrace, splashing in pools of their own making, running like tears down the trunks of trees. "I don't want to be alone," she said again, and looked at the empty chair to her right. She wanted Max.

In the afternoon she lit a fire in the library and curled up in a leather chair, leafing through a book of French paintings and sculpture. But when she heard Madame Besset return, she rushed to the kitchen for companionship. "Oh, how wet you are!" she cried.

"Like a duck, Madame Sabrina," Madame Besset said cheerfully. "One would think the good Lord had turned the ocean upside down, just over Cavaillon. A strange thing for the Lord to do, but then, many things connected with the Lord frequently seem strange, do they not?" She dropped her raincoat on the tile floor and toweled her hair vigorously until it stood up like a black fringe above her round black eyes and high brows. Her face was round with full cheeks, her figure was round and ample, and her arms were muscled from working on her family's farm. "Perhaps, in the spring, I will grow tall, like our crops, from all this good rain." She laughed as she began to put away her purchases.

"Let me help," Stephanie said.

"Ah, no, madame, you sit there. Perhaps you would like a café au lait?"

"No, I want to do something; I want to help you put everything away."

Madame Besset tilted her head to the side in thought. "No, madame. It is not right."

"But I want it and that makes it right."

"Madame, forgive me, but some things are correct and some are not. I was taught very thoroughly what was correct, and you must not ask me to forget all that I was taught."

"What is correct on your farm may not be correct in this

house. While you work here, all you need to remember is that what monsieur and I say is correct. And I'm tired of sitting around and doing nothing, Madame Besset, and you will make me very happy if you move to one side so that I can work with you.''

It was the most authoritative speech Stephanie had made, and Madame Besset's eyes were wide with surprise. Until now she had felt she worked for the husband, since he was the only one who gave orders. Now she saw that there would be two people to please: a man of strong opinions and a woman who changed with the rain and wind. But the position was good and paid well and so of course Madame Besset would adapt; she came from a line of French farmers and vintners who had learned, through the bloody centuries of Provence's history, to adapt and adapt again, and survive. She smiled. ''You are recovered, Madame Sabrina. I am pleased to see it. And I would find it pleasant to share this task.''

Madame Besset hummed a folk tune as they emptied the large woven baskets she carried to the market three times a week. The kitchen was cozy and cheerful, with a white tiled floor and white cabinets. The countertops were tiled in red, and so was the large island with a built-in grill, and Stephanie took pleasure in the colors as she and Madame Besset piled up the food they took from the baskets: shiny purple eggplants, oranges, lemons, leeks, russet potatoes, red cabbage, wrinkled black marinated olives, pale green endive, and dark green spinach and chard. All the lights were on, and the food and the copper-bottomed utensils and the jars of jam and vinegar shone brightly against the leaden windows streaming with rain. Stephanie felt a long, slow sense of comfort fill her as she and Madame Besset worked together. I wonder if I had many women friends, she thought as she put away green-gold olive oil and goat cheese wrapped in chestnut leaves. I'm sure I did. I'm sure I had a very close woman friend. Sometimes that's the best thing of all.

''Madame will have chicken stew for dinner,'' Madame

Besset pronounced as she closely examined two pale chickens spread-eagled on the counter, searching for feathers the butcher had overlooked. "And endive salad. Is there anything else madame would like?"

Stephanie was piling tiny white potatoes in a basket. "I would like it if you would stop calling me madame."

"But then what would I call you, madame?"

"I have a name."

"Call you by your given name? Oh, madame, that would be very wrong. It is as I said: I was taught what is correct and what is not correct, and that is most definitely not correct. Your name would be a piece of glue on my tongue. No, madame, it is not possible."

Stephanie sighed. "So many rules, so much formality . . ." Two of the potatoes fell to the floor and she bent to retrieve them. "You and Mrs. Thirkell, you're just the same: so strict with formality . . ."

"Who, madame?"

Stephanie stood up. Her eyes were bright. "Mrs. Thirkell," she repeated.

"And who is that, madame?"

"Oh . . . someone I once knew." She spoke casually, but inwardly she was filled with excitement. *Mrs. Thirkell. She must have been a housekeeper, like Madame Besset. Where was that? I don't know, but it doesn't matter for now, because I'm remembering. I'm remembering.*

"It does not sound like a French name," Madame Besset said dismissively. She found a feather and plucked it vehemently. "One cannot trust a butcher these days."

Stephanie watched her. "I want to learn to drive," she said.

Madame Besset looked up. "Yes, madame."

"And I would like you to teach me."

"Oh, madame, Monsieur Lacoste would be angry. He would say that that is his responsibility, not mine."

Stephanie piled more potatoes into the basket. Max did not want her to leave the house. He found reasons for her to stay at home whenever she suggested an excursion to

Cavaillon or the surrounding countryside or even to the Auberge de la Colline, the small café at the far end of their street.

They had been there once for dinner, seated near the huge open fireplace with its grill jutting over the raised brick hearth, but that was all, only once. But Robert had said it was possible that she would remember more if she saw more. I need to see and hear, Stephanie thought; anything to jog my memory. I've got to see more than this house and these gardens; I've got to be part of the world. Then the world will come back to me. I've got to get away from here. So I have to be able to drive.

"Ask him, madame," said Madame Besset gently. "All women drive now. Even the most backward men get used to it."

Stephanie laughed. "I will ask him. But he's not here, and I don't know for sure how long he'll be gone, and I'm anxious to start. I want this very much," she said strongly.

"Well. It is of course very difficult, living here, so far from town. One does need a car. Well, madame." She pondered it. "We could begin, and then monsieur, as soon as he returns, would continue. You never drove, madame? At all?"

I must have driven a car; I must have cooked. Women do those things. But I don't remember . . . Oh, God, if I could only remember . . . "No," she said to Madame Besset. "I never learned. But I want to. Right away. This afternoon."

"But the rain, madame! It is not the best—"

"We'll go slowly. Just up here. Please; it's very important to me. We won't drive into Cavaillon today."

"I should hope not," Madame Besset said under her breath. She shrugged. "Well, then, if you will wait just a moment . . ." She dropped the chickens into an iron pot with chopped vegetables and water, threw in a handful of herbs, propped a lid halfway over the pot, and turned on a low flame beneath it. "Now, madame. The chickens cook and we drive."

Max had taken the large Renault, leaving a small low-slung Alfa Romeo in the garage. Madame Besset shook her head as she and Stephanie walked past it. "Most definitely not that one." She opened the garage door and the two of them, wearing slick raincoats and hoods, ran the few steps to Madame Besset's small Citroën.

Stephanie sat behind the wheel. "Now, madame," said Madame Besset, and visibly began to swell with the importance of what she was doing. She sat straighter, her fingers emphatically jabbing. "The key. The clutch. The brake. The gas pedal. The gearshift. The radio. Ignore the radio, madame; you must not be distracted." She named all the parts of the car, pointed out the five positions for the gearshift, then told Stephanie to turn the key. "Fortunately, I have backed into the driveway, so you have only to drive forward."

For the next hour, in the pounding rain, the small Citroën lurched along the main street that circled the plateau above Cavaillon. Stephanie sat rigidly, her hands gripping the wheel, her face set with concentration, lifting her foot too fast or not fast enough, pressing too lightly or slamming the brake or releasing the clutch with a jerk that caused Madame Besset to cry out, turning too sharply on the curves or not sharply enough, yanking the steering wheel to left or right when a tree loomed ahead. But soon the drive became smoother, Stephanie's movements grew more sure, her body began to relax.

"Very good, madame," said Madame Besset. "One would think you had done this before, you learn so quickly."

"Yes," Stephanie murmured, "it feels very comfortable." In fact, it felt wonderful. The bulk of the car, its steady hum and enclosed warmth in the pouring rain made her feel strong and powerful, and exhilaration filled her as the Citroën obeyed her commands, spurting forward, stopping, turning to left or right or forging straight ahead. She sat tall and looked straight ahead. She was going ten miles an hour; the drenched stone walls and iron gates guarding stone houses, the sodden gardens, heavy bushes and tall trees moved past in dignified slow motion, but Stephanie felt she was flying. I can go anywhere, she thought. To Cavaillon and all the other places Max and Madame Besset and Robert talk about: Aix-en-Provence, Roussillon, Arles, Saint-Rémy, Gordes, Avignon. I can go anywhere. I'm free.

She drove one more smooth circuit, then came to a gentle stop at the driveway of the Auberge de la Colline. "Well done, madame," said Madame Besset. "A good, smooth stop. But we are not home yet."

"We're not ready to go home," Stephanie replied firmly. She contemplated the driveway, gauging its width between two stone pillars, then took a deep breath and drove between the pillars into the parking area. There were only a few cars at this time of day, but Stephanie had not considered maneuvering into a parking place, and while she tried to consider it now, the car kept moving forward.

"Madame!" Madame Besset said, alarmed, and Stephanie turned to ask her a question, but there was no time: the car reached a row of bushes at the far end of the lot and came to an abrupt stop with its headlights in the branches.

"Oh, no! Oh, how could I—" Stephanie's shoulders slumped as she looked at the bushes embracing the front end of the car. "I'm so sorry, Madame Besset; look what I've done to your car. I'm so sorry—"

"Please, madame, do not be upset. You did so well—"

"But look what I've done. Why didn't I step on the brake? I just forgot about it." Her voice rose. "Forgot, forgot, can't remember . . . that's what's wrong with me!"

"Madame, please!"

"We'll buy you a new car, I'm so sorry, I should have known I couldn't drive—"

"*Madame.*"

Stephanie turned and Madame Besset put a hand on her arm.

"You drove very well. You did excellently for one who has never driven. I am sure you have not destroyed my car; it perhaps will need some new paint. It does not worry me, and it must not worry you, either. It is a small matter and all will be well."

In a minute, Stephanie gave a small smile. "Thank you. I think I'd better back out of here."

"Ah, no, madame; do not attempt any more right now. We have not practiced driving in reverse. I will get us out of here and then perhaps I should drive home."

Stephanie shook her head. I did do well, she thought, I did excellently, and I'm not going to give up. "I'll get us out of here and I'll drive home. But not right away. First we're going to have a glass of wine. We've earned it. Poor Madame Besset; were you afraid for your life?"

Madame Besset opened her mouth to object, then closed it. They were in her car and it certainly was not proper for her to drink wine with madame in a café—or anywhere!—but she worked for madame and madame had become very stubborn suddenly, and more sure of herself, and it seemed unlikely that madame would change her mind about the wine, or perhaps about anything, just because Madame Besset objected.

The café was almost empty, the tables neatly set with pink patterned tablecloths and napkins, the ladder-back chairs pushed in, the stone floor swept clean, poised for the dinner crowd. Stephanie and Madame Besset sat near the fireplace, the flames rising inside a tepee of logs, plates warming on the brick hearth. "Red wine," Stephanie said and looked at Madame Besset, who, after a moment, nodded. They were silent, gazing at the fire, Madame Besset with her mouth in a thin line of resignation, Stephanie smiling to herself, once again feeling wonderful.

The owner of the café brought the wine and two slices of pear tatin—"to fortify two lovely ladies on a very wet day, with my compliments."

Stephanie watched him walk away. "What a nice thing to do."

"He most likely remembers madame from her dinner here with monsieur and is looking for more visits," said Madame Besset, knowing that there was only one lovely lady at the table.

"Oh, how hard you are. I think he was just feeling generous and wanted to brighten a rainy day." Stephanie tasted the wine. "This is very good. Well, we will come back. I like this room and I like the owner and this wine is excellent." She took a bite of the pear tatin. "Everything is excellent. I think we'll come here often for dinner, certainly on your days off, Madame Besset."

The room was quiet. Two men sat at a table in the back, reading Provençal newspapers; two men nearby were playing chess while a third watched; in a corner a man sat alone with a carafe of wine and a small dish of walnuts. The clatter of dishes and pots and pans could be heard from the kitchen. Stephanie saw herself and Madame Besset sitting at their small table, two women sharing a glass of wine on a winter afternoon, the warmth of the fire curling around them, their rain slickers and hats dripping from a nearby coat tree, and she felt a rush of affection for Madame Besset. This is how women become friends, she thought, and asked, "Madame Besset, are you married?"

"Yes, madame."

"And? Do you have children?"

"Yes, madame."

"Are they young? Do they still live at home?"

"No, madame."

"Oh, I will not have this!" Stephanie exclaimed. "I want a conversation, not questions and answers as if you're a student taking a test. Surely we can talk to each other as two women; what would be wrong with that? I promise to ignore you when we're at home, if that's what you would like. I could even order you around quite haughtily, if that is what you were taught to think of as correct."

A smile flickered on Madame Besset's lips and the muscles in her face began to relax. She was aware of the warmth of the fire and the excellent red wine and pear tatin, and she liked—more today than before—this very beautiful and kind lady who was so strangely childlike one moment, seeming lost and bewildered, and so much a woman the next. And always lonely, Madame Besset thought, and found herself leaning forward. Two women having a conversation; there could be nothing wrong in that. In fact, it could be very pleasant. "Well, madame, I have seven children, three boys and four girls, born between the time I was sixteen and twenty-eight. Of course they are grown now, and four of them have families of their own, but still one thinks always of one's children as children."

"And your husband? He owns the farm where you live?"

"He and my father and uncle. It is large enough to support two families—my uncle's and ours—"

"Your mother is dead?"

"For thirty years. Some tumor . . . no one knew what it was and she did not trust doctors. And then it was too late."

"So she was not with you to help with the children."

"No one helped me with the children. I am fortunate in that I have a large lap, madame, and much good humor. And I know what is correct, so I could teach my little ones and then they knew how to behave and they were no trouble."

Stephanie smiled. "It sounds so simple."

"It is simple, madame, if one is firm and has a loving heart."

"And do you—"

"Pardon, madame, do you wish more wine?" The café owner had materialized beside their table, his balding head shining beneath the ceiling lights, his curved black brows raised in inquiry.

"Not for me," Stephanie said. "But Madame Besset . . . ?"

"No, no, I am content, madame."

"You are, aren't you?" Stephanie asked. "I mean, with your life and your family and your farm."

"Of course, madame; I am greatly blessed. I was born on my farm; I have traveled a little—"

"Where?"

"What, madame?"

"How far have you traveled?"

"Oh, I went once to the sea, to Nice and to Marseilles, but they were far too crowded; I like fields and hills and the sky without interruption. I have been to Orange and Vence, but nowhere was any better than right here; in fact, nowhere was as good. You see, madame, we all have a place that is right for us, with people who are right for us, and when we find it, and recognize it, it is foolish to waste time searching for something else. I know there may be many excitements in other places that I have never even dreamed of, and perhaps riches and perhaps sorrows, but I think I would lose myself if I were not in my own place, and then what would I be?"

Tears stung Stephanie's eyes and she looked away, staring at the fire.

"Madame?" Madame Besset was leaning forward. "I have said something wrong?"

"No, of course not." Stephanie turned back, and met Madame Besset's worried frown. "I was just thinking that I envy you. Your life is so clear, to you and to your family; you all know yourselves: where you come from and where you're going, where you belong and . . . who you are."

Madame Besset gave a slight shrug. "It is of no great difficulty; we are ourselves and we do not try to behave like others. We are comfortable together. As for me, I have a good husband and good children, a good position with you and monsieur, and good health. That is enough to make anyone content."

"But why do you work for us? Didn't you say the farm takes care of your uncle's family and yours?"

"Indeed it does, but our sons and their families will want it soon for themselves; always the younger generation itches to pull free of the old. My uncle has no children, so our three boys will take the farm and we will retire to a house we have bought, with a large garden, in Saint-Saturnin-lès-Apt, perhaps thirty kilometers from here. So I put away the money monsieur pays me, for that future time. And you know, madame, I enjoy my work. It gives me pleasure to make a home—it is what I do best—and you and monsieur need me. So there you are."

"Why do we need you?" Stephanie asked curiously.

"Because I think you have not found your place yet. Monsieur, perhaps, but you are still searching. So it seems that you do not know what to expect of each other, almost as if you are strangers, getting acquainted. And of course you do not— But forgive me; that is not to be spoken of."

"We do not sleep together. Is that what you were about to say?"

"It is not for me to speak of that, madame."

"But surely there have been times in your married life when you did not sleep with your husband."

"Madame!"

"Oh, I didn't mean . . . I didn't mean you were sleeping with someone else. I meant, you might have been ill, or your husband was, and one of you went to a different room, so the other could sleep."

"Well. Perhaps, now and then . . ."

"And that is how it is with monsieur and me. I was injured, and I was sleeping badly, and so we thought it would be better for me to have a separate room."

"Forever, madame?" asked Madame Besset boldly.

Stephanie shrank from the question. "Everything changes. Perhaps not for you and your family, but for most of us. I can't predict next week or next month, as you can." She looked at her watch, the gold watch Max had given her when they arrived in Cavaillon, saying that now she would want to know the time, to make her own schedule instead of following the one the hospital made for her. "We should go home. Monsieur will be calling, and he will worry if I am not home."

"Yes, madame." Her lips pressed tightly together again, Madame Besset withdrew into her earlier stiffness. "If madame wishes me to drive—"

"No, I want to drive home. And I have to learn to back out, don't I? I can't drive forward all my life."

Madame Besset smiled slightly. "That is true, madame."

"Then you'll teach me. Madame Besset, I have many things to thank you for." Stephanie took her hand, clasping it against Madame Besset's instinctive withdrawal. "But mostly for this afternoon. I've had a wonderful time. And I think we're friends. Perhaps sometime you'll take me to your farm. I'd like to see it. And meet your family."

"If madame wishes . . ."

"I just said I did," said Stephanie impatiently, and went to get her rain slicker. The mood of the afternoon had been lost: they were simply two women in a café with a fire that was dying and the sound of dishes in the kitchen, and it was time to go home.

Outside, darkness had fallen and they scurried across the parking area beneath tall light poles that illuminated the rain still splashing in puddles and bouncing off leaves. Stephanie sat behind the wheel, thinking of driving in the dark, of driving in the rain, of driving backwards, and she turned to Madame Besset, to suggest that perhaps, after all . . .

No, she thought. This woman has never been more than fifty kilometers from her home. If she can drive, so can I.

And so, with Madame Besset giving instructions, Stephanie put the car in reverse, pressed cautiously on the accelerator and very slowly released the clutch. Looking over her shoulder, she backed the car in a half circle until she faced the stucco pillars at the entrance. She looked at

Madame Besset, who nodded solemnly and repeated her instructions about first and second and third gear. And Stephanie drove through the gates and turned right onto the main street.

Her headlights pierced the darkness and streaming rain only a few yards ahead, and there were no streetlights, but she drove steadily, guided by the stone walls on her right that led her to her own wall, her own gate, and she drove through it and stopped just short of the garage door. She turned the key in the ignition, and a long sigh broke from her. *I did it. Without crashing into anything. Maybe a few scratches, but I didn't destroy this wonderful, wonderful car.*

They ran the few steps from the car into the garage. Madame Besset went on into the kitchen, but Stephanie stayed in the garage, standing beside Max's sports car. I'll drive this one, too, she thought. And his Renault. Or . . . why shouldn't I have my own? I can't ask his permission every time I want to go to the market. I'll ask him as soon as he gets back.

She laid her hand on the shiny car and stroked it gently, as if it were alive. *I'll go everywhere, I'll meet people, I'll go into shops, I'll buy things for myself. I'll talk to everyone. And after a while I'll find out where my place is, the place that is right for me. And then I won't be lost anymore.*

*M*adame Besset was away, and Robert and Stephanie had the bright kitchen to themselves. A March wind rattled the windows, but the sun shone, flowers were thrusting up through newly raked gardens, and tiny buds had appeared on the short stumps of plane tree branches, pruned back in the fall and ready now to grow again, and spread out. In Provence, summer was almost here. Robert stood before the stove, Stephanie beside him, and he dipped a spoon into the pot of simmering sauce and blew on it lightly. "Now, Sabrina, let us see what we have wrought." He took a small sip. "Ah, yes. It is a miracle, how a few ingredients can blend to such sublime harmony. What a pity people and their governments cannot learn to do the same."

"If it's a miracle, how can they learn it?" Stephanie asked.

He chuckled. "You have me there. They can only pray. But that seems an inadequate solution for the problems of the world."

"Robert, you must believe in prayer."

"And so I do. But I do not trust prayer on its own strength and fervor to bring about the great changes the world needs. People must take action if there is to be progress and hope. Now, taste this and tell me if there is some way we can improve it."

Stephanie took the spoon and sipped from it. "Oh, wonderful. But . . . perhaps a little flat?"

"Good. Very good. What a pleasure to have such a quick student. We shall add a soupçon of lemon juice"—he was slicing a lemon as he spoke—"and then a touch more salt and pepper . . ."

"Robert, don't you ever measure anything? It's always a handful of sugar or a touch of cayenne or a soupçon of lemon juice or a few capers . . . How can I follow recipes like that?"

"You will not follow recipes; you will create by understanding the relationship of one ingredient to the other. Cooking is like life, you know: you do not strive for rigidity and absolutism; you seek variety, flexibility, freedom. Without them, you cook insipid dishes and live a narrow life. You are already learning this in our lessons. I think, my dear, that you have done a considerable amount of cooking in your life, probably not haute cuisine, but simple everyday meals that were most likely very good, because you are comfortable in a kitchen. Do you not feel this?"

"No. Everything is new." She picked up a lemon zester. "You had to tell me what to do with this, and I thought the poultry shears were just an odd kind of scissors, and I didn't know how to use a boning knife, and"—her voice caught—"*I couldn't even peel a potato until you showed me how to hold—*"

"Hush, now, hush, my dear Sabrina." He took the zester from her and put his arms around her, holding her gently. "I know this is terrible for you, and worrisome, but you are doing well. This is only our second lesson, and look how much you've learned. As for your past, I don't think you can force it or command it to return to you; it will come in its own way, in its own time. You must have patience. Do not try so hard. Relax and enjoy this lovely home and the people who care for you." He moved away from her in a way that made it seem they had simultaneously stepped apart. "So. Max will be here in two hours and we have not finished our dinner. Now that we have the sauce for the coquilles Saint-Jacques, we will make coq au vin, and then marquise au chocolat for dessert. You understand, I do not eat this way every day; if I did I would have a paunch that would be memorable, even in Provence. But for a small party, to welcome Max home and to celebrate your second very successful cooking lesson, it is a good menu. Now, my dear, we first reduce the chicken stock, and while it is cooking we prepare the pearl onions."

I love Robert, Stephanie thought. And I love Madame Besset and I love this room, all white and red and shining, and I love the sun after a week of rain. She felt light and happy, moving purposefully about the kitchen, using her hands, thinking, planning, creating. She found it incomprehensible and frightening that her moods swung so wildly from fear and depression to happiness and then back again without warning, as just now, when the full weight of what she did not know about a kitchen had struck her, but as soon as Robert comforted her, she swung again to joy. She felt now just as she had the week before, driving Madame Besset's car: she was a real person, a whole person, thinking about now and not about a past that was lost to her.

She watched Robert's hands move surely and swiftly, with perfect economy of movement, and she tried to match him. As he worked, he described each step, and even told her the history of the foods and spices they were using and anecdotes about them. "It was Lewis Carroll, you know, in *Alice in Wonderland,* who had the walrus say that a loaf of bread and pepper and vinegar would—"

"Alice in wonderland? What is that? A story? About a

talking walrus? How strange; do you have it? I'd like to read it.''

Robert was sliding a covered dish into the oven and he waited until he turned around to answer. He was filled with pity for this woman, so strikingly beautiful, so full of life and curiosity, her mind quick and open . . . but with nothing to cling to but the things of here and now. How much we take the past for granted, he thought; without being aware of it, each day we stand on top of yesterday, reaching back a week, a month, years, perhaps, to pluck out memories that give us assurance of our place in the world and a foundation for tomorrow. How would it be to awaken and have nothing to reach back and grasp, not even my own name? I cannot imagine it; it seems it would be a form of death.

But this lovely woman was not dead: she was young and vibrant and she was making a life. With our help, Robert thought. We must all be very good to her, and very careful; she is dependent on us for all of the todays that will become her yesterdays, for the foundation she is building for the future. We can give her security and time to become a new Sabrina Lacoste. We can give her love. And if we are steadfast in that, she will remake herself with the grace and style that are hers, even if she never recovers her past.

His thoughts had been swift, and he was speaking even as he turned back from the oven. ''I think I have a copy of *Alice in Wonderland;* I'll look for it. It is a fantasy filled with wisdom, written by a British mathematician who knew a great deal about human foibles, including his own. If you have questions when you read it, you must ask me. Or Max, of course. Now, my dear, everything has been prepared, and I am going to clean the kitchen while you change into something festive. We'll have drinks in the library as soon as Max arrives.''

''Madame Besset will clean up tomorrow,'' Stephanie said.

He smiled. ''I'm sure she would. But I have invaded

her kitchen, and the only way to ensure a pleasant encounter the next time is to leave it as I found it. Better, if possible, though with Madame Besset that is very difficult. Go on, now, get ready; Max said six o'clock and he is always punctual."

"You like him, don't you?" Stephanie asked. She was reluctant to leave.

"Very much. He is a man of his word."

"Do you know . . ." She hesitated. "Do you know what he does on his business trips?"

"He tells me he exports farm and construction equipment."

"Do you believe that?"

"I have no reason not to. Do you?"

"I don't know. He keeps a wall around himself; I never know what he's thinking."

"He loves you. You know that."

Stephanie was silent. After a moment she said, "I think you don't really believe him when he tells you what his business is."

"Sabrina, I do not call my good friend a liar."

"But you said, 'He *tells* me he exports equipment.' "

"Ah. You have a quick mind; you hear subtleties. Well, he does tell me that and I do not doubt it, but I think Max is a man who would not be content with that, and so it seems possible to me, even likely, that he also is involved in other endeavors that challenge his wits more than construction equipment."

"He said he gives money to you and other priests around the world."

"He does. We have some programs that are very important to us and Max helps fund them. In fact, I rely on him greatly for the money he contributes; it is substantial."

"Programs of education and job training."

"Yes, for young people. And finding housing for them, helping them help their parents and younger brothers and

141

sisters, teaching them to be involved in the political system, if there is one.''

''If there is one?''

''Many countries have only a dictatorship.''

''So you don't teach them about politics in those countries?''

''Well, we do, in a different way. My dear Sabrina, if you do not get cleaned up, Max will find you looking like the chef instead of the mistress of this house. He might even confuse you with Madame Besset.''

Stephanie did not return his smile; she was looking at him closely. ''All right, I will, but I'm not through asking you questions. It seems to me you go into the tiniest details when you talk about food and cooking, but as soon as I ask you about yourself, you get very vague.''

''Go on, now,'' Robert said gently. ''This has been a good day, filled with many lessons.''

''Oh.'' Stephanie made a gesture of frustration. ''You and Max, so mysterious sometimes.''

But when she was taking her bath she forgot Robert and thought only of Max. He had been gone for eight days, and the house had seemed to grow larger and more silent with each day. Well, I got used to him, Stephanie thought, stepping out of the tub and reaching for her bath sheet. He's a big man; he takes up a lot of space. And he's interesting to talk to.

She dressed in an ivory silk sweater and wide ivory silk pants that Max had bought one day in a boutique in Aix-en-Provence while she was in the hospital. It was the first time she had worn them, and the cool, clinging smoothness of the sweater and the swirl of the pants felt so good that she spun about in a brief whirl of pleasure. Very sexy clothes, she thought, fastening a gold necklace that Max had given her just before he left for Marseilles. Whatever that means: sexy clothes.

She ran a comb through her hair; it was beginning to grow long. Max had mentioned it a few times after she had asked him about it—how magnificent it had been—and she had known it would please him if she wore it long, but that was not the reason she was letting it grow. She wanted to see the other person she was, the one she could not reach or even imagine.

She lifted her hair to look at her forehead. The scar was long, but tight and neat, and it was fading; the doctor had said it would become silvery in a few months and then almost disappear. Her cheeks and neck and the area around her eyes were still scarred, but each week the lines grew fainter; by now, from a distance, they were barely visible. Pretty soon I'll look as good as new, Stephanie thought, stepping into ivory silk shoes. All patched up. The only thing missing will be my real self.

She looked at her image in the mirror and knew that she was beautiful and that she had dressed to make the most of her slender figure. She picked up a heavy gold link belt and threaded it through the loops on her pants. It fastened intricately in front, with a cluster of pearls. "Smashing," she said aloud, in English, and saw her eyes in the mirror grow wide with surprise. "Smashing," she repeated. "Where was I that people said *'smashing'*?"

The glare of headlights swept across her window; she heard a car stop and a door slam. I'll think about it later, she thought. Max is here. She ran from her room and was in the foyer when the front door opened and he walked in. She was in his arms before the door had swung shut. "Too long," he said, his mouth on hers. "Much too long away from you."

Stephanie's body awoke. Within her, small flames flickered, reached higher, then caught in a burst of heat and light. They danced wildly inside her; her fingers dug into Max's back, and she gave herself to the crush of his arms, feeling herself dissolve into wanting him.

"My God," he muttered and swept her off the floor. "You're back, my magnificent Sabrina . . ."

He turned to the stairs, cradling Stephanie in his arms, her face buried against his neck. But just then, faintly, came the sound of a casserole lid being replaced and an oven door closing. Stephanie's head came up; her body tightened. "Oh, Max, I forgot. Wait. Robert is in the kitchen—"

"The hell with him."

"No, you don't understand; he and I made dinner. He's waiting for us."

"Let him wait."

"*No!*" She was struggling to stand up.

He let her go. "Well, what the hell do you want, then?"

"Robert and I made dinner. It's very special, he cared very much about making a special meal for you, to welcome you home, and I want us to eat it together. And then, when Robert goes . . ."

"Dinner. One fucking dinner is so goddam important you put it ahead of—"

"Don't talk like that!" She was trembling with wanting him, but angry at him for not caring about Robert. "This is important to Robert and he's the best friend we've got, and we are not going to keep him sitting in the kitchen like a servant after he spent a whole day teaching me and cooking for you and telling me how much he likes you. Dinner will take two or three hours, and if you can't wait that long to go to bed with me, then we won't go to bed at all."

Max stood at the bottom of the stairs, looking at her through narrowed eyes. Stephanie gazed back at him steadily. After a minute he smiled and lifted her hand to his lips. "My fiery Sabrina. You've come back to me. What happened this week to wake you up?"

So I was like this before, Stephanie thought. Standing up for things; saying what I think, even if it isn't convenient. I'm glad. I hated feeling helpless all these months.

"I learned to drive," she said, and turned her hand within Max's to twine her fingers in his and lead him to the kitchen.

He watched her all through dinner. At first he let Robert do much of the talking, about events in Cavaillon, but after the soup he opened up, praising the food and the chefs who had prepared it, admiring the choice of wines, talking easily and amusingly about Marseilles. At one time he mentioned a trade representative from Guatemala whom he had met there, named Carlos Figueros. Stephanie thought there was a quick look between him and Robert when he talked about him, but she could not be sure. What she was aware of mostly was Max watching her, his eyes on her face for the two and a half hours they sat at dinner.

Then Robert left, promising to come back in two days for another cooking lesson, and the instant Max locked the front door Stephanie was in his arms and then, for the first time, they went upstairs together, to his room.

He pulled her sweater over her head, caressing her breasts as he did; then he fumbled with the clasp of the gold and pearl belt. "Why the hell you wore this . . ." he muttered, and Stephanie broke into nervous laughter. "Maybe I wanted a chastity belt." Panic was rising inside her. *I don't know what to do; I'm not even sure I want this.* But he bent to take her breast in his mouth, and a gasp broke from her. She opened the belt and stepped out of her pants and then, wide-eyed, stared unseeing across the room while he undressed her completely. She kept her gaze away from him, hearing him take off his own clothes, until he pulled her to him and she gave a start at the shock of his skin on hers. Her breasts were flattened against the thick hair on his chest; his large hands moved over her back, her buttocks, her waist, her thighs, as if shaping clay, and then her long sigh broke the silence. She remembered nothing about making love to him in the past, but his hands were insistent and her body, fervid and open, rose to meet his. It knew what to do.

At dawn they put on two of Max's silk robes, Stephanie rolling the sleeves up to her elbows, and they went downstairs to the breakfast room and ate cold coq au vin and slices of marquise au chocolat, and finished a bottle of burgundy. "An excellent dinner twice excellent," Max said. "I'm in Robert's debt, and even more in yours. I haven't been this hungry or this satisfied since October twenty-fourth.''

"What was October twenty-fourth?" Stephanie asked idly. She was drifting on the languor of the night, remembering how it had felt to live fully in the moment, as if neither of them had a past and so finally were equals.

"Nothing. It was a slip of the tongue."

"No, it wasn't. It was a specific date. Tell me what it was.''

"It can wait."

"Max."

"Well. That was the day the yacht exploded. Since then I haven't been sure when we would find each other again, and so I haven't felt satisfied. Until tonight. That was all I meant."

"But you've never told me what happened. Every time I ask, you put me off."

"There's no rush; it might be a shock to you to hear the details. Anyway, this is not the time to dredge it up; I'm sorry I mentioned it. You talk to me instead. Tell me what you meant about learning to drive; a joke, I assume, but I seem to have missed the point."

"It wasn't a joke. Madame Besset taught me to drive."

"Madame—" He frowned. "I told you I would teach you when the time came."

"Well, the time came, and you weren't here." A spark of annoyance cut through her languor. "Max, I'm not a child, and I'm not a prisoner. Am I? Do you plan to keep me locked up forever?"

"Of course not; don't be absurd. I wanted to make sure you were well and strong."

"I've been well and strong for at least a month."

"But you still get headaches, and you're frequently depressed—"

"And driving makes me feel better. It makes me feel wonderful."

After a moment he shrugged. "Where have you driven?"

"Only up here. Twice. Once in a torrential rain and once with blue sky and puffy clouds and birds flying all around us and I felt as if I was flying with them. It was absolutely wonderful; I loved it. I didn't want to stop. I wanted to go into Cavaillon, but Madame Besset thought it would be best to wait for you."

"The first sensible thing I've heard about her tonight. I should fire her; she had no right—"

"Max, you will not fire her! She taught me because I insisted, and I like her and I want her here. And I don't know what we'd do without her."

He gazed at her for a long moment. "Well, then, this time she stays. But you understand, Sabrina, I will not have servants breaking my rules in my home. I do not give directions frivolously, and I expect everyone to understand that they are to be scrupulously followed at all times."

"Everyone?" Stephanie sat back in her chair, putting space between them. "You're not talking only about servants; you're talking about me, too, isn't that right? I'm to obey all your orders, *scrupulously*, in your home. Isn't this my home, too?"

"Of course it is. We share it as we share our lives, which gives both of us satisfaction and enormous pleasure. But you have no knowledge of the world, Sabrina; you know that you have everything to learn. Until you do, you're in my care and you'll defer to me and let me guide you. Good God, do you know how I worried about you in the hospital—that without me to watch over you, you would die? You've been entrusted to me, Sabrina, and I will decide how to protect you so that nothing can harm you."

She was stunned, almost buffeted, by the force of his words.

"And I need order in my life," he went on. "This house is a refuge for me, and for you, too. I promise I'll take care of you; you will never lack for anything. Whatever I can do to make you happy and content, I will do; I

147

promise you that. But you can't fight me, Sabrina; I've lived by my own rules for a long time, I've never lived with anyone else, and I have no interest in learning to live with chaos.''

"All I did was learn to drive. What does that have to do with chaos?''

"Nothing; you're right, of course. I exaggerate. But I will not have a breakdown of authority.''

"Your authority.''

"My dear, you can't believe that I would bend to anyone else's. As for your driving, would it have been so painful to wait another week or two? If you had asked me, I would have been delighted to teach you. In fact, I was looking forward to it.''

Stephanie was silent. Her week-long exhilaration at learning to drive, her pleasure in standing up to Max regarding dinner with Robert, the night's sensual languors were all gone. She felt as helpless and vulnerable and alone as she had in the hospital and in the weeks after Max brought her to this house.

I will decide how to protect you so that nothing can harm you.

I've lived by my own rules for a long time.

I will not have a breakdown of authority.

She looked at her hands, folded compliantly in her lap. The only thing he hadn't said was that if she didn't like it she could leave.

But where would I go? I don't know anything, I have no money, I have no other place. I have no one but Max to take care of me.

Her throat tightened and she closed her eyes to prevent tears from forming. No one but Max. Robert was there and he cared for her, but he had his own life, restricted in many ways; Madame Besset was there, but she had a husband, a family, a farm, and she knew what was correct and what was not, and her employer coming to live with her, even temporarily, would definitely not be correct.

The silence dragged on; Max would not break it, and

Stephanie could not. The sky was brightening. She could see the kitchen come to life, but what she saw most clearly was that she was alone with a man she barely knew in a small town nestled in the fields and hills of southern France, and she had nothing of her own, not even a name. She had only what Max gave her. Somewhere in the world there were people who knew her and who were wondering what had happened to her, but she had lost them. She had no connections, except to Max. She had no family, except for Max. She was lost to everyone, even to herself, except for Max.

"My dear," he said at last, and took her clasped hands between his. "We will do many things together, go many places. You will learn so much it will be as if you never forgot anything. You will never feel deprived. Now come. We're going to move your things into my room."

She followed him from the breakfast room, the fine silk of his robe brushing her skin, wrapping her, enfolding her. I belong to him, she thought, and shivered.

In the small room that had been hers, Max pulled clothes from the closet and laid them on the bed. He piled cosmetics into one box, shoes into another, lingerie and sweaters into a third. "We can do this in two trips." He draped clothes over Stephanie's outstretched arms and picked up two boxes. "You'll decide where everything goes; I bought an extra armoire and bureau for you."

Surprised, she stopped on the bottom stair and looked back at him. "I didn't see them."

"I put them in the dressing room. If you want them in the bedroom, we'll move them."

On the second trip, Max paused beside the wide arch to the living room. It was daylight now, and he saw the room for the first time. "What have you done here?"

Behind him, Stephanie stopped short. "I changed a few things."

"So I see." He put down the box he was carrying and walked forward. Stephanie watched from the doorway. He strolled around the room, examining the arrangement of the furniture, the lamps and bowls of fruit, the groupings of small sculptures, the paintings and patterned rugs, as if he had never seen them before. He came back to the center of the room. "Why did you do this?"

"It wasn't right before."

"What was wrong with it?"

"It wasn't harmonious."

"What made you think that?"

"I don't know. I just knew it."

"You just knew it? The idea just came to you out of nowhere that this room wasn't harmonious?"

"It wasn't an idea. I felt it. I *knew* it. And I knew I could make it better. I would have liked to change some of the furniture, but I worked with what was here and a couple of pieces I found in the attic."

"What made you think you could make it better?"

"*I don't know!* That's just what I thought!"

"Based on nothing else?"

"Oh." She caught her breath. "You think I did this before. You think I knew what to do because it was my profession. But you said I never talked about a profession. Did I ever say anything about designing rooms?"

"No," he said flatly. "And I have no reason to think that was your profession. You might have done it as a hobby, but we have no way of knowing that. We'll have to see what other inspirations you come up with. Did you have any while you were cooking with Robert?"

"He says he's sure I've spent a lot of time in kitchens."

"An easy guess, true of most women. Where did you get the rug in front of the fireplace?"

"In the attic. Madame Besset took me up there. I think it may be very fine; the weave is tight and the colors . . ." Her voice trailed off.

"Why didn't you wait for me, to ask me if you could do this?"

Anger flared within Stephanie. She had worked hard to make this room beautiful, and she knew she had succeeded. He had not thanked her, or even acknowledged that she had improved it. Instead he had put her through a quiz and treated her like an ignorant servant. *Whatever I can do to make you happy and content, I will do, I promise you that.* Well, he has a hell of a lot to learn, she thought, and snapped, "Change it back."

"No," he said musingly. "I wouldn't do that. It is indeed far better, far more pleasant than it was. In fact, it is superb. You have an excellent eye. Thank you, my dear. I hope you'll look at the other rooms of the house without waiting for me to go away again."

Stephanie's anger simmered, with nowhere to go. Damn him, she thought, and wondered if she had been able to keep ahead of him before she lost her memory. But they had known each other for only a few days. *I didn't know him then, and I don't know him now. I wonder how long it will be before I figure him out.*

He was looking at her, waiting for her to respond. "Of course," she said. "I'd like that," and followed him up the stairs.

It took only half an hour to make her a part of his bedroom. Max hung her clothes in one of the closets in his dressing room and in the new armoire; Stephanie laid sweaters and silk underclothes in the new bureau and arranged her jewelry box and cosmetics on the dressing table. Max replaced the burned-out bulb in the lamp on one of the nightstands. "Max," Stephanie said, piling her books beside the lamp, "do we have a copy of *Alice in Wonderland?*"

"I have no idea; I don't read fantasy. Why?"

"Robert mentioned it. I'd like to read it."

"Then we'll buy a copy if we don't have one."

Stephanie yawned, her eyelids suddenly so heavy she could not keep them open. "I think I need to go to sleep." She looked at him curiously. "Aren't you even tired?"

"No, I've stayed up all night many times. You lie down; I'll be downstairs in my office."

Stephanie wanted to say, *Stayed up for what?* but she was too sleepy; her body was shutting down, legs, arms, neck, eyelids, all drooping, letting go. She lay down on Max's bed—*no, now it's my bed, too*—and felt him cover her with the quilt before she sank into sleep.

Max stood over her, gazing at her beauty, still astonishing to him when he came back to her, even from another room of the house. His face darkened when he focused on the small scars on her face and the large one on her forehead, partially visible through her hair; that anything should diminish her beauty enraged him. He saw her beauty as art, and he was a collector of art; he had studied it all his life and had made acquaintances around the world with whom he could talk in the private vocabulary of those who were familiar with art and could afford the greatest works of the present and the past.

And art had been his business, too, for two decades, until last October. He had been perhaps the world's most successful smuggler, arranging for his people in Central and South America and the Middle East and Far East to rob museums, tombs and ancient temples—sometimes whole sections of the temples themselves, dismantled for shipment—and to smuggle them out of their countries and into Europe and America, where collectors willing to pay huge fees were waiting. He had been preeminently successful because he was far more than a businessman: like his clients, he knew the intrinsic value of what he was obtaining, and often they came to him for advice on filling out a collection or selling something they had tired of.

Now, as he looked down upon the woman in his bed, his rage was the same rage he would feel if one of those irreplaceable works of art had been damaged, not grossly, but enough to cast a pall over its perfection and reduce its value to anyone who might have wanted it.

Still, he felt a certain satisfaction in that: the scars on her face and her loss of memory made her less perfect and therefore more dependent on him. And he needed her dependence. His love for her had grown in the past months to an obsession, desire eating at him wherever he was, whatever he was doing, and he had known, through the night just ended, that he had to possess her completely and permanently, and to receive from her a passion equal to his.

He was sure that would come, had already begun, and so when she came to his office after her nap, and he stood up and confidently took her in his arms, he was stunned and then infuriated by her instinctive withdrawal. His arms tightened. "Well?"

Stephanie saw the flat coldness in his eyes and her body went slack; she stood passively within his arms. "I don't know. I was just . . . surprised."

"By your husband embracing you in the house you share after a night of making love."

She did not answer. He made it sound absurd, but something in the way he had taken her to him, as if he had the right . . .

But didn't he have the right? She had married him. She lived with him. She had made love to him all night.

"Well?" he demanded again.

"I don't know." She moved away from him, and he did not try to hold her. "I don't *know* you," she burst out. "You never let me know who you are, inside."

His eyebrows rose. "What would you like to know?"

"Oh . . . so many things. What you really want, what worries you, what makes you happy, what you're afraid of."

"Are *you* afraid? Is that what's worrying you?"

"No, should I be? Of what? The explosion on the yacht? You won't tell me about it. Or everything you know about me—"

"Why do you think I haven't told you everything I know about you?"

"I don't know. I feel it."

"The way you felt the living room was not harmonious?"

He was smiling, but Stephanie's face was somber. "Yes. Exactly. Something between us isn't harmonious, and there has to be a reason for that. And there are other things I want to know. I think you're hiding something, and I want to know what it is and why you're doing it; I want to know if maybe you're not as absolutely sure of yourself as you pretend to be, if you're worried about not always being in control of things around you, of what happens to you.''

"I'm not afraid, I'm not worried, I'm not hiding anything," he said flatly. "You know as much about me as anyone does, probably more. I don't show my feelings the way Robert does; you'll have to accept that. Now, that's enough; I don't fritter my time away speculating about motives. What would you like to do today?''

She thought of trying again to make him understand how important this was to her: that as long as she felt he was hiding things, as long as she felt they were not harmonious, she could not love him. Then, with a small gesture of resignation, she dropped it. Later, she thought, as she seemed to think so often with Max. Later she'd make him understand, and then, perhaps, she would love him.

"Could we go for a drive?" she asked. "I mean, would you come with me while I drive into Cavaillon? We could have lunch and I could see the town; I haven't seen it at all.''

"Whatever you'd like. Give me a few minutes to finish up here.''

He went to his desk and began to sort through papers spread out on the large blotter. Stephanie watched for a minute, trying to see from his face if he was angry, but he showed nothing but concentration, and after a moment she left and went to the kitchen. Madame Besset was opening and closing cabinets, a deep frown on her face. "Is something wrong?" Stephanie asked.

"No, madame, though I had my fears. Everything is exactly where it belongs and nothing is broken. I am very pleased.''

"I'm glad you're pleased," Stephanie said gravely. "We didn't want you to think we'd invaded your kitchen.''

"An army invades, madame. Two people simply displace. I felt displaced. Do you anticipate that it will happen often?"

"As often as possible," Stephanie said, more sharply than she intended. Everyone wanted to be in charge of something: Madame Besset wanted to be in charge of the kitchen; Robert wanted to be in charge of the school he headed and of their cooking lessons; Max wanted to be in charge of her and of the house. And I ought to be in charge of something, she thought. But I don't know what that would be. If I were really good at something—if I'd earned my living in some profession—wouldn't it have come back to me by now? Some hints, at least?

Well, maybe I did have a hint. I redesigned the living room and Max said I had a good eye. An excellent eye, he said. *You might have done it as a hobby*. But even if it was only a hobby, I still knew exactly how I wanted everything to look. And it looked just the way I'd hoped and I felt so happy doing it . . .

Maybe I could get a job. I could help people make their homes beautiful. I wouldn't even charge them; I'd do it just because it makes me happy. And because it would give me another name—interior designer —an identity. I'd know exactly who I am.

Maybe then, what I would be in charge of is myself.

She became aware of Madame Besset's scowl. "I'm sorry," she said gently. "I meant, I enjoy learning from Father Chalon—you remember I told you he'd been a three-star chef?—and I hope he'll come often to give me lessons."

"I know who he is, madame; Chalon's was famous everywhere. People mourned its disappearance. I would not have allowed anyone else in my kitchen."

Oh, wouldn't you? Stephanie thought. This is my house and my kitchen and I'll decide who occupies it. I saved your job today.

But she heard Max walking down the gallery and knew it was not worth arguing about. She and Madame Besset would get along most easily by skirting difficult issues, letting things slide into place almost as if arranged by someone else, and finding ways not to dwell on who really made the decisions in that house.

I wonder if that's how other people do it, she thought, and then Max was there and they were on their way to the garage. "If you could, we need flour for tonight," Madame Besset called after them. "I thought I had more than enough, but for a pie, and bread—"

Max closed the door on her voice. "Shall we bring flour for our chef?"

"Oh, absolutely," Stephanie said. "She needs to shine tonight, to outperform Robert. I predict a memorable dinner."

"The battle of the foie gras." Max opened the car door on the driver's side. "Well, let's see what you can do."

Stephanie sat behind the wheel, momentarily frozen. She felt Max's eyes on her face and hands and she could not remember the first thing to do.

"The key," he said.

"I know," she retorted coldly, and then everything came back, and she was all right. She started the car, backed smoothly out of the garage, and drove through their gates to the street. "But I don't know how to get to Cavaillon."

"Turn right just beyond the gateposts and follow the road down the hill." He was amused, and Stephanie realized that her hands were gripping the steering wheel and she was gritting her teeth. I probably look like a warrior about to scale the ramparts, she thought. I'll feel better if I can pretend it's Madame Besset sitting beside me. A laugh broke from her.

"What is it?" Max asked.

"I was trying to pretend you're Madame Besset, but that was more than my imagination could manage."

He chuckled. "I'm relieved to hear it."

The exchange had relaxed her; now her hands lay lightly on the wheel and, for the first time, she let herself look at the landscape. Her eyes darted to left and right, hungrily taking in scenes she had glimpsed only once, when Max brought her here from the hospital.

From their terrace, her view had been of Cavaillon from above: a jumble of orange tile roofs, a few concrete apartment buildings, a highway. Beyond lay a valley where small, neat fields of grapes and melons and potatoes nestled between Cavaillon and the gentle hills of the Lubéron range. Now she saw the town and the fields from the street: new shapes, new colors, a real town.

She slowed down as she drove into town and along its tree-lined streets. "Where shall I go?"

"Wherever you like."

She smiled and drove at random, turning wherever it pleased her. She passed the Grand Marché supermarket, its parking lot filled with cars, and the trailer park behind it, some with added porches and tiny gardens; she passed small shops and bistros, homes and apartments, and then saw the shops change: their windows sparkled; they displayed elegant gowns and shoes, jewelry and kitchenware. Then Cavaillon's main square opened up before them, with its fountain topped with a sculpture of metal spikes like the rays of the sun. Trying to see everything, Stephanie drove more slowly, barely crawling, and soon other drivers were honking angrily, shouting at her, throwing up their hands in Gallic frustration and telling her in various ways where she should go and what she should do with herself.

"Ignore them," Max said, and she nodded, but in fact she barely heard him or the shouts of the other drivers; she was in her own small shell, trembling with the rapture of discovery. Oh, the people, so many people, old and young, skinny and fat, strolling or striding purposefully along the sidewalks, pulling off jackets and coats in the March sun to reveal a kaleidoscope of patterned shirts and plaid pants like flashes of light amid sober business suits and casual dresses. And so many cars crazily swerving around her, the drivers gesticulating when her eyes met theirs; and so many cyclists weaving casually and cheerfully through the treacherous traffic; and the shop windows beckoning with bright displays, and sidewalk cafés with white-aproned waiters holding trays high as they slid sideways between crammed tables where people sat reading the newspaper or talking, their heads close together, striking the table to make an important point . . . how wonderful it all was, how noisy and alive and *busy* after the silence of the stone house on the hill.

Stephanie was buoyant, as if she had broken free and had just been born into this wonderful world. *I love it; I love being part of the world, I love being alive and being me, here, now . . . whoever I am.*

Joyous, growing confident, she drove more easily, speeding up to join the movement of traffic. She turned into the main shopping areas of town, no longer fearful that she would scrape the sides of parked cars or run over curbs when she turned corners. By the time she turned onto the cours Gambetta, she was allowing herself swift glances into the windows of the shops on both sides of the wide street. And then she looked, and looked again, into the windows of a shop in the middle of the block and stepped on the brake. "Max, I have to stop; where can I park?"

"Nowhere," he said dryly, looking up and down the street. "Well, perhaps over there. Have you ever parked anywhere but in our garage?"

"Not really. Would you do it? I'll wait for you in that shop."

He followed her glance. It was the largest shop on the street, its slightly dusty windows flanking a wide door beneath the name Jacqueline en Provence spelled out in tall gold decorative letters. In the windows Max saw furniture and ceramics, floor pillows, dishes, draperies and tall glass hurricane lamps crammed together. "For refurnishing our house?"

"Oh. Yes, if there's anything . . ." She opened the door and stepped from the car. She had not thought of furnishings for their house; she had not thought of anything except seeing what was inside the shop. It fascinated her, and she did not even hear Max's grunt of annoyance as he circled the car and sat in the driver's seat.

"Wait for me there," he said. "Don't wander off."

"Yes." She was already crossing the sidewalk, heading for the door.

Just inside, she stopped and looked around. There was barely room to move: antique sideboards and hutches held displays of old translucent china and vases; antique sofas, chairs and rockers were grouped around tables and desks mellowed by age, set with silver and glass bowls filled with old marbles, napkin rings, candle snuffers, salt cellars. Wherever a few inches of space had been found on the floor there were baskets holding folded tablecloths and sets of place mats and napkins. Everything in the shop contained something which contained something else; the floor was carpeted, the walls were hung with draperies and tapestries, chandeliers hung from the ceiling. The air smelled of silk and wool and freshly ironed cotton, the lemony scent of furniture polish, and the sweet, slightly musty scent of old velvet and tapestries and faded rugs. Like someone's attic, Stephanie thought, and she knew that this was the most wonderful place in the world and that she felt she had come home.

"Yes, madame." A tall, slender woman, austerely beautiful, had come from another room. She wore a gray silk dress, perfect in its simplicity, and her ash blond hair was held loosely back from her face. "What may I show you?"

"Oh, the desk," Stephanie said, choosing a piece at random. "It looks very old."

"Seventeen-thirty, perhaps -forty. The construction of the drawers and the curve of the legs . . ." She pulled open a drawer and Stephanie bent to look. The dusty smell of the wood enveloped her and suddenly she felt dizzy. Without thinking, she knelt on the floor and ran her hand over the smooth wood of the legs and around the carvings of the feet, like a blind person identifying features. "It's in very fine condition," she said at last, standing up.

"Yes." The woman was peering at her closely. "Madame knows something about furniture?"

"No, I don't know anything, but I'd like to. I like old pieces, working with them, arranging them . . ." She moved to a bureau and touched a candelabrum centered on it. Fanciful animals played at its base and its arms stretched upward like tree branches, holding eleven candles. "Can you tell me about this? And what it costs?"

"It was made by Ladatte, about 1770. As you see, it is gilt bronze and the candles seem to rise out of flowers. It is a favorite piece of mine; its twin is in the Palazzo Reale in Turin."

"And the price?"

"Fifty thousand francs, madame."

Stephanie touched the candelabrum again. "Is that a good price?"

The woman smiled. "It is a very rare piece."

Stephanie turned. "And it will be perfect for someone's home, and then cost will not be an issue."

"As madame says." They shared a smile. "Is there anything else I can tell you, madame?"

"Oh, I want to know about everything. I love this place, just being here . . . I never want to leave."

She looked everywhere, her gaze coming to rest on a coat tree hung with boldly designed tablecloths in brilliant yellows and blues, ochers and splashes of vermilion. "Would you let me work here?" she asked abruptly. "I'd do anything, whatever you need, and I know I could learn, I'm *sure* I could learn and be useful, and I want to be here so much; I want it more than—" She saw Max pushing open the door and lowered her voice. "Well, I don't really know if I could . . . I mean, I'd have to ask . . . someone, but if I could work here, would you let me?"

The woman watched Max walk toward them; then she turned her back to him, facing Stephanie as if forming an alliance. "I wish I could, madame. I like you very much, but you see I have two women who help me now and I cannot afford anyone else, especially someone I must train. I am truly sorry. Perhaps you would wish to ask me again in a few months. Who knows? Something may have changed."

Max heard the last few words. "Ask what in a few months?" he asked Stephanie.

"If I can work here."

"Why?"

"Because I love it, I love being here . . ." She was holding back tears, feeling as if a door, briefly opened on enchantment, had swung shut. "I don't have anything to do, Max, and I want to do something, and it would be so wonderful if I could work here . . ."

"Just here, or anywhere?"

"Just here."

"There are other shops."

"Not like this one."

"You said you would redesign our house, buy new furniture; that should keep you busy for a long time."

"I can still do that. But I want to be here, too."

"I'd rather you were at home. Now that you can drive, you can visit other towns, buy anything you want for the house and for yourself. There's no need for you to work."

"Oh, you're talking about money. I'm talking about something else. I want to work. I want to work here."

"Why?"

"I don't know. What difference does it make? Max, I want this so much. Is it that you don't want me to work? Why shouldn't I? I'd like to find something I'm really good at, something I can be proud of. It really isn't the money, you know; I'd work for nothing just to be here."

There was a silence. Max looked past her, seeing nothing of the shop, seeing instead Ambassadors, Sabrina Longworth's shop in London. He had considered from the time she was in the hospital the possibility that she would regain her memory, and he had worked out several scenarios for dealing with that if it happened, all of them built around the central fact that there had been a bomb on his yacht and he—and probably she, too—had been the target.

He did not know how much she had known of the forged porcelains that had been a private sideline for Ivan Lazlo and Rory Carr, who had worked in his smuggling operation; for some time he had not known himself. He wondered if Sabrina had unknowingly bought one of the forgeries and then found out about it; if she had, and if she then confronted Lazlo or Carr, they would have been delighted to get rid of both Max and Sabrina with the same bomb. But it did not really matter if she had known something or not: she was with him and therefore Carr and Lazlo probably thought she was a danger to them, too.

He could tell her that much: that she had been a target because of him. But he could not explain why he did not want her to work in a public place, even in a town as small as Cavaillon, the center of the region's melon farming, not a place where tourist buses or hordes of visitors came in the summer.

Because he had realized, soon after they moved there, that they were not home free after all. As long as there was no body of Max Stuyvesant, whoever actually set the bomb would be wondering whether he really was dead. And looking for him.

He could not tell her that because she knew nothing of Max Stuyvesant. She did not know that Max Lacoste had dyed his hair and grown a beard to go with his new name, and lived more quietly than ever before and avoided places popular with English tourists. There was no reason for her to know any of that. But now she was asking him for something that seemed so simple he did not know how to continue to refuse. Something had broken free of the locked rooms of her amnesia and brought her here. Inwardly he shrugged. One more risk. And it will please her.

"Well, madame," he said to the proprietor, who had walked a few steps away to give them privacy, "my wife seems to want to be an apprentice in your shop. For no salary. That eliminates the problem of your payroll. I would expect, however, that you would reopen the discussion of a salary in six months or so, when you both know what she can do.''

Stephanie looked at him with such gratitude that the woman drew in her breath. What made a beautiful young woman so dependent on a man? She stood before him, her face as eager as a child's, her body bent forward slightly as if she could draw from him the answer she longed for. There is no way I can say no, the woman thought; I have to help her get away from her husband, if only for a few hours a day.

''It would give me great pleasure to have you here, madame,'' she said. ''My name is Jacqueline Lapautre; you will call me Jacqueline and I am sure we will work together in perfect harmony.''

''Oh.'' Stephanie's breath came out in a long sigh. She held out her hand. ''Sabrina Lacoste. Thank you, thank you; I'll do anything you want. Could I come every day?''

''Two days a week would be sufficient,'' Max said.

Jacqueline glanced at him. ''For stability and continuity, monsieur, it would be best if Sabrina came in every day for a few hours.''

''Well, we'll try it for a month. I want you at home for lunch, Sabrina.''

Stephanie's eyes met Jacqueline's; then she looked at Max. ''I can't do that if I'm working. But you said you'd be traveling more . . . and we'll still have dinner . . . and breakfast. That's really quite enough, Max.''

''Is it,'' he said. ''Make your arrangements, then; I'll be in the car, just down the street.''

When he was gone, the two women looked at each other. ''He wants to protect me,'' Stephanie said.

Jacqueline smiled. ''To my knowledge, there are no threats here.'' She held out her hands and Stephanie took them. ''Welcome, my dear. I think we are going to have a very good time.''

CHAPTER *9*

---

*S*abrina climbed down from the ladder in the window of Collectibles and adjusted the antique lace curtains she had just hung from a rod at the ceiling. They filtered the April sunlight streaming through the glass, patterning the Italian silk armchair and needlepoint footstool she had placed in front of them. She contemplated the arrangement, then brought a heavy bronze Art Deco lamp to a spot beside the chair.

"Oh, Stephanie, I like that," Madeline Kane said, coming from the back room. She was small and slender, with a thin, delicate face dominated by sharp black eyes. "I wouldn't have thought they'd go together at all."

"It still needs something. What did we do with those old eyeglasses someone brought in last month?"

"They're on the Louis Quinze desk, aren't they? I'll get them."

When she brought them back, Sabrina hung them over the arm of the chair, their round, spidery wire frames and glass lenses glinting in the sun. "And a book," she murmured, and went into the shop and found an 1870 leather-

164

bound copy of *Alice in Wonderland* with faded gilt lettering and frayed edges. "Stephanie and I loved this book," she murmured, and leafed through it until she found a page she liked, then laid it on the seat of the chair, opened to an illustration of Alice and the Caterpillar.

"What did you say?" Madeline asked.

"Oh, I was just talking to myself. I loved this book when I was growing up and I was thinking that I haven't read it in years. I'm not even sure Penny and Cliff have read it. I'll ask them." She glanced at her watch. "I've got to change and get out of here; how did it get so late?"

"You were having fun. I like what you've done; it's so cozy I could move right in."

Sabrina laughed. "You're our best customer." She heard the telephone. "I'll get it; I'm going back there anyway."

At the refectory table they used as a desk in the back room she picked up the telephone.

"Stephanie, it's Brian."

"Oh." It took her a minute to switch from Evanston to London, from Collectibles to Ambassadors. "Brian, I'm running late; can I call you back?"

"I just wondered when you'd be coming to see us."

"I've been thinking about it; in fact, I'd planned on coming in February, but I couldn't get away. Is anything wrong?"

"I think it might be a good idea for you to pay us a visit. It is your shop, you know. I mean, I'm sure you're busy with your own life, but you said you'd be able to handle both, and if you expect me to manage here and deal with Nicholas—"

"Just a minute." They're not getting along, she thought, and Brian is working himself up to hysteria, and who knows what Nicholas is working himself up to? "Brian, I'll be there; I'm just not sure when. I'll call you tomorrow; I'm sure we can handle this over the telephone, whatever it is."

"Stephanie, I really would prefer it if you were here."

I can't get away; I have too much to do. This had happened in February, when she had told Garth she was going to London: everything in Evanston had tugged at her and so she had canceled her plans. I'll go in March, she had thought, but that was the month she began the Koner Building, and so March had come and gone. And now it was April and Brian said he needed her and all she felt was impatience with his demands.

It occurred to her, as it had before, that it might be a good idea to sell Ambassadors and cut her ties to London altogether. But immediately she thought, No, not yet. Some time in the future, maybe, but not yet. It's too soon. I want to know they're there for me.

She was ashamed of the thought and pushed it away. It was too soon to decide anything; there was plenty of time. But for now, with Brian's voice rising in anguish, she could not turn her back on her shop and on Blackford's, Nicholas's shop. "I'll do my best to get there, Brian. I have a project here. Can you wait a couple of weeks?"

There was a pause. "If absolutely necessary."

"Good heavens, Brian, all these intimations of disaster . . . I can't imagine that you'll be unable to cope with Nicholas or anything else for two more weeks. I rely on you for your skill and ingenuity, you know."

"Well. Yes, of course. I do know that. I'll do my best. When do you think—"

"I don't know. I'll call you when I've decided."

In the dressing room she and Madeline had carved out of their work space, she washed her face and hands, pulled off her blue jeans and sweatshirt and opened the small overnight bag she had brought to work that morning. In a few minutes she came out wearing a red tweed suit and a pale gray silk blouse. "I'll be back at two," she said as she walked past the refectory table where Madeline sat, a sandwich and a thermos in front of her.

"Have a good lunch."

Sabrina caught the wistful note in her voice and turned

back. "Am I keeping you from something you wanted to do?"

"No, of course not. You told me about this date last week."

"But something's bothering you."

"Is it that obvious? What a lousy poker player I'd make. It's not important, Stephanie."

"It's important if it bothers you. *Is* it my lunch date?"

"Oh, in a way. It's more who it's with. In fact, it's *all* the people you know. They're so interesting and important; they do things, they make things happen. I don't know anyone like that. I don't have one friend who's ever had his picture in the paper."

Sabrina smiled. "Criminals get their pictures in the paper."

"You know what I mean. It's all right. I'm jealous, but I'm glad for you. You have fun at everything you do; you make your own excitement. That's an art, and I guess I never learned it. I keep thinking that if I just knew how to go about it, my life would be a lot more exciting and fun. It isn't that my life is bad, you know; it's just that I know there are adventures out there, but I don't know how to grab them. Well, what the hell, you shouldn't have to listen to me complaining; go on, now, Stephanie; you don't want to keep a college president waiting."

Sabrina bent down and kissed her cheek. "I'll be back soon."

Claudia Beyer lived a few blocks from the campus, and as Sabrina approached her house, she saw her walking toward it from the other direction. They smiled from a distance. "Perfect timing," Claudia said as they shook hands. "I'm glad to see you. I hope you don't mind coming here; it's the only place I can be sure of privacy."

"I like it here." Sabrina followed her through the cool house into the bright solarium. "And it's nice to see it in the daytime; we've only been here at night."

"For faculty functions that are too big, but absolutely

necessary. I'm hoping to get you and Garth here for a small dinner party one of these nights."

"We'd like that." Sabrina breathed deeply of roses and geraniums, basil, thyme, and seedlings ready to be transplanted to the garden. "This is a wonderful room."

"My therapy center. It always restores my soul, no matter how frustrated or furious I get at work. But it needs new furniture and I'm hoping you'll help me with it."

A young girl in a white dress put a bowl of salade niçoise on a table near a tall fig tree. Beside it she put a basket of bread and a small decanter of green olive oil. "*Merci*, Violette," Claudia said. "*Nous aurons notre dessert immédiatement après, s'il vous plaît, et ensuite notre café.*"

"*Est-ce que madame désire du vin?*"

"*Non, merci*," Sabrina said, smiling, and went on, still in French: "I couldn't work in the afternoon if I drank wine at lunch."

"Once again you amaze me," Claudia said as Violette left and they sat at the table. "Your French is perfect."

"I grew up in Europe. It was fun to slip into it; I don't get to speak it often. And how lucky you are to have a little bit of France in your house."

"And you, I understand, have a little bit of London."

Sabrina's eyebrows rose. "News of Mrs. Thirkell has even reached your office?"

"I hope I hear everything, at one time or another."

"And did you hear it from someone who resented it?"

"Yes, but also from others who didn't. There will always be those who think that it somehow dilutes the purity of research if professors have fun or indulge in luxuries. And there are those, not all of them on campus, who question where the money to pay for a housekeeper comes from."

"Where it comes from? I don't understand."

"Well, we'll talk about that later. Help yourself to salad, please."

Sabrina considered pursuing it, then let it go. She was a guest here. "Tell me about Violette."

"When Philip and I were first married, we lived in Paris while he studied at the Sorbonne and we made many good friends. We see them when we visit France, and all of them seem to have at least one daughter who wants to come to America and learn English and go to college and, of course, live with us. And so we've had several helpers over the years. I like it, you know; they're lovely girls. Violette arrived just last week, which is why we're still speaking French. You'd told me you grew up in Europe, but you didn't tell me much more. You talk about yourself very little."

"I'd rather listen to other people."

"Yes, you're good at that. So am I, but it's part of my job. I get the feeling you've cultivated it because you have a past you don't want to discuss."

Sabrina smiled faintly and poured a small pool of the fragrant olive oil on her plate. "I'm very happily involved in the present; it's quite full enough without bringing in the past. Sometimes I think the present is like walking through the Luxembourg Gardens in Paris: so many choices of where to go and how to get there, so many new sights and things to think about around every corner, with such beauty everywhere that it's almost possible to forget there are such things as ugliness and sadness in the world, and pain and loss."

"I like that image. Life as the Luxembourg Gardens. And yours must be very happy indeed if that's how you see it. But ugliness and sadness and pain do exist beyond the gardens; you can't wish them away. And perhaps you've had your share."

Violette returned with a carafe of mineral water and two stemmed glasses, and Sabrina watched her arrange them. "We all have our share; I think the hard part is finding a way to balance them, or the memory of them, with the wonderful things around us. It seems to me we spend most of our lives searching for something to balance pain and then something else to balance happiness, because we feel just as disoriented by perfection as we do by sorrow. My work is all about balance, you know; every house I design depends upon it. And I'd like very much to help you with this room. In fact, I've got a glass-and-steel Italian table that would be perfect in here."

"You do balance your life; I've watched you. You're young, but you have a strong sense of who you are and how you want to direct your life. Too many people, too many women, take a long time to discover that; some of them never do."

"You must have discovered it very early. Not many major universities have a woman as president. Were you always aiming for that?"

"Not anything like it. When we married I had much more traditional goals. Did you expect to be married to a professor and have your own career?"

"I'm not sure what any of us expected; we had so many different dreams. Did Philip go along with your traditional goals or was he the one who expected them?"

Claudia laughed. "That's very perceptive. He and his family expected them, and I was young and didn't fight back. His family descends from the French nobility going back to the Crusades, and they know exactly how the world should be ordered, so they simply assumed I'd be a perfect wife and mother and fit in with their twenty-odd generations of women. I found them completely daunting. Did you and Garth agree on all your goals from the beginning?"

"Not in the way we do now. We've changed, and so has everything around us. Did you get along with Philip's parents?"

"I was very good with them and they approved of me. I was writing poetry in my spare time, and they thought that was a sweet, rather feminine hobby. But I began to publish, you see, and then I went back to school, and then taught poetry and eventually became dean of students at

Massachusetts College for Women and then president of Midwestern, and here I am."

"And Philip? Did he approve of all that motion on your part?"

"Oh, I like that. *All that motion.* Philip would like it, too, now; in the old days he would have scowled, thinking you were being flippant about his attitudes."

"He would have been right." Their eyes met and they laughed. "But now he applauds your success?"

"More or less. It isn't easy for a man, French or American or otherwise, to stand in the shadows, so to speak, while his wife gives the speeches and gets the attention and earns considerably more than he does."

"And has more power."

"To the extent that anyone connected with a university has power."

"But within the campus."

"Yes. It's interesting that you see that; so many people think only of the public position and of the fact that I make more money than he does."

"But you've worked it out; he doesn't resent the fact that you have your own life. You're happy together."

Claudia smiled slightly, as if looking into herself. "It depends on the day of the week. Men seem to need predictability more than women do. They like life to be a sheet of graph paper with clear lines showing directions and trends and everything staying close to center: as it was, as it will be. If they suddenly find those lines not so clear and not in the center—you know what Yeats wrote: 'Things fall apart; the center cannot hold'—then they feel caught in something that defies the laws of nature, or at least the laws that they want to live by, and they have trouble facing it, much less accepting it."

"And then what happens?"

"I think that must be a subject for another day. As it is, I've spent our time talking about myself, and I planned this lunch so that I could listen to you. I give up, for now;

you're too stubborn for me. Tell me about the Italian table you want to put in this room.''

Sabrina described the table she had bought at an estate sale in Lake Forest, and then they talked of other things. Their low voices were the only sounds in the sun-washed room. Beyond the glass walls two puppies played on a flagstone terrace and robins and sparrows flew circles around each other above a broad lawn bounded by honeysuckle and lilac bushes, their branches bent low beneath the weight of their flowers. Sabrina felt a deep sense of well-being. The beauty around her, her family, her home and work, her health, the strength of her body when she played tennis and bicycled and climbed ladders at Collectibles, and her friends, including the intelligent and powerful woman sitting across from her, all buoyed her up. *Our perfect time.* Garth had been right. Because even her grief over Stephanie's death, which ran like a subterranean stream beneath all her thoughts, could not drown out all that was wonderful in her life. She was too young, too resilient, too vibrant not to embrace such an exhilarating world.

That was why she was reluctant to go to London, she thought, even though that life of freedom still called to her on occasion, like the siren's song. She did not need London; this life was enough. *Our perfect time.*

''And we treasure Garth,'' Claudia said as they finished their espresso and biscotti. ''He brings prestige to the university, not to mention a lot of money in research grants. Does he ever talk to you about them?''

Sabrina heard the too-casual note behind the question and her head came up, as if a warning bell had sounded. ''Sometimes. He's very proud of them, but I think he's just as proud of the money he's raising for the new institute.''

''Yes, he's doing an extraordinary job.'' There was a silence. ''This is a difficult time for universities, Stephanie. I don't know how much you and Garth talk about it, but it's a time to be cautious. And careful.''

"Of what?"

"Of what others think of us. A lot of people don't understand what we do, and if some self-styled crusader says we're wasting money on foolish projects—wasting taxpayers' dollars, that is—they tend to believe it."

"And then what?"

"Then the crusader gets more attention from television and the press and after a while Congress backpedals when it comes time to renew funding for research. Congressmen don't know the first thing about research, of course; they can't think further than the next election, so how can they understand projects that can take years and sometimes result in something as dramatic as a polio vaccine, and other times turn out to be a dead end with no payoff at all?"

"You're talking about Congressman Leglind," Sabrina said.

"You've been reading your newspapers, I see. Yes, Oliver Leglind, but he's only one of several. He's the worst, but without others he'd have no influence at all."

Sabrina set her coffee cup in its saucer. "What does this have to do with Garth?"

"I'm not singling out Garth; it has to do with all of us. But the professors on the front line, so to speak—the most visible, the most involved in government-funded projects—should be the most aware of what is at stake and how vulnerable the university can be."

"You think Garth is not aware of these dangerous times?"

"I didn't say dangerous; I said difficult. And I'm sure he's aware of them."

"Then I don't understand this conversation," Sabrina said flatly. It seemed clear that there was a threat somewhere in Claudia's remarks, but she could not identify it; it was as if shadows had closed in: a warning of something to be fought off.

Claudia sighed. "You know, Stephanie, it isn't only Garth we treasure; I'm very glad to count you as a friend.

There aren't many people a university president can talk to openly.''

"But you're not being open."

"I've told you that I'm concerned about influential congressmen who single out universities to attack when they're looking for a hot issue dealing with money. I don't know how serious this might be; I'm trying to be prepared, in case it is serious, so I need to talk, even though I have nothing specific to say right now."

"Do you talk to Philip about it?"

"Philip is easily bored by administrative matters."

Sabrina felt a little jolt. So that was one of the problems between them. Either Philip was genuinely bored by administrative matters and not willing to endure boredom for his wife's sake, or he fabricated boredom to keep his wife from discussing her work at home, because even now, after all this time, he still could not acknowledge her position, more visible than his, more powerful, robbing his world of predictability. And so, in this lovely home made by two people of intelligence and grace and sophistication, Claudia could not talk about her work or her worries, because her husband would not listen. And Claudia had to wonder who would listen sympathetically and not repeat to others what was said in the quiet of her solarium. She was taking a chance today, but she was not ready to take a bigger one and be as honest as she could be. As she might be, Sabrina thought, if our friendship grows.

She stood and held out her hand. "I must get back; Madeline expects me. Thank you for lunch and for our conversation. I hope we can do this often."

Claudia stood with her, their hands clasped. " 'Often' is a word I like. I'll call you soon."

"I hope you'll come to my house next time. Mrs. Thirkell knows no French, but she'd be delighted to cook for us."

"Thank you, I'd like that."

Sabrina strode down the sun-dappled street through flickering shadows cast by new leaves unfolding on the maples and elms arching overhead. Shadows, she thought. I'll have to tell Garth. The spring air was soft and smelled of freshly turned earth and clipped grass, lilacs and daffodils, and she felt again the sense of well-being that had come to her in Claudia's home. But now a dark thread ran through it. I'll have to tell Garth.

She waved to the owner of the pharmacy across the street and stopped briefly to greet the manager of Sorenson's Fireplaces. In the next block she met a neighbor shopping for a dress for her granddaughter. "Eighty dollars is too much, don't you think?" the neighbor asked when Sabrina stopped in the doorway of the shop. "For a three-year-old, I mean."

"It's a very impressive price."

"My daughter would say I threw my money away, because how long will a three-year-old wear it? But it is pretty, isn't it? The French are so good with fabrics; it's from Provence, you know, and I love it."

"Then you should buy it. Dresses like that aren't really made for children or even for their parents; they're made for grandparents."

"You mean we're soft touches."

"What's wrong with that, if it's for someone you cherish?"

"Not a thing. Well, I'll do it. Thank you, Stephanie; I'm glad you were here."

I'm glad I'm here, too, Sabrina thought, walking on. Claudia said it: I've made a place here.

She was half a block from Collectibles when she saw a young boy standing on the corner, kicking stones, waiting. Her heart lurched. "Cliff, what's wrong? What's happened?"

"Nothing much."

" 'Nothing much'? What does that mean? If nothing much is happening, why are you standing around waiting for me—you are waiting for me, aren't you?" When he nodded, she said, "And why are you doing that when you ought to be in . . . math, isn't it? Next to last period, and then American history. And then soccer practice."

"Jeez, Mom, you remember everything."

"I don't remember this being a holiday."

He kicked another stone. "I got bored."

"Bored?"

"I knew all the stuff they were doing."

Sabrina studied his closed face. "Let's take a walk," she said, and they turned toward the lake. Cliff was almost as tall as she, and she felt a rush of pride in her handsome son, striding along beside her, still a boy but with a sense of decency and honesty and humor that showed what kind of man he would be. But there was no humor in his face now, though Sabrina thought he looked more confused than angry. "You walked out of class because you were bored?"

"I didn't go. I knew what they'd be doing."

"Because of the homework you did last night?"

"I didn't do— I didn't have any homework last night."

"I thought you always had homework."

He shrugged.

"Well, how did you know what they'd be doing in class today?"

"Somebody told me."

"Who?"

He shrugged again.

"Cliff, a shrug is not a good conversational tool."

"I don't remember who told me. Somebody."

A string of sailboats on the lake stretched out like the tail of a kite, white triangles against the dark blue water: a sailing class. I miss sailing, Sabrina thought. Maybe we'll teach Cliff; he seems ready for something new.

"You think school isn't as good this year as last year?" she asked as they began to walk along the lake.

Cliff shrugged.

"Cut it out, Cliff; I won't tolerate that. If I talk to you with respect for your ideas and feelings, you can do the same for me."

He threw her a sidelong glance, almost of relief, she thought, that she would not allow him to be rude to her. "It's okay. The same as ever, I guess."

"But last year you seemed more enthusiastic."

He started to shrug, caught himself, and mumbled something.

"I didn't hear that."

"Sometimes things change."

"Do you want to tell me what things you're talking about?"

"Not really."

"Why not?"

"You wouldn't understand."

"I could try. Sometimes I'm pretty good at understanding. And weren't you waiting for me so you could talk to me?"

"It's . . ." Cliff struggled. "It's that guy."

Sabrina started to ask which guy, but then she knew. "You mean Lu Zhen." She paused. "I know you don't like him, Cliff, but he's a pretty small part of your life, isn't he? He's your dad's student, but he's here only until he gets his Ph.D. and goes back to China. He really doesn't have much to do with you."

"He's coming to dinner next week."

"Well, is that so terrible? He's in a strange country and your dad thinks it's nice to give him a feeling of family once in a while. He's always very pleasant, even though he's so uptight about his work it's hard to get him to relax. You don't think we should welcome him?"

"I hate him."

"That's hard," Sabrina said after a moment. "Hatred is awfully heavy to carry around, like an overloaded backpack. Or it gets inside you and it's always there, whatever else you're doing; even when you wake up in the morning, there's a lump inside you and you know something's really wrong and after a minute you remember what it is: you hate someone."

Cliff was staring at her. "How do you know all that?"

She put a casual arm around his shoulders. "I've had a few bad times of my own: things I was afraid of, people I didn't like, people I thought I hated . . . mostly people I envied."

"I don't envy him," Cliff said in a rush.

"Well, then, what is it?"

"I just hate him. I don't want him around. He doesn't belong in our family. He's too different."

"Cliff! You mean because he's Chinese?"

"He's too different. We should just be with people like us; that's best for everybody. All the kids in school say that."

"Good heavens." They walked in silence for a moment. "I find that pretty surprising. Do you mean that if somebody from Antarctica or New Zealand—or how about a Martian or somebody from Venus?—if any of them showed up, you wouldn't let them in the front door because they're different from us?"

"That's different."

"How is it different?"

"They could tell us about where they come from."

"Lu Zhen does that. He tells us about growing up in Beijing, and how his government sent him here to—"

"That's right! He talks and talks and everybody listens and you think he's so *fascinating* just because he comes from somewhere else!"

Sabrina's arm was still around Cliff's shoulders and they walked slowly, their steps synchronized. "I guess we do give him a lot of attention. Maybe we feel sorry for him because he's lonely and we have each other."

"He's not lonely!"

"Oh, I think he is. It seems to me that when somebody talks a lot, it's because he doesn't have many people who'll listen to him. So he stores things up until he finds himself at a table with friendly people and then everything just pours out."

Cliff kicked a stone and watched it skitter along the path

and into the grass. "I can't help it if he's lonely. I still hate him."

They came to an intersection and Sabrina turned to circle back toward Collectibles, bringing Cliff with her. "I'm not asking you to love him, Cliff, or even like him. But it's important to your dad that we help him. I gather that he's a brilliant student, and your dad—"

"Right! And I'll never be as brilliant as him, or even close, so it doesn't matter what I want; nobody gives a damn!"

"We do give a damn, though I'm not really thrilled when you use that word. We love you, Cliff, and we want you to be happy. Just because a student is brilliant—"

"And I'm not!"

"What does that have to do with whether we love you or not?"

"It just does. 'Cause the people Dad likes best are big deals, high grades and scholarships and super special research, all that shit."

"Oh, Cliff." She stopped and put her hands on his shoulders. "You know perfectly well your dad loves you more than any student he's ever had or any he will have. Do you really think there's a chance that some student is going to sit down in one of Professor Andersen's classes and Professor Andersen is going to say, 'Well, how about that, I've found somebody to love more than my son'?"

A short laugh broke from Cliff. "Well, but—"

"Because if you think there is, you're dumber than I think you are, and I think you're pretty smart."

"Not as smart as what's-his-name."

"I don't know exactly how smart you can be, and neither do you; you haven't really pushed yourself yet. You're a good student, Cliff; you're curious about the world, and when you put your mind to it, you learn a lot and I think you have a good time doing it. But I don't see how you can be any kind of student—good, bad, or brilliant—if you walk out of school in the middle of the afternoon and if you're not honest about how much homework you have.''

Cliff shot a glance at her. ''Like what?''

''Like last night. I think you had homework. I think you didn't do it. And then a little while ago you told me you didn't have any.''

''Well, I might have had a little, but not a—''

''Cliff.''

''I just didn't feel like doing it! Don't you ever feel like not going to work?''

''Well, I love my work, so that's not a good comparison. But sure, there are lots of things I don't feel like doing.''

''So you don't do them.''

''Unless I have to. Homework is something you have to do.''

They walked again, to the next corner, and turned left. Cliff saw where they were headed. ''Are you going back to work?''

''I have to stop by and see if Madeline needs anything. She's been alone all afternoon.''

''Can I come?''

''Sure. But I think you'd better stop at school on your way home and get your books, don't you? And you can find out what your homework is for math and American history.''

''I don't know what to tell them.''

''Tell them you had to talk to me. That's pretty much the truth, isn't it?''

''But you're not supposed to leave without permission.''

''That would have been a good thing to remember before you took off. You'll have to deal with that yourself, Cliff.''

''What about soccer practice?''

''What about it?''

''Can I go?''

''It's all right with me if it's all right with your school.''

"But what if they say I can't because I sort of . . . walked out?"

"That's something else you'll have to deal with. As far as I can tell, you were upset and you wanted to talk to me and you didn't want to wait, so you left without thinking it through. But you've never done it before and you won't do it again, so I'm not worried about it. That doesn't mean that's how they'll see it at your school."

They had reached Collectibles. Cliff scuffed his feet. "You could call the principal and tell him it was an emergency."

"I won't do that, Cliff. This is your problem." Sabrina put her arm around him again and kissed his cheek. "You'll do fine. I have great confidence in you. And I love you and I'm very proud of you."

"You are?"

"Of course I am. You're a big deal and very super special in our house."

Cliff grinned weakly. "Yeh, but you're a mom." After a moment, his head down, he turned and walked slowly away. Sabrina watched him; at the next corner, his head came up and his stride lengthened. *Good boy; always go in with your head high.*

And that was how she described Cliff—striding away with his head high—when she told Garth about it later that night. Everyone had gone off, Penny and Cliff and Mrs. Thirkell tucked into their bedrooms, and the two of them were sitting alone in the living room, a thermos of coffee and the rest of the wine from dinner on the low table before them. Sabrina was wearing a dark blue velvet robe Garth had given her when he brought her back from London at Christmas.

"I like the feel of this," Garth said, his arm around her as she rested against his shoulder.

"The velvet?"

"The lady inside the velvet."

She gave a low laugh and looked up, and they kissed, quietly at first, a kiss of companionship, then more deeply:

two people still discovering each other. "I love you," Garth said.

Sabrina sighed. "I spend a whole day running around, being busy, talking to people, and as soon as I slow down, the first thing I think about is you."

"Scientifically speaking, I'd say that's the right reaction." Without taking his arm from her shoulders, he leaned forward and filled their wineglasses. "I thought about you today while I was playing tennis with Nat, and while I was lecturing on autoimmune diseases, and when I met with Lu Zhen to talk about his research, and when I was eating lunch with the dean, and when I was walking home."

"It sounds like the professor is having trouble concentrating. It must be his advanced age."

"If it is, it means I've grown mature enough not to let small matters interfere with my passion for my wife. Do you want to tell me about your day?"

"Oh, not really."

"Problems?"

"There are always problems. Just when I think I have Penny pretty much taken care of, there's Cliff."

"Other than being a short-tempered and sullen twelve-year-old, what's wrong with Cliff?"

"He was never short-tempered and sullen before, Garth. He's not happy about your favorite student."

"He's jealous. He'll get over it. I tried to talk to him but he wouldn't listen."

"He'll listen if you get him in a quiet corner. He's unhappy and he needs you and all he sees is Lu Zhen getting your attention when he's here for dinner."

"He's our guest. Cliff knows I haven't forgotten him just because I don't coddle him for one evening. My God, he's my son; he doesn't need proof every single day that I love him."

"We all need proof every single day that we're loved."

Garth gazed at her. "Do I give you that proof?"

"Yes, always, it's part of what is so wonderful between

us. And you give it to Cliff and Penny, too, but they don't always see it. I think you can't be subtle about love with children that age.''

"Well, I'll talk to him. I'm not sure what I'll say, other than to tell him again that I love him, but I'll try."

"He wants you to think he's special."

"I do. He must know that. I look at him sometimes and wonder how I was so blessed to have such wonderful kids. And not just to love them but to like them. In fact, I think it's the most special blessing of all: to like our children as companions."

"Have you ever told him any of that?"

"Probably not in those words," Garth said after a minute. "I assumed it showed in everything we did together."

"A big assumption."

"But they don't like to be slobbered over, you know. Twelve isn't a great age for expressing lots of emotion."

"Do you think you could find a middle ground between praise and slobber?"

He chuckled. "I'll work on it. Anything else about Cliff?"

"He's picked up from his friends at school the idea that we should only be with our own kind."

"Good God. Don't they teach kids about a shrinking world these days? And about getting fresh ideas and making a leap forward from being a melting pot and all that sort of thing?"

"I'm not sure what they're teaching; I guess I'll have to find out. It is dismaying; you might bring it up sometime. I mentioned Martians at the door and whether he'd let them in and so on; you could build on that."

He chuckled again and kissed her. "A good place to start. Didn't you have lunch with Claudia today? How was that?"

"Wonderful. I like her so much. She needs someone to talk to; I hope I don't disappoint her in that."

"Why would you?"

"I might not have good answers when she needs them. Right now she's worried about Congress, among other things."

"University presidents always worry about Congress. Too many congressmen vote on whims and political fears, so they can't be reasoned with or predicted. That confuses anyone who believes in a life spent training minds to think clearly, and it worries the hell out of anyone who relies on them for funding. Is there anything special she's concerned about?"

"Oliver Leglind. And she thinks you ought to be aware of the dangers. Difficulties, she calls them."

"Does she think I'm not?"

"She says she's sure you are. It's just one more thing, though, distracting you. And us."

"It's not earthshaking, my love; it's part of the crazy political and academic climate I work in. You're not worried, are you?"

"A little. Claudia told me to be watchful; she had a reason for that. And she's worried; that was pretty clear."

"Well, we're always watchful where government grants are concerned, and there are a lot of us keeping our eyes open: we'd lose too many projects if we lost that funding. But it's not something that has to invade our home; we have enough people demanding this or that from us without adding Oliver Leglind to the list."

"Oh. That reminds me. People making demands of us. There seems to be a crisis at Ambassadors. Or at least Brian thinks there's one."

"So you want to go to London."

"I don't, really, but I think I'd better. I didn't go in February, you know, and—"

"My love, you don't have to explain it. Just don't stay away too long."

"I can't; I have to work on the first spec sheets for Billy Koner, and Madeline and I are expecting a new shipment in about ten days. Oh, but why don't you come with me? We could make it a holiday."

"Not this time. You'll be worrying about Brian and Nicholas and Billy Koner and I'd be thinking about Lu Zhen's research project and Cliff and maybe even Oliver Leglind. We'll go soon, though; I'd like some time in Europe with you. When we're both ready, just the two of us and no projects dangling like loose ends back home."

He put his arms around Sabrina and brought her to lie back against him. They were quiet for a long time in the quiet house that drowsed in the late night hush when creaking floors were silent, the busy kitchen put to rest, the day's voices and laughter stilled; when the street in front was a clear black ribbon running straight through the sleeping town; when lampposts cast blue-white circles of light on deserted sidewalks and the houses across the way stood like dark sentinels against a cloudy sky faintly pink from the glow of Chicago's skyscrapers, just a few miles away.

"Isn't it amazing," Garth murmured, "how every lover thinks he's invented love? People fall in love in the most unlikely times and places, and they wonder at the magic of it, and sing with the joy of it, and think no one else has ever known what they have discovered." He held Sabrina close, one hand inside her robe holding her warm breast. "And everyone who thinks that is absolutely right. We've invented it, we've created the words for it; it's our love and no one else's. It becomes a mirror of the two of us, and no matter how many poets write about it, it can never be fully shared with anyone but the two people in the mirror." He kissed her, his mouth opening hers. Sabrina turned within his arms and they fitted their bodies to each other like travelers coming home, knowing the door would always be open to them. When they pulled apart they were smiling, letting desire fill them, and they held it close, wondrous and wild and theirs alone.

"Whatever else happens in our life," Garth said, "whatever the intrusions, we've created ourselves as we are to each other, part of each other, and nothing can diminish that. Nothing can ever take that from us."

185

"Garth," Sabrina said, her hand along his face, "it's time to go to bed."

He stood, bringing her with him, and they walked to the foot of the stairs, their arms around each other. *You have a strong sense of who you are and how you want to direct your life.* Oh, yes, Sabrina thought, remembering what Claudia had said. Yes, with this man, in this place, and with no one else, ever.

They climbed the stairs, their steps in unison, and the lights of their house, the last to be illuminated on the street where they lived, went out one by one.

CHAPTER 10

Stephanie was making a life. Each day, each week, became part of a new past, and when she woke each morning with Max beside her and the sun streaming through uncurtained windows over the familiar contours of the bedroom, she no longer had the sinking feeling of being lost and alone in emptiness; now she had yesterday to remember and today to plan and tomorrow to anticipate.

She had a schedule. Five days a week, from nine to one, she worked at Jacqueline en Provence. One afternoon a week she cooked with Robert. The other afternoons were for Max, unless he was away, and then she worked on redesigning the rooms of the house or chatted with Madame Besset or lay on the chaise in the sitting room, reading books from Max's library.

She had found an illustrated copy of *Alice in Wonderland* on a high shelf, an old leather-bound copy in perfect condition, with a gold ribbon for a marker, and she opened it one day after lunch, when Madame Besset was at the market. She began to read and it was a moment before she looked up, her heart pounding. She had read ten pages, in English, without hesitating or stumbling over a word.

But why would she be surprised? In the hospital they had discovered that she was fluent in three languages.

But it's so easy, she thought, and looked again at the page before her.

Alice took up the fan and gloves and, as the hall was very hot, she kept fanning herself all the time she went on talking. "Dear, dear! How queer everything is today! And yesterday things went on just as usual. I wonder if I've been changed in the night? Let me think: *was* I the same when I got up this morning? I almost think I can remember feeling a little different. But if I'm not the same, the next question is, 'Who in the world am I?' Ah, *that's* the great puzzle!"

Stephanie drew in her breath. *I guess I'm not the only one who wonders that.* She read the book through, then turned back to the beginning and read it again, stopping for a long time at a page in the middle.

The Gryphon added, "Come, let's hear some of *your* adventures."

"I could tell you my adventures—beginning from this morning," said Alice a little timidly; "but it's no use going back to yesterday, because I was a different person then."

Maybe there are a lot of ways we can lose ourselves, Stephanie thought, gazing at the picture of the Gryphon. And Alice finds herself at the end; she gets back to where she started. Maybe that's what Robert wanted me to discover when he talked about this book.

She put the book on the table in the library and kept it there, where she could pick it up and read it whenever she felt like it. *I wonder if I read this before. Maybe, if I just concentrate, it will remind me of something.*

She was always trying to be reminded of something, straining to dredge up memories from associations. "House," she would say aloud, and close her eyes, picturing a house, rooms, furniture, gardens . . . but the only rooms and gardens she could picture were her own. When she thought "house" she tried to picture a family, but no faces came to her and she felt a great sadness. But as the weeks went by, she stopped struggling to tear down the curtain that hid her past. The doctors at the hospital had said everything might come back to her someday; Robert had said the same thing. Until then she had a life, and that would have to be enough.

When Max was home, they spent the afternoons driving to nearby towns, exploring twisting streets and browsing in the shops and talking. As Stephanie built a new store of memories and worked and drove and felt her life building around her, she became bolder. "You don't really tell me anything about yourself," she said one afternoon as they took shelter from an April rain in Les Deux Garçons in Aix-en-Provence. "You always put me off, as if I'm a child."

"What do you want to know?" he asked. They were sitting just inside the café, facing the cours Mirabeau, and he watched Stephanie's profile as she gazed at the fanciful ironwork on the balconies of the buildings across the wide, tree-lined street. She was wearing white jeans and a black turtleneck sweater with a silver necklace and long earrings he had bought only an hour before; her scars were barely visible, her beauty almost as pure and striking as before, and Max felt a surge of pride. He had done this. He had saved Sabrina Longworth from death and the destruction of her beauty, and he had re-created her as Sabrina Lacoste, whose beauty and spirit were now truly his. Sitting in the café, he felt relaxed and expansive; everything was going so well he could almost believe it would always be this way. "I've told you about my mother's death and my wanderings with my father . . . you do remember all that?"

"Yes, of course," she said impatiently, as if memory had never been a problem. "And Holland and Belgium and Germany and Spain . . . of course I remember. And then you went to London. But how did you feel when it was just you and your father? Did you love him?"

"I can't remember. We stayed together because we didn't have anyone else. I was afraid of him for a while; he had a bad temper and he hated staying in one place for long; a bad combination because he was always looking for excuses to move on and the excuse was usually a fight with someone. Once I got in the middle, I don't remember how, and was thoroughly beaten up. He took me to London, and when I recovered, I left him."

"Such a cold listing of facts," Stephanie said. "No feelings, nothing but facts. Wasn't there any love or fun in your life?"

"There was necessity. That's what gets most people through their days; how many do you think are fortunate enough to find love?" He took her hand. "When it comes, and comes late, it's all the better."

"And the fun?"

"I've never been sure what that is. I don't ask myself if I'm having fun. I take great pleasure in what I do; is that good enough?"

"What do you do?"

"I live with you and introduce you to Provence; I spend time with Robert and business associates in Marseilles—"

"I meant, what do you do for a living?"

"I told you. I export farm and construction equipment to developing countries."

"Did you tell me that before I lost my memory?"

"I don't remember. It's possible, but as I told you, we talked mostly about the future."

"Well, I think you do more than export equipment."

"Do you indeed. And why do you think that?"

"Because you take great pleasure in what you do. And you're not a dull man; you like challenges. So I think you do something more interesting than exporting machinery, and I'd like to know what it is."

The waiter brought their coffee and Max waited until he left. "Do you know, Sabrina, that is the first compliment you have paid me since you were injured."

She looked startled. "Is it? I'm sorry; you've been very good to me."

"There is a difference between compliments and gratitude."

"You mean you want me to admire the person you are. I do, from what I know. Robert says you're a man of your word. I admire that. But how do I know whether there is more to admire, or less?"

Max was growing bored. He loved her, he was obsessed with her, but not even she would know any more about him than he was willing to share. He had never been open with anyone; he had no intention of starting now. But what would she say, he wondered idly, if he told her what he did? *My dear Sabrina, I own a small printing job shop in Marseilles where we print party invitations and letterhead stationery and thousands of other innocuous jobs, but our main job is to print money. We ship the equivalent of hundreds of millions of francs' worth of counterfeit money to customers all over the world, packed neatly and efficiently inside farm and construction equipment . . .* He had no idea how she would react.

But it was only an idle thought. He would not tell her; he would not tell anyone, because he trusted no one but the few men who worked with him. And it would have no effect on their life together; they would be happy and she would love him, knowing exactly as much as she knew and no more. It was as much as she needed to know.

But for now he was not interested in playing games; he would not waste time dancing around her questions. "I'll try to make sure you find more to admire, the longer we're together. Now tell me about your work; what did you do this morning?"

"Oh, stop it!" Stephanie cried. "I'm not a child; I

won't be treated like one. You build a wall of secrets around yourself; do you expect me to admire that? I hate secrets—my whole past is a secret—and I refuse to live with them now.''

She pulled on her raincoat and rushed out of the café. The rain had stopped, and she made her way between the few soggy tourists sitting doggedly at the rows of tables and chairs lined up as if in a theater. On the broad sidewalk that ran the length of the street she turned toward the main square, walking rapidly, pulling on her rain hat as protection against the drops falling from the trees. When she reached the main square with its enormous fountain, gray-green with wet moss, she sat on the broad stone edge, looking away from the direction Max would come when he followed her.

Her back was rigid, her hands clenched, and it was a moment before she realized that what she felt was not aloneness or anxiety, as so often before, but a cold, hard anger. She sat in the windswept square, the gray plumes of water behind her splashing invisibly into the gray sky, wet stones gleaming faintly beneath dripping trees, and let her anger grow, knowing that it was important to her: that anger at being treated like a child was the beginning of standing alone in this new life she was making. She remembered that she had felt like a child the day she met Robert, as she sat between him and Max at lunch; she remembered feeling like a child when she first began to cook in the kitchen, when she first sat behind the wheel of the car, when she first moved into Max's arms and grew panic-stricken at the thought of making love to him.

But I'm growing up, she thought; I'm learning my way around. And Max and everyone else will have to treat me like an adult, like one of them.

In front of her, three women led a long line of schoolchildren across the square. The children, wearing yellow slickers, were strung together like beads, holding on to a bright red rope that trailed on the wet stones behind the last child. Their high-pitched voices rang excitedly through the square above the sound of the splashing fountain. Stephanie watched them, and suddenly she was swept by a wave of longing so powerful she stood up and started toward them, following them partway across the square before she realized what she was doing and came to a stop. *What a crazy thing to do; why am I doing this?* She watched them file into a narrow street and disappear around a bend. *I wonder how old they are. Eight? Nine? Such a lovely age, so open and full of love.*

A child ran past her, one child alone, wearing a yellow slicker, tears streaming down her face. Without thinking, Stephanie reached out and stopped her, and knelt down to hold her close. "It's all right, I'll help you, don't cry. Tell me what happened. Did you lose your friends?"

The child nodded, gulping through her tears. "I saw a puppy and I stopped to pet it . . . I wasn't supposed to . . . they said hold on to the rope . . . and now I don't know where they are!"

"I saw them go past. We'll find them." Stephanie smoothed the child's hair from her wet face and kissed her forehead and her cheeks. Through the bulky slicker she felt the trembling of the small, wiry body and she tightened her arms and felt that the child had become part of her. She could not hold her close enough; she never wanted to let her go.

"But where are they?" the child cried. "They will be so angry . . . and my mama and papa will punish me if they find out . . ."

Reluctantly Stephanie stood up and took her hand. "What is your name?"

"Lisa Vernet."

"Well, Lisa, let's find your class and perhaps no one will tell your mama and papa that this happened."

Lisa looked up, her eyes wide. "Is that possible?"

"I don't know. But we'll try." They set off, walking rapidly toward the street where the class had gone. The buildings here were of old mottled stucco with shutters streaked and faded from rain and sun, the heavy wooden doors deeply grained and scarred with age. The street was barely wide enough for a small car and there was no sidewalk. Stephanie and Lisa walked down the center on wet cobblestones until they came to a tiny square with three streets leading from it. Lisa looked up, waiting for Stephanie to show her which way to go. Stephanie had no idea. "This way," she said firmly, and took the street to the left, in every way identical to the one they had just been on.

"—and we always go somewhere on Thursday," Lisa chattered as they walked. "Madame Frontenac, she's our teacher, you'll like her, she's very pretty, like you, and she has a daughter of her own, so she is very kind to the girls, very understanding, you know, and then she *was* one, too, when she was growing up and she remembers what it was like, but with the boys she is much more firm, but then that is proper, they need it, they are very rough— some of them are bullies—and they need to be told—"

Stephanie was walking as fast as she could with Lisa clutching her hand. There was no sign of the class. How far ahead could they be? It had only been a few minutes . . . . Her heart was pounding; she could have guessed wrong, she could have gotten them both lost. Lisa would stop her cheerful chattering and become frightened again, and it would be Stephanie's fault for pretending she was grown up and could take care of a child.

The street bent to the right and they followed it and then, above Lisa's chattering, Stephanie thought she heard the babble of young voices.

"Hush, Penny, just a minute," she said. "I want to listen."

"What?" Lisa asked.

"Wait," Stephanie said, and they stood still and heard the sound of voices and laughter.

"Oh, we found them!" Lisa cried and ran on ahead, around another corner. Stephanie followed and found the class clustered around Lisa, everyone talking at once.

One of the teachers stepped forward. "Are you the good person who found our naughty girl?"

"Oh, but she isn't naughty at all," Stephanie said. She held out her hand. "Sabrina Lacoste."

"Marie Frontenac," the teacher said.

Stephanie smiled. "And you have a daughter, so you are very understanding with the young girls and very firm with the boys, especially the bullies."

"Ah, Lisa is a chatterbox. But how interesting that she thinks that I am gentler with the girls because of my daughter. Do they all, I wonder? Probably, if Lisa talks of it. And perhaps I am. Well, but now we must do something." She looked at Lisa, surrounded by her friends, all of them talking at a high pitch of excitement. "We cannot let our young people wander off; she must be punished."

"She was terrified," Stephanie said. "She felt alone and lost, and the square seemed strange to her, like a world she didn't know. Isn't that punishment enough?"

"Perhaps, but I cannot let the incident vanish. I must say something to the others."

"Ask Lisa to tell them how frightened she was. She'll probably exaggerate—they all do, at that age—and it will become a better lesson than anything you could say."

Their eyes met and they laughed. "Ah, Madame Lacoste, how well you know children," said Marie Frontenac. "Are you a teacher?"

"No."

"But of course you have children of your own."

"No. And I didn't think I knew . . ." Her voice trailed away. "I work in an antique shop in Cavaillon," she said abruptly. "Jacqueline en Provence."

"Ah, I know that shop, it is exquisite. Oh, madame, perhaps you will consent to speak to our class sometime on what that means—antiques. Children cannot comprehend the past, and perhaps you can help them understand how it still lives and comes to us in furniture and buildings and art and other antiquities."

"I'm not an expert," Stephanie said. "I'm just beginning."

"But you know more than we do. Would you consider it?"

Stephanie thought about it. She wanted to see Lisa again; she wanted to be with children. *Maybe I was a teacher. Or I did have children after all. No, Max said I didn't. How strange this is.* "Maybe I will," she said. "I'll call you when I decide."

"My address and telephone . . ." Marie Frontenac wrote on a pad of paper and tore the top sheet off. "I look forward to it. Now I must leave. I thank you from my heart, Madame Lacoste—"

"Please. Call me Sabrina."

"Ah, Sabrina. I thank you from my heart for returning Lisa to us. Lisa, come here; you of course wish to say goodbye to this good lady who rescued you."

Stephanie bent down and Lisa kissed her on one cheek, then the other, then back to the first. "Thank you, madame. But could I ask you a question?"

"Of course." Stephanie's arms were around her and she was thinking of nothing but the good feeling of that slender body against hers.

"Why did you call me Penny?"

Stephanie pulled back. "I didn't know I did. I called you Penny?"

"When you told me to hush. You said, 'Hush, Penny.' I think you were trying very hard to hear if my class was nearby. And it was."

"Yes. I don't know, Lisa. Perhaps you reminded me of someone named Penny. But I do know your name and I'm coming back to see you one day."

"Oh, how lovely." She looked at Stephanie searchingly. "And no one is going to tell . . ."

"It doesn't seem at all necessary to tell Lisa's parents, does it?" Stephanie asked Marie Frontenac. "If Lisa talks to the class as we discussed . . ."

"Well, no, I think this time it will not be necessary. Of

course if Lisa makes a habit of running off whenever she feels like—"

"I didn't run off!" Lisa cried. "I stopped to pet a puppy, but then I got lost and it was terrible!"

"Yes, that is what we are counting on." Marie Frontenac held out her hand. "Thank you again, Sabrina. I hope, when you return, we will have time to get acquainted."

"I'd like that very much." Stephanie bent down and kissed Lisa's forehead. "I'll see you soon." She turned and went back the way she had come, trying to remember the twists they had taken. Here and there, like guideposts, she saw a broken shutter, a strange pink door, a toppled flowerpot, and she followed them, thinking, I remember, I remember; I remember everything now.

But in a few minutes the silence of the narrow streets closed in upon her. No one was about; she turned and turned, but behind her and ahead of her the street was deserted. There were no clues in this part of the walk, nothing that looked familiar; she could have been ten miles from the square or a few feet from it. Fear built inside her. *She felt alone and lost, and the square seemed strange to her, like a world she didn't know. Isn't that punishment enough?*

But I'm not being punished, she thought. I haven't done anything wrong. Or have I? What did I do, in those years I can't remember, that led me here?

She began to run, turning a corner, then turning another and another, looking for anything familiar, but by now all the buildings looked identical, and there were no guideposts, and she wondered if perhaps she only thought she was running but in fact she was standing still. The thought made her dizzy and she leaned against a building. *I don't know where I am or where I'm going.*

The fear grew inside her and she ran again, trailing one hand on the stucco buildings crammed together, leaning into the street. And then abruptly, as she turned another corner, she saw, framed by the buildings on all sides, the square opening before her, with the fountain, and Max standing beside it.

"Well? Did you have a satisfactory excursion?" he asked coldly.

"I'm glad to see you," Stephanie said, her breathing beginning to slow with relief. She kissed him. "I took a lost child back to the group she'd been with. I hope you weren't worried."

"It occurred to me that you might not come back."

She looked at him somberly. "Where would I go?"

"I have no idea. Do you stay with me only because you have nowhere else to go?"

She gave him a long look. "I don't know."

He took her hand and they walked toward the side street where he had parked the car. "I told you, you will love me. You did once; you will again."

"Not if you treat me like a child."

"I treat you like a woman. I do not talk about myself, Sabrina."

"You told me about your mother, about Holland, about Spain—"

"And that should have been enough."

As he unlocked the car, Stephanie asked, "Is it criminal? Is that it? You don't tell me what you do because it's illegal?"

"Would it make a difference?"

"And that explosion on the ship? Was that part of it?"

He sat behind the wheel, rubbing the car key with his thumb as Stephanie sat beside him. "I've told you that the explosion was an accident."

"But you said, in the hospital, that you would keep me safe."

"You remember that," he said musingly. "You forgot so much else in those early days."

"I remember your voice saying it. I thought about it every day I was there. That you said you would keep me safe."

"And so I will." He started the car. "In a world where

people are cold and hungry and without the help of friends, I will make sure you are warm and fed and close to people who care for you."

"And is it illegal, what you do?"

"Would it make a difference?"

"No. If I loved you, it would."

"Brutal but honest. Well, you will love me, Sabrina, and someday I may tell you what I do, but not today. Tell me about the child you found."

This time, when he brushed aside her questions, there was nowhere to run; nor did she want to. She did not want to be alone, in Aix or anywhere else. Max was her anchor and the center of her life. He took care of her and was a good companion; they had a marriage even if she did not love him. At least for now, she thought. At least for now.

"Max, did I ever mention someone named Penny?"

"No." He drove around the main square and headed out of town. "Do you know someone named Penny?"

"I think I did. And I'm sure she was a child. Someone I taught, perhaps, or . . . perhaps my daughter."

"You told me you had no children. And you never mentioned being a teacher."

Stephanie sighed. "I don't know."

"What was the name of the child you found?"

"Lisa." She told him about the class of children holding on to a red rope, and about Lisa Vernet and Marie Frontenac, and the invitation to speak to their class. "Marie Frontenac said children can't comprehend the past; it seems strange that I would be asked to talk about it, when I don't have one."

"She didn't ask for a personal history; she asked for a discussion of how the past comes to us in antiques."

"She said, 'how it still lives and comes to us.' It does still live, doesn't it? It's there somewhere, like another floor in a house, but closed off. If I could find the way to it . . ."

They were silent. They were driving through a misty landscape, the distant colors muted but the nearby fields bright green beside vineyards of rich black earth, where skeletal grape plants stood like sentinels in perfect rows. Along the road, the plane trees were sending out new shoots, the first irises were blooming along stone walls, and the *genêt* bushes were just beginning to bloom, pale yellow but already hinting at the deep canary they would become, with a pungent fragrance that would fill the air for miles.

"I've collected art and antiques for thirty years," Max said casually. "The pieces in our house are mine."

"Oh." Stephanie nodded, as if to herself. That was the way she would learn about him, in small bits of information that came out almost incidentally. Except, she thought, that Max never does anything incidentally. "You could help me, then. I don't know how to talk about antiques."

They discussed paintings and furniture, silver, porcelain, old lace and cut glass, as Max took back roads, extending their drive. Stephanie was astonished by the extent of his knowledge; it was as if he had spent a lifetime studying these things. "There are a number of books in the library that will help you," he said. "I'll give you a list."

The late afternoon sun broke through the clouds, spilling over the houses of Roussillon, nestled high in the hills, intensifying their color: vivid orange, pink, red, ocher climbing the slope like a construction of children's playing blocks. "Robert's son lives there," she murmured. "I'd like to meet him someday."

"Don't count on it. Robert keeps his lives carefully separated."

Stephanie smiled. "How many does he have?"

"A few that I know of."

More secrets, she thought. What is the matter with these men?

But she could not be angry, not with so much beauty all around her: the sun-burnished houses of Roussillon and the tree-covered hills where it perched, the fields and gardens bursting with new life, the clouds pulling apart like curtains on a stage to reveal blue sky and a pale crescent moon. Her earlier anger was gone as well, wiped out by the adventure with Lisa and Marie Frontenac. As they approached Cavaillon, she was feeling lighthearted, all her fears gone. Everything would be all right; everything she wanted could truly come to pass.

And Max was beside her: she was safe and protected, enclosed in his car as if she were in his arms. As if she were that crescent moon, shining because of the light from the sun, she felt herself absorb and reflect his confidence and power, and make it her own.

But I don't want to be a reflection of Max. I want to be myself.

And what if he is a criminal?

Oh, of course he's not, she thought, without pause. He likes to be dramatic and he was angry at me for walking out on him, and so he hints and pretends and tries to make me nervous. But Robert wouldn't be his friend if he were a criminal.

But still she could not give Max the trust he wanted. She could not brush aside the feeling that even though he was exciting and passionate and seemed truly to love her, there was something dangerous about him. Today was the first time she had thought he might be doing something criminal, but every day something about him made her think that he lived with danger or put others in danger, or perhaps both.

And every day she thought he lied to her about what he knew of her past.

And so she did not trust him or love him. She reserved the small self she had—the few months of experience that were her entire history—for herself.

I don't even know if I can really love anyone until I'm a whole person again, she thought. And who would it be, even if I could? I don't know anyone. I'd like to, though; I want so much to know what love feels like.

She remembered greeting Max after his first trip away

from her. She had been sure she loved him and wanted him and was happy to be his wife. But that was the only time; she hadn't been able to feel that way again.

So if I did love him and trust him once—and I must have if I married him—it's gone.

"You're very quiet," Max said as he drove up the hill to their house.

"There's so much to think about," she said vaguely.

"Well, right now let's think about dinner. Would you like to go to Goult? You liked La Bartavelle last time we were there."

"Oh, I loved it. Yes, that would be wonderful. But we shouldn't go if Madame Besset has already begun dinner."

"She has not; I called her from Aix."

"Oh. This was planned in advance?"

"I wanted to make sure we did something special. I'm leaving tomorrow, for a week."

"Where are you going?"

"Marseilles and Nice."

"Why can't I come with you? I haven't really been to either one."

"I'd like to have you with me; I hate the idea of a week away from you. But we couldn't be together; I have meetings day and night. And I want to show you those cities in my own way, when we have plenty of time. We'll go soon, when I have only you to think about." In the garage, he turned off the engine and took her in his arms. "Sabrina, you know I love you. If I could change my life to be with you all the time I would." He kissed her, his hand on her breast, his arm enclosing her so that she felt submerged within him. Stephanie let herself respond; it was easier than debating with herself whether she really wanted to make love to him, and it was much, much easier than telling him she wanted to think about it. So her body warmed and opened to him even as her thoughts were cool and separate, and as they walked upstairs to his room she told herself that she was his wife and he took care of her and she owed this to him. She knew there was something wrong with that, but she let it go; she could think about it when he was gone.

Max watched the shore recede as Carlos Figueros raced his small motorboat out to sea, past sailboats, past other motorboats, past yachts moving with stately grace through the choppy water. "Now we have absolute privacy," Figueros said, cutting the motor. He leaned forward. "What do you have for me?"

"A list of shipments." Max took from inside his slicker a sheaf of papers clipped together. "And you have for me . . ."

"Payment for the last load of counterfeit we shipped. And a record of what has been donated." He searched in his pocket and brought out a business envelope and a small notebook, no larger than his palm. He gave the envelope to Max. "Eighty-five thousand francs."

"How much was donated?"

"Max." Figueros pouted. "You think I am not honest? We donated eight thousand five hundred. Ten percent. Were not those your orders? Ten percent of your share for the priest's people, the rest to you."

Max held out his hand and Figueros put the notebook in it. He leafed through the small pages, squinting to read the tiny handwriting. "Guatemala, Haiti, Chile. Nothing in Africa this time?"

"No, nor in Russia or Eastern Europe or the Middle East or China. Father Chalon said he didn't want us to spread the money too thin; he says that would be almost the same as giving them nothing at all. Do you want us to do it a different way?"

"No, it's Father Chalon's game; you'll do whatever he says." He pocketed the money without counting it, as well as the page he had been reading, and gave Figueros the sheaf of papers. "The schedule. It begins next month, the first of May, and runs through the end of July. You should be able to handle that."

Figueros turned the pages slowly, reading each line. Max watched a nearby sailboat with four young people practicing raising the spinnaker. He was impatient to get back to shore, but he kept it well hidden; Carlos Figueros was valuable to him.

"There is no figure for the shipment to England," Figueros said at last.

Max took the sheaf. "It should be here. My secretary was supposed to get it before she typed this. I'll talk to her when we get to shore."

"She is not there."

"In her office? You checked?"

"I stopped in to say good morning before I met you. The office was locked."

"That doesn't mean she isn't there now. She's never missed a day. Well, let's go back and find out. If she's ill we can call her or go to her home."

"Good." Figueros started the motor. The boat vibrated beneath them, then shot forward, making a wide arc as he pointed it toward shore. They wove through other boats, and Max recalled the last time he had been in a motorboat, speeding from Monte Carlo to Nice with Sabrina bleeding and unconscious and the sunken remains of his yacht behind them. No more danger from there, he thought; they think we're dead.

On shore, he and Figueros went to the Lacoste et fils warehouse at the end of the dock. The office was in a small building attached to one side. Max turned the knob, but the door was locked. "Peculiar," he muttered and took out his key. Inside, the room was damp and still; the desk empty, the files locked, telephone directories and atlases and maps neatly lined up on the bookshelves. Max looked at the calendar on the desk. "Saturday, four days ago. We talked that day; it was the day I left for Nice. Where the hell is she? I don't remember any talk about a vacation."

He picked up the telephone and dialed her home number and heard her voice on her answering machine. Without leaving a message, he hung up. "She lives not far from here; I think I'll run over there."

Figueros nodded. "I'll come with you."

There was no answer when they knocked on the door of the apartment in a tall concrete building a few blocks from the harbor. But as Max knocked again, the door across the hall opened. "It will do no good, monsieur," said the small man standing there. His eyes looked up at them with sadness. "The police were here; the young lady was in an automobile accident, she and her young man, and they are both dead."

"These are Valdrôme," Jacqueline said, unwrapping a package of quilted place mats. "Excellent quality, as is this . . ." She tore open another wrapping from the shipment that had arrived that morning. "Martine Nourissat: some of the finest tablecloths I have found."

Stephanie ran her hand over the fabric, cotton as smooth as silk, the patterns ranging from a small floral on the place mats to bold stylized flowers and branches on the tablecloths. She and Jacqueline were sitting on the floor beside stacks of packages, a knife and scissors and café au lait on a low table nearby. The shop was not yet open and the high-ceilinged room was in shadows where lights had not been turned on. Beyond the windows, the cours Gambetta was crowded with office workers leaving the cafés to go to work, shopkeepers unlocking their doors, and trucks and cars and motorcycles jamming the street in an early morning rush punctuated by horns and the squeal of brakes.

Inside Jacqueline en Provence, all was hushed and peaceful, the furniture and fabrics crowded together as if in a warm, familiar living room, Jacqueline and Stephanie talking in low voices and sipping their hot coffee. Jacqueline had asked her to come in early to unwrap the shipment, and so for the first time in the two weeks Stephanie had worked there, they had a quiet time for talking. Two women talking together, Stephanie thought. Two friends.

At first there was only Madame Besset; now there is Jacqueline.

"Of course these are all new," Jacqueline went on as they unwrapped other packages and laid the folded tablecloths and place mats in baskets for display. "The old pieces, mostly lace but a few silk and linen, are in the armoire across the room. We'll talk about them next."

"I looked at them yesterday when you were out," Stephanie said. "And I found a book in the back room on antique fabrics; I read it last night."

Jacqueline smiled. "Soon I'll have nothing to teach you. But, my dear, it wasn't necessary to read the whole book in one night; you don't have to study as if I'm going to give you a test."

"Oh, but I liked doing it. I always read late when my husband is out of town."

"He's an impressive man, your husband; I'd like to know him better." Jacqueline folded a large tablecloth, laid eight matching napkins on top and tied them all together with a wide green crepe ribbon. "I was sorry you couldn't come to my dinner party the other night."

"Dinner party?"

"On Saturday. I mailed the invitation; it was foolish, of course, since I see you every morning, but I like the formality of written invitations, and the element of surprise." She tilted her head and contemplated Stephanie. "And you *are* surprised, but not the way I anticipated."

"Max didn't tell me. We were in Aix on Saturday, but we had plenty of time . . . in fact, we went out to dinner that night. He wanted us to be together because he was leaving the next day. But he should have told me."

"Husbands often think their decisions need no explanation."

Their eyes met and they smiled. "I didn't know you were married," Stephanie said.

"I am not. But I have been, twice. It embarrasses me to say it. Marriage is not like folding tablecloths: it is of such greater proportions that one should take care to learn from one's first mistake and never repeat it. But I did. When I realized it, two years into my second marriage, I could not believe it. I have always been proud of my intelligence. How could it fail me so completely? I did not even have youth as a defense; I was over fifty. I had no excuse at all.''

Stephanie gazed at her in surprise. "How old are you?''

"Sixty-two in a few weeks. A very good age in most regards, though I find I am not as patient with fools as I once was, and every year it seems that there are more fools than one would have thought possible.''

"You don't look sixty-two.''

"And what does sixty-two look like?''

Stephanie laughed. "I don't know. Just . . . older. Someone who doesn't move furniture around the way you do, and climb ladders and talk about skiing off-piste at Chamonix and keep moving for hours without sitting down. And, I suppose, gray hair.''

"Ah, well, as for the hair, that needs some help, which I give it regularly; otherwise you would see gray, perhaps not all, but enough to create an impression. The rest, however, is me. I am blessed with health and energy. And sixty-two, you know, is, after all, quite young; there is nothing one stops enjoying at that age. And you, my dear? How old—''

"Do you think you'll marry again?'' Stephanie asked.

Jacqueline looked at her curiously; already she knew enough about this woman to know that she would not be deliberately rude. But now she was rude. Why would it bother her to be asked her age, when she was clearly so much younger than Jacqueline? Well, another time, perhaps; meanwhile the question was easily answered. "No, most certainly not. I do not need the financial support of a man and there is always the possibility of another failure. And I like living alone; I like to live to a pattern and rhythm I make for myself. I don't get lonely; I have many friends and resources. And a man, of course. It is essential to have a man when one wants him. Or men, on occasion, though I prefer one at a time, and at the moment there is only one.''

Stephanie had stopped opening packages and was sitting very still, her eyes fixed on the fine sculpted lines of Jacqueline's face. She felt very happy because Jacqueline was being so open, and in that way making her a part of her life. Stephanie felt that she was learning what it really meant to have a woman friend. She thought of Max and realized how alone she had been until now, without a woman to talk to and learn from. And so, thinking still of Max, she asked what would have seemed an impermissibly intimate question but now was not, because Jacqueline had made it permissible. "And do you love him?"

"No, nor does he love me," Jacqueline said easily. "That part of it definitely is not essential. We like each other and we have a pleasant time together, and that is quite enough.''

"But you trust him.''

"Trust? I think that is a word for marriage, not for an arrangement of convenience. It is a question I have not asked. Do you ask it about your husband?''

"Yes," Stephanie said, and felt a wonderful sense of relief as the word came out and she knew that Jacqueline had made it possible for her to say many things. "Not that he won't take care of me; I know he will. But that he is . . . what he says he is.''

"Oh, well, my dear, how many of us are what we say we are? We all have hidden pasts, hidden lusts or fears or hatreds or loves . . .'' She gazed at Stephanie for a moment. "But you mean more than that. You mean you think he is not as honorable as he seems.''

Stephanie nodded.

"That should become clear the longer you live with him. One thing I discovered about marriage was that almost always one learns far more about a spouse than one ever wished to know.''

"I want to know everything," Stephanie said. "I don't like blank spaces.''

"Well, we all have our own needs. I think a little mystery keeps us on a fine edge of interest. It is like the sun slipping in and out of great dark clouds; suddenly the world is brilliantly transformed, and if we have been drowsing or inattentive we are brought back instantly to beauty, and to life."

"Do you feel that way about the man you're with now?"

"Ah, no. If I did, we would have a grand passion instead of a pleasant friendship. We are very different, and neither of us feels the need to share too much or to enjoy the mystery of each other. That does not mean we do not have a good time and, in fact, need each other. If we parted tomorrow I would miss him very much for a while, but I would wish him well for the pleasure we have had, and he would do the same for me. That is all I want."

Jacqueline picked up another package and slit the wrapping paper carefully along one end to avoid cutting the fabric inside. "Have you been married long?" she asked.

"No. A few months." Stephanie's hands rested in her lap; a small frown was between her eyes.

"Well, you will find how very much you learn in the first year. Probably you will fill in most of those blank spaces you don't like." She slipped the fabric from the wrapper and began to separate the tablecloths and the napkins. Without looking up, she asked casually, "How old are you, my dear?"

There was a silence. "I don't know," Stephanie said at last.

Jacqueline's head shot up. "Why is that?"

"Because I don't know anything about myself except what I've done since October. Because I have no memory. Because I've lost myself."

"Oh, my poor little one." Jacqueline swept aside the tablecloths and place mats and took Stephanie in her arms. "What a terrible thing. You remember nothing? Nothing comes back to you?"

"A few bits and pieces. I think my mother's name was

Laura. I knew someone named Penny, probably a little girl. I never lived alone. I cut roses with a silver scissors."

"And you know design."

"Maybe. Just because I rearranged—" Stephanie pulled back within Jacqueline's arms. "How did you know I rearranged our living room?"

"I didn't know it. But I'm not surprised. I've been watching you in the two weeks you've been here; you've been moving things around the shop since the day you arrived."

"Oh. I didn't realize . . . I'm sorry."

"Why should you be?"

"Because it's your shop, not my living room."

"But the more you treat it as your living room, the better it looks. Sabrina, I could have stopped you at any time; I did not, because you have a very good eye and an excellent sense of harmony. I like everything you have done. I would guess that you were an interior designer once, or at least you worked with furnishings. Tell me what happened. Did you have an accident? You were injured?"

Stephanie brushed aside her hair to expose the scar on her forehead. "There was an explosion on a boat. Max got me away and held me in the water until another boat picked us up. That's what he says; I don't remember any of it. I was in a hospital in Marseilles for two months; there was a wonderful plastic surgeon there and Max says I look the same now as I did before. But . . . ."

"Yes? There is more?"

Stephanie nodded. She had not told this to Robert or to Max, but she wanted to tell Jacqueline. "About a week ago I called the hospital in Marseilles and spoke to one of the doctors who took care of me. I can't remember most of what happened there, either, you see, and I wanted to know what he had said about my memory. And he said he thought it wasn't only that I was struck on the head, but that there's something I don't want to remember, something I want to block out, so I've blocked out everything. He called it psychogenic amnesia.''

"He cannot be sure of that.''

"He said they had discussed my case and they all agreed.''

"Well. And how do you feel about that?''

"I don't know. I think about it all the time; what could I have done that made me so ashamed I forced myself to forget it?''

"Perhaps it was something else, something you saw or heard,'' Jacqueline said gently. "Why do you blame yourself?''

"Because I feel that something is my fault.'' The words were almost inaudible. "I can't explain it, but I wake up in the morning and the first thing I think is that I've done something wrong. And I can't remember what it was. Because I can't remember anything.''

"My poor little one,'' Jacqueline said again, and held Stephanie close. Stephanie let herself sink into Jacqueline's strong embrace; she felt safe and protected and wished she could stay there forever, not having to worry about who she was or what she had done, just staying close and soaking up Jacqueline's assurance and control of her life.

A knock on the door made them start. "Oh, my Lord, look at the time, and these packages not finished.'' Jacqueline put Stephanie gently from her and stood up, smoothing her wool skirt, adjusting her silk blouse, sweeping her palms along her perfectly smooth hair. "I'll unlock the door, Sabrina; would you take the rest of these packages to the back room and open them? We'll put everything away later. And, my dear''—she put her hand on Stephanie's arm—"we'll talk again. This time together has meant a great deal to me.''

Stephanie was trembling with the shock of returning to the normal day. "Yes, it was wonderful. Thank you.'' She scooped up the remaining brown-wrapped packages and made her way through the crowded room to the back. "I'll turn on the lights."

"Good." Jacqueline was at the front door, and as she swung it open, Stephanie flicked the switches and all the lights came on, illuminating the curves and angles of the furniture, the translucent china displayed in old painted armoires, the small stitches of cashmere throws and the worn threads of antique tapestries. *It is like the sun slipping in and out of great dark clouds; suddenly the world is brilliantly transformed, and if we have been drowsing or inattentive we are brought back instantly to beauty, and to life.*

Oh, I'd like that, Stephanie thought, filled suddenly with a longing that took in the whole world beyond Cavaillon and Max's house and Max's bed. I wish I could know what it's like to feel that.

She stood beside a long oak table in the back room amid the clutter of gifts to be wrapped, lamps to be repaired, draperies to be hung, and unopened boxes that had arrived in that morning's shipment. On a small desk was a computer used for recording and ringing up sales, an empty coffee can holding pencils and pens, and a mug half full of coffee left over from the day before. Absently, Stephanie took the mug to the sink in the corner and washed it and set it on the edge to drain. She picked up a spool of iridescent ribbon that had fallen to the floor and dropped it into a box with others like it. She pushed lamps and vases and memo pads aside to make a place on the oak table and used the space to open the packages she had carried in. And all the time she was thinking, I'll never know what that feels like as long as I'm with Max. But I'm tied to him; the only life I know is with him. And it's a good life; I should be grateful; I haven't any right to complain.

Besides, how can I think of not being with Max? I'm too afraid. I don't know how I'd manage without protection. She remembered feeling safe and protected in Max's car, driving back from Aix, as if she were the moon reflecting his sun, making his confidence and power her own. And then she had wanted to stay in Jacqueline's embrace forever, soaking up her assurance and control.

When am I going to be myself, with my own strength? When am I going to be more adventurous?

She heard voices from the shop: two women talking animatedly about an eighteenth-century sofa, a man's voice saying something about a group of paintings, and Jacqueline saying, "Good, very good, we sold all the last ones so quickly, and I have customers waiting. They want especially the landscapes."

The man chuckled. "Too bad. The new ones are abstracts. I've brought slides of them; if they're not right for your shop I can take them to Galerie Le Fèvre."

"You will not! Léon, good heavens, I represent you; you agreed to that."

Someone was standing in the door to the back room. "If you please, madame, this tablecloth, what is the price?"

Stephanie looked at the cloth draped over the woman's arm. "Fifteen hundred francs. That includes the napkins, of course."

"Well, I adore it and I must have it. And I want one for a housewarming gift; which would you suggest? Something a little smaller. And definitely not as expensive."

Stephanie suppressed a smile as she led the customer into the shop. "We have several on this rack; if you wish to look through them . . ."

"Oh, whatever you choose. She won't invite me to dinner so often that I'll have to look at it very much. Here, what about this? Yellow. A color I detest, but she'll probably like it."

"Not just yellow; aureolin," said a man's voice, "deep, luscious, lustrous, filled with sunlight and fresh breezes, youth, love, and the promise of good food and wine."

Stephanie and the customer had turned around. He leaned against the wall, smiling easily, a small man barely taller than Stephanie and about her age, lean, broad-shouldered, blond and deeply tanned, wearing blue jeans and an open-necked white shirt. His face was thin, with

213

faintly hollowed cheeks; his eyes were green and they met Stephanie's with a look of amused conspiracy. His voice was the one she had heard in the shop, talking to Jacqueline about paintings.

They stood looking at each other while the customer said, "Aureolin? Aureolin? I never heard of it. I don't even know how to pronounce it. What is it?"

"Chrome yellow," said Jacqueline, coming up to them. "A pigment painters often use. You wish to buy these two tablecloths, the red and the yellow?"

Stephanie took them from the customer. "I'll wrap them for you."

"Unless there is something else madame wishes," Jacqueline said.

Stephanie flushed. She was not concentrating; she still felt the man's eyes on her and she wanted to look at him. "Yes, please look around; I'll have these for you when you're ready."

"Well, I will; I saw a vase I rather liked . . ." The customer drifted away.

"I'm sorry," Stephanie said to Jacqueline.

"Oh, Léon has a way of derailing conversations. Sabrina Lacoste, Léon Dumas. You may have seen some of Léon's paintings in the shop, Sabrina; I think the last one sold just after you began to work here."

"I did see it and we have one in our living room," Stephanie said as she and Léon shook hands.

"Which one?" he asked.

"The Alpilles. The little house in it reminds me of van Gogh's painting of them."

His eyes brightened. "I put it there in homage to him. Have you been there? Or climbed them?"

"No." Stephanie was confused and she took a step back, and then another. "Excuse me, I have to take care of this; I have to wrap these . . ." She turned and fled to the back room. *I know about van Gogh. I know about his painting of the Alpilles. But in all the months I've lived with Max and looked at that painting, I never thought of*

214

van Gogh. Maybe I'm beginning to remember. Maybe it's coming back.

Léon was in the doorway. "Was it something I said?"

"No." She pulled out a length of wrapping paper and cut it off. "I just wanted to take care of this."

"Not quite true, I think, but we'll let it go for now." He watched her wrap the red tablecloth and napkins. In the silence, they could hear Jacqueline's voice in the shop. "You said, '*We* have one in *our* living room.' Are you married?"

"Yes."

"And who bought the painting? You or your husband?"

"My husband. Before we met."

"I admire his good judgment." He came into the room and held out his hand. "I'm happy we met. I hope to see you again."

"Yes," Stephanie said. Once again they shook hands, and their hands stayed clasped while their eyes met. He was not handsome, Stephanie thought, but she liked his looks; his face was alive with curiosity and intelligence and humor, and he looked at everything with intensity. Right now he was looking at her as if he wanted to know all about her, not just in a casual way with carelessly spoken social phrases—*I hope to see you again*—but in a way that took what he said and did seriously. And Max had said he was one of the finest young painters in the country. He held her hand too tightly, but then, she was not trying to pull away. They looked at each other steadily, as if they were speaking together, getting acquainted.

When am I going to be more adventurous?

Oh, Stephanie thought, perhaps beginning right now.

CHAPTER 11

Mrs. Thirkell pushed forward the platter of roast chicken and potatoes she was holding at Lu Zhen's right hand. "Of course you'll have seconds," she scolded. "A growing boy is an engine that needs a constant supply of petrol. Especially if he's also a student, and a skinny one at that. Come on, now, two or three slices, young man, you'll be the better for them. And more potatoes, too."

"He doesn't want any more," Cliff growled.

"Yes, he does," Penny said, watching Lu. "He's just being polite. Can I have some more, Mrs. Thirkell? After Lu?"

Sabrina and Garth exchanged a smile. "Our diplomat," Garth said. "Go on, Lu, dig in; you're outnumbered and Penny's made it accepted practice."

Lu smiled his thin, cautious smile and heaped chicken and potatoes on his plate. Mrs. Thirkell sighed with exaggerated gratification and took the platter to Penny. "It's really delicious," Penny said. "Is it different from the chicken in China?"

"Their eyes are different," Cliff said.

216

"Cliff—" Garth began, but Sabrina forestalled him. "Not a good joke," she said lightly.

"Do you know, I think they look exactly like your chickens," Lu said seriously. "I lived in a village once and I saw them being slaughtered, and they seemed quite ordinary to me."

"I thought you grew up in Beijing," Sabrina said. "When did you live in a village?"

"When I was a child. There was a time when the government ordered people from cities to work in the fields and villages, and I went with my family to the west."

"Masses of people uprooted," Garth said, "whoever they were, whatever their profession. Including Lu's father, who's a physicist, and his mother, who teaches English."

Lu smiled again, the smile that barely stretched his lips. "My father shoveled manure for five years; my mother did laundry."

"Why?" Cliff asked, curiosity cutting through his sullenness.

"The government felt that intellectuals and professionals should return to the people because they'd forgotten who they were."

"What does that mean?"

"The government said intellectuals and professionals thought of themselves as better than the peasants when really everybody should be the same."

"But people aren't the same," Penny said.

"The government said they were."

"But they were wrong. Didn't anybody complain? People here complain about the government all the time."

"That is not the way in China."

"Well, I know you can't complain out loud; we learned about that at school. But don't you, when you're at home? You know, when you talk about things at the dinner table, the way we do."

"Sometimes."

"Does the government still think everybody's the same?" Cliff asked.

"Not so much, it seems."

"So where are your parents now?"

"In Beijing. My father teaches at the university and my mother is in a middle school."

"Did your mother teach you English?" Penny asked.

"Yes, but I also studied it in school. Everyone wants to learn English. Especially if you want to go into science. English is the language of science all over the world."

"I'd like to learn Chinese," Penny said. "It sounds sort of like singing."

"I could teach you some words, if you like."

"Really? Would you? That would be so neat; nobody at school knows any Chinese at all. Tell me a word now."

"*Ma.*"

"What does that mean?"

"Mother."

"But that's the same as English. Who cares about that? Tell me a *Chinese* word."

"That is the Chinese word. But I will give you this one: *hen hao chi.*"

"What's that?"

"Tasty. That's what this dinner is. And here's another one: *youyi.* It means friendship."

Penny repeated them. "Will you teach me lots more?"

"If you like."

"Lots. So I can talk, you know, not just words and stuff, but a few sentences that really sound like I'm talking in Chinese. Then I can do it at school and everybody else will just be *totally out of it.*"

Sabrina looked at Penny thoughtfully, wondering which problems, old or new, were behind her vehemence. She'd bring it up when they were alone; right now she was enjoying the conversation, pleased that Cliff had joined in. There had been a swift moment of pain when Lu first arrived—it happened every time he entered their house—when, looking at him and hearing his accent, she was swept back to China last September, China for two weeks with Stephanie, ending in Hong Kong when the two of them took the first step in the game they had decided to play and handed each other the keys to their front doors. China: the last place she had seen her sister alive.

The pain subsided when they sat at the table; it always did, when the conversation began and she was once again Stephanie Andersen, making a foreign student feel at home. "Does speaking English all the time make you feel different about yourself?" she asked Lu. "Language seems to me to be so deeply a part of our identity: the way we view the world, the way we see ourselves, the subtleties of words that can't ever be perfectly translated . . . Would any of us be the same person if we spoke another language all the time?"

"You did, Mom," Cliff said. "You told us you and Aunt Sabrina talked French when you were in school in Switzerland."

"Yes, but only in classes and whenever we were with the faculty. In our rooms we always went back to English. I think if I were living in Switzerland now, or France, and speaking only French, I might be confused about my identity. Lu, what do you think?"

"I speak Chinese to other Chinese students at school. It is very important to me; it makes me feel I am not drowning in America and the sloppiness of English."

"Sloppy!" Cliff exclaimed.

"So it seems to me. It is very casual, very fluid, like the American people. Chinese is very specific, very rigid, very clear at all times."

"English isn't sloppy," Cliff insisted.

" 'Sloppy' probably isn't the best word," Garth said. "I'd think 'casual' is better. But whatever English is, I'm glad Lu learned it, because if his research comes out as we hope it will, he has a brilliant future as a scientist."

Lu gazed fixedly at Garth. "Thank you."

There was a silence. "Can you tell us about it?" Sabrina asked.

"I think you would not find it interesting."

"Make it interesting," Garth said. "The other day you told me you want to do research when you go home, and run an institute of genetic engineering and teach. The most successful teachers are those who make their subject interesting for everyone, even people who aren't in their field."

Lu gave a barely perceptible shrug. "I am interested in problems in immunology. The lymphocytes—the white blood cells—are some of the best understood cells in the body and this is a field where some very advanced research is being done. For my postdoctoral project I am working on autoimmune disease. This is when the body's B and T cells—"

"The what?" Penny asked.

"I'm sorry. B and T cells are the names of lymphocytes that recognize foreign cells in our bodies and destroy them. It is because of them that we recover from a cold or the flu—that is, when they do what they are supposed to do. But it is a very complex system and it can fail if certain genetic defects exist, and then the system turns against the body."

"Turns against the body?" Sabrina repeated. "What does that mean?"

"The B and T cells can no longer tell the difference between foreign cells that invade our body, and our body itself." Penny was frowning, and Lu said, "I mean, the lymphocytes that are supposed to save us by attacking invading cells turn on us and start attacking *us*. Then we get diseases like rheumatoid arthritis, diabetes mellitus, multiple sclerosis, myasthenia gravis, and Addison's disease. These are all autoimmune diseases. The one I am working on is rheumatoid arthritis; I am trying to find out if we can replace the defective gene that controls the growth of lymphocytes with a healthy one so that the body can produce new lymphocytes that won't attack joint tissue."

"Could you cure AIDS that way?" Cliff asked.

"No, AIDS is caused by HIV. Anyway, I am not working on AIDS."

"Why not? AIDS is killing people."

"And rheumatoid arthritis is crippling millions . . . including my mother. I promised her I would bring back to China a cure for her and so many others."

"It would be a medical revolution," Garth said. "There's tremendous excitement in the department; this is the frontier of research in how genes specify the immune system, and Lu is doing the kind of work that will push it even further ahead. We're very proud of him; his research program is excellent and he has good ideas about the nature of the problem and ways to attack it. If his experiments pan out, it will be a very big feather in the cap of our new institute."

Sabrina saw Lu's face close up. He wants the glory for himself, she thought—not for the department, not for the institute, certainly not for Garth Andersen, just for Lu. He probably thinks he's going to get the Nobel Prize. And from what Garth says, maybe he could. "But others must be working on this, too," she said to Garth.

"At least a dozen, but I don't think they're as close as we are. Farver Labs in San Francisco is probably the closest; I talked to Bill Farver a couple of weeks ago and he sounded about as excited as we are. Of course they don't have Lu, which puts them at a distinct disadvantage."

Cliff made a retching sound. "Oh, Cliff," Sabrina sighed, but at the same time she felt a rush of pity for him. She met Garth's eyes and shook her head slightly. She didn't know why he always seemed to go overboard about Lu, as if he had to make him feel loved and admired over and over again, as if it weren't enough to tell him once that he was on his way to being a fine scientist and leave it there.

Well, if he has to, for whatever reason, he can do it on campus, she thought; he doesn't have to do it at home, especially in front of Cliff. We just talked about this; I guess we'll have to do it again.

"I did want to ask you, Professor," Lu said, "about the polymorphisms within the peptide-binding cleft: how much of the variation in individuals is determined by the ability of the MHC protein to bind different antigens . . ."

They slipped into their own language, their own world. Smiling, Sabrina watched them, feeling a great tenderness for Garth, a man driven by so many passions, and for Lu, never capable, perhaps, of passions as intense as Garth's, but somehow understanding how rare and wonderful they were. His face was absorbed and even adoring, she thought, as he kept his eyes locked on Garth's face.

She looked around the table, set by Mrs. Thirkell with a patterned Provençal cloth, yellow candles, white and yellow daffodils, and bright blue and yellow Provençal pottery that Sabrina had found years before at the marché aux puces outside Paris. It was as if the sun shone within the room, bringing a brightness to the faces around the table, and Sabrina felt a tenderness for all of them—her husband, her children, Mrs. Thirkell, Lu—and for the place where she was: the dining room with its furniture rubbed golden and satiny from centuries of loving hands, the house that enclosed her in well-worn comfort, the town where she greeted friends as she walked down the street.

Oh, everything is so good, she thought. The good things in her life piled up ever higher, never erasing the sadness inside her but dulling it, keeping it out of sight except for the quiet times of very early morning, when she often woke and ached for Stephanie. But at times like this, with her family around her in their bright dining room, she felt herself stretching inside, like a cat in a warm circle of sunlight, and thinking, Oh, everything is so good.

It struck her that she thought that more and more often lately, so often that it had become a refrain beneath everything she did. It was almost as if she were cataloguing and memorizing the glories of autumn, knowing they would be snatched away in the cold sweep of winter. But that was a foolish fantasy, and she brushed it aside. I'm happy, she thought, and I'm grateful for happiness, and I thank goodness for that. The riskiest thing one can do with happiness is to take it for granted.

But Garth and Lu had talked long enough in their private jargon; Cliff's face had tightened and Penny was fidgeting. "We're feeling a little left out, here," Sabrina said lightly. "The conversation has gotten a trifle technical."

"More than a trifle," Garth said ruefully. "I'm sorry. The problem is that I'm so busy with the new institute I don't get much time with Lu. In fact, I haven't been paying much attention to him at all. So it was fun to catch up." Then, as if going back over their dinner and hearing himself praise Lu and withdraw with him into a scientific discussion, he turned to Cliff. "We haven't heard much about your work lately; what are you doing in your lab course these days?"

"Nothing much. It's pretty boring."

"I thought you liked it."

Cliff shrugged, then threw a glance at Sabrina and hunched his shoulders. "Can I be excused?"

"Before dessert?" Garth asked. "That's a first. I think you should hang around, Cliff. We have a guest and it would be nice if we could finish dinner together."

"I *know* we have a guest!"

Mrs. Thirkell came in and began to clear the dishes. "Cliff, how about helping out?"

"Do I have to stay?" Cliff asked Sabrina.

She nodded. "I agree with your father."

"Jeez," he muttered, and began to stack plates.

"Not too high," said Mrs. Thirkell, and the two of them went into the kitchen.

"Cliff does not like me," Lu said. "Have I done something to offend him?"

"A lot of ideas and feelings get stirred up in a twelve-year-old," Sabrina replied. "Cliff will work them out. Didn't you have a lot of mixed-up feelings when you were twelve?"

He shook his head. "We don't have time for things like that. We owe our country all our energy and attention. It is making it possible for us to be educated so we can lead productive lives, and we have no right to fritter away any of our time."

"*What?*" Penny asked.

"Well, we feel honored that you took time out for dinner," Sabrina said, amused, and then was ashamed as she saw confusion on Lu's face.

"I take it very seriously. My government and my family expect me to bring great credit to our country, and then to come home to help all of China."

"Quite a burden for anyone, much less a young man of twenty-two," Garth said. "I hope you don't feel that all of China will condemn you if you do less than brilliantly."

"But why would I do less? You told me I have a brilliant future."

"If everything goes well, I think you do. But I'm sure that your government will support you, and your family will always be behind you whatever—" Garth saw the confusion deepen on Lu's face, and he cut his sentence off. "That's enough shop talk for tonight, I think. Let's have coffee. Lu?"

"Yes, thank you." His voice was muted, and then he was silent as Garth poured coffee and talked about plans for the groundbreaking ceremony for the Institute of Genetic Engineering.

"A little over three weeks away and Claudia and I haven't written our speeches," he said as Mrs. Thirkell and Cliff finished clearing the table and brought in a cake. "The hope is that the longer we wait the shorter they'll be. Do you know, if we could find the gene for brevity we could create universal happiness by shortening ceremonies all over the world."

Sabrina smiled. She cut the cake and handed around the dessert plates, and as they talked of other things, Lu's face relaxed, though he remained quiet. But when he stood up to leave, he stopped beside Cliff's chair. "I guess you don't want to learn Chinese, but I played soccer in China and we could talk about some things I learned from my coach. I mean, if you want to. They're a little different from the stuff you're doing.''

Sabrina heard the plea in his voice and held her breath, watching Cliff struggle between jealousy and his love of soccer. ''I guess,'' he said at last; then, as if he was ashamed of his grudging reply, he added, ''Sure. Thanks.'' Sabrina breathed a sigh of relief. She met Garth's eyes. He needs our help, she thought, and then, as they stood and went with Lu to the front door, she wondered which young man, Lu or Cliff, she had meant.

Garth watched Lu walk down the porch steps. A light May rain was falling; there was no breeze and the warm air was soft on their skin. Lu put up an umbrella and turned to wave goodbye, and then Garth closed the door and put his arm around Sabrina as they went back to the dining room. ''Thank you. It is a joy to watch you keep a conversation going.''

''Everyone helped. He loves you, you know.''

''Lu? Why do you think that?''

''I saw it in his face.''

''I haven't seen it. Or much of anything else; he hides most of his feelings. I've known him for two years and he's never talked to me before tonight about proving himself worthy of his government's expectations.''

''Still, I think he thinks of you as a father.''

''Well, I can live with that if Cliff can.''

''We'll talk to Cliff. But, Garth, you really do go on about Lu; does he need all that stroking all the time?''

''I don't know. You're right; I realized I did it again tonight, but he's so tense most of the time I find myself trying to make him feel better about himself. There's a kind of desperation to him, almost a recklessness. He can't really relax; he can't really enjoy himself. One time when he was in my office I wanted to hold him on my lap and tell him everything would be all right.''

Sabrina smiled. ''He would have been very surprised.''

"He would have thought the eminent professor had lost his mind. Well, I'll be careful at home from now on, and I'll talk to Cliff." At the door to the dining room, he stopped and took her in his arms. "I love you."

"I'm so glad of that." They glanced into the room and saw an empty table, and heard Penny and Cliff talking to Mrs. Thirkell in the kitchen, and they held each other close and kissed.

"Stolen kisses," Garth murmured as the kitchen door swung open and Penny and Cliff came back.

Sabrina stayed in his arms. "It's when parents stop kissing that children get upset."

"Not a problem, then, since kissing you is the first item on my agenda for the next fifty or sixty years."

"What's the joke?" Cliff asked as Sabrina and Garth smiled together.

"Sixty years of kissing," Sabrina said, and as Cliff came close she put her hand on his hair, chestnut-colored, the same as her own, and pulled him closer. "We plan to kiss you and Penny for at least the next sixty years."

"You'll be ninety-three," Penny said. "That's really old."

"Not too old to kiss."

"We're hot on the trail of a gene that makes kissing as potent at ninety-three as it is at thirty-three," Garth said, and he stood in his dining room with his wife in his arms and his children close by, and felt the abundance of his world and of his own powers: he was just forty years old, healthy, respected in his field, loved in his home. He had everything he wanted; there was nothing he could not do.

A week later he reached back to retrieve that feeling as he sat in his office facing a staff attorney for Congressman Oliver Leglind.

"Roy Stroud," the attorney had said as he walked in. "Glad to meet you, Professor; I've been wanting to for a long time. Ah, this must be the grand new building we've heard so much about." He walked to a square table beneath the window and looked down at a model of the Institute for Genetic Engineering. He was short and stout, with a small brush mustache, wire-rimmed glasses that slid down his small round nose, and a watch chain across his paunch, and he rocked back and forth from toes to heels to toes as he contemplated the Styrofoam model set in Styrofoam-landscaped grounds. "Very handsome. Handsome indeed. That's a handsome monument to you, Professor."

"To science," Garth said.

Stroud was moving a model car along the road circling the institute. "Takes me back, oh, it does take me back. I had a collection once: every model car they made. I don't think I missed one. Not one model car did I miss. Well." He turned back to Garth. "Let's sit down, Professor, I don't want to take too much of your time."

Garth pulled out a chair for Stroud, debated briefly taking the one next to it, then sat in his leather swivel chair instead, putting his desk between them. "It would be helpful if I knew what this is about."

"Well, it's about universities; I guess you could guess that. Congressman Leglind, as I'm sure you know, is chairman of the House Committee on Science, Space and Technology, and he's been bombarded lately with a flood of mail from constituents who are worried about balancing the budget and wondering if maybe Congress is giving too much money to universities. Nobody watches over universities, you know; there's nobody out there signing off on how you spend the funding you get from your government, so nobody really knows where the money goes. So the congressman thought, in response to this avalanche of mail—an outcry from the people if we ever saw one—that he'd hold hearings on the way universities use the money Congress gives them."

"A bombardment, a flood, and an avalanche," Garth said reflectively. "How much mail is that, exactly?"

Stroud guffawed. "I do use a lot of words; I confess it.

I don't have an exact count, Professor, but I assure you it was definitely a torrent.''

Garth did not smile. ''And what is it you want from me?''

''Information. The hearings start next month and you're on the list of those we'll probably call to testify, but right now we're just gathering information. The congressman likes information up front; he doesn't like a lot of surprises, so we're into fieldwork in a heavy way before the hearings begin. We're curious people, Professor, and we're mainly curious about the way other people spend the government's money. So what I want first is to ask—''

''It is not the government's money. It's our money; it comes from our taxes. The government wasn't transplanted here from Mars: the government is us, all of us who vote and pay taxes. And the government doesn't give our money away; it invests it. In this university, the government invests in genetic research that can change people's lives: how long they live, how comfortably they live, how productive they are, how secure an environment they can provide for their children—the next generation. Most people would call that a wise investment.''

''And indeed it might be, it might indeed be, if the money is used wisely. The wise use of money, as of course you know, is numero uno when there isn't enough to go around. So, Professor, I'd ask you first about a party you gave at the Shedd Aquarium in Chicago on February twentieth of this year.''

Garth stared at him. ''You can't be serious.''

''I am always serious, Professor.''

''You come in here talking about balancing the federal budget and then you ask me about a fund-raising event that cost five thousand dollars.''

''Is that what you call it? A fund-raising event? I understood that it was a party.''

''Who called it that?''

''Well, it doesn't really matter. Someone who heard about it. Renting the aquarium, you know, that's a class act, and class acts tend to get around. Good food, music, limos to take some of you home . . . doesn't sound very academic, does it? I mean, I went to college and law school and I never heard of my professors dancing around with fish and catered dinners and riding home in limos."

"Entertainment is in the budget," Garth said, and heard himself saying it to Claudia at the aquarium. "People who give substantial sums of money like to be appreciated. We hold these events in the most pleasant atmosphere we can find to thank those who've helped fund our programs and to describe to them and to prospective donors the programs that still need funding. Our guests always know we'll be coming back to them for more at some time in the future; a convivial evening is part of the whole process."

"But you've got the government giving you—sorry, investing in you. That money is supposed to be used for research, not for renting the aquarium. And not for putting on a dinner at the Ritz-Carlton last December eighth, or for a dinner at Le Français on January the twentieth, or for renting a cruise ship on Lake Michigan for dinner on March tenth. One thing we've noticed, Professor, is how well you all eat."

Garth gazed at him. "The entertainment budget is one half of one percent of the money we spend on research. It pays for itself many times over."

"So far. You don't know that, going in; that's just a hope and hopes sometimes crash; hope is not a way to do business. Especially with the government's money. But I agree: these aren't the biggest items. The biggest—no contest—is this handsome institute you're building for yourself."

"For the university. And for science."

"But there's a kitchen in this building, and a lounge that's sort of like a faculty club, and an auditorium, and some pretty nice offices and reception rooms. So what we're curious about here, Professor, is what does all that have to do with science?"

Garth was so still it seemed he barely breathed. Anyone

who knew him would have known how his anger was building. "Since we're asking questions, I have some for you. Why is Congressman Leglind hostile to science? Is he afraid of it? Does he think that attacking science somehow makes this a better country? Or does he believe that the fortunes of his political career rest on finding something to destroy?"

He was on his feet now, leaning over the desk, his voice rising. "Or is he simply the kind of politician who makes Congress a laughingstock, the kind who creates circuses instead of legislation, the kind who believes in nothing but getting reelected by means of whatever demagoguery it takes?" He paused. "I'm waiting for an answer."

Stroud shook his head. "Shame on you, Professor. You're talking about a congressman who spends his life in the service of his country and doesn't have anything like the cushy life you professors have, and you still can't leave him alone. Congressman Leglind cares about science, he cares deeply about it, but he also cares about the government's money, how it gets spread around college campuses and frittered away on dinner parties and fancy buildings. He's determined to root out anybody who isn't doing science. Real scientists spend the government's money on equipment, not fripperies; they don't need kitchens and lounges and auditoriums and fancy parties. Real scientists care about science. Period. And that's what the congressman cares about."

Garth circled his desk and went to the door of his office. "If your congressman gave a damn about science, you'd be asking what that institute is for, how many students and faculty will use it, what lab facilities it will have and what kind of a library, what guest speakers will use the auditorium and who will be in the audience from local high schools and other universities, what space it will free up in other buildings that can then be used for other branches of science."

Stroud had turned to face him, and Garth opened the door. "That's what an inquiring mind would ask; that's what a truly curious person would want to know. A curious person would not spend his time fabricating plots to whip up the anger of voters. A curious person would want to search out the best ways he and his constituents can make this a more informed, more intelligent nation. And there are people like that around: people who understand the value of science and how desperately this country needs to increase its commitment to it, for our own good and for our place in the world. They know that if some universities are guilty of excesses, that's not a reason to undermine all the work that's being done by serious scientists across the country, and I can't believe those people will let you get away with a slash-and-burn rampage across the campuses.''

He looked at his watch. Be polite, he told himself. At least be polite from now on. ''When we made this appointment I thought I'd have another hour, but as it happens, I have to take a class in a few minutes for a colleague who is ill. If you think we need a follow-up, my secretary will find a date.''

Slowly Stroud stood and retrieved his briefcase, which he had not opened, from beneath his chair. ''I'd be more respectful, Professor, when you testify before the committee. Just a friendly warning. If the congressman wants me to come back, I'll call.''

Garth watched him disappear where the corridor turned a corner, and after waiting another minute he too went out, turning the other direction to a door that led to a small courtyard behind the science building. Patches of May sunlight dappled a stone bench beneath spreading trees; beside it was a dry stone fountain, its basin filled with last fall's papery maple leaves and brittle black locust pods. In a warm corner beside a brick wall, a student slept, his head on his outstretched arm, his book face down in the grass. Garth watched two butterflies chase each other in fluttering circles around his motionless body; then he sat on the stone bench, legs outstretched, and put his face up to the sun, letting his anger seep away.

For all his intelligence and sophistication, his world travels to scientific conferences, his work and friendships with an international array of biologists and chemists, he still had a naive astonishment that he could not lead the simple life he wanted without interruptions from people who had no idea what he did and had not the slightest interest in finding out. He had thought he was insulated on a campus, secure behind walls that enclosed a community dedicated to the life of the mind, but in that, too, he was naive: campus walls were easily breached and universities had become big business, involved with corporations and the government and a host of government agencies like NASA and the National Science Foundation and the National Institutes of Health, contracting with them for research and development with huge sums of money involved.

But still Garth Andersen, professor, came to work each day and returned home each night thinking that his clearly defined life was all he needed to concentrate on: his work and his family, the two passions that drove and exhilarated him and made him whole. He had never cared about the fray of competition. He knew Sabrina missed it and was looking forward to returning to it when she went to London, and he knew that his children were learning to handle it in school, from necessity if not from desire. But he was bored by it and did all he could to avoid it.

He always had done, in his own way, what he wanted to do and what he was best at. And, because he had always excelled, he had never known failure or even second place; he had not had to consider what they would mean in his life. He knew he was lucky, but he was also confident: he knew himself and he knew what he could do excellently and what he could not do at all, like painting, sculpting, singing on key, or building a fine cabinet, though he admired, extravagantly and sometimes with envy, those who did all those things. He was interested in politics and sports; he loved literature, movies, theater, the opera, but none of them were absolutely essential to his idea of a complete life. His family and his work were.

And so when a little round man with a watch chain across his paunch walked into his office looking like a bill collector from the London of Charles Dickens, Garth's immediate reaction was to brush him aside. The hell with it, he thought; it will die away. They'll probably find something on other campuses to spice up their hearings, but there's nothing here and they know it. It was a fishing expedition and it's over.

He checked his watch. Five minutes before his first class. As he stood up, he glanced at the student on the grass. He was awake, stuffing his book into his backpack, preparing to leave. The sun had moved behind the corner of the building, and the courtyard was in shadow. Garth turned toward the door of his building, then glanced back one more time. The student had left, and the butterflies were gone.

. .

It was raining in London, wet streaks on gray buildings, gusty May winds flinging sheets of water against the windows of Ambassadors. Sabrina opened the front door, snapping her umbrella shut as she backed into the shop. She stood on the Bokhara rug just inside the door shaking the water from her hair, feeling exhilarated, as if she had confronted Poseidon and won. Or at least prevailed, she thought; one never defeats the gods—they always have another trick up their sleeve.

"Mrs. Andersen!" Brian said, coming from the back room. His voice was surprised and also relieved. So whatever it is, it's still going on, Sabrina thought, and everything else fell away: she became alert, thinking of possible problems, noticing changes in the shop: a new Empire sofa and Directoire chair, a pair of French clocks . . . with a price tag visible on one of them. She went to it and tucked it out of sight, knowing Brian was watching, knowing he would remember and not let it happen again.

She unbuttoned her raincoat and waited for Brian to

help her slip out of it. He held it, dripping, in front of him, and carried it to the back of the shop, partitioned into her office and a smaller one for him, and hung it on an antique coat tree in the corner. Sabrina eyed it. "Where did that come from?"

"Nicholas found it. Or rather, Amelia did, for Blackford's, but he doesn't acknowledge that. Such a strange marriage, you know: I almost never see them together, and the few times I do, they pay absolutely no attention to each other."

"We will not discuss Nicholas's marriage," Sabrina said calmly, though she was angry. Brian would never have made that statement had he thought she was Lady Longworth; he said it only because he knew her as Stephanie Andersen, American, and therefore eager for gossip and unaware of the fine distinctions of social status. She sat at her cherrywood desk. "I'll look at the ledgers now."

His face flushed, Brian brought them from his office. "Is there anything else you need, Mrs. Andersen?"

"Yes, sit down." She flipped the pages back to December, when she had last been there. She ran a finger down the columns of purchases and sales, then looked at Brian, seated across from her. "I'll go over it more closely later on, but at first glance everything looks fine. All right, Brian, let's talk about your problem."

He shifted in his chair. "Nicholas wants to fire me."

"Oh, I doubt it; he'd have to deal with me on that, and he hasn't said a word. Why would he want to?"

"He thinks I'm spying on him."

Sabrina kept her gaze level. "Are you?"

"Well, yes, as a matter of fact. But only on behalf of Ambassadors."

"And what activity requires you to spy on him?"

"I think he's buying very special pieces and shipping them directly to clients, not bringing them through Ambassadors or Blackford's."

"You'd hear from the clients. They always call to discuss a piece they've bought."

"Not if Nicholas told them we've slipped badly, lost our touch, our expertise, since Lady Longworth's death."

"*Is* Nicholas telling them that?"

"I've heard that he is."

It was possible, Sabrina thought. Once before, in the turmoil after Stephanie's funeral, Nicholas had tried to take Ambassadors from her. She had stopped him then: stunned him by understanding immediately what he was doing and cutting him off exactly as Sabrina would have done. If he was trying again, he must believe Stephanie Andersen was too absorbed with her life in America to pay attention. Or to care. Stubborn Nicholas, she thought. But perhaps formidable.

"Olivia knows it's not true that we've lost our touch," she said. "Her friends know it's not true."

"Some of them are loyal," Brian replied gloomily.

"I'll talk to Olivia; she'll take care of it," Sabrina said at last. "It used to be Alexandra who stopped rumors for me; now it has to be Olivia."

"For Lady Longworth," Brian murmured, almost apologetic at reminding her that Alexandra had stopped rumors for her sister, not for her.

Sabrina ignored it. "Is there anything else I should know about?"

"There's an auction on Thursday, Lord Midgeford—"

"Riscombe Park? You didn't send me the catalogue."

"I was late mailing it; I imagine it's arriving in Evanston about now."

"Well, I'll be here on Thursday, so I'll go. Please get another catalogue and reserve a seat for me. And I'll need a limousine."

"Nicholas will have his, my la— I'm sorry. Mrs. Andersen."

"If what you tell me is true, I don't want to be in Nicholas's limousine; I want him to be in mine. I'd like the names of clients you think will be interested in specific pieces at Riscombe, especially Regency silver; Abner Midgeford collected it. I've lost touch with a lot of the people who will want it.'' She wondered if Brian would correct her again, asking how Stephanie Andersen could have lost touch with anyone when it was Sabrina Longworth who had lived in London and owned Ambassadors and known the people who collected Regency silver. But he was silent. He probably thinks I've gone crazy, Sabrina thought; what a test of Brian's reserve. ''Please call Nicholas; tell him I'd like him to have dinner with me tomorrow night at the Savoy. Eight o'clock; please take care of the reservation.''

She spent the afternoon at her desk, going more deliberately through the ledgers, reading the mail. She kept looking at her watch, and when it was dinnertime in Evanston she called Garth and the children, and closed her eyes, seeing them, feeling their arms around her. ''Soon,'' she told them. ''I'll be home very soon.''

Brian left early for a dentist's appointment, but Sabrina stayed on. She was not in a hurry to return to the empty house on Cadogan Square and she liked the atmosphere of her shop, the faintly cloying scent of furniture polish in the still air, the stuffy smell of old wood and old fabrics. They were odors she remembered from the shopping expeditions of her childhood, with her mother and Stephanie, and they were exactly the same as those at Collectibles in Evanston. The universal air of antique shops, she mused with a smile; one could be anywhere in the world and always be at home.

She heard the front bell ring and the door open. Brian should have locked it, she thought, and stood up quickly to go into the shop. ''I'm sorry, we're closed for the— good heavens,'' she said as she saw who it was. ''Denton.'' She walked toward him. *I'm Stephanie; I'm not Sabrina. He'd expect* . . . She held out her hand and Denton took it and pumped it up and down.

''Delighted to see you again, Stephanie; how well you look. Much better than the last time we met, at Sabrina's funeral. In fact . . .'' He leaned forward, scanning her face. ''My God, you could be Sabrina. I never realized . . . It's quite amazing, you know; it quite takes one aback. Did you look like this all those years ago when she and I were at that barbecue at your house in . . . where was it? Evansville?''

"Evanston."

"Of course. I didn't think I'd ever forget that day. Years ago, of course, but if you'd looked like this . . . well, I would have noticed . . . said something . . . I didn't say anything, did I? No, of course I didn't; I would have remembered. Well, then, that's the answer. You didn't look like this. You couldn't have.''

Sabrina gazed at him in silence.

Denton cleared his throat. His sharp black eyes slid left and right and he wandered vaguely around the shop, trailing delicate fingers across clocks and lamps and furniture. "Wonderful things. Sabrina had superb taste, and so do you, I see. I always admired her taste.''

That is a lie. You paid no attention to it at all.

He looked at her from across the room, bouncing slightly on his toes. "Look here, why don't we dine together? It would please me very much. I was passing by and I saw you in here, and it occurred to me that you probably don't know many people in town, and I have a free evening, and why should you be lonely?''

Dinner with Denton? What a depressing thought; it would be like seeing my life go by in reverse. "Thank you, no, Denton; I have too much to do in the short time I'm here. I'll work right through dinner at home.''

"Alone? You can't do that. The worst thing for your digestion, you know, and for your state of mind. People have gone mad from eating alone.''

Involuntarily she smiled. She wondered how he had managed to stay exactly the same for almost fifteen years. His round face and rosy cheeks, his little mustache, his fascination with himself, his desperate need to be surrounded by people at all times to convince himself that he was happy . . . they were all familiar to her. As if pre-

237

served in plaster of paris, Denton seemed the same today as on the day she married him.

"There, that's the ticket; you're magnificent when you smile, you should never frown or even look too serious. Sabrina had the same smile, you know—well, of course you know; you knew her better than anyone—it was one of the reasons I adored her and could never tear myself from her." Sabrina's eyebrows rose. "Truth," Denton said, raising his hand. "I couldn't look at another woman when I had my Sabrina."

That is a lie. You slept with any woman close enough for you to sniff her perfume.

"And we were incredibly happy, you know. Two people—"

That is a lie.

"—who adored each other. We were the talk of London society, the envy of everyone because we were perfect."

That is a lie.

"I miss her, you know. In spite of the fact that we couldn't make it, I loved her and admired her; I still do. I want you to know that."

Why are you telling me these lies?

"And it was unbelievably ghastly, you know, when they asked me to identify her. I could barely look at her; I broke down like a baby, shaking all over; I nearly fainted away."

I'd be willing to bet that's a lie, too.

"It was bad enough that it was my own wife they were telling me to identify. But dead bodies, you know . . . I never could look at them; I can't even think about death, much less look at it . . ."

That part I believe.

"Stephanie, forgive me. I didn't mean to talk about this, but seeing you . . . My God, it's even worse for you than for me and I go on and on . . . I'm a blithering ass. I do beg your forgiveness; I am truly contrite. Tell me I'm forgiven. Tell me it won't stop you from having dinner with me. Tell me we're still friends."

"I forgive you, Denton, but we've never been friends, and I think it highly unlikely that we ever will be. And I won't have dinner with you because I would much rather be at home."

There was a pause. "You sound just like her, do you know that? The same voice, the same odd accent that nobody could ever place, the same way of saying 'I think it highly unlikely . . .' Of course with twins it's hard to fathom . . ."

"I'm closing the shop now. Good night, Denton."

"You'd really rather eat alone?"

"Yes."

"She was like that, too, you know. Sometimes she'd say she just didn't want to go to another dinner; she wanted to be by herself. She said it quite a lot after a while, and then I'd go by myself . . . of course we were having some problems by then."

"Good night, Denton."

"Well, then. Good night, Stephanie." At the door he turned back casually, as if something had just occurred to him. "I don't suppose you've heard from Max Stuyvesant, have you?"

Sabrina froze in shock. "Max? What are you talking about? He's dead."

"Presumed dead. They never found a body. I thought if he turned up somewhere he might have tried to contact someone. You know."

"No, I don't know. If he were alive he would have come home; where else would he go? He would have called you; you were one of his friends. You introduced u . . . them, didn't you? I thought Sabrina told me you took her on a cruise on his yacht and that's when she met him. That must have been the same yacht—" She took a breath. "He would have called you, not me."

Denton nodded. "I suppose so. But you know, Stephanie, if he does surface—good Lord, what an unfortunate choice of words; I'm so sorry. But if he does come back—it probably won't happen, of course, everyone else was killed; they found everyone else—but if he does and if he happens to call you, would you let me know? I would appreciate it. I somehow can't believe he's really dead, you know. He always seemed indestructible to me.''

''I'll let you know, Denton.'' She said it almost soothingly. ''Now I'd like to lock up.''

''Yes, right, sorry.'' He opened the front door, then reared back as wind and rain gusted in. He slammed it shut. ''Damn, I can't go out in this.''

''You did it once, to get here; you can do it again,'' she said coldly. ''Go home, Denton. I don't want you here.''

''Yes, well, that is abundantly clear, isn't it? It's too bad, you know, Stephanie; I did think we could be friends. I might stop in again sometime, just to make sure you're all right. I feel a sense of responsibility . . . Sabrina's sister . . .'' He waited for her to say something. When she did not, he girded himself, ducked his head as he opened the door, and flung himself into the storm.

Sabrina was shaking. What was going on? What was he looking for? Or afraid of, she thought suddenly, recalling the quivering of his mustache and the nervous thrust of his lower lip as he said, ''I might stop in again sometime . . .''

Still shaking, she pulled on her raincoat. My hat, she thought; I had one, a long time ago . . . Oh, it can't be here; Stephanie would have found it, or someone . . . She reached up to a high shelf in the supply closet and her hand closed on a Burberry rain hat, neatly folded. Oh, Stephanie, you left it for me.

She was crying. She grabbed her umbrella, turned out the lights and left the shop, the hat pulled low over her eyes, her open umbrella close to the top of her head. She walked to the taxi stand and stood there for a long time until, through the rain, she saw one of the familiar tall black cars pull along the curb. She got in and put her hat and umbrella on the floor. ''Kensington Cemetery.''

''They close pretty soon, miss, and it's no place to be in a rainstorm.''

"I want to go. I won't stay long; can you wait for me?"

"If you was my daughter, I wouldn't let—"

"Please."

He looked at her closely. "All right, then."

Inside the cemetery, the taxi moved slowly along the curved road until Sabrina told the driver to stop. "You will wait?"

"Not likely I'd leave you, miss."

"Thank you."

She walked along the road. She had thought she would come here the next morning, but she found she could not wait. It was strange, but she found more of Stephanie in London than in Evanston: this was where she had spent the last month of her life and Sabrina felt her presence everywhere. Now she looked for her as the rain stung her face and whipped her coat about her ankles. It had been gray last October during the funeral, the clouds lowering against skeletal trees, the cold wind cutting through the mourners' coats. But why should the sun ever shine on Stephanie's grave?

Sabrina tilted her umbrella against the wind and walked slowly along the road until she found the white marble stone. She had ordered it in February and sent to the stonemason the lines to be carved on it from Yeats's poem, one of Stephanie's favorites. This was the first time she had seen it, and she ran her wet hand over the deeply chiseled letters.

LADY SABRINA LONGWORTH

Through hollow lands and hilly lands,
I will find out where she has gone,
And kiss her lips and take her hands;
And walk among long dappled grass,
And pluck till time and times are done
The silver apples of the moon,
The golden apples of the sun.

Rain streaked the marble like cold tears. Sabrina knelt on the sodden grass, the umbrella resting on her bent head, and wept.

"Miss," the taxi driver said. He put his hand on her shoulder. She had been there for ten minutes and she was shivering so violently she could barely look up at him. "They're closing, miss, and you're going to catch your death."

She let him help her up and stumbled beside him back to the taxi. She was not aware of the streets through which they drove: the sidewalks undulating ribbons of black umbrellas, the lights of shop windows and apartments wavering drunkenly through the rain-lashed windows of the taxi. Sabrina huddled in the back seat, numb and cold, the tears flowing silently down her face.

She let herself into the empty house on Cadogan Square and dropped her umbrella and drenched coat and hat in the foyer. A stream ran from them to the serape rug in the center. She looked at it with unconcern and climbed the stairs to her sitting room. The fireplace was dark. On my own, Sabrina thought ruefully. I told Denton that was what I wanted.

She laid a fire and lit it, then turned on both faucets in her tub, pouring in a stream of bath oil. She boiled water in an electric teakettle in her sitting room and stripped off her clothes while the tea was steeping, then carried the cup and teapot into the bathroom and lowered herself slowly into the fragrant, steaming water. Her tears had stopped and now, gradually, her shivering stopped. Her body soaked up the heat and the slow caress of the bath oil; she put her head back until only her face was exposed, her hair floating on the surface of the water.

Stephanie was here, too: it was as if Sabrina could see her coming in that first night, walking around the room, opening closets and drawers, discovering all that would be hers for the one week they had crazily decided to steal from their lives, standing before the mirror in a dress from the closet that made her look, suddenly and astonishingly, exactly like Sabrina, the same tilt of the head, the same confident pose . . .

I can't do this, Sabrina thought; it's so real it's as if she's alive.

She forced herself to think of London, of Ambassadors and Brian, and of Nicholas. Dinner with Nicholas tomorrow, and she had to be prepared. She thought often of selling Ambassadors and she knew she would one day, but no one, certainly not Nicholas, was going to steal it from her.

And so when she met him at the Savoy the next evening, she was cool and watchful. At first Nicholas was not aware of it. "A small gift, Stephanie," he said, handing her a box wrapped in silver and gold paper. "Sabrina found them amusing." They were sitting at a small table beside a window looking out on the Thames and the long span of Waterloo Bridge. The view was framed by velvet draperies and figured wallpaper, and Nicholas, in suit and vest and starched cuffs, had settled into his upholstered chair with a sigh; it was his favorite room, as Sabrina had known. "I thought you might find it amusing, too. It's a little gift to welcome you to London. It was a surprise to hear from Brian—you never told us the exact date you'd be coming—but how pleasant, Stephanie . . . and of course you have a birthday coming up—in September, isn't it?—and you may not be here then. And I always remembered Sabrina's birthday with some little token."

No, you did not. And this is only May; a very long time to September. Sabrina opened the box. "Well, Nicholas," she said after a moment. "A Fabergé egg is more than a little token." She lifted it from its box, a golden egg decorated with jewels that swung open beneath her fingers to reveal a tiny basket of flowers carved from precious stones. "In perfect condition," she murmured.

"Well, only the best," said Nicholas gaily.

"Thank you. It's very generous of you." And not bad, she thought, as an attempted bribe. She smiled at him, suddenly enjoying herself, reveling in being back in the fray, fencing with people who always had hidden motives. "Such a clever idea, to open a conversation with such a gift."

Nicholas's look sharpened; he never liked it when people understood him.

"Tell me about the winter season," she said. "I've gone over our books and it seems to have been rather quiet."

"Yes, rather. The economy, you know, people are holding back, waiting for a clue to the future. I wouldn't worry, though, dear Stephanie; we're solvent and we can wait out a bad season, or even two, if we have to."

"Even two," Sabrina repeated thoughtfully. "And what are you doing to change a bad season to a successful one?"

"Well, you know, one talks to clients, as always, one meets new people, one gathers information for the future; the main thing is to make sure that one's clients and their friends don't forget one."

"You mean you continue to build goodwill for Blackford's and Ambassadors."

"Exactly. Exactly. One is always at work, always."

"But the question seems to be, Nicholas, for whom?"

"I beg your pardon?" He finished his martini, waved to the waiter for another, and picked up his soup spoon, absently tapping it on the table. "You tend to talk in riddles, dear Stephanie; many of us find it disconcerting— even, on occasion, unpleasant."

My God, Sabrina thought, is that the best he can do to try to make me afraid of him? "If that's true, I regret it," she said evenly. "I've not heard that from anyone, but of course you deal with rumors far more frequently than I do." She watched several expressions flit across his face. "I'm concerned about our reputation, Nicholas. I've been thinking of expanding from our three shops, adding two more, in New York and Paris"—she had not been thinking of any such thing, but as she said it, she thought, Why not?—"and I will not tolerate anything that might tarnish our good name. There are only two things we have to offer our clients: expertise and trust—you know that as well as I do—and it takes a long time to establish both of them. I worked too hard to create that for Ambassadors to allow anyone—"

"Well, but my dear Stephanie, surely you mean your sister did."

Abruptly, Sabrina struck the table with her hand. "It's the same thing!" She stopped, astounded at her lack of control. Nicholas was staring at her in amazement. And, in fact, she had never before raised her voice in a business discussion, nor had she done anything as untoward as striking the table in a discreet restaurant. *It's being back here for the first time in months, but not really being back, because I have another life now.*

"Stephanie?"

"I'm sorry," she said. "That was uncalled for. Of course my sister built Ambassadors, but I often find myself speaking for both of us, especially when it comes to business. As you know, we were very close. My point remains, Nicholas: I will not tolerate anyone making the slightest attempt to undermine my reputation or that of the shop."

"Of course, of course." His head tilted, Nicholas looked at her through narrowed eyes. "Forgive me for getting a trifle personal, Stephanie, but you seem to be under a strain; I think you're trying to do too much. Why don't you go back to your husband and children—you're obviously a fine housewife and mother—and let me manage Ambassadors? I'll continue to report to you at regular intervals, and I assure you, you will be quite satisfied."

"What satisfies me," Sabrina said softly, "is working with the three shops we have now, and any others we decide to purchase, and being kept informed on all major purchases and sales at Ambassadors and Blackford's. What satisfies me, Nicholas, is trust."

"Yes, yes, of course, but really, Stephanie, you cannot run a business from across the ocean. There are major decisions that must be made every day involving hundreds of thousands of pounds—millions, on occasion. These are not small dealings such as you handle from your little shop in Chicago—"

"Evanston."

"Evanston, yes, of course." The waiter placed another martini in front of him and refilled Sabrina's wineglass from the bottle on the table. "The point remains—"

"And I intend to keep doing it, Nicholas, with help and cooperation from you and Brian. I do own Ambassadors, as I hope you remember. I think there's nothing more to be said about that."

"*Nothing more to be said?* My dear Stephanie, that is not for you to decide." He took a long swallow of his martini. "The fact is, I am bringing new clients to Ambassadors far more prominent than those Sabrina dealt with before her death. I am commissioned to locate and purchase pieces of furniture, jewelry and paintings that are among the most precious in the world."

"I thought business was down. The economy and so forth."

"Even in a slow season, I am finding the best clients. And you are in no position to deal with them. Sabrina might have been able to, but beyond the physical resemblance you are nothing like her. You are quite out of your depth here; London is really no place for you. You're far better off in Evanston with your family and friends. I promise you, at regular intervals, your share of the profits—"

"Excuse me, Nicholas," Sabrina said as the waiter approached again, "may we order now?"

His face was flushed. "I haven't decided . . . well, what are you having?"

"Scallops and then the duck."

He nodded. "Fine. The same."

The sommelier had joined them. "And perhaps a red wine to accompany the duck?"

"Châteauneuf-du-Pape," said Sabrina. "Do you still have any of the 'fifty-eight?"

"Ah," he said approvingly. "We have a few bottles, madame."

As he left, Nicholas spread his hands. "Did she tell you everything?"

"Yes. Now, if I heard you correctly, you were talking about profits. You alone would send my checks? With no one else looking at the account books?"

"A ship has one captain, Stephanie. I will take care of you, I promise."

Sabrina laughed. "Oh, Nicholas, a Fabergé egg isn't enough."

His face reddened again. "Don't play games with me. You're a very pleasant woman, Stephanie, but—I regret having to repeat this, but it is important—you do not have your sister's class and sophistication. You're a housewife and a mother, both admirable occupations, but they do not prepare you for dealing with wealth and royalty. You can wear Sabrina's clothes and live in her house, you can even order wine that she told you about, but you're still a poor imitation of Sabrina Longworth. You're not as experienced as she was, not as socially adept, and because of that, I am the one who should be concerned about our reputation, and I cannot allow you to continue to interfere in the workings of these shops, putting everything at risk. Too much is at stake."

Sabrina had leaned forward so that their faces were a few inches apart. "A poor imitation?" she echoed seriously. "Everyone else has trouble believing I'm not really Sabrina." She held his gaze for a long moment, then slowly shook her head. "Poor Nicholas, to be so desperate. I won't ask you what is at stake; you'll have to deal with whatever you've done that has made you so anxious to be rid of me. But I will tell you what I've decided. I'm going to write letters to all our clients and to others—those prominent people you mentioned—assuring them that our services are as complete as ever and that we act on their behalf from the moment an item is purchased to the time it is delivered. That means we will not allow any item, however small or large, to be shipped to a customer without a thorough inspection of its condition and a search of its provenance in our shop. Any sale at auction is contingent on the item's condition being as stated in the catalogue—you know that, Nicholas, but many clients do not—and one of our most important duties is to fulfill that part of the sale. Those letters will go out this week over my signature. It would be appropriate, if we are to remain partners, for your signature to be there as well."

His face had darkened; his eyes were bulging. "You can't do that."

"Why not?"

"It undermines my integrity; it makes me look a fool."

"How does it do that if your signature is on the letter?"

"You must not write it; it would be a mistake."

"I don't think so."

"You don't have to explain yourself to clients who already know what you can do for them."

"I think perhaps I do."

"You are absolutely determined to do this?"

"Absolutely."

He sat frozen, then abruptly shoved back his chair. "We have nothing to talk about." And with only the slightest hesitation as he realized he was deserting a woman in the middle of his favorite restaurant, he turned and walked out.

Sabrina sat alone. The sommelier brought the red wine and held the bottle for her to read the label. She nodded and he uncorked it. The minutes passed. The waiter put a dish of scallops before her and set another at Nicholas's place. "You may remove that," she said. "Mr. Blackford has been taken ill and has gone home."

The waiter's brows went up. In a moment, the maître d' sped to her table. "If madame is uncomfortable and wishes to leave, we would understand . . . there would be no charge . . ."

Sabrina smiled at him. "I'm not at all uncomfortable. But I am very hungry."

He stood looking at her, wondering why a beautiful woman forced to eat alone in a fine restaurant was not uncomfortable. But she continued to smile at him, and so, after a moment, he bowed. "If there is anything I can do . . ."

"Not at the moment." She watched him walk away. In fact, she was very uncomfortable, but not for the reason he thought. Nicholas's hostility had shaken her; it wound itself around her and made London seem unpleasant, even treacherous. She sipped the superb red wine and felt depressed. She didn't really love being back in the fray, fencing with people who had hidden motives; it was a terrible waste of energy and she resented having to do it when she could be concentrating on making a marriage, building a home, bringing up children, spending her time loving instead of parrying thrusts from greedy or frightened people.

The waiter brought a plate of duck and wild rice and she contemplated it. She had no appetite but she would eat some of it, to prove to Nicholas and Denton and the waiters at the Savoy that she could eat alone anywhere. But she missed her family. She missed her home. She missed Garth. She wanted to look up and meet his eyes down the length of the dinner table. She wanted to hear her children chatter and even squabble over the things of their day. She wanted her house to creak about her and know that the windows were tight and the doors secure. I don't want two lives, she thought. I only want one.

But she would not let Nicholas win. She would find someone to buy Ambassadors and she would withdraw from her participation in Blackford's. She had known the time would come to do this; now that it had come, she realized how anxious she was to cut these ties. But she would not rush: now that she knew what she wanted, she would do it properly, even if it took a few months. I'll sell the house, too, she thought. Maybe by September I'll have sold them both.

September. My birthday. And I'll be home for good.

249

CHAPTER *12*

Stephanie and Léon met on the sidewalk on the cours Gambetta as she was wheeling her bicycle from the shop and he was striding toward her.

"I was watching for you," he said as they shook hands. "Perhaps you will let me join you on your ride."

Her heart had lifted when she saw him and she was smiling. "But you have no bicycle."

"Behind you, in the shop. We use the same repairman; it's a good sign, I think. May I join you?"

"Yes, I'd like that."

"I'll be right back."

In a moment he was wheeling his bicycle from the shop, unhooking his helmet from the handlebars as he stopped beside her. "Have you a destination?"

"No. I thought perhaps some of the hill towns. I've only ridden to three of them."

"Have you been to Fontaine-de-Vaucluse?"

"No. I haven't even heard of it."

"Then that is where we go. No, I'm sorry; that was high-handed. I'd like to show you one of my favorite spots, but since what I want most is to spend the afternoon with you, I'll go wherever you choose.''

"Fontaine. Is it really a fountain?''

''An underground one, a spring that is the source of the river Sorgue. A beautiful spot; magical, I think.''

"Then that is where we go.''

He chuckled and they put on their helmets and began to walk the bicycles to the corner. ''I saw you leave your shop; have you had lunch?''

''No, I didn't want to take the time. I brought an apple.''

''Have you the time when we get to Fontaine-de-Vaucluse? I'd like to show you Café Philip; another of my special places.''

Stephanie thought about it only a moment. ''Yes. Not all afternoon, but for a little while.''

''Good.'' They parted to allow a woman with a baby buggy to pass between them. ''Where have you ridden around here?''

''Mainly around the vineyards, but last week I rode to Maubec and Robion and up to Oppède-le-Vieux.''

''A steep hill; you're very strong. But isn't it a wonderful ride? And beyond, to Ménerbes and Bonnieux as well.''

''How do you ride so much, and paint?''

''I almost always ride in the morning, seven, six, even five o'clock. I recommend it; perhaps we'll do it together. The traffic is light; the air is cool. By now, the end of June, it really is too hot to—'' He stopped. ''I just realized. Have you recently come to Cavaillon?''

''Yes, a few months ago. Doesn't the traffic seem worse than usual today?'' They had reached the corner and stood on the curb, waiting for the light to change.

''It is bad, but I try to ignore it when I'm riding. My theory is that since no driver is anxious to hit me, nor I him, we'll manage to take appropriate action to avoid each other. So far that's been the case. When we cross, we'll ride straight ahead and turn at the first cross street; it will be quieter then. I'll go first if you'd like.''

Stephanie nodded. She was feeling young and free and very happy. She had not seen Léon since the day they had met six weeks ago. He had not come again to Jacqueline en Provence; his new paintings were delivered by his friend who owned a large van. As she and Jacqueline had unwrapped them, Stephanie had asked casually if Léon would come to see how they were displayed in the shop, or if he would be bringing new ones.

"Oh, one cannot be sure," Jacqueline replied. "He is totally unpredictable. But aren't these fine? So different from the landscapes, but with that same power, as if he could cut with his brush through all pretense . . .''

That was the last time Stephanie mentioned him. And after a while she stopped thinking about him; she was ashamed of feeling she could be adventurous with him. I'm married, she told herself; how did I plan to be adventurous with Léon? Just what did I have in mind?

But I shouldn't use Léon or anyone else to break away from Max; I have to do that by myself. I have to learn to do everything by myself; I can't always let other people clear a path for me.

"Green light," Léon said, smiling at her, knowing her thoughts were far away.

They rode across the highway, then stayed close to the edge of the road as cars and trucks whizzed past. Stephanie gritted her teeth, her eyes on Léon's back, willing herself to ignore the noise and the rumble of the pavement as trucks barreled down upon her from behind. Her muscles were knotted and she cringed as she rode, certain every moment that the next truck would fling her aside like a piece of debris. But nothing happened; she and Léon pedaled furiously and it was only a few moments before he turned, and she followed, onto a narrow road that cut a straight line between high solid walls of cypress trees.

The sounds of the highway stopped as if a door had slammed; the air was still and hushed. Stephanie heard the

swish of their tires, the slow drone of bees, the distant call
of a rooster, the descending scales of birds silhouetted
against the silvery blue sky. She relaxed and caught up to
Léon, who had slowed for her.

"Better?" he asked.

"Much. This is lovely."

They rode in silence to the end of the cypresses, then
between vineyards whose rows of vines, sprouting new
leaves, seemed to radiate in perfectly straight lines from
the farmhouse in the center. The sun blazed upon them
and Stephanie wiped her forehead with the back of her
bicycle glove, then reached down for her water bottle and
drank from it as they rode. She liked Léon's silence and
his smile when their eyes met; she liked letting her
thoughts float, absorbing all that surrounded her: sprin-
klers spraying high arcs of water that glittered in the sun,
wild thyme lining the road with tiny pale purple flowers,
and rosemary bushes blossoming with pink flowers amid
their pinelike needles, men walking on the road wearing
undershirts and black pants that fell in folds over the tops
of their boots and calling out an amiable *bonjour* as they
passed, cherry trees with lush bunches of fruit peering
through the dense foliage, the small postal wagon scooting
along back roads like a child's toy. She felt strong and
healthy, part of the earth, propelling herself through a
landscape so serene and timeless that she could believe
nothing existed beyond it, and she and Léon were the only
two people in the world.

Oh, how happy I am, she thought, and she knew that
whatever else she had felt, with Max and Robert, with
Madame Besset and with Jacqueline, she had not said
those words to herself in that way before.

The road widened, became busier; soon it was bordered
by a low stone wall and there were power lines, light
poles, signs of a town. Stephanie and Léon rode around a
curve and saw just ahead an enormous stone bridge of tall
arches, and they flew beneath it and then past high dark

gray cliffs pocked with deep caves that led directly into Fontaine-de-Vaucluse.

"We can leave the bicycles in the square," Léon said, and asked a policeman where they could lock them. "Now we walk." They skirted the crowded square shaded by ancient trees and strolled up a long inclined promenade with the river on one side and booths on the other filled with souvenirs to catch unwary tourists. When they reached a row of cafés, Léon stopped at the one with a sign that said Café Philip. "One moment." He ran down a small stone stairway and quickly returned. "We have a reservation for lunch in half an hour."

As they came to the top of the promenade, Stephanie caught her breath and moved ahead, forgetting Léon. She stood beside a pond as still as a mirror, reflecting a giant curved cliff behind it. But the stillness was only in the pond; at the edge, where the earth fell away, the water plunged straight down in a thunderous fall, flinging spray high in the air, churning foam over huge boulders and spinning in whirlpools and eddies as it roared down the steep grade. Then, as the land leveled, the river widened, moving in rapid currents, and then widened still more, tossing up little waves that caught the sun. Small waterfalls like silver ribbons lined its banks and it grew steadily calmer as it flowed: one of the mighty rivers of Provence, the Sorgue River.

Stephanie sat on the rocks beside the edge of the pond where the still water fell into the deafening waterfall. Around her, children ran and shouted, dancing on the rocks, daring the water, screaming to make themselves heard; their parents clicked cameras and dragged the children back, warning of danger. Stephanie was unaware of them. She stared at small rainbows in the river's dancing droplets, at rocks glistening purple and brown and black from centuries of polishing by that relentless flow, and she felt herself become part of it, merging with it, fighting it, being carried away by it. It was as if she were back in the hospital, imprisoned in a fog, unable to break out or even move; it was as if she were in bed in Cavaillon in those early morning hours when she would wake from a dream and try to recapture it, to find in it a clue to her past, but would find instead an emptiness as loud, in its way, as the roaring water beside her.

Standing a few feet away, Léon watched her. She was very beautiful and he knew he wanted to paint her, but he was more interested in the impression she made of tentativeness: a woman unsure of herself, of who she was, where she was, even how she got here. He knew that was fanciful, but Léon believed in fancy: he believed in the furthest stretches of the imagination, in coincidence and unlikely circumstances, in events that seemed impossible or, more likely, unexplainable.

He knew that art could not be created or enjoyed without the unexplainable, nor could love and friendship grow, and so he trusted his emotions and his senses, his imagination, and his delight in complexity and perverseness to lead him, ultimately, to some kind of truth. Because of that, when he saw Sabrina Lacoste, stunningly beautiful, charming and intelligent, looking in this pensive moment like a woman who did not know who she was or where she belonged, he believed it was possible that indeed she did not know those things, and instead of brushing that idea aside, he found himself wondering about her past, and what part he could play in helping her, if help was what she wanted.

His painter's eye framed the landscape: a woman sitting on gray-white rock in front of a dark cliff where tenacious trees grew outward to catch the sun, the black water of the still pond, and the woman herself, wearing dark blue bicycle shorts and a white bicycle shirt open at the neck, her chestnut hair barely brushing her shoulders—it had been shorter when he met her six weeks ago—her slender body, her long legs, and a regal bearing that must have been drilled into her when she was young, so natural did it seem. Her gaze was fixed on the tumbling water, and he wondered what compelling memory it had brought to life.

And then he saw that her hands were clenched, the muscles of her arms taut, as if she were trying to swim against that fierce current, or to escape whatever thoughts were roiling within her.

He took a small sketch pad and a piece of charcoal from his backpack and drew swiftly and surely, first the landscape—crowds milling about the motionless woman, leaving a small private place for her as she stared at the water—and then the woman herself. Sabrina, he thought. A lovely name. A lovely mystery. Tantalizing and irresistible.

And married.

But I am involved with someone, too, Léon thought. Not a marriage, but still complicated. So we shall not look too far ahead, Sabrina and I. Not yet.

After a time, he went to her and put a hand on her shoulder. "If you're ready, we can go to lunch."

"Yes." She came out of her reverie and took his hand and stood up. "Thank you for bringing me here; you were right: it is magical."

"It reminds you of something." Their heads were close together, in order to hear each other. "Something beautiful . . . or overwhelming?"

"It's overwhelming on its own—don't you think?—without reminding anyone of anything. How deep is the spring beneath the pool?"

"No one has found it yet, though Cousteau and many others have tried."

"No one has found it? But isn't that amazing, that its beginnings are hidden, that only part of it is revealed, but still it has such strength and beauty . . ."

Léon was looking at her with curiosity. "Most of us reveal only parts of ourselves."

"Yes. Of course." As they turned, she looked back at the torrent. "I wish we didn't have to leave."

"But we aren't leaving. You'll see."

They walked back the way they had come, down the stone staircase to a glassed-in restaurant, and beyond it, a broad flagstone terrace shaded by an awning and extending over the water. "Oh, perfect," Stephanie said as they were shown to a table at the railing, with the river just below them. "What a lovely discovery."

"It often seems that most of the world has discovered it," Léon said with a smile as the waitress brought their menus. "When I want to be truly alone here, I come in the winter; it's truly magical then, with steam and snow and not a human voice to be heard, nor any presence but my own. Except, of course, for whatever gnomes and elves inhabit the caves in the cliffs."

"Gnomes and elves. Do you see them? And have conversations with them?"

"Not so far. But one doesn't have to do either to believe."

Stephanie rested her chin on her folded hands. "You believe in things that are invisible."

"I believe that there are things beyond our knowing: mysteries, magic, the shape of the future, the whole meaning of the past."

"And that doesn't frighten you?"

"It makes me very happy. How poor life would be without mysteries and miracles. And they fill my life, so I must believe in them."

"You mean your painting."

He took her hand. "Do you know, you are the first person who has understood immediately what I mean when I say that. Most people think I take a brush and paint what I see in front of me, just as they think writers write about people they know and scientists weigh and measure what they can pick up or trip over. Which is all nonsense. We paint and write and study what we cannot see; we leave the rest to the camera and the journalist. And we don't even know how we do it. Something inside us—or outside of us, who knows?—guides the brush and the pen and the scientist's thoughts, and we never fully understand what that force is, where our vision comes from. Why should we even try? We should only be grateful that it's there. I think our waitress would like us to order. I recommend the omelet with truffles and the Provençal tomatoes, unless you don't like—"

"It sounds perfect."

Léon ordered, and chose a bottle of Côtes du Rhône, and in the flurry of ordering and the setting of cutlery and napkins at their places and the pouring of wine, their hands came apart, and when they were alone again, Stephanie was holding her wineglass, and her other hand was in her lap.

They gazed at the water in a comfortable silence. "Have you been to the top of Mont Ventoux?" Léon asked.

"No. I'm waiting until I can do it on my bicycle."

"A formidable trip."

"I have a friend who does it every week. He says in a month or two I'll be strong enough if I work at it."

"And is it so important that you ride to the top?"

"Yes."

"It would be a triumph over . . . what?"

"It would be a triumph. Tell me about your painting. Have you always been a painter?"

"Since I was four. In fact, I remember the day and my first box of colored chalk, a birthday present. I took it to my room and stayed up through my naptime covering the walls as high as I could reach—and standing on chairs—with drawings of people, pets, animals in the zoo, and of course goblins and elves. I think they all may have looked alike; that part I can't remember. I do know that I used up every bit of the chalk."

"Your parents told you about that later."

"No, it's quite astonishing, but I remember it. No one was with me, but later I described the room exactly as they saw it when they walked in. As far as I know now, that's the only day I remember from my early years, but I do remember it: one ecstatic afternoon with four blank walls and a fresh box of colored chalk. The dream of every painter, and the birth of this one. I'm sure I have never been more perfectly happy."

Stephanie's eyes were on his, but she was seeing beyond him. "Wonderful," she said softly.

"It is a wonderful memory." He knew, without being able to define it, that they were talking about different things, but he had decided that he would ask her nothing about herself. It seemed clear that she would fend off any personal questions, as she had several times today, and so he let it go. Next time, perhaps, or the time after that. He would wait until she was ready.

"And you went on drawing and painting?" she asked. "No time out for sports or mischief?"

"None. I was an exceedingly dull boy. I was an only child and my parents had many ambitions for me, but I had only one for myself and I never wavered, though, for their sake, I did give some thought to medicine, law, science . . . all the respectable professions. It did no good; I always came back to what my mother called 'making pictures.' "

"Are they pleased now with your success?"

"They're very pleased that I'm successful, but they think I've come to it by a dubious route, through play rather than hard work and purposeful activity."

Stephanie smiled. "Where do they live?"

"In Lyon."

"Is that where you were born?"

"Born and grew up." Léon sat back as the waitress refilled their wineglasses and served their lunch. "I left high school after my second year and hitchhiked and worked on freighters—Europe, England, America, Africa, India—and then settled in Goult, which astonishes my friends and dismays my parents."

"I've been to Goult, to La Bartavelle, for dinner."

"An excellent restaurant. You were a few blocks from my house when you were there."

"It's a strange town. So tiny and . . . ghostly. It makes me think of a medieval town that everyone has fled because marauders are storming the walls."

He chuckled. "A perfect description, and the very rea-

son my parents are dismayed. They think I've holed myself up in a village of stone walls, shuttered windows and
hermits, cutting myself off from the world. In fact, I've
found a perch from which to view it, and swoop down
now and then to capture what takes my fancy.''

''And what is it that takes your fancy?''

''You do,'' he said quietly.

Stephanie caught her breath and looked away, to the
blue-green river with sunlit froth dancing on the surface.
Léon's eyes were the color of the river, green and blue;
she could see them in her mind and feel them watching
her. He had let her lead the conversation and she had been
lulled by that, thinking it extraordinary but somehow natural that he knew she did not want questions about herself.
A few times he had tried to turn the conversation to her,
but when she changed the subject, he had moved smoothly
on, and had not asked again.

She felt a small twinge of disappointment. If he had
persevered, she might have answered. But that's foolish,
she thought. I made it clear I wouldn't answer; I changed
the subject and he allowed me my privacy. But that odd
disappointment lingered. She felt again the warmth of his
hand on her shoulder as she sat beside the waterfall, and
his hand holding hers on the table, and she knew she
wanted to talk to him.

*I want to confide in him and trust him. I want to tell him
whatever is inside me. Because I think he'll understand.*

I want to make love to him.

She felt a sinking within her. I can't think that. I'm
married to Max. I have a home with him, he's given me
the only life I know. I owe him—

''And opera,'' Léon went on easily. ''Theater, the circus, market days, bookstores, toy shops, antique shops,
bicycle riding, hiking, good movies, good food, and good
friends. Not, of course, in that order.'' He saw Stephanie
watching him with a small frown. ''You did ask what
takes my fancy.''

''A long list for someone who was a dull boy.''

He smiled. "I picked things up along the way."

"And you didn't finish high school or go to college?"

"No, I couldn't handle it—classrooms, teachers, assignments. I'm sorry now, because there is so much about literature and history and science I'd like to know in an organized way instead of the haphazard way I teach myself, but when I was young I couldn't do it. I hated having other people organize the world for me. I knew that when I painted I created worlds and images that made sense to me and I knew, even when I was very young, that I had to believe in myself and my way of doing things or I would never be a painter. I still believe that, but I went too far, and with all the arrogance of a young person, I decided that the only worthwhile and important thing in the world was my painting. So, in school, I got myself into trouble, doing my damnedest to get expelled, and though my father tried everything he knew, even threatening the principal with the wrath of God—as if my father could direct God's wrath—and giving me regular whippings—"

"He whipped you?"

"He thought that would make me understand that life is harsh, filled with obstacles, pain and disappointment, and that the only way I could make my way in its tangles was with diligence, concentration, constant application, and automatic obedience to authority. I could handle the first three if I could apply them to art, but of course that wasn't the lesson he was trying to teach me. And then, as you may imagine, I was a total flop when it came to automatic obedience."

Stephanie laughed. "I can't imagine that you even tried."

He smiled. "I didn't. It seemed to me that obedience would require great amounts of energy and offer a meager reward. I was working and saving my money to buy paints; that was where my energy went."

"Where were you working?"

"I modeled for other artists from the time I was ten. The pay was not bad and I liked being around them. They gave me things, too—sketch pads, canvases, extra tubes of paint—and introduced me to dealers and gallery owners. After I was expelled—because of course I was—and came back from my travels, I showed the paintings I'd been making to some of the dealers I'd met and they took almost all of them. It was a very lucky time for me."

"Or the paintings were very good."

"Luck always plays a part. The fates play tricks on us, and all our talent and experience piled up together often can't deflect them. We forget that at our peril."

The sunlit river ran swiftly past their table, the restaurant emptied, the waitress served coffee with small wrapped squares of bittersweet chocolate, and Léon and Stephanie rested their arms on the table, leaned toward each other, and talked all through that long summer afternoon.

Max waited in a dim corner of a café in Carpentras, drinking marc and cursing silently as the time dragged on. Everyone who worked for him knew that he was never kept waiting, but Doerner was—he looked at his watch—four minutes late. Only four minutes, he thought; it had seemed like twenty. He told himself to relax, but he could not; he had not relaxed since the death of his secretary, and that was why he was here now, waiting for Hermann Doerner, whom he had sent to find out what the police knew about it.

He had told Sabrina he would be late, but would be home for dinner. She had gone bicycling the day before—to Fontaine-de-Vaucluse, she had told him—but today she was working on their house, and he pictured her walking through the rooms, making sketches, talking to Madame Besset, gesturing as she described to the gardener new plants she wanted along the terrace. His body strained to escape from the grimy booth, the secretive dark, and go to her. But he sat, locked in place, waiting for a fool who was late, because he had to know what had happened to his secretary before he could decide what to do next.

"*Es tut mir leid.*" Doerner slid into the opposite side of the booth. He was as tall as Max, slightly stooped and balding; he wore square glasses and his mouth was wide, with a full lower lip.

Max nodded shortly; apologies sounded the same in any language. He signaled for two drinks. "Well?"

They spoke German, falling silent when the bartender brought their beers.

"They think it was an accident. No sign of foul play."

"They *think?*"

Doerner drew an envelope from inside his jacket and held it out to Max. "They'd been to a party in Toulon. They were driving back to Marseilles, late, and they'd told their friends they'd take A-Fifty, but for some reason they took N-Eight instead. Probably not thinking; they'd had a lot to drink. It looks like they realized their mistake and tried to cut back to the highway at Le Beausset, but they never made it; just outside town they lost control of the car. It turned over a few times and they were both thrown out and killed. Instantly, the postmortem says."

"No witnesses."

"No, but someone who was on the road behind them said a car came toward him and slowed down at the place where they were thrown out and then turned and went back the way it had come. You know, as if making sure . . ."

"The police think someone followed them from the party?"

"They don't know. Everyone denies it, all the guests. They all say it had to be an accident; you know, three a.m., lots to drink, a difficult road. But the police are leaving it open."

"Were all the guests from Toulon?"

"Most. A few from Marseilles, a couple from Aix, three people from Nice. Some of them stayed the night."

"Did you talk to any of them yourself?"

"Eleven of them: the names checked on that list. I couldn't tell if anybody was lying."

Max read the list of names. None of them were known to him. "No one else was at the party?"

"That's the whole bunch."

"Are the police going to watch them?"

"They said they would. But who knows? Most of them think it was an accident."

"But they're not sure."

"They won't say they're sure."

Max tossed down the glass of marc, letting the fumes fill his head. "Is there anything else in the report?"

"Details. Nothing I haven't told you."

He drummed his fingers on the table. "Keep in touch with them; they may find something else. Meanwhile, you're interviewing secretaries?"

"I may have found one. I'll know by the time you come to Marseilles."

"Thursday. I'll see you then."

Max put money on the table for their drinks, and left. Doerner would follow later. *They won't say they're sure. I couldn't tell if anybody was lying.*

He drove through the town. None of the names had been known to him, but that meant nothing; Denton could have sent someone who'd never been in the area, someone who could follow a secretary, get friendly with her, get invited to a party . . . or not be at the party at all, but simply follow the secretary to Toulon and wait until she and her boyfriend came out to drive home.

He knew no more than he had before.

Outside Carpentras he picked up speed. He turned on the air conditioning, found some music on the radio, and settled into the seat, absently watching the needle climb to 175 kilometers an hour. Speed helped him make decisions. And he was not far beyond Carpentras when he knew that he would have to leave Provence.

He did not believe in coincidences, and so he did not

believe that his secretary's death was accidental. Somehow Denton had arranged it, probably as a warning.

But perhaps not. It had been eight months since the explosion, and not a sign of anyone interested in him. How could Denton have found him? There was no way he—

There was always a way.

But Denton was a fool and a dilettante; he'd preen himself on successfully blowing up Max and Sabrina, and wander off to another playground.

He was also stubborn and vindictive and afraid. A dangerous combination.

Max had known all this from the beginning, when he began making his plans to disappear, and so he had never expected to stay in France for more than a few months. He had started Lacoste et fils and had run it from London for a year; he had planned to leave it in the hands of Hermann Doerner and Carlos Figueros as soon as he was convinced they could run it without his close presence. Then he would move on, open another company, probably in the United States or Latin America, and settle there.

There had been no room in that plan for buying a house and living with Sabrina Longworth. But once he made that decision, he had been lulled into complacency. His business was thriving, he had a comfortable home, and he knew Sabrina would want to stay there.

But he was not in a position to be lulled into complacency. Not with Denton; not even completely with Sabrina. He had carefully rehearsed what he would tell her if her memory suddenly returned, but she would accept his story of danger only if she loved him. And he knew that, still, she did not.

He believed that the longer her amnesia lasted, the more likely it was that it would be permanent. But he could not rely on that: there was nothing scientific to support it. It seemed he could rely on less and less lately. All his life he had trusted his tough instincts; now, suddenly, instincts, toughness, even brutality, seemed feeble tools for survival.

We'll get out of here, he thought. Robert will sell the house and everything in it; we can't risk a trail of furniture. Carlos will buy a new place for us—Buenos Aires? Los Angeles? Maybe Toronto—and rent a warehouse and create a life for us to step into. We can't change our names; I couldn't explain that to Sabrina. But it doesn't matter. It's not certain that we're running away from anything. Not yet.

I won't tell her tonight, he thought as he turned into their driveway and saw the house waiting for him, the windows brilliantly lit. It can wait for a week or two, until I have a schedule, a place, a plan.

A question came to him, but he brushed it aside. Of course she would go with him. There was nothing else she could do.

She was very quiet at dinner, but it suited him not to talk. And that night he could not sleep, and so spent the hours in his study and, in the morning, had locked the door, as he always did when he was working, before she was awake. Later he caught a glimpse of her car as she drove to work, and then he left the study to greet Robert when he arrived.

"You look tired," Robert said. "Another night of insomnia?"

"It has nothing to do with insomnia; I had work to do. You can analyze and prescribe for your students and your flock, Robert, and for your revolutionaries, but not for me."

"Not revolutionaries, my friend, though the vocabulary is often similar. And so is the need for money; thank you for your last deposit; it was an extraordinarily generous one."

"We had a good quarter. And I added some of my own."

"I thought so. I didn't see how you could reap such profits from your small printing shop and your exports.

But obviously I know nothing about it. Max, as usual when I come to you, I need help."

"What do you need?"

"A passport, a visa, a driver's license, two or three letters with envelopes canceled at post offices in Haiti."

"A difficult country, Robert."

"The easy ones don't need me."

"What name for the passport and visa?"

"Wallace Lambert. Does that sound sufficiently stuffy for the son of a successful British businessman?"

"Is he?"

"Of course not. But the people in Haiti will think he is. Is the name a good choice?"

"Very good. You want the letters addressed to him, I suppose."

"Yes."

"And when do you need all these documents?"

"Is one week too soon?"

"Can the letters be waiting for your person in Haiti?"

"No, they must be here."

"Then I need two weeks. Everything else is easy, but that takes time."

"Two weeks, then. Thank you, Max. And something else. There will be someone coming out of Chile soon. I don't know if you have current business there . . ."

"I do, as it happens. We'll be shipping them two front-end loaders in a month or so, about the end of July, and bringing back one that was the wrong model. Will that fit in with your plans?"

"We'll make it fit. It's a young woman, Jana Corley. She's quite small; I think she would manage easily if the equipment is of a size that requires a large crate. And a front-end loader would, I imagine."

"A woman. I hadn't thought of women; it's always been men, until now."

"More women are coming to us lately. They're as idealistic as men, you know, probably more so, and certainly they like adventure as much as men. And they're very good: they speak softly, but they work with the local priests—"

"*Your* local priests."

"The ones in our network, yes, of course. They work with them to help the people in these countries feel they have some power."

"Starting a kindergarten," Max said, amused.

"Does that surprise you? In a village where no one provides education, a kindergarten is a victory. If they can add another grade each year—"

"A revolution would be faster."

"And bloodier, and not at all certain of victory."

"But you're moving an inch at a time. You help these peasants protest when the government stockpiles food for the wealthy; you open clinics where their kids can be vaccinated. It's window dressing; it doesn't change a damn thing."

"It changes the way they feel about themselves: they begin to think they can have some power over their lives. Until they think that, what can they do for themselves? They rely on outsiders."

"Your idealistic boys and girls."

"Young men and women. Children of God. If you could work with them you would not be so cynical. They are so beautiful, Max, and they truly become part of the poor people's lives."

"Until the governments come after them, and you have to smuggle them out."

"You and I smuggle them out. You know all this, Max; we've talked about it before. I think you like hearing me repeat it as a child likes a familiar bedtime story told over and over."

Max smiled thinly. "Perhaps."

Robert shook his head. "Max, you should not be so angry when someone understands you. There is no attempt to understand where there is no love." Max was silent. "Look, my friend, I don't pry into the dark corners of your life. Whatever you may regret or fear or try to deny is your affair, unless you ask me for guidance. I would rejoice if I could help you with any troubles you have, should you ever ask me. But I see your pleasure in helping me in my cause, however small and slow you think it, and I think that your pleasure comes from doing good, perhaps because it balances other things that you do or have done. And so you ask to hear about it now and then for comfort or for reassurance that your money and your help are still doing good."

Max said nothing. He was angry, with the visceral defensive withdrawal that came whenever anyone saw beneath his surface, but he was also impressed. And for the first time he felt a warming toward Robert far different from the casual affinity he had felt until now. *There is no attempt to understand where there is no love.* It occurred to him that Robert might—in time, and if he let him— become more than the kind of arm's-length acquaintance Max had had all his life; he might become a friend.

Except, of course, that soon Max would be half a world away.

"Well." Robert sighed. "I'll have the details about Jana in a couple of weeks; I'll tell you as soon as I have them. Last time, when it was Afghanistan, you used a cargo plane; I assume this time you'll use a freighter."

"Since it's Chile, yes."

Robert grinned. "I feel sometimes that we are like two boys smoking behind the barn. Smuggling . . . Not something one learns in the kitchen or the seminary. You handle it well, you and Carlos and Hermann. I could almost guess you had done it before, but I know nothing about these things. I should simply thank you for using what you know to help me. I seem to be thanking you all the time. What can I do for you? I'm going to Marseilles this afternoon; is there anything I can do for you there?"

"Stop by the shop and tell them exactly what you want for whomever you're sending to Haiti. I'll call to tell them you're coming. You know, a post office canceling machine isn't a bad idea. I'll look into it."

Robert laughed. "You'd need one from every dictatorship in the world."

"Not impossible."

They shook hands, smiling, more comfortable with each other than at any time in their year-long acquaintance. "By the way," Robert said. "I saw Sabrina in town this morning, on her way to work. She looks very well; beautiful, as always, and also happy."

"Hasn't she been happy in your cooking lessons?"

"It seems so, but when we're together I sometimes wonder whether she might be pretending so I won't worry about her. This morning, however, she was alone in her car and her face had a lovely brightness I haven't seen before. So things go well with the two of you?"

"Very well."

Robert searched his face. "You know, Max, I love her. She has so many needs, but she doesn't demand that we satisfy them; she doesn't cling or complain. I admire her and I want her to be content, with herself and with the world. I hope indeed that things go well with the two of you. I do know that she is happy in Cavaillon; in such a short time she has truly made it her home."

"I'll see you out," Max said abruptly, and led Robert to the door. "I have some calls to make," he said in a kind of apology. "I'll see you tomorrow, won't I? Isn't that the next cooking lesson?"

"Not this week; I'll still be in Marseilles. Next week."

They shook hands and Max watched Robert walk to his car. It was probably a good thing that he was leaving: Robert often understood too much. Max felt a sinking in his heart. It did not really matter where he was or how comfortable he might begin to feel with another person; there never would be a time when he could completely relax.

Watching the small car follow the curve in the road and disappear, he wondered for the first time if Robert might be in danger. Probably not; there was no trail leading to a small, quiet priest in Cavaillon who organized a network of activist priests all around the world and smuggled other activists, mostly students, into and out of their countries. We're two of a kind, Max thought; that's probably why we get along so well. Two smugglers in a world of police, border guards and identity papers. And if my smuggling has always been to increase my own wealth, and Robert's is to enhance the lives of the poor and the helpless, we still have our bond. And we need each other. He saw that, even if I didn't want him to.

The telephone was ringing in his study and he went to answer it.

"The contract came, from Bimerji in Iran," Carlos said. "Will you be here soon, or shall I send it up?"

"I'll be there Thursday." Iran, he thought with satisfaction. He had been talking to the Iranians for months, and now they'd taken the last steps, bringing in Bimerji to buy the construction equipment, and sending the contract to Lacoste et fils in Marseilles. He'd known they would come through; everyone knew there were factions in Iran trying to undermine the government, and what better way to start than to flood the country with counterfeit currency? But to know the contract was there . . . that was the satisfaction he had waited for.

He pictured Carlos sitting in the office that everyone, including Robert, thought was a small print shop connected to Lacoste et fils. Carlos would be at his small desk behind the counter beside steel shelves stacked with paper, envelopes, inks and rubber stamps. Through a nearby door one could glimpse the large copy camera with its anachronistic-looking bellows, two offset printers, and a small laser scanner; the closed door of the darkroom was just beyond. On the walls of the front room, with its counter for customers, hung samples of party invitations, announcements, business cards, letterhead and printed envelopes: the kind of careful work the shop did so well.

Everything was neat, orderly, modest: an unobtrusive windowless wooden building jutting from one side of his warehouse. But in a room behind the darkroom sat Andrew Frick, an American of genius—so the judge had called him when sentencing him the last time—a man who called himself a true artist. Frick was passionately absorbed in the romance of copying, engraving and printing money in dozens of currencies. He had invented an ink mixed with magnetic metal powder that duplicated the inks used throughout the world, and he had found a way to use nonfluorescent pigments to simulate the whiteness of cotton fiber instead of using the bleach that less artistic counterfeiters used, which fluoresced beneath ultraviolet light, showing them instantly to be counterfeit.

Andrew Frick's counterfeit money was so fine it had been compared by experts to the delicate purity of a Botticelli. And Andrew Frick had never been as happy in his life as he was in Max Lacoste's back room, where he could make his own hours and have the most modern equipment to do what he loved best, and receive in return generous pay, an apartment near the harbor and a charge account, billed to Max, at Fauchon and Galeries Lafayette.

Frick had burned all his bridges in America, moved everything he owned to France, and thrown in his lot for all time with Max Lacoste. He never wanted to be anywhere else.

Seeing all of it in his mind as he stood at his desk in Cavaillon, Max thought ahead to Thursday. "How much do they want in Iran?" he asked Carlos.

"One hundred fifty million rials."

"When?"

"A month. I suggested a shipment of three backhoes about the end of July. If they find they don't need one of them after all, the contract specifies that they can send it back."

A hundred fifty million rials would take no more than two or three cubic feet of space, Max calculated. The Iranians would convert thirty-seven and a half million rials—his fee—to francs and ship them to him in the backhoe that they would find they did not, after all, need.

"You're satisfied?" he asked Carlos.

"I think everything is there. I want you to go over it."

"Good. I'll be there early on Thursday, eight or eight-thirty. By the way, Father Chalon will be there tomorrow. He needs identity papers; he'll tell you about them. I'd like them rushed through."

"They always are, for him. Anything else?"

"No, I'll see you Thursday."

He stood beside his desk after he hung up. Of course Robert is in danger, just as I am. There is always the chance that someone will talk, someone will recognize a face, someone will follow a trail that seems so faint as to be invisible but that, to just one person, is as clear and straight as an arrow.

Which is why I have to move.

And which is why a priest in Cavaillon, who believes prayer is good but prayer with action is better, might also have to move one day.

Maybe three of us will go, Max thought. Or Robert will join us later. That would make leaving Cavaillon easier for Sabrina to accept. I'll mention that to her as a possibility. He locked his door and went back to his desk, to return to work.

"I thought perhaps a hike and picnic," Léon said on the telephone. "It's been five days since Fontaine-de-Vaucluse and I am badly in need of exercise."

"No five a.m. bicycle rides?" Stephanie asked. She was in the back room of Jacqueline en Provence an hour before the shop would open. She had begun coming in early every morning, to work alone and to feel, for that brief, wonderful time, that it was her shop, her own place, to mold any way she wished. It was like a secret she carried with her. And now Léon was another secret. It was the first time he had called since their afternoon at Fontaine-de-Vaucluse.

"I haven't even thought about bicycling; I've been working on a new series of paintings, very different and exciting. Perhaps you'll come to the studio to see them.''

"I'd like that."

"After our picnic, then. Are you free this afternoon?"

"No. I'm sorry. But on Thursday . . ."

"Three more days."

Stephanie was silent.

"Well, then, Thursday. You choose the place; I'll bring the food. I'll call you the day before, about this time, if that's all right. I've missed you, Sabrina; I've replayed last Tuesday in my head a dozen times. It was a very special day."

"Yes. For me, too." Stephanie's hand shook as she hung up. Max was going to Marseilles on Thursday. She had made a date with Léon for a day when Max would be away.

"You're very quiet," Jacqueline said later that morning as they unpacked and arranged a display of china. "Is something troubling you?"

Stephanie nodded. "But it's something I have to work out; it's complicated."

"Then it involves love. And it is probably less complicated than you think. Love always seems to create so many tangles, but in fact there is usually a single thread that can be pulled to make everything clear. Though I admit that finding the thread is sometimes difficult and painful."

"And have you found it, with your friend?"

"Certainly, but he and I have no tangle. The thread is friendship. Are you worried about finding it with Max?"

"I don't know what it would be. I couldn't give it a name."

Jacqueline looked at her thoughtfully. "Perhaps because you don't know what you have: marriage, friendship, companionship, a living arrangement, a business relationship—"

"Business!"

"Well, because he offers you his home and his name and his protection and you offer him eight months of mem-

274

ory, and affection but not love. I don't know how many men would consider that satisfactory for a marriage, though for a business transaction it would do.''

"I think he likes it that I have no memory.''

"Indeed? Why?''

"I don't know. But he doesn't urge me to make connections, to try to reach back, the way Robert does.''

"And you do not . . . when you are making love, at that time when we are most open and most receptive to stimuli, you do not recall anything?''

Stephanie concentrated on aligning pearl-handled knives and forks with the china. "I'm . . . not open then.''

"Ah. And what keeps you guarded?''

"What I told you before. I can't believe what he says. I can't trust him.''

"Yes, but just for the pleasure of it . . . Well I see that that is not enough for you. You need more. I hope you find it with someone, my dear. Or . . . perhaps you have found it and that is the tangle that bothers you now?'' She waited, but Stephanie did not answer. "You know you can always talk to me, Sabrina.''

"I know. I love talking to you. And I will, but I have too much to sort out.''

The doorbell rang as a customer came into the shop, and Stephanie went to greet her with relief. She did not know why she was uncomfortable; she could always talk to Jacqueline. But today the words stayed inside her.

"And what have you planned while I'm gone?'' Max asked that night at dinner.

"To work on this room,'' Stephanie said. "If you don't mind, I want to get rid of most of the furniture; it's too heavy for a dining room, especially this one. We've got a table in the shop that I'd like to try, and Jacqueline told me about some places that may have chairs and a sideboard.''

He did not want to hear about her plans for the house. "And what else?''

"A chandelier—''

"No, I mean what else will you be doing?''

"Max, we go through this every time you leave. I haven't planned every minute of every day, and even if I had, I don't see why I'd give you an itinerary. You don't give me one for your time in Marseilles."

"More bicycling?"

"I may ride to Roussillon with Robert."

"And what else?"

"And I'm going to hike. I haven't done that yet."

"Where?"

"I don't know."

"If madame will forgive me for intruding," Madame Besset said, bringing the cheese tray, "there is an excellent hike above Saint-Saturnin. That is the town, if you remember, we will move to after we sell the farm to our son. I know it well. If you park in the square and walk behind the church, you will find a stairway of Roman steps. I think you will be very pleased with what is at the top."

"What is at the top?" Max asked.

"A medieval town now in ruins. Collapsed castles, homes, an old roadway."

"It sounds wonderful," Stephanie said. "That's where I'll go."

"Take a camera," Max said. "I'd like to see pictures."

"Yes."

I am deceiving Max. I'm doing it very easily. I wonder if I ever deceived anyone before.

She began to tremble and could not stop. *Something is wrong; what is wrong with me?*

"Sabrina, what is it?"

"Madame!"

Max helped her to her feet, waving Madame Besset away. "We'll be in the library; you can bring our coffee there."

He led Stephanie to a couch and held her so she would not collapse while she sat down. "Can you tell me what it is?"

"No." She was breathless, as if she had been running.

He sat beside her. "Close your eyes. Lie back. Shall I call the doctor?"

"No."

"Do you feel ill?"

"No. I don't know how I feel." She lay against him, her eyes closed. Gradually her trembling eased. She opened her eyes. *Alice in Wonderland* lay open on the table in front of her.

"I could tell you my adventures—beginning from this morning," said Alice . . . "but it's no use going back to yesterday, because I was a different person then."

That has something to do with the way I feel. But I don't know what.

I was a different person then.

Yes, of course. I knew who I was; I had a name, memories, a past, a future.

But is that really what it means?

I don't know. I have to think, I have to try to understand—

"Feeling better?" Max asked.

"Yes. Thank you." She sat up. *Later. When I'm alone.* Madame Besset brought in a tray with coffee and slices of tarte tatin. "Tell me what you'll be doing in Marseilles."

She poured coffee, they talked quietly in the library, and it became an evening like any other. And then it faded from her mind, more quickly than she would have thought possible. She was busy with Jacqueline; she and Max drove to Saint-Rémy where she shopped for clothes; she drew plans for the redesign of the dining room. And she thought about Thursday. And then Max was gone. And Thursday had come.

"Your Madame Besset is wonderful," Léon said. "I've never been here."

They were walking on a wide, rocky path, the remains of a Roman road far above the town of Saint-Saturnin. On either side was a tumbled stone wall, here and there intact: black stones carefully set atop each other almost a thousand years earlier to mark the main road of the fortified town. The road began at a ruined castle overlooking the fertile valley far below, and stretched for more than two miles, past dozens of *bories* where families had lived, now little more than heaps of mute black stones.

"I wish I could bring the people back," Stephanie said, "and watch them farm and go shopping and play and . . . Where did they get water?"

"There may have been a river down there." They peered over the cliff into the valley below. "Dried up now, but we know that without water there could have been no town."

"So many people, so many stories." They walked slowly, beneath the blazing sun. They wore shorts, lightweight T-shirts and billed caps, and small backpacks. Léon had a sketch pad in his pocket and Stephanie's camera was hooked to her belt. "Did anyone write their stories? Is there a history of Saint-Saturnin?"

"I don't know of one. But I have histories of Provence in my library; I'll see what I can find."

"All gone," Stephanie murmured. "We should write everything down, everything, every day. We don't think about it, but otherwise it can vanish so completely . . ."

"Nothing vanishes." Léon's voice was casual, but he was being careful, searching for the words that would allow her to talk about herself. "Everything is here surrounding us, wherever we are. It's what I try to show in my paintings: the other lives and memories that are part of us even though they're voiceless and invisible. They haven't vanished; it's just that we haven't figured out how to find the key that will open all those locked doors."

They were alone in the ruined village. Bushes and flowers grew out of walls, clinging to bits of earth between the stones, lizards whipped across the road and into the shade of shrubs, birds flew protectively about their nests in the crevices of shattered homes, and the *genêt* bushes were in bloom, perfuming the air.

"My life has vanished," Stephanie said. She did not look at Léon. "You're right, of course, it's somewhere, in letters I wrote or work I accomplished or in people's memories. But not in mine. Not in my memory. I have none."

Thank you, Léon breathed silently, and knew then how desperately he had wanted her to be open to him, and knew, too, in that moment that he loved her. But, my God, he thought, my God, to live without memory: such terrible loneliness . . . "And Max?" he asked.

"He says he can't help me."

"Tell me all of it—can you?—from the beginning."

"The beginning," Stephanie said wryly. "A very recent one. Eight months ago. October."

They walked a little apart from each other, drinking from their water bottles as the sun moved higher, and she told him everything, even her faintness of three nights earlier, and the passage from *Alice in Wonderland*. By the time she finished, they had left the ruined village behind and were in open fields of tall wild grass, hot and dry, dotted with low scrub bushes. A small farm was in a hollow on their right, with a donkey in a small fenced enclosure and a child throwing a ball against white sheets swaying on a clothesline. Ahead was the edge of a forest.

Léon took Stephanie's hand. "We'll find a place to sit and have our picnic."

Stephanie felt his firm clasp and the rhythm of their matched steps. She was relaxed now, and happy, and there was a singing inside her. She had told him more than she had told Robert; more than she had told Jacqueline. She had talked to him as if she had been talking to herself.

The path led into the forest and they gave a small gasp at the sudden coolness. In a few minutes Léon stopped. "Grass, leaves, a small room. A place for lunch." He ducked into a grove of trees near the path and when Stephanie followed, she found herself in a small green space with walls of leafy branches and a ceiling of cloudless sky. Pale forest grasses covered the ground, drooping over the fallen leaves of many seasons, black and weathered to pliant softness.

Léon took from his backpack cheeses, saucisson, a container of wrinkled black olives in herbs, and a round loaf of roughly shaped bread. "Wine," he murmured, finding a flat place for the bottle, "glasses, knives, napkins. And grapes. Whenever we're ready. Now?"

"Not yet. It's so cool and quiet; I'd just like to sit for a while."

"Well, then." He pulled from his pocket his sketch pad and a crayon and with swift, easy strokes began drawing her. She sat a few feet away, her back against a tree, her legs stretched out, her head turned to watch him.

"As you will see when you visit my studio," he said, his eyes on his paper, "I have painted little else but you since our bicycle trip. If that displeases you, you must tell me."

"It pleases me."

He looked up quickly. "Why?"

"Because people in paintings have a life of their own. I know they're frozen in time, but they reflect what they were and hint at what they will be. If you paint me, I think it will be me and . . . not me. It might be the person I was. I'd like to see what she looks like."

He nodded, as if to himself. "An interesting idea. But is that the only reason you are pleased?"

"No. I like knowing that you think about me."

He laughed. "Most of the time, it seems. And do you think of me?"

"Yes. I shouldn't. I have a husband, a home . . . I shouldn't be . . . I have responsibilities and obligations—"

"But you see I have not asked you about them—nothing about your marriage or your home—nor have I told you about my own involvements. And you have not asked me. None of that has any place here."

"Why not?"

"Because there is too much we don't know yet."

"You mean I'm hurrying things along."

"I mean you are not joining me in holding them back. Come," he said, seeing the confusion on her face, "we'll have our lunch. And I want to talk to you about memory."

"What about it?"

He filled their wineglasses, then broke off a piece of bread and spread it with cheese and handed it to her. "Often, when I'm in the middle of a painting, I stand back from the canvas and look at what I've done and see something very good—an arrangement of shapes or colors, an altered landscape, a portrait—and I have no idea where that good thing came from. I didn't think about it before I painted it; I hadn't done it before. It just appeared."

Stephanie nodded. "From all your experiences for— how many years? How old are you?"

"Thirty-six."

"All your experiences for thirty-six years, stored in your memory, waiting for you. Because you remember everything, back to the time you were four years old."

"I don't remember everything; no one does. You're right that the experiences are waiting for me, but that's what I'm saying: they're waiting for all of us. Yours are waiting for you. And you'll find them. They'll come unbidden, as mine do when I paint, or you'll make connections with things you see and hear and read. In fact, some already have come to you, when you called the little girl Penny and mentioned Mrs. Thirkell. And you said you told Max that you'd moved around a lot, and you told me my painting reminded you of van Gogh. It's all there, Sabrina, everything you've ever done, your thoughts, your loves, your hates and fears and the wonders of your—how many years? How old are you?"

"I don't know."

"Ah. Of course. Well, we will declare your age. What do you think? I think thirty-one, perhaps thirty-two. Would one of those suit you?"

She was smiling. "And when is my birthday?"

"Oh, today. Why not? What better way to celebrate than this? Today, June thirtieth, you are thirty-one years old and this is a celebration." He refilled their wine-glasses. "So you have thirty-one years of loves and hates and fears and wonders and maybe a few things you'd like to forget permanently, all inside you, waiting for you, like an attic in an old house, dusty and whispering of secrets. Everything from the past is piled up, stacked away, pushed back to make room for more. But a wind comes, a hurricane, an earthquake, and things in the attic shift: some reach the top and come to us with no rhyme or reason, or we reach in and pluck something out—"

"*I can't do that!* Don't you understand? I can't reach in—"

"I know that. I'm sorry; I do understand that. But I believe that you will."

"Why?"

"Because you are young and strong. Because you try very hard and don't accept what has happened with tears or resignation. Because you have already remembered some things."

"And because you believe in gnomes and elves."

"And magic."

They shared a smile. The grove where they sat was hushed and still. The leaves drooped; the birds slept in the afternoon heat. No voice, no sounds from farm or city broke the silence. Stephanie bit into the earthy crust of the bread; the cool, smooth cheese melted on her tongue; the cold Chablis flowed to the back of her throat, and it all had the slow grace of a dream. She watched Léon begin drawing again, his crayon making a faint swish on the heavy paper. She liked the way he looked: his short blond hair almost white against his deep tan; his lean, muscular body a little tensed as he drew, as if every nerve was concentrating, as if all his energy nourished the fingers that moved so swiftly and surely over the paper. His blue shirt was streaked with perspiration, his mouth was faintly smiling, his green eyes were looking down—

He looked up and met her gaze and their eyes held. And that was like a dream, too, Stephanie thought, because it did not need logic to be natural and right that he was all she saw, or wanted to see.

He did not move, but it was as if he reached out to her. "I would like to help you find your past if you will let me."

"Yes." She stretched out her hand, and he took it. *This is where I belong; here and nowhere else.*

They sat that way for a long time, their hands clasped. Léon's sketchbook lay at his side. The hot, still air held them suspended, the grass and leaves felt moist beneath Stephanie's bare legs, a trickle of perspiration ran down the side of her face. Within her, the turmoil of the past months stilled. Her thoughts drifted, her breathing was light, a small pulse beat in her palm where Léon held it clasped to his.

After a time he stirred. "I was wrong. I do need to know about your marriage."

Stephanie's heart took a small lurch, as if she had been walking on level ground but had fallen suddenly down a step she had not seen. *My life is full of beginnings, and this is one of them.*

But she did not know how to begin, and the silence stretched out.

"You don't remember anything about marrying him," Léon said finally. "Or talking about a future with him. Or being in a motorboat after the explosion. But you do remember some of the things the doctors told you in the hospital. Did you talk to them about Max? Or your marriage?"

"I don't remember. Max bought all my clothes, I remember that; and they were always perfect, the right colors, the right size. And he stayed with me until he knew I would recover; then he went back to his company, and came and went. Then Robert found the house in Cavaillon and Max furnished it with pieces he'd had in storage somewhere, and his art collection. He'd owned your painting of the Alpilles for ten years, he said; he'd bought it at Galeries de Rohan in Paris.''

"That was when I painted it. It was in my first show at the gallery. I've shown there ever since."

"In Paris? But we have your paintings at Jacqueline en Provence."

"I do that for Jacqueline. A few only. Most go to Rohan. But you are only giving me information that anyone can see. I want to know about what is unseen."

"I know." And then it came, more easily than she would have thought. "I don't love him. I've tried, but there is such a gulf between us of *not knowing* . . . I mean, I think he knows more about my past than he tells me, but I have no way of proving that, or even testing him. It's a feeling, no more, but so strong that I can't trust him. I believe him when he says he loves me and he's very good to me: he's let me do things he'd rather I didn't do, like work in the shop with Jacqueline and cook with Robert—''

"Why should you not do those things?"

"I don't know. He certainly doesn't want a helpless woman who lolls on a chaise all day eating bonbons and humming French love songs—''

Léon was laughing. "A charming picture. Did he tell you that was what he didn't want?"

"No, I asked him one day if that was what he was waiting for. He found it amusing, too, but he didn't tell me what was wrong with working with Jacqueline and cooking with Robert. He does like it, though, that I'm redecorating the house and adding on a studio for myself."

"Because you are at home when you do it."

"Yes. And because . . . it fixes me more permanently there."

"Have you given him reason to doubt your permanence?"

"I haven't given him any reasons to be sure of me."

Léon's hand tightened on hers, and she shook her head.

"I'm not proud of that. I owe him everything: my life, a home, a chance to make a real person of myself, Robert's friendship . . . I'd have nothing if it weren't for Max."

"But you think he is lying to you."

"Oh . . . such a harsh word. I don't know. I just can't be sure of anything with Max. I like him, you know; he's a good companion and he's a bulwark when I'm frightened or feeling lost, but there's something about him that makes me think of danger, or of dangerous people . . . maybe both. I know that sounds foolish; I know he'd be astonished if I told him that, but I feel it and it won't go away, even when I'm relying on him the most."

She paused. "I can't imagine myself changing the way I feel about him. Ever."

Léon's breath came out in a long sigh. "And what will you do?"

"I don't know. I've thought of leaving him, but there are so many reasons not to . . . I don't want to hurt him; he's done nothing to deserve that. And I'm afraid. I know so little about anything, I don't know where I'd even begin if I were on my own. Now that I have a job, soon perhaps I can think more seriously about leaving. But not yet. And there is one more thing . . ."

She looked at their clasped hands. Her voice was very low. "I will not move from being dependent on Max to being dependent on someone else. I will not exchange one protector for another."

"No, that would not be good. And there is no reason for you to do it. But what of us?"

She looked up at him and gave a slow, impish smile. "You're not offering to be my protector?"

"No. Though I would protect you if the need arose."

Oh, I like that, Stephanie thought. That he knows there is a difference. And then she took a long breath and plunged into the future. "I want to be with you."

"Then we'll be together. We'll discover all that we do not know and create our own memories." It was as solemn as a ceremony, Stephanie thought, with their clasped hands to mark it.

After a moment Léon said, "I've been with someone for a few months. I'll end it as soon as I can."

"I'm not asking you to do that. And I'm not—"

"You're not leaving Max. But it would not be fair to my friend to continue; we don't love each other, but we're good friends and I've always been honest with her."

"Jacqueline said the same thing about the man she sees. It sounds so simple."

He looked at her curiously. "Did she tell you the name of the man?"

"No, just that they have a good—" Stephanie stared at him and caught her breath. "No. It can't be. Léon, it can't be!"

"Why not?" His voice was gentle. "I told you my paintings were at her shop because of her; we've helped each other for a long time. And about a year ago we were both at a place in our lives when we needed companionship. We didn't want love; we wanted warmth and solace, and that was what we gave each other. She's a remarkable woman, you know; a very dear friend."

"She's been a friend to *me*. She gave me a job, she teaches me every day, we talk . . . about everything. I can't hurt her; I can't do anything that might hurt her."

"Sabrina, this is not between you and Jacqueline; it is between Jacqueline and me."

"No, no, don't you understand? I talk to her about Max and she told me about you; we were two women, talking, trusting each other. She's the only woman friend I have— well, there's Madame Besset, but that isn't at all the same—and I won't take and take from her and then steal someone away, someone she cares about . . ."

"You cannot steal me; what are you thinking? That I am like one of those silver spoons in your shop that you can tuck inside your coat and carry away on tiptoe?"

A small laugh broke from Stephanie. "I'm sorry; that wasn't a good word, but—"

"And as for Jacqueline caring about me, she does so as a friend, not as a serious lover. I told you that. Evidently, so did she."

"She told me you need each other."

His eyebrows rose. "She said that?"

"Yes."

"Just like that?"

"She said that you have a good time and need each other and if you parted tomorrow she would miss you very much."

Léon contemplated her. "Sabrina, I know Jacqueline well. I do not believe that was all she said."

Stephanie looked away from him. What did she owe Jacqueline? Loyalty, gratitude, love . . . but not a lie. "She said she would miss you very much for a while, but she would wish you well for the pleasure you had together. And you would do the same for her."

"She was right. Now please listen to me. Jacqueline and I have not looked for love from each other, and so we have not expected permanence. Each of us knew that what we had could change at any time, and then we would be friends of a different kind. That's what she told you: we would wish each other well. How many people are lucky enough to find that when they need it? A loving friend who brightens a dark corner of our life, who chases shadows away, who strives to make us feel better about who we are and what we are doing. Jacqueline and I did that for each other. But we never touched the mystery in each other, or even tried—" He saw Stephanie's eyes widen. "So she told you that, too. It seems she told you everything that was important about us. Now I will tell you what is important about you and me."

He turned Stephanie's hand within his and kissed the palm. It sent a shock through her and she gasped, and he kissed the same spot again, feeling her tremble. "I love you, Sabrina. I want to be with you and help you rediscover the world and yourself, and you will help me discover the world from this day on. We will be together as little or as much as you want, I'll do whatever you want, and someday . . . Well, that's enough. Predictions are folly; we have enough to learn about each other to fill the present. We'll build the future as we go.''

A powerful joy flared within Stephanie. She had no past, and no real belief that she ever would find it, but now she saw the outlines of a future, a place to belong, where she would not be lost again. She felt a delight in herself that she had not felt before: delight in her youth and strength, in her mind that could learn and remember what it learned, in her work, in the affection of friends, and in this man's love. Exhilaration buoyed her up: she was part of the earth and the sky, in this place, at this time. She was whole, and she was happy.

Almost without moving, they were in each other's arms. Stephanie put back her head. ''I love you,'' she said, and the words were a song that had been locked within her, waiting for a chance to soar. When they kissed, her mouth opened to Léon's and her arms drew him down to lie on her. She desired and she loved, and for Sabrina Lacoste, whose memory was eight months old, it was the first time.

CHAPTER 13

"*M*orning, Mrs. Andersen," the garage attendant said. "How long for you today?"

"About three hours, Juan." Sabrina slipped the ticket he gave her into her purse and took her briefcase and small suitcase of samples from the back seat. "How was your friend's wedding?"

"Oh, that was one great party. They better stay married after that send-off. Nice of you to remember. You want your car washed today? I've got time."

She started to say no, because that was Cliff's job, but Cliff was at soccer camp every day, coming home exhausted from some fierce determination that drove him from morning to night, and why not have someone else do it? "Yes, please. And would you try to get the stain off the back seat? I think it's ice cream, or maybe pizza."

He grinned. "Yes, ma'am. Kids, they are a trial. And put it on your bill?"

"Yes."

She walked from the cool garage to the heat of Dearborn Street, humid air heavy with fumes from cars and trucks, the smell of chickens turning on spits in a nearby restaurant, the faint spicy scent of carnations at the florist next door. The end of July, she thought. This has to be as hot as it gets. But then, why did Madeline say August is usually worse?

At the Koner Building the door swung open as she tried it. Vern was there, she thought, surprised; usually he sauntered in after she and Koner had been waiting for fifteen minutes.

Her footsteps echoed as she climbed the stairs to the room they had cleaned out to use as an office. "Good morning," Vernon Stern said. "Have I impressed you?"

"You have." She smiled at his grin, self-deprecating but eager, like that of a small boy who had lain in wait to spring a surprise. He was extraordinarily handsome, she thought as she did each time she saw him: his blond hair curlier than usual in the humidity, but still looking perfectly groomed. He was carefully craggy but polished, wearing jeans and cowboy boots and a blue silk shirt open at the neck.

"That's the goal: to impress." He took her suitcase and laid it on the folding steel table in the center of the room beside his rolls of drawings and the morning newspaper. "What is this? It feels like you packed rocks."

"A few wood samples and paint chips; mostly tiles and quartzite. So, yes, basically I packed rocks."

They laughed together as Sabrina opened her briefcase and took out three thick loose-leaf binders. "These are the specs; I finished them late last night, so I haven't gone over them. I'd appreciate it if you'd let me have your comments within a week."

He was scanning one of them. "Very good. Looks very complete. Quartzite in the foyers of the double apartments. I like that. And in the foyers of the smaller ones?" He leafed back. "Slate. Verde. Good choice. And six-inch floor moldings; wonderful. I hope Billy goes for the expense; they're the only ones that look right in a vintage building. You have a good sense of tradition—the best of it, anyway. I haven't met many designers who do; it's more European than American." He looked up at her. "You've had fun doing this."

"The best designs come when it's fun."

"I agree. I wasn't criticizing. My dullest buildings are the ones designed to clients' idiosyncrasies; no fun at all. In fact, I detest them."

"Why do you do them?"

"Because when you're on your own and dependent on the whims and whispers of the public, you keep your eye on what's truly important, which is keeping your name visible and memorable while doing your best to create excellence. Success and fame are wondrous things, though; they do make it possible to say no. And I think I'll be there in a few years."

"I hope you will. It gives you such a feeling of strength, of being in control of who you are through what you're doing."

He looked at her curiously. "Now, how would you know what it is to depend for survival on the vagaries of fickle, wealthy, slightly bored socialites and know-it-all corporate types?"

"I've read about it."

"Which means you don't want to tell me. Hints of a colorful past. I'd like to hear about it." Sabrina was silent. "I'm serious; I really would. You're a fascinating woman, Stephanie; I can't find a category for you. Suburban housewife, antique dealer, terrific interior designer . . . but more than that, much more, and I'm damned if I can put my finger on it."

"Why should you?" she asked coolly.

"Because I don't like mysteries. I'm a very literal guy: I design buildings, I don't write poetry. You told me you'd grown up in Europe, so that explains your accent, and I suppose your feel for tradition, but there's something else, sort of a second person somewhere; you're so guarded, almost secretive. It's a challenge, getting close to you." He waited, but Sabrina met his eyes and said nothing.

"You know, that's hard to do: to say nothing. Most people try to fill a silence. You're not a babbler; I find that fascinating, too." He paused again. "Well, someday, perhaps; I don't give up easily, you know." He looked again at the notebook and skimmed more pages. "Double doors into the master bedroom suite?"

"I know you drew a single door, but it's at the end of the gallery, with a vestibule behind it, and I thought if we could find old stained glass it would be more dramatic from both sides."

"It would. Nice idea. Have you some ideas for locating the glass?"

"I'd try Salvage One first. And I have a list of other possibilities."

"So you know Salvage One. A designer's dream."

"Yes, but a nightmare, too, don't you think? All those bits and pieces of buildings that have been torn down—doors, windows, fireplace surrounds, sinks, grates, wall sconces—fragments of people's hopes and dreams and tragedies. I always feel as if a whisper follows me through all the floors, saying that everything is fragile, everything dies, and we should write down everything we do and think; otherwise it will vanish so completely . . ."

"Yes, I've felt that. But more than that: that we shouldn't believe in anything too devoutly, because it will soon be gone."

"Oh, no. It has nothing to do with trust and belief and love; just because something is fragile is no reason not to believe in it. Maybe it's a reason to believe in it even more; then we'll try to protect it."

"You have faith. I admire that."

Their eyes met and they smiled. Sabrina thought how much she liked him, and liked working with him. "Is there anything else in the specs you want to talk about now?"

"Well, let's see." He turned more pages. "What are the question marks? Decisions you haven't made?"

"Items where you and Billy and I disagree. He thinks

the quartzite is too expensive, for example. I hope we can settle most of them today.''

"I'm sure we can." Stern closed the book and laid it down. He sat on the edge of the table, lightly swinging one foot. "Where do you do your work? Do you have an office?"

"I'm using our attic until we figure something out. Why?"

"Our firm has an extra room; it's yours if you want it."

Her eyebrows rose. "That's very generous."

"No, it's quite selfish. I want to see more of you." His eyes, improbably blue, gazed at her, and Sabrina was conscious of her Indian gauze skirt over bare legs, and her sheer cotton blouse with a deep V neck. He took her hand. "I enjoy talking to you, Stephanie, and working with you. I think about you when we're not together; you sneak up on me while I'm doing other things and then you stay there and I like it, I like the idea of your being with me. I like your quietness and your mysteries, I like the way you think, and you are wonderfully beautiful. Every time we finish up here I feel cheated because I want more of you, and it's seemed to me that you feel the same, that you wished you could stay." He paused briefly, as if waiting for her to agree. When she did not, he added, "And we make a good team; I can see us working on a lot of jobs together, even bigger than this one."

Sabrina nodded thoughtfully. "We do work well together.'" She was thinking how astonishing it was that a man so smoothly put together could be so crude. That shows how far I've come from London: it wouldn't have surprised me at all in those days to find a perfectly groomed member of a perfectly groomed society making a proposition and dangling at the end of it the temptation of more and bigger jobs through his influence.

She thought of Garth and smiled to herself. The idea of any other man in her life was incomprehensible. Once she had been able to visualize herself at dinner or the theater or in bed with a man she met; now she could not even imagine it. No one, ever, but Garth, she thought; how ridiculous for Vernon Stern to fantasize that I long to stay with him when it's time to go home.

I liked him, she thought; and now I don't. Now I just admire his work.

"Good," he said and smiled his boyish smile once again. "You can move into that room whenever you want; just let me know so I can tell the secretary you're coming."

"Oh, I won't be using it." She slipped her hand from his and moved away. "I do thank you, Vern, but I'm quite happy where I am."

She thought of stopping there, since that said everything about her life, but she went on, her voice friendly but a little distant, as if she were thinking aloud about an abstract problem that had nothing to do with him; as if, in fact, she had already forgotten what he had said. It gave them a chance, she thought, to continue to work together comfortably, on this job or any other.

"I do believe in things; I do have faith in what I can do. But I have faith in luck, too, and in magic. Because it seems to me that the world is so complicated, with twists and turns that can transform whole lives in an instant, if we find love and work and a family and a home, and if we can hold them together, a lot of it is because of luck and magic. And that's too special and rare to toss away for an adventure. It would be like daring the gods to repeat a miracle, and I'm not brave enough to do that."

There was a silence. Stern turned to the table and slowly unrolled his plans, as if taking comfort from the reality of them. He anchored the corners with a large stapler and a tape dispenser, and in another minute turned back to Sabrina.

"Lucky lady," he said lightly. "It seems those gods used my allotment of luck and magic to make me an architect. A good one, a great one, some people say, but when it comes to all those other good things—love and family and home—I haven't done so— Stephanie? What is it?"

She was looking past him, at the table. He had pushed the copy of the *Chicago Tribune* to one side when he unrolled his plans, and Sabrina was reading the headline of the article in the center of the front page, over a picture of the Administration Building of Midwestern University: "House Committee to Investigate University Use of Government Funds."

"Excuse me," she said, and picked up the paper.

Congressman Oliver Leglind, chairman of the House Committee on Science, Space and Technology, announced today that he is launching an investigation into college and university use of government grants in response to complaints that the system is rife with irregularities, waste and fraud.

One of the universities under investigation is Midwestern University in Evanston.

Roy Stroud, chief counsel to the committee, listed MU's Professor Garth Andersen as one of those who will be asked to testify. "Professor Andersen has admitted that some universities are guilty of excesses," Mr. Stroud said today, "but he also accused the committee—before a single witness has been heard—of 'fabricating plots to whip up the anger of voters with a slash-and-burn rampage across the campuses.' "

Other professors who will be asked to testify, according to Mr. Stroud, are . . .

"Excuse me," Sabrina said again and rushed into the corridor where they had hooked up a portable telephone. Billy Koner was walking up the stairs. "Vern's in the office," she said, and dialed Garth's number at the university.

"He's here? He's turned over a new leaf?"

"I doubt it." The ringing went on; she pictured Garth's

office, empty. "Billy, I won't be able to stay this morning. The specs are in the office. You and Vern can go over them and call me."

"No, no, that won't—" He stopped as she bent her head to talk privately on the telephone. "I'll wait for you in the office," he muttered and left her alone.

"He's in the lab, Mrs. Andersen," the secretary said. "Professor Collins had to go out of town and asked Professor Andersen to take his lab class and it's an especially long one; it's the last of the summer session. Is something happening? Three reporters have called this morning."

"Can you get a message to him in the lab?"

"I can go over there. Is that what you want me to do?"

"Yes. Please. Tell him to call me . . . no, I'll be on my way home." *I wanted a phone in the car, but Garth said it was an extravagance. I thought, after Mrs. Thirkell, a car phone would look like nothing, but I thought wrong.* "Tell him I'll call him in his office in fifteen minutes. And, Dalia, keep the reporters away. Can you do that?"

"Why don't I suggest he use Professor Collins's office? No one will find him there."

"Oh, very good." *Wonderful, unquestioning Dalia; she should get a raise,* Sabrina thought. "Do you have that phone number?"

She wrote it down, then, starting back to the office, had another idea and dialed her home number. "Mrs. Thirkell, have any reporters called this morning?"

"Three or four, my lady. All wanting Professor Andersen. I told them I had no idea when he would be home."

"Thank you." *We are blessed with discreet women,* she thought. "You can continue to say that all day. And if I'm not back when Penny and Cliff get home from camp, please tell them to stay home and wait for me."

Billy Koner and Stern were waiting for her, the *Tribune* spread out before them.

"This is your husband?"

"Yes. I'm sorry, Billy, but I have to leave."

"Because of this? What's the problem? He goes to D.C., tells them he spent the money on research or whatever, and he comes home. 'Course he shouldn't have said that about fabricating plots, that wasn't smart, if you'll forgive my saying so, but they don't hang people for that. So how come you have to hold his hand?"

"I want to be with him. When Roy Stroud was here he made it clear that he and Leglind are looking for a very big story with heroes and villains. Leglind is the hero; who do you think will be the villains?"

"Your husband? He's just a professor. These guys like bigger fish: CEOs, bank presidents, stockbrokers . . . they make good stories because the dollars are bigger and nobody loves them except maybe their dogs. You're too uptight, Stephanie; it comes from being connected to a university. You people lose touch with reality."

Impatiently she shook her head. "Leglind wants a ladder to climb on and he thinks he's going to get it from universities. He doesn't like professors and they're an easy target because they're so insulated they don't see what's coming until they've been run over by it."

"He doesn't need a ladder; he's head of one of the most powerful committees . . . Listen. I know Oliver Leglind; we grew up together. I put more money into his campaigns than people in his own state, than anybody, probably. He isn't going to run over anybody, and whatever you mean by a ladder, he isn't looking for it."

"I didn't realize you knew him. Then you'd know better than most people what he's thinking. He is a powerful man, but maybe the House isn't enough for him. Does he want to be in the Senate? Has he ever talked about the White House?"

Koner's face changed. After a minute he said, "They all talk about the White House."

"Really? All of them? Well, that may be, but right now I'm only interested in what Oliver Leglind talks about. He's built a reputation for being hard-nosed about the budget, except for projects in his own state, and now it looks as if he's going to get hard-nosed about professors with government grants. And they're sitting ducks because they can't show that every dollar they get leads to a product that you can buy at Wal-Mart. And if I can be of any help to my husband when Leglind goes after him, that's where I'll be, for as long as it takes.''

There was a pause. Koner picked up the newspaper. ''It says here, 'Professor Andersen has admitted that some universities are guilty of excesses.' ''

''That was Roy Stroud supposedly quoting Garth; I wouldn't take it on faith. But suppose he did say it. There are excesses everywhere. One definition of government is excess.''

Koner laughed. ''Right. They do know a lot about excess in Washington. So. Your husband isn't going to whip up some genes that I can buy at Wal-Mart?''

Sabrina smiled. ''I'm afraid not.''

''But he could change cattle or whatever, you know, getting more milk or leaner beef or whatever. Things we eat, right?''

''There are researchers working in those areas.''

''At your husband's university?''

''Yes. As long as they have the money. You can't have research unless someone pays for it.''

''Why don't the universities pay for it?''

''They do, as much as they can.''

''And they don't waste the government's money?''

''They probably do; I don't think anybody's found a way to make every penny productive. Have you, at home, or in remodeling this building?''

''I watch every penny.''

''That isn't what I asked. No waste, Billy, anywhere, in any of your projects?'' She waited. ''Well, that's not the main point anyway. I want to be with my husband, now that your friend has gone after him, and that's where I'm going. I'll call you—''

Koner grunted. ''Maybe I'll have a talk with Ollie. See

what he's up to. He's gonna be looking for money pretty soon; they always are, in the House. Damnedest thing; they get elected and they haven't even warmed their chairs before they're asking for money for the next campaign. I don't know how he has time to go after professors or anybody else. But what the hell, you're right: there's plenty of waste around. He could find it blindfolded; he doesn't have to go after it here. Listen. I'll talk to him. So today you can stay with Vern and get the specs finished. Right?''

''No, today I'm going to be with Garth. If you want—''

''It's Friday! You'll be with him all weekend!''

''If you want to talk to the congressman, Billy, you'll be doing it on your own, not as our representative. But I'll be interested in what he has to say. Call me at home. Anytime.''

She shook hands with him and with Stern, picked up her briefcase and ran from the building, then walked quickly the half block to the garage.

''I never washed it, Mrs. Andersen; you said three hours.''

''It's all right, Juan; next time.''

On Sheridan Road she pulled into a gas station and called Garth. ''Have you seen today's *Tribune?*''

''Just now. There was a copy in Chuck's office. Don't worry about it; it's a nuisance but we'll handle it.''

''I'm on my way home.''

''You don't have to do that.''

''I want to. Garth, I think it's more than a nuisance.''

She heard him tapping a pencil on the desk. ''Well, so do I. But I haven't had time to think it through. There are exciting things happening here; I saw Lu this morning, and his paper . . . well, I'll tell you about it later.''

''Is it finished? Are you submitting it?''

''It's finished; I'll send it in next week. I'm glad you're coming home. There's a lot to talk about.''

''Garth, you won't talk to any reporters, will you? I should tell you about Billy Koner before you do.''

"What about him?"

"He knows Leglind; in fact, it sounds like he's Leglind's pot of gold. He says he's going to talk to him. I'll tell you about it at home."

But when she parked the car in the driveway and walked up the front walk, Garth and Lu were sitting on the front porch swing, deep in conversation. Garth came down the steps and kissed her. "I couldn't send him away; he's too keyed up. It's a defining moment for him; he really isn't a student anymore: he's a scientist."

Sabrina turned to smile at Lu. "But he doesn't look happy."

"I know. I asked him if something was wrong. He said no. He could be worrying about the journal accepting his paper, but I've told him a dozen times I'm sure they'll accept it, which means it could be published before the end of the year. I don't know what's bothering him; I haven't pursued it."

"No, we have other things to think about."

Lu came down the steps. "I'll be going. If we could talk again, Professor—tomorrow, perhaps . . ."

"Lu, this weekend won't be a good time. But we've covered everything; there's nothing to do now but wait to hear from the editors."

"Once you submit the paper."

"I told you I'd do that next week."

Lu hesitated, then nodded. "Thank you." His voice was polite, flat, almost distant.

"How odd," Sabrina said, watching him walk away. "You're far more excited than he is. Did you say he was keyed up?"

"Almost manic when he arrived. Almost sleepwalking when he left. Maybe I will try to see him tomorrow."

"Garth, how about paying some attention to Professor Andersen and the crusading Oliver Leglind?"

He chuckled and put his arm around her as they walked up the porch steps. "I'm glad you're home. I'm glad you're with me. I love you."

They held each other and kissed. "Oh, your arms feel good," Sabrina sighed. "I miss them when they're not around me. I miss you, too." But after a minute she pulled away with a smile. "Too hot for extended kissing. Oh, iced tea. How wonderful."

"Courtesy of Mrs. Thirkell. She was making it when I got home."

"Is she here?"

"Shopping. Back soon." He dropped ice cubes into two glasses and filled them from the pitcher, beaded with moisture in the heat. They sat close together on the swing, holding hands. "What did your Billy Koner say?"

"I gather he's going to tell Leglind to take his fangs somewhere else."

"Why would Koner do that?"

"Either because I convinced him that universities aren't cesspools of waste and corruption, or because he thinks I won't spend time on his building if you're being hounded."

"And why would Leglind listen to him? You said something about a pot of gold."

"He made it sound as if he single-handedly funds Leglind's career. That could mean giving a lot or raising a lot; probably both."

"Did you ask him to talk to Leglind?"

"Garth, of course not! In the first place, I'm not even sure it's the best thing to do."

"It may not be. What did you tell him?"

"That if he did talk to Leglind he was doing it on his own, not as our representative, but of course I'd be interested in what he has to say."

"That sounds fine." Garth drained his glass and refilled it, and they sat in silence.

"You lost your temper with Stroud," Sabrina said.

"I was imprudent. I told myself to be polite, but that was after I hadn't been."

"And the quote about excesses in universities?"

"Not accurate. I said if there were excesses, that still wouldn't be an excuse to attack all research."

"A slash-and-burn rampage."

"Not the best choice of words."

"No." She smiled at him. "I love you, and you shouldn't have talked to him when you knew how angry you were."

"You're right. It's happened before. I should know better."

"When do you think they'll call you to testify?"

"September, October, maybe later. They don't seem to be in a hurry. They're concentrating on maximum publicity for a while."

"You've got the money for the institute, though."

"Most of it. It would be worse if we'd just begun our fund-raising. Still, I'd rather all those people of goodwill wouldn't be reading in their newspapers for the next couple of months about money going down the drain at Midwestern U."

"Is that what you're worried about?"

"That's part of it. I suppose my job as director would be on the line if they decided the institute is a boondoggle."

"Not for you; no one would accuse you of enriching yourself."

"Glory and fame. Keeping my name visible."

Sabrina thought of Vernon Stern. "That's important for some people; it's never been for you."

"Tell that to the congressman."

They were silent again. Beyond the shaded porch the humid air hung from the sky like a faintly rippling curtain, making the street look like an old painting, faded with time. Sabrina stirred, turning her hand within Garth's. "I said something today about writing down what we do and think: that we should write it all down because without warning it could vanish."

"An unhappy thought. What we have won't vanish."

"I was thinking of our street, our solid, secure, comfortable street. And it really is . . . but it's also a place where bad things can happen.''

"Which we will face together. And vanquish." They heard the telephone. "Damn, where is Mrs. Thirkell when we need her? I'll be right back.''

Sabrina gazed at the ripples of heat. *Bad things happen. But not as bad as if we weren't together, all of us, our family.*

Garth came back and refilled their glasses. "That was Claudia. Your Billy Koner doesn't waste time. He called Leglind, evidently before you'd even left the building, and Leglind has called Claudia to say that their interviews have shown that the irregularities at Midwestern are innocuous compared to those at other institutions and because his time is limited he will be dealing only with the most egregious cases; therefore, none of us will be called to testify.''

"What an easily bought congressman he is.''

Garth put his arm around her and kissed her. "You're wonderful; have I told you that recently? Of course that's the real issue: not whether we have to testify or not, but whether a congressman is for sale. Claudia is furious; so am I. It's bad enough that he's for sale, but the other half of it is that he's letting that newspaper story dribble off into silence, leaving the innuendos floating around with a life of their own. We're not going to let him get away with it.''

She pulled back to look at him. "You're going to demand a retraction. But you don't have any leverage. Unless you're going to use Billy again, and I can't believe either one of you would do that.''

"Of course not; aiding and abetting the purchase of a congressman? Not the kind of thing we're known for. No, we're going to Washington. The congressman needs to have a conversation instead of issuing decrees. Claudia's secretary is setting it up, probably sometime next week.''

"Do you think the congressman wants a conversation?''

"No, but he's going to have one. It wouldn't be smart

to refuse to see the president of a major university and the director of its Institute for Genetic Engineering whom you have vaguely accused of malfeasance, if not fraud. Now, that would be a juicy story for the newspapers.''

''I'm glad you're going. Both of you. If we could put this whole thing behind us—''

''It would be a brushfire, not a conflagration. That's the idea. You know, it seems our lives are made up of brushfires: little crises that could scorch a life, even burn holes in parts of it, but not do long-term damage, even though when we're in the middle it seems that they might.''

''We spend our time putting out fires? It sounds awful. And frenetic.''

''Call it problem-solving. It sounds better.''

They laughed quietly, then sat, relaxed, gazing at the street, drinking the ice-cold tea, their clasped hands a little sweaty, their bodies languid in the heat. ''We could go inside where it's cool,'' Garth said.

Sabrina shook her head. ''Not yet. I like the idea of sitting with my husband on a front-porch swing in the middle of the afternoon; it feels very peaceful and old-fashioned.''

''Like courting.'' They smiled and kissed lightly, then sat again in silence, watching cars pass and neighbors come and go and the smudged shadows of trees lengthen across the pavement. Then the summer camp buses pulled up at the corner and children ran from them, backpacks bulging, hands full of trophies and projects. Penny was one of the first, and she was sitting on the steps near Sabrina and Garth when Cliff dragged his feet up the walk, scowling.

''I didn't think you'd be home,'' he said to them.

Garth's eyebrows rose. ''That's our greeting?''

''Sorry. Hi. Why are you sitting out here? It's too hot.''

''It seemed like a good idea, for a while,'' Sabrina said. ''Did the heat get to you?''

Cliff squinted as he looked at her from under the thatch of hair falling over his forehead. ''Why?''

"You look pretty grim for someone who's just come from camp. I thought you liked it."

"It's okay."

"It was fantastic two days ago," Garth said.

Cliff shrugged, then shot a glance at Sabrina. He leaned against the step railing, kicking at small stones on the front walk.

"Lu Zhen was there," said Penny. "He said he came to watch Cliff play."

"I didn't think he ever took time off," Garth said. "But he did say he'd talk about soccer in China; has he been doing that, Cliff?"

"A few times."

"He said he finished his paper," Penny said. "Does that mean he's going back to China?"

"Soon," Garth replied. "He's finished his postdoctoral work with me, and he's said he'll go back as soon as his paper is accepted for publication."

"Did you send it to *Newsweek* or *Time* or *People* or what?" Penny asked.

Garth smiled. "None of the above. Papers like Lu's go to professional journals, in this case *Science*. But I haven't sent it in yet. I'll do it next week, after I go over it."

"Again?" Sabrina asked. "I thought it was finished."

"It probably is, but I've only read it in pieces; I haven't had time to read the whole thing, start to finish. If it hangs together as Lu's described it, it will be a major break-through, something to make us all very proud of him."

Cliff kicked a stone and banged his shin against the porch railing. "Fuck it!" he cried and sat down, rubbing his leg.

Sabrina met Garth's eyes. "Why don't you and Cliff go inside where it's cool?" she said. "Maybe you'll make us a pitcher of lemonade; we seem to be out of iced tea."

"Good idea. Come on, Cliff, let's resupply the family with cooling beverages. I'm sorry," he said to Sabrina in a low voice. "I got carried away. It *is* an amazing project, you know; I'll tell you about it later."

He kissed her and stood up. "Cliff?"

"Yeh." He slouched through the door as Garth held it, then followed his father into the kitchen. The air in the house was cool and dry, and spontaneously they grinned at each other as they felt it buoy them up. "*Crazy* to sit out there," Cliff said.

Garth took lemons from the refrigerator. "I'll cut and you squeeze. Okay?"

"Sure."

They worked in silence, Cliff pulling down on the juicer's handle with such vigor that lemon juice splashed on the counter and on his shirt. Garth made no comment. He finished slicing the lemons, then scooped sugar into a tall glass pitcher. In a few minutes Cliff poured lemon juice and water into the pitcher. Garth stirred with a long spoon. They stood side by side, gazing intently at the sugar dissolving in the pale yellow liquid and at the small bits of lemon swirling wildly, chased by Garth's spoon.

Cliff went to the freezer, filled his cupped hands at the ice maker, and dumped the cubes into the pitcher, splashing lemonade on the counter. He looked at Garth, waiting for comments about the messy counter, about the splashes on his shirt, about his unwashed hands putting ice in the lemonade.

"Let's sit in here," Garth said. "I imagine your mother and Penny will be along soon."

Cliff did not move. "I've got some stuff to do in my room."

"In a while. I want to talk to you. It's important, Cliff."

Cliff shrugged and walked to the couch. Garth took glasses and the lemonade pitcher and followed him. "I thought we'd talk about Lu Zhen, since he seems to be a sore point in our house."

"It doesn't matter."

"Why not?"

"You said he was going back."

"Of course he is; that's been the idea from the beginning."

"I mean, like next week or something."

"I'm pretty sure it won't be that soon. I think he'll wait to hear if his paper is accepted for publication, and that usually takes a few weeks."

"You said it would be faster this time."

"It may be; I hope it is. But what difference does it make, Cliff? Lu is a student of mine and a guest in this house and no more than that; why can't we talk about him and even have him to dinner without your behaving as if war's been declared?"

Cliff shrugged.

"Am I supposed to know what that means?"

"I don't like him!"

"Well, that's something we've all noticed. The question is, why?" Garth poured lemonade, letting a few ice cubes slip into each glass. He looked at the tight muscles of his son's face and the disconsolate look in his eyes, and he ached for him, twelve years old, trying to find his place in the world, afraid of losing the place he had and that, until recently, he had never doubted. "I'll tell you something about Lu," Garth said reflectively. "Most of the time he's afraid. Some of my students are driven by ambition, some by a desire to do good, a few by greed. Lu is driven by fear. Everyone at home seems to have laid the most appalling expectations on him; it's a little like a Brothers Grimm fairy tale where the prince is sent out to slay the dragon, defeat the trolls, find the treasure, win the princess and get back to the palace in time for dinner."

Cliff gave a reluctant laugh. "He could just tell them to leave him alone; he's not their slave."

"I don't think he can tell them that. The government is paying his tuition and his rent, and his parents scrape up whatever they can spare for his food and clothes. The point is, he's a good scientist driven by fear, and I'm his advisor, and I want to help him. But that has nothing to do with how I feel about my own son."

"Yeh, it does," Cliff said after a moment. " 'Cause you get all excited when things happen in the lab; you talk about lymphocytes and all that stuff like they're people, I mean, you know, like you think they're terrific, and him, too, and you sit and talk and use words I never heard of, and I'm not smart enough to do any of that and I never will be—''

"Hold on." Garth set down his glass and turned to face Cliff on the couch. Why haven't we ever had this talk? he wondered. Is there something wrong with me, have I been too absorbed in my work and, lately, with my wife, or do other fathers and sons go along the same way for years without talking about their feelings, taking love for granted and assuming everything is fine? "You don't know how smart you are or how smart you will be. You're still trying things out and discovering things about yourself. I expect you to do that for a lot of years. If you pointed to something tomorrow and said, 'That's the kind of person I am and that's what I want to do for the rest of my life,' I'd be disappointed. I don't want—''

"You'd be *disappointed?*''

"Very disappointed. I don't want you to be like Lu, Cliff; I want you to be young for a while and not lock yourself into a room that may not be right for you. Even if it is right, I don't want you to settle into it too soon. You know"—he sat back, looking at Cliff with a smile—"you already have more confidence in yourself than I had at your age, and you're more balanced. All I ever wanted was to be a scientist; I was absolutely convinced that nothing else was interesting or worth my time. Then, later, I realized how many empty spaces there were in my life and I started spending time on history and literature and art, and having a good time with them. You're ahead of me in that.''

Cliff shook his head. "I'm no good in school.''

"You're okay. You're not giving it your full attention yet. We don't know what kind of a student you'll be when you decide that school deserves as much attention as soccer. But there's no hurry; you're giving yourself a chance to try everything. I admire that.''

"Admire . . ." Cliff's voice trailed off. He was eyeing his father as if weighing his seriousness.

"Because it means you're curious, open to new ideas, ready to take on the whole world. I'm trying to tell you, Cliff: that makes me prouder of you than anything, even winning at soccer. I'd always love you, but on top of that I admire you for the kind of person you are. And I like you. I like to be with you. I'm grateful for that. I think it's the most special blessing of all: to like our children as companions."

Cliff was staring at him intently. The muscles in his face had relaxed; the disconsolate look was gone. He was absorbed in everything Garth said, reorganizing the way he thought about their relationship. "What about Lu?"

"What about him?"

"Well, you could say all that about him: you like him and you like to be with him and he's like a companion 'cause he's smart and he can talk about the things you want to talk about . . ."

"Cliff, I have a son. I love you and I like you and you're the only son I want. You're one of my three favorite people in the whole world and I want to talk to you about whatever you're interested in and I want you to listen to me when I talk about whatever I'm interested in. That sounds like a good deal to me; in fact, it makes me feel pretty lucky whenever I think about it."

There was a long silence. "You don't care what grades I get?"

Garth smiled to himself at his son's pushing to find the boundaries of his father's love. "I'd rather you didn't fail any courses."

"But if I did?"

"I'd be sorry."

"Why?"

"Because I'm unhappy when you're unhappy and I think you would be: you don't like to fail at anything. And then it would mess up your soccer; they don't let you play, do they, if you fail a course?"

"Uh . . . no." He picked at a scab on his knuckle. "Mom said that stuff once; she said I was curious about the world and I could learn a lot if I tried."

"Well, sometimes if we hear something twice it's easier to believe it. Maybe you'll believe it now."

"But when I asked her to go to the principal, you know, tell him something for me, she wouldn't do it. She said it was my problem, like she didn't care."

"She didn't tell me that. *Was* it your problem?"

"Well, yeh, but, you know, she used to go to school and explain things . . ."

"And now she doesn't. Do you really think that means she doesn't care about you and love you? Or just that she thinks you're so smart and grown up you can handle a lot of things without your mother running interference for you?"

"I suppose."

"You suppose what?"

"That she thinks I could do it without her."

"And did you?"

Cliff nodded.

"It sounds to me as if your mother thinks you're pretty special, the way I do. Look, Cliff . . ." Garth put his arm around his son. "Why don't we relax around here? We've got a wonderful family, one of the best, and we live in a good house in a good town, and we have a lot of fun together. I guess if we looked for problems hard enough we'd find some, but why should we? Let the scientists look for problems; they thrive on them. All the scientists in the world would vanish in a cloud of bewilderment if suddenly there weren't any problems. But right here, in our house, in our family, I love you and your mother loves you and what we all ought to be doing is enjoying each other, not growling about *maybe*s and *what-if*s. What do you think?"

Cliff sighed. He was resting against his father, still picking at the scab on his knuckle. "Sounds okay to me. Are you going to invite him to dinner again?"

Frustration rose in Garth. Cliff felt it in the tension of his body and he shrank into himself.

"Much too hot," Sabrina said, coming in with Penny close behind her. "I do like being outside, but there's a limit, and we've passed it." She made a swift survey of Garth's arm around Cliff, and of their faces. "Did I miss something?"

"Cliff wondered if we'd be inviting Lu to dinner again," Garth said, his voice carefully neutral.

"Oh." Stubborn Cliff, Sabrina thought. A long talk with your father, a good one, it looks like, but everything you heard will have to be absorbed over time, and meanwhile you have to push and prod, at least once more. "Well, I'm sure we will," she said matter-of-factly. "We'll probably have a farewell dinner for him when he's ready to go back to China. We always do that for visitors, don't we?"

She smiled at Cliff. "We'll have to be very nice to him, so he'll know we wish him all the success he's hoping for." She poured lemonade for herself and Penny and decided to do a little pushing and prodding of her own. "I think you might be especially nice to him, Cliff, since you haven't been in the past."

Cliff scowled.

"You're a host here, too, you know; this is your house as much as ours, and hosts have responsibilities to their guests."

"Yeh, but—"

"And it's always a good idea to be extra nice to someone when you're pretty sure you won't ever see him again."

"Oh." The scowl faded. "Well, yeah. Sure."

The back door opened and Mrs. Thirkell came in, struggling with shopping bags. "Cliff, could you—"

"Sure." He jumped up. His face was bright. He pried two bags from her grasp. "How come you don't drive? It'd be a lot easier."

"Because in this country you drive on the wrong side of

the street and it's unnatural and I want no part of it.'' The telephone rang and she swooped down on it. ''Put everything on the counter, Cliff, if you please.''

Garth stood and put his arm around Sabrina. ''Thank you. Maybe, between the two of us, we've taken care of it.''

''Mommy,'' Penny said, ''did you forget? You were going to ask Daddy about the party tonight.''

''Party?'' Garth asked.

''Penny's been invited to Carla Shelton's house and she doesn't know who else is going.''

''Shelton? Is that a new name? I haven't heard it.''

''They're new in town.''

''It's Carla's birthday,'' Penny said. ''Can I go? She lives in that big house that we walked past, the huge one that was for sale for such a long time.''

''But you don't know who's been invited, Penny, and we talked about that, remember?''

''My lady,'' Mrs. Thirkell said, ''Princess Alexandra is on the telephone.''

Sabrina looked at her uncomprehendingly. Alexandra?

I am standing in a kitchen in Evanston, Illinois, talking to my molecular-scientist husband and our eleven-year-old daughter about a party that perhaps she shouldn't go to, while our twelve-year-old son unloads groceries. What place does Princess Alexandra Martova have here, even on the telephone?

''My lady?''

''Yes. Thank you, Mrs. Thirkell.'' She took the telephone into the breakfast room. ''Alexandra? Where are you?''

''Chicago, the Fairchild. Honey, I know this is unforgivable, but we're just here overnight, and would you and your husband come down and have dinner with me? Antonio's doing business from now to midnight and I'd love to see you. I didn't know we'd be here; we were flying from London to somewhere—Detroit? Pittsburgh?—where Antonio had people to see, and all of a sudden he told our pilot to go to Chicago instead. So I thought . . . You know, I miss Sabrina, and I thought how nice it would be to be with you for a while. Do you mind my saying that?"

"No." Sabrina closed her eyes and for a moment was Sabrina Longworth again, in London, talking to Alexandra about plans to go to a restaurant that night, talking about the next party, the next country weekend, the next cruise . . . the next cruise, Max's yacht, a cruise off Monaco, an explosion . . .

"Honey? If you're too busy—"

"No, I'd like to see you. But why don't you come here? We'll have dinner and talk as long as we want."

"At your house? But you don't live in Chicago."

"I don't live in the next county, either. It's about twenty minutes by taxi. Or . . . don't tell me Antonio hasn't hired a limousine; that was always the first thing—" She stopped. *Why do I do that? I slip back so easily; you'd think by now . . .*

"It is amazing to me," Alexandra said into the silence, "the little things Sabrina told you about us. Yes, we've got a limo, and I'd love to come to your house. Eight o'clock?"

Sabrina smiled, thinking how long it had been since eight o'clock was the earliest anyone would consider having dinner. "Fine. I'll see you then."

"*Mommy,*" Penny said. She had come into the breakfast room. "Can I go? Barbara's going."

Sabrina switched her attention. "You didn't tell me that before."

"I forgot."

Garth had joined them and he and Sabrina exchanged a glance. "It sounds all right," he said. "Vivian wouldn't let Barbara go if she was worried."

Sabrina nodded slowly. "Ten o'clock, Penny."

"*Ten o'clock!* Mommy, it's Friday night!"

"You're right. Ten-thirty."

"Mommy!"

313

"That's the deadline, Penny, and you know it. When you're twelve you can add half an hour."

"Barbara has till midnight."

"I don't believe it."

"Well . . . when she's home and they're having a party . . ."

"But when she goes out?"

"Ten-thirty," Penny said reluctantly, then impulsively threw her arms around Sabrina. "It's okay, I don't mind. Can I wear my new dress?"

"Yes, but it needs hemming. Ask Mrs. Thirkell."

Penny ran to Mrs. Thirkell and Garth and Sabrina turned to each other. "You're wonderful with her," Garth said. "She wants restraints—they all do, really, especially and mostly the indulged ones—and somehow you've always known that."

Always. Since September. At first it was easy to be strict because it's always easier with another woman's children, but then it was because they were mine and I worried about them and feared for them and, mostly, loved them.

"I love her. I love Cliff. I love you." She put her arms around him and kissed him.

"What did Alexandra want?"

"An evening of talk. She's coming to dinner—at eight o'clock, which shows that she has no children. I can't imagine her in this house, but it seems she wants to reminisce. You don't have to stay and listen."

"I thought I'd go to my office. It would be a quiet time to go over Lu's paper. Would you mind?"

"Of course not. Can you pick up Penny at ten-thirty, or be home so I can?"

"I'll pick her up."

They kissed again and stood in each other's arms as the sun streamed into the breakfast room and the bright voices of their children danced around Mrs. Thirkell's directions and words of advice. My home, my place, my love, Sabrina thought. The thought was sharper because she had slipped into her London self as soon as she heard Alexandra's voice, and for a moment it had seemed as if she held both lives in her hands and then, without hesitation or regret, had opened the London hand and let that life slip away.

"No, I won't live there ever," she said to Alexandra that night. They were alone in the library, a pot of coffee and the last of Mrs. Thirkell's apple pie on the table before them. "That was Sabrina Longworth's life, and my life is here."

Alexandra contemplated her. "You look gorgeous; night and day from the way you looked in London last time I saw you. Of course that was a ghastly time, that funeral, and then everybody gorging themselves at her house as if they were afraid they might never eat again . . ."

"Or be alive," Sabrina said quietly. "People eat after funerals to convince themselves they're still alive and healthy, everything functioning, death unthinkable."

"God, you sound just like her; that's something she'd say, in just that voice." Alexandra tilted her head and studied her. "You look like her and you don't. After the funeral, when the hordes were descending on the food, I kept watching you, and I thought I was crazy because I was sure you were Sabrina. I would have laid bets on it. But now I wouldn't be so sure. You're . . . oh, I don't know . . . softer than Sabrina was. No, that's not it. Quieter, not as much on edge."

"Happier, maybe."

"Oh, I don't know. Sabrina had some worries—didn't we all—but she was pretty happy, you know; we had a good time."

"I know." Sabrina smiled at her, glad to be with her. She was tall and willowy, with light blue eyes that turned up at the corners and pale blond hair falling sleekly down her back. She wore cream-colored silk pants and a matching short-sleeved blouse, and emeralds and diamonds at her neck and ears and wrists. Sabrina pictured herself in her French cotton sundress, with a Katherine Hayward amber necklace and earrings, and ballet slippers on her bare feet, and knew she was as perfectly dressed as Alexandra, but she also knew that she had lost the sleekness that radiated from Alexandra: a final polish that had been part of her London life when she was always on display. And I don't miss it, she thought, smiling at Alexandra. "You look perfect. Are you as happy as you look?"

"Honey, I find this hard to believe, but I am. I like building towns in Brazil; it's the first time in my life I've really felt useful. And I've fallen in love with Antonio, which is a good thing to do with your husband. I have Sabrina to thank for that; he learned a lot from her before she sent him packing."

"Antonio learned . . . ?" Sabrina was amazed; he had seemed impervious to any influences when she knew him. But it was Stephanie who broke with him, and she must have done it with a kind of innocent finality that Sabrina never had been able to muster. "What did he learn?"

"That other people, even women, have their own ideas and their own agendas that are as legitimate as his. I don't mean it's a heartfelt belief all the time, only sporadically, so I need to remind him, but he's doing better, and I've never had as much fun as I'm having now. I wish Sabrina could have known."

"She would have been glad for both of you."

"So what are you going to do about London? I thought you'd merged your shops, there and here."

"I did, but it isn't what I really want. It's incredible how much energy a house and a family take—"

"You're just finding that out? How old are your kids?"

"Eleven and twelve. No, of course I knew it, but everything doubled or tripled when I tried to juggle all of it with London. And when I thought about it, I realized I didn't want to be a juggler."

"No, I see that. Sabrina would have tried it; she probably could have made it work. But you're more focused here; you're really wrapped up in all this. I'm sorry Garth couldn't stay tonight; I like his looks. Smart and sexy, and, my God, the way he looks at you . . . every woman's dream. And I thought we'd have your kids, too; are your nights always this quiet?''

Sabrina laughed. "Hardly. Penny's at a party; Cliff is upstairs with a friend, playing computer games."

"And Garth's at work."

"He thought we'd like some time alone."

"He was right, actually; I like this." There was a pause. "I have a question."

"I thought so."

"You *thought* so?"

"I thought there was a reason you came to Chicago. Straight from London."

"You know, you're really unbelievable. Sabrina used to do that: just about read my mind. It's disconcerting, honey; it was then and it is now."

"But you still have a question."

"I do. Is Ambassadors for sale?"

"The only one who could have told you that is Sidney Jones, and I asked him not to tell anyone yet."

"Well, some lawyers have generous hearts. I called him because I knew he was your solicitor and I told him it has been my lifelong dream to own Ambassadors and I would be crushed if you sold it—"

"Your lifelong dream?"

"A small exaggeration. I've been dreaming about it for the past couple of months. Honey, I could run it—I'm back and forth from Brazil all the time—and I want to do it. I want something of my own, apart from Antonio, and also . . . it would be like keeping Sabrina with me. I'll need some experts to help me until I learn a lot more than I know now, but London is crawling with experts. And wouldn't you rather sell to me than to a stranger?"

"Yes. I'd be very happy if you owned Ambassadors. The price is one million pounds."

Alexandra burst into laughter. "You don't waste time,

do you? You even converted the money into pounds. That's without the inventory?"

"With the inventory."

"Then you're cheating yourself."

"I don't know the market in London these days. If you think I've cheated myself when you sell the pieces in the shop, send me half the purchase price. Then you're on your own."

"Honey, am I missing something? You've got it all thought out. Did you know I was going to do this? How could you?"

"I didn't know, but I think it's wonderful. You're right: I didn't want to sell to a stranger. I feel the same way about my house, but that probably—"

"Yes, Sidney told me about the house. I don't need it; I have my own and you made it so wonderful I wouldn't give it up. But I have some friends who are looking for a place; would you mind if I told them about it?"

Sabrina felt a moment of panic. It was all being taken from her. She had thought it would be a slow process, interviewing people, checking references, cataloguing inventory, all giving her time to let go slowly, to say farewell to what she had been. Now it was being snatched away from her and instinctively she put out a hand to hold it back.

But I don't want to. And as soon as she thought it, her panic was gone; her reluctance vanished. "That would be fine," she said. Her hand was still out and she put it on Alexandra's arm, and then they were holding each other, and both of them were thinking about Sabrina Longworth. "Thank you," she said at last. "I thought it would be so hard to do all that, cut the ties and turn my back on it . . . but this way it's almost like keeping it in the family. Do you think we could do all the paperwork by September? I'd like to have it done by my birthday."

"The nineteenth, right? Well, why not? Even lawyers ought to get through the paperwork in six weeks." She stood up and went to the small bar in the corner of the room and, as casually as if she were, in fact, a member of the family, she poured two glasses of port. "I'd like to drink to that."

"Yes. And to more visits. Would you come to Chicago again?"

"Honey, Antonio believes there are two places in the world: Brazil and Europe. Why don't you come to see me? I'm in Paris a lot; I'll be in London more than ever now; and we just bought a house in Provence, between Cavaillon and Gordes. You'd be welcome; you and your family. Oh, what a great idea! The kids would love it. Say you'll come. Not now; it's too hot. But in the fall . . ."

"I'll talk to Garth. He has to be at the Hague in October and we're going to be in Paris for a week after that, just the two of us. We might come to Provence for a couple of days; we'll talk about it."

The telephone rang and Sabrina looked at her watch in surprise. "Ten o'clock; maybe Penny wants to come home early. Excuse me."

When she answered it, Garth's voice was hurried, abstracted. "I have to stay later than I'd expected. Can you get Penny?"

"I don't like to leave Cliff alone."

"I thought Alexandra would still be there."

"Garth, what is it? What's wrong?"

"I'm not sure yet. I'll tell you about it when I get home."

"Is it Lu's paper?"

"It may be. *Is* Alexandra still there? Can she stay while you get Penny?"

"I'm sure she will. I'll take care of it, Garth. And I'll wait for you."

"I'll be home as soon as I can. I love you." Garth hung up and turned back to his desk, where the neatly printed pages of Lu's paper, with perfectly spaced paragraphs, formulas, and footnotes, were spread out before him.

Lu had been working for two years to find a way to produce mice with rheumatoid arthritis identical to that in humans so that scientists could rapidly test new treatments to alleviate and cure arthritis. To do this he had begun with a person who had rheumatoid arthritis, and isolated and removed genes that controlled the formation of joint tissue. Once the genes were isolated, he cloned them, collected fertilized mouse eggs and injected the cloned genes into the eggs, and then transferred the eggs to the oviduct of a foster mother mouse.

He went through the same procedure with the same person to isolate and remove genes that produced lymphocytes that attacked the joint tissue, causing arthritis. When he had two strains of mice with the two kinds of genes, he mated them. His theory was that their progeny would have rheumatoid arthritis identical to that of humans.

Garth had worked with Lu on his program of isolating and cloning the genes, and of producing two strains of mice that could be mated. They had celebrated together when Lu succeeded in producing a mouse with the gene that controlled the formation of human joint tissue. But after that Lu had withdrawn into the harder part of the project: producing a mouse with the gene with instructions for producing lymphocytes that would attack joint tissue.

And I was busy with the institute, Garth thought, hunched over the papers on his desk. And with my wife. And for a year I haven't paid enough attention.

He had thought from the beginning, two years earlier, that Lu would find it was not a single gene that controlled the development of lymphocytes, but two, perhaps more, which would complicate the project even further. But Lu had created his transgenic mice—mice with foreign genes—with a single gene controlling the development of joint tissue and a single gene controlling the development of lymphocytes. That was the reason Garth thought Lu had taken such a giant step forward.

But something nagged at him as he read the paper. He remembered other experiments with lymphocytes that had been ambiguous as to the number of genes involved; he recalled conversations with other researchers who said there had to be several genes, and papers that concluded there was much still to be learned.

But Lu's paper, elegantly constructed, said the issue was resolved.

Well, hallelujah, Garth had thought since Lu had told him. But beneath the celebrating, questions remained, and they became insistent in the silence of his office in the empty Molecular Biology Building at nine o'clock on a Friday night. And so, after reading the paper a third time, he reached for the telephone to call his friend Bill Farver. Seven o'clock in San Francisco, he thought; probably still at work. He called Farver's office at Farver Labs and found him there. "I thought you'd like to be the first to know that Lu Zhen says he's done it. I'm going over his paper now."

Farver's voice rumbled over the telephone, sounding as if he were in the next office. "Transgenic progeny with human rheumatoid arthritis? Garth, that's fantastic. Hats off; a hundred hats off. Of course I'm crushed; I don't like coming in second."

"How close are you?"

"Well, we're having trouble with the second gene for the lymphocytes; I don't know how long it'll be. I'd like to see Lu's paper; see how he did it."

Garth stared into the dark corners of his office. He and Farver had not talked about details; in a real sense they were competitors and only now, when he thought this part of the race was won, had Farver been so specific. "What have you tried?" he asked casually.

They compared notes on experimental techniques, Lu's and Farver's and others in Farver's lab, and then Farver said, "I just don't see how he did it, Garth. Two of my researchers swear there has to be a second gene, that there's no way you could end up with rheumatoid arthritis in a mouse with only one gene; you've got to have both. 'Course that's not the word of God from Jerusalem, but they've done a hell of a lot of work on this and I'm inclined to think they're right. Have you checked out Lu's work?''

Garth started to snap that of course he had; that that was his job as Lu's advisor and the director of his postdoctoral research project . . . but he got no further than opening his mouth. He hadn't checked out Lu's research as it progressed. He'd been busy, he'd trusted Lu, and he'd wanted him to succeed. ''I'll look at it again,'' he said.

''Your name is on Lu's paper, right? Have you sent it anywhere?''

''No. I wasn't ready.''

''Good thing. I always knew caution deserved more credit than we usually give it. Listen, let me know what you find, will you? If he's right, if we've missed something here, you could help get us back on track.''

''You'll hear from me. And, Bill, thanks. I appreciate your sharing all this.''

He gathered the pages of Lu's paper together and absently squared the corners. If Farver was right, the progeny of Lu's transgenic mice would be perfectly healthy: no sign of rheumatoid arthritis. Their parents would have had the gene for producing joint tissue, but they wouldn't have had two genes for lymphocytes. And therefore . . .

He left the light on in his office and walked through the building to Lu's laboratory. The mice slept or scampered or sat meditatively as he moved past them, reading the labels on their cages. When he found the ones he wanted, he drew blood from the tails of five of them and took the samples one floor down, to the testing lab. He glanced at his watch as he placed the test tubes in an agitator. Almost ten. He wouldn't be finished in time to get Penny. He called home from the telephone on the wall, gazing at the test tubes as he listened to Sabrina's voice and pictured the two women in the library, curled up on the couch, comparing lives, reminiscing.

''I'll take care of it, Garth. And I'll wait for you.''

''I'll be home as soon as I can,'' he said. ''I love you.''
His thoughts were on the test tubes, shining at him, light

from the ceiling fixtures flashing off the glass and the bright red fluid as the agitator tilted the tubes up and down, like a playground seesaw.

He put the blood into the analyzer, then stood at the computer printer, waiting. A watched printer never prints, he thought, and strolled around the lab, stretching his neck, clenching and opening his fists. He did not come here often, though in his student days and the early days of his teaching at Columbia he had spent as much time analyzing blood as had all the other researchers. I'm getting away from the real work, he thought, and there isn't anything I can do about it. Not if I want to run an institute and advise students. And pay more attention to them than I've paid to Lu in the past year.

He heard the printer start up and he crossed the room to watch the paper roll from the machine. The columns of numbers printed out, one slow line at a time. And even before the printer stopped, even before he tore the page at its perforations to take it back to his office, Garth knew that the blood samples showed no sign of arthritis, or of any disease. The mice were healthy . . . and Lu's paper was a fraud.

CHAPTER *14*

Stephanie heard a key turn, the front door open and close, the key locking it again, and she pictured Jacqueline walking into the coolness of the shop from the July heat on the cours Gambetta, adjusting a vase here, a lamp there as she approached the back room.

"Good morning, did you have a pleasant weekend?" Her voice seemed preoccupied. "Did you and Max do something exciting?" She opened a closet in the corner and exchanged her walking shoes for high heels. "You're very quiet, my dear. Is something bothering you?"

"Yes." *This is not between you and Jacqueline; it is between Jacqueline and me.* She heard Léon's voice, felt his arms around her in the cool forest clearing where they had made love. But it had been four days since then, with a weekend in between, and she could not stand it any longer; she had to talk to Jacqueline. Because it *is* between us, she thought, and she and Léon must have been together this weekend, and I can't go on pretending everything is the same, because nothing is.

"Well, then, we must talk about it." Jacqueline sat on

the edge of the table and reached out to put her arm around Stephanie.

"No, wait, please. I have to tell you . . . I thought, this weekend, you might have . . . you would have seen . . ."

"I was not here. I was in Paris from Friday afternoon to late last night. What would I have seen if I had been here?"

"Léon."

Jacqueline's body stilled, as if poised to listen, perhaps to flee. "So." Her voice was a murmur. "I did not guess it was you."

"What do you mean? You said you weren't here; you didn't talk to him."

"But he came to my house on Saturday and when he found I was gone he left flowers and a letter. I did not open the letter; it was late when I returned and I was tired and I left it for this evening. Because when a man leaves flowers and a letter, my dear, it means only one thing. Come now, don't hide your face; let me look at you."

Stephanie met her eyes. "I didn't know. And then he told me, but by then everything had changed."

"By then you were in love with him. And he with you, of course, since he has written me a letter." She smiled faintly. "Léon and I once promised each other we would not linger, half in and half out of the door, if we met someone else."

"I'm sorry, Jacqueline, please believe that. I wouldn't have—"

"Of course you would have. It is clear that this was meant to be; you could not have fought it without destroying yourself. You must not even think that you would have turned away from it; that would have been wrong. And what are you sorry for? Loving Léon? There is no better man anywhere; why would you be sorry you love him?"

"I'm not sorry I love him. I'm sorry that you must be hurt by it."

"Oh, well, hurt . . . we all are hurt now and then; otherwise we are dead. I am glad—" Her voice caught on the word, and she cleared her throat. "I am very glad for both of you, but for you especially, my dear Sabrina, because you are young and—"

"So are you!"

"Yes, but not as young as you. And not in so much need."

"We all need companionship and love, and someone to—" Stephanie broke into a nervous laugh. "Jacqueline, doesn't it seem to you that this is a very odd conversation?"

"Odd? I don't think so. I would say civilized."

"But neither of us has said anything about my husband."

"Well, no, but we are talking about you, what you need, which does not necessarily have anything to do with you and Max."

"But I'm *married*."

"But that is a problem only if you wish to marry someone else and have children. But I suppose . . . well, I suppose you do. Is that it?"

"We haven't talked about marrying or having children. It's just . . . loving him. Making love to him. Wanting to be with him even when I'm with Max, and I'm *married* to Max, I have responsibilities to him . . ."

"Oh, my dear, you sound like an American." Jacqueline paused. "Maybe you are; wouldn't that be a surprise? No, really, you can't be; no American speaks French as you do. But to have such ideas . . . Why can't you love someone besides your husband, especially when your marriage is not what you would like it to be? Are you being less kind to Max? Are you hurting him?"

"I will. Just as Léon hurt you."

Imperceptibly, Jacqueline's face became harder, almost masklike. And Stephanie understood that for the past few minutes she had been playing a part, conversing animatedly about Stephanie and Léon as if they were characters on a stage and she could analyze them, even help write

326

their script while all the time staying apart, coolly interested but uninvolved.

But she was not uninvolved. *That is a problem only if you wish to marry someone else and have children.* She had not been able to say Léon's name. Stephanie saw how carefully she held herself, her back straight, her head high, as if she might shatter like a piece of rare porcelain if she let one muscle relax or one emotion burst to the surface. There was a desolate pride in that straight back and high head and Stephanie thought of how she would feel if Léon had written her a letter and sent flowers, and tears came to her eyes.

"Ah, you will not cry," Jacqueline said. "Neither of us will cry. Instead we—" There was a knock at the front door. Jacqueline and Stephanie exchanged a glance: they knew who it was, and for just a moment they were two women sharing a secret and, because of that, closer to each other than they could be to any man. But then it was gone. Jacqueline sighed. "I'll let him in." But Stephanie stood with her and they walked together into the showroom.

When the door swung open, Léon saw them both at the same time. "Good morning," Jacqueline said formally and stood aside.

He walked into the dimly lit shop and stopped beside a table where one of his smaller paintings stood on an easel. His voice was neutral as he greeted both of them. "It occurred to me," he said to Jacqueline, "that you might not have read my letter."

She smiled faintly. "How well you know me, Léon."

Stephanie winced. "I should leave. I'll be in back."

"I want you to stay," Jacqueline said. "We are all friends, isn't that so? And of course, Léon, you are right; I did not read the letter. I left it for tonight."

Léon looked at both of them. "It seems that by now it isn't necessary."

"Of course it is necessary. I will have it as a memento. In that sense it is far better than a conversation on a

Saturday morning, which would have left me only with echoes.''

"I called again on Sunday," he said quietly.

"My maid told me. That was very thoughtful, to make sure I had not come home early and faced Sunday afternoon alone, with only flowers and a letter. It was very like you; you have always been the most thoughtful—'' She took a few steps from them and stood with her back to them, one hand resting lightly on a gilded desk.

Stephanie started toward her, but Léon put his hand on her arm, and at that moment Jacqueline turned. The mask was gone from her face, but Stephanie thought she looked almost austere, her bones chiseled and sharply shadowed. There might have been tears in her eyes, but it was hard to tell in the dim light; they had forgotten to turn on the lights in the shop when they came to answer the front door. She contemplated Stephanie and Léon, who stood close together, his hand still on her arm. "How lovely you are together. You make each other more beautiful. That is a gift that love brings . . . and its mystery, of course. It is so special, that part: sharing and enjoying the mystery of each other.''

She put her hands lightly on their arms, an embrace, a blessing. "I like knowing that you have found each other; I like being reminded that there are mysteries and discoveries always waiting for us.'' She kissed each of them on the cheek. "I love you both. I wish you much joy.''

Stephanie breathed a sigh of gratitude and started to put her arms around Jacqueline, then hesitated.

"Oh, come," Jacqueline said. "We love each other, yes?''

"Yes. Oh, yes." They held each other. "I do love you. You've been so wonderful to talk to. I want you to be happy. I want you to have everything you want.''

Jacqueline gave a small laugh. "So do I. And we still will talk, yes? As often as before. I would miss it if we did not.''

"Yes." Stephanie concealed her doubt. She could talk

to Jacqueline about Max, but never about Léon. There are always compartments and hidden places, she thought, where we allow some people in and keep others out; our lives are tangled webs of secrets and deceptions.

A shudder ran through her. "What is it?" Jacqueline asked, feeling it in Stephanie's body, but before Stephanie could answer, another knock came at the front door, and they saw a face peering in.

"Oh, damn," Jacqueline said crossly. "Ten o'clock. Why can't people come late to do their shopping, the way they are always late for dinner parties?"

"I'll turn on the lights," Stephanie said, and went to the back room to flick on all the switches and bring the shop to life.

"And I will go to work," Léon said, joining her. "Are you all right? For a minute you looked faint."

"I'm fine. It was that feeling I've had before. But it goes away."

In a corner of the room they embraced and kissed, and Stephanie let herself flow into him, part of him as he was part of her. "I love you. I'm glad you came this morning."

He kissed her eyes and the corners of her mouth. "I adore you, I want you, I want to be inside you and next to you and across the table from you, and running through fields of lavender with you, and bicycling with you to every spring that is the source of every river, of life, of love . . . My God, I am running on like a drunken amateur poet. My love, we have many things to talk about."

"Yes." She was so happy she thought she could not contain it all inside her. "I'll call you, is that all right? I don't know when I can—"

"Yes, yes, call me. At my studio or at home. Anytime. Midnight, dawn, noon, I'll be awake, thinking about you, wanting you, most likely painting you. Call me. I love you."

Stephanie watched him walk through the shop. He stopped to speak briefly to Jacqueline and kiss her cheek, and then he was gone. She stayed where she was, giving herself another minute before going to work, holding on to his voice and his touch and the look in his eyes.

"Sabrina," Jacqueline called, her low voice carrying through the shop, "would you please bring the Terre d'Homme pitchers that came in this morning?"

And at that moment, Stephanie thought of Max, and her exhilaration vanished. I have to tell him, she thought. Tonight. Whatever Jacqueline says, what I'm doing is wrong, and I have to tell him . . . tell him I want to move out of his house, get a divorce, be free to . . . to do whatever I decide to do. *My love, we have many things to talk about.*

She carried the box of pitchers into the shop. Several customers were there, and then more came, and Stephanie thought of Max again only when she was driving out of Cavaillon and up the hill to their small enclave at the top. Her hands were tight on the wheel; she was rehearsing.

I'm sorry, Max; you gave me a life, but now I have to make my own.

I'm sorry, Max; I like you and I'm grateful to you, but I've fallen in love with—

I'm sorry, Max, but I think it's time I lived alone.

I'm sorry, Max; I don't want to hurt you, but I've met someone else and I have to be with—

I'm sorry, Max, but I can't live with you any longer because I don't love you and I think you're keeping things from me; you're not honest with me; I think you don't even want me to remember who I am, or anything about my past . . .

That was it, she thought as she drove into the garage. That was the reason she wanted to leave. She turned off the engine. It was all true, but it wasn't why she was leaving. She was leaving so she could be in Léon's bed, and spend her days and nights with him, and love him. She didn't love Max or trust him, and that had been true from the beginning, in the hospital, but she had stayed with him, because it had been secure. She felt a wave of despair. *I haven't grown up at all. I'm going from one safe haven to another, just the way I did when I went from my father to school to Garth.*

Garth.

The name echoed within her. Garth, Garth, Garth. Stephanie concentrated on it, trying to hold it still, trying to connect it to something else. But there was nothing; it meant nothing to her. Garth, Garth, Garth. Not a name she heard in Cavaillon; not an ordinary name. *Was I married to him? Maybe I just lived with him. Who was he? Who was I?*

"Damn it!" she cried, and hammered the steering wheel with her fists. One fist struck the horn and the sound blasted through the garage. In an instant the door opened and Madame Besset ran to her.

"Madame, madame, what is it?" She opened the car door. "Oh, how pale you are. You are ill, you have hurt yourself . . . Here, let me help you . . ."

"No, no, it's all right."

"It is not all right, madame, you are trembling. My God, what has happened? Come, take my arm . . ."

Stephanie held on to Madame Besset's ample arm and stepped out of the car. When she looked up, Max was there. "I'll take her, Madame Besset; please bring us something cold to drink." He put an arm around Stephanie's shoulders and led her into the house and into the living room, cool and shaded from the afternoon heat. "Sit down. Now tell me what happened."

"Max, who is Garth?"

"Garth? I have no idea."

"I never talked about him?"

"No. Does he have a last name?"

"I don't know."

"That's what happened in the car just now? You thought of a name?"

"Yes, and it was so clear . . . I never mentioned him? You're sure?"

"Sabrina, I've never heard that name. I would have

remembered if I had; it's not a common one. You think you knew someone named Garth? Have you any idea who it might have been?''

Stephanie searched his face. His arm was around her, and his eyes were close and steady. She knew he was telling the truth. Often she was not sure; there was a flicker in his eyes or a slight tightening of his mouth that she thought meant he was lying or hiding something, but now there was none of that. The name meant no more to him than it did to her.

"I think I was married to him. Or lived with him."

"Impossible."

"Why?"

"Because, my dear Sabrina, you would have told me. That much we did talk about."

Madame Besset brought a tray with bottled water, a small ice bucket, and a bowl of fruit. "Lunch is ready, monsieur, but I did not know if madame would be hungry."

"Shall we have lunch?" Max asked. "I have something to talk to you about, but I won't until you feel ready."

Stephanie felt a chill. "Is something wrong?"

"Something might be, but it is manageable. Come; shall we have lunch?"

Subdued, Stephanie followed him onto the terrace, where the table had been moved to a corner shaded by a plane tree. They looked out on their small grove of cherry trees, stepping down the hill and, far below, the roofs of Cavaillon and the green valley beyond, shimmering in the heat. Climbing roses covered the wall behind them, white and pale pink, flickering with butterflies. "Such a beautiful spot," Stephanie murmured.

Max served them from platters of cold sliced pheasant and marinated vegetables. "There are thousands of beautiful spots in the world. So many places you haven't seen that I'd like to show you."

"You mean you want to travel? Why? We haven't been here very long." Her eyes widened. "Because of something that's gone wrong? You want to run away, is that it? Max, tell me what's happening.''

He saw the fear in her eyes and backed off from what he had planned to say. She was already confused about this name that had popped up. And who the hell was Garth? Max Stuyvesant and Sabrina Longworth had moved in the same social circles in London and nowhere in those circles was there anyone named Garth. Well, probably someone from her childhood. He wondered if it was a good sign or a bad one that she would retrieve a memory from that far back. Did that mean less chance or more that she would remember everything? But it had been eight months; surely if amnesia lasted this long, it was unlikely—

"Max, tell me what is happening!''

"Nothing that you have to worry about.'' He filled their wineglasses and made his voice casual, almost indifferent. He'd have to prepare her: lay some groundwork. He could wait a couple of weeks before telling her they were leaving Cavaillon, and he would use that time to make sure everything was organized for him to operate from another place. "I told you, I can manage it. We don't have to talk about it today; it can wait.''

"What can wait?''

"Talking about what we're going to do. It's not urgent; I want you to forget I said anything.''

"I don't forget anymore. And if you're in trouble I should know about it.''

"I'm not in trouble.''

"You said something might be wrong.''

"Well, it might be. But nothing has happened that you need to know about or worry about.'' He took her hand between his. "I'm touched by your concern. It means a great deal to me.''

I've fallen in love with someone else. I'm leaving you.
She looked away, trying to find a way to begin.
You think, because I'm worried about you, I must love you. But I don't. I'm concerned because you've been good to me and I don't want you to be in danger, but I don't

love you. I love someone else and I want to be with him, so I'm leaving you.

She could not say it. If Max was in trouble or in danger she would not walk out on him. And there had been something in his voice today that she had not heard before, something in his face she had not seen, just a flicker, but it was so startling to see even that tiny flare of anxiety in Max's eyes and to hear it in his voice that she could not say she was leaving, or even let him know that she was thinking about it.

But I can't share his bed and go on as his wife . . .

"I'll be away for a couple of weeks," he said as Stephanie remained silent. "I hate to leave you, but I have to see some of my people in a few places and I'll be on the move the whole time; otherwise I'd take you with me."

Relief swept through her and she looked down so he would not see it in her eyes. "Your export and import people?"

"Yes."

"And will they help you solve your problems?"

"I expect to have all the information I need after I talk to them. You'll be all right, won't you? You have Madame Besset and you seem to be close to Jacqueline; and you can finish the house while I'm gone. Surprise me. You can give me a tour when I get back."

Two weeks, Stephanie thought; two whole weeks. He'll work out whatever is wrong, and when he comes back, I'll tell him I'm leaving. And in the meantime I'll find a place to live. Because I have to do that. I'll be with Léon, but I have to be by myself, too.

Maybe, if I'm alone, I can concentrate and put things together and remember. Laura. Mrs. Thirkell. Penny. Garth.

She repeated the names to herself. They meant nothing. No faces came with them, no voices or conversations, no clasping of hands or sharing of smiles. Laura. Mrs. Thirkell. Penny. Garth.

Nothing.

But I will remember, she thought. Robert thinks I will; Léon thinks I will. One day it will all come back.

"—worried about my being gone?" Max was asking. "If you're really upset I can try to break it into shorter trips and be home in between."

"No, I'm not worried; I'll be fine. And I will finish the house; I think I can do it in two weeks. I need to find curtains for the bedroom; I think sailcloth . . ." And they talked about the house, and the orders Max wanted her to give the maintenance man and the gardener, and how she should forward his mail to the Marseilles office, and a dozen other topics, and buried in their conversation was the fact that both of them had decided that day not to tell the other what was most urgent to each of them. And in protecting each other by keeping silent, they were perhaps closer than at any time since Stephanie had awakened in the hospital and Max had told her he was her husband.

Stephanie held that closeness to her when he left the next day. He had bent over the bed to kiss her goodbye before the sky was fully light, telling her he loved her and would miss her and would call every evening. "Take care of yourself," she had said, and when he saw the worry in her eyes, he bent down and kissed her again, and then took his suitcase and was gone.

Stephanie and Madame Besset conferred on what they would need in the house for the next two weeks, she gave Max's instructions to the maintenance man and the gardener, and then she went to work early, and when the telephone rang she picked it up on the first ring.

"May I see you this afternoon?" Léon asked.

"Yes."

"I'll be outside at one. Or earlier, if you can."

"No, Jacqueline expects me to work until one."

And exactly at one he was outside the shop in his small car. "I want you to see my studio. And I've prepared a feast for you. Will you come with me or follow me in your car?"

"I'll follow you."

"How much time do we have?"

"As much as we want."

"As much . . . Max is away?"

"Yes."

He touched her hand, then waited while she went to her car, and in a few minutes they had left Cavaillon behind. They drove on narrow, curving roads past neat fields of melon and potato plants and stubby grapevines sprouting new leaves; past stretches of pale green wild grass slashed by brilliant swaths of orange-red poppies. Here and there painters wearing broad-brimmed straw hats sat in folding chairs before large canvases. Their arms were stretched straight out, extended by brushes that swirled, dabbed, swooped across the canvas to create visions of vivid poppies against a backdrop of green-black trees that marked the corners of farmers' fields and, on the horizon, the softly rounded hills and terra-cotta hill towns of the Vaucluse.

Oh, it is so beautiful, Stephanie thought, as if she had never seen the valley before. In the stillness of the fields that drowsed beneath a blue-white summer sky she felt herself moving soundlessly, without volition, dreamlike, suspended above the earth. The landscape floated past her, and the heat and molten light and piercing color of the poppies were inside her and enveloping her at the same time. She was part of everything, she took everything into her, and as she watched the back of Léon's head as he drove, she felt how wonderful and wondrous it was to be alive.

Léon turned onto a road that climbed above the valley floor, and she recognized the way to Goult, where she and Max had had dinner. But before they reached the center of the tiny medieval town, Léon turned onto an even narrower road and then, sharply, into a driveway barely wide enough for the car, walled on both sides by an impenetrable mass of trees and bushes and vines.

Once inside the wild tangle of that natural wall, Stephanie drew in her breath at the riot of color in flower gardens that seemed to have sprung up naturally but were in fact planned by an artist for harmony and scale. And tucked among them were small patches of herbs, vegetables, and salad greens: tall spires of frisée, feathery mizuna, white-flowered arugula, red oak leaf, pea vines, fronds of fennel. Sectioned by flagstone walks, the gardens filled every inch between the roadside hedge and the house.

Stephanie parked behind Léon and stood beside him, looking up at the house. It was built of rough-hewn weathered stone and was perfectly square, two stories high, with windows evenly spaced and three chimneys in the sloping tile roof. A child's drawing, Stephanie thought with amusement, and wondered briefly where she had seen a child's drawing of a house. But she let it go as Léon took her hand and led her to the heavy wooden door. "The studio is in back, but I want you to see the house first."

They walked into a central hall that cut through the house to the back door. Square, high-ceilinged rooms opened off either side of the hall, with polished stone floors, fringed Moroccan rugs, and couches and chairs of leather or intricately patterned wool. Huge paintings hung on the walls, abstracts by Tàpies and Rothko, a great blue horse by Rothenberg, drawings by de Kooning and Morisot. "My favorites," Léon said. "I don't hang my own work in my house."

They went through the back door to another building, a smaller version of the house, set amid more gardens and shaded by cypress trees. Léon unlocked the door and stood aside for Stephanie to go ahead of him. He stayed back, watching her as she stood in the center of the room beneath a twenty-foot ceiling. Under a hard bright light from a north-facing glass wall, there was color everywhere: canvases covered with an explosion of colors in slashing angles and flowing curves that spilled over into a confusion of paint-spattered chairs, tables, ladders, easels, high stools, and benches. Fluorescent fixtures hung from the ceiling, two potted tree geraniums covered with blooms stood near the window, a radio played Mozart, an armchair and daybed were covered with fabrics designed by Claire Goddard. Rolls of canvas stood in a corner near a coat tree missing an arm, a coffeepot stood on a small sink, and the tables were buried beneath books, thumbed and tattered magazines, pots of brushes and pencils, and stacks of sketch pads.

And on all the walls, tacked close together, were pictures of Stephanie.

Stunned, she turned in place, seeing herself repeated in charcoal sketches of a few swift lines, in washes of watercolor, in the bolder lines of crayon, in pencil, in pastel. She was sitting on the rocks at Fontaine-de-Vaucluse and in the forest at Saint-Saturnin; she was pensively drinking coffee at an outdoor café, lighting a lamp at Jacqueline en Provence, reading a book, daydreaming beside an open window. But most of the pictures were portraits, her face filling the canvas in full view, in profile, or turning away, the painter desperately trying to stop her before she escaped.

And always, in the curve of her mouth, the angle of her head, the shadow in her eyes, there was a sadness, a sense of loss underlying every other mood that Léon had caught. "Even when I smile," Stephanie said wonderingly, and looked back at him. "Is that true? It's always there?"

"So far. Sometimes more strongly than others."

Their eyes met across the studio and she wondered that he saw so deeply into her. He had not moved since she walked into the room and she realized how great was his capacity for stillness. She recalled it from their picnic at Saint-Saturnin: he settled into place, observing and reflecting, his imagination transforming what he saw, creating paintings in his mind so that, when he stood before a canvas, it was as if he played it all out, like a fisherman with his line.

"How do you see that in me? No one else sees it: Robert, Max, Jacqueline . . ."

"Perhaps I look more closely because I love you."

"But you see more than most people, in everything."

He smiled. "You're right; there's more to it than love."
He closed the door and walked into the studio, absently
picking up a tube of paint and replacing it in its rack. "The
first law of painting—I'm sure writers would say the same
thing about their work—is to take in everything unfiltered,
without thinking about order or even meaning. The important thing is to concentrate and absorb. When we're
young we hear only our own voice and we pay our most
ardent attention to what touches us; many people never get
beyond that, no matter how old they are. But anyone who
wants to create must learn to see and hear more than the
obvious and the personal. It's like sitting by a lake and
suddenly seeing a trout break the water and leap up to
catch an insect. When it leaps, you realize you've been
seeing ripples all along—faint, but enough to let you know
the trout was there. So you train your eye and you concentrate, and after a while, under calm surfaces you see
other worlds, parallel to the visible one, and far more
complex." He gave a rueful laugh. "I'm sorry; I'm sounding pompous."

"You sound like a man who thinks about what he does
and understands it and loves it."

"In this case, with these drawings, I love you. I've
been waking up at night and drawing you, and drawing
you while I eat and walk in the woods, and when I'm
supposed to be working on two paintings I've promised
my gallery in Paris by the first of September. I found great
joy in it, perhaps because I imagined you were thinking of
me all those times I reached for chalk and pencil and
paint."

"Yes."

Stephanie moved closer to the paintings and studied
each one, walking slowly around the room. And suddenly
she found herself before an oil painting, the only one in
the collection, and it was of two of her.

"My two Sabrinas," Léon said, standing beside her.

In the painting, two women, identical except for their
dress, faced each other, faintly smiling, so absorbed in

each other that they had shut out the rest of the world. The light slanted across them at such an angle that one Sabrina was in sunlight while the other was in shadow.

Stephanie gazed at the painting for a long, silent time. She felt strangely happy, almost buoyant, held fast by the two women; she did not want to walk away from them. "It's very strange," she said at last. "I know I've seen this before. But that can't be, can it?"

"No. I painted it yesterday and last night. Perhaps you dreamed there were two of you? The Sabrina you can't remember and the Sabrina you are today?"

"I suppose . . . That must be it; what else could it be? Léon, I want to buy this. May I?"

"You will not buy it, what are you thinking? It's yours, all of these are yours. You need not ask; take what you wish."

"Thank you. Just this one. It makes me feel at home. That's where I'll hang it: in my own place."

"Your own place?"

Still looking at the painting, Stephanie said, "I'm going to find a place to live in Cavaillon. I can't live with Max anymore."

Léon drew in his breath. He turned her to him. "You're sure? You must not leave him because it is what I want."

"You didn't tell me you wanted it."

"No, of course not; how could I do that? I thought of it all weekend, but I knew it had to come from you. And you must be very sure, because you've lived with him and you feel loyal to him."

"But I don't want to spend my life with him. I want to spend it with you."

He studied her face, then sighed as if he had been holding his breath, and he kissed her, his mouth opening hers as his arms tightened. Stephanie felt their bodies fit together, shift and nestle in small adjustments until there was no space between them. She felt again the heat she had felt in the car, the dreamlike suspension, the brilliant colors exploding soundlessly around her. Heat and light and colors were all inside her and enclosing her; she was open to everything, part of the hugeness of life. Her arms were around Léon, her hand on the back of his head as they kissed, and suddenly a fleeting image came, of a white hospital room and a fog of nothingness. But it vanished as soon as it had come: there was no room for it in what surged through her now: the unfathomable vivid wonder of loving and of being alive.

"We could delay lunch," Léon murmured.

"Yes. Later."

They moved together to the daybed in the corner and lay on it and took off each other's clothes, Stephanie's gauze skirt over bare legs and her sheer cotton blouse with a deep V neck, and Léon's duck pants and short-sleeved shirt. "Thank God for summer," he said, "so little, and so easily removed."

Stephanie laughed with the joy of their bodies touching. This time, with hours before them, they explored each other, tasted each other, learned the outlines of each other's body. Léon's hands, a painter's hands, moved over her body as if he were discovering and revealing her at the same time. And Stephanie's hands, which had learned to identify the carvings of antique furniture and jewelry by touch as well as by sight, curved around the muscles and bones and hollows of Léon's body, memorizing him, making him hers.

In the wash of white light that poured through the glass wall, every angle of their bodies was accentuated, every pore, every fine hair, every pale vein that pulsed beneath their touch. "This is what I am doing when I draw you," Léon murmured, his mouth moving down Stephanie's body from her lips to her throat to her breasts. "I am kissing you and whispering to you and feeling the silk of your skin under my brush, and then"—he moved to lie on her—"I am inside you and you are pulling me deeper, making me one with you . . ."

A low laugh rippled in Stephanie's throat. "You can't do all that and go on drawing."

"No. Which is why I am not drawing now."

"I love you," Stephanie said, and touched his face.
And then their bodies moved together and spoke for them,
and they were silent.

Max and Robert sat in the small motorboat, sharing
sandwiches and a thermos of coffee. They could not make
out each other's face in the faint light from the distant
shore, but they talked casually, like good friends. The
intense heat of the early evening had eased, and they sat
back, in shirtsleeves and chino pants, breathing deeply of
the fresh sea air.

"Thank you for being here," Robert said. "I would
have asked someone else, but my friend got sick so late,
the time was getting short—"

"It's all right, Robert. You needed help and you knew
I'd be here."

"But you were on your way home."

"I'll still go tonight; you know that. As soon as we've
finished, we'll all drive back."

"It's not difficult, you know, but it always goes more
smoothly with two. So I do thank you, and so will Jana
when she gets here; it is a great favor to both of us.
Sabrina will be glad to see you; this has been a long trip,
has it not?"

"Two weeks."

"A long time away from her."

"Too long. It's the damnedest thing: I think I go a little
crazy without her. After a few days it gets hard to eat and
sleep. I don't understand it; I act like a smitten adolescent." He heard himself with surprise. It must be the
darkness, he thought; otherwise I'd never have said that.
But this is almost like talking to myself. And Robert is
never judgmental. "Anyway, I won't leave her again. We
may even go away."

"You mean take a trip? No, that was not in your voice.
What did you mean, Max?"

Max considered telling him, then decided against it. He

had changed some of his plans and made new ones in the two weeks just ended, so it was impossible that Denton or anyone else would know them, but still, the fewer who had any information at all—even including Robert—the safer he would feel. "I meant a trip. We haven't traveled together. Is that the freighter?"

"Ah. Yes. On time."

They watched through binoculars as the freighter from Chile made its slow way toward them. "Five minutes," Robert said. "Ten at the most."

Max heard the tremor in his voice. "Why are you nervous? You just said it wasn't difficult. And you've done it often enough; it ought to be as simple as a game of croquet."

"My friend, croquet is filled with snares for the unwary."

"But you're not unwary."

"No. And I'm not usually this nervous. I suppose it's because she's so small, almost like a child, and so I think of her as a child, as vulnerable as a child."

"Robert, she's been teaching peasants how to fight for their rights in a country that tears people like her to pieces; she wanted to go there and you wouldn't have sent her if you'd thought she was as vulnerable as a child."

"I know. But still, so small, in such a harsh world . . ."

"Which she thinks she can make better."

"She is making it better. She knows that; they all do, all the young people who go off so bravely to wherever there is injustice. They all come from privileged families; have I told you that? They are wealthy, well educated, accustomed to luxury and the indulgences of a world that admires and rewards wealth more than poverty. But they find their way to me because they need something more, something they can point to and say, 'I did this and in my own small way I made the world a better place.' "

Max was silent, thinking of his life: smuggling and amassing wealth. The boat rocked gently; the freighter was almost up to them. Robert leaned down and lit a lantern, shading it with his cap.

"And that is why you help me, my friend. So that you can say in the cold hours before dawn when all of us are most anxious about ourselves, 'I did this and it helped Robert, who helps many others; in my own small way, I made the world a better place.' And now we must signal." He looked back for a moment. "We're lined up with the last dock?"

"We're exactly where you wanted to be."

"Then she will know where to look."

He balanced the lantern on the gunwale of the boat and slid his cap across it and away, four times, then waited a moment and did it twice again. He and Max stowed the thermos and unfolded a large blanket. Robert repeated the signal with the lantern three times, and then they waited.

This was the first time Max had come with Robert to pick up one of the fugitives, though he knew of many of them, since they often hid in a Lacoste et fils crate when a piece of equipment was being returned to Marseilles. Max's people fitted the crate with a small amount of food and water, and evacuation bags, and when the freighter was at sea a bribed crew member would open it. Freighters always carried thirty or forty passengers—travelers willing to forgo the comforts of a regular sailing ship for a bargain price and whatever romance they found in traveling on a working freighter and eating with the captain and crew—and Robert's young people, staying quietly in the background, blended unobtrusively with them until, approaching France, it was time to rendezvous with Robert in his small boat.

But this night, as Robert handed Max the binoculars and then took them back to focus on the freighter, no figure slipped over the side; no one swam to them to be hauled into their boat and wrapped in the large blanket. Max took the binoculars from Robert, and when the freighter slid silently past and he turned to watch it, he saw uniformed men on the dock. "Something's wrong. We're going in."

"A few more minutes." Robert's voice trembled. "Give her a few more minutes."

Max started the engine and kept it at a low idle while the freighter docked. He was furious. He was the one who bore all the risk: his company, his shipment, himself. "You're sure she left Chile?"

"I'm sure. I had a telephone call. You're right, Max, we must go in. My friend, don't be so angry yet. She may be hidden."

"She damned well better be." He revved the engine and swung the boat around. "What the hell made you think you could trust a girl to do something like this?"

"Max, she is a woman, not a girl, and of course I trust her. You yourself said she has been living a life of danger in a country where they tear people like her to pieces. Why should she not be successful as a stowaway?"

Max did not answer. They docked at the Lacoste et fils warehouse, and from there they went to a bar near the docked freighter. It was jammed with crews from freighters up and down the Marseilles dock, the air thick with cigarette smoke, the noise deafening. Robert, less noticeable and memorable than Max, slipped through the crowd, listening, asking questions. He returned to Max, who had bought two beers, and they found a place to lean against the wall. "Customs. They'll make a special search of the cargo. They choose at random; they chose this one. We have to—"

"They just happened to choose this one the night your girl is on board? How do we know they weren't tipped off?"

"We don't. But it would have had to come from Chile—"

"Or whomever they bribed on board."

"Yes, but then they would be looking for a stowaway, and the police would be here. All they're talking about is a routine customs check. Well, not routine, but a more thorough one, and they do those often. At random. We have to think about—"

345

"Fuck it," Max muttered.

"Max, this is not like you. You knew there was a risk; there's always been a risk, every time you've helped us bring someone out or in. Why is this night different from all other nights?"

"I don't know."

But he did. He felt things were closing in. For the first time he wondered if going to Los Angeles was realistic, or Rio, or Buenos Aires, or anywhere else. Since October he had behaved as if he was living a normal life, married, working, relaxing in short car trips around Provence. Not hiding, not on the run. But it was all pretense. Nothing about his life was normal. He was not married, he was in hiding, and soon he would be on the run. He had brushed all that aside because he wanted what he wanted, and he had ignored reality. *Like a smitten adolescent.*

Christ, he thought, I've got to get out of here.

And he meant all of it: Marseilles, Cavaillon, France, Europe.

While there was still time.

"We have to think about Jana," Robert said. "But we have to know what they're planning. I'll be back."

He made his way toward the bar again while Max stayed where he was, jostled by the crowd, watching through the swirling haze of smoke until two customs officers pushed into the room and fought their way to the bar. Robert stood near them, then motioned to Max to meet him outside.

"They're searching the cargo tomorrow; all they did tonight was stay with it until it was unloaded and locked in their warehouse. Max, she's in there, I know it. If we can get her out, no one will know. But of course the warehouse will be locked . . . and guarded." He turned to look down the dock. "Do you know which one it is?"

"At the end. No, the other end, the farthest from mine. One entrance and one guard. We'd have to take care of him."

Their eyes met. "I'll do that," Robert said. "But first I need the key to your car."

346

Max gave it to him. "I'll wait here."

He walked around the corner and leaned against the wall, away from the entrance to the bar. When Robert returned, dressed in his cassock, his hair and beard neatly combed, Max's eyebrows rose. "This requires prayer?"

"My friend, prayer and clothing have nothing to do with each other. I have been praying since Jana failed to appear. But what I am going to do requires trust, and this garb inspires trust, even though, sadly, in this case it will be misplaced. Now, you will leave the guard to me and I will tell you when we are ready for the next step."

Max put his hand on Robert's arm. "You'll be careful."

"I try always to be careful. Thank you, Max, for your concern."

They walked the length of the dock to a row of darkened warehouses, each with a lighted window beside the entrance. Robert went to the window, leaving Max behind. He pulled a bottle of cognac from beneath his cassock, took a drink, then struck the window with his knuckles and let himself fall just below it, flinging himself against the building.

The door swung wide and the guard stood in the opening. "Who's there?" He was short, with a broad chest and shoulders, hugely muscled arms and a paunch that hung over a wide belt. "What the hell . . . Father? Father, you shouldn't be here."

"Just celebrating," Robert said thickly. "Nothing wrong; just a little tired after all the celebrating." He grinned at the guard. "Getting transferred to Paris."

"Paris," the guard snorted. "That's no reason to celebrate. Full of fags and weaklings, and they take you for everything you got. You know what's good for you, you'll stay here."

"Well, but I have to go." Robert struggled to sit up, and held out the bottle. "Have a drink in my honor, even if you don't like Paris."

"Can't, Father, I'm working."

"Just one, to wish me well. Now you've got me worried about how I'll get along there."

"Well, one . . . what the hell." He took a swig from the bottle and wiped his mouth with the back of his hand. "But that was to you, Father; not to Paris or anywhere but Marseilles."

"Then we should drink to Marseilles. A great city."

"Well, why not?"

Another bottle appeared from beneath Robert's cassock. The two men sat together beneath the illuminated window, drinking to the guard's wife, to his four sons and three daughters, to his brothers and sisters, to his grandfather who worked in an olive oil cooperative, and then to the olive oil cooperative. Robert was faking it with small sips but still he thought perhaps he could not hold out against the guard, until at last he saw the guard's head nod, jerk up, nod again, and at last stay down, his chin on his chest, gentle snores lifting the edge of his undershirt.

Robert walked to the corner of the warehouse, and Max joined him. "That gentleman has a capacity of truly staggering proportions. He has a key ring but I don't think we can get it off his belt."

"Then we'll take the belt. But first bring him inside."

They dragged the guard into his room, then unfastened his belt and pulled it through his pants loops. He snorted as they took off the key ring and the keys clattered together.

Max bent over him. "Sound asleep. How much did he drink?"

"Just under one bottle."

"He'll have a good time explaining that tomorrow; more likely he'll fabricate a sudden attack of flu. Hold on while I check the logbook."

He ran down the columned entries in the book on the guard's desk until he found the shipment being returned to Lacoste et fils. "Fifth floor. We'll walk; I don't want to chance the elevator. And we'll move fast, Robert; I don't know how often someone comes to check on the guards."

He unlocked the warehouse door and they used the light from the guard's office to locate the stairway before locking the door behind them. Max jammed the key ring into his pants pocket and they made their way to the stairs. The staircase had windows at each landing, so they kept their flashlights off, guiding themselves in the blackness by keeping a hand on the wall. They climbed fast and steadily, counting five floors until they came to a steel door that Max eased open. "Ten minutes; less if possible." He was breathing hard and thought fleetingly that he was out of shape; he ought to ride a bicycle like Robert, whose breathing had barely changed.

The windowless floor was pitch black and they turned on their small flashlights. There was a sudden scratching, and then a scampering sound. Robert spun around. "Who is that? It may be—"

"It's not your girl. It's a rat. The warehouses are full of them. You start on the left; I'll go to the right. Hurry."

Narrow aisles stretched the length of the huge room between ghostly crates that loomed up in the narrow beams from their flashlights: crates as big as rooms and smaller ones stacked to the ceiling. Playing the flashlight beams on the shipper and destination stamped on each crate, they moved swiftly up and down the aisles, in dead silence. No sound penetrated from the dock below; the scampering had stopped. Max thought he might have suddenly gone deaf and he tapped his flashlight on a crate, for reassurance. Then, in the next aisle, he found his crate, and said, "Robert. Here. Quickly."

"Where are you?"

"Here." He shone the flashlight on the ceiling and Robert used the pinpoint of light as a guide to make his way up and down the aisles to him. "The crate is here; there's no sound from inside."

"She doesn't know your voice. She'd be very still. Keep talking. It helps me find you."

"Shall I recite poetry? Or tell tales from the Arabian Nights? Hurry, damn it; I want to get out of here."

"Max, I can't leap over these crates and fly to you."

"You haven't tried."

Robert chuckled. He felt very close to Max, their voices mingling in the darkness, danger hanging in the air. He turned a corner and saw Max holding his flashlight up to the ceiling, and he grinned, even knowing Max could not see him, because he had found him and they were together. "Thank you for the beacon. But what now? How do we open the crate?"

"With this." Max handed Robert his flashlight, took a chisel from his pocket, and began to pry open the side facing them.

Robert held the flashlight. "Do you remember the time I said I felt that we were two boys smoking behind the barn where the grown-ups couldn't find us?"

"How does it happen that a priest understands the rush one gets from danger? Most priests live unnaturally secluded lives; you're an anomaly, and even you—"

"There are more of us than you think, my friend, who believe that God looks kindly on action."

"But even you don't court danger; you simply do good."

"There is nothing simple about it. No, I don't court danger, Max, but I recognize its seductive nature. One could get hooked, as the young people say."

"Well, maybe you do court it; probably we all do. No game would seem worth the candle if it had no danger and we weren't sure that it had the potential to explode in our faces." He eased the heavy wood from the crate; it screeched faintly as it pulled away from its nails.

"Jana!" Robert exclaimed. He knelt as Max pulled the wood aside. "My dear, dear Jana!"

She was sitting between the wheels of the front-end loader, her knees to her chin, her arms around her legs. "Robert?" Her eyes, enormous in her small thin face, looked up at them blindly and Robert lowered his flashlight and reached in to help her out. She staggered a little, holding on to him. "I'm sorry; I've been here for a while."

"When did you hear about customs?"

"About six hours ago, and I got back in here right away; I thought I shouldn't wait."

"Very wise. Jana, this is my friend, Max Lacoste. We have him to thank for getting you here. Max, this is Jana Corley."

"We'll talk later," Max said impatiently. "Is anything left in here? Food? Water? Evacuation bags?"

"No. We cleaned it out on board. We thought they might have dogs."

"So if we hadn't found you . . ."

"I would have been very uncomfortable."

"Admirable." He made a swift survey of the interior of the crate, then took a hammer from his belt and hammered the crate shut. "Hurry." He led the way to the staircase and they ran down it in the darkness, their hands on the walls for guidance.

They had been in the warehouse for seven minutes.

Max locked the door and handed Robert the key ring. "You and Jana put it on him; I'll watch at the corner." He was breathing hard again; his legs felt rubbery. Damn it, I'm in lousy shape. He looked to left and right along the empty stretch of dock. I'll go with Sabrina on her bike rides; maybe go back to tennis. When we leave France, I'll get back in shape.

Robert and Jana joined him and he led them around the corner of the warehouse to the street behind it, and then through an alley to another street, this one brightly lit, lined with bars, cafés and strip joints. Prostitutes stood at street corners, couples strolled, a family with a baby in a backpack stood debating where to eat. Music blared from open doors to the sidewalks where men sat at tables drinking beer, playing cards, bantering with passersby and with the prostitutes who wandered over for companionship, then drifted back to their corners.

"The car is this way," Max said, but Robert put a hand on his arm.

"Perhaps we could get Jana something to eat before we leave. It's a long ride to Cavaillon."

"I'd rather get started; it's after midnight. Jana, can you wait a couple of hours?"

He looked down at her. It had been dark in the warehouse but now they were standing beside the brightly lit window of a café. Customers on the other side of the glass were only a few inches from them, talking and gesticulating, but Jana was not looking at them; she was looking at Max and as their eyes met, he knew she recognized him.

They all come from privileged families; have I told you that?

Jana Corley, Max thought. Small, blond, thin, extremely pretty, with a tilt to her head and an easy walk that showed she had been brought up with wealth.

They are wealthy, well educated, accustomed to luxury and the indulgences of a world that admires and rewards wealth more than poverty.

In other words, she came from the social circles in which Max Stuyvesant had been visible and prominent. Corley, he thought again. He had met a Corley—Richard, Ramsay, Ralph, something like that. He owned factories in Manchester, Max remembered, and had a home somewhere outside London. They had met, he thought, once or twice at Olivia Chasson's garden parties. And Jana could have been there.

What were the chances that one of Robert's idealistic young people would know Max Stuyvesant and would be smuggled into France in one of Max's crates on the one night that Max was there?

Not one chance in a million.

Except that it had happened. Because such things did happen all the time. People marveled at such coincidences, but they shrugged them off, saying "Small world" . . . one more proof that life was strange.

And so Max Stuyvesant, with a new name and newly

bearded, his hair dyed since he had last been in London almost a year before, stood on a raucous harbor street in Marseilles at twelve-thirty in the morning in the middle of July, and looked into the eyes of a blond radical activist and knew that she knew him.

Jana's eyes widened as their look held. "What did you say your name was?" she asked.

"Max Lacoste." His large body was very still. He expects me to expose him, Jana thought. She felt the unreality of everything that was happening: she was tired and stiff and keyed up from the last twenty-four hours, and now she was talking to a man she had last seen drinking champagne at a garden party in Kent, a man who was allowing everyone to believe him dead. And now he expected her to expose him. But why would I? she thought. He's helping Robert, and Robert is the best man in the world and he probably knows what's going on with him a lot better than I do, and Robert says he got me out of Chile. I'm not going to mess up his story, whatever it is. What good would it do?

She held out her thin hand. "How do you do. It's because of you that I'm here?"

"It was my company's shipment."

"And it was your people who gave me food and water in Chile?"

"Yes."

"And you were here to open my prison. I do thank you. You must think very highly of Robert and of what he's doing."

"We are good friends," Robert said. "Jana, shall we get you something to eat?"

"No, thank you, Robert, but I can wait. How long is it to . . . where are we going?"

"To Cavaillon. You'll come home with me just for tonight; tomorrow you return to London. It's two hours to Cavaillon, probably less, with Max driving. But you should have something—"

"Robert, I'm fine."

"Just a minute." Max went into the café. He returned shortly and handed her a paper bag. "Ham sandwiches and coffee. You can eat in the car."

"Thank you." But he was walking ahead and she and Robert walked quickly to catch up to him.

In the car, she devoured a sandwich, drank the coffee, then curled up on the back seat and fell asleep. She woke only long enough to realize they were in Cavaillon, to see Max's long look as she said goodbye, and to feel Robert's hand under her arm as he helped her up some stairs and onto a couch already made up with sheets and a light blanket.

The next morning there was barely time to discuss her work as they drove to Avignon, where she would catch a plane for Paris and then London. "A vacation," Robert said. "We will not talk about any more work for you for a while. You were in Chile for eight months; that is a long stint."

"I just want to know what you're thinking of, for me."

"I'm not, not yet. There is time, Jana; don't you want to play for a little while? Don't you have a young man to see?"

"Yes, but—"

"Then for now that is what you should be doing." He kissed her on both cheeks and held her close. "I am so proud of you. And grateful; you keep my hope alive. Now go; you'll miss your plane. I'll call you in a few weeks."

He is so good, Jana thought, and that was what she told Alan that night, when they were in his bed in London. "He doesn't want anything for himself; he just wants people to be happy. And to see justice done."

"I'll bet he gets a kick out of it, though," Alan said lazily. He lay beside her, his head propped on his arm, stroking her body. "God, you're thin. It looks as if you haven't eaten for eight months."

"I ate what the peasants ate. What does that mean: he gets a kick out of it?"

"Oh, cops and robbers, cowboys and Indians, bad guys

and good guys. It's a lot more exciting than sprinkling holy water."

"He does more than that; he runs a school."

"So it's more exciting than running a school."

"Well, of course it is. But he really thinks he can make the world better. For everybody, but especially for poor people."

"I know, you tell me that all the time. But everybody likes excitement, you know: danger or just a few thrills. You do, or you wouldn't go to those places. In fact, I want to talk to you about that."

No, Jana thought; not now. I like you, someday I might love you, but right now I don't want to get married; I don't want to stop what I'm doing. I'm only twenty-six; I'm not ready to settle down.

She cast about for something to change the subject. "Alan, do you remember Max Stuyvesant?"

"Sure; he was killed when his boat blew up. Last year, wasn't it?"

"Well, I'll tell you something if you promise to keep it to yourself."

"Whatever you want."

"No, I mean it, Alan; I think we should keep it a secret."

"Then you shouldn't tell me. I tend to talk."

"Do you? I never thought that. Well, then, I won't."

"I only do sometimes. For you I'd keep quiet. And now you've started; you have to finish it. Something to do with Max? A sly fellow, you know; he owned Westbridge. Remember that story?"

"Yes. Would you really keep it to yourself?"

"Word of honor on my titled ancestors' graves."

"You don't have titled ancestors."

"One of them was a duke, somewhere in there; I never paid much attention; it always seemed overrated to me. I mean, look at Denton Longworth, for God's sake; does he look like nobility to you?"

Jana laughed. "No, nothing like the fairy tales. Have you seen him lately?"

"Oh, here and there. We belong to the same club and you know how everybody goes to the same parties. They're all incredibly dull, I might add, when you're not around. Denton's all right, you know; he and Max were close friends."

"I didn't know that."

"Well, actually I didn't either, but he went ballistic when Max was killed. He kept after the police to find out if Max was really dead or not, kept saying Max wasn't the type to die, he had the luck of fifteen cats, that kind of thing, on and on. I never saw anybody as cut up as he was. Are you going to tell me the secret about old Max?"

"Well . . . I saw him in France."

"You mean his ghost? Come on, Jana, you don't believe in ghosts."

"I saw Max Stuyvesant. He isn't dead. He's alive and living in a little town called Cavaillon . . . well, actually, I'm not sure he lives there; he took Robert and me there and then drove off. But he must live around there, because when we left Marseilles he said he was going home, and he looks just the same except of course for his beard and I think he's dyed his hair. Wasn't it red?"

"With lots of gray," Alan said absently. "You're sure it was Max?"

"Of course I'm sure. I saw him at Olivia's a few times . . . in fact, the first time I saw him there was years ago, and Denton was there with Sabrina—you know, his wife? Before they were divorced. Anyway, I saw Max at Olivia's a few times, and then his picture was in the paper in all those stories about Westbridge. It's very strange—"

"Strange! It's crazy. Why would he let everybody think he's dead? Maybe he doesn't know who he is; maybe he lost his memory."

"No, he knew I recognized him. He was waiting for me to say something."

"Well, did you?"

"No. Alan, he was helping Robert; he got me out. I owed him something. And it was his company's crate that I was hiding in; if I'd been found, he could have been prosecuted."

"He could have wriggled out of it. Said he didn't know how you got in there."

"Still, it would have been hard for him. I mean, I'm sure his company is reputable and he isn't doing any smuggling like he did with Westbridge—"

"He smuggled you."

"That's different. That's doing good. For Robert."

"Well, that part's crazy, too, if you ask me. It doesn't sound like Max Stuyvesant, cozying up to a priest and helping him fight for the rights of poor people."

"Well, it was Max and he is doing good and that's why I didn't say anything. I mean, maybe he's trying to make up for what he did with Westbridge, so why not let him? I mean, I haven't any right to give him away, and I'm not going to. And neither are you."

"No, right, of course not. Except, you know, it isn't really fair to people who really care about him not to let them know—"

"Alan! You promised!"

"I know, but, you know, reporters . . . police . . . people like that shouldn't know. But what about his friends?"

"If he wanted them to know he would have told them himself."

"Well, it's hard to pick up the telephone and say, 'I say, old chap, this is Max Stuyvesant and I know you think I've been dead for lo these many months, but the fact is . . .' "

Jana was laughing, but she was uncomfortable. "You promised you'd keep it a secret."

He shrugged. "Whatever. Now, how about if we stop talking about Max? I haven't seen you in eight months and I think—"

"Yes," Jana said, and put her arms up to encircle his neck. "Yes, that would be lovely."

"And you'll stay with me through the weekend?"

"Till Monday. I told my parents I'd be home then."

"Oh, well, we can put it out of our minds, then. Monday is three whole days away."

And so it was not until the middle of the next week, when he went to his club, that Alan ran into Denton Longworth at the bar and told him, in absolute confidence, that he'd be pleased to hear that his good friend Max Stuyvesant was alive and well after all, and living in France, somewhere around Cavaillon.

*G*arth locked the blood samples from Lu Zhen's mice in the refrigerator in his office, locked the office and left the biology building, letting the door slam shut and lock behind him. Anger and pain propelled him across the campus; he was almost running, furious at Lu, furious at himself, and as hurt by the betrayal as if he had been dealt a body blow. The air was heavy and hot even now, at one in the morning, with no breeze from the lake to lighten it; the streetlights were softly smudged in the humidity and the trees seemed to droop and sleep. The campus was so quiet Garth's steps were loud on the paved walk. Lights burned in dormitory windows and he pictured students at Friday night parties or hunched over their desks or in armchairs, reading. Lu Zhen was behind one of those windows, perhaps writing to his family that his esteemed Professor Andersen would soon send his paper to a professional journal; that the years of study and sacrifice were about to culminate in widespread applause and a triumphant return to China.

Almost triumphant, Garth thought. Almost. The esteemed professor was careless, put his name on a fraud, and came close to sending it out for the world to see.

Lu should know. He pulled up in his headlong rush across the campus. *Why wait until tomorrow? I should tell him what I've found, that his paper won't be published, that he's through here.* He turned back toward the dormitories, but this time his steps dragged and soon he stopped again. He wanted to go home first; he wanted to talk to Sabrina.

He turned again and strode through the high Gothic gate at the corner of the campus and then past darkened houses through empty streets to his home. His house was not dark: the porch lights blazed and the curved windows of the upstairs bedroom shone for him. He let himself in the front door and took the stairs two at a time. Sabrina met him in the center of the room and put her arms around him and kissed him, and the tension in his body began to ease.

She smiled at him. "Coffee and cake in the library. Unless you want a drink."

"A drink and then coffee. Thank you, my love."

They walked downstairs, arms around each other. Garth felt her fine bones beneath her light silk robe, the smooth grace of her muscles as she moved, the strength of her body holding him, matching his steps. He was filled with the continuing wonder of it: that there was a door always open to him, lamps lit for him, and love to welcome him. "God, it's good to be here. I was so damned furious, and all I wanted was to talk to you about it."

In the library, he mixed Scotch and water and added ice. Sabrina had turned on a table lamp, and its soft light picked out the familiar shapes of furniture and books and stacks of magazines and journals on the tables and the floor, and Garth sighed, as if he had come to sanctuary. "Oh, what about Penny? Alexandra stayed while you picked her up?"

"Yes. I hope she had a good time; she didn't talk much. I'll ask her about it tomorrow." She poured coffee from a thermos and curled up in a corner of the couch. "Now tell me. What happened with Lu?"

"He faked his results. The experiment didn't work, but he wrote it up as if it had. Brilliantly conceived, beautifully constructed, and every word a lie."

"The experiment didn't work or he made mistakes in doing it?"

"It didn't work. It couldn't have." He gazed at her thoughtfully. "You don't seem surprised."

"I am surprised."

"But not shocked. You never did trust him, did you?"

"Not lately. But I wouldn't have guessed anything like this. I just thought he'd grab all the credit, use you to get ahead, that kind of thing."

"That kind of thing and a lot more is exactly what he did. And I should have caught it earlier. I'd been worried about his results off and on, but he had such confidence and I had confidence in *him* and I didn't watch closely enough. Then tonight I called Bill Farver and he told me they'd been having exactly the problems I'd been worried about. Lu knew about them—I'd mentioned them and he had to come up against them in his work—but he evidently brushed them aside. He could have called Bill or other biologists around the country to compare notes, but he was too damned arrogant—"

"Would they have told him? Isn't there a lot of competition in research?"

"Yes. You're right: they might not have told him. But if he'd asked, I could have called Bill a long time ago. I wasn't paying enough attention, I know that now, but all Lu had to do was ask me to find out what directions other researchers were going . . . he knows I would have done that. But he was so damn sure his way was the only way . . ."

"Or he was afraid."

There was a pause. "Could be, but I think more likely he was so convinced he'd found the answer that he was like a horse wearing blinders. Or maybe it was both: he was afraid and he isn't someone who lets himself question his own theories. But then, when the experiment failed . . .''

He stood and paced the length of the room. He felt Sabrina's eyes following him as he prowled. He loved that feeling of being in her sight, as if he were being held, caressed, encouraged to be himself without posturing, because she loved him as he was, and always would. An uncritical love, he thought, meeting her clear look, that made him far better than he would have been without it.

He moved restlessly back and forth, fingering objects on shelves and tables, skirting piles of books on the floor. "The damnedest thing is that he thought he could get away with it. He's working in one of the hottest fields in science today, along with hundreds of others, all of them ready to replicate experiments the minute they're published, to build on them and take the research even further. He knew that no one could replicate his experiment, because it didn't work, but he went ahead; he built an elegant structure over a rotten foundation, as if elegance were all that mattered. And I wasn't watching. I should have been meeting with him every week, forcing him to explain and defend every step of his experiment. But I trusted him. And I was careless.''

"I don't suppose,'' Sabrina said thoughtfully, "that this is the first time this has ever happened in scientific research.''

Garth gave a rueful laugh. "No, you're right; of course it's not the first time. Or the last: there are always people who will fake results if they're at a dead end. I've never understood how they can do it, any more than I can understand Lu, but I know they're out there. Some of them land on the front page of the *New York Times,* which is where I would have been if I'd sent in Lu's paper. And I wouldn't have been director of a genetics institute, here or anywhere else. I'd have been lucky to keep on teaching; Claudia would have been under a lot of pressure to get rid of me.''

He contemplated the dark fireplace, neatly swept for the summer. "I was so proud of him."

Sabrina heard the despair in his voice, and ached for him. "He gave you every reason to be proud. There was no way you could have known that he'd do this."

"But he lied about more than his work. He not only faked his research and put his career at risk, he put mine at risk as well, and that would have harmed all of us. All those nights he sat at our table, acting as if he liked being part of our family . . . that was another lie."

"He did like it." Sabrina went to him. "He missed his family, he liked being part of ours, and he likes all of us. He adores you, Garth; remember when I told you that? I've watched him looking at you and I know he loves you. It makes me wonder . . . are you sure he really knew all the implications of what he was doing?"

"He's been working with other scientists; he's very smart. He knew."

"But when you talk to him, you might try to find out what he was thinking, instead of straight out accusing him. He may not have thought it through. I just can't believe he'd purposely put you in danger."

Garth thought about it. "I don't know. Maybe. More likely he knew what he was doing and regretted it, but whatever he felt for me wasn't strong enough to overcome the pressures from his family and his government. Well, I'll know tomorrow morning." He took her in his arms. "Do you know, the only thing that cut through my anger tonight was knowing I could come home to you. No one else helps make my world as clear as you do. It's hard to keep believing that we can create order when things get messy, but somehow you do that for me; you help me believe it—"

As no one else has ever done. He thought that but could not say it, could never say it. He could never say that he and Stephanie had lost their way so long ago that for years they had been unable to make for each other, as he and

Sabrina had done, a place to belong and a sense of self that was fixed and solid in a shifting world.

"—and I keep wanting to thank you," he said, "to tell you what you give me each day, every day . . ."

"But you do the same for me. And it always seems new and wonderful and even surprising, and then I feel so grateful, because I'm where I want to be, and I'm with you, and I never want to be with anyone else, and it is so good to love you—"

His mouth met hers, and Sabrina closed her eyes as her arms curved around the familiar shape of his shoulders and his body fitted itself to hers. It was all familiar now, as welcoming as the rooms and lighted windows of their home, and they grew more confident in their coming together with each week and month of knowing that what they had was solidly theirs, not something balanced precariously on the edge of a deception. They kissed and held each other with the effortless merging of a swimmer slipping through water, weightless, almost without form, but at the same time sharply aware of an individual self, exultant and powerful, independent but still buoyed up and stronger for what was shared.

"Upstairs," Garth murmured, "or it's going to be the carpet right here. I've been wanting you all evening."

Sabrina laughed. "You were thinking about faked DNA all evening."

"Part of me was. The other part wanted you. There's always a part that wants you." He turned, his arm still around her, and started for the stairs.

"The lights . . ."

"Mrs. Thirkell will get them in the morning. You wanted me to get used to being coddled; look how well I've done."

Sabrina laughed again and Garth heard in her laugh love and contentment and delight, and felt a rush of well-being, that he had brought all that to life. *If a man can give that to the woman he loves, he ought to be able to do anything.*

Moonlight filled their bedroom, the shadowed corners

black against the pure white light, the patchwork quilt on the bed a soft pattern of pastels, the only color in the room. Sabrina threw back the quilt and they lay on the cool sheet in the cool room, their mouths and hands rediscovering each other, and then Garth was inside her, so easily, so naturally it was like a conversation, their bodies weaving together as had their voices in the library. But it is a conversation, Sabrina thought fleetingly. Whatever we do, wherever we are, we're talking to each other. But it's complete only when we're together.

Garth smiled at her and said, "Yes, my love," and brought his mouth to hers.

They were awake until almost dawn, and all those hours together were, to Garth, another affirmation of his need for her, not only when something terrible happened, but also when everything was good. He held her with a fierceness that came from knowing how devastating it would be to lose her, and he knew from her response that the same lurking possibility also haunted her—that something would separate them: illness, death, or the kind of unforeseen event or mad idea that had brought them together less than a year before. And, caught in the whimsical tangle of chance and probability, they made love with an intensity that seemed greater with each passing week, as the stakes grew higher and their defenses disappeared.

Garth could still feel that intensity and see Sabrina's smile the next morning as he crossed the campus, lightheaded from lack of sleep, so deeply in love that it seemed impossible that he inhabited a world in which there was fraud and fear and confrontation. And the buying of congressmen, he mused, thinking beyond his meeting with Lu Zhen, in a few minutes, to two weeks ahead when he and Claudia would go to Washington, and then thinking beyond that to the politics of a university, the rituals of grant applications, the research projects that were fruitful and the others that ran aground, the time-consuming needs of students who deserved the best he could give them. All of it was part of the world he and Sabrina inhabited, but none of it, he told himself in what was almost a vow, no major problems or minutiae, would come between them. They would be vigilant, they would be protective, and whatever attention and energy it required, they would not let anything come between them.

He had called earlier, telling Lu to meet him at ten, and when he bounded up the stairs he saw him waiting beside his office door.

"Professor, good morning." Lu smiled broadly and held out his hand. "Are we going to discuss the note to *Science* announcing my discovery? I wrote it last night; I have it to show to you. They will publish it in their next issue, yes? And then, later, publish the paper. Of course that should not take long, as you said: major discoveries are published quickly. So"—he took a sheet of paper from his briefcase—"here it is; I think you will find it says everything it should."

"Perhaps not everything." Garth unlocked his office door, propped it open, and sat at his desk.

Lu brought a chair close to the corner of the desk, his favorite spot, and leaned forward, still holding his letter, still smiling. "And what is it I have left out?"

"An explanation of how you expect other scientists to replicate your experiment."

Lu's eyes widened in surprise. "Replicate? But of course . . ." And then, as Garth gazed at him steadily, the words sank in, and very slowly his smile faded.

Garth unlocked his top drawer and took out the bound copy of Lu's paper. He went to the refrigerator in the corner of the office and brought to the desk the vials of blood samples he had taken the night before. Finally, he took from a drawer in a file cabinet the computer printout from the blood analyzer. He lined everything up on the blotter on his desk. Lu watched his fingers as he squared them.

"I won't submit your paper to *Science,* or the note you've written. I'm sure you know why."

"No. I don't understand. You put your name on the paper; you said you would submit it on Monday."

"I also told you I'd go over it this weekend. I read it through last night and something in it bothered me, an assumption about a single gene. We did discuss this, you know, several times, though I didn't follow it up; I was distracted by other things."

"But it is a single gene! If you read my paper, you know that I proved it!"

He looked bewildered and painfully earnest, and for a brief second Garth wondered if he could be mistaken: if he had taken blood from the wrong mice, if the blood analyzer had malfunctioned, if Bill Farver had been wrong . . .

Impossible. Every one of those things would have had to occur simultaneously last night, and that was so unlikely as to be impossible. Lu Zhen was a consummate actor; he knew that, too. "I took these blood samples from your mice last night. This is the blood analyzer printout. You know what it says; you've probably got stacks of identical ones in your files. Or did you destroy them when they kept showing that your mice were healthy?" There was a silence. "Perhaps you'd like to read this one." He held out the long sheet of paper for Lu to take.

Lu's hands remained in his lap. He gave an almost imperceptible shrug. "Well, but you know, Professor, it doesn't matter. Somewhere in going through the experiment, I made a mistake. That was not good, I acknowledge that, but it was only procedural. Of course it affected my results, but not the research project itself; all I have to do is repeat the experiment correctly and the results will be exactly as my paper says. And other scientists will be able to replicate it and see its truth. Professor, I *know* I am right, and that is what is important: the theory and the experiment, not my procedural mistakes. So you see, there is nothing to worry about."

Garth was stunned into silence. He contemplated Lu Zhen as if trying to identify a new species. Lu gazed back at him confidently, one scientist to another. The silence lengthened. A ball thumped against the building just below the office window; students clattered past the open door on their way to the laboratories at the end of the corridor. There was no other sound. It was Saturday; most students were studying; most professors were mowing lawns or doing errands or lying in a hammock with a beer and a book: for them it was a normal weekend. But for Garth it was the end of a dream, and the pain and anger he had felt the night before stabbed at him again.

He showed none of that. He sat motionless, and the minutes passed, and soon Lu could not endure the silence. "So you will send in the paper. And the note."

"No, of course not; you don't know what you're talking about. You've written a fairy tale and called it a scientific paper and called yourself a scientist. You're not a scientist; you have no right to be part of the scientific community. We spend our lives dedicated to research, with absolute fidelity to that which can be proven; we search for connections—cause and effect, beginning and ending, living and dying—and follow them wherever they lead us, and if they take us down blind alleys we look for other paths, and when we find what we're looking for, or come upon something serendipitously, we stay with it until we've proven and proven again that it works, that it's correct and others can follow us, that we've made an advance, however small, in the long journey of science and a new beginning for—"

"Professor, this is the talk you give to freshmen; I've heard you. It is also in the introduction to your book. It's very impressive. But very little in the real world is so clear-cut. You know this; you deal with politicians and businesspeople and they always bend the rules. I bent some information, that is all, because I *know* my experiment will work; I know the results will be found by others. This is my truth and I *am* a scientist and I am as serious about it as you say all scientists should be."

"You would throw science out the window," Garth

said evenly, though his anger was growing, more so since he had been caught repeating himself, something every professor dreads. "You'd publish a lie because of a crazy arrogance that you know the truth in spite of experimental findings that show you're wrong."

"I'm not wrong! Professor, Professor, this works! You have been so excited . . . and now it will bring great glory to you and your institute . . . you will be famous! Even the Nobel Prize!"

Garth felt a flash of contempt. "I called Bill Farver last night, in Berkeley. He's been working on the same premise as you; remember we talked about that? He and his team have concluded that there must be at least two genes, perhaps more . . ." He laid it out, describing other theories and experiments, each deliberate word carefully chosen to leave no doubt. When he finished, Lu was looking past him, out the window, his face drawn, his cheeks hollow, as if he had grown old while listening.

"I had no evidence of that," he murmured. "All the steps I went through, and there was no sign . . ."

"There were signs, and we talked about them," Garth said flatly. "You chose another direction."

"All scientists do that." Lu looked at Garth, and now he was pleading. "We decide what we'll pay attention to and what we'll ignore. I did the same thing every scientist does. Professor, I can use so much of what I've done; it wouldn't take me long to go back and develop a new approach. I know I could find the answer and beat those people in Berkeley; I know more than they do—"

"You don't know a damn thing. You've got a good mind, Lu, but you're driven by arrogance and ambition and fear, and even the best mind isn't a match for all that. You're right: we do decide what we'll focus on, but we don't do it at the beginning; we do it when we know more about our options. You were in a hurry, so you decided at the beginning what you'd find and then you tailored your experiments to find it. And when it didn't work, you wrote down a bunch of fake blood-test results and let me put my name on it.''

"But I thought . . . when I did it again, without whatever mistakes I'd made—"

"The whole goddam project was a mistake! Don't you understand that? And what the hell does that have to do with letting me put my name on a paper that was full of faked numbers? Even if you were right and the experiment worked the next time, I'd be listed as advisor and coauthor of a fraud. That was the bonus you were going to leave me with when you went back to China.''

Lu's eyes narrowed. "You'd survive. You're famous. Everyone says you're one of the best, and you've got your institute and your family . . . you've got everything. But if you don't send in my paper, you rob me of everything. I couldn't go home; I couldn't go anywhere. I couldn't even get a job without a reference from you. I'd have nothing!''

Troubled by the desperation and resentment in Lu's voice, Garth said, "I think you should go back to China. You have your doctorate; you can get a job there. Perhaps some of your other professors will give you a reference. I won't pursue you or tell anyone what you've done, but if anyone—''

"You mean you'll write a reference for me?''

"Good God, after today? I said perhaps others would. If you go back to China I won't publicize what you've done. But if others ask me, I won't lie.''

"You don't have to tell them. No one would be forcing you.''

"Science would force me, my belief in science and in myself as a scientist. If you understood that, none of this would have happened.'' He stood up. "I have to leave now; I promised my family I'd spend the afternoon with them. Here's your paper; there are a number of things in it that you can use again, especially in the first half of the experiment. You did that part well. I admired you. I'm sorry''—he cleared his throat—"I'm sorrier than you will ever know that you couldn't be the kind of scientist I thought you were.''

Lu gave him a long look of pure hatred. He took the bound pages from Garth's hand and left.

Garth let out his breath and realized he was shaking. Damn him, he thought; damn him for the brutality of his stupidity and arrogance. But stupidity and arrogance were always brutal; Garth knew that. He just had not expected it in a young man of such brilliance.

He returned the blood samples to the refrigerator and locked it, then locked his office door. Outside, the heat rose up like a wall to meet him. He was wearing a short-sleeved shirt and khaki pants, and before he reached the campus gate they were wet. It was like swimming underwater, and he imagined himself doing a butterfly stroke, pushing the humid air aside so that he could reach his home.

And forget Lu, he thought, at least for a while. Forget the disappointment and my own failures, and how close I came to disaster. He walked down the somnolent streets. The houses and trees seemed to fade away in the heat, and Garth felt like a ghost in an abandoned town. He met no one else on his walk, though he heard shouts and laughter and splashes from backyard swimming pools, and a few blocks ahead he saw the mail truck making its slow way toward him. He turned up the walk to his house and opened the front door. Cool air curled about him, drawing him inside. What a good place to be, he thought as he closed the door. In so many ways.

He passed Mrs. Thirkell, humming in the kitchen, and went to the second floor. Young voices came from Penny's room. He glanced inside and saw Barbara Goodman and Penny facing each other cross-legged on the floor between the twin Jenny Lind beds, so absorbed they did not look up. A few feet away, Sabrina was sitting on the curved window seat in the round turret at the end of the hall, partially hidden behind a folding screen. She put her finger to her lips and he walked quietly to her and kissed her.

"Was it very hard?" she asked, her voice low.

"Sad and infuriating. Are you eavesdropping on Penny and Barbara?"

"Yes." She moved over so he could sit beside her. "I couldn't get her to talk about the party last night, and then I heard them—"

"—Tinkertoys," Penny was saying. "You know, gears and wheels and stuff, but nothing inside."

Barbara giggled, then her voice came, as earnest as Penny's. "But they're not really like that; they look fantastic, and they wear, you know, these great clothes that my mom won't buy for me, and they do everything! Nobody stops them the way everybody stops us!"

"I know. Except that . . . well, it's like nobody's paying any attention to them."

"Right! They're so lucky . . . I mean, don't you hate it when people are always telling you what to do and when to be home and whatever *they* want?"

"Well, yes, but . . . well, you know . . . maybe nobody cares about what they do. Or cares about them. Or loves them."

"Who doesn't?"

"Well, their parents."

"Oh, sure they do. Parents always love their kids. It's in the genes. Ask your dad."

"But my mom says they're like Tinkertoys because they're sort of empty inside. And she says they don't know anything."

"Oh, come on, Penny, they know everything! And they have all the fun, and you know it. I mean, didn't you want to go upstairs with them at the party last night?"

There was a pause. "Sort of."

"You did! I saw you watching them. And when they asked you, you said you'd be up later."

"Well, you know, if you say no, they make fun of you. And I didn't tell my mom and dad that they were going to be at the party. I mean, I just said you were going. So I thought . . . if something happened, I couldn't talk to my mom about it. I mean, if I did, she'd know I lied—''

"You didn't lie, you just didn't tell her everything. You shouldn't tell her everything anyway; it's babyish.''

"It's not! I tell you things!''

"It's different with friends.''

"Well, she's my friend, too. She always says the right thing.''

"Yeh, like Tinkertoys.''

"Well, it made sense when she said it. Why wouldn't you tell me last night what they were doing upstairs?''

" 'Cause you didn't come up and I wanted you to. I mean, *I* went up there when they asked me and you said you would and then you didn't. It was like you didn't care about me.''

"I kept thinking about it . . . I wanted to but I didn't want to, I mean, I really wanted to, but they scare me, you know, I can't help it. They talk so loud and they tell jokes I don't get and they make me feel stupid. What were they *doing*?''

"Oh, lying around on those leather couches and sort of sliding off them and laughing and telling jokes and drinking beer and stuff, and the TV was on. They were in that little room, you know, with all that leather furniture.''

"I didn't see it.''

"And Arnie and Vera had sex.''

"They did? Right there?''

"No, of course not. I mean, somebody said they should, but they said they weren't into that. They went into one of the bedrooms.''

"I hate Arnie. He was one of the ones who threw me around that day at recess. I hate Vera, too. She laughs at me. What . . . what did *you* do upstairs?''

There was a silence.

"Barbara! You didn't!''

"No. I really wanted to, you know, see what it's like—I mean, it's all they talk about, practically—and they only like the kids who do it, but Joey started pulling me out, you know, to this bedroom, and then he, uh, put his hand here and he stuck his tongue in my mouth and it was so awful, he tasted like beer and he was *sucking* and I thought he'd pull my tongue out . . . yech! I hated it!''

"He was sucking on your tongue? That's gross."

"Right. It was."

"So what did you do?"

"Knocked him down."

"Knocked him *down*?"

"Well, I pushed him and he fell backwards. There was this hassock behind him, you know, and he fell over it."

"Was he mad?"

"What do you think?"

"Well, what did he do?"

"He called me things. And everybody laughed."

"At Joey?"

"No! At me!" Her voice fell away. "They said I was stupid and a tease and a cunt. And they made this circle around me and you know, kind of danced? And I was in the middle, and they were saying cunt, cunt, cunt . . . I hate that word. It was so awful; they were so *mean*. They were never like that before."

"Not to you. Because you always sort of hang around them, like you like them. I hate it when you do that."

"I don't like them, not really. I mean, I mostly hate them. And I never went with them after school or anything, when they asked me, but, you know, I couldn't stand it if they laughed at me all the time the way they did last night. The way they laugh at you. And they really are cool, Penny, and I really do wish I was like them and they liked me."

"They turn lovemaking into fucking."

"What? That's really weird. What does it mean?"

"They make it not loving. You know, ordinary, like a handshake. Or scratching an itch."

"An itch!" Barbara giggled. "Who says it's like an itch?"

374

"My mother."

"Oh, you're always talking about your mother! I mean, she's really nice, but she doesn't know anything about sex; she's too old."

"She knows everything. About sex, too, I'll bet; she and my dad are always kissing. And one time he had his hand here, you know, sort of moving his fingers over it, and my mom said, 'Wonderful hands,' real low, and gave this little laugh like she was *so* happy, and I wished I could feel that way . . . someday. They thought they were alone, you know, in the kitchen, and lots of times, on Saturday and Sunday mornings, their bedroom door's shut and one time Cliff and I listened and we heard them talking and making all these . . . sounds, you know?"

Garth tightened his arm around Sabrina as she rested against him on the window seat. "Maybe a soundproof door?"

She smiled. "I think as long as it's part of our loving each other, there isn't anything she shouldn't hear."

"And I knew they were . . . doing it," Penny finished triumphantly.

Barbara sighed. "I never get to hear anything like that. My parents don't kiss much, at least not that I can see. And they close their door at night, and they get up early, before me. It'd be neat to hear them sometime. I guess they don't do it a lot." There was a pause. "She said it was an itch?"

"It shouldn't be like scratching one, she said. But when kids do it, that's what it's like. And she said it was like something else, too . . . I forget. Oh, like an after-school sport."

They giggled. "Soccer and softball and gymnastics and fucking," Barbara said, her voice rising. "They could put it on the bulletin board and we could check off which one we—"

"Sssssh!" Penny said.

Barbara's voice dropped only slightly. "But wouldn't you like to try it? I mean, find out what it's really *like*? I mean, they talk like it's the greatest thing and I don't know what they're talking about and it makes me feel *little*, like they're grown up and I'm still a baby.''

"My mother says we should wait to find somebody we really love and share things with him; then it would be making love instead of, you know, fucking.''

Garth kissed Sabrina's cheek. "What a smart mother Penny has,'' he murmured.

"She didn't say that!'' Barbara exclaimed. "Did she? Does your mother really say 'fucking' to you?''

"Sure. Well, not a lot, she says it's not a good word, but you know, one time I said the kids at school were talking about fucking and masturbating and . . . you know. So we talked about it.''

"Well, it's easy for her; she can talk about itches and stuff because she doesn't have to go to school with those kids, so what good is that?''

"She says they're infants,'' Penny went on doggedly, "and the reason they laugh at us is probably because they're scared but they can't admit it.''

There was a pause. "She thinks they're scared?''

"That's what she said. That they got in too deep and don't know how to get out and don't know where they're going. Something like that.''

"Well . . . I don't know. They don't look scared to me. They didn't look scared last night.''

"I bet they were, though.''

"They didn't look like it. And when Arnie and Vera went into the bedroom, they didn't, either.''

"Did you watch them?''

"They closed the door.''

"So how do you know they did it?''

"They said so, when they came back.''

"So what did you do then? You didn't come downstairs right away. Did you try anything?''

"Sort of.''

"*You did?* You didn't tell me!''

"I meant to. I was going to today.''

"What did you try?"

"Uh, coke. They were snorting it."

"You did *coke*?"

"A little."

"How much?"

"I don't know. It didn't look like very much."

"Could you feel it? I mean, how did you *feel*?"

"It sort of tickled my nose."

"But how did you *feel*?"

"Nice. Like everything was fine. They stopped laughing at me and they liked me and I felt grown up and . . . good. It was really nice."

"Then what did you do?"

"Oh, sort of hung out, but they didn't seem so nice after a while. They got mean, like always, and they were telling jokes that I didn't get, so I came downstairs and that's when, you know, they opened the dining room and everybody started eating, so I did, too."

"And that was all?"

"Yeh, it wasn't, you know, fabulous or anything. It just felt nice for a little while. You could try it and see for yourself, they'd give you some, they've got lots. Or, you know, if we wanted to do the rest of it, we could ask Vera or somebody and they'd, you know, tell us where they'd be after school or on weekends."

"And do coke, you mean?"

"Well, sex, too. You know. I mean, I don't know about itches and all that stuff, but they keep saying it's so much fun and we could find out what it's like. They'd let us; they told me they like virgins."

"Oh." It came out as a terrified gasp and Sabrina started up, but Garth held her back. "She doesn't need us," he murmured, and slowly she settled back, but her hands were clenched. "I can't believe they're saying these things."

"So what do you think?" Barbara asked.

"I guess not," Penny said, her voice becoming stronger as she spoke. "I mean, I really don't want to. My mother says those kids are messing up a lot of things because they don't know who they are or how—"

"They know who they are! That's dumb!"

"No, like, they don't know what they can be, you know, how they'll feel about things when they grow up. Really grow up, you know, because there's all those things waiting for us—love and adventures and stuff—and we don't know what we'll really want later on, so we should wait. You know, be really grown up before we do grown-up things. So I guess I'll wait."

Sabrina sighed. *Maybe that's the best thing I've ever done.* She tilted back her head and met Garth's eyes, and they kissed, as lovers and parents, and Sabrina felt a rush of thankfulness for everything that was so good.

"Anyway," Penny finished, putting forward her last argument, "if my mother ever found out, she'd ground me for a year."

"A year! That's awful! That's not fair!"

"I know. She thinks it is, though. She says it's important for my growing up. And I guess I . . . sort of . . . believe her."

"You do?"

"Well, you know, when she's talking she makes everything sound like she's right."

"That's just because she's your mother."

There was a pause. "Maybe it's because she's really right."

Garth chuckled. "I like the way Penny thinks."

"Well," Barbara said, drawing it out. "Well, I guess . . ."

"What?"

"I guess I won't do it if you won't. Like, if we did it together we could, you know, talk about it. But I don't want to do it without you."

"Any of it?"

"I guess. But then they'll start laughing at me again."

"Oh, well. We could talk Chinese at them."

"Chinese? How? We don't know any."

378

"I know a little bit. Lu Zhen taught me; he's really nice. When he comes for dinner again, I'll ask him for more words and then I'll teach you."

"It's a lot harder than French, isn't it?"

Their voices changed; now they were relaxed, with no residue of their earlier tension that had seemed to Sabrina to be close to hysteria. They talked about their French teacher for the school year beginning in just a few weeks, and the sixth grade play, and some sweaters that Barbara wanted to buy because all the girls were buying them. A few minutes more and they were on their feet, talking about food. "Mrs. Thirkell always has something; she's wonderful," said Penny. "My dad says she's like the sun and the British Empire, that she never sets. I guess that means she never sits down, or she's always there, something like that."

"You're so lucky," Barbara said. "I mean, having her is like being rich, isn't it? Or a princess or something."

Their voices moved down the hall to the stairs and faded away. Sabrina was laughing softly. "You didn't tell me about Mrs. Thirkell never setting."

"I'd forgotten I said it. How nice that Penny understood it. I hope she understands how much she owes you."

"She understands that she got help when she needed it. And she isn't afraid to acknowledge it. I'm so proud of her."

"So am I. But mostly of her mother." They sat quietly, gazing through the turret's curved windows at the front yard below, shimmering in the heat. A neighbor, looking wilted, walked a wilted Dalmatian on a long leash; another neighbor gazed at a lawn mower in his front yard, gazed at the sky, then shrugged and put the lawn mower away. "It's better inside," Garth said. "It's amazing how many reasons I find to say that. Which reminds me: Claudia and I will be going to Washington week after next, just for the day."

"Yes, she called me. We had a long talk. It was very strange; she asked me how I'd handle them."

"Leglind?"

"And his sidekick. I can't believe that she really needs help with them."

"What did she say?"

"That she was looking for something that would lead to a public retraction, and she had some ideas but she wondered how I'd handle it."

"She didn't say why?"

Sabrina gestured slightly with her hand. "It seems that Lloyd Strauss told her I'd had something to do with solving a sex-for-grades scandal last year."

"A little more than something, my love. You did it all. Of course Claudia would have heard about that. And she likes you; she told me she values your friendship. Well, did you give her any suggestions?"

"We talked through a few of them, and there was only one that we thought might work, though we weren't happy about it. And of course everything could change when you're there."

"What was it?"

"Well, it was very simple, if you can ever call blackmail simple. I thought she might tell Leglind about the publicity you're working on for the institute: the donors and so on, and the opening ceremonies with guest speakers and politicians, and that you'd like him to be part of it, but if he's on record calling for an investigation of the institute as a waste of money, and then the university publicly applauds him for his support, it would sound like a bribe, even though everyone knows how interested he is in science . . . well, you get the idea."

"I do. As blackmail it's very good."

"You don't like it."

"Not any more than you do; it's a depressing way to get things done. It doesn't even matter that people use blackmail all their lives, mild forms of it—well, maybe not quite so mild—and find prettier names for it than blackmail or bribery or whatever it comes down to."

"But what you mostly don't like is that it probably will work."

"That's the most depressing part. In spite of all the good people who find their way to Congress, the ones who usually leave the biggest impression are the corrupt and craven ones. I know it's not only Congress, it's everywhere, and my friends in the social sciences say it's naive to expect anything else, but still it's depressing. And Claudia thought it was a good idea?"

"She thought it sounded more practical than appealing to Leglind's better instincts."

"Since he has none. She's right. Well, we have an appointment a week from Monday; we'll know then."

"Are you dividing up what you're going to say?"

"She wants to do most of the talking. I'm looking forward to it; I've never even heard her raise her voice, much less lecture a congressman."

As it happened, Claudia did not raise her voice in Oliver Leglind's office; she spoke so softly that the congressman had to strain to hear her. "We appreciate your seeing us on such short notice," she said, and watched with quiet amusement as Leglind and Stroud exchanged a quick glance of surprise at the gentle voice issuing from a woman six feet tall with slicked-back gray hair and oversize glasses. "It was, of course, gratifying to hear from Mr. Stroud that we had been exonerated, but it was quite dismaying as well."

The congressman frowned. He was a small man oddly out of proportion, his arms too long for his torso, his legs too short, his eyes peering narrowly from beneath heavy brows. He had thick hair so carefully waved it was clear it was his pride and joy. Garth knew he could be mesmerizing in front of a crowd, working it to a frenzied pitch with dark tales of government waste so dire it threatened the very core of the American way of life. But he was not swaying a crowd now; he was looking puzzled and a little impatient. "I thought you'd be pleased. I was told that you weren't happy with us, that you'd told Professor Andersen not to testify—"

"No one told me any such thing," Garth said. "I was prepared to testify; Mr. Stroud and I discussed that."

"Right. I heard about that discussion, Professor. You seem to think I'm not a curious person. You said *if* I gave a damn about science. You made some comments about my making up plots."

"I did, and I apologize. Those were ill-considered remarks that I regret making. I'm ashamed of them."

Leglind was silent. Garth was amused, as he always was at how disarming an apology is. Few people, poised for battle, can charge forward after those simple words: *I'm sorry. I'm ashamed.*

"Well, now, that's generous," Roy Stroud said. "Not too many people are manly enough to admit their mistakes. But I think the congressman hasn't been told why you're not happy with our decision. And why you're here."

"Because you've left us hanging," Claudia said. "We're in limbo out there where accusations float around but never quite come to earth."

"What? I'm sorry, I don't quite get that."

"She means we didn't say we were wrong about their university," said Leglind flatly. "But nobody can say that, because there hasn't been any testimony, and there isn't going to be any because that's the way you want it. At least that's what we were told. So if that's why you came, you've made the trip for nothing."

"Oh, I don't think so. We came because we want to discuss with you the opening ceremonies for the Institute for Genetic Engineering." Garth saw the twist of distaste in the corners of her mouth as she spoke the lines she and Sabrina had discussed, painting in glowing terms a picture of national and international attention, of wealthy donors including Billy Koner, of guest speakers who included Nobel Prize winners and political leaders from around the world. She held out a list of names. "They're confidential for now, but we brought them for you, because of course you belong among them.''

She paused, then reminded them of Leglind's call for an investigation of the institute as a waste of money. "So how can we include you in this group of supporters whom we are publicly applauding? Others would say we were trying to bribe you. Everyone knows of your deep concern for science, and of course the institute is on the cutting edge of research and teaching, but still, we can't ignore your public statements. Of course,'' she added, ''a retraction now, almost ten months before the May dedication and opening ceremonies, would stand on its own. But that is not in our hands. We came all this way, Congressman, in the hope that you could help us resolve this dilemma.''

Delicately, almost reverently, Leglind took the list of names and held it at arm's length. Stroud handed him his reading glasses. He read it several times, top to bottom. ''Roy,'' he said at last, ''you didn't offer coffee to our guests.''

The *Chicago Tribune* for August 20 lay on Sabrina's attic worktable as she worked on the final set of specifications for the Koner Building. It had been ten days since the paper appeared with Oliver Leglind's statement printed on the front page, and Sabrina still glanced at it now and then as she worked.

It is the duty of all of us who are dedicated to democracy to study and investigate the information that comes to us. When, in our diligent and relentless search for truth, some information turns out to be false, to protect the reputation and integrity of all those involved, we must be swift to admit our error. Such was the case recently with Midwestern University and its Institute for Genetic Engineering. This institute, on the cutting edge of research and teaching, when opened next year will be a beacon to sci-

ence and the world. The House Committee on
Science, Space and Technology received information
questioning the financial underpinnings of the institute and the university's handling of government
grants. The committee would have been derelict in its
duty had it not investigated those allegations. Having
done so, committee staff found the institute, under
Professor Garth Andersen, to be a model for other
institutions; it found Midwestern University's use of
government grants to be fully documented. There is
much that is wrong in this great country of ours, and
it is our duty to find it and root it out, but we must
also applaud all that is magnificent, and make
sure . . .

*All those high-flown words, all that dancing around, to
hide the fact that he cares only about his own power, his
own publicity, his own agenda. And that he's for sale.*

Sabrina turned back to the long table in front of her,
covered with samples of carpeting and drapery fabrics,
tiles, wood flooring, faucets, textured plaster for walls,
and cut sheets of lighting fixtures. The specification books
that she had first shown to Vernon Stern and Billy Koner
had grown to twice their original thickness as the design of
each room of each apartment was described, with samples
of materials pasted in, and the names of the manufacturers
and dealers who sold them. She had just inserted into the
book the latest changes, and now she was packing the
samples in boxes to be sent to the contractor for ordering.
It was the biggest job she had ever done, and as she taped
shut the last box, she felt content and a little sad that it was
over. On the floors below, her empty house drowsed in the
dense August heat, and Sabrina felt as if she were protecting it, like a bird nurturing the eggs in her nest. Everything was silent and still, Mrs. Thirkell on her day off,
Penny and Cliff visiting friends, Garth in Chicago on a
mysterious errand, which Penny had predicted at breakfast
was probably to buy Mommy a birthday present. "Be-

cause it's only two weeks," she said, "and Cliff and I already did ours."

Two weeks, and it will be one full year that I've lived here, one year that I've been Stephanie Andersen, one year since I began to love this family and feel that it was mine.

But a year ago she had had two lives, two homes, two businesses. Soon she would have only one, when she signed the papers transferring ownership of Ambassadors to Alexandra. The house in Cadogan Square was still Sabrina's, but Alexandra's friends had agreed to buy it and would take possession in December. And then I will have one place, Sabrina thought: one home, one family, one business, one center to my life.

Shafts of late afternoon sunlight dancing with dust motes lay like white ribbons across the worktable, empty now except for the boxes she had just packed. Finished, she thought; so many things are being finished. But so many are being started. That's the fun of a family: never knowing what will be around the next corner.

She carried the boxes to the head of the stairs for the UPS driver to take them to his truck, took a last look at the bare worktable, and left the attic, running lightly down the stairs. The telephone rang as she reached the kitchen.

"Stephanie, Vern Stern; I'm just checking on the samples."

"They're ready; I'll send them tomorrow."

"Good. I wasn't worried, but I like to check."

"You don't have to apologize. I'd do the same thing."

There was a pause. "I hope we connect again soon," he said. "I'll miss working with you."

"I've enjoyed it. And I've learned a lot from you; I was going to write to thank you for all you've taught me."

"Write? So formal. We could have had dinner; you could have told me then."

"No, we couldn't," Sabrina said easily, "unless you'll come here. I've invited you often enough."

"Someday I might take you up on it. You know, there's

a downside to being watched over by your friends; there's always the end of the evening when they wave goodbye from their cozy hearth and you go off alone. I'm not saying I'm not glad to have a place at my friends' tables; I am. But you're different, for me, and right now I'd rather not see you happily married and ensconced and ensnared."

"Friends are glad to see that in their friends' lives. I'd be glad to see it in yours if you found it."

"Well, who knows? I do envy you, Stephanie; you make the most of where you are. So many people don't, you know; they keep running after something else: money or fame or a bigger house or car or a new wife or husband . . . if it's there to want, they'll want it. But there's a serenity in you, like a fixed star; you know who you are and what you want to do with your life and whom you want to do it with. I was hoping some of that would rub off on me. Maybe if we do a few jobs together, it will."

A fixed star, Sabrina thought as they hung up. After a lifetime of feeling unconnected. Garth doesn't have to buy me a birthday present; he's given me the best I could ever have. He's helped me find my place.

She heard the front door open. They're home early, she thought. She went to the living room and stopped abruptly in the doorway. Lu Zhen stood in the middle of the room. His face was haggard, his eyes were huge and darting, his tie dangled around his neck, and in his hand was a small black gun. He stared at her in shock and anger. "You weren't supposed to be here."

"Lu, for heaven's sake, what are you doing?" He waved the gun toward her tentatively, as if waiting for someone to tell him what to do next. "*Lu, what are you doing?*"

His head jerked back, his arm stiffened. "Mrs. Andersen, sit down. Please."

"Not until you put down that gun. Lu Zhen, what is the matter with you?"

"You must sit down, Mrs. Andersen. I order you to sit down."

"I will, Lu, we both will, but first give me the gun."
Her heart was pounding. This couldn't be happening; such
things didn't happen to anyone they knew. "Give it to
me." Her voice came out hoarsely and she cleared her
throat. "I'll put it away and I won't tell anyone about it.
Professor Andersen won't know—"

"Professor Andersen!" He spat the name. "He's the
one I came to see. You were supposed to be at your work;
no one was supposed to be home." He raised the gun.
"Sit down!"

Sabrina sat on the arm of a chair. "Why do you—"

"*In* the chair! *In* the chair!"

She let herself down, her eyes fixed on him. "Why do
you need a gun when you come to this house?"

"Because there's nothing else to do. But I will not talk
to you; I will talk to the professor and no one else."

"I don't know when he'll be home. Why don't you sit
down while you wait?"

"I will not sit in your house anymore!"

"Oh, won't you!" she flared, forgetting the gun for a
moment. "We've been good to you, we've made you
welcome here as if you were a member of our family—"

"I have never been a member of your family! No one
ever cared a damn for me!"

"That's not true and you know it; for two years we
cared greatly for you. I know you miss your family and
haven't made many friends; you're alone far too much.
But why do you blame us, when we've tried to give you
a family and a home to come to?"

"That isn't it," he muttered.

"What is it, then? Lu, I'll try to help you, but not if you
threaten me with a gun. Good heavens, is that the way you
treat your friends?"

"I have no friends in this house."

"Well, whose fault is that? We were all your friends
once, and you liked it here: you couldn't wait for the next
invitation. Now put that gun down; I can't talk to you
while you're holding it."

"I need it."

"For what? To shoot me?"

He shook his head. He was very pale and his hand hung at his side, the gun pointing at the floor. "I don't want to shoot you."

"You don't want to shoot anyone. You know it would only make things worse. Lu, give me the gun. It's a terrible thing to stand there like that: it makes us enemies."

He stared at her and she thought she saw him waver, but then the front door opened and Garth came in, followed by Cliff and Penny.

"What the hell—!" Garth exclaimed.

"Stay back!" Lu cried. "Move over there, all of you!"

"Lu, what are you doing with a toy gun?" Penny demanded.

Cliff shoved her with his shoulder, moving her with him toward the stairs. "Maybe it's not a toy."

Garth stormed in, his hand outstretched. "Give it to me. God damn it, *give me that gun!*"

"Don't come any closer!" Lu's voice rose in hysteria. "Stay away from me!"

Garth stopped, his body straining forward. "You will not hurt anyone here, do you understand that? *I'm* the one you're angry at; you leave them alone or I swear I'll tear you to pieces. Come outside; we can talk—"

"I won't go anywhere with you! You want to ruin my life!" He swung around as Penny and Cliff reached the stairs. "Come back! You can't go anywhere! You'll call the police; do you think I'm stupid?"

"Leave them alone!" Garth started for him, but Lu swung back, pointing the gun at Garth's head.

"I hate you!" Penny screamed. "I thought you were nice, you were going to teach me Chinese, but you're mean and I hate you!" She ran to Sabrina and flung herself in her lap, crying. "Why do people have to be mean?"

"I'm not mean," Lu said, the child in him breaking through, but the gun was steady and his face was as steely as before. "*You're* the ones . . ." His voice rose. "You think you can take somebody and smash him . . . *ruin him!*"

Cliff saw him bring the gun up. "Don't!" he shouted. "Don't! Don't! Don't!"

Sabrina cradled Penny, bending over her to shield her small body. She was terrified. He could kill them. The television news was full of stories about angry, irrational people who thought the solution was to kill and who found it too easy to get hold of a gun. She tightened her arms around Penny. *They can't die. Penny and Cliff can't die; they're just beginning their lives.* Panic filled her and she stretched forward to cover Penny's tense, wiry body, which was pressing into her lap, straining to disappear into her mother. *Don't let her die, don't let Cliff die, please, please don't let my children die.*

"DROP THE GUN!" Garth roared and lunged forward.

Lu scuttled sideways, to the far corner of the room, waving the gun at them. "What will you do if I don't? You can't do anything!"

"I told you, we'll go outside and talk—"

"Talk! What good is talking? We talked in your office and I hear your voice all the time, telling me what you'll do and what you won't do, and I know you won't do a fucking thing to help me. You're jealous of me; you *want* me to fail. You think I'll get ahead of you, I'll get a Nobel Prize and be famous, and you'll be stuck here in your goddam institute. But I deserve to get ahead of you! Do you know how I worked for two years on my project? Harder than you ever worked in your life. You don't know what it is to work like that; you have everything, you Americans, you think the world comes to you and gives you everything and you take and take and take and what do you give? You do whatever you want, and if you don't like what somebody does, you throw him away, like a piece of trash! Well, I'm not trash! I'm as good a scientist as you are—better!—and I did my research and my experiment and *you said they were brilliant*, and now you fucking will do what I tell you because now I have the power! You will call the people at *Science* and tell them you are sending in my paper and it is very important and they should publish it right away.''

"All right, I'll do that, I'll call them, but only after you come outside. Come on, we'll go outside; I'll take the telephone with me and I'll call them from the porch.''

Lu narrowed his eyes. "You don't really mean that. You're just saying it to get me out of here. You think you're so smart, you think you can fool me, but you wouldn't call them, I know you wouldn't, because you're too jealous, you know my paper is better than anything you've ever done in your whole life.''

"That paper is a fraud,'' Garth snapped before he could stop himself.

"It is not a fraud! It is not a fraud! *You said it was important!* You were wrong to listen to those other researchers; they lied to keep secret what they're doing. They're jealous, too, because I'm young and just beginning; you should have known that. Because my paper is not a fraud, and I have to get it published so I can go home!''

"No one will be able to replicate the experiment. Can't you get that through your head? The whole scientific community will know it won't work.''

"It will work. They just have to do it right. Anyway . . .''

"Anyway, by then you'll be in China, is that it? And you think Chinese scientists won't know what's going on in molecular biology in the rest of the world?''

"I'll take care of that when I'm there.''

"How?''

"I don't know!'' His voice rose in fury and frustration and without warning he pointed the gun at the ceiling and fired. Instinctively Garth leaped back. Penny screamed; Sabrina cried, "Lu!'' The sound of the shot rocketed around the room; flakes of plaster fell on their heads.

"Lu, *listen,* please listen,'' Sabrina said urgently. "It

won't do any good if you hurt us; it will be worse for you. Put down the gun. Lu, *put down the gun.*"

But Lu barely heard her. For a moment he had looked stunned, but then desperation again held him in its grip. "See, it's not a toy, see, Professor, I mean it and you'll do what I tell you because you're afraid, aren't you? The big professor is afraid! You think everybody is afraid of you, all the little students, but some of us are as big as you, and now you're the one who's afraid! How does it feel? Does it hurt? I'll make you hurt if you don't do what I tell you and call the journal. Call them! Right now!"

"And after I call them, what will you do? Just walk out of here? Or will you think you should shoot us because we'll come after you?" Garth took a step forward. "You've boxed yourself in, Lu, and if you don't give it up now you'll do yourself incalculable harm." He took another step.

"Stop!" Lu cried.

"Think about China; you have a chance there. Your academic record is excellent; you'll get a teaching job there; you have a future. But not if you use that gun." He took another step. "Think about China, Lu; they'll know, they'll hear—"

Oh, Garth, my darling Garth, Sabrina thought through her fear. Always believing in reason. But there are so many times when reason isn't enough.

"Don't come any closer!" Lu yelled. "You don't know a damn thing about China. I'll be fine there; I'll take care of everything. But first I have to have my paper published! I have to have a name!"

"Based on a deception."

"NO! It's good science. And if you don't do what I say"—he took a long step forward and swung the gun toward Sabrina—"I will kill all of you. You don't think I will, but I will, because I don't care!"

His eyes followed the barrel of the gun and for an instant he was looking at Sabrina and Penny. And in that instant, Garth and Cliff flung themselves at him and slammed him to the floor. The gun went off and Penny screamed.

"Garth!" Sabrina leaped up, leaving Penny cringing in a corner of the chair. "Oh my God, my God . . . Garth! Cliff!"

"All right," Garth said. He sat up and knelt beside Lu, who was crumpled beneath Cliff. His body shook with silent sobs. Cliff straddled him, stunned by what he and his father had done.

"How did we do that?" he asked Garth. "How did we know, so we jumped him at the same time?"

"We make a good team." Garth took the gun from Lu's limp fingers and stood up. "All right," he said again, and took Sabrina in his arms. "I thought I might lose you. My God, the thought of anyone hurting you . . . or Penny or Cliff . . ."

"I know." She laid her head on his chest and felt the pounding of his heart. "We were all afraid for each other."

"Daddy?" Penny asked. "What will he do when Cliff lets him up?"

"He won't do anything. He's outnumbered." Garth realized he was still holding the gun. "Cliff, put this in the library. We'll get rid of it later."

Cliff's eyes were wide. "Sure," he said, awed by his father's trust. He eased himself away from Lu's body, waiting to see if he would move, but Lu stayed where he was, his head in his arms, his shoulders heaving. Cliff took the gun from Garth and held it gingerly by the handle, pointing it at the floor and walking almost on tiptoe to the library.

"He can't do anything," Garth said again to Penny. "It's over."

"But the gun went off."

"We'll look for the bullet later; it's probably in some furniture. The most important thing is that we're all right."

Sabrina knelt beside the chair where Penny still huddled. "It's over, sweetheart. Lu did a terrible thing, but he's sorry and no one was hurt. All of us who love each other are still here; we have each other and we're fine."

"I was so *scared* . . ."

"We all were. It was very scary. But now we don't have to be because everything is all right. Penny, listen, now we can say it's over, and feel safe again."

Penny's eyes were still wide with apprehension. "I thought our house was always safe."

"Well, it is, isn't it? Here we are; we're all fine, thanks to your dad and Cliff's amazing flying tackle. We'll talk about it at dinner, all right? But first we have to take care of Lu Zhen, and maybe you'd like to go upstairs while we do that. Okay?"

"Is Cliff coming up, too?"

"Why don't you ask him? I have a feeling he's in the library, thinking about everything that's happened."

"If he's not there, can I come back?"

"Of course."

She went off, and Sabrina sighed. There were tears in her eyes. "It isn't safe. We pretend it is, but the world is full of dangers and they can invade our most private places, the ones we trust to protect us. How can we tell Penny that?"

Garth held her close again. "We tell her we'll do our best to protect each other, wherever we are. That has to be good enough for all of us. I suppose the only true sanctuary is in love and responsibility, but even they go only so far. After that, we have to rely on caution and luck. My love, you were wonderful."

"I was terrified."

"So was I."

They held each other quietly, their heads bowed. Thank you, Sabrina said in a silent prayer. Thank you for this gift of time, more time for us to love each other and help our children grow up.

"I suppose I should call the police," Garth said at last, "but I don't really want to. What do you think?"

"I don't know. He's so unstable I don't think we can just let him go. What he ought to do is go home right away and let his parents take care of him until he can sort out everything that's happened and make a fresh start. But someone should be with him until he leaves; do you know of anyone?"

"I don't know of any friends . . . Oh, there's a chemistry professor from Hong Kong, unmarried, young; Lu's spent some time with him. I'll call him. He's completely reliable; I can tell him the whole story."

"No!" Lu jumped up. "Don't tell anyone. Please. Especially Professor Shao Meng; he . . . he thinks highly of me."

"You can't be alone," Garth said flatly. "Shao Meng is a good man and he could have been your friend if you'd gone to him. He may keep this to himself; it will be up to him how many other people know about it. You have no choice in this; you've forfeited the choices you once had."

"He won't like me anymore."

"You'll have to deal with that. Sit down while I call him. Sit down! And stay there."

Lu slumped onto the edge of a chair, his hands dangling between his knees. When Garth went to the telephone in the hall, Lu shot a glance at Sabrina. "You don't care that he's destroying me."

"Oh, what a fool you are. He's saving you. What future would you have had as a scientist after your fraud was discovered? This way, you'll go home with your Ph.D. and a clean slate."

Lu muttered something.

"What did you say?"

"There are lots of Ph.D.'s. I wanted to be famous."

"Maybe you still will be. But not if you keep on lying to yourself."

"I didn't lie. The others did. Professor Andersen was wrong to listen to them."

Sabrina gazed at him in amazement. *Still clinging to it, after all that's happened. There is no limit to people's capacity for deceiving themselves. And perhaps that is the most devastating deception of all.*

"And now you don't like me anymore," Lu said.

"Of course I don't. You almost ruined my husband and then you came here threatening to shoot me and my whole family. Why should I like you?"

"I didn't almost ruin him."

"Lu, stop lying to yourself! My God, can't you face the world as it is and stop retreating into fantasy?" She looked closely at his bleak face. "I'll bet you can. Late at night when no one is around and there's nothing in the silence but your thoughts, I'll bet you admit to yourself that your research was no good. You may push it away in the daytime, but I'll bet you tell yourself the truth late at night, when there's no one to face but yourself."

He glared at her. "What I tell myself late at night is my own business."

"Yes," Sabrina said quietly. "We both know it is."

In a few minutes Garth returned. "Shao Meng is on his way. Tomorrow he'll put you on a plane for China," he said to Lu. "As soon as you get to his house, you'll call your parents and tell them. If you give him any trouble, we'll call the police."

They all waited together, without speaking, until they heard a car turn into the driveway. Sabrina and Garth flanked Lu and walked him to the front door, then watched Shao Meng's car disappear down the street.

"God, what a waste, what an unbelievably self-destructive waste," Garth murmured. "So much promise, so much hope . . ."

"There's still promise, and hope, too," Sabrina said, and took his hand as they walked back to the living room. "It could be that he'll grow up after this."

"It takes a long stretch to believe that."

"I don't mind stretching. Right now I feel rather optimistic."

"An amazing feat."

"Oh, it's not so hard. Look what we've come through.

Leglind, Penny's and Cliff's crises, and now Lu. I think we've done pretty well. Especially in this Wild West scene; no one got hurt and there's only one small scar on the ceiling. We have a lot to be grateful for."

He smiled. "Yes, we do." He sat in an armchair and brought Sabrina to sit in his lap. "I think of that a lot. How much we have, and how we should always be aware of that, never let it fade into the background."

They kissed, and then Sabrina sat straight, her hands on his shoulders. "I have something to tell you. I probably should have earlier, but I was waiting to be sure everything would go through. I'm selling Ambassadors, Garth. Alexandra is buying it, and Blackford's, too, as a matter of fact; we'll sign the papers in a couple of weeks. And some friends of hers are buying the Cadogan Square house. We'll close on that in December."

Garth studied her face. "The shop and the house. A clean sweep. You're sure this is what you want?"

"Very sure. I've thought about it for a long time. I don't want two lives, my darling; I can barely keep up with all the drama in this one."

He chuckled and they were kissing again when Penny and Cliff ran down the stairs. "Oh, sorry," Cliff said, and took an awkward step back.

"For what? You're not bothering us; we're having a good time." Garth smiled at his children, their faces flushed, their eyes bright with that strange combination of pleasure and embarrassment that children feel when they see their parents embrace. His gaze took in the quiet living room and he saw in his mind the other rooms of his house and he knew that for most of the time they were indeed a haven against most of the winds of chance. Then he turned to his wife, who had just chosen their life as the only one she wanted. He held her close again until she lay against his chest. "A man's castle," he murmured.

Sabrina smiled. "A family's," she said.

CHAPTER *16*

---

*I*t was early September, two weeks after Max's trip to Marseilles, when Stephanie walked into the living room and saw that three paintings, among them Léon Dumas's painting of the Alpilles, had disappeared. Max was talking on the telephone in his office and she stood in the doorway, waiting until he hung up. "Max, what happened to the paintings?"

He looked surprised, as if whatever he did should be obvious to everyone. "I sent them away."

"What for?"

There was a pause. "To be cleaned."

"*Cleaned*?"

"Well, stored." He shoved back his chair. "Sit down, Sabrina; I want to talk to you."

"Oh, not here." Instinctively she had tightened inside, fending off something that sounded unpleasant. "Why don't we take a walk? We never do, and it's such a beautiful morning, I hate to stay inside."

He shrugged. "If you like." He put his arm around her and they walked outside, along the terrace to the flagstone

397

walk that led to the front gate. The sun was burning off an early morning haze, and as they walked at the side of the road, the air was soft and warm and scented with lavender and thyme and late summer roses. "I've left you alone too much lately; I apologize for that."

"You've been so busy." Stephanie had been grateful for his late nights; they had freed her from refusing to make love to him. But now, glancing at him, she saw new lines in his face, accentuated by the sun's glare, and she felt a rush of concern. "You're worried about something. Is that what you wanted to talk about?"

"Yes, but not walking; I can't talk to you this way."

"Oh, Max, of course you can. You just prefer to do it the way you planned, in your office. You always have to be in control." She waited, but he made no response. "Where did you send the paintings?"

He took her hand, surprised once again by her quick perception. Somehow he had assumed that a woman with no memory would be slow to understand hidden meanings and the trail of clues that devious behavior left behind, but instead, he was always dodging her instinctive understanding.

"I'm sorry," he said. "I've been making plans that include you, but I didn't want to tell you about them all at once. I thought you'd be uncomfortable with change."

"Sometimes I am. What change?"

"My business. And our home."

They reached the end of the road and turned to walk along the edge of the plateau. Beside them the cliff fell steeply away, studded with low bushes, stunted trees, and pocked gray boulders deeply embedded in the earth. After a few minutes they came to an ancient church, straight-sided and windowless in gray stone with a small steeple and bell tower. A wooden gate was at one side; Max pushed it open and they walked into a tiny courtyard dominated by a wide spreading tree. A row of tombstones worn smooth by the centuries stretched along the stone wall. They sat on a small bench beneath the tree and Max put his arm around Stephanie. He kissed the top of her head, and they sat quietly for a moment, but he was too restless to stay still; he moved back so he could look at her. "You've been here before."

"Yes. Robert told me about it. It's a good place to think. Max, tell me what this is all about."

"I never knew it was here. Is the church locked?"

"Yes."

Beneath the tree the air was cool and still; not a sound broke the silence. "A hideaway," he murmured. "Except, of course, that it's a dead end."

"Do we need a hideaway?" In the silence, Stephanie sighed with impatience. "Where did you send the paintings?"

"To a warehouse in Marseilles."

"Why?"

He looked around as a man came into the courtyard wearing a leather vest, black work pants and a slouch-brimmed black hat. He nodded when he met Max's eye, and ambled over to the stone wall, looking over it at the roofs of Cavaillon.

"We'll go back." Holding her hand, Max led her to the wooden gate and back to the road, and looked over his shoulder as they walked toward their house. They walked between stone walls and high wrought-iron gates that allowed glimpses of stone houses set amid broad gardens, fountains, statues and towering trees. The sun-washed stones seemed luminous beneath the deepening blue sky; the roses were gold and pink, the leaves of the plane trees dark green, almost black. Max was touched by the purity and soft harmony of the scene. He looked back again and saw that the road behind them remained empty, but still he could not relax; he hurried on toward their gate. "I'm putting a number of things in storage to be sent to us wherever we are."

"You're planning to leave? Why? You'd leave Cavaillon?"

"Sabrina, we talked about this: all the places you haven't seen, places far more wonderful than this. We should start thinking about them, about other countries, other cities . . . Why would you want to stay cooped up in this little corner of the world?''

"I'm not cooped up. I like Cavaillon; it's my home. It's the only home I know.''

"You'll make others. We'll make them together.''

"I don't want others.''

"You may not have that choice.''

Stephanie pulled her hand from his. "I do have a choice.'' They reached their gate and Max turned in. "Can't we stay outside? Why are we going in?''

He took her arm. "I'm more comfortable inside.''

"I'm not.'' Stephanie thought of Léon: of making love beneath the trees of Saint-Saturnin, eating lunch beside the sunlit waves of the Sorgue, bicycling past gnarled vines bowed down with grapes. Léon was fresh air, sunlight, the silver sheen of the moon, the warm, moist earth, and when they were together they were part of the earth, taking their strength from it and from each other. She could never say that about Max. Max was enclosures, interiors, secrets, manipulations, artificiality. Max was not part of the earth because he was determined to twist it to his purposes.

In the living room he sat on one of the couches, making room for Stephanie, but she perched on the arm of a nearby chair. "I won't leave Cavaillon, Max.''

"You will.'' He held her gaze as if he could bend her to his will. "You have nothing but me. Do you think that that woman in the shop will carry you indefinitely while you learn a trade? Do you think anyone in town gives a damn whether you live or die?''

"Robert cares.''

"Robert may not be here.''

She looked up at him sharply. "*Robert* is leaving Cavaillon?''

"Not right away. But he may have to. ''

"Why?''

"For his own reasons.''

"And what are yours?"

Max went to the bar and poured a drink. Stephanie raised her eyebrows. "You don't drink in the morning."

"This morning I do."

"You're only doing it to keep from talking to me. Max, tell me whatever you have to say; you can't put it off forever. I want to hear all of it. Including," she added abruptly, suddenly seeing everything as part of a pattern, "how you make your money."

She had taken him by surprise; he shot her a look. "You didn't believe what I told you?"

"No. Well, partly. But I never believed that you told me everything. And now I want you to."

He paused, then shrugged. "Well, then." He returned to his chair and contemplated his drink. "There is a man who works for me in Marseilles, an artist, a brilliant engraver who—"

"What is his name?"

Max paused again. "Andrew Frick. I protect him; that name must not be repeated."

"Protect him from what? The police?"

"Among others. Andrew engraves money. Superbly. And I sell it, in large quantities, to people all over the world. Some of them use it for personal needs; some use it to bring down a government by undermining their country's currency; some use it to get prisoners out of jail, to arm private armies, sometimes to build schools."

"You make and sell counterfeit money." She remembered his locked desk, his secretiveness, the times she had wondered whether he was involved in something criminal. She felt sick. And then something else occurred to her. "How do you get it to them?" He did not answer, and after a moment she said, "You ship it to them. In construction equipment."

"Yes."

"You smuggle it."

"Yes."

"Why?"

401

"Because the amounts are too bulky to carry, and in luggage they could be found by customs—"

"No, I mean, why do you do it?" She forced herself to look at him, trying to see what he was thinking. She had lived with him for more than eight months, enjoying his companionship, depending on him, but she did not know what he was thinking. His gray eyes were as flat and unrevealing as they always were, even when they were making love. "Why, Max? You don't really need to, do you? Couldn't you make as much money—or, anyway, enough to live on—doing something that isn't criminal?"

He went to her and took her hands, kissing the palms. "I love you, Sabrina; you've made these months the best I've ever known. You've made a home for me. You gave me a place to belong. You're the most beautiful woman I've ever known, and the most intriguing, and I want you with me, wherever I am, whatever I'm doing."

"Why do you do it?" she asked again, her voice cool.

He hesitated, then smiled faintly, a little sadly. "Because, my dear, smuggling is all I've ever known. It's the way I live; it's what I do best."

"But that's ridiculous; you know so many things, you could do almost anything."

"Well, then, it's what I like best."

"But it's the reason you're in trouble, is that right? Because the police found out? Or someone else did, someone who could expose you. That's why you want to leave Cavaillon."

"Partly."

"Well, what else is it? What else have you done? You haven't"—she caught her breath—"you haven't killed anyone."

"No." The irony of it made Max furious. He could not tell the truth, even now, when he was ready to because he loved her. He could not tell her about Denton, or that they were both in danger because Denton had tried to kill them once, because to do so would be to tell her about Sabrina Longworth, about the past he had kept from her. "I haven't killed anyone; I'm not at all sure that I could. We'll leave Cavaillon because we have to, because my business requires it.''

''That's not true. You're running away. But you'll always be running, won't you, and hiding inside houses instead of being free? Something will always come along that will make you run and hide. I won't be part of that. Even if I wanted to leave Cavaillon, I wouldn't run away with you.''

''We won't be running. We'll buy another house; we'll discover a new place. We'll be together. My God, Sabrina, as long as we're together . . .'' He looked at her and knew, with a heavy sinking inside him, that their being together was not an argument that would move her. But he went on, pushing the words at her, trying to make her feel what he felt, if only by the force of his voice. ''I thought of California, perhaps Los Angeles. You'd have mountains there, and the desert and the ocean as well. Far more than you have here. Or Rio de Janeiro. I know some people there; they'd help you find another antique shop, or you could start your own. We'll make a new home. And we'll be together.''

Stephanie shook her head. She tried to stand up, but Max still held her hands and pinned her in place. ''Am I a prisoner?'' she asked angrily.

''You can't walk out on me when I'm talking to you.''

''I can walk out any time! Good God, Max, I've just begun to make a life and you're trying to force me to run away from it. I won't do it! I want to stay here. This is my home and I love it, and *it's familiar to me* and that's the most important thing in the world right now, to be surrounded by things that are familiar. Just because I went to China once and decided to try a new life for a while doesn't mean I want to do it forever! It was just— Max!''

She was staring wildly at him. There was a ringing in her ears . . . *To try a new life for a while.* What does that mean? *What does that mean?* ''Max, did I go to China some time before the explosion?''

"I have no idea. If you did, you never told me about it."

"Why would I go? Max, help me! Didn't I tell you anything that might be a reason for me to go there?"

"No. And I don't believe you went there. Perhaps a friend . . . or perhaps you were thinking about it."

"I went there," she said flatly. "And I was running away." But that was all she knew; the fog had closed in and nothing was left. She had pulled her hands from Max's, and now, caught in the fog and the frustration of trying to cut through it, she went to the door.

Max stopped her. "You're not walking out on me. We're still talking about this."

She saw a flicker of emotion in his eyes: fear, she thought, or perhaps only worry. The lines in his face seemed to deepen as she gazed at him; behind the mask of his beard he looked almost drawn. He's sixty, she thought; it can't be easy to think about moving to a new country and changing life at sixty. Especially alone.

And so, once again, she knew she could not tell him about Léon. Not then, not ever. He would leave alone, knowing the partial truth that she could not bear the uncertainties of a new place or of a life on the run. He could live with that far more easily than with knowing she had fallen in love with another man.

She shook her head again. "I won't leave Cavaillon. Everything I want is here."

"You don't even know what you want. You don't know anything yet."

"I've learned enough to know what I want."

"Nothing lasts; don't you understand? What you think you have is only what you see today. It won't be the same tomorrow or next week or next year."

"Yes, that's how you live. I understand that. But I believe things do last. This town, my friends, this house, this—"

"You won't have this house."

"You'll take it away from me?"

"You can't afford it."

"Oh. Well, then, I'll find something small. Robert or . . . or Jacqueline will help me. And I'll get another job if she can't use me full time. And Madame Besset can always find a new position; she knows everyone."

"You belong with me." He heard the plea in his voice and silently cursed himself. Max Stuyvesant did not plead with anyone. Once again he turned away from her, and as he did he saw on the terrace the man in the leather vest and slouch-brimmed hat who had been in the churchyard. He was leaning against a tree, lighting a cigarette. As he flicked away the match, he looked up and met Max's eyes.

"Christ, she told someone. That damned girl, Robert's fucking do-gooder . . ." He strode to the terrace door. *Confront them; they can't think I'm afraid.* "What the hell are you doing here? Get out! Marcel!" he shouted, and the gardener appeared around the corner of the house. "Get him out of here; he's lost or drunk. And after this, God damn it, keep the gate locked."

He turned back, his hands jammed in his pockets. "I'm sorry."

"What did you mean? What girl?" Stephanie was frightened by the fury in his voice and by the fear, naked now, that lay beneath it.

"Sabrina, listen to me. We don't have much time. I've made my plans; I'm ready to leave, and you're coming with me. You're my wife; you belong with me. There's nothing keeping us here. You've built up a fantasy about Cavaillon because it's all you know, but that's the way an infant thinks of its crib. Any place in the world can be home; there's nothing, anywhere, that can't be duplicated. Come." Without moving from his place by the door, he held out his hand. "Come with me. I love you; I'll take care of you. You're my wife, Sabrina; you belong with me. I'll give you everything you want; I'll make you happy. Sabrina, I promise you I'll make you happy; we'll have a good life."

"No." She stood near the door at the far side of the

room. She pitied him for pleading when she knew he thought of himself as a man who never asked for anything, and she feared for him because of his sudden desperation. But another part of her felt detached, already cut off from him, wanting to have nothing to do with him. "You talk as if I belong to you. But I don't. And I don't belong with you. I don't like the kind of life you make for yourself, Max."

"You don't have to like it; you don't even have to know about it."

"If I stayed with you, I'd be as involved as you are because I'd be living on what you make. I can't be part of that, Max; I won't be part of it. And I can't be on the run all the time, hiding, looking over my shoulder—"

"God damn it, I'm leaving, do you understand that?" He was furious with her for fighting him, for refusing his pleas, his logic, his love. "This isn't a game, Sabrina, it's real, and I'm leaving. Do you know what that means? Do you know what it will mean to you to be alone? You have no idea what that's like."

"I won't be alone."

"You're depending on Robert—"

"I'm depending on myself."

"You can't."

"I can! Stop telling me I can't! You've tried to keep me dependent on you, Max; I know that. You haven't wanted me to recover my memory; you've wanted me to be a little girl, needing you for everything. But I'm not a little girl and I won't be your little girl ever again, and that's not a game, either; that is real."

He waited another minute, his eyes locked fiercely on hers; then he wheeled and left the room. Stephanie stayed where she was, trembling from his intensity and her own. But with him gone, the room was silent, as hushed as the land after a storm, and gradually her trembling stopped. It was over. *I'm depending on myself.* Soon she and Max would part, probably never to meet again. She was touched by sadness. He had been good to her; they had made a home. But everything she had heard and felt that morning wiped out the sadness, and let her think with equanimity of the moment of his departure, when she would touch his hand and kiss him goodbye for the last time.

But she did not touch him or kiss him goodbye. He stayed in his locked office for the rest of that day, and when she awoke the next morning he was gone. It was five o'clock; she had set her alarm because she had planned a bicycle trip up Mont Ventoux and had to start before the day became too hot.

Madame Besset was already in the kitchen, kneading bread dough. "Monsieur must have left very early, madame; he was gone when I arrived a little while ago. Will he be away long this time?"

"I don't know." Stephanie stood in the kitchen, holding her cup of espresso, feeling as if the earth had shifted beneath her feet. He was gone. Not just a short business trip this time; he would go thousands of miles, and he would stay there. She was alone. No, not alone, she thought, but she felt the emptiness of the house, its high-ceilinged rooms, the furnishings that she had bought and arranged over the past months, the gardens heavy with fall blooms, the well-stocked kitchen with Madame Besset its focal point.

You won't have this house. You can't afford it.

She walked to the back door and looked through the glass at Marcel, cutting that day's flowers for Madame Besset to arrange.

Who owns this house?

For the first time in months she was engulfed in the emptiness of not knowing who she was or where she belonged. The fog closed in and panic rose inside her. I don't belong here. I don't belong anywhere.

"A few days, madame?" pressed Madame Besset. "It would help in my marketing if you could tell me—"

"I told you I don't know!" She took a breath. "I'm sorry, Madame Besset; I really don't know. I'll tell you as soon as I can." She wanted to get away from Madame Besset's bright black eyes that saw so much and guessed much more. "I'm going to ride up Mont Ventoux on my bicycle; would you make a sandwich and fill two water bottles for me?"

"Yes, madame. That is a formidable ride."

"I know. I may drive the lower part of it." She went back to the bedroom and swiftly dressed in skintight bicycle shorts, a loose short-sleeved shirt, and bicycle shoes. In a small waist pack she stowed her wallet and car keys, sunscreen and a lightweight jacket, and the sandwich and grapes Madame Besset had given her. She slipped the two water bottles into the sleeves on either side of the pack. "I'll be back by midafternoon," she said to Madame Besset.

In the garage she strapped her bicycle to the rack on the back of the car, tossed her helmet and gloves into the front seat, and backed out of the driveway. A car was parked nearby with a man in the driver's seat wearing a black hat pulled low over his eyes. He seemed vaguely familiar and Stephanie nodded to him as she drove off. It was five-thirty in the morning.

The air was cool, the sky a faint blue-pink, and every leaf and blade of grass seemed clear and sparkling in this brief crisp interlude before the day's heat descended. Stephanie drove fast and easily, passing the trucks that barreled down the narrow roads. Once they had terrified her; now she thought of them only as obstacles to be calculated so that she had time to pull back in front of them before an oncoming car reached her. For such an early hour, the roads were busy, and she concentrated on driving, glancing now and then at farmers in the fields, women hanging out wash in the early coolness, and schoolchildren walking along the roads with yapping dogs chasing each other about their heels. Ahead of her loomed the chalky summit of Mont Ventoux with its radar station and huge television mast outlined against the pale sky.

She slowed when she reached the village of Bédoin, built on a small hill with Mont Ventoux rising majestically behind it. The narrow streets were deserted at this hour, except for the market area where men and women in long aprons were setting up tables and arranging on them fruits and vegetables or stacks of baskets and tablecloths while others hung newly killed chickens upside down, set out rows of cheeses in refrigerated cases, with long curving sausages dangling above, opened barrels and jars of a dozen kinds of marinated and herb-infused olives, and stacked loaves of bread of all sizes and shapes, some almost three feet across. Near the market area was the main square with the mayor's house at one end and the soaring stone church at the other; in the other houses that faced the square people slept or rose to make their breakfast. Everything was normal; for this village, the earth had not shifted. But Stephanie saw all of it as if for the first time because for the first time she was alone.

The summit of Mont Ventoux towered more than four thousand feet above the valley floor, and Stephanie drove partway up its heavily wooded flank before beginning her ride. At a curve in the road she pulled into a grove of cedars, out of the way of other cars, almost hidden from view. She put on her helmet and bicycle gloves and fastened her pack around her waist. It was six-fifteen when she began the ride up the paved road that cut back and forth between cherry and peach orchards and forests of beech and oak, cedar and pine that gradually gave way to scrub that thinned with the thinning air. Through the leaves Stephanie caught glimpses of the TV tower at the top, beckoning her on.

Her body had settled into a rhythm that made her feel she was flowing up the mountain, breathing hard, muscles straining, but exhilarated with her own energy and the cool air swirling about her. Thoughts and images drifted through her mind and she let them come and go without trying to hold on to them.

Max is gone.

I have the house.

But who owns it?

Robert will know; he found it for Max.

Robert will tell me what I can do. Stay for a while, then sell it.

Max should have the money, but how will I get it to him?

And where will I go?

I could live with Léon. He wants that. And I want it.

No, not yet. I told him I was going to live alone. *I'm depending on myself.*

He understood; he always understands.

I love Léon. I love Léon. I love Léon.

The words sang within her to the rhythm of her body. Her muscles began to ache; she downshifted until she was in the lowest gear and rode more slowly. She pulled out her water bottle and squeezed a stream of cold water into her mouth as she rode, then twisted to replace it in her pack. As she turned back, a car passed her, surprising her; she barely saw the driver's black hat as she swerved to the right, skidding in the gravel at the side of the road. *Have to be careful; I might break my wrist.*

What an odd idea, she thought, but her mind was slowing to the same speed as her legs, and she let the thought go and pushed steadily upward, keeping her eyes on the summit. It was closer now and the trees were almost gone; soon they would disappear entirely and only the white stone of the highest elevation would remain, a white cap with the television mast like a feather in its center. The sun was higher, but as she climbed, the air grew cooler. She breathed deeply and thought of nothing but one more revolution of her legs, one more and then one more, and then she made the final turn in the road and she was at the top.

Gasping, she leaned her bicycle against the low stone wall and drank deeply from her water bottle, draining it, then opening the other. It was eight o'clock in the morning and at the base of the mountain the heat was building, but here, at six thousand feet, the air was cold and Stephanie began to shiver. She pulled out her jacket and put it on, zipping it up to the collar. She was alone; it was too early for tourists, and the restaurant was not yet open. The only sound was the steady rush of wind that gave the mountain its name. Stephanie left the bicycle and, nibbling a bunch of grapes, walked slowly around the summit, circling the white and red air force radar station and the long, low building housing scientific and television equipment, gazing at the scene below.

The Provençal plain spread on all sides like a verdant ring, and beyond it in a great circle of green and buff and blue were the Alps, capped with snow, the Lubéron, the Pyrenees, the Rhône Valley with its broad river winding in lazy curves to the horizon, shining silver in the sun, Marseilles and the lighthouses of the Berre lagoon, and the Alpilles chain that Stephanie had first seen in Léon's painting. *Léon should be here; we should be seeing this together. So much beauty, so much magnificence, such a glorious world.*

She felt a piercing happiness. Everything is waiting for me: a new life, a whole life, with Léon. Because I will remember, however long it takes, and then I'll be the person I was and the person I am now. And I'll have everything I could ever want.

She was smiling to herself, in love with Léon, with life, with all the possibilities that awaited her, when a shadow fell near her and she looked up into the face of a man who had come up behind her. He held a gun, so small it looked like a shiny silver toy palmed in his gloved hand, but it was aimed at her, and it was so close that her arm brushed it in turning. She gave a sharp cry and he gripped her arm with his other hand.

"Shut up. Don't say anything, just stand here, just the way you are, like you're looking at the view. People may come."

"What do you want?" Her voice sounded strange to her. "I don't have much money, you can have what I've got, it's in my pack. Take—"

"Shut up! Keep your voice down!" His black slouch hat almost touched Stephanie's forehead and their bodies were so close she could see small scratches in his leather vest. "I don't want your money. I want your husband. Where is he?"

"I saw you yesterday! In the churchyard. And this morning you were outside our house, in your car."

"*Where is he?*"

"I don't know."

"The fuck you don't." He pushed the gun upward into Stephanie's breast and she gasped. "I was outside your house all night; he didn't leave, but he's not there now. Where is he?"

"He did leave. He's gone." Now it was real, the man, the gun, the darkening sky. She was trembling and breathing rapidly; the gun cut into her breast and the man's face, so oddly cherubic with a tiny nose above full, red lips, was so close to hers she could feel his breath. Léon, Léon, Léon, she thought wildly; I can't die; we haven't even begun. "You're hurting me. What do you want?"

"Where did he go?"

"I told you, I don't know! I can't tell you! Please stop . . . you're hurting me."

"You stupid cunt, I'll stop when you tell me where the fuck he is. He didn't go to Marseilles; I checked. *Where is he?*"

"I don't know!" *He knows about Max's warehouse in Marseilles. What else does he know? Where does he come from?* "What do you want him for? What do you want of us?"

"I want him. I don't give a fuck for you if you tell me where he is."

"I can't tell you. He left while I was asleep; he didn't tell me where he—"

"You're lying." He tightened his grip on her arm, twisting it until she cried out.

"I'm not, I'm not. Please, that hurts, please leave me alone, there's nothing I—"

"Christ, this is like a fucking conversation. Okay, you're coming with me; if you won't talk, you'll take me to him."

"I can't!" Her fear exploded. "Damn you, I don't know where he is! We don't live together anymore!"

He was taken aback. The gun relaxed slightly against Stephanie's breast. "Since when?"

"Last night. He left and he's not coming back and that's all I know."

"Bullshit. I saw you at that church, all lovey-dovey; there's no way he was about to walk out on you."

Stephanie looked at him in despair, not knowing what else to say. "He's gone. He's not coming back."

"Fuck." He looked around as a tour bus pulled into the parking area a hundred feet away. "Come on, we're getting out of here."

"Why? I can't tell you anything! Can't you just leave, please, just go away? I told you, *I swear*, there's nothing—"

"Shut up!"

Men and women in straw hats and brightly printed cotton shirts and dresses, with cameras slung around their necks, were streaming out of the tour bus. The man pushed Stephanie before him along the low wall until they had rounded a corner and were behind the radar station. "My car's over there, around the corner," he said and gestured with the gun toward the end of the viewing area where Stephanie had left her bicycle. "You walk nice and quiet right next to me, and keep your mouth shut."

"Where are we going?"

"To your husband, like I said." He eyed Stephanie's long bare legs, then once again nudged her breast with his gun, this time a little playfully. "We might stop and have some fun on the way, though." Swiftly he reached down and shoved his hand between her legs. "Nice. Real nice. There's no hurry, is there? He'll be waiting for you, wherever he is."

"No!" Stephanie cried, and in desperation said, "If you touch me I'll never tell you where he is."

The man cocked an eyebrow. "See? I knew all along. And you'll tell me, you little cunt; you think you won't, but when I get through with you, you'll—'' Raised voices came from the direction of the tour bus. "Get going, to the car." He jammed the gun against Stephanie's ribs and edged her with him to the corner of the radar station. He stopped there, gripping Stephanie's arm to keep her out of sight, and casually looked around. A few feet away stood the low building housing television and scientific equipment, its door closed. It was built in the shape of an L, and he pushed Stephanie before him across the small open space to the sheltered corner at the back of the low building.

They stood there, waiting. Stephanie's body was like ice, her breathing shallow, her muscles taut. She was terrified of the cheerful smile on the man's cherubic face and the way his eyes raked her. She could still feel the pressure of the gun barrel pushing into her breast and his hand between her legs. She looked around, but there was nowhere to run; the rock-strewn, treeless summit was bare except for the two vacant buildings and the tourists cheerfully exclaiming in German over the view, their cameras clicking.

But within a few minutes they were leaving. Cameras and binoculars were put away and they climbed inside the bus, the driver counting as they mounted the steps. The door swung shut with a hydraulic hiss and they were gone.

"Now." The man pulled Stephanie's hand through his arm, like a gentleman taking a stroll with his lady. But at that moment a car sped up the road, careened across the parking area, and scraped the man's car as it stopped beside it. "What the fuck—" he began and then he saw, around the corner of the building, as Stephanie did, that the driver was Max.

"Hey. How about that." As Max opened the door and stepped from his car, Stephanie felt the arm clamping hers relax, and she whipped her hand free and ran toward Max.

"Max, go back!" she screamed.

"Sabrina! Where are—" Stephanie heard a pop behind her, like a firecracker, and saw Max stagger and fall against the car.

"Max!" She stumbled and fell to one knee, then got up and ran on. Her knee stung and she saw blood running down her leg. "Max, go away, he's after you—"

"Get down!" Max's voice was a grunt, and as the gun fired again he and Stephanie dropped to the ground at the same time. Stephanie crawled rapidly along the pavement, grimacing with the sharp pain of her cut knee, until she turned the corner of the building. She heard the gun fire again, twice, as Max made a dash from his car to the other side of the building; then there was silence. She moved farther until she came to a recessed doorway and she huddled within it, holding her legs to her chest. She could not see either man; there was no sound but the steady rush of the wind. Then suddenly Max was there, silently putting his arm around her, pulling her against him. Blood from her knee stained the front of his shirt, but there was blood, too, soaking the upper part of his sleeve.

"Max, he hit you—"

"Hush." He kissed her, a brief, despairing kiss. "I love you. I couldn't leave you. Stay here. *Stay here.*" And then, his bloodied arm dangling, he left the doorway. He searched along the edge of the building until he found a large rounded stone, and took it with him as he moved away from Stephanie, back in the direction from which he had come. She watched him as he moved crablike, keeping his right side close to the building, until he reached the far corner. He turned and threw the rock the length of the building to the corner closer to Stephanie. It struck the wall, and as it took a bounce on the pavement, he disappeared around the corner.

Stephanie waited. Drawn back into the doorway, she saw only the shadow of the man as he peered around the corner where the rock had struck. Almost at the same time, another shadow joined it and then both shadows disappeared as Max threw himself on the man's back and they crashed to the ground. They fought on the pavement amid the sharp stones, grunting, cursing, rolling over each other.

Max felt the man trying to choke him, one hand driving knifelike against his larynx, and he slammed his knee into the man's crotch and heard him yowl as he relaxed his hand on Max's throat. Max was older but taller and heavier and so driven by terror—*he'll kill her; he won't be satisfied with me because she can identify him*—that nothing could hold him down. The man's black slouch-brimmed hat went flying, blood streaked the pavement, and then the shiny silver gun skidded along the ground.

Stephanie leaped from the doorway and swept it up. "Max!" She crawled closer to the writhing men. "Max, the gun!"

"*Merde!*" Max roared at the man and flung him off. He grabbed the gun from Stephanie's outstretched hand, aimed it shakily with his left hand—but he's right-handed, Stephanie thought, and then realized that it was his right arm that had been hit—and fired.

The man screamed and clutched his stomach. Max fired again, but his body was sagging and the bullet hit the building. "*Merde,*" he whispered, this time to himself.

Stephanie crawled to him and put her arms around him, cradling him. "We've got to get to the car; get you to a doctor. Can you—"

"No, wait. Have to rest." His breath was rasping in his chest and he slumped against her. "Too damn . . . old for . . . this sort of . . . thing."

"Max, who is he?"

"Sent by . . . someone. To kill me. Sabrina, get out . . . out of Cavaillon; they want you, too."

"No, he said it was only you . . ."

". . . a lackey . . . doesn't know anything. That's why I . . . came back. To get you. Couldn't leave you." He shifted his arm, grunting with the pain. "He was . . . at the house?"

"Yes, in his car, when I left this morning. He was in the churchyard yesterday, too; you saw him. Max, *who sent him?*"

". . . doesn't matter. As long as you get out . . . get away . . ."

"What good will it do? He found you this time."

"Chance. A stupid accident. A favor for a friend . . . a good deed . . . should have known better . . . not the type to do good deeds . . . and it backfired. It won't happen to you. Listen to me—"

"How did you know I was up here?"

"Madame Besset. And he'd been on our terrace, so I knew he was around. Went out the back at midnight; didn't see him, but I knew he was . . . somewhere . . . so I had to come back . . . couldn't leave you. Then I saw his car. Christ, so close . . . he could have killed you . . . shouldn't have left you alone. Sabrina, get out, get out, you're not safe!"

"You didn't say that yesterday."

He gave a weak bark of laughter. "I thought . . . love . . . and being together . . . Christ, what a fool, to think that love was enough."

Stephanie was crying. She held him to her breast, her head bent over his. She had never cared for him so much. "Max, I've got to get you to a doctor. You can crawl, can't you? Where are the keys to your car?"

"Left them in it." He raised his good hand and caressed Stephanie's face. "So beautiful . . . made my life bright. Sabrina, listen . . . listen . . . if I don't make it—"

"Don't say that! Max, we're going to your car. Come on, now, I'll help—"

"—call Robert. He'll take care of you. He knows what to do. *Call Robert.* Say you will."

"Of course I will; I'll call him anyway; he'll help us. Now come on, Max, please, I can't carry you . . ."

"Try . . ." Grunting, he tried to push himself up, using his good arm, and at that moment the other man gathered himself together and leaped upon them, knocking them backwards. Stephanie's head hit the pavement and for a moment the world was black. Max was on top of her, crushing her, and she could not breathe; blood throbbed in her head, bursting against her eyeballs. She dragged breath into her lungs and tried to scream, but no sound came. I'm going to die, she thought, and heard the gun fire, and fire again, and with a fierce effort she thrust herself up and pushed Max off her.

She opened her eyes and saw the building nearby, blurred and wavering, and clouds trailing like torn ribbons across the deep blue sky. She felt cool air on her face and a terrible pain at the back of her head, and then her vision cleared and she saw Max's head near her own, unmoving.

She took long gasping breaths and slowly came to her hands and knees. She stayed there, swaying a little, her head down, then moved stiffly to Max. Blood covered the front of his shirt; he was staring at nothing. "No, no, no," Stephanie whispered, and laid her face against his and held her fingers to the side of his neck to find a pulse. "Max, please be alive, please be alive." But there was no response; there was no pulse. She stayed there for a long time, until she told herself that he was dead.

She sat up and gazed at his face, the deep lines that had only recently appeared, his halo of grizzled hair, his tight gray beard. She put her hand over his eyes and closed them. "You didn't have to stay," she whispered. She was crying again. "Oh, Max, you didn't have to stay. You were gone; he didn't know where. You were safe. And even when you came back, when you saw his car, you could have turned around. You could have run."

A few feet away, the other man sprawled across piles of rocks, blood soaking his pants. His eyes stared at the sky. And from the other side of the building came the sound of a tourist bus lumbering up the hill.

They were hidden from the main parking lot and viewing platform by the long side of the building. Without thinking it through, Stephanie knew she had to hide them. She did not know what Max had done or who had sent his murderer and still might want to kill her, and since she could explain nothing she knew she had to keep this a secret, at least until she could talk to Robert. Robert would know what to do. Robert knew more than she did.

So, crying, gasping with pain as she struggled with their deadweight, she dragged Max and then the gunman around the corner to the inside angle of the L-shaped building, and piled rocks in front of them. If tourists came around to see the view from this side of the summit, it would be almost impossible to make anything out in the deeply shadowed rock-filled niche where they lay.

She bent over Max and touched his face. She kissed his closed eyes and his mouth. "I'm sorry, Max. I'm sorry I couldn't love you; I'm sorry I couldn't stay with you. I'm sorry I can't stay with you now or take you down with me. If I could . . ."

The brakes of the tour bus squealed; the pneumatic door hissed as it opened. In Spanish the driver told his passengers how long they had to admire the view, and not to wander down the mountain or stand too close to the edge. Over his voice came the sound of another bus, close behind, with another load of tourists.

Stephanie took off her torn jacket and brushed herself off, wiping her bloody knee with tissue from her pocket. She ran her fingers through her hair and took deep breaths, trying to still her trembling. She wanted someone to hold her, she wanted to cry in someone's lap, but there was no one. *I'm depending on myself.*

But Robert will help me, she thought again. Max said he'd know what to do. I have Robert to help me with everything. And Léon . . . oh, Léon, my love, when I feel a little stronger, when I don't come to you as a child, then we'll be together.

It had been only a few minutes since the buses had arrived. She was still trembling, but she was able to stand straight, her head high, and she walked away from the protection of the building, moving quickly, purposefully, to Max's car, ignoring the buses and anyone who might be looking. The key was in the ignition; she turned it, backed out of the lot and drove down the mountain.

*   *   *

It was after nine o'clock that night before it was dark enough for Robert and Stephanie and Andrew Frick to drive up Mont Ventoux unobserved. When Stephanie had arrived that morning after driving recklessly, almost blindly, through the streets of Cavaillon, she and Robert had held each other and wept together, wrenching tears that were perhaps the only ones that had ever been shed for Max. Then, exhausted, she had fallen asleep on the couch in Robert's apartment, and Robert struggled with the tears that would not stop and with a sense of unreality as he called Andrew and made the arrangements Max had laid out for him.

Confident Max, invulnerable Max, the consummate schemer and manipulator and survivor . . . how could he be gone? For all that he had done that forced Robert to turn a blind eye, for all that he had been that Robert bemoaned—what a great man he might have been had he turned his talents and energy to true leadership!—for all that, he had helped Robert when Robert needed him; they had been friends; they had loved each other.

Robert did not know what job Andrew Frick had with Max, but his name and telephone number were among Max's instructions, and so it was Andrew, crying, cursing Max's killer, who drove Robert and Stephanie in his van up Mont Ventoux as the sky darkened and a sliver of a moon rose over the Alps. "The main thing is, the police can't know," he said.

"No," Robert agreed. He had wrestled with that problem all day, and concluded that there was too much at stake for the police to investigate the shooting death of Max and his assassin. Robert's obligation now was to Sabrina, and Max had told him that she could be in danger. A police investigation would expose her, her picture would be in the newspapers, other unknown men might come for her. And whatever Max's business had been, it was obviously not one that would withstand police scrutiny, and that could harm Sabrina, too. There was Max's

Swiss bank account, which Robert would turn over to Sabrina, there was the title to the house and the cars, there were valuable antiques, all of them hers now. But perhaps not so easily hers if the police were brought in. She could be left with nothing but the taint of having been Max's wife.

So, my dear friend, we will give you a private funeral, and make our private farewells. And since you were a private man, it seems right that that is what we do.

"Neither of them can be found," he said to Andrew.

"Right. We'll have to take care of both of them."

On the summit of Mont Ventoux, so dark when they turned off their headlights that they could not see each other, they found the bodies where Stephanie had left them, behind crude piles of rocks. Andrew drove close to them and the three of them lifted them into the back, dimly lit by the van's ceiling light. Then Andrew retrieved Stephanie's bicycle and helmet and locked them in the rack on the back of the van.

"That man's car," Stephanie said. "There may be something in it."

"He never gave you a name?" Robert asked.

She shook her head. "Or where he came from. But Max knew. He wouldn't tell me, but he knew who sent him. He knew who wanted him . . . dead."

Andrew put his arm around her and squeezed, thinking that this was the most gorgeous woman he'd ever seen, and trust Max to keep her a secret. Old Max, sixty, he'd said once, sixty years old and good enough to get this incredible woman. Christ, he thought, what the hell am I going to do without Max? Not that I can't find work—I can always do that—but he made it so much fun.

They found the car still parked unobtrusively in a corner of the parking lot, a rental agency sticker on its license plate. Inside, they found another gun, three passports with different names and countries of origin, a map of Provence, a thermos of coffee, a half-eaten sandwich, and a photo of Max torn out of a glossy magazine.

"But he has no beard," Robert exclaimed.

"And his hair is red; I never knew it was red," Stephanie said. "He looks so much younger." She felt a deep sadness; she had known almost nothing about him.

"I liked the beard," Andrew said. "He always seemed a little wild, you know, outside everybody's predictable lives."

"Yes, that was Max," Robert said softly. "He wouldn't let himself fit into a category. Or a way of life."

"Come on," Andrew said impatiently. He gathered up everything but the thermos and sandwich and put it all in the glove compartment of his van. "Let's get out of here."

They drove down the mountain and pulled into the grove of cedar and pine trees where Stephanie's car was still parked. Only this morning, she thought. A lifetime ago. Fifty feet into the woods, while Stephanie held a small flashlight, the men took shovels from the van and dug two graves. "Not close to each other," Robert said. "I don't want that man lying beside Max."

"Wherever," grunted Andrew. "Just so the son of a bitch who sent him doesn't know where he is. Hey, that'll keep him awake, right? His guy disappears, no sign of Max, no nothing. He won't know what the hell happened. I hope it drives him crazy."

It was midnight when they laid the two bodies in the graves. A light breeze whispered through the small clearing, lightly touching the perspiring men and Stephanie's tearful face.

"Our Father," Robert said quietly. He took the flashlight from Stephanie and turned it off, and the three of them stood in the pitch-black silence, holding hands. "We bring you Max Lacoste, in an unconventional way, but nonetheless in a spirit of love and grace. He was a man who wandered far from your path, a man who lived a life we would not emulate but for which we cannot entirely condemn him. He was a complicated man, a devious man, but a caring man. He was a man who, even when outside the law, cared for others, did good, and shared what he had in money and energy and talents. He could have been much more . . . or much less. He was never able to be completely happy, though he knew happiness as well as sadness, wealth and loss, love and fear. He was my friend and the friend of others. Had he lived, he might have turned his great talents to the service of others. I will always believe that that might have happened, if he had lived. Now we commend his soul to you. In the name of the Father, the Son, and the Holy Ghost . . . amen."

Stephanie, crying, heard Andrew crying. Then she saw the flashlight's thin beam move to the other grave, and heard Robert say a brief prayer for the soul of the murderer. "Now," Robert said, and with Stephanie again holding the flashlight the men shoveled earth into the graves, tamped it down, then dragged branches and fallen leaves over them.

Stephanie knelt where Max was buried and pressed her palm to the earth. My husband, she thought. Somehow it never seemed right to me that we were married, just as it doesn't seem right, even now, that Sabrina is my name, but he cared for me as a husband would, and that was what mattered.

"My dear." Robert's hand was on her shoulder, and she rose and went with him to her car, and he drove it while Andrew followed in the van, all of them locked in their thoughts as they drove through a sleeping Bédoin, past the darkened villages and farmhouses that dotted the rolling plain, and so back to Cavaillon. "And you will stay with me tonight," Robert said to Stephanie. "I don't want you to be alone in your house."

She looked at him through drooping eyes. "You think there are others, and when they don't hear from that man they'll come looking for me."

"We don't know that."

"But you think it. That's why you want me to stay with you."

"It's possible. I don't want to take the chance."

She was too tired to argue. "But I want to talk to Andrew first."

Robert left them alone in his small living room, and she asked Andrew about what Max did in Marseilles, and he told her. "There's a huge market all over the world for counterfeit money, hundreds of millions of dollars a year. Max was providing a service, and I was honored to be part of it. He was a hell of a guy to work for, Sabrina, and a hell of a good friend. I mean, he cared about people and he loved being alive and making things happen. I thought he was like a puppet master, you know, sort of keeping the rest of us dancing."

"Yes," Stephanie murmured. "What was the good deed he did?"

"Good deed? No idea."

"He said the reason they found him was some kind of coincidence. He was doing a favor for a friend and it backfired."

Andrew shrugged. "Got me. He didn't talk to me about his private life."

"Does Robert know?"

"About the good deed?"

"About any of it. The counterfeiting, the smuggling . . ."

"Christ, no. Max told me never to tell him. He really cared about Robert, you know; he wouldn't have laid that on him. Anyway, he didn't really trust anybody, even the people he cared about. Oh, sorry, I didn't mean—"

"It's all right. I know he was like that."

"Look, Sabrina, if you need help, if you need anything . . . I'll get you out of here, I'll take care of you; I mean, if you'd let me—"

"Thank you, Andrew, but I'm fine. I have Robert and . . . I have friends."

Robert. Friends. She thought about them all night, sleeping fitfully on the small couch, waking with a start, thinking she heard Max's voice, or Léon's or Jacqueline's, or Madame Besset beating egg whites for a soufflé, or the bell at Jacqueline en Provence announcing a customer. Sometimes she was sure she heard the dull thud of soil being flung into graves. At dawn she stayed awake, and that was how Robert found her, curled up, one hand under her cheek, her eyes wide and thoughtful.

"What is it you look at so intently?" he asked.

"I'm trying to see the future." She wore a pair of Robert's pajamas that were only slightly too big, and as she sat up, her hair tousled, her cheek red with the imprint of her fingers, Robert thought she looked like an innocent child.

"Part of your future is secure," he said, and told her about Max's money. "You're a wealthy woman, Sabrina; you'll need someone to help you handle your money and Max's investments. I know two people, one in Marseilles, one in Paris. Let me give you their names."

Stephanie took the cards he held out. *A wealthy woman. But all I want is what I have: a home, a job, friends . . . and Léon.* "Robert, I have a friend. Someone very important to me. I'd like you to meet him."

He gazed at her without expression. "Did Max know?"

"I never found a way to tell him. I wanted to, but . . . You see, he was leaving Cavaillon. And I was staying."

"He told me you were leaving together. But not for a while."

"He left last night. I wouldn't go with him."

"Because of your friend?"

"Partly. But mostly because this is my home and I didn't want to start all over again somewhere else."

"Max was your husband."

"I couldn't go with him, Robert. He told me things about his life, things I couldn't be part of . . ." A shiver went through her. "I can't believe we're talking about him like this; I keep thinking he'll walk in the door and be angry because we're talking about him. He didn't like people to talk about him, or to know anything about him."

"But I knew him, at least I knew some sides of him, and I don't believe he would have left you behind."

"He didn't want to. He tried to persuade me to go. But he knew I didn't love him—I think you knew it, too, Robert—and when I refused, he had to leave. He knew they'd found him, whoever they were, and he didn't have much time. But then he came back. He said I was in danger, too."

"And so you must leave after all. As soon as possible."

"Where will I go? Robert, I have nowhere to go; I don't know anyone anywhere but here."

"I have friends; I can send you to them. Or is the real reason that your friend does not want to leave?"

"I haven't asked him. I love him, Robert, and I want to marry him, but I have to know what kind of life I can lead before I ask him to be with me."

"But you must leave. How can you hesitate, after yesterday? If you want your friend with you, you must ask him to leave Cavaillon, but in any event, Sabrina, *you cannot stay here.*"

"Yes, I know, I know, I just can't decide right now . . . Robert, right now I just want you to meet him and get to know him."

"To give you my blessing."

"Yes."

"And to marry you?"

"When we're ready . . . if you would . . . there's no one else I want."

"But then what is it you want now?"

"I want you to tell me you're happy for me. I want you to be glad that I've found someone to love." Tears came to her eyes. "I want you to be my family."

Robert kissed her forehead. "This afternoon, then. Can you reach him that quickly? We'll have lunch at Café Hélène. A family lunch."

Café Hélène was a converted house, white stucco, square and solid on its street corner, its tables shielded from the traffic by a high stucco wall. Stephanie and Robert were led through a narrow arch to a tiny walled courtyard fragrant with roses, with a single table set for three.

When Léon arrived, he took Stephanie's hands and kissed them. "I was worried. I called all day yesterday. I even called Jacqueline, who said she does not keep track of you on Sundays."

"So much has happened . . . I have so much to tell you. Léon, this is Father Robert Chalon."

They shook hands, taking stock of each other, liking each other. "I've seen your work," Robert said. "You have a great talent."

"But what has happened?" Léon took Stephanie's hand again, and sat beside her while Robert told him what had happened on Mont Ventoux. As he talked, Léon moved his chair closer to Stephanie's, his grip tightening on her hand. "Terrible, terrible. How terrifying to be there . . . alone. With the winds and the dead. Dead," he repeated, his voice barely a murmur. "Dead. So suddenly, so crazily. We never thought . . ." He put his arm around Stephanie and turned her face to his. "All I want is to be with you always, to help you when you need it, to shield you from danger so that never again could you be alone on a mountaintop in such terror . . . my God, I would do anything to keep you from that."

"I thought of you," Stephanie said. "I talked to you. I said I couldn't die because we had barely begun."

He laughed quietly. "We'll take care of each other from now on. And Father Chalon will watch over us both."

"Wherever you are," Robert said, and then they talked about all that had happened and all that might happen. They sat at the small round table for the whole afternoon, remembering Max, learning about Robert's work and how Max had helped it, trying to imagine the danger facing Stephanie.

"We'll leave," Léon said at last. "Why would we stay where there is any danger at all? Nothing keeps us here; we'll choose a town where we can begin everything new, where we can be as private as we wish. Oh. I know the place. I have friends in Vézelay; I use their guest house and studio whenever I visit Burgundy. We'll go there. No one looks for anyone in Vézelay; there are too many tourists. Everyone becomes anonymous.''

"A beautiful town," said Robert. "But close to Paris. Less than two hundred kilometers, I believe."

"Far enough," Léon said. "We can slip in and out for theater and music and galleries, and live as we wish in Vézelay. Sabrina, does that sound good to you?"

"Yes," she said. And she did not say that there might be people in Vézelay who knew her, or in Paris, or anywhere else they might go. Until she remembered who she was, there was nowhere she could be sure she would be anonymous. But why talk about that now? She was with Léon. The terror of yesterday and the black sorrow of the burial in the forest were behind her. She remembered her piercing happiness on the summit of Mont Ventoux just before the murderer arrived. *Everything is waiting for me . . . a new life, a whole life, with Léon. Because I will remember, and then I'll be the person I was and the person I am now. And I'll have everything I could ever want.*

It would never seem that simple again, she thought. She knew now how the calm of a sunlit day could be shattered and happiness swept away. She knew there would be other shadows in the years to come, new discoveries, sudden meetings that she could not even imagine. But if they held on to each other, to what they would build together, nothing would be as terrible as that lonely moment on the summit of Mont Ventoux. *Because we'll be together. And we won't let anything tear us apart.*

"Well, then, Vézelay," Léon said. "A very special place. A good place for us. How soon can you be ready?"

"The house . . ." Stephanie said. "Madame Besset. I can't just walk out."

"Madame Besset and I will pack up everything in the house and send it to you when you're ready," Robert said. "You should leave very soon. You should not go back to that house at all."

"No, you'll stay with me," Léon said. They talked about storing the antiques and the art from the house, and paying Madame Besset and moving Léon's furnishings and his studio. "Formidable but not impossible," Léon said to Stephanie with a smile. "And we start with a visit to Avignon. I have some supplies to pick up; can you come with me? We can make lists of everything we need to do."

Stephanie shook her head. "I can't just walk out of Jacqueline's shop. I'll ask her how long she needs me."

"It is more important that you leave," Robert said. "I could tell her for you."

"No. Thank you, Robert, but Jacqueline is my friend. I'll tell her I'm leaving in . . . one week."

Léon met Robert's eyes. "Less," he said. "We'll go the day after tomorrow. What we cannot pack, Father Chalon and Madame Besset will finish for us. But first Avignon, yes? Will you come with me tomorrow afternoon after you finish in the shop?"

"Yes," Stephanie said. She was remembering a shop Max had shown her, filled with antique maps. She would buy one for Léon. She had not yet given him a gift and suddenly, urgently, she wanted to.

"I'll pick you up at one," Léon said, but when he arrived at the shop the next afternoon Stephanie was still inside, helping a customer. He watched through the window as she appeared and disappeared, moving from the front of the shop to the back. Seen through the glass and the cluttered window display, she seemed dreamlike, a beautiful woman wearing a white summer dress, drifting among fragile antiques. Nothing lasts, Léon thought. He gripped the steering wheel. The hell it doesn't. This will last. What we create will last.

Stephanie opened the car door and leaned across to kiss him. "I'm sorry; we were so busy. Jacqueline was wonderful. I hope we can ask her to visit us in Vézelay. Do you think she'll come?"

"Someday. I went to your house today. Madame Besset and I packed your clothes and I paid her for September. I told her you'd left town."

"What did she say?"

"That she'd always thought you and monsieur had many secrets and she would not be surprised at anything you did. She hopes you remember her fondly."

"She knows I will. She taught me to drive."

"And Robert taught you to cook."

"And you taught me to love. How long will we be in Avignon?"

"Not long. And tomorrow we go home to Vézelay."

Stephanie sighed. "Once I thought I should live alone for a while before coming to you. I thought I needed to learn how to do that."

"And now?"

"I want to be with you. I like to hear you say *home*. And I don't know what all the tomorrows will be like."

"Whatever they're like, we'll face them together." They drove in the hazy heat through villages with a row of shops, a church, and a square where men in black played *boules*, rolling the silver balls across the smoothly swept dirt while families watched and applauded, and then they were driving through one of the gates in the old stone wall that encircled Avignon. In the distance they saw the great towers and domes of the Palace of the Popes. Léon found a parking place near the river and got out, stretching his legs. Stephanie reached into the back seat and put on a wide-brimmed straw hat with a long red and orange scarf tied around the crown. Léon drew in his breath. "So lovely . . . I'll paint you like that, in Vézelay, beside a wall of bougainvillaea. Is the hat new?"

"I just bought it; I loved the colors. Where are we going?"

"To Monet Fournitures Artistiques. This way." They walked to the Place de l'Horloge, and stopped for a moment beside the carousel of brightly painted horses and elephants and great thronelike seats, turning to the accompaniment of hurdy-gurdy music. Stephanie gazed at it, unable to tear herself away. "Isn't it wonderful? Such a happy place for children."

Léon took her arm and they moved on. The heat built up in the square; people took off their jackets and draped them over their arms. Stephanie took off her hat, combed her hair with her fingers, and put it on again. They left the square and came to a cobbled street along the Sorgue River, the air cooler here, mossy waterwheels turning lazily at the river's edge and, on the other side of the Rue des Teinturiers, a row of antique shops.

Stephanie recognized one of them. "Léon, we have to go in here. I want to buy you something."

Inside, she moved around a large table, lifting heavy folios, each one holding a map encased in protective sheets of plastic. "Oh, this one. Do you like it?"

Léon's eyebrows rose. "It's quite wonderful. Very rare. A Tavernier. But do you have any idea what it costs?"

"It doesn't matter. I want to buy you a present. I want to buy you this."

A small man, stooped over a cane, came through the doorway. His white hair was in disarray; his white beard was trimmed to a neat point. "Yes, madame?" He quoted a price.

"Fine," Stephanie said.

Léon was poring over the map. "Superb. I've always looked for one." He and the shop owner compared the map to others; Léon said that he was a painter and looked at ancient maps as works of art. They talked for a long time, answering Stephanie's questions, enjoying each other. Then Léon said to Stephanie, "I'd like to wait. Do you mind very much if we don't buy it today? I'd like to be sure where we'll be living before I start dragging it around. It could be sent to us later."

"Oh. If that's the reason . . . yes, of course. But I do want to buy it for you. And I won't forget. We'll wait," Stephanie said to the owner of the shop.

"I can hold it for you. If you have a card, monsieur . . . ?"

"No, plenty of canvases, but no cards."

"We'll call you," Stephanie said, and as they left,

Léon took a final glance at the map, lovingly put back in its case by the little man with white hair.

"You're wonderful," he said as they walked to Monet Fournitures Artistiques, the art supply shop. "I've wanted one of those all my life." Inside, Léon greeted a tall woman with broad shoulders, round cheeks and oversize glasses that made her look like an amiable owl. They talked about oils and watercolors while Stephanie wandered around the shop, enjoying the riot of colors, the display of brushes lined up by size like a military formation, stacks of canvases in graduated sizes, and palettes hanging from long rods. When the woman went in back to find some gesso, Léon put his arm around Stephanie. "My darling Sabrina, you are very patient."

"I'm having a good time. Max never liked to browse in shops. He just looked in windows."

"Husbands aren't supposed to love shopping."

"Some husbands might."

He smiled. "Perhaps we'll come across one."

The woman came back and wrapped Léon's order. "Thank you, monsieur. I hope to see you again soon."

"I hope so. But the next shop will be in Paris," he said to Stephanie when they were outside again. "I'll have to find a whole new set of shopkeepers."

Stephanie stopped in the street. "You're turning your life upside down because of me."

"There is no better reason in all the world."

They kissed beneath the trees of Avignon, and then they walked on, arm in arm, in love, free of the tentacles that seemed to reach for them in Cavaillon. "Soon," Léon murmured. "A new life. I feel like an explorer beginning a new adventure."

Two adventures, Stephanie thought. The one we make together and the one I still travel alone: finding the other half of myself. And I will. Soon. Léon will help me. And who knows what I'll find in Vézelay or Paris that will be the key I've been looking for all this time?

Part III

Part III

CHAPTER 17

*I*n Avignon, on a hot October afternoon, Sabrina stood at the counter of Monet Fournitures Artistiques. She wore a wide-brimmed straw hat with a long red and orange scarf tied around the crown, and she spoke with the owner of the shop about two people who had been there a few weeks before.

"The woman did not tell me her name," the owner said. "But when I was in the other room, she and her friend were talking together and he called her by her name. And she spoke her husband's name."

Sabrina looked at her, waiting.

"Her name was Sabrina," the woman said. "And the husband's name was Max."

The colorful shelves seemed to tilt around her and Sabrina put a hand on the counter to steady herself. *Sabrina and Max.* She had come to Avignon looking for a ghost. And she had found two of them.

It could not be coincidence. Someone was deliberately impersonating Sabrina Longworth, even going so far as to create a man named Max. But why? Everyone thought

Sabrina Longworth was dead; why would anyone impersonate a dead woman? It made no sense. Unless . . .

Unless . . .

Unless she was Stephanie. Stephanie Andersen, still playing the role of her sister Sabrina. Stephanie . . . alive.

She couldn't be. There was no way . . .

But who else would look exactly like her and be named Sabrina and be with a man named Max?

What if she hadn't been killed? What if she was alive?

Oh, my God, Stephanie, if you really could be . . .

"Madame," said the woman, and Sabrina saw that she was offering a glass of water.

"Thank you." The glass was heavy and deeply ridged, a bistro glass, comforting in the hand. "I need to know more about them. Please believe me, I was not that woman."

"Then, madame, she could only have been your twin sister; such an astonishing resemblance—"

"I must know more about them. Please, is there nothing else you can tell me?"

"Nothing, madame. I had not seen them before. The man, the painter, most likely does not live in Avignon; otherwise, I am sure he would have been in my shop many times. I would guess he is from a nearby town, perhaps Les Baux; many artists live there."

"And . . . the woman? Where might she live?"

"I cannot say. But even though they spoke of a husband, they seemed to me like two people who live together. Or perhaps . . ."

"Yes?"

"I did think that perhaps they were running away together. There was a kind of urgency—" A customer came into the shop and the woman put her hand briefly on Sabrina's. "That is all I can tell you, madame; I wish I could be more helpful."

"Yes. Thank you." And then she was in the street again, in the early afternoon heat. Crowds walked past, heading purposefully to cafés; shopkeepers hung Closed signs in doors and windows. Lunchtime, Sabrina thought vaguely. One o'clock. My flight from Marseilles to London. And tomorrow, to Chicago.

But she could not move. She stood in the shade of a plane tree, her thoughts chasing each other.

Her name was Sabrina. And the husband's name was Max.

Sabrina and Max. Not so many miles from Monte Carlo, where there had been an explosion . . .

The street emptied. She leaned against the tree, breathing rapidly.

To live another life. Stephanie in Hong Kong, one year ago. *An adventure, Sabrina! A week. Just one incredible week.*

And Sabrina hesitating: *You might get greedy.*

Was that what had happened? Had she wanted more? Had she wanted a lifetime, and so she and Max had arranged to disappear?

Stephanie would never do that.

Her name was Sabrina. And the husband's name was Max. Not so many miles from Monte Carlo.

And the man in the map store, angry because she insisted she had never been there, had said, *I understand that you are not especially interested in maps—that you deal with antique furniture instead . . .*

"Dear God," Sabrina said aloud. "I don't understand.".

But . . . if Stephanie was alive . . .

Stephanie. Alive.

Her other half, the part of her that she had lost a year earlier and still mourned, still ached for, even in the midst of the greatest happiness she had ever known.

Stephanie. Stephanie. Stephanie.

She had to find her. Whatever she found, whatever it meant, whoever that woman was, she had to find her.

You deal with antique furniture.

Almost running, she retraced her steps through the sun-baked streets to the shaded stone courtyard of L'Europe.

Lunch was being served to well-dressed guests who looked up in surprise at Sabrina's flushed face and hurried footsteps, and she walked more slowly into the lobby and upstairs to her room.

I'll call, she thought. I haven't time to run all over the countryside from one antique shop to another—

Time. The flight from Marseilles to London. And tomorrow morning, from London to Chicago.

She looked at her watch. One-thirty in Avignon. Seventhirty in Evanston. They'll be at breakfast. My family will be at breakfast. My husband and children will be at breakfast.

The words sank like stones. *My family. My husband and children.*

Garth, Garth, Garth.

She clamped down on the thought. Not now. Later. Now is for Stephanie.

Stephanie. Alive.

Oh, Stephanie, I love you, I've missed you, sometimes I've felt so empty . . .

But if she is, what does that mean? She's been gone for a year. She let us think she was dead.

Why would she do that? Because she still wants to be Sabrina Longworth? Married to Max?

Max would want to disappear. That would not surprise anyone who knew him and could imagine what he would do when he heard that reporters were working on a series of stories exposing Westbridge Imports, art forgeries, and smuggled antiquities. Max Stuyvesant would have made careful plans and then, one day, vanished, and no one would have been surprised.

But would Stephanie have wanted to share that exile with him? Could she be so much in love . . . ?

But her husband. Her children. Her sister. *How could she let us think she was dead?*

Wait . . . wait. She's not alive. How could she be? It's all a coincidence . . . an impostor . . .

But there were too many coincidences, and the longer

she thought of Stephanie alive, the more real it became.

She hunched over in her chair, her hand trembling as she waited for the hotel operator to connect her to Evanston. Mrs. Thirkell answered, solid and comforting, and then Garth was there.

"Oh, my love, my love," Sabrina said, the words breaking loose before she could stop them.

"What is it? What's wrong?" His voice, quick with concern, resonated inside her; she shut her eyes and felt his warmth, his lips on hers, the weight of him . . .

"Nothing." But she was trembling so violently the word was barely a whisper. I'm sorry, she told him silently. I haven't lied to you since you found out the truth about me; I believed I never would lie to you again. But I can't tell you about this. I have to follow it myself; I have to find out what happened, because, in the deepest way, this is between Stephanie and me. I'm sorry, my love, I'm sorry, but I have to talk to Stephanie by myself—

Talk to Stephanie?

I can't talk to her; she's dead. She's been dead for a year and I've had to get used to being without her. But if . . . if somehow she's alive, then I have to talk to her by myself and find out why she's done this. She'll talk to me; we always could talk, about everything.

She took a breath. "Nothing's wrong; it's just that I miss you, I love you . . . I miss all of you. I hate being away; nothing is any fun without you."

"Well, that's easily solved."

"I know. I'm working on it. Now tell me what's happening at home."

"You're not coming back tomorrow."

Oh, Garth, you know me so well, you understand things before I say them.

"No, I'm staying on for a few days. There are some things I want to look at, for Collectibles."

"Are you still in London?"

"No, in Avignon. I'm going to call some antique dealers in Provence; I don't know how long it will take."

439

He was silent. He knows I'm lying, Sabrina thought. I came to Provence without telling him; I'm not being forthcoming now. He'll wonder if I'm being pulled back to Europe, to my old life; if a year of domesticity was enough.

"Garth, this came up all of a sudden; I hadn't planned it." She heard the pleading in her voice, but there was nothing she could do about it; she was pleading with fate, that everything would be fine. "Nothing's really changed. I'll meet you in Paris in two weeks, after your conference, just the way we planned it. Cliff and Penny will go to Vivian's and you and I will have our week alone."

"Of course we will," he said easily. "Now tell me what else you've been doing."

Sabrina sat back in her chair, breathing more easily. What was wrong with her that the first thing she thought of was that Garth would be angry or fearful? He knew that she had sold Ambassadors and her house on Cadogan Square; he knew she no longer wanted even a partial life in Europe. I'm seeing plots everywhere, she thought. "I saw Sidney Jones and signed the papers for Ambassadors; it's all Alexandra's now. But I spent a lot of time there, going over the books, talking to Brian, checking the inventory . . ."

"Handling withdrawal pangs."

She smiled. "Something like that. It wasn't hard; it just had a sort of melancholy about it. Like graduation."

He chuckled. "I like that. By the way, do you know what hotels you'll be staying in before you get to Paris?"

"Not yet. I'll let you know as soon as I do."

"Good. Our children are clamoring to talk to you; this is fair warning before the sound you hear goes up a few decibels."

"Thank you. I love you, Garth."

"I love you, my dear one."

Then Penny and Cliff were on extension phones, chattering about school and sports and friends, their voices riding over each other, evoking their life in Evanston: the three-story frame house with high-ceilinged rooms, polished wood floors, tiled fireplaces, shelves of books, a basement and an attic where unexpected treasures could be found, the kitchen with its sagging couch where everyone sat at some time during the day. *My* house, Sabrina thought, remembering the warm embrace with which it held their family together.

Still, she felt a tug of impatience as the children talked and as soon as she hung up she opened the telephone book to antique shops and galleries, and thought of nothing else but this task. This search. For Stephanie.

She began with shops in Avignon. She had admired Arjuna earlier that day, and so she called it first and asked if a woman named Sabrina Longworth worked there.

"No, no one by that name," said the owner, and was about to hang up when Sabrina said quickly, "Or anyone named Sabrina? Whatever the last name?"

Again the answer was no. But now Sabrina knew what to ask: there was no reason to think that Stephanie would have continued to call herself Sabrina Longworth if she was in hiding with Max. They would have taken a new name.

If it really is Stephanie. If she really is alive.

But that thought was growing fainter. By now Sabrina was searching not for a ghost but for her sister.

She telephoned antique shops in Avignon, Arles, Les Baux, and Saint- Rémy all that afternoon and evening—"Is there someone working in your shop named Sabrina?"—with no success. The next day, on a chance, she skipped to the east and called shops in Aix-en-Provence and Saint-Saturnin, but again had no success. After a quick lunch, with the map before her, she called shops in the small towns between Aix and Avignon: Apt, Fontaine-de-Vaucluse, Carpentras, Orange, Gordes, Roussillon. And late in the afternoon she came to Cavaillon, and called Jacqueline en Provence.

When a woman answered, Sabrina asked the question automatically; she had repeated it so often she barely heard herself say the words. "Is there someone working in your shop named Sabrina?"

"Sabrina? Is that you?" asked the woman.

Sabrina's heart pounded. "You know her?"

"Is this a joke? Sabrina, where are you?"

"Please, does Sabrina work there?"

"Well, I don't understand . . . I could have sworn it was your voice . . . No, Sabrina no longer works here; she's left town. Who is—"

"Can you tell me where she went?"

"No. Who is this?"

"A . . . friend. I must talk to you about her. I'll come to see you. What time do you open tomorrow?"

"Ten. But I would not tell a stranger—"

"I'll see you then."

That night she did not sleep. She sat in a café in the Place de l'Horloge, watching the carousel revolve, watching the people, watching the hours pass on the clock tower. *I'll know tomorrow. They worked together; they would have talked. This woman will know her.* At dawn she packed and checked out of the hotel and took a taxi to the train station, where she rented a car and drove the forty miles to Cavaillon. She pretended she was Stephanie, looking at farmers preparing their small fields for winter, driving along high walls of meticulously pruned cypress trees that stopped abruptly to reveal snug stone farmhouses set back from the road, each with its own swimming pool and neat gardens. She heard a rooster crow, and then another, as the sky grew bright. If Stephanie had been in Avignon, and worked in Cavaillon, she would have driven on this road. She would have seen these fields, these houses, heard these roosters. So different from Evanston, so different from London . . .

The traffic became heavier as she approached Cavaillon, and it took her a while to find the center of town. She reached it just before ten, driving around the central square with its fountain topped with a sculpture of metal spikes like the rays of the sun. Exuberant drops of water flew out from the fountain, sparkling in the morning sun, landing on Sabrina's car. She barely noticed; her gaze was fixed ahead or glancing down briefly at the map on the seat beside her. Following it, she drove past small shops and cafés to the cours Gambetta and, turning onto it, saw Jacqueline en Provence, in the center of the block, its gold lettering beckoning her on.

There was no place to park; she left the car jutting into an alley and rushed to the shop, pushing open the front door and stopping only when she found herself in a narrow space with furniture, floor lamps, and baskets of linens blocking her way. The air was faintly musty, the light soft and diffuse, the furnishings mellow with the polish of generations. *My favorite kind of shop. And Stephanie's, too.*

"Sabrina! My dear, I thought you had gone. You've changed your plans?"

A tall woman, austerely beautiful, her ash blond hair pinned loosely back from her face, came from the rear of the shop, her hands outstretched. "I was worried about you; such a quick farewell, without an address or an explanation . . . you and Léon both. I couldn't imagine that he would leave his studio, just like that . . . and what of Max? I was quite concerned. You both just vanished. So much mystery."

Sabrina's hands were held tightly and she was silent for a moment, caught in the absurdity of what was happening. *Sabrina, who is playing Stephanie, being mistaken for Sabrina.* She shook her head in despair. *Will there ever be an end to this deception?*

"Not a mystery?" the woman asked, seeing Sabrina shake her head. "Then what is it?"

She wished she could tell her the truth; she liked her. But there was nothing she could learn here. *Without an address or an explanation . . . you and Léon both.* Léon would be the artist buying supplies in Avignon. Both gone, vanished, and this woman knew nothing about it.

Sabrina felt a sinking within her. Stephanie—if it is Stephanie—didn't want this woman to know anything. They worked together, but she left without an address or an explanation. *I can't even ask her what Sabrina's last name is.*

443

"My dear, what happened?"

"Oh, it's so complicated," she said in frustration. "I came to find out . . . a few things."

The woman frowned. "This is very strange. A woman telephoned yesterday, asking about you. I would have sworn it was your voice."

Sabrina shook her head, and then remembered that both the woman at Monet Fournitures Artistiques and this woman had spoken of an urgency: *Perhaps they were running away together.* "Has anyone else been asking about me?"

"No one. Well, your friend the priest, Robert, came to retrieve a jacket you had left here. He was quite evasive when I asked him if he knew where you'd gone. But that's not what you meant. Sabrina, are you afraid of someone?"

Someone else to ask. A priest who knows more than he wants to tell. I can find a priest named Robert; that shouldn't be hard. She moved toward the door, impatient to be gone. "I don't know. There are so many things I don't understand. I'm sorry; I'd tell you everything if I could. Perhaps later I'll come back and tell you everything. I'm sorry . . ." She opened the door and rushed to her car.

She looked for steeples and drove toward the one that seemed nearest and in a few minutes she came to a large church with an attached rectory and school. I'll ask inside, she thought; they'll know every priest in town.

She saw no one in the church, so she went to the school. Its double doors opened onto a large corridor stretching to left and right; directly opposite was a door with a translucent glass window, and the word "Director." Sabrina knocked once and went in, and found herself in a small anteroom with an empty desk. An open door led to an office where a small man with a neatly trimmed beard shot with gray sat at a desk. He looked up, then leaped to his feet. "Sabrina! My dear, what can you be thinking of?

Why have you come back? Where is Léon? Have you both gone mad?''

He knows. He knows everything. Sabrina walked into his office and closed the door behind her. ''I must talk to you. Is it all right to talk here, or will we be interrupted?''

''What is it? Has something happened to Léon?''

''That's not why I'm here. Please, I must talk to you and it will take quite a while.''

Frowning deeply, he studied her. ''My dear, you are very strange. Well, then, come. My apartment is the quietest place, and for a change no one is sleeping on the sofa.''

He glanced at her with a smile, but Sabrina did not even pretend to understand. She would tell him the truth. And he would take her to Stephanie.

He led her outside and along the building to a door that led upstairs to a tiny apartment: a living room with a couch, a chair, a lamp, and a small sink and hot plate in a corner. A narrow bed could be seen through a partially opened door. ''Would you like tea? Or coffee?''

''Tea. Thank you.''

He brewed it on the hot plate, his back to her. They were silent; both tense, both expecting a surprise.

''So, my dear.'' He put two thick white mugs on a small bench in front of the sofa and sat beside Sabrina. ''What is it that you wish to tell me?''

''A complicated story. And I will ask you to help me when I've finished.''

''I will always help you when you need me, Sabrina; you know that.''

''Yes.'' She gazed at him. A good friend. A good man. She sipped her tea, then put down the mug and folded her hands in her lap. ''First I must ask you to tell me your name.''

''You are serious?''

''Yes.''

''Well, then. Robert Chalon. As you have known for almost a year.''

445

"Thank you. Now I would be grateful if you will let me speak without interruption."

His eyebrows rose. "So authoritative suddenly. But of course, my dear, if you wish, I will not interrupt."

"Well, then. My name is Sabrina Longworth. I was born in—"

"Sabrina! Your memory has returned! Oh, what a wonderful gift; why did you not tell me immediately?"

Sabrina stared at him. *Your memory has returned.* Why had she never thought of that? It explained everything. And it seemed so obvious: the yacht, the explosion, injuries . . . and a year of silence because Stephanie did not know who she was.

But why did she think her name was Sabrina?

Max.

Both of them had survived and he'd told her that her name was Sabrina. Sabrina what?

"My dear Sabrina, please go on. I'm sorry; I did promise not to interrupt."

Not Longworth; the name was new to Robert. So something else.

"Sabrina?"

"It's not what you think. Please, let me tell the whole story. I was born in America and grew up in Europe. I lived in London, I was married and divorced, I owned an antique shop. My sister married a professor in America and had two children. Her name was—is—Stephanie Andersen; she is my identical twin, and she is the woman who was on the yacht with Max."

Robert's face was frozen, stunned; he leaned forward, his eyes locked on hers.

"One day, in September of last year, we took a trip to China together and decided to change places, just for a week. We both needed to get away and we thought it would be a lark, an adventure, and no one would know and no one would be hurt. But deceptions"—the word caught in her throat—"deceptions don't work that way."

She told it all then, from her broken wrist to the explo-

446

sion on the yacht, her mourning for her sister, the passionate love that had grown between her and Garth and the children, the life they had made together.

"Last month a friend called and said she had seen me in Europe. She said it had to be"—the words caught again—"my sister or a ghost."

"And it was both," said Robert when she did not go on.

She nodded. After a moment Robert poured their cold tea into the sink and brewed another pot. "A most incredible story."

"I know. So fantastic it seems to have nothing to do with everyday life. But it's all true."

He unwrapped two tea bags. "All of us lead fantastic lives, you know. I would not deny the drama of any life." He tilted the teapot and refilled their cups. "Of course your story goes beyond that: it is fantastic and outrageous. I believe it and I am sorry for it—from a whim you have reaped a maelstrom—but it is not productive to talk about that now." He sat beside her. "The explosion on the yacht. You don't know what happened before it?"

"No. Stephanie called from London the day before she left. That was the last time I talked to her. The next day . . . a telephone call . . ." A tremor ran through her.

"You miss her greatly."

"We were so much a part of each other; it was as if a piece of me had died, as if something inside me had been torn away. That didn't change, no matter how happy I was . . ."

"My poor child," Robert said, understanding what torments crouched, waiting, for both sisters. But he had said enough; it was not the time to say more. This woman still had to come to terms with the reality of a sister who lived, and how she would welcome her back.

Sabrina had fallen silent again. She was exhausted, but pleasantly comfortable. "You're very easy to talk to."

"I hope so. Sabrina always thought so. But it is Stephanie, isn't it? I can't think of her that way."

"Please tell me where to find her."

"She and Léon have gone to Vézelay."

"Vézelay? In Burgundy?"

"Yes, fairly near Paris. A lovely town filled with tourists. They thought they could be anonymous there."

"Why should they be? What are they afraid of? Are they hiding?"

"Yes . . . perhaps. We're not sure, but it is possible that Sabrina—Stephanie—is in danger and it seemed wise for them to leave. They wanted to start a new life since Max—"

"Max. Is he here?"

"No, he—"

"He was the one who told her she was Sabrina, wasn't he? When she lost her memory. Of course he had only known her as Sabrina. What did he say her last name was?"

"Lacoste. The same as his."

"The same? Why?"

"Because she was his wife."

"But she wasn't. She wouldn't have married him; she couldn't have."

Startled, Robert said, "No, of course not. Of course not; she couldn't have married Max. But he told her he was her husband, and she had no information that would contradict that. Although she told me often that she did not *feel* married to him, even though he was deeply in love with her and she was grateful to him for the home he gave her. But I should tell you that Max—"

"I have to find her. How do I get to Vézelay? I have a car; I can drive. If I leave now—"

"My dear, wait until tomorrow. You look worn out. One more night won't make a difference and I could help you by telling you something of her life, of the things that have happened to her."

"No, I know you want to help, but I want to see her, I want to hear it from her. And I can't wait another night; my God, to know that she's alive—I have to find her!"

448

"But there is something else. I told you that your sister may be in danger. Things have happened here—"

"Danger from whom?"

"We don't know. But—"

"You don't know? Then why are we wasting time talking about it? Good heavens, are you saying I should be frightened? Whatever it is, Stephanie will tell me about it. And we'll share it."

"Léon is with her."

"That doesn't matter! It never has. Whoever else came into our lives, there was still the two of us. Nothing ever changed that."

But now something could. Garth . . . Penny . . . Cliff . . .

She shook her head roughly. Not now. Later.

"Please, I can't stay and talk; please tell me how to get there. And where she lives."

"Well, then." Robert rummaged in his desk and found a map of France. In the margin he wrote an address and telephone number. "It's a little more than five hundred kilometers, and you are not familiar with the roads. If you would like, I can come with you."

"No. Thank you, but I can't . . . no one but the two of us."

He nodded. "I understand. Now let me show you . . ." They bent over the map and Robert marked the route. "It is not a difficult drive, but some of it may be tedious. And if you get tired, you must rest; don't push yourself." He met her eyes. "But of course you will. My dear, I wish you well."

Tears came to Sabrina's eyes. He feared for her, and for Stephanie, too. She bowed her head and he took her in his arms like a child and held her with a slight rocking motion.

"You are a strong woman, my dear, but sometimes strength is not enough. If you need me, I am here. For both of you. I hope you will always remember that."

"I will. Thank you." Sabrina took the map, with the

most direct route to Vézelay brightly outlined with a yellow marker. "You must have been a very good friend to Stephanie."

"And to you," Robert said and they exchanged a smile as Sabrina gently closed the door, then ran down the stairs and down the street to her car.

Stephanie and Léon lingered over coffee in the long, slow evening, drifting in reverie, reaching out now and then to touch each other and exchange a smile of wonder. They were together, and no one but Robert knew where they were.

Cavaillon, and the violence and fear that had come to it, had been left behind. They sat in the courtyard of a small, square two-story stone house with a steeply pitched orange tile roof, hidden from the street by a high, rough stone wall covered on both sides with bougainvillaea. The pale purple blossoms hung in lacy clusters from long looping branches that tumbled over the stones and the white wooden gate set deep into the wall. The scent of the flowers mingled with that of the roses and wisteria in the courtyard, the coffee in small porcelain cups, the spicy pears in a glass bowl on the table.

"Like honeysuckle and red wine," Stephanie murmured.

Léon looked at her quickly. "Yes. Where? A garden?"

She tried to hold on to the brief flash of memory. "It must have been. Honeysuckle bushes and red wine. And people, lots of people. A party. Léon, there was a party! And it was in a yard, not a garden, a yard, and the bushes, the honeysuckle bushes, were all around it."

"Yes, good, and who was at the party? Who were the people, Sabrina?"

After a moment she shook her head. "I don't know. I can't even see myself there. Oh, I hate this, I feel so unconnected when I see a flash of something and then nothing else; it's like finding a sliver of china and never knowing what the bowl or vase it came from looked like."

"But you're not unconnected."

"No." She smiled at him, grateful for his quiet presence, and his love. "Not anymore."

They held hands on the table and the calm of the evening enfolded them and they returned to their reverie and sense of wonder. The sun had gone down, but still the light held, shadows more sharply creased, the sky above their small enclosed courtyard arching gray-blue, streaked with peach and lilac clouds. Muted voices came from beyond the wall; somewhere a violin sang a plaintive folk song of Burgundy. Stephanie, fully in the present, breathed deeply, sensually, and stretched her arms above her head. "I love you," she said, and Léon stood behind her and bent to kiss her neck, his hands on her breasts.

"We've come home," he murmured. "My darling Sabrina, we have come home."

Later, they cleared the table together, stacking the dishes in the sink, and went out, to walk through the town. Vézelay was built on a hill, the streets leading steeply to the great basilica of La Madeleine at the top. In the growing darkness, Stephanie and Léon strolled past low stucco buildings, holding hands, looking into shops and art galleries so tiny they were barely wider than their open doorways. Above were apartments, shutters open wide in the soft air. Geraniums bloomed on windowsills and in wooden planters and clay flowerpots spaced along the stone sidewalk and beside every entrance. Interspersed with the shops were houses turning a blank face to the street, showing to the throngs of tourists only their locked front doors and garage doors so old they were deeply fissured, held together in wildly random patterns by the square handmade nails of another age.

The tourists were leaving, walking down the hill to their buses, and the higher Stephanie and Léon walked, the quieter the town became. Soon, at the top, they were alone. "Now, briefly, Vézelay is ours," Léon said in amusement. "Until tomorrow when the buses return."

"I like it both ways," Stephanie said. "Even when it's

so crowded we can't walk up the street, everyone is so happy. They like being here and they're always smiling."

He kissed her lightly. "And so am I, it seems." They walked around the great church with its tiled conical roof topped with a cross and the narrow arched windows that reminded Stephanie of eyes open in surprise. At the far end of the flat summit was a stone wall overgrown with grasses and wildflowers, and Stephanie and Léon perched on it and looked over it, down the long, long slope to the flat green fields of Burgundy outlined by rows of trees and the lazy bend of the Cure River, a sinuous ghost in the fading light. In the two weeks they had been in Vézelay, it had become their favorite spot. "A destination for pilgrims over a thousand years ago," Léon had said when they first visited it. "And still today, for aren't we on a pilgrimage to find safe haven and a home?"

They sat there until it was almost too dark to see; then they turned and walked back the way they had come. "Come to the studio," Léon said suddenly when they were near their house. "I want to show you something. I was going to wait, but I want you to see them now."

He had rented a studio above a wineshop and charcuterie; it was flooded with light from the north and east and large enough for the wide canvases he had begun painting in his studio in Goult. At the top of the stairs he unlocked the door and threw the light switch. From the doorway, Stephanie saw the two portraits of her that he had almost finished when they left Provence and, on another wall, a series of paintings that were new. Léon stepped back and she went up to them, moving slowly from one to the next.

They were blocks and fragments of color, but within the abstract breakdown of form could be seen the essence of each painting: four children playing, sitting, hiding, sharing secrets, urgently racing to a destination unseen.

"Of course they'll get more abstract, more essential," Léon said as Stephanie gazed at them for a long time. "But this is the beginning." He put his arm around her. "What is bothering you?"

"A dozen paintings of children."

"Yes?"

"We've never talked about children."

"Of course not. We were getting acquainted. And you were married. I never felt it was urgent, did you?"

"But you've never even said you like children. Or that you want them. I still don't know if you want them."

"I've always liked them. I find them baffling and secretive, and it's a little daunting the way they often make one feel extraneous, but they're really quite fascinating and likable, even lovable. Why are you laughing at me?"

"Because you're so solemn, as if you're analyzing aliens. Children are just like us; they're just more open about everything. Even when they're secretive, they're more honest about it than we are."

"I don't know what that means."

"Oh, that they want to be found out." She had moved closer to the row of paintings pinned to the wall, so engrossed in them she was almost talking to herself. "They leave clues so others will stop them from doing something they know is wrong. Cliff made sure I'd find that radio and those other things in his room; he didn't even try to hide—"

She turned slowly. She was pale, her eyes as startled as those of a sleeper awakened by sudden light.

"Who is Cliff?" Léon asked.

"I don't know. It sounds as if he's . . . my son."

"Or a brother?"

"Oh. Yes, I suppose . . . But he would have to be much younger."

"That would not be so unusual." He drew her to him. Her face was against his neck; he could feel her quick short breaths, the trembling of her slender body. He held her until the trembling subsided and she drew back.

"What if he's my son?"

"Then we have a greatly complicated situation. And I think we will know, one way or another, before much more time passes; it seems to me you are remembering more these days, are you not?"

She made a gesture of frustration. "As I said: flashes. Bits and pieces."

"But from them you will build a past; one day they will all fall into place, like the chips of marble an artist embeds into a mosaic. Each is valuable but meaningless; then suddenly it is part of a whole and tells a story. Do you believe this?"

"Yes." And, hearing him say it, she did. One day she would know.

"But we will not let ghosts and fancies interfere," he said, and kissed her again. "We are going to make our own life, and take what comes each day and conquer it. We will talk about having children, because of course I want them. I never did before, but now I do, and I think that must be why I made these paintings. Often I find my dreams on paper before I know I have dreamed them. What do you think?"

"Yes." She felt herself curl up inside, as if she had told a lie, and she knew she should not do this; she had no right to take Léon into the emptiness that was always with her, no matter how happy and content she was. But she loved him and he was her whole world, and so she kissed him and said, "Yes, I want to have our children."

"And Robert will marry us here, in Vézelay. My love?" His face was close to Stephanie's; he kissed her almost chastely. "Will you marry me? Do you know, I have never asked you that."

"Yes," Stephanie said once again. "Yes, yes, I want to marry you. But . . . not yet. We don't know what I'll remember. We could wait a few months, a year, even more; what difference does it make as long as we're living together?"

"I want to marry you," he said quietly. "I don't want to wait. I don't want to live with you in a way that makes it impossible for us to build a family. I want everything with you, Sabrina, not just a living arrangement. I will not force you, but I feel strongly about this."

And that was enough. Whatever lay ahead, they would

share it. "Then we should invite Robert to Vézelay," she said.

"We'll call him tonight."

He turned off the light switches and locked the door. They walked down the narrow stairway to the dark sidewalk, faintly lit, and made their way down the middle of the deserted street to their gate. Léon pushed it open and they walked into the courtyard, where one candle still burned on the olivewood table where they had eaten their dinner. Golden light spilled from the windows of their house, turning to gold the wisteria vines climbing around them, the bougainvillaea on the stone wall, the single rose on their dinner table, their faces as they turned to each other. "I love this house," Stephanie said. "I love you. Thank you for giving me all this."

He gave a small laugh. "I'm the one who is grateful. Once my only center was painting; everything else revolved on the periphery, casual, not essential. You've given me everything that is essential. You've made me complete."

He unlocked the heavy wooden front door and they went inside and up the stairs. "The dishes," Stephanie murmured.

"Terribly important," Léon said dryly, his long thin fingers unbuttoning her white shirt. "I greatly fear they will wait for us."

They lay on the bed and came together with a passion that had been growing since they left Cavaillon. Nothing they had known before was as powerful as the love they shared and the response of their bodies in their own home, together in a small town where no one knew them. When, much later, they lay side by side, smiling at each other in the lamplight, Stephanie kissed him and said, "I think I could be content with this and nothing else. If I never know any more about myself than I know now, it might be enough."

"Not forever, I think. But it doesn't matter. Whatever you discover, I can't imagine it changing what we have.

Something this powerful can't be shattered easily. Or at all. Good heavens, is that the doorbell? No one in Vézelay is up this late.''

Stephanie felt a stab of fear. "Could someone have followed us?''

"No, no, there is no chance. You know that. Robert's friend has been watching your house; no stranger has been near it. And we left from my house in Goult, not from Cavaillon. Perhaps it is a peddler; shall we ignore it?''

"Yes.'' But when the bell rang again and then again, Stephanie unaccountably began to tremble. "It's something else. Something . . . something . . . oh, what's wrong with me?''

Léon sat up. "You're afraid. I'll go.''

"No, I'm not afraid, that's not it. It's just . . .'' She leaped out of bed. "I have to go. It's for me.''

His eyebrows rose. "How do you know that?''

"I don't know.'' She pulled on a silk robe of peacock blue and green that Léon had bought for her in Avignon, and ran her fingers through her long hair. "I'll be right back.''

"I'm coming too. Wait for me. Where did I put my robe?''

"I think it's in the other closet. It's all right, Léon; don't bother. I'll only be a minute.''

She ran down the stairs. She heard Léon go into the other room and open the closet and pictured him fumbling through clothes they had not yet completely organized. At the bottom of the stairs she crossed the small foyer and opened the door. "Yes, what can I—''

She was looking at herself.

"Stephanie!'' said the vision. "Oh, Stephanie, thank God—''

A long scream broke from her, shattering the quiet night. And then the world went black.

CHAPTER 18

"*S*abrina!"

Léon, at the bend in the stairs, heard Stephanie's scream and hurtled the rest of the way down and into the foyer. In the dim light he saw Stephanie on the floor and a woman bending over her, her long chestnut hair falling over her face. *Just like Sabrina's hair . . .* The thought came and was gone as Léon shoved her aside. "Get away from her!" He took Stephanie into his arms and lifted her. He heard the woman say, "Léon, please, let me help," and thought, as fleetingly as before, *How the hell does she know my name?* before he carried Stephanie into the living room and laid her on the couch.

"Sabrina, my love, my love." He sat with her, cradling her against his chest. And then he looked up at the woman, who had followed him, and felt his body go rigid with shock. "My God. My God. Who the devil—" The woman reached out to touch Stephanie's hair. "Get away from her! Leave her alone!"

Leave *us* alone, he thought, because he was filled with fear. Sabrina in his arms; Sabrina standing beside him.

457

The room seemed to tilt; he could not think. And so he denied the other woman and bent over Stephanie, seeing only her, murmuring to her. "Wake up, Sabrina, wake up, my love; it will be all right. Whatever it is . . ." He breathed in the scent of her hair and brushed his lips across her cheek, watching her eyelids flutter. He felt he was holding his whole world in his arms, this woman who was the core of his life, and he was filled with terror because he knew her past had come into their home and could take her from him.

How lightly he had talked of it! How easily he had told her she would remember everything and then they would deal with it together. Fool, fool, fool, to be so naive. Now, at this moment, he knew that the past could never be so casually dismissed: it could always twist and shatter the present, and only a fool would think otherwise.

"My love, my love, it will be all right." Like a child trying to ward off invisible dangers in the scary corners of his room, he repeated it. "You'll be all right. *We'll* be all right." And, like a child, he added to himself, *We will, we will, we will.*

"Léon, please, please let me . . ."

The woman was standing close by, reaching toward Stephanie, *yearning* toward her, Léon thought, and he could deny her no longer. He looked up. "You're her sister."

"Yes."

"She didn't know she had one. And a twin . . ." He stared at her, his artist's eye comparing them. "It's uncanny. I could have mistaken you for her."

She nodded gravely. "Many people have." Once again she reached out, and this time Léon did not stop her as she took Stephanie's hand in hers and bent to kiss her. And then, suddenly, as her lips touched the warmth of Stephanie's cheek, her legs buckled and she sank to her knees beside the couch and laid her cheek on Stephanie's.

Stephanie, Stephanie . . . She wept and it seemed she could not stop. She looked at Stephanie through her tears and gently brushed her hair back from her face. *I did that before, in the funeral home, a year ago. I laid my head on the side of Stephanie's coffin and wept in that awful dark room until I thought I would tear apart. How can she be here now?*

"I don't know, I don't know," she murmured. She kissed Stephanie's forehead, her cheek, her closed eyes. "So wonderful . . . magical . . ." She looked at Léon. "I thought she was dead."

Instinctively he had tightened his arms as if to keep Stephanie to himself, safe from even the touch of the past. But the past was here: the past was this woman, kneeling beside the couch, her hand on her sister's hair, her body leaning toward her as if desperate to take her from Léon into her own embrace.

"Is she married?" he burst out. "Does she have children?"

Sabrina froze. Her hand fell to her side; she swayed a little, away from him. Her mouth opened, then closed. The words would not come.

Stephanie stirred and Léon bent to her. "My love, my love . . ."

Her eyes opened. She saw only his face. "Léon? I thought Sabrina was here. I saw her and everything came back . . . it was like a flood . . . I couldn't stand it; it hurt. Isn't she here?"

"Sabrina? But, my love, you're Sabrina."

"Stephanie," Sabrina said.

Stephanie turned. A low cry broke from her. She wrenched free of Léon's embrace, and then she and Sabrina were in each other's arms.

Two identical faces, wet with tears, pressed together as they embraced so tightly it seemed they had merged into one. They held each other for a long time, not moving, silent tears falling softly in the silence of the house, the silence of the night.

Quietly Léon moved away, through an archway that led to a small library. He could see them sitting on the couch, but he stayed in the shadows and watched them. He could not believe it even now: two stunning women, identical in every way, even to the curve of their arms and fingers as they embraced, the lashes on their closed eyes, their voices murmuring each other's names, saying they loved each other.

Stephanie, he thought. Her name is Stephanie. But Max called her Sabrina, and so we all did. And they were speaking English. American English, not British. Effortlessly, without an accent, Sabrina—*no, her name is Stephanie*—was speaking to her sister in English. American, he thought. She's American. I never guessed.

"I love you," Sabrina said. "I couldn't bear it that you were gone; I've missed you so much."

Stephanie shuddered within her sister's arms. "I didn't remember anything about you. I remembered other things, other people—flashes, really, not connected to anything—but I never remembered you. I love you, I love you, but I didn't remember you. Why didn't I? Oh, Sabrina, so much has happened! How will we ever put it all together?"

Sabrina gave a shaky laugh. "We'll start at the beginning. But not yet. Let's not talk yet; let's just be together—"

"No, we have to talk. We have to. I lost everything—did you know that? It was so awful: like walking through a fog, through *nothing*, just—"

"—emptiness," Sabrina said. "I thought of that when I thought about you, everything gone: an awful—"

"Nothingness. That was it. I knew the names of things, and languages—isn't that odd?—or maybe not. One of the doctors told me I was repressing things about myself because I'd had some kind of conflict that caused pain or guilt . . ." She and Sabrina exchanged a quick look; then Stephanie veered away from it. "So there was nothing about myself. Nothing. Except, somehow there must have been something, because it never seemed right that my name was Sabrina. And Léon painted a portrait of me, a double portrait, and when I looked at it, it made me feel so happy . . ." She shook her head. "I can't believe it. It's all back, as if nothing had happened. But I don't know anything about you, what you did, what's happened— Oh! Penny and Cliff! Have you seen them? Do you know how they are?"

There was a pause barely the length of a heartbeat. "Yes. They're fine. You're right; we have to talk. Do you think we could make some tea?"

"Oh, yes, let's. We can't just stay here; I want to know everything. Let's go to the kitchen. Oh, but Léon—" Stephanie looked for him. "Léon?"

"Yes." He was beside her, thinking: Penny and Cliff, Penny and Cliff. She said those names once and wondered if they were her children. "What would you like? Shall I make you some tea and then"—he forced himself to say it—"then I'll leave the two of you alone."

A look of confusion swept over Stephanie's face. "No." She stood up, and Sabrina stood with her; they clung to each other, arms around each other's waists. "Would you mind?" she asked Sabrina. "I want Léon to know everything."

"If that's what you want."

"I know you'd rather it's just the two of us, after so much time . . ."

"Yes. But we'll do what you want." Sabrina extended her hand. "Hello, Léon. I'm glad to meet you."

Through his bewilderment and cold fear, he saw the swift understanding between them, the unspoken assumptions, the powerful love, and knew he could not break that bond, nor would he even try. It was theirs alone, and it changed everything: it turned his world and Stephanie's upside down. But he liked this woman: the love she had for her sister; her warmth and directness. She would not lie or participate in others' lies, he thought. He took the hand Sabrina held out to him and saw the shadowed look in her eyes and wondered what part of this incredible meeting was causing her pain. "Léon Dumas," he said. "But I don't know your name."

461

"Sabrina . . . Longworth." Her tongue tripped on it. "But also . . . Stephanie Andersen."

Stephanie frowned. "That was a long time ago . . . and it wasn't for real."

"But they told us you were dead and I couldn't—"

"*Dead*?" Stephanie stared at her and suddenly all the events of the past year seemed to surround her, pieces fitting into place. "Lacoste . . . Max Lacoste. Sabrina Lacoste. But he was Max Stuyvesant, and I was Stephanie Andersen. He didn't know that, of course; he thought I was you, so when he told me my name was Sabrina, when he said I never had children and he'd never heard of Garth, that was the truth, as far as he knew it. But he said we were married, and I never married him; how could I? He made that up, I suppose, when the yacht exploded, and he changed his name and let everyone think we'd been killed. He made us disappear. Of course you thought we were dead; what else could you think? And then"—she looked wildly at Sabrina—"*then you couldn't change back.*"

"You and Max weren't married?" Léon asked. He could make sense of nothing but that.

"No. Oh, Sabrina, that's what you meant about my being gone." She kissed Sabrina's cheek. They were still standing together, their arms around each other, their hands moving, stroking, caressing in constant reminders that this was real. "You meant you thought I was dead. But there wasn't a . . . body. How could you think—?"

"I don't know. We have to figure that out. But first I want to know about you. Everything. Robert wanted to tell me but I—"

"You know Robert?"

"That was how I found you. I'll tell you the whole story when you tell me yours . . . or we can take turns, but—"

"But not standing in the living room." Léon felt he had to do something, say something, to restore a sense of reality. He felt he was losing Sabrina . . . no, he thought, Stephanie. I must remember, her name is Stephanie. It seemed to him she was disappearing into her sister, the two of them merging as their voices, identical voices, overlapped and they held each other as if they could not ever again be torn apart. And what they said made no sense. "Come; we'll make tea and then you can talk. I'll stay if you wish."

This time Stephanie hesitated. She glanced at Sabrina. "It might be better if we're alone."

Léon's fear rose again, but he only nodded. "I thought so." He led the way to the kitchen, a long narrow room with tall wood cabinets, a worn wood floor, and a high window at one end above a planked table and four wooden chairs with rush seats. Léon switched on the ship's lantern above the table and went to the stove.

"Léon, I'll do it." Stephanie finally left her sister's side and went to him, her arm around his waist, her head on his shoulder. "I'm sorry. I love you; I don't want to hurt you. But there's so much . . . everything is so mixed up and I can't tell you about it, not yet . . . or maybe I should . . . Oh, I don't know what I should do!"

Léon hesitated, afraid of confusing her even more. But then he thought, the hell with it. He had his fear to deal with, and he had to try to balance the sisters' almost mystical closeness. He took Stephanie in his arms. "I love you. And you love me. We haven't dreamed this; we haven't chased a fantasy or clung to each other out of desperation. We came together freely and offered to each other all that we had and all that we were, and it didn't matter what we had been before. From the moment we loved, our past had nothing to do with the life we were building together. We knew that we would change each other, and our lives would change, and *that was what we wanted*. That was what made us happy. I want you to remember that."

"I will," Stephanie said gravely. "I couldn't forget it." She reached up and touched his face. "I love you. But everything is so complicated . . . I'll tell you about it later, I promise. I'll tell you all of it. But Sabrina and I have to fill in our lives, and we have to do it in our own way, and I don't see how you can be part of that."

She was changing as he watched her, growing stronger, more positive, more sure of herself. Because now she has a self, he thought. The recovery of her memory and her sister beside her have filled in all the empty spaces that I alone, and all the love in the world, could not fill.

"I'll be upstairs," he said, and kissed her, and felt her respond with the passion she had shown earlier that night, and that was what he took with him when he left the room, a passion that could not—if there was any meaning in the world—be taken from them.

Stephanie stood at the stove, her back to Sabrina, waiting for the water to boil. As soon as Léon left, she had begun trembling and now she could barely lift the kettle. "Let me help," Sabrina said at her shoulder.

Stephanie did not turn around. "I'm afraid."

"We both are."

The words they had not said, the questions they had not asked in the rush of emotions in rediscovering each other, hung in the room.

Will you try to take your children? What will you do about Garth? Do you want to come home? It's my home now, my . . .

Will you walk away from my family? Will you make room for me with them or will you fight? It's my family, my home, my . . .

But they could not say them aloud.

Sabrina poured steaming water into a red-patterned teapot. "Tea bags," she murmured, and Stephanie opened a drawer and took out a handful, then reached up and brought down two mugs in a red and white pattern that matched the teapot. "Oh, it's not fair!" Sabrina cried. She stared through sudden tears at the cheerful mugs. "You're back, we're together . . . we shouldn't have anything to be afraid of; we should be rejoicing, celebrating, singing, dancing . . ."

But there was too much between them besides joy and

discovery: they were mired in the quicksand of what they had begun one year ago.

At the table they held hands, their heads close together. "Tell me what happened to you," Sabrina said. "Where were you when you couldn't remember anything?"

"In a hospital in Marseilles. I woke up and Max was there and I didn't know who I was. But I don't want to talk about—"

"And that's when everything seemed empty. Like a fog. That was how I thought of you. As if you'd disappeared into a fog, a cloud, an emptiness, all of space."

"Yes, yes, that's what it was! And everything was muffled and I felt so *alone*. Even later, when I'd feel happy . . ."

"Yes, even then," Sabrina murmured.

"You know; of course you know. You always know. What were you doing? Sabrina, I don't want to talk about me; I want to know about my family and what you've been doing, where you've been—"

"I'll tell you later. I want to know about you, and about Robert and Léon and that shop you worked in, and everything else. All of it."

"No!" She jerked her hand from Sabrina's. "I have to know about my children! How did you tell them? Do they hate me? They thought I was dead! They thought I'd run off from them and then I was killed—"

"So did Garth."

"Yes, but . . ."

"What?"

"He wouldn't have cared. Things were so bad between us . . . you must have found that out right away. I was afraid to tell you in Hong Kong; I was afraid if you knew, you wouldn't change places. But it must have been obvious. He barely knew I existed, and all I wanted was to get away from him. And when you broke your wrist and I stayed in London, I was so relieved; I just didn't want to go back to him."

Sabrina tightened her muscles, trying to still the tremors that ran through her.

"What's wrong?" Stephanie leaned forward and took Sabrina's hands in hers. "What's wrong? Why are you shaking?"

Sabrina shook her head. "I'll be all right. Just give me a minute—"

But Stephanie's fingers were moving over Sabrina's, feeling the rings on her left hand. She spread her sister's fingers across her palm. "You're married! You didn't tell me. We've been talking all this time and you never said a word. Who is it?"

Sabrina looked at the dark window giving back their reflections: the only people in a darkened world. She took a breath, as if plunging off a cliff into the unknown, because there was no way to hide it or to soften it.

"Garth," she said.

Stephanie dropped her sister's hands and shoved her chair back, the legs scraping on the wood floor. "What are you talking about? *Married to Garth?* That's crazy; you couldn't be. You didn't even like him. It's been a year; there's no way you could live with him that long, much less marry him. And anyway, why would he—" Her breath came in short bursts; her face was flushed. "Why would you make up something like that? You're not married!"

"We were married last Christmas. Stephanie, listen—"

"I don't believe it. Why? *Why would you?*"

"Because we love each other." Sabrina's tremors had stopped; her body was cold, her voice flat. She would tell the whole story and then somehow they would go on; they would decide about the rest of their lives. She wished she could have put it off and enjoyed the miracle of being with Stephanie, but that was like a child's prayer that everything would be easy. "I told you I couldn't change back. The world thought Sabrina Longworth was dead, so I couldn't be her, ever again. I was living Stephanie Andersen's life and I knew it was wrong, that it couldn't go on,

466

and I tried to leave Garth, over and over again, but something always came up, something with the university or the children or the trip to Stamford, and then he figured out who I was and . . . kicked me out.''

"He figured it out? When?"

"Just before Christmas."

"*Christmas?* From September? All that time he didn't know? Didn't even have a suspicion?"

"He had reasons for overlooking things, for finding explanations. He wanted to believe I was his wife."

Stephanie flinched. After a moment she said, "Was there a funeral?"

"Yes. In London."

"And you didn't tell him then?"

"I tried to. Stephanie, let me tell it all, from the beginning."

"So he finally got it and kicked you out." Abruptly her thoughts switched to Sabrina, and, as it had been through all their lives, it was as if she were inside her. "What a terrible time for you; what an awful thing, to lose everything, to have someone tell you you can't have it anymore or even come close . . . But you didn't lose it, did you? You're still there?"

"I went back. Garth came—"

But Stephanie had plunged into herself again. "So when he kicked you out, he told Penny and Cliff, and they hated me. Didn't they? I know they hated me. He told them I'd left them to play a silly game because they weren't as important as—"

"Stephanie, he didn't—"

"But it was only going to be for a week! They could understand that, couldn't they? And then later they thought I was dead, so maybe . . . maybe they didn't hate me so much."

"He didn't tell them. We've never told them. They don't know."

Stephanie stared at her. "They don't know I've been gone all this time? They think you're their mother?"

"Well, damn it, that was the idea, wasn't it? You wanted me to convince them of that when you asked me to take your place." Sabrina drew in her breath. "I'm sorry. Yes, they think I'm their mother. They *know* I'm their mother; I have been, you know, for over a year. And I've been Garth's wife since December. Stephanie, I'll tell you the whole story, but please let me tell it all; don't say anything until I'm finished. Please."

"You took over my family. *You stole my family!*"

"What are you talking about? I didn't steal anyone! They weren't sitting on a shelf waiting to be stolen; they're human beings who love and who need love, and I went to them because you asked me to, and I stayed because—"

"Because you wanted them for yourself!"

"Because I love them! Because you were dead. Because they became my family!"

The kitchen was silent. The two women sat so still they might have been sculpted in their chairs, leaning slightly forward as if wanting to touch but unable to; as if a barrier, more formidable than anyone could measure, kept them apart. Stephanie could not make sense of it. For over a year, with so many chances for mistakes and blunders and nostalgia for another way of life, Sabrina had played a part so brilliantly she had swept a whole family into her embrace and they had loved it enough to make her a part of them without ever wondering if she belonged there. Well, she doesn't, Stephanie thought. She's an impostor. She's only been filling in.

From upstairs came the sound of something being moved across the floor, a lamp, perhaps, or a chair. Oh, Léon, Stephanie thought, what are we going to do? She pictured him upstairs, unable to sleep. "He's sketching," she murmured. "He does that when he's worried about something or he can't sleep. He fills pages: people, landscapes, fantasies, dreams . . ."

"You love him very much."

"More than . . . almost more than anyone. We were going to ask Robert to marry us."

Sabrina burst through the barrier between them; she jumped up and put her arms around Stephanie, holding her close. Stephanie's head was against her breast; she felt her tears and her warm breath through her blouse. "I'll tell you everything that's happened. And then you'll tell me. We can't think about what comes next until we do. Oh, I wish it was just the—"

"—two of us. I know. We could have such a good time, just being together. Finding out again—"

"—how wonderful it is. How perfect. Whatever else happens—"

"It is perfect." Stephanie looked up at Sabrina and instinctively they laughed together. "It's not the same with anyone else; how could it be?"

"I know." But Sabrina's smile faded and she stood with her head bent. Because it had been perfect when they were growing up and, later, when they had separate homes and separate lives and had turned to each other for support and encouragement, but now, when they were caught in a tangle of conflicting needs, she did not see how it could ever be perfect again.

Stephanie went to the stove. "We'd better have more tea. It's going to be a long night."

Sabrina watched her fill the teakettle, and then she began to talk, even before Stephanie returned to the table. She began with Brooks's call from London, telling them the yacht had exploded off the coast of Monte Carlo and everyone aboard had been killed. She described the funeral and her frantic attempts to tell everyone that it wasn't Sabrina who had died; it was Stephanie. "But they all said I was in shock; poor Stephanie Andersen, in shock, distraught, incoherent. And I suppose I was. I broke down and said sometimes I couldn't tell who I was, Sabrina or Stephanie, and that was when Garth took me away."

In her mind Stephanie saw Sabrina fall beside the open grave, crying, *It wasn't Sabrina! It wasn't Sabrina who died!*; she heard people gasping and saw Garth leading Sabrina away. But Sabrina had left something out. "Before that, before the funeral, why did you think it was me, in the coffin?''

"I don't know. The room was dark and I was crying, everything was blurred . . . but it did look like you. I remember how dark it was—there were a few candles, that was all—and everything seemed hazy because I couldn't stop crying . . . but still . . . I don't know. Maybe we'll be able to find out sometime . . ." She fell silent. "Shall I go on?''

"Yes.''

She told Stephanie everything in that long year: how she had helped Garth in the sex-for-grades scandal at the university that had almost cost him his job; the job offer from a company in Connecticut and their visit there; her growing love for Garth and the children, their love for her. And then she came to Gabrielle's telephone call—*I know what the two of you look like and I'm telling you, I saw you, or her. Or a ghost*—and her trip to Avignon, and then Cavaillon.

It was dawn when she finished: the sky over Vézelay lightening to pearl gray and then a soft wash of color that turned the bougainvillaea to pink and gold. From upstairs came the sound of a door closing, footsteps, another door.

Stephanie sighed. "Why did you come looking for me? You didn't have to. You could have gone back, to Garth and Penny and Cliff. I might never have remembered who I was:"

"You don't mean that. You know why I came here. I had to find you; you're part of me."

"Yes." Stephanie smiled faintly. "Thank you. What an odd thing to say. Thank you for finding me, for giving me back my past. Thank you for loving me."

But now what? Will you walk away from my family? Will you make room for me with them or will you fight? It's my family, my home, my . . .

They sat quietly, staring blankly ahead, and turned together as Léon came in. He stopped short, arrested by the sight of those identical faces, identical poses, even an identical exhausted droop to their shoulders.

"I'm going to the studio," he said casually, as if this were an ordinary morning, with an unremarkable visitor. "I'll be there all day, if you'd like to walk over later on."

Stephanie tried to focus on him. Nothing in Sabrina's story seemed to have any connection with Sabrina Lacoste and the life she lived in France, or with Léon Dumas, whom she loved and wanted to live with for the rest of her life. She felt a sinking inside as she thought of her two lives, each like a seamless sphere. *How will I ever put them together?*

"Come at one; we'll go to lunch." He said nothing about the bewilderment on Stephanie's face; he ached to hold her and comfort her but at the same time his anger was growing because she seemed to be shutting him out, his beloved Sabrina who . . . *No, damn it, why can't I remember? Stephanie, Stephanie, Stephanie.* He wanted to demand information, but he knew she had to tell him freely who she was and what she had been, and whether she wanted his help in patching her two lives together. He could not force any of that on her. "One o'clock," he said again. "We'll go to Melanie's."

Sabrina glanced at Stephanie's frozen face and said, "We'd like that. And I'd like very much to see your studio."

Léon walked the length of the room and kissed Stephanie. "I love you." He nodded to Sabrina. "I'll see you at one."

Then they were alone again. "Are you too tired to go on?" Sabrina asked. "Should we wait?"

"No, I don't want to wait. I want you to know what I've done, what it's been like . . ."

They made coffee, and Stephanie warmed croissants in the small oven and filled a dish with red pears. "Let's sit outside; I like it there."

They sat at the table where she and Léon had eaten dinner . . . a lifetime ago, she thought. The sun was higher

471

now, lifting over the houses across the street, warming the old stone wall, the painted wooden gate set deep within it, the rough flagstones of the courtyard. A nuthatch sang in the chestnut tree spreading above them; blue jays swept across the open sky. From the street beyond the wall came the clang of iron shutters being raised by merchants opening their shops, the laughter of children skipping down the hill to school, the rumble of German and Spanish, English, French, Italian, Swedish that accompanied groups of tourists, cameras clicking, making an early pilgrimage to the basilica at the top of the hill. "What a lovely place," Sabrina said. "No wonder you chose it."

"We chose it because Léon has a friend here who found us the house and the studio. We didn't have time to look around."

"Why not?"

"Wait. I'll tell you the whole thing. I don't understand all of it; there's so much we don't know. But . . ."

She told Sabrina everything, from the moment she'd awakened in the hospital and looked up into Max's face to the day she and Léon left Cavaillon. Sabrina listened with a sense of wonder that they had been so far apart for a year, living in different cultures, speaking different languages, and yet they both had worked in antique shops, had made new friends and fallen deeply in love, and had been in danger, had faced a man with a gun and felt the helplessness that comes when reason is not enough.

When Stephanie finished, Sabrina stirred. "Terrible, terrible. What you went through . . ."

"It was worse for Max," said Stephanie, almost coolly, and Sabrina drew back a little.

"Are you mourning him?"

"He was good to me and he—"

"He lied to you about being his wife; he hid your past from you—at least what he thought was your past—"

"I don't forgive him for that. But he cared about me, he was good to me, and he died in a terrible way."

"And almost took you with him."

"He saved my life!"

"But what got you there in the first place? He was running, Stephanie, hiding . . . from what? Most of us aren't living with men who are being stalked; what was he up to? Probably some scheme like Westbridge; there's no reason to suppose he'd do anything legal for a change."

"Westbridge? Max's company? What about it?"

"Oh, you don't know. No, how could you? The stories came out last December. They smuggled antiquities out of Third World countries; they had customers who paid millions of dollars for a vase or a funerary sculpture or a piece of a mosaic floor . . . anything and everything. They faked rare porcelains, too, but that was almost a sideline. If Max was doing the same kind of thing in Marseilles . . . what did he do there?"

Stephanie hesitated, strangely reluctant to expose Max, even in death, even to Sabrina. But they had to talk about it; too much hinged on Max, in London and perhaps in Marseilles. "He made counterfeit money and sold it around the world."

"Good Lord, he never changed, did he? I suppose he smuggled it in; how else would he do it?"

"Yes."

"What was his company?"

"Lacoste et fils."

"He never had sons."

"He liked the sound of it. I suppose he thought that any company with a father and sons had to sound respectable."

"And who worked with him?"

"Oh, he had people in a lot of countries. I don't know who was here, except for Andrew. Andrew Frick. The engraver. An artist, Max said. A genius."

"Where is he? We ought to talk to him."

"I don't know. He's disappeared."

"You mean you called or went there?"

"Robert tried to find him after Max was killed, but he'd vanished. The telephone at Lacoste et fils was discon-

473

nected, and there was nothing in the office or the warehouse: Robert called the police and they broke in and found nothing. Not even a piece of paper.''

"Frick cleaned it out?''

"Or someone else; I don't know how many people worked there.''

"You never went there?''

"No. Max said I'd find it dull. And then, after I met Léon . . .''

"You wanted to stay home when Max went to Marseilles.''

Stephanie nodded. Their eyes met. "It was never right between us. I tried, because I knew he cared for me and I was grateful for all that he'd done, but I never felt really married to him.''

"Because you weren't. Even Max Stuyvesant couldn't fool you completely.''

They smiled together, sharing the small joke about Max—always so certain of his irresistible powers of persuasion—and it struck Sabrina that for this brief time she and her sister were living entirely in the moment: being together and puzzling something out, as they had done through all their growing up when they had relied on each other for companionship and love and understanding.

But her thoughts were moving ahead. "So Max could have been killed because of what he did in Marseilles. But he said you were in danger, too. Meaning Sabrina Longworth was in danger. And that could only have been because of something that had happened in London. And London was Westbridge.''

"I didn't have anything to do with Westbridge.''

"You're sure? You were there for five weeks. Long enough to hear something or repeat something.''

"I didn't. You were there for years, it was your life; I was only borrowing it.''

"Wait, maybe it was this. Do you remember, just before you left for the cruise, you wrote a letter to me. You thought I'd read it after we switched back. I found it at

Ambassadors after you'd—after I thought you'd died. You said in the letter that you'd told Rory Carr he could tell you nothing you didn't already know."

"I remember that. He was taken aback when I said it. But . . . *Rory Carr?* You think he was working with Max?"

"He confessed to that. It was part of the whole Westbridge story. You said in your letter that he'd been fishing for information about Olivia Chasson's Meissen stork, the one that turned out to be a forgery."

"The one I broke."

"That was brilliant, Stephanie. I wouldn't have thought of it; I'd been going crazy trying to figure out how to tell Olivia I'd sold her a fake."

"Oh, it was such fun. I made it look like an accident and I felt so good about doing it for you . . ."

"And Rory asked you about it."

"Yes."

"So he probably thought maybe it wasn't an accident, that you'd broken it deliberately, and then he would have panicked, thinking you knew all about Westbridge."

"I didn't."

"But you implied that you did when you said you knew everything there was to know. When I read your letter about that, I was sure that was why they blew up the yacht; they were after—"

"*Blew it up?* Max said it was the boiler."

Sabrina put her hand on Stephanie's. "That's the one part I didn't tell you. It was a bomb. Under your stateroom."

"A bomb . . . But all those other people . . ."

"Whoever did it wasn't concerned about other people."

Instinctively Stephanie curled her shoulders against a world that had such people in it. After a moment she said, "But it couldn't have been Rory. If he worked with Max he wouldn't have killed him; he would have picked a time when I was alone."

"Rory and Ivan Lazlo—"

"Ivan Lazlo?"

"Max's secretary, years and years ago; he was in with Rory in Westbridge. These people seem to hang around forever. They confessed that they'd planned to blow up the yacht and one or both of them set the bomb. And they were after both Max and Sabrina Longworth. They said they'd had some quarrel with Max, but I don't believe that anymore. I think they were working for someone."

"Someone else was after us? Why?"

"I don't know. But Rory and Ivan are in jail, and someone found out that Max was alive and learned where he was living and sent someone to kill him, and I don't think Rory and Ivan are smart enough for that, or have the right connections. But someone did it, and we have to find out who it was. Because . . ."

Sabrina turned her hand and Stephanie clasped it, and suddenly they were girls again, with Sabrina explaining something and Stephanie putting her trust in her sister. Their handclasp tightened and Sabrina closed her eyes, treasuring the warmth that flowed between them.

She opened her eyes to the cloudless sky and the bright sun filtering through chestnut leaves and the song of the nuthatch descending in sweet trills. "Because now there are two of us. And you can't stay in hiding forever. And however all this works out between us, one of the first things that's going to happen is that the news will get back to London that Sabrina Longworth is alive. And Max could be, too, as far as that goes."

"Max is dead!"

"Who knows that? You and I and Robert and Andrew Frick, who's disappeared. The murderer couldn't exactly report back: he's dead and buried. So whoever gave the order will be wondering about Max, and then he'll hear that Sabrina Longworth is alive. And he'll probably try again."

Stephanie froze, her coffee cup halfway to her mouth. "But then, which one of us . . . ?"

"I suppose whichever one he sees first, you or me. So we have to find him and stop him before he hears that you're alive."

"How?"

"I don't know. We'll have to figure that out. I think we'd better go to London, though; that's where it starts."

Their eyes met.

"I'll call Garth. He wants to know where I'll be staying. He's leaving tomorrow for a conference in The Hague; we're meeting—we're supposed to meet—in Paris next week."

"You won't tell him!" Stephanie exclaimed.

"I can't lie to him. I've already—"

"Sabrina, please! You don't have to lie; you just don't have to tell him! Please, please; you've got to give me some time. It's too soon; it's all happened so fast, I don't know what to . . . What am I going to tell Penny and Cliff? I've got to think about it; I've got to think about what I'm . . . what I can . . . I mean, I can't just walk in and pretend I've been there all this—" She stopped. That was what they could not talk about; not yet. That was what Sabrina had done: walked into a house that was not her own and built a life of love and cherishing . . . built a family.

He wants to know where I'll be staying. Léon will want to know where I am, Stephanie thought. And I want to be with him. But my children are with Garth.

Sabrina had pulled back, her body shrinking away. Stephanie saw the bleak emptiness on her face and knew she was thinking of Stephanie Andersen reclaiming her life: slipping smoothly into the house in Evanston, into her family, leaving Sabrina to return to London. Alone. As if the past year had never been.

But I couldn't do that, Stephanie thought. Garth would know. I couldn't fool Garth.

She looked again at Sabrina's desolate face, and tears came to her eyes. "I'm sorry, I'm sorry, I don't know what to think or what to say . . ." She leaped up and walked around the small courtyard, arms crossed, hugging herself as if to hold inside all the emotions that were clamoring for attention. She looked at Sabrina across the space between them. "Please don't tell him, Sabrina. *Please*. Not until I know what to do, what to say . . . how to talk to Penny and Cliff. Oh, God, it seemed so simple when we started . . . remember? But what do I tell them now? That I left them because I wanted a little adventure all to myself but now I'm back and ready to be their mother again? I can't say that; I have to think of something else, another way to . . . I can't do it! I can't face them! Please, Sabrina, please, I beg you, please give me some time!"

"All right." Sabrina's voice was so low that Stephanie did not hear the despair in it. "But just for a week. Just until we meet in Paris." Until who meets in Paris? an inner voice asked, but she pushed it away. She felt drained. She would keep the secret for Stephanie, but it could destroy everything she and Garth had built when he learned that she had kept it from him for a week that her sister was alive.

But isn't it destroyed anyway if Stephanie wants her family back?

"Then we can go to London right away." Stephanie's voice was calm now; she had averted a crisis and put off a decision. "That's the most important thing right now, isn't it? If you're right, if someone really will come after me . . . or you . . . or us . . ."

Her voice took on another kind of anxiety, the kind Sabrina recognized from when they were young: fearful, edgy, but also oddly confident, because Sabrina was there and Sabrina had always been the one to lead the way into adventures and find the way out of them. "We'll find them, won't we? We've got to! You're right, I can't stay in hiding forever, but I can't go through anything like that again . . . If you knew what it was like on that mountain, watching that man and Max and feeling so helpless . . . It comes back at night, you know; I wake up and I'm up there again and that man is so close to me, and then Max is telling me I'm in danger . . . Oh, you're right, you're right, we have to find out who it is and . . . stop it. Somehow. What shall we do in London? Talk to Rory Carr? We could make a list of people Max knew—''

Sabrina stood up. "I'm going to call home. They'll just be getting up."

"Home," Stephanie murmured. Her rush of words stopped; she stood, drooping, beside the wooden gate, holding a trailing vine of bougainvillaea. My home is with Léon, she thought.

And Sabrina paused at the door to the house and looked back at her sister, gazing intently at the tangled vines of pale purple flowers, fragile-looking but tough. My enemy, my love, Sabrina thought. We've spun a web that has no way out.

*L*éon drove them to the airport and Sabrina went alone onto the plane, leaving them to say goodbye.

They stood in a corner, away from the crowds. The sun streamed through the glass wall, and Stephanie closed her eyes against it. Léon held her to him with a kind of fatalism. "Through this whole mad story, this remains: I love you. And I'll be here. I'll wait as long as you need."

"But not forever," she murmured.

He smiled faintly. "Forever has a great deal of flexibility. I don't know how long mine would be. But you're right: I won't wait if you show no sign of being able to make up your mind to come to me."

She opened her eyes. "I love you, Léon. I want to marry you. I can't imagine living with Garth ever again. But . . ."

"But Penny and Cliff. I understand that. They're wonderful in those pictures; she showed us so many I felt I almost knew them."

"So many," Stephanie echoed, remembering the shock of seeing the small leather-bound album that Sabrina carried in her purse. Twenty photographs of Penny and Cliff playing, studying, reading, digging in the garden, grinning into the camera or making gargoyle faces and striking poses, Cliff in a muddy soccer uniform, Penny painting at an easel on the screened-in back porch, the two of them on bicycles with Garth. Stephanie barely looked at Garth, but she could not take her eyes off her children. How could they have grown so much in only a year? They had a poise, a confident stance, a lift to the head that she did not remember. She had not even recognized their clothes. She had ached to hold them and she had studied each picture for some sign of unhappiness or insecurity. But she had found none. They were all prospering, she had thought: secure, comfortable, loved. And the house had looked neater than she remembered it: newly painted, the warped boards on the front porch replaced and stained, the bushes trimmed. So many pictures, she had mused, leafing through them again and again. Most parents are satisfied with one or two. And then she remembered that Sabrina was not even a parent. Or maybe . . .

She shook off the memory and kissed Léon, clinging to him, afraid to let him go. "I'll call you. I can't decide anything until we know what we can do in London, but I'll call you, I promise, every day."

"I can still come with you; there are seats on this plane. It might be better—"

Stephanie was shaking her head. "I told you before, Léon, we have to be together and figure out who we are and what we're going to do, and no one can help us with that. We got ourselves into this and somehow we'll get ourselves out."

"You may. You may find it impossible. And meanwhile you could be in danger. If you would go to the police—"

"We can't. I told you: if we went to them the whole story would come out and Penny and Cliff would . . . oh, God, read about me in the newspapers, hear about me on television, that I left them . . . You said you understood that, Léon; I have to tell them myself."

"And when will you do that?"

"When I know what to say. And how to say it."

"But first you'll go off on this crazy adventure in London, the two of you, after you told me you'd had enough of crazy adventures."

"But we're in danger. You just said that. We have to do this."

"Yes, all right, I understand that. But at least let me come with you. I don't know how much good I'd be at protecting you, but you might need help; how do you know what you're getting into?"

They heard the final boarding call for the plane. "We'll be careful; we'll be all right." She kissed him. "I'll call you, I love you, please don't forget. I love you."

He held her for one last moment. "I want to do so much for you. But you'll have to let me."

"I know." She tried to promise him that she would, that they would do so much for each other, but she could not promise. "Thank you for saying that; thank you for wanting it for me. Please trust me; I'll try . . . I love you."

In the plane, Sabrina was sitting in the aisle seat, her hands folded loosely in her lap. She looked up. "I thought you might want the window." A glass of orange juice was on the small tray between the wide leather seats, and she held it while Stephanie slid past.

"Thank you. I would like to see Paris again, even if only from above; it's been so long. Do I look all right?"

Sabrina smiled. "Like a woman in disguise."

"But it's all right?"

"Yes, of course; you look wonderful." They had chosen their clothes the night before, dressing for London in October: Stephanie in a gray wool pants suit Max had bought for her, perfectly tailored, with a high-necked sweater and a wide-brimmed felt hat pulled low over her forehead, almost touching her dark glasses. Her hair was in a braid tucked beneath the hat. She wore no makeup. Sabrina wore a wine-red wool dress with a long triple strand of pearls and carried a matching cape; her hair fell in long waves below her shoulders, her makeup was distinctive. "We look perfect," she said and looked up as the steward came with his tray of drinks.

"*Madame Lacoste, voulez-vous un jus de fruit ou du champagne?*"

"*Jus,*" Stephanie said, looking directly at him, and when he had served her and left, she grinned at Sabrina and lowered her voice as she switched to English. "He didn't even look twice."

"Because we don't look the same, not much, anyway. But we shouldn't push it in London. I don't think we should be seen together at all."

"Until we feel safe. And then—" An amplified voice gave instructions in French and English as the plane moved away from the gate, and Sabrina leaned closer to hear her sister's faint voice. "And then I won't be Sabrina Lacoste anymore."

Sabrina looked past her, out the window. They had made an unspoken agreement not to talk about the future. First they would do whatever they could in London and then they would confront themselves. They both knew it was cowardly, but they wanted these few days together, to rediscover what they had been to each other in the past. *Because whatever we do, it's going to change again. And we don't have any idea how much we can salvage.*

She saw the vast sprawl of Paris tilt as the plane banked and turned north. The gold dome of the Invalides gleamed in the morning sunlight, the Eiffel Tower's web of girders was silhouetted against a pale blue sky. She thought of Garth at The Hague, giving his talk, joining in seminars, part of a community of scientists. "Yes, it's a good conference, one of the best," he had said on the telephone the night before. "But I'm having trouble concentrating. All I want to do is meet my wife at L'Hôtel on Sunday."

Five days from now. I have five more days to be Stepha-

nie Andersen, Garth's wife, Penny and Cliff's mother, a homemaker and interior designer from Evanston, Illinois.

The silver ribbon of the Seine meandered out of Paris into the green countryside and suddenly Sabrina felt a rush of relief. They were free. The land and its entanglements lay thousands of feet below, they floated through sparkling sunlit space in a cocoon of leather and tapestry and shining metal, and they were together.

Stephanie turned from the window and met her eyes. "We're free. Isn't it amazing? And wonderful? I wish we could just keep flying for . . . oh, a long time."

Their hands met, their fingers twined. "We'll have to figure out how to feel this way on the ground," Sabrina said.

"Oh, if we could."

The steward returned. *"Madame Lacoste, Madame Andersen, voulez-vous du vin? Du café? Nous avons une variété de pâtisseries . . ."*

"Café et pâtisseries," Sabrina said, and Stephanie nodded. They held hands until he brought trays set with linen, crystal and china and offered them a choice of pastries in a woven basket. He filled their coffee cups.

"Merci," Stephanie said and turned to Sabrina. "I do like being waited on. Part of the magic of London was Mrs. Thirkell. And even though I loved being alone with Léon in Vézelay, sometimes I missed Madame Besset."

"They sound like two of a kind. Another thing we shared all year. I like your friend Robert."

"Oh, yes. Wasn't it wonderful that he came to Vézelay before we left?"

"Yes, but that was no accident. He came to help. He was afraid he'd find chaos and disarray—"

"Léon furious or perhaps even gone—"

"And the two of us at swords' points, or something like that; anyway, having a lot of trouble loving each other."

They laughed softly, remembering Robert as he had stood in the doorway, dressed in a bright red shirt and blue jeans, gazing solemnly from one of them to the other, then smiling and holding out his hands. "Two amazing women. Beautiful, intelligent, energetic, and very, very foolish."

"Yes," Sabrina had said. "If you came to tell us that, we've already discussed it more than once."

"I came to help. But you seem to be fine. I'm comforted by the way you look at each other; you haven't lost love or trust." He looked around. "And Léon?"

"At his studio," Stephanie said. "He'll be here soon for dinner. You'll stay with us, Robert, won't you? We have an extra room."

"Gladly." He looked closely at her. "No more nightmares about Mont Ventoux?"

"Yes, but Léon is wonderful, and getting away from Cavaillon helped. But I've missed you."

"And I've missed you. Our little town is quite dull without our talks and our cooking lessons. And without Max. I loved him, you know. We talked often; he called almost every day, sometimes on business, but usually just to chat."

"What kind of business?" Sabrina asked.

Robert hesitated only a moment. "He helped me smuggle young people into countries of great poverty and political repression, and, when necessary, out of them."

Stephanie stared at him. "But he was smuggling counterfeit money; that was why I wouldn't go away with him."

"Wait." Robert closed his eyes briefly. "Money. In those large pieces of equipment. He always had huge crates coming and going: returns, he said. I thought the returns were high. And Frick . . . Frick made the money. Max once called him his Dürer. I thought he was joking, but I should have caught on: Dürer was a brilliant engraver. Oh, Max, Max, I made use of you, I loved you, and you were everything I didn't want to think you were. All the clues were there and I ignored them because I chose not to know."

Sabrina thought of Garth in the beginning, ignoring clues so that he could believe Sabrina was his wife. *We*

485

*shape the world to our own needs and desires, and when
we can't, sometimes we call it a disappointment and other
times we call it tragedy.*

"Smuggling young people?" Stephanie asked. "For
what?"

"To help poor people resist despots. To help them organize and protest, sometimes to take the land that rightfully should be theirs, sometimes simply to manage their
own villages without interference. All those activities are,
of course, illegal in those countries, and so, when the
governments begin to close in, we bring the young people
home. Max helped me bring a young woman out shortly
before he was killed. That was an adventure: we were like
two boys."

"A good deed," Stephanie said suddenly.

"Yes, he did many."

"No. I mean, I know he did, but I meant something
else. He told me that he did a good deed and, because of
it, that man found him and killed him. He said it was some
kind of coincidence."

Robert stood with clasped hands, his head bowed.
"Jana," he said at last.

"What?"

"The young woman we brought out. Jana Corley. I
thought she and Max looked at each other in a way that
seemed . . . well, it was just a passing thought, but it
seemed to me that they knew each other."

"Corley," Sabrina said. "I know a Tabitha and Ramsay Corley. He owns factories in Manchester; they have a
home in Kent."

"Her mother's name is Tabitha," Robert said slowly.
"She told me that once. But Jana is discreet; she doesn't
talk about our work. I can't believe she would talk to
anyone about someone helping me, as Max was that
night."

"Well, we'll find out," Sabrina said decisively. "We
wondered where we'd start in London. Now we know."

Robert held their hands. "Take care, my children. You

are so lovely and full of life, but you know that there is evil in the world. You did a foolhardy and dangerous thing when you traded places; now you must be exceedingly wise and cautious and thoughtful.'' He kissed their foreheads and Sabrina felt it was a blessing. ''I wish you well. You must write to me, or call. We must not lose each other.''

The plane flew over the flat fields of Normandy and then the English Channel, speckled with tiny whitecaps like flecks of snow. The coast of England was visible at the top of Sabrina's window. London, she thought. Home for so many years. Home, work, friends.

''Will we stay at Cadogan Square?'' Stephanie asked.

''Yes, for the last time. I sold it to Alexandra's friends, but they won't take possession until—''

''You sold it? You sold your house?''

''I have another one.'' The words whipped out before Sabrina could stop them. She set down her coffee cup with a shaking hand. *How are we going to keep from talking about who we are and what we're going to do?*

The steward removed their trays; there was a bustle in the cabin as passengers slid their tables into the slots in the arms of the seats, put away computers and briefcases and prepared to land.

''Do you want to be the one to talk to Jana?'' she asked. ''You were living with Max; it makes sense for you to do it.''

''Oh. Yes, if you'd like.'' And they both knew that by veering away from it they had decided, once again, that they could keep from talking about it as long as they both wanted to.

Stephanie's face was averted; she was watching the land come up to meet them, and thinking about touching down at Heathrow. It was so nice up there, she thought; now I have to face things. Except . . . not alone. Sabrina will help me. She'll get us through this. Somehow.

The house on Cadogan Square was dark and chilly, huddling against the rain that drummed from a leaden sky.

Sabrina made a fire in the sitting room while Stephanie ran to the market and brought back food for lunch and dinner. They both were at home in the neighborhood and in the house, moving easily through its rooms, and both felt the strangeness of that but did not comment on it.

"Shall I call her?" Stephanie asked. "I don't want to go all the way to Kent if she's out of town."

"She might have a flat in town." Sabrina paged through the telephone directory. "There's a J. Corley in London, near Berkeley Square. It's worth a try."

"That's so close. I think I won't call; I'll just take a chance."

"I'll have lunch ready when you get back."

Stephanie called for a taxi and Sabrina watched her, marveling that she was so comfortable in London and Cadogan Square after such a brief time. But why not? she thought. How long did it take me, in Evanston?

Stephanie found a raincoat and hat and umbrella in the foyer closet and dashed from the front door to the taxi. As they crawled through the traffic, she looked at the streets and buildings and undulating lines of black umbrellas with bewilderment. London, ageless and familiar, felt like home. But she had felt the tug of belonging as she looked at the scenes of Evanston in Sabrina's photograph album. And Cavaillon had been home. And Vézelay was home now—or anywhere, with Léon.

What's wrong with me? Can't I even say where I belong?

Jana Corley's apartment was in a curved row of flats, gray and dripping in the rain. Stephanie rang the bell and when a young voice came over the intercom, she said, "I'm a friend of Robert Chalon."

A buzzer sounded; she opened the door and climbed two flights of stairs. Jana was waiting, thin and blond, wearing a sweatsuit and heavy socks, her eyebrows still raised in surprise at Stephanie's announcement.

Stephanie held out her hand. "Sabrina Lacoste. And you're Jana Corley?" She kept her hand in Jana's and walked her back into the flat. All the lamps were on, and a small gas fire burned in the grate. The bewilderment Stephanie had felt in the taxi was gone: she felt strong and purposeful because she was doing something she and Sabrina had planned together. "I'm a friend of Robert's; I lived in Cavaillon until a short while ago. I lived with a man named Max Lacoste. But I think you knew him as Max Stuyvesant."

Jana's face became wary and she pulled away. "Max Stuyvesant is dead."

"He was thought to be dead. He's been living in Cavaillon. You know that. You met him there, when you were with Robert."

"But I didn't say anything. I mean, I didn't tell him I recognized him; it was obvious that he didn't want me to. I guess Robert didn't know. And I could understand it, you know; if I'd been mixed up in that Westbridge business I'd have wanted to duck out, too. And I figured maybe he was sort of doing penance for it."

"Penance?" Stephanie asked.

"Well, you know, he was working with Robert; you do know they brought me out of Chile? They even did this routine, it was like a movie, when I was locked up in a warehouse in Marseilles: Robert got the guard drunk so Max could take his keys, and they broke open the crate I was hiding in . . . I was never so glad to see anybody in my life. So if Max was working with Robert, he was doing good, and I thought it might be to sort of balance Westbridge and whatever else he'd done. You know, after Westbridge everybody laid the most incredible exploits on him; it was mostly envy, I think. Like he'd lived out their fantasies. I'm sorry, I didn't offer you anything. Would you like tea? Or soup? I'm heating some for lunch; anything to keep warm. I hate October; all of a sudden it's winter. What do you take in your tea?"

"Nothing, I don't want anything, thanks. I have an engagement for lunch. I need to ask you something."

"About Max? Did he send you here?"

489

"I'm trying to find out if you told anyone you'd seen him in Marseilles."

"No, of course I— Oh. Well, I did, as a matter of fact. I shouldn't have, but Alan absolutely promised he wouldn't tell anyone. We hadn't seen each other in a long time and I was . . . well, you know, I was very relaxed and I sort of let it out. That didn't get back to Max, did it? I can't imagine how it would."

"Who is Alan?"

"My fiancé. Alan Lethridge. Well, he's not exactly my fiancé, but I call him that sometimes, when I'm feeling fond of him. But, you know, he promised he wouldn't tell anyone and I'm sure he didn't. I'll ask him, if you like."

"I'd like to ask him myself. If you'll tell me where to find him . . ."

Jana frowned. "Did something happen?"

"I'm just looking for information. And it would be helpful if I could talk to Alan."

"Well." She went to the desk and stood beside it indecisively, then shrugged. "I guess Alan can take care of himself." She wrote on a pad of paper and handed the sheet to Stephanie. "He's usually home by four."

"Thank you."

Jana followed her to the door. "Say hello to Max for me when you see him. I don't care whether he wants to stay in hiding or not. He did a good thing for me and I'll always be grateful."

"Thank you," Stephanie said again. "I'm glad to hear it."

In the taxi she gazed unseeing at the streaming window, thinking of Max, whom Robert had loved and Jana admired, who tried to control everything and everyone around him, who lived by his own rules whether he was doing good or breaking the law. *They even did this routine, it was like a movie.* I couldn't love him, she thought, but I could have tried to get to know him better, to understand him. I wish I had.

Sabrina had set the small table in the sitting room, and

Stephanie warmed herself at the fire before sitting down. The lashing wind and rain made the room hushed in dry snugness, and Stephanie sighed as Sabrina poured a white wine. "So lovely. Maybe we could make time stop for a while."

"Yes, we keep thinking that."

Sabrina filled their bowls from the soup tureen, and it occurred to Stephanie that her sister was acting as hostess, pouring wine, serving soup in her own home. *Has she already decided to come back here? What is it she wants?*

"Tell me about Jana," Sabrina said, and as she listened to Stephanie's brief report she thought how well Stephanie looked, how confident in relating her conversation. *Does she think she can do whatever she wants, with Penny and Cliff, with Garth, with Léon? With me? She can't believe I'll just walk away from them; she knows now what they are to me.* "So Alan is next," she said when Stephanie finished. "Do you want to talk to him?"

"Oh, no, it's your turn. Unless you'd rather not. Have you ever met him?"

"I've met his mother, but I never liked her. Xanthia Lethridge. As I recall, no one ever talked to her because she couldn't keep anything to herself; it would be all over London the next—" Her eyes met Stephanie's. "Maybe it runs in the family. I'll call him; if he's in town I'll see him tomorrow."

Alan Lethridge lived in a town house filled with his parents' discarded furniture. "Awful stuff, isn't it?" he said to Sabrina, leading her into the drawing room. He was tall and thin, with a handsome, eager face and long hair; he wore blue jeans and an oversize sweater. "No wonder they got rid of it. But I'm too lazy to shop and I wouldn't know what to buy anyway. I'm waiting for a princess to rescue me and turn the place into a palace. Won't you sit down, Mrs. Andersen? What can I do for you? I remember I met your sister somewhere a long time ago, but I don't know where."

Sabrina sat on the edge of a hassock and waited until he

sat nearby. "I'm trying to find Max Stuyvesant and I thought you might be able to help me."

"Max? *Max Stuyvesant?* What are you talking about?" There was a clamorous silence; Sabrina could almost hear options running through his mind. "Is this some kind of a joke? Max is dead."

"He was presumed dead. But didn't you find out that he was alive?"

"Me? I didn't find out anything. How could I? I didn't know him; I never saw him. I mean, I did once in a while, I mean, people do, you know, at parties or the races, but we never talked; the fact is, I'd barely know him if I saw him."

"But I think you heard he was alive and told someone."

"I didn't." He looked at the ceiling, seeking help. "I mean, I didn't hear he was alive, so naturally I couldn't tell anyone anything."

"I think you did tell someone. And it's important that you tell me who it was."

"Nobody! Look, I'm sorry, Mrs. Andersen, but obviously I can't help you, so if you don't have anything else . . . I mean, I'm sorry to be rude, but . . ." He stood and looked down at her.

Sabrina stood beside him. He was indeed being rude, and the only reason for that was fear. "This isn't a game, Alan. It's very important; in fact, someone could be in danger—" Panic flared in his eyes, his mouth tightened stubbornly and he strode to the door. A mistake, Sabrina thought, at least a mistake until she and Stephanie decided how much to tell him. She followed him to the door, her voice casual now. "If you remember something, please call me. I'm staying at Lady Longworth's house and I'll be there for a few more days."

"There's nothing to remember." Sabrina thought he sounded like Cliff, mumbling, grouchy, guilty.

"He's lying and he's not very good at it," she said to Stephanie, at home.

"Is he afraid?" Stephanie asked. "What would he be afraid of?"

"Maybe Jana. If she's the princess he's waiting for, he wouldn't want her to know he broke his promise, especially if there are serious consequences. We have to decide how much to tell him, in case we want to talk to him again."

"Why can't we just tell him what happened to Max?"

"Because . . ." Sabrina got up to add a log to the fire. They were in the upstairs sitting room, where they spent most of their time, the drapes pulled shut, the fire casting a flickering copper glow on their faces, cashmere afghans lying lightly over their laps as Sabrina lay on the chaise and Stephanie curled up in a deep armchair. A tea service was on the table between them, and now and then they exchanged a smile because it was so good to be together in this warm, private place. "Because I don't think we should tell anyone."

"But why not? How can we find out who sent that man if we don't tell people what happened?"

"I don't know. I just think it's best not to tell anyone, at least for now. It's just a feeling I have. We can talk about it some more if you want; I'm sorry I can't give you a reason."

"No, it's all right. I trust you." Stephanie leaned forward and lifted the quilted cozy off the teapot to refill their cups. "But if Alan won't tell you anything, what do we do now?"

"Talk to Lazlo and Carr. I don't know how close they were to Max, but we do know they worked for him and they quarreled over their forgery business. Maybe somebody talked to them about Max, or asked questions that seemed unusual, or . . . Oh."

"What?"

"I just remembered. The oddest thing. One day last spring, when I was over here, Denton came into Ambassadors and asked me if I'd heard from Max."

"*Heard from Max?*"

"Yes, I thought he'd gone crazy. But when I said Max was dead, he said he was *presumed* dead, that they'd never found a body. And he thought he might have called me."

"That's sort of scary, isn't it? What did you tell him?"

"That Max was his friend, so if he were alive he would have called him, not Stephanie Andersen in America. And then he said . . . wait a minute, I'll try to remember . . . He said, 'Well, if he does surface—' and then he apologized for putting it that way—'if he does and if he happens to call you, would you let me know? I somehow can't believe he's really dead, you know. He always seemed indestructible to me.' And there was something else, Stephanie. I think he was afraid."

"Of what?"

"I don't know. But I'm going to call him."

She spoke briefly on the telephone, then hung up. "Hunting in Germany. Back on Friday."

"Well, but he couldn't really know anything, could he? It was just some kind of weird thing. Does Denton do weird things?"

"He wasn't crazy when I was married to him, if that's what you mean. And he wouldn't be frightened without a reason. Well, I'll talk to him on Friday. Or maybe you'll do it; you might be better with him. But first we'll find Rory Carr or Ivan Lazlo. Maybe both of them."

At her desk, Sabrina called Michel Bernard and Jolie Fantôme, who had written the newspaper articles exposing Westbridge Imports and Max Stuyvesant. "They're on assignment in Canada, Mrs. Andersen," said their assistant. "Can I help?" And when Sabrina told him what she wanted, he said, "Carr and Lazlo are London, both of them, at Wormwood Scrubs Prison in Shepherds Bush. They're in the lifers unit, you know, so they get only one VO—sorry, visiting order—a month, and it's only for ninety minutes. So you'll have to find out if they've had a visitor for October. They may not have, since it's early in the month. If you need me for anything else, please call. Good luck."

"They're in London," Sabrina said. "Wormwood Scrubs Prison. Not far: Shepherds Bush, on the west side. Shall we each take one?"

"Oh. Yes, why not?" They looked at each other and burst out laughing. "Remember Dmitri?" Stephanie asked.

"And Theo, poor Theo, our—"

"—chauffeur. And those swimming parties when one of us would dive in and nobody knew—"

"—which one of us came up at which end of the pool."

"And one of the embassy secretaries giving us a lecture and getting us mixed up and you'd say—"

" *'I'm* Sabrina, Miss Derringer, that's Stephanie,' and she'd get so furious she'd just about choke on those eighteen strands of pearls she wore every day . . ."

They were laughing and they moved into each other's arms, holding each other tightly in the sheer joy of being together. "It's the same," Stephanie whispered. "We haven't lost any of it."

Yes, we have, Sabrina thought bleakly, but she did not say it because she did not want to shatter this time together. Right now they were caught up in the hunt, following it with the closeness and delight that had once been the most important things in their lives, and so this brief time itself became the most important thing in their lives, for as long as it lasted.

But too much has changed. And this is the last time. We'll never have it again.

The visiting room at Wormwood Scrubs Prison was narrow and low-ceilinged, with a long table for prisoners and their visitors. Impassive guards watched for the slightest movement that was out of the ordinary. The noise increased as visitors arrived; voices bounced off gray walls and the gray floor and ceiling. As she walked into the room Sabrina felt that the world had turned to gray, leaching the color from her blue and green plaid suit, her blue hat and blue leather gloves. And when she took off her gloves her hands looked pasty beneath the unforgiving lights.

Through a far door, Rory Carr walked in, dressed in gray. His silver hair was slicked back, but that was all that was left of the impeccable art dealer Sabrina remembered. The skin of his neck hung in folds, his eyes were sunken and restless, the pouches beneath them puffed half-moons sliding down his cheeks. But his voice was almost the same: as unctuous as if he oiled it regularly. "Mrs. Andersen, I am very glad to see you. I've wanted for a long time to express to you my profound regret at the death of Lady Longworth. I sincerely hope you will believe me when I say that I had nothing but admiration and affection for her. I never knew she would be on the yacht when Ivan proposed his mad scheme. Of course I had no influence on his infantile and destructive behavior, but had I known, I could have tried to stop him. It haunts me that I might at least have tried."

"No influence," Sabrina murmured. The newspapers had reported that Rory Carr had been indicted as a principal—an accomplice, aider and abettor in the heinous crime—and found guilty of murder.

"None whatsoever." Carr's voice deepened. "Lazlo is an animal; no one can deal with him. But foolishly I believed him and trusted him, and I am paying for my foolishness by being forced to greet you in these depressing surroundings."

Sabrina sat in the hard straight chair and folded her hands on the table. The room was filling up and the clamor of dozens of voices crying, swearing, demanding, begging, forced everyone to speak even louder to be heard across the width of the table. She looked at Rory Carr's ruined face and told herself that he had been a partner with Lazlo in murdering fourteen people and in trying to murder her sister. She waited to feel hatred for him, but she felt nothing. Stephanie was alive and Carr's life was over.

So she could talk to him and make him feel she was not an enemy. "No one can deal with Ivan? I thought Max Stuyvesant dealt with him. And with you."

"Well, Max . . . Ivan worked for Max for many, many years. At least fifteen. He did Max's bidding."

"Except when he put a bomb under his stateroom."

"Please." Carr held up his hand. "I can't bear to think of it. Max was one of my favorite people, a good friend, a superb art aficionado, an absolute genius in smuggling. I admired him enormously."

"Then it will please you to know that there is a rumor that he is alive."

"*Alive?*" Carr's body seemed to surge across the table. A guard moved forward and he sat straight again, staring at a far wall. In a moment he smiled a gentle smile. "Dear Mrs. Andersen, that is not possible. Your credulity is charming—very American—but whatever you have heard cannot be true. I would be delighted if it were, but really, there is no way that Max could be alive. He was killed on his yacht last October. Everyone knows that."

"There is speculation that in fact he wasn't killed; that he's been living in France."

"Speculation? A vague word. What does it mean?" His condescending voice roughened at the edges. "Believe me, Mrs. Andersen, he is not alive!"

"You mean no one else has suggested to you that he might be living in Provence, running an export company in Marseilles, perhaps smuggling counterfeit money into Third World countries?"

At the addition of each new detail, Carr's face sagged farther, like taffy oozing off the edge of a spoon. "Of course not. Of course not." In the surrounding din, a small pool of silence spread between them. "My God . . . could that be possible?" His glance raced around the room. "You're serious? There is evidence that Max is alive? Mrs. Andersen, you must tell me! Is he alive or not?"

He had skidded from patronizing to terrified, and it

seemed clear to Sabrina that he was telling the truth: no one had told him. So he was not the one who had sent an assassin to Provence. Someone else had, most likely the same person who had ordered Lazlo and Carr to kill Max on his yacht, someone so powerful that Carr was terrified. Of what? Of being punished, perhaps killed, even inside Wormwood Scrubs Prison, for failing to kill Max on his yacht?

"Well?" he demanded. "Is he alive or not?"

"I can't tell you. But if he is, he would be very grateful if you cooperated with the police and told them who ordered you and Lazlo to set the bomb—"

"What? What's that? No one ordered us—my God, what are you saying? Ivan set the bomb because he was afraid of Max, afraid Max might kill us. We'd had our little business, you know, small forgeries, nothing major, but it was a nice living. But Max thought it would lead the police to Westbridge, and we quarreled . . . But you know all that; you read it in the papers. What did you mean about someone ordering us?"

"Perhaps I'm wrong. But suppose there is someone. He's not in prison; we'd know about it. So he's outside. How did he manage to put you and Ivan here for years while he went on with his life as if nothing had happened? I know Ivan isn't too bright, but I thought you'd be too smart for that."

"I am. I know what I'm doing."

Sabrina tilted her head thoughtfully. "So someone has promised to take care of you when you get out. Money or a job, maybe a house in some warm climate? Come on, Rory, what did he promise you? Even lifers can apply for parole after enough years; you'd still have time to enjoy being set up somewhere. Who was it?"

"I don't know what you're talking about."

"Well," Sabrina said after a silence, and stood up.

"You're not going!" Carr exclaimed. "Our ninety minutes aren't up."

"I might as well, if you can't tell me anything."

"Tell you what?"

"Whom you're working for."

"I just told you! Is that why you came? Because you imagined . . . Mrs. Andersen, Ivan did it! By himself! I did nothing, though I confess I knew about it. But no one else is involved! I assure you, I swear to you, no one else!"

His face was shiny with terror and Sabrina felt a rush of triumph because she knew she was right. But there was no pleasure in reducing Rory Carr to terror; she was sick of the whole thing. "Well, as I said, I may be wrong. But I certainly thought there were signs that pointed to someone else."

Carr's head jutted forward. "Why?"

"Oh, rumors; you know how people talk."

"More rumors? My God . . . But no one has anything to talk about."

"Would Max, if he were alive?"

"No. Nothing."

"How about the man who told you to kill Max?"

"*I told you* there wasn't anyone."

"But just as a hypothesis. If someone ordered you and Ivan to kill Max, he'd have something to talk about, wouldn't he? Maybe in bed with someone or in a bar or at a party where everyone was bragging about something or other . . ."

"No! It's a crazy hypothesis."

"Well, crazy or not, perhaps he sends you money and writes to you and does what he can to make you more comfortable. *Does* anyone write to you or send you money?"

"No."

"I'm sorry to hear it. You have indeed been abandoned. How about visits?"

"No."

"No visits?"

"Not since—" Carr pressed his lips together, struggled with the idea of saying more, then shrugged. "Not for a couple of months. Nicholas used to visit both of us, but he stopped. Of course he's having financial troubles and I gather he and Amelia have gone their separate ways, but still, he's a free man and I'm in here and it's quite selfish of him to worry about himself so much that he has no time for me. I miss our talks about art. I should think he misses them, too; he doesn't have so many friends, you know; he's not generally a lovable person."

"Perhaps he'll come back." Sabrina stood up again, anxious to leave. Her heart was pounding. Nicholas. Nicholas, who had tried twice to wrest Ambassadors from her and had been worried about her looking too closely at the finances of Ambassadors and Blackford's . . . Nicholas might have known about the forgeries, might have joined forces with Rory and Ivan to add to his income and then decided to kill Max if Max had threatened to expose him.

No. He isn't smart enough, she thought. Also, he's a coward.

But he knows something. He must, or why would he have come here? Why would fastidious, self-centered Nicholas have come to Wormwood Scrubs Prison month after month to talk about art with Rory Carr?

She started to ask Carr if Nicholas had worked with him, but changed her mind. It would be best to go to Nicholas.

"No one comes back," said Carr mournfully. "No one cares. And Max isn't alive. No one could have survived that bomb. The police said the same thing, you know; no one could have survived."

"Goodbye, Rory." Following a guard, Sabrina hurried through the prison to the cold sunshine outside, the clear air, the distant horizon. She drove to a hotel where Stephanie waited, and while she told Stephanie about the conversation she changed into black slacks and a black sweater while Stephanie put on the blue and green plaid suit, the blue hat, the leather gloves. "He's terrified," Sabrina said. "I'd guess Ivan will be, too. And if he doesn't mention Nicholas, be sure you do.'' And then she waited for Stephanie to return.

It was almost an hour before she did. "He's mean and stupid,'' Stephanie said contemptuously. "And he looks like a ferret or a weasel or whatever they are: as thin as a rope and he *slinks*; he almost bends around corners. Why would Max have anything to do with him?''

"I gather he was efficient. Did he say anything about Nicholas?''

"He talked about everybody but himself. Can't we talk in the car? I really want to get out of here.''

"Give me a minute.'' Sabrina twisted her hair on top of her head and pulled on a black hat with a floppy brim that left only her long, graceful neck exposed. She fastened a black fur-lined cape at her throat and put on oversize dark glasses. She and Stephanie stood before the mirror while Stephanie applied more lipstick, combed her hair so that it fell loosely over her shoulders and down her back, and adjusted the small blue hat at a sharp angle, leaving her face free. "Pretty good,'' Sabrina said, looking at their distinct images with approval. "I'll pick you up in front in about twenty minutes.''

Dressing up and playacting, she thought as she went to a taxi stand and directed the driver to take her to the hotel. For all the seriousness of what they were doing, and the deadly crime at the core of it, they were having fun, like children playing a game. Having an adventure. Doing something for a lark. A shiver went through her. *Just this time. We won't do it again. Whatever happens, after this we'll never playact anymore.*

Stephanie was waiting in front of the hotel, and stepped quickly into the taxi as it pulled up. "I never want to go to a prison again,'' she said as the driver turned around for the drive back to Cadogan Square. "Nobody seemed to like anybody; most of them were blaming each other for everything.''

"You mean Ivan?''

"Everybody. The prisoners blamed their families and

the families blamed the prisoners, and they all blamed somebody else for whatever they'd done, like the landlord or the police or the foreman at the factory . . . Oh, Lord, what an unhappy place. It makes me feel so lucky . . ."

"Yes." They fell silent and only began talking again when they reached the green expanse of Kensington Gardens, alive with the cheerful voices of children playing, and turned onto Gloucester Road to go home. "Did Ivan say anything about Nicholas?" Sabrina asked.

"Mostly he blamed everything on Rory Carr. He said no one could deal with him. I said that Max had, and he said Rory did Max's bidding, and I said, 'Except when he planted the bomb under his stateroom,' and he said—"

"Did you really? That's exactly what I said. What did he say about Nicholas?"

"That he didn't come to visit anymore. Amelia left him, he said, and he's got financial problems, but it's a dirty trick to think only of himself and let Ivan rot. I was going to ask him if Nicholas had worked with them— could that be possible? It seems incredible to me—but I thought if they *did* work together they could still get in touch, and why let Ivan know I was even thinking that?"

"Yes, that's what I thought. And I just wanted to get out of there."

"Let's go see Nicholas, shall we? Right now." Stephanie saw Sabrina smile and she laughed a little self-consciously. "I know how it sounds—like somebody on a hunt—but that's how I feel, and now we have a new clue and I can't wait to do something about it."

Sabrina looked at her watch. "He usually leaves at three. We'd better wait till morning. Do you want to be the one to talk to him?"

"I don't know. We should think about what we'll say."

"Maybe . . ." Sabrina smiled to herself. "Maybe we should take turns. Shake him up a little."

"Would it? Maybe we should."

"Oh, I don't know. It was just a thought. Another game."

They turned to look at each other. "We're getting so good at them," Stephanie said.

"Yes." In a minute Sabrina leaned forward. "There used to be a little grocery store here, but I don't see it; I guess we'll go to Harrods."

"What for?"

"Dinner. We didn't buy enough yesterday."

"Oh, Sabrina, can't we go out? There must be lots of places in London where nobody knew you and it won't mean anything to them if they see us together. Please, can't we?"

"I thought the whole idea was that we wouldn't be seen together."

"I know, but now that we're here it doesn't seem that anything could hurt us. Doesn't it seem that way to you? I know that Max was killed, probably by somebody from here, but that doesn't really mean we're in danger."

"I think we could be."

"Well, maybe. It's hard to believe, though, when everything is so normal, people going about their business . . . What do you think could happen? Do you think someone is going to shoot us if he sees us together?"

"I don't know. But that part of it isn't a game. You saw Max get killed, Stephanie; whoever caused that to happen isn't a normal person just going about his business; he's somebody who thinks he has to kill to protect himself. Do you really want him to know Sabrina Longworth is alive?"

Stephanie was silent. "Well." She sighed. "I just thought it would be nice to go out together. It's fun to playact, but it's been so long since we did things together, and I was thinking that we might not be together like this again . . . at least, not for quite a while."

"Oh. Well, we'll think about it. I suppose we could go out of town. Maybe tomorrow night. First we have to decide what we're going to say to Nicholas."

At dinner in the sitting room, before the fire, they wrote out questions and practiced asking them, as if they were rehearsing a play. But the next morning, when Stephanie walked into Blackford's, Nicholas gave her no chance to ask any of them.

He came to greet her, bouncing on his small feet, hands outstretched, a merry smile on his face that did not reach his eyes. "My dear Stephanie, what a surprise, a splendid surprise, to be sure, but still . . . why didn't you let me know you were coming? I would have arranged a festive board at the Savoy to make up for last time."

Stephanie gazed at him, frowning slightly; she had no idea what he was talking about.

"Well, of course you would prefer to forget it; I assure you, so would I. Believe me, Stephanie, never have I done anything like that. To walk away and leave a woman alone in a restaurant . . . good Lord, it twists like a knife inside me whenever I think about it. You have my apology, my heartfelt, *agonized* apology; I can't imagine how I could have done it; it's not in my character—but of course you know that; we've been good friends since your dear sister left us, and you know it is not my way to do such things. Well, now we can put that behind us and go on as before. Let me show you what I've done with the shop . . . a few new pieces, not as many as I'd like, but the economy, you know, and a slow summer—"

"Is that the real reason, Nicholas? Are you sure it has nothing to do with your finances?"

He swung around. "Good heavens, what a question. Has someone been talking about me? Might you have gone to Amelia before coming here? I hadn't thought you were close to her. But if you did, you heard many falsehoods and I should tell you . . ."

Stephanie was silent until his litany of complaints about Amelia, which slid smoothly into mistrust of Brian's work at Ambassadors, ran down. When at last it did, she said, "I haven't talked to Amelia. I'd rather hear from you what your finances are."

"But they're fine, why wouldn't they be? Business is always slow in the summer; by now you should know that. I'm quite dismayed, Stephanie; I thought we understood that it was to our mutual benefit to be friends in a trusting association, and not allow suspicion to cloud our relationship.''

''Suspicion? All I did was ask about your finances. I thought if you've been in trouble for a few years—''

''I have not been in trouble! Good Lord, Stephanie, you Americans see dark plots everywhere . . . it must be all those gangster movies. Have you really nothing else to think about?''

Frustrated, Stephanie contemplated him. ''You're doing well; everything is fine—''

''Exactly. Exactly.'' A jovial smile creased his face.

''—and there's been no reason in the past few years for you to look for other sources of income.''

His smile faded. ''What an odd thing to say. Are you fabricating another plot?''

''Plots depend on secrets, Nicholas, and if anyone has them, you do. You'll have to excuse me; I have another appointment.''

Stymied, angry, she took a taxi to Cadogan Square. ''I was no good at all. I didn't get anything out of him.''

Sabrina stepped into the skirt Stephanie had taken off. ''You can't be subtle with Nicholas; he sees it as weakness.'' She buttoned Stephanie's blouse and pulled on her tweed blazer. ''You wore a hat, didn't you?''

''Your brown cloche. It's amazing how many clothes you still have here.''

''I only took the ones that are right for Evanston.'' She veered away from that subject. ''Have you told me everything he said?''

''Yes. It wasn't exactly a long conversation.''

''Well, we're about to begin the second act.''

She studied Blackford's windows before going in. They were dusty and the displays were the same she had seen when she was there in the spring. Sloppy or uninterested or broke, she thought. Maybe all three. She pushed open the door and a small bell announced her arrival.

Nicholas appeared from the back room. Annoyance

spread over his face. "My dear Stephanie, more questions? This does begin to resemble an interrogation."

Sabrina took note of the dust on the furniture, the visible price tags that should have been tucked away, the ragged displays of books and cushions, a lampshade askew. "What an interesting choice of words, Nicholas. One thinks of prisoners being interrogated. Is that what you see in your future?"

His bouncing feet stilled. He sighed. "We're back to gangster films again. Really, my dear Stephanie, you have a narrow, uninformed view of the world, quite American, of course, but I thought some of your sister's knowledge and sophistication would have rubbed off on you."

"I would have thought 'narrow and uninformed' describes anyone whose main vocabulary is insults. Is that the only way you can talk to me, Nicholas? I came back because we never discussed your finances, or how you augmented them when Blackford's started to go down—"

"*Augmented?* I told you—"

"You told me nothing that was true or useful. Your shop looks as if you've abandoned it already; I assume, in your mind, you have."

"Ridiculous. Blackford's is my life. I would have nothing if I lost it. This is a temporary slowdown, nothing else. I'll recover from it; I always do."

"You've lost the ability to recover. At one time you were a good dealer, Nicholas; you knew antiques and you had a real love for them. But now you're just hanging on: a frightened, failed businessman stupid enough to ride on the coattails of the wrong people."

"Good heavens, what's happened to you? You were quite reasonable this morning. It's quite confusing, Stephanie, and I haven't the faintest idea what you're talking about."

"Your partnership with Rory Carr and Ivan Lazlo."

Nicholas took a step back. Dust motes hung in the air and he seemed to waver in their midst. "I don't know anything about Rory Carr and Ivan Lazlo."

"You know everything about them. I've just been to Wormwood Scrubs. They told me you'd stopped—"

"*You went to Wormwood Scrubs?*"

"—visiting them. They're angry that you're free and they're locked up. They say you're being selfish and only worrying about yourself. Rory says he misses your talks about art."

Nicholas's face was ashen. "They shouldn't have said anything."

"Why not? What did you promise them?"

He shook his head. His hands twisted around each other; one toe tapped spastically on the wooden floor. He looked at it as if willing it to stop, but it had a life of its own. Still looking at it, he said, "You see, it was a brief madness, Stephanie. Madness. I knew it, but I couldn't stop it."

Sabrina's steady gaze betrayed none of the relief that swept through her. Not a bad bluff, she thought. "Yes," she said, encouraging him.

"That's all." He looked up and backed farther away. "There's nothing else to say. It's over."

"Hardly. I have contacts in London, you know, through my sister. I think the authorities would listen to me if I went to them."

"But you wouldn't! What would you gain? I told you: it's over. Westbridge is gone, and in any event I would have stopped; I worried about it, you know, all of it."

"All but the money. And that was much more important than your integrity and your honesty with your customers."

He flinched. "I didn't *want* to do it, you know. That's what I meant about a madness . . . You won't tell anyone, will you?"

"Not today. Today I'm looking for information."

"About what?" It was a whisper.

"How it worked. All of it."

"And you'll keep it to yourself?"

"At least for today."

"That's not very reassuring, Stephanie." He waited.

"Well, of course there's no proof . . . it would be your word against mine. And who would believe you? You're an American."

Sabrina burst out laughing. It unnerved Nicholas, and his hands fluttered, but in another minute he brightened, as if he had convinced himself that now they were friends. "Come on, Nicholas," Sabrina said. "Tell me how it worked."

"Well." His foot tapped; he put both hands on his thigh to still it. "It really wasn't so much, you know. I did need money, and they needed a reputable gallery for the forged pieces Rory couldn't sell anywhere else. I did fret over it, but it was so absurdly easy and no one questioned the authenticity of the pieces and after a while it was just another business. Of course it was wrong—I knew that—but we all do wrong things in our lives and I wasn't really harming anyone; I'm really a very productive member of society. I certainly don't deserve to be punished; I provided a service and ran my little business very quietly. It really was quite little, you know; quite tiny compared to Max's. He and his partner were the important part of Westbridge: Rory and Ivan and I were little cogs in a very big wheel."

"Partner? There was nothing in the newspapers about a partner."

"Well, I don't know absolutely that there was one." Nicholas was talking faster, the words spurting out as if they had been bottled up and now, at last, shot forth to point in the direction of this anonymous person left over from Westbridge, still free, still without worries. "But, you know, I was puzzled by how easily Max found clients—princes, kings, presidents, the wealthiest of the international set—and he always knew what art they wanted for their collections. I asked him about it once, but he brushed me off as if I were a fractious child; he was quite abrupt. So after a time it occurred to me that he must have someone high up, perhaps even a member of royalty, who had access to these people all around the world and could set things up. Of course I had no proof, but it seemed to make sense.''

''Yes.'' Each person leads to another, she thought. All of them tangled in webs of secrets and schemes . . . and murder. ''And I'm sure you found out who it was.''

''To my deep regret I did not. It wasn't as if one could ask his secretary if Max had a silent partner; as far as I could tell, he kept his records in his head and did most of his business at his club. One never knew whether he was mingling socially or doing business there.''

''What was his club?''

''The Monarch. On Regency Street.''

''Thank you.'' She turned to the door, then turned back. ''By the way, Princess Alexandra Martova is buying Ambassadors from me. I think it would be best if you sold her Blackford's.''

''Sell Blackford's? Never. You're being quite high-handed, Stephanie. Sabrina never would have spoken to me in such a way; she would have understood that this shop is all I have left in the world. I'm not surprised you're selling Ambassadors; after all, it's not as if you're really part of London. But I will not even discuss selling Blackford's.''

''You may change your mind. As you say, what you did was wrong, in fact it was criminal, and Rory and Ivan may not keep that to themselves forever.''

''They have no reason to talk about me. None.''

''Because you promised to take care of them? Money, a house, a warm climate?''

''Good God, no! I said I'd do what I could if they needed help, but I don't have the resources to support them for the rest of their lives.''

True, Sabrina thought. So it was someone else who had made that promise.

''But what if you can't give them any help at all? They already feel betrayed by you, Nicholas; would they tell the police about you if you gave them nothing?'' She opened the door. ''Of course, if you sold Blackford's you'd have enough money to protect yourself, maybe even to start another shop, something on a smaller scale.''

Nicholas stood with his head bowed, his hands clasped beneath his chin, as if in prayer. He stood there for a long time. ''What would she pay?''

''Fifty thousand pounds for the inventory and your client list. I'm sure that list is quite small by now.''

His head came up. ''Fifty thousand! That's nothing. The reputation of Blackford's—''

''Has gone steadily downhill. And it will be worth nothing if your involvement in the forgeries comes out. Fifty thousand is what I will suggest that Princess Martova pay.''

Nicholas looked around his shop. The tapping of his foot was loud in the silence. ''I'll have nothing left.''

An appropriate punishment for the forgeries, which, after all, no one can prove.

At last a long sigh came from his slack lips. ''Have her solicitor call me. I'll talk to him. I don't promise that I'll accept such an absurd offer, but I'll talk to him.''

''Goodbye, Nicholas.'' She closed the door softly behind her.

In the gathering darkness, she hesitated; then, on impulse, she took a taxi to the Monarch Club on Regency Street. ''Wait for me,'' she said, and started up the steps of the gray stone town house, one of three, side by side, that made up the exclusive men's club. Women were not allowed inside, but she planned to talk to the concierge at the doorway.

She stopped halfway up the steps. Above her, Alan Lethridge was coming through the door, laughing heartily at a friend's remark. He met Sabrina's eyes. ''Hello again,'' he said, still smiling, and then he remembered their conversation and his smile faded. He stood a few steps above her while his companion went on, not realizing Alan had remained behind.

''Alan,'' Sabrina said pleasantly. ''I think we should have a talk.''

His companion turned. "What's up, Alan? They're waiting for us."

"I'm late," Alan said to Sabrina. "I'm meeting Jana."

Once again she thought how much like Cliff he was: sullen, angry, but unable to push past her, held by the authority in her voice and stance.

"This shouldn't take long," she said. "We'll just take a short walk."

He looked helplessly at his companion. "I guess I'll meet you. Tell Jana I'll be there in a minute. As soon as I can."

Sabrina took his arm and they strolled along the street, past the shops closing for the evening, past restaurants poised for the evening to begin. "You didn't tell me you were a member of Max's club."

"Why should I? I don't see why you give a damn whether I am or not."

"I give a damn because you told me you'd barely recognize Max if you saw him, that you never saw him except at parties and maybe the races, and you never talked to him. And I'm wondering why you lied about that."

Alan walked beside her, slouching, his hands in his pockets.

"You knew Max," Sabrina said, so softly that Alan had to lean sideways to hear her. "And Jana told you that Max was alive when everyone thought he was dead. And you passed that on. But you weren't thinking about what you were doing. Why do you think he was hiding in France? What if his life was in danger? Max has always had enemies; everyone knows that. What if you put him in danger by talking? Do you know what you've done?"

"I haven't done anything!"

"You broke a promise. You exposed someone who was hiding from danger. You put him at risk."

"You don't know that for sure!"

"How do you know? You don't know very much, Alan. You talk too much without thinking about possible consequences. Now I'm asking you one more time. Who was it? Whom did you tell?''

"Christ, why do you care so much? What difference does it make?''

"It makes a difference. You don't need to know why.''

"*Why?* Is he dead or something?''

"Do you want that on your conscience?''

"I just want you to leave me alone!'' He stopped walking and stared at his shoes. "I promised Jana . . .'' He scuffed one shoe on the sidewalk. "Denton,'' he blurted. "He'd been out of his mind, you know, wondering if Max was really dead—they didn't find the body, he kept saying that—so I thought he ought to know that Max was alive. Put his mind at rest. I told him in confidence. Absolute confidence. I'm sure he kept it to himself.''

Sabrina was staring past him at the trees spaced along the street.

It occurred to me that he must have someone high up, perhaps even a member of royalty . . .

Max and his partner were the important part of West-bridge.

He'd been out of his mind, you know, wondering if Max was really dead—they didn't find the body, he kept saying that.

Kept saying that. Denton Longworth, frantic about whether Max was really dead or not.

Maybe Rory Carr and Ivan Lazlo hadn't been the only ones who were worried about Max getting rid of them because they were endangering his business.

Maybe Denton had had a falling-out with him; maybe Denton was trying to take over Westbridge; maybe Denton had threatened to shut the business down if it didn't go his way.

Crooks could find so many things to quarrel about.

Denton would have heard from Rory Carr that Sabrina Longworth had told him, one day in her shop, that there was nothing he could tell her that she did not already know. He would think she'd figured out the forgeries for herself, or that Max had told her.

Plenty of reasons for Denton to want both of them gone.

But then, after the explosion, why did Denton identify someone's body as that of Sabrina Longworth? He'd been married to her; he knew what she looked like.

Something we'll have to ask him. Among a lot of other questions.

She dismissed Alan, who was gone in an instant, and stopped at a telephone to call Stephanie. "I'm on my way home. I have a lot to tell you. And tomorrow Denton will be back from his hunting, and we're going to pay him a visit."

CHAPTER *20*

"*I* expect him by noon tomorrow, Mrs. Andersen," Denton's butler told Sabrina when she called. "If you wish to call then . . ."

"No, that won't be possible. Just tell him I'll be there at two. It's very important that I see him; make sure he understands that."

"If you could tell me the nature of your call . . . he likes to know in advance . . ."

"I know he does. This is confidential and urgent. He'll know what it's about."

She turned to Stephanie. "That should get him. He'll think I've heard from Max. That was the last thing he asked me: to call him if I did." She ran a finger around the rim of her teacup. They were sitting in their usual places in the upstairs sitting room; in three days it had become a habit, one they already looked forward to. How quickly we make nests for ourselves, Sabrina thought. And settle into them, and mold ourselves to them and make them our definition of happiness. We didn't think about that a year ago when we started this caper.

"He'll be upset," Stephanie said.

"I'd guess that panicked would be more like it. You know, I can't really believe it. In spite of everything we've heard, how could it be Denton? He wasn't brought up on the streets; he had everything anyone could want. And besides, he's such a lightweight."

"Is he really? I always thought he had power; a viscount and all that."

"Titles don't mean power. Anyway, I don't think Denton would know what to do with power if he had it. As far as I know, he only cares about himself and making his world pleasant."

Their eyes met. "That's why it could be Denton," said Stephanie. "Protecting his pleasant world." They gazed at the leaping flames in the fireplace. "Do you know, almost the first thing you ever told me about him, when I came to your wedding at Treveston, was that he strolled through the world as if it were one of his Treveston gardens."

Sabrina smiled faintly. "I remember. I thought it was wonderful, that kind of confidence. But in fact it's far different from confidence; it's a supreme arrogance that I suppose makes just about anything possible. Including murder."

Stephanie put down her cup. "Let's go somewhere. We can't sit around and think about Denton all night; how incredibly depressing. And you did say you'd think about going out to dinner. Did you find a restaurant?"

"Yes, but—"

"Sabrina, please!"

"Well, I read about a new Italian place in Cambridge. I haven't been there for years and I don't know anyone there. It's about an hour and a half away; if you don't mind the drive, I think we'd be all right."

"Then let's go."

They dressed in evening suits with short skirts and long jackets with beaded lapels, Sabrina in black, Stephanie in deep blue. They took capes from Sabrina's closet, and then Sabrina called a limousine. "The first rule for strange places is, always make sure you have a way to get home."

Their eyes met in the mirror. They had not done that when they traded lives. Such a simple rule, and they had forgotten it.

They looked away. "Time to go," Sabrina said.

The limousine drove slowly through the early evening traffic, weaving among high black taxis and small MGs and Volkswagens that skittered along the road like children thumbing their noses at authority. At intersections, streams of workers flowed past and vanished as they plunged into the earth, descending on escalators to tube stations far below. Locked in their thoughts, Sabrina and Stephanie watched through tinted windows as the neighborhoods changed, the crowds thinned and then disappeared, and only a few cars moved through the streets.

They were in the suburbs: neat cottages and half-timbered houses, blocks of apartments sprouting forests of television antennas, children playing in front yards, shops, schools, a hospital. And then open fields and dense forests, deep green in the fading light. Sabrina remembered a line from Blake—"England's green and pleasant land"—and she thought of how long it had been her green and pleasant home but now was a country for others. She could not imagine living there again.

She glanced at Stephanie, gazing out her window, absorbed in . . . what? Her children? Her husband? Léon? How far away she is, Sabrina thought, and touched Stephanie's hand lying on the seat between them. Stephanie turned and smiled briefly, and then they turned away again, into their own thoughts.

The limousine slowed as it reached Cambridge, driving past the mellowed red brick buildings of the university and through narrow streets lit by gas lamps and the illuminated windows of shops. "Wait, could we stop?" Stephanie asked suddenly. "Look, Sabrina, what a lovely shop. Ballard's. Have you ever heard of it?"

"No, it must be new."

"Let's go in, shall we?" When Sabrina hesitated, she said, "Please, Sabrina, we're so far from London, what harm could it do?"

"Oh, I suppose it's all right. It's been a long time since we went to an antique shop together. We'll be about half an hour," she said to the driver, and they walked to the shop.

The entrance door, of old leaded and stained glass, opened into a wide, shallow room, dimly lit and filled with European and American furniture, clocks and chandeliers from three centuries. "What an incredible collection," Stephanie said. "Jacqueline would love it." There was no shopkeeper in sight and she and Sabrina moved slowly through the room, looking at telltale details that could distinguish a genuine piece from a reproduction. "Georgian," Sabrina murmured. "Just right for Billy Koner's lobby. Vern would love it, but Billy would say it's too old-fashioned."

"Who are they? Billy Koner and Vern."

"Billy owns the building I told you I designed. The one in Printer's Row. Vern is the architect."

"And Vern likes Georgian furniture? Isn't that strange, for an American architect?"

"He's more interesting than most of them." She looked up as an enormous man came into the store, his bald head shining as he flipped a light switch near the entrance.

"So sorry, my dear," he said to Sabrina, peering at her through his glasses. "I stepped out for a pint and ran into some friends." He did not see Stephanie, who was shielded by a large armoire. "Closing in half an hour; I'll be in the office back there if you need me."

"Tell me about Vern and Billy Koner," Stephanie said when he was gone. Sabrina described them, and her designs for the apartments, the lobby, the elevators and stairwells. "I loved that job; it was the biggest I've ever done, and the most fun because of Vern. And Billy, too; I like him. Vern and I played a game, guessing how long it would take to convince him of something we both knew was perfect.''

''Did you convince him?''

''Most of the time. Sometimes he dug in his heels, but then, why not? It's his building.''

''It sounds wonderful. Much bigger than Max's town house, and that's the only job I've ever done.''

''But you had a good time. Did you buy all the furniture?''

''Good heavens, no; he had tons of it in storage. He took me to see it one day and I couldn't believe it; he had so many pallets in the warehouse it was like opening one treasure chest after another.''

They were sitting on one of the sofas now, close together, their voices low. Stephanie described her remodeling of Max's house around his massive furniture, covering the walls with suede, adding Oriental rugs and bringing in low lamps because he liked the rooms dim at night. ''It wasn't as good as your design of Alexandra's house—I couldn't get the same light touch you had—but Max was pleased. He said it was the best house he'd ever had.''

After a moment Sabrina said, ''You really became me, didn't you? I didn't realize, from our telephone calls, how perfectly you made my life your own. I knew you were having a good time, but it was more than that, wasn't it?''

''It was magical; it was a fairy tale that I'd dreamed about and envied as long as I could remember. And the most incredible thing was that I couldn't seem to do anything wrong. It was the only time in my life when everything went perfectly: I went to auctions and parties and dinners and I did what you would have done, and I did it well. I don't understand how that happened, but it did and it was so wonderful I didn't want to give it up. The problem is, I became you, but you did better: you became both of us. I don't know how that happened, either, but somehow the whole time you were Stephanie Andersen, you never stopped being Sabrina Longworth. I was so sure you'd be bored and furious that you had to stay there, but you were happy. So what happened? You changed them; is that it? Somehow you changed Garth and Penny and Cliff so they fit in with the way you wanted to live. How did you do that?"

"I didn't change them. They changed me."

"No, don't you understand? You were still Sabrina. You are now. You're both of us. So who am I?" Her eyes were pleading for an answer. "Who am I, Sabrina? You know who you are, but I've lost myself."

Sabrina took Stephanie in her arms. "You're my sister and I love you." Stephanie laid her head on Sabrina's chest like a child, her breathing slowing as if she would settle there for good.

"Closing, my dears, sorry, but it's time."

The voice came from the office and Stephanie shot upright with a small laugh. "The voice of doom. *Closing.* Coming to an end. Oh, Lord, I'm getting morbid. Let's go to dinner."

The Italian restaurant had a small front room with a bar and a larger room with tables and high-backed booths. Sabrina had requested a booth and they were led to one in the corner, drawing stares as they walked to it. "Not one familiar face," Sabrina said as they sat opposite each other.

"You didn't expect any." Stephanie leaned out of the booth to look behind her. "I like the room."

Sabrina, facing the room, nodded. The walls were of rough plaster hung with watercolors of Italian hill towns and harbors; the floor was tiled in white stone, crisp paper covered the cloth on their table. "It could be Italy; they've done a nice job."

The waiter, wearing an open-necked shirt, black pants, and a towel wrapped around his waist as an apron, brought glasses and a bottle of Chianti and took their order. "Tell me again about Penny's puppets," said Stephanie, and Sabrina thought how like a child she sounded, asking for a bedtime story. Over the past three nights, in their long evenings together before the fire, she had told Stephanie everything about Penny and Cliff she could think of, but still Stephanie asked for more.

As if she's memorizing things for her return, Sabrina thought, but she talked to Stephanie calmly and steadily, as if the thought had never been.

"—so somehow her teacher arranged with Kroch's to display Penny's puppets in the window with her name on a card in front of them—" She stopped, looking across the restaurant, her face frozen.

"What is it?" Stephanie's voice rose in alarm. "What's wrong?" She turned, but the booth was too high for her to see over it, and before she could slide to the front to look out, Alexandra was there, bending down, hugging Sabrina.

"My God, Stephanie, what a place to find you! Is this for antiques or academics? Garth giving lectures—" She turned to the other side of the booth and sucked in a loud breath. She staggered and grabbed the table, staring at Stephanie. Her mouth moved but no words came.

"Sit down, Alexandra." Sabrina held her arm and pulled her down beside her.

She sat, her eyes on Stephanie. She looked from one sister to the other. "I don't . . . How could . . . *Who are you?*"

As she asked that of each of them, the waiter arrived with bowls of risotto. "Ah, there are three signorinas for dinner?"

"Later," Sabrina said and waited until he left. She pushed away her dinner and held Alexandra's hand between hers. "My sister wasn't killed on Max's yacht; she escaped, but she lost her memory and only regained it two weeks ago. But that's only—"

"Sabrina!" She rose to lean over the table, stretching her hand to Stephanie. "Oh, my God, my God, I can't believe it . . . Sabrina!"

"No, wait," Stephanie said. "That's only the beginning."

"We'll tell you all of it," Sabrina said, "but first we owe you an apology."

Alexandra turned to her. "For what? You don't owe me anything. Sabrina was the best friend I ever had, and when she was gone, it was as if you took her place. I mean, when I visited you in Evanston I almost felt—"

"You were in Evanston?" Stephanie exclaimed in surprise.

"I forgot to tell you about that," Sabrina said to Stephanie.

"So what's the apology for?" asked Alexandra.

Sabrina and Stephanie exchanged a look. "You tell it," Stephanie said.

The waiter returned. "Is there anything—?"

"More wine," Sabrina said.

"Just a minute." Alexandra took a pad of paper from her purse and wrote a brief note. "Give this to Mr. Tarleton when he comes in, with my apologies. My would-be dinner companion," she said to Sabrina and Stephanie. "Now, go ahead. You're apologizing—for what?"

"We played a trick on you. You were a loving friend and we tricked you, and both of us hated doing it, but we were in so deep by then—"

"Am I supposed to know what you're talking about?"

"No. I'm about to tell you." Sabrina paused impatiently while the waiter filled three wineglasses. He looked at them curiously. "That's all," Sabrina said, and, reluctantly, he left. "First of all, I'm Sabrina; that's my sister, Stephanie. Thirteen months ago we took a trip to China . . ."

Gradually the restaurant emptied. The waiter drifted by as he crisscrossed the room. He removed the cold risotto. Unasked, he brought espresso for three. Soon all the waiters were clustered near the kitchen door, relaxing. Talk and laughter still came from the bar and a few diners dallied at tables near them, but Stephanie felt the change in the atmosphere: the evening coming slowly to an end, busboys clearing the last dishes and spreading fresh tablecloths and white paper on the tables, waiters changing into their street clothes, the owner preparing to make a final swift appraisal of his domain before closing and locking the door.

Closing. Coming to an end.

She shook her head and turned back to Alexandra, who, all through Sabrina's story, had looked back and forth from one of them to the other, listening, looking, wondering. By now she was no longer disbelieving, as she had been when Sabrina began, but she was still stunned, clinging to every word.

"—and we came to London a couple of days ago, to try to figure out what happened. We never went anywhere together, but we thought we were safe in Cambridge, that no one would know us. What in heaven's name you're doing here—"

"A new restaurant, and the owner is a friend and he asked me to show up so he'd get a mention in the gossip columns. You and I used to do this a lot; we did it a year ago, as I have good reason to remember, since that was the night you introduced me to Antonio. Oh. But it wasn't you, was it? It was Stephanie, and you were in America, being her." Alexandra's eyes flashed to the ring on Sabrina's left hand. "You haven't said anything about that."

"That's a separate story."

"But I visited you, and you had the most wonderful family . . ." She saw Stephanie wince. "I'm sorry, I didn't mean . . . well, yes, I did; that's what I saw. And all that time you'd found Léon. I have one of his paintings, by the way; I bought it at Galeries de Rohan. I liked the way Sabrina described him. Is he really that wonderful?"

"Yes."

"And you've told him all of this?"

"Yes."

"I can't believe it. It is the most fantastic, unbelievable, incredible story . . ." A slow smile lit her face. "You two are amazing. You know, I don't even mind it that you fooled me; good Lord, how many times have I wished I could do the same thing? I've looked at other women and wanted to be them, just for a little while . . . What the hell, there was a time, some years back, when I wanted to be Sabrina.''

"A tangled web," Sabrina murmured.

"Yes, a good way to put it. But who could have guessed the things that would happen?"

"We never even tried to predict what could happen," said Stephanie. "We just talked about how to make it work for a week."

"Well, it did. And for a lot longer. You were perfect. And you must have been having a good time; everybody in London said how happy you looked all that fall." She looked at Sabrina. "Both of you, right? Building new lives. Well, I have to hand it to you; you'd win best actress at Cannes hands down." She saw Sabrina's face harden and glanced again to her left hand. "Sorry, that was dumb. You weren't acting, were you? Not after a while. But why didn't you tell *me*?" she suddenly demanded. "We were as close as friends could be. When we all thought you'd been killed, and you came back as Stephanie to bury her— oh. For God's sake, *whom did we bury that day?*"

"We don't know. We can't understand it. I was in the funeral home for a long time; I sat by the coffin . . ."

"But you said it was dark," Stephanie said. "Just a few candles. And you were crying."

"Yes, but my own sister . . . Well, maybe that was it; I really didn't see anything clearly. I saw what I expected to see." Slowly she repeated it. "What I expected. Everyone does that, you know; that's why Stephanie and I were so successful; people arrange reality to fit their expectations, and they'll go through all sorts of contortions to make the world seem logical rather than take something seriously that doesn't make sense at all."

"I did that," Alexandra said to Stephanie. "Remember, at my dinner party, you told a story about Greece, when you were young, and you said, 'Sabrina saved me.'

We all thought it was very odd, but you covered it up
somehow and that was that. It never occurred to any of
us . . ."

"Why would it?" Stephanie said with a faint smile.
"Who would try such a crazy trick?"

"Yes, but wait a minute. Didn't Denton identify the
body?"

"He did, and that really doesn't make sense," Sabrina
said. "I'm sure he wasn't crying his eyes out when he did
it. That's one of the things we're going to ask him."

"Both of you? Didn't you tell me you'd been taking
turns?"

"Yes, up to now." She and Stephanie smiled at each
other. "But I think this time we'll go together."

Alexandra's eyes gleamed. "Won't that be something
to see. You know, I was never fond of Denton; he didn't
seem to connect with anybody, me included: we were all
background to whatever he was doing to make himself
happy. But I never would have pegged him for a murderer. It makes me wonder about some other people I
know in the upper ranks, so to speak, of society, here,
South America, everywhere. Do you think it's dangerous,
going to see him?"

Sabrina thought about it. She met Stephanie's worried
frown. "He'll be confused when he sees us; we'll definitely have the advantage. And I'll bet he never does his
own dirty work. I think we'll be all right."

"You're just going to walk up there, both of you, and
ring the bell?"

"That's the idea."

"It has great possibilities. I'd love to see it. Can I go
along? I promise I'll stay in the background; you won't
even know I'm there."

"No, but we'll tell you what happens. Where are you
staying?"

"Claridge's. I've been meeting with Brian at Ambassadors. I love that shop, Sabrina. I love owning it."

"You're probably going to own Blackford's, too. I'll tell you all about it later."

"Blackford's? It's gone downhill."

"That's one of the reasons you're getting it for fifty thousand pounds. You'll do wonders with it; even from Brazil, you'll do better than Nicholas has."

"Probably, but I didn't even know I wanted it. Well, good Lord, another mystery. You're sure you won't take me with you to see Denton?"

"No, and you didn't really expect us to. We'll call you tomorrow, after we see him. It may be late afternoon."

"Then I won't be here. I'm going to Paris."

"Oh." *So am I, to have a week with my husband. But when he finds out I've lied to him, when he finds out that Stephanie is alive—*

And what happens before that, when Stephanie and I finally talk about everything we've avoided for three days?

"We're going, too," Stephanie said, and avoided Sabrina's swift, surprised glance. "We'll be in Paris tomorrow night. We can call you there."

"Oh, good. Why don't we have dinner together? And really eat it this time. I'll be at Relais Christine; where will you be?"

Stephanie looked at Sabrina.

"L'Hôtel," Sabrina said. Her hands were clenched in her lap.

"Perfect; we'll be just a few blocks from each other. I'll call you tomorrow night. No, Antonio meets me tomorrow night, and it's beyond his understanding that I'd be able to think of anything but him on the night of our reunion. How about Saturday morning?"

"Fine," Stephanie said. "We have all day Saturday."

Sabrina was silent. *All day Saturday. Before Garth arrives on Sunday. All day to talk, to decide what will happen on Sunday, at least the part of Sunday we have any control over.*

Sabrina signaled for the check. "Listen," Alexandra said abruptly, "I want you to know I love you both. I guess if I knew Stephanie better I'd see differences between you. but to me. right now. you're both Sabrina and I love you. I'm sorry. I know how crazy that sounds. but—"

"It's all right." Stephanie said. She put her hand on Alexandra's arm. almost as if to steady herself. "I don't know who I am. either."

That night. as she did every night at midnight. Sabrina called home. They were ready for her: Cliff on the couch in the kitchen. Penny in Garth's study. and Mrs. Thirkell waiting nearby to say a few words when Cliff let her have the telephone.

"You sound excited." Sabrina said to Cliff. "What's going on?"

"Nothing." There was a warning note in his voice that was clearly meant for Penny on the other telephone. and Sabrina knew that something was indeed going on. Her heart sank. because she was sure it was some kind of homecoming surprise. and there might not be a homecoming if Garth would not allow it. Maybe he'll banish me as he did before. she thought. as he has a right to do. and I'll lose them. lose them all. and Penny and Cliff will think I deserted them. just as I did last December.

But if she did not come home. would Penny and Cliff know it?

If Stephanie went home with Garth. would Penny and Cliff know it?

Would they see differences even greater than the ones they had found excuses for a year ago?

Would they demand an explanation because they'd know something was wrong. that the mother they loved had changed?

Tears stung her eyes. "Cliff, if you're planning something for when I come home—"

"We're not." he said. sounding relieved. and Sabrina was taken aback. What were they up to?

She listened to their talk about school and friends and a

painting contest Penny had entered, and she laughed at their small jokes and puns, and when she hung up, she told herself that she wouldn't think about whatever they were planning. It was probably a present they were making at school, and there was nothing she could do about that. *They'll give it to me or they won't. I'll know on Sunday.*

At six the next morning, as she did every morning, she called Garth in his hotel at The Hague. Seven in the morning there; his only time to talk before his conference sessions began. Curled up in her sitting room, with Stephanie in the guest room down the hall, Sabrina knew that her voice was subdued, almost strained with the effort of measuring every word, but she could not make herself sound carefree and lively, even when she concentrated on trying.

"A lot of talking to people," she said, avoiding outright lies. "Nicholas is selling Blackford's . . . Oh, Alexandra is here, getting organized at Ambassadors with Brian, and she's buying Blackford's, too." She talked about London and the weather and packing up the furnishings and art at Cadogan Square and shipping them to Evanston, and then she said, "I don't really want to talk about me; tell me what you've been doing."

As he talked, she could tell, because she was so familiar with every nuance of his voice, that he knew something was bothering her. But after the first night, when she had been evasive, he had not pressed her. He described the scientists at the conference and their papers, the attention his own talk had received and the little sight-seeing he had been able to do; he told her he had heard from Claudia that the *Chicago Tribune* was doing an investigative series on Congressman Leglind and the effect congressional hearings had on university research, and Sabrina asked enough questions to keep him talking about all of that and more for almost an hour.

"And that's enough," he said at last. "Everything else will wait. You haven't told me your hotel in Paris."

"L'Hôtel. It's on the Left Bank, near the Boulevard Saint-Germain. Do you know what time you'll be there?"

"Early. Probably about nine-thirty. I have a surprise for you; I'm telling you now so you can wonder about it for a couple of days."

"You too? Penny and Cliff are planning something . . . Garth, what's going on?"

"Were they mysterious? I'll have to ask them about that. My love, you'll have to wait until Sunday. I've started counting the hours."

"It will be here before we know it," Sabrina murmured. "Oh, Garth, I love you; you're so much a part of me, my life, my dreams . . . I'm sorry," she said and willed her voice to lightness. "I'm being dramatic. I miss you. I love you. I'll call you tomorrow from Paris."

When she came downstairs, Stephanie was waiting in the kitchen with café au lait and croissants. "Not exactly an American breakfast," she mused. "Isn't it odd how French I've become? Do you know, for ten months I didn't speak English or hear English spoken. Now and then a word would break through and I'd find that scary because I had no idea what it meant, but otherwise everything I said and thought was in French and I never thought twice about it. Isn't that unbelievable? Even my language was lost." She was concentrating on carefully folding napkins. "Were you talking to Garth this morning? I came down early and I heard your voice when I went past your room."

"Yes. And I talked to Penny and Cliff last night. They're fine: busy and happy and brewing some kind of mischief."

"Mischief?"

"They denied it, but I could hear it in Cliff's voice. I suppose they're making something in school; they've done that before."

"Yes, I remember."

Withdrawn again, they ate their breakfast and then the telephone rang. Stephanie went to answer it, because every morning at ten—how ritualized we have become, Sabrina thought—Léon called.

She looked up when Stephanie returned. "What is it?"

"He wants to buy a house." She sat down and held her cup in both hands. "He found an old house high up, near the basilica, and he wants to renovate it. There's a building about fifty feet away that would be perfect for his studio; he'd make a covered passage to connect it to the house. It's very big, the house is; he says it has . . . plenty of room for children."

With a small gasp, Sabrina shrank into herself. Stephanie was staring out the window, her thoughts far away. And then the telephone rang again and after a minute Sabrina rose to answer it.

"Stephanie? Denton Longworth here. I understand you called, you wanted to come over at two? Of course you can, but you could just tell me now what it is you want; you don't have to come all the way here . . ."

Alert now, hearing the thread of alarm in his voice, Sabrina glanced at Stephanie, and mouthed, *Denton*, before saying calmly, "It's not that far, and I don't like to have important conversations on the telephone."

"Well, then, why not come right away? You don't have to wait; I mean, I'm here, and I don't have any plans . . . I got back early, you know, and there's nothing on my calendar until later . . . You can come now!"

"What a good idea. I'll be there in twenty minutes."

In the entrance hall, she and Stephanie stood before the tall mirror. They were wearing tweed slacks and gray cashmere sweaters they had found in Sabrina's bureaus: not identical, but close enough. They both wore a strand of pearls and pearl earrings; they both pulled on long charcoal gray coats, one belted, the other not—"but he'll never notice," Sabrina said. Their makeup was identical; their long chestnut hair, falling below their shoulders, was identical. "We'll do fine," Stephanie said. And they left the house to walk to the taxi stand.

Denton's tall gray town house was so narrow it reminded Stephanie of a passenger on a crowded bus, his arms clamped to his sides. It stood on a street of equally narrow houses near Saint James's Square and within walking distance of the Monarch, the club where Sabrina had seen Alan Lethridge. Closed drapes and a deeply carved front door made it look as if it were fending off visitors, but before Sabrina and Stephanie had a chance to lift the brass knocker, the door was opened wide and the butler stood before them.

"Mrs. Ander— Good God!"

Decidedly un-butlerlike, Stephanie thought in amusement. She had been tense and fearful, in spite of Sabrina's confidence, but the thought came to her that this, too, was a game, another game among all those they had played as children and in the past year, and alongside her fear a spark of anticipation flared up.

"Good afternoon, Bunter," said Sabrina. "I believe we're expected."

"Mrs. Andersen?" His eyes, wide and staring, slid back and forth so he did not have to declare himself speaking to one or the other.

"Yes," Sabrina said simply and walked past him into the house.

She remembered it so well it was as if she had been there the day before. Nothing had changed; it was furnished exactly as it had been when Denton's parents bought it for them as a wedding gift. Even the floral arrangements seemed the same. With Stephanie close behind, she walked through the echoing marble foyer, ignoring an archway that led to the main salon, heading instead for a closed door that, she knew, led to a small study. *Less room for Denton to maneuver.*

"Please, if you would . . ." the butler said helplessly, standing in the archway, indicating they should follow him into the salon.

"We'll wait in here." Sabrina opened the door. Across the room, standing beside a leather-topped desk, Denton was on the telephone, his back to them. He heard the door open and turned and saw Sabrina and Stephanie side by side. There was a suspended moment that seemed to stretch endlessly; then a small sound escaped him, the telephone fell from his hand, and he crumpled to the floor.

"My lord!" The butler sprang to Denton's side, lifting him to a sitting position on the floor. "My lord, my lord!"

Still wearing their coats, Sabrina and Stephanie sat on one of the leather couches and waited. The room felt like a cave, Stephanie thought, with brown velvet drapes pulled tight across the high windows and a brown and black Bokhara rug stretching from the heavy mahogany door to the brown marble hearth of the cold fireplace. She watched Denton's head roll against the butler's arm, and saw his eyes open and look toward the doorway where he had seen them. When he found it empty, he looked slowly to the left and saw them sitting together on the couch, two identical women, their heads tilted at exactly the same angle, watching him with interest.

He closed his eyes, then slowly opened them, willing the vision to disappear. "Denton, we want to talk to you," Sabrina said briskly. "Get up now. Perhaps Bunter will bring you some tea."

"Scotch," Denton said automatically. He stayed where he was, his eyes moving from Sabrina to Stephanie, his small mustache quivering in the round face that usually was rosy and smiling but now was stiff and pale, the lips barely moving. "You were dead. I saw you."

"My lord, let me help you up." The butler stood, bringing Denton with him. He lowered him onto the other leather couch, then hung up the telephone, which had been dangling over the edge of the desk. "I'll bring tea, my lord."

"*Scotch.*" His eyes were on Sabrina and Stephanie. "You found someone—a double—God, it's a perfect match. What was it, plastic surgery? What for? Christ, you could have killed me . . . the shock . . . I could have died. What the hell do you think you're doing?"

"But we didn't die," Sabrina said.

"We're both here," Stephanie said.

"Stephanie Andersen and Sabrina Longworth."

"You see, two people got off the yacht before it went down."

"And they've been living in France."

"Quite well, and very anxious to talk to you."

They looked at Denton expectantly.

"Got off the yacht . . ." Denton echoed hoarsely. He cleared his throat. "It's a lie. I saw your body. I identified you."

"Yes, we've been wondering why you did that," Sabrina said. "How closely did you look at the body?"

He stared at them helplessly. "I don't know."

"Oh, come now, Denton, of course you do. What did you see? Hair that looked like mine? A face that looked a little like mine?"

"But it would have been bruised and swollen," Stephanie said. "And there would have been cuts all over it. That's what we've been forgetting; that's how I looked when they took me to the hospital. It took weeks for the bruises to disappear and the swelling to go down."

"So someone could have resembled you—"

"There was someone!" Stephanie turned to Sabrina. "There was a woman on the yacht who did look like me. She was taller and thinner, but there was definitely a resemblance, and her hair was almost the same as mine—in fact, Max teased her: he said she'd obviously found my hairdresser and had it colored and styled like mine, and someone else asked her if she'd hired my dressmaker so she could look like me. If she was badly bruised—"

"*Two people*?" Denton demanded, and they turned to him.

"What did you tell the undertaker?" Sabrina asked.

"*Two* people got off the boat?" he asked. "Who was the other one?"

"One thing at a time," Stephanie said. "What did you tell the undertaker?"

"*Who was the other one?*"

The butler came in, carrying a tray with glasses, an ice

bucket and a bottle of Scotch. "If the ladies wish a drink, or tea . . . ?"

"Nothing," Sabrina said. "And I think we won't need to be disturbed again."

"Christ, you sound just like her. Christ, I can't believe—it can't be . . . you really are Sabrina?"

"Really," Stephanie said solemnly. "I got off the yacht before it sank. What did you tell the undertaker?"

"Christ. Sabrina. Christ. I was so sure . . . It looked like you. Not a lot, I suppose; you're right, the face was all bruised, the eyes were swollen shut, and they'd cut your—her—hair; it was so matted they couldn't comb it, they said, and there was a lot of confusion, people all around, the press, you know, and relatives of all those other people, so I just glanced—you know I can't stand the sight of dead people, it makes me sick—and said it was you, and then I gave them a picture of you and told them to do the best they could with makeup and whatever tricks they have, for the funeral, you know. I thought it was the least I could do."

He took a breath, adjusting, adapting. "But this is fantastic! Incredible! Wonderful! It was a terrible shock, terrible, terrible, to all of us, Sabrina"—he looked from one sister to the other, reluctant to ask outright which of them had once been his wife—"everyone felt it; we all were devastated. What happy news we have to tell everyone now! A miracle! I'm glad you came to tell me, though I must say it was not kind of you to play that shocking trick, showing up without warning . . . I really might have had a heart attack, you know, and there was no reason for it. We're not enemies, you know. By the way"—it came out carelessly now—"who *was* the other person who escaped from the yacht?"

"But you already know the answer," Stephanie said. "You know that Max escaped and you know he's been living in France ever since it happened."

"*Max?* Good God, how would I know that? Escaped? Alive? My God, my God, another miracle. It's almost too much to believe. But of course I knew nothing about it; how could I? Why would you think that?"

"Because we know a great deal about you," Sabrina said. "We've talked to Nicholas about Westbridge Imports and he told us about Max's partner—"

"Partner? Wait, this is . . . Nicholas said Max had a partner? He's lying. I knew Max and I never heard him talk about a partner. Never. Westbridge was all his: his money, his ideas . . ."

"Nicholas didn't say anyone else had money in Westbridge. He said someone was lining up customers for smuggled antiquities and giving Max information about them, and places to find specific works of art to be stolen and smuggled out . . . that sort of thing. Someone who moved in wealthy circles. Someone like you."

"I would never do such a thing. It would be a betrayal of my class."

Sabrina and Stephanie gazed at him in contempt. Denton poured more Scotch, the neck of the bottle rattling against the edge of the glass. "Max and I were friends. That was all."

"You worked together," Stephanie said, and coldly lied. "Max told me that."

"When? What are you talking about?"

"When we were living together," Sabrina said and watched with amusement as Denton's eyes swiveled to her. "I lived with Max for almost a year; surely you knew that, Denton. When you tracked him down, didn't anyone tell you he had a wife?"

"Wait. Wait. One thing at a . . . Lived with him? You lived with him? And what does that mean . . . *tracked him down*? What are you talking about?"

"I lost my memory in the explosion," Stephanie said, and Denton's eyes swung back to her. "Max told me I was his wife, and I believed him and lived with him. He told me everything. He told me about you. He told me we were in danger."

Denton's glass stopped halfway to his mouth. "Why?"

"Because," said Sabrina, and Denton's eyes jerked from Stephanie's face to hers, "you'd tried to kill him once, with the bomb on the yacht. He knew it—"

"*I* tried to kill him? You're mad. I had no reason, no reason, no reason to kill anyone. What do you think you—"

"That's why he was living in France under another name. And he knew that if you found him, you'd try again. So he told me we were in danger, and in fact—"

"Stop it! This is insane. You're making this up, the two of you . . . What is it, some kind of game? Going back and forth . . . what the hell for? Making these outrageous statements . . ." He seemed to gain strength as he talked. "Absolutely outrageous. Based on nothing but some kind of fantasy. You're still trying to get back at me, Sabrina, is that it?" He looked at Stephanie, then at Sabrina, then back again, and finally settled on some neutral point between them so he would not have to decide which sister was which. "Haven't we been divorced long enough to become friends? What do you want? Money? Is that what you're here for? I don't pay blackmail. Even if I did, I haven't anything to give you, so you're wasting your time. Wasting your time! Coming in here . . . how dare you come into my home and brazenly accuse me of . . . of . . ."

"Murder," Sabrina said. "We're not interested in money, Denton; we're interested in what you've done. You see, we also talked to Ivan Lazlo and Rory Carr."

His face darkened. He put down his glass. "You bitch. You didn't talk to them. Even if you did, they wouldn't tell you anything."

"You seem so sure of that. I suppose that's because you promised to take care of them when they get paroled. Even if it took another ten or fifteen years, they'd still be young enough to enjoy whatever you've promised them."

"This isn't a game," Stephanie said. "You and Max quarreled about Westbridge, and Rory told you I'd made a foolish remark that I knew everything there was to know about the forged ceramics. So you had reason to want us both gone, and you told Ivan and Rory to get rid of us. Was the bomb their idea or yours? It really doesn't matter; you gave them an order and they carried it out, which makes you guilty of murder."

"But Max wasn't killed!"

"Fourteen other people were on that yacht. They were all killed."

"And then," Sabrina went on, "you found out that Max was alive, in Cavaillon, and you sent another one of your henchmen to kill him. You're not very creative, Denton; you always think of killing when you feel threatened. Of course, as you've discovered, what seems to be an obvious solution doesn't always work."

"I have no henchmen; I sent no one! How the hell many times do I have to tell you that? As far as I knew, Max was dead."

"You were never sure of that. You weren't sure last May, when you came to Ambassadors and asked me if I'd heard from him. I thought he was dead, Denton; you weren't sure. And then, a few weeks ago, you heard that he was alive. You heard it from someone in your club. You see, we've talked to him, too. We've talked to all of them. Rory Carr, Ivan Lazlo, Alan Lethridge, and of course Nicholas. No one is lying for you, Denton; they're all quite willing to talk."

Denton sagged. His chin was embedded in his chest and he looked at them from beneath heavy eyelids and saw them close together on the couch, arms touching, bodies touching, wearing the same clothes, their voices overlapping. They seemed to be one person, vengeful, relentless, implacable. He lowered his eyes and looked at his hands, twisted in his lap, and tried to think of a way to ask if Max was still alive.

"I saw the man you sent," Stephanie said casually. "He followed us home once, from a church we'd visited. He hung around our house. He was still there after Max left."

"Left," Denton echoed. He looked up. "*Left?*"

"Yes. I woke up one morning and he was gone. He'd told me he was leaving, so I wasn't surprised; it was just more sudden than I'd expected. I left Cavaillon after that; Max had told me your man might be after me, too. The way Rory and Ivan had been when we were on the yacht." She gazed at Denton. "Max told me," she added dreamily, "that he would always come back."

With a grunt, as if the breath had been knocked out of him, Denton slid all the way down on the leather couch. His heels dug into the rug, his head sank lower onto his chest. Burt, the man he had sent to Cavaillon, had called to say he had located Max, and that was the last Denton had heard. He had not called again; he had not checked out of his hotel. But he was never there when Denton called, again and again. There was no way to know what had happened: if he had tried to kill Max and failed, or if he had given up without trying because Max seemed invulnerable.

He *was* invulnerable. The son of a bitch wouldn't die.

Denton had always been in awe of Max Stuyvesant. He believed there was something mystical about him, as if he were a djin, larger than life, moving among them but not one of them, ruthless, unstoppable, untouchable, a force that Denton never could emulate or even understand. After the yacht had exploded and he had identified the body of Lady Longworth, Denton had haunted the waterfront for days, pestering the police for information about any bodies found far from the sunken ship, insisting that the search continue, that he would pay for it, that he had to know whether the one man still unaccounted for had survived or not.

In the end, he had left Monte Carlo without knowing anything, and slowly, in the following months, as nothing was heard of Max, he began to believe he had indeed been killed, blown to pieces in the explosion, or trapped somewhere at the bottom of the Mediterranean, beyond everyone's reach. Until Alan Lethridge had told him that Max was alive.

He knew then that he had been right all along. Max was a djin: a creature of magic who either had come through that powerful explosion unscarred or else had died and then come back to life.

Max told me that he would always come back.

And either he had escaped Burt's gun in Cavaillon or Burt had killed him and once again he had come back to life, scaring the hell out of Burt, who took off, never to be seen again.

At the moment, Denton could believe either one.

He'll be after me.

His head came up as if the words had been spoken aloud.

He knows I've tried twice; he'll kill me before I can try again. And there is no place I can hide.

Sabrina and Stephanie were watching him intently, following the expressions that raced across his face. "Of course you can tell the police what happened," Sabrina said conversationally. "You'll go to prison, of course, but I suppose you have as much chance for parole as Rory and Ivan. And you're a young man—forty-one, isn't it? When you get out, you'll still have many happy years with your friends."

I'll never have any happy years. I'll always wonder where he is, when he'll show up. I'll always be looking over my shoulder . . .

"I think you should call the police," Stephanie said seriously, her voice warm and encouraging. "You'll feel much better about everything."

But not safer. Even prison isn't safe from his reach.

"Call them," Sabrina said firmly: it was an order. "Of course we could do it, but it would be better if you did. Or would you rather call your solicitor? Yes, I'm sure you would; you always find other people to do the difficult work for you. Call him, Denton; let him take care of informing the police."

But even prison is safer than this house or anywhere I might go: cruises, the races, country houses, ski resorts . . . Prison would be much harder for him, and it would give me time to think of some way to get to him before he can get to me. That's what I need—time—and I know I'll figure out a way to beat him.

As if in a dream, he rose from the couch and went to the desk. It was out of his hands. He saw Sabrina and Stephanie exchange a look and knew they had triumphed completely, but it was too late to care about that. He turned his back and picked up the telephone, and with a leaden finger slowly dialed his solicitor's office.

C H A P T E R *21*

*A*t last, in Paris, they talked.

They arrived on Friday evening and left their luggage in the sitting room of their suite at L'Hôtel. "Let's walk before dinner, shall we?" Sabrina asked, and they went out as they were, in the walking shoes and pants suits that they had put on for travel after coming back to Cadogan Square from Denton's house, Sabrina's a sleek gray with a thin stripe and Stephanie's a brown and black tweed. They walked a little apart from each other in the mild evening air beneath the bright lights of Paris. The closeness, the oneness they had felt in Denton's study, was gone. Sabrina tried to find a way to recapture it, remembering their pleasure in sharing London, wishing they could share the magic of Paris in the same way, but she could not do it. There were too many words waiting to be said. Say them! she cried silently to Stephanie. We only have tonight and tomorrow before Garth arrives. Tell me what you want. I don't know what I can do, what rights I have . . . Tell me what you want so we can talk about it.

But Stephanie was silent and so they walked in silence,

crossing the Seine on the Pont Neuf and turning to follow the river past the ancient Palais de Justice and the extravagantly sculptured Hôtel de Ville. The apartment buildings of Paris crowded in upon each other and upon the river. Their steep roofs, punctuated by dormers, hung like heavy eyebrows over gray or buff stone facades; scrolled ironwork curved around balconies or guarded high arched windows, and at the windows lace curtains or fringed draperies framed a small sculpture, a lamp, an arrangement of flowers.

"And behind every window a private story," Sabrina mused aloud, providing an opening to conversation. But Stephanie did not answer, and so they walked on, amid the crowds strolling on the riverbank past lighted boats tied up below, some decked out as restaurants. Then they left the river and turned down a quiet side street until they came to the Rue de Rivoli and turned once again.

"Where are we going?" It was the first Stephanie had spoken since they left the hotel.

"This was always one of my favorite walks," Sabrina said. "From the Left Bank to the Place des Vosges. It's so old it's almost a history of Paris. I used to walk here all the time, when I was at school. There was a little café called Trumilou on the Right Bank; I wonder if it's still here."

Stephanie put a little more space between them. *You were at the Sorbonne and I was at Bryn Mawr. Later, that was one of the things I envied, part of your whole life that I envied. And never stopped envying, so that when I thought of changing places, it seemed I'd wanted to do that all my life.*

And now what? What do I want from you now?

The Place des Vosges lay before them, a vast square of four-story town houses, once the homes of royalty, surrounding a fenced park. "It was in ruins," Sabrina said, "but most of the houses have been renovated and it's become very chic. Vern Stern told me that an American, Ross Hayward, did one of them: brilliantly, he said. It was unusual to have an American architect working here."

Stephanie gazed at the elegant buildings with steep mansard roofs and shuttered windows. "Did you ever design any houses in Paris?"

"No, just in London and the countryside."

"But you could. You know French interiors as well as English, and you have contacts here."

"I do, but I'm not working in Europe anymore."

They stopped in the middle of the sidewalk and the crowds parted around them, giving them quick sideways glances as if feeling the tension building between them. "Let's go back," Stephanie said.

They walked back and crossed the Pont d'Arcole to Notre-Dame. They stopped on the broad plaza facing the great gray mass of the church, tilting their heads back to gaze at the towers and flying buttresses illuminated against low clouds that shone a pale gray from the lights of the city. No other city, Sabrina thought, had such beauty at every turn, such a wealth of evidence of the brilliance of the human imagination. So the two of us ought to be able to solve our little problem, she thought wryly. Compared to the conception and building of Paris, it should be a breeze.

"It's nine o'clock," she said as they turned to walk again along the Seine. "I made a reservation for dinner, if you feel like it."

Stephanie's eyebrows rose. "When did you do that?"

"Before we left London."

"Where?"

"Laperouse."

"I've never been there."

"The food is good and it's very quiet."

"You're always arranging things." A faint note of resentment trailed through the words, and Sabrina said quickly, "We can go anywhere; what would you like?"

"I don't know. I don't know Paris."

"Well, a bistro?"

"Yes. Something small."

542

"Let's see if we can get into Benoît. Do you want to walk? We'd have to go back the way we came."

"Yes, I love to walk."

It's such a good way to put off talking, Sabrina thought, and in fact they did not speak again until they were seated across from each other in Benoît's tiny dining room with figured wallpaper, lace curtains stretched across the bottom half of the windows, and a few small tables, most of them along a banquette that stretched the length of the room. The maître d' led them to the only unoccupied table and Stephanie slid onto the banquette. Briefly, Sabrina debated sitting beside her, but instead took the chair the maître d' was holding for her on the other side of the table.

"We'll order right away," she said, "and we'll have a bottle of the Pichon-Lalande." She looked quickly at Stephanie. "Unless you'd rather have something else."

"No, that's fine." The maître d' brought the wine, displayed the label to Sabrina, poured it, waited for her to taste it and nod her approval, and all the while Stephanie seemed to be gathering herself to begin, like a diver in the moment when every muscle is tensed to push off from the board and into the air. "Everything should be fine, shouldn't it?" she said at last. "We don't have to be afraid anymore that someone is after us; we're together, we're in Paris, we have people who love us . . ."

"What do you want to do?" It came out so abruptly that Sabrina repeated it more softly. "What do you want, Stephanie?"

"Everything. I want all of it." She gave a rueful laugh. "That's what got us into this mess, isn't it? I wanted everything. To be Sabrina Longworth just for a little while and to have my own life waiting for me so that I could go back whenever I wished. As if the world would stand still for me while I lived all the fantasies I'd ever dreamed of. Like a child. Children see the world that way."

"I wanted it, too," Sabrina murmured.

"But your world changed and you changed with it and

543

made it all yours. I didn't change, not enough anyway, and now I don't know where I belong."

"Where do you want to belong?"

"I don't know. But wherever it is, I want Léon to be part of it. I can't imagine living with Garth again. We had nothing together when I left for China, only misunderstandings and anger and frustration, and we both wanted out. I know he was relieved when I left; he probably hoped I wouldn't come back."

"He hoped you'd come back and make your marriage work."

Stephanie shrugged. "I didn't see any sign of that. I'm not even sure he felt that way until you came and somehow made him want it. But it doesn't matter, don't you understand? I don't care what he wanted." She leaned forward, the words, after so long a silence, pouring out. "I did care once, but after a while it seemed that his work was more important to him than I was, much more interesting and . . . *valuable*, and that just wore me down. I suppose I wore him down, too; maybe that's what happens in marriages that fail: people grind each other down until they just don't fit together anymore. I don't know what you found in him; maybe he changed after I left, or you're better for him, so *he* was better. Maybe because you weren't Stephanie, he wasn't Garth. Wouldn't that be odd? But it doesn't matter. We can't ever live together again. I'd feel that way about him even without Léon. But I want my children."

A long sigh escaped Sabrina; that was what had been lurking at the edges of all their conversations in all the days they had been together.

"I think about them all the time, you know. When I saw those pictures in your album I almost couldn't stand it. I wanted to hold them and hear their voices, the way they talk so fast, both at once, sort of tumbling over each other, so excited, so in love with being alive . . . Oh, God, Sabrina, I miss them, I feel empty without them . . . Do you know, once, in London, Gabrielle was having trouble with Brooks and she came and sat in my lap and I said without thinking, 'Hush, dear Penny' . . . Oh, why didn't I go back then, why did I have to go on that cruise . . .''

"One last fling," Sabrina reminded her, knowing she was being cruel.

"I know, I know, I still thought I could have it all; I thought I could push it a little further, and then still further, and nothing would change: there wouldn't be any price to pay. That was a fantasy too, but I wouldn't let myself think about it because I didn't want to go back to being myself. Because it was myself that I didn't like; I never stopped loving my children and I never forgot them when I lost my memory; they were always inside me. One day, when I was in Aix, there were some schoolchildren on an outing and a little girl got separated from them and I was taking her back to her group and I called her Penny. She asked me why and I didn't know why, but I thought—I even told Max—I thought that must be my daughter. He'd told me I wasn't married when we met—and of course that was the truth as far as he knew it, since he thought I was you—but after I met that little girl I thought he'd lied or something, and I must have been married. Another time I told Léon that Cliff had made sure I'd find a stolen radio in his room. It was so strange, I had no idea what it meant, except that it sounded as if I had a son named Cliff. I even remembered Garth's name once. It came out of nowhere.''

The waiter brought their dinners, sliding them deftly onto the table, though they were leaning so close to each other there was barely room. He glanced at their identical faces, so beautiful it was difficult to believe that there could be two of them, but he did not linger; he refilled their wineglasses and left. He respected discreet conversations.

"I'm not even sure I want to live in America again. I could live in France, you know, with Léon and Penny and Cliff. That's what Léon wants. He wants us to have children—so do I—but that doesn't change anything: I want Penny and Cliff.''

The words were hammer blows, shattering the crystal of Sabrina's life. She felt numb, as if the only way to keep her life intact was to cut off all feeling. She sat back and took a sip of wine and looked at Stephanie without expression. "And what will you tell them?"

Stephanie flushed. "I thought . . . I thought you would . . ."

"Tell them for you? No. I won't do that. Or were you thinking I'd walk away and let you walk in, in my place? Why should I? They're not a set of dolls to be passed back and forth, depending on the day of the week and what suits us. We fooled them once and it took Garth a long time to be able to live with that, and I won't be a party to trying to fool him again. I love him, Stephanie, I love all of them, they shape my life, but even if that weren't true . . . good God, you can't play with people that way!"

"You said Penny and Cliff still don't know."

"It doesn't matter. They're human beings and you can't toy with them as if they're not. Besides, they've grown up in the past year and I'm not at all sure they could be fooled again. Maybe at first, but not over time. They're still as self-absorbed as most children, but they're smarter than most, they're curious and observant and loving, they see a lot and they listen and they try to fit what they see and hear into a view of the world that makes sense. And after a while, if things don't make sense, they ask a lot of very tricky questions. Stephanie, I know them! And I won't have them hurt!"

"*You* won't have them hurt? They're my children, not yours! You were the one who said they aren't dolls to be passed back and forth . . . Who do you think you are to tell *me* you know them, as if you can just walk in and take over and be their mother—"

"I am their mother," Sabrina said icily. "I did walk in and take over. I did it because you begged me to."

A shudder swept over Stephanie. She pushed her untasted food away. Her mouth drooped. "That's what I'd have to tell them, isn't it? That their mother wanted to be somebody else and so she . . . walked out on them.''

The pain in her sister's voice cut across Sabrina's anger and she started to reach out to comfort her. But her hand fell back to her lap. My enemy, my love, she thought, as she had before. They faced each other as if they were strangers.

"Yes," she said bluntly. "That's what you'd have to tell them."

"But there must be some way to say it so that it doesn't sound so awful . . ." Stephanie clasped her hands as her thoughts swung wildly from one side to the other. "There has to be a way to make them understand. Everybody has crazy ideas; they'd understand that. Kids always think about doing things that seem crazy and impossible . . . If I could make them feel what I was feeling at the time, I know they'd forgive me. It might be hard for them, but they would, I'm sure they would."

She looked at her hands. "No, they probably wouldn't. They probably couldn't. It would destroy everything they believe in, the goodness of their mother"—she looked at Sabrina—"*both their mothers*. They'd hate us both, wouldn't they? Children believe the world is reliable and predictable, and if I told them what I'd done, what *we'd* done, the world would seem crazy. Not reliable. Not something they could count on."

Around them was the murmur of quiet conversations, an occasional boisterous laugh, the chime of wineglasses meeting in a toast, the clatter of dishes from behind the swinging doors that led to the kitchen. But a hush enclosed Stephanie and Sabrina's table, and even as they faced each other it seemed to Sabrina that they were speeding away from each other, faster and faster, like a film gone haywire, and soon they would only be small specks, no longer, or ever again, recognizable to each other. And she did not know how to stop it; she thought perhaps there was nothing they could do but watch each other disappear.

Stephanie shifted in her chair. "But I have to tell them,

547

don't I? Denton's solicitor will go to the police, and the whole story will come out; everyone will know I'm alive—I mean, Sabrina Longworth is alive—and Penny and Cliff will hear it from television or newspapers or other people if they don't hear it from me. Or from you.'' She looked at Sabrina's face. ''No, you said you wouldn't do that. And I couldn't ask you to. I couldn't ask you to tell them you're not their real mother.''

I am their real mother; I've become their real mother.

''But they'll hear it anyway; an hour, a few hours after Denton's solicitor goes to the police the news will be everywhere and that would be the worst way of all; then they really wouldn't forgive me. If I told them, at least they'd know I'd been honest . . . finally. But honesty isn't really something we can claim, is it?''

I've been honest in my year with them. Everything I've done has been done through my love for them; they know that.

''No, I'll have to tell them, that's all there is to it. They're my children, and I want them, and if they're hurt, they'll get over it. Children are resilient; they bounce right back. Anyway, I don't believe they're really completely happy; they must know, deep down, that something isn't the way it ought to be. When they—''

''They are happy,'' Sabrina said sharply, unable once again to hold back the words. ''They've had a wonderful year. They've been happy and loving and loved. They haven't felt anything was missing—'' Not fair, she thought. She had no right to claim her sister's children just because they had had a good year.

''I don't believe that,'' Stephanie said firmly. ''They must have a feeling, even if they don't understand it, that something is wrong. And when they know I'm their real mother they'll be happy because things will seem right again and they'll want to be with me and no one else.''

The waiter came with raised eyebrows, and when Sabrina nodded, he removed their full plates. ''It was not good, madame?'' he asked each of them.

"*C'était excellent. Malheureusement nous étions distraites.*"

"*Nous reviendrons,*" Stephanie said. She looked at Sabrina, her eyes bewildered. "It feels so natural to speak French, but it feels right to speak English, too. It's as if I'm always caught somewhere between two people, whatever I do. Whatever I decide."

Outside, in the mild evening, they retraced their steps back to L'Hôtel. Stephanie walked past the fine antiques furnishing the sitting room of their suite, past a table with fruit and a bottle of champagne sent by the manager, to the terrace, filled with late autumn flowers. She leaned against the low wall, gazing at the steeple of the church of Saint-Germain-des-Prés. "It's terrible, what we're doing," she murmured. "I hate it, I hate it, but I don't know what else to do."

Sabrina was in the doorway behind her. "What do you hate?"

"Hurting you." She did not turn around. "You knew that's what I meant; you always know what I mean. I hate hurting you. But wouldn't it be enough if you kept Garth and I took Penny and Cliff?" She heard Sabrina's sharp intake of breath and she swung around. "I'm sorry, oh, God, Sabrina, I'm sorry, I don't know what's wrong with me, I sound like a vendor haggling in the market. It's just that I feel so trapped . . . that there's no good way to untangle what we've done . . . and I love you and I know you love me and I need you—we've always needed each other; we've always been closer to each other than anybody, anywhere—but still . . ."

"Still we're further apart than we've ever been."

"Yes."

The width of the terrace stretched between them. Sabrina's arms came up and Stephanie leaned forward, as if to move into her embrace. But at the same moment, Sabrina's arms fell to her sides and Stephanie leaned back against the wall. The terrace seemed to widen between them. They looked at each other in the faint light, identical faces, beloved faces, separated by all that they themselves had set in motion. Around them, the scent of chrysanthemums and stock seemed painfully sharp; the distant sounds of traffic suddenly rose to a clamor.

"I'm going to bed," Stephanie said and, in a flurry of movement, crossed the terrace, passed Sabrina in the doorway, and disappeared into the bedroom. Sabrina stood where she was, watching the church steeple fade as the lights of the city went out one by one. It was very late; the hotel slumbered. On the street below, a dog barked, a man said good night to friends, a pair of motorcyclists revved their engines and roared off into the distance. In the silence that followed, as clearly as if they were beside her, she heard her children's laughter and the clatter of their feet as they dashed about the house. She closed her eyes. I won't give them up. I won't give them up. I won't give them up.

What does that mean? I have no way to keep them without destroying their love for me and for Stephanie.

She was crying. She turned from the terrace and walked blindly to the closed door of the bedroom. The lamp beside her double bed was on; in the other bed, Stephanie lay curled·up on her side, her back to the room. Silently, Sabrina closed the door of the marble bathroom and washed her face and undressed, then slipped between the cool sheets of her bed. She could hear Stephanie's irregular breathing and knew she was awake, but she said nothing; in her separate space, she lay awake through the night, thinking of home and imagining Garth holding her hand, as he did every night as they fell asleep and every morning as they awoke and turned to each other to begin a new day.

When the sun reached their room, Stephanie threw back the covers and stood up. She glanced at Sabrina's closed eyes and thought, She isn't asleep, I know she isn't, she didn't sleep any more than I did, but she doesn't want to talk. And even if she did, what can we say to each other?

She walked past her sister without speaking and closed the bathroom door quietly behind her.

She showered and washed her hair and dried it, combing it with her fingers. She dressed in the clothes she had brought into the bathroom with her, then eased open the door and went back into the bedroom. Sabrina was not there.

She's gone! Stephanie thought wildly. Garth will be here tomorrow, and she's left me to face him. I can't, I can't, I'm not ready! I don't know what to say to him; I don't know what to say to Penny and Cliff. I'm not ready; she can't leave me here alone!

She ran into the sitting room. Sabrina was sitting on the terrace, wearing her silk robe. Coffee and a covered basket were on the table beside her next to a folded copy of *Le Figaro*; she had not opened it.

"Oh, thank God," Stephanie said. "I thought you'd gone."

"Not yet." Sabrina's face was pale and Stephanie saw a reflection of her own sleeplessness and uncertainty in her sister's eyes.

"Are you going to wait for Garth?"

"I haven't decided anything about tomorrow. Have you called Léon?"

"Not yet."

"What will you tell him?"

"I don't know. I don't know!" She stood in the doorway. "What should we do today? We have to do something, don't we?"

"Alexandra called while you were in the shower; she wanted to have lunch. I told her I was thinking of Giverny or the Marmottan for today, and she said she'd like to go along and she'd be here about ten."

"Giverny or the Marmottan?"

"Well, anything to do with Monet. When I was in school here, whenever I had a problem I took refuge in his garden or his paintings. There's something about their perfection, even while it's not quite real, that always made me feel there was a core of serenity I could reach, even if it took a long time.''

''A core of serenity. Oh, if only . . .'' Stephanie shook her head and, after a moment, said, ''Is there more coffee?''

''Of course. And croissants. I'll take a shower and then we'll ask the concierge for the train schedule to Giverny.''

Stephanie sat down as Sabrina went to the French doors. But as she reached for the pot of coffee, Sabrina came back and bent down and kissed her on both cheeks.

''Good morning, Stephanie. I love you.''

Stephanie turned and put her arms up. ''Oh, I do love you, Sabrina. I love you and I'm sorry, I'm so sorry, but there's nothing I can do about it! I wish . . . I wish . . . oh, God, I don't even know what I wish!''

Sabrina knelt beside the chair and they embraced, their cheeks together, their eyes closed. The sun warmed them. ''I'll get ready,'' she said, and left quickly, while Stephanie's eyes were still closed.

Stephanie poured coffee and bit into a croissant, barely tasting it. She gazed for a long time at the church of Saint-Germain-des-Prés, thinking of people stopping in on their way to work, looking for something. *A core of serenity.* And maybe they find it, she thought, unless they've gotten themselves into the kind of mess we have.

But if we hadn't started this whole crazy thing a year ago, I never would have met Léon. I wouldn't have met Robert or Jacqueline; I wouldn't have found out all the things I could do in London; I wouldn't have been Alexandra's friend.

But I would have had my children.

And taken them for granted, the way I used to do.

She was dizzy. She closed her eyes and opened them to the brilliant sun and still nothing was clear. I want it all, she thought again, with despair—*all, all, all*—haven't I learned anything? She felt herself tense with the impossibility of it, and then she thought, Well, no one can have it all, I know that, but it would be a lot easier to accept whatever I can have if Sabrina would decide what we're going to do, so I wouldn't have to—

She was ashamed, and she gripped her hands in her lap. *I'm sorry, Sabrina: I'm still trying to get you to take the responsibility for my life.*

The knocker on the door of their suite startled her. The maids, she thought, walking through the sitting room. They can come back when we're gone. She opened the door.

"Mom!" Cliff yelled, and flung himself against her, pushing her backwards into the room.

"Mommy, *bonjour, bonjour!*" Penny was dancing up and down in her excitement as she burrowed against Stephanie under Cliff's widespread arms. "Daddy taught me that, did we surprise you? We did, didn't we? That was our surprise! You didn't know we were coming!"

Stephanie staggered beneath the onslaught of her children. Joy flooded through her and she bent her head and clasped them in her arms.

"You didn't know, did you?" Cliff demanded. "We kept it a secret, didn't we?"

"Yes, you did," Stephanie whispered. "Oh, I love you, I love you, I love you, I love you . . ." She could not stop saying it. Her lips were against the upraised faces of her children, her body opened to their warmth and electric energy, and she felt faint and stumbled backwards again.

She heard the door close and looked up, over the heads of the children, into Garth's eyes.

Shock struck her like a wave, and she looked quickly away. She had cut him so completely out of her life that it was incredible to see him this close, with the children there, almost as if they were the family group she had long since denied. And he had been reaching toward her with a love in his eyes she had not seen since their first years together, sending a stab of jealousy through her that her sister had brought that out in him where she herself had been incapable of it.

553

She shook her head as if to fling off her thoughts. She had registered, in one swift second, that there was more gray in his hair than she remembered, that his lean face had a gentleness she did not remember and that he was far handsomer than she remembered, but then she withdrew from him and returned to the clamor of her children. That outstretched hand, the love in his eyes, were not for her, and she could not tell him she wasn't Sabrina. She wasn't ready. She could not even greet him as if she were his wife. If he didn't like it, that was too bad; what right did he have to spring this surprise on her? She would deal with it later. Maybe he would just go away and leave her with her children.

With the children and Léon.

"You smell different," Penny said accusingly. "Are you wearing perfume? You told me you don't like perfume."

"Oh. Well, most perfumes . . . Maybe it's my shampoo; it's a new kind. Tell me about your plane trip. And how come you're here. I thought . . ."

Huddled together, they moved past the closed bedroom door and onto the terrace, Penny and Cliff's high, excited voices propelling them along. Garth stayed where he was, cold with shock and fury. This woman was not his wife. He had known it the moment their eyes met. He had lived with Sabrina for thirteen months and he knew her as he had never known another human being, and this woman was not Sabrina.

This woman was Stephanie.

Not killed in an explosion. Not buried in London. Not mourned for a year. Instead, living in . . . well, wherever the hell she'd been living; what difference did it make? Wherever it was, she would have had to be in hiding, since she was supposed to be dead. But here she was, traveling with Sabrina, sharing a hotel suite, having a couple of weeks together—was that why Sabrina had come to London so often in the past year, to visit her sister?— then going back to whatever life she was living now.

Sending Sabrina back to Evanston.

They hadn't been satisfied with playing at a new life for a few months; they'd wanted it for good. And so the deception had never ended.

He watched Stephanie's radiant face as his children chattered about O'Hare Airport in Chicago and De Gaulle in Paris, and about their trip. They were so full of new adventures that they asked her nothing about herself; they looked directly at her but always through the haze of their self-absorption, adjusting reality—if indeed they needed to—automatically as they went along.

As I did once, Garth thought. *But never again.*

"Look, Mom, they gave us these neat little kits; see, the toothbrush folds up—"

"And there's a mask, Mommy, look, and some of the people wore them when they went to sleep and they looked so weird!"

Garth watched them, his face frozen. *Why didn't she tell me? If they wanted to make it permanent, that was what I wanted, too. Why in God's name didn't she tell me so we could deal with it together, make our marriage valid, live an open life . . .*

Because she would have had to tell the children.

But we could have done that together.

Could we?

What would we have told them?

That the woman they thought was their mother had fooled them. That their real mother had waltzed off one fine September day and stayed away for a month before she was killed—well, supposedly killed—without making any effort to see her children or talk to them in all that time. Could we have told that to Penny and Cliff?

"And a comb and these funny slippers. Why would you wear slippers on a *plane*?"

"And they gave us a book of crossword puzzles and we did *six* of them!"

Of course we could have told them. They're strong children, and with enough love we could have found a way to help them deal with it. It would have been better than living a lie. If she'd told me from the beginning, she and I could have worked everything out, made a life together. And now we can't. Now we have nothing together.

I will never be deceived by her again.

His muscles were taut beneath his cold skin, like wires wound on a spool almost to the breaking point. His face was rigid, his eyes blank, hiding the turmoil of his thoughts as he watched Stephanie and his children. She never looked at him.

God damn it, look at me! Look at what you've done to us, to all of us . . . He took a long step toward her and saw her flinch—so she was aware of him; she knew exactly how much distance was between them— and he stopped. There would be no confrontation in front of Penny and Cliff. Not now, not until he'd had time to think of some way to bring them up to date on how their mother and their aunt had made fools of all of them again and again and then, most devastatingly, again. He felt he would explode with the rage within him; he wanted to tear his children from that woman's arms and take them away, cradled protectively, shielded even from the sight of her. But he did not move. He would wait until he could get her alone.

Or get Sabrina alone.

Where was she? It was no longer a question of his dealing with one impostor or the other; now, for the first time since this damned game had begun, he would face them together.

But he could not ask Stephanie where her sister was until he could get her away from Penny and Cliff. And how the hell was he going to manage that?

There was a knock on the door behind him and he jerked around. If that was her— No, of course it wasn't; she wouldn't knock. The maids, he thought. Good; they might distract Penny and Cliff. He opened the door.

"Garth!" Alexandra exclaimed. "Good heavens, a day early? Husbands should never do that to wives, you know, it's—'' She saw his stony face and his rigid stance. ''Oh, my God.'' She looked beyond him, at Stephanie and the children close together on the terrace, and turned back to him. ''I gather that's Stephanie, and she told you.''

''Does the whole world know?''

''Almost no one. Did she tell the whole story? Where she's been?''

''She told me nothing. We haven't spoken.''

''Then how did you know?''

He gazed at her in silence.

The color rose in her face. ''Well, I guess, if you really do find that kind of love with someone . . .'' She looked again at the terrace. ''Where's Sabrina?''

''I don't know.''

''And from the sound of your voice you don't care. But I don't believe that, and I'll bet you don't either.'' She gazed at Penny and Cliff. ''I think we've got to get the youngsters out of here so you can explode. I do believe you're going to any minute now.'' She strode past him, to the terrace. ''Penny and Cliff! What a fabulous surprise!''

''Is *everybody* in Paris?'' Cliff demanded.

''The whole world, at least. Don't I get a hug?''

They ran to hug her, and Stephanie looked up, as if just awakening. ''I forgot. Giverny . . . the Marmottan . . .''

''Slight change in plans. The grown-ups have a lot to talk about so the younger generation is going to be whisked away.'' Casually she put her arms around Penny's and Cliff's shoulders. ''Come on, you two, we're going to give your parents some time together. I'm taking you to my favorite café, a few blocks from here, as it happens; there's a magician there every day at eleven-thirty, and I'll treat you to lunch and café au lait.''

''A magician?'' Cliff echoed. ''A French magician?''

''Probably. I think nationality doesn't have much to do with it.''

''We're too young for coffee,'' Penny said.

''Maybe in Evanston, but not in Paris.'' She was shepherding them through the sitting room.

"What kinds of tricks does he do?" Cliff asked.

"You should never ask that, Cliff; most of the magic of a magic show is surprise. It's like love," she added, fixing her gaze on Garth until he met her eyes. "There are always surprises; love is supposed to be able to roll with them, instead of getting knocked out. That's the magic part: something to hold on to even when you're not sure what's going on around you."

"Can we really have coffee?" Penny asked. "I mean, we're not any older, just because we're in Paris."

"You're older than you were yesterday. Anyway, it's half hot milk. That's what café au lait is: coffee with milk. If you don't like it, we'll switch to hot chocolate."

"How about wine?" Cliff demanded. "I mean, as long as we're in Paris . . ."

Alexandra laughed. "That's a bolder step. We'll discuss it on the way. Garth, you and Stephanie take your time; you can join us later."

"No!" Stephanie had moved swiftly from the terrace, terrified of being alone with Garth and having to tell him who she really was. "We'll go with you." She was so nervous her movements were jerky as she sidled past Garth and opened the door. "Come on, let's go, let's go."

Alexandra looked at Garth. "I'd be glad to take them; it would be a treat for me."

"No!" Stephanie cried. "*Come on!*"

"Come on, Daddy." Penny took Garth's hand. "Isn't it amazing to see Alexandra in Paris? And we'll all have café au lait!"

"Half milk," said Cliff. "It sounds awesomely boring. Can't we do something else, Dad, until time for the magician? Like climb the Eiffel Tower?"

"And walk off all our angst," Garth murmured, and only Alexandra heard the bitterness in his voice.

Cliff frowned. "What's an angst?"

"Anxiety, depression, worries, problems."

"I haven't got any. So can we *go*?"

"Daddy, let's go!" Penny cried.

They were tugging at his hands, and Garth saw beneath their excitement the first faint signs of worry that something was wrong: their mother wanted to go with them to the café and their father was holding back, and why was that? And they hadn't even kissed, and they always kissed, all the time, even when they hadn't been apart for two weeks. Garth met their eyes, tinged with apprehension, and gave in. He let them lead him out the door behind Alexandra, who, with a brief shrug of resignation, had followed Stephanie into the corridor.

L'Hôtel was lavish with antiques, marble and velvet; Garth had noted them peripherally when he arrived, thinking mostly of Sabrina and the surprise he and the children had planned: two days in Paris for the four of them and then a week for the two of them alone while Penny and Cliff flew to London, where Mrs. Thirkell waited at Cadogan Square to take them under her wing for a few days before taking them home to Evanston. It had seemed like such a good idea at the time. Now, taking the velvet-lined elevator to the lobby and walking blindly past pink marble and a soaring curved staircase, he knew that it was clearly the worst idea in the world.

No, it was a good idea. Based on what I thought . . .

Not thought. Knew. I knew the way things were between us. I didn't dream it or willingly deceive myself. I brought Penny and Cliff to Paris because we were a family in the best sense of the word.

The sun's glare stopped him just outside the entrance and he shaded his eyes, watching the others a few paces ahead. Alexandra and the children looked back when they realized he was not with them, but Stephanie looked fixedly ahead, her back stiff. And in that stiff back, Garth saw the Stephanie of their last quarrel, thirteen months ago, just before she went to China: the Stephanie who had not returned.

Sabrina had returned. Sabrina, who had shown again and again how deeply she loved them.

She wouldn't do this to us. She wouldn't live a lie,

pretending to mourn her dead sister—pretending to marry me!—pretending in every way that made us lovers and friends and husband and wife, and brought magic into our home.

I don't believe that. I do not believe that.

But . . . magic and surprise, Alexandra says.

Well, I am surprised.

"Daddy, come on! It's just a few blocks, Alexandra said!"

"Garth." Alexandra waited until he caught up to her. "Tell me what you want. We've got to do something to help Penny and Cliff; they keep asking me if everything is all right. They ask Stephanie, too."

"And what does she say?"

"That everything is fine and she loves them."

Garth shaded his eyes again and looked at his children. "Can't you think up a story about my wanting to be alone with . . . their mother? You've already said it once; add some window dressing. Make it sound romantic, if you don't mind stretching the truth to the breaking point."

"Garth, don't pass judgment yet. And don't be so bitter. You don't know the whole story. You don't know what she's been through."

"I don't give a damn what she's been through. Nothing would justify the lies, the pretense—"

"Wait a minute." Alexandra's eyes were wide with surprise. "I didn't mean Sabrina. I meant Stephanie. You don't know anything about her."

"I don't want to. Why the hell should I? You think that after she's been romping around the world for more than a year without a sign that she gave a damn for her family, I should start worrying about what she's been through? Oh, Christ, Alexandra, I'm sorry; I shouldn't dump it on you. If you still want to take Penny and Cliff for a while and give them some story to explain it, I'd be very grateful."

"I'll take care of it; I love being with them. We'll be at Le Petit Prince, on the Seine; keep going to the river, then turn left. You can't miss it. Take as long as you need; we'll be very happy watching the magician.''

Garth watched her stride ahead and scoop Penny and Cliff into her orbit. But already his thoughts had moved on.

She identified the body. She went through the funeral. If she wasn't pretending, how did that happen?

Whom did we bury that day?

They had always been so close, Sabrina and Stephanie; in some ways mystically close. Had he ever really known either of them? Had he really been a part of Sabrina, or had he deluded himself about the magic of this past year, fabricating what he wanted to believe just as he had willed his belief that she was Stephanie those first three months before he figured out the deception?

No, damn it; she loves me as I love her. I know that. I know that. Some things can't be faked.

Once before, he had felt this unraveling of certainty in a world gone haywire: last Christmas, after he had kicked Sabrina out and she had fled to London. Alone, in the late night stillness, he had thought, *Things fall apart; the center cannot hold.* Now, on the Rue de Seine on a brilliantly sunny day in October, he longed for a center that could hold, a stable center, a place where trust could live.

He could hear Alexandra pronouncing French phrases and his children repeating them, frowning in concentration. But they kept looking back, too, and their frowns then were for Stephanie and Garth, a little distance back, not near each other. Garth lengthened his stride and caught up to her. "We're going to talk. Alexandra is taking care of Penny and Cliff.''

"Not now, later, please, not now.'' Stephanie looked to left and right, into tiny ateliers and shops, as if some place might offer escape. She could not talk to Garth. He thought she was Sabrina and she did not know how to act like Sabrina with him; she had no idea what they were like together.

I just want my children. I just want to be with them and think that everything will be all right from now on.

"Not now," she repeated to Garth, her voice rising. "Later, later, not now." Sabrina wouldn't have said that, of course; Sabrina would have greeted him with the same love that he'd had in his eyes when he came in the door. He'll think I'm angry, tired of him, maybe he'll think I've met someone else. Well, that's too bad. I'm doing the best I can. I can't face anger and accusations and . . . hatred. She shook her head again—"Not now!"—and walked swiftly on.

Sabrina sat in the bedroom of the hotel suite, behind the closed door, her hands limp in her lap. Why hadn't he told her he was coming a day early? Why hadn't he said he was bringing the children? She could have planned for it; she and Stephanie could have been prepared. Why had he thought it should be a surprise?

But those weren't the important questions.

How could he have believed I was the woman who answered the door? How could he have been fooled again, after the year we've had together?

But it seemed he did believe it. And had gone off to a café with his children and with Stephanie. The Andersen family, on an outing in Paris.

She sat beside the window overlooking the street and the church steeple, but what she saw was the house in Evanston, the bedroom she shared with Garth, the kitchen where Mrs. Thirkell reigned and Penny and Cliff helped make dinner and brought their schoolwork to their parents for help or admiration, the dining room where they had welcomed Lu Zhen because he had no love in his life and they had so much.

I helped Garth with Lu Zhen. I helped Cliff with some of his problems and I made it easier for Garth to talk to him. I helped Penny believe in herself enough to withstand the sexual pressures at school. I was a friend to Claudia and helped her put the squeeze on a disreputable congress-man. I finished the design of the Koner Building.

I could say that I've done a good job in Evanston; I wrapped things up nicely, no loose ends dangling. I could say that my story there is finished; that it's time for me to leave.

In her mind she saw Garth's smile of greeting as it would have looked when Stephanie opened the door to their suite. She sat in the bedroom, seeing his smile, feeling his touch. *Oh, my dear love, forgive me. Everything got so complicated . . . The only thing that stayed simple and clear was my love for you and the children, but I couldn't separate it out from all the rest. I'm sorry, I'm sorry. I love you.*

Alexandra swept the children into the café and in a flurry of energy held their attention by commandeering a table and imperiously demanding menus, sparkling water and café au lait. While they waited for the magician, she wove elaborate stories about the posters that covered the walls; she told them how one of the waiters got his large red nose, why madame peeked out from the kitchen but never took a step into the café, why the dog was curled up in a corner looking so mournful. She was exhausted by the need for such continuous creativity, but she was exhilarated by their enthralled faces, and so she went on and on, silently wondering why the magician had chosen this day of all days to be late.

Outside, Stephanie stood at the window and watched the backs of her children's heads, bent forward to be close to Alexandra. Once in a while Penny jumped a little in her chair; she always did that, Stephanie thought, when something brought her a special delight. The minutes passed, the crowds flowed around her, leaving her a little space of her own. Behind her, couples strolled along the Seine or sat on benches, eating lunches from paper bags. Through the glass, Stephanie watched Alexandra talk and caught glimpses of her children's laughing faces. They looked up eagerly as a red-mustached man in a tuxedo and top hat came to their table. He carried a large basket, and after saying something to Penny and Cliff, he gestured over the basket with a white-gloved hand, and instantly a hat made of brilliantly colored feathers appeared on Penny's head. Her eyes wide with wonder, Penny reached up to touch it. She took it off, and she and Cliff turned it this way and that, looking inside it, trying to find the secret to the trick. Like their father, Stephanie thought. Believing everything has an explanation. But then she saw them look at Alexandra and the magician, laughing with delight, and she knew they believed in magic, too.

She put her hands on the warm glass window. Something was happening to her: she felt like a stranger. Outside, looking in, not able to hear what her children were saying, not able to share their laughter and wonder and delight. But I'm not a stranger, she thought; I'm their mother. She repeated it aloud. "I'm their mother. They love me. I'm their mother. *I'm* their mother."

But still, she was standing outside the window, cut off from them, from their thoughts, from their excitement, from their animated conversation with the magician and with Alexandra. How did they know Alexandra? Oh, yes, Sabrina had said she'd been in Evanston. Why? Sabrina hadn't said. Something else that had happened while Stephanie was gone, one of dozens, hundreds—too many, perhaps, for her ever to know them all.

I'm not part of their life anymore. And it's my own fault, nobody else's; I walked away and never thought that I might lose them.

But I can find my way back; I can be the center of their lives again, really and truly their mother again, I know I can. It will just take time, and I'll have to be so careful . . .

But what if I can't? What if I've changed so much—or they have—that they'll know that I don't belong with them? How will I explain that?

Maybe I wouldn't have to. I could just tell them how

much I love them and how sorry I am that I left them; wouldn't that be enough?

She saw her children waver through her tears. *It ought to be enough to tell your children that you love them. Love ought to be enough to smooth over anything.*

But if it isn't . . .

Abruptly she turned and walked back the way she had come, her head bowed, tears running down her face. Garth, watching from a few feet away, took her arm, gripping it so that she had no choice but to walk with him toward the hotel. "Where is she?"

Still crying, Stephanie barely heard him. "What?"

"Sabrina. Where is she?"

She looked at him wildly. "What are you talking about?"

"You know damn well what I'm talking about. For God's sake, Stephanie, you can't believe you two could fool me again." He stopped and stared into her frantic eyes. Stephanie. The real Stephanie. But Sabrina had been his Stephanie for so long, the only woman he . . .

I can't think about that now.

He walked on, almost dragging Stephanie with him. "Whatever you've been up to, however the two of you managed to make everyone think you've been dead all this time, I won't be part of your games anymore."

"Wait, you're wrong." Relief flooded her. He knew. She didn't have to tell him. "Sabrina didn't—"

"Wrong? You didn't let all of us think you were dead? You haven't been living another life for the past year? And Sabrina wasn't having a good time fooling me again— another deception, a very successful one? She's been calling me every night for the past two weeks, lying about what she was doing and whom she was with." His voice shook with fury. "Lying . . . my God, you're both experts at that. And now you want something else, so you've come back. A year ago you wanted out and you got out, you did whatever the hell you wanted to do, and now you want something else. Well, what is it? If you think for one minute you're going to take those children away from me—''

"You're hurting my arm!"

"Hurt isn't something you have much right to talk about." He stopped beside the iron fence that ran along the Seine, and held her in front of him, once again staring into her face. The image of Sabrina. Uncanny, he thought; even now she could be Sabrina. But there was something that made her Stephanie, a woman he did not love, a woman he could despise for what she had done.

She tried to pry his fingers loose. "I never meant to hurt you. I did want to get away, to have another life . . . I wasn't happy—you knew that!—but all I wanted was a few days; I thought I'd be back in a week and we could try to start again. I never wanted to hurt you!"

"You chose a peculiar way to demonstrate it." He eased his grip on her arm. "But nobody forced it on you; you chose it and went through with it and now it's done. And if you've come back to take Penny and Cliff, you can forget it. They're staying with me. I don't know what you've done for the past thirteen months or whom you've done it with, but you've managed to go all that time without a single phone call or letter to your children, and as far as I'm concerned—as far as any judge would be concerned—that disqualifies you from having anything to do with them. Are you listening to me? Damn it, look at me! They're the most important thing in the world to me right now, and I'm going to make sure they don't know what's been going on: you're not going to tell them and neither is Sabrina. My God, you two bitches, toying with a couple of children who never did anything to you but love you and depend on you—''

"Garth, stop, stop . . . Listen to me! Sabrina didn't know I was alive. She didn't toy with Penny and Cliff, or with you. She loves you. It was terrible for her to lie to you every night, but she did it for me, because I begged her to. I couldn't face you and the children; I didn't know what to do, so I asked her for a little time . . . and then we had to find out who was after us . . . Oh, God, it's so complicated; I can't explain it all."

"She didn't know you were alive?"

"No. My God, Garth, she thought she'd buried me!"

Before he could stop it, joy flooded him. *She didn't know.* He had barely heard the rest—someone was after them?—all he knew was that Sabrina had not lied, had not pretended to be his wife, his love . . .

But then, looking past Stephanie at the sun-speckled crowds beneath tall horse chestnut trees, he thought, Why should I believe that? It's too easy. They lie too well, both of them. "She sat beside a coffin for a whole afternoon and said goodbye to her sister."

"I know; we've talked about that and we think we know how it must have happened. It's part of everything else, the whole year that I was in London and then France . . . Garth?" She looked into his eyes, trying to read them. She thought there was less anger; he seemed to be listening, weighing what she said, and she remembered how he always took time to repeat to himself what he heard so that he could incorporate it into what he knew, and evaluate it. The scientist, Stephanie thought, and knew she had never tried to understand that part of him. "I could tell you the whole story, but it would take so long . . . and Sabrina ought to help me tell it."

"Where is she?"

"I don't know. She was in our bedroom at the hotel."

"While the rest of us were there?"

"Yes."

"There was a closed door; was that it? Could she hear us through it?"

"I'm pretty sure . . . yes, she could. I forgot she was there. The children, the shock of seeing you . . . I didn't think. But she can tell you . . . we can tell you everything, if you'll just listen. Garth, believe me. She didn't know. She thought I was dead and she was in love with you. She is in love with you."

He studied her face. "Can you think of any reason why I should believe you?"

"You're a scientist; you ought to be able to recognize the truth."

He gave a short laugh. "Scientists are often fools."

"But you aren't. Sabrina said once that you weren't a fool, but we fooled you; she was trying to get me to come back because she was worried about what we'd done. I think she loved you then, though of course she wouldn't tell me. But I wanted more time; I wanted one last cruise"—a shiver swept over her—"and she gave it to me." Her voice dropped, and Garth leaned closer to hear her. "She's always done that. All our lives she's done what she could to make me happy. And I've relied on her to do it. I've never been as strong as she is; I've never had the same kind of belief in myself; I've never been as free in my imagination or my friendships or my work, or any other way. That was why I envied her. So I . . . used her. And she let me, because she loves me."

They stood on a cobblestone walk beneath a wide-spreading chestnut tree. On the far side of the Seine the massive gray stones of the Louvre seemed almost black, silhouetted against the cloudless sky. "Let's go," Garth said abruptly, and turned her with him and they walked quickly the remaining short blocks to the hotel. They took the elevator in silence to the top floor and in silence they stood at the door of the suite.

Stephanie raised a tentative hand to knock, but Garth reached around her and turned the knob and they walked in.

Sabrina was in an armchair on the terrace, her hands folded in her lap. She had moved from the bedroom, and that was all she had done. She looked up at the sound of the door; her eyes met Garth's and what should have been a joyous reunion after two weeks apart was instead a long look of doubt and anger, smoldering resentment, apology, and an attraction between them so powerful that even Stephanie felt it.

568

Sabrina stood up. "Where are Penny and Cliff?"

"At the café with Alexandra," Stephanie said, "and a magician to entertain them." She rushed to Sabrina, as if she had to move quickly to keep from changing her mind, and put her arms around her. "Too much is happening. It must have been awful for you, listening to us and then hearing us leave. I'm sorry we did that, but I couldn't stay here alone with— I mean, I was afraid. Everything happened too fast for me to think straight."

Sabrina's eyes again went to Garth.

"He knew right away," Stephanie said. "I thought he didn't, but he knew the minute he saw me. And then we all dragged him off to the café."

"You knew," Sabrina said to Garth. "You knew." And for the first time a small smile lit her face. "And did Stephanie tell you what happened to her?"

"No." Garth was looking from one to the other with the sense of unreality he had had since arriving that morning. Seen together, except for the clothes they wore, the sisters could have been one woman standing before a mirror, and as he looked at them his anger revived. It may have been true that Sabrina believed her sister to be dead, but, for all the love she professed for him, she kept from him the shattering revelation of Stephanie's survival. And now, seeing them together, he wondered if anyone ever could become as important to them as they were to each other. He did not know what to say to them, how to talk to them together. He told himself he did not want to talk to them; he would take his children home and get the hell out of both of their lives.

But Sabrina had taken a step forward, her hands out. "I'm sorry. I promised once never to lie to you again. I broke my promise and I can't tell you how sorry—"

"You broke more than that." Fighting against the ache to hold her, to kiss her, to awaken the smile that illuminated her face, he ignored her hands. He watched them drop to her sides and then he let his anger overflow. "I thought we had an understanding in our family that we

569

wouldn't hurt each other, that our home was a place of safety, a refuge in a world that sometimes seemed cold and complicated and threatening. We got past your first lies—I thought we'd gotten past them—but now we're back where we started. There were dozens of chances for you to tell me what you were doing these past two weeks, but you'd decided—the two of you had decided—again!— how much truth the rest of us were entitled to.''

Stephanie had crept into a corner of the sitting room, shrinking from the anger in Garth's voice as if it were aimed at her. She stood there tentatively, wanting to escape into the bedroom but afraid to leave. Garth saw her behind him in the shadows, and he saw Sabrina in front of him on the sunlit terrace, and his rage built as he thought of them flanking him as they had flanked a year of his life without his knowing it. Impostors shaping his life. ''Well, it's over and I'm leaving and I'm taking Penny and Cliff with me. Neither of you will have them. It's monstrous to think that a family could be incidental to the whims of two bored women, that children could be passed back and forth like playthings, enjoyed for a while then tossed aside until at some point they're remembered and maybe longed for. I won't—''

''I didn't toss them aside!'' Stephanie cried. ''I knew Sabrina would take care of them; I knew she'd keep them healthy and happy until I came back, and she did, and now—''

''*Now*? You think you're coming back now?''

''Not to you. I couldn't do that. You don't want me and I don't want to live with you, Garth, not anymore. But I want my children. They're mine, Garth, I'm their mother! Doesn't that mean anything to you?''

''No. Should it? It hasn't meant anything to you.''

''That's not true; it has! I've wanted them every minute since I got my memory back—'' Garth's head swung sharply to her. ''That's what happened! You never asked, you never cared, but that's what happened to me, and we haven't had a chance to tell you about it, but if you'd let us, you'd understand; you'd change your mind. Sabrina"—she went to the terrace where Sabrina stood—"you've got to help me. I don't want to tell it alone; I want us both to do it."

" 'The whims of two bored women,' " Sabrina said icily, looking at Garth. "You know better than that. You're working yourself up to a rage—you tend to do that—and if you don't stop, we won't be able to talk at all."

"God damn it, don't tell me what I 'tend' to do. You knew for two weeks that Stephanie was alive, that you were making our whole life a sham—"

"Our whole life?"

"—and that nothing would ever be the same. You knew it and kept it to yourself. Because you loved your sister. That's a hell of an excuse. You say you love us, too. Is that the dividing line of your loyalties? If it's us and a stranger, you'll choose us; if it's us and your sister, you choose her."

"That's not fair."

"Why not? You did choose her."

"Briefly. And only once. I knew we'd see you soon—"

"More than once. There was the big one. You chose her when you faked being her so we wouldn't know she'd left."

"I didn't love you then. I haven't chosen anyone but you and the children since then. I did lie on the telephone, but I didn't see how I could do anything else, and it was only for a few days. I thought, on Sunday, tomorrow, I'd meet your plane and we'd be able to talk and . . . work things out . . ."

"You thought you'd have time to manipulate me again."

"Garth, please stop. I know you're hurt and angry, and you have good reason to be, but I never wanted to manipulate you and you know it. All I wanted was to live with you and make a life with our children that was good and loving and rewarding. I never wanted to fool you

571

beyond that first week; I fell in love with you. And our house really was a refuge for me, a haven, and I did my damnedest to make it one for you and Penny and Cliff, too. As far as I know, I never hurt you, or them; I tried to make the three of you feel loved and cared for and protected. You know all this, you've known it for months, and I'd appreciate it if you'd try to remember what we've had together instead of sliding back to what you were feeling last December and reliving that whole awful time as if nothing had changed."

"How much has changed if you could lie to me for the past two weeks?" He heard himself fling the words at her and wondered why he could not let it go, why he kept harping on it. *I love you. I know you love me, I know you get trapped by Stephanie's demands. I need you; I don't want to live a life without you.* But still his anger fueled him and the harsh words poured out. He turned from the pain in Sabrina's eyes and looked at Stephanie. "You both think you can pick up wherever you want, whatever you've done, and go right on, like kids who break a window and then pretend it wasn't their fault. But this time you're not picking up where you left off; you can't blame someone else for what happened. I don't give a damn what you do with your life, but Penny and Cliff won't be part of it."

"You can't say that! I'll fight you for them!"

"With what? Your passionate desire for a fling in London? A year away from them? They're staying with me. You won't see them again. Neither one of you will see them again."

"Oh, don't keep going on like that," Sabrina said angrily. "Be angry, hold on to your anger if that's all you can do, but you don't know the whole story and you can't even think rationally about what to do until you've heard it. Why did you ignore Stephanie when she told you she'd lost her memory? Didn't you believe her? Or don't you want to hear anything that might change your mind about us? All we're asking is that you listen to us. Will you do that? If nothing else, it will satisfy your scientific curiosity."

He smiled, then caught himself. He looked at his watch. A little after noon; his children were still being entertained by the magician. And by Alexandra. Our guardian angel, he thought.

"It won't take too much of your time," Sabrina said coldly.

He nodded. "All right."

"Let's sit out here." Her voice had changed again. Now that she knew that the whole story would come out, she let herself feel Garth's sense of betrayal and vulnerability in the unstable world he had discovered when he came to their hotel room, and her voice shook with her love for him and her desire to protect him. "It's so beautiful; the terrace is so wonderful . . . and I'll get us something to eat; I think we need it." She picked up the telephone and asked for wine and coffee. "And lunch," she added, and ordered seafood salad for three. "I don't know if we'll eat it; probably not. Stephanie and I mostly send our food back these days: we haven't finished a meal in so long I can't remember it; I suppose if we were on a diet it would be . . . But we're not; we're just . . . Well, anyway, we can try." She was talking too fast and too much, but she was so nervous she thought she would fly apart. Garth had slowly followed them to the terrace, and as he did, she felt she could barely grasp the fact that the three of them were together, their roles so oddly skewed, all the secrets exposed, the future still unknown. *Except that Garth may, at any time, tell me to leave so he and Stephanie can work out how they'll share their children.*

Stephanie sat on the edge of a chair near Sabrina. Garth pushed a chair farther away from them before sitting down. "Well?"

"Max got me off the ship," Stephanie said without preamble, and she told the whole story in a level voice, now and then looking at Sabrina, never at Garth, mostly gazing past both of them at the nearby steeple and at tall thunderheads building on the horizon. Rain tonight, she thought absently even as she talked on, occasionally turning to Sabrina to ask her to take part, but for the most part speaking by herself for almost an hour.

When the waiter brought their order, Garth directed him to the terrace and, when he had left, closed and locked the door. That was their only distraction; the rest of the time Stephanie talked, and as she told her story, all the parts of her life came together: her years growing up with Sabrina, college, marriage to Garth, the birth of her children, her brief time in London pretending to be Sabrina, the months in France with Max, Robert, Jacqueline, and then Léon. And she saw herself standing outside the café, watching her children with Alexandra; she felt again the warm window beneath her palms, saw Penny and Cliff waver through her tears. It was the first time she had seen everything at once, and she began to realize that there were some parts of her that she could never recapture.

When she finished her story, they sat in silence. One of the bottles of wine was empty; the coffeepot on its warmer was half full. The seafood salad was untouched.

"But there's something else," Stephanie said at last, looking at her hands, clasped in her lap. "I'm having trouble making sense of who I am. I used to know, when I lived in Evanston, but I didn't like myself very much; that was why I wanted Sabrina's life. I wanted to be her a lot more than she wanted to be me; I really believed that I could put on a new life like a new coat, and then I'd be everything I wanted to be."

"And were you?" Garth asked. It was the first time he had spoken, and when Sabrina heard in his voice the curiosity of the scientist, she breathed a sigh of relief.

Stephanie's glance flickered toward him, then away. "It seemed that way. I knew I was only playing a part, but I was almost perfect because I'd been longing for it for so many years, and because Sabrina was inside me somehow, helping me without my realizing it." For a brief moment she looked directly at Garth. "I know we did a terrible thing, and I'm sorry, but for a little while I was so happy. I forgot how overwhelming the world had seemed every morning when I woke up; I felt I could do anything. But of course I knew, underneath, that I couldn't; I knew I was only playing a part, that I couldn't really be Sabrina because I'd left too much behind that I really cared about.'' Her glance slid past Garth's eyes again. ''I kept wanting more and more adventures because I thought that was the way to stay happy, to forget the person I'd been, the one I didn't like. So I held on to being Sabrina; I couldn't let go. But, underneath, I knew I couldn't ever really step into Sabrina's life because of everything I'd left behind. I'd had so much, much more than I'd realized, and then I'd abandoned it, but it was always there, whatever else I did.''

''You got what you wanted,'' Garth said, still with the absorbed air of the scientist. ''You wanted to forget who you were, and you did.''

Stephanie stared at him. ''Yes, but I didn't plan to forget. The doctors told me I was repressing my life because I felt guilty about something I'd done. And they were right, but that didn't help me remember. But now, when I do remember, I don't seem to be anyone. I mean, I don't seem to fit in anywhere.''

Sabrina took her hand. ''You will. You haven't had enough time to get used to remembering.''

''No, it's more than that.'' She took her hand from Sabrina's and turned her empty glass between her fingers. ''I told you the other day that you kept on being yourself all the time you were being me. This whole year, you've been both of us. You knew what you wanted, you knew where you belonged and you trusted yourself to shape your future. I guess most people know those things and don't wonder about them at all, as if they've built a house and furnished it and they can go from room to room with their eyes closed, they know it so well, and they know it belongs to them and no one else, so it becomes a reflection of them and they see themselves every time they walk in the door.''

She looked again at Garth and saw an intense interest in his eyes. For the first time since their early years together, she felt the stirrings of pleasure that she had caught Garth Andersen's attention. ''But when I was in London all I wanted was to be Sabrina: I kept pushing Stephanie Andersen away. And then, in France, I was Sabrina Lacoste, and I made a life there, as whole as I could make it. So many lives, so many feelings, all mixed up inside me and I've lost whoever I was and I don't know who I am now. Or where I belong.''

A wren flew down to the terrace wall, pecked at a stone, hopped a few exploratory feet, and then, with a rush of small wings, flew off.

''All I have are my children. Don't you see? You've got to understand this: they're all I'm really sure of! I think about them and everything seems clear. I know they could give me what I don't have: I'd be their mother, so I'd know who I am, and we'd make a life together, and I'd know where I belong.''

Sabrina leaned forward to pour from the second bottle of wine. She waited a moment to steady her hand before she refilled their glasses. ''I thought it was the parents' job to help children find out who they are and where they belong.''

Stephanie flushed. ''That's a cruel thing to say. I'm trying to be honest.''

''So am I. Penny and Cliff already have what you're looking for. They've learned a lot in the past year. Or haven't you noticed?''

''Yes, I've noticed! Damn you, damn you, you know I have!'' She stared angrily at Sabrina through sudden tears. ''They're so different; how could I miss it? They're . . . stronger than they were.'' Her voice faltered. ''Bolder. More adventurous.'' And then she spoke aloud the words that had been gnawing at her since she had been with her children that morning. ''Like you.''

"Like both of us," Sabrina said quickly. "You brought them up for all those years before I got there."

"No. You know what I mean. All those years I envied you, it wasn't just for the life you led, it was because you were the one who reached out for adventures. You helped me come along when we were young, you even led me, and I was grateful . . . but it isn't easy being grateful. And then when I was living in Evanston, I'd get angry with myself for holding back when I knew you would have gone out of your way to meet somebody new or handle a problem or face a crisis instead of running from it. That's what you've given to Penny and Cliff. They won't grow up feeling angry at themselves for being afraid of adventures. They'll forge ahead. Like you."

For the first time, Garth felt a stab of pity for Stephanie. He knew she was right: in one year with Sabrina his children had grown more eager to rush forward and embrace whatever might lie ahead, more confident of their future. They were no smarter or nicer than they had been when they lived with Stephanie, but they were more able to take on the world. And Stephanie knew it.

Sabrina was conscious of Garth observing them. It was the first time, she thought, that an outsider had watched them work out the tensions and love and unfathomable closeness between them. But then she caught herself. An outsider? Her beloved Garth; Penny and Cliff's father. Sitting back in his chair, looking relaxed and casually interested, as Sabrina had seen him look many times when he was in fact intently listening, weighing new information, analyzing it and incorporating it into his world. There was nothing sloppy or careless about her beloved Garth: he was passionately curious about everything and, except when angry, willing to listen to anything, but it was facts he trusted; he relied on emotions only when they did not create havoc with an orderly world. He was not an outsider; he was part of whatever order she and Stephanie would create from the confusion they had wrought. He belonged with them; they were all part of each other now.

As if she were looking down from above, she saw the three of them held together as if by the strands of a spiderweb, invisible until the sun struck it at the right angle. Then, briefly, the connections and strength of the bonds became clear. Three of us, she thought, sitting together in Paris beneath a brilliant sun and a clear blue sky and a little wren who keeps swooping by to check us out: three people caught in a drama infinitesimally small on the world's stage but so enormous within the boundaries of our lives that it overwhelms us with its possibilities for happiness or despair. We are being very civilized about it all. But we are very frightened.

As the silence stretched out, Stephanie jumped up and stood a little distance away, leaning against the terrace wall, her arms folded protectively across her chest. "You've all changed, you know; it's obvious. You're not as hard as you used to be," she said to Garth, "even with all the terrible things you've said today. The way I remember you, your face always looked so stern, as if you were about to give a lecture or scold somebody. And, it's funny, but you seem more sure of yourself, too, like Penny and Cliff. I don't know what that means: maybe it means you've discovered there's more to life than genetics."

She saw him look at Sabrina; she saw their eyes meet and hold. "I guess," she sighed. "I guess that's it. And you're in love," she said to Sabrina. "I've never seen you when you really loved someone. I thought you loved Denton when you married him, but that was just excitement, wasn't it? You're different now. As if everything is in the right place and you can reach out beyond yourself and . . . soar."

Sabrina smiled. "I like that. It's what I thought about you, in Vézelay."

"Oh. I seemed that way to you? It seems like such a long time ago."

She paced with short, nervous steps, trailing her hand along the stone wall. "Maybe I was that way. I think I felt that way before I remembered everything. Then I got so confused . . ."

In the corner of the terrace she turned and faced them. "You've made a new family," she said, almost accusingly. "You've all changed so much, especially Penny and Cliff; they're so . . . oh, God, *they're so happy*. And I don't know if . . . if it would be best for them . . . I'm not sure . . ." She closed her eyes. "I don't know if I can do this," she whispered.

"Stephanie." Sabrina began to stand up to go to her, but Garth leaned forward and put a hand on her arm. She turned and met his eyes again, and in that moment, with the warmth of his hand holding them together, she chose to stay with him and let Stephanie find her own way, alone.

Stephanie opened her eyes. "I don't think . . . when children are happy, anybody should take that from them. They're so beautiful, aren't they—Penny and Cliff? So full of life and joy and fun . . . They were dancing down the street with Alexandra as if they were going off to conquer Paris. They weren't afraid of anything! Well, yes, they were: they were afraid their parents weren't being loving to each other. And I guess they're used to seeing loving parents, aren't they? They're used to that. A house filled with love. *Aren't they?*"

"Yes," Sabrina said quietly.

Stephanie bent her head. She picked at a stone on the wall, just as the wren had pecked at it earlier, concentrating on it. "All last night, when neither of us was sleeping, I was thinking about the four of you in Evanston, in that awful old house that always creaked and needed fixing somewhere, and in the kitchen, making dinner and eating together . . . I could see all the rooms so clearly, and all of you in them, being together . . . All those things you told me when we were in London, about their school and Cliff's soccer and Penny's painting and their friends, and that Chinese boy . . . all night I thought about you, the four of you, but mostly about Penny and Cliff, and I knew they were happy, and then when I saw them, it was more than I'd ever imagined . . . how happy and secure and loving they are in a . . . in a loving family.''

There was a long silence. The sounds of traffic were like ocean waves in the background, isolating the terrace with its three motionless people. ''What I mean is, I couldn't . . . I couldn't imagine . . . forcing myself into that. Into what you've created. Because they don't think anything is wrong, anything is missing. I wanted to believe they thought that, but they don't. They're happy. Their world is solid and familiar and . . . stable. They're full of trust, not fear. As long as . . . as long as I . . . as long as I keep quiet.''

She looked at Garth. ''I asked for them today because I thought if you said yes, we could work something out. I thought it would be so wonderful to have them that I'd do anything to make them happy and then they would be.'' A rueful smile touched her lips. ''Instant happiness. I didn't have any new ideas about how we'd do it or what I'd tell them when they knew I wasn't Sabrina—because of course they would know; there's no way I could fool them for more than a few hours—I just wanted it to happen because it would be so wonderful. The same way I wanted to be Sabrina because that would be wonderful. As if I could wish into being a world that was wonderful. But what would I do when they started wondering why I wasn't like the mother they knew? I couldn't tell them the truth. I thought I could think of a way to do it, but there isn't one. They'd never trust me again. Children think their parents will always be there for them. I guess they find ways to handle divorce, but this wasn't a divorce: this was a game—Robert called it foolhardy and dangerous—and we played it so carelessly, as if we were playing with a deck of cards. How do you make children believe their world is stable and reliable after that? I can't do it. I can't take them away and pretend to be their—'' Her lips moved, but no sound came. And then, her voice almost inaudible, she said, "—pretend to be their mother, when they've already got one."

Sabrina felt a rush of wonder and joy that left her breathless, and then a terrible sadness. *Stephanie, you can't walk away from them forever; you love them so.*

But isn't that exactly what I want her to do?

Garth went to Stephanie and took her in his arms. She looked at him through her tears and then laid her head on his shoulder like a child. "I'm sorry, Garth, I'm so sorry, I'm so sorry; I didn't think about what I was doing, I just went ahead, and you deserved better, and so did Penny and Cliff; I'm sorry, I'm sorry—"

"Hush, it's over, it's over." Garth stroked her hair. "It's done; we can't go back." Over Stephanie's head, he met Sabrina's eyes and, jubilantly, felt once again the unalloyed wonder he had felt for a year whenever he looked at her and knew she was part of his life, part of him, and nothing could shatter that. "We wouldn't go back, even if we could," he said to her. "We've traveled too far; we've made too many discoveries."

"But we have to find a way," Sabrina said to him. "The three of us."

"Yes. We will." His love for her seemed to him so transcendent, their understanding so instinctive and complete, that he knew there could be no room, ever again, for a deception between them: no room, no need, no place in what they would build on that which they had already begun. In the damnedest way possible, he thought wryly, but we have made a beginning, and a good one, and from now on we'll . . . what had Stephanie said? Soar. From now on, we'll soar.

The wren had returned and was swooping in narrowing circles, looking for a place to land. Garth smiled. Stubborn bird. He'll find his place. We all do, if we're lucky.

He held Stephanie away from him. "Listen to me. You're not going to walk completely out of Penny and Cliff's life. We won't be a party to that. We'll tell them the same truth we'll tell everyone else: that their Aunt

Sabrina wasn't killed in the explosion, that she lost her memory and has been living in France since January, that she's recovered her memory and loves them and wants to see them as often as possible, even more often than she used to. And that we'll visit her in Vézelay or wherever she's living, as often as we can.''

Stephanie was staring at him, standing stiffly within his loose embrace. With a sharp movement, she pulled away and walked to the other end of the terrace and stood there, her head bent, her hands over her ears. *There is no end to a deception once it begins.*

She saw Sabrina walking toward her and turned her back, leaning her forehead against the stone wall, still holding her ears. *On and on and on: endless ramifications, circles and more circles, layers and layers piling up, until it becomes a new truth.*

And this was the new truth: that she would play a part in her children's life. Not the part a mother expected to play, but a part that would allow her to see her children grow, and give her opportunities over the years to tell them how much she loved them and wanted what was best for them, wanted them to be the strongest, happiest people they could be.

On the fringes, Stephanie thought. I'll always be on the fringes of the Andersen family, the one to wave goodbye when they go off together to their home, their shared experiences, their private stories and jokes, their plans for tomorrow and the next day and the next.

It isn't enough.

It's better than nothing.

And in that moment she gave up Stephanie Andersen and took to herself Sabrina Longworth. Not the Sabrina she had replaced in London, but a new one, entirely hers. Somehow she would make a life from that name.

Garth saw the slight straightening of her shoulders and knew she had made up her mind. It occurred to him briefly that they would have to find a way to get a divorce. We don't really have to, he thought: if she's going to be Sabrina, she's been divorced from Denton for years and she's never been married to me. But I think we'll all want to do it as soon as possible, and put an end to as much as we can of this crazy adventure.

"Stephanie," Sabrina said.

Stephanie turned. "Wrong name," she said shakily, trying to smile, and then they were in each other's arms. And if their world had turned upside down and they could not yet fathom how they would deal with the twists and turns of the coming years, they were still together, they had not lost each other, there would still be a voice at the other end of the telephone line, saying, "You understand, you always understand."

Stephanie held her sister as if she could never let her go, but then, steeling herself, she kissed Sabrina on both cheeks and stepped back. "I can't see Penny and Cliff now; I can't talk to them yet. I have to get ready to be their Aunt Sabrina, and that's going to take a while."

Sabrina studied her face. "You're not going back to Vézelay?"

"Not yet. I'll call Léon; he'll understand that nothing has changed between us, that I want to spend my life with him, but right now I have to be alone for a while. I think I'll stay in Paris for a few days and then probably go to Cavaillon to spend some time with Robert. I'll let you know where I am." She stepped back farther, putting more distance between them, until she was beside Garth. "Thank you for forgiving me. And for letting me be part of Penny and Cliff's life. I promise I'll be very good to them. A good aunt. I've never been an aunt. An adventure, Sabrina!"

She turned to the French doors that led to the living room and looked from Garth to Sabrina with a wavering smile. "I think you'd better go, don't you? Your children are waiting."

"Yes," Sabrina said, "in a minute." She walked past Stephanie into the sitting room and took from her purse the small photo album she carried at all times. "This is for you. I'll send more as we take them."

Stephanie held the album in both hands. She opened it and turned the pages. "My sweet Penny," she whispered. "And my very handsome, grown-up Cliff." She rested her fingers on a picture of the two of them grinning at her from the backyard of their house. "Thank you," she said to Sabrina. "I love you."

Sabrina kissed her. "I love you . . . Sabrina. You'll come to visit us in a little while. Please. Please."

Garth put his arm around her. "Time to go." He kissed Stephanie's cheek. "We'll talk to you soon. And see you soon."

His arm around Sabrina, they walked to the door and into the corridor without looking back. But Sabrina could not help it. She glanced quickly into the room as the door closed and saw Stephanie standing alone, one hand clutching the photo album, the other raised in farewell.

Then she and Garth were in each other's arms for a long silent moment until, together, they turned to walk down the corridor. Hand in hand, Garth and Stephanie Andersen walked to the elevator, to the lobby, to the street, where, a few blocks away, their children waited.